陳善偉
Chan Sin-wai

粵普英
順逆序辭典

A New Comprehensive
Cantonese-Putonghua-English
Dictionary

商務印書館
The Commercial Press

粵普英順逆序辭典
A New Comprehensive Cantonese-Putonghua-English Dictionary

作者 Author	陳善偉 Chan Sin-wai
責任編輯 Editors	黃家麗　　黃稔茵 Betty Wong　Tracy Wong
封面設計 Graphic Designer	涂　慧 Tina Tu
出版 Published by	商務印書館 (香港) 有限公司 香港筲箕灣耀興道 3 號東滙廣場 8 樓 http://www.commercialpress.com.hk The Commercial Press (H.K.) Limited 8/F, Eastern Central Plaza, 3 Yiu Hing Road, Shau Kei Wan, Hong Kong http://www.commercialpress.com.hk
發行 Distributed by	香港聯合書刊物流有限公司 香港新界大埔汀麗路 36 號中華商務印刷大廈 3 字樓 The SUP Publishing Logistics (HK) Limited 3/F, C & C Building, 36 Ting Lai Road, Tai Po, N.T., Hong Kong
印刷 Printed by	中華商務彩色印刷有限公司 香港新界大埔汀麗路 36 號中華商務印刷大廈 14 字樓 C & C Offset Printing Co., Ltd. 14/F, C & C Building, 36 Ting Lai Road, Tai Po, N.T., Hong Kong
版次 Edition	2019 年 10 月第 1 版第 1 次印刷 © 2019 商務印書館 (香港) 有限公司 ISBN 978 962 07 0545 8 Printed in Hong Kong 版權所有 不得翻印 First Edition, First Publishing, October 2019 © 2019 The Commercial Press (H.K.) Limited ISBN 978 962 07 0545 8 Printed in Hong Kong All rights reserved.

辭典編纂者 Lexicographer

陳善偉　為明愛專上學院人文及語言學院院長及教授，歷任香港中文大學 (深圳) 人文社科學院教授，香港中文大學翻譯系教授、系主任、電腦輔助翻譯碩士課程主任及翻譯科技研究中心主任。主要研究範圍為電腦輔助翻譯、雙語辭典學及漢英翻譯。曾編輯《翻譯學百科全書》，審訂《朗文當代大辭典》、《朗文簡明漢英辭典》及撰寫《翻譯科技辭典》。漢英翻譯著作有《仁學英譯》、《紫禁城宮殿》、《近代名人手扎精選》、《饒宗頤書畫集》、《高陽小說選譯》及《中國古代印刷史圖冊》。英漢翻譯著作有《我的兒子馬友友》。著書六十一部，共八十冊。

Chan Sin-wai　is Dean and Professor of the School of Humanities and Languages of Caritas Institute of Higher Education. He was Professor in the School of Humanities and Social Sciences, The Chinese University of Hong Kong, Shenzhen, Professor and Chairman of the Department of Translation, The Chinese University of Hong Kong. He was also Director of the Master of Arts in Computer-aided Translation Programme and Director of the Centre for Translation Technology. His research interests include computer-aided translation, bilingual lexicography, and Chinese-English translation. He edited *An Encyclopaedia of Translation*, revised *Longman Dictionary of English Language and Culture (bilingual edition)* and *Longman Concise Chinese-English Dictionary* and authored *A Dictionary of Translation Technology*. His books in Chinese-English translation include *An Exposition of Benevolence, Palaces of the Forbidden City, Letters of Prominent Figures in Modern China, Paintings and Calligraphy of Jao Tsung-I, Stories by Gao Yang*, and *An Illustrated History of Printing in Ancient China*. He has also translated *My Son Yo Yo* from English into Chinese. He has, to date, published sixty-one books, in eighty volumes.

目錄 Table of Contents

字頭索引 Headword Index

注釋：所有字頭僅顯示首個頁碼，如：頁 31、32【中】。

Note: Only the first page number is shown for all headwords, for example, 【中】 on page 31 and 32.

Introduction

Reasons for preparing this dictionary

This new Cantonese-Putonghua-English dictionary, containing 2,925 headwords, over 15,000 entries, and over 490,000 characters and words, has been prepared for people who are interested in learning Chinese and English, the two major languages of the world, and Cantonese, a major dialect in southern China. It is particularly relevant to Hong Kong where the government promotes a "bilingual and triliterate" approach in administration, education, and communication.

Chinese, or to be precise, Putonghua, is a language spoken by about one fifth of the world's population as China is a vast country with a huge population. According to statistics, the number of Chinese language speakers exceeds 1.4 billion, which includes 50 million people who have Chinese as their second language. The case of English is more or less the same. Though the number of native speakers of English is much smaller than that of Chinese, English is ranked second in the world of languages in terms of speakers, totalling around 700 million in 2017. As for Cantonese, it is the major dialect in the southern part of China, with around 59 million speakers in 2017. Though Cantonese, by virtue of its designation, is the speech of Canton, present-day Guangzhou, its usage goes far beyond a single city in the Guangdong province. Cantonese nowadays generally refers to a dialect that is commonly used in Guangzhou, Hong Kong, Macau, and Cantonese-speaking communities in other parts of the world, such as Malaysia and Singapore in Southeast Asia, Toronto and Vancouver in Canada, London in the United Kingdom, and New York and San Francisco in the United States.

This dictionary therefore deals with words and expressions which might be of considerable interest to around two billion speakers of English, Putonghua, and Cantonese in the world.

Aims of this dictionary

There are several aims. First, it aims to provide multiple Putonghua (where appropriate) and English equivalents of Cantonese words and expressions so that users know how to convey what they want to say in Cantonese in either Putonghua or English or both in a number of ways. Second, as this dictionary does not aim to be a comprehensive bilingual dictionary, it focuses on indigenous Cantonese expressions, including common expressions, colloquialisms, idioms, common sayings, and end-clippers. Third, as this dictionary is educational in its approach and dictionary users include both sexes and people of all ages, vulgar or swear words in Cantonese, which are rather commonplace, have not been included.

Lexical, cultural, and phonological differences between Cantonese and Putonghua

Cantonese, a southern dialect, and Putonghua, a northern dialect and a national language, differ in many ways. As dictionaries are mainly about characters or words, phrases, and set expressions, we will discuss the differences between Cantonese and Putonghua in terms of lexical, cultural, and phonological variations. Lexical differences are about single words or compound expressions; cultural differences are about idioms; and phonological differences are closely related to transliteration systems.

Lexical differences

Lexically, Cantonese (hereafter abbreviated as (c)) differs from Putonghua (hereafter abbreviated as (p)) in fourteen ways, which deserve our attention.

(1) Cantonese retains more classical Chinese elements than Putonghua

Despite the fact that Cantonese is a southern dialect, it has retained more elements of ancient Chinese than Putonghua. In the case of verbs, 食 (c) (eat) is 吃 (p), 睇 (c) (look) is 看 (p), and 諗 (c) (think) is 想 (p). In the case of nouns, 髀 (c) (leg) is 腿 (p), and 頸 (c) (neck) is 脖子 (p). In the case of adjectives, 晏 (c) (late) is 晚 (p). In the case of pronouns, 佢 (c) (he/she/it) is 他 (p) (he/him), 她 (p) (she/her) and 它 (p) (it). In the case of measure words, 餐 (meal) is 頓 (p). In the case of conjunctions, 抑或 (c) (or) is 或者 (p), and 故此 (c) (therefore) is 所以 (p).

The Cantonese words cited above are expressions used in classical Chinese, which are no longer used in Putonghua. This shows that Cantonese retains a large number of terms which were used in classical Chinese.

(2) Cantonese words have a larger semantic scope than Putonghua words

The semantic scope of Cantonese words tends to be larger than that of Putonghua words. Take the word 扮 (p) as an example. In *A New Comprehensive Chinese-English Dictionary* (Chan 2016: page 67), 扮 is defined as: "(1) be dressed up as; disguise oneself as; dress up; play the part of; (2) put on an expression." There are six entries under the headword 扮 , including 扮戲 , 扮相 , 扮演 , 扮裝 , and 扮作 . In this dictionary, the headword 扮 (c) is defined as: "pretend", which has eight entries, including 扮串 (arrogant; vain), 扮傻 (play the fool); 扮嘢 (pretend; strike an attitude), 扮靚 (make oneself pretty), 扮豬食老虎 (wolf in sheep's clothing), 扮懵 (play the fool), 扮蟹 (act cool; pretend ignorance), and 扮蠢 (pretend ignorance; pretend to be stupid).

(3) Cantonese has more abbreviations than Putonghua

Abbreviations in Putonghua are rather formal. There are contracted forms for proper nouns, such as Zhong De 中德 (China and Germany), and common nouns, such as *ke ji* 科技 (science and technology).

Abbreviations in Cantonese are more commonly used. 西方人 (p) (Westerner) is abbreviated as 西人 (c), 游泳池 (p) (swimming pool) as 泳池 (c), and 洗衣粉 (p) (detergent powder) as 洗粉 (c).

(4) Cantonese has a larger number of coined words than Putonghua

Cantonese has a large number of words which are not found in Putonghua, such as 甲由 (c) (cockroach) 蟑螂 (p), 冚 (c) (cover) 蓋 (p), 脷 (c) (tongue) 舌頭 (p), and 嗰 (c) (that) 那 (p).

(5) Cantonese and Putonghua differ in the number of characters and word-order

Cantonese and Putonghua differ in four ways in terms of the number of characters in an expression: first, Cantonese expressions may have one character less than Putonghua expressions; second, Cantonese expressions may have one character more than Putonghua expressions; third, Cantonese expressions may vary from Putonghua expressions in one character; and fourth, the characters in Cantonese expressions and those in Putonghua expressions are in reverse order.

Cantonese expressions with one character less than Putonghua expressions

There is a large number of monosyllabic Cantonese words which are disyllabic in Putonghua. These disyllabic Putonghua expressions are normally formed by adding the suffix 子 . The following are examples: 叉 (c) (fork) （叉子） (p), 杯 (c) (cup) （杯子） (p), 釘 (c) (nail) （釘子） (p), 裙 (c) (skirt) （裙子） (p), 鞋 (c) (shoe) （鞋子） (p), 竹 (c) (bamboo) （竹子） (p), 旺 (c) (prosperous) （興旺） (p), 鏡 (c) (mirror) （鏡子） (p), 梳 (c) (comb) （梳子） (p), 被 (c) (quilt) （被子） (p), 凳 (c) (chair) （椅子） (p), (stool) （凳子） (p), 襪 (c) (socks) （襪子） (p), 珠 (c) (pearl) （珠子） (p), 葉 (c) (leaf) （葉子） (p), and 刀 (c) (knife) （刀子） (p).

There are, nevertheless, exceptions, such as 蛇 (snake), 貓 (cat), 狗 (dog), 牛 (cow), 羊 (goat), 豬 (pig), 筆 (pen), and 錶 (watch).

Another word that is often used as a substitute for 子 is the retroflex 兒 . For example, 杏 (c) (apricot) （杏兒） (p), 香味 (c) (fragrance) 香味兒 (p), 刀 (c) (knife) 刀兒 (p), 繩 (c) (rope) 繩兒 (p), 浪 (c) (wave) 浪花兒 (p), and 蟲 (c) (worm) 蟲兒 (p).

There are also common monosyllabic words in Cantonese which are often disyllabic in Putonghua. This is the case with common nouns, verbs and adjectives, either with a prefix or a suffix. Nouns with a prefix include 爆 (c) (quick fry) and 爆炒 (p), 痛 (c) (pain) 疼痛 (p), 咳 (c) (cough) 咳嗽 (p), 筍 (c) (bamboo shoot) 竹筍 (p), 雁 (c) (wild goose) and 大雁 (p), 袋 (c) (pocket) 口袋 (p), 柴 (c) (firewood) 木柴 (p), 絨 (c) (woollen cloth) 呢絨 (p), 蔗 (c) (sugarcane) 甘蔗 (p), 飯 (c) (rice) 米飯 (p), 蟻 (c) (ant) 螞蟻 (p), 蟹 (c) (crab) 螃蟹 (p), and 窿 (c) (hole) 窟窿 (p).

Nouns with a suffix include 木 (c) (wood) 木頭 , 骨 (c) (bone) 骨頭 (p), 尾 (c) (tail) 尾巴 (p), 耳 (c) (ear) 耳朵 (p), and 眼 (c) (eye) 眼睛 (p).

The following are examples of verbs. Verbs with a prefix include 累 (c) (burden) 連累 (p), and 知 (c) (know) 知道 (p). Verbs with a suffix include 曉 (c) (learn about) 曉得 (p), and 掛住 (c) (miss sb) 掛念 (p). This is also the case with adjectives. Adjectives with a prefix include 易 (c) (easy) 容易 (p), and 同 (c) (same) 相同 (p). An example of adjectives with a suffix is 孱 (c) (weak) 孱弱 (p).

Cantonese expressions with one character more than Putonghua expressions

Cantonese expressions in general have fewer characters than Putonghua. But there are exceptions, such as 交叉 (c) (cross) 叉 (p); 鴨嘴梨 (c) (pear) 鴨梨 (p), 暈車浪 (c) (carsickness) 暈車 (p), 暈船浪 (c) (seasickness) 暈船 (p), 然之後 (c) (and then) 然後 (p), 左手邊 (c) (left-hand side) 左面 (p), 右手邊 (c) (right-hand side) 右面 (p), 角落頭 (c) (corner) 角落 (p), 大笨象 (c) (elephant) 大象 (p), 抹枱布 (table-cleaning cloth) (c) 抹布 (p), and 於是乎 (c) (hence) 於是 (p).

Cantonese expressions with one character different from Putonghua expressions

There are many Cantonese words and expressions which are different from their counterparts in Putonghua in just one character. This character may appear as the first character, such as 唐裝 (c) (Chinese-style clothes) 中裝 (p), 撈麵 (c) (noodles in mixed sauces) 拌麵 (p), 青瓜 (c) (cucumber) 黃瓜 (p), 合桃 (c) (shelled walnut) 核桃 (p), and 銀包 (c) (purse) 錢包 (p). This character may occur as the last character, such as 毛冷 (c) (sheep's wool) (毛線) (p), 棉衲 (c) (cotton-packed jacket) 棉襖 (p), 塑膠 (c) (plastics) (p) 塑料 , and 指甲鉗 (c) (nail-clipper) 指甲刀 (p).

Cantonese and Putonghua expressions with semantic sameness differ in their word-order

There are Cantonese and Putonghua expressions with the same meanings but with a different word-order, such as 經已 (c) (has already) 已經 (p), 人客 (c) (guest) 客人 (p), 怪責 (c) (blame) 責怪 (p), 擠擁 (c) (crowded) 擁擠 (p), 緊要 (c) (important) 要緊 (p), and 質素 (c) (quality) 素質 (p).

(6) Cantonese tends to appear as the first word and Putonghua the second word in two-word expressions

Examples of this phenomenon include 肥 (c) and 胖 (p) in 肥胖 (fat) (p), 憎 (c) and 恨 (p) in 憎恨 (hate) (p), 憂 (c) and 愁 (p) in 憂愁 (worried) (p), and 計 (c) and 算 (p) in 計算 (calculate) (p).

(7) Cantonese and Putonghua expressions refer to the same things with different words

Different words have been used in Cantonese and Putonghua to refer to the same things. Though it is true that the different use of words is understandable, their acceptability is determined by convention and popularity. In other words, it depends on how the things are commonly expressed in Cantonese or Putonghua.

Examples of the differences in vocabulary include 滾水 (c) (boiled water) 開水 (p), 皮蛋 (c) (century egg) 松花蛋 (p), 香片 (c) (jasmine tea) 茉莉花茶 (p), 合約 (c) (contract) 合同 (p), and 水準 (c) (standard) 水平 (p).

(8) Cantonese and Putonghua homographs have different meanings

Characters written in the same way are known as homographs. They do not necessarily have the same meanings. An example of homographs is 功夫 which means 武術 (martial art) in Cantonese, but 本領 (ability) in Putonghua. Another example of homographs is 班房 , which literally means "house of detention" in Putonghua, whereas it means "classroom" in Cantonese.

(9) Cantonese has more loanwords than Putonghua

Words taken from foreign languages are loanwords. These words become neologisms in the target language, which is one major way of expanding its vocabulary and enriching the target language and culture. Cantonese, especially Cantonese spoken in Hong Kong, has been greatly influenced by English as Hong Kong was under British colonial rule for over one hundred and fifty years.

Examples of loanwords are abundant, such as 巴士 (c) (bus) 公共汽車 (p), 冧巴 (c) (number) 號碼 (p), 波 (c) (ball) 球 (p), 嘜 (c) (mark) 商標 (p), and 啤令 (c) (bearing) 軸承 (p).

(10) Cantonese and Putonghua differ in transliteration

As Cantonese and Putonghua are phonologically different, the transliteration of foreign words, mainly English words or words with Anglicised pronunciation, is different. Examples of such include sofa as 梳化 (c) and 沙發 (p), motor as 摩打 (c) and 馬達 (p), microphone as 米高峯 (c) and 麥克風 (p), and sandwich as 三文治 (c) and 三明治 (p).

(11) Cantonese and Putonghua have different ways of paraphrasing words

When transliteration cannot convey the meaning of a word or an expression in the source language, the method of paraphrasing is used. To paraphrase means free rendering of the meaning of an expression or a sentence. It also means replacing a word in the source with a group of words or phrases in the target text. Paraphrasing is a common translation technique when there are no formal equivalents.

Cantonese and Putonghua differ in paraphrasing, such as "chewing gum" is 香口膠 (c) and 口香糖 (p), "refrigerator" is 雪櫃 (c) and 冰箱 (p), and "sweater" is 冷衫 (c) and 毛衣 (p).

When paraphrasing alone cannot convey the original meaning, the method of transliteration plus paraphrasing is used, such as "motorcycle" as 電單車 (c) and 摩托車 (p), and "miniskirt" as 迷你裙 (c) and 超短裙 (p). Yet another method is to paraphrase and transliterate, such as "dining car" as 餐卡 (c) and 餐車 (p).

(12) Cantonese has more expressions with an English component than Putonghua expressions

Cantonese has a considerable number of expressions which have English components. Some Cantonese expressions start with an English word, such as "dump 時間" (kill time) 磨時間 (p). Others have an English component in the middle position, such as "發 T 騰" (frightened) 膽戰心驚 (p). Others have an English component in the final position, such as "打 tie" (wear a tie) 繫領帶 (p), "去 BBQ" (go to a barbeque) 去燒烤 (p), "低 B" (feeble-mindedness; incompetent; mental deficiency; retarded) 低能 , 愚蠢 (p), "做 facial" (have a facial) 臉部美容 (p), and "落 club" (go to a nightclub) 去夜總會 (p).

There are also Cantonese expressions which are half transliterated and half-English, such as "sale 史" (salesperson) 售貨員 (p), and "實 Q" (security guard; security personnel) 保安員 (p).

(13) Cantonese has more taboos than Putonghua

Cantonese people are in general superstitious, and they tend to use words which sound auspicious and avoid using words which have bad connotations. This being the case, a number of expressions have been changed from inauspicious to auspicious connotations. 空房 is changed to 吉房 as 空 is homophonic with 兇 (evil); 豬舌 (pig's tongue) is changed to 豬脷 as 舌 is homophonic to 蝕 (loss) and 脷 is homophonic to 利 (profit). By the same token, 通書 is changed to 通勝 as 書 sounds the same as 輸 , meaning "loss".

(14) Cantonese and Putonghua differ greatly in measure words

A measure word is a type of classifier in Chinese that is placed between a numeral and a noun to indicate the unit of the object, a linguistic feature which is characteristic of the Sino-Tibetan language family.

There are several ways to classify measure words. In terms of their formation, measure words can be of three types: (1) weights and measurements, such as 尺 (foot), 斗 (decalitre), 斤 (catty) and 畝 (one fifteenth of a hectare); (2) the way things have habitually be counted, such as 條 (piece), 張 (sheet) and 塊 (piece); (3) the way things have been contained or held, such as 碗 (bowl), 桶 (barrel) and 瓶 (bottle). In terms of their grammatical structure, measure words can be divided into: (1) simple measure words, such as 張 (sheet) and 尺 (foot); and (2) compound measure words, such as 人次 (person-time) and 架次 (sortie). In terms of their usage, Chinese measure words can be divided into two types: nominal measure words（名量詞 / 物量詞）, which refer to the ways things are counted, e.g. 一本書 (a book), 三頭牛 (three cows); and verbal measure words 動量詞 , which refer to the ways actions are counted, e.g. 說一遍 (say it again) and 走一趟 (go over once).

Cantonese and Putonghua measure words differ greatly. The following examples serve to illustrate the vast differences between them: 一口井 (c) (a well) 一眼井 (p); 一口釘 (c) (a nail) 一顆釘子 (p); 一支竹 (c) (a bamboo stick) 一根竹子 (p); 一支酒 (c) (a bottle of wine) 一瓶酒 (p); 一支針 (c) (a needle) 一根針 (p); 一支旗 (c) (a flag) 一面旗 (p); 一把梳 (c) (a comb) 一個梳子 (p); 一把秤 (c) (a steelyard) 一桿秤 (p); 一把嘴 (c) (a mouth) 一張嘴 (p); 一把聲 (c) (a voice) 一種聲音 (p); 一啉磚頭 (c) (a heap of bricks) 一堆磚頭 (p), 一嚿磚頭 (c) (a brick) 一塊磚 (p), 一舊蒜頭 (c) (a bulb of garlic) 一頭蒜 (p); and 一粒蒜頭 (c) (a clove of garlic) 一瓣蒜 (p).

Cultural differences

The cultural differences between Cantonese and Putonghua are best shown in folk sayings, which reflect to a great extent Cantonese culture and people's viewpoints. This dictionary has over 1,600 entries of Cantonese folk sayings (熟語), which can be divided into three types: idioms (成語), common sayings (俗語), and end-clippers (*xiehouyu*) (歇後語).

(1) Idioms

According to *Webster's Third New International Dictionary of the English Language*, there are several definitions of "idiom", the understanding of which can help the work of translation:

1a: the language proper or peculiar to a people or to a district, community or class;
 b: the syntactical, grammatical, or structural form peculiar to a language: the genius, habit, or cast of a language;
2: an expression established in the usage of a language that is peculiar to itself either in the grammatical construction or in having a meaning that cannot be derived as a whole from the conjoined meanings of its elements.
3: a style or form of artistic expression that is characteristic of an individual, a period or movement, or a medium or instrument.

Cantonese idioms are mostly four-character expressions whose meanings are more than the sum of the parts. The four-character idioms can be parsed into two groups. They are conventional and fixed and usually have an implicit meaning. The major sources of idioms are allusions, literary quotations and common sayings.

(2) Common sayings

Common Cantonese sayings, which have no set length or form, also include proverbs (諺語), which in general have five or seven characters, and slang (俚語), which is a type of colloquial speech with dialectical characteristics, colloquialisms (口語), and wisecracks (俏皮語). Common sayings are usually complete sentences which express a kind of attitude one takes toward life, loss, love, etc, or the mentality of a person expressed in an old or metaphorical saying, such as

做一日和尚撞一日鐘
So long as I remain a bonze, I go on tolling the bell.
老虎頭上釘虱嫲
Only fools will pin fleas on a tiger's head.

(3) End-clippers (*xiehouyu*)

End-clippers, or *xiehouyu* in Putonghua, are metaphorical folk sayings, the first part of which will lead logically or phonetically to the meaning expressed in the second part. End-clippers are used to convey intended meanings in a vivid, jovial, or satirical way.

肉包子打狗——有去無回
Pelting a dog with meat dumplings——once gone, never to return.
狗咬呂洞賓——不識好人心
Like the dog that bit Lu Dongbin——you bite the hand that feeds you.

Sources of Cantonese common sayings

Cantonese sayings come from a number of sources, which include historical stories, such as 事後孔明 (be wise after an event); fables, such as 姜太公封神——漏咗自己 (leave out oneself); symmetrical structures, such as ABCD 甜酸苦辣 (all the sweet and bitter experiences of life) and 酒色財氣 (wine, sex, money, and power), and ACBD 七零八落 (in disorder); partially symmetrical structures, such as AABB 凹凹凸凸 (bumpy; full of bumps and holes; full of lumps; lumpy; rough; scraggy, uneven) and 混混噩噩 (ignorant; muddle-headed; without a clear aim), AABC 官官相衞 (devils help devils), and ABCC 官仔骨骨 (well-dressed); antithetical structures, such as 三長兩短 (die; unexpected misfortune that results in death) and 三衰六旺 (ups and downs of life); alliteration, such as 玲 (ling) 瓏 (lung) 浮凸 (curvaceous); assonance, such as 冇厘搭 (daap) 霎 (saap) (unreliable; irresponsible); juxtaposition of synonyms, such as 知書識禮 (educated and polite); juxtaposition of antonyms, such as 山高水低 (unexpected misfortune); similes, such as 穩如泰山 (as firm as Mount Tai); and famous sayings, such as 天網恢恢，疏而不漏 (justice has long arms).

Culture reflected by Cantonese idioms and common sayings

It is often said that language and culture are two sides of the same coin. Idioms are condensed and concise sayings that reflect the various cultures of a locality. What then is culture? According to *The American Heritage Dictionary*, culture is the totality of socially transmitted behaviour patterns, arts, beliefs, institutions and all other products of human work and thought characteristic of a community or population. Burton Raffel (1988: 3) says that "Culture is a basic aspect of human existence, a set of ways of living specific to a group of human beings and usually passed by them from generation to generation". Culture therefore can mean (1) a general process of intellectual, spiritual, and aesthetic development; (2) a particular way of life, whether of a people, a period or a group; (3) works and practices of intellectual and especially artistic activity, such as music, literature, painting, and film.

Culture in idioms will be discussed according to the definitions given above and related topics in alphabetical order.

Human characteristics

There are many sayings which are related to human characteristics. In this section, they will be grouped according to human characteristics as a whole and body parts. The former refers to ability, achievement, action, age, appearance, manners, personality, death, education, effort, experience, family, fortune, misfortune, friendships, gains and losses, health, jobs, life, livelihood, marriage, dealing with matters, popularity, power, practice, relationships, responsibility, retribution, resources, trouble, wealth and work, whereas body parts will be discussed in a top-down fashion from head to toe, or to be exact, from hair to nail.

Ability

Ability is highly prized in Cantonese culture. A capable person is described as one who has 三頭六臂 (three heads and six arms, meaning extraordinarily able or very capable). For people with comparable abilities, they are 半斤八兩 (as broad as it is long; fifty-fifty; half a pound of one and eight ounces of the other; much of a muchness; not much to choose between the two; nothing to choose between the two; six of one and half a dozen of the other; tweedledum and tweedledee; well-match in ability), or 你有半斤，我有八兩 (six of one and half a dozen of the other). For people who have different kinds of ability to show off, they are described as 八仙過海——各顯神通 (each displays their ability; each has their merits; try to outshine each other; vie with each other). Leaders are admired as 蛇無頭不行 (without a person in the lead, all the others move no farther). It is also true that everyone vies to be a leader (行船爭解纜 take the lead), and the existence of more than one leader is not a desirable situation (一山不能藏二虎 at daggers drawn).

But there are also people who are not so capable and are known as 空心老倌 (a person without real ability and learning; gorgeous in appearance but inwardly insubstantial). They lack the ability to do anything (有心無力 be unable to do what one wants to do), or defend themselves (有招架之功，無還手之力 can only ward off blows) as they do not have any special skills (周身刀冇張利 jack-of-all-trades, master of none).

Achievement

Achievers are always admired. People respect those who achieve through hard work (白手興家 achieve success in life with one's own hands; start from scratch). They believe that if one works hard, one can be outstanding in any trade (行行出狀元), or they would become 高不成，低不就 (neither fit for a higher position nor willing to take a lower one). Achievers respect achievers (識英雄重英雄 like knows like), and the offsprings of achievers are equally outstanding (虎父無犬子 like father, like son).

Action

Action can be slow or quick, proper or improper, decisive or indecisive. If action is preemptive, then it is said to be 先下手為強 (catch the ball before the rebound), 先斬後奏 (act before reporting), or 先禮後兵 (a dog often barks before it bites). Some believe that perhaps it would be best not to 打草驚蛇 (wake a sleeping dog).

Things should be done quickly as it is believed that 執輸行頭，慘過敗家 (it would be disadvantageous not to take an immediate action in time). There are idioms that describe hurried actions, such as 一扑一碌 (in a great hurry), 三扒二撥 (hurry through; in no time at all), 左騰右騰 (rushing about), 鈴鈴霖霖 (in a big hurry), 滾水淥腳 (go quickly; hurry off), 趕頭趕命 (in a great hurry), 頻頻倫倫 (in great hurry), 臨急臨忙 (in a great rush), 臨時臨急 (at the last moment; be hard pressed for time), 騰上騰落 (rush around), 頻倫唔得入城 (more haste, less speed), and 裙拉褲甩 (in a great hurry).

Things could be done slowly (他他條條 go easy; 咪咪嚀嚀 very slow and clumsy; 姿姿整整 dally; dawdle; move slowly), instantly (打鐵趁熱 strike the iron while it is hot), promptly (撇撇脫脫 prompt in action), decisively (快刀斬亂麻 take decisive action). But actions done recklessly are mocked as 盲頭烏蠅，亂碰亂闖 (act like blind flies; act helter-skelter; act in a chaotic manner), or 橫衝直撞 (collide in every direction). Actions done stealthily are 偷偷摸摸 (act stealthily).

There are a number of expressions on clumsiness in action 論論盡盡 (very clumsy), usually with the metaphor of hands and feet, such as 笨手笨腳 (stumblebum), 粗手粗腳 (have clumsy fingers), 雞手鴨腳 (clumsy; have two left feet), 姐手姐腳 (clumsy because she is not accustomed in doing heavy work), and 陀手唔腳 (clumsy).

Action in a negative form could result in fighting (五行欠打 deserve a beating; 五行欠炳 deserve a scolding). Internecine fighting is described as 狗咬狗骨 (fighting among members of the same group; put up an internecine fight). Fighting is sometimes provoked (撩是鬥非 provoke a fight; stir up a quarrel; sow the seeds of discord). When there is a fight, the one who is beaten could be in a very bad shape, so much so that one could be 打到阿媽都唔認得 (get so badly beaten up that not even his mum can recognise him) or 打到豬頭咁 (be beaten to the shape of a pig's head, which means being beaten severely). There is also an amusing saying that comes probably from boxing circles: 後備拳師——聽打 (substitute boxer——waiting to be beaten, meaning sb who is waiting to be beaten by others).

Advantages/disadvantages

Advantages and disadvantages, or pros or cons, are of concern to people. There are naturally advantages and disadvantages, 有一利必有一害 (no rose without a thorn). One can gain an initial advantage (飲頭啖湯 gain the initial advantage), which should not be accompanied by a disadvantage (食砒霜土狗 at a disadvantage before gaining an advantage). Or one can be at a disadvantage accompanied by an advantage (除笨有精 problems apart, there are still advantages to a particular activity).

It is thought that advantages can be obtained through a person, which is known as 借艇割禾 (to borrow a boat for harvest, meaning to make use of sb to profit oneself). Proximity, however, is not the best guarantee of getting an advantage, which is expressed by the idiom 蜑家雞——見水唔飲得 (the Tanka chicken——sees water but can't drink it, which refers to the person who fails to obtain an advantage in spite of being in a favourable position), and 幡竿燈籠——照遠唔照近 (丈八燈台——照遠不照近 benefit any other person than close ones).

Advice

People need advice from time to time. There are people who offer good advice (循循善導 good at giving methodical and patient guidance; lead one gradually into good practices; teach with skill and patience; lead sb gradually and patiently on the right path). The elderly, with their rich experience, could also give good advice to people, which explains why there is an idiom 家有一老, 如有一寶 (an old-timer in the family is an advisor of rich experience). Good advice could be offered in a sincere way (苦口婆心 exhort sb repeatedly with good intentions; words importunate but heart compassionate), and it could bring good results (一言驚醒夢中人 a person suddenly becomes clear-minded upon listening to a word of wisdom; give a wise word to a fool).

There are also people whose advice is not acceptable, and they are known as 紅鬚軍師 (mis-advisor; thoughtless advisor) and 蠱蟲師爺 (a person who always offers bad solutions to problems; a person who is caught in his own trap).

The decision to take or not to take advice from others rests with the recipients. When they do not take others' advice, it is 借咗聾陳隻耳 (turn a deaf ear to sb) or 亞聾送殯──唔聽枝死人笛 (turn a deaf ear to sb).

Age

It is noted that idioms on age have a lot to do with old age and little to do with youth. Of all the six idioms on age, all are on the elderly people, which include 七老八十 (aged; elderly; in one's seventies or eighties; live to a great age; old), 恃老賣老 (act like a Dutch uncle; flaunt one's seniority) or alternatively 倚老賣老 (act like a Dutch uncle; flaunt one's seniority), 寧欺白鬚公, 莫欺鼻涕蟲 (a colt may make a good horse), 老人成嫩仔 (once a man and twice a child), and 人老心不老 (young in spirit for one's old age).

What deserves mentioning is that some elderly people attempt to learn new skills at an old age (臨老學吹打 an old dog begins to learn new tricks; an old man learning a new skill) without any concern about success or failure.

Appearance

In Cantonese, a tall person is described as 牛高馬大 (tall as an ox and big as a horse; stand like a giant; tall and big; well-grown), 神高神大 (tall and big as a god; well-built), or 肥屍大隻 (strongly-built; big as a corpse). A short person is described as 矮矮細細 (short and small); a strong person as 銅皮鐵骨 (iron constitution; brass muscles and iron bones; strong and solid body; tough and strong as iron and steel; with vigorous skin and bones and strong muscles); a fat person as 肥肥白白 (fair and plump) and 腰圓背厚 (plump); a skinny person as 奀挑鬼命 (extremely skinny and frail), 膊頭高過耳 (one's shoulders are above one's ears; skinny), 膝頭大過髀 (one's knees are bigger than one's thighs; very skinny); and a woman with a good figure as 玲瓏浮凸 (curvaceous).

Appearance also refers to how one looks. People who look alike are 一模一樣 (be exactly alike). People with devilish looks are 兇神惡煞 (fiendish and devilish; look furious). People who look miserable are 苦口苦面 (look bitter), or 苦瓜乾咁嘅面口 (a face of a dried balsam pear, meaning a face of woe). People who look vulgar are 頭尖額窄 (person with a pointed face and a narrow forehead looks vulgar). People who look out of sorts are 冇厘神氣 (looking out of sorts). People who look stealthy are 賊眉賊眼 (look like a thief).

There are also people who have impressive looks (係威係勢 look impressive; 大模斯樣 haughty) or affected looks (裝模作樣 pretend to be a know-it-all). What appears to be imposing may not be equally so inside, just like 繡花枕頭 (embroidered pillow──beautiful in appearance but lacking inner talent), 屎坑關刀──聞唔聞得, 武唔武得 (sword in a shit pit──having imposing looks but useless). Some people are more concerned about looks than health (愛靚唔愛命 be more concerned about looking good than being healthy).

In Chinese society, much importance is attached to dressing up oneself to look impressive as people tend to focus on what one wears (先敬羅衣後敬人 people usually open doors to fine clothes), which explains the saying 人要衣裝, 佛要金裝 (humans need fine clothing as Buddha needs to be gilded, meaning fine feathers make fine birds).

People who are dressed up are described as 身光頸靚 (dressed up and look sharp) and 官仔骨骨 (well dressed as an official). When one wears shabby clothes, then one is 爛身爛世 (looks torn in shabby clothes) and 賣花姑娘插竹葉 (the girl selling flowers adorns herself with a bamboo leaf, meaning a tailor makes the man but he dresses himself in rags). A dress does not always make the person look gorgeous, for there is a saying 着起龍袍唔似太子 (a beggar in a dress-suit still looks like a beggar). Sometimes, a dressed-up person may not have anywhere to go (喺門角落頭燒炮仗 set off firecrackers in a corner, meaning one is all dressed up but has nowhere to go).

Behaviour

We will divide Cantonese idioms into idioms on good and bad behaviour.

Good behaviour

Idioms on good behaviour are few and far between.

(1) By example

Sometimes we act by following what others do (有樣學樣 follow a bad example; 入鄉隨俗 , 出水隨灣 do in Rome as the Romans do), or what others own (年晚煎堆 —— 人有我有 jian dui at year's end —— to possess the same as others do). But what should be avoided is to follow a bad example (上樑唔正下樑歪 those below will follow the bad example set by those above).

(2) Help

It is always commendable to look after one's own business without seeking help from others (求人不如求己 applying to others for help is not as good as applying to oneself; 馬死落地行 when your horse dies you walk on your own —— to have to get oneself through a difficulty without help). When offering help to others, sometimes we help them by 睇頭睇尾 (see the beginning and the end —— lending a hand), and we should 為人為到底 (when one helps others, help them to the end). What is to be avoided is to seek help in extreme urgency (臨急抱佛腳 / 急時抱佛腳 hug Buddha's feet in emergency —— to seek help at the last moment).

(3) Propriety

We say one's behaviour is good when action is done in a proper way (有分有寸 know what to do; 行得正 , 企得正 act in a totally proper manner; play fair and square; 安份守己 abide by laws and behave oneself well).

Bad behaviour

Bad behaviour are abundant and are listed below in alphabetical order for discussion.

(1) Bullying

Cantonese society, as with all other societies, is full of bullies, whose behaviour is described by idioms such as 恃勢欺人 (abuse one's power and bully the people), 欺善怕惡 (bully the good people, fear the evil ones), 蝦蝦霸霸 (bully; bully and humiliate), 橫行霸道 (play the bully), and 聲大夾惡 (a bully is loudmouthed). Even strong people from other places will be bullied by the local people, as expressed by the idioms 龍游淺水遭蝦戲 (when a dragon swims in shallow water it is bullied by shrimps —— no man is a hero to his valet) and 虎落平陽被犬欺 (when a tiger goes downhill to flat land it will be bullied by a dog —— out of one's sphere of influence, out of one's power).

(2) Cheating

People cheat others by 呃呃騙騙 (deceive; cheat), 呃神騙鬼 (deceive both gods and ghosts —— lure sb into a trap), 招搖撞騙 (put on a good bluff), 偷呃拐騙 (steal, cheat, kidnap, and swindle) and (一味靠滾 always rely on cheating). Their tactics include 隻手遮天 (cover the sky with one hand —— hide the truth from the masses; hoodwink the public; pull the wool over the eyes of the public) and 掛羊頭賣狗肉 (hang out a sheep's head when what one is selling is dog's meat——swindle others by making false claims). People who have been cheated have the feeling of being taken in by swindlers (畀人賣豬仔 be transported overseas and sold as coolies——be cheated and taken advantage of by others; 呃鬼食豆腐 coax a ghost to eat tofu——cheat sb into the belief), but the fact is cheating can never last long as the truth will be revealed in time (風水佬呃你十年八年，唔呃得一世 a fengshui master can deceive you for eight to ten years but not for life——time can witness to a fact).

People who cheat will pick those who could be easily deceived, such as friends (黃皮樹了哥——唔熟唔食 / 黃皮樹了哥——熟嗰個食嗰個 the crested myna on a wampi tree only eats those pieces of wampi fruit that are ripe——the person who swindles money out of his friends) and the ignorant (低頭切肉，把眼看人 choose a pigeon to cheat). What is most interesting is that sometimes swindlers swindle swindlers and they gain nothing from their cheating tactics (光棍遇着冇皮柴 a bachelor meets with barkless firewood——a swindler takes in a swindler; 銅銀買病豬——大家偷歡喜 buy a sick pig with gold and silver——each of the two hugs himself on having cheated the other).

(3) Gambling
Cantonese people, and the Chinese people on the whole, like gambling despite the fact it is considered a bad thing. One might 盡地一煲 (risk everything on one bet), and believe that it would be 有殺冇賠 (net profits without any loss). But in gambling, it is always 十賭九輸 (nine out of ten cases lose in gambling), like what is said in an end-clipper (*xiehouyu*) 秀才手巾——包書（輸）(stand to lose).

This is also the case with playing mahjong, a popular form of gambling for Cantonese people. It is said that 食頭糊，輸甩褲 (the first game winner in player mahjong will be the biggest loser in the end) and 衰家食尾糊 (the unlucky mahjong player wins the last game).

(4) Laziness
Another behaviour which is considered bad is laziness. Idioms related to laziness are numerous, such as 死蛇爛蟮 (like a dead snake and rotten eel——(1) too lazy to stir a finger; (2) lazy person, 懶到出汁 (one is so lazy that one leaks juice——be extremely lazy), 懶懶散散 (languid; lethargic; listless), 懶人多屎尿 (a lazy person has more faeces and urine——a lazybone cooks up many lame excuses), 眼眉毛長過辮 (one's eyebrow is longer than one's braid——not to stir a finger; very lazy), 好食懶飛 (eat but do nothing; eat one's head off; lazy), and the end-clipper (*xiehouyu*) 四方木——踢一踢，郁一郁 (a wooden man never moves without a rush on it; lazybones).

(5) Lust
In Cantonese, being lustful is bad as lustful men are 滾紅滾綠 (lecherous). They grope women (摸身摸勢 grope a woman) and show their lustful manner (飛擒大咬 take a big bite——show one's lustful manner).

Another aspect of lust is womanising. Those who womanise are known as 花心大少 (playboy), 花心蘿蔔 (playboy), or 花花公子 (dandy; playboy).

Yet another aspect of lust is sexual attraction (神魂顛倒 be out of one's head; 暈晒大浪 fall under sb's spell; 放路溪錢——引死人 money put on the street for the dead——very attractive).

(6) Obstructive behaviour
There are people who act to obstruct others from achieving their goals. Their behaviour is 刁橋扭擰 (deliberately create obstructions for sb), 阻頭阻勢 (decline with all sorts of excuses; fob sb off with excuses; get in the way; give the runaround; make excuses and put obstacles in the way), or 阻手阻腳 (a hindrance to sb; a nuisance to sb; an encumbrance to sb; cumbersome; cumbrous; get in the way of sb; hinder; impede; in the way; obstructive; one too many; stand in sb's way; stand in the way of). People may even occupy a position just to stop others from getting it (生人霸死地 a living person occupies land for the dead——block the path of others).

(7) Pretence
There is no lack of idioms on pretence in Cantonese, such as 詐詐帝帝 (feign; pretend), 詐傻扮懵 (act stupid; play the fool), 裝傻扮懵 (play the fool), 賊喊捉賊 (a thief crying "stop the thief"), 整古做怪 (wrap sth in mystery),

整色整水 (put on a show; put on an act), 扮豬食老虎 (play a pig to eat a tiger——feign ignorance; play the fool; pretend to be a fool but to be actually very clever), 貓哭老鼠——假慈悲 (a cat crying over a rat——shed crocodile tears), and 豉油撈飯——整色整水 (eat rice with soya sauce——put on a show; put on an act).

(8) Stealing

Stealing may be done secretly, as in 順手牽羊 (go on the scamp; make away with sth), or become a habit hard to kick off, as expressed by the idiom 細時偷針，大時偷牛 (young pilferer, old robber). Cantonese has idioms about stealthy behaviour, such as 鬼鬼鼠鼠 (like ghosts and rats——furtive; sneaky; stealthy). We should, however, note that 若要人不知，除非己莫為 (there are eyes even in the dark; what is done by night will appear by day).

Personality

The character of a person is determined by birth (三歲定八十 the child is father to the man), unless there is a change of character for a reason (亞崩養狗——轉性 have a change of nature). Otherwise, there is no way to change a person's character (死性不改 as stubborn as a mule; not change for the better). There is also a saying that when one becomes rich, one should start to cultivate one's character (發財立品 cultivate one's character when one becomes rich).

There are several traits in one's character which are considered to be good, including forgiveness, good temper, honesty, integrity, patience, and straightforwardness. People who are forgiving are generous (大人有大量 an important person is forgiving). People who are good-tempered can easily get along with people (隔夜油炸鬼 a fried dough stick which is put aside overnight——good-tempered person). Honest people are those who remain honest in whatever situation they are in (擔屎都唔偷食 won't eat the faeces that one is carrying with a pole—— very honest), but they might end up in poverty (忠忠直直，終須乞食 an honest person will end up begging for their livelihood). People with integrity can stand severe tests (真金不怕洪爐火，石獅不怕雨滂沱 real gold can be tested by fire and a stone lion can stand the test of heavy rain——a person of integrity can stand severe tests). Patient people are praiseworthy (百忍成金 patience is a plaster for all sores). People who are straightforward do not mince their words (該釘就釘，該鐵就鐵 call a spade a spade). What is so special about people with good character is that they remain composed in spite of what happens (修游淡定 calm and composed; 滋油淡定 calm; not panic; slow coach; 滋滋油油 unhurriedly; 定過抬油 be completely composed; have full confidence in; have the game in one's hands).

People with a bad personality, on the other hand, are said to be 縮頭烏龜 (a tortoise hiding its head——a coward), 惡死能登 (ferocious; harsh; vicious), 狼過華秀隻狗 (more fierce than Wah Sau's dog——very ferocious), 炮仗頸——一點就着 (be ignited easily like the neck of a firecracker——being hot-tempered), 唔三唔四 (immoral in character; neither fish, flesh nor fowl), 死牛一便頸 (stick to one's guns; stubborn), 死雞撐飯蓋 (dead chicken still props up the lid of a rice pot——being shabby-genteel), and 生蟲拐杖——靠唔住 (a rail made of rotten rushes——a broken reed; unreliable).

Death

Human beings know that life will come to an end when death knocks at the door. Since some Cantonese people still regard the mention of death as a taboo, a number of end-clippers have been used to make indirect references to death, which explains why death idioms are somewhat different from other idioms.

The Cantonese dialect has idioms expressing the idea of death as being the end of a life journey, such as 大限難逃 (meet one's fate; pay one's debt to nature), 生死有命 (life and death are predestined; every bullet has its billet), 三長兩短 (unexpected misfortune that results in death), and 賣鹹鴨蛋 (sell salted duck eggs——die; pass away). People may die one after another, which is like 豬欄報數——又一隻 (count off at the pigpen——another one again, meaning one more has died), or a long time ago (骨頭打鼓 bones drumming——died a long time ago), but no one can 死過番生 (be saved from death), saving the ritual of 擔幡買水 (carry the hearse and escort a funeral).

For people who are about to die, they are described as 聞見棺材香 (smell the coffin——at death's door; have one's foot in the grave), 條命凍過水 (one's life is colder than water——be in danger), 劏豬櫈——上嚟就死 (a fat pig going to the butchery——sure to die), 浮頭魚——死梗 (taking poison and hanging oneself——sure to die), 老虎頭上釘蝨乸——自尋死路 (pin a flea on a tiger's head; bread the lion in his den; defy the mighty; offend powerful people; provoke a powerful person; provoke sb far superior in power), 雞春砍石頭 (like an egg dashing itself against a rock——courting destruction), and 獵狗終須山上喪 (a hound will eventually die on the hill——he who plays with fire will get burned at last).

There are also situations in which people court death, such as 激死老豆搵山拜 (unfilial son who infuriates his father to death is only looking for a tomb to sweep), 壽星公吊頸——嫌命長 (Old Man of the South Pole hanging himself——tempt one's fate), 閻羅王探病——問你死未 (drive sb to his death; like the King of Hell dispatching invitation cards), 棺材舖拜神——想人死啫嘛 (gritting one's teeth in a coffin shop——laying a curse upon all who are not dying), 水浸眼眉——唔知死 (a tortoise eating croton-oil seeds——unaware of the death ahead), and 老鼠拉鯰魚——一命搏一命 (a mouse tugging at a catfish——risking one's life).

People can end their lives in different ways, such as 攬住一齊死 (end in common ruin), 送羊入虎口 (a lamb to the tiger's mouth; put sb to death), 借刀殺人 (murder with a borrowed knife), 食咗人隻車 (take the wind out of sb's sails), and 橫死掂死 (it doesn't make any difference either way). People may die in discontent, such as 死唔眼閉 (die without closing one's eyes; turn in one's grave), or 剝皮田雞——死都唔閉眼 (skinned frog——die without closing one's eyes). Sometimes even death cannot expiate our crimes (死有餘辜 death would not expiate all one's crimes).

Education

Education in China and likewise in Guangdong has been based on Confucian teachings. People are trained to be educated and well-mannered (知書識禮), and it is believed that education can change one's destiny (一命二運三風水，四積陰德五讀書 fate first, luck second, fengshui third, virtue fourth, education fifth).

Education must start young, like 初歸心抱，落地孩兒 (bend a tree while it is still young), and there are people who simply cannot be changed through education (爛泥扶唔上壁 bad mud can't be plastered on walls——people of bad character will not be able to change). Home education is also important, otherwise it would become 有爺生無乸教 (have parents but have no parental guidance; lack home education). Lastly, no matter how educated one is, one should never 喺孔夫子面前賣文章 (show off one's writing in front of Confucius——teach one's grandmother how to suck eggs).

Effort

People make enormous efforts to get what they want (出盡八寶 have exerted one's utmost skill). Sometimes, one needs to make very little effort (慳水慳力 save money and effort) to achieve one's goal. It can be as easy as asking for fire (易過借火). At other times, much effort is needed, like 拉牛上樹 (pull an ox up a tree——a vain attempt to do sth), 拉拉扯扯 (prevaricate), 沬水舂牆 (go through fire and water), and 二叔婆養豬——夠晒好心機 (grandaunt rearing pigs——having so much patience; sitting on a pit to count sesame seeds——it requires meticulous work). With such efforts, we can 鐵杵磨成針 (grind an iron pestle into a needle; little strokes fell great oaks) and 燈芯擰成鐵 (a wick can be wringed until it becomes an iron rod; a straw shows its weight when it is carried a long way).

If anything goes wrong, sometimes it would be impossible to make changes (船到江心補漏遲 it is too late to repair the boat when it reaches the middle of a river; it is too late to mend), and all our efforts will be lost (前功盡廢 all efforts go down the drain). Or others can enjoy what we have achieved without sweating (開埋井俾人食水 you drill the well but others simply take the water), which can be compared to 牛耕田馬食穀——父賺錢仔享福 (the father earns, the son spends).

Experience

Experience is closely related to age. One who has seen much of the world (經風雨，見世面 brave the storm and face the world), 食鹽多過食飯，行橋多過行路 (eat more salt than rice and walk on more bridges than roads——have seen more elephants), which explains why 人老精，鬼老靈 (humans become smarter and ghosts have greater power when they age; experience teaches).

Experience has to be gone through, just like 唔同床唔知被爛 (only those on the same bed know the quilt is torn) and 唔見過鬼都唔怕黑 (ones dreads darkness after seeing a ghost). We should bear in mind, however, that experience can fail, which is described by the idiom 老貓燒鬚 (an old cat has her whisker burnt; a good horse stumbles) and the saying 盲拳打死老師傅 (a poor hand may put the old master to death).

Family

Family is an important pillar of a society. Harmony in a family is essential (家和萬事興 harmony makes a family prosperous). Family life centers around home, and people feel strongly attached to home (龍床唔似狗竇 an emperor's bed is not as good as a dog's den——there is no place sweeter than home). When there is any dispute between or among members of a family (相見好，同住難 it's nice to see each other from time to time; but to live together is difficult; familiarity breeds contempt), even a judge could not help (清官難審家庭事 outsiders find it hard to understand the cause of a family quarrel; 家家有本難唸的經 each and every family has its own problems). When one is away from home, one always wants to return home, for 樹高千丈，落葉歸根 (no matter how tall a tree is, its fallen leaves return to its root——whether it is east or west, home is the best).

Family background is also crucial. Some are born rich (身嬌肉貴 come from a rich family), and they are considered to be born with a good fate (條命生得正). When one is successful in their career, people always say 英雄莫問出處 (no need to ask a hero his family background; not every great person was born with a silver spoon in his/her mouth), for talents do not have to come from a rich family.

A house is where a family lives (有瓦遮頭 have a place to live). If there is not enough space for everyone to have a room to stay, then a foldable bed would be used (朝行晚拆 a bed set up in the morning and dismantled at the evening; 朝拆晚行 a bed set up at the evening and dismantled in the morning). There are all sorts of things needed to run a family, including pots and bottles (砂煲罌罉 pots and bottles) and other necessities (柴米油鹽醬醋茶 firewood, rice, oil, salt, soya sauce, vinegar, and tea). And there are all sorts of things to do (家頭細務 household chores).

Fortune/misfortune

It is believed that fortunes change (世界輪流轉 everybody has the turn of the wheel; fortunes change; 風水輪流轉 every dog has his day; fortunes change). Fortune will not be with one forever (人無千日好 no person is fortunate forever; 人有三衰六旺 a person suffers misfortunes and other times strokes of good fortune). Sometimes, you have fortune (行運一條龍 fortunes come one after another; 神主牌都會郁 even a memorial tablet moves——meet with one's fortune). At other times, you have misfortune (山高水低 tall hills and low water——unexpected misfortune; 冬瓜豆腐 winter gourd and tofu——die; 行運一條龍，失運一條蟲 a person in luck walks heavy but a person out of luck cowers with humility; 黑過墨斗 blacker than a chalk box-have bad luck; 風吹芫荽——衰 (垂) 到貼地 winds blowing the coriander——reach the pitch of bad fortune). And misfortune never comes singly (行路打倒褪 when one is luckless one walks backward——fortunes never come singly; 屋漏兼逢夜雨 it never rains but pours; misfortunes never come singly), and everybody has their fortune and misfortune (同遮唔同柄，同人唔同命 the same group of people have different lot; 同人唔同命，同遮唔同柄 no man has the same fortune; no two people's fate is the same).

As fortune or misfortune is with one all the time, it is the way one deals with it that matters. Nobody likes misfortune (唔怕米貴，至怕運滯 not afraid of the price of rice going up, but afraid of being unlucky; 亞駝賣蝦米——大家都唔掂 a humpback sells dried shrimps——all play in hard luck). The sooner one overcomes misfortune, the better (大步躂過 escape from misfortune). It would be good if one has others to stand against misfortune (有福同享，有禍同當 for better or for worse; go through thick and thin together). People believe that when misfortune goes away, fortune will come (終須有日龍穿鳳 every cloud has a silver lining; every dog has his day; 大難不死，必有後福 one's escape from death will certainly bring one good fortune), and one might have an unexpected stroke of good fortune (跛腳鷯哥自有飛來蜢 a lame hill myna will have grasshopers fly to him——God tempers the wind to the shorn lamb; 冷手執個熱煎堆 a cold hand picks a hot deep-fried sesame ball——have an unexpected stroke of good fortune). But one's good wishes would not apply to one's enemies (幸災樂禍 chuckle at sb's discomfiture or misfortune; 攞景定贈慶 take advantage of one's vulnerability; 頭髮尾浸浸涼 ends of hair feeling cool——gloat over sb's enemy's misfortune).

Friendships

A person is judged by the company he or she keeps. This is very much the case with the Cantonese people (未觀其人，先觀其友 you can judge a person by the friends they keep). Friends with similar interests get together easily (物以類聚 birds of a feather flock together) and closely (筲箕冚鬼——一窩神 ghosts covered by a winnow basket——a basket of gods, meaning to be hand and glove with each other). This is particularly true with bad companions (豬朋狗友 pig and dog friends——bad companions) and when you have money to spend (有酒有肉多兄弟 a heavy purse makes friends come).

Strangers (三九唔識七 numbers three and nine know not number seven——be a stranger to each other; 三唔識七 number three knows not number seven——strangers) can become friends easily due to one's character (單料銅煲 thin copper pot——the person who instantly makes friends with a stranger; 人夾人緣 whether people get along with one another or not depends on the compatibility of their characters; 曹操都有知心友，關公亦有對頭人 a devil has friends to support with and a saint has foes worthy of his steel), and through discord (唔打唔相識 no discord, no concord; no fight, no acquaintance; 不打不相識 build up friendship after an exchange of blows). Friends are to be treasured as they could help one when one is in predicament (患難見真情 a friend in need is a friend indeed), or away from home (在家靠父母，出外靠朋友 at home, you rely on parents; away from home, you rely on friends).

Gains and losses

Cantonese people take gains and losses rather philosophically. It would certainly be ideal if both or all parties win (一家便宜兩家着 both sides benefit; win-win situation), everything comes off well (掂過碌蔗 come off well; really good; 實食冇黐牙 all eaten without having some stick to the teeth——sure win), with everyone getting what they want (得償所願 attain one's end; obtain one's heart's desire; 盤滿缽滿 full to the brim).

People certainly know that efforts are needed to get what one wants (力不到不為財 no pain, no gain). One might be able to do that because of one's favourable position (近廚得食 you get things to eat if you are near the kitchen, meaning being in a favourable position to gain advantage). One might have to lose before one gains (小財唔出，大財唔入 an empty hand is no lure for a hawk; nothing venture, nothing gain; 跌咗個橙，執番個桔 you drop an orange but pick up a mandarin orange; lose at sunrise and gain at sunset; 未見官先打三十大板 before seeing the official one is hit with a rod thirty times; suffer a loss before the gain; 未見其利，先見其害 suffer a loss before an uncertain gain) and one should be content with what one can get (邊有咁大隻蛤乸隨街跳 a big toad won't be seen jumping on the street——good cheap is dear; 得些好意須回手 stop before going too far; 密食當三番 a lot of small gains is as good as one big gain).

It is not advisable to be too aggressive (得寸進尺 give sb an inch and they will take a mile), for very often, one's loss is much greater than one's gain (因小失大 spoil a ship for a halfpenny worth of tar; 賺粒糖，蝕間廠 for gaining a cube of sugar you lost a whole factory; while seeking a small gain, one could suffer a big loss; 執到襪帶累身家 lose a pound for gaining a penny; 滾水淥豬腸——兩頭縮 boil a pig's intestines——both ends shrink, meaning to become less; lose out on both sides; 水瓜打狗——唔見咗一撅 to beat a dog with a water melon——part of it will disappear; half of sth is lost; 盲佬貼符——倒貼 not getting but giving away money). What is most undesirable would be to suffer a great loss (損手爛腳 bruise one's hands and feet——suffer heavy losses; 鈴鈴鎈鎈都丟埋 meet with a crushing defeat; 筲箕打水——一場空 draw water with a sieve; 阿聾燒炮仗——散晒 a deaf person sets off firecrackers——all go apart, meaning to meet with a failure; 坑渠浸死鴨 a duck gets drowned in a ditch——fail miserably in a very easy task).

It may offer one some comfort to call the person who incurs losses 倒米壽星 (person who causes others to suffer losses; person who stands in his own light), or console oneself with the words 羊毛出在羊身上 (whatever is given is paid for), 針冇兩頭利 (a needle can't be pointed at both ends——one cannot have it both ways; there's no rose without a thorn), 留得青山在, 哪怕冇柴燒 (no need to worry about having no firewood when the mountain is still there; life is safe and gains will surely be safe), 一眼針冇兩頭尖 (a needle can't be pointed at both ends; sugar cane is never sweet at both ends——one cannot have it both ways). To others, what one is actually doing is 跌倒捯番揸沙 (one falls down but still grabs a handful of sand——put one's fault in the right side) or 偷雞唔倒蝕揸米 (lost a handful of rice without stealing a chicken——end up with nothing; go for wool and come back shorn).

Health

Everyone wants to enjoy good health (身壯力健 have a strong body; in good health; in vigorous health). Illness, nevertheless, is unavoidable. If one has a chronic disease, it will make one a doctor (久病成醫 prolonged illness makes a doctor of a patient).

Symptoms of illness include vomiting and diarrhea (又屙又嘔), headaches (頭痛發燒), and pain in the neck and shoulder (頸梗膞痛). In treating these illnesses, a doctor should not cure only the symptoms, but also the illnesses (頭痛醫頭, 腳痛醫腳 treat the head when the head aches, treat the foot when the foot hurts——take a defensive stopgap measure; sporadic and piecemeal steps; take only palliative measures for one's illness).

In treating illnesses, patients would be unlucky if they are treated by a doctor who treats them slowly (急驚風遇着慢郎中 meet with a slow doctor when having an urgent illness). Doctors would be lucky if they cure a patient who has almost recovered before treatment (行運醫生醫病尾 a lucky doctor cures a patient who is in the last stage of recovery).

Job

A job is needed to maintain one's livelihood. When one is employed, one has to work hard to complete one's tasks (受人二分四 work as an employee; 受人二分四, 做到索晒氣 one toils for just a low wage; 受人錢財, 替人消災 one must be committed to completing a task for which one has been paid; 食君之祿, 擔君之憂 do one's duty as one is paid). If one does one's job well, one gets promotion (矮仔上樓梯——步步高升 climb up step by step in one's career).

If one is unhappy with one's job, one could look for another job while having one (騎牛搵馬 look out for a horse when riding a cow——seek the better while holding on to one; work in one job but look out for a better one) or simply quit one's job (劈炮唔撈 give up one's job) as jobs are always available in other places (東家唔打打西家 lose employment in one place but get a job in another). One tends to think that the work situation in another place could be better (隔籬飯香 neighbour's rice smells better; the grass is greener on the other side of the fence).

Life

One is the master of one's own life. The kind of life one leads very much depends on one's viewpoint. Some think that since it is 人一世, 物一世 (you only live once), they should enjoy life as much as possible (自斟自酌 drink without company——in the enjoyment of one's own life all by oneself; 火燒棺材——大歎 (炭) enjoy life as much as possible; 火燒旗竿——長歎 (炭) enjoy life as long as possible; live in clover forever). Others may hold the view that since their life is worthless (爛命一條 live a worthless life and have nothing to lose), and life is full of ups and downs (三衰六旺 ups and downs of life; 甜酸苦辣 all the sweet and bitter experiences of life), the best course to take is to lead an aimless life (胡胡混混 live an aimless life; 做慣乞兒懶做官 get used to living a life of a beggar and doesn't bother to be an official) as you have only a life to live (一世流流長 as long as one lives) and you might not be able to live long enough to spend all your money (有錢冇命享 have a lot of money but no life in which to spend it).

Livelihood

To earn a living is important and that is why people have to work (為口奔馳 work hard to make a living; 拋頭露面 make a living in the public eye) for if people do not work, they have no food to eat (手停口停 if a person doesn't work he/she has no food to eat; no work no food), or they will eat up what they have stored up (坐食山崩 sit idle without work and the whole fortune will be at last used up).

Most of the idioms on livelihood are about people failing to earn enough to make a living, such as 餐搵餐食 (live from hand to mouth), 飽唔死餓唔嚟 (earn no more than what one needs), 搵朝唔得晚 (live from hand to mouth), 朝種樹，晚剝板 (grow a tree in the morning and cut a wooden board at night — live from hand to mouth), 睇餸食飯 (live within one's means), 睇餸食飯，睇燭喃嘸 (live within one's means), and 手搵口食 (live from hand to mouth).

The situation people face is that they fail to make both ends meet (十個甕缸九個蓋 nine lids for ten urns — fail to make both ends meet) and have to tighten their belts (勒緊褲頭), and therefore not able to have a family (餓死老婆瘟臭屋 starve one's wife to death and make the house smelly; cannot earn enough bread to get married or raise a family). This is why there is a saying 冇咁大嘅頭就唔好戴咁大頂帽 (don't wear a hat which is larger than your head — don't live beyond one's means).

Mistakes

To err is human. People make mistakes (行差踏錯 take a wrong step; make a mistake; 人有失手，馬有失蹄 there's always many a slip-up in a person's job; 撞板多過食飯 mistakes are made more frequently than rice is eaten — keep making mistakes), at times serious ones (晒晒大板 make a serious mistake). Sometimes mistakes are made even before work begins (落筆打三更 / 落手打三更 begin with a wrong move; make mistakes when starting to do sth; ruin sth as soon as it starts).

There are various ways to handle mistakes. Other than shedding tears over mistakes one has committed (膝頭哥撟眼淚 wipe tears with your knees — make a big mistake and shed tears), one can shift the blame to others (屙屎唔出賴地硬 blame the ground for being hard when one cannot defecate; blame others for your own mistakes), or make the best of a mistake (將錯就錯 make the best of a bad job; make the best of a mistake; over shoes over boots), believing that mistakes could offer a lesson to the maker (錯有錯着 have a fault on the right side; mistakes can turn out to be useful).

Marriage

When a man is single, he is a bachelor (單身寡仔). In traditional China, arranged marriages through match-makers were commonplace, and hence there is a saying 唔做中唔做保，唔做媒人三代好 (one who does not engage himself in the business of a middleman or a guarantor will have worthy descendants for three generations).

When a man and a woman get married, they are expected to marry to someone from a similar background (門當戶對 let beggars match with beggars). In some cases, men and women have shotgun weddings (奉旨 (子) 成婚) when the woman is pregnant before the wedding. After the wedding, the wife is expected to become subordinate to her husband (嫁雞隨雞，嫁狗隨狗 follow a cock or a dog when you marry a cock or a dog — become a subordinate to one's husband once married).

Dealing with matters

Matters can be big or small (可大可小 it may be either serious or unimportant), serious (講笑搵第樣 this is no laughing matter) or trivial (雞毛蒜皮 like a chicken feather or skin of garlic).

Matters are dealt with in different ways. Matters can be left undealt with (兩個和尚擔水食，三個和尚冇水食 everybody's business is nobody's business; 不了了之 allow sth to remain unresolved; conclude without conclusion; end up with nothing definite; settle a matter by leaving it unsettled; 一三五七九——無傷 (雙) (一二三五六——沒事 (四)) one, two, three, five, and six — nothing goes amiss; 一棟都冇 cannot do anything). Matters can be dealt with according to prioritisation (大雞唔食細米 a big chicken won't eat small rice — care naught for trifles;

important person does not bother with trivial matters; 妹仔大過主人婆 a maid being ranked higher than her master——have one's priority wrong; put the trivial above the important; the tail wags the dog). Matters can be dealt with seriously based on their importance (大蛇痾尿 / 大蛇痾屎 a big snake urinates/shits——important deal). Matters can be dealt with openly (明人不做暗事) or separately (一件還一件). One can 煮到嚟就食 (deal with things in due course; submit oneself to the circumstances). And there are people who want to get to the bottom of the matter (打爛砂盆問到篤).

Popularity

Popularity refers to how well artists in the entertainment business are received. Artists who are very popular are said to be 大紅大紫 (in bright red and purple——at the height of one's power and influence; at the zenith of one's fame), 紅到發紫 (in deep red which is akin to purple——enjoy great popularity), or 當時得令 (in season; win popularity). Artists who are neither popular nor unpopular are said to be 唔紅唔黑 (not red or black). For artists who are no longer popular, they are said to be 過氣老倌 (actor/actress who has passed their primes).

Power

Power is what people look for as power allows one to fulfil one's wishes (要風得風，要雨得雨 get wind or rain as one wishes——be able to get what one wants). A person in power could flaunt their power (也文也武).

But power is not absolute as there is always one who is above the person in power (斧頭打鑿鑿打木 the axe strikes the chisel, and the chisel strikes the wood——everything has its vanquisher; there is always one thing to conquer another). A person who does not use his power is sometimes regarded as a powerless person (老虎唔發威當病貓 mistake a tiger for a sick cat), and there are powerless people who pretend to be in power by stealing the show of an authority (揸住雞毛當令箭 pretend to hold an arrow with a chicken feather).

Practice

Practice makes perfect (工多藝熟；曲不離口；熟能生巧). A person learns skill through practice (熟讀唐詩三百首，唔會吟詩也會偷 be familiar with the 300 Tang poems and even if you don't know how to write a poem you can steal one——skill comes from constant practice; 一次生兩次熟 clumsy at first but skilful later on; people get used to things quickly).

Relationships

Relationships have been highly emphasised in China, and Guangdong is no exception. Cantonese people attach great importance to human relationships, holding the view that blood is thicker than water (切肉不離皮 one can't sever meat from skin——blood is thicker than water; 打死不離親兄弟 blood is thicker than water; 一世人兩兄弟 we're brothers all our lives). Father's sisters and mother's sisters 姨媽姑姐 in a family and relatives on one's mother's side are to be highly respected (天上雷公，地下舅公 brothers of the mother have the same status as the god of thunder in human relations). According to tradition, it is absolutely wrong to turn one's back on all one's relations (六親不認). Sometimes, disputes between one's relatives put one in a difficult position (手板係肉，手背又係肉 difficult to decide in taking sides as you are on good terms with both parties). If one sides with outsiders, one is considered to be improper (手指拗出唔拗入 bend one's fingers out——help outsiders at the expense of insiders).

Other kinds of relationships, which could be rather entangled (藤揗瓜，瓜揗藤 vines get entangled with the melon), could be divided into close and hostile. A close relationship is one that is tight (打風都打唔甩 won't be blown apart by wind) whereas a hostile relationship can be applied to enemies (貼錯門神 at odds with each other; become hostile; 督眼督鼻 a thorn in one's eye; eyesore; irritate the eyes; 前世撈亂骨頭 got each other's bones mixed up in the previous lives——be hostile to each other), but one should avoid making enemies (冤家宜解不宜結 it is better to bury the hatchet). It is said that enemies are bound to meet (冤家路窄 enemies are bound to meet; 不是冤家不聚頭 dogs and cats are sure to meet). When enemies meet, it would be advisable not to push them too hard (窮寇莫追 not to try to run after the hard-pressed enemy).

Responsibility

Cantonese people consider responsibility important (一人做事一人當 one is responsible for what one does; 萬大有我 even if the sky falls down, I'll hold it up).

Responsibility could in some context be burdensome (砣手唔腳 burdensome) as burden could become heavy (落雨賣風爐 ── 越擔越重 one's burden becomes greater), drag in others (亞蘭嫁亞瑞 ── 大家累鬥累 drag in one another), and be lifelong (一生兒女債, 半世老婆奴 a wife and children are a man's burdens).

Retribution

The majority of Cantonese people are Buddhists who believe in the Buddhist idea of retribution or karma, meaning that what one does will be rewarded accordingly. When things do not go well, people would say 前世唔修 (pitiful; suffer retribution for all ill deeds done in the previous existence). People are therefore reminded that good will be rewarded with good, evil, with evil (惡有惡報 curses come home to roost; sow the wind and reap the whirl-wind; 惡人自有惡人磨 devils devil devils; 善有善報, 惡有惡報 get what's coming to one; fortune is the good man's price, but the bad man's bane; good has its reward and evil has its recompense; good will be rewarded with good and evil with evil; if you do good, good will be done to you; but if do ill, the same will be measured back to you).

Resources

Things cannot be achieved without resources (鳳凰無寶不落 a phoenix won't land on barren land ── draw water to one's mill). When there is a lack of resources (山窮水盡 at the end of one's rope; 萬事俱備, 只欠東風 ready to the last gaiter button), one can only obtain them from other sources (拉上補下 make up for the deficit in one area by using resources from another), which is like 人哋出雞, 你出豉油 (while others offer a chicken you offer soya sauce, meaning while the larger part of the expenses is borne by others, one still has to bear a small part of the expenses).

Trouble

Everyone has to deal with all sorts of troubles as there are people who are keen to make troubles (攪是攪非 cause trouble between people; 攪風攪雨 cause wind and rain-stir up troubles; 無事生非 make trouble out of nothing; 煽風點火 stir up troubles; whip up waves; 無風三尺浪 make trouble out of nothing; 掘尾龍 ── 攪風攪雨 a tailless dragon ── the person who stirs up strife). Sometimes, troubles are created by oneself (唔衰攞嚟衰; 惹屎上身 stain oneself with feces). At other times, troubles may be caused by verbosity (是非只為多開口), nosiness (是非皆因強出頭 a nosy person often invites troubles), or fame (人怕出名豬怕肥 a person fears fame as pigs fear being fat ── fame brings troubles). Troubles might also come unexpectedly (唔食羊肉一身臊 miss the goat meat and just get the smell of the goat; 白蟮上沙灘 ── 唔死一身潺 an eel stranded on the beach ── even if it survives it will be seriously sick, meaning that one gets out of distress but into trouble), and they come one after another (一波未平, 一波又起 troubles come one after another)

As a result of trouble, everything is in a mess (家嘈屋閉 cause trouble at home; 頭都大埋 addle one's head; 攪出個大頭佛 put all the fat in the fire). The course to follow is to settle trouble. When troubles are over, things will get better (一天光晒 all is bright and clear; the trouble is over). Otherwise, there will be trouble in the future (放虎歸山 release a tghter back to the hill ── lay trouble for the future).

Wealth

People want to make a lot of money or get rich (發過豬頭 fatter than a pig head; 發過豬蹄 fatter than a pig foot; 風生水起 wind stirs and water runs ── get rich; 盆滿缽滿 with money full to the brim ── make a lot of money; 豬籠入水 have lots of money pouring in; have many different ways to make money; hit the jackpot; 大把世界 have many chances to make money). That, however, depends on how one makes money. Some are born rich (家肥屋潤 well-off family; 老豆大把 one's father is loaded); others accumulate wealth through frugality (死慳死抵 pinch and screw; tighten one's belt; 知慳識儉 (1) eat sparingly and spend frugally; go slow with, pinch and scrape; scrape and screw; skimp and save; (2) careful calculation and strict budgeting; 袋袋平安 acquire and keep safe a sum of money). When one gets rich, one has power (財可通神 money makes the world go round; money talks; 有錢使得鬼推磨 money makes the mare go; money makes the world go round; 有錢佬話事 money talks; 見錢開眼 be moved at the sight of money; be tempted by money; care for nothing but money; open the eyes wide at the sight of money; one's eyes grow round with delight at the sight of money; 跪地餵豬乸──睇錢份上 kneel on the ground to feed the swine──all for money; money makes the mare go; suffer disgrace and insults in order to get money).

One, nevertheless, may not be rich forever as one's wealth may come and go (三更窮，四更富), 搵得嚟使得去 (easy come, easy go), 左手嚟，右手去 (in at one hand and out at the other). When one is rich, one should also avoid flaunting one's wealth (財不可露眼 don't flaunt your wealth; opportunity makes the thief), and one should pretend to be poor (禾稈冚珍珠 cover the pearl with straws). People have the general impression that most bald men are rich (十個光頭九個富 nine out of ten bald men are rich), rich people are not healthy (財多身子弱), and money only goes to the right person (唔係你財唔入你袋).

To stay rich, one should not overspend. But this is certainly not the case with many rich people as they feel more comfortable to spend a lot, sometimes unnecessarily (風吹雞蛋殼──財散人安樂 pay a price for one's safety; when money is spent, peace of mind is possible; 有錢就身痕 money burns a hole in one's pocket; 倒吊荷包 hang one's purse upside down──invite losses for oneself; 洗腳唔抹腳 wash one's feet without wiping them──spend lavishly or extravagantly; squander). This leads to the reduction of their wealth slowly (神前桔──陰乾).

The poor, not the rich, are the majority. Many people are short of money (五行欠水 / 五行缺水 / 五行欠金──冇錢 / 乾時緊月 / 仙都唔仙吓). Some borrow money from people (船頭尺──度水 a measuring tape at the front of a boat──someone who is always asking others for money). Many borrowers, however, do not settle debts with their lenders (劉備借荊州──一借冇回頭 money or things borrowed are never returned; the loan once given never comes back; 財到光棍手──有去冇回頭 give a bone to a dog; 財到光棍手──易放難收 once money goes to the hands of a conman, it's difficult to get it back from him) and make the excuse that debts could be settled in the long run (長命債，長命還 a life-long debt is to be settled by a life time). It should be realised that debts are to be settled, regardless of one's relationship with the lender (數還數路還路 balance accounts with sb no matter who they are) and the clearance of debts will bring peace of mind (無債一身輕 feel relieved if one is not in debt; out of debt, out of burden).

Work

Cantonese people are hardworking (做牛做馬 toil like oxen and horses; 捱生捱死 work extremely hard; 捱更抵夜 sit up all night to work; work night and day; 死做爛做 tire oneself out through overwork; work oneself to death; 輕枷重罪 be burdened with the work of a moment; 日捱夜捱 work hard night and day), and they are so busy that they do not have time to take a rest (得閒死，唔得閒病 have time for death but not time for falling ill; 鐵腳馬眼神仙肚 one who has iron legs, a horse's eyes and a deity's stomach──energetic person who can work long hours without sitting, sleeping or eating; 忙到七個一皮 frantically busy). A rest, nevertheless, is always desirable (吊頸都要透氣 one needs to take a breath even when one is hanging himself; need to have an opportunity to relax no matter how busy one is).

There are people who do not take work very seriously (做一日和尚唸一日經 wear through the day; 做又三十六，唔做又三十六 one gets the same pay whether one is hardworking or lazy). They just fool around, idling away their time (行行企企 saunter or stand there).

Team work enhances efficiency (夾手夾腳 co-operate closely with each other; 人多好做作 many hands make light work), but at the same time it might cause problems (人多手腳亂 / 人多熠唔焾 too many cooks spoil the broth).

Body parts

In this part, idioms relating to the functions of different parts of the body are arranged alphabetically and discussed in detail.

The brain

Idioms about the brain are not to be taken clinically or physiologically. The brain to the Chinese people is the same as the mind, which has a set of faculties or functions, including attitude, consciousness, imagination, perception, reasoning, recognition, thoughts, thinking, judgment, and memory. The brain is to be distinguished from the heart, which has the functions of feelings and emotions.

The brain as the mind is illustrated by a large number of Cantonese idioms: 十五十六 (in two minds; indecisive), 三心兩意 (dillydally; in two minds), 心大心細 (hesitate to do sth; indecisive), 心中有屎 (have a guilty conscience), 心中有數 (know what is what), 密底算盤 (penny pincher), 幫理不幫親 (fair-minded), 寡母婆咁多心 (in two minds like a single mother), 知人口面不知心 (be familiar with sb but ignorant of his true nature), 五時花六時變 (change one's mind easily; changeable; have an unstable temperament), and 事不關己, 己不勞心 (mind one's own business).

Other functions of the mind are given below, in alphabetical order.

(1) Attention

Attention could be concentrated (埋頭埋腦 full attention; all ears; all eyes; all eyes and ears; 迷頭迷腦 indulge oneself in; immerse oneself in), distributed (一眼關七 attend to several things at the same time; keep one's eyes open; on the alert), lost (神不守舍 absent-minded), lacking (粗心大意 careless; inadvertent; negligent; scatter-brain; 老虎都會瞌眼瞓 even a watchful person will fall asleep), or negligent (顧得頭嚟腳反筋 attend to one thing and neglect another).

(2) Attitude

One of the functions of the brain is attitude. Attitude covers arrogance (沙塵白霍 consider oneself a world above others; consider oneself unexcelled in the world; insufferably arrogant; on the high ropes; ride the high horse; swagger like a conquering hero; 招搖過市 be fond of showing oneself in the streets); carelessness (唔理 三七廿一 regardless of the consequences; 唔理得咁多 cast all caution to the wind; 有理冇理 forget about it and let it rip); fence-sitting (豆腐刀——兩便面 a bean curd knife is sharp on both sides——a fence-sitter); indifference (隔岸觀火 watch the fire on the other side of the river——show indifference towards sb's trouble; 闊佬懶理 not interested; not to bother with others; won't bother to heed it); ingratitude (有事鍾無艷, 無事夏迎春 once out of danger, cast the deliverer behind one's back; 打完齋唔要和尚 kick down the ladder); middle-course (亞駝行路—— 舂舂地 take a mean course); non-involvement (企喺城樓睇馬打 stand on top of the gate tower and watch horses fight——keep oneself out of the affair; make oneself stay out of the matter); selfishness (潮州音樂—— 自己顧自 己 (老西兒拉胡琴——自顧自) Chiu Chow music——everyone for themselves; pay one's bill for oneself; 田雞過 河——各有各撐 each goes their own way like frogs in the field; each takes to their own legs); sloppiness (是是但 但 anybody will do; as you like it; anything is alright/all right; anything will do; 馬馬虎虎 not serious; perfunctory; sloppy; 唔嗲唔吊 careless; casual; 得過且過 muddle along; 點話點好 as you please); snobbery (見高就拜, 見低 就踩 (軟的欺負硬的怕) flatter those above and bully those below; snobbish); take-it-easy attitude (天跌落嚟當 被冚 treat the fallen sky as a quilt; 大安旨意 choose to ignore any risk or danger).

(3) Clarity of mind

To have a clear mind is important. When one's mind works fast, one is said to be 挑通眼眉 (clear-headed and clever), 眉精眼企 (know a trick or two; smart), 精乖伶俐 (clever and quick-witted; quick on the uptake) and 話 頭醒尾 (able to take a hint). When one's mind works in a clever way, one is said to have 眼眉毛雕通瓏 (sharp-witted; up to snuff) or 靈機一觸 (a flash of wit; a sudden inspiration; hit on a bright idea; suddenly have a brain wave). Wisdom has to be gained through time and experience (事後孔明 be wise after an event; 靈神不用多致燭,

響鼓不用重錘／好鼓不用多槌 a word is enough to the wise; 薑越老越辣 the older, the wiser; 唔信命都信吓塊鏡 it is wise to know oneself; 多一事長一智 by every affair a person transacts; in doing, one learns; one learns from experience; wisdom comes from experience; 人急智生 have quick wits in an emergency).

To have a confused mind is undesirable. When one's mind is unclear, one is said to be insane or crazy (神神經經／癲癲痱痱／癲癲得得／阿駝都俾你激直 you make sb crazy). When one's mind is muddled, one is said to be muddle-headed (見山就拜 taking A for B without making sure; 混混噩噩 ignorant; muddle-headed; without a clear aim; 壽頭壽腦 muddle-headed; 瘟瘟沌沌 lose one's consciousness; 騎牛搵牛 look for an ox while sitting on one; 南嘸佬遇鬼迷 an old horse loses its way; 聰明一世，蠢鈍一時 clever all the time but become a fool this once; 精埋一便 clever only at ill doings). When one's mind works unwell, one is said to be dumb (吽吽豆豆), stupid (人頭豬腦 as stupid as a pig; 肥頭耷耳 have a fat head and drooping ears; 頭大冇腦 brainless with a big head; 腦大生草 a big head grows grass; 薯頭薯腦 dumb like a potato; 獻醜不如藏拙 it is wiser to conceal one's stupidity than it is to show oneself up; 傻傻庚庚 foolish; 人蠢冇藥醫 there's no remedy to cure the stupidity of a person; 笨頭笨腦 block-headed).

To have a wicked mind is in general not acceptable (老奸巨猾 as cunning as an old fox; 陰陰濕濕 cunning; treacherous; vicious; 精到出骨 act cleverly from selfish motives; 蛇頭鼠眼 as crafty as a fox; 有心裝冇心人 set a trap for sb; 明槍易擋，暗箭難防 it is easy to dodge a spear but difficult to guard against an arrow in the dark).

(4) Intention

Intention is sometimes hard to gauge (生仔唔知仔心肝 it is hard to know even one's own son's intention) and likely to be misunderstood (捉錯用神). Evil intention has, nevertheless, received more attention (端端度度 have an evil intention; 鱸魚探蝦毛——冇好心 a weasel giving new year's greetings to a hen has ulterior motives; a yellow weasel goes to pay New Year's call to a hen——not with the best of intentions; the weasel goes to pay its respects to the hen——not with the best of intentions); 墨魚肝肚雞泡心腸——黑夾毒 the belly and intestines of a cuttlefish and the liver of a puff fish——they are all black and poisonous).

(5) Perception

Perception is about how one sees things. It is therefore related to one's views (同聲同氣 of the same opinion; 同一鼻哥窿出氣 breathe through the same nostrils; have the same opinion; in tune with; sing the same tune; talk exactly one like the other).

Perception is about one's assessment of things. One's assessment could be biased (先入為主 have a prejudice against), critical (有彈冇讚 just criticism without praise; 有彈有讚 criticise and praise; 濕水棉胎——冇得彈 above criticism; beyond reproach), or fussy (奄尖聲悶 choosy; fussy; 婆婆媽媽 womanishly fussy; 腌尖腥悶 hard to please).

(6) Reasoning

There are idioms expressing things happening without a reason (無情白事／無端白事 without reason or cause; 橫蠻無理 savage like a beast), people losing their reasons (唔係人咁品 lose one's reason; 秀才遇着兵——有理講唔清 be unable to persuade sb with reason), and people clinging to their own reasons (公說公有理，婆說婆有理 each clings to his own view).

One of the important functions of reasoning is to provide an excuse for something, which is otherwise known as pretexts. Idioms on pretexts include 借頭借路 (cook up a lame excuse; use any pretext), 借題發揮 (make use of the subject under discussion to put across one's ideas), and 推三推四 (cock up a lame excuse; reluctant to do sth; stall).

Another function of reasoning is bargaining, which is to haggle over prices. Idioms on bargaining include 打死狗講價 (bargain over a dog beaten to death——fish in troubled waters), 開天索價／開天殺價 (ask a sky-high price; ask an exorbitant price), 聽價唔聽斗 (care for whether the price is cheap or high but neglect the quality or quantity), 開天索價／開天殺價，落地還錢 (drive a hard bargain over sth), and 亞蘭賣豬——一千唔賣，賣八百 (Ah Lan sells a pig for eight hundred instead of one thousand——bargain away sth; be forced to devalue sth).

(7) Recognition

Recognition is related to knowledge and understanding. Cantonese idioms on knowledge include 知子莫若父 (no one knows a boy better than his father) and 知其一不知其二 (have a smattering of sth or sb). Idioms on understanding include 知己知彼 (it needs to understand both oneself and others), 帶眼識人 (know a person with one's own eyes), 對牛彈琴 (sing to a mule; speak to the wrong audience), 又聾又啞 (can neither understand or speak the native language when in a foreign country), 唔使劃公仔劃出腸 (it goes without saying), 雞啄放光蟲——心知肚明 (a turtledove eating up a firefly——bright in the belly; have a clear understanding of things), 牛皮燈籠——點極都唔明 (a lantern made of cow leather——thick-headed), 半夜食黃瓜——不知頭定尾 (eat a cucumber at midnight——make neither head nor tail of sth), 一理通，百理明 (once one has mastered the basic idea, the rest is easy); 日久見人心 (time makes one understand a person), and 水洗都唔清 (not even water can wash it clean——the misunderstanding is beyond repair).

Recognition is related to one's ability to distinguish differences so that one would not be confused (一頭霧水 a head surrounded by mist——in bewilderment; in confusion). Examples of confusion are evident in the idioms 顛倒是非 (confound right and wrong; confuse truth and falsehood; distort truth; give a false account of the true facts; invert justice; stand facts on their heads; swear black is white), 唔湯唔水 (neither fish nor fowl), and 戾横折曲 (swear black is white).

(8) Thinking

One of the most important functions of a human brain is thinking, which generates confusion, decisions, determination, imagination, strategies, and actions such as cunningness and madness.

Thinking could be imaginative or wishful, which is expressed by the idioms 妙想天開 (a flight of fancy; a stretch of the imagination; ask for the moon), and 痴心妄想 (fond dream; wishful thinking).

One's thinking could be shown by one's facial expression (眉頭眼額 eyebrows, eyes and forehead). When one thinks about long-term (從長計議 give a matter further deliberation and discuss it later), one may have to weigh the pros and cons (患得患失 be swayed by considerations of success and failure) and its significance (嗒落有味 the significance of sth becomes clear after careful consideration). Attention must be paid to its results in future (落雨擔遮——顧前唔顧後 use an umbrella in the rain——tend to the front but not the rear, meaning one pays no regard to the future).

Decisions have to be made after thinking. There might be the case where one does not have the right to make a decision (杉木靈牌——唔做得主 manage a family but without the right to make any decisions). One might incline to make a decision based on preference (獨沽一味 have a strong preference for only one thing). There might be too many choices for one to make a right decision (千揀萬揀 select carefully; 花多眼亂 have a dazzling array of choices before one), and one might end up making a bad decision (千揀萬揀，揀着個爛燈盞 choose a broken lamp after making a thousand and ten thousand choices——the most careful choice is often the worst choice; 打錯算盤 make a wrong calculation). When one has grown-up children, they could make their own decisions (仔大仔世界 children who are grown-up should make their own decisions).

Strategies are schemes that come from thinking. One might think out a strategy by oneself (山人自有妙計 I've an excellent solution; 眉頭一皺，計上心頭 have a sudden inspiration; hit upon an idea). Generally, it is believed that two heads are better than one when it comes to working out strategies (一人計短，二人計長), short persons are good at working out strategies (矮仔多計), and thieves are good strategists (賊公計，狀元才).

One might hammer out a strategy that takes things as they come (見步行步), achieves two goals at one go (一弓射兩箭 kill two birds with one stone), plays safe (穩打穩紮), matches the strategies of one's player (棋逢敵手 nip and tuck; well-matched; 你有張良計，我有過牆梯 be evenly matched; 棋高一着 be a stroke above sb), or outplays one's counterpart (將計就計 turn sb's tricks against him). One might run out of wit in working out strategies (三十六度板斧都出齊 at the end of one's wits). One tactic that could be considered is to run away (三十六着，走為上着 of all the thirty-six tactics, to "running away" is the best one). If one makes a bad move, things will fall apart (一子錯滿盤皆落索 a wrong step causes a messy tumble; one careless move loses the whole game; 棋差一着 lose a move to sb).

The ear

The only idiom for the ear is 左耳入，右耳出 (go in one ear and out the other).

The eye

Eyes are for looking at things. There is a small number of end-clippers on taking a glance (單眼仔睇老婆——一眼見晒／單眼佬睇榜——一目了然 clear at a glance; see with half an eye;), and a small number of idioms on gazing (走馬看花 take a scamper through sth; 眈天望地 glance at the sky and the ground——look this way and that; 睇東睇西 gaze this way and that; stare about; watch out furtively to the east and west; 二叔公割禾——望下截 granduncle harvesting grains——to look at the lower part of the stalk, meaning one looks back on).

Other eye idioms are related to blindness (有眼無珠 blind; undervalue sb; 隻眼開，隻眼閉 shut one's eyes to; turn a blind eye to), red eyes due to overwork (金睛火眼 (1) eyes tired from intense concentration; very attentive eyes; (2) have red eyes due to overwork), sore eyes (眼唔見為伶俐 out of sight, out of mind; 鞋底沙——拃乾淨至安樂 you won't feel comfortable until the sting in one's eyes is pulled out), carelessness in seeing things (眼大睇過籠 be too careless to see anything), and things to be seen at a later stage (好戲在後頭 there will be sth interesting to see a little later).

The face

Idioms on the face could be related to colour of the complexion (紅光滿面 one's face glows with health; 面紅耳熱 as red as a turkey-cook; blush to the roots; blush up to the ears; colour up; crimson with rage; flush with shame; red with anger; 黃泡髧熟 a swollen face with yellow complexion), condition of health (面青心紅 look weak but actually strong and loyal), expression of one's mental state (木口木面 expressionless; slow-witted; wooden-faced; 嘆口嘆面 look upset; 面不改容 not to change colour; one's countenance betrays nothing; one's face is untroubled; remain calm; undismayed; without batting an eyelid; without changing countenance; without turning a hair; 灶君老爺——黑口黑面 fierce demon and devils), face-to-face situations (二口六面／三口六面 face-to-face; two parties and witness confront in court), appearance (熟口熟面 familiar face; 面黃骨瘦 skinny and look pale; 面懵心精 appear to be stupid but is actually very smart; play the fool), authority (睇人口面 be dependent on other's pleasure; 賣鹹酸菜——畀面 give face to sb; 人要面，樹要皮 a person needs face just like a tree needs bark; 唔睇僧面，都睇吓佛面 not for everybody's sake but for sb's sake).

Feet

Idioms on feet are related to ways of walking, including 大搖大擺 (swagger about), 行路唔帶眼 (jaywalk), 冷巷擔竹竿——直出直入 (walking in a lane with a plank on one's shoulder——taking an arrow-straight course), and 出出入入 coming in and out; in and out; shuttle in and out) or 行出行入 (come in and out; in and out; shuttle in and out).

The hand

A notable characteristic of idioms on hands is that most of these idioms mention hands and feet together instead of just mentioning hands alone (手多腳多 touch things when one should not; 手忙腳亂 all in a hustle of excitement; be thrown into a panic; be thrown into confusion; in a great flurry; in disarray; 乾手淨腳 (1) crispy; dapper; efficient; neat; neat and tidy; neatly; smooth and clean; trim; very efficient; (2) finished and done with, once for all; and 毛手毛腳 (inappropriate fondling or touching).

In this dictionary, the only exception is 手急眼快 (quick eye and deft hand).

The head

Literally, the head is always mentioned together with the tail, while figuratively, the head is interpreted as a beginning and the tail, an ending. This is why there is a number of idioms containing heads and tails being translated as the beginning and the end, such as 一頭一尾 ((1) both ends; (2) here and there), 由頭到尾 (all the way; from the beginning to the end; from end to end; from first to last; from hub to tire; from soup to nuts; from start to finish; from stem to stern; from the egg to the apple; from the head to the tail; from the sole of the foot to the crown of the head; from tip to toe; from top to bottom; from top to toe; the whole way; through and through; through the whole length), 好頭好尾 (a good beginning and a good ending), 頭頭尾尾 ((1) odd pieces; (2) altogether), and 有頭威 , 冇尾陣 (a brave beginning and weak ending; a brave beginning but a poor ending; a tiger's head and a snake's tail; begin with tigerish energy but peter out towards the end; come out at the small end of the horn; do sth by halves; fine start and poor finish; in like a lion, out like a lamb).

In this dictionary, there are three idioms on heads that do not have tails, including 頭重腳輕 (top-heavy), 萬事起頭難 (it is difficult to begin a new business), and 頭崩額裂 (be scorched by the flames; badly battered; beat sb's head off; in a sorry plight; in a terrible fix; smash heads and scorch brows; utterly exhausted from overwork).

The heart

In contrast to the brain, or mind, which is about thinking, the heart is about feelings and emotions. There are twenty idioms which are about the heart, including 人面獸心 (a wolf in lamb's skin), 入心入肺 (take sth to heart), 心服口服 (be sincerely convinced), 心知肚明 (know in one's heart), 死心不息 (as obstinate as a mule), 佛口蛇心 (talk like Buddha but with a heart of a snake——kind-mouthed but vicious-hearted; with a human face and the heart of a beast), 死心塌地 (hell-bent on sb), 抆心抆肺 (break sb's heart), 將心比己 (measure another's foot by one's own last), 提心吊膽 (have one's heart in one's mouth), 開心見誠 (open-hearted), 好眉好貌生沙蝨 (a fair face hides a foul heart), 狼心狗肺 (be ungrateful for a favour and regard it as a disservice), 芋頭點糖——心淡 (one's heart sinks), 狗咬呂洞賓——不識好人心 (not know chalk from cheese), 人心肉做 (have a good conscience; people are by nature compassionate), 好心有好報 (a good act will be well rewarded; fortune is the companion of virtue; good will be rewarded with good; goodness will have a good reward; kind deeds pay rich dividends to the doer), 好心唔怕做 (not afraid to do good deeds; have one's heart in the right place), 好心唔得好報 (recompense good with evil), and 好心着雷劈 (bite the hand that feeds one; recompense good with evil).

Feelings and emotions related to the heart have been arranged alphabetically and discussed separately.

(1) Anger

There is a large number of expressions on anger as a human emotion, which include 佛都有火 (it would try the patience of a saint), 熱過火屎 (hotter than soot–very angry), 熱過烙雞 (hotter than a soldering iron——very angry), and 激到一把火 (a stomachful of anger). Sometimes, it is not possible to withhold one's anger (劏住度氣 be compelled to hold back one's rage; be forced to submit to humiliation; be forced to swallow the leek).

Anger can be expressed through body movements, such as 七竅生煙 (smoke comes out of the seven orifices of one's body——fly into a rage), 頭殼頂出煙 (smoke comes out of one's head——get very angry), 嬲到彈起 (hit the roof), 激到生蝦咁跳 (be infuriated and jump up like a shrimp——tremble with anger), 吹鬚碌眼 (blow a fuse; blow a gasket; fall into a rage; foam with rage; froth at the mouth and glare with rage; scowl and growl; snort and stare in anger), or through facial expressions, such as 黑口黑面 / 口黑面黑 / 黑埋口面 ((1) very angry; (2) look displeased; pull a long face).

(2) Courage

Courage is interchangeable with audacity, which carries with an appreciative connotation (膽大心細 bold but cautious; courageous and cautious; 膽大心細面皮厚 bold, cautious, and thick-skinned).

Courage could be monstrous (狗膽包天 monstrous audacity). People who are extremely audacious do not care for their own lives (膽正命平 have too much spunk to care for one's own life) and would come with ill intentions (來者不善 , 善者不來 he/she could not have come with good intentions; those who fear the gallows shall never be a good thief; those who have come, they come with ill intent, certainly not on virtue bent; those who come are surely strong or they would never come along).

There are naturally people who are not so audacious (生人唔生膽 born without a gall bladder——as timid as a hare; be intimidated).

(3) Desire

Desire is what one is after. It can be achieved through the power of others, just like what is said in the end-clipper (*xiehouyu*) 黃大仙——有求必應 (Wong Tai Sin——one gives whatever you ask for; one who always accepts others' requests). The fulfilment of desire is without limits (坐一望二 hope for another after gaining one) and without self-knowledge (癩蛤蟆想食天鵝肉 overestimate oneself; overreach oneself). But one's desire may not be fulfilled, just like 寡母婆死仔——冇晒希望 (a widow who lost her son——be driven to despair), or simply 冇鼕聲氣 (hear nothing of; beyond hope).

(4) Fear

Fear is a negative human emotion. Extreme fear could make the sufferer 鼻哥窿冇肉 (be extremely terrified), 魂魄都唔齊／三魂唔見咗七魄 (be entranced with fear; be frightened out of one's wits; be scared to death), or 有得震冇得瞓 (tremble with fear).

People who have experienced fear would be afraid of fear, as expressed by the idioms 見過鬼就怕黑 (once bitten, twice shy), 一朝俾蛇咬，三年怕草繩 (once bitten by a snake, one shies at a coiled rope for the next three years). These people become timid and overcautious (船頭驚賊，船尾驚鬼 fear pirates at the bow and ghosts at stern; get into a hobble). Regrettably, there is no cure for fear (人嚇人冇藥醫 there's no remedy to cure a person horrified by others).

Fear gives rise to nervousness or panic (慌慌失失 nervous; 失驚無神 be seized with panic). One trembles when seized with fear (手騰腳震 tremble all over), becoming nervous (踩着芋莢都當蛇 one thinks that he steps on a snake but actually it is just a pod; take every bush for a bugbear) and a nervous person (緊張大師 nervous person).

(5) Feelings

Feelings are complicated. It is said that empathy is universal (人同此心，心同此理 everybody feels the same). There are bad feelings, such as 牽腸掛肚 (feel deep anxiety about sb), 週身唔自然／週身唔聚財 (uneasy all over), and 針唔拮到肉唔知痛 (no one but the wearer knows better where the shoe pinches). There are also good feelings (關公細佬——亦得（翼德）as you like; 千里送鵝毛，物輕情意重 the trifling gift sent from afar conveys deep affection).

(6) Greed

Greed carries the derogatory connotation of having a strong desire to have a lot of things out of selfishness or which are unfair to other people (恨到發燒 want sth desperately; feverish).

Cantonese idioms on greed are 貪得無厭 (too greedy for gains) and 食人唔矃骨 (eat up sb without even spitting the bones). Greed could end in poverty (貪字得個貧), and the advice is 光棍佬教仔——便宜莫貪 (don't be covetous of things on the cheap).

(7) Hate

Hate is not greatly emphasised in Cantonese culture. A typical idiom that expresses hate is 神憎鬼厭 (hated by both gods and ghosts; accused target; person who is hated by all), or in the form of an end-clipper (*xiehouyu*) 神枱貓屎——神憎鬼厭 (cat feces on the altar——accused target; person who is hated by all).

(8) Jealousy

People tend to envy those who are rich (憎人富貴厭人貧 envy the rich people and despise the poor), or famous (樹大招風 a tall tree catches winds——a person of reputation is liable to become the envy of others), which explains why they become the envy of others (恨死隔離 become the envy of others; object of great envy). Lovers, moreover, are also jealous (打爛醋醰).

(9) Joy

People believe that joy or happiness is not limited to any class of people, for 辣撻人有辣撻福 (happiness often comes to mediocre persons). And when it comes to making a choice between wealth and happiness, people prefer happiness (寧食開眉粥，莫食愁眉飯 would rather be poor but happy than become rich but anxious), and they will burst with joy when they have happiness (鬆毛鬆翼).

(10) Love

A man could be attracted to a woman at first sight (生滋貓入眼), for love is essentially blind (情人眼裏出西施 beauty exists in a lover's eyes) and 冤豬頭都有盟鼻菩薩 (a lover has no judge of beauty). Lovers could have amorous behaviour (依依挹挹) and they should be loyal to each other like 桃椰樹——一條心 (love sb heart and soul; single-minded in love). But this might not be the case. People could have two or more than two lovers (一腳踏兩船 (1) attempt to make a profit two ways; seek benefits from two sides; (2) have two lovers at the same time; 一腳踏幾船 have several lovers at the same time), and a woman could have a few lovers (勾三搭四).

In a family, parents dote on the youngest son or youngest daughter (孻仔拉心肝，孻女拉五臟 parents lavish most affection on their youngest son, but they also lavish just as much affection on their youngest daughter), and the youngest sons and daughters are likely to be spoiled (生骨大頭菜——縱 (種) 壞晒 be spoiled).

(11) Loyalty

Idioms on loyalty seem to be giving a negative impression, which include 樹倒猢猻散 (rats leave a sinking ship), 義氣搏兒戲 (take the risk of being loyal to a potential traitor), and 食碗面，反碗底 (betray a friend; ungrateful).

(12) Mood

Idioms on moods are generally negative (六神無主 be thrown into confusion; 拾吓拾吓 swaying; unstable; 耷頭耷腦 listless; 要生要死 hysterical; 嘅口嘅面 in a bad mood; 有神冇氣 breath is present but vigour is absent; faint; feeble; listless; slack; weak; wearily).

(13) Regrets

Life is full of regrets. One might regret what one did a long time ago (早知今日，何必當初 it is too late to ask oneself why one has gone astray when one knows the consequence to be so serious; 早知今日，悔不當初 it is too late to repent having gone astray when one knows the consequence to be so serious), or regret having to sell one's favourite son (賣仔莫摸頭 express regret at being forced to sell one's favourite), and regret having paid for something worthless (呻到樹葉都落埋 express one's repentance for having paid for sth worthless).

No matter how deep one's regret is (扰心扰肺 (很後悔)), there is no point in banging one's head against the wall to show one's repentance for having been so foolish (撼頭埋牆).

(14) Satisfaction

People are often not easily satisfied (人心冇厭足 one is never content; one is never satisfied; 到喉唔到肺 be half satisfied; insufficient; not enough to satisfy one's appetite; unsatisfying). They always want more (人心不足蛇吞象 a snake swallows an elephant——human beings are never satisfied with what they have; no person is contented with their own possessions). When they are not satisfied, they move in a certain way (郁身郁勢 show discontent with one's position). When they are satisfied, they nod in self-approbation (擰頭擰髻 nod one's head——assume an air of self-approbation).

(15) Sorrow

Sorrow seems to be a synonym for suffering. There are two idioms that express sorrow in terms of suffering, which include 貼錢買難受 (get bad service; pay for troubles) and 啞仔食黃蓮——有苦自己知 (swallow the leek).

(16) Spirits

One's spirits could be high or low. When one's spirits are high, one is said to be 精神爽利 (brisk and neat; full of spirit and energy; in good feather; in great feather; in high feather), 龍馬精神 (as vigorous as a dragon or a horse), 龍精虎猛 (as vigorous as a dragon and a tiger——full of energy; full of strength), 打醒十二分精神 (raise one's spirits; attentive; focused), and 鬼打都冇咁醒 (be on the alert). When one's spirits are low, then one is said to be 冇厘精神 (a cup too low; disheartened; dispirited and discouraged; have a fit of blues; in low spirits; in the blues; in the dumps; lackadaisical; listless; out of humour; out of sorts; out of spirits; seedy; spiritless; with little enthusiasm; with the wind taken out of one's sails), and 頭耷耷眼濕濕 (become dejected and despondent; blue about the gills; bury one's head in dejection; down at the mouth; down in the chops; down in the dumps; down in the mouth; hang one's head; have one's tail down; in low spirits; in the dumps; look downcast; mope about; one's crest falls; out of heart; out of spirits; out of sorts; sing the blues; take the heart out of sb).

(17) Tolerance

Tolerance tests one's ability to accept things or people one disagrees with (忍無可忍 be out of patience with; 捱頸就命 patient with the current situation; bear and forbear to save life; have no choice but to comply). Very often, one has to put up with the situation in order to achieve one's goal (食得鹹魚抵得渴 if you eat salted fish you should be able to bear thirst——since one has the courage of one's convictions, one must be prepared to accept the consequences).

Beards

There is one idiom on beards, which is 鬍鬚勒突 (heavy-bearded).

Lungs

There are two idioms related to lungs: 氣來氣喘 (gasp for breath; out of breath) and 上氣唔接下氣 (be out of breath; pant).

The mouth

One uses one's mouth to do a lot of actions: drinking, eating, smiling, and speaking.

(1) Drinking

Drinking in Cantonese idioms refers to drinking wine. This dictionary has three idioms related to wine drinking, including 花天酒地 (attend a dinner with sing-song girls; be in the world of wine and women; be on the loose; be on the tiles; be out on the tiles; go on the loose; go on the racket; go on the tiles; guzzle and carouse to one's heart content; guzzle and have a good time; have one's fling; indulge in fast life and debauchery; led a decadent and dissolute life; lead a fast life; live in the world of wine and women; sow a large crop of wild oats), 酒醉三分醒 (be in wine but still a little conscious), and 酒後吐真言 (truth is exposed in wine).

(2) Eating

Chinese people in general and Cantonese people in particular are fond of eating good food. People believe in working hard and eating at leisure (辛苦搵嚟自在食 work hard in order to eat at leisure). Life is about eating and drinking (飲飲食食 eat and drink; wine and dine with sb). People are choosy in eating (揀飲擇食 be particular about one's food; choose one's food; fussy about food; fussy eater) and know how to enjoy good food (識飲識食 enjoy life to the full; have a good palate for food; know how to enjoy food and drink; 飲飽食醉 good meal and many drinks).

For ordinary people, a home meal with simple food is good enough (粗茶淡飯 plain tea and simple meal; 家常便飯 homely food; ordinary meal; 鹹魚白菜 salted fish and Chinese cabbage). With a good appetite, they eat up all the dishes (食七咁食 eat and drink as much as one can; gorge oneself; have a good stomach; 美人照鏡 eat up all the food on the dish) despite the small size of their stomachs (眼闊肚窄 bite off more than one can chew), just like a hungry ghost swallowing up everything (餓鬼投胎). They would like to have more to eat the next time around (食過翻尋味) though the food might not be healthy (利口唔利腹 good for mouth but bad for health).

When one's appetite is poor (翳翳滯滯) or they have no food to eat (食西北風 eat the winter wind), the situation would be different.

(3) Smiling

There is a number of idioms on different ways people smile. One could smile in a stupid way (焓熟狗頭 smiling stupidly like a cooked dog head), broadly (焓熟狗頭 on the broad grin), in a radiant way (笑口吟吟), constantly (笑口常開), mischievously (笑騎騎), uproariously (捧腹大笑 roar with laughter; uproarious laughter), sweetly (蓮子蓉咁口), and insincerely (皮笑肉不笑).

(4) Speaking

The contents of what one speaks vary. Included in this topic are arguing, badmouthing, chattering, commanding, complaining, contradicting, demanding, empty talk, exaggerating, gossiping, hesitating, innuendo, lying, nagging, oath-taking, praising, promising, having a ready tongue, repetition, scolding, stammering, straight talking, talking, and vulgarism.

(a) Arguing

When one argues over nothing, this is 口同鼻拗 (the mouth argues with the nose). When one argues unreasonably, this is 死都要拗番生 (argue that the dead is still living).

(b) Badmouthing

Badmouthing is American English, meaning to speak badly of something or somebody. Badmouthing in Cantonese is 煮人一鑊.

(c) Chattering

To chatter is to talk about something unimportant or trivial for a long time. Chattering in Cantonese is 囉囉嗦嗦 and 吱吱喳喳. Sometimes when women get together, they talk a lot (七嘴八舌 all talking at once) and chatter without stopping (雞啄唔斷), which explains why there is a saying 三個女人一個墟 (when women get together they make a market).

(d) Commanding

There are occasions when one makes commands to others, such as 躝屍趌路 or 躝屍趷路, either meaning "get out" or "go away".

(e) Complaining

There are people who frequently complain about something (呻呢呻嘮), often with a murmur (禀神咁聲 / 拜神唔見雞).

(f) Contradicting

People may say something which contradicts what they say, this is 前言不對後語 (one's remarks are incoherent; one's words do not hang together) or 自打嘴巴 (contradict oneself).

(g) Demanding

When one makes a huge demand, it is 獅子開大口 (open one's mouth like a lion) and demands without reasonable awards is described as 一句語該使死人 (make excessive demands on sb without offering a reasonable reward).

(h) Empty talk

Cantonese idioms for empty talk are 空口講白話 (all mouth and no action; boasting; words pay no debts), 口水多過茶 (have more saliva than tea──all mouth and no action; shoot off one's mouth; talk too much; very talkative; wag one's tongue), 見雷響唔見雨落 (there is just thunder but no rain──all talk but no action), and 煲冇米粥 (congee without rice──all talk; discuss something that will never amount to anything; make an idle talk).

The Cantonese end-clipper (*xiehouyu*) for empty talk is 冇柄士巴拿──得棚牙 (a teapot without a handle──only the spout is left).

(i) Exaggerating

Cantonese idioms have 加鹽加醋 (add in salt and vinegar) and 死人燈籠報大數 (draw a long bow).

(j) Gossiping

People like to gossip. Cantonese idioms for gossiping are 講是講非, 講三講四, and 噏三噏四. People are warned against gossipers 來說是非者，便是是非人 (the person who speaks ill of others will speak ill of you).

(k) Hesitating

When one halts in speech, one shows one's hesitation. Idioms on hesitation include 半吞半吐 (hesitate in speaking), 吞吞吐吐 (hem and haw; hesitate in speech; hum and haw; mince words; mutter and mumble; prunes and prism speak of things with scruple; speak with reservation; stumbe over one's words; tick over), 依依哦哦 (hem and haw; hesitate in speech; hum and haw; mince words; mutter and mumble; runes and prism; say hesitantly; speak in a halting way; speak of things with scruple; speak with reservation; stumble over one's words; tick over).

(l) Innuendo

Cantonese idioms are full of insinuating remarks, such as 單單打打 (criticise sb harshly; make oblique accusations at sb).

(m) Lying

Idioms on lying include 稟神都冇句真 (lie to gods) and 講大話，甩大牙 (to a child) if you lie, your molar will fall out).

(n) Nagging

Nagging is annoying, such as 開口及着脷 (one bites one's tongue as soon as he opens his mouth──annoy others as soon as one starts talking), 窒頭窒勢 (interrupt with discouraging comments), 頂心頂肺 (be hurt by others by what they say about one; pain in the neck), 含血噴人 (smite with the tongue), and 日鵝夜鵝 (nag day and night).

(o) Oath-taking

Oaths must not be interpreted in a legal sense, for they are made as promises to a god. When one takes an oath, a god is called to witness it (誓神劈願 swear solemn oath; take an oath and call a god to witness). When an oath is realised, one has to thank one's god for being able to achieve it (還得神落 can redeem a vow to a god).

There are people who take oaths lightly and their attitude is described as 誓願當食生菜 (treat an oath as eating lettuce).

(p) Praising

When one sings one's own praises, it is 賣花讚花香 (make a boast of oneself; sing one's own praises) and 老鼠跌落天平──自己秤自己 (sing one's own praise), believing that one is like 扁鼻佬戴眼鏡──冇得頂 (without equal).

When praise is followed by criticism, it is 一啖砂糖一啖屎 (praise is followed by criticism).

(q) Promising

Promises are to be kept, not to be broken. When one keeps one's word, it is 牙齒當金使 (one's teeth are true as gold), 講咗就算 (one means what one says), and 講過算數 (a verbal promise has to be kept; as good as one's word; honour one's own words; keep one's word; live up to one's word; one means what one says; true to one's word). When one promises without conditions, one is 托塔都應承 (one even promises to shoulder a toilet bowl).

Those who break their promises are said to be 反口覆舌 (break one's promise; inconsistent with what one says), 出爾反爾 (go back on one's words), 打退堂鼓 (back out one's promise), and 三口兩脷 (play fast and loose).

(r) Having a ready tongue

People with a ready tongue say something smoothly and easily. Idioms describing ready tongues include 出口成文 / 出口成章 (keep a civil tongue in one's head), 利口便辭 (have a ready tongue), 倒掛臘鴨——滿嘴油 (have a glib tongue).

A ready tongue is sometimes synonymous with a sweet tongue, which is 口甜舌滑 (oil one's tongue; sweet talk) and 花言巧語 (fine words; have a sweet tongue).

(s) Repetition

In Cantonese, repetition is expressed as〔三番五次 again and again; many a time). It is rather boring to hear something being said repeatedly〔講嚟講去都係三幅被 sing the song of burden; 講明就陳顯南 it is tiresome repetition to make oneself clear; 開口埋口 always talk about; 人講你又講 parrot what other people say).

(t) Scolding

Cantonese idioms on scolding add finger-pointing: 篤口篤鼻 (scold sb while pointing your finger at him) and 篤眼篤鼻 (scold sb with the finger pointing at him, or refer to an eyesore).

(u) Stammering

Idioms on stammering include 勒勒卡卡 (hesitate in speaking; stammer; stammer out; stumble over; stutter) and 窒口窒舌 (stammer nervously).

(v) Straight Talking

When one says something in a direct, honest, and frank manner, one is said to be 快人快語 (a person of straightforward disposition is outspoken; a straight talk from an honest person; a straightforward talk from a straightforward person; an outspoken person speaks his mind; sb who does not mince his words), 單刀直入 (come straight to the point; speak out without beating about the bush), 開門見山 (come straight to the point; not to mince one's words; put it bluntly), 擺明車馬 (open-hearted; state one's intention openly), 心嗰句, 口嗰句 (say what one thinks; speak one's mind), 好話唔好聽 (frankly speaking; to be blunt), 灶君上天——有句講句 (be frank with one's opinions; outspoken; say whatever one likes), 有碗話碗, 有碟話碟 (call a spade a spade), 直腸直肚 (straight-talking), 直腸直腦 (straight-talking), 知無不言, 言無不盡 (say all what one knows), and 食齋不如講正話 (it is better to be straight talking).

(w) Talking

According to grammarians, there is not much difference between "talking" and "speaking" as they carry the same meaning in most situations. In Cantonese, talking, which is rendered as 講 , is less formal than speaking, which is 說 . This is well illustrated by the idioms beginning with the character "講", such as 講多無謂 (talk is cheap), 講多錯多 (the least said, the soonest mended; the more one says, the more mistakes one makes), 講咁易咩 (it's easy to talk so), 講到做到 (do what one says), 講唔埋欄 (unable to reach a consensus), 講得口響 (fine words; make an unpleasant fact sound attractive; says you; talk fine; use fine-sounding phrases), 講開又講 (by the way), 講就易 , 做就難 (easier said than done), 講得出就講 (have a loose tongue), 講起嚟一疋布咁長 (it is like telling a long story), 嘢可以亂食，說話唔可以亂講 (watch what one says), 冇咁衰講到咁衰 (paint a grim picture of sb/sth), and 見人講人話，見鬼講鬼話 (speak to a saint like a saint, to a devil like a devil), 一講曹操，曹操就到 (speak/talk of the devil and here he/she is), and 吐口水講過 (take back words that are unlucky).

There are other idioms about talking which deserve our attention. When one says something that one does not mean, it is 口不對心 (speak with one's tongue in one's cheek). When one talks at random, it is 紙紮下扒——口輕輕 . When one says things which are superfluous, it is 老人院都唔收 (one's remarks are too superfluous). When one does not want to mention something, it is 黃腫腳——不消蹄（提）, and when one is forced to keep silent, it is 亞崩劏羊——咩都冇得咩 .

Talking back is not infrequent, and the idioms for this behaviour are 駁嘴駁舌 (talk back) and 阿吱阿咗 (argue; moan; talk back; whine). And when people talk nonsense, Cantonese people would say that they are 指天篤地 (point at the sky and the ground), 亂噏廿四 , 亂噏無為 , 噏得就噏 , and 聲大夾冇準 (much cry and little wool).

(x) Vulgarism

The Cantonese dialect is known for its vulgarisms. The dialect has a large number of swear words that are used commonly in social discourse, such as conversations, dialogues, and colloquial writings.

The vulgar language used is described as 炒蝦嚓蟹 (use vulgar language), 粗口爛舌 (speak coarse language; use a lot of bad language), and 粗口橫飛 (use a lot of bad language).

The nose

All the three idioms related to the nose carry derogatory meanings, including 冤崩爛臭 (smelly; stinking), 臭坑出臭草 (a smelly ditch grows smelly grass), and 唔埋得個鼻 (have an unpleasant smell).

Skin

People with smooth skin are well liked and this is reflected in the two idioms on skin collected in this dictionary, including 青靚白淨 (young, handsome, and have a fresh complexion) and 皮光肉滑 (smooth skin).

The throat

From the throat comes voice and the ability of singing. Voice can be strange （怪聲怪氣 ; 鬼聲鬼氣 (1) （陰陽怪氣）speak in a strange voice; (2) speak with a foreign accent), alluring （嗲聲嗲）, effeminate （姆聲姆氣）, and soft （陰聲細氣）.

Singing, on the other hand, can be awful, and this is described as 劏豬咁聲 (sing in a terrible way, like a pig being slaughtered).

The tongue

In Cantonese, the tongue is for tasting food and producing speech. Cantonese idioms on the tongue include 翻渣茶葉——冇釐味道 (as insipid as water) and 牛嚼牡丹——唔知花定草 (cannot appreciate good food; not know chalk from cheese; pigsy eating ginseng fruit——no flavour).

The tongue for producing speech is described by the idiom 牙尖嘴利 (have a caustic and flippant tongue; have a caustic tongue; have a sharp tongue).

Teeth

Though teeth serve the important function of biting food, there is only one idiom on teeth, which is 依牙鬆槓 (clench one's teeth).

The womb

An idiom related to the womb in a woman's body is 粗身大細 (pregnant).

Non-body topics

Bureaucracy

In traditional China, officials were powerful people who could say whatever they liked (官字兩個口 the character *guan* (official) has two mouths——officials can say whatever they like; speak in bureaucratese) and they protected each other to gain benefits (官官相衛 devils help devils). The officials who were one's immediate superiors were most fearful (唔怕官，至怕管 a mouse fears nobody but the cat that would catch it; one's immediate superior is more fearful than the person in charge). Since officials were so powerful, a friend in court could help enormously (近官得力).

Politics, nevertheless, is not an easy game to play. A new official would remove old officials and replace them with his trusted followers (一朝天子一朝臣 a new chief brings in his own trusted followers). When a new official took up his post, he would put in strict measures to exert his authority (新官上場三把火 a new broom sweeps clean; a new official applies strict measures; 新官上場整色水 a new broom sweeps clean; a new official applies strict measures). Some officials might be fed up with bureaucracy and wanted to withdraw from it to regain their freedom (無官一身輕 free from office, free from care; without burden, without worry).

Business

In business management, cost is an important factor. The overheads of a company are known, in traditional China as 燈油火蠟 (lamp, oil, fire, and wax). If business is very poor, it is 水靜河飛 (have no business; the market is dull). Some companies will close down, and new companies will be set up (一雞死一雞鳴 successors come forth one after another; when one person leaves a business, another will take it up).

Chances

Chances (or opportunities) could be small (大海撈針 look for a needle in a haystack; 萬中無一 one in a million; most unlikely; 陪太子讀書 bear sb company; some not given much chance of winning; 年三十晚有月光 it's impossible; 老糠搾出油 get oil out of rocks), great (萬無一失 as sure as a surefooted horse; 穩如鐵塔 as firm as it is founded on the rock; 坐定粒六 be sure about sth; have full confidence), or rare (十年唔逢一閏 a chance of lifetime; once in a blue moon; 好水冇幾多朝 there is not much of such a good opportunity in one's life).

People should make the most of an opportunity that comes along to achieve one's goals (無孔不入 seize every opportunity; 順水推舟 make use of an opportunity to win one's end; 順風駛𰗉 avail oneself of an opportunity; trim the sails; 打蛇隨棍上 capitalise on one's opportunity; grasp an opportunity; leap at the chance; leap at the opportunity; seize an opportunity; seize the right time; take advantage of an opportunity; take advantage of the tide; 有風駛盡𰗉 avail oneself of an opportunity to the fullest extent; take advantage of an opportunity to the full extent). Otherwise, an opportunity that is missed might not come back (蘇州過後冇艇搭 after you leave Suzhou you won't be able to take a boat ride), and one lets the opportunity slip (捉到鹿唔識脫角 you get hold of the deer but fail to take the antler).

Change

Things constantly undergo changes. Though things could be fickle (一時一樣), yet they are based on their origins (萬變不離宗).

People should not adhere to the old ways (一本通書睇到老) and believe that nothing is unchangeable (二四六八單——冇得變).

To make changes, resources are needed; otherwise, changes are impossible (無氈無扇，神仙難變 no one can make bricks without straw).

Colour

Idioms on colour include 五顏六色 (a riot of colour; colourful; play of colours) and 花花碌碌 (colourful). Idioms on other colours include bright red (紅粉緋緋) and black (黑古勒特).

Comparison

No comparison would be possible if things are two of a kind (一個願打，一個願捱 well-matched couple; 你唔嫌我囉嗦，我唔嫌你米碎 be two of a kind; 叮噹馬頭 difficult to tell which one has outdone the other; very hard to tell which one is better). Since nothing is the same, comparisons are odious (十隻手指有長短 among the ten fingers there are long and short ones; 比上不足比下有餘 be worse as compared with the best but better as compared with the worst; 人比人，比死人 comparisons are odious; it is harmful to compare oneself with others; 你走你嘅陽關路，我過我嘅獨木橋 each goes their own way).

When comparisons are made, the difference could be huge (蚊髀同牛髀 a mosquito's thigh vs an elephant's thigh; no comparison between; one cannot be compared to the other; pale into insignificance by comparison; the moon is not seen where the sun shines; when the sun shines, the light of stars is not seen; when the sun shines, the moon has nothing to do with it; 唔係我嗰皮 not my match).

Competition

The outcome of a competition depends on a number of factors, one of which is strength (石地堂鐵掃把—硬打硬 an iron broom pounding a stone ground—a case of the tough confronting the tough). When things are on a par, there is no competition (你有乾坤，我有日月 be on a par with). There will be competition as soon as new things are created (瘦田冇人耕，耕開有人爭 once a wasteland is inhabited, a rush for an occupation is insisted; 餓狗搶屎 hunger dogs fight for shit; compete against each other for sth; 好食爭崩頭 grab sth when it is cheap; 多隻香爐多隻鬼 one more incense burner, one more ghost; the more the competitors, the keener the competition).

The results of a competition sometimes are hard to predict as it is always the tough against the tough (強中自有強中手 catch a tartar; fight a strong enemy) and the locals might lose out to outsiders (猛虎不及地頭蟲 a mighty dragon is no match for the native serpent). Winning a complete victory is 羅通掃北 (make a clean sweep of everything). When one comes out last, it is 包尾大番, or 番鬼佬睇榜——倒數第一 (the first from the bottom).

Control

Control is not possible if things or people are remote from the authority (山高皇帝遠 run one's own affairs without interference from a distant centre of authority). Nevertheless, everything has its superior (一物治一物；一物治一物，糯米治木蝨). Sometimes, a master-mind is in control of everything behind the scenes (幕後主腦 master-mind; 幕後黑手 person who controls everything from behind the scenes).

Dilemma

People are often in a dilemma where decisions are hard to make (兩頭唔到岸 in a situation where whichever way one turns one will lose out; neither sink nor swim in the middle of the sea; on the horns of a dilemma). People would be in an awkward predicament (左右做人難), and find it difficult to remain impartial (順得哥情失嫂意).

Dirtiness

There are two idioms on dirtiness: 又鹹又臭 (dirty and stinky) and 污糟邋遢 (dirty; soiled).

Goods

People prefer goods which are cheap but good (又平又靚). But it is always the case that one gets what one pays for (一分錢一分貨). If the name of a piece of goods does not match what it claims to be (貨不對辦), nobody woud buy it (閻羅王揸攤——鬼買).

Rare goods are expensive (物以罕為貴). One should not buy goods without seeing them (隔山買牛 buy a cow over the mountain), and it would be safer to buy goods from a familiar shop (買生不如買熟).

Order

In this dictionary, all idioms on order are actually about disorder, which include 七國咁亂 (chaotic; in a disorderly situation; in a very confused and messy situation; messy; very messy), 七零八落 (in disorder), 四分五裂 (be rent by disunity; be smashed to bits; be split up; be torn apart; break into pieces come apart at the seams; come to pieces; fall apart; fall to pieces; scattered and disunited), 倒瀉籮蟹 (drop a basket of crabs——in a muddle; messy; troublesome), 烏喱馬扠 (illegible and sloppy; in a mess), 烏喱單刀 (chaotic; disorder; get everything mixed up; in a mess; muddled), 烏煙瘴氣 (all in a muddle; foul atmosphere), 鬼五馬六 (messy), 亂晒大籠 (in great chaos; in great disorder), 零星落索 (all in a hideous mess; all upside down; at sixes and sevens; chaotic; everything is upside down; fall apart into seven or eight pieces; in a state of confusion; in disorder; in great disorder; in ruin; in scattered confusion; scatter about in all directions), 攦頭撒尾 (always getting things; always losing this and forgetting that; forget this, that, and the other; miss this and that), 捔手唔成勢 (be tied up in knots due to lack of indecision), and 一隻筷子食豆腐——攪喎晒 (use one chopstick to eat tofu——make a mess of things).

People

There are all sorts of people (一樣米養百樣人 one type of rice feeds different kinds of people; many people, many minds; 木蝨狷入花生殼——硬充好人（仁）chewing melon seeds with the appearance of a bug——there are all sorts of people): the young and the old (有老有幼), famous and titled (有頭有面), and people on the street (亞保亞勝 every Tom, Dick, and Harry; 阿福阿壽 any person in the street).

There might be many people crowding together (人頭湧湧 a mass of people; 人山人海 a sea of faces; huge crowds of people; 聯羣結隊 band together; in crowds; in flocks; in groups; in throngs). There might be people grouping together (三羣五隊 in groups; 蛇鼠一窩 a group of bad people; act in collusion with; collude in doing evil; conspire for illegal ends; gang up for evil purposes; gang up with each other; join in plotting reason; play booty; work hand in glove with sb for evil doings). There might be only a few people (三九兩丁七 only a few people). Regardless of the ways of how people are put together, there are good and bad people in every group (樹大有枯枝 there is deadwood in every tree; 樹大有枯枝, 族大有乞兒 there's a black sheep in every fold).

Places

A remote place is said to be 冇雷公咁遠, a cool place, 風涼水冷 (has cool winds and water), and a place where people are free to come and go is known as 冇掩雞籠 (a coop without a flap).

Quantity

There are different ways to express quantity in Cantonese. Small quantity is expressed as 濕濕碎 (miscellaneous and trifling things; miscellaneous trifles; odds and ends; scattered and disorderly), 雞碎咁多 (a few; a little; a small amount of sth), 做薑唔辣, 做醋唔酸 (not spicy enough to be a ginger nor sour enough to be vinegar—— it is far from sufficient for the purpose), and 老鼠尾生瘡——大極有限 (a sore on a mouse's tail——there's a ceiling for sth). Increases in quantity are expressed as 小數怕長計 (carelessness with small amounts leads to big money problems in the long term), 山大斬埋有柴 (achieve a lot by proceeding in small steps; many a little makes a mickle), and such increases are well received (韓信點兵——多多益善 the more, the better). Approximation is expressed as 大大話話 (estimate approximately; roughly).

Situations

To Chinese people, a favourable situation is important to the accomplishment of goals (近水樓台先得月 a pavilion close to water will catch a glimpse of the moon first, meaning that one is in a favourable situation).

Situations may be bad (雞毛鴨血), acceptable (阿駝行路——中中哋 the state of being in the middle), desperate (上天無路, 入地無門 in desperate straits), chaotic (六國大封相), urgent (風頭火勢 at full throttle; in the state of full blast), or worsening (一蟹不如一蟹 the next crab is worse).

When the situation is urgent, illegal means might have to be used (事急馬行田). Very often, a situation is determined by fate (人算不如天算).

Time

Time is precious as even gold cannot buy time (寸金難買寸光陰). Punctuality therefore is much treasured (依時不誤 on time; 依時依候 on schedule; on time; punctual). When one is late, try one's best to make it up, for it is better late than never (遲到好過冇到 better late than never; 有心唔怕遲, 十月都係拜年時 it's never too late to do sth if you really want to do it; you can pay New Year visits to your friends even in the tenth month of the year). Sometimes, the late-comer may become a forerunner (遲嚟先上岸).

Weather

Weather in southern China is capricious. It has myriad changes (翻風落雨 windy and rainy) and much is under the mercy of God (摩囉差拜神——睇天 (小碗吃飯——靠天 (添)).

People are advised not to put aside one's winter clothes before the fifth month of the year as weather is so unpredictable (未食五月粽, 寒衣不入櫳).

Women

Women who get together to gossip are referred to as 三姑六婆 (a bevy of shrewish women; gossipy women). Men who are attractive to women, on the other hand, are known as 女人湯丸 or 女人湯圓 (attractive man with many female admirers).

Phonological differences

The pronunciation of Cantonese is different from that of Putonghua for the mere fact that Cantonese has nine tones, including 陰平 (dark flat), 陰上 (dark rising), 陰去 (dark departing), 陽平 (light flat), 陽上 (light rising), 陽去 (light departing), 陰入 (dark entering), 中入 (middle entering), and 陽入 (light entering), whereas Putonghua has four, including the first tone 陰平 (dark flat), second tone 陽平 (light flat), third tone 上聲 (rising tone), and fourth tone 去聲 (departing tone). The way we pronounce Cantonese obviously is different from the way we pronounce Putonghua.

For Putonghua, the Hanyu Pinyin Romanisation system is widely used. There are a number of transliteration systems for Cantonese, such as the Yale system. In this dictionary, the transliteration of all the Cantonese characters in this dictionary is based on《廣州話正音字典》(*Cantonese Pronunciation Dictionary*), edited by Zhan Bohui 詹伯慧 and published by Guangdong People's Publishing House 廣東人民出版社 .

After a detailed explanation of the lexical, cultural, and phonological differences between Cantonese and Putonghua, it is necessary to explain briefly the arrangement of entries in this dictionary. Entries in this dictionary are arranged as follows: (1) all entries are arranged according to their number of strokes; (2) entries with the same number of strokes are arranged according to the order of radicals; (3) all entries are arranged in normal and reverse sequences; and (4) whenever possible, entries are arranged in the order of Cantonese expressions, Putonghua equivalents, and English equivalents. Putonghua equivalents will not be provided if the entries can be used in both Cantonese and Putonghua.

Lastly, I would like to express my thanks to Mr Mao Yong-bo and Ms Betty K.L. Wong of The Commercial Press (H.K.) for their great efforts in the publication of this dictionary. My gratitude also goes to Professor Kenneth Young, Professor Xu Yangsheng, Dr Kim Mak, Dr Kat Leung, and Ms Florence Li for their support and encouragement in my academic endeavours.

Chan Sin-wai
September 2019

1 劃

【一】jat⁷ one

一一 one by one; one after another

一丁人（一個人）a person

一丁人都有（一個人都沒有）there isn't anyone

一了百了 when sth ends, all things end

一人 one man; one person

　一人計短，二人計長（一人不如兩人議）two heads are better than one

　一人做事一人當 one is responsible for what one does

　一人得道，雞犬升天 when a person gets to the top, all their friends and relatives get there with them

一刀兩斷 make a clean break; sever ties with sb

一三五七九一無傷（雙）（一二三五六——沒事（四））one, two, three, five, and six – nothing goes amiss

一下子 all at once

一千 one thousand

　一千尺 one thousand square feet

　一千蚊（一千塊）one thousand dollars

　一千零一 the only one

　千幾尺 more than one thousand square feet

一口 flatly; readily; promise without hesitation; with certainty

　一口井（一眼井）a well

　一口咬實（一口咬定）hold firm to one's stance; speak in an assertive tone

　一口氣 a breath; at a breath; at a stretch; at a whack; at one fling; at one go; at one sitting; in one breath; right off/straight off the reel; without a break; without stopping

　一口釘（一顆釘子）a nail

　一口針（一根針）a needle

一子錯滿盤皆落索 a wrong step causes a masty tumble; one careless move loses the whole game

一山不能藏二虎 at daggers drawn

一嚿 measure word, meaning a lump

　一嚿水（一百元）one hundred dollars

一弓射兩箭（一石二鳥）kill two birds with one stone

一不做，二不休 not to stop half way once a thing is started

　一不離二，二不離三（接二連三）another yet another; coming in quick succession; in rapid sequence; one after another; repeatedly; thick and fast; thick and threefold

一五一十 blow-by-blow; in full details; with all the details

一分（一分錢）one cent

　一分錢一分貨 one gets what one pays for

一分鐘 one minute

一天光晒（一天雲霧散）all is bright and clear; the trouble is over

一手 ① all by oneself ② firsthand

　一手購入 purchase firsthand

一支 a piece of; a stick of

　一支公 ①（獨個兒）alone ②（光棍兒一個）a bachelor; an unmarried man

　一支竹（一根竹子）a bamboo stick

　一支酒（一瓶酒）a bottle of wine

　一支針（一根針）a needle

　一支煙 a cigarette

　一支旗（一面旗）a flag

一日（一天）one day

　一日千里 advance by leaps and bounds

　一日到黑（一天到晚）all day(long); as the day is long; from dawn to dusk; from morning till night; the whole day

　總有一日 someday in the future

一世（人）（一輩子）a lifetime; all one's life; as long as one lives; man and boy; one's whole lifetime; throughout one's life

　一世人兩兄弟（一輩子就咱哥倆）we're brothers all our lives

　一世流流長（一輩子這麼長）as long as one lives

　不可一世 consider oneself unexcelled in the world; get on your high horse; insufferably arrogant; swagger like a conquering hero; think oneself supreme in the world

　捱一世（熬一輩子）toil all one's life

一仙（一分錢）one cent

一半 half; half of it; one half

　一半一半 fifty fifty

　另一半 other half; spouse

一去不返 be gone without returning

一句 a line; a word

　一句語該使死人 make excessive demands on sb without offering reasonable reward; make sb toil for you with just a word of thanks

　一句講晒（總言之）in a word

一粒鐘（一小時）one hour

一扑一碌 stumble and roll, meaning in a great hurry

一本 a book (of); a copy (of); a reel (of); a volume (of)

　一本書 a book

　一本／部通書睇到老（墨守成規）adhere to the old ways; cling conservatively to the old system; devote to conventions; follow a stereotypical routine; get into/move in/stay in/be stuck in a rut; go round like a horse in a mill; inflexible; stick-in-the-mud; stick to

accustomed rules/conventions/established practice/
outdated ways and regulations/the old ways

一本萬利 ① a small investment brings a ten-thousand-
fold profit; gain big profits with a small capital; gain
enormous profits out of a small capital investment;
make a ten-thousand-fold profit; make big profits with
a small capital ② wish you a profitable business

一生 all one's life

一生坎坷 a lifetime of frustrations; have hard luck all
one's life

一生兒女債，半世老婆奴 a wife and children are
a man's burdens

一氹水 (一灘水) a puddle of water

一疋布咁長 it's a long story

一蚊 (一塊錢) one dollar

一石二鳥 answer/serve a double purpose; kill two birds
with one stone

一份 one portion of

一件 one piece

一件事 a matter

一件衫 (一件衣服) an item of clothing

一件頭 one-piece outfit

一件還一件 things should be dealt with separately

一向 all along; consistently; up to now

一向都 always been

一地兩檢 co-location clearance

一字咁淺 (一加一那麼簡單／非常淺易) as easy as ABC;
as simple as the character "one"; extremely simple

一字馬 (一字腿) the splits

擘一字馬 (又一字腿／扒一字腿) do the splits

一孖梘 (兩塊肥皂) two bars of soap

一年 one year

一年一度 annual; once a year

一年到晚 (一年到頭) all the year round; at all seasons;
in season and out of season; the whole year round/
through; throughout the year; year in and year out;
year-round

一年容易又中秋 days in the year go by swiftly and it is
mid-autumn again

一早 early in the morning; very early

一次 once; one time

一次生兩次熟 clumsy at first but skilful the second time;
get used to things quickly

一次過 all at once; at one dash; at one go; in one breath;
once for all

唔該你講多一次 (請你說多一遍) pardon me

一死了之 death pays all debts

一百 one hundred

一百蚊 (一百塊) one hundred dollars

一竹篙打死一船人 (一棍子通通打死) can't take a bad
one for all; paint everybody with the same brush

一自 (一邊…一邊) at the same time

一行 a line of

一行字 a line of characters

排成一行 stand in a line

一坎炮 (一尊炮) a canon

一成 (百分之十) ten per-cent

一把 a bunch of; a bundle of; a handful of; a pair of;
a wisp of

一把刀 a knife

一把尺 a foot-rule

一把火 (一肚子火) be filled with rage; hot with rage

一把梳 (一個梳子) a comb

一把秤 (一桿秤) a steelyard

一把梯 a ladder

一把劍 a sword

一把嘴 (一張嘴) a mouth

一把遮 an umbrella

一把聲 (一種聲音) a voice

一把鎖 a lock

一步 one step

一步一步 step by step

一人行一步 (雙方讓步) have both sides make a
concession

一沉百踩 (牆倒眾人推) everybody hits a person who is
down; once sb falls from power, other people are eager
to criticise/step on him

一甫路 (十里路) a distance of ten miles

一肚氣 (一肚子氣) a stomachful of grudge; full of
complaints/grievances; strong emotions

一見鍾情 love at first sight

一言 a word; a single word

一言為定 that's a deal

一言難盡 it's a long story

一言驚醒夢中人 a person suddenly becomes clear-
minded upon listening to a word of wisdom

一身蟻 (一身躁／惹來一大堆麻煩) get into trouble; in a
great deal of trouble

一兩 one tael

一味 ① (總是) always; as a rule; commonly; constantly;
generally; invariably; usually; without exception ② (一道
菜) a dish ③ ingredient

一味靠指 (總是靠指) rely solely on talking nonsense

一味靠滾 (總是靠騙) always rely on cheating

一味餸 (一樣菜) a dish of food

一命二運三風水，四積陰德五讀書 Fate first, luck
second, fengshui third, virtue fourth, and education fifth

一坺 (一攤) a soft mass of

一坺泥 (一攤泥) a soft mass of mud

一坺泏 (一攤兒) as thick as paste; be all muddled up; make a mess of sth

一夜情 one-night stand

一定 certainly, must

一定要 must

一定唔 (一定不) must not

不一定 not necessarily so; not sure; uncertain

一底 (一大塊) a large piece of

一底糕 (一大盤糕) a tray of cake

一拃米 (一把米) a handful of rice

一抽 (一串) a bunch of; a cluster of; a rope of; a strand of; a string of

一抽二㩧 (拿着很多東西) carrying lots of different things

一抽臘腸 a string of Chinese sausages

一於 (就) even; even if; so

一於咁話 (就這樣了) so it's settled

一杯 a cup

一杯水 a cup of water; a glass of water

一杯茶 a cup of tea

一沓 ① (一疊) pile ② (棟) pillar

一沓樓 (一棟樓) a building

一枝 (一根 / 一條) a piece of; a stalk of

一枝公 ① (獨自一人 / 獨個兒) alone ② (光棍兒一個) a bachelor; an unmarried man

一枝竹 (一根竹子 / 一條竹子) a bamboo stick

一枝花 a spray of flower

一枝笛 a flute

一枝筆 ① a pen ② a writing brush

一枝旗 (一面旗) a banner; a flag

一枝墨 (一錠墨) a slab of ink

一波三折 meet with difficulties one after another

一波未平，一波又起 one trouble is followed by another

一泡氣 (一肚子氣) a stomachful of grudge; full of complaints; full of grievances

一物治一物 (一物降一物) everything has its superior; one thing is always controlled or conquered by another

一係 (或者 / 要不然) or

一封 measure word for a letter

一封信 a letter

一道門 (一扇門) a door

一度橋 (一座橋) a bridge

一律 alike; all; without exception

一架 measure word for vehicles

一架車 (一輛車) a car

一流 (第一流 / 頭等) first rate; superb; top class

真係一流 (真棒) excellent

一盆水 (一萬元) ten thousand dollars

一秒 one second

一秒鐘 one second

一面 ① one aspect; one side; a look ② at the same time

一面之詞 one-sided statement

一面之緣 have a face-to-face meeting with sb

一面屁 (一鼻子灰) be rebuffed; meet frustration, humiliation or rejection; run into a stone wall

最後一面 take a last look at a dying person

一個 ① a; an; one ② a piece of; a word of

一個二個 (所有人) all of you

一個人 a person

一個井 (一口井) a well

一個仔 (一個兒子) a son

一個仙 (一分錢) one cent

一個字 (五分鐘) five minutes

一個杯 a cup; a glass

一個咪 (一個麥克風) a microphone

一個缸 (一口缸) a large bowl

一個骨 ① (一刻 / 一刻鐘) fifteen minutes ② a quarter

一個做好一個做醜 (一個唱紅臉一個唱白臉) one plays the role of a gentleman while the other plays the role of a villain

一個袋 a bag

一個湯 a soup

一個煲 a pot

一個碟 ① a plate ② a saucer

一個蜆一個肉 (一個蘿蔔一個坑) each has their own task, and there is nobody to spare; (literally) every hole has its own turnip

一個對 (二十四小時) twenty-four hours

一個橙 an orange

一個碼 one size

一個箱 a case

一個樽 a bottle

一個錶 (一塊錶) a watch

一個鎚 (一把鎚子) a hammer

一個願打，一個願捱 one likes to hurt and the other is willing to suffer; a well-matched couple

一個鏡 (一面鏡子) a mirror

一個餸 (一個菜) a dish of food

一個罌 (一個廣口瓶) an earthen jar

一個鐘 ① (一個鐘頭) one hour ② (一座鐘 / 一個時鐘) a clock

上一個 one ahead of you

下一個 next in line

一哥 ① (老大 / 第一把手 / 頭頭) chief; head; number-one person ② (警務署長) Police Commissioner

一浸／嗲（一層）a bed of; a blanket of; a cloak of; a coat of; a curtain of; a deck of; a film of; a flake of; a layer of; a level of; a line of ; a mantle of; a ring of; a veil of
　一浸／嗲 浸皮（一層皮）a layer of skin
　一浸／嗲 浸煙（一股煙／一縷煙）a trail of smoke
　一浸／嗲 浸𦟌（一股味）a trail of bad smell
一埕酒（一壜子酒）a jar of wine
一埲／郴牆（一道／堵牆）a wall
一套 a set; a suit
　一套衫 an outfit
　一套戲（一齣戲）a movie; a play
　另搞一套 go one's own way
　老一套 the same old methods or stories
一家 a family; one family
　一家人 whole family
　一家便宜兩家着（一面砌牆兩面光）both sides benefit; win-win situation
一座山 a mountain
一息間 a little while; in a moment
一戚（一堞）a pile of; a stack of
　一戚書（一摞書）a pile of books
　一戚都冇（一點兒轍也沒有）at one's wits end; at a loss of what to do
　一戚嘢（一百塊）one hundred dollars
　一戚磚（一堞磚）a stack of bricks
一時 a period of time; briefly; for a short while; momentarily
　一時一樣 fickle
　一時口快 speak too quickly
　一時唔偷雞做保長（一時不做壞事便周圍教訓人）a rogue goes so far as to moralise to another rogue
　一時時 sometimes; for a single moment
一氣 at one go; in one breath; without a break
一浪接一浪 waves after waves
一班（一夥）a class of; a group of; a squad of; a troupe of
　一班人 a class of people; a group of people; a squad of people; a troupe of performers (dancers/singers)
一紮花（一束花）a bundle of flowers
一般 common; general
　一般嚟講 generally speaking; usually
一蚊（雞）（一塊錢）one dollar
一陣（間）（一會兒／一陣子）a little while; a short while; (informal) in a jiffy; in a moment; presently
　一陣見（稍後再見）see you soon
　一陣陣（有時候）sometimes; for a single moment
　阻你一陣（請你等一下）keep you for a moment
　等一陣間（等一下）wait for a moment
一隻 a; an; one
　一隻叉（一支叉）a fork

一隻牙（一顆牙齒）a tooth
一隻牛（一條牛／一頭牛）a cow
一隻字（一個字）a character
一隻狗（一條狗）a dog
一隻梳（一把梳子）a comb
一隻馬（一匹馬）a horse
一隻眼（一隻眼睛）an eye
一隻蛋（一個雞蛋）an egg
一隻窗（一扇窗戶）a window
一隻碗（一個碗）a bowl
一隻腳（一條腿）a leg
一隻豬（一口豬／一頭豬）a pig
一隻貓 a cat
一隻鴨 a duck
一隻雞 a chicken
一隻藥（一種藥）a kind of medicine
一隻鑊（一口鍋）a pan
一兜飯（一碟飯）a plate of cooked rice
一副 measure word for spectacles, games, etc.
一啖（一口）a mouthful of
　一啖砂糖一啖屎 praise is followed by criticism
　一啖氣（一口氣）at one breath
　一啖飯（一口飯）a mouthful of rice
　呷一啖（喝一口）take a sip
　咬一啖 have a bite
一嗿布（一小塊布）a small piece of cloth
一啲（一點兒）some
一執 ①（一把）a handful of ②（一撮）a tuft of
　一執毛（一撮毛）a tuft of hair
　一執米（一把米）a handful of rice
一堂 a period of; a pair of
　一堂眉（兩條眉）a pair of eyebrows
　一堂課（一節課）a class
一張 a piece of; a sheet of; a slip of
　一張刀（一把刀）a knife
　一張枱（一張桌子）a table
　一張氈（一條毯子）a blanket
　一張相（一張照片）a photo
　一張飛（一張票）a ticket
　一張紙 a sheet of paper
　一張被（一條被子）a quilt
　一張椅（一把椅子）a chair
　一張蓆（一領蓆）a straw mattress
　一張櫈（一個櫈子）a stool
一排（一段時間）a row; a period of time
一桶 a bucket of
　一桶水 a bucket of water
一條 a bar of; a carton of; a loaf of; a pair of; a piece of
　一條心（全心全意）whole-heartedly

一條毛（一根毛）a hair

一條呔（一條領帶）a tie

一條屍（一具死屍）a corpse

一條氣（一口氣）at a breath; at a stretch; at a whack; at one fling; at one go; at one sitting; in one breath; right off the reel; without a break

一條痕（一道印兒）a scar

一條蛇 a snake

一條魚 a fish

一條街 a street

一條葱（一根葱）a piece of green onion

一條裙（一條裙子）a skirt

一條路 a road

一條嘢（一百塊錢）one hundred dollars

一條數（一筆賬）a sum of money

一條橋（一座橋）a bridge

一條褲（一條褲子）a pair of trousers

一條龍 ① one queue ② one-way through ③ one-stop service

一條罅（一道縫兒）a gap

一條／碌蔗（一根甘蔗／一條甘蔗）a sugar cane

一條繩（一條繩子）a string

一條鎖匙聞唔聲，兩條鎖匙冷冷響（一個碗不響，兩個碗叮噹）(literally) one key (bowl) is quiet while two keys (bowls) give out ding-dong sounds

一梳蕉（一串／一把香蕉）a bunch of bananas; a hand of bananas

一埲／桸牆（一道／堵牆）a wall

一毫（紙）（一毛（錢））ten cents

一理通，百理明 once one has mastered the basic idea, the rest is easy

一眼 ① a glance ② measure word for needles, nails and wells

一眼井（一口井）a well

一眼釘（一根釘子）a nail

一眼針（一支／一根針）a needle

一眼針冇兩頭尖（甘蔗沒有兩頭甜）(literally) a needle can't be sharp at both ends; (a sugar cane is never sweet at both ends) – one cannot have it both ways

一眼燈（一盞燈）a lamp

一眼關七（眼觀六路）attend to several things at the same time; keep one's eyes open; on the alert

一笪（一塊）a block of; a chunk of; a lump of; a piece of; a plot of; a slab of; a slice of; an area of

一笪地（一塊地）a plot of land

一笪瘌（一塊疤）a scar

一粒 a grain of; a piece of

一粒仔（一個兒子）a son

一粒米 a grain of rice

一粒色（小個子）short person

一粒沙 a grain of sand

一粒豆 a bean

一粒星（一顆星）a star

一粒珠（一顆珠子）a pearl

一粒嘢（一萬塊）ten thousand dollars

一粒糖（一顆糖）a sweet

一粒鐘（一小時）one hour

一紮 a bouquet of; a bunch of; a bundle of; a cluster of; a hank of

一紮花（一束花）a bunch of flowers

一紮草（一捆草）a bundle of grass

一脫人（一輩人）a certain kind of people

一造禾（一熟稻）a harvest of rice

一連 in a row

一部 a volume of; a work of

一部書 a book

一部通書睇到老 stick in the mud

一圍 a table of

一圍台（一桌）a table

一圍酒（一桌酒席）a table for a Chinese banquet

一喺（要麼）or

一場歡喜一場空 draw water with a sieve

一就一，二就二 (literally) one is one, two is two; be straightforward; unequivocal

一幅（一塊）a piece of

一幅地（一塊地）a piece of land

一幅相（一張照片）a photo

一幅畫 a drawing; a painting; a picture

一揸米（一把米）a handful of rice

一棟 a building

一棟／戙都冇 cannot do anything

一棟樓 a building

一棚 a bag of; a heap of; a row of

一棚牙（一排牙齒）a row of teeth

一棚骨（一把骨頭）a bag of bones

一棚渣（一堆渣）a heap of dregs

一棵 measure word for plants

一棵菜 a vegetable

一棵樹 a tree

一朝俾蛇咬，三年怕草繩（一朝被蛇咬，三年怕井繩）a burnt child dreads the fire; (literally) once bitten by a snake, one shies at a coiled rope for the next three years; once bitten, twice shy; the scalded dog fears cold water

一朝天子一朝臣 a new chief brings in his own trusted followers

一殼（一勺）a ladle of

一殼水（一瓢水）a ladle of water

一殼飯（一勺飯）a ladle of rice

一劃一戙（一橫一豎）a horizontal stroke and a vertical stroke

一筆 one sum; one stroke
　一筆還一筆 treat two things separately

一等（第一流／頭等）first class

一間 measure word for rooms
　一間舖／舖頭（一家店）a shop
　一間房（一個房間）a room
　一間屋（一所房子）a house

一傳十，十傳百 news travels fast; spread from mouth to mouth

一塊 a piece of; a sheet of; a slice of; a tablet of
　一塊布 a piece of cloth
　一塊田 a field
　一塊面（一張臉）a face
　一塊葉（一片葉子）a leaf
　一塊鏡（一面鏡子）a mirror

一煲（一鍋）a pot of
　一煲水 a pot of water
　一煲粥（一鍋稀飯）a pot of congee
　一煲飯（一鍋飯）a pot of rice

一盞 measure word for lamps and lights
　一盞燈 a lamp

一督尿（一泡尿）pass water

一碌 measure word
　一碌木（一根木頭）a log; a long piece of wood
　一碌蔗（一段甘蔗）a segment of sugar cane; a stick of sugar cane

一窟（一小塊）a small piece of
　一窟布（一小塊布）a small piece of cloth

一經 as soon as; once

一腳 one foot
　一腳踏兩／幾船（腳踩兩條船）have two/ several lovers at the same time
　一腳踢（一人班）do everything by oneself; one-man band
　凌空一腳 kick the ball high up in the air

一萬 ten thousand
　一萬蚊（一萬塊）ten thousand dollars

一路 ① （一直）all along; all the time/way/while; all through; always; as ever; as the day is long; constantly; continuously; ever since; from...till now; hold; keep; on end; to this day; used to be ② during the whole journey
　一路平安 a safe journey
　一路發 getting rich all the time

一道 a beam of; a flash of; a line of; a shaft of; a streak of
　一道門（一扇門）a door

一嘜米（一鐵罐米）a can of rice

一夥 a company of

一夥人（一戶人家）a group of people

一對（副／雙）pair
　一對手（一雙手）a pair of hands
　一對眼（一雙眼睛）a pair of eyes
　一對腳（一雙腿）a pair of legs
　一對鞋（一雙鞋）a pair of shoes
　一對襪（一雙襪子）a pair of socks

一箸夾中（一擊即中）hit the right nail on the head; make a right guess

一網打盡 make a clean sweep

一辣（一排）a row of
　一辣屋（一排房子）a row of houses

一齊（一同／一起／一道／一塊兒）all together; at the same time; in company; in union; simultaneously; together
　一齊包（一起包）pack things together; wrap things together
　一齊去（一起去）go together
　擺埋一齊 bring together

一墩（一座）a block of stone
　一墩樓（一座樓／一棟樓）a building

一層 ① one floor; one storey ② a stratum ③ a bed of; a blanket of; a cloak of; a coat of; a curtain of; a deck of; a film of; a flake of; a floor of; a floor of; a layer; a layer of; a level of; a line of; a mantle of; a ring of; a storey; a storey of; a veil of
　一層樓 ① a flat ② a storey

一撇 one thousand
　一撇水／一叉嘢（一千塊）one thousand dollars

一樓一鳳（一個住宅住一個妓女）one-woman brothel

一樣 same
　一樣米養百樣人（一娘生九種，種種不同）there are all kinds of people in the world

一箒（一棵）a stalk of; a tuft of
　一箒菜（一棵菜）a vegetable

一盤水（一萬塊）ten thousand dollars

一趟 a ride; a trip

一輪嘴 a volley of words; talk continuously; wag one's tongue

一舖棋（一盤棋）a game of chess

一劑（一服）a dose of
　一劑藥（一服藥）a dose of medicine

一擔菜（一挑兒菜）two baskets of vegetables carried on a shoulder pole
　一擔擔（半斤八兩）two of a kind

一樽（一瓶）a bottle of
　一樽水 a bottle of water
　一樽酒（一瓶酒）a bottle of wine

一橫一棟（一橫一豎）one horizontal stroke and one

vertical stroke

一橛（一段／一節）a section of
　一橛蔗（一節甘蔗）a section of sugar cane
一篤（一泡／一堆）a puddle
　一篤尿（一泡尿）pass water
　一篤屎（一堆屎）dung
　一篤痰（一口痰）a glob of phlegm; a spit of phlegm
一舉成名 famous overnight
一頭 ① a head of ②（個）a; an; one
　一頭半個月 half of a month
　一頭家（一個家庭）a family
　一頭煙 extremely busy
一頸血（賠很多錢）lose a great deal of money
一餐飯（一頓飯）a meal
一龍去，二龍追（眾人聚會，甲未到，乙去找）(literally)
while one goes to look for sb along one route, that
person comes back along the other
一窿蛇（一班壞傢伙／蛇鼠一窩）a group of gangsters
一餅（一盒）a cassette of
一餅帶（一盒帶子）a cassette of recording tape
　一餅錄音帶（一盒錄音帶）a cassette of recording tape
一點 ① one o'clock ② a little bit
　一點一 five past one
　一點一個字 five past one
　一點一個骨 a quarter past one; one fifteen
　一點七 one thirty-five; twenty-five to two
　一點七個字 one thirty-five; twenty-five to two
　一點九 a quarter to two; one forty-five
　一點九個字 a quarter to two; one forty-five
　一點二 ten past one
　一點二十五分 one twenty-five; twenty-five past one
　一點二十分 one twenty; twenty past one
　一點八 one forty; twenty to two
　一點八個字 one forty; twenty to two
　一點十 one fifty; ten to two
　一點十一 five to two; one fifty-five
　一點十五分 a quarter past one; one fifteen
　一點十分 ten past one
　一點十個字 one fifty; ten to two
　一點三 a quarter past one; one fifteen
　一點三十五分 one thirty-five; twenty-five to two
　一點三十分 half past one; one thirty
　一點三個字 a quarter past one; one fifteen
　一點三個骨 a quarter to two; one forty-five
　一點五 one twenty-five; twenty-five past one
　一點五十五分 five to two; one fifty-five
　一點五十分 one fifty; ten to two
　一點五個字 one twenty-five; twenty-five past one
　一點半 half past one; one thirty

　一點四 one twenty; twenty past one
　一點四十五分 a quarter to two; one forty-five
　一點四十分 one forty; twenty to two
　一點四個字 one twenty; twenty past one
　一點兩個字 ten past one
　一點嗒一 five past one
　一點嗒七 one thirty-five; twenty-five to two
　一點嗒九 a quarter to two; one forty-five
　一點嗒二 ten past one
　一點嗒八 one forty; twenty to two
　一點嗒十 one fifty; ten to two
　一點嗒十一 five to two; one fifty-five
　一點嗒三 a quarter past one; one fifteen
　一點嗒五 one twenty-five; twenty-five past one
　一點嗒四 one twenty; twenty past one
　一點零五分 five past one
　一點鐘 one o'clock
一轆（一根／一條）a stick of
　一轆木（一根木頭）a log; a long piece of wood
　一轆蔗（一根／一條甘蔗）a segment of sugar cane; a
　stick of sugar cane
一額汗（一頭汗）a sweat-covered head
一雙 a pair of
　一雙一對 a couple
一雞死一雞鳴 persons of a kind come forth in
succession; successors come forth one after another;
when one person leaves a business, another will take
it up
一蟹不如一蟹（每況愈下）become worse and worse; go
downhill; go from bad to worse; on the decline; steadily
deteriorate; take a bad turn
一竇（一窩）a brood of; a litter of
　一竇豬（一窩豬）a nest of pigs
一罌鹽（一瓦罐鹽）an earthen jar of salt
一嚿（一塊）a cake of; a piece of; a lump of
　一嚿木（一塊木頭）a piece of wood
　一嚿木咁 look dumb
　一嚿水（一百塊）one hundred dollars
　一嚿肉（一塊肉）a piece of meat
　一嚿泥（一團泥土）a lump of mud
　一嚿炭 a piece of charcoal
　一嚿嚿（一塊／一團）a lump
　一嚿骨（一塊骨）a bone
　一嚿梘（一塊肥皂）a cake of soap
　一嚿雲 all at sea
　一嚿電（一節電池）a battery
　一嚿飯 ①（一團飯）a lump of cooked rice ②（呆子／
　笨蛋／飯桶）stupid person
　一嚿薑 a piece of ginger

一籠 a basket of; a small steamer basket of; a cage of

一鑊 a wok of

　　一鑊泡 (一塌糊塗) (literally) a wok of bubbles, meaning chaotic or unmanageable

　　一鑊粥 (literally) a wok of congee, meaning a chaotic situation

　　一鑊熟 ① (大鍋熬) cook everything in one wok/pot ② (同歸於盡) all come to an end; all perish together

　　一鑊翹起 (麻煩很大) cause sb a lot of trouble

一千零一 the only one

二分之一 half; one half

十一 eleven

三分之一 one third

三比一 three to one

三合一 three in one

三缺一 one player short for a game of mahjong

三對一 three to one

不一 differ; vary

牛一 (生日) birthday

加一 ten percent service charge

加零一 in the extreme; to the utmost

四分之一 a quarter

正一 really

年初一 the first day of the Chinese Lunar New Year

百分一 one percent

免加一 waive the ten-percent service charge

言行不一 actions repugnant to one's words; one does not do what one preaches; one's actions are not in keeping with one's promises; one's acts belie one's words; talk one way and behave another

阿一 ① boss ② leader ③ person-in-charge

星期一 Monday

唔怕一萬，至怕萬一 a contingency is what we are afraid of

唔理三七廿一 (不理三七二十一) fling caution to the winds; regardless of the consequences

第一 the first

番鬼佬睇榜——倒數第一 the first from the bottom

統一 unification

買一送一 buy one get one free

萬一 in case

萬中無一 one in a million

零點一 zero point one

歸一 neat; tidy

禮拜一 Monday

壞到加零一 extremely bad

2 劃

【丁】ding¹ man

丁丁 Hong Kong tram

丁字 T-shaped

丁屋 indigenous villager's house

丁香 lilac

丁點 a tiny bit

尼古丁 nicotine

豆丁 kid; tiny

添丁 have a baby born into the family

單丁 alone; single

搵丁 trick

零丁 odd cents

零零丁丁 scattered; solitary

諸事丁 meddler; nosy person

雞丁 chicken cube

【七】tsat⁷ seven

七七八八 (八九不離十 / 差不多 / 接近完成) ① the great majority of sth ② almost done

七月 ① July ② the seventh month of the lunar year

七老八十 (年紀大 / 年邁) aged; elderly; in one's seventies or eighties

七姐誕 (七夕) Double Seventh Festival; Seven Sisters Festival

七除八拆 (七折八扣) various deductions; big discounts

七國咁亂 (大混亂 / 亂成一圍 / 亂得一塌糊塗) chaotic; in a mess

七彩 ① colourful ② severe

七零八落 in disorder

七嘴八舌 all talking at once

七點 (鐘) seven o'clock

七竅生煙 fly into a rage

一眼關七 attend to several things at the same time; keep one's eyes open; on the alert

十七 seventeen

三 (九) 唔識七 (完全不認識) be stranger to each other; don't know him/her

尾七 the ninth seven after one's death

做七 memorial ceremony for the dead seven weeks after their death

墨七 (匪徒) burglar; thief

錢七 (舊車) old car

頭七 the first seven days after sb's death

【乜】 mat⁷ what

乜乜物物（等等／甚麼的）and so on and so forth

乜水（誰）who

乜東東（甚麼東西）(informal) thingummy; what is it

乜料 ①（甚麼東西）what is it ②（有甚麼特別）what is special

乜鬼（甚麼鬼名堂）what is it

乜都有（甚麼都有）have everything

乜都係假（其他全不重要）all else is unimportant; none is the point

乜嘢（甚麼）what; whatever

　乜嘢色（甚麼顏色）what colour

　乜嘢事（甚麼事）what is the matter

　　發生乜嘢事（發生甚麼事）what's going on

　乜嘢物嘢（等等／甚麼的）and so on and so forth

　　想食啲乜嘢（想吃些甚麼東西）what would you like to have

冇乜（不要緊）it doesn't matter; it's nothing; never mind; that's all right

使乜（沒必要）need not; why is it necessary to

為／做乜（為甚麼要這樣）how come; how is it that; what for; why; why is it that

唔知老豆姓乜（literally) forget even the surname of one's father, meaning one is totally immersed in sth that one doesn't remember anything at all

驚乜（害怕甚麼）what is to be feared

【九】 gau² nine

九大簋 lavish banquet

　食九大簋 have a sumptuous meal

九月 ① September ② the ninth month of the lunar year

九因歌（乘法口訣）multiplication table rhyme

九成九（百分之九十九）ninety-nine percent

九折 10% discount

九流 poor quality

九個字 forty-five minutes

九唔搭八（牛頭不對馬嘴）illogical or irrelevant answer

九點（鐘）nine o'clock

八八九九 almost completed

十九 ① nineteen ② nine and ten

十之八九 ① eight or nine out of ten ② most likely

【了】 liu⁵ ① end; finish ② settle

了結 bring to an end/conclusion; finish; get through with; settle; wind up

了解 know clearly; understand

　直接了解 know directly

一了百了 when sth ends, all things end

大不了 at worst; it's not a big deal

不了 without end

不得了 ① desperately serious; horrible; terrible ② exceedingly; extremely

免不了 be bound to be; hard to avoid; inevitable; it is only natural that

咁仲得了（怎能這樣）how could this be

唔得了（不得了）exceedingly; extremely; terrible

【二】 ji⁶ two

二一添作五 divide sth equally; go fifty-fifty

二人 two persons

　二人餐 two-person meal

二五仔 ①（叛徒）traitor ②（舉報人）whistleblower

二分之一 half; one half

二手 second-hand; used

　二手市場 secondary market

　二手交投 secondary transaction

　二手成交 second-hand transactions completed

　二手車 second-hand car; used car

　二手衫 second-hand clothes

　二手貨 second-hand goods; used goods

　二手買賣 secondaryhand trade

　二手樓 second-hand property

二月 ① February ② the second month of the lunar year

二水貨（次等貨）second-rate goods

二世祖（不肖子／敗家子）big-spending son; fop

二四六八單 — 有得變 it is unchangeable

二奶（小老婆／少奶奶／姘婦／情婦／小三）mistress; number-two wife

　二奶命 always have to settle for second best

　包二奶 keep a mistress

二打六（小人物）low-level person; unimportant person

二叔公 pawn shop

　二叔公割禾——望下截（拉縴的瞧活兒——往後看）(literally) granduncle harvesting grains——to look at the lower part of the stalk (boat tracker tending to his job), meaning to look back on

　二叔婆養豬 — 夠晒好心機（坐在坑頭數芝麻 — 用上細工了）(literally) grandaunt rearing pigs——having so much patience (sitting on a pit to count sesame seeds – it requires meticulous work)

二等 second class

二撇雞／鬚（八字鬚）man with a beard

一就一，二就二 (literally) one is one, two is two, meaning distinctions should be clearly made; straightforward; unequivocal

一點二 (一時十分) ten past one

十二 twelve

年初二 the second day of the Chinese Lunar New Year

坐一望二 hope for another after gaining one

尾二 the second last

知其一不知其二 have a smattering of sth or sb

阿二 ① number two ② mistress; second wife

星期二 Tuesday

第二 ① another; the other ② second ③ next

數一數二 reckon as one of the very best; the best; the most famous

獨一無二 unique

禮拜二 (星期二／週二) Tuesday

【人】 jan⁴ person

人一世，物一世 (人生幾何) you only live once

人力 human power
　　人力資源 human resources

人又老，錢又冇 (又窮又沒錢) old and penniless; old and poor

人口 population
　　人口密集 be densely populated

人士 person
　　知名人士 famous person

人山人海 a sea of faces; huge crowds of people

人工 ① (工錢／工資／薪金) salary; wage ② artificial
　　人工好灰 (工錢少得可憐) the salary is miserable
　　加人工 (加工資) have a pay rise
　　扣人工 (扣工資) deduct wages

人才 talented people
　　人才流失 brain drain
　　人才過剩 an excess of talented people

人不為己，天誅地滅 everyone for themselves; look after one's own interests

人心 a person's heart
　　人心不足蛇吞象 human beings are never satisfied with what they have
　　人心冇厭足 (心無厭足／貪得無厭) one is never contented; one is never satisfied
　　人心肉做 have a good conscience; people are by nature compassionate
　　不得人心 contrary to the will of the people; fail to gain popular support; fall into disfavour among the people; go against the will of the people; have no popular support
　　迷惑人心 confuse the masses

人日 Birthday of Human Beings; Everybody's Birthday

人比人，比死人 (人比人氣死人) comparisons are odious; it is harmful to compare oneself with others

人民 people
　　人民幣 Renminbi

人生 life
　　人生路不熟 (人生地不熟) be a complete stranger
　　美好人生 happy life

人同此心，心同此理 everybody feels the same

人在人情在 while a person lives, his favours are remembered

人多 many people
　　人多手腳亂 too many cooks spoil the broth
　　人多好做作 many hands make light work
　　人多車多 a large population with lots of traffic

人有三急 go for a pee; need to go to the toilet; take a leak
　　人有三衰六旺 a person suffers misfortunes and other times strokes of good fortune
　　人有失手，馬有失蹄 there's always many a slip-up in a person's job

人老心不老 young in spirit for one's old age
　　人老精，鬼老靈 (薑是老的辣) experience teaches

人夾人緣 (有人緣才有朋友) whether people get along with one another or not depends on the compatibility of their characters

人妖 (兩性人) transvestite

人事 (關係) relationship

人命 life
　　攪出人命 (意外懷孕) have a baby unexpectedly

人怕出名豬怕肥 (人怕出名豬怕壯) (literally) a person fears fame as a pig fears fat, meaning fame brings trouble

人爭一口氣，佛爭一爐香 make a good show of oneself

人物 people
　　大人物 great person; important person; somebody
　　小人物 cipher; nobody; (informal) small beer; small fry; small potato
　　幕後人物 wirepuller

人哋 (人家／別人) other people; others
　　人哋出雞，你出豉油 While the larger part of the expenses is borne by others, one still has to bear a small part of the expenses

人客 (客人) guest

人急智生 have quick wits in an emergency

人要衣裝，佛要金裝 (literally) a person needs clothing while Buddha needs gilding, meaning fine feathers make fine birds; the tailor makes the man
　　人要面，樹要皮 (人要臉，樹要皮) a person needs face just like a tree needs bark

人面 (人際關係) personal relations

人面廣（人脈廣／交遊廣闊）be well connected

人面獸心 a wolf in lamb's skin/sheep's clothing

人格 personality

　　人格分裂 disintegration of personality

人氣 ①（知名度）popularity ②（有生氣）liveliness ③（熱鬧）with lots of people

人情 ① human relationship ② gift; gratuity money

　　人情物理 gifts in general

　　人情緊過債（送禮比還債緊急）giving a gift is more urgent than settling a debt

　　人情薄過紙（人情如紙薄）kindness and compassion are rare in relationships between people

　　　做人情（送禮）give gratuity money at weddings; send a gift

人望高處，水往低流 everybody looks up

人細鬼大（人小點子多）a young boy with the mind and maturity of an adult; young but tricky

人蛇（水路偷渡者／偷渡者）illegal immigrant

人造 man-made

人渣（敗類）dreg; scum

人無千日好 no person is fortunate forever

人間蒸發 disappear without a trace

人道毀滅 euthanasia

人算不如天算 circumstances often defeat humans' expectations; man proposes, God disposes; the fate decides all

人影 human shadow

　　人影都冇隻（一個人影都沒有）there's nobody

人潮 crowds of people

人窮志不窮 poor but ambitious

人窮志短 humble oneself for being poor

人質 hostage

人頭 head

　　人頭湧湧 a mass of people

　　人頭豬腦 as stupid as a pig; stupid

人講你又講（人云亦云）parrot what other people say

人類 mankind

人權 human rights

一世人 all one's life

一竹篙打死一船人 can't take a bad one for all; paint everybody with the same brush

一言驚醒夢中人 a person suddenly becomes clear-minded upon listening to a word of wisdom; give a wise word to a fool

一家人 whole family

一班人 a class of people; a group of people; a squad of people; a troupe of performers (singers/dancers)

一脫人 a certain kind of people

一夥人 a group of people

一樣米養百樣人 there are all kinds of people in the world

十年樹木，百年樹人 it takes ten years to grow a tree, but a hundred years to bring up a generation of people

丈人 wife's father

凡人 ① ordinary person ② mortal

大人（成年人）① adult ② important person

大男人 chauvinist; domineering man

大美人 very beautiful lady

女人 woman; women

小人 base person; villain

工人 ① amah;（保姆）②（家傭）domestic helper ③ worker ④ servant

工廠工人 factory worker

才子佳人 a gifted scholar and a beautiful lady

不求人 back scratcher

中國人 Chinese

介紹人 introducer

內向的人 introvert

內行人 expert; insider

王人 artful person

太空人 ①（宇航員／航天員）astronaut; spaceman ② one whose wife is abroad

好迫人（太擠）overcrowded

夫人 wife

冇人（沒有人／無人）nobody

冇呢個人（沒有這個人）there's no one by that name

冇面見人（羞愧得不想見人）feel too ashamed to face people

主人 ① master ② owner

主持人 chairperson; host; presenter; quizmaster

他人 another person; other people; others; sb else

仗勢欺人 abuse one's power and bully people; ; take advantage of one's own position or power to bully people

代理人 agent

令人（使人）arouse; cause; make

北方人 northerner

古人 ancients; old friend

召集人 convener

失禮死人（真失禮）it is totally disgraceful

巨人 giant

打小人 beat the little person

本人 ① I; me; myself ② in person; in the flesh; oneself

本地人 local

犯人 convict; criminal; prisoner; the guilty

生人 living person

生保人（陌生人）stranger

目擊證人 eyewitness

先人 ancestor

先敬羅衣後敬人 people usually open doors to fine clothes

同人 with people

名人 celebrity; famous person

好人 good/nice person; goody; goodie

大忙人 busy person; busy bee

有心裝冇心人 (設下陷阱) set a trap for sb

有錢人 rich people

死人 dead person

百年樹人 education of people takes many many years to bear fruit; it takes a hundred years to rear people

老人 old person; old people; the aged; the elderly

自己人 one of us; our own mate

路人 (行人) pedestrian

行內人 expert; insider

西人 Westerner

低頭切肉，把眼看人 (勢利的人看人行事) choose a pigeon to cheat

住家男人 family man

冷落人 give sb the cold shoulder

初戀情人 first love; first lover

別人 ① another person; sb else ② other people; others

含血噴人 smite with the tongue

呃人 (騙人) deceive sb

局中人 player

局內人 insider

局外人 outsider

成棚人 (一輩人／一堆人) a large group of people

成拃人 (一整群人／一堆人) a group of people

每個人 everyone

求人 seek help from others

狂人 ① kook; lunatic; madman; maniac ② an extremely arrogant and conceited person

走人 leave stealthily; scarper; slink; slip away; slope off

車死人 (車撞死人) car running over people causing death

車嘜人 (車撞傷人) run over sb

邑人 people of the same county

佳人 beautiful woman

來說是非者，便是是非人 the person who speaks ill of others will speak ill of you

卑鄙小人 creep

呢世人 (這一生人) this lifetime

呢個人 (這個人) this person

呢挺人 (這種人) this kind of people

怕人 ① (怕生) shy; timid ② (挺嚇人) awful; frightening; horrible; terrifying

怪人 strange guy

拉人 (拘捕／逮捕／捉拿) arrest sb

抬棺材甩褲——失禮死人 one's trousers drop when carrying a coffin – very embarrassing

放路溪錢——引死人 very attractive

明人 honest person

明白人 perceptive person

明眼人 discerning person

枉作小人 play the villain, but fail to gain any profit

枕邊人 wife

泥水佬開門口——過得自己過得人 live and let live

炒人 (解僱) be dismissed; fire an employee

俗人 vulgarian; ordinary person

前無古人 have no parallel in history

屋企人 (家人) family member

後人 descendants

急急腳走人 (匆匆離去) go away in a hurry; leave in a hurry

恰人 (欺負別人) bully others

皇天不負有心人 God tempers the wind to the shorn lamb

紅人 a favourite of the person in power

達人 expert

要人 important person

俾人 (讓人) allow sb; give sb

個個人 (每一個人／每人) everybody

借刀殺人 murder with a borrowed knife

冧人 (討人歡心) please others

哲人 philosopher; sage

唐人 Chinese

娛人 (娛樂別人) make sb happy

差人 (警察) cop; police

恩人 benefactor

捉兒人 (捉迷藏) play hide-and-seek

旁人 other people; others

真人 (本人) the person himself/herself

能人 able person

衰人 (壞人) bad guy; bad person

迷人 charming; enchanting

偉人 great man; great personage

做人 behave as a person; conduct oneself

做咗鬼會迷人 once a beggar is set on horse back, he will work for devils

做衰人 play the villain

做醜人 carry the can

唱衰人 (詆譭別人) bad-mouth others; speak ill of

問吓人 ask people there

圈中人 insider

圈外人 outsider

婦人 married woman

專登撚化人 (特地捉弄人) deliberately play tricks on others

帶眼識人 (小心交友) know a person with one's own eyes

常人 common people; man in the street; ordinary people

情人 lover

探人（探望）pay a visit to sb

曹操都有知心友，關公亦有對頭人 a devil has friends to sup with and a saint has foes worthy of his steel

猛人 powerful people

窒人（搶白）make others wordless

第一夫人 first lady; president's wife

第二啲人（別的人）other people

粗人 vulgar person; vulgarian

陰人（暗中傷人）do secret injury to others

嘓人（胳肢）tickle sb

單企人（單人旁）the "man" 人 radical

圍內人 insider; people within our circle

幾好人（人挺好）a nice person

無聲狗，咬死人 barking dog never bites

睇人（看人）watch one's look

睇小人／睇低人（輕看人）look down on people

睇衰人（不看好）look down on people

蛙人 frogman

貴人 people who can help

順德（得）人 a person who never refuses

黑市夫人 mistress

嗌人 cry for sb

嫂夫人 your wife

意中人 the person one is in love with

搵人 look for sb

搣人（捏）pinch others

撠滿晒人 be crowded with people; be jammed with people; be packed with people; full of people; swarm with people

新人 newly-wed

楚楚動人 delicate and attractive; lovingly pathetic; moving the heart of all those who see her

歲月不待／饒人 time and tide wait for no man; time marches on

話人（說別人）bad-mouth others; talk behind one's back

話事人（負責人）person in charge

跣人（陷害）trick sb

路人 passer-by

夢中情人 dream lover

熊人 black bear

誘人 attractive

誤人 harm people; mislead

齊人（到齊／都到了）all the people are present

彈人（批評）criticise others

熟人 acquaintance; friend

線人 informer

蝦人（欺負人）bully others

請人（招聘）recruit people

鬧人（罵）give sb a good dressing down/a good wigging/a scolding

整蠱人（捉弄）play tricks on people

激死人（令人生氣）annoying; irritating

篙人 boatman

鬆人（溜）flee an unpleasant situation

賴人（推諉）blame others

鮑人 scholar; the name of an official in Zhou Dynasty

雙面人 double-dealer; double-faced person

雞仔媒人（中間人）go-between; nosy intermediator

藝人 actor

識人 make friends

麗人 beauty

鐘點工人 part-time maid

攝石人 sb who tries to hog the limelight

蠢人（笨人）blockhead; fool; idiot; stupid person

鐵人 strong man

靈舍唔同過人（與眾不同）be entirely and totally different from others

【入】jap⁹ ① （進）enter ② （裝）put into

入口 ① entrance ② import

入心入肺 take sth to heart

入水（灌水）pour in water

入主 become the master

入冊（坐牢）be imprisoned

入去（進去）enter; get in; go in

入市 ① （進入市場）get into the market ② （開始交易）initiate transactions
　入市追擊 profit by entering transactions

入伙（搬入／搬新居）move in
　入伙紙（入住許可證）occupation certificate

入行 enter a field; join a profession

入房（進房子）enter the room

入油（加油）refuel

入波（進球）score a goal

入門女婿（贅婿）son-in-law who lives in the home of his wife's parents

入面（裏面／裏邊）inside

入屋（進屋子）enter the house
　入屋叫人，入廟拜神 (literally) greet people when you enter a house, worship the god when you enter a temple, meaning to do whatever you're supposed to do

入倉（進倉）entre a warehouse

入席 start the banquet
　五時恭候，八時入席 reception at 5 p.m. and banquet at 8 p.m.

入息（收入）income
　入息稅 income tax

入院／入廠（住進醫院）be admitted to hospital; be hospitalised

入廠大修 be hospitalised for a serious illness

入票（存支票）deposit a cheque

入袋（放進口袋）put into the pocket

入貨（進貨）stock with goods

入圍（入選）on the shortlist

入睡 go to sleep
　　難以入睡 hard to go to sleep

入鄉隨俗，出水隨灣 do in Rome as the Romans do

入閘（進閘）pass through an entry gate

入境問禁 do in Rome as the Romans do; to ask about the do's and don'ts when you arrive in a place or country

入數 ① （放入錢）deposit money ② （入賬／登賬）put it to one's account ③ （算在頭上）put the blame on
　　入我數 my treat; put it to my account

入學 enter a school
　　入學年齡 age of admission
　　入學試 entrance examination

入樽 ① （倒進瓶子）pour into a bottle ② slam-dunk

入錢（放錢進去／把錢放進去）put money into

入牆櫃（壁櫃／壁櫥）built-in wardrobe

入嚟（進來）come in

一手購入 purchase firsthand

刀槍不入 neither swords nor spears can enter

小財唔出，大財唔入 an empty hand is no lure for a hawk; nothing ventured, nothing gained

引入 call; draw into; introduce; lead into

手指拗出唔拗入 help outsiders at the expense of insiders

月入 monthly income

出入 ① in and out ② difference

出出入入／行出行入 coming in and out; in and out; shuttle in and out

冷巷擔竹竿——直出直入 walking in a lane with a plank on one's shoulder – taking an arrow-straight course

咬唔入（奈何不了）cannot take one's advantage; can't be brought to justice

乘虛而入 break through at a weak point; get or seize a chance to step in

格格不入 alien to; cannot get along with others; ill-adapted to; incompatible with; jar with

單刀直入 come straight to the point; speak out without beating about the bush

無孔不入 seize every opportunity

登入 log on

買入 buy in

裝入（裝進）install

踩入（一頭栽進）step into

鐵沙梨——咬唔入 very stingy

【几】gei¹ small table

茶几 coffee table

牀頭几 bedside table

【八】bat⁸ ① eight ② nosy

八八九九 eighty or ninety percent; almost done

八月 ① August ② the eighth month of the lunar year
　　八月十五 ① 15 August ② the fifteenth day of the eighth month ③ （屁股／臀部）bottom; buttocks

八爪魚（章魚）octopus
　　打八爪 take fingerprints

八仙 Eight Immortals
　　八仙枱（八仙桌）square table with Eight Immortals

八字 The Eight Characters relating to the celestial stems and earth branches of the year, month, day, and hour of one's birth
　　八字馬（八字腿）splayed feet
　　　擘八字馬（叉八字腿）split the splayed feet
　　八字鬚 moustache that resembles the Chinese character "eight"
　　睇八字（合八字）match and compare the Eight Characters before marriage

八卦 ① Eight Trigram ② （三八／好事／好管閒事／愛打探人家秘密／饒舌）gossipy; nosy
　　八卦婆（好管閒事的女人／長舌婦／饒舌婦）gossipy woman; meddling woman; nosy parker; shrewish woman

八妹 nosy girl
　　八妹仔 nosy girl

八號波（八號風球）typhoon signal 8

八達通 Octopus; Octopus card

八點 eight o'clock

七七八八 ① the great majority of sth ② extremely likely; possibly; probably

九唔搭八 illogical answer; irrelevant answer

阿八 duck

臭八 nasty person; unpleasant person

【刀】dou¹（刀子／大刀）knife

刀口（刀鋒）blade point

刀仔（小刀）small knife
　　刀仔鋸大樹（以小搏大／以弱贏強）manage to cut down a big tree with a small knife

刀好鈍（刀子很鈍）the knife is really blunt

刀字邊（立刀兒／立刀旁）the "knife" 刀 radical

刀唔利（刀子不快）the knife is blunt

刀殼（刀鞘）sheath

刀槍 sword and spear; weapons

　　刀槍不入 neither swords nor spears can enter/hurt

　　明刀明槍 in real earnest; real swords and spears – the real thing; with swords out of sheaths

刀劍 knives and swords

　　刀光劍影 be engaged in fierce battle; flashing with knives and swords; sabre-rattling; the flashes and shadows of swords

刀嘴（刀尖兒）point of a knife

色字頭上一把刀 womanising is dangerous

豆腐刀 indecisive person

烏喱單刀（亂七八糟）chaotic; get everything mixed up; in a mess

單刀 solo effort

開刀 ① perform an operation on a patient ② take action

【刁】diu¹ put on

刁時（平分）(transliteration) deuce

刁眼角 make eyes at sb

刁橋扭擰（裝模作樣）put on affected manners

刁難 create difficulties; deliberately put obstacles in sb's way; make things difficult

　　故意刁難 deliberately place obstacles

刁蠻 impervious to reason; obstinate; unruly

【力】lik⁷ strength

力不到不為財 no pain, no gain

力量 ① physical strength ②（火力）force; power; strength

冇牙力（沒有份量）fail to bring over

出全力 exert all one's strength; spare no effort; devote/concentrate one's energy

同心協力 all of one mind; cooperate with one heart; make concerted efforts

好力（有力）have great strength

有心無力 be unable to do what one wants to do

有招架之功，無還手之力 can only ward off blows

朱古力（巧克力）chocolate

兵力 armed forces; military strength; troops

定力 perserverance

武力 ① force ② military force; military might

近官得力 it is much more convenient to have a friend in court

唔夠力（不夠力）not have enough strength

效力 ① render a service to; serve ② effect; efficacy; potence ③ avail; effect; force

動力 dynamic power; motivation

眼力（視力）eyesight; power of vision; sight; vision

量力 do sth according to one's capability

羣策羣力 club ideas and exertions; collective wisdom and efforts; work as a team

腳骨力（腳力）strength of one's legs

落力（用力／盡力）spare no effort

逼力（煞車掣）brake

慳力（省力）save efforts

慳水慳力（省力）shoddy

【十】sap⁹ ten

十之八九 ① eight or nine out of ten ② most likely

十拿九穩 a sure thing for; almost certain; as sure as a gun; hold the cards in one's hand; in the bag; it's dollars to buttons; ninety percent sure; very sure of success

十二 twelve

　　十二月 ① December ② the twelfth month of the lunar year

　　十二碼 penalty kick

　　十二點 twelve o'clock

十八 eighteen

　　十八般武藝 (literally) be skilled in wielding the eighteen kinds of weapons, meaning to be skilled in various types of combat

　　女大十八變 (literally) a girl changes eighteen times before reaching womanhood, meaning that a girl changes fast in physical appearance from childhood to adulthood

十三 baker's dozen; thirteen

　　十三不祥 thirteen is an unlucky number

　　十三點（半瘋不癲）giggly; not ladylike

十五 fifteen

　　十五十六（遲疑不決）in two minds; indecisive

十六 sixteen

　　十六座 mini-bus

十分之（十分）very

十月 ① October ② the tenth month of the lunar year

　　十月芥菜起晒心（臘月的白菜——動（凍）了心）of an age when one's thoughts turn to courtship and sex

十全 all complete; full; perfect; utterly

　　十全十美 perfect; be all roses

　　十項全能 decathlon; all-round

十字 cross; cross-shaped

　　十字車（救護車）ambulance

　　十字架 cross

十年 decade; ten years
十年唔逢一閏（很罕見）a chance of a lifetime; once in a blue moon; very rare
十年樹木，百年樹人 it takes ten years to grow a tree, but a hundred years to bring up a generation of people

十足 ① exact ② all
十足十 ① one hundred percent ② be completely alike; look completely alike

十個甕缸九個蓋 fail to make both ends meet

十蚊（十塊錢）ten dollars
十幾蚊 ten odd dollars
幾十蚊 tens of dollars

十隻手指有長短（十個指頭不一般齊）(literally) among the ten fingers there are long and short ones, meaning that since nothing is the same, comparison is odious

十萬 one hundred thousand
十萬火急 very urgent

十號波 typhoon signal 10

十劃 ten strokes
十劃都冇一撇（八字沒一撇）have barely started a large project

十賭九輸 nine out of ten cases lose in gambling
七老八十（一把年紀）aged; elderly; in one's seventies or eighties; live to a great age; old

十足十（活脫）look completely alike
三歲定八十 the child is father to the man
大喊十 cry-baby; loud mouth
屈尾十（轉過頭）turn round and go back; things take a different course after a turn
橫九掂十（橫豎都是一樣）in any case; such being the case

【卜】buk⁷（預約）book

卜卜脆 / 脆卜卜（鬆脆 / 脆脆的）crispy
卜卜跳（呼呼亂跳）heart beating
卜臣（拳擊）boxing
打卜臣（打拳擊）practise boxing

生蘿卜（凍傷）have frostbite
紅卜卜（紅紅的 / 紅通通）red
脹卜卜（脹鼓鼓）bulging out

【又】jau⁶（再）again; also; in addition to

又平又靚（又便宜又好）cheap but good
又好（也好 / 好吧）all right; as well and good; it may not be a bad idea; that is fine
又係 / 又係嘅（也是 / 可也是）also the same; this is also the same

咁又係（那倒也是）that is also true
又食又拎（貪得無厭）have it both ways; greedy
又會咁嘅（怎麼會這樣的）how can this be
又嚟（又 / 再）again; also; in addition to; once again
又點呀（又怎麼樣）so what
又關我事（怎麼又算到我頭上）has this anything to do with me
又鹹又臭（又髒又臭）dirty and stinky

3 劃

【丈】dzoeng⁶ husband

丈夫 ①（informal）hubby; husband; one's better half ② real man
大丈夫 man; real man; true man
大丈夫能屈能伸 a great man knows when to yield and when not
大丈夫講得出做得到 a real man does what he says
無毒不丈夫（literally）a man who is not ruthless is not a truly great man, meaning ruthlessness is the mark of a truly great man

你敬我一尺，我敬你一丈 you scratch my back and I'll scratch yours
姑丈（姑父）uncle
姨丈（姨父）husband of one's maternal aunt
道高一尺魔高一丈 offenders are a stroke above law-makers

【三】saam¹ three

三九兩丁七（沒幾個人）only a few people
三九唔識七 be a stranger to each other
三十 thirty
三十火（三十瓦）thirty watt
三十六度板斧都出齊（山窮水盡）at the end of one's wits
三十六着，走為上着（literally）of all the thirty-six tactics, to "run away" is the best one
三三不盡，六六無窮 never-ending
三口兩脷 play fast and loose
三不管 nobody's business
三五知己 a few close friends; several bosom friends
三六（狗肉）dog meat
三六滾一滾，神仙都企唔穩（難以抗拒）(literally) when dog meat is cooked, even a god is attracted to the fragrance and cannot stand firm
三心兩意（三心二意）dillydally; in two minds

三文治（三明治）sandwich
　　公司三文治 club sandwich
三文魚（鮭魚）(transliteration) salmon
三扒二撥（叮噹五四）hurry through; in no time at all
三件頭（三件套）three-piece suit
三合一 three in one
三合會 triad society
三字經（粗話）foul language; swear words
三尖八角（凹凹凸凸）of irregular shape
三行（建造業）construction business
　　三行仔（建築工匠）constructor
三更 midnight; third watch of the day
　　三更半夜 in the middle of the night
　　三更窮，四更富 one's poverty or wealth fluctuates
三兩吓手勢／三扒兩撥（快手快腳）quickly and
　　skilfully
三姑六婆 ① a bevy of shrewish women ② gossipy
　　women
三長兩短 die; unexpected misfortune that results
　　in death
三急 go for a pee; need to go to the toilet
三個 three
　　三個女人一個墟 when woman get together they make a
　　　　lot of noise chattering
　　三個字（一刻鐘）fifteen minutes
　　三個骨（三刻鐘）forty-five minutes; three quarters of
　　　　an hour
三唔識七（誰也不認識誰）don't know him/her;
　　strangers
三級（淫穢不雅）Category III; X-rated
　　三級片 Category III movie; X-rated movie
　　三級跳 ① hop, skip, and jump; triple jump ② quick
　　　　promotion
三缺一 one player short for a game of mahjong
三衰六旺（高低起伏）ups and downs of life
三隻手（小偷）pickpocket
三張野（三十來歲）thirty something
三造（三季）three crops a year
三圍 measurements of the bust, waist, and hips
三幅被（老調重彈）harp on the same string
三番四次 repeatedly
三等 third class
三歲定八十（三歲看大七歲看老）the child is father to
　　the man
三羣五隊 in groups
三腳凳 ① unreliable ②（不靠譜的人）unreliable
　　person
三腳雞（機動三輪車）car with three wheels
三號波 typhoon signal 3

三頭六臂 extraordinarily able person; very capable person
三點 ① three points ② three o'clock
　　三點三 ① 3:15 p.m. ②（下午茶）afternoon tea
　　三點式 bikini

一不離二，二不離三 another yet another; coming in quick
　　succession
年初三 ① the third day of the Chinese New Year ② the third
　　day of the first month of the lunar year

【上】soeng⁵ ① go up ② screw

上工 start working
上晝（上午）morning
上天無路，入地無門 in desperate straits
上市 listed; listed in the stock exchange
上位（升職）be promoted; get promoted
上身 one's body being possessed; obsessed with
　　鬼上身 possessed by a ghost
上車 ① get in the car; get on a vehicle ②（初次置業）first-
　　time flat buyer
　　上車盤 first-time flat
上咗岸（上了岸）have made one's fortune
上門（登門）house call
上契（認乾親）enter into an adoptive relationship
上馬（開展工程）take on a job
上堂 ①（上課）attend a class; attend class; go to a class;
　　take a class ② conduct a class; give a lesson
上得山多終遇虎 the fist that nibbles at every bait will
　　be caught
上船（登船）board a ship; embark a ship
上莊 join a committee
上期 ① advance payment of wage ② advance payment
　　of rent
上畫（上映）on screen; run
上當 be duped; be taken in
上路 ① set off ② die
上網 access the internet; surf the net
上膊（上肩）over the shoulder
上樓（住樓房）live in a building
上機（登機）board a plane
上嚟（上來）come up
上鏈（上發條）wind
上鏡 photogenic
上癮（成癮）be addicted
上 course attend a course
上 seminar attend a seminar

比得上（堪配／匹配）bear comparison with; can compare
　　with; compare favourably with

北上 go north (to mainland China)

打孖上（雙份）have two of sth at the same time

打蛇隨棍上 capitalise on one's opportunity; take advantage of the tide

迎難而上 advance against difficulties; press ahead in face of difficulties

追唔上（追不上／落後）can't catch up with

追得上（追上）can catch up with

頂硬上（硬着頭皮）brace oneself up and bear with sth; hang tough

【上】soeng⁶ above

上下（大約／左右）about; almost; approximate to

上司 direct boss; superior officer

上年（去年）last year

上便／上邊（上面）above; on the surface of; on top of; over; top; upper surface

上衫（女裝上衣）blouse

上屋搬下屋，唔見一籮穀（東搬西搬虧了一半）moving from upstairs to downstairs – one spends a basket of grains; a rolling stone gathers no moss

上氣唔接下氣（氣喘吁吁）be out of breath; pant

上高（上面／上頭／上邊）authorities

上畫（上午）forenoon; morning

上湯（高湯）superior broth

上訴 appeal to a higher court

上樑唔正下樑歪（上樑不正下樑歪）those below will follow the bad examples set by those above

上頭 ①（上司）direct boss; superior ②（上面）above; on the surface of; on top of; over; top; upper surface

手頭上（手上）on hand

羊毛出在羊身上 whatever is given is paid for

肉隨砧板上 be led by the nose

府上 your family; your home

馬上 at once; immediately; right away

跪地餵豬乸——睇錢份上 money makes the mare go; money makes the world go round

網上 online

樓上 the floor above; upstairs

【下】haa⁶ ① underneath ② next

下下（次次／每次／每時每刻／經常）at every turn; every time

下午 afternoon

下午茶 afternoon tea

飲下午茶 have afternoon tea

下水（去水／排水）drain

下水禮 launching ceremony

下扒（下巴）chin

下扒輕輕（言而無信／隨便許諾）make promises too easily

下年（明年）next year

下次（下一次）next time

下低／下邊／下便／下面（下頭）low; under; below

下更（中班）middle switch

下個（下一個）next

下氣 humble oneself; humble one's pride

下海 ① give up one's career and go into business ② begin one's career as a prostitute

下馬威 display one's authority soon after one comes into power

下欄 ①（外快）extra income; tips ②（剩菜）leftovers

下欄錢 tips

一下 all at once

天下 heaven and earth

手下（下屬）subordinate; (derogatory) underling

以下 below; less than; no more than; under

打天下 conquer; take over

全家上上下下 the whole family

全國上下 the whole nation from the leadship to the masses

名下 under sb's name

名滿天下 gain a world reputation

地下 ①（地面／地上）ground floor; the ground/floor ②（地面以下）underground

行下（走一走／散步去）take a walk; take an airing

低下（低端）low; lowly

私下 in private; in secret; privately; under the rose

咁上下（差不多）about; approximately; more or less

拉上補下 make up for the deficit in one area by using resources from another

返鄉下（回鄉）go to one's home town; return home

度下／吓（量度）take a measurement of sth

計下／吓 figure out; make out

時下 nowadays

鄉下（農村）① countryside ② home village

滾下／吓 boil for a minute

撩下／吓 ① stir ② tease

樓下 ① downstairs; the floor below ② (said of prices) below

遲下／吓 later; later on

【丫】aa¹ branch; fork

丫杈（分枝）forked branch

丫烏（夜叉）ugly devil

丫鬟（丫頭）servant girl

【丸】jyn⁴⁻² pill
丸仔 ①（丸）small pill ②（毒品）drugs

女人湯丸 lady's man; attractive man with many female admirers

肉丸 meat ball

臭丸（樟腦丸）moth ball

湯丸 dumpling in sweet soup

暈浪丸 motion sickness medicine; seasick pill

維他命丸 vitamin pill

藥丸 pill; tablet

【久】gau² for a long time
久仰 I'm pleased to meet you

久而久之（時間久了）in the course of time; with the passage of time

久唔久（久不久）at times; every now and then; from time to time

久病成醫 prolonged illness makes a doctor of a patient

永久 everlasting

恆／持久 constant; endurable; forever; lasting; protracted

【之】dzi¹ ① modifier ② 's (possessive)
之不過（不過／可是／但）but; just that

之字形 zigzag

之後 after; then

之唔係（不就是）isn't that

之嘛（罷了）only; that's all

一死了之 death pays all debts

十分之（十分）very

久而久之（時間久了）in the course of time; with the passage of time

不了了之 allow sth to remain unresolved; conclude without conclusion; end up with nothing definite; settle a matter by leaving it unsettled

卒之（終於）at last; end in; eventually; finally; in the end; result in; ultimately

取而代之 replace

固然之（固然）indeed; it is true; of course; really

姑妄言之（即係咁講呀（講是這樣講）just talk for the sake of talking; just venture an opinion

姑妄聽之／聽住先（聽說是這樣）just listen to sth without taking it seriously; to hear is not to believe

非常之（十分／非常）very; very much

既來之，則安之 let's cross the bridge when we come to it; since we are here, we may as well stay and make the best of it

相當之（相當）about; considerably; fairly; quite; rather;

somewhat; to a great extent; very

唔怪得之（難怪／怪不得）little wonder that; no wonder; 極之（很／十分／非常）exceedingly; extremely; very

總而言之／總之 all things considered; to sum up

【乞】hat⁷（乞求／乞討）beg
乞人憎（可恨／令人討厭）disgusting; nuisance

乞米 very poor

乞兒（乞丐／叫化子）beggar

　乞兒婆（女乞丐）bag lady

　　大種乞兒 a person who disregards small gains; scrounger

　　做慣乞兒懶做官（討飯三年懶做官）get used to living in idleness

　　喺乞兒兜揦飯食 rob the poor

乞食（要飯／討飯）beg for food

乞錢（討錢）beg for money

【也】jaa⁵ also
也文也武（耀武揚威）flaunt one's power; make a show of power

吊威也（吊威亞）hanging from a wire

【亡】mong⁴ die
亡羊補牢 better late than never

亡命 ①（流亡／逃亡）flee; go into exile; seek refuge ②（拼了命）desperate

　亡命之徒 badmen; dead rabbits; desperado; fugitive; ruffian

亡國 ① fall of a nation ② conquered nation

存亡 live or die; survive or perish; survive and downfall

死亡 death

身亡 die

妻離子散，家破人亡 cause the break-up by death or separation of countless families

陣亡 be killed/fall in action; fall in battle

滅亡 become extinct; die out

【兀】ngak⁹ upright
兀立 stand rigidly without motion

突兀 exceed

【凡】faan⁴ ordinary
凡人 ① ordinary person ② mortal

凡係／但凡（凡是）all; any; every

不平凡（唔簡單）unusual

仙女下凡 a fairy descending to the mundane world

平凡 / 平平凡凡 normal and usual

【千】tsin¹ thousand

千百 hundreds and thousands

千方百計 by hook and by crook; by every conceivable means

千年道行一朝喪 all the good deeds are spoilt by only an ill doing

千里送鵝毛，物輕情意重 the trifling gift sent from afar conveys deep affection

千金 ① a thousand pieces of gold ② daughter ③ extremely precious

千金小姐 well-off lady

千金難買向南樓 south-facing flats are hard to buy

千祈 (一定要 / 千萬 / 必須) by all means; don't ever; earnestly; it is imperative that; must; sure; whatever you do,

千祈唔好 (千萬不要 / 千萬別) never ever

千真萬確 as sure as fate

千揀萬揀 (千挑萬選) select carefully

千揀萬揀，揀着個爛燈盞 the most careful choice is often the worst choice

千層糕 multi-layered cake

出千 cheat

老千 (騙子) trickster

【叉】tsaa¹ (叉子) fork

叉腸 / 叉燒腸粉 (紅燒肉粉條) steamed rice roll with barbeque pork

叉燒 (紅燒肉 / 烤肉) barbeque pork

叉燒包 barbeque pork bun

一籠叉燒包 a basket of barbeque pork buns

叉燒酥 barbeque pork pastry

叉燒餐包 baked barbeque pork bun

打交叉 (劃去 / 打叉) cross out

交叉 (叉) cross

開叉 slit

【口】hau² (嘴) mouth

口不 / 唔對心 (口是心非) speak with one's tongue in one's cheek

口水 ① talkative ② (唾液 / 涎) saliva

口水多過茶 (大耍嘴皮子) all mouth and no action; shoot off one's mouth; talk too much; very talkative; wag one's tongue

口水尾 (吐沫星子) saliva drops

口水佬 (長篇大論的人) talkative person

口水肩 (圍嘴) bib; cloth necklet

口水花 (唾沫) saliva drops

一督口水 (一口唾沫) a dribble of saliva

吐口水 spit

吐口水講過 (收回不吉利的話) take back words that are unlucky

吞口水養命 (撐下去) hope to linger out longer

流口水 ① (流涎) make sb's mouth water; mouth-watering ② (垂涎) covet; drool over; gloat over; hanker after; slaver over

執人口水尾 (拾人牙慧) parrot sb's words

嘥口水 (浪費唇舌) waste one's words

口同鼻拗 argue over nothing; it's useless to argue

口多多 (多嘴 / 多嘴多舌 / 喜歡搶白) like to gossip; shoot off one's mouth; talk too much

口快快 (口直心快) say sth quickly without thinking

口乖 (嘴甜) honey-mouthed

口供 (供詞) evidence; statement; verbal statement

口味 (品味 / 喜好) taste

啱口味 (合口味) be to one's taste; suit one's taste

重口味 like food with strong flavours

口花花 (多嘴 / 浪嘴輕舌 / 嘴巴花巧) like to tease others; loose-tongued when flirting with girls; sweet talk; talk frivolously

口信 message

口面 (面容 / 臉色 / 臉型) one's look

好熟口面 / 熟口熟面 (面善 / 面熟) look familiar

國字口面 (國字臉) square face

鵝蛋口面 (鵝蛋臉) oval face

口唇 (嘴唇) lip

口唇膏 (口紅) lippy; lipstick

口臭 ① (口氣) bad breath ② (惹人討厭) irritating

口臭仔 foul-mouthed boy

口衰 foul-mouthed

口訊 ① message ② voice message

口乾 (口渴) thirsty

口啞 (啞) tongue-tied

口啞啞 (啞口無言) tongue-tied

口密 (嘴嚴) able to keep a secret; cautious about speech; discreet in speech

口淡淡 (沒胃口) have no appetite

口窒窒 (有點兒口吃 / 吞吐吐 / 結結巴巴) stammer a little

口爽 (心直口快 / 順口) say without thinking; slip out of one's tongue; speak casually; speak without much thought

口甜舌滑 oil one's tongue; sweet talk

口痕 a desire to eat or say sth; talkative

口疏（疏）（不能保密／走漏風聲／嘴快）have a loose tongue; incapable of keeping secrets; rash in speech; loose-lipped

口硬（嘴硬）① refuse to admit a mistake; stubborn and reluctant to admit mistakes or defeats ② talk toughly

口滑（油嘴滑舌）flattering tongue; glib; glib-tongued; slimy-tongued

口罩 mask
　除口罩（脫下口罩）take off a mask
　戴口罩 wear a mask

口碑 word of mouth

口腫面腫 swollen face

口號 slogan

口輕輕（輕嘴薄舌）glib; make easy promises

口噏噏（喃喃／喃喃自語）murmur

口數（心算）do sums in one's head; mental arithmetic

口齒（信用／承諾）guarantee; promise
　冇口齒（不守諾言／沒信用）break one's promise; untrustworthy
　有／講口齒（講信用）keep one's promise; keep one's word

口響（響亮）glib

一口 flatly; readily; promise without hesitation; with certainty

人口 population

入口 ① entrance ② import

刀口 blade point

十字路口 at crossroads

三岔路口 fork in the road; junction of three roads

大門口 main doorway

仇口 animosity; enmity; grudge; hostility

反口 deny one's promise

心口（胸口）chest

戶口 an account

胃口 appetite

出入口 import and export

出口 ① export ② exit ③ what comes out from the mouth

加把口 give verbal support to a person; speak in support of sb

可口 dainty; delectable; delicious; good to eat; luscious; palatable; savoury; tasty

四萬咁口（笑容可掬）wear a big smile

生口（活口）survivor of a murder attempt

生面口（面生）look unfamiliar

好唱口 ①（唱個不停／吱吱喳喳）never stop singing ② good singing

好難開口（說不出口）be too embarrassed to say

收口（閉嘴）shut up

死剩把口（愛爭論）never yield and keep arguing with others

戒口 avoid certain food; on diet

把口 one's mouth

扰心口（捶胸口）nurse a grief; regret; regret doing sth

官字兩個口（literally）officials have two mouths, meaning that they can say whatever they like; speak in bureaucratese/officialese

拍心口（保證）guarantee; readily promise to undertake responsibility

河口 estuary; firth; river mouth

虎口 ① tiger's mouth ② an acupuncture point between the thumb and the index finger

門口 door; doorway

守／看門口 to have medicine to get prepared for common illnesses; brace oneself for (illness)

青口 mussel

巷口 entrance to a lane

是非只為多開口（言多必失）loquacity leads to trouble

牲口 livestock

可口 delicious and tasty

苦瓜乾咁嘅面 have a look like a dried balsam pear, meaning a face of woe

面口（面色）a look

唔停口（說個不停）talkative

啷口（嗽口）gargle; rinse the mouth

埋口（癒合）heal (wounds)

息口（利率）interest rate

拳不離手，曲不離口 boxing cannot dispense with the hand, nor songs the mouth; practice makes perfect; the boxer's fist must stick to its task, and the singer's mouth no rest must ask

破口 ① cut ② get a cut

笑口 in smile

笑大人個口（貽笑大方）very embarrassing

笑笑口 ① joking ② with a smiling face

缺口 ① breach; gap; loophole; opening ② deficiency; insufficiency; shortage

袖口 cuff; wristband

送羊入虎口 a lamb to slaughter; put sb to death

堂口 underworld gang

崩口（兔唇）harelipped person

得把口（會講不會做）all mouth and no action; boasting; go on cackling without laying an egg

爽口（爽脆）crispy

眾口 what people say

粗口（粗／髒話）foul language

講粗口 speak foul language

喊咁口 look like crying

港口 harbour

窗口 window

答口 pick up the thread of a conversation and take part in it

街口 corner of the street; road junction; street intersection; street junction

裂口 crack; gap; split

開口 ① open one's mouth ② unsealed

開口埋口 (一張嘴就說 / 開口閉口也說) always talk about

順口 read smoothly

傷口 wound

溜口 stammer; stutter

獅子開大口 over-demanding

誇口 boast; brag; talk big

路口 crossing; road intersection; road junction

閘口 gate

滯口 ① poor appetite ② not smooth

漏口 (口吃) stammer; stutter

緊急出口 emergency exit

數口 quick with figures

槽口 notch

糊口 eke out a living; make a living to feed the family

線口 end of a thread

蓮子蓉咁口 (滿臉笑容) very sweet smile

幫口 put in a few words for sb

擘大口 (張開口) open one's mouth wide

檔口 booth; stall; vendor's stand

澀口 (澀) astringent; pucker

膾炙人口 on everybody's lips

儲蓄戶口 savings account

繑口 (拗 / 不順口) awkward-sounding; hard to pronounce; twist the tongue

藉口 excuse

改口 withdraw one's previous remark

懵到上心口 (非常愚笨) extremely foolish

爆響口 (洩漏秘密) disclose a secret

竇口 (家) den; home

爛口 (常說粗話) swearing all the time

讚不絕口 praise without stopping

【土】 tou² land

土地 ① land ② (田地) field

土狗 (螻蛄) mole cricket

土炮 (廉價的酒) cheap rice wine

老土 (土氣) rustic; old-fashioned

領土 territory

【士】 si⁶ person

士巴拿 (扳子 / 扳手 / 螺絲刀) spanner

士多 (小商店 / 雜貨店) grocery store

　士多房 (雜物房) storeroom

　士多啤梨 strawberry

士兵 soldier

士的 (手杖 / 拐杖) (transliteration) stick

士急馬行田 act according to the circumstances

士氣 morale

士啤 (後備) spare

　士啤呔 (後備車輪 / 肚腩) spare tyre; pot belly

士碌架 (桌球) snooker

士撻打 (起動器) (transliteration) starter

士擔 (郵票) (transliteration) stamp

多士 (吐司 / 烘麵包) a piece of toast

安士 ounce

巴士 (公車) a bus

的士 (計程車) a taxi

芝士 (奶酪) a piece of cheese

人士 person

11 號巴士 walk

卡士 (陣容) cast

文學士 bachelor of arts

牛油多士 toast with butter

右翼人士 right-winger

灰士 /fill 士 (保險絲) (transliteration) fuse

西多士 French toast

甫士 (姿勢) posture

波士 (老闆) boss

直通巴士 non-stop bus

空中巴士 air bus

穿梭巴士 shuttle bus

飛士 (面子) face

茶博士 teahouse waiter

烈士 martyr

院士 academician

助產士 midwife

接駁巴士 feeder bus

術士 ① one who practises occult arts ② scholars

博士 ① doctorate ② scholar or professional

貼士 (提示) ① tips ② hint; prompt

煙士 (王牌) ace

畸士 (案例 / 例子) case

喱士 (花邊 / 蕾絲) lace

唦士 (尺碼) size

雙層巴士 double-decker bus

爵士 ① sir ② jazz

護士 nurse
觀光巴士（觀光公車）tour bus

【夕】dzik⁶ eve

夕陽 setting sun
　夕陽西下 the sun sets in the west
　夕陽無限好 the sunset is magnificient
　夕陽工業 / 夕陽行業 declining industries

旦夕 in a short while
危在旦夕 at death's door; at the last gasp
除夕 Chinese New Year's Eve

【大】daai⁶ ① big; large ② great

大人 ① adult ② important person
　大人有大量 an important person is forgiving
　　大小通吃（通吃）sweep all before one
大少（大少爺）① eldest son of a rich family ② eldest son of one's master ③ spoilt son of a rich family
大方 ① liberal; generous ② dignified; sophisticated; tasteful
大牙（槽牙）molar
大牛（五百塊錢紙幣）five-hundred-dollar note
大仔（大兒子）eldest son
大出血（血拼）spend big
大石 big rock
　大石責死蟹 be crushed by force; pressure sb into doing sth
大份（個兒大）hulk
大件（塊兒大）hulky
　大件事（大事件 / 出大事兒）a big event
大光燈（汽燈）gas lamp
大吉大利 may you be fortunate
　大吉利是 touch wood
大字（毛筆字）Chinese characters written with a writing brush
　　寫大字（寫毛筆字）do Chinese calligraphy
大早 ①（剛才）just now ②（很久以前）a long time ago
大汗疊細汗（汗流浹背）very sweaty
大老倌（著名演員）famous actor
大行其道 in the trend; prevail throughout
大亨 tycoon
大妗姐（媒人 / 媒婆）go-between; match-maker
大把（多的是 / 很多 / 許多）a great deal of
大步躐過（逃出厄運）escape from misfortune
大沙蹄（象皮腿）elephantiasic crus
大肚（懷孕）heavy with child; pregnant
　大肚婆（孕婦）pregnant woman
大豆（黃豆芽）bean sprout

大事化小，小事化無 bring a problem to naught
大使（揮霍 / 大手大腳）big-spending
大花筒 big spender; spendthrift
大佬 ①（大哥 / 哥哥）elder brother ②（老兄）big brother ③（黑幫首領）gang leader; triad boss
大哥大（archaic）the first generation mobile phone
大命（命大）escape with bare life
大姐 big sister
　大姐大 female boss
　大姐仔（小姑娘）young girl
　　大人大姐（成年人）adult; grown-up
大姑奶（大姑姑）the eldest aunt on father's side
大 / 高官 high-ranking official
大抵（大概）generally; generally speaking
大押（當舖）pawnshop
大枝野（耍大牌的人）arrogant person
大泡和（二百五）① muddle-headed ② absent-minded person
大牀 ①（雙人牀）double bed ② a kind of double decker bus
大狀（大律師）barrister
大門（正門）main door
大姨（大姨子）aunt
大屋（大宅）big house
大帝（大爺）① gluttonous idler ② lazy, arrogant, and willful man
大炮 ① lie ② cannon
　大炮友 / 鬼（牛皮大王）braggard; liar; teller of tall stories
　　一坎大炮（一門大炮）a cannon
大紅大紫（紅得發紫）at the height of one's power and influence; at the zenith of one's fame; enjoy great popularity
大限到（大限難逃）meet one's fate; pay one's debt to nature
大風（風大）windy
大飛（快艇）speedboat
大食（食量大）big-eating; gluttonous
　大食有旨意 have a firm backing to do such a deed for one's extravagance
　大食佬（大胃王）big eater
　大食細（大吃小）the big swallowing up the small
　大食會（聚餐）food feast
　大食懶（好吃懶做 / 懶骨頭）lazybone
大唔透（孩子氣）person who is old in age but young at heart
大家 ① everyone ② you ③ all of us; we ④ together
　大家咁話 same to you

大師 master
大拿拿（挺多的）quite a large amount
大海 big sea
大海茫茫 a vast expanse of sea
大海撈針 look for a needle in a haystack
過大海 go to Macau
大班 boss
大病 serious illness
大致上 / 大抵上 in general
大茶飯 big deal
大草（大寫）block letter; capital letter
大陣仗 ①（大排場 / 排場大）go in for an ostentation ② big deal; big fuss
大隻（個兒大 / 塊頭足）big build; hulky; muscular; well built
大隻佬（身型高大的人）big guy; hulk; muscular guy; strongly-built person
大隻講（只講不做的）① all talk and no action ② boastful person
大隻騾騾（膀大腰圓的）as big as a mule; strongly-built man
大鬼（大王）joker
大偈（大副）chief officer; first mate
大堂（大廳）lobby; lounge
大堆頭（大量）in a large quantity
大婆（大老婆）legal wife
大排檔（飲食攤）Cantonese open-air restaurant
大眼雞（大眼鯛）big eye
大笪地 night market
大笨象 ①（大象）elephant ② fat person
一隻大笨象（一頭大象）an elephant
大粒（有權有勢）big-shot; important
大粒佬（有影響力的人）big-shot; influential person; very important person
大粒癦（大官 / 高官 / 大人物）(literally) person with a big mole, meaing high-ranking official; very important person
大粒嘢（大人物）important person
大細 ① size ② adults and children ③ risk; uncertainty
大細超（偏心 / 偏好）show favouritism
一家大細（一家人）whole family
心大心細（三心二意 / 拿不定主意）hesitate to do sth; indecisive
兩大一細 two adults and one child
粗身大細（雙身大肚子的 / 腹大便便）pregnant
賭大細（冒險）take a risk
大赦 amnesty
大造（大年）bumper year; good year; on year
大陸 mainland; mainland China
大魚（鱅魚）bighead carp
大喊十 cry-baby; loud mouth
大單（大宗）a large amount; a large quantity
大掣（總閘）main switch
大棚（大羣）a large group
大牌（派頭挺足 / 擺架子）big-shot; self-important person
大牌檔 Cantonese open-air restaurant
讕大牌（耍大牌）act like a top-billing actor
大黃魚 Crocine croaker
大嗌（大叫 / 喊）yell out
大廈 building
大意 ① careless ② gist
大搖大擺 swagger about
大煲 / 大鑊（大事件）big problem
大話（謊話）lie
大話鬼 / 精 liar
大大話話（不下）estimate approximately; roughly
講大話（說 / 撒謊）lie; tell a lie
講大話甩大牙 (to a child) (literally) if you lie, your molar will fall off
大舅 / 大舅爺（大舅子）one's wife's elder brother
大葵扇（媒人 / 媒婆）go-between; match-maker
大支嘢（傲慢）arrogant person
大電（一號電池）D-size battery
大嘥（浪費）extravagant
大熱 / 大熱門（很火）big hit
大熱症（傷寒）typhoid fever
大碟 ①（大盤子）large saucer ②（大唱片）large album
大綱 outline
大髀（大腿）thigh
大鼻 ① arrogant; haughty; putting on airs; snob; snobbish ② big nose
大廚 chef
大碼（大號）large size
大蝦 prawn
大蝦細（以大欺小）bully
大賣特賣（熱賣）sell like hot cakes
大劑（麻煩很大）big trouble
大學 university
大學畢業 graduate from the university
名牌大學 prestigious university
讀緊大學（唸大學）be studying in university
大蕉（芭蕉）banana; plantain
大褸（大衣）overcloth; overcoat; topcloth
大頭 big head
大頭佛 (literally) big-headed Buddha, meaning a series of trouble
搞出個大頭佛（惹很大麻煩）make a mess; cause lots of trouble

大頭針 pin

大頭鬼 (揮霍的人) big-spending person

　充大頭鬼 (裝闊氣) pretend to be rich

大頭魚 (鱅魚) bighead carp

大頭蝦 (馬大哈) absent-minded person

大頸泡 (大脖子) ① big neck ② goiter

大戲 Cantonese opera

大檔 gambling den

大糠 (粗糠) chaff

大聲 in a loud voice; loud

　大聲公 ① (揚聲器) loud-speaker megaphone

　② (大嗓門) man with a loud voice

大膽 daring; very brave

大餅 (一塊錢硬幣) one-dollar coin

　洗大餅 (洗碗碟) clean dishes

大轆竹 (水煙筒) Chinese water pipe

大雞唔食細米 (literally) big chicken doesn't eat small rice, meaning not to care about trifles; important person does not bother with trivial matters

大懶蛇 (懶人) lazy person

大懵 (非常糊塗) absent-minded person; blunder head; muddle-headed

　大懵鬼 (糊塗的人) absent-minded person

大難 death

　大難不死，必有後福 one's escape from death will certainly bring one good fortune

　大難友 idler

大霧 foggy

　博大霧 (佔便宜 / 混水摸魚) to profit at other people's expense

大餸王 glutton

大隻佬 (身材高大的人) hulk; strongly-built person

大隻衰 (身材高大而愚笨的人) big bully

大疊水 very rich

大鑊 (出大事兒) big trouble

　大鑊飯 ① (大鍋飯) cooked rice in a big pot ② big mess

　大鑊嘢 big mess

　　食大鑊飯 use resources from the government

大驚小怪 a storm in a tea cup

大癲大廢 (嘻嘻哈哈地 / 愛笑鬧) act in a crazy manner; playsome

大纜 (拔河繩 / 粗纜繩) thick rope

　大纜都扯唔埋 cannot meet sb half-way; people or groups who are always in conflict

　扯 / 拉大纜 (拔河) tug-of-war

大鱷 master swindler

人細鬼大 a young boy with the mind and maturity of an adult; young but tricky

月大 ① solar month of thirty-one days ② lunar month of thirty days

牛高馬大 stand like a giant; tall and big; well-grown

加大 (特大) extra large

目光遠大 have a broad vision

因小失大 spoil a ship for a halfpenny worth of tar

妄自尊大 aggrandise oneself; arrogant and overweening

年紀大 old

老大 boss; leader

自大 arrogant

作大 (誇大) exaggerate

壯大 ① robust; strong; sturdy; vigorous ② make better; strengthen

快高長大 may you grow tall and strong

命大 lucky

長大 grow up; mature

阿大 gang boss

係咁大 it's game over

保你大 (服了你) I concede

架子大 arrogant; assume an air of importance

海上無魚蝦自大 a dwarf in Lilliput would be thought a superbeing

神高神大 (高大) well-built

門面大 have a large shop front

偉大 great; mighty

幾大 ① (年紀多大) how old ② 幾大就幾大 (無論付出任何代價) at all costs; howsoever; for good or for evil; rain or shine; whatever the consequences

煲大 play up

飲大 (喝醉) get drunk

遠大 ambitious; broad; long-range; very promising

養大 bring up

頭大 / 都大 ① have a trouble ② difficult to solve; knotty; troublesome

雙加大 double extra large size

自大 be bloated with pride; be puffed up

【女】 noey⁵⁻² ① girl ② (女兒) daughter ③ (閨女) maiden ④ girlfriend ⑤ club girl

女人 woman; women

　女人湯圓 lady's man; attractive man with many female admirers

　女人纏腳布 —— 又長又臭 foot-binding cloths – long and tiresome

　玩女人 play around with women

女女 (女兒) daughter

女友 girlfriend

女仔 (女孩 / 女孩子 / 女孩兒) girl

　女仔之家 (女兒家) as a proper girl

追女仔 (追求女孩) chase after girls

睇女仔 (看女孩) look at girls

撩女仔 (逗女孩子) tease a girl

女性 female

女神 goddess

女婿 son-in-law

女廁 women's toilet

女傭 maid

女裝 women's wear

女警 policewoman

才女 a girl of many accomplishments; accomplished lady; gifted female scholar; talented woman

少女 (archaic) damsel; lass; maid; maiden; young girl

世界女 woman of the world; worldly girl; worldly woman

仔女 (子女) children; offspring; sons and daughters

仙女 fairy

叻女 (聰明的女孩) clever girl; smart girl

打女 (功夫女演員) martial art actress

母女 mother and daughter

玉女 (優雅的女孩) well-mannered girl

生女 give birth to a girl

生兒育女 give birth to children and raise them

後生女 young girl

孖女 twin girls; twin sisters

孖辮女 girl with hair in twin braids

竹升女 (生於外國的中國女孩) young overseas Chinese girl

自梳女 a maid making up her mind not to marry all her life

吧女 bargirl

妓女 prostitute

孝女 bereaved daughter

侄女 brother's daughter; nephew

兒甥女 niece

油脂女 / 飛女 teddy girl

油瓶女 step-daughter

契女 (義女 / 誼女) adopted daughter

後生女 (年輕女子) lass; miss; young girl; 靚女 (美女) beautiful girl; beautiful woman

美少女 nymph

修女 nun; sister

孫女 granddaughter

書院女 schoolgirl

神女 ① deities in Chinese mythology ② prostitute

索女 babe; dazzling girl; hottie

衰女 (壞女孩) naughty girl

淫人妻女 violate another's wife and daughters

細路女 (小女孩) little girl

處女 virgin

無兒無女 childless; have neither sons nor daughters

絕世美女 a girl of unparalleled beauty

傻女 silly girl

稚女 young girl

飲食男女 men and women interested in eating and drinking

壽星女 birthday girl

舞女 nightclub hostess

撈女 prostitute; street-walker

獨女 (獨生女) only daughter

醒目女 (聰明的女孩) smart girl/lady

孻女 (最小的女兒) youngest daughter

靚妹靚妹仔 (少女) teenager girl

蘇蝦女 /BB 女 baby girl

【子】dzi² son

子女 children; offspring; sons and daughters

獨生子女 only child

子弟 children; juniors; young dependants

子弟兵 army made up of the sons of the people

子夜 midnight

子孫 children and grandchildren; descendants

子孫滿堂 have many children and grandchildren

子子孫孫 children and grandchildren; descendants; posterity

百子千孫 have many siblings

子宮 uterus; womb

子宮頸癌 cervical cancer

子宮癌 cancer of the uterus/the womb; uterine cancer

子彈 ① bullet ② money

子鴨 (童子鴨) green duck

子薑 (嫩薑) tender ginger; young ginger

才子 genius; gifted scholar

不法份子 law breakers

冇法子 (沒法) it can't be helped; nothing can be done; there's no way

太子 crown prince

夫子 ancient form of address to a Confucian scholar

引子 introduction; introductory music

日子 life; time

父子 father and son

仙子 ① fairy maiden; female celestial ② celestial being; fairy; immortal

冊子 book; volume

句子 sentence

瓜子 melon seed

甲子 a cycle of sixty years

白馬王子 prince charming

份子 one's share of expenses for a joint undertaking

先小人後君子 make sure of every trifling matter before generosity

有仇不報非君子 demand blood for blood

有其父必有其子 like father, like son

老夫子 tutor in a private school; unpractical scholar

老媽子 mum

老頭子 father

母子 ① mother and child ② mother and son

君子 gentleman

孝子 ① devoted child; dutiful son; submissive and obedient son ② bereaved son

弟子 disciple; follower; pupil

戒子 (指環) ring

杈子 forked branch

杆子 pole; rod

杞子 fruit of Chinese wolfberry

男子 man

身子 body

車厘子 (櫻桃) cherry

沫子 foam; froth

法子 method; way

例子 case; example; instance

花花公子 dandy; playboy

波子 ① a glass marble ② Porche

虎父無犬子 like father, like son

架子 airs

恐怖份子 terrorist

面子 face

風流才子 talented and romantic scholar

原子 atomic

核子 ① nuclear ② nucleon

骨子 delicate and exquisite

帶子 (扇貝) scallop

毫子 coin

梅子 plum

浪子 bum; dissipater; loafer; prodigal; rakehell; rounder; wastrel

淥吓筷子 (泡筷子) rinse the chopsticks in hot water

粒子 grain; granule; particle

魚子 roe

揸筷子 (拿筷子) hold a pair of chopsticks

極力子 (transliteration) clutch

痧子 (俗稱痲疹) measles

着起龍袍唔似太子 (literally) a beggar wearing a dragon robe still doesn't look like a prince

牌子 brand; brand name; trademark

椰子 coconut

獅子 lion

筷子 chopstick

褂子 Chinese gown; robe

電子 electronic

樑上君子 ① (賊) thief ② (脫離實際的人) a person who does not face reality

種子 seed

蒿子 herb of sweet wormwood

蓮子 lotus seed

醒子 earthern jar

燕子 swallow

孺子 (最小的兒子) boy; child

戲子 actor

雞子 chicken's kidney

蟶子 razor clam

騙子 blackleg; blagger; charlatan; cheater; con artist; conman; crook; double crosser; faker; fiddler; flimflammer; humbug; hustler; imposter; phony; swindler; trickster

【寸】 tsyn³ ① inch ② arrogant; cheeky

寸心 feelings

　　聊表寸心 as a small token of my feelings; just to show my appreciation or gratitude

寸步 single step; tiny step

　　寸步難行 cannot do anything; cannot go a step

寸金難買寸光陰 gold cannot buy time

尺寸 measurement

分寸 a sense of propriety

有分寸 have a sense of propriety; know how far to go and when to stop

明寸 deliberately cocky

【小】 siu² little

小人 base person; creep; little person; villain

　　打小人 (literally) beat the little person

　　枉作小人 play the villain, but fail to gain any profit

　　卑鄙小人 creep

小丑 ① buffoon; clown; knave ② contemptible wretch

小巴 (小公共汽車／中巴) minibus; public light bus

　　小巴站 minibus station

　　一架小巴 (一輛小公車) a minibus

小心 ① careful; cautious; precaution ② take care ③ be careful

　　小心地滑 beware of slippery floor

　　小心車門 mind the door of the vehicle

　　小心眼 (心胸狹窄) narrow-minded

　　小心駛得萬年船 take care and care will prevail

　　唔小心 (不小心) not careful

小半 lesser part

小白臉 a man who lives off the earnings of a woman

小兒科 peanuts; trivial matters

小姐 miss
　　空中小姐 air hostess
小姓 one's surname is
　　小姓陳 my surname is Chan
小便 urinate; urine
小食 (小吃／零食) snack
　　小食店 snack shop
小家 mean-spirited
　　小家器 mean-spirited
　　小家種 (小心眼兒) miserly person
小恩小惠 petty favours
小氣 narrow-minded; petty
小茴香 cumin
小財唔出，大財唔入 an empty hand is no lure for a
　　hawk; nothing ventured, nothing gained
小鬼頭 (小鬼) buster; little devil; mischievous child; imp
小產 (流產) abortion
小組 team
小造 (小年) off year
小販 hawker; pedlar; street vendor; vendor
小提琴 violin
小棠菜 Shanghai cabbage
小菜 common dishes; plain dishes; side dishes
小腌 (肋下) subcostal
小腸氣 (疝氣) hernia
小道 pass; passageway; path; pathway; trail
　　小道消息 hearsay; rumour; grapevine gossip
小說 fiction; novel
　　武俠小說 martial art novel
小數怕長計 carelessness with small amounts leads to big
　　money problems in the long term
小輪 (渡輪) ferry; ferry boat
小氣 (小心眼兒／氣量窄) narrow-minded
小學 primary school
　　小學雞 (初級／入門) elementary; layman
小貓 kitten
　　得小貓三四隻 only a few people
小籠包 steamed meat dumpling

中小 (企) small and medium-sized business
月小 ① solar month of thirty days ② lunar month of
　　twenty-nine days
可大可小 it may be either serious or unimportant
幼小 young and small
妻小 one's wife and children
妻兒老小 one's parents, wife and children; a married man's
　　entire family; wife and family
窄小 small and narrow
睇小 (輕看) belittle sb; look down on sb

【山】 saan¹ mountain

山大斬埋有柴 (積少成多) achieve a lot by proceeding
　　in small steps; many a little makes a mickle; look
　　after the pennies and the pounds will look after
　　themselves
山火 hill fire
山卡罅 ① deserted place ② (山谷) mountain valley
山泥 mountain clay
　　山泥傾瀉 landslide
山背 (山後) back of a mountain
山埃 (氰化鉀) (transliteration) potassium cyanide
山草藥 (草藥) herbal medicine
　　山草樂——嗡得就嗡 speak light of
山高水低 unexpected misfortune
山高皇帝遠 (literally) run one's own affairs without
　　interference from a distant centre of authority; while the
　　cat is away, the mice will play
山腳 (山麓) base/bottom/foot of a mountain
山寨廠 (小作坊) cottage factory; squatter factory
山窮水盡 at the end of one's rope
山墳 (墳墓) grave
山豬 (野豬) boar; wild boar
山窿 (山洞) cave; cavern
山罅 (石縫) crack; cranny
山雞 (野雞) pheasant

火山 volcano
出山 take up a job; carry a coffin to the cemetery to hold
　　a funeral procession; work at public office or other
　　organisations after withdrawing from society for some
　　time; go back to the outside world after reclusion (for
　　monks)
古老石山 ① old-fashioned ② old fogy
收山 ① live in retirement; retire ② quit
有眼不識泰山 fail to recognise an important person; too
　　blind to recognise the sun
江山 ① landscape; rivers and mountains ② country; state
　　power; territories
行山 hiking; take a walk on the hills; walk the hills
爬山 mountain climbing
放虎歸山 lay trouble for the future
金山 the United States
拜山 (掃墓／上墳) visit a grave
淮山 Chinese yam
開門見山 come straight to the point; not to mince one's
　　words; put it bluntly
搵靠山 (找有力人士支持) look for a powerful supporter
靠山 sponsor; supporter
舊金山 San Francisco

【川】tsyn¹ river

川菜 Sichuan food

川劇 Sichuan opera

四川 Sichuan

【工】gung¹ (工作) work

工人 ① (保姆) amah; maid ② domestic helper ③ worker ④ servant

　工人房 room for domestic helpers

工友 (工人) worker

工夫 (事情) work

　　做足工夫 be well prepared

　　慳工夫 (省事) save trouble

工多藝熟 practice makes perfect

工作 ① work ② job

　工作人員 working staff

　工作表 spreadsheet

　工作愉快 happy work

　工作簽證 working visa

　　一份工 (一份工作) a job

　　全職工 (全職工作) full-time job

　　輪班 / 輪更 (輪流工作) work in shifts

工具 instrument; tool

　　一副工具 (一套工具) a set of tools

工時 working hours

　　標準工時 standard working hours

工商舖 industrial and commercial premises

工場 (車間) workshop

工程 engineering

　工程師 engineer

　　一項工程 a construction

工業 industry

　工業家 industrialist

工廠 factory

　工廠工人 factory worker

　　一間工廠 (一家工廠) a factory

工模 (模子) mould

工頭 (監工) foreman; overlooker; overseer; supervisor; task master

上工 start working

分工 divide the work

手工 workmanship

加人工 (加工資) have a pay rise

打工 (工作) take up employment; work

打住家工 (當家傭) work as a housemaid

返工 (上班) go to work very early

扣人工 (減工資) deduct wages

收工 / 放工 (下班) clock off; come off work; go off work

技工 artificer; artisan; mechanic; skilled worker; technician

見工 (面試) be interviewed for a job; job interview

社工 social worker

員工 staff

校工 manual worker in a school

笋工 dream job

做義工 (當義工) do volunteer work

義工 volunteer worker

散工 casual labourer; hourly-paid job; odd-job man; part-timer; seasonal worker; temporary worker

替工 ① fill in; work as a substitute ② substititute worker

異曲同工 achieve the same goal with different means

黑工 illegal worker

傭工 hired labourer; servant

搵工 (找工作 / 求職) find a job; job-hunting; look for a job

搵緊工 (正在找工作) looking for a job; trying to find a job

電工 electrician

管工 foreman

趕工 work overtime

雕工 carver; grinder

臨時工 temporary worker

轉工 (轉職) change a job

鐘點工 worker paid by the hour

【己】gei² self

己見 one's own opinion

　　各抒己見 each airs their own view; each has their say

人在江湖，身不由己 one's life is bound by rules of the underworld

三五知己 a few close friends; several bosom friends

佢自己 (他自己) ① himself ② herself

安份守己 abide by laws and behave oneself well

老鼠跌落天平——自己秤自己 sing one's own praise

自己 oneself

你自己 yourself

作賤自己 (糟踐自己) run oneself down

我自己 myself

求人不如求己 ask another for help is not as good as to help oneself; better depend on oneself than ask for help from others

私己 private resources; private savings

盲公竹——督人唔督己 a white cane – one who is always strict with others but never with himself

信自己 believe in yourself

姜太公封神——漏咗自己 leave out oneself

律己 discipline oneself; self-restraint

害人（終）害己 harm both oneself and others; curses come home to roost; harm set, harm get; harm watch; harm catch

將心比己 measure another's foot by one's own last

潮州音樂——自己顧自己 Chiu Chow music——everyone for themselves; pay one's bill for oneself

【已】ji¹ have already
已婚 married

不得已 act against one's will; have no alternative but to

【干】gon¹ concern; involve
干貝（乾貝）dried scallop
干涉 intervene in; meddle in; poke one's nose into sth
　干涉內政 interference in domestic affairs; meddle in a country's internal affairs
干擾 disturb; interfere; lapse; obstruct; tamper; trouble; upset

一干 (a measure-word)
冇相干（不礙事 / 不要緊）never mind; nothing serious
相干 relation
若干 certain
唔相干（沒有關係）have nothing to do with; no concern; no relationship; unconcerned

【巾】gan¹ towel
巾幗 ① ancient woman's headdress ② woman
　巾幗英雄 female hero; heroine
　巾幗鬚眉 women who act and talk like men

紙巾 tissue paper
毛巾 towel
頸巾 scarf
手巾 handkerchief
面巾 (face) towel; washcloth
浴巾 bath towel
腳巾 foot-cleaning cloth
衛生巾（衛生棉）sanitary napkin
餐巾 napkin
擘網巾（翻臉 / 拆夥）break off friendly relations with sb; sever connections with sb
濕紙巾 wet tissue
纏頸巾（圍頸巾）wear a scarf

【弓】gung¹ bow
弓形 bow-shaped
弓鼻（嗆鼻子）irritate the nose

弓箭 bows and arrows

裝彈弓（設圈套 / 坑人）make an ambush; set a trap
彈弓（彈簧）spring
攣弓 coil; curl; hump up

【才】tsoi⁴ ability; talent
才女 a girl of many accomplishments; accomplished lady; gifted female scholar; talented woman
才子 genius; gifted scholar
　才子佳人 a gifted scholar and a beautiful lady; genius and beauty
　風流才子 talented and romantic scholar
才能 talent
才幹 ability; caliber; capability; competence; management ability
才華 talent
才藝 talent and skill
　多才多藝 versatile

人才 talented people
天才 talent
天妒英才 heaven envies talented people
奴才 flunkey; lackey
忌才 jealous of other people's talent; resent people who are more able than oneself
作育英才 nurture talented people
秀才 county graduate
英才 talented person
剛才 a moment ago; a while ago; just now
賊公計，狀元才 know a trick worth two of that
酸秀才 county graduate who is envious of others' achievement

4 劃

【不】bat⁷ not
不一 differ; vary
　不一而足 by no means an isolated case
不了 without end
　不了了之 allow sth to remain unresolved; conclude without conclusion; end up with nothing definite; settle a matter by leaving it unsettled
　大不了 at worst; it's not a big deal
　免不了 be bound to be; hard to avoid; inevitable; it is ony natural that; unavoidable
不二價 one price only

不可 be forbidden; cannot; must not; not allowed; should not
　　缺一不可 none of them can be dispensed with; not a single one can be omitted or excluded
不必 need not; no need to; not have to; not necessary
不打不相識 build up friendship after an exchange of blows
不打自招 make a confession without duress
不如 how about; it would be better if
不安 disquiet; disturbed; restless; uneasy
不妨 could as well; may as well; might as well; doesn't matter; there is no harm in
不見 ① have not met; have not seen ② disappear; missing
　　不見不散 don't leave until we are all there; not to leave without seeing each other
　　不見天日 live in dark oppression; live in darkness
　　不見三日，如隔三秋 not seeing each other for just three days feels like being separated for three years
不到黃河心不死 there is no stopping me until I reach the Yellow River, meaning to go to great lengths to do sth
不和 at cross-purposes; at loggerheads with sb; at odds with sb; discord
不宜 inadvisable; inappropriate
　　兒童不宜 not suitable for children
不法 illegal; unlawful
　　不法份子 law breakers
　　不法行為 illegality
不知 not know
　　不知不覺 unconsciously; without realising it
　　不知幾 extremely
　　不知幾開心 extremely happy
　　有所不知 there are things one doesn't know
不是冤家不聚頭 dogs and cats are sure to meet
不特止 (不僅僅) not only
不嬲 (一向) all along; consistently; frequently; for always
不至於 it is unlikely that; unlikely to go so far
不停 (咁) non-stop
不得 may not; must not; not be allowed
　　不得了 ① desperately serious; horrible; terrible ② exceedingly; extremely; terrible
不堪 ① cannot bear; cannot stand ② extremely; utterly
　　不堪一擊 be finished off at one blow; cannot withstand a single blow
不敵 be defeated; no match for
不舉 sexually impotent
不斷 unceasingly
不歡而散 break up in disagreement; break up in discord; disperse with ill feelings

永不 never
　　永不錄用 never to be employed again

點解唔 (何不) not see any harm in; why not

【丑】 tsau² clown
丑生 (丑角 / 丑腳) clown; comedian

小丑 ① buffoon; clown; knave ② contemptible wretch

【中】 dzung¹ middle
中小 (企) small- and medium-sized enterprises
中午 high noon; midday; noon; noonday
中心 centre; core; crux; heart; hub; kernel
中文 Chinese
中立 neither on one side nor the other; neutral
　　中立國 neutral nation
　　　　保持中立 adhere to/maintain neutrality; remain neutral; sit on the fence
中西 Chinese and Western
　　中西文化 Chinese and Western cultures
中坑 (中年男人) middle-aged man
中更 (中班) middle switch
中挺 (中等) medium
中度 medium
中秋 mid-autumn
　　中秋節 Mid-autumn Festival
　　　　月到中秋份外明 the harvest moon is exceptionally bright; the mid-autumn moon is exceptionally bright
中氣 (literary) lung power
中國 China
　　中國人 Chinese
　　中國大陸 mainland China
　　中國茶 Chinese tea
　　中國菜 / 中菜 Chinese dishes; Chinese food
中途 halfway; midway; on the way
中湯 Chinese soup
中等 middle class
中間 centre; in the middle of; middle
　　中間人 middle-man
　　中間位 middle seat
中意 (喜歡) like; satisfied
中電 (二號電池) C-size battery
中華 China
中碼 (中號) medium; medium size
中學 secondary school
中檔 average
中褸 (短大衣) short overcoat

中醫 Chinese medicine
　　中醫師 Chinese medicine practitioner
　　　睇中醫（看中醫）see a doctor of Chinese medicine

月中 middle of the month
年中 during the year; middle of the year
秀外慧中 beautiful and intelligent; pretty and intelligent
盲中中 absent-minded
急驚風遇着慢郎中 meet with a slow doctor when having
　　an urgent illness, meaning to be too slow for the
　　demand
耐唔中／間唔中／間中（偶爾／有時候）occasionally;
　　sometimes
郎中 doctor; physician trained in herbal medicine
高中 senior middle school
從中 from among; out of; therefrom
途中 en route; on passage; on the way
無意中 unintentionally

【中】dzung³ make a direct hit

中招（上當）be caught in a trap; get hit
中毒 poison
中計 fall into a set-up; fall into a trap
中風 stroke
中暑 sun stroke
中傷 defame

一箸夾中（一擊即中）hit the right nail on the head; make a
　　right guess
打中 hit
估中（猜中／對）one's guess is right
估唔中（猜不對／錯）cannot guess; miss one's guess;
　　unable to make out the right answer
批中（測對）as expected
命中 hit the target; score a hit
睇中（看中）be interested in; take a fancy to
擊中 hit the target
講中（說準／中）as expected

【予】jy⁵ give

予以 give; grant

准予 approve; authorise; grant; permit

【丹】daan¹ red

丹心 loyal heart; loyalty
　　一片丹心 a heart of pure loyalty; a loyal heart
丹田 pubic region
　　丹田之氣 deep breath controlled by the diaphragm

牡丹 peony

【互】wu⁶ mutual

互助 mutual help
互補 complement each other; supplement each other
互聯網 internet

【五】ng⁵ five

五五波（一半）a fifty-fifty chance
五月 ① May ② the fifth month of the lunar year
　　五月節（端午節）Dragon Boat Festival
五行 five basic elements
　　五行欠水／五行缺水（缺錢）in need of money
　　五行欠打 deserve a beating
　　五行欠金 —— 冇錢（羅鍋兒上山 —— 錢（前）緊）broke;
　　　in need of money; penniless
　　五行欠炳 in need of a beating
五更 the fifth watch of the night
　　三更窮五更富（literally）at the third watch of the night
　　　one is poor, by the fifth watch of the night one is
　　　rich, meaning that things are uncertain
五花 five-flower
　　五花八門 a motley; a variety of; all kinds of
　　五花茶 five-flower tea
　　五花腩（五花肉）pork belly; streaky pork
　　五花大縛
五金 hardware; metals in general
　　五金舖 hardware store
五星（級）five-star
五時花六時變 change one's mind easily
五張嘢（五十來歲）fifty something
五湖四海 different places of the country
五筒櫃（五屜櫃）five-drawer cabinet
五線譜 musical score using the staff notation; staff
五顏六色 ①（五光十色／彩色繽紛）a riot of colour;
　　colourful; gaudy; a play of colours ②（said of illness）
　　critical
　　病到五顏六色 be critically ill

二一添作五 divide sth equally; go fifty-fifty
八月十五 ① 15 August ② the fifteenth day of the eighth
　　month ③（屁股／臀部）bottom; buttocks
王老五 bachelor; bachelor guy; unmarried man
你做初一，我做十五（literally）you be the first day of the
　　lunar month, I be the fifteen of the month, meaning a
　　tooth for a tooth; an eye for an eye; answer blows with
　　blows
禮拜五 Friday（星期五／週五）Friday
朝九晚五 working from nine to five

【井】dzeng² well
井水 well water
> 河水不犯井水 (literally) well water does not interfere with river water, meaning each one minds their own business

井號 pound sign

一個井（一眼井／一口井）a well
天井 courtyard; open yard; patio
沙井 seepage pit
掏古井 marry a rich widow for her money
掘井 dig a well
臨渴掘井 (literally) begin to dig a well when feeling thirsty, meaning that a person fails to make timely preparations
龍井 Longjing tea
離鄉別井 away from one's home-town

【仁】jan⁴ ① (仁兒) core ② benevolence
仁兄／仁弟 my dear friend
仁義 kindheartedness and justice
> 仁義道德 benevolence, righteousness, and virtue

仁慈 kind; merciful

杏仁 almond

【仃】ding¹ lonely; solitary

孤苦伶仃／伶伶仃仃 lonely and poor

【仄】dzak⁷ cheque
仄紙（支票）(archaic) cheque

【仆】puk⁹ (摔) fall down
仆喺度（摔在這兒）fall down here
仆轉（反轉東西）turn sth over

【仇】sau⁴ hatred
仇人 personal enemy
> 仇人見面，分外眼紅 meeting enemies opens old wounds; when two foes meet, there is no mistaking each other

仇口（仇恨／怨恨／積怨）animosity; enmity; grudge; hatred; hostility
仇家 enemy

恩仇 debt of gratitude and of revenge

【今】gam¹ ① this ② now
今勻（這次）this time
今日（今天）today
> 今時今日 nowadays
> 早知今日，何必當初 it is too late to ask oneself why one has gone astray when one knows the consequence to be so serious

今年 this year
今次（這次）current; present; this time
今後 along the road; down the road; from now on; henceforth; hereafter; in the days to come
今時唔同往日（今非昔比）times have changed
今晚（今天晚上）tonight
> 今晚黑（今天晚上）tonight

今朝（今天早上）this morning
> 今朝早（今天早上）this morning
> 今朝有酒今朝醉 don't worry today about what you're going to eat tomorrow; enjoy the pleasures of drinking wine here and now; enjoy while one can

古今 the ancient and the modern
於今 at present; now; since; up to the present
是古非今 admire everything ancient and belittle present-day achievements; consider anything old as good and reject everything that is modern

【介】gaai³ introduce
介乎（介於）in between
介紹 introduce
> 介紹人 ① introducer ② referee
> 介紹信 letter of introduction
> > 自我介紹 self-introduction

介詞 preposition
介意 mind
> 不必介意 please don't mind

介懷（介意）care about; get annoyed; mind; take offence

大眾媒介 mass media
媒介 medium; vehicle
轉介 medical referral

【元】jyn⁴ first
元月 first month of the lunar year
元旦 New Year
元老 doyen; senior statesmen
元宵節／元宵佳節 Lantern Fstival
元氣 strength; vigor; vitality
> 元氣大傷 one's constitution is greatly undermined; sap one's vitality

元蹄 (豬肘子) pig's elbow
元寶 paper ingot
　元寶蠟燭 paper ingots and candles

行行出狀元 every profession produces its own leading
　authority or specialists; one can be outstanding in any trade
狀元 first in the civil service examination

【內】noi⁶ inside

內心 in one's mind
　內心世界 one's inner world
內外 ① inside and outside ② domestic and foreign
內向 introversion
　內向的人 introvert
內因 internal cause
內在 inherent; inner; internal; intrinsic
　內在因素 internal factor
　內在美 inner beauty
內地 mainland China
內行 expert
　內行人 expert; insider
　　充內行 pass oneself off as an expert; pose as
　　　an expert
內定 designated
　內定名額 officially decided quota
內疚 compunction; guilty conscience
內政 home affairs; internal affairs
內科 internal medicine
內容 content
　內容枯燥 / 內容乏味 dull in content
　內容豐富 rich in content
內鬼 spy on the inside
內部 ① inside; interior ② restricted
　內部矛盾 internal contradictions
內陸 hinterland; inland
內亂 civil strife; internal disorder
　平息內亂 suppress the internal disorder
內幕 inside story
　內幕消息 inside information
　泄漏內幕 give the show away
內閣 cabinet
　解散內閣 disband the cabinet
內線 extension
內戰 civil war
內鬨 internal conflict
　挑起內鬨 stir up internal strife
內牆 internal wall
內籠 internal
　內籠面積 internal floor area

內臟 intestines

宇內 ① (中國疆域之內) in the country ② (整個世界) in
　the world
室內 indoors
懼內 henpecked

【公】gung¹ ① (雄) male ② husband ③ (公公) old man

公不離婆，秤不離砣 husbands are in pair with wives,
　just like sliding weights are inseparable from scales
公仔 ① (洋娃娃 / 模型人兒) doll ② (連環圖 / 漫畫)
　cartoon
　公仔書 (小人書 / 連環圖 / 漫畫書) ① (小人書)
　　children's book ② (連環畫 / 連環圖 / 漫畫書) comics
　公仔箱 (電視) television set
　公仔麵 (快速麵 / 即食麵 / 速食麵) instant noodles
　　孖公仔 two people who are constantly together
　　扯線公仔 (牽線木偶) puppet
公司 company; firm; shop
　公司三文治 club sandwich
　　分公司 branch
　　百貨公司 (百貨大樓) department store
　　行公司 (逛商店) go shopping; visit department stores
　　返公司 (去單位) go to office
　　返到公司 (回到單位) arrive at the office
　　國貨公司 Chinese products emporium
　　總公司 head office
公平 fair; just
　唔公平 (不公平) unfair
公正 justice
公民 citizen
　公民責任 civic responsibilities
　公民權利 civic rights
公用事務 utilities
公共 public
　公共秩序 public order
公事 official business
　公事包 briefcase
　公事喼 (手提箱) suitcase
公務員 civil servant; government servant
公婆 husband and wife
　兩公婆 (兩口子) husband and wife; married couple
　兩公婆扒艇 —— 你有你事 (各顧各) mind your own
　　business
　兩公婆見鬼 —— 唔係你就係我 either of the two
公眾 public
　公眾假期 public holiday
　公眾場所 public places

公園 park
　　行公園 (到公園散步) walk in the park
公路 road
　　高速公路 highway
公道 (合理) reasonable
　　主持公道 uphold justice
公說公有理，婆說婆有理 each clings to his own view
公關 public relations

一支公 ① alone ② a bachelor; an unmarried man
二叔公 pawn shop
大聲公 ① loud-speaker megaphone ② man with a
　　loud voice
天上雷公，地下舅公 brothers of the mother has a high
　　status in human relations
太公 (曾祖父) great-grandfather
老公 husband
廿四考老公 caring husband
手指公 (拇指) thumb
包租公 landlord
(去) 搵周公 (睡覺) go to bed; go to sleep
阿公 (外公) maternal grandfather; maternal grandpa
石狗公 sea ruffle
伯爺公 old chap; old man
叔公 (叔祖) grand uncle
家公 father-in-law
陰公 pitiful
壽星公 birthday boy
蝦公 prawn
豬公 (公豬／雄豬) boar
貓公 (公貓／雄貓) tomcat
辦公 ① attend to business; do office work ② (上廁所) go to
　　the toilet (in cantonese meaning)
鴨公 (公鴨／雄鴨) drake
雞公 (公雞) cock
關公 Lord Kwan

【六】 luk⁹ six
六六無窮 never-ending
六月 ① June ② the sixth month of the lunar year
六合彩 Mark Six
六安 Lu'an tea
六耳不同謀 two's company, three's none
六畜 six domestic animals
六神無主 be thrown into confusion; don't know what to do
六國大封相 chaotic situation
六親 one's kin; the six relations: father, mother, elder
　　brothers, younger brothers, wife, and children
　　六親不認 turn one's back on all one's relations

二打六 low-level person; unimportant person
十五十六 (literally) fifteen or sixteen, meaning in two minds;
　　indecisive
三六 doq meat
坐定粒六 have 6 dots on a six-sided dice for sure, meaning
　　to be sure about sth; have full confidence
鬼五馬六 (亂七八糟) ① act in a grotesque way; act
　　strangely ② frivolous ③ messy
做又三十六，唔做又三十六 one gets the same pay whether
　　one is hardworking or lazy
禮拜六 (星期六) Saturday

【分】 fan¹ ① share ② cent
分寸 a sense of propriety
　　有分寸 have a sense of propriety; know how far to go
　　　　and when to stop
　　有分有寸 know what to do
分工 divide the work
　　分工合作 divide labour and join in work
分分鐘 (每時每刻／隨時) all the time; any time
分化 become divided; break up; split up
分心 distract
分手 break up
分外 (格外) all the more; especially; exceptionally;
　　extraordinarily
分甘同味 (共享甜頭) share and share alike
分行 branch
分別 ① leave each other; part; separate ② discriminate;
　　differentiate; distinguish ③ differently ④ respectively;
　　separately
分居 live apart; separate without a legal divorce; separation
分娩 give birth
　　自然分娩 natural childbirth
　　無痛分娩 painless delivery
分裂 break up; cleavage; disintegrate; dissociate; disunity;
　　divide; split
　　四分五裂 be rent by disunity; be smashed to bits;
　　　　break into pieces
分開 break up; divide; isolate; part; partition; segregate;
　　separate; sort
　　分開包 pack things separately; wrap things separately
分號 ① semicolon ② branch of a firm
分解 ① break down; decompose; resolution; resolve
　　② disclose; recount
分隔開 be separated from
分數 (分寸) propriety
　　有分數 (有數) have a good sense of propriety; know
　　　　how to manage sth; know what to do and what not
　　　　to do

分擔 share the responsibility
分類 classify; ledger; sort; sorting; taxonomy
　　分門別類 categorise

一分 one cent
十分 completely; extremely; fully; utterly; very
是非不分 cannot tell right from wrong; confuse truth and falsehood
區分 demarcate; differentiate
績分 credit

【切】 tsit[8] cut

切勿 be sure not to; do not by any means
切件（切塊）cut into pieces
切肉不離皮 (literally) one can't sever meat from skin, meaning blood is thicker than water
切身 ① directly affect a person; of immediate concern to oneself ② first-hand; one's own; personal
切菜刀剃頭——牙煙（剃頭刀擦屁股——懸得乎）clean the buttocks with a barber's knife – dangerous enough

走唔切（來不及逃走）do not have enough time to go
食唔切 do not have enough time to eat up
做唔切（來不及完成）do not have enough time to complete the tasks
趕唔切（趕不上）do not have enough time to do sth; out of time; too late to catch
趕得切（趕上）have enough time to do sth; just in time
密切 close
薄切切（很薄）very thin
嚟唔切（來不及）can't make it; won't make it
嚟得切（趕及）can make it; in time

【切】 tsai[3] all

一切 everything

【勻】 wan[4] even

勻巡（勻和／均勻）even
勻淨 even; uniform

今勻（這次）this time
行一勻 take a walk
行勻（走遍）do the rounds
均勻 even; well-matched
拉勻（平均計算）average; balance up
搖勻 shake up
頭一勻（第一次／首次）the first time
攪勻（拌勻）mix; mix thoroughly

【勾】 ngau[1] entice

勾佬（勾引男人）pick up a man
勾搭 find a lover; pick up someone
　　勾三搭四 (said of a woman) have many lovers
勾當 business; deal
勾銷 eliminate
　　一筆勾銷 eliminate at one stroke
勾爛 hang on and break sth

四十幾勾 forty sth; in one's forties; more than forty years old
生勾勾（活生生）alive; have great vitality; lively

【勿】 mat[9] not

勿歇 unceasingly
勿論 non-negotiable
　　姑勿論（不用說／且不說）let alone; not to mention; not to speak of; to say nothing of
　　格殺勿論 capture and summarily execute

切勿 be sure not to; do not by any means

【化】 faa[3] transform

化身 embodiment; incarnate; incarnation
化晒（看破紅塵）be disillusioned with this human world; see through the emptiness of the material world; see through the vanity of life
化骨龍 dependent child
化粧 apply cosmetics or make up
　　化粧間 powder room
　　化粧師 make-up artist
化痰 reduce phlegm
化算（上算／划算）deserving; worthwhile
　　唔化算（不合算）not worthwhile
化學 ① chemistry ②（不耐用／易壞的／靠不住）feeble; fragile; not long-lasting; undurable
化驗 laboratory test
　　化驗室 laboratory

千變萬化 full of changes
分化 become divided; break up; split up
文化 culture
炭化 carbonise
美化 beautify; embellish; prettify
活化 revitalise
梳化（沙發）sofa
淨化 purify
唔化（看不開）too stubborn
消化 digest

神化 strange
神神化化 not quite right in the mind; silly and curious; strange
焚化 cremate; incinerate
睇化 (看開) accept calmly whatever comes along; realise why life should be so
歐化 Europeanised
鬆化 (酥脆) crisp
變化 change

【升】sing¹ go up; raise; rise

升天 ascend to heaven; go up to the heaven
升水 (升值) appreciation; positive evaluation
升仙 die; pass away
升降 hoist and lower; rise and fall
　　升降機 lift
升值 appreciate; revaluation
升級 advance to a higher grade; be promoted to a higher class; go up one grade in school
升起 rise
升跌 rise and fall
　　無升跌 constant
升職 promotion
升 cup increase bust size

一公升 a litre
竹升 ① bamboo carrying pole ② overseas Chinese
筆升 brush pot; pen container
矮仔上樓梯——步步高升 climb up step by step in one's career

【午】ng⁵ noon

午安 good afternoon
午夜 midnight
　　午夜場 midnight movie
　　　　捱近午夜 near midnight
午餐 (午飯) lunch; luncheon
　　午餐肉 luncheon meat
　　　　自助午餐 lunch buffet
　　　　免費午餐 free lunch

上午 morning
下午 afternoon
中午 high noon; midday; noon; noonday
傍午 about noon; near noontime; shortly before noon

【及】kap⁹ and

及早 as soon as possible; at an early date; before it is too late
　　及早回頭 lose no time in mending one's ways; make haste to reform; mend one's ways without delay; repent before it is too late
及時 at a most opportune moment; at the right time; in due course; in due time; in good season; in good time; in season; in the nick of time; in time; promptly; timely; without delay
　　及時雨 a much-needed rain; a seasonable rain; a timely help; a timely rain; an opportune rain; help rendered in the nick of time
及格 pass an examination
　　唔及格 clutch the gunny; fail; fail in an examination

埃及 Egypt
旁及 take up
涉及 deal with; involve; refer to; relate to; touch upon
莫及 beyond reach
望塵莫及 a far cry from; be left far behind; be left in the dust; be thrown into the shade; cannot hold a candle to; fall far behind; hopelessly behindhand; lay a long way behind; too far behind to catch up; too inferior to bear comparison; unable to keep pace with; unequal to
愚不可及 abysmal ignorance; could not be more foolish; crass stupidity; hopelessly stupid; most foolish; the height of folly
與及 along with; and; as well as; including; together with
憶及 call to mind; recollect; remember
鞭長莫及 beyond one's influence; beyond one's reach; beyond the range of one's ability; beyond the reach of one's power; cannot do it much as I would like to; out of range; too far away for one to be able to help

【及】gap⁹ watch

及住 watch closely
及野 peep

【友】jau⁵ ① (朋友) friend ② guy

友仔 (小子／傢伙) that guy
友好 ① close friend; friend ② amicable; amity; buddy-buddy; congenial friends
友情 fraternal love; friendly sentiments; friendship
友善 friendly
　　好友善 very friendly
友誼 friendship
　　友誼賽 friendly match
　　　　促進友誼 promote friendship

口痕友 prater
大炮友 braggard; liar; teller of tall stories
大難友 idler
小朋友 ① little boys; little friends; little girls ② one's children

女友 girlfriend

女朋友 girlfriend

工友 worker

牙較友 chin-wagger

古惑友 tricky person

未觀其人，先觀其友 you can know a man by the friends he keeps

在家靠父母，出外靠朋友 at home, you rely on parents; away from home, you rely on friends

好老友 very friendly

有少少朋友 have a few friends

老友 ① good friend ② old friend

自己友 one of us

行友 hiker

西裝友 man in a suit

男友 boyfriend

男朋友 boyfriend

呢條友 this guy

拖友 lover

朋友 friend

炒友 speculator

飛機友 a person who always breaks appointments

唔夠老友 not friendly enough

書友 ex-classmate

益友 beneficial friends; helping friends; useful friends

麻雀友 mahjong enthusiast; mahjong fan

密友 close friend

啤友 lovers

探朋友 visit a friend

傍友 hanger-on; person who sponges on his boss

幾個朋友 several friends

發燒友 fan; fanatic; maniac

硯友 (同學) classmate; fellow student

嗰條友 (那傢伙) that guy

損友 vicious companion

道友 (吸毒者) drug addict; druggie

滾友 ① (到色情樂場所的人) one who visits prostitutes ② imposter; swindler ③ irresponsible person ④ (騙子) liar

網友 internet friend

影友 (攝影愛好者) shutterbug

賤友 vulgar person

豬朋狗友 bad companions; bad friends; bad mates; friends of bad character; friends with bad habits or low morals

親朋戚友 friends and relatives

親戚朋友 friends and relatives

難友 (難兄難弟) fellow sufferer

蠱惑友 (奸詐的人) tricky person

【反】 faan² rebel

反口 (出爾反爾) deny one's promise

　　反口咬一啖 (反咬一口) turn around and hit back

　　反口覆舌 (否認前言) inconsistent with what one says

反文邊 (反文兒／反文旁) the "rap" 攵 radical

反斗 (淘氣／頑皮／調皮／搞蛋) mischievous; naughty

　　反斗仔 (小淘氣／搞蛋鬼) naughty boy

　　反斗星 (小淘氣／搞蛋鬼) naughty boy

反而 but; instead; on the contrary; rather than

反抗 resist

反肚 (肚皮朝天) die

反昂瞓 (俯睡) lie on one's back in sleeping

反為 (反而) but; instead; on the contrary; rather than

反胃 (噁心) ① stomach upset ② disgusting

　　令人反胃 (令人噁心的) nasty

　　好反胃 (很噁心) very disgusting

反面 ① (相反的情況) reverse side ② (鬧翻) fall out; not on good terms with one; suddenly turn out to be hostile to sb

反骨 (吃裏爬外／恩將仇報) bite the hand that feeds one; quit love with hate; rebellious; repay love with hate; requite kindness with enmity; return evil for good; return kindness with ingratitude; treat one's benefactor as one's enemy

　　反骨仔 (白眼兒狼) a snake in sb's bosom; rebel; traitor

反常 aberrant; abnormal; paradoxical; perverse; strange; unusual

反艇 (死) die

反對 argue against; be against; be opposed to; buck against; combat; come out against; conspire against; cry against; cry out against; declare against; decry; demonstrate against; demur at; fight; fight against; go against; have an objection to; have an opposition to; in opposition to; make an objection to; object to; objection; oppose; protest against; react against; set against; set one's face against; set oneself against; show opposition to; side against; speak against; stand against; take opposition to; vote against

　　反對黨 opposition party

反駁 confute; contradict; controvert; countercharge; counterplea; disprove; gainsay; refute; retort

反彈 bounce back; rebound

反戰 anti-war

反應 reaction; response

　　反應靈敏 be quick on the draw

反擊 counter-attack

反覆 again and again; once and again; over and over; over and over again; iterative; time after time; time and again

　　反反覆覆 again and again; like the burden of a song; over and over again; repeatedly

反轉 (反過來／翻過來) reverse
反轉豬肚就係屎 (翻臉不認人) change friendship into
　　anger

作反 (造反) rebel; revolt; rise up against
相反 opposite
違反 act against; contradict; disregard; infringe; run counter
　　to; transgress; violate
籠裏雞作反 (內訌) have an internal dissension;
　　internal rift

【壬】 jam⁴ the ninth heavenly stem
壬人 (奸佞之人) artful person

扭六壬 (千方百計) rack one's brains

【天】 tin¹ ① heaven ② sky
天一半，地一半 all over the place
天上雷公，地下舅公 brothers of the mother has a high
　　status in human relations
天下 heaven
　　打天下 (努力闖蕩) conquer; take over
　　名滿天下 gain a world reputation; world-renowned
　　威振天下 the entire world is overwhelmed
天口 (天氣) weather
天才 talent
天井 (庭院) courtyard; open yard; patio
天分 talent
天有眼 (老天無眼) this is so unfair
　　天有眼 (老天有眼) the wicked are punished
天文台 ① observatory ② (通風報訊的人) look-out
天主教 Catholicism
天台 (曬台) roof
天光 (天亮／天明) dawn; daybreak
　　天光早 (光亮的大清早) bright and early; early in the
　　　morning; the crack of dawn
　　六點天光 (六點天亮) the day breaks at six a.m.
天各一方 be separated far apart
天后 Heaven Queen
　　天后誕 Birthday of the Heaven Queen
天地 heaven and earth
　　天地不容 heaven and earth do not tolerate; heaven
　　　forbid
　　天地良心 from the bottom of one's heart; in all fairness;
　　　in all justice; in fact; in my soul of souls; speak the
　　　truth
　　天寒地凍 freezing; severe cold and frozen land;
　　　the weather is so cold that the ground is frozen;
　　　very cold

車天車地 (侃大山) have an idle talk with sb
呼天搶地 cry bitterly and loudly in excessive grief; utter
　　cries of anguish
花天酒地 attend a dinner with sing-song girls; be in
　　the world of wine and women; be on the loose; be
　　on the tiles; be out on the tiles; go on the loose; go
　　on the racket; go on the tiles; guzzle and carouse to
　　one's heart content; guzzle and have a good time;
　　have one's fling; indulge in fast life and
　　debauchery; indulge oneself in dissipation; lead a
　　decadent and dissolute life; lead a fast life; live in
　　the world of wine and women; sow a large crop
　　of wild oats
謝天謝地 God be praised; God be thanked; thank God;
　　thank goodness; thank heavens; thank one's stars;
　　thank the Lord
驚天動地 earthshaking; shake heaven and earth; startle
　　the world; surprise the world; titanic; tremendous;
　　worldshaking
天收佢 (老天會懲罰他) heaven will punish him
天使 angel
　　白衣天使 (護士) nurse
天空 sky
　　天空海闊 of boundless capacity
天花 ① (痘瘡) smallpox ② (天花板) ceiling
　　天花板 ceiling
　　天花板滲水 (天花板漏水) water seepage from the
　　　ceiling
　　天花龍鳳 (虛張聲勢) bluff
天皇 (巨星) celebrity
天拿水 (稀釋劑) thinner
天時 (天氣) climate; weather
　　天時冷 (天氣冷) the weather is cold
　　天時暑熱 (天氣熱) the weather is hot
　　天時熱 (夏天) summer time
天書 success key book
天氣 weather
　　天氣好好 (天氣很好) it's a nice day; the weather is
　　　beautiful
　　天氣好差 (天氣很糟) the weather is very bad
　　天氣炎熱 it's hot
　　天氣麻麻 (天氣挺差) the weather is horrible
　　天氣報告 weather report
　　天氣酷熱 it's very hot
　　天氣轉涼 it's getting cooler
天堂 heaven
天眼 (望遠鏡) telescope
天陰 cloudy
　　天陰陰 (天色陰沉) cloudy

天晴 (天氣晴朗) the sky is clear
　　雨過天晴 after a shower, the sky clears; after a storm comes a calm; after black clouds, clear weather; after rain comes fair weather; after rain comes sunshine; the rain stops and the sky clears up; the skies clear up after a storm; the storm subsides and the sky clears; the sun shines again after the rain

天棚 (天台／曬台) flat roof

天無絕人之路 it is a long lane that has no turning; there is always a way out

天跌落嚟當被冚 (天塌下來當被蓋) take it easy

天黑 the sky becomes dark
　　幾點天黑 what time will it get dark

天意 destiny; fate

天腳底 (天腳底下／天邊兒) ends of the earth

天網恢恢，疏而不漏 (作惡的人總會落網) justice has long arms

天線 antenna

天賜 endowed by heaven; given by heaven
　　天賜良緣 heaven-sent marriage

天橋 flyover
　　行人天橋 (人行天橋) footbridge
　　行天橋 (走貓步) catwalk
　　行車天橋 (立體交叉橋) flyover

天藍色 sky blue

天鵝 swan
　　一隻天鵝 a swan
　　黑天鵝 black swan

天曚光 (天剛亮／黎明) at dawn; daybreak

天體 (裸體) naked

一人得道，雞犬升天 (一人得勢，跟着他的人也沾光) when a person gets to the top, all his friends and relatives get there with him; to ride on sb else's success

升天 ascend to the heaven; go up to the heaven

冬天 winter

民以食為天 people regard food as important as heaven

仰天 look up to heaven

好天 (晴天) fine day; good clear day

好好天 (天氣很好) it's a nice day; the weather is beautiful

冷天 (天冷) ① winter ② cold weather

狗膽包天 (膽大妄為) monstrous audacity

春天 spring

秋天 autumn

胡帝胡天 (言語荒唐，行為放肆) behave foolishly; run wild

夏天 summer

隻手遮天 (一手遮天) hide the truth from the masses; hoodwink the public; pull the wool over the eye of the public

聊天 (聊天兒) bat the breeze; chat; chew the fat; chinwag; chit-chat; fan the breeze; have a chat; have a chin; have a chinwag; have a dish of gossip; shoot the breeze; shoot the bull; swap lies; visit with

通天 expose sth without any reserve

晴天 cloudless day; fine day; sunny day

嘈到拆天 (大吵大鬧) extremely noisy

熱天 summer time

摩囉差拜神——睇天 (凡事皆有天意) it depends on the weather; under the mercy of God

擎天 (高聳入雲) prop up the sky

霜天 bleak sky

鬎鬁頭擔遮——無法 (髮) 無天 (和尚打傘——無法 (髮) 無天) a Buddhist monk opens an umbrella – no hair, no sky (pun) lawless and godless

露天 (戶外) in the open; in the open air; outdoors

【太】 taai³ too

太大 too big

太子 crown prince
　　太子爺 ① (少東) young master ② (大公子) (i) eldest son of a rich family (ii) eldest son of one's master ③ spoilt son of a rich family

太公 (老祖父) great-grandfather
　　太公分豬肉 (每人平等佔一份) distribution money where every body gets an equal share

太太 ① madam ② married woman ③ Mrs. ④ one's wife
　　我太太 my wife

太空 outer space
　　太空人 ① (宇航員) astronaut; spaceman ② one whose wife is abroad
　　太空館 space museum

太肥 (太胖) too fat

太長 too long

太重 too heavy

太座 (尊夫人) your wife

太婆 (老祖母) great-grandmother

太淡 too weak
　　茶太淡 the tea is too weak

太細 (太小) too small

太短 too short

太陽 sun
　　太陽油 (防曬油) suntan lotion
　　太陽眼鏡 sunglasses
　　太陽蛋 (煎蛋煎一面) sunny-side-up
　　太陽鏡 (墨鏡) sunglasses
　　好好太陽 very sunny

曬太陽（日光浴）sunbathe

太極 Tai Chi; Chinese shadow boxing
    耍太極 ① practise Tai Chi ② （推來推去）give the
      runaround

太過（太）excessively; much; over; too

太嘈（太吵）too noisy

太緊 too tight

太濃 too strong

茶太濃 the tea is too strong

太鬆（太寬）too loose

姨太太（妾）concubine

師太 ① （老師的太太）wife of one's teacher ② female
    Daoist priest/monk

靚太（漂亮的太太）beautiful wife

闊太 big-spending woman

【夫】fu¹ husband

夫人 wife
    第一夫人 first lady; president's wife
    黑市夫人（情婦）mistress

夫子 ① （學者）ancient form of address to a Confucian
    scholar ② pedant ③ husband ④ husband and children
    老夫子 tutor in a private school; unpractical scholar

夫妻 husband and wife
    老夫老妻 an old married couple
    兩夫妻（夫妻倆 / 兩人）husband and wife

夫婦 husband and wife
    一對夫婦 a couple
    兩夫婦（夫婦倆）married couple

下功夫（花心血）concentrate one's efforts; devote time and
    effort to a task; put in time and energy

大丈夫（英雄好漢）man; real man; true man

丈夫 ① hubby; husband; one's worse half ② real man

工夫 work

中國功夫 Chinese kung fu

功夫（transliteration）kung fu; martial art

打功夫（練功夫）practise martial art

未婚夫 fiancé

役夫（服役的人）labourer; servant

更夫（打更巡夜的人）night watchman

使出真功夫（拖渾身解數）show one's real power

妹夫 ① brother-in-law ② younger sister's husband

姐夫 ① brother-in-law ② elder sister's husband

枉費工夫（徒然）spend time and work in vain; waste time
    and energy

姦夫 adulterer; intrigant; paramour

哥爾夫（高爾夫）（transliteration）golf

柴可夫（司機）chauffeur; driver

做工夫 do things

做足工夫（準備充足）be well prepared

粗重工夫 heavy work

屠夫 ① （屠工）butcher; slaughterer; slaughterman; sticker
    ② ruthless ruler

無毒不丈夫（不對敵人狠毒，成不了漢子（屠工）a man
    who is not ruthless is not a truly great man; ruthlessness
    is the mark of a truly great man

硬功夫（真本領）great proficiency

漁夫 fisher; fisherman

農夫 farmer

慳工夫（省工夫）save the trouble

懦夫（膽小鬼）coward

懶佬工夫（不費勁的工作）the work that saves labour

【孔】hung² opening

孔雀 peacock

孔聖誕（孔聖節）Birthday of Confucius

天使面孔（天使臉）angel face

毛孔 pore

面孔（臉孔）face

【少】siu² little

少少（一點兒 / 有點兒）little
    早少少走（早點兒走）leave a little bit earlier
    有少少（有點兒）slightly

少有 rare

少見 rare; seldom seen; unique
    少見多怪 a man who has seen little regards many things
    as strange; comment excitedly on a commonplace
    thing; consider sth remarkable simply because one
    has not seen it before; having seen little, one gets
    excited easily; he who has little experience has many
    surprises; ignorant people are easily surprised; kick up
    a fuss; the less a man has seen, the more he has to
    wonder at; things rarely seen are regarded as
    strange; things seldom seen seem strange; wonder at
    what one has not seen; wonder is the daughter
    of ignorance

少甜（少點兒甜）less syrup

少量 a few; a little; a small amount; a sprinkling of

少過 less than

少數 minority

打得少（欠湊）deserve a beating up; deserve further
    beating; haven't hit sb enough

多少 a little

好少 rarely; very few
老少 old and young
老老少少 old and young; people old and young
老來少 old in age but young at heart
些少 (一點兒) a bit; a bit of; a little; a morsel of; a shade; a streak of; a trifle; faintly; slightly something
或多或少 (多少有點) more or less
計少 (算少了) short-charge
唔係嘢少 (沒那麼簡單) it's not that simple
缺少 absence; deficient in; lack; short of
減少 decrease; reduce
稀少 few; few and far between; little; rare; scarce; sparse
買少見少 become increasingly scarce
最少 at least

【少】 siu³ young

少女 damsel; lass; maid; maiden; young girl
　少女時期 girlhood
　　美少女 nymph
　　時髦少女 teenybopper
少奶 / 少奶奶 ① lady of leisure ② young mistress of the house ③ daughter-in-law
少東 (少東家) young boss; young master
少爺 young master of the house
　　大少爺 ① eldest son of a rich family ② eldest son of one's master ③ spendthrift; spoilt son of a rich family;
　　大少爺作風 behaviour typical of the spoiled son of a rich family; extravagant ways

大少 ① eldest son of a rich family ② eldest son of one's master ③ spoilt son of a rich family
空少 (空中少爺) air steward
花心大少 (花花公子) playboy

【尤】 jau⁴ particularly

尤其 especially
　尤其是 especially
尤物 ① uncommon person ② rare beauty; woman of extraordinary beauty

以儆效尤 as a warning to others; in order to warn against bad examples; so as to deter anyone from committing the same crime; warn others against following a bad example; warn others against making the same mistake
效尤 follow a bad example
儆尤 emulate

【尺】 cek³ ① ruler ② unit of measurement

尺寸 measurement
　　得寸進尺 give sb an inch and they will take an ell; give sb an inch and they will take a mile; much will have more; reach out for a yard after taking an inch; the more one gets, the more one wants
　　量尺寸 take the measurements
尺碼 size

一千尺 (一千平方尺) one thousand square feet
一把尺 (一把直尺長度) a foot-rule
一把間尺 (一把直尺) a ruler
千幾尺 (千多尺) more than one thousand square feet
垂涎三尺 bring the water to one's mouth; cast a covetous eye at sth; cast greedy eyes at; cannot hide one's greed; drool with envy; gape after; gape for; hanker for; have one's mouth made up for; lick one's chops; lick one's lips; make sb's mouth water; one's mouth waters after; smack one's lips
拉尺 band tape; tape measure
唔合何尺 (不合尺寸) mismatch
軟尺 (捲尺) tape-measure
間尺 (直尺) ruler

【巴】 baa¹ hope for

巴士 (公共汽車 / 公車) (transliteration) bus
　巴士佬 (公共汽車司機) bus driver
　巴士服務 (公共汽車服務) bus services
　巴士站 (公車站) bus stop
　　行去巴士站 (走去公車站) walk to the bus stop
　巴士總站 (公車總站) bus terminal
　　一架巴士 (一輛公共汽車) a bus
　　11 號巴士 (11 號公共汽車) no.11 bus
　　冷氣巴士 (空調公共汽車) air-conditioned bus
　　空中巴士 (空中客機) air bus
　　空調巴士 (空調公共汽車) air-conditioned bus
　　迫巴士 (擠公車) in a crowded bus
　　直通巴士 (直達公車) through bus
　　穿梭巴士 (穿梭車) shuttle bus
　　接駁巴士 (接駁車) feeder bus
　　等緊巴士 (等候公車) waiting for the bus
　　搭巴士 (乘公車) by bus; take a bus
　　雙層巴士 (雙層公車) double-decker bus
　　觀光巴士 (觀光車) tour bus
巴仙 (百分之) percent
巴閉 (了不起 / 有能耐 / 排場大) arrogant; far from common; flashy; impressive; proud and overweening; showy

巴巴閉閉 (吵吵鬧鬧) arrogant; flashy; showy
巴屎閉 (了不得) arrogant; flashy; showy
巴掌 (耳光) ① palm of the hand ② slap
　一巴掌 (一記耳光) slap
巴渣 (咋呼 / 話多) gossipy
巴結 be all over sb; bootlick; brown-nose; buddy up; butter up sb; cotton up to; cozy up to; curry favour with sb; fawn on; flatter; get in with sb; lay on the butter; lay the butter on; lick sb's boots; lick sb's shoes; make up to; play up to; polish the apple; soak sb down; stand in with sb; suck up to; toady to sb; try hard to please
巴辣 (潑辣) fierce
巴黎帽 (貝雷帽) (transliteration) beret

一架小巴 (一輛公共汽車) a minibus
小巴 (公共小巴) minibus; public light bus
自打嘴巴 contradict oneself
直通巴 (直通車) shuttle bus
城巴 city bus
冧巴 (號碼) number
旅遊巴 (旅遊車) sightseeing bus
校巴 (校車) school bus
淋巴 lymph
通淋巴 (推淋巴) lymph circulation
摑佢一巴 (給他一記耳光) give sb a slap
嘴巴 mouth
諗巴 (號碼) number
隧巴 (隧道車) tunnel bus

【幻】waan⁶ fantasy
幻想 fantasy; imagine
　充滿幻想 full of fancies
幻燈 ① slide show ② magic lantern; slide project
　幻燈片 slide; transparency
幻覺 delusion; hallucination; illusion
　產生幻覺 (出現幻覺) has an illusion; see things

夢幻 illusion; reverie
變幻 change

【廿】jaa⁶ twenty
廿一點 (二十一點) blackjack; pontoon
廿四 (二十四) twenty-four
　廿四史 (二十四史) twenty-four histories
　廿四孝 ① twenty-four paragons of filial piety
　　② caring
　　廿四孝老公 caring husband
　廿四味 tea boiled with twenty-four kinds of herbs

【引】jan⁵ attract
引入 (傳入 / 進來) call; draw into; introduce; lead into; import
引子 (開場) introduction; introductory music
引用 ① cite; quote ② appoint; recommend
引起 arise from; arise out of; arouse; bring about; bring down the house; bring on; bring to; call forth; cause; create; engender; evoke; give rise to; induce; kick up; lead to; lead up to; produce; set off; stir up; touch off; trigger
引蛇入屋 (引狼入室) court disaster
引號 inverted comma; quotation mark; speech mar
　單引號 single quotation marks
　雙引號 double quotation marks
引誘 (誘惑) accost; attract; cajole; entice; induce; lead on; lure; persuade; seduce; tempt
引擎 (發動機) engine

吸引 attract
指引 (領着) guide

【心】sam¹ ① heart ② feeling; mind ③ centre; core ④ conscience; moral nature
心口 (胸口) chest
　心口針 (胸針) brooch
　心口翳 (胸悶) chest distress
　　扰心口 (捶胸) ① (後悔) nurse a grief; regret; regret doing sth ② (勒索) extort money from sb
　　拍心口 (拍胸膛) guarantee; readily promise to undertake responsibility
　　懵到上心口 (糊塗極了) extremely foolish
心不在焉 absent-minded
心中有屎 (心存牛糞) have a guilty conscience
心中有數 (心裏曉分寸) know what is what
心水 (心意) idea; opinion; point of view; thought
　心水清 careful
　　合心水 (稱心) after one's own heart; be satisfied with sth; exactly what is required; one's cup of tea; to one's liking
　　合晒心水 (稱心如意) after one's own heart; be satisfied with sth; exactly what is required; one's cup of tea; to one's own liking
　　啱心水 (稱心) after one's own heart; be satisfied with sth; exactly what is required; one's cup of tea; to one's liking
　　疊埋心水 (一意) at one; be bent on; concentrate on sth; have one's heart in sth; make up one's mind in doing sth; put one's whole heart into; with all one's heart and mind; with body and soul; with one heart and one mind; with wholehearted devotion

心火盛 (煩躁) irritable

心甘 (甘心) ① readily; willing ② be content with; be reconciled; resign oneself to

心甘命抵 (心甘情願) of one's own accord; willing to follow a course of action whatever the consequences

心地 (心眼兒) disposition; heart
好心地 (心眼兒好 / 心很善良) kind-hearted

心多 (多心) over-suspicious
心多多 (三心兩意 / 拿不定主意 / 左顧右盼) in two minds

心字底 the "heart bottom" 心 radical

心灰 (灰心) disheartened

心灰意冷 feel disheartened

心肝 heart
心肝椗 (心肝寶貝) one's darling
冇心肝 (沒心沒肺 / 沒有記性) forgetful; inattentive; negligent
生仔唔知仔心肝 (猜不透) it is hard to know people's hidden intention
的起心肝 (下定決心) be determined to; bestir oneself; brace up; come to a determination; come to a resolution; decide; determine; have one's mind made up; make a firm decision; make a firm resolve to do sth; make a resolution; make up one's mind; pull up one's socks; resolve
諗爛心肝 (絞盡腦汁) chew the cud

心足 (心滿意足 / 滿足) complacent; contented; feel very pleased with; fully contented; fully satisfied; in the pride of one's heart; perfectly content; rest satisfied; solid satisfaction; to one's heart's content; very contented

心抱 (兒媳婦 / 媳婦) daughter-in-law
娶心抱 (娶媳婦) get a daughter-in-law

心服 be convinced
心服口服 be sincerely convinced
令人心服 (讓人心服) carry conviction

心知肚明 (心照不宣) know in one's heart

心思思 (心癢癢 / 老惦念着 / 老想着) have a mind to do sth; keep thinking of; trying to do sth; long for sth

心急 anxious; short-tempered

心肺病 cardiac-pulmonary disease

心郁郁 (心動 / 起了心 / 動了心) one's desire is aroused

心息 (死心) give up one's hope forever; have no more illusions about the matter; think no more of sth

心氣痛 (胸口痛) chest pain

心病 (不和) sore point; secret trouble

心神 mood; state of mind
心神不定 a confused state of mind; a restless mood; agitated; an unstable mood; anxious and preoccupied; distracted; feel restless; have no peace of mind; ill at ease; in a state of discomposure; indisposed; out of sorts; wandering in thought
心神恍惚 lose one's presence of mind

心胸 mind
心胸狹窄 (氣量小) narrow-minded

心得 experience

心掛掛 (掛心 / 牽掛) be anxious about; be concerned for; care; feel anxious about; worry; worry about; worry over

心涼 (解氣) gloat over one's enemy's misfortune
心都涼晒 (真解氣啊) gloat over one's enemy's misfortune

心淡 (心灰意冷 / 心涼) lose confidence in; lose heart
心都淡晒 (心都涼了) lose heart

心甜 (心都甜了) gloat

心軟 give in to sb's plea

心寒 (寒心) feel terrible

心散 (精神不集中) inattentive

心都實 (心已灰死) downhearted
心都實晒 (心已灰死) downhearted

心亂如麻 one's mind is in a tangle

心喗句，口喗句 (說話坦白) say what one thinks; speak one's mind

心想事成 may your wishes come true

心煩 (心緒不寧) be vexed; flutter; in a disturbed state of mind; in a flutter; in a state of agitation; one's state of mind is not at ease

心照 understand what is meant without needing explicit explanation
心照不宣 have a tacit understanding
大家心照 (你懂的) have a tacit understanding

心腸 heart
心腸軟 (心腸兒軟) soft-hearted
立實心腸 (硬起心腸) make up one's mind

心跳 heart beating

心實 (心灰) disappointed

心態 (心理) mentality

心酸 (悲傷) be deeply grieved

心領 no, thank you

心諗 (心裏想) I think to myself

心機 (心思) mood
二叔婆養豬 —— 夠晒好心機 (好心思) sitting on a pit to count sesame seeds – it requires meticulous work
冇心機 / 冇厘心機 (沒心思 / 沒勁兒) in no mood; looking out of sorts
白費心機 waste one's efforts
有心機 (有心情) in the mood for sth

好心機（耐心／細心）patient

俾心機（下功夫／用心）devote one's time and effort to

俾心機做人（好好做人）behave well in society

俾心機讀書（努力學習）devote one's time and
effort to one's study

嘥心機（白費時間）plough the sand; waste
one's time

嘥心機，捱眼瞓（白賠辛苦）waste one's time

心頭好 one's favourite thing

心頭高（心志太高）expecting too much; over-ambitious;
set one's goal too high

心翳（胸悶）depressed

心臟 heart

心臟有問題 heart problem

心臟病 heart disease

心臟病發 heart attack

一片丹心 a heart of pure loyalty; a loyal heart; a piece of
loyalty

一條心 whole-heartedly

一籠點心 a basket of dim sum

人心 a person's heart

人面獸心 a wolf in lamb's skin; a wolf in sheep's clothing

力不從心 ability falling short of one's wishes; ability not
equal to one's ambition; beyond one's power; bite off
more than one can chew; lacking the ability to do what
one would like to do; one's strength does not match
one's ambitions; the spirit is willing but the flesh is weak;
unable to do as well as one would wish

十月芥菜起晒心（春心萌動）of an age when one's thoughts
turn to courtship and sex

口不對心（口是心非）speak with one's tongue in one's
cheek

小心 ① careful; cautious; precaution ② take care ③ be
careful

寸心（寸衷）feelings

不知幾開心（多開心）extremely happy

不得人心 contrary to the will of the people; fail to gain
popular support; fall into disfavor among the people; go
against the will of the people; have no popular support;
not enjoy popular support; unable to win popular support;
unpopular

不得民心 very unpopular

中心 centre; core; crux; heart; hub; kernel

丹心 loyal heart; loyalty

內心 in one's mind; mental

分心 distract

天地良心 from the bottom of one's heart; in all fairness; in
all justice; in fact; in my soul of souls; speak the truth

日久見人心 time makes one understand a person

手板心（手掌心）palm of the hand

冇心（非故意）not deliberate; unintentional

冇本心（沒良心）heartless; ungrateful; without conscience

冇良心（沒良心）have no conscience

令人痛心（讓人心疼）cut one to the heart

市中心 town centre

本心（良心）conscience

民心 popular feelings

甘心 ① readily; willing ② be content with; be reconciled;
resign oneself to

立心（決心）determination

同情心 sympathy

同理心 empathy

多心 change one's mind constantly; have two minds; in two
minds; infirm of purpose; irresolute; of two minds; play
the field; undecided; vacillating

好心 good-heartedness

好奇心 curiosity

好開心 really happy

宅心（存心）intention

有口無心 not really mean what one says

有心 ① with the intention ② thank you ③ kind of you to
ask; you're very kind ④ show concern

死心 have no more illusions about sth/sb

死咗條心（死心吧）abandoned; have no more illusions
about sth/sb; heartless; in a state of stupor

你真係有心（你真有心）thank you for your care

你真係有我心（你真關心我）you really care about me

佛口蛇心 a beast in human shape; a brute of a man; a brute
under a human mask; a fiend in human shape; a man's
face but the heart of a beast; a wolf in sheep's clothing;
bear the semblance of a man but have the heart of a
beast; gentle in appearance but cruel at heart; have the
face of a man but the heart of a beast; kind-mouthed
but vicious-hearted; with a human face and the heart of
a beast

孝心 filial piety; love and devotion to one's parents; love
toward one's parents

忍心 hardhearted; have the heart to; merciless; steel one's
heart; unfeeling

決心 all set; bent on; bent upon; bound; decide;
determination; determine; determined; from a resolution;
make a resolution; make up one's mind; out to; pass a
resolution; resolve; resolved; set on; set oneself to; set
one's heart on; set one's mind on; take a resolution

良心 good heart

身心 body and mind

事不關己，己不勞心（獨善其身）mind one's own business

枋榔樹一條心（一心一意）love sb heart and soul; single-minded in love

狗咬呂洞賓——不識好人心 not know chalk from cheese

知人口面不知心（白天不懂夜的黑）be familiar with sb but ignorant of his true nature

居心 harbour evil intentions

忠心 devotion; faithfulness; loyalty; sincerity

放心 breathe easy; feel relieved; free from cares; have one's heart at ease; put one's heart at ease; rest assured; rest one's heart; set one's mind at rest; with no worries

空心 hollow

花心 disloyal; have many lovers; not to give one's mind to one's lover

信心 ① confidence ② faith

耐心 patient

恒心（毅力）perseverance

苦口婆心 exhort sb repeatedly with good intentions; words importunate but heart compassionate

哽心 break one's heart

唔小心（不小心）not careful

唔甘心（不甘心）① unwilling ② not content with

唔忍心（不忍心）compassionate

核心 centre; core; crux; heart; kernel; nucleus

桄榔樹——一條心（一心一意）love sb heart and soul; single-minded in love

留心 be careful; be cautious; bear in mind; pay attention to; take care; take heed; take note

神心（虔誠）devout; pious

衷心 cordial; heartfelt

迷惑人心 confuse the masses

偏心 show partiality to sb

做磨心（當磨心）in a dilemma

動心（心動）one's desire is aroused

從心 follow one's wishes

細心 attentive to sb

聊表寸心 as a small token of my feelings; it is a mere proof of my regard; just to show my appreciation; just to show my gratitude

貪心 greedy

通心（空心）hollow

野心 ambition

掌心 centre of the palm

揞住個良心（瞞着良心）against one's conscience

揪心 ① anxious ② agonising

湖心 middle of a lake

菜心 flowering Chinese cabbage

痛心 sad

虛榮心 vanity

軸心 axis

開心 happy

開開心心 very happy

黑心 wicked-minded

傷心 sad; sorrowful

暗住良心（瞞着良心）go aginst one's conscience

當心 beware of

痴心 infatuation

誠心 sincere desire; wholeheartedness

靶心 bull's-eye

嘔心 distressed; grieved; painful

寡母婆咁多心（寡婦再嫁心思多）in two minds

對你有信心 have confidence in you

窩心 feel irritated; feel vexed

擔心 feel worried; worried

憂心 worry

熱心 enthusiastic; zeal

磨心 mediator suffering from complaints from disputants

蔗心 centre stem of a cane

點心（transliteration）dimsum; light refreshments

獸醫中心 veterinary centre

藝術中心 arts centre

關心 care about

癡心 ① blind love; blind passion; infatuation ② silly wish

鱸魚探蝦毛——冇好心（黃鼠狼給雞拜年——不懷好意）a weasel giving new year's greetings to a hen has ulterior motives; a yellow weasel goes to pay New Year's call to a hen – not with the best of intentions; the weasel goes to pay its respects to the hen – not with the best of intentions

【戶】wu[6] ① door ② household

戶口 ①（賬戶）account ②（賬號）account number
戶口名（賬戶名）account name
一個戶口（一個賬戶）an account
往來戶口（往來賬戶）current account
儲蓄戶口（儲蓄賬戶）savings account

戶主（房東）head of a household

另立門戶 live in a separate house

用戶 consumer; customer; subscriber; user

住戶（住客）resident

門戶 ① door ② family status

客戶 client

【手】sau[2] hand

手力（手勁兒）strength of the hands

手下（下屬）subordinate; underling

手工（工藝）workmanship

手工藝 handicraft

手巾 (手帕／手絹) handkerchief
　手巾仔 (手帕／手絹) handkerchief
　　一條手巾仔 (一條手帕) a handkerchief
　　一兜手巾仔 (一條手絹) a handkerchief

手瓜 (上臂) biceps
　手瓜起脹 (胳膊很粗) have strong and muscular arms
　手瓜硬 (胳膊粗) have power; have real power
　　拗手瓜 ① (扳手腕／掰腕子) arm-wrestling
　　② compete with; show power against another

手甲 (手指甲／指甲) fingernail

手多 (多手) touch things when one should not
　手多多 (多手多腳) touch things when one should not
　手多腳多 (多手多腳) touch things when one
　　should not

手忙腳亂 (慌手慌腳) all in a hustle of excitement; be
　thrown into a panic; be thrown into confusion; in a great
　flurry; in disarray

手扣 (手銬) handcuffs

手作 (手工藝) handicraft
　手作仔 (手藝人) craftsman
　手作佬 (工藝師) craftsman

手尾 ① (剩下的活兒) unfinished job left by sb
　② (麻煩事) troubles left behind
　手尾長 (麻煩事可多) the trouble lasts long
　　冇手尾 (有頭沒尾) fail to put things back after use;
　　　leave things about
　　冇釐手尾 (東西亂放) fail to put things back after use;
　　　leave things about
　　有手尾 (有頭有尾) there's a beginning and an end
　　執手尾 (善後) clean up; deal with the work left over;
　　　finish a job for sb; wind up
　　跟手尾 complete an unfinshed job left by sb

手快有，手慢冇 (先到先得) first come, first served

手拖手 (手拉手) hand in hand
　時時手拖手 (經常手拉手) always hand in hand

手足 (搭檔) brothers (secret society slang)

手車 (手推車) trolley

手板 (手掌) palm
　手板心 (手掌心) palm of the hand
　手板係肉，手背又係肉 (手心是肉，手背也是肉)
　　difficult to decide in taking sides as both parties are on
　　good terms; have friendly relation with both parties
　手板堂 (手心) palm of the hand
　手板眼見功夫 (輕而易舉) a job that does not require
　　any special training
　　打手板 (打手心兒) hit the palm of the hand
　　攤大手板 (張開雙手要錢) open up one's hands to ask
　　　for money

手信 (禮物) souvenir; sourvenir bought as a gift

手急眼快 (眼明手快) quick of eye and deft of hand

手指 finger
　手指公 (大指／大姆指) thumb
　手指甲 nail
　手指尾 (小指／小姆指) little finger
　手指指 (指着) gesture with the finger as if to lecture sb
　手指拗出唔拗入 (胳膊肘往裏不往外) help outsiders
　　at the expense of insiders
　手指模 (指印) finger-print
　手指罅 (手指縫) space between two fingers
　　手指罅疏 big-spender; spend money like water
　　飛唔過我手指罅 (逃不過我手心) can't escape from
　　　my control
　　勾手指 make a promise by hooking each other's little
　　　finger
　　多到十隻手指都數唔晒 (多得數不過來) too many to
　　　be counted
　　金手指 (告密者) ① (police) informer ② backbiter;
　　　backstabber
　　斬手指 (戒賭) give up gambling
　　鎅嚫隻手指 (切傷了手指) cut one's finger

手套 gloves
　　一對手套 a pair of gloves

手睜 (老繭) callus on the hand

手風 (手氣) luck
　手風順 (好手氣) have luck

手氣 luck; luck in gambling
　　好手氣 good luck in gambling

手神 (手氣) one's luck

手紋 (掌紋) palm print

手袖 (袖套) oversleeve

手停口停 (不做事就沒飯吃) if a person doesn't work
　he/she has no food to eat; no work no food

手動 manual
　手動波 (手動檔) manual shift

手痕 ① (手癢) itching hand ② (想隨便亂碰亂弄) cannot
　resist doing sth; eager to try
　手痕痕 (手癢癢) cannot resist doing sth; eager to have a
　　go; eager to try

手術 operation
　手術室 operation theatre

手袋 (包／提包) handbag
　　一個手袋 (一個手提包) a handbag
　　挽住個手袋 (提着手提包) carry a handbag on
　　　the arm

手軟 very busy
　　寫到手軟 (手都寫酸了) one's hands get sore for
　　　writing

手掌 palm
　　拍手掌 (拍掌) clap one's hands
　　拍爛手掌 (手掌都拍紅了) clap one's hands so long
　　　　that they become red, meaning to show approval
　　　　and give great praise
手掣 hand brake
手提 ① portable ② (流動電話／手機) mobile phone
　　打我手提 (打我手機) call me on my mobile phone
手疏 (大手大腳) big-spender
手硬 (有本事／有辦法) smart person
手腕 wrist
手鈪 (手鐲) bracelet
手勢 ① skill at cooking ② (手氣) one's luck
手搵口食 (現掙現吃) live from hand to mouth
手痺 (手發麻) paralysis of hands
手腳 hands and feet
　　手腳唔好 (手腳不乾淨) have a tendency of stealing
　　一手一腳 do sth all by oneself
　　小手小腳 stingy; timid
　　毛手毛腳 inappropriate fondling or touching
　　有人做咗手腳 (有人做了手腳) sb has secretly got up
　　　　to little tricks
　　夾手夾腳 (一起動手) co-operate closely with each
　　　　other; work well together
　　阻手阻腳 (阻礙／礙手礙腳) a hindrance to sb; a
　　　　nuisance to sb; an encumbrance to sb; cumbersome;
　　　　cumbrous; get in the way of sb; hinder; impede; in
　　　　the way; obstructive; one too many; stand in sb's
　　　　way; stand in the way of
　　唔好手腳 (手腳不乾淨) have a tendency of stealing
　　唔係我手腳 (不是我對手) not one's equal
　　砣手嘥腳 (累累贅贅) burdensome
　　做咗手腳 (搞了鬼把戲) do some tricks
　　笨手笨腳 stumblebum
　　粗手粗腳 have clumsy fingers
　　乾手淨腳 ① (乾淨利落) crispy; dapper; efficient; neat;
　　　　neat and tidy; neatly; smooth and clean; trim; very
　　　　efficient ② finished and done with, once for all
　　落手落腳 (親力親為) do sth oneself; do the actual
　　　　work oneself
　　雞手鴨腳 (笨手笨腳) clumsy; have two left feet
手槍 handgun; pistol
手緊 (手頭緊／缺錢) out at elbows; short of money
手踭 (胳膊肘) elbow
　　托手踭 (推託／攔胳膊) give sb a flat refusal; refuse
　　　　sb's request; refuse to help
手機 (移動電話／手提電話) cell; cellular phone; hand
　　phone; mobile; mobile phone
　　手機冇電 (手機沒電) one's mobile phone battery is

dead; one's mobile phone battery died
　　打我手機 call me on my mobile phone
　　熄手機 (關手機) switch off the mobile phone; turn off
　　　　your mobile
手瘸 (手僵硬) paralysis of the hands
手錶 watch
　　一隻手錶 a watch
　　一個手錶 (一塊手錶) a watch
手頭 the money one has at a certain time
　　手頭上 on hand
手骹 (手腕) wrist
手臂 (胳膊) arm
手鍊 bracelet
　　一條手鍊 a bracelet
手騰腳震 (渾身哆嗦) tremble all over
手鐐 (手銬) cuffs; handcuffs
手續 handling; procedure
手襪 (手套) gloves
　　一對手襪 (一副手套) a pair of gloves

一手 ① (親身) all by oneself ② (第一手的) firsthand
一對手 (一雙手) a pair of hands
二手 second-hand; used
三隻手 (扒手) pickpocket
大顯身手 bring one's talents into full play; come out strong;
　　cut a dashing figure; display one's skill to the full;
　　distinguish oneself; give a good account of oneself; give
　　full play to one's abilities; play one's prize; show one's
　　best; turn one's talents to full account
小手 (扒手) pickpocket; shoplifter
分手 break up
水手 sailor
生手 ① inexperienced ② inexperienced worker
出手 ① (出錢) money ② (提出) offer ③ (打) hit out
叫起手 (想要用的時候) anytime; as the occasion demands;
　　at all times; at any time; whenever
右手 right hand
左手 left hand
左右手 helpful assistant; right-hand man
平手 draw; tie
扒手 pickpocket
打手 bodyguard; fighter
打平手 break even; come out even; draw; draw a game; end
　　in a draw; fight to a standoff; play even; tie it up; tie the
　　score
甩手 (脫手) dishoard; dispose of
兇手 assassin; killer; murderer
多手 (手多) touch things out of curiosity
好熱手 (好燙手) it really scalds one's hand

收手（住手／洗手不幹）quit; stop doing sth
有兩下散手（有兩下子）know one's stuff
有兩手（有兩下子）have real skill; know one's stuff; one really knows a thing or two
老手 experienced person; expert; old hand; old stager
老鼠拉龜——冇埞埋手（狗咬刺蝟——下不得嘴／無從下手）at one's wit's end; have no way of doing sth; not know how to start
伸手 hold out one's hand; reach out one's hand; stretch out one's hand
伸出援手 lend a helping hand
助手 assistant
扶手 handrail
快手 ①（手快）deft of hand ②（幹活很迅速）nimble-handed person; quick worker
束手 have one's hands tied; helpless
身手 ① skills; talent ② agility; dexterity
使唔使幫手（需不需要幫手）do you need any help
使橫手（使出不光彩的手段）accomplish sth by underhand methods; use dirty methods
到手 come to one's hands; in one's hands; in one's possession
垂手 ① obtain sth hands down; within easy reach ② let the hands hang by one's sides; stand with one's hands hanging by the sides
戾手（轉手）at once; right away
拍手 applaud; clap hands
拖拉手（拖手）hand in hand
易手 change hands
泳手（游泳手）swimmer
金盆洗手 hang up one's axe
非常搶手 go like hot cakes; sell like hot cakes; the cat's meow
耍手（揮手）wave one's hand
要起手（需要的時候）when needed
武林高手 master in the world of martial art
洗手 wash one's hands
拳手 boxer
流行歌手 pop singer
郁手（動手）take action
埋手 ①（入手）take as the point of departure ② tackle
師奶殺手 housewife killer
徒手 bare-handed; empty-handed; freehand; unarmed
拿手 good at; strong suit
挹手（擺手）wave one's hand
時時手拖手（常常手拉手）always hand in hand
隻手（單手）single-handed
高手 expert; master
做槍手（請人槍替）ask sb to do sth for a person

副手 deputy
挽下／起手（忽然／突然）abruptly; all at once; all of a sudden; by the run; cap the climax; out of the blue; suddenly; unexpectedly; with a run; with suddenness; without any warning
挽手（扶手）handle
密密手（孜孜不倦）diligent; hardworking; industrious
得些好意須回手（見好就收）stop before going too far
情場老手 veteran womaniser
爽手 ①（爽利）quickly ②（出手大方）generous
着手 proceed
頂手（頂讓）transfer ownership; transfer possession
鹿死誰手 who will win in the struggle
嘟手（動手）make motions to start a fight
就手（稱手）① at one's convenience ② smooth
強中自有強中手 catch a tartar; fight a strong enemy
提防小手（提防扒手）beware of pickpockets
揮手 wave; wave one's hand
援手 ① aid; extend a helping hand; rescue; save ② helper
揸手 ①（在手／掌管）have sth in hand as an assurance ②（握手）shake hands
揦手（棘手）difficult to handle; knotty; thorny; ticklish; troublesome
散手 ①（技能）have a special skill ②（小本領）expertise
棋逢敵手 nip and tuck; well-matched
棘手 difficult to handle; knotty; thorny; ticklish; troublesome
翕手（招手）beckon with the hand; wave one's hand
趁手（趁機）take the opportunity
順手 handy; sth that can be done easily in the course of things; without extra trouble
損手（有傷）injured
搭手（幫忙）assist; help
搶手 big hit; in great demand; sell like hot cakes; sell well; the cat's meow
搵鬼幫手（無人願意來幫忙）no one is willing to help someone in need
新手 beginner; novice
落手（開始／着手）begin; put one's hand to the plough
過手（經手）deal with; handle
跟手（跟着）carry on; follow; go on; in the wake of; proceed
剳嚫手（扎破了手）get a thorn in one's hand
對手 competitor
幕後黑手 person who controls everything from behind the scenes
慢手（手慢）slow
慢吓手（手太慢的話）if things are messed up
槍手（替槍）① ghost-writer ② one who does homework, sit examinations, or write essays for someone else
歌手 singer

精人出口，笨人出手 smart people get stupid people to do annoying tasks for them; words are cleverer than action

辣手 hard to deal with

撚手 (拿手) of high quality

熟手 adept at a particular task; experienced; skilled

緊握扶手 hold the handrail tightly

擔高手 (抬高手) raise one's hand

整損手 (弄傷手) one's hand is injured

橫手 (不光彩的手段) the person who acts underhand for sb

豬手 pork knuckle

親手 with one's own hand

選手 player

幫手 (幫忙) assist; help

幫吓手 (幫忙一下) lend sb a hand

幫幫手 (幫幫忙) lend sb a hand

縮手 draw back one's hand

賽車手 racing driver

壘手 baseman

繑起對手 (翹起雙手) cross one's arms

熱嗯手 ① (燙傷手) scald one's hand; one's hand is burnt ② (棘手) difficult to manage

蹺口杉手 (棘手／難處理) hard to deal with

攬手 ① (主辦者) sponsor ② (發起人) initiator

【扎】 zaat³ ① with a start ② (束) a bundle of

扎扎跳 (跑跑跳跳／蹦蹦跳) bouncing and vivacious; hot with rage

扎炮 (捱餓) have nothing to eat; suffer from hunger

扎營 (紮營) encamp; pitch a camp; pitch a tent

扎醒 (驚醒) wake up with a start

垂死掙扎 conduct desperate struggles; deathbed struggle; flounder desperately before dying; give dying kicks; in one's death throes; in the throes of one's deathbed; make a last desperate stand; on one's last legs; put up a last-ditch fight

雞扎 chicken bundle

【支】 zi¹ ① (分支) branch ② (支撐) prop up

支出 ① disburse; expend; pay ② expenditure; outlay

支持 at sb's back; at the back of sb; backing; bear; buttress; countenance; for; hold out; stand up for; support; sustain

支持者 backer; camp follower; follower; supporter; sympathiser

支票 cheque

支票簿 (支票本) cheque book

空頭支票 ① dishonoured cheque ② empty promise

旅行支票 traveller's cheque

現金支票 cash cheque

支撐 bracing; crutch; prop up; support; sustain; timbering

支質 (囉嗦的) wordy

支整 (好打扮) like to be affected

一支 a piece of; a stick of

旁支 collateral branch

透支 overdraft; overdraw

【文】 man⁴ language

文化 culture

文件 document

文件夾 file

文字 ① character; word ② language

文字處理 word processing

文具 stationery

文法 (語法) grammar

文員 clerk

文雀 (三合會術語：扒手) pickpocket

文學 literature

文憑 diploma

中文 Chinese

日文 Japanese

出口成文 keep a civil tongue in one's head

序文 foreword; preface

法文 French

科文 (工頭) foreman

英文 English

國文 Chinese

斯文 cultured; elegant; gentle; refined

意大利文 Italian

碑文 inscription on a tablet

德文 German

論文 thesis

【斗】 dau² ① (穀物等的乾糧量度單位) Chinese peck ② (中國古代掏水容器) container

斗零 (五分錢) five cents

斗膽 make bold; of great courage; venture

反斗 (淘氣) mischievous; naughty

打關斗 (翻筋斗) somersault; take a somersault

正斗 (優質) excellent; good; terrific

灰斗 (裝石灰漿的斗) lime bucket

吼斗 (發呆) take a fancy to

苴斗 (低質素／差勁) of low quality; poor

觔斗 (筋斗) somersault

黑過墨斗 (倒霉／不走運) have bad luck

燙斗 iron
翻觔斗 somersault; take a somersault
關斗 (筋斗) somersault
聽價唔聽斗 (只重價錢，不重質量) care for whether the
　　price is cheap or high but neglect the quality or quantity

【斤】gan¹ catty

斤斤 fuss about; haggle over
　　斤斤計較 calculating; calculating and unwilling to make
　　　the smallest sacrifice; excessively mean in one's
　　　dealings; haggle over every ounce; mindful of narrow
　　　personal gains and losses; palter with a person
　　　about sth; particular about; reckon up every iota;
　　　split hairs; split straws; stand on little points; skin a
　　　flint; weigh and balance every detail; weigh up
　　　every detail
斤半 one and a half catties
斤兩 ① catty and tael ② (能力) ability
　　冇斤兩 (沒能耐) have no skill in sth
　　有斤兩 (有本事) capable

一公斤 a kilogram
一斤 one catty
半斤 half catty
幾錢斤 (多少錢斤) how much is one catty

【方】fong¹ square

方包 (方麵包 / 白麵包) white bread
方向 direction; orientation
方法 means; method; way
　　用盡方法 by all means
方便 ① convenient; handy ② go to the bath; go to the
　　bathroom to tidy; go to the toilet
　　提供方便 provide convenience
方枱 (方桌) square table
方面 aspect
　　一方面 on one hand
　　另一方面 on the other hand
　　有關方面 concerned parties
方框 (方框兒) the "square" 口 radical
方針 guiding principle; orientation; policy

一笪地方 a place
大方 ① liberal; generous ② dignified; sophisticated; tasteful
天各一方 be separated far apart
北方 north
四方 four directions
地方 place
西方 west

老地方 the same old place
見笑大方 be laughed at by experts; become a laughingstock
　　of the learned people; expose oneself to ridicule; give an
　　expert cause for laughter; incur the ridicule of experts;
　　make a laughingstock of oneself before experts
官方 authority; by the government; of the government;
　　official
東方 ① east ② East; Orient
南方 south
開方 write out a prescription
搬去新地方 move to a new place
對方 counterpart; opposite side
嗰笪地方 (那個地方) that place
遠方 distant place; remote place
雙方 both sides

【日】jat⁶ (天) day

日久見人心 time makes one understand a person
日子 life; time
　　日子難過 have a hard time; lead a hard life
日文 Japanese
日日 (天天) daily; day in, day out; every day
日出 sunrise
日本 Japan
　　日本人 Japanese
　　日本菜 Japanese food
日用品 articles in daily use
日光 sunlight
　　日光日白 (大白天) in broad daylight
日字邊 (日字旁) the "sun" 日 radical
日更 (早班) morning shift
日夜 day and night
　　日捱夜捱 (拼死拼活) work hard night and day
　　日鵝夜鵝 (絮叨不停) nag day and night
日記 diary
日期 date
日圓 (日元) Japanese yen
日落 sunset
日數 number of days
　　平均持貨日數 average holding days
日劇 Japanese drama
日曆 calender
日頭 ① (太陽) sun ② (白天) day; day time
　　日頭唔好講人，夜晚唔好講神 (一說曹操，曹操就到)
　　　speak/talk of the devil and here he/she is

一日 (一天) one day
人日 Birthday of Human Beings; Everybody's Birthday
不見天日 live in dark oppression; live in darkness

今日（今天）today

今時今日（現在／如今）nowadays

今時唔同往日（時代變了）times have changed

水殼仔──唔浮得幾日（兔子尾巴──長不了）a hare's tail – can't be long; the tail of a rabbit can't be long – won't last long

半日（半天）half a day; half day

平日 ① usually ②（星期一至五）weekdays

末日 ① doomsday; Judgment Day ② doom; end

民間節日 folk festival

生日 birthday

有日（有一天）one day

有朝一日（某一天）one day; some day

成日 ①（整天）all day long ②（總是）always

吉日 auspicious day; good day

你幾時生日（你何時生日）when is your birthday

即日 that very day; the same day

投票日 polling day

每日（每天）each day; everyday

來日 ①（來臨的日子）coming days; days ahead; days to come; time ahead ②（明天）tomorrow

兩三日（兩三天／幾天）a couple of days

到期日 ① expiry date ② maturity date

往日 previously

昔日 in former days

前日（前天）day before yesterday

後日（後天）day after tomorrow

昨日（昨天）yesterday

星期日（星期天）Sunday

烈日 burning sun; scorching sun

做生日 celebrate one's birthday

第日（改天）another day; some other day

連氣幾日（連續幾天）for days on end

喜慶節日 festive days

尋日（昨天）yesterday

幾時幾日（何時）when

節日 festival

閒日（平日）Monday to Friday; weekdays

琴日（昨天）yesterday

過幾日（過幾天）for a couple of days

隔日（每隔一天）every other day

噚日（昨天）yesterday

嗟日（昨天）yesterday

擇吉日 choose a good day

褪一日（推遲一天）put off a day accordingly

頭尾三日（來回三天）about three days altogether

總有一日（總有一天）someday in the future

禮拜日（星期天）Sunday

聽日（明天）tomorrow

【月】jyut⁶ ① moon ② months of the year

月入（每月收入）monthly income

月大（大月）① solar month of thirty-one days ② lunar month of thirty days

月小（小月）① solar month of thirty days ② lunar month of twenty-nine days

月中 middle of the month

月份牌（月曆）monthly calendar

月光 ①（月亮）moon ②（月光）moonlight; moonshine ③（屁股）bottom
　　晒月光（戀人在晚上約會）date under the moonlight; lovers basking in the moonlight

月字邊（月字旁）the "moon" 月 radical

月尾（月底）end of the month

月亮 moon

月桂葉 bay leaf

月票 monthly ticket

月費 monthly fee

月經 period
　　月經痛 menstrual cramps

月餅 moon cake
　　食月餅（吃月餅）eat moon cakes

月曆 calendar

月頭（月初）beginning of the month

一月 ① January ② the first month of the lunar year

一頭半個月（半個月）half of a month

七月 ① July ② the seventh month of the lunar year

九月 ① September ② the ninth month of the lunar year

二月 ① February ② the second month of the lunar year

八月 ① August ② the eighth month of the lunar year

十一月 ① November ② the eleventh month of the lunar year

十二月 ① December ② the twelfth month of the lunar year

十月 ① October ② the tenth month of the lunar year

三月 ① March ② the third month of the lunar year

上月 last month

上個月 last month

下個月 next month

五月 ① May ② the fifth month of the lunar year

今個月（這個月）this month

元月 the first month of the lunar year

六月 ① June ② the sixth month of the lunar year

四月 ① April ② the fourth month of the lunar year

年月 days and years

戌月 the ninth month of the lunar year

肉月（鮮肉月餅）mooncake stuffed with meat

你有乾坤，我有日月 be on a par with

坐月 confinement in childbirth; lying-in

成個月（整個月）the whole month

每月 every month; monthly

呢個月（這個月）this month

明月 bright moon

近水樓台先得月 in a favourable situation

個個月 every month

個零月（一個多月）more than a month

素月（素月餅）vegetarian mooncake

乾時緊月（缺錢）hard up for money

幾多月（哪個月份）which month

閏月 intercalary month

歲月 ① times and seasons ② years

滿月 a baby's completion of its first month of life

蜜月 honey moon

賞月 enjoy the moonlight

蹉跎歲月 dawdle one's life; dawdle one's time; fool one's time away; fritter one's time away; idle about; idle away one's time; lead an idle life; let time slip by without accomplishing anything; live an idle life; live in idleness; on the racket; profane the precious time; spend one's time in dissipation; spend one's time in frolic; trifle away one's time; waste time; while away one's time

邊個月（哪個月份）which month

【木】muk⁶ ① (木頭) wood; timber ② (木獨) socially inept

木瓜 papaya; pawpaw

木字邊（木字旁）the "tree" 木 radical

木耳 wood-ear fungus

木屐（木拖鞋）wooden slippers

木偶 puppet

木蝨（臭蟲）bedbug

　木蝨狙入花生殼 —— 硬充好人（仁）（嗑瓜子出個臭蟲 —— 甚麼人（仁）都有）(literally) chewing melon seeds with the appearance of a bug – there are all sorts of people

　一物治一物，糯米治木蝨 one thing is always controlled by another

　捉木蝨（抓木蝨 / 臭蟲）catch the bedbug

木獨（木訥 / 遲鈍）(transliteration) moody; socially inept; unsocial

　木木獨獨（木無表情）expressionless

木頭車（手推車）handcart; wheelbarrow

木糠（鋸末）sawdust

一碌 / 轆木（一塊木頭）a log; a long piece of wood

一嚿木（一塊木頭）a piece of wood

杉木 fir

斧頭打鑿鑿打木（斧頭吃鑿子，鑿子吃木頭 / 一物降一物）the axe strikes the chisel, and the chisel strikes the wood – everything has its vanquisher; there is always one thing to conquer another

枕木 railway sleeper; sleeper; tie

林木 ① forest; woods ② crop; forest tree

柚木 teakwood

砌積木（搭積木）juggle; pile up the building blocks

桃木 peachwood

鬥木（木工）carpentry; woodwork

棺木 coffin

碌木（傻子 / 呆子）idiot

鋸木 saw wood

鎅木（鋸木塊）saw a piece of wood

【欠】him³ owe

欠債 behind with; fall into debt; get into debt; in debt; in debt to; in deficit; in hock; in hock to sb; in the hole; in sb's debt; in the red; owe a debt; owe sb money for; promise a debt; run into debt (to sb)

欠錢 owe sb a debt

　欠人錢 owe sb a debt

欠薪 salary in arrears

【止】zi² stop

止汗劑 deodorant

止血 stanch bleeding; stop bleeding

止咳 temporary solution to a problem

　止咳水 cough mixture

　止咳糖 cough drop/lozenge/sweet

止渴 quench thirst

　止渴生津 quench thirst and help produce saliva

止痛 assuage pain; kill pain; relieve pain; stop pain

　止痛藥 painkiller

止嘔（止吐藥）antinausea drug

止瀉藥 anti-diarrhoea

到此為止 leave it at that; let's call it a day; rest here; so much for; that's all for

到而家為止（到目前為止）up to now

制止 check; curb; face down; prevent; put an end to; stop

唔（單）止（不僅）not only

停止 stop

欲言又止 about to speak, but say nothing; bite one's lip; hold back the words which spring to one's lips; swallow back the words on the tip of one's tongue; wish to speak but not do so on second thought

禁止 prohibit

截止 close; end

舉止 demeanour

【比】 bei² compare

比上不足比下有餘 be worse as compared with the best but better as compared with the worst

比例 proportion
　　按比例 pro-rata basis

比起 compare to

比得上 bear comparison with; can compare with; compare favourably with

比率 ratio

比堅尼 (比基尼) (transliteration) bikini

比較 ① compare ② comparatively

比對 (對比) balance; comparison; contrast

比數 (比分) score

比賽 competition; match
　　打比賽 (進行比賽) have a game
　　參加比賽 participate in a competition

百份比 percentage

倫比 equal; rival

無與倫比 beyond compare; beyond comparison; defy all comparison; head and shoulders above the rest; incomparable; matchless; out of comparison; past compare; peerless; stand alone; there is no comparison with; there is none to compare to; unbeatable; unequalled; unique; unparalleled; unrivalled; untouched; without compare; without comparison; without equal; without parallel; without peer; without rival

【毛】 mou⁴ hair

毛巾 towel
　　一條毛巾 a towel

毛孔 pore

毛毛雨 drizzle
　　落毛毛雨 (下毛毛雨) drizzle

毛布 (絨布) lint

毛冷 (毛線 / 羊毛絨) sheep's wool

毛病 ① breakdown ② defect; fault; mistake; shortcoming ③ bad habit ④ illness
　　小毛病 glitch

毛神神 (毛茸茸) downy; hairy

毛筆 writing brush
　　一枝毛筆 a writing brush

毛管 (毛孔) sweat pores
　　毛管戙 (起鷄皮疙瘩) get the creeps; make one's flesh crawl

毛氈 (毛毯子) blanket

一條毛 a hair

一執毛 (一撮毛) a tuft of hair

用毛 (掉毛) loss of hair

汗毛 fine hair on the human body

羊毛 wool

羽毛 down; feathers; plumes

長毛 long hair

胸毛 chest hair

掹毛 (拔毛) pluck out hairs

梳毛 (刷毛 / 理毛) grooming

眼眉毛 eyebrow

眼㼼毛 (眼睫毛) eyelashes

短毛 short hair

發毛 (發霉) go mouldy

黃毛 yellow-haired

腿毛 hair on legs

蝦毛 ① (蝦米) small shrimps ② (小人物) unimportant person

膽生毛 (膽子大) audacious

擘 / 摩毛 (捲髮) curled

【氏】 si⁶ family name

氏族 clan; family

你真係好人氏 (你人真好) you're very nice

【水】 seoy² ① water ② (錢) money ③ (差) inferior; poor

水分 ① moisture content ② (有誇大成份) exaggeration

水手 (船員) sailor

水仙 narcissus
　　水仙茶 narcissus tea

水平 level
　　水平線 horizon

水氹 (水坑) small puddle

水瓜打狗——唔見咗一撅 (損失慘重) half of sth is lost

水田 (稻田) paddy field; rice field

水皮 ① (差勁) inferior; poor ② sloppy

水位 (價格) price

水吧 bar

水坑 (水溝 / 水渠) ditch; drain; gaw; gole; gool; gutterway

水尾 ① (剩貨 / 殘貨) leftover goods; leftovers; remaining goods ② (黃金時間的末段) end of a prime time

水汪汪 (不牢靠) have only a forlorn hope

水災 flood

水抱 ① (水疱) blister ② (救生圈) life buoy

水杯 glass

水松塞 (軟木塞) cork

水泡 (救生圈) life buoy

水泥 cement

水客（水路走私者）parallel trader

水柿（柿子）persimmon

水洗都唔清（跳到黃河也洗不清）the misunderstanding is beyond repair

水泵 water pump

水炮 water-cannon

水為財 water is money

水浸（水淹）flood

　　水浸眼眉（火燒眉毛）a matter of the utmost urgency; about to meet with disaster; at death's door; fire catches the eyebrows – in imminent danger

　　水浸眼眉——唔知死（烏龜吃巴豆——不知死活）a tortoise eating croton-oil seeds – unaware of the death ahead

　　　銀行水浸（銀行儲備超額）too much money is deposited in the bank

水草 waterweed

　　一條水草（一根水草）a blade of waterweed

水馬（充氣式護欄）water-filled plastic barricade

水鬼升城隍（升遷）get a promotion

水桶 water bucket

水蛇春咁長（非常長）lengthy

水貨（私貨）goods illegally obtained and sold; parallel import

　　水貨客 parallel trader

水魚①（甲魚）freshwater tortoise ②（容易被利用的人）person who could be easily taken advantage of

水喉（水管兒）water pipe; water tap

　　水喉師傅（水管兒技工）plumber

　　水喉通（水管兒）water pipe

　　水喉掣（自來水開關）water supply lock

　　水喉鐵（鐵水管兒）iron water pipe

　　　閂水喉（關水龍頭）turn off the tap

　　　爆水喉（水管兒爆裂）water pipe burst

水廁（沖水馬桶）flush toilet

水掣（水閘／水總閘）sluice; water supply main switch

水晶 crystal

　　水晶燈 crystal light

　　　紫水晶 amethyst

水渠 ditch

水殼（水舀子／水瓢）dipper; ladle; scoop

　　水殼仔——唔浮得幾日（兔子尾巴——長不了）a hare's tail – can't be long; the tail of a rabbit can't be long – won't last long

水牌（商場名錄／指示牌）signboard

水痘 chickenpox

水費 water bill

　　水費站（洗手間）toilet

　　　交水費（上洗手間）urinate

水塘①（水庫）reservoir ②（池塘）pool

水溝油（合不來）cannot get along with each other; unfriendly

水煲（水鍋）kettle

水腳（路費／運費）freight

水落石出 come out in the wash

水過鴨背（健忘）forgetful of sth

水靴（雨靴）rubber boots for wet weather

水嘢（次貨）defective goods; inferior goods; substandard goods

水漬 water stain

水撥（撥水器）wiper

水槽（泄水管）downpipe; downspout

水線（地線）ground wire

水鞋（雨鞋）rainshoes

水餃（餃子）dumpling

水樽（水瓶兒）water bottle

水靜河飛①have no business; the market is dull ②（冷冷清清的）silence reigns in the place

水頭（錢款）money

　　水頭足（錢款充足）a large amount of money

　　　夠水頭（夠錢）have enough money

水龍頭 faucet

水翼船 hydrofoil

一干水（一千塊）one thousand dollars

一公升水 a litre of water

一支汽水（一瓶汽水）a bottle of beverage

一氹水（一灘水）a puddle of water

一杯水 a cup of water; a glass of water

一盆水（一萬塊）ten thousand dollars

一桶水 a bucket of water

一壺滾水 a pot of boiling water; a pot of hot water

一殼水（一勺水）a ladle of water

一煲水（一鍋水）a pot of water

一撇水（一千塊）one thousand dollars

一頭霧水 be confused; be puzzled; become lost; cannot understand; can't make the head or tail of sth; in bewilderment; in confusion

一樽水（一瓶水）a bottle of water

一樽香水（一瓶香水）a bottle of perfume

一樽藥水（一瓶藥水）a bottle of liquid medicine

一盤水（一萬塊）ten thousand dollars

一嚿水（一百塊）one hundred dollars

乜水（誰）who

入水（進水）pour in water

口水①（健談）talkative ②saliva

下水（去水／排水）drain

大疊水（很有錢）very rich

五行缺水（缺錢）no money

井水 well water

井水不犯河水 each one minds their own business; well water does not interfere with river water

升水（漲價）appreciation; positive evaluation

天花板滲水 water seepage from the ceiling

天拿水 thinner

心水（心意）idea; opinion; point of view; thought

止咳水（止咳藥）cough mixture

火水（煤油）kerosene

冇水 ① （沒有水）no water ② （缺錢）be short of money; broke; no money

加水 refill the teapot

半桶水（半瓶醋 / 半懂不懂）a little knowledge of sth

去水 drain

生粉水 cornstarch solution

白滾水（白開水）plain boiled water

四點水（四點底）the "fire" 火 radical

奶水（牛奶）milk

合心水（合心意）after one's own heart; be satisfied with sth; exactly what is required; one's cup of tea; to one's liking

合晒心水（真合心意）after one's own heart; be satisfied with sth; exactly what is required; one's cup of tea; to one's liking

吊鹽水 ① （打點滴）transfusion ② （開工不足）under-employment

回水（退款）refund

地水（盲人）blind person

好威水（好厲害）it's really impressive

好猛水（水很澎湃）the water is strong

收水（收錢）collect money

有水（有錢）loaded; rich; wealthy; well-heeled; well-off; well-to-do

有咳同流鼻水（有咳嗽，也有流鼻涕）have a cough and a runny nose

汗水 perspiration; sweat

池水 pond water

米水（洗米水）rice-washing water

灰水 paint

色水（顏色）colour

冷水 cold water

吹一輪水（閒聊一會兒）have a chat

忍住淚水 hold back one's tears

扭乾啲水（扭乾水）wring out the water

扯落水（拉下水）drag sb down

改錯水（塗改液）correction fluid

汽水 ① aerated water ② soft drink

沖水 fill with water; pour water

沖滾水（燒開水）pour boiled water

足水（滿足）be contented with one's luck; be pleased with oneself

防水 waterproof

供水 water supply

制水（限制用水）water rationing

油水 ① grease ② profit

油灰水 ① （石灰水）whitewash ② （化濃粧）do make-up

河水 river water

命水（命運）fate

屈水（敲詐金錢）extort money

拉埋…落水（拉…下水）drag sb in; include sb in the subject of conversation

拉落水（牽連）put the blame on

抽水 ① draw water ② （佔便宜）fool around with a girl; take advantage of a girl ③ （賭博術語：賭場集團從每局賭博中抽取的費用）take a percentage out of the winnings in gambling

拖泥帶水 be sloppy in one's work; indecisive

放水 ① （小便）urinate ② （暗中給予某人不正當的利益）make an exception to favour sb

河水不犯井水 each follows their own bent; each minds their own business; river water does not mix with well water

近山不可燒枉柴，近河不可洗枉水 waste not, want not

度水（借錢）ask for money; borrow money from others

侵水（加水）add water

威水（威風 / 厲害）awe-inspiring; imposing; impressive; majestic-looking; spirited

咳藥水 cough syrup

昧水（潛水）dive; go under water

洗頭水（洗髮露）shampoo

洱水 a river in Yunnan

流口水 ① make sb's mouth water; mouth-watering ② covet; drool over; gloat over; hanker after; slaver over

流鼻水（流鼻涕）have a runny nose

紅豆水 red bean soup

紅汞水 mercurochrome

紅藥水 mecurochrome solution

風水 ① geomancy ② fortune

食水 ① drinking water ② （謀利）absorb water

香水 perfume

倒吊冇滴墨水（胸無點墨）be illiterate

倒瀉水（打翻了水）spill water

凍水（冷水）cold water

凍過水（沒有希望了）past salvation

凍滾水（冷開水）cold boiled water

凍檸水（冰檸檬水）cold lemon water

挽水（提水）carry water

唔湯唔水（不倫不類）neither fish nor fowl

校水（調試水溫）adjust the warmth of the water

浸水 flood; submerge

浸（過）鹹水（放洋讀書）spent time abroad; studied abroad

涉水 wade; wade into the water

消毒藥水 antiseptic liquid

索水（吸水）absorb water

茶水 tea or boiled water

逆水 go against the current

高水（價格高）premium

啱心水（合心意）after one's own heart; be satisfied with sth; exactly what is required; one's cup of tea; to one's liking

掃灰水 ①（抹石灰水）whitewash ②（化濃粧）do make-up

掠水 ①（騙水）take advantage of sb's money; trick sb out of money ②（多收錢）overcharge

條命凍過水（大難臨頭）be in danger

梳打水（炭酸水）soda water

梘水 ①（肥皂水）soap water ②（鹼性水）alkali water

淋水（澆水）water

淚水 tears

眼水（淚水）tears

眼淚水 tears

眼藥水 eye drop

豉油撈飯——整色整水 ①（裝模作樣）put on airs; put on a show; put on an act ②（賣弄）flirt; play the coquette

通水（通消息）disclose secret information; give information to sb; give a tip

速速過水（快快給錢）pay up quick

雪水 iced water

船頭尺——度水（借錢）someone who is always asking others for money

喺泳池游水（在游泳池游泳）swim in the pool

揩油水（從中取利）profit at others' expense

提水（提詞兒）prompt

插水（假摔）take a dive

散水（解散／離開）disperse; escape in every direction; everybody takes his way; leave a place; scatter away

游水 ①（游泳）swim ②（活生生）fresh and alive

游乾水（打麻將）play mahjong

游龍舟水（划龍舟）swim while dragonboating

睇水（看風聲）keep watch; stand watch; take a sharp lookout

睇風水（看風水）practise geomancy

粥水 congee soup

跌落水（跌下水）fall into water

開埋井俾人食水（自己努力以後讓別人坐享其成）do pioneering work with labour but let sb sit with folded arms and enjoy the results

黃藥水 acrinol solution

搆水（摻水）mix with water

搵水（掙錢）make money

揀地游水（安全至上）play for safety; play safe

斟水 pour water

新官上場整色水（新官上任裝模作樣）a new broom sweeps clean; a new official applies strict measures; new brooms sweep clean

暖水（溫水）warm water

溪水 water of a mountain stream

滑水 water ski

煲水 ①（燒水）boil water ②（醞釀小道消息）indulge in petty gossip

補水（補錢）payment for overtime work

過水 ①（給錢）give sb money; grease sb's hand; pay sb ②（沖洗）rinse

椰青水 coconut water

跳水 diving

飲水（喝水）drink water

飲冰水（喝冰水）drink iced water

飲滾水（喝開水）drink boiled water

慳水（省水）save water

搦住桶水（拿着一桶水）carry a bucket of water

摻啲水（摻些水）mix with some water

滲水 water leakage; water seepage

滴水（鬢髮）hair on the temples

滾水（開心）①boiling water ②boiled water ③hot water

漏水 leak

漱口水（漱口藥）mouthwash

潑冷水（挫傷別人的熱情）dampen sb's enthusiasm; dampen sth; discourage sb from doing sth; pour/throw cold water on sth/sb

潭水 deep water

綠豆水 green bean soup

銀紙縮水（貨幣貶值）currency depreciation/devaluation

墨水 ink

撈靜水（吃獨門兒）live on one's special skill

撲水（借錢）go for rush money; raise money

標水（噴水）water spray

潛水 diving

潲水（餿水）hogwash; swill

熱水 hot water

熱檸水 hot lemon water

賠水（賠錢）pay compensation

磅水（給錢）give sb the money; pay cash; pay sb; pay up

膠水 glue

蒸餾水 distilled water

踩水 tread water

蝕水（蝕錢）lose money

隱形眼鏡藥水 contact lens solution

整色整水 ① (裝模作樣) put on a show; put on an act
　　② (賣弄風情) flirt; play the coquette
擔水 (揹水) carry water
擔擔買水 (擔擔買水是喪事儀式的術語) carry the hearse
　　and escort a funeral
糖水 sweet soup
豬籠入水 have lots of money pouring in; have many different
　　ways to make money; hit the jackpot; make wads of
　　money; one's financial resources come from all directions
醒水 ① (機靈) quick to realise ② (警覺) alarmed; alert
濕咗水 (沾濕了水) has soaked in water
縮水 ① (降低成本) reduce one's costs ② (收縮) shrink
　　③ (貶值) depreciation
薪水 earnings; pay; salary; wage
雙氧水 oxydol
薑水 ginger water
檸水 lemon water
檸檬水 lemon water
藍藥水 gentian violet solution; methyl violet solution
藥水 liquid medicine; syrup
霧水 dew
礦泉水 mineral water
鹹水 (外國) foreign
疊埋心水 (專心一意) at one; be bent on; concentrate on
　　sth; have one's heart in sth; make up one's mind in doing
　　sth; put one's whole heart into; with all one's heart and
　　mind; with body and soul; with one heart and one mind;
　　with wholehearted devotion
鬚後水 after-shave; shaving lotion
灣水 (待業) be unemployed

【火】 fo² ① fire ② (生氣) anger

火上加油 add oil to the flames; pour oil on fire
火山 volcano
火水 (煤油) kerosene
　　火水燈 (煤油燈) kerosene lamp
　　火水爐 (煤油爐) kerosene stove
　　火水罐 (煤油罐) kerosene container
火牛 (變壓器 / 鎮流器) adapter
火字邊 (火字旁) the "fire" 火 radical
火車 train
　　火車站 train station
　　火車頭 engine
　　　　上火車 get on a train
　　　　搭火車 (乘火車) take a train
火油 (煤油) kerosene
火屎 (火灰) spark
火星 Mars
　　火星撞地球 be on a collision course

火柴 match
　　一支火柴 (一根火柴) a match
　　一盒火柴 a box of matches
火紅火綠 (怒氣大) in a frenzy
火氣 bad temper; temper
火起 (冒火兒 / 生氣 / 發火 / 惱火) angry; be ablaze
　　with anger; fire up; fit to be tied; flare up; get angry; get
　　shirty; lose one's temper
火酒 (酒精) alcohol
火猛 (火旺) fierceness of the fire
火船 (汽船) steam boat; steamer
火葬 cremation
火路 (火候) duration and degree of cooking
火滾 (生氣 / 發火 / 氣憤 / 惱火) angry; indignant
火腿 ham
　　火腿通粉 macaroni with ham
　　火腿絲 shredded ham
火嘴 (火花塞) ignition plug; spark plug; sparking plug
火箭 rocket
火遮眼 (氣糊塗了) blind with fury; eyes blaze
　　with anger
火機 (打火機) lighter
火燒旗竿——長炭 (歎) (慢慢享受) enjoy life as long
　　as possible; live in clover forever
火頭軍 (炊事員) cook
火燭 (火災 / 着火) fire; on fire
　　火燭呀 (着火呀) fire
　　火燭車 (消防車 / 救火車) fire engine
火鍋 hotpot
　　食火鍋 (吃火鍋) have hotpot
火爆 ① (激烈) intense; sharp ② (急躁) impetuous; lose
　　one's temper
火爐 fire place
火警 fire
　　火警路線圖 fire safety route
　　走火警 (火警演習) fire drill
火藥 gunpowder
　　吞咗火藥 / 食咗火藥 (吃槍藥了 / 火氣大) be hot
　　　　with rage; fly into a fury
火鑽 (紅寶石) ruby

一把火 be filled with rage; extremely angry; hot with rage
三十火 (三十瓦) thirty watt
山火 hill fire
好猛火 (火很旺) the fire is fierce
死火 ① (拋錨) breakdown ② (糟糕) damn it
佛都有火 (性子再好的人也受不了) it would try the
　　patience of a saint
扯火 (冒火兒) get angry; lose one's temper

把火（發怒）be filled with rage; extremely angry; hot with rage

把鬼火（怒火燒心）extremely angry

把幾火（怒火燒心）burn with anger; extremely angry

肝火 ①（脾氣暴躁）irascibility ②（中醫用語：肝的疏泄功能太過旺盛）liver fire

走火 run away from fire

防火 fire prevention; fire safety

易過借火（易如反掌）a piece of cake; as easy as ABC; as easy as child's play; as easy as damn it; as easy as falling off a log; as easy as pie; as easy as turning one's palm over; as easy as turning over one's hand; as easy as winking; easy job

玩火 play with fire

挑起把火（挑起怒火）arouse sb's anger

烤火 warm oneself by a fire

烏燈黑火（黑燈瞎火）completely dark; pitch-dark

停火 ceasefire

透火（生火）start a fire

焙火（烤火／圍着火取暖）warm oneself by a fire

發火 burst into anger

開火（槍戰）argue; fight; start a war; start gunfire

新官上場三把火（新官上任三把火）a new broom sweeps clean; a new official applies strict measures; new brooms sweep clean

惹火 sexy

痰火 phlegm-fire

過火（過份）go too far; overstep the bounds

隔岸觀火 show indifference towards sb's trouble

煽風點火 stir up troubles; whip up waves

膏火（燈火）lamp oil

駁火 fire fight

墜火（敗火／去火）relieve heat; relieve inflammation

慾火 passion; the fire of lust

撞火（生氣）angry; be ablazed with anger; feel angry; fire up; fit to be tied; flare up; get angry; get shirty; lose one's temper

撻火（點火）ignite

激到一把火（氣到一肚子火）a stomachful of anger

燂火（烤火／圍着火取暖）warm oneself by a fire

燥火（發怒）get angry

爆火（發脾氣）angry; be ablaze with anger; fire up; fit to be tied; flare up; get angry; get shirty; lose one's temper

躁火 dryness-heat

【爪】zaau² claw

爪牙 lackeys; retainers

爪印 nail mark; print; trace

八爪 octopus

打八爪（留下指紋）take fingerprints

百足咁多爪（多才多藝）put nobody on one's track

鳳爪（雞爪子）chicken feet

【父】fu⁶ father

父子 father and son

　父子關係 relationship between father and son

　　有其父必有其子 like father, like son

父母 parents

　父母官 local officials

　父母親 parents

　　在家靠父母，出外靠朋友 at home, you rely on parents; away from home, you rely on friends

父老 elders

　　一時唔偷雞做父老 a rogue goes so far as to moralise to another rogue

　　鄉親父老 elders and folks

父親 father

　父親節 Father's Day

外父（岳父）father-in-law; wife's father

叔父 uncle

知子莫若父 no one knows a boy better than his father

岳父 one's father-in-law; one's wife's father

師父 master

神父 father

舅父 mother's brother; uncle

慈父 loving father; father

嚴父 stern father

【片】pin³ film

片段 bit; extract; fragment; part; passage; section; segment

　預告片段 trailer

片面 ① one-sided; single-faceted; unilateral ② lopsided

　片面之詞 one-sided statement

片場（電影製片廠）film studio

一套三級片（一部三級片）a Category III movie; an X-rated movie

一張卡片（一張名片）a name card

一張明信片 a postcard

一張相片 a photo

一壺香片 a pot of jasmine tea

三級片 Category III movie; X-rated movie

幻燈片 slide; transparency

卡片（名片）name card

古裝片（古裝戲）ancient-costume drama

白金唱片 platinum record
交換名片 exchange name cards
名片 name card
西片（外國片兒）Western movie
成人尿片（成人尿布）adult diaper
尿片（尿布）diaper; nappy
呢張係我嘅咭片（這是我的名片）this is my name card
拍片（拍電影）make/produce/shoot a movie
明信片 postcard
芯片 microchip
金唱片 golden record
相片 photo; photograph
香片 jasmine tea
留下名片 leave one's name card
唱片 record
國語片 Mandarin movie
魚片 ① fish filet ② fish slices
換尿片（換尿布）change the baby's diaper
晶片 chip; crystal plate
港產片（港產電影）Hong Kong movie
賀歲片 movies shown during the Chinese Lunar
　　New Year
開片（打羣架）fight with weapons between groups of
　　people; scuffle
預告片 trailer
像片 photo; photograph
鴨片 duck slice
薯片 potato chips
簧片 reed
鏡片（眼鏡鏡片）plate
警匪片 detective movie
鹹片（色情影片）pornographic film
攬尿片（穿尿布）wear the diaper
鱗片 scales

【片】pin³ blade
片車（賽車）race cars
片過（打架）have a fight

卡通片 cartoon
咭片（名片）name card

【牙】ngaa⁴（牙齒）tooth
牙力（說服力）power
　　冇牙力（說不服）fail to bring over
牙尖嘴利（口齒伶俐 / 尖嘴薄舌 / 說話尖銳）have a
　　caustic and flippant tongue; have a caustic tongue; have
　　a sharp tongue
牙肉（牙齦）gum

牙刷 toothbrush
　　一枝 / 個牙刷（一把牙刷）a toothbrush
牙周病 periodontal disease; periodonotosis
牙屎（牙垢）tartar
牙科 dentistry
　　牙科診所 dental clinic; the dentist; the dentist's
　　牙科醫生 dental surgeon; dentist
牙帶（帶魚）hairtail
　　牙帶魚（帶魚）hairtail
牙斬斬（嘴巴耍強 / 貧嘴薄舌）garrulous and sharp-
　　tongued; have a caustic and flippant tongue; light and
　　airy utterance; wag one's tongue too freely
牙痛 toothache
　　牙痛咁聲（直哼哼 / 嚷嚷）（形容人不願意做但又不
　　得不做某事的神態）groan with pain to show one's
　　reluctance to do sth; grumble to show one's reluctance
　　to do sth
牙煙（危險）dangerous; horrible
　　切菜刀剃頭 —— 牙煙（剃頭刀擦屁股 —— 懸得乎）
　　clean the buttocks with a barber's knife –
　　dangerous enough
　　睇見就牙煙（看着真危險）it looks dangerous
牙較（牙關）jaw
　　牙較友（碎嘴子）chin-wagger
　　打牙較（閒聊）bull session; chat; chat idly; chew the
　　rag; chinwag; gossip; have a chat; have small talk;
　　natter; schmooze; shoot the breeze
　　甩牙較（下巴脫臼）dislocated jaw
牙膏 toothpaste
　　唧牙膏（擠牙膏）squeeze tooth paste out from the
　　tube
牙齒 tooth
　　牙齒印痕（雙方有心結）a score to settle
　　牙齒當金使（信守承諾 / 言而有信）always true in word
　　and resolute in deed; as good as one's words; keep
　　one's promise; keep one's word
牙線 dental floss
牙擦 ①（浮誇 / 愛炫耀自己 / 傲慢）boastful
　　②（牙刷）toothbrush
　　牙擦擦（浮誇 / 炫耀自己）boastful
　　牙擦蘇（誇大其辭的人）boastful person
牙罅（牙縫）crevice between teeth
牙醫 dental surgeon; dentist
　　睇牙醫（看牙醫）see a dentist
牙籤 toothpick
　　一枝牙籤（一根牙籤）a toothpick

一隻牙（一顆牙齒）a tooth
一隻假牙（一顆假牙）a false tooth

一隻爛牙（一顆蟲牙）a decayed tooth; a rotten tooth

一棚牙（一排牙齒）a row of teeth

大牙 front tooth

冇柄士巴拿——得棚牙（茶壺沒有把兒——光剩嘴兒了）
　　a teapot without a handle – only the spout is left

爪牙 lackeys; retainers

以牙還牙 a tooth for a tooth; an eye for an eye; answer
　　blows with blows; fight fire with fire; give as good
　　as one gets; like for like; repay evil with evil; return
　　blow for blow; return like for like; tit for tat; tooth
　　for tooth

出牙 teethe; tooth eruption

甩牙（掉牙）a tooth drops off

西班牙 Spain

刷牙 brush one's teeth

剝牙（拔牙）extract a tooth; pull out a tooth

咬牙 ① grit one's teeth ② grind one's teech

唔咬啱牙（合不來）not get along well

哨牙（齙牙）protruding tooth

假牙 false teeth

啱牙（合得來）get along well with people; hit it off

崩牙（缺齒／螺絲桿破損）goofy teeth

得棚牙（光會說）have a loose tongue

搣牙（拔牙）extract a tooth

脫牙 extract a tooth; pull out a tooth

滑牙（擰不緊）stripping

象牙 ivory

落牙（拔牙）extract a tooth; pull out a tooth

實食冇黐牙（有十足把握）sure win

撩牙（剔牙）pick one's teeth

擦牙（刷牙）brush one's teeth

黐牙 stick to one's teeth

講大話，甩大牙（說謊會掉門牙）（用來嚇小朋友別要說謊）
　　(to a child) (literally) if you lie, your molar will fall off

爛牙（蟲牙）carious tooth; decayed tooth; rotten tooth

【牛】ngau⁴ bull; cow

牛一（生日／生辰）birthday

牛王（倔強／蠻不講理）obstinate; stubborn; unbending;
　　unyielding

　　牛王頭（橫行霸道的人）unreasonable person

牛仔 ①（牛犢）calf ② cowboy

　　牛仔褲 jeans

　　　　一條牛仔褲 a pair of jeans

　　牛仔褸（牛仔外套）denim jacket

牛奶 milk

　　牛奶麥皮 oatmeal with milk

　　牛奶嗲（牛奶罐兒）milk jar

牛扒（牛排）steak

牛扒刀（牛排刀）steak knife

牛扒飯（牛排飯）rice with beef steak

牛皮 ①（疲弱／疲軟）fatigued and weak; tired and weak
　　②（頑皮）naughty

　　牛皮燈籠——點極都唔明（牛皮燈籠——點不透）thick-
　　headed

牛年 Year of the Ox

牛死送牛喪（某種損失導致另一種損失）flog a dead
　　horse

牛肉 beef

　　牛肉球 beef meatball

　　牛肉乾 ① beef jerky ②（違例停車告票）parking ticket

　　牛肉粥 congee with beef

　　牛肉麵 beef noodles

　　牛肉漢堡 beef burger

　　　山竹牛肉 beef ball with bean curd skin

牛舌 ox tongue

牛尾 ox tail

牛咁眼（凝視）gape at

牛房（牛欄）cattle pen

牛油（黃油）butter

　　牛油刀（黃油刀）butter spreader

　　牛油多士 toast with butter

　　　人造牛油（人造黃油）margarine

牛乸（母牛）cow

牛屎（牛糞）cowpat

牛柳 beef tenderloin

牛牯（公牛）bull; ox

牛唔飲水，唔撳得牛頭低（凡事靠自願／不可強迫）
　　(literally) one cannot press down the head of a cow if it
　　does not want to drink water

牛栢葉（牛胃）beef tripe

牛耕田馬食穀——父賺錢仔享福（老子打洞——兒
　　子受用）the father earns, the son spends

牛記（牛仔褲）jeans

　　牛記笠記（牛仔褲配上T恤）casual style of dress

牛高馬大（長得非常高大）stand like a giant; tall and big;
　　well-grown

牛脷（牛舌）ox tongue

牛黃 ①（蠻不講理）bad-tempered ②（不聽教的小孩）
　　little rogue

牛腱 beef gristle

牛腸（牛肉腸粉）steamed rice roll with beef

牛腩 beef brisket; belly beef; brisket

　　牛腩麵 beef brisket noodles

牛精（牛脾氣／倔小子／倔強）behave like a bully;
　　unreasonable

牛頭 cow's head

　　牛頭唔對馬嘴（毫無關係）beside the point

牛頭馬面（牛馬將軍——鬼差）devils

牛頭褲 jeans

牛頸（倔強／固執）obstinate; stubborn; unbending; unyielding

牛嚼牡丹——唔知花定草（豬八戒吃人參果——不知啥滋味）cannot appreciate good food; not know chalk from cheese; pigsy eating ginseng fruit – no flavour

牛輾（牛腱子）beef shank

牛雜（牛下水）beef offal

牛髀肉（牛腿肉）round steak

牛欄 cattle pen

一隻大牛（舊時港幣五百元的鈔票）five-hundred note

一隻牛（一頭牛）a cow

一隻金牛（舊時港幣一千元的鈔票）one-thousand dollar note

大牛（舊時港幣一千元的鈔票）five-hundred-dollar note

火牛（變壓器）adapter

死牛 dead cow

吹牛 baloney; blow one's own horn; blow one's own trumpet; boast; brag; draw a long bow; eyewash; hot air; plume oneself; shoot the breeze; swing the lead; talk big; talk in high language; tell lies

乳牛 dairy cattle; milk cow

兩騎牛（兩面派）double dealer; sit on the fence

波牛（足球發燒友）person who is always playing football

金牛（舊時港幣一千元的鈔票）one-thousand-dollar note

剝皮牛（馬面魨）black scraper

牯牛 ①（公牛）cow ②（閹割過的公牛）castrated cow

細時偷針，大時偷牛（小時候偷針，長大偷牛）young pilferer, old robber

睇牛（牧牛者）cowherd

開荒牛（辛勞的創業者）pioneer in a particular field

黃牛（牟取暴利的人）profiteer

隔山買牛（靠瞎猜）buy sth without seeing it first

劏牛（牢牛）slaughter a cow

劏死牛（劫持／綁架）highjack; mug; rob

駛牛（騎牛）drive a cow

騎牛搵牛（騎牛找牛（不安心於本職））look for an ox while sitting on one

【犬】hyun² dog

犬字邊（狗爪邊／反犬旁／犬猶兒）the "dog"（犬）radical

犬吠 bark; bark of a dog

黃犬（蚯蚓／黃蟮）earthworm

謀犬（獵狗）setter

警犬 police dog

【王】wong⁴ king

王母娘娘 Heaven Queen

王字邊（王字旁／玉部）the "king" 王 radical

王老五（光棍／單身漢）bachelor; bachelor guy; unmarried man

王朝 ① imperial court; royal curt ② dynasty

大餟王（大胃王）glutton

牛王（固執）obstinate; stubborn; unbending; unyielding

花王（園丁／花匠）gardener

帝王 emperor; monarch

拳王 boxing champion

烏龍王（糊塗蟲）addle-brained; airhead; muddled person; nitwit

混世魔王 devil incarnate

殺人王（讓許多學生考試不合格的老師的暱稱）nickname for a teacher who fails a large number of students in his class

蛇王（偷懶）abscond; absence without leave; decamp; go over the hill; jump the track; shirker; slink away; sneak off

蜂王 ① queen bee ② queen wasp

稱王 declare oneself king

賭王 gambling king

閻羅王 the King of Hell

霸王 overbearing; high-handed; rule by force

【冇】mou⁵（沒／沒有）not to have; no; without

冇一定（不一定）it is unfixable

冇人（沒人）nobody

　冇人有（沒見過）have never seen

　冇人吼（沒人有興趣）nobody is interested

　冇人接（沒人接）no answer

　冇人搪（沒人搭理）nobody pays any attention to sb

冇乜（沒事兒／沒甚麼）it doesn't matter; it's nothing; never mind; that's all right

　冇乜兩句（不投緣）have no relationship with

　冇乜嘢（沒事兒／沒甚麼）it doesn't matter; it's nothing; never mind; that's all right

　冇乜點（沒甚麼特別）nothing out of the ordinary; nothing special; nothing unusual

冇大冇細（沒大沒小）not respecting hierarchy and status

冇心（不是故意的）not deliberate; unintentional

冇水 ①（沒水）no water ②（沒錢）be short of money; broke; no money

冇王管（沒人管）a chaotic situation where there is no one in charge

　有王管（有人管）someone is in charge

冇用（不中用／沒用）useless

　冇鬼用（真不中用）bloody useless

冇份（沒份兒）have no involvement in sth

冇收（沒轍）at loose ends
冇佢收（拿他沒辦法）can't do anything about him;
there's nothing one can do

冇冇怕（別怕／沒甚麼可怕的）don't be afraid

冇死（必定了）sure winner

冇米粥（沒有結果的事情）sth that will never amount to
anything

冇耳性（健忘）forgetful; have a memory like a sieve

冇耳聽（不想聽）do not want to hear sth

冇行（沒戲／沒門兒）it is hopeless; unsuccessful in a
venture

冇尾飛鉈（斷線風箏／跟影難覓的人）a person without
any trace

冇走雞（十拿九穩／有把握）have everything in
the bag

冇事／冇事嘅（沒事兒／沒事的）it's alright/all right

冇來由（沒根據）no evidence
有來由（有根據）there's evidence

冇咁大嘅頭就唔好戴咁大頂帽（不要不自量力）
don't live beyond one's means

冇咁衰講到咁衰（抹黑別人）paint a grim picture of
sb/sth

冇呢枝歌仔唱（現在沒有這回好事了）such a good thing
is a thing of the past

冇咗 ①（流產）abortion ②（去世／死了）dead

冇定準（不一定／沒準兒）not sure; the chances of success
are uncertain

冇性（沒人性的／殘忍）savaged and absurd; unreasonable

冇姆教（沒娘教育）lack the education of one's mother

冇厘頭（莫名其妙）pointless behaviour or talk

冇柄士巴拿——得棚牙（茶壺沒有把兒——光剩嘴兒
了）a teapot without a handle – only the spout is left

冇穿冇爛（無病無災）everything is alright/all right;
without a scratch

冇計（沒法子／沒辦法／沒轍）be unable to find a way
out; can't be helped; can do nothing about it; can't help
it; have no choice but; have no way out but to do sth;
nothing can be done about it
冇計啦（沒法子）can't be helped
冇計嘅（沒說的）have nothing to be criticised
冇晒計（完全沒法子／完全沒辦法）can't do anything
about it

冇訂企（沒有地方立足）be pushed out

冇面（沒面子／沒臉／丟臉）have no face; lose face
冇晒面（沒一點兒面子）lose face completely

冇修（沒治／別提了）hopeless; nothing can be done; past
remedy

冇哪更（無緣無故）not to the point

冇哪嗌（沒關係）have nothing to do with

冇害（沒害）harmless

冇效（沒效）null

冇料 ①（沒本事／沒本領）nothing special
②（沒學問）ill-educated
冇料到（沒用）useless
冇乜料（沒有甚麼特別的）nothing special

冇時（無時無刻）all the time; at all times; every hour and
moment; every minute; incessantly; without a moment's
pause
冇時定（不固定）changeful; fluid; unfixed; unstable;
unsteadfast

冇晒（完了）come to an end

冇氣 ①（喘不過氣）exhausted; out of breath
②（死了）die; pass away

冇益（沒好處）do no good; not beneficial

冇紋路（沒正經／沒章法）have no sense of propriety

冇得（不能）be unable to
冇得救（救不了）it's beyond remedy
冇得揮（打不垮）unbeatable
冇得彈 ①（沒說的／無法挑剔的）above criticism;
beyond reproach ②（好極了）couldn't be better;
excellent; second to none; very good; wonderful
冇得頂（好極了）couldn't be better; excellent; second to
none; wonderful
冇得傾（沒得說）unnegotiable
冇得撓（無法挽回）past remedy
冇得諗（想也不用想）leave sth out of consideration
冇得斟（沒甚麼可談的）no room for discussion
冇得撈（沒活兒幹）be unemployed

冇掩雞籠（沒有掩上門的雞籠——隨意出入）a coop
without a flap; a place where people are free to come
and go

冇眼睇（看不下去）too disappointed to see; turn a blind
eye to

冇符 ①（沒咒兒唸／沒辦法）at one's wit's end; nothing
can be done; there's nothing one can do ②it's hopeless
冇晒符 ①（完全沒法子／完全沒辦法）at one's wit's
end; nothing can be done; there's nothing one can do
②it's hopeless

冇細藝（沒事兒幹）at a loose end; have nothing to do

冇貨（沒貨）out of stock

冇陰功（多可憐）how sad

冇渣嘜（沒有保證）gain no guarantee against loss; no
guarantee

冇睇頭（沒看頭兒）nothing interesting to see

冇嗰樣整嗰樣（沒事找事做）do sth unnecessary

冇準（不一定／沒準兒）not sure; the chances of success
are uncertain

冇腦（沒腦子）brainless
冇解（不像話／沒道理）it is unreasonable that
冇話（從不／沒說）never ever
　　冇話好講（無話可說）be stuck for an answer
　　冇話頭（沒得說）nothing to be said
冇雷公咁遠（偏遠地方）remote place
冇嘢（沒事兒／沒甚麼）it doesn't matter; it's nothing;
　　never mind; that's all right
　　冇嘢到（沒料到）have no benefit
冇樣叻（沒有一點長處）good for nothing
冇錢（沒錢）no money
　　冇錢買嘢食（沒錢買東西吃）no money to buy food
冇錯 ①（沒有錯誤）no mistake ②（對的）it's right; that's
　　right; you're right
冇膽（膽小）chicken; do not have the guts; no guts
冇壞嘅（沒有壞處的）there's no harm in doing sth
冇礙（沒關係的／不礙事兒）nothng is seriously wrong
冇譜（不像話／亂來）break the routine; incoherent
冇藥醫（無可救藥）no remedy for one's behaviour
　　人嚇人冇藥醫（人嚇人無藥醫）there's no remedy to
　　　cure a person horrified by others
　　人蠢冇藥醫（棒槌）there's no remedy to cure the
　　　stupidity of a person
冇彎轉（沒辦法打開僵局）there is no way to break a
　　deadlock
冇癮 ①（沒興趣／沒趣）bored ②（沒勁）disappointed
　　冇釐癮頭 ①（沒趣）bored ②（沒勁）disappointed
冇 cash（沒現金）have no cash
冇 face（丟臉）lose one's face

一丁人都冇（一個人也沒有）there isn't anyone
一戙都冇／一棟都冇（無言而對／一敗塗地）left
　　speechless; cannot do anything
人又老，錢又冇 old and penniless; old and poor
手快有，手慢冇（先到先得）first come, first served
問和尚借梳——實冇／問師姑攞梳——實冇（向和尚借
　　梳——所託非人）ask the wrong person for sth; come to
　　the wrong shop

5 劃

【且】ce²
且住（停住）hold it; stop it
且慢 hold it; wait a minute

姑且 for the time being
尚且 ① even ② still; yet

況且 furthermore

【世】sai³ world
世代 generation
　　世世代代 generation after generation
世伯 uncle (polite way of addressing a friend's father)
世事 affairs of human life; affairs of the world
　　世事無常 affairs of the world are inconstant
世故 experienced
　　人情世故 ways of the world
　　老於世故 be experienced in the ways of the world;
　　　have seen much of the world
世界 world
　　世界女／仔（阿諛奉承的女士／男士／面面俱到的
　　　女孩／男孩）woman/man of the world; worldly girl/
　　　boy; worldly woman/man
　　世界各地 places all over the world
　　世界波（美妙的進球）good shot at goal
　　世界輪流轉（一生不會只有好運或一帆風順）everybody
　　　has the turn of the wheel; fortunes change
　　大把世界（很多機會掙錢）have many chances to
　　　make money
　　全世界 all over the whole
　　好世界（好日子）happy life
　　做世界（去偷去搶）become involved in illegal
　　　activities in order to make money
　　捱世界（熬日子）struggle hard to make a living
　　搵世界（找生活）earn a living
　　撈世界 ①（混日子）make a living through crime
　　　②（闖蕩世界）earn a living
　　歎世界（享受人生／享樂／享福）enjoy life; have a
　　　comfortable existence; live in luxury
　　歎大把世界（享受生活）live in luxury
　　環遊世界 travel around the world
世紀 century
世態 ways of the world
　　世態炎涼 fickleness of the world; inconstancy of human
　　　relationships; snobbishness of human relationships; the
　　　aspects of worldly affairs are now hot and now cold

一世 a lifetime; all one's life; as long as one lives; man and
　　boy; one's whole lifetime; throughout one's life
人一世，物一世 you only live once
不可一世 come the heavy swell over sb; consider oneself a
　　world above others; consider oneself unexcelled in the
　　world; insufferably arrogant; on the high ropes; ride the
　　high horse; swagger like a conquering hero; think oneself
　　supreme in the world
出世 born

成世（一輩子）a lifetime; all one's life; as long as one lives; man and boy; one's whole lifetime; throughout one's life

呢世（今世）all one's life

前世（上一世）previous life

風水佬呃你十年八年，唔呃得一世（風水師傅騙你十年八年，不能騙你一輩子／時間會證明一切）a feng shui master can deceive you for eight to ten year but not for life – time can witness to a fact

捱一世（捱一輩子）toil all one's life

第世（下一世）life after death; the life to come; the next incarnation; the next life

逝世 die; pass away

棄世 ① die; pass away ② abandon worldly life; lift one's head above ordinary things; look far and high

幾世 several generations

蓋世 matchless; uparalleled

獻世 be disgraced; bring shame on oneself; lose face; make a fool of oneself; make a spectacle of oneself

爛身爛世（破破爛爛）wear shabby clothes

【丙】bing² (打) hit; (transliteration) punch; scold

丙門（蠢人）stupid person

丙等 C grade; the third class

丙鑊（痛毆）beat up

　丙一鑊（痛毆一頓）beat up thoroughly

娘丙（過時）old-fashioned

【主】zyu² ① host ② master

主人 ① master ② owner

　主人房（主卧室）master bedroom

主任 chairman; director; head; minister

主角 lead; leading character; leading player; leading role; main actor; main actress; major character protagonist

　女主角 actress; female lead; leading lady

　男主角 actor; chief actor; leading man; male lead; male title role

主板 main board

主持 direct; manage; take charge of

　主持人 chairperson; host; presenter; quizmaster

主要 chief; main; major

主家席 head table

主席 chairman; chairperson

　名譽主席 honorary chairman; honorary chairperson

主動 of one's own accord; take the initiative

　採取主動 take the initiative

主菜 main course; main dish

主意 idea

另打主意 make some other plans

打錯主意 get a wrong idea into one's head

好主意 good idea; that's a brilliant idea; that's a good idea; that's a marvellous idea; that's a practical idea; that's a wonderful idea; that's an excellent idea; what a capital idea

改變主意 change one's mind

揸主意（拿主意）make a decision; make up one's mind

主腦（主謀／頭目）chief; leader; mastermind

主管 ①（領導）leader ② supervisor; boss

主播 anchor of the show

　新聞主播 news anchor

　電視主播 TV anchor

主顧 client; customer

主觀 subjective

入主 become the master

六神無主 be thrown into confusion; don't know what to do

戶主 head of a household

民主 democracy

先入為主 have a prejudice against

米飯班主 people from whom one earns a living

作主 ① decide; have the say; make the decision; take the responsibility for a decision ② back up; support

君主 crowned head; monarch; sovereign

杉木靈牌——唔做得主（杉木靈牌——遇事做不了主）manage a family but without the right to make any decisions

身不由主 do sth not of one's own free will; helpless; incapable of resistance; involuntarily; lose control of oneself; unable to contain oneself; one's limbs no longer obey one; unable to act according to one's own will; unable to contain oneself; under compulsion

事主 boss

易主 change masters; change owners

狗主 dog owner

客家佔地主（外地來的人佔了作主人家的地方）reverse the positions of the host and the guest

屋主 landlady; landlord

原業主 original owner; original property owner

馬主 horse owner

堂主 underworld gang leader

冤有頭，債有主 there must be an agent for what is done; sb is responsible for a wrong and they will pay for it

物主 owner

買主 buyer; purchaser

當家作主 master in one's own house

過主（滾開）go away

業主 ① property owner ② landlord
僱主 employer

【乎】fu⁴ (近乎) almost

介乎 in between
似乎 as if; as it appears; it appears that; it looks as if; it looks like; it seems; seem; seemingly
危危乎 (懸得乎) precarious
於是乎 as a result; consequently; hence; so; then; thereafter; therefore; thereupon; thus
甚至乎 as ...as; enough; even; even if; far from; go so far as to; if anything; if not more; in fact; indeed; nay; nor yet; not a; not a single; not once; not one; not to say; or more; so far from; so much so that; such...that; very
梳／疏乎 (享受) comfortable; cosy
幾乎 almost; nearly
關乎 bear upon; relate to

【乏】fat⁶ lack

乏力 feeble; lacking in strength; weak
乏善可陳 have nothing good to report

缺乏 lack of

【仔】dzai² ① (兒子) son ② (孩子) children ③ boyfriend ④ young ⑤ (年輕人) young guy ⑥ surname-prefix to show friendliness or intimacy

仔大仔世界 (兒孫自有兒孫福) children who are grown-up should make their own decsions
仔女 (子女／兒女／孩子) one's children; sons and daughters
　　有兩個仔女 (有兩個子女) have two children
　　獨生仔女 (獨生子女) the only son and the only daughter
仔仔 (兒子) one's son
仔乸 (母子) mother and son
仔爺 (父子) father and son
　　兩仔爺 (父子兩人) father and son

一包煙仔 (一包香煙) a pack of cigarettes
一個仔 (一個兒子) a son
一個細路仔 (一個小孩) a child
一個碗仔 (一個小碗) a small bowl
一隻耳仔 (一隻耳朵) a ear
一隻兔仔 (一隻兔子) a rabbit
一隻碗仔 (一隻小碗) a small bowl
一條手巾仔 (一條小手帕) a handkerchief

一粒仔 (一個兒子) a son
一架 van 仔 (一輛小巴) a minibus
一竇貓仔 (一窩小貓) a litter of kitten
二五仔 (叛徒) ① traitor ② informer
八妹仔 (八卦的女生) nosy girl
刀仔 (小刀) small knife
三行仔 (泥水、木工和搭棚師傅) constructor
丸仔 (小藥丸) small pill
大仔 (大兒子) eldest son
大姐仔 (姑娘) young girl
大客仔 (重要的客戶) important client
女仔 (女子) girl
公仔 ① (洋娃娃) doll ② (卡通) cartoon
反斗仔 (搗蛋鬼) naughty boy
反骨仔 (吃裏爬外的人) a snake in sb's bosom; rebel; traitor
手巾仔 (手絹) handkerchief
手作仔 (手藝人) craftsman
牛仔 ① calf ② cowboy
世界仔 (阿諛奉承的人) man of the world; worldly boy; worldly man
仔仔 (兒子) one's son
氹細蚊仔 (哄小孩子) coax a child
出計仔 (出點子) offer advice; work out a way to deal with sth/sb
叻仔 (聰明的傢伙) smart chap; smart guy
古仔 (故事) story
古惑仔 (小混混) gangster; young villain
四眼仔 (戴眼鏡的男孩) a boy who wears glasses; a guy who wears spectacles; short-sighted boy
左優仔 (左撇子) left-hander
扒艇仔 (划船) row a boat
打工仔 (做工的人) employee; jobber boy; worker
打仔 (打手) body-guard; fighter
生仔 (生孩子) give birth to a boy
白痴仔 (白痴子) fool; stupid person
石仔 (小石) pebble
右耳仔 (左耳旁) the "town" (阝) radical
左耳仔 (右耳旁) the "mound" (阝) radical
光頭仔 (光頭的男人) bald man
后生仔 (年輕人) young lad
好靚仔 (好帥) very handsome
孖公仔 (經常在一起的兩人) two people who are constantly together
孖仔 (雙胞胎) twin boys; twin brothers
百厭仔 (淘氣鬼) naughty boy; naughty rascal; urchin
竹升仔 (放洋的中國男孩) young overseas Chinese boy
老人成嫩仔 (越活越年輕) once a man and twice a child
老土仔 (落伍的年輕人) old-fashioned boy
老公仔 steady boyfriend

老豆養仔仔養仔（爸爸養子，兒子卻只理會自己的兒子／
　有私心，無孝心）sons who support their fathers are rare

老婆仔 steady girlfriend

老鼠仔 ①（小老鼠）little mouse ②（小偷）thief
　③（二頭肌）bulging bicepts

耳仔（耳朵）ear

色仔（骰子）dice

吹波仔（呼氣酒精測試）breath alcohol test

奀仔（瘦弱的男孩）thin boy

我個仔（我的兒子）my son

扭耳仔（擰耳朵）bully sb

扯線公仔（木偶／傀儡）puppet

扰色仔（擲骰子）throw the dice

男仔（男孩子）boy; guy

芋頭仔（芋頭）eddoes

車仔 ①（人力車）rickshaw ②（手推車）trolley

乖仔（乖孩子）good child

侄仔（侄子）brother's son; nephew

侍仔（服務員）waiter

兒甥仔 ①（外甥）nephew ②　daughter's son

兔仔（兔子）rabbit

卒仔 ①（跟隨者）follower ②（小人物）small potato

叔仔（小叔子）brother-in-law

妹仔（丫頭／婢女）servant girl

姑仔（姑姑）aunt; father's younger sister

姑爺仔（老鴇）pimp

拉手仔／拖手仔（談戀愛）be occupied with finding a match;
　go steady; be in love; fall in love; be in a relationship; be
　in a loving relationship

孭仔（懷孕）pregnant

招積仔（傲慢的孩子）arrogant child; arrogant guy

果仔（水果）fruit

油脂仔（舉止浮誇、不切實際的早熟男孩）teddy boy

油瓶仔（繼子）step-son

狗仔（小狗）puppy

玩煮飯仔（玩家家酒）cooking for fun

畀人賣豬仔（被人賣豬仔）be cheated and taken advantage
　of by others; sb being sold like a piglet

肥仔（小胖子）fat boy; fatty

花靚／嘅仔（小伙子）little boy; little rascal; youngster of
　rascality

青頭仔（童男）virgin male

咬耳仔（耳語）have a word in one's ear; talk secretly;
　whisper to sb

契仔（乾兒子）adoptive son

姨仔（小姨子）aunt; sister-in-law

姪仔（姪子）nephew; the son of one's brother

客仔（客人）client; customer; patient; punter; shopper

巷仔（小巷）by-street; lane

後生仔（年輕人）chap; chappy; kiddo; lad; laddie; laddy;
　little fellow; sonny; stripling; young chap; young fellow;
　young lad; young man; youngster

恨仔（想生兒子）want to have a son

屋仔（小房子）small house

星軍仔（淘氣鬼）naughty child; urchin

紅簿仔（銀行存摺）bank passbook

缸仔（小杯）mug

計仔（點子）stratagem; trick; way

飛仔（小混混）gangster; teddy boy

食煙仔（抽煙）smoke; smoke a cigarette

個仔（的兒子）one's son

哥哥仔（年輕人）young man

孫仔（孫子）grandson

揹仔（揹孩子）carry one's child on the back

挽油瓶仔（喪夫攜子女再嫁）a woman's children by previous
　marriage; step-children

格仔（格子）check

桔仔（桔子）small mandarin orange

書仔（小冊子）booklet

蚊仔（蚊子）mosquito

衰仔（壞小子）little brat; little rascal

唔係三歲細路仔（不是三歲小孩）I wasn't born yesterday

釘仔（小釘子）small nail

追女仔（追女孩）chase after girls

馬仔 ①（侍從）attendant ②（跑腿／打手）bodyguard;
　hatchet man; henchman ③（低級職員）junior employee;
　subordinate ④（沙琪馬）candied rice fritter

鬼仔（年輕外國人）young foreigner/Westerner

鬼頭仔（內鬼）hidden traitor; informer; quisling

啞仔（啞巴）dumb

執仔（接生）practise midwifery

捱騾仔（當牛做馬）labour up to live on; work like a horse

排骨仔（瘦骨嶙峋的男孩）skinny boy

敗家仔（敗家子）black sheep; disgrace to the family;
　prodigal son; spendthrift; wastrel

眼公仔（眸子）pupil (of the eye)

細仔（細兒子）youngest son

細蚊／路仔（小孩子）child; kid

野仔（私生子）child born out of wedlock; illegitimate child;
　love child

雀仔（小鳥）bird

喫煙仔（喫煙）smoke; smoke a cigarette

單耳仔（單耳旁）the "single ear" 耳 radical

單身寡仔（單身漢）a man who is still unmarried; bachelor

㗎仔（日本男孩）Japanese boy

揞住耳仔（掩着耳朵）cover one's ears

散仔 ①（散工）job-work; odd jobs ②（臨時工）odd hand

棍仔（筷子）chopsticks

湊仔（帶孩子）babysit; look after one's child

睇女仔（看女孩子）look at girls

裙腳仔（媽寶）a boy who is dependent on his family mother

番鬼仔（西洋小孩）young foreigner/Westerner

跎仔（懷孕）be pregnant

黑仔（倒霉）① unlucky ② bad-luck guy

債仔（債務人）debtor

傻仔（傻子）① silly boy; silly fellow ② fool; simpleton

新仔（菜鳥）new recruit

煙仔（煙）cigarette

煮飯仔（擺家家）cook a simple meal

煲仔（小鍋）clay pot

矮仔（矮子）dwarf; short person

碗仔（小碗）small bowl

舅仔（舅舅）brother-in-law; wife's younger brother

腸仔 sausage

艇仔（小船）boat; small boat

落仔（墮胎）induced abortion

鉗仔（鉗子）forceps; pincers; pliers

賊仔（小偷）thief

辣椒仔（脾氣暴躁的男孩）short and sharp person

壽星仔（生日的男孩）birthday boy

歌仔（歌曲）song

碟仔（淺碟）saucer

綿羊仔 ①（綿羊）sheep ②（摩托車）motorcycle

精仔（精明的人）smart guy

趕鴨仔（導遊帶着一羣遊客走馬觀花）hurry along a group

銀仔（碎錢）coin; hard currency

閣仔（閣樓）attic; penthouse

喙石仔（打麻將）play mahjong

撈家仔（小流氓）person earning dishonest profits; racketeer

撩女仔（調戲女子）tease a girl

撩耳仔（挖耳朵）clean one's ears; pick the ears

熟客仔（熟客）frequent customer; old customer; regular customer

諗計仔（想點子）work out a way

賣豬仔（讓人誘騙去做苦工）sell sb like a piglet

靚／嘅（妹）仔（小伙子）little boy/girl; little rascal

靚仔（帥哥）handsome boy/guy/man

學友仔（同學）classmate

學師仔（學徒）apprentice; trainee

搣耳仔（扯耳朵）pull one's ear

樽仔（小瓶子）small bottle

獨生仔（獨生子）only son

錘仔（錘子）hammer

豬仔（小豬）piglet

貓仔（小貓）kitten

賭仔（賭徒）gambler

醒目仔（小機靈）clever boy; smart guy; smart kid

鴨仔 ①（小鴨）duckling ②（旅行團遊客）member of a tour group ③（學生遊客）student passengers taking a nanny van

孻仔（最細的兒子）youngest son

擦鞋仔（馬屁精）flunky

窿仔（小洞）small hole

膔蝦仔（男嬰兒）baby boy

講古仔（說故事）tell a story

擲色仔（擲骰子）throw the dice

櫈仔（櫈子）stool

薯仔 ①（土豆）potato ②（傻子）fool

蟲仔（蟲害）pest

雞仔（小雞）chicken; springer

雞春咁密都褓出仔（紙包不住火）no secret can be kept

鎚仔（鎚子）hammer

懵仔（傻子）fool

矇眼仔（蠢子）stupid boy

繩仔（繩子）small cord; small string

蘇蝦仔（男嬰兒）baby boy

爛仔（流氓）hooligan

蘿蔔仔（凍瘡）chilblain

蠱惑仔（小混混）gangster; young villain

BB 仔（男嬰兒）baby boy

van 仔（小型貨車）van

【他】taa¹ he; him

他人 another person; other people; others; sb else
　　尊重他人 respect for others

他條（優哉遊哉／從容／舒坦／優閒）go easy
　　他他條條（優哉游哉／從容不迫）go easy

他鄉 alien land; other lands; place far away from home
　　客死他鄉 die abroad; die in a strange land

其他 other

結他 guitar

彈結他 play the guitar

【仗】zoeng⁶ battle

仗勢 take advantage of one's power or connection with influential people
　　仗勢欺人 abuse one's power and bully the people; bully others because one has power; bully people on the strength of one's powerful connections; bully the weak on one's power; make use of sb's position to bully others; pull one's rank on others; rely on sb else's power to bully people; take advantage of one's own power to bully people; take one's position to lord it over and insult people; throw one's weight about; trust to one's power and insult people

仗義 rely on a sense of justice
　仗義執言 speak boldly in defence of justice; speak in accordance with justice; speak out from a sense of justice/to uphold justice; speak straightforwardly for justice

大陣仗 ① （排場大）go in for an ostentation ② （大件事）big deal; big fuss
炮仗 （鞭炮）firecracker
喺門角落頭燒炮仗 （打扮整齊卻無處可去）all dressed up and have nowhere to go
燒炮仗 （放鞭炮）let off firecrackers

【付】fu⁶ pay
付出 pay sth off
　付出代價 pay a price
付款 payment
　分期付款 instalment

兌付 cash a cheque
拒付 refuse payment
應付 deal with

【仙】sin¹ （分）cent
仙子 ① fairy maiden; female celestial ② celestial being; fairy; immortal
仙女 fairy
　仙女下凡 a fairy descending to the mundane world
仙屎 （分）(transliteration) cents
　一個仙屎 （一分錢）one cent
仙都唔仙吓 （一分錢也沒有）very poor

一仙 （一分錢）one cent
一個仙 （一分錢）one cent
八仙 Eight Immortals
巴仙 （百分之）percent
升仙 （上天堂了）die; pass away
水仙 narcissus
生神仙 （算命師傅）fortune-telling person
神仙 fairy
過咗海就係神仙 （過了關便成了）using whatever means would be alright/all right as long as goals are achieved
瘦骨仙 （很瘦的人）very thin

【代】doi⁶ represent
代表 represent
　代表作 magnum opus; representative work
　代表團 contingent; delegation; deputation; mission

代理 agency
　代理人 agent
　　單邊代理 （單方代理）single agency
　　雙邊代理 （雙方代理）dual agency
代詞 pronoun
代價 cost; price
代課 substitute teacher

九十年代 the nineties
世代 generation
世世代代 generation after generation
交代 ① account for; brief; explain; justify oneself; make clear; tell ② hand over; transfer; turn over
年代 ① age ② generation
取代 displace; replace; step into sb's shoes; substitute for; supersede; supplant; take for
後代 descendants
現代 modern
朝代 dynasty
幾代 （幾世代）several generations

【令】ling⁶ ① （使）make ② （您的）your
令人 arouse; cause; make; make people
令郎 your son
令尊 your father

下命令 issue an order
司令 commander; commanding officer
打令 （親愛的）darling
命令 order
服從命令 obey orders
花士令 （凡士林）(transliteration) vaseline
急口令 （繞口令）tongue twister
省到立立令 （口頭上狠狠地教訓一頓）give sb a dressing down
夏令 ① summer; summertime ② summer weather
啤令 （軸承）bearing
接受命令 take orders
執行命令 carry out orders; execute orders
赦令 decree for pardon
當時得令 （行時）in season; win popularity
號令 order; verbal command; whistle
總司令 commander-in-chief

【以】ji⁵ because of
以上 above; and upwards; in excess of; more than; or above; over; upwards up
以下 below; less than; no more than; under
以牙還牙 a tooth for a tooth; an eye for an eye; answer

blows with blows; fight fire with fire; give as good as one
gets; like for like; repay evil with evil; return blow for
blow; return like for like; tit for tat; tooth for tooth

以和為貴 make peace

以物換物 barter; exchange of goods; exchange of
one commodity for another; trade one thing
against another

以前 ago; before; ex-; former; formerly; in the past; old;
once; past; previous; prior to; since; used to be
以前嘅事 (以前的事) things of the past
好耐以前 (很久以前) a long time ago; long
ago; (informal) since the year dot; time out
of mind

以後 ① after; afterward; from then on; hereafter; later;
later on; since then; subsequent to ② at a later date
從今以後 from now on

以為 assume; regard as; think

以寡敵眾 a few against many

予以 give; grant
可以 be able to; can
所以 hence; therefore
唔可以 (不可以) be unable to; cannot
難以 difficult to; hard to

【兄】 hing¹ elder brother

兄台 (閣下) you
兄弟 brothers
兄弟姐妹 brothers and sisters
好兄弟 good mates
叔伯兄弟 cousins; sons of paternal uncles
堂兄弟 cousins
襟兄弟 (連襟) husbands of two sisters
難兄難弟 fellow sufferers; two of a kind
兄嫂 one's elder brother and his wife

仁兄 my dear friend
弟兄 brothers
師兄 ① senior male apprentice ② senior male schoolmate
③ son of one's master
堂兄 elder male cousin; first cousin
硯兄 (學長) elder classmate

【冚】 ham⁶ all

冚唪唥 / 辦欄 (全部) all; all of a lump; any and
every; by the lump; complete; entire; full; in a lump/
one/the lump; lock, stock, and barrel; one and all;
the entire shoot; the whole; total; without
exception

【冚】 kam² cover

冚冚 (蓋緊) cover tightly
冚住 (遮蔽 / 蓋着 / 覆蓋) cover up
冚到密 (封鎖消息) block the passage of information; keep
one's mouth shut
冚到實 (不走漏風聲) not to breathe a word about sth
冚埋 (蓋住) cover up
冚被 (蓋被子) cover with a blanket
冚蓋 (蓋蓋兒) cover with a lid
冚旗 ① (死) die ② (不載乘客) (taxi) out of service
冚國旗 (死) die
冚賭 (抓賭博) smash a gambling party
冚檔 / 竇 (查封 / 停業 / 倒閉) close down

天跌落嚟當被冚 (心態從容) take it easy
沙冚 (擋泥板) fender board
牀冚 (牀罩) bedspread
被冚 (被罩) bedsheet
墟冚 (亂哄哄) as bustling as a market; in a bustle
鏈冚 (鏈罩) chain cover; chain guard

【冊】 caak³ volume

冊子 book; volume
冊頁 album of calligraphy/paintings

入冊 (入獄) be imprisoned; be jailed; be shut behind the
bars; be taken off to prison; commit a person to prison;
go to prison; in jail; in prison; lay sb by the heels; put into
prison; run in; send to prison
出冊 (出獄) be discharged/released from prison
註冊 register
簿冊 books and files; lists

【冬】 dung¹ winter

冬大過年 Winter Solstice is more important than the
Chinese New Year
冬天 winter
冬瓜 winter melon
冬瓜豆腐 (三長兩短) die
冬瓜盅 winter melon soup
大冬瓜 fat man
煲 / 刨冬瓜 (普通話) Putonghua
倒瓤冬瓜 (身體不好) a person who is strong in
appearance but poor in health
冬甩 (甜甜圈) (transliteration) doughnut
冬至 Winter Solstice
冬泳 winter swimming
冬菇 dried mushroom
冬菇湯 dried mushroom soup

燉冬菇（降職）demotion

冬筍 bamboo shoot

做冬（過冬至節）celebrate the Winter Solstice Festival

【凸】dat⁶ convex

凸出嚟（凸出來）stick out

凸字（盲文）braille character

凸起 convex

凸點 smarties

凹凹凸凸 bumpy; full of bumps and holes; lumpy; rough

有凸（有餘）have a surplus; have enough to spare

眼凸凸（眼瞪瞪）with bulging eyes

激到眼凸凸（氣得眼瞪瞪）the anger is swelling

【凹】nap¹ concave

凹凹凸凸（坑坑注注）bumpy; full of bumps and holes; lumpy; rough

凹凸印（鋼印）steel seal

凹咗／落去（凹了進去）cave in; concave

酒凹（酒鍋）dimple

【出】ceot¹ ①（外）out ②（出來）come out

出人頭地 come out first

出入 ① in and out ② difference

　出入口（進出口）import and export

　　出入口公司（進出口公司）import and export company

　出入平安 may you be safe wherever you go

　出出入入／行出行入（出出進進／進進出出）coming in and out; in and out; shuttle in and out

　自由出入 free to go or stay

出力（用力／使勁兒）exert all one's strength; put in energy

出千（出騙術）cheat

出口 ① export ② exit ③ what comes out from the mouth

　出口成文／章 be eloquent

　　緊急出口 emergency exit

　　難以出口（難以啟齒）be too embarrassed to say

出山（出殯）carry a coffin to the cemetery to hold a funeral procession

出公數（公家報銷）apply for reimbursement from an organisation

出手 ①（出錢）money ②（提出／給予）offer ③（打）hit out

　出手低 ① low offer ②（出錢少）not so generous with one's money

出水紙（提貨單）bill of lading

出牙（長牙）teethe; tooth eruption

出世（出生）born

　出世紙（出生證明）birth certificate

出冊（出獄）be discharged/released from prison

出去 get out

出名 famous; well-known

出年（明年）next year

出色 outstanding

出血 bleed

　大出血（大減價）big sale

出身 ① one's family background ②（自食其力）begin the world; start earning one's living

出車（掙快錢）make easy money

出事 ① cause the accident; ① cause the problem

出招 make a strategic move

出奇（特別）extraordinarily; unusually

　唔出奇（沒奇怪的）not surprising

　唔出奇吖（沒甚麼奇怪的）there's nothing strange about sth

出版 come off the press; come out; give to the world; publish; see the light of day

出返啖氣（出口氣）vent one's spleen on

出門 ①（外出）away from home; go out ②（嫁出去）marry off

出便（出面／外邊）outside

出面（站出來代人處理問題）act as a mediator

出風癩（起風疙瘩）urticarial

出差（公幹）on a business trip

出息 ① promising ② high-minded

　冇出息（沒出息）futureless

出氣 ① release gas ② let off steam by losing one's temper; vent one's anger; vent one's disgust on sb; vent one's spleen

出番啖氣（出一口氣）get one's own back

出恭（上廁所／大便／拉屎）① clear one's bowel; defecate; dump; egest; empty/move/evacuate the bowels; go boom-boom; go number two; go potty; have a bowel movement/loose bowels; relieve oneself/the bowels; the bowel moves; void excrement ② faeces; human excrement; shit; stool; turd

出海 go out to the sea

出疹（出疹子／出麻疹）suffer from measles

出租 for rent; to let

出院 be discharged from the hospital

出馬（出動）deal with; tackle a problem/a situation; take the field

出骨（不掩飾的／明顯）undisguised

出售 sale

　出售面積 saleable area

出術（耍花招）device means

出麻（出疹子／出麻疹）suffer from measles

出痘（出水痘）suffer from chickenpox

出街 ①（上街／外出）go out; go out into the street
　　②（said of TV show）（播映）broadcast; on air
　　③（said of publications）put on the market for sale
　　出街食（在外面吃）dine out; eat out
　　　一個人出街（一個人逛街）go out into the street alone
　　　出咗街（去了街）has gone out

出爾反爾 go back on one's words

出盡八寶（使盡法寶）have exerted one's utmost skill

出價 offer

出賣 betray

出貓（考試作弊）cheat in an examination; exercise fraud in
　　an examination

出頭 become successful

出聲 ①（吭聲）raise one's voice; voice; utter a word
　　② speak out
　　唔出聲（不作聲）keep silent; remain silent
　　唔好出聲（不要作聲）keep quiet; keep silent
　　驚到唔識出聲（嚇得說不出話來）too panic to make
　　　any utterance

出醜 incur disgrace

出嚟（出來）go out
　　出嚟做（做妓女）start a career as a prostitute
　　出嚟撈 ①（走江湖）drift about in the world to engage in
　　　dishonest work ②（做妓女）prostitute oneself
　　出嚟蒲（走江湖）make a living in the criminal
　　　underworld
　　出嚟擺（做妓女）be a prostitute

出糧（發工資／發薪）pay salary; pay wages

出邊 outside

出爐 come out newly
　　新鮮出爐 fresh from the oven

出籠（上名）product released on the market

出鶴哥 plot a conspiracy

支出 ① disburse; expend; pay ② expenditure; outlay

日出 sunrise

水落石出 come out in the wash

付出 pay sth off

外出 be out

左耳入，右耳出（literally）go in one ear and out the other,
　　meaning that one does not pay any attention

打出 reveal; show

矛盾百出 full of contradictions

列出 list; make out; write out

伸出 extend; project; overhang; reach; runout

使出 exert; use

拔出 draw out; extract; pull out

沽出（賣出）sell

保釋外出 release on bail

指出 point out

查出 detect; find out

突出 outstanding

娩出 be delivered of a child; give birth to

展出 exhibit; put on display; on show

挺身而出 bell the cat; bolster oneself up; come forward
　　courageously; come out boldly; stand up and volunteer
　　to help; step forth bravely; step forward boldly/bravely;
　　thrust oneself forward to face a challenge

破綻百出 full of flaws/holes/loopholes; ragged; in tatters

售出 sell; succeed in selling

登出 log off

屙唔出（拉不出來）cannot pull out the excrement

粒聲唔出（一聲不吭）keep quiet; not to utter a
　　single sound

復出 come out again; come out of retirement again

揪出 ferret out

勝出 win/achieve/gain a victory

量入為出 keep one's expenditures within one's limits of income;
　　live within one's means; measure one's needs to one's
　　income

湧出 spring out; well out

搾出 squeeze out

撤出 evacuate; withraw

播出 airing; broadcast

衝出 rush out

輩出 appear one after another; come forth in large numbers;
　　come out in succession

褪出（溜出去）slip out

講唔出（講不出）cannot say

飄出 blow out

【出】tsoet[7] go out

出位 ①（破格兒）make a name for oneself ②（出格）
　　exceed proper limits for speech or action; exceed what is
　　proper; go too far; overdo sth
　　出晒位（出風頭）beyond expectations
　　　搏出位（搶風頭）try and make a name for oneself

【刊】hon[2] publish

刊行 print and publish

刊物 publication

刊登 carry; publish

週刊 weekly magazine

季刊 quarterly; quarterly publication

【功】 gung[1] merit

功夫 (transliteration) kung fu; (武術) martial art
　　下功夫 concentrate one's efforts; devote time and effort to a task; put in time and energy
　　中國功夫 Chinese kung fu
　　打功夫 practise martial art
　　使出真功夫 (展示實力) show one's real power
　　硬功夫 (紮實的本領) great proficiency

功名 scholarly honour and official rank
　　功名富貴 fame and fortune; fame, riches, and honours; officialdom, wealth, and fame; rank, success, fame, and riches

功利 material gains; utility
　　急功近利 anxious to achieve quick success and get instant benefits; eager for quick success and instant benefits; seek quick success and instant benefits

功能 function

功過 merits and demerits

功課 (家課) homework
　　做功課 do schoolwork

冇陰功 (多可憐) how sad

成功 success

見功 (見效果) become effective; provide the desired effect

徒勞無功 an ass for one's pains; beat the air; draw water in a sieve; drop a bucket into an empty well; flog a dead horse; labour in vain; labour to no purpose; make a futile effort; make useless trouble; milk a he-goat; not to succeed after trying hard; prove futile; sow the sands; use vain efforts; wasted effort; work to no avail; work without achieving anything

陰功 (可憐) pitiful

邀功 take credit for sb else's achievements

【加】 gaa[1] add

加一 (加一成收費) ten percent surcharge; ten percent service charge
　　加一服務費 (加一成服務費) ten per-cent service charge
　　　免加一 (免加一成收費) waive the ten-percent service charge

加大 extra large
　　加大碼 (加大號) extra large size

加元 (加拿大元) Canadian dollar

加水 refill the teapot

加多個位 (加一個位子) put in an extra seat

加把口 (幫腔) give verbal support to a person; speak in support of sb

加底 (白飯或麵粉要加倍份量) increase the bulk of food

加油 ① (吶喊鼓勵) go for it ② (加把勁) make extra efforts ③ (給汽車補加燃料) refuel

加長 lengthen

加埋 (加起來) add up to...
　　加埋晒 (全加起來) add up to
　　加加埋埋 (全都加起來) add together

加拿大 Canada
　　加拿大人 Canadian

加班 work overtime

加料 (加勁兒) make a greater effort

加細 (加小) extra small
　　加細碼 (加小號) extra small

加零一 (透頂) in the extreme; to the utmost

加價 (漲價) increase the price; raise prices; rise in price

加餸 (加菜) add more dishes

加鹽加醋 (誇張誇大) exaggerate; lay on thicker colours

仲加 (更) all the more; even more; further; more; still more

倍加 double; extraordinarily; increase by one fold

參加 participate; take part in

增加 increase

【包】 baau[1] ① wrap up ② bun

包尾大番 (最後一名) come out last

包底 (包圓兒) promise to pay money until it's enough

包保 (準保) guarantee

包括 include

包埋 (包括在內) include

包租公 (男房東) sub-landlord

包租婆 (女房東) sub-landlady

包剪揼 (包剪錘) scissors and stones

包紮 (包紮) bandage

包單 (承擔 / 保證) guarantee
　　打包單 / 寫包單 (保證) guarantee; vouch

包袱 ① a bundle wrapped in cloth ② burden; liability; load; weight
　　執包袱 (革職) be fired

包粟 millet

包裹 parcel

包斷尾 (保證根治) guarantee to remove the root of an illness

包羅萬有 (各式各樣) all-embracing; all-inclusive; cover a wide range; cover and contain everything; inclusive of everything

一個書包 a school bag

一個銀包 a purse

一齊包 (包起來) pack things together; wrap things together

一籠叉燒包 a basket of barbeque pork buns
一籠奶皇包 a basket of sweet cream buns
一籠蓮蓉包 a basket of lotus-seed paste buns
叉燒包 barbeque pork bun
叉燒餐包 baked barbeque pork bun
上海小籠包 Shanghai steamed meat dumpling
小籠包 steamed meat dumpling
公事包 suitcase
分開包 pack things separately; wrap things separately
方包 (白麵包) white bread
奶皇包 sweet cream bun
打包 put the leftovers into a doggy bag
打荷包 (搶錢包) pick a pocket; pick-pocket; purse
　　snatching
生菜包 lettuce wrap
拋書包 (賣弄學問) show off one's knowledge
承包 contract
枕頭包 pillow-shaped bread
炕麵包 (烘麵包) bake bread
紅包 red packet
陋包 (粗笨) bulky; cumbersome; heavy; unwieldy
倒吊荷包 (花冤枉錢而無可奈何) invite losses for oneself
書包 school bag
流沙包 bun with creamy egg yolk
茶包 tea bag
捱麵包 (捱窮) struggle to make a living
荷包 (錢包) purse; wallet
眼淚包 (愛哭鬼) crying baby
頂包 (冒名頂替) pass sb off as
魚柳包 fish burger
麥包 wheat bread
喊包 (愛哭鬼) children who like crying; crying baby
菠蘿包 pineapple-shaped bun
漢堡包 hamburger
銀包 (錢包) purse; wallet
賣大包 (便宜售出) bargain away; off a good bargain to
　　buyers; sell sth cheaply
錢包 purse; wallet
豬油包 (不機靈的人) someone who moves or
　　reacts slowly
蓮蓉包 lotus-seed paste bun
雞尾包 cocktail bun

【匆】cung¹ hurry
匆匆 (匆匆 / 匆忙) hastily; hurriedly
　　匆匆而去 hurry away; leave in a hurry; pop off;
　　　　scoot off
　　匆匆而來 come in great haste
匆忙 hurry; in a hurry

【北】bak⁷ ① north ② northern
北上 (去國內) go north (to mainland China)
北方 north
　　北方人 northerner
北京 Beijing; Peking
　　北京菜 Beijing food
　　北京填鴨 Peking duck
北邊 ① (北方) north ② (北部) northern part

東北 ① (東北方) northeast ② (中國東北) northeast China
羅通掃北 (掃清光) make a clean sweep of everything

【半】bun³ half
半山坳 (山腰) mid-slope of a mountain
半天吊 (不上不下的) hang in the balance; in a
　　stalemate
半斤 half catty
　　半斤八兩 as broad as it is long; as long as it is broad;
　　　　fifty-fifty; half a pound of one and eight ounces of
　　　　the other; much of a muchness; not much to choose
　　　　between the two; nothing to choose between the two;
　　　　six of one and half a dozen of the other; tweedledum
　　　　and tweedledee; well-match in ability
　　　　你有半斤，我有八兩 six of one and half a dozen of
　　　　　the other
半日 (半天) half a day; half day
半生熟 (不生不熟) medium; medium-cooked
半杯茶 half a cup of tea
半夜 (夜半) midnight
　　半夜三更 in the depth of night; late at night
　　半夜食黃瓜 —— 不知頭定尾 (不知頭尾) make neither
　　　　head nor tail of sth
半信半疑 be not quite convinced
半個鐘 (半小時) half an hour
半唐番 (中外混血兒) Westernised Chinese
半勒卡 incomplete; unfinished
半桶水 (一知半解) a little knowledge of sth
半粒鐘 (半小時) half an hour
半晝 (中午) noon
半價 half price
半截裙 (半身裙) skirt
半點鐘 (半小時) half an hour
半鹹淡 (不標準) sub-standard

一半 half; half of it; one half
一半一半 fifty fifty
一點半 (一點半鐘) half past one; one thirty
小半 lesser part
天一半，地一半 (分散四處) all over the place

斤半 (一斤半) one and a half catties
另一半 other half; spouse
四塊半 (棺材) coffin
夜半 midnight
兩點半 half past two
個半 (一個半) one dollar and fifty cents; one dollar fifty

【占】zim¹ ① divine ② jam

占卜 fortune-telling
占卦 divination; divine by the Eight Diagrams; tell by divination
　　占卦算命 (占卦算命) divine one's fortune

果占 (果醬) jam

【卡】kaa¹ ① car; carriage ② card

卡士 (演員表 / 陣容) (transliteration) cast
　　大卡士 (陣容頂盛) all-star cast
卡片 (名片) name card
　　一張卡片 (一張名片) a name card
卡式 (transliteration) cassette
卡曲 (車皮套) (transliteration) car coat
卡位 (廂座) balcony seat; booth
卡住 get stuck; seize
卡車 autotruck; lorry; truck
卡拉 OK (Japanese) karaoke
　　唱卡拉 OK sing in the karaoke
卡紙 cardboard
卡通片 (動畫片) cartoon
　　卡通片集 (動畫片集) cartoon series
卡路里 (transliteration) calorie
卡罅 ① (模棱兩可) equivocal ② (裂縫 / 縫隙) the crevice between two things

一卡車卡 a railway carriage; a train
半勒卡 (未完成) incomplete; unfinished
生日卡 birthday card
甩卡 (不連貫的) be disjointed
投票通知卡 poll card
車卡 (車廂) car; carriage; coach; compartment
拖卡 (拖車) trailer
勒勒卡卡 (口吃) hesitate in speaking; stammer; stumble over; stutter
貨卡 (貨車) freight train; goods train
聖誕卡 Christmas card
電話卡 (手機卡) calling card
蒲士卡 (明信片) (transliteration) post card
餐卡 (餐車) buffet car; dining car; restaurant car
IDD 電話卡 (國際直撥卡) IDD (International Direct Dialling) calling card

【去】heoi³ go

去一趟 (去一次 / 去一回) make a trip
去水 (排水) drain
　　去水渠 (排水溝) drain
去死 go to hell
　　去死啦 go to hell
去咗 ① (去了) has gone to ② (去世) has passed away
　　去咗 trip (到外地出差) be on a business trip
去威 (吃喝玩樂) go out for a good time; hang about; hang around; hang out; hang round
去馬 (上馬) go ahead
去骨 (剔去骨頭) boned
　　去骨肉 (剔去骨頭和肉) boned meat
去街 ① (溜街) go into the street; go on the street ② (外出) go out
去揾周公 (去睡覺) go to bed; go to sleep
去飲 (喝喜酒 / 赴宴) go to a wedding banquet
去蒲 (去玩 / 吃喝玩樂) go onto the streets to hang out; go out for a good time; hang about; hang around; hang out; hang round
去 ball (參加舞會) go to a ball
去 BBQ (去燒烤) go for a barbeque
去 cocktail (參加雞尾酒會) go to a cocktail party
去 disco (泡的士高) go to the discotheque
去 wet (去玩 / 吃喝玩樂) go out for a good time; go out for fun

一齊去 (一起去) go together
入去 (進去) enter; get in; go in
上去 go up
下去 descend; go down
凹落去 (塌落) cave in; concave
出去 get out
匆匆而去 hurry away; leave in a hurry; pop off; scoot off
左手嚟，右手去 (漏走) in at one hand and out at the other
由佢去 (由他 / 她去) do as one's like
行路去 (走路) go on foot
車入去 (開車進去) drive in
爬上去 climb up
直去 (往直走) go straight
返去 (回去) go back
飛個電話去 (撥個號碼) give sb a quick call
飛嚟飛去 (飛來飛去) flying to and fro
埋去 (靠近) go near; go over
留戀過去 (戀舊) yearn for the past
跂個頭出去 (伸出頭來) stretch out one's head
略去 (刪去) delete; leave out; omit
逝去 be gone; depart; pass
冤枉嚟瘟疫去 (不義之財永無久享) ill gotten, ill spent

舂入去（闖進去）rush in
舂落去（栽進）crash down
嵌入去（深深地固定）set sth in
睇上去（看上去）it seems; look
想去 wish to go to
搬入去（搬進去）move in
搬去（搬進）move to
搵得嚟使得去（來得容易去得快）easy come, easy go; light come, light go
㩧入去（塞進去）stuff sth into sth
落去（下去）go down
落狗屎都要去（多壞的天氣也要去）will go regardless of weather conditions
跟埋我去（跟我一起去）come along with me
過去 in the past
過得去（還可以）not too bad; passable
撳上去（爬上去）climb up
澎出去（突然出現）go up and dash out suddenly
監硬揾我去（強行拉着我去）drag me in by force
㩧出去（把某人攆走）drive sb away; drive sb out of the door; expel; kick out of; kick sb downstairs; oust; put sb to the door; see the back of sb; send sb about his business; send sb packing; send sb to the right-abut about; show sb the door; throw out; turn out sb; turn sb out of doors; turn sb out of the house
瞓個身落去（全身心投進去）put all one's investment into sth
擒上去（爬上去）climb up
擒嚟擒去（爬來爬去）climb all over furniture
搵埋佢去（找他／她一起去）get him along
踭得過去（挺過去）can overcome sth
剟入去（擠進去）stuff in
講得過去（說得還可以）justifiable
鯁落去（嚥下去）swallow sth in a hard way
辭去 resign
躝出去（滾出去）go away

【叻】lek[1] ① (棒／有本事／了不起／厲害／機靈) smart ② (專長) good at sth

叻女（聰明的女孩）clever girl; smart girl
叻仔（聰明的小伙子）smart chap; smart guy

冇樣叻（不濟／沒有一樣好）good for nothing
好叻（真了不起）① very good ② very smart
真係叻（真厲害）you're great
鬥叻（比本事）measure one's skill against one's rival
精叻（精明靈活）bright; capable; intelligent; smart
認叻（自誇）boast; brag
懶叻（想拔尖兒）play the smart guy

逞叻（逞強）act up; parade one's ability; show off one's ability or skill

【古】gu[2] ① (舊) old ② (故事) story

古人 ancients
前無古人 have no parallel in history; no one has ever attempted anything of this kind; peerless; unknown in history; unparallelled in history; unprecedented in history; without parallel in history; without precedent in history
古今 the ancient and the modern
古今中外 at all times and in all countries; both ancient and modern, Chinese and foreign; classical and modern, Chinese and foreign; in China or elsewhere, in modern or ancient times; in the past or present, in China or anywhere else in the world; past and present, at home and abroad; whether in China or other lands, in ancient or today
古月粉（胡椒粉）ground pepper
古仔（故事）story
古老 ① ancient ② old-fashioned
古老石山（古老石山）① old-fashioned ② old fogy
古老當時興（古老當時髦）the old-fashioned is treated as the trendy
古色古香 air of antiquity; antique; quaint; be beautiful in the traditional style; classic beauty; having an antique flavour; in ancient styles; of ancient flavour; smack of sth classical in its design
古典 ① (古典的) classical ② (典故) classical allusions
古怪（蹊蹺）odd; strange
古古怪怪（古怪）bats; bizzare; cranky; eccentric; erratic; flaky; funky; gnarled; odd; ornery; quaint; queer; quizzical; strange; uncouth; wacky; wayward; whimsical; whimsy; wonder
有古怪（有蹊蹺）that's very extraordinary
古惑（古惑）crafty; cunning; tricksy
古惑女（女小滑頭）young female villain
古惑友（鬼計多端的人）tricky person
古惑仔（小滑頭）gangster; young villain
古董 ① antique; curio ② (老頑固) old fogey
古董店 antique shop
一件古董 an antique
老古董 ① antique; museum piece; old-fashioned article ② (老頑固) fuddy-duddy; old fogey; ultra-conservative
古裝（古裝）ancient costume
古裝片（古裝戲劇）ancient-costume drama
古裝電影（古裝戲）costume movie
古裝劇 costume drama

古裝戲（古裝劇）costume play

古銅色（赤褐色）sun-tanned colour

古縮（古板）conservative; old-fashioned; old-fashioned and inflexible; quiet and unsocial

古靈精怪（稀奇古怪）bizarre; funny; queer

仿古 model after an antique

鬼古（鬼故事）ghost story

整古（作弄）trick

講古（講故事）storytelling

講鬼古（講鬼故事）tell a ghost story

鹹古（色情故事）pornographic story

覽古 tour ancient relics

【句】goei³ sentence

句子 sentence

句法 ① sentence structure ② syntax

句號 full point; full stop; period

一句 a line; a word

心嗰句，口嗰句（大馬金刀）say what one thinks; speak one's mind

冇七兩句（不大熟落）have no relationship with

同人冇七兩句（與那人沒有啥好說的）one does not have any argument with another person

灶君上天——有句講句（與君坦白）be frank with one's opinions; outspoken; say whatever one likes

佳句 beautiful lines in a poem; well-turned phrases

砌句（造句）build sentences

請你為我美言幾句（請替我講好話）please put in a good word for me

【另】ling⁶ separate

另外 moreover

另行 at some other time; separately

【叩】kau³ knock

叩門（敲門）knock at the door

叩門求見（叩門求見）knock at the door and ask for an interview

叩門磚（敲門磚）a means to find favour with an influential person; a stepping stone to one's purpose

叩頭（磕頭）kowtow

【只】zi² only

只可（只能）can only

只因 for the simple reason that; only because

只好 have to; the next best thing to do is to; the only alternative is to

只有 ① alone; only ② have to

只是 ① but; yet ② just; merely; only

只要 ① want only ② all one has to do is to

只得 be obliged to; have to; there is no alternative

唔淨只（不單）not only

【叫】giu³ call

叫座（賣座）appeal to the audience; draw a large audience; draw well

叫起手（隨時）anytime; as the occasion demands; at all times; at any time; whenever

叫做（叫）is called; so-called

叫菜 order dishes

叫多個菜（叫多一碟菜）order one more dish

叫價（售價）asked price; asking price

每方呎叫價（每方呎售價）asked price per square foot

叫雞（召妓）visit a prostitute

尖叫 scream

呱呱叫 ① complain ② make a lot of noise

呼叫 ① call out; shout ② call; ring

【召】ziu⁶ summon

召回 recall

召集 call together; convene; draw together

召集人 convener

召開 convene; convoke

提前召開 convene before the due date

號召 appeal; call; draw

應召 work as a prostitute

【叮】ding¹ exhort repeatedly

叮叮（電車）tram

搭叮叮（乘電車）take the tram

叮噹 clank; clatter

叮噹馬頭（不相伯仲）difficult to tell which one has outdone the other; very hard to tell which one is better

叮囑 exhort; repeatedly advise; urge again and again; warn

千叮萬囑 exhort sb repeatedly; give advice repeatedly; give many exhortations to sb; warn again and again

【可】ho² can

可口 dainty; delectable; delicious; good to eat; luscious; palatable; savoury; tasty

可大可小 it may be either serious or unimportant

可以 be able to; can

唔可以（不能夠）be unable to; cannot

可怕 terrible
可能 possible
　　冇乜可能 (沒可能) it's out of the question; unlikely
　　冇可能 (不可能) it's out of the question; unlikely
　　好可能 likely
　　有可能 be on the cards
可惜 pity
可愛 likable; lovable; lovely
可憐 miserable; pity
　　扮可憐 (裝可憐) ① play pitiful; pretend to be pitiful
　　　② play miserable; pretend to be miserable
　　唔抵可憐 (不值得可憐) not deserving one's sympathy
可靠 dependable; reliable; trustworthy

不可 (不能夠 / 禁止) be forbidden; cannot; must not; not
　　allowed; should not
只可 (只能) can only
尚可 ① acceptable; passable ② still permissible; still possible
缺一不可 (一個都不能少) none of them can be dispensed
　　with; not a single one can be omitted; not one of them
　　can be excluded
許可 allow; approve; clearance; consent; give permission;
　　licence; licensing; permit
寧可 would rather

【台】 toi⁴ ① raised platform ② (桌子) table

台型 good-looking
台柱 ① (戲班中的主要演員) important actor in a troupe
　　② important person in an organisation
台風 stage manners
台灣 Taiwan
　　台灣菜 Taiwanese food

一圍台 (一桌) a table
大陽台 terrace
天台 (曬台) roof
天文台 ① observatory ② look-out
兄台 (閣下) you
平台 flat roof
打對台 act the opposite; challenge sb with opposing views;
　　compete with sb with a countermeasure; enter into
　　rivalry; put on a rival show; set oneself up against; set up
　　a rival stage in opposition to
打擂台 (要求與某人決鬥) rise to the challenge; take up the
　　challenge
有後台 (背後有人撐腰) have support behind the scenes
地台 (地面) flooring
收銀台 cashier
後台 (背後有連繫) contacts behind the scenes

茅台 Maotai
柴台 (喝倒采) boo; discourage sb; hoot; make catcalls
趴台 (俯身於桌上) bend over the table
校台 (調校頻道) tune the channels
追台 (調校頻道) tune the channels
窗台 ① bay window ② window ledge; windowsill
陽台 veranda
落台 (下台) step down
電台 radio station
舞台 stage
寫字台 (寫字桌) writing desk
擂台 arena; ring
燭台 candlestick
露台 (陽台) balcony
櫃台 bar; counter
擺擂台 (比武較量) give an open challenge
轉台 (轉台 / 轉頻道) switch over
臨時舞台 (臨時替代的舞台) makeshift stage

【史】 si² history

史料 historical data; historical materials
史實 historical facts
史學 historiography

廿四史 (二十四史) twenty-four histories
血淚史 heart-rending story; sad story
歪曲歷史 distort history; garble history
威水史 (豐功偉績) famous achievements
歷史 history

【右】 jau⁶ right

右手 right hand
　　右手便 / 手面 (右邊) right-hand side
右便 (在右邊) on the right side
右軚 (右邊駕駛盤) right-hand drive
右軚車 (右邊駕駛盤汽車) right-hand drive vehicle
右翼 right wing
　　右翼人士 (右翼份子) right-winger
右轉 (右拐) turn right
右邊 (在右方) on the right; right-hand side; right side

左右 ① (左與右) left and right ② (大約 / 差不多) about;
　　around
隔籬左右 (左右四鄰) neighbours
轉右 (右轉 / 右拐 / 向右) turn right

【司】 si¹ preside over

司令 commander; commanding officer
　　總司令 commander-in-chief

司法 administration of justice; judicature
司法部門 judicial department
司機 (師傅) driver

上司 direct boss; superior officer
公司 company; firm; shop
分公司 branch
出入口公司 (進出口公司) import and export company
百貨公司 department store
色司 (性感的) (transliteration) sexy
行公司 (逛公司) ① (逛百貨公司) go shopping; visit department stores ② (溜街) strolling around the streets ③ (逛街看櫥窗) window shopping
行吓公司 (逛街看櫥窗) do some window shopping
奉承上司 play up to one's superiors
官司 lawsuit
返公司 (回公司) go to office
返到公司 (回到公司) arrive at the office
金融公司 finance company
派司 (合格) (transliteration) pass
建築公司 (建築公司 / 工程商) construction company
國貨公司 Chinese products emporium
頂頭上司 direct boss; direct superior; immediate superior; superior officer
裁判司 (執法官) magistrate
運輸公司 transport company
電腦公司 computer company
壽司 (Japanese) sushi
蒙騙上司 deceive one's superior
總公司 head office
爆人陰司 (泄露別人的秘密) reveal the secrets of others

【叭】 baa¹ trumpet
叭叭聲 (片刻) in a flash

【四】 sei³ four
四十 ① (數字：四十) forty ② (年紀：四十) forty years old
四十幾勾 (四十多歲) forty sth; in one's forties; more than forty years old
四十幾歲 (四十多歲) forty sth; in one's forties; more than forty years old
四川 Sichuan
四川擔擔麵 Sichuan spicy noodle
四分之一 a quarter
四分之三 three quarters
四分五散 (四分五裂) be rent by disunity; be smashed to bits; be split up; be torn apart; break into pieces; come apart at the seams; come to pieces; fall apart; fall to

pieces; scattered and disunited; split up
四方 four directions
四方木——踢一踢，郁一郁 (木頭人——推一推，動一動) a wooden person never moves without a rush on it; lazybones
四方框 (方框兒) the "square" 口 radical
四月 ① April ② fourth month of the lunar year
四正 ① (方正) regular-featured ② (整齊) neat and tidy
四四正正 ① (方正) regular-featured ② (整齊) neat and tidy
四季 four seasons
四季平安 wish you safe all year round
四季豆 seasonal pea
一年四季 four seasons of the year
四便 (四周 / 四邊) all round; all sides; four sides; on all sides; on four sides
四隻腳 (打麻將的四位玩家兒) four players of a game of mahjong
四張嘢 (四十多歲) forty something
四眼 (戴眼鏡的) four eyes
四眼仔 (小四眼兒) a boy who wears glasses; a guy who wears spectacles; short-sighted boy
四眼佬 (戴眼鏡的人) a man wearing glasses; short-sighted guy
四眼婆 (四眼兒) a woman wearing glasses; short-sighted woman
四圍 (四圍 / 到處 / 周圍) all around; everywhere; surrounding area
四圍行吓 (四處遊盪) wander around
四圍貢 (到處走動) go around everywhere
四圍望 (四下張望) look around
四圍蒲 (溜街 / 到處遊盪) hang around on the streets
四塊半 (棺材) coffin
四腳蛇 (蜥蜴) lizard
四萬 (露齒而笑) huge grin
四萬咁口 (笑容可掬) wear a big smile
四點 (四點) four o'clock
四點水 (四點底) the "fire" (火) radical
四點鐘 four o'clock

一點四 (一點二十分) one twenty; twenty past one
一點嗒四 (一點二十分) one twenty; twenty past one
勾三搭四 have many lovers
廿四 (二十四) twenty-four
受人二分四 (受僱於人) work as an employee
阿四 (傭人) maid servant
星期四 Thursday
唔三唔四 (不倫不類) indecent; immoral in character; improper; neither fish, flesh nor fowl

推三推四（藉故推搪）cock up a lame excuse; reluctant to do sth; stall

亂噏／講廿四（胡言亂語）talk nonsense; talk rubbish

噏三噏四（流言蜚語／小道消息）chatter away; gossip

講三講四（流言蜚語／小道消息）gossip

禮拜四（星期四）Thursday

【外】ngoi⁶ outside

外公（外祖父）maternal grandfather; maternal grandpa

外父（岳父）father-in-law; wife's father

外出 be out

外母（岳母）mother-in-law; wife's mother

外交 diplomacy

　外交禮節 diplomatic propriety

外江（外省）province other than one's own

　外江佬（外省來的人）people from other provinces

外快 income from an extra job

外表 appearance

外便（外面／外邊）outside

外家（娘家）parents' home of a married woman

外套 coat; jacket

冷外套（毛衣）cardigan

外國 foreign country

　外國人（外地人）foreigner

外婆（姥姥）maternal grandma; maternal grandmother

外圍（非法賭博）illegal betting

外匯 foreign exchange

　賭外匯 gamble on foreign exchange

外幣（國外元）foreign currency

　換外幣（換外元）exchange foreign currency

外賣 takeaway

外牆 external wall

　粉飾外牆（抹牆）paint external walls

外邊（外面）outside

內外 ①（裏面與外面）inside and outside ②（內地與國外）domestic and foreign

分外 all the more; especially; exceptionally; extraordinarily

古今中外 at all times and in all countries; both ancient and modern, Chinese and foreign; classical and modern, Chinese and foreign; in China or elsewhere, in modern or ancient times; in the past or present, in China or anywhere else in the world; past and present, at home and abroad; whether in China or other lands, in ancient or today

另外 moreover

交通意外（車禍）traffic accident

老外（洋鬼子）foreigner

例外 exception

室外（戶外）outdoor; outside

格外（尤其／特別）all the more; especially; exceptionally; extraordinarily

媚外 fawn on foreign powers

號外 extra of a newspaper

擔保出外（交保釋放）bail

額外 extra

【失】sat¹ lost

失身 lose one's virginity

失車（車子丟了）① lost car ② lost a car

失咗（丟／掉）lose

失音（嗓子啞了）lose one's voice

失威（丟面子）humiliate oneself; lose face

失眠 insomnia

失婚（離婚）divorce

失望 disappointment

失敗（輸掉）failure

失散 be separated and lose contact

失業 out of job; unemployed

失魂（冒失）absent-minded; distracted; in a trance; lose one's soul

　失魂魚（冒失鬼）absent-minded person; distracted; rash person

　失魂落魄（心神恍惚）stand aghast

　　嚇失魂（嚇破了膽）be scared out of one's wits; be scared stiff

失憶（失憶）lapse of memory

失禮（不禮貌／丟人／丟臉）be disgraced; bring shame on oneself; lose face; lose one's decorum; make a breach of etiquette

　失禮死人（活現世）it is totally disgraceful

失戀 be crossed in love

失驚無神（冷不防）be seized with panic

失靈（故障）break down

人才流失（人才外流）brain drain

流失（外流）drain; erosion; loss

消失 disappear

患得患失 be swayed by considerations of success and failure

慌失失（慌慌張張）all in a fluster; higgledy-piggledy; in a hurried and confused manner; in a rush; lose one's head; nervous; on the rush; nervous

萬無一失 as sure as a surefooted horse

【奴】nou⁴ slave

奴才 flunkey; lackey

奴役 enslave; keep in bondage; slavery

一生兒女債，半世老婆奴（一輩兒子女債，半輩兒老婆奴）
　　a wife and children are a man's burdens
守財奴 cheapskate; miser; niggard

【奶】naai⁵ ① milk ② (乳房) breast ③ 中年婦人 middle-aged married woman

奶水（乳汁）milk
奶奶（婆婆）grandma
　　親家奶奶（親家母）one's child's mother-in-law
奶白色（乳白色）beige
奶昔 milkshake
　　士多啤梨奶昔（草莓奶昔）strawberry milkshake
奶油多（奶油多士）toast with butter and concentrated milk
奶皇包 sweet cream bun
　　一籠奶皇包 a basket of sweet cream buns
奶茶 milk tea; tea with milk
　　珍珠奶茶 pearl milk tea
　　凍奶茶（冰奶茶）iced tea with milk
　　飲奶茶（喝奶茶）drink tea with milk
　　熱奶茶 hot tea with milk
奶粉 dried milk; milk powder; powdered milk
奶媽（乳母）wet nurse
　　奶媽抱仔 — 人家物（老媽抱孩子 — 人家的）a wet nurse holding a baby – sb else's child
奶罩（胸罩）bra
奶嘴（奶頭）dummy
奶樽（奶瓶）baby's bottle; milk bottle
奶頭（乳頭）nipple; teat

二奶（小老婆）mistress
少奶 ①（休閒淑女）lady of leisure ②（少奶奶）young mistress of the house ③（兒媳婦）daughter-in-law
包二奶 keep a mistress; provide for a mistress
吮奶（啜奶）① suck milk ② suck the breast
戒奶（離乳）wean
谷奶（製造乳汁）stimulate the secretion of milk
豆奶 soy milk
走奶（去奶）no milk added please
姑奶（姑姑）aunt; father's elder sister
食奶（喝奶）suck the breast
師奶（大嬸）housewife; middle-aged married woman
校奶（泡奶：特別指溫度上的調校）adjust the warmth of the milk
啜奶（吮奶）suck milk
娶二奶（包二奶）keep a mistress
開奶（泡奶）adjust the warmth of the milk
椰奶 coconut milk

煉奶 condensed milk
嘔奶（吐奶）throw up milk; vomit milk from repletion
鮮奶（牛奶）fresh milk
雙皮奶 double-boiled milk and egg white
餵奶（餵奶／母乳餵養）breastfeed

【孕】jan⁶ conceive; pregnant

孕育 foster; nurse; nurture
孕婦 pregnant woman
　　孕婦裝 maternity clothes

避孕 contraception
懷孕 pregnant

【尼】nei⁴ Buddhist nun

尼古丁 nicotine
尼姑 Buddhist nun
尼龍 nylon

比堅尼 (transliteration) bikini

【左】zo² left

左手 left hand
　　左手便／面（左邊）left-hand side; to the left
　　左手嚟，右手去（漏走）in at one hand and out at the other
左右 ①（左與右）left and right ②（大約／差不多）about; around
　　左右手（好幫手／助手）helpful assistant; right-hand man
　　左右做人難（左右為難／順得哥情失嫂意）be stuck between a rock and a hard place; between the devil and the deep blue sea; between two fires; get into a fix; in a bind; in a box; in a dilemma; in a quandary about; in an awkward predicament; in the middle; on the horns of a dilemma; stand at a nonplus; torn between
　　左耳入，右耳出（聽不進）go in one ear and out the other
左近 ①（附近）around the corner; in the vicinity; neighbouring; nearby; round the corner ②（大約／左右）about; almost; a matter of; approximate to; around; before or after; circa; in the neighbourhood of; in the region of; in the rough; in the vicinity of; more or less; nearly; or so; or thereabout; probably; round about; some; something like; somewhere about; somewhere around; somehere round; something like; thereabout; towards
左便（在左邊）on the left side
左軚（左邊駕駛盤）left-hand drive
　　左軚車（左邊駕駛盤汽車）left-hand drive vehicle

左優（左撇子）left-hander
　　左優仔（左撇子）left-hander
左轉（左轉／向左拐個彎）turn left
左騰右騰（東奔西走）rushing about

面左左（不願見面）be at odds with one another
轉左（左轉／向左拐個彎）turn left

【巧】haau² skilful
巧合 by chance; by coincidence
巧妙（靈巧）clever; ingenious; skilful; smart; wonderful
巧婦 clever woman
　　巧婦難為無米之炊（再聰明的女人，沒米也煮不出飯來）even a clever woman cannot cook a meal without rice; even the cleverest housewife can't cook a meal without rice; if you have no hand, you can't make a fist; one cannot make a silk purse out of a sow's ear; one cannot realise a certain purpose without the necessary means; one can't make bricks without straw; the French would be the best cooks in Europe if they had got any butcher's meat; you cannot make an omelette without breaking eggs; you can't make sth out of nothing

佻巧（輕浮）frivolous and tricky
技巧 technique
投機取巧 opportunistic; resort to dubious shifts to further one's interests; seek private gain by dishonest means; seize every chance to gain advantage by trickery; speculate and take advantage of an opportunity; use every trick in shortcuts and finesse; wheel and deal; wheeling and dealing
乖巧 clever; lovely
啱巧（碰巧）by chance
熟能生巧 practice makes perfect

【巨】goei⁶ huge
巨人 giant
巨星 big star
　　巨星殞落 death of a big star
　　　一代巨星 big star of the generation
　　　粒粒巨星（星光熠熠）everyone is a big star
巨著 great work; monumental work
巨頭（大亨）baron; magnate; tycoon

【市】si⁵ market
市中心 town centre
市民 citizen

普通市民 ordinary citizen
市區 urban area
市場（菜市場）market
　　超級市場 supermarket
　　漁市場 fish market
　　壟斷市場 corner the market
市道（商情／行情）market conditions
　　睇市道（留意商情／看行情）watch the market conditions
市價 market price
市儈（唯利是圖）materialistic
市鎮 town

入市（投資）① get into the market ② initiate transactions
上市 listed; listed in the stock exchange
大城市 big city
好市（暢銷的）sell well
行花市（逛花市）visit the flower market
利市 ① （紅包）red pocket ② （如意）luck
招搖過市 be fond of showing oneself in the streets
花市 ① （花市）flower market ② （年宵）Lunar New Year flower market
股市 stock market
城市 city
脫市 out of stock; sold out
頂爛市（賤賣）drive down the market
渴市（熱賣）bestseller; command a ready sale; command a good sale; enjoy a huge circulation; find a ready market; go like hot cakes; go off like hot cakes; have a good sale; have a ready market; have a ready sale; in good demand; in great demand; in great request; meet with a good sale; meet with a ready sale; sell like hot cakes; sell well; well-received
發市 ① open one's account ② conclude an initial transaction of the day
街市（菜市場）market
黑市 black market
樓市（房產市場）property market
濕貨街市（菜市場）wet market
斷市（售罄）be out of stock; be sold out
爛市（滯市）dull of sale

【布】bou³ cloth
布甸（布丁）pudding
布梾（李子）(transliteration) plum
布辦（布樣品）cloth sample

一㘄／窟布（一塊兒布）a small piece of cloth

一張枱布（一幅枱布）a table cloth
一塊布（一匹布）a piece of cloth
毛布（絨毛棉布）lint
帆布 canvas
尿布（紙尿褲）diaper; napkin; nappy
抹枱布（抹布）table-cleaning cloth
枱布 table cloth
洗碗布 dish-washing cloth
紗布 gauge
窗簾布（窗簾）curtains
絨布 cotton flannel
墩布（拖把）mop; swab
膠布 ① plastic cloth ② sticking plaster

【平】ping⁴ level

平凡 normal and usual
　　不平凡 unusual
　　平平凡凡 normal and usual
平手 draw; tie
　　打和手（打成平局）break even; come out even; draw;
　　　　draw a game; end in a draw; fight to a standoff; play
　　　　even; tie it up; tie the score
平日 ①（平常）usually ②（星期一至五）weekdays
平台 flat roof
平白 for no reason
平安 safe
　　平安夜 Christmas Eve
　　平平安安 safe
平均 average; on average
　　唔平均（不平均）uneven
平時（平常）usually
　　平時一樣（平常一般）as usual
　　好似平時咁（好像平常一般）as usual
平郵 surface mail
平衡 balance

公平 fair; just
水平 level
和平 peace
忿忿不平 indignant and disturbed
促進和平 promote peace
持平 fair; unbiased
唔公平（不公平）unfair
教育水平 level of education
剷平 level; level to the ground
墊平 level up
擺平 ①（平息）calm a situation; settle an argument
　　② （懲罰）punish

【平】peng⁴（便宜）cheap

平到爛（便宜極了）very cheap
平啲（便宜點兒）cheaper
　　平啲得唔得呀（可以便宜點兒嗎）can it be cheaper; can
　　　　you make it cheaper
　　平啲啦（便宜點兒吧）cheaper, please; make it cheaper
平貨（便宜貨）cheap goods
平嘢（便宜貨）bargain; cheap stuff; schlock
　　平嘢冇好，好嘢冇平（便宜沒好貨，好貨沒便宜）cheap
　　　　things are not good, and good things are not cheap
　　平嘢冇好嘢（便宜沒好貨）cheap things are not good
　　　　things
平價（廉價）cheap; inexpensive
　　平價市場（跳蚤市場／廉價市場）flea market
　　平價貨（便宜貨）bargain; cheap goods
平賣（甩賣）selling cheap
平靚正（價廉物美）cheap, good, and first-rate

平嘢冇好，好嘢冇平（便宜沒好貨，好貨沒便宜）cheap
　　things are not good, and good things are not cheap
膽正命平（為正義不怕死）have too much spunk to care for
　　one's own life

【幼】jau³（細）fine

幼小（細小）young and small
幼沙（細沙）fine sand
幼兒 child; infant; nestling
　　幼兒園 kindergarten; nursery school; preschool
幼砂（幼砂糖）castor sugar
幼紗（細紗線）fine thread
幼細（精巧）fine
幼稚（孩子氣的）childish; naive; puerile
　　幼稚園（幼兒園）kindergarten; nursery school; pre-school
幼糠（細糠）bran shorts
幼鹽（細鹽）fine salt

有老有幼（有老有嫩）there are the young and the old
老幼 the old and the young
自幼 as a child; from childhood
扶老攜幼 bring along the old and the young

【弗】fat¹ not

弗如（不如）not as good as; not equal to; worse than
弗克 unable

出符弗（想出一些壞主義）plot a conspiracy
花弗 ①（愛調情的）flirtatious ②（花俏）gaudy like a
　　peacock

符弗（鬼點子）clever tricks; incantations
揸弗（負責）be in charge

【必】bit⁷ beat

必定 bound to; sure to
必要 indispensable; necessary; need
必須 cannot do without; have to; it is imperative for; it is necessary that; must; ought to
必需 essential; indispensable
　必需品 necessity

不必 need not; no need to; not have to; not necessary
未必（可能不一樣）may not; not always; not necessarily; not sure
行必（巡邏）walk the beat
行仔必／仔必（兩名警察拍檔巡邏）two policemen patrolling in pairs
何必 there is no need; why
定必 bound to; sure to
是必 have to; must
務必 be sure to; by all means; must
勢必 be bound to; certainly will; undoubtedly

【扑】pok³ strike

扑濕（襲擊）(rude) assault physically

【扒】paa⁴ paddle

扒手（小偷）pickpocket
　提防扒手（謹防扒手）beware of pickpockets
扒飯（動筷子）eat one's rice very fast
扒艇（划船）boating; go boating; paddle a boat; row a boat
扒頭（超車）overtake; overtaking

下扒（下巴）chin
牛扒 steak
用下扒（下巴脫臼）dislocated jaw
豬扒 ①（豬排）pork chop ②（肥胖的女性）(offensive) fat woman; nottie

【扒】paa⁴ steak

扒房 ①（牛排餐館）steak house ②很多醜女的地方 place with lots of ugly women

【打】daa³ assault; hit

打一下 give sb a punch
打一身（痛打一頓）beat up
打乞嗤（打噴嚏）sneeze
打大赤肋（赤着上身）be stripped to the waist; strip oneself to the waist

打大翻（打空翻）forward somersault
打女（女武打演員）martial art actress
打工（做工）take up employment; work
　打工仔（小工人）employee; jobber boy; salary man; worker
　打工皇帝 highly-paid worker
　打工階級 working class
　打住家工（做女傭）work as a maid-servant
打中（擊中）hit
打手（拳擊手）bodyguard; fighter
打水片（打水漂兒）play ducks and drakes
打火機 lighter
打牙祭 eat one's fill
打牙骹（打牙涮嘴）chat; engage in friendly banter; have a chat with friends; have a chat with sb; tattle
打仔（男武打演員）body-guard; fighter
打令（心上人／愛人）darling
打出（露出）reveal; show
打包 put the leftovers into a doggy bag
打打殺殺（打架殺人）fighting and killing
打瓜（打死）(rude) beat to death
打交 brawling; fight
打印機 printer
　標籤打印機（標籤打印機）label maker
　噴墨打印機 inkjet printer
　鐳射打印機 laser printer
打地鋪（睡地鋪）make up a bed on the ground; sleep on the floor
打孖（成雙）in pairs
　打孖上（一雙／一對）have two of sth at the same time
打字 type
　打字員 typist
　打字機 typewriter
打尖（插隊）jump the queue
打早（吃早餐）have breakfast
打死 beat to death
　打死不離親兄弟 blood is thicker than water
　打死狗講價（混水摸魚／趁火打劫）fish in troubled waters
打色（擲骰子）throw the dice
打低（打倒）defeat
打冷 have a night snack in the Chiu Chow style
打劫 rob; robbery
　俾人打劫（被人打劫）be robbed
打吠（繫領帶）tie a tie
打呃（打嗝兒）hiccup
打屁（放屁）backfire; beef-hearts; break wind; fart; have gas; lay fart; make a noise; pass air; pass wind; rip off a fart; set a fart; shoot rabbits

打折 give a discount
　　打八折 give a 20% discount

打和 (平手) draw; tie

打底 (墊底) give sb a hint beforehand

打店 (出門在外住宿旅店) put up for the night in an inn or a hotel

打斧頭 (偷工減料) cook up an expense account to line one's pockets

打昂瞓 (俯睡) lie on one's back in sleeping

打波 (打球) play a ball game
　　打茅波 (不遵守規則) ① bend the rules ② cheat ③ act dumb; pretend to be ignorant of something in order to gloss it over ④ play dirty in a ball game
　　打假波 (控制賽果) cheat at soccer
　　好打波 (好打球 / 愛打球) fond of playing ball games

打的 take a taxi

打直 (垂直) vertical

打芡 (勻芡) starching

打咭 (打卡) punch a card
　　打咭鐘 (考勤機) roll machine

打思臆 (打噎兒) ① burp ② get hiccups; have hiccups; hiccup

打穿頭 (打破腦袋) break one's head

打風 ① (颱風) typhoon ② (颳颱風) have a typhoon
　　打風車 (側手翻) cartwheel
　　打風都打唔甩 (很牢固) very tight

打個白鴿轉 (打個轉兒就回來) turn around

打個突 (感到吃驚) be surprised; surprise

打倒 (打着) knock down
　　打唔倒 (打不倒 / 打不着) can't knock down
　　打得倒 (打倒了 / 打着了) can knock down

打剔 (打鈎) (transliteration) tick

打拳 (拳擊) boxing; play boxing; spar

打書釘 (打書釘) spend a long time in a bookstore to read books

打戙 (豎放) set upright

打烊 (關店門) finish business

打特 (吃驚) be startled

打草驚蛇 wake a sleeping dog

打退堂鼓 back out one's promise

打針 (注射) give an injection; have an injection
　　打針紙 (注射證明) injection record
　　快過打針 (快極了) very fast

打側 (向旁邊的 / 側放) sidelong; slant
　　打側瞓 (側臥) lie on the side in sleeping

打啤 (打撲克) play poker

打崩頭 (打破了頭) break one's head

打巢 (擊敗) defeat

打得 ① (能打的) beatable ② can be beaten

打得少 (欠揍) deserve a beating up; deserve further beating; haven't hit sb enough
打得更多夜又長 (夜長夢多) it wastes time only to talk
　　唔打得 (不能打) cannot be beaten

打恬 (豎着) put sth upright

打掃 dust; tidy up

打探 (打聽) ask about; find out; get a line on; inquire about

打救 (搭救) save

打理 (管理 / 掌管) in charge of; manage; take care of

打窒 (痛打) beat up

打蛇 (大學術語：校方巡查有沒有人非法留宿) The school makes a patrol of the dormitory if anyone staying overnight illegally
打蛇餅 (很長的人龍) line up with many people; long queue
　　打晒蛇餅 (人龍像長蛇捲起來) line up with many people like a curling snake
打蛇隨棍上 (順勢而為) capitalize on one's opportunity; grasp an opportunity; leap at the chance; leap at the opportunity; seize an opportunity; seize the right time; take advantage of an opportunity; take advantage of the tide; take an opportunity that comes along; take opportunity; use opportunity

打雀 (監房術語：抽煙) smoke
打雀咁眼 (目不轉睛) keep a close eye on

打喊路 (打哈欠 / 打呵欠) yawn

打單 (打秋風 / 勒索) blackmail; practice extortion
打單信 (勒索信) invitation

打牌 (打麻將) play mahjong

打腳骨 (敲竹槓) extort money; fleece; fleece sb of his money; make advantage of sb's being in a weak position to overcharge him; take an exorbitant charge for services rendered; make sb pay through the nose; make sb squeal; overcharge; put the lug on; soak; sponge a person; sponge on sb; squeeze a person for money; sting; that is as good as blackmail; that is highway robbery

打靶 (槍決 / 槍斃) execute by shooting; shoot to death
打靶仔 (不得好死的傢伙) (offensive) useless person
打靶鬼 (不得好死的傢伙) (offensive) useless person

打對台 (唱對台戲) act the opposite; challenge sb with opposing views; compete with sb with a countermeasure; enter into rivalry; put on a rival show; set oneself up against; set up a rival stage in opposition to

打碟 (播歌) play disks

打種 (配種) breed

打算 intend; plan
　　另有打算 have some other plans; try to find some other ways

打骰（負責／作主）be in charge

打鳳眼（鎖眼）work buttonholes

打價（定價）fix a price

打噎（打嗝）① hiccup ② belch; burp
　　打思噎 ① burp ②（打嗝兒）get hiccups; have
　　　hiccups; hiccup

打賞（給賞錢）give tips

打震（發抖／顫抖）quiver; shake; shiver; tremble

打冷震（發抖／顫抖）shiver; tremble

打機（打遊戲機）play video games

打橫（橫放／橫着放）lie horizontally
　　打橫嚟（不講理）impervious to all reasons

打燕（踢毽子）kick the shuttlecock

打貓（偷吃）nibble; snack

打輸（擊敗）be defeated
　　打輸數（預算失敗）give up for loss
　　打咗／定輸數（預先做好不成功準備）be mentally
　　　prepared for a loss

打錯（打錯號碼）wrong number

打頭陣（帶頭）take the lead

打龍通（串通）act in collusion with each other; collaborate
　　in a scheme; collude; collude with; conspire with; gang
　　up; in collusion with; work hand in glove with

打擊 hit
　　大受打擊 suffer a big shock

打窿機（打孔機／打洞機）hole-puncher; puncher

打齋（做法事）perform Buddhist rites

打瀉茶（望門寡）widowed maiden

打雜 ① do odd jobs ② odd-job man

打爆（毆打）beat up; destroy
　　打爆機（玩電子遊戲破紀錄）get to the highest level of a
　　　video game

打邊爐（涮鍋子）have hot-pot

打躉（長時間停留某地方）frequent a place

打簿 update passbook

打響頭炮 meet with a first success

打爛（弄破）break
　　打爛咗（打破了）be broken; be smashed
　　打爛砂盆問到篤（打破沙鍋問到底）go to the bottom of
　　　the matter
　　打爛齋砵（開齋）break one's fast

打鐵（造鐵）strike the iron
　　打鐵佬（鐵匠）ironsmith
　　打鐵趁熱（趁熱打鐵）strike the iron while it is hot

打攪（打擾）bother; disturb

打鑼（敲鑼）beat the gong
　　打鑼咁搵你（提着燈籠找你）take a lantern to look
　　　for you

打 band（組織樂隊玩音樂）play in a band

打 golf（打高爾夫球）play golf

打 tennis（打網球）play tennis

打 tie（繫領帶）wear a tie

士撻打（頭盤）(transliteration) starter

五行欠打（欠揍）(rude) deserve a beating

企喺城樓睇馬打（袖手旁觀）keep oneself out of the affair;
　　make oneself stay out of the matter

好打（能打的）good at fighting

死纏爛打（死皮賴臉）pester sb endlessly for sth

吹吶打（吹嗩吶）play the souna horn

忌廉梳打 cream soda

攻打 assail; assault; attack

抵打（欠揍）deserve punishment

易打 easy to beat

後備拳師──聽打（將會被人打）sb who will be beaten by
　　others

柯打（訂單）order

唔好打（很難打）not easy to beat

吶打（嗩吶）suona horn

拳打 strike with fists

梳打（炭酸水）(transliteration) soda

單打 criticise sb with strong language

單單打打（暗諷）criticise sb harshly for sth; make oblique
　　accusations at sb

硬打（硬碰硬）confront the tough with toughness; diamond
　　cut diamond

搏打（欠揍）put oneself in danger of being punched

當打（功夫泰斗）formidable

落柯打（下單）place an order

摟打（做出搏人辱罵的行為）want to engage in a fight

摩打（馬達）motor

撩交打（找交架）provoke sb into fighting

毆打 beat up

臨老學吹打（臨老了再學新行當）an old dog begins to learn
　　new tricks; an old man learning a new skill

鞭打 flagellate; flog; lash; thrash; whip

難打 not easy to beat

蘇打（梳打／氣泡水）(transliteration) soda

爛打（好鬥的）bellicose

【打】daa¹ dozen

每打 every dozen

【扐】lik⁷（拿）take

扐住（拿住／拿着）holding; taking
　　扐唔住（拿不住）can't hold it
　　扐得住（拿得住）can hold it

扐倒 (拿到) can get it; have got
　扐唔倒 (拿不了／拿不到) can't get it
　扐得倒 (拿得了／拿得到) can get it

扐唔嘟 (拿不動) can't move
　扐得嘟 (拿得動) can be moved

扐晒 (拿光／拿完) be all taken; be taken up
　扐唔晒 (拿不完) can't take all; too many to be
　　taken away

【旦】daan³ daybreak
旦夕 in a short while
　危在旦夕 at death's door; at the last gasp; death
　　is expected at any moment in deadly danger; in
　　imminent danger; not worth a day's purchase; on the
　　verge of death; on the verge of destruction

元旦 New Year

【甲】gaat⁶ cockroach
甲由 (蟑螂) cockroach
　蠱甲由 (毒蟑螂) eliminate the cockroach

【未】mei⁶ have not; not yet
未必 (未必／不肯定) may not; not always; not necessarily;
　not sure

未有 (還有) have never been; have never had
　未有耐 (早着呢／還早) it is still a long time before...

未見 have not seen; not yet seen
　未見官先打三十大板 suffer a loss before the gain
　未見其利，先見其害 suffer a loss before an uncertain gain
　前所未見 have never seen before

未來 future
　美好未來 glorious future

未到六十六，唔好笑人手指曲 (即使年老也不可嘲
　笑別人的短處) don't tease others too soon

未食五月粽，寒衣不入櫃 (未食過端午節的粽，寒衣
　不要收起) don't put one's winter clothes into the chest
　before the fifth month of the year

未夠班 (不夠格) not good enough

未夠秤 (年紀未夠／年紀太輕) not old enough

未夠喉 (不滿足) not satisfied

未婚夫 fiancé
　未婚妻 fiancée

未曾 (沒) have not; have never

未學行先學走 (沒學爬就學走) learn to run before
　learning to walk

未驚過 (怕甚麼) know no fear

未觀其人，先觀其友 you can judge a person by the
　friends he keeps

仲未 (還未) has not; not yet; still not yet

好番未 (痊癒了嗎) have you recovered

重未 (還未) has not; not yet; still not yet

做起未 (完成了沒) have you finished doing sth

從未 (從來沒有) never

問你死未 (問你怎麼辦) we'll see how you would handle it

得未 (可以了沒有／還好嗎) is it alright/all right

從來未 (不曾) never before

着咗衫未 (穿了衣服沒有) have you put on your clothes

閻羅王探病——問你死未 (快死了) drive sb to his death;
　like the King of Hell dispatching invitation cards

【末】mut⁶ end
末日 ① doomsday; Judgment Day ② doom; end

末路 (死胡同) dead end; impasse

週末 weekend

始末 ① from beginning to end ② ins and outs; whole story

珠末 (珍珠末) pearl powder

【本】bun² ① local ② measure word for books, magazines, and writing pads
本人 ① I; me; myself ② in person; in the flesh; oneself

本分 one's duty; one's part; one's role

本心 (良心) conscience
　冇本心 (沒良心) heartless; ungrateful; without
　　conscience

本地 (原住) indigenous; local; native
　本地人 (原住民) local
　本地薑唔辣 (牆裏開花牆外香) grass is always greener
　　on the other side of the fence; local things or talents
　　are not as valued as foreign ones

本年 current year; present year; this year

本行 one's line; one's profession; one's specialty; one's
　trade
　　三句不離本行 cadgers speak of lead saddles; talk
　　　about nothing but one's own interests; talk
　　　always about one's own line; talk shop; talk shop all
　　　the time
　　老本行 old hand

本身 in itself; itself; oneself; personally

本事 ability; be capable
　冇本事 (沒本事) of no ability
　有本事 capable

本性 instincts; one's natural character; real nature

本金 (本錢) principal

本能 instinct
　出於本能 by instinct

本票 bank cheque; cashier's order; promissory note

本銀（本錢）principal
本應 ought to have; should have
本嚟（本來）at first; from the beginning; in itself; in the first place; it goes without saying; original; originally; properly speaking; should have; used to be

一本 ① a book; a copy; a reel; a volume ② a book of; a copy of; a reel of; a volume of
日本 Japan
老本 original principal
助人為快樂之本 happiness lies in rendering help to others; service begets happiness
成本 cost
治本 deal with a trouble at the source; effect a permanent cure; get at the root; get at the root of a problem; provide fundamental solutions to the problems; take radical measures; treat a matter thoroughly
治標不治本 cure the symptoms, not the disease; palliatives
版本 edition
原本 at first; from the beginning; in itself; in the first place; it goes without saying; original; originally; properly speaking; should have; used to be
根本 at all; essence; fundamental; not care a hoot; not give a damn; not the least; once for all; simply; thoroughly
副本 copy
夠本（足夠）enough; enough to cover the costs; have had enough; sufficient
棺材本 money put aside for one's old age
源本（根源）origin of an event
落本（下本錢）put in time, money, and effort
資本 capital
劇本 drama; play; script
槧本（刻本）books made of engravings
範本 model for calligraphy or painting
課本 textbook
蝕大本（蝕了老本）lose money greatly in business
蝕本（蝕本）lose money in business; lose one's capital; suffer a deficit
藍本 blueprint

【正】zing¹ formal
正月頭（過年／正月）during the New Year
正將（老千行動主腦）sting

【正】zing³ ①（正是）exactly ②（棒）great; terrific ③（地道）local
正斗（好的／美麗的／漂亮的）excellent; good; terrific
正式 formal
正常 normal

正貨（好貨／好東西）genuine stuff; great stuff
正菜（正妹）good-looking girl
正話 ①（剛才）just now ②（正在）in the midst of doing sth
正野（正品／好東西／好貨）genuine stuff; great stuff
正確 correct; exact; right
正爆（火辣）irresistibly sexy

公正 justice
四四正正 ①（方正）regular-featured ②（整潔）neat and tidy
四正 ①（方正）regular-featured ②（整潔）neat and tidy
平靚正（價廉物美）cheap, good, and first-rate
好正（很棒）gorgeous; very good
行得正，企得正（光明正大）act in a totally proper manner; play fair and square
坐正（扶正）become head of a unit
味道好正（味道很棒）the taste is superb
斧正（斧正／斧削／斧正）make corrections
真正 real
純正 pure; unadulterated
執正／執到正（打扮得那麼漂亮）dress properly
條命生得正（好命）born in a good family
發音好正（發音很標準）one's pronunciation is standard
嘈正（整潔）neat
端正 ① regular; upright ② correct; proper ③ correct; rectify; straighten
撞正（正撞上／正碰上）by a curious coincidence; by chance
撞到正（正撞上／正碰上）by chance
踏正（剛剛）exactly; just in time
擔正（當主角／作正選）act the leading role
樣靚身材正（樣子漂亮／身材又好）pretty face with a nice body
斷正（被揭發／穿幫）be caught red-handed

【正】zing³ ① exactly ② great; terrific
正一（真的）really
正方形 square
正係（正是）just happens to be
正經 serious
　　冇釐正經（沒正經）joke about serious matters; not so decent as one should be
　　調正經（裝正經／假正經）pretend to be serious

更正 amend; make corrections
計正（照正理說）in the ordinary course of things; under normal circumstances
郁不得其正（動彈不得）cannot move at all

【母】mou⁵ mother

母女 mother and daughter
母子 ① (母親和孩子) mother and child ② (母親和兒子)
　　mother and son
　　母子平安 after the birth, mother and child were
　　　doing well
母校 alma mater
母愛 maternal love; mother love
母語 mother tongue
母親 mother
　　母親節 Mother's Day

父母 parents
外母 (岳母) mother-in-law; wife's mother
字母 alphabet
老母 (母親 / 媽媽) (rude) mother
衣食父母 (穿的和吃的都靠父母) employer; those on whom
　　one's livelihood depends
伯母 auntie
你老母 (你娘親) (rude) your mother
佢老母 (他 / 她娘親) (rude) his mother
妗母 (舅母) (aunt; wife of mother's brother)
叔母 wife of one's father's younger brother
姑母 aunt
岳母 one's mother-in-law; one's wife's mother
姻母 aunt by marriage
師母 teacher's wife
舅母 aunt; wife of mother's brother
慈母 loving mother
鴇母 procuress
嬸母 aunt; wife of father's younger brother

【民】man⁴ people

民心 popular feelings
　　不得民心 very unpopular
民主 democracy
民以食為天 (民以吃為天) people regard food as
　　important as heaven
民生 people's livelihood
民事 civil
　　民事訴訟 civil lawsuit
民居 local dwelling houses
民情 ① condition of the people ② public feeling
　　了解民情 know public feelings
民族 nationality
　　民族自決 national self-determination
　　民族尊嚴 national dignity
民眾 general public
民間 ① among the people ② non-governmental

民間流傳 circulate among the people
民意 popular sentiment; will of the people
　　順從民意 obey the will of the people
民歌 (民謠 / 民歌 / 俚謠) folk song
　　唱民歌 sing folk songs
民辦 be run by the local people
民權 civil rights
　　保障民權 safeguard civil rights

人民 people
公民 / 市民 citizen
回民 people of the Hui nationality
居民 resident
移民 ① migrate ② immigration ③ emigration
殖民 colonize
普通市民 ordinary citizen
遣返難民 repatriate refugees
農民 farmer
漁民 fisherman
澤民 benefit the people
擾民 harass the people
難民 refugee
蟹民 people who lost money in the stock market

【永】wing⁵ forever

永久 constant; durable; endless; enduring; everlasting; for
　　good; forever; lasting; long-lasting; permanent; perpetual;
　　unchanging; unending
永不 never
永世 ① eternity; forever ② whole lifetime
　　永世不忘 remember sth for life; will bear sth in mind
　　　for life; will never forget sth
永遠 forever

【汁】zap¹ sauce

汁液 juice; sap
汁都撈埋 (打淨撈乾) consume every possible thing
　　on offer

石榴汁 pomegranate juice
冷飯菜汁 (殘羹剩菜) leftovers
茄汁 (茄醬) ketchup; tomato sauce
喼汁 (transliteration) ketchup; Worcestershire sauce
絞盡腦汁 rack one's brains
榨汁 liquidise
腦汁 (腦汁 / 腦筋) brain
撈汁 (菜湯汁拌飯) stir and mix with sauce from
　　the dishes
橙汁 orange juice

蕃石榴汁 guava juice
蕃茄汁 tomato juice
菠蘿汁 (鳳梨汁) pineapple juice
蔗汁 (甘蔗汁) cane juice; sugarcane juice
鮮橙汁 fresh orange juice
薑汁 ginger sauce
醬汁 sauce
懶到出汁 be extremely lazy
蘋果汁 apple juice
蘸汁 (水蘸汁 / 甜魚露) dipping sauce

【汀】ding¹ island

汀洲 islet in a river

洲汀 island in a river

【冰】tam⁵ (哄) coax

冰冰轉 (圍圍轉) in a confused haste; turn round and round

水冰 (水坑) small puddle
泥冰 (泥潭) mire; morass; quagmire
填冰 (償債) replace money that one has taken secretly

【犯】faan⁶ offend

犯人 convict; criminal; prisoner; the guilty
犯法 break the law; violate the law
　　知法犯法 deliberately break the law; know the law and violate it; know the law but break it; knowingly violate the law; transgress a law knowingly; wilfully commit an offence
犯規 ① breach of rules; break the rules; offend; violation of rules ② foul
犯眾憎 (犯眾怒) someone who is hated by everyone
犯罪 commit a crime; commit an offence; crime; offence
犯賤 demean oneself

押犯 escort a criminal; send a criminal away under escort
明知故犯 break a law on purpose
侵犯 encroach upon; in violation of; infringe upon; intrude; molestation; violate
故意冒犯 offend sb on purpose
冒犯 affront; offend
罪犯 criminal
獄犯 convict
疑犯 suspect
監犯 (囚犯) prisoner

【玉】juk⁶ jade

玉女 well-mannered girl
玉字邊 (王部 / 玉字旁) the "jade" (玉) radical
玉鈪 (玉鐲子) jade bracelet
玉器 jadeware
玉糠 (細糠) bran shorts

璧玉 jade

【瓜】gwaa¹ ① (瓜) melon ② (死了) die

瓜子 (瓜子兒) melon seeds
　　瓜子面 (瓜子臉) oval face
　　瓜子殼 (瓜子皮) skin of a melon seed
瓜老襯 (伸腿瞪眼了) die; fall flat; meet with one's death
瓜豆 (死) die
瓜咗 (去世 / 死了) dead; die; pass away
瓜直 (死了) die
瓜柴 (伸腿兒) collapse completely; die
瓜得 (要命) be done for; meet one's fate

一嚿西瓜 (一片西瓜) a slice of water melon
大冬瓜 (胖子) fat man
大腳瓜 (象皮腿) elephantiasic crus
手瓜 (二頭肌) biceps
木瓜 papaya; pawpaw
冬瓜 winter melon
打瓜 (打死) beat to death
刨冬瓜 (普通話) Putonghua
西瓜 water melon
拗手瓜 ① (掰腕子) arm-wrestling ② (較量) compete with; show power against another
金瓜 (南瓜) pumpkin
青瓜 cucumber
信瓜 (茄子) eggplant
哈蜜瓜 Hami melon
苦瓜 bitter gourd
倒瓤冬瓜 (冬瓜裏全都是壞水 (身體不好)) a person who is strong in appearance but poor in health
茶瓜 (醬瓜) pickled cucumber
做瓜 (殺) kill
涼瓜 (苦瓜) bitter gourd
頂瓜瓜 (頂呱呱 / 超棒) excellent
番瓜 (南瓜) pumpkin
勝瓜 (絲瓜) sponge gourd; towel gourd
矮瓜 (茄子) eggplant
菜瓜 snake melon
腳瓜 (小腿肚) calf of the leg
蜜瓜 honey dew melon
蒸生瓜 (笨頭笨腦) not alert

節瓜（毛瓜）fuzzy melon; hairy gourd
傻瓜 dopey; fool; silly fool
醬瓜 soy sauced cucumber

【瓦】ngaa⁵ tile

瓦坑（瓦溝）concave channels of tiling
瓦背（房頂）roof
　瓦背頂（房頂）roof
瓦通紙（瓦楞紙）corrugated paper
瓦煲（砂鍋）earthenware pot
瓦解 breakdown; collapse; crumble; disintegrate;
　disorganised; fall apart; fall into pieces
瓦檐（屋簷）tile eaves
瓦罉（瓦鍋／砂鍋）clay pot

缸瓦（陶器瓷）earthenware
瓷器碰缸瓦（不要跟人一般見識）not worth struggling with
　people of lower status
燒壞瓦（不合羣）cannot mate with others
磚瓦 bricks and tiles

【甘】gam¹（甘甜／甜）sweet

甘心 ① readily; willing ② be content with; be reconciled;
　resign oneself to
　唔甘心（不甘心）① unwilling ② not content with
甘草 licorice

心甘 ① readily; willing ② be content with; be reconciled;
　resign oneself to
令人眼甘甘（讓人一眼不眨）poke sb's eyes out
眼甘甘（一眼不眨）fix one's eyes on; never take one's eyes
　off sb

【生】saang¹ live

生人 living person
　生人勿近 stay away from an obnocious person
　生人唔生膽（膽小怕事）as timid as a hare; be
　　intimidated
　生人霸死地（佔着毛坑不拉屎）block the path of others
生女（生女孩）give birth to a girl
生口（活口）survivor of a murder attempt
生勾勾（活生生的）alive; have great vitality; lively
生手 ① inexperienced ② inexperienced worker
生日 birthday
　生日卡（生日賀卡）birthday card
　生日快樂 happy birthday
　生日咭（生日賀卡）birthday card
　生日派對（生日派對／生日慶祝會）birthday party
　生日會 birthday party

　開生日會（辦生日會）hold a birthday party
　生日禮物 birthday gift
　　你幾時生日（你哪一天生日）when is your birthday
　　做生日（慶祝生日）celebrate one's birthday
生仔（生男孩兒）give birth to a boy
生字 vocabulary
　生字表 vocabulary list
生安白做（生造／捏造）fabricate; invent a story
生死 life and death
　生死有定 every bullet has its billet
　　打生打死（拼命求存）fight for survival
　　捱生捱死（拼死拼活）work extremely hard
生肉（長肉）put on weight
　唔生肉（不長肉）lose weight
生色 add colour to; add lustre to
生冷 raw or cold food
生事（惹事）make trouble
生命 life
　生命線 lifeline
生定（注定）destined; predestined
生性（爭氣／有出息／懂事）have a grown-up
　understanding
　　生吓性喇（爭點兒氣吧）try to win credit for
　　真係生性（真有出息）promising
　　唔生性（不懂事／沒出息）unpromising
生抽（白醬油／淡醬油）light soy sauce
生果（水果）fruit
　生果金（老齡津貼）old age allowance
　生果檔（水果攤）fruit stall
　生果盤 fresh fruit platter
　一籃生果 a basket of fruit
生油（煮食油）cooking oil
生物 biology
　生物學 biology
生花（鮮花）flowers; fresh flowers
生保（陌生）strange; unfamiliar
　生保人（陌生人）stranger
生活 ① life ② living ③ livelihood
　生活方式 lifestyle
　生活刻苦 lead a simple and frugal life
　生活美滿 lead a happy life
　生活緊張 one's life is stressful
生面（陌生）unfamiliar
生埗（陌生）strange; unfamiliar
生息 bear interest
生痄腮（患腮腺炎）have mumps; suffer from epidemic
　parotitis
生粉（淀粉／芡粉）cornflour
　生粉水（水淀粉）cornstarch solution

生草藥 (中草藥) Chinese herbal medicine

生骨大頭菜——縱 (種) 壞晒 (茄子開黃花——縱 (種) 壞了) be spoiled

生鬼 (詼諧 / 活潑有趣) comical; funny; jocular

生啤 (紮啤) draught beer

生得歪 (長得瘦小) skinny

生猛 / 生生猛猛 (活潑 / 活蹦亂跳 / 鮮活 / 活生生) alive; lively; very fresh

生理痛 (生理痛 / 月經痛 / 女人之苦) dysmenorrhea

生眼挑針 (長針眼) have a sty

生粒粒 (長暗粒) get acne

生蛋 (下蛋) lay an egg

生魚 (烏魚) snakehead

生番晒 (復活了) resume one's spirits

生菜 lettuce
　　生菜包 lettuce wrap
　　　　一棵生菜 a lettuce
　　　　食生菜 as easy as pie; sth easy to do
　　　　食生菜咁食 (白玩兒) it is as easy as rolling a log
　　　　唐生菜 Chinese lettuce

生意 business
　　生意人 / 生意佬 (商人) merchant; businessman; trader
　　生意旺 business is blooming
　　生意淡 business is poor
　　生意興隆 wish you a blooming business
　　　　一單生意 (一筆生意 / 一號買賣) a business transaction
　　　　入口生意 import business
　　　　小本生意 small business
　　　　出入口生意 (進出口生意) import and export business
　　　　出口生意 export business
　　　　好生意 (生意好) do a brisk business; good business
　　　　做生意 (做生意 / 做買賣) conduct business; do business; do business transactions; run a business
　　　　傾生意 (談生意) solicit business
　　　　斟生意 (談生意) negotiate business
　　　　摟生意 (兜生意) solicit business; solicit trade

生滋貓入眼 (一見鍾情) love at first sight

生漬 (生污漬) generate stains

生劏 (活殺) kill alive

生熟 (熟的程度) a stranger and a friend
　　　　一次生，二次熟 (第一次生手，第二次便熟習起來) clumsy at first but skillful later on; people get used to things quickly

生蝦咁跳 (跳起來像生蝦一樣) dance with rage; furious; have ants in one's pants

生瘡 (長瘡) form a boil

生蝨 (生疥瘡 / 得瘡積病) have scabies

生積 (有積) have digestive disorders

生鋰 (生鏽) get rusty

生蟲 (長蟲子) have a parasitic disease

生雞 (小公雞) chick; cockalorum; cockerel
　　生雞精 (對女生有特別表現的男生) luster

生癪 (瘡積 / 得瘡積病) infantile malnutrition

生曬 (在太陽底下曬) be dried in the sun while sth is alive

生蘿卜 (長凍瘡) have frostbite

生鹽 (粗鹽) coarse salt

生 BB (生孩子) give birth to a baby

生 cancer (患癌) have cancer

一生 all one's life

一粒花生 a peanut

人生 life

人急智生 have quick wits in an emergency

大學生 university student

小學生 primary school student

丑生 (丑角) clown; comedian

中學生 secondary school student

牙科醫生 dental surgeon; dentist

民生 people's livelihood

丟生 (荒廢) out of practice; rusty

先生 ① (老師) teacher ② (男士的稱謂) mister; Mr. ③ (老公) husband

在生 (在人世間) alive

好好先生 Mr Goody Goody; Mr Nice Guy

好後生 (很年輕) very young

孖生 (孿生) twins

收生 (招攬學生) student recruitment

此生 (此生 / 今生) one's life

死人都要拗番生 (死的也要說活) argue that the dead is still living

死裏逃生 be saved from death; be snatched from the jaws of death; close call; close shave; escape by a hairbreadth; escape by the skin of one's teeth; escape death by a narrow margin; escape with one's bare life; hairbreadth escape; have a close bout with death; miss death by a hair's breadth; narrow escape from death; narrow shave; near thing

死過番生 (死裏逃生) be saved from death; be snatched from the jaws of death; close call; close shave; escape by a hairbreadth; escape by the skin of one's teeth; escape death by a narrow margin; escape with one's bare life; hairbreadth escape; have a close bout with death; miss death by a hairs breadth; narrow escape from death; narrow shave; near thing

自己執生（靠自己應變）tread carefully; use one's own judgment and do what one deems best
更生 ① regenerate; revive ② renew
男生 ① schoolboy ② male; man
私家醫生 private doctor
侍應生（服務員）waiter
放生 ①（照他／她喜歡）as one likes ②（由他／她去吧）let sb go
返生（復活）bring back to life; come alive again; resurgence; resuscitate; revive
長生 long life
花生 peanut
冒牌醫生 quack doctor
後生（年輕）① young ② young people; youngster; youth ③ apprentice; assistant
架生 ①（道具／工具）tools ②（武器）weapons
活生生 living; real
美好人生 happy life
家生 ①（道具／工具）tools ②（武器）weapons
逃生 escape; escape with one's life; flee for one's life
接生 deliver; deliver a child; practice midwifery
執生（隨機應變）act according to circumstances; act as circumstances dictate; act as the occasion demands; act on seeing an opportunity; adapt oneself to circumstances; do as one sees fit; play sth by ear; lay to the score; profit by the occasion; see one's chance and act; take things as they come; use one's own judgment and do what one deemed best
畢生 all one's life; in one's whole life; lifelong; lifetime; throughout one's lifetime
發生 happen
睇醫生（看醫生）consult a doctor; go to see a doctor; see a doctor
孳生 grow and multiply
黃綠醫生（庸醫／江湖醫生）charlatan; quack; quack physician
媽媽生（風月場所中的女性領班）female pimp
電話接線生 telephone operator
誕生 birth
監生（活生生）alive
衛生 hygiene
學生 student
謀生 make a living
隨時發生 imminent
險象環生 beset with danger; dangers lurking on all sides; incessant crises; incessant occurrence of crises; signs of danger appearing everywhere
優異生 excellent student
翻生（復活）bring back to life; resuscitate

舊生 former student
醫生 doctor; medical doctor; physician
鹹魚翻生（鹹魚又復活了）①（起死回生）escape unexpectedly from a difficulty ② a person back in favour
爛生（粗生）easy to grow

【用】jung⁶ expenses; use
用戶 consumer; customer subscriber; user
用具 tool
用途 usage
用腦（動腦／動腦筋）use one's brain
　用腦過度（過度動腦筋）overtax one's brain
用盡（用盡／耗盡）run out; use up
分擔費用 share the expenses

引用 ① cite; quote ② appoint; recommend
冇用（沒用）useless
冇鬼用（真沒有）bloody useless
充分利用 make the best use of
共用 common; sharing
吃飯時服用 to be taken during a meal
有用 useful
有信用 trustworthy
好使好用（聽使喚）good to use
作用 effect
利用 make use of
享用 enjoy; enjoy the use of
受用 ① enjoy ② comfortable; feel good
服用 take the medicine
信用 ① trust ② credit
耐用 durable
美觀耐用 beautiful and durable
家用（家用／生活費）family allowance; family expenses
唔中用（沒有用）good-for-nothing; useless
效用 effectiveness; utility; usefulness
租用 rent
副作用 side-effect
啱用（合適）convenient to use; fit for use; work well
常用 in common use
費用 cost; expenses; fee
飯前服用 to be taken before a meal
飯後服用 to be taken after a meal
誤用 misuse
實用 practical
模範作用 exemplary role
錄用 employ; take sb on the staff
襟用（耐用）durable
襲用（沿用）follow a practice; take over

【甩】lat¹ (掉 / 脫落 / 掉落) get rid of; lose

甩手 (脫手) dishoard; dispose of

甩毛 (掉毛) loss of hair

甩牙 (掉牙) a tooth drops off

甩卡 (火車脫節) be disjointed

甩皮 (脫皮) decrustation
　甩皮甩骨 (皮開骨散 / 缺頭短尾) in bad shape

甩色 (褪色 / 掉色) fade; lose colour

甩身 (脫身 / 擺脫) get away from; get rid of a problem

甩底 ① (失信 / 爽約) break one's appointment; fail to turn up; not turn up for an appointment; stand someone up ② the bottom part of a shoe looses off

甩咗 (掉下) fall off

甩拖 (分手 / 吹了) break up a relationship; lovers no longer dating each other

甩肺 (被人打得很厲害) be beaten up badly

甩鈎 (脫鈎) disconnect; unhook

甩期 (失期) miss the deadline

甩骹 (脫臼 / 脫骹) broken joint; dislocate

甩難 (脫離困境) got out of trouble

甩鬚 (出醜 / 丟臉 / 失面子) feel ashamed; lose face; unbecoming

冬甩 (甜甜圈) (transliteration) doughnut

打風都打唔甩 (鐵着呢) very tight

尖筆甩 (尖尖的) pointed; sharp

吟詩都吟唔甩 (跳進黃河也洗不清) fail to shirk

秀才遇老虎—— 吟詩都吟唔甩 (跳進黃河也洗不清) fail to shirk

走甩 (逃脫) get away

走唔甩 (逃脫了) cannot escape; cannot get away

走得甩 (逃脫不了) can escape; can get away

直畢甩 (筆直) very straight

唔要斧頭唔得柄甩 (騎虎難下 / 進退兩難) hold a wolf by the ears

搇甩 (拔出) pull out; pull up

掏甩 (扔掉) throw away

揩得甩 (能刷得乾淨) erasable

裙拉褲甩 (匆匆忙忙) in a great hurry

撇甩 (甩掉) dump; get rid of

撟甩 (撬開) pry away

糖不甩 (糖不甩 / 麻糬) glutinous rice flour balls with peanuts and coconuts in syrup

【田】tin⁴ field

田地 ① (農田) agricultural land; farmland; field
　② (困境) plight; wretched situation

田基 (田埂) balk; rand

田園 countryside; fields and gardens

田雞 (青蛙) frog
　田雞過河 —— 各有各撐 (青蛙過河 —— 自己蹬自己的) each goes their own way; each takes to their own legs

田螺 river snail

一塊田 a field

士急馬行田 (因地制宜) act according to the circumstances

丹田 pubic region

水田 paddy field; rice field

禾田 paddy field; rice field

事急馬行田 (和尚要錢經也賣) use illegal means in urgent situations

桑田 plantation of mulberry trees

耕田 farm; till

買田 buy land

落田 (落田 / 下田) go farming in the field

稻田 paddy field; rice field

駛田 (犁田) till fields

【由】jau⁴ ① (原由) reason ② (從) from

由此 from this; therefore; therefrom; thus

由佢 (讓它去 / 放開) let go
　由佢去 (由他 / 她去) do as one likes

由於 as; as a result of; because of; by virtue of; considering; due to; for; for-as-much-as; in consequence of; in consideration of; in that; in the light of; in view of; in virtue of; inasmuch as; on account of; owing to; seeing that; since; take into consideration; thanks to; through; with; with a view to

由得你 (隨便你) as you please; as you think fit; do as you like; it's up to you; please yourself; suit yourself; whatever you say

由得佢 (算了吧 / 讓它去) leave him alone; leave it; let him be; let him please himself; let it be

由朝到晚 (從早到晚) from dawn to dusk; from morning till night

冇來由 (沒來由) no evidence

冇理由 (沒可能的) without reason

正當理由 justifiable reasons

任由 as one sees fit

因由 reason

有來由 there's evidence

自由 free; freedom

來由 reason

理由 reason

雙重理由 double cause

【甲】 gaap³ nail

甲子 a cycle of sixty years
甲板 deck; deck armour
甲狀腺 thyroid gland
甲魚 freshwater tortoise
甲蟲 beetle

手甲 fingernail
披甲 put on an armour
指甲 nail
剪指甲 cut the nail
趾甲 toenail
腳甲 toenail

【申】 san¹ stretch

申報 ① report to a high body ② declare sth
申訴 appeal; complain
申請 apply

【甴】 zaat⁶ cockroach

甲甴 (蟑螂) cockroach
蟲甲甴 (消滅蟑螂) eliminate the cockroach

【白】 baak⁶ white

白切雞 poached chicken; steamed chicken
白手興家 (白手起家) achieve success in life with one's own hands; start from scratch
白白 (徒勞無功) beat the air; draw water in a sieve; drop a bucket into an empty well; flag a dead horse; labour in vain; labour to no purpose; make a futile effort; make useless trouble; milk a he-goat; not to succeed after trying hard; plough the waves; ploughing the wave; prove futile; sow the sands; use vain efforts; wasted effort; work to no avail; work without achieving anything
白色 white; white colour
白灼 (焯) blanch
　白灼蝦 (白焯蝦) blanched shrimps
　　一斤白灼蝦 (一斤白焯蝦) a catty of blanched shrimps
白豆 (大豆 / 黃豆) yellow bean
白車 (救護車) ambulance
　叫白車 (召喚救護車) call an ambulance
白果 ① (銀杏) gingko; gingko nut ② (沒結果) no business
　生白果 —— 腥夾悶 (雞蛋裏挑骨頭 —— 沒茬找茬) fault-finding; nitpick; picking bones in an egg – overcritical
　食白果 ① (徒勞的) rewardless ② (沒結果) no business
白油 (改正液 / 塗改液) correction fluid
白金 platinum

白炸 ① (水母) jellyfish ② (交警) traffic policeman; traffic warden
白食 (吃免費的) get a free meal; have a free meal
白晒晒 (過於白皙) just white
白焓 (用清水煮) boil without seasoning
　白焓蛋 (水煮蛋) boiled egg
白粉 (白面) heroin
　食白粉 (吸白面) take heroin
白紙黑字 in black and white; in print; in writing
白酒 white wine
白馬王子 prince charming
白鬼 (白種人) Caucasians
白淨 (白嫩) delicate
　青靚白淨 (一般用於男子) (面孔白淨 / 樣子俊俏) young, handsome, and have a fresh complexion
白斬雞 (白切雞) poached chicken; steamed chicken
白雪 snow
　白雪公主 snow white
　白雪雪 (白淨淨的 / 雪白 / 白皙) snowy white
白粥 (稀飯) congee; gruel; plain congee; plain rice congee; porridge
　白粥油炸鬼 (白粥油條) plain rice congee with deep-fried dough stick
白菜 Chinese cabbage
　一棵白菜 a Chinese cabbage
白痴 idiot; stupid
　白痴仔 (蠢笨) fool; stupid person
白裏透紅 (白裏透紅) rosy chin
白飯 plain cooked rice
　白飯魚 ① (銀魚) salangidae ② (白布鞋) white cloth shoes ③ (傻子) stupid person
　一碗白飯 a bowl of steamed rice
白銀 silver
白鼻哥 ① (丑角) clown; comedian ② (考試失敗者) person who fails in an examination ③ (狡猾的人) cunning person; wicked person
白撞 (擅闖的) pass off as sb in order to cheat others
　白撞雨 (驟雨 / 陣雨) occasional drizzle; passing shower; rain shower; shower; shower of rain
白醋 white vinegar
白蝕 (白斑病) leukoderma; white spots
白頭佬 (白頭翁) Chinese bulbul; grey starling
白霍 (好出風頭 / 臭顯 / 輕浮) make a boast of oneself
白濛濛 (白茫茫) all white
白鴿 (鴿子) dove; pigeon
　白鴿眼 (勢利眼) look down on people; snobbish
　打個白鴿轉 (出外走走) go for a quick walk around the block
　放白鴿 (串通行騙) conspire to trick

白蟻上沙灘 —— 唔死一身潺 (開水淋臭蟲 —— 不死也夠受) get out of distress but into trouble

白蘭 (玉蘭花) gardenia flower
白蘭地 brandy

白曬曬 (白淨淨的 / 雪白 / 白皙) snowy white

白欖 (青橄欖) Chinese white olive

日光日白 (光天化日) in broad daylight

平白 for no reason

灰白 ashen; greyish; hoary; ale; white

含冤莫白 suffer an unrighted wrong

告白 (廣告) advertisement

身家清白 have a clean record

坦白 candid; confess; frank; honest; tell the truth

明白 be clear about; realise; understand

明明白白 as clear as noonday

肥肥白白 (白白胖胖的) fair and plump

直白 (坦率) candid; forthright; frank; outspoken; straightforward

青白 (蒼白的) pale

洗白白 (洗澡) take a child for a bath

面青口唇白 (唇青臉白) white with fear

唇紅齒白 have rosy lips and pretty white teeth

旁白 aside; narration; speak aside; voice-over

清白 not guilty

眼白 whites of the eyes

眼白白 (眼巴巴地) look on helplessly

蛋白 egg white

雪白 snowy white

雪咁白 (像雪一般白) as white as snow

斑白 grizzled; greying

睇白 (看得出) it is apparent; it is obvious; stand to one's assertion that

黃牙白 / 黃芽白 (大白菜) Chinese lettuce

腦海一片空白 have a blank mind

葱白 (大葱) scallion

跟紅頂白 (勢利眼) flatter those in power and hurt those in bad luck

潔白 clean and white

賣告白 (賣廣告) advertise

頭髮灰白 have grizzled hair

【皮】pei⁴ ① (皮膚) skin ② (錢) money ③ (費用) expenditure ⑤ (皮革) leather

皮光肉滑 (外皮光滑) smooth skin

皮具 leather goods

皮笑肉不笑 (裝出一副笑臉) put on a false smile; insincere smile

皮帶 belt

皮蛋 (松花蛋) century egg
皮蛋瘦肉粥 (松花蛋瘦肉粥) congee with lean pork and century egg

皮喼 (皮箱) suitcase

皮費 (費用 / 開支) expenses; overheads

皮膚 skin
皮膚敏感 skin allergy

皮箧 (皮箱) leather case

皮鞋 leather shoes

皮褸 (皮大衣) leather overcoat

一皮 (一元) one dollar

一褸 / 嘪 / 浸皮 (一層皮) a layer of skin

人心隔肚皮 (知人口面不知心) no one can read the mind of another person

人要面，樹要皮 (要面子) a person needs face just like a tree needs bark

切肉不離皮 (血濃於水) blood is thicker than water

水皮 ① (差勁) inferior; poor ② (馬馬虎虎的) sloppy

牛皮 ① (疲弱) fatigued and weak; tired and weak ② (頑皮) naughty

牛奶麥皮 oatmeal with milk

甩皮 (脫皮) decrustation

忙到七個一皮 (忙得手腳朝天) frantically busy

收皮 (滾開) go away

夭皮 (頑皮) naughty

批皮 (削皮) peel

肚皮 belly

豆 / 痘皮 ① (有麻子的) pockmarked ② (麻子臉) a pockmarked face

刮損皮 (刮傷了皮膚) hurt one's skin with scraping

炒地皮 speculate in land

炸魚皮 deep-fried fish skin

香蕉皮 (陷阱) trap

為皮 (算成本) cost

重皮 (貴) costly; expensive

面皮 (臉皮) face; sb's feelings; self-respect

唔係我嗰皮 (不是我的對手) not my match

唔夠皮 (入不敷出 / 不夠) not enough to spend

桂皮 cinnamon bark

差一皮 (差一等) a bit worse; on a lower level

差皮 (差勁) poor

揦高肚皮 (醜事拿出來讓人看) reveal one's privacy

海皮 (海邊 / 海濱) seafront; seaside; waterfront

海蜇皮 jellyfish

紙皮 straw board

脆皮 (鬆脆的) crispy

草皮 grass

粉皮 bean jelly sheet

夠皮（足夠）enough; enough to cover the costs; have had enough; sufficient

眼皮（眼皮兒）upper eyelid

豹死留皮（人死了／精神永在）a leopard leaves behind its skin when it dies

陳皮 ①（陳皮）aged tangerine peel ②（陳舊）old-fashioned

魚皮 fish skin

麥皮 oatmeal

捌高肚皮（洩露內幕）give the show away

揦皮 skin

痘皮（凹洞臉）pockmark face

睇差一皮（預測失準）form a wrong estimation of sth

韌皮（多用於小孩）（頑皮／不怕打）naughty

搣皮（剝皮）peel; peel off the skin

撽損皮（抓傷了皮膚）scrap the skin

瘀皮（窘）lose face

落皮（下本錢）put in time, money, and effort

蜇皮 jellyfish

跳皮（調皮）mischievous; naughty

頑皮 naughty

慳皮（節省）save money

摟錯人皮（表現得像隻野獸）behave oneself like a beast

腐皮（油皮）bean curd sheet

鋪草皮（賽馬術語：輸的金錢足以代替草皮鋪滿馬場跑道）lose money in horse-racing

樹皮 bark

頭皮（頭屑）dandruff

縮皮（削減開支）cut back expenses

薄皮（臉皮子薄）prone to; blush

謝皮（沒生氣了／死）die

雞毛蒜皮 trivial matter

雞皮 ① chicken skin ② goosebumps

【目】muk⁶ eye

目光 ①（遠見）vision ②（凝視）gaze
目光呆滯 have fishy eyes; have glassy eyes
目光遠大 have a broad vision
目光銳利 have a sharp eye

目字邊（目字旁）the "eye"（目）radical

目定口呆（目瞪口呆）be struck dumb; be dumbfounded; be dumbstruck; gape; gaping; stand aghast; stare in mute amazement; stare openmouthed; stare with astonishment; strike sb dumb; stunned; stupefied

目的 aim; purpose
目的地 destination
達到目的 attain one's goal
漫無目的 aimless

目前 at present; at the moment

目標 target

長遠目標 long-term goal
追求目標 pursue one's goal

目錄 catalogue

目擊 see with one's own eyes; witness
目擊證人 eyewitness

一條題目 a question

盲目 blind

面目 appearance; face

眠目 close one's eyes

閉目 close one's eyes

發展項目 development project

項目 item; project

節目 programme

蔽目 blindfold; cover the eyes

醒目（機靈）① catch the eye ② clever; intelligent; quick-witted; smart

題目 question

耀目 dazzle

【矛】maau⁴ spear

矛盾 contradiction
矛盾百出 full of contradictions
矛盾重重 with many contradictions
自相矛盾 self-contradictory
解決矛盾 solve a problem
避免矛盾 avoid conflicts

矛頭 bunt; spearhead; spearpoint

【石】sek⁶ ①（大石／石頭）rock ②（石子／石塊）pebble; strone

石山（假山）rockery; rockwork

石仔（石子）pebble

石地堂鐵掃把 —— 硬打硬（石板上甩烏龜 —— 硬碰硬）a tortoise pounding a slabstone – a case of the tough confronting the tough

石字邊（石字旁）the "stone"（石）radical

石米（碎石）crushed stones

石油 petroleum
石油氣 butane gas

石狗公（裝闊佬）poor person pretending to be a rich one

石屋（磚房）brick house

石屎（混凝土）concrete
石屎樓（水泥房屋）building constructed of concrete and steel

石春（卵石／鵝卵石）cobble

石英 quartz

石級（台階）staircase; steps; stone steps

石棉 asbestos; cotton asbestos

石斑 garoupa
　　石斑魚 garoupa
　　　　清蒸石斑 steamed garoupa
石榴 pomegranate
　　石榴汁 pomegranate juice
　　石榴紅 garnet
石膏 plaster cast
　　　打石膏 apply a plaster cast
石頭 rock; stone
　　　一嚿石頭 (一塊石頭) a rock

大石 big rock
放下心頭大石 (鬆一口氣) free from anxiety
紅寶石 ruby
紙皮石 (馬賽克) mosaic
麻石 (花崗岩) granite
晶石 spar
雲石 marble
戥穿石 (結婚當天陪伴新郎的一羣男士) men helping the
　　bridegroom at his wedding
落井下石 persecute sb while he is down
磁石 magnetic iron
膽生石 (膽石症) cholelithiasis
膽石 gallstone
藍寶石 sapphire
爆石 (大解) have a poo
寶石 gem; precious stone
攝石 (磁石) magnet
鑽石 diamond

【示】 si⁶ show

示威 demonstration
示眾 exhibit to the public; publicly expose; put before the
　　public; show to the public
示意 drop a hint; give a sign; hint; indicate one's wish;
　　motion; signal

告示 bulletin; official notice; placard
指示 indication
展示 display; exhibit; lay bare; open up before one's eyes;
　　reveal; show
訓示 ① (告誡) admonish ② (指導) instructions
暗示 infer
顯示 show

【禾】 wo⁴ (稻子) rice paddy

禾田 (稻田) paddy field; rice field
禾字邊 (禾字旁) the "rice straw" (禾) radical
禾尾 (稻穗) ear of rice; spike of rice

禾苗 (秧苗 / 稻秧) rice seedlings; rice shoot
禾草 (稻草) rice straw
禾秧 (秧苗 / 稻秧) rice seedlings; rice shoot
禾堂 (曬穀場) grain-sunning ground
禾稈 (稻草) rice straw
　　禾稈冚珍珠 (富人裝窮) hide one's true wealth; rich
　　　　people pretending to be poor
　　禾稈草 (稻草) rice straw
　　禾稈堆 (稻草垛) stack of rice straw
　　禾稈頭 (稻荏兒) rice straw
禾塘 (曬穀場) grain-sunning ground
禾頭 (稻荏兒) rice straw
禾鐮 (鐮刀) sickle for cutting rice straws

一造禾 a harvest of rice
早禾 (早稻) early season rice
借艇割禾 (借他人之力來獲利) make use of sb to profit oneself
執禾 (撿拾遺漏的稻穗) pick up the ears of rice
割禾 (割稻子) reap the rice
晚禾 (晚稻) late season rice

【穴】 jyut⁶ den

穴位 acupuncture point
穴居 cave-dwelling; live in caves

洞穴 burrow; cave; cavern
巢穴 den; hideout; lair; nest

【立】 lap⁶ stand

立心 (決心) determination
　　立心不良 have an evil plan; ill-disposed
立即 at once; immediately; off hand; promptly
立足 achieve a status
立刻 as soon as; as quick as a flash; at once; at one stroke;
　　at the drop of a hat; before one could say Jack Johnson;
　　before you found where you are; directly; first thing off
　　the bat; here and now; immediately; in a brace of shakes;
　　in a crack; in a flash; in a jiffy; in a minute; in a moment;
　　in no time; just now; lose no time in; off hand; on the
　　moment; on the nail; out of hand; promptly; pronto;
　　right away; right now; right off the bat; straight away;
　　straight off; thereupon; this instant; this moment; without
　　a moment's delay; without delay; without hesitation;
　　without loss of time; without thinking much longer
立定 (停止) halt
立法 legislate
立場 position; stand; standpoint
　　立場堅定 be firm in one's stand; keep one's stand; take a
　　　firm stand

改變立場 shift one's position

表明立場 make one's position clear

立雜野 (零食) junk food

兀立 stand rigidly without motion

中立 neither on one side nor the other; neutral

屹立 stand erect; stand towering like a giant

成立 establish

林立 a forest of; stand in great numbers

亭亭玉立 slim and graceful; stand gracefully erect; tall and straight

保持中立 adhere to neutrality; maintain neutrality; remain neutral; sit on the fence; sit on the hedge

建立 establish; set up

站立 on one's feet; stand

勢不兩立 absolutely antagonistic; at daggers drawn; at enmity; at the opposite pole to; completely incompatible; diametrically opposed to; extremely antagonistic to; implacable hostility; irreconcilable with; swear not to coexist with; unable to coexist

罪名成立 be proved to be guilty

豎立 erect; set upright; stand

獨立 independent

【立】laap⁶ grab

立立吟 (繡亮) glossy; shiny

黐立立 (黏黏的) sticky

【立】lap⁶ establish

立亂 (胡亂／凌亂／雜亂) messy

立立亂 (亂糟糟) all in a muddle; messy

亂立立 (亂七八糟) messy

立孻 (溫溫吞吞的) slow to react

亂立立 (亂糟糟) in a hubbub; in an uproar; in noisy disorder; tumultuous

6劃

【丟】diu¹ lose

丟生 (生疏) out of practice; rusty

丟生晒 (生疏) out of practice; show neglect of one's skill

丟架 (丟人／丟臉) lose face

丟假 (丟人／丟臉) lose face

丟疏咗 (生疏) have one's skills go rusty; out of practice

【乒】bing¹ table-tennis

乒乓 (transliteration) ping pong; table tennis

乒乓波 (乒乓球) ping pong; table tennis

打乒乓波 (打乒乓球) play table-tennis

【交】gaau¹ connect

交叉 cross

交叉點 crossing; intersection; junction

打交叉 (打叉兒) cross out

交代 ① account for; brief; explain; justify oneself; make clear; tell ② hand over; transfer; turn over

交白卷 (無功而返) fail to accomplish anything

交吉 (交房) hand over a completed unit

交低 (留下來) leave behind

交更 (交班兒) change shift

交往 communicate

秘密交往 communicate secretly

交波 (傳球) pass the ball; passing

交易 dealing; make a deal; transaction

冇交易 (沒得做) no dealing can be concluded

有交易 (有得做) dealings can be concluded

枱底交易 (私下交易) under-the-table transaction

幕後交易 behind-the-scenes deal

交投 (買賣交易) transactions

交投暢旺 (成交量暢旺) a lot of transactions

交待 ① account for ② hand over; turn over

老實交待 come clean; make a clean breast of everything

坦白交待 come clean; make a clean breast of one's crimes

交租 (交房租) pay the rent

交差 work without enthusiasm

交俾 (交給) hand to sb

交流 exchange; interchange; interflow

交情 friendly relation; friendship

交配 mating

交帶 (可靠的) responsible

交通 ① traffic ② transport

交通工具 transportation

交通差 (交警) traffic policeman

交通規則 traffic regulations

交通費 transportation fee

交通意外 traffic accident

交通標誌 traffic sign

交通燈 (紅綠燈／信號燈) traffic lights

交通燈——點紅點綠 (瞎指揮／說這說那) person who fools others into doing sth at one time and other things at other times

交通警／交通警察 (交警) traffic policeman

妨礙交通 block the traffic; obstruct the traffic

交貨 consignment; deliver goods
交換 exchange
交際 social intercourse
　　交際舞（交誼舞）social dance
交樓（交房）hand over a completed unit
交還 return
交關（極度／非常）extremely; exceedingly
交 report（交報告）hand in a report

二手成交 second-hand transactions completed
外交 diplomacy
打交（打架）brawling; fight
忘年交 a friendship in which the difference of years is
　　forgotten; friendship between generations; friendship
　　between old and young people; good friends despite
　　great difference in age; the best of friends in spite of the
　　difference in ages
爭交（勸架）stop people from fighting with each other
社交 social intercourse
性交 act of love; action; sexual intercourse; sexual intimacy;
　　sleep together; venereal act; what Eve did with Adam
絕交 break off friendship
嗌交（吵架）argument; bicker; make a row;
　　quarrel; wrangle
嘈交（爭執）have a row; quarrel; wrangle
遞交 deliver; hand over
締交（訂交）① establish diplomatic relations ② contract a
　　friendship; form a friendship
鬧交（吵架）argue; quarrel
舊交 old acquaintance
勸交 mediate a quarrel; mediate between two quarrelling
　　parties; try to patch up a quarrel; try to stop people from
　　fighting each other
擲交（把東西交給別人）hand over
斷交 ① break off a friendship ② break off diplomatic
　　relations; sever diplomatic relations

【亦】jik⁶（也）also
亦即 namely; that is; viz.; i.e.
亦然 also; similarly; too
亦都（也）also

【仰】joeng⁵ ① look up ② admire ② lean on
仰天 look up to heaven
仰泳 backstroke
仰慕 admire; admire and respect; adore; look up to; regard
　　with admiration

久仰 I'm pleased to meet you

素仰 have always admired; have always looked up to
景仰 hold in deep respect; respect and admire

【仲】zung⁶（還）still
仲加（更加／還要）all the more; even more; further; more;
　　still more
仲未（還沒有）has not; not yet; still not yet
仲好（更好）so much the better
　　仲好講添（還說呢）don't tell me
仲有（還有）there's still
仲係（仍然／還是）still
仲兼（而且）what's more
仲差／衰（差多了）worse

不相伯仲 about the same
伯仲（兄弟長幼）brothers; older and younger brothers
咁仲（這還／豈能）how could

【伕】fu¹（勞動者）laborer

馬伕 pander; pimp; procure for prostitutes

【仵】ng⁵ similar
仵作佬（殯儀員／仵作）undertaker

【件】gin⁶ ① piece ② measure word for upper body items of clothing
件件俱全 all are complete
件號 piece number

一件 one piece
一件還一件（一件一件來）things should be dealt with
　　separately
大件 hulky
文件 document
切件（切塊兒）cut into pieces
汽車零件 automobile parts
事件 matter
案件 case
條件 condition
軟件 software
硬件 hardware
郵件 mail
備用零件 spare parts
零件 component parts; part; spare parts
電子郵件 email
電腦軟件 computer software
稿件 manuscript
緊急事件 emergency

歷史事件 historical event
類似事件 similar incidents

【任】jam⁶ (隨便) as you like

任由 as one sees fit
任何 any; whatever; whichever
任命 appoint; commission; designate; nominate
任務 assignment; duties; job; mission; responsibility; task
任揀 (隨便挑) choose whatever you like

公民責任 civic responsibilities
主任 chairman; director; head; minister
委任 appoint
兼任 ① hold a concurrent post ② part-time
責任 duty; obligation; responsibility
連任 be reappointed successively; be relected consecutively; renew one's terms of office
離任 leave office; leave one's post; resign from one's office; retire from one's office

【仿】fong² imitate

仿古 model after an antique
仿傚 after the model of; follow the example of; imitate; model oneself upon sb; on the model of
仿製 be modelled

模仿 imitate

【企】kei⁵ (站) stand

企一陣 (站一會兒) stand for a while
企人邊 (單人旁 / 單立人) the "person" (人) radical
企入啲 (往裏點兒) stand a little inside
企住 (站住) halt; stand one's ground; stop
企身 (立式) vertical
　企起身 (站起來) stand up
企定 (站住) stand still
企直 (站直) stand upright
企埋一邊 (站在一旁) stand back
企埋啲 (站裏邊點兒) stand closer to each other
企堂 (侍應生) ① waiter ② waitress
企理 (有條理 / 利落 / 整齊 / 整潔) neat; neat and clean; neat and tidy
企硬 (立場堅定 / 強硬) stand firm
企喺城樓睇馬打 (袖手旁觀) keep oneself out of the affair; make oneself stay out of the matter
企圖 intention
企業 corporation
　企業金融 corporate finance
企領 (豎領) stand collar; stand-up collar

企鵝 penguin
企穩 (站穩) come to a stop; stand firm; take a firm stand

中小企 small- and medium-sized enterprises
冇訂企 (沒有地方立足) be pushed out
行行企企 (不重要) at a loose end; an an idle end; at loose ends; be engaged in nothing; be occupied with nothing; dilly dally; do nothing; eat one's head off; fool about; fool around; goof; goof off; hang about; hang around; have nothing to do; idle about; idle along; idle away one's time; kick one's heels; loaf; lost and bewildered; mess about; mess around; moon about; not to do a hand's turn; not to do a stitch of work; not to lift a hand; play about in a foolish way; saunter; stroll; twiddle one's thumbs; twirl one's thumbs
返屋企 (回家) go home; return home
屋企 ① (家) home ② (家庭) family
眉精眼企 (長相精明機靈) know a trick or two; smart
息口持續低企 (金融業專有詞：指利息處於低的位置) interest rate being continuously low
戚企 (直立) stand upright
戚篤企 (站着) place upright
湊佢返屋企 (帶他 / 她回家) take sb home
喺屋企 (在家裏) at home
罰企 (罰站) to be made to stand still as a punishment

【伍】ng⁵ ① military unit ② associate with ③ five

伍長 lead of a five-soldier unit

落伍 outdated

【伏】fuk⁶ (趴) lie

伏低 (趴下) lie down
伏擊 ambuscade; ambush; still-hunt; waylay

【休】jau¹ ① rest ② cease

休克 coma
休息 rest; take a rest
　休息一吓 (休息一下) take a rest
休會 adjourn a meeting
休假 ① go on a vacation; have a holiday; take a cavation ② on leave; take a leave
休憩處 sitting-out area

一不做，二不休 (要麼不做，要做便做到底) not to stop half way once a thing is started
退休 retire
簝休 (不修邊幅的) slovenly

【伙】 fo² colleague

伙計 (店員／服務員／催員) waiter
伙食 board; fare; food; meal; mess; table
伙記 ① (員工) employee ② (服務員) waiter
伙頭 (廚師／大師傅) cook
　　伙頭將軍 (廚師) cook

入伙 move in
私伙 (私家物品) privately owned things
弊傢伙 (糟了) how terrible; oh dear; what a bad luck

【充】 cung¹ pose

充大頭鬼 (裝富／裝闊氣) pretend that one is rich or
　　powerful; put on the appearance of a man of wealth
充生晒 (假晚得) pretend to know sth
充電 ① recharge ② (休息) take a break
充撑場面 (撐場面) give one's support

冒充 pass off as; pretend to be

【份】 fan⁶ share

份子 one's share of expenses for a joint undertaking
份額 share

一份 one portion of
冇份 (沒有份) have no involvement in sth
孖份 (合伙) club together; make up the full amount of
　　money; pool shares
安份 know one's lot
夾份 (湊份子) club together; make up the full amount of
　　money; pool shares
見者有份 the seer has a share of sth
身份 identity
敆份 (湊份子) club together; make up the full amount of
　　money; pool shares
部份 part; portion; section
過份 go too far; overstep the bounds
緣份 destiny; fate
輩份 difference in seniority; seniority in a clan; seniority in a
　　family
應份 ought to; should

【佢】 koei⁵ ① (他) he ② (她) she ③ (它) it

佢份人幾好 (他為人挺好) he is quite nice
佢死佢賤 (管他／她的) not give a damn
佢哋 (他們／她們／它們) them; they
　　佢哋嘅 (他們的／她們的／它們的) their
佢話乜呀 (他說甚麼) what does he say
佢嘅 ① (他的) his ② (她的) her ③ (它的) its

天收佢 (他會遭天譴的) heaven will punish him
由佢 (讓它走) let go
由得佢 (由他) leave him alone; leave it; let him be; let him
　　please himself; let it be
好憎佢 (很恨他／她) hate sb very much
扙咗佢 (畫掉) wipe it off
吼實佢 (盯着他) keep a watch on him
困住佢 (把他關起來) confine him
扔咗佢 (扔掉) throw away
扰咗佢 (扔掉) throw it away
扰爛佢 (擊碎) smash it
呵吓佢 (安撫一下他) soothe him
直頭搵佢 (直接找他) contact him directly
咪爭住佢 (不要偏幫某人了) don't side with sb who is in
　　the wrong
吸住佢 (盯着他) keep a close watch on him
飛咗佢 (甩掉他) get rid of him
唔睬佢 (不理會他／她) pay no heed to sb
浸吓佢 (浸它一下) soak it
捉住佢 (抓住他) catch him
粉板字——唔啱就抹咗佢 (抹去了就是) forget it if what is
　　said is incorrect
唱衰佢 (到處說某人的壞話) saying that sb is worthless
啤啤佢 (喝一杯) let's have beer
掂佢 (碰他／她) touch him/her
掂到佢 (碰倒他／她) touched him/her
掟佢 (與他／她分手) break up with him/her
陪住佢 (陪住他／她) accompany sb; keep sb company; get
　　around sb
殺咗佢 (殺了他) kill him
眄吓佢 (瞥他一眼) glance at him
話之佢 (管他的) ① as you like; as you please
　　② couldn't care less
話吓佢 (訓斥某人) lecture sb
飲勝佢 (乾杯) bottoms up; cheers; drink a toast; drink to;
　　let's drink up; propose a toast; to
蔣咗佢 (得到她) get her
憎死佢 (恨透某人) hate sb deeply
撈勻佢 (拌勻) mix sth thoroughly
撇甩佢 (甩掉他) get rid of him
撇開佢 (撇開他) get rid of him
潤吓佢 (嘲諷一下他) give him a pleasant flavor
撻低佢 (打倒他) knock him down
操吓佢 (鍛鍊一下) help to drill him
擗咗佢 (扔掉它) throw it away
篤吓佢 (戳一下佢) stab him once
嬲死佢 (很生某人的氣) very angry with sb
擺平佢 (把某人搞定) punish sb
識得佢 (認識他) know him

【兆】siu⁶ omen
兆頭 omen; portent; sign

祥兆 good omen; propitious sign

【兇】hung¹ fearsome
兇手 assassin; killer; murderer
兇惡 evil; ferocious; malignant; wicked
兇神惡煞 (氣勢洶洶) fiendish and devilish; look furious

【先】sin¹ first
先人 ancestor
先入為主 have a prejudice against
先下手為強 catch the ball before the rebound
先生 ① (老師) teacher ② (男士的稱謂) mister; Mr.
　　③ (老公) husband
先先 (最先 / 起先) at first
先至 ① (才) just; not until; only; then and only then
　　② (剛剛) just now
　　幾難先至 (好不容易才…) by the skin of one's teeth;
　　　go to a lot of trouble; have a hard time; it takes a lot
　　　of time to; not easy at all; with much difficulty
先例 precedent
先到先得 first come, first served
先時 (以前 / 從前) ago; before; former; formerly; in the
　　past; once; previous; prior; used to be
先排 (早些天 / 前一陣子) earlier on; early on; not long ago
　　先一排 (早些天 / 前一陣子) earlier on; early on; not
　　　long ago
　　先嗰排 (早些天 / 前一陣子) earlier on; early on; not
　　　long ago
先斬後奏 act before reporting
先進 advanced
先嗰輪 (前一陣子) earlier on; early on; not long ago
先敬羅衣後敬人 (人靠衣裝) people usually open doors
　　to fine clothes
先頭 (起先 / 起初) at first; in the beginning
先禮後兵 a dog often barks before it bites

多謝先 (先謝謝你) thank you in advance
行先 (請) go first
你先 (請先) after you
我行先 (我先走) I'll go first
求先 (剛剛) a moment ago; just now
找數先 (先結賬) pay the bill first
抖吓先 (休息一會兒) have a short rest
爭先 compete
爭住先 (先欠某人) owe sb sth temporarily
係咁先 (就這樣了) that's all for now

咪住先 (等一等) hold on
祖先 ancestor
喏先 (剛剛) just now
頂住檔先 (臨時做) improvise
睇定啲先 (瞧着看) let's wait and see
睇過先 (先看一看) see what is going to happen before
　　making a decision
稍稍領先 have a slight lead
預先 in advance
領先 have a lead; lead; take the lead
閂住先 (先停一下) block it first
諗過先 (先想一想) think about it first
諗過度過先 (好好想一想) think it through first
優先 priority
頭先 (剛剛) a little while ago; a moment ago; just now

【光】gwong¹ ① (亮) bright ② light
光猛 (光亮 / 明亮 / 窗亮) bright; roomy and bright
光脫脫 (光溜溜) naked
光棍 ① (騙子) conman; swindler; trickster ② (單身漢)
　　bachelor; unmarried man
　　光棍佬 (騙子) trickster
　　光棍佬教仔 —— 便宜莫貪 don't be covetous of things on
　　　the cheap
　　光棍遇着冇皮柴 (騙子撞正騙子) a swindler takes in a
　　　swindler
光滑 glossy; sleek; slick; smooth
光管 (日光燈 / 管燈 / 燈管) fluorescent lamp; tube light
光碟 (光盤) light disk
光瞪瞪 (光耀奪目) dazzling; very bright
光頭 bald
　　光頭仔 (禿子) bald man
　　光頭佬 (禿子) bald man
　　光頭剔 (禿子) bald man
　　十個光頭九個富 (十個禿九個富) nine out of ten bald
　　　men are rich
光臨 arrive
光鮮 (簇新 / 光潔 / 新鮮 / 整潔) clean and tidy; neat;
　　neat and clean; prim; tidy and pretty

六點天光 (六點天亮) the day breaks at six a.m.
天光 (天亮) dawn; daybreak
天矇光 (天亮) at dawn; daybreak
日光 sunlight
月光 ① moon ② moonlight ③ bottom
目光 ① vision ② gaze
好光 very bright
好好陽光 very sunny
年三十晚有月光 (年三十晚出現月光 —— 冇可能) it's impossible

走光 a woman's underwear is shown due to careless dressing or posture

走清光 (全部都走了) all gone away

兩面光 (圓滑) please both parties

亮光 light

唔見得光 (不能見光) cannot be exposed to the light of day; keep sth secret

晒月光 (戀人在晚上約會) date under the moonlight; lovers basking in the moonlight

容光 facial expression; general appearance

清光 with nothing left

眼光光 (眼睜睜地) stare vacantly

發光 glow

發青光 (害青光眼) ① stare fixedly ② glaucoma

陽光 sunlight

間房好光 (房間很光亮) this room is very bright

賣面光 (賣好) curry favour with sb

螢光 fluorescence

濛濛光 (天亮) daybreak

燭光 candlelight

耀光 sparkle; sparkling

觀光 sightseeing

【全】cyun⁴ full

全力 all one's strength; all-out; do everything in one's power; in full strength; spare no effort; with all one's strength; with wholehearted dedication

　全力以赴 at full blast; at full stretch; boots and all; call forth all one's energy; dedicate oneself to; devote every effort to; do all in one's power; do everything in one's power; do one's best; do one's damnedest; do one's level best; do one's utmost; flat out; full sail; full steam ahead; full speed ahead; go all out; go for broke; go nap; go to all lengths; hammer and tongs; horse and foot; in full sail; like billy-o; make all-out efforts; make every effort to; muster all one's strength to cope with a given situation; overcome difficulties with one's entire energy; put all one's effort into; pull out all stops; put one's back into; put one's best foot forward; put one's best leg forward; put one's foot forward; put forth every effort; put one's heart into; spare no efforts; straight from the shoulder; strain every nerve; strive with all one's might for; tooth and nail; with both hands; with might and main; with teeth and all

全走 (去油 / 去蠔油) no oil and oyster sauce

全家 the whole family

　全家上上下下 the whole family

全國 countrywide; nation-wide; national; the entire country; throughout the country

全國上下 the whole nation from the leadship to the masses

全部 all; all of a lump; any and every; by the lump; complete; entire; full; in a lump; in one lump; in the lump; lock, stock, and barrel; one and all; the entire shoot; the whole; whole; total; without exception; whole

十全 all complete; full; perfect; utterly

件件俱全 all are complete

安全 safe; safety

完全 absolutely; complete; completely; entirely; fully; mere; perfectly; pure; thorough; totally; whole

成全 help

麻雀雖小，五臟俱全 (小但齊備) there is a life in a mussel though it is small

齊全 complete

【共】gung⁶ ① common; general ② altogether

共用 common; sharing

共同 common; in common; jointly; side by side

共計 add up to

共埋 (湊在一起 / 合起來) add up to; amount to; together

共處 coexist

公共 public

攏共 all told; altogether; in all

【再】zoi³ again

再三 again and again; over and over again; repeatedly; time and again

再次 a second time; again; another time

再見 adieu; adios; bye; bye-bye; cheerio; good day to you; goodbye; have a nice day; see you; see you again; see you around; so long

再造紙 (再生紙) recycled paper

再會 goodbye; see you again

再試 (又 / 再) again; also; in addition to; once again

【冰】bing¹ ice

冰水 ice water

　飲冰水 (喝冰水) drink iced water

冰室 (冷飲店) cold drinks shop

冰凍 freeze; frost; frozen

冰糖 rock sugar

多啲冰 (多一點兒冰) more ice

冷冰冰 cold; icy

刨冰 water ice

走冰（去冰）no ice
食冰（喝冰飲）have cold drinks
唔要冰（去冰）no ice
飲冰（喝冰飲）have cold drinks
溜冰 skate; skate on the ice; staking
踩冰（溜冰）ice-skate

【刑】jing⁴ sentence
刑事 criminal; penal
刑罰 criminal penalty; penalty; punishment

判刑 pass a sentence; sentence

【列】lit⁶ list
列入 be included in; be incorporated in; enter in a list; list
　　列入計劃 be incorporated in the plan
列出 list; make out; write out
列隊 fall into rank; file; line up; rank
　　列隊歡迎 line up to welcome
列舉 cite; enumerate; list
　　列舉如下 as listed below
　　列舉事實 cite facts

吉列（炸）deep-fried
並列 be juxtaposed; put sth on a par with; put sth on an equal footing; put side by side; stand side by side
庵列（煎蛋捲）omelette

【劣】lyut³ bad; inferior; of low quality
劣等 low-grade; of inferior quality; poor
劣勢 inferior position; inferior strength
劣質 of poor quality

拙劣 clumsy; inferior

【印】jan³ ①（圖章）imprint ② print
印水紙（吸水紙／吸墨紙）absorbent paper
印印腳 ①（輕輕鬆鬆）relaxed ②（享受人生）enjoy life
印刷 printing
　　印刷品 printed matter
印花 stamp
　　印花稅 stamp duty
印度 India
　　印度菜 Indian food
印章 chop
印象 impression
　　冇乜印象（沒有甚麼印象）not have any impression of sth or sb
印嘢（打印）print

印傭（印尼傭人）Indonesian maid

餅印（一模一樣）a copy of sb; a splitting image of sb; as like as two peas; cut from the same cloth; exactly alike; exactly the same; identical; like two peas in a pod; look the same
牙齒印（仇恨）a score to settle
爪印 nail mark; print; trace
凹凸印（鋼印）steel seal
扰印（打印／蓋圖章）stamp a chop
搬印（蓋印）affix one's seal
影印 copy; photocopy
複印 copy; duplicate; photocopy; xerox

【危】ngai⁴ danger
危危乎（危險）precarious
危急 hazardous; in a desperate situation; in a state of emergency; urgent
危機 crisis
危險 danger

生命垂危 at the gasp
岌岌可危 be placed in jeopardy; between the beetle and the block; extremely hazardous; hang by a hair; hang by a single thread; in a critical situation; in a precarious situation; in a tottering position; in great peril; in imminent danger
垂危 approaching death; at one's last gasp; close to death; critically ill; near one's end; terminally ill
乘人之危 capitalize on sb's difficulties; make use of sb's dilemma; take advantage of sb's precarious position

【合】hap⁶ join
合作 cooperate
　　搵人合作（找某人合作／找伙伴）find sb to cooperate
合併 merger
合法 legal
合約 contract
合格 pass
　　勉強合格 scrape through the examination
　　唔合格（不合格）fail
合桃（核桃）shelled walnut; walnut
　　合桃酥（桃酥）walnut cake
　　合桃露（合桃糊）sweet walnut soup
合時（當造）in season
　　邊啲最合時呀（哪些是當造的）what is in season
合得嚟（合得來）get along well
合理 reasonable

唔合理（不合理）unreasonable

合適 appropriate

合襯（配合／相襯／配得上）well-matched

巧合 by chance; by coincidence

回合 round

百合 lily

百年好合 have a long and harmonious married life

吻合 coincide; dovetail; fit; identical; tally; tally with

志同道合 cherish the same ideals and follow the same path; have a common goal; hit if off well together; in the same camp; of one mind; share the same ambition and purpose; share the same view; two minds with but a single thought

投資組合 investment portfolio

併合（合併）integrate; unite

宙合（包羅萬有的）all-embracing; all-encompassing

沓合（加上去）pile one upon another; superimpose

迎合 cater to; pander to; play up to

音響組合 hi-fi set

唔適合（不適合）inappropriate

珠聯璧合 excellent combination; excellent match; happy combination; perfect pair; strings of pearls and girdles of jade

組合 composition; compose; constitute; make up

場合 occasion; situation

集合 assemble

聚合 ① get together ② polymerization

適合 appropriate; suitable

融合 amalgamate; blend; coalesce; compromise; fuse; harmonize; mix together

聯合 united

縫合 sew up

璧合 perfect match

【吃】hek³（口吃）stammer; stutter

吃力 entail strenuous effort; laborious; strain

吃喝 eat and drink

吃喝玩樂 beer and skittles; cakes and ale; eat, drink, and be merry; feasting and reveling; gluttony and pleasure-seeking; idle away one's time in pleasure-seeking

吃虧 ① come to grief; get a beating; get the worst of it; suffer losses; take a beating ② at a disadvantage; in an unfavourable situation

口吃吃（結結巴巴）stammer a little

大小通吃 sweep all before one

黐餐飯吃（擾頓飯吃）get a free meal

【各】gok³ each

各自為政 each one minds their own business

各花入各眼（各人口味不同）beauty exists in the eyes of the beholder; beauty is just subjective; people have different tastes and preferences

各適其適（愛做甚麼就做甚麼）each takes what he needs

【吉】gat¹ ① lucky ②（空）empty

吉日 auspicious day; good day

　　擇吉日 choose a good day

吉列（炸）deep-fried

吉利 auspicious; lucky

吉車（空車）empty car

吉屋（空房子）unoccupied flat; unoccupied house

交吉（騰空了）hand over a completed unit

阿吉（雞）chicken

得個吉（一場空）come to nothing; draw water with a sieve; end up with nothing; get nothing

混吉（糊弄／瞎忙）fool around

【吋】cyun³ inch

腰圍廿三吋（腰圍二十三吋）one's waist measures twenty-three inches

【同】tung⁴ ①（一樣）same ②（和）and ③（替）for

同一鼻哥窿出氣（同聲同氣）breathe through the same nostrils; have the same opinion; in tune with; sing the same tune; talk exactly one like the other

同人（和人）with people

　　同人冇乜兩句（沒跟別人怒容相對）one does not have any argument with another person

　　同人唔同命，同遮唔同柄（同是人，命運卻各有不同）no man has the same fortune; no two people's fate is the same

同…有路（與某人有曖昧關係）have illicit intercourse with sb

同行 ①（內行）of the same trade ②（同一項專業）of the same profession

　　同行如敵國（內行人就如敵方）bitter rivalry and hatred exist among people in the same profession; two of a trade never agree

　　同…行得好埋（與某人很相熟）on very familiar terms with sb

　　同…行埋咗（與某人發生關係）have made love with sb

同志（同性戀者）gay; homosexual

女同志 (女同性戀者) les; lesbian
男同志 (男同性戀者) male homosexual
同事 colleague
同姓三分親 people with the same surname are somehow related
同性戀 gay love; homosexuality
同花順 straight flush
同枱食飯，各自修行 each does what he thinks is right
同埋 ① (和) and ② (一起) all together; at the same time; in company; in unison; simultaneously; together; together with
同時 at the same time; simultaneously
同班 classmate
同情 sympathy
同情心 sympathy
同理心 empathy
同意 agree; consent
同撈同煲 (患難與共) live together through fair and foul; stick together through adversity
同遮唔同柄，同人唔同命 (同是人，命運卻各有不同) the same group of people have different lot
同學 fellow student
　　同班同學 classmate
　　舊同學 (老同學) former classmate

小胡同 by-street
共同 common; in common; jointly; side by side
死胡同 blind alley; cul-de-sac; dead end; impasse
咁又唔同 (那又不一樣) it is different
胡同 alley; alleyway; lane; side road
英雄所見略同 great minds think alike
唔同 (不同 / 不一樣) different; various
與別不同 different from all others; different from other people; different from the common run; different from the rest; distinctive; extraordinary; flaky; not like others; not the same as others; out of the common; out of the ordinary; peculiar; uncommon; unlike others; unusual
零舍唔同 (特別不一樣) in a different class
贊同 agree with; approve of; be all for; consent to; countenance; endorse; go along with
靈舍唔同 (特別不一樣) entirely and totally different; quite a different pair of shoes

【名】ming⁴ (名字) name

名人 celebrity; famous person
　　成為名人 become a celebrity
名下 under sb's name
名片 calling card

交換名片 exchange name cards
留下名片 leave one's name card
名字 name
名次 position in a name list
名利 fame and fortune; fame and gain; fame and wealth
　　名利雙收 gain both fame and wealth
　　　名成利就 gain both fame and fortune
　　　追求名利 court fame and fortune
名言 famous remark; well-known saying
名門 illustrious family
　　名門之後 descendant of a notable family
　　名門望族 notable family and great clan
　　　出身名門 come from an illustrious family
名氣 fame; name; reputation
　　有啲名氣 (有點兒名氣) enjoy some reputation
名單 name list
　　列出名單 compile a name list
名堂 item
名勝 scenic spots
　　名勝古蹟 scenic spots and historical relics
名著 famous work
名貴 famous and precious
名牌 famous brand; luxury brand
　　名牌貨 branded product
名義 name
　　名義上 in name
名實 name and reality
　　名符其實 the name matches the reality
　　　有名無實 in name but not in reality
名銜 (姓名官銜 / 姓名職稱) designation
名模 famous model
名聲 reputation
名額 quota of people
　　名額有限 limited quota
名譽 ① fame; reputation ② honorary
　　名譽地位 fame and status
　　名譽掃地 be discredited

一舉成名 famous overnight
功名 scholarly honour and official rank
更改姓名 change one's name
乳名 child's pet name; infant name
命名 name
姓名 name
易名 change one's name
冒名 assume another's name
英名 good reputation
匿名 anonymous
域名 domain name

排名 ① listing ② ranking
莫名 indescribable; inexpressible
提名 nominate
揚名 become famous; become known; have one's name up; make a name for oneself
筆名 pen-name
貴姓名 what's your name
罪名 accusation; charge
著名 famous
虛名 bubble reputation; empty reputation; false reputation; undeserved reputation
馳名 ① spread one's fame ② famous; renowned; well-known
聞名 ① distinguished; famous; renowned; well-known ② familiar with sb's name; know sb by repute
慕名 long for fame
講低姓名 (留下姓名) leave one's name
題名 ① autograph; inscribe one's name ② subject; title; topic ③ entitle; name a work

【名】meng² (名字) name

戶口名 (帳號名) account name
出名 famous; well-known
有名 famous
改名 (取名字) ① give a name; name ② change a name
改／起花名 (改／起綽號) give sb a nickname
花名 (綽號) nickname
掛名 (名義上) in name; nominally
喺呢度簽名 (在這裏簽署) sign here
落名 (放上某人的簽字) put down one's signature
落你個名 (放上你的名字) put down your name
話名 (名義上) in name; nominally
寫低你個名 (寫下你的名字) write down your name
點名 call the roll; make a roll-call; roll-call
轉名 change the name of owner; transfer
簽名 affix one's signature to; attach one's signature to; autograph; put a signature to; put down one's signature; put one's name to; put one's signature to; set one's hand to; set one's name to; sign; sign one's name to; signature
幫我簽個名 could I have your autograph
藝名 professional name; stage name

【后】hau⁶ step

后冠 tiara

天后 Heaven Queen

皇后 queen

【吐】tou³ spit; vomit

吐明珠 brush the teeth
吐氣 give vent to pent-up feelings
　　吐氣揚眉 blow off steam in rejoicing; elated; feel proud; feel proud and elated after one suddenly comes to fame; rpoud and elated; wealth or good luck; happy and proud; hold one's head high; stand up with head high
吐痰 spit
　　禁止吐痰 spitting is prohibited
吐露 confess; disclose; reveal; tell

引起嘔吐 cause vomiting
半吞半吐 hesitate in speaking
吞吐 hesitant in speaking
吞吞吐吐 hem and haw; hesitate in speech; hum and haw; mince words; mutter and mumble; prunes and prism; say hesitantly; speak in a halting way; speak of things with scruple; speak with reservation; stumble over one's words; tick over
嘔吐 vomit
談吐 manner of speaking; style of conversation; the way a person talks

【向】hoeng³ direction

向上 ① up; upward ② make progress; strive upward; try to improve oneself
　　向上爬 ambitious; be intent on personal advancement; careerist; climb to the upper echelon of society; climb up the social ladder; intent on personal advancement; office seeker; social climber
向來 (一向) all along; consistently
向前 ahead; forward; go forward; onward
向後 ① backward; towards the back; turn around ② in the future

一向 all along; consistently; up to now
內向 introversion
方向 direction; orientation
相反方向 opposite direction
動向 tendency; trend
路向 direction
趨向 ① direction; tendency; trend ② incline to; tend to

【吏】lei⁶ official

污吏 corrupt officials

【吔】jaa¹ ① (吃) eat ② (呀) oh

吔吔烏 (很糟糕) very bad

吔飯 (吃飯) eat

**【吔】jaa⁵ (威吔是英文 "wire" 的音譯)
transliteration of "re" (from "wire")**

吊威吔 (吊鋼絲) hanging from wire

威吔 (鋼絲) (transliteration) wire

【吊】diu³ hang

吊尾 (跟蹤) follow sb

吊沙煲 (斷頓兒) can't afford the next meal; go
hungry; starve

吊味 (調味兒) add to the taste; adjust the taste

吊命 (依靠一小撮金錢來活命) depend on some source of
money to survive

吊起嚟賣 (提高身價) hoard up for a higher price; increase
prices when things are in great demand; speculate by
hoarding a commodity

吊帳 (圓頂蚊帳) hanging mosquito net

吊煲 (斷炊) go hungry

吊靴鬼 (跟尾蟲) limpet

吊嘴 (垂飾) pendant

吊燈 pendant lamp

吊頸 (上吊 / 自縊) commit suicide by hanging; hang
oneself

　　吊頸都要透氣 (再忙也要休息) need to have an
opportunity to relax no matter how busy one is; need
to take a rest

吊櫃 hanging cabinet

吊雞 (吊車 / 吊機) hoist

吊鐘 ① (小舌兒) little red tongue; uvula ② (倒掛金鐘)
fuchsia

吊癮 (吊胃口 / 搯了癮頭) not to satisfy the craving for the
time being; run out of drugs

吊鹽水 ① (打點滴 / 鹽水注射) transfusion ② (就業不足)
under-employment

半天吊 (不上不下的) hang in the balance; in a stalemate

唔嗲唔吊 (拖拖拉拉) careless; casual

單吊 (麻將術語：在牌戰中剩下來的一張) single piece

發羊吊 (發羊癇) epilepsy

嗲吊 (拖拖拉拉) sluggish and dilatory

嗲嗲吊 (拖泥帶水) irresponsible

【吓】haa⁵ a final particle

吓吓要 (動不動就要) apt to

　　吓吓要使錢 (動不動便揮霍) apt to spend money

仙都唔仙吓 (一分錢都沒有) very poor

四圍行吓 (四周走走) wander around

休息一吓 (休息一下) take a rest

死死吓 (半死) not lively

估估吓 (瞎猜) calculate roughly

抖吓 (休息一下) rest a while; take a rest

玩玩吓 (玩一玩) horse around; joke

威 (水) 吓 (威風一下) show one's prowess; show off one's
power and influence

威番吓 (顯威風) show off

拾吓拾吓 (傻呼呼) foolish

泵泵吓 (拖延) procrastinate

砐吓砐吓 (搖晃的) swaying; unstable

烏吓烏吓 (亂糟糟) messy

眨吓眨吓 (閃閃的) wink

眨眨吓 (一閃一閃) twinkle

笑吓 (笑一下) smile

眼尾都唔望吓 (不屑一顧) deliberately ignore sb

郁吓 (動一動) at every move; at every turn; at the drop of
a hat; at the slightest provocation; easily; frequently; on
every occasion

睇吓 (看一看) ① take a look ② depend on

傾吓 (談談) have a chat

傾吓問吓 (談問一下) ask and answer

試吓 (試試) have a try

歎吓 (享受一下) enjoy

瞓 (一) 吓 (打盹) take a nap

遲吓 (遲點兒) later; later on

霎吓霎吓 (一晃一晃) appear and disappear very quickly

濕吓濕吓 (零碎東西) odds and ends

講講吓 (光說不做) as one talks

攝高枕頭想吓 (把事情想清楚) sleep over it

【吖】aa¹ a final particle

有幾何吖 (能有幾回呀) this is infrequent

阻唔阻你吖 (打擾你嗎) excuse me

唔出奇吖 (有甚麼奇怪) there's nothing strange about sth

睇住嚟吖 (瞧着看) just wait and see

睇落幾好吖 (看起來不錯啊) it looks fine

曉未吖 (曉得了沒有 / 懂了嗎) have you understood

擦飽未吖 (吃飽了沒有) have you eaten to the full

點得吖 (怎樣可以) how can it be

【回】wui⁴ (退) return

回水 (退錢) refund

回民 people of the Hui nationality

回合 round

回扣 (賠錢) pay damages

回佣 (回扣) kick-back; rebate
回尾 (退回) give back; return; send back
回南 (天氣轉暖) the weather gets warm
回流 back-flow
回馬槍 (槍法的一種：坐在馬背上面裝逃走，突然調頭襲擊對方) back thrust
回教寺 (清真寺) mosque
回報 return
回樽 (退瓶子) return the bottle
回應 (反應) response
回贈 rebate
回禮 ① send a return gift ② return the courtesy of sb

召回 recall
即日來回 same day return
來回 ① to and fro ② make a return jouney; make a round trip

【因】jan¹ ① (因為) because ② (估計 / 估量 / 算算) estimate

因小失大 spoil a ship for a halfpenny worth of tar
因加得減 (弄巧反拙) cunning outwits itself; get into trouble through clever means; in trying to be smart, one makes oneself look foolish; make a fool of oneself in trying to be smart; outsmart oneself; overreach oneself; overshoot oneself; overshoot the mark; suffer from being too smart; try to be clever but end in being a fool; try to be clever but end up a fool; try to be clever but turn out the contrary; try to be clever only to end up with a blunder; turn out to the clumsy sleight of hand
因由 (原因 / 根據) reason
因此 for this reason; on this account
因住 ① (限著) not to exceed the limit ② (小心) take care of oneself ③ control one's emotions ④ (提防) beware of one's life; watch out
　因住使錢 (量入為出) don't overspend
　因住遲到 make sure you're on time
因何 (為何 / 為甚麼) how is it that; what for; why; why is it that; why oh why
因果 cause and effect
因為 because

內因 internal cause
只因 for the simple reason that; only because
事出有因 a thing has its cause; everything has its seed; it is by no means accidental; no smoke without fire; not devoid of truth; there is a reason for it; there is good cause for it; there is no smoke without fire; this happens not without reason; where there's smoke there's fire

事因 after; as; as a result of; at; because; because of; by; by dint of; by reason of; by right of; by virtue of; due to; failing; for; from; in; in consequence of; in consideration of; in default of; in right of; in that; in the absence of; in view of; in virtue of; inasmuch as; of; on; on account of; on the ground of; on the ground that; on the score of; out of; over; owing to; seeing that; since; thanks to; that; through; wanting; what with; with
皆因 (全因為) because of; due to
捉依因 (捉迷藏) play hide-and-seek
誘因 incentive; inducement; remote cause

【在】zoi⁶ exist

在生 (活著 / 健在) alive
在行 (內行) be skilled; be well acquainted with a task
在我嚟講 (對我來說) as for me; for me
在所不免 (在所難免) can hardly be avoided; impossible to be avoided; scarcely avoidable; unavoidable
在場 on the scene; on the spot; present
在意 use caution
　唔在意 (不留心) not careful
在職 at one's post; hold a position; in-service; on the job

人在人情在 while a person lives, his favours are remembered
內在 inherent; inner; internal; intrinsic
好在 (幸好) as luck would have it; but for; fortunately; luckily; thanks to
好唔自在 (很別扭) feel very uncomfortable
存在 existence
旨在 with the intention of
自在 ① free ② relaxing
志在 aim at; with the intention of
唔自在 (很別扭) ① not feeling comfortable ② not care a bit
唔志在 (不在乎) not to care a fig
唔爭在 (不差) can do without

【地】dei⁶ ① ground ② (土地) land

地上執到寶，問天問地攞唔倒 (街上拾得喜愛的東西，捨不得分給別人) things that one picks up from the ground cannot be taken away by any means
地下 ① (一樓 / 底層) ground floor ② (地下的) underground
　地下情 secret love affair
　地下鐵 MTR (Mass Transit Railway)
地中海 ① Mediterranean Sea ② (禿子) bald in the middle of the head
地少人多 a small place with a large population
地心吸力 gravity
地方 place

一笪地方（一個地方）a place
老地方 the same old place
嗰笪地方（那個地方）that place

地水（盲人）blind person
地台 flooring
地位 status
地址 address
　　改地址 change of address
地牢（地下室）basement
　　地牢商場 underground shopping mall
地底泥 ①（不受尊敬的人）sb not worthy of respect
　　②（劣質的物品）sth cheap and nasty
地拖（拖把）mop; swop
地板 floor
柚木地板 teak floor
地庫（地下室）basement
地區 area
　　局部地區 parts of an area
　　鄰近地區 neighbourhood
地球 earth
地理 geography
地產 real estate
　　地產公司 real estate company
　　地產代理 estate agent
　　　　持牌地產代理 licensed estate agent
　　地產新聞 property news
　　地產經紀 real estate agent; property agent
　　地產樓盤 units for sale
地勤 ground service
地稅 rates bill
地圖 map
　　一幅地圖（一張地圖）a map
地痞（土霸）local gangster
地塘（曬穀場）grain-sunning ground
地雷 ① mine ②（動物的糞便）animal shit on the road
地腳（地基）foundation; ground
地獄 hell
地踎（廉宜的餐廳）very cheap restaurant
地價 land price
　　補地價 pay a premium to the government
地盤 ①（工地 / 建築地盤）building site; construction site
　　②（黑幫控制的地方）triad society district
　　地盤工人 construction worker
　　地盤佬（建築工人）construction worker
　　爭地盤 fight for territory
　　建築地盤（建築工地）building site; construction site
地震 ① earthquake ② shake-up in a large company
地頭（地方 / 地盤）sphere of operation; territory
　　地頭蛇 sb who knows a particular area well

地頭龍 powerful figure in a particular area
地頭蟲（地頭蛇）sb who knows a particular area well
地檔（地攤兒）street-floor stall
地膽 ①（地頭蛇）sb who knows a particular area well
　　② local gangster ③ a cock on its own dunghill
地氈（地毯）carpet
　　一張 / 塊地氈 a carpet
地點 location
地 / 港鐵 ① MTR (Mass Transit Railway) ② subway; underground railway
地 / 港鐵站 MTR (Mass Transit Railway) station

近地 / 港鐵站 close to the MTR station
搭地 / 港鐵（乘地 / 港鐵）take the MTR (Mass Transit Railway)
一笪 / 幅（一塊地）a plot of land; a piece of land
一幅草地（一片草地）a piece of grassland
土地 field
內地 mainland
分居兩地 live in two separate places
天地 heaven and earth
心地（心腸）disposition; heart
世界各地 places all over the world
出人頭地 come out first
本地 indigenous; local; native
生人霸死地（佔着茅坑不拉屎）block the path of others
田地 ① agricultural land; farmland; field ② plight; wretched situation
白蘭地 brandy
目的地 destination
名譽掃地 be discredited
好心地（好心腸）kind-hearted
好地地（好端端的）in good order; in perfectly good condition
死心塌地 hell-bent on sb
扰地（跺腳）stamp the ground
甸子地 marshy grassland
車天車地（吹牛吹得天花亂墜）have an idle talk with sb
亞駝行路——春春地（比上不足比下有餘）take a mean course
呼天搶地 cry bitterly and loudly in excessive grief; utter cries of anguish
拔蘭地 (transliteration) brandy
拖地 / 抹地 mop the floor
旺地 good land; prosperous place
波地（足球場）football field
花天酒地 attend a dinner with sing-song girls; be in the world of wine and women; be on the loose; be on the tiles; be out on the tiles; go on the loose; go on the

racket; go on the tiles; guzzle and carouse to one's heart content; guzzle and have a good time; have one's fling; indulge in fast life and debauchery; led a decadent and dissolute life; lead a fast life; live in the world of wine and women; sow a large crop of wild oats

采地 fief

陀地 (土霸) protection

指天篤地 sheer rubbish; talk nonsense

眈天望地 (東張西望) glance this way and that way

風吹芫荽——衰 (垂) 到貼地 (倒霉 / 楣) reach the pitch of bad fortune

席地 on the ground

旅遊勝地 tourist resort

笑到轆地 (笑得打跌) burst out laughing

茫茫大地 boundless land

衰到貼地 (倒楣) extremely nasty

草地 grassland

陣地 battle field; position

揆 / 睩 / 碌 / 轆 / 擸地 (在地上打滾兒) roll on the ground

掘地 turn up the soil

荒地 no man's land; wasteland

清清地 (清淡的) plain and refreshing taste

陸地 dry land; land

場地 place; site; space

揼落地 (扔在地上) throw to the ground

移民外地 emigration

殖民地 colony

量地 (沒做工的) be out of job; be unemployed

園地 ① garden plot ② field; scope

遍地 everywhere; throughout the land

飲到大大地 (喝到醉了) drink and get drunk

墓地 cemetery

彈丸之地 tiny little place

質地 quality; texture

趣趣地 (些微) for fun

擔天望地 (東張西望) gaze this way and that; stare about; watch out furtively to the east and west

餘地 alternative; leeway; margin; room; spare space; latitude

濕濕地 (濕濕的) damp

謝天謝地 God be praised; God be thanked; thank God; thank goodness; thank heavens; thank one's stars; thank the Lord

驚天動地 earthshaking; shake heaven and earth; startle the world; surprise the world; titanic; tremendous; worldshaking

【多】 do[1] many; much

多一事長一智 (經一事長一智) by every affair a person transacts; in doing, one learns; one learns from experience; wisdom comes from experience

多士 (吐司 / 烤麵包) (transliteration) toast

多士爐 (烤箱) toaster

　一件多士 a piece of toast

　一塊多士 (一件多士) a piece of toast

　西多士 French toast

多少 (一點兒) a little

　或多或少 more or less

多心 (三心兩意) change one's mind constantly; have two minds; in two minds; infirm of purpose; irresolute; of two minds; play the field; undecided; vacillating

多手 touch things out of curiosity

　多手多腳 touch things one likes

多多 (很多) many

多事 ① nosy ② (事兒媽) nosy girls

　多事實 (事兒媽) nosy girls

多計 (點子多) full of wicked ideas

多個香爐多隻鬼 (多一個香爐多一位神道) the more the competitors, the keener the competition

多除少補 (多退少補) return the overcharge and demand payment of the shortage; return the surplus and charge the balance; the balances will be paid to either side as the case may be

多得 (多虧 / 幸虧) thanks to

　多得你嗰 (多虧你了) thanks to you; it owes much to you

多啲 (多點兒) more

　多啲冰 (多點兒冰) more ice

多數 (大多 / 大部份) for the most part; mostly

多餘 (多此一舉) redundant

多謝 (謝謝) thank you

　多謝先 (先謝謝) thank you in advance

　多謝晒 (太謝謝了) thank you so much

多籮籮 (多得很) many; very much

人多 many people

人多車多 a large population with lots of traffic

口多多 (多嘴多舌) like to gossip; shoot off one's mouth; talk too much

士多 store

心多 (心眼兒多) over-suspicious

心多多 (三心兩意) in two minds

手多 (多手) touch things when one should not

手多 (腳) 多 (多手) touch things when one should not

奶油多 (奶油多士) toast with butter and concentrated milk

地少人多 a small place with a large population

好多 a lot of; many; plenty

好番好多 (好多了) (be) much better (now)

老竇都要多 (貪小便宜) be greedy for gains

至多 at most; the most

爭好多 (差很多) much difference

夜長夢多 too long a delay causes hitches

油占多 (牛油果醬多士) toast with butter and jam

油多 (牛油多士) toast with butter

計多 (算多了) over-charge

食得禾米多 (多行不義) have made lots of people fall into one's foolery

唔多 (不太) don't...very much

唔理得咁多 (不能理會太多) cast all caution to the wind

唔論幾多 (無論多少) ① no matter how much ② no matter how many

差好多 entirely different; very different

差唔多 (差很多) ① almost; around; nearly ② about the same; more or less; much of a muchness; similar

啲咁多 (一點點) a little bit; a wee bit

理佢咁多 (算了吧) forget it

眾多 multitudinous; numerous

許多 a big percentage of; a crowd of; a flock of; a good deal of; a good few of; a great deal of; a great many; a heap of; a host of; a hundred and one; a large amount of; a large body of; a large number of; a large quantity of; a lot; a lot of; a mass of; a number of; a pile of; a power of; a sight of; a store of; a thousand and one; a wealth of; a world of; all manner of; an army of; bags of; heaps of; hundreds of; in profusion; lots and lots of; lots of; many; many in number; much; no end of; not a few; numbers of; numerous; plenty; plenty of; quite a few; stacks of; thousands of; volumes of

幾多 (多少 / 幾) ① how many ② how much

越嚟越多 (越來越) more and more

路少車多 many vehicles and few roads

講多錯多 (說得多錯得多) the least said, the soonest mended; the more one says, the more mistakes one makes

雞碎咁多 (一點點兒) a few; a little; a small amount of sth; chicken feed; peanuts

薩爾瓦多 (transliteration) El Salvador

【奸】gaan¹ cunning

奸茅 (賴皮) rascally; shameless; shameless behaviour; unreasonable

奸笑 sinister smile

奸賴 (耍賴 / 耍花招) cunning; dishonest; tricky

奸賴貓 (賴皮) cunning; dishonest; tricky

姑息養奸 excessive indulgence breeds traitors; indulge the evildoers; lenient towards villains and let them grow; overindulgence nurtures evil; pardon makes offenders; to tolerate evil is to abet it; tolerant and indulgent

朋比為奸 act in collusion with; claw me and I will claw thee; claw me, claw thee; collude in doing evil; conspire for illegal ends; gang up for evil purposes; join in plotting reason; play booty; scratch me and I'll scratch you; scratch my back and I'll scratch yours; work hand in glove with sb for evil doings

漢奸 traitor

【好】hou² ① good; nice ② very

好人 (人好) good person; goodie; goody; nice person

好人有限 far from being a good person

好人事 (友善 / 和藹可親) affable; helpful; kind-hearted

好人難做 a sage is often regarded as a savage

幾好人 (人挺好) a nice person

好力 (力氣大) have great strength

好大筆錢 (很大筆錢) large amount of money

好女兩頭瞞 (兩面討好) make the best of both worlds

好天 (好天氣 / 晴天 / 晴朗) fine day; good clear day

好天搵埋落雨米 (未雨綢繆) gather hay against a rainy day

好少 rarely; very few

好少何 (很少) rarely

好少理 ① (不過問) not look into ② (不管) couldn't be bothered

好心 good-heartedness

好心有好報 (善有善報) a good act will be well rewarded; fortune is the companion of virtue; good will be rewarded with good; goodness will have a good reward; kind deeds pay rich dividends to the doer

好心唔怕做 (好心不怕做) not afraid to do good deeds; have one's heart in the right place

好心唔得好報 (好心沒善報) recompense good with evil

好心着雷殛 (好心當作驢肝肺) bite the hand that feeds one; recompense good with evil

好水有幾多朝 (人生沒幾回好機會) there is not much of such a good opportunity in one's life

好叻 (了不起) ① very good ② very smart

好失威 (殺了威風) take sb down a peg or two

好市 (賣得好) sell well

好打 good at fighting

好正 (好棒 / 超讚) gorgeous; very good

好光 (很亮) very bright

間房好光 (房間很亮) this room is very bright

好在 (幸虧) as luck would have it; but for; fortunately; luckily; thanks to

好地地 (好好地 / 好端端) in good order; in perfectly good condition

好多 (很多) a lot of; many; plenty

好多時 (很多時) very often

好好 ① well ② very good
　好好天 (天氣很好) it's a nice day; the weather is beautiful
　好好先生 Mr Goody Goody; Mr Nice Guy
　好好多 (好多了) much better

好忙 very busy

好死 (好心) with good intentions

好老 (很老) very old

好耳 (耳朵好) have sharp ears

好肉 (肉多) fleshy

好行 (慢走 / 好走) goodbye; take care

好串 (很囂張) ① cocky ② stuck-up

好似 (似乎 / 好像 / 很像) as if; look like; resemble; seem; seem like
　好似咁 (好像這樣) like this

好夾 (很合得來) get along well; hit it off

好乖 very good; very obedient

好事不出門，壞事傳千里 good news goes on clutchers but ill news flies apace

好使好用 (聽使喚) good to use

好佬怕爛佬 (好人怕壞人) a pigeon makes no friends with a hawk

好到極 (好極了) excellent; great

好味 (味道很好) delicious
　好好味 (味道好棒) very tasty

好定當 (不慌不忙) calmly; deliberately; keep a level head; keep one's head; neither alarmed nor excited; take one's time; unhurried; with full composure; without haste or confusion; without hurry or bustle

好物沉歸底 the best comes last; the best fish swim near the bottom

好玩 (好玩兒) amusing; enjoyable; funny; interesting

好返晒 (完全痊癒了 / 全好了) be fully recovered

好勁 (帶勁) excellent

好型 (時髦) very stylish

好眉好貌生沙蝨 (相貌堂堂，滿肚子壞水) a fair face hides a foul heart

好紅 ① very red ② very popular

好耐 (很久) for a long time; for yonks; yonks ago
　好耐冇見 (很久沒見) haven't seen each other for a long time; haven't seen you for ages; long time no see

好苦 (很苦) very bitter

好食 (好吃) delicious; good to eat; tasty; yummy
　好食爭崩頭 (見便宜就搶) grab sth when it is cheap
　冇啖好食 (吃也沒有一口好吃的) ① nothing good to eat ② no profits to be gained ③ struggle to make a living
　好好食 (味道好棒) delicious; good to eat; tasty; very tasty; yummy

好難食 (好難吃) hard to eat
　鬼咁好食 (怪好吃的) quite delicious

好香 (很香) it smells good; very fragrant

好凍 (很冷) very cold

好氣 ① (説個不停 / 囉嗦) talkative ② (有耐性) patient

好臭 (很臭) very smelly

好衰唔衰 (真倒霉 / 運氣不好 / 最糟糕的是) unfortunately; unluckily

好馬不食回頭草 a bird flying away from the cage will never come back to be fed

好鬼 (非常) very

好做唔做 (好幹不幹) not doing what needs to be done

好啱傾 (談得來) be congenial to each other

好唱口 ① (唱不停) never stop singing ② (唱得好聽) good singing

好啲 (好些了) better

好彩 ① (幸好 / 幸運 / 幸虧) fortunately; luckily ② (好在) just as well
　大話夾好彩 (吹牛過骨) all by good luck

好掂 (很不錯) quite good
　呢排好掂 (這些天很不錯) quite good these days

好涼 (很涼) very cool

好淡 (很淡) too light in taste

好焗 (很悶) stuffy; suffocating; very stuffy

好猛 (很 / 非常) very
　好猛水 (水很衝) the water is strong
　好猛火 (火很旺) the fire is fierce
　好猛風 (風勢很猛) the wind is strong
　好猛鬼 (鬼很多) full of ghosts

好甜 (很甜) very sweet

好眼 (眼力好) have good eyesight

好景 (景氣好) prosperity

好番 (痊癒) recover
　好番未 (痊癒了沒有) have you recovered
　好番好多 (好多了) be much better now
　好番嘞 (已痊癒) have recovered

好痛 (很痛) very painful
　對眼好痛 (雙眼很痛) my eyes hurt

好睇 ① (好看) good-looking ② interesting to watch ③ interesting to read
　好睇唔好食 (好看不好吃) good looking but of no practical use
　好好睇睇 (像像樣樣地) decently

好悶 (很悶) very boring
　覺得好悶 (覺得很悶) feel very bored

好閒 (小意思 / 小事兒 / 不要緊) it's nothing; never mind
　好閒啫 (沒甚麼 / 沒關係) it doesn't matter; it's nothing; never mind; that's all right

好黑 (很黑) ① it's dark ② very dark

好亂（很亂）very messy
　　個腦好亂（腦袋一片糟）cannot think straight
　　間屋好亂（屋子很亂）the house is really messy
好傾（談得來）get along with sb
好想 eager to
好感 favourable impression
好搵（賺很多）make a lot of money
好暖（很暖）very warm
好腥行（慢走）goodbye; take care
好話 not at all; you're welcome
　　好話唔好聽（說了別見怪／說句不好聽的）frankly
　　　　speaking; to be blunt
　　好話為（好說）that can be settled easily
　　好話嘅（對了／沒錯）that's right
好逼（很擠）① very crowded ② cramped
好運（好運氣）good fortune
　　交好運（趕上好運氣）run into good fortune
　　祝你好運 good luck; good luck to you
好過 be better than
　　好過去搶（比搶更好）what one gets is better than
　　　　robbing others
好飲（好喝）tasty
　　好好飲（很好喝）very tasty
好憎佢（好討厭他／她）hate sb very much
好嘞（好了）well
好嘢 ①（好極了）great ②（好東西）good stuff; good things
　　你好嘢（你真可以）you're really great
　　真好嘢（真棒）it's really great
好漢不吃眼前虧 it is better to avoid visible loss than it is
　　to brave it out
好辣（很辣）very spicy
好酸（很酸）very sour
好遠（很遠）very far
　　相距好遠（相距很遠）far away from
好樣（樣子好）good-looking
好熱（很熱）very hot
好窮（很窮）very poor
好瞓（好睡）sound sleep
好賣 sell well
　　好好賣 sell very well
好靚（很漂亮）very beautiful; very pretty
　　生得好靚（長得很漂亮）sb is beautiful
　　你好靚（你很漂亮）you are very beautiful
　　彩色好靚（彩色很漂亮）the colours are beautiful
好橋（好點子）good tactic
好遲（很晚）very late
好醒（很機靈）very smart
好靜（很寧靜）very quiet
好戲在後頭 there will be sth interesting to see a little later

好聲（小心／當心）careful; take care
　　好聲行（慢走）goodbye; take care
好懶（很懶）very lazy
好鹹（很鹹）very salty
好襯（很相襯）good match; match well with
好 cool（很酷）in fashion; so cool
好 man（很男子氣）very manly; very masculine

人無千日好 no person is fortunate forever
十分好 very good
又好 all right; as well and good; it may not be a bad idea;
　　may be well; that is fine
千祈唔好 never ever
友好 ① close friend; friend ② amicable; amity; buddy-
　　buddy; congenial friendly
天氣好好 it's a nice day; the weather is beautiful
只好 have to; the next best thing to do is to; the only
　　alternative is to
手腳唔好（愛偷東西）have a tendency of stealing
仲好（更好）so much the better
至好 had better; it might as well
老相好 ex-lover
佢份人幾好（他為人挺好的）he is quite nice
利好 advantage
良好 fine; good; well
言歸於好 be reconciled; become reconciled; bury the
　　hatchet; bury the tomahawk; heal the breach; kiss and
　　be friends; maintain amicable relations hereafter; make
　　friends again; make it up with sb; make one's peace with
　　sb; make peace with; make sb's peace with; make up a
　　quarrel; on good terms again; put up the sword; reconcile;
　　resume friendship; shake and be friends; sink a feud;
　　smoke the pipe of peace; square oneself with; start with
　　a clean slate
兩面討好 please both parties
咁好（那麼好）so nice
奉承討好 fawn upon sb; flatter; lick the feet of sb; toady
幸好 fortunately; just as well; luckily
美好 fine; glorious; happy
面色唔好（臉色不好）look blue about the gills; look green
　　about the gills; look white about the gills; look yellow
　　about the gills; look pale; not to look oneself; off colour
起好（完成建工）complete the construction
唔好（不要／不好）do not; not good
唔做中唔做保，唔做媒人三代好（不做中間人）one who
　　does not engage himself in the business of a middleman
　　or a guarantor will have worthy descendants for three
　　generations
唔夠好（不夠好）not good enough

唔睇好（不被看好）not optimistic about sth

討好 blandish; butter up; cotton up to; curry favour with; fawn on; fawn upon; get in with; ingratiate oneself with; keep sb sweet; make up to; play up to; please; polish the apple; shine up to; suck up to; sweeten up; throw oneself at; throw oneself at sb's head; toady to

鬼咁好（非常好）very good

做得好 well done

做得好好 well done

唱好（說好話）say sth good about sth/sb

啱好（剛好）by chance

啱啱好（剛剛好）as right as nails; just right

執好（整理）make neat; tidy up

最好 best

幾好 not bad; quite good

睇好（看好）be optimistic about sth

腳頭好（人生的運氣好）bring good fortune

越多越好 as much as possible; the more, the better

對身體好 good for health

瞓得唔好（睡得不好）did not sleep very well

講好（說定了）come to an agreement

點話點好（你決定）as you please

點算好（怎麼辦）what shall we do

點解唔好（為甚麼不好）why not

疊好 fold up

【好】hou³ be fond of

好色 lecherous; sex-obsessed

好奇 curious

　　好奇心 curiosity

好玩（愛玩兒）fond of playing

好食（好吃／愛吃）fond of eating

　　好食懶飛（好吃懶做）eat but do nothing; eat one's head off; lazy

　　好酒（好喝酒／愛喝酒）fond of the bottle

好煙（愛抽煙）fond of smoking

好靚（好打扮／愛打扮）fond of making oneself pretty

好賭（愛賭）fond of gambling

心頭好 one's favourite thing

各有所好 each follows their own bent; each has their hobby; each has their likes and dislikes; every person has their hobby-horse; everyone to their own taste; every person to their taste; tastes differ; there is no accounting for tastes

投其所好 cater to sb's likes; cater to sb's pleasure; cater to sb's tastes; cater to sb's wishes; cater to the needs of sb; give sb exactly what they like; hit on what sb likes; offer what sb is hankering after; rub sb the right way; suit one's fancy; take a fancy to; take sb's fancy; tickle the ear of sb; to one's liking

【如】jyu⁴ if

如此類推 so on and so forth

如果 if

　　如果係咁（如果是這樣）if it were so; if that's the case; in that case

　　如果唔係（如果不是）otherwise

如意吉祥 may your wishes come true and you be fortunate

不如 how about; it would be better if

弗如 not as good as; not equal to; worse than

例如 for example; for instance; such as

【妄】mong⁵ reckless

妄自 excess presumptuous

　　妄自菲薄 excessively humble; have a sense of inferiority; have too low an opinion of oneself; improperly belittle oneself; look down upon oneself; think lightly of oneself; think too lowly of oneself; underestimate oneself; undervalue oneself; unduly humble oneself

　　妄自尊大 aggrandize oneself; arrogant and overweening; be eaten up with pride; be given to swaggering; be puffed up with pride; be puffed up with self-importance; be well wadded with conceit; boast wildly of oneself; get too big for one's boots; get too big for one's breeches; get too big for one's shoes; get too big for one's trousers; give oneself airs; grow too big for one's boots; have too high an opinion of oneself; indulge in foolish display; overbearing; overweening; put on the ritz; self-conceited; self-glorification; self-important; set oneself up as superior to everyone; swell with pride; think no end of oneself; think no small beer of oneself

妄想 absurd pursuit; daydream; delusion; forlorn hope; kink; vain hope; wishful thinking

狂妄 arrogant; presumptuous

姑妄 see no harm in sth

【字】zi⁶ ① character ② word

字母 alphabet

字典 dictionary

　　一本字典 a dictionary

字紙笠（字紙簍／廢紙簍）waste basket; waste paper basket

字粒（鉛字）lead type

　　執字粒（排字）typesetting

字詞 words and phrases
字號 company
　　老字號 established company
字幕 caption; subtitle; title

一行字 a line of characters
一隻字 a character
一個字（五分鐘）five minutes
一點一個字（一點零五分）five past one
一點七個字（一點三十五分）one thirty-five; twenty-five
　　to two
一點九個字（一點四十五分）a quarter to two; one forty-five
一點八個字（一點四十分）one forty; twenty to two
一點十個字（一點五十分）one fifty; ten to two
一點三個字（一點十五分）a quarter past one; one fifteen
一點五個字（一點二十五分）one twenty-five; twenty-five
　　past one
一點四個字（一點二十分）one twenty; twenty past one
一點兩個字（一點十分）ten past one
丁字 T-shaped
九個字（四十五分鐘）forty-five minutes; three quarters of
　　an hour
八字 The Eight Characters relating to the celestial stems
　　and earth branches of the year, month, day, and hour of
　　one's birth
十字 cross; cross-shaped
三個字（十五分鐘）fifteen minutes
大字（書法）Chinese characters written with a
　　writing brush
文字 ① character; word ② language
白紙黑字 in black and white; in print; in writing
凸字（點字）braille character
打字 type
生字 vocabulary
名字 name
串字（拼寫）transliterate
別字 ① mispronounced character; wrongly written character
　　② alias
赤字 deficit; in the red
刻字 carve characters on a seal
咬字 enunciate
隻字（一個字）brief note; single character; single word
鬥字 orthography
得個睇字（光靠外表）not practical
得個講字（光靠一把口）all talk and no action
深筆字（繁體字）traditional Chinese character
植字 typeset
睇八字（看八字）match and compare the Eight Characters
　　before marriage

漢字 Chinese character
寫大字（書法）do Chinese calligraphy
寫字 writing
數字 figure
簡筆字（簡體字）simplified Chinese character
簽字 affix one's signature to; attach one's signature to;
　　autograph; put a signature to; put down one's signature;
　　put one's name to; put one's signature to; set one's
　　hand to; set one's name to; sign; sign one's name to;
　　signature
雞㕮咁大隻字（字體碩大）very large characters
識字 literate

【存】cyun⁴ save
存亡 live or die; survive or perish; survive and downfall
存在 existence
存款 ① deposit; deposit money ② bank savings
存貨 inventory
存摺（存折／存款簿）bankbook; passbook
存錢 ① deposit ② save

並存 co-exist
逆境求存 try to survive in adverse circumstances
庫存 inventory; repertory; reserve; stock
現金結存 cash balance
惠存（請保存）please keep it as a souvenir
儲存 deposit

【孖】maa¹（兩個人）twin
孖女（雙生女／雙胞胎／孿生姐妹）twin girls;
　　twin sisters
　　　一對孖女（一雙孿生姐妹）twin sisters
孖仔（雙生子／雙胞胎／孿生兄弟）twin boys; twin
　　brothers
　　　一對孖仔（一雙孿生兄弟）twin brothers
孖必（兩名警察拍檔巡邏）policemen patrolling in pairs
孖生（孿生）twins
孖份（合夥／湊份子／湊份兒）club together; make up the
　　full amount of money; pool shares
孖指（六指兒）hand with six fingers
孖展（保證金）(transliteration) margin
孖站（共站）co-station
孖煙通（平內褲）boxer shorts
孖鋪（合睡／兩人同睡一張床）two persons sleeping on
　　one bed
孖辮女（辮子女孩）girl with hair in braids

打孖（成對）in pairs
黑孖孖（黑漆漆）very dark

【宅】zaak⁶ residence

宅心 intention
　　宅心仁厚 of a kindly disposition; settle the mind with
　　　　benevolence and honesty
宅院 house with a courtyard
宅園 private garden

住宅 apartment
坤宅 bride's family
服務式住宅（公寓）serviced apartment
查家宅（查戶口）make a through and detailed inquiry
　　into sb
買豪宅 buy a luxurious apartment
豪宅 luxurious apartment

【宇】jyu⁵ building; house

宇內 in the country; in the world
宇宙 cosmos; universe
　　宇宙萬物 myriad things in the universe
　　　　大宇宙 macrocosmos
宇航 astronautical; space travel

廟宇 temple
樓宇 building

【守】sau² guard

守口如瓶 as close as an oyster; as dumb as an oyster; as
　　silent as the grave; as silent as the tomb; be buttoned
　　up; be tight-mouthed; breathe not a word of a secret;
　　button up one's lip; button up one's mouth; hold one's
　　cards close to one's chest; keep a still tongue in one's
　　head; keep dumb as an oyster; keep mum; keep one's
　　lips buttoned; keep one's mouth closed; keep one's
　　mouth shut; keep one's mouth tight as a jar; keep one's
　　tongue between one's teeth; keep the mouth closed like
　　a bottle; keep the mouth shut as that of a jar; one's lips
　　are sealed; stay tight-lipped; tight-mouthed
守法 abide by the law; keep the law; law-abiding; observe
　　the law
守夜（守靈）keep vigil beside the coffin; stand as guards at
　　the bier
守時 on time; punctual
守財奴 cheapskate; miser; niggard
守得雲開見月明 wait till the clouds roll by
守寡 keep living as a widow; live in widowhood; remain a
　　widow; remain in widowhood
守舊 adhere to past practices; conservative; resistant to
　　advances; stick to old ways

死守 defend desperately; defend to death
防守 defend; defence; guard; parry
駐守 garrison

【安】on¹ ① obligation ② safety ③（安裝）install

安士（盎司）ounce
　　一安士（一盎司）one ounce
安份 know one's lot
　　安份守己 abide by laws and behave oneself well
安全 safe; safety
　　安全套（避孕套）condom
　　安全帶 seat belt
　　　　攬安全帶（繫好安全帶）fasten your seat belt
　　安全第一 safety first
　　安全掣（安全閥）safe valve
安老院 home for the elderly
安排 arrange
　　另行安排 make other arrangements
安樂 comfortable
　　安樂窩 home sweet home
安慰 comfort; console

一路平安 a safe journey
不安 ① uneasy; uncomfortable; unpeaceful; unstable ②
　　disquiet; disturbed; restless; uneasy
六安 Lu'an tea
午安 good afternoon
出入平安 may you be safe wherever you go
四季平安 wish you safe all year round
平平安安 safe
平安 safe
母子平安 after the birth, mother and child were
　　doing well
治安 peace and order of a nation; public order;
　　public security
保安 security
袋袋平安 acquire and keep safe a sum of money
感到不安 be abashed; be disturbed; feel disturbed; feel
　　uncomfortable; not be at ease

【寺】zi⁶ temple

寺門（寺院）temple
寺院 monastery; temple
寺廟 house of god; temple
寺觀 Buddhist and Daoist temples

回教寺 mosque

【尖】 zim¹ tip

尖叫 scream

尖筆甩 (尖的) pointed; sharp

尖端 ① acme; external centre; peak; tip ② apex; frontier; leading edge; the most advanced; the sophisticated

尖酸刻薄 mean and cruel

尖嘴 ① sharp mouth ② particular about food
尖嘴辣椒 (秦椒) long and thin pepper

尖銳 incisive; keen; penetrating; sharp; sharp-pointed

一眼針冇兩頭尖 (針只有一頭尖──沒有十全十美) sugar cane is never sweet at both ends – one cannot have it both ways

打尖 (插隊) jump the queue

舌尖 tip of the tongue

奄尖／腍尖／醃尖 (挑剔) fussy; cavil; choosy; fastidious; fussy; hypercritical; nitpick; pick and choose; find fault; picky; upbraid

笋尖 tips of bamboo shoots

趾尖 tiptoe

頂尖 choose the best

鼻哥尖 (鼻頭) tip of the nose

嘴尖 (嘴叼／挑食) particular about food

【屹】 ngat⁶ rise

屹立 stand erect; stand towering like a giant

屹起身 (欠起身子) half rise from one's seat

屹然 majestic; towering

【州】 zau¹ county

州治 state government

州長 governor of a state

州際 interstate

廣州 Guangzhou

潮州 Chiu Chow

【帆】 faan⁴ sail

帆布 canvas

帆船 junk

滑浪風帆 windsurfing

【年】 nin⁴ year

年三十晚 (大年三十／農曆除夕) Chinese New Year's Eve
年三十晚有月光 (沒可能) it's impossible
年三十晚謝竈 ── 好做唔做 (不合時宜) do not do what one should do

年中 during the year; middle of the year

年廿八，洗邋遢 (臘月二八大清掃) do the year-end clean-up two days before the Lunar New Year

年月 days and years

年代 ① age ② generation
九十年代 the nineties

年年 every year
年年有今日，歲歲有今朝 happy birthday; many happy returns of the day
年年有餘 may there be surpluses every year
年年係咁 (年復一年／年年如是) year in and year out

年老 aged; old
年老多病 old and be troubled by illness

年初一 Lunar New Year's Day
年初二 ① the second day of the Chinese New Year ② the second day of the first month of the lunar year
年初三 ① the third day of the Chinese New Year ② the third day of the first month of the lunar year

年尾 (年底) end of the year; year-end

年事 age
年事已高 be advanced in years

年青 young
年青有為 young and have good future; young and promising

年紀 age
年紀大 old
年紀細 young

年限 fixed number of years

年宵 Lunar New Year's Eve
年宵市場 Lunar New Year's Eve market

年級 grade; year
低年級 junior grade
高年級 senior grade

年假 annual leave

年晚 end of the year
年晚錢，飯後煙 things that ordinary people enjoy

年終 year-end

年貨 Spring Festival goods
辦年貨 do Spring Festival shopping

年華 time; year
年華虛度 spend idly the best of one's days

年費 annual fee

年輕 young
年輕力壯 young and vigorous
年輕有為 young and capable
年輕貌美 young and pretty

年糕 rice cake

年頭 (年初) beginning of the year

年齡 age
　　法定年齡 legal age
年關 end of the year
　　年關難過 it is difficult to pass the end of the year

一年 one year
十年 decade; ten years
上年 last year
下年 next year
大我十幾年 (比我大十多歲) more than ten years older
　　than I
今年 this year
牛年 Year of the Ox
冬大過年 Winter Solstice is more important than the Chinese
　　New Year
出年 (明年) next year
本年 current year; present year; this year
早年 ① one's early years ② in bygone years; many years
　　ago; years ago
百年 ① century; hundred years ② one's lifetime; one's
　　whole life
羊年 Year of the Sheep; Year of the Goat
壯年 prime of one's life
成年 all the year round; the whole year; throughout
　　the year
每年 every year; per annum
兩三年 a couple of years
往年 in bygone years; in former years; in the years past
狗年 Year of the Dog
兔年 Year of the Rabbit
虎年 Year of the Tiger
青少年 adolescent
前年 year before last
前幾年 a few years ago
後年 year after next
拜年 pay a New Year visit
蛇年 Year of the Snake
馬年 Year of the Horse
連續幾年 for years in a row; for years on end; for years
　　running
幾 (多) 年 how many years
猴年 Year of the Monkey
開年 scold sb during the lunar new year time
閏年 leap year; intercalary year
新年 new year
新曆 (新) 年 New Year's Day
鼠年 Year of the Rat
農曆新年 lunar new year
豬年 Year of the Pig

團年 New Year Eve's dinner
髫年 childhood; youth
龍年 Year of the Dragon
舊年 (去年) last year
舊曆年 lunar calendar
邊年 (哪一年) which year
雞年 Year of the Chicken; Year of the Rooster

【式】sik¹ style
式微 decline
式樣 mode; model; style; type
　　式樣美觀 attractive fashion
　　式樣新穎 in a novel style; stylish
　　　各式各樣 all kinds of; all sorts of; every kind of; in
　　　　every shape and form; of every description; of every
　　　　hue; of various descriptions

三點式 (比基尼) bikini
卡式 (transliteration) cassette
正式 formal
生活方式 lifestyle
自由式 (自由泳) free strokes
形式 form; format; formation; layout; modality; shape
的式 / 的的式式 (小巧) delicate; small; tiny
格式 form; format; layout; mode; style
盒式 (卡式) cassette
港式 Hong Kong style
款式 pattern; style
程式 ① form; pattern ② programme; programming
蛙式 (蛙泳) breast stroke
粵式 Cantonese style
儀式 ceremony
蝴蝶式 (蝴蝶泳) butterfly stroke
簽字儀式 signing ceremony

【忙】mong⁴ ① busy ② hurry; rush
忙人 busy person
忙中有錯 error is always made in haste; haste is of the
　　devil; haste makes waste
忙到七個一皮 (忙得手腳朝天) frantically busy
忙碌 all go; be engaged in doing sth; be engaged in sth;
　　be occupied with; be swamped with work; bustle; bustle
　　about; busy; get one's hands full; have much to do; have
　　one's hands full; on one's toes; on the go; on the run;
　　one's hands are full; up to one's eyes in work; up to the
　　ears in work
　　忙忙碌碌 as busy as a bee; busy going about one's work

匆忙 hurry; in a hurry

好忙 very busy

狼忙 in a hurry; in a hurry-skurry

無事忙 (沒事忙) busy with nothing; make much ado about nothing

樂於幫忙 be glad to help; be willing to give a hand

幫忙 help

臨急臨忙 in a great rush

繁忙 busy

【戌】seot¹ (門閂) bolt

戌月 the ninth month of the lunar year

戌時 the period between seven and nine p.m.

門戌 bolt

【扣】kau³ ring

扣住 (別上 / 別着) pin; pin up

扣底 (白飯或麵粉要減少份量) smaller portion of rice or noodle

扣留 be caught and detained by police

扣起 (扣下來) deduct

扣針 (別針兒) brooch

扣除 deduct; take off

扣殺 smash

扣鈕 (扣鈕扣) button up

手扣 handcuffs

回扣 rebate

克扣 embezzle part of what should be issued

利息回扣 interest rebate

折扣 discount

鎖匙扣 key holder; key ring

【托】tok³ (扛 / 抬) carry on the shoulder

托大腳 (吹捧奉承 / 拍馬屁 / 抱粗腿) adulate; brown-nose; butter sb up; crawl to; curry favour; curry favour with sb; eat sb's toads; fawn on; flatter; give sb the soft-soap; ingratiate oneself with; kiss sb's ass; lay it on thick; lay it on with a trowel; lick sb's boots; lick sb's shoes; lick sb's spittle; lick the boots of sb; obsequious; play up to; polish the apple; soft-soap; suck up to; sycophancy; toady sb

托水龍 (替人收款或交款時私吞款項) embezzle; embezzle sb's money; run away with the money entrusted to sb

托住 (扛着) carry sth on the shoulder

托住啲嘢 (扛着點東西) carry sth on the shoulder

用膊頭托住 (用膊頭扛着) carry sth on the shoulder

托兒所 child-care centre; nursery; nursery school

托派 (馬屁精) flunky

托塔都應承 (上刀山都答應) promise without conditions

托夢 appear in one's dream and make a request

托賴 (托福) be indebted to

【劼】gui⁶ (累) exhausted; tired

劼劼哋 (有點兒累) a little tired

劼到死 (累透了) very tired

【扠】caa³ (劃) delete

扠到花晒 (劃得亂七八糟) delete totally

扠咗 (擦掉) erase; rub off; rub out; wipe off

扠咗佢 (把它擦掉) wipe it off

扠禍 (弄壞 / 搞亂) ruin

烏喱馬扠 (亂七八糟) illegible and sloppy; in a mess

【收】sau¹ receive

收入 income

收口 shut up

收山 ① (退隱) live in retirement; retire ② (辭退) quit

收工 (下班) clock off; come off work; go off work; knock off; leave off

五點收工 (五點下班) knock off at five

收手 (住手 / 停手) quit; stop doing sth; throw in one's hands

收水 (收錢) collect money

收市價 closing price

收生 (招生) student recruitment

收皮 (滾開) go away

收尾 (最後) at last; finally; lastly

收兵 withdraw troops

收到 ① receive ② (知道了) got it

收拾 ① clear away; gather up; put in order; tidy ② get things ready; pack ③ mend; repair ④ punish; settle with; torture

收拾殘局 clear up a messy situation; clear up the mess; pick up the pieces; settle a disturbed situation

收音機 radio

一架收音機 (一台收音機) a radio

開收音機 turn on the radio

收科 (完工 / 結束) clean up a mess; end up

收風 / 收到風 (得到消息) gather information about sth; get wind of sth

收埋 (收起來) hide; put aside

收爹 (住口 / 閉嘴) shut up

收料 (得到情報) get some information

收得 (受歡迎 / 賣座) a success with the public

唔收得 (不受歡迎 / 不賣座) the tickets sell badly

收條 receipt
收細音量 (調低音量) turn down the sound volume
收規 (受賄) accept bribes
收買佬 (收破爛的) junk collector
收嗲 (住口 / 閉嘴) shut up
收銀 (收款) collect cash
　收銀台 (收款台) cashier
　收銀員 (收款員) cashier
收數 (收錢 / 收賬) collect debts
收線 (掛上電話 / 掛斷電話) hang up; hang up the phone
收盤 (停業 / 歇業) close a business; close down; go out of business; stop doing business; suspense of business; termination of business; wind up business
收據 receipt
收錢 charge
收檔 ① (收攤兒 / 關店) close the shop for the night ② (結束營業) shut down a business ③ (辭退) not to do it any more ④ (死) die
收獲 harvest
收聲 (住嘴 / 閉嘴 / 住口) shut up; stop talking

冇收 (沒事做) at loose ends
冇佢收 (拿他沒辦法) can't do anything about him; there's nothing one can do
名利雙收 gain both fame and wealth
老人院都唔收 (絮叨) one's remarks are too superfluous
沒收 confiscate
前人種果後人收 descendants reap wheat their ancestors sowed
財到光棍手——易放難收 once money goes to the hands of a conman, it's difficult to get it back from him
豐收 abundant harvest; bumper harvest

【旨】zi² rely on
旨在 with the intention of
旨意 (完全投靠) depend on; rely on
　大安旨意 (過份放心而不過問) choose to ignore any risk or danger
　大食有旨意 (有後台) have a firm backing to do such a deed for one's extravagance
旨趣 objective; purport

奉旨 take things for granted
宗旨 aim; objective; purpose

【早】zou² early
早禾 (早稻) early season rice
早年 ① one's early years ② in bygone years; many years ago; years ago

早到 arrive ahead of time; arrive early
早唞 ① (住口) shut up ② (晚安) good night ③ (滾開) go away
早班 morning shift
早晨 (早 / 早上好) good morning
　早晨流流 (大清早的) bright and early; early in the morning; the crack of dawn
早排 (早些時候 / 前一陣子) earlier on; early on; not long ago
早造 (早稻) early season rice
　早造米 (早稻米) early season rice
早晚 ① morning and evening ② sooner or later ③ time ④ (將來某天) some day; some time in the future
早熟 ① ripen early ② reach puberty early ③ precocious
早餐 (早飯) breakfast
　一個早餐 (一份早飯 / 一份早餐) a breakfast
　食早餐 (吃早飯 / 吃早餐) have breakfast

一早 early in the morning; very early
大早 ① (剛剛) just now ② (很久以前) a long time ago
及早 as soon as possible; at an early date; before it is too late
天光早 (天亮) bright and early; early in the morning; the crack of dawn
打早 (吃早飯 / 吃早餐) have breakfast
老早 long ago; very early
成朝早 (整天早上) the whole morning
倒塔咁早 (一大清早) very early in the morning
晨早 (清早) dawn; early in the morning; early morning
提早 in advance
發夢冇咁早 (白日做夢) not to have a fond dream in the day time
朝早 (上午) morning
朝頭早 (早上) early in the morning; early morning; morning
預早 (預先) ahead of schedule; in advance; shift to an earlier time
遲早 (早晚) sooner or later
聽朝早 (明天) tomorrow morning

【曲】kuk¹ ① (使彎曲) bend ② (歌曲) song ③ transliteration
曲不離口 practice makes perfect
曲折 ① circuitous; curving; intricate; tortuous; ups and downs; winding; zigzag ② complications; intricacy; not smooth; not straightforward
曲奇 (transliteration) cookie
　曲奇餅 cookie
曲意 (奉迎) make a special concession to achieve others' goals
　曲意逢迎 curry favour with others by roundabout

methods; do everything to please sb; flatter by hook or by crook; flatter sb in a hundred and one ways; go out of one's way to curry favour with sb; gratify sb's every whim; lick sb's boots; ply sb with assiduous flattery; submit obsequiously to sb's will

曲線 curve

未到六十六，唔好笑人手指曲 (不可嘲笑別人的短處) don't tease others too soon

卡曲 (車皮套) (transliteration) car coat

扭曲 contort

屈曲 twist sth until it is bent

奏鳴曲 sonata

流行歌曲 popular songs

歪曲 distort; misrepresent; twist

捩橫折曲 (是非不分) swear black is white

歌曲 song

彎曲 meandering; winding; zigzag

戲曲 Chinese opera

【有】jau⁵ have

有之 (有可能 / 或者會) maybe; perhaps; possible

有口無心 not really mean what one says

有口難言 find it hard to say

有心 ① (故意) with the intention ② (多謝關心) thank you ③ kind of you to ask; you're very kind ④ (關心) show concern

有心唔怕遲 (有心不怕遲) do sth even though they are late

有心唔怕遲，十月都係拜年時 (有心不怕遲，十月也是拜年的時節) it's never too late to do sth if you really want to do it; you can pay New Year visits to your friends even in the tenth month of the year

有心無力 be unable to do what one wants to do

有心裝冇心人 (中傷某人) set a trap for sb

有日 (有一天) one day

有毛有翼 (翅膀長硬了) independent; uncontrollable

有水 (有錢) loaded; rich; wealthy; well-heeled; well-off; well-to-do

有凸 (有餘) have a surplus; have enough to spare

有奶便是娘 he that serves God for money will serve the devil for better wages

有平有貴 (有便宜也有貴的) have expensive ones and cheap ones

有瓦遮頭 (有容身處) have a place to live

有用 useful

有名 famous

有米 (有錢) rich

有老有幼 (有老有少 / 有老有嫩) there are the young and the old

有行 (有希望) there is hope

有尾學人跳，冇尾又學人跳 (盲目跟從) blindly imitate sb

有事 there's trouble

有事鍾無艷，無事夏迎春 once out of danger, cast the deliverer behind one's back

有兩手 (有兩下子) have real skill; know one's stuff; one really knows a thing or two

有咗 (懷孕) be pregnant

有咗身紀 (有了身子 / 懷孕) pregnant

有咗 BB (懷孕) pregnant

有咁啱得咁橋 (無巧不成書) as luck would have it

有味 (變味兒) revert

有女人味 feminine

有男人味 manly; masculine

有書卷味 have an intellectual demeanour

有怪莫怪 (懇求原諒) beg for one's apology

有型 (瀟灑) cool; handsome; stylish

有型有款 (又帥又酷) cool and stylish; handsome and stylish

好有型 (好瀟灑) really cool

懶有型 (裝酷) have pretensions to be stylish

有突 (多出 / 有餘 / 超出) exceed; odd

有面 (有面子 / 有臉) enjoy due respect

有風駛盡哩 (小車不倒儘管推) avail oneself of an opportunity to the fullest extent; take advantage of an opportunity to the full extent

有效 effective

有料 (有本事) capable

有料到 (有本事) be really something

有時 (有時候) sometimes

有陣時 (有時候) sometimes

有益 (有好處) advantageous

有骨 (帶刺兒) have a sting in one's words; sarcastic

有鬼 (有內奸) there's sth fishy

有啲 ① (有些) some ② (有點兒) rather; somewhat

有冤無路訴 (有冤無處伸) have no one to complain about one's injustice

有得 (可以得到) can

有得飲 (有宴請) have a banquet to attend

有得震冇得瞓 (膽戰心驚) tremble with fear

有得諗 (值得考慮) be worth consideration

有得講 (可以商量) negotiable

有得醫 (可醫治的) can be cured; curable

有情飲水飽 (有情喝水飽) people in love could satisfy their hunger by drinking water

有排 (還要待很久) a long time to go; a long time to wait; for ages; for an age; very long

有晚 (有一天晚上) one evening; one night

有殺有賠 (淨贏不輸) net profits without any loss

有理冇理 (不管三七二十一) foreget about it and let it rip

有眼不識泰山 fail to recognise an important person; too blind to recognise the sun

有眼無珠 blind; misvalue sb

有剩 (有餘) have a surplus; have enough to spare

有幾何 (難得) rare; seldom
　　有幾何吖 (能有幾回呀) this is infrequent

有朝一日 (有一天) one day; some day

有番兩度 (有兩下子) have it in one; have real skill; have a thing or two; know a few tricks of the trade; know one's staff

有爺生無乸教 (有爺生沒娘教) have parents but have no parental guidance; lack home education

有碗話碗，有碟話碟 (有一說一 / 有二說二) call a spade a spade

有腦 (腦子靈) have quick wits; keen and sharp in thinking

有落 (要下車) want to get off a bus
　　巴士站有落 (在公車站下車) get off a bus at the bus stop
　　前面有落 (前面下車) please stop in front; please stop over there; would like to get off a bus over there
　　路口有落 (路口下車) I want to get off a bus at the intersection
　　轉彎有落 (轉彎後要下車) I want to get off a bus at the corner

有路 (有染) have an affair with sb

有辣有唔辣 (有利有弊) each has its own advantages and weak points; there are pros and cons

有彈冇讚 (有批評沒有稱讚) just criticism without praise

有彈有讚 (有稱讚有批評) criticise and praise

有樣學樣 (見誰學誰) follow a bad example

有辦睇 (有榜樣 / 有樣品看) have an example to see

有錢 have money
　　有錢人 rich people
　　有錢冇命享 (有錢沒命享) have a lot of money but no life in which to spend it
　　有錢使得鬼推磨 (只要有錢，萬事皆能辦到) money makes the mare go; money makes the world go round
　　有錢佬 (有錢人 / 富豪) rich man
　　有錢佬話事 (富豪作主) money talks
　　有錢就身痕 (有錢便想揮霍) money burns a hole in one's pocket
　　好有錢 (很富有) very rich

有頭髮冇人想生鬎鬁 (沒有選擇) be driven to such a stupid move

有頭有面 ① (有派頭) be famous and titled ② (有社會地位的人) person with social status

有頭威，冇尾陣 (虎頭蛇尾) a brave beginning and a weak ending; a brave beginning but a poor ending; a tiger's head and a snake's tail; begin well but fall of towards the close; begin with tigerish energy but peter out towards the end; come out at the small end of the horn; do sth by halves; fine start and poor finish; in like a lion, out like a lamb; start out well but not continue; with a fine start but a poor finish

有膽 (有種 / 夠種) have the guts

有寶 (了不起) amazing; extraordinary; far from common; proud and overweening; terrific
　　懶有寶 (裝作很了不起) have a high opinion of oneself; play the big-shot
　　瀾有寶 (自以為了不起) as if one's far from common

有麝自然香 (好酒客自來) good wine needs no bush

有癮 (有興趣 / 有意思 / 過癮) do sth to one's heart's content; enjoy oneself to the full; satisfy a carving

有讚冇彈 (有稱讚沒有批評) just praise without criticism

七都有 (甚麼也有) have everything

少有 rare

包羅萬有 all-embracing; all-inclusive; cover a wide range; cover and contain everything; inclusive of everything

只有 ① alone; only ② have to

未有 have never been; have never had

仲有 (還有) there's still

年晚煎堆——人有我有 possess oneself of the same as others do

佔有 ① have; own; posses ② hold; occupy

罕有 exceptional; rare; unusual

所有 ① owe; possess ② possessions ③ all

具有 be provided with; have; possess

衰到冇人有 (非常差) extremely bad

祇有 (只有) only

都有 it's possible

富有 rich

稀有 one in a million; rare; uncommon; unusual

擁有 be armed with; come into possession of; come into sb's possession; conquer; get possession of sth; have; hold; in possession of; in the possession of; occupy; own

據為己有 appropriate to oneself; have all to oneself; make sth his own; pocket; seize sth for oneself; take forcible possession of sth for oneself

【朱】 zyu¹ red

朱古力 (巧克力) chocolate

朱唇 red lips

朱義盛 ① (假首飾) fake jewellry ② (假貨) fake product

【朵】 do² measure-word for flowers

朵朵白雲 clusters of cloud

圓揼朵 (圓胖的) chubby

撻朵 (說出自己的名字) name dropping

爛朵朵 (快要倒塌的) dilapidated

響朵 (說出自己的名字或身份) give props to

【次】 ci³ time

次次 (每次) every time

次序 arrangement; order; sequence

次要 less important; minor; next in importance; secondary; subordinate

次按 sub-prime mortgage

次貨 defective goods

次等 inferior; second-class; second-rate

一次 once; one time

三番四次 (一次又一次) again and again; many a time; over and over again; repeatedly; time after time; time and again; time and time again

上次 last time

下 (一) 次 next time

今次 current; present; this time

名次 position in a name list

再次 a second time; again; another time

每日四次 (每天四次) four times a day

每次 at every turn; each time; every time

呢次 (這次) current; present; this time

兩次 twice

其次 ① besides; next; secondly; the next in order; then ② next in importance; of minor importance; secondary

唔該你講多一次 (麻煩你再說一遍) pardon me

退而求其次 be left with nothing better than the second choice; have no alternative but to give up one's preference; have to be content with the second best; seek what is less attractive than one's original objective; the next best thing

第次 (下次) next time

嗰次 (那次) that time

語無倫次 babble in one's statement; babble like an idiot; go off at score; ramble in one's statement; speak incoherently; use indecent language; want of order in one's speech

檔次 gradation; scale

【此】 ci² ① this ② thus

此生 one's life

此地無銀三百兩 reveal one's secret unintentionally

此時 at present; for the time being; now; right now; this moment

由此 from this; therefore; therefrom; thus

因此 for this reason; on this account

到此 so far

彼此 both parties; each other; one another; this and that; you and me

彼此彼此 the feeling is mutual; we are alike; we are in a similar position

故此 as a result; because of this; consequently; for that reason; hence; on that account; so; therefore; thus

於此 here; in this place

為此 for this reason; to this end

無分彼此 one for all and all for one

【死】 sei² die

死人 dead person

死人都要拗番生 (死的也要說活) argue that the dead is still living

死人尋舊路 (重覆走老路) follow one's own old tracks

死人燈籠報大數 (誇大其詞) pull a long bow

車死人 (軋死人) car running over people causing death

死口咬實 (一口咬定) stand by one's guns; stick to what one says

死亡 death

死亡證 (死亡通知書) death certificate

死心 have no more illusions about sth/sb

死心不息 as obstinate as a mule

死心塌地 hell-bent on sb

死咗條心 (不抱希望) abandoned; have no more illusions about sth/sb; heartless; in a state of stupor

死火 ① (拋錨) breakdown ② (可壞了 / 糟糕) damn it

死牛 dead cow

死牛一便頸 (固執己見 / 板板六十四 / 倔強 / 執拗 / 硬性子) stick to one's guns; stubborn; unyielding

死守 defend desperately; defend to death

死有餘辜 death would not expiate all one's crimes

死死吓 (累極了) not lively

死死氣 (灰溜溜) reluctant but have no alternative

死死地 / 自氣 (灰溜溜的) reluctant but have no alternative

死估估 (毫無生氣的) poor-witted

死角 (死胡同) dead angle; dead space

死咕咕 (毫無生氣的) not lively

死咗 (去世 / 死了) dead

死性不改 as stubborn as a mule; not change for the better

死唔眼閉（死不瞑目）die discontent; die dissatisfied; die with an everlasting regret; die with injustice unredressed; die without closing one's eyes; turn in one's grave

死者 the deceased

死記硬背 mechanical memorizing

死鬼 ① deceased ② devil

死做爛做（拼命幹活兒／累死累活）tire oneself out through overwork; work oneself to death

死冤（跟屁蟲）stick like a limpet

死蛇爛蟮 ①（懶洋洋）too lazy to stir a finger ②（懶人）lazy person

死剩把口（強辯不服輸）never yield and keep arguing with others

死硬（沒希望／死定了）have no hope

死結 fast knot

死路 blind alley; the road to ruin
　　死路一條 blind alley; doomed; no way out; the road to extinction

死過番生（死裏逃生）be saved from death; be snatched from the jaws of death; close call; close shave; escape by a hairbreadth; escape by the skin of one's teeth; escape death by a narrow margin; escape with one's bare life; hair breadth escape; have a close bout with death; miss death by a hair's breadth; narrow escape from death; narrow shave; near thing

死嘞（壞了／糟糕）damn it

死對頭 rival

死慳死抵（拼命節省）pinch and screw; tighten one's belt

死撐（嘴硬）refuse to admit a mistake; stubborn and reluctant to admit mistakes or defeats

死敵 arch rival; deadly enemy

死線 deadline

死雞撐飯蓋（不認輸）shabby-genteel

死黨（閨蜜（女）／哥兒們（男）／好朋友／莫逆之交）best friend; bosom friend; very close friend

死纏爛打 pester sb endlessly for sth

水浸眼眉——唔知死（烏龜吃巴豆——不知死活）a tortoise eating croton-oil seeds – unaware of the death ahead

冇死（肯定／必勝）sure winner

去死 go to hell

打生打死 fight for survival

打死 beat to death

生死 life and death

劫到死（累得要命）very tired

好死（有心）with good intentions

老死（老朋友）buddy

作死（自找死路）take the road to ruin oneself; threat

見死（大難臨頭）seeing sb in mortal danger

車死（輾斃）be knocked down to death by a car

垂死 at the last breath; dying; expiring; fading fast; going; going belly up; going for your tea; have one foot in the grave; knocking on heaven's door; on one's last legs

怕死 fear death

抵死（該死）serve sb right; you deserve it

抵你死（你真的該死）have only oneself to thank; serve sb right; you deserve it

抵佢死（他真的該死）have only himself to thank; he deserves it; serve him right

枉死 be wronged and driven to death; die through injustice

玩死 play tricks on sb to cause him/her trouble; play with sb until they are dead or finished

要生要死（要死要活）hysterical

畏死 afraid of dying; fear death

唔知死（不知大限已到）unaware of the death ahead

殊死 desperate; life-and-death

浸死（淹死）drown

狼死（兇狠的）unscrupulous

衰到死（壞透了）extremely bad

捱生捱死（拼死拼活／拼命幹活兒）work extremely hard

責死（給砸死了）be crashed to death

蛇都死（甚麼辦法也不行啦）hard to deal with

惡（到）死（兇巴巴的）fiendish; fierce; harsh; not easy to get along with

替死 sacrifice oneself for someone

睇死（看不起）① look down on sb ② stand to one's assertion that; sure

慌死（生怕）for fear that; lest; so as not to

煮死（當場就擒）catch

溺死 be drowned

該死 deserve it

監生打死（活生生打死）be beaten to death alive

誓死 pledge one's life

飽死 be exasperated against sb; feel disgusted

寧死 would rather die

劏豬櫈——上嚟就死（死定了）a fat pig toing to the butchery – sure to die

㩧死（揰死）kill

靚到死（漂亮極了）absolutely gorgeous; stunning; very beautiful

橫死掂死（幾大就幾大了）it doesn't make any difference either way

激死（氣死了）annoy sb

賴死 reluctant to do sth one is supposed to

餓死 starve to death

嚇死 scare to death

嬲死（很生氣）very angry

癐到死（累得要命）be tired to death

壓死（砸死）press to death

鮻魚骨炒飯——唔食餓死，食又哽死（怎麼樣也要死）just like Wu Dalang taking poison – he will die anyway

聽死（受死吧）get into trouble

驚死（生怕）be terrified

攬住一齊死（同歸於盡）end in common ruin

攬住死（一起遭殃）get into trouble together

【汗】hon⁶ persperation

汗水 perspiration; sweat

汗毛 fine hair on the human body

汗流（流汗）sweat

汗腺 apocrine sweat gland; sweat gland

一額汗 a sweat-covered head

大汗疊細汗 very sweaty

血汗 blood and sweat; sweat and toil

冷汗 cold sweat

身水身汗 all of a sweat; be running with sweat; be soaked with sweat; drip with perspiration; perspire all over; pouring with sweat; stream with sweat; sweat like a pig; sweat like a trooper; sweating heavily; wet through with perspiration; wringing wet

抒汗 be embarrassed

淡汗（虛汗）cold insulation

焗汗 induce perspiration

捏一把汗（嚇得出一身汗）break out into cold perspiration

擺汗（出汗）sweat

擺冷汗（出虛汗）break out in a cold sweat

標汗（出汗）perspire; sweat

澎汗（出汗）sweat

【池】ci⁴ pool

池中物 person of mediocre abilities

池水 pond water

池魚 fish in the pond

池塘 pond

沙池 ① sandpit; sand trap ② bunker

泳池 swimming pool

差池（失誤）error; fault; miscalculation; mistake; slip

游水池（游泳池）swimming pool

游泳池 swimming pool

電池 car battery

露天泳池 open-air swimming pool

【江】gong¹ river

江山 ① landscape; rivers and mountains ② country; state power; territories

江山易改，本性難移 a fox may grow grey but never good; a leopard cannot change its spots; a sow, when washed, returns to the muck; clipping a tiger's claws never makes him lose his taste for blood; it is difficult to change one's skin; it is easier to move a mountain than change a person's character; it is easy to move rivers and mountains, but difficult to change a person's nature; the wolf may lose its teeth, but never his nature; what is bred in the bone will come out of the flesh; you can change mountains and rivers but not a person's nature; you cannot make a crab walk straight

江湖 ① rivers and lakes ② all corners of the country ③ underworld

江湖大佬 underworld big boss

江湖地位 status in the underworld

江湖道義 code of ethics of the underworld

江湖情 a feeling of loyalty in underworld culture

人在江湖，身不由己 one's life is bound by rules of the underworld

老江湖 experienced person in the underworld

江瑤柱（乾貝）dried scallop

外江 province other than one's own

【污】wu¹ dirty

污吏 corrupt officials

污染 pollution

污染指數 pollution index

減低污染 reduce pollution

污煙障氣 chaos

污點 black mark; blemish; blot; defect; flaw; flick; smear; smirch; smotch; smudge; smut; smutch; spot; stain

污糟（骯髒）dirty; soiled

污糟辣撻／邋遢（骯髒的）dirty; soiled

污糟貓（骯髒的人）untidy person

整污糟（弄骯髒了）stain

貪污 corruption

【灰】fui¹ ① ash ② grey

灰士（保險絲）(transliteration) fuse

燒灰士（燒保險絲）fuse blowing

灰斗（石灰斗）lime bucket

灰水（石灰漿）paint

油灰水／掃灰水 ①（掃石灰水）whitewash ②（化很濃厚的粧）do make-up

灰白 ashen; greyish; hoary; ale; white

灰色 grey; grey colour

灰掃 (石灰刷子) lime brush

灰桶 (石灰桶) lime barrel

灰塵 ① ash; dirt; dust ② spindrift

心灰 disheartened

炮灰 cannon fodder

香爐灰 incense ashes

桐油灰 putty

跳灰 (賣海洛因) sell heroin

【百】 baak³ hundred

百分 per-cent

　百分一 (百分之一) one per-cent

　百分之九十九 ninety-nine per-cent

　百分之五 five per-cent

　百分百 (百分之百) one-hundred per-cent

　百份比 percentage

百合 lily

　百合花 lily

百年 ① century; hundred years ② one's lifetime; one's whole life

　百年好合 have a long and harmonious married life

　百年老店 century-old shop

　百年樹人 education of people takes many many years to bear fruit; it takes a hundred years to rear people

　百年歸老 die of old age

百忍成金 patience is a plaster for all sores

百足 (蜈蚣) centipede

百足咁多爪 (身兼數職) put nobody on one's track

百姓 common people; people

　平民百姓 common people

　老百姓 civilians; common people; folks; ordinary

百貨 general merchandise

百幾蚊 (百多元) a hundred something dollars

百爺公 (老大爺 / 老伯 / 老漢 / 老頭兒) old chap; old codger; old fogey; old man

百爺婆 (老大姑 / 老太太 / 老婆婆) old lady; old woman

百葉簾 (百葉窗) shutter

百厭 (淘氣 / 頑皮 / 調皮) mischievous; naughty; playful

　百厭仔 (淘氣包) naughty boy; naughty rascal; urchin

　百厭星 (小淘氣 / 淘氣鬼 / 搗蛋鬼) little horror; mischievous imp; naughty kid

一百 one hundred

一傳十，十傳百 news travels fast; spread from mouth to mouth

千百 hundreds and thousands

亞蘭賣豬——一千唔賣，賣八百 (自以為聰明) bargain away sth; be forced to devalue sth

幾百 hundreds; several hundred

【竹】 zuk¹ (竹子) bamboo

竹升 ① (竹杠 / 竹竿) bamboo carrying pole ② (外國回流的中國人) overseas Chinese

　竹升女 (外國回流的中國女孩) young overseas Chinese girl

　竹升仔 (外國回流的中國男孩) young overseas Chinese boy

　竹升妹 (外國回流的中國女孩) young overseas Chinese girl

竹板 (竹片兒) bamboo lath

竹枝 ① (竹枝兒) bamboo pole ② (腐竹) dried beancurd stick

竹牀 bamboo bed

竹花頭 (竹字頭) the "bamboo" (竹) radical

竹門對竹門，木門對木門 choose a husband/wife with a similar background

竹筍 bamboo shoot

竹篙 (竹竿) bamboo pole; bamboo stick

竹戰 (打麻將) play mahjong

　打竹戰 (打麻將) play mahjong

竹館 (麻將館) mahjong parlour

竹簾 bamboo curtain; bamboo screen

竹籃 bamboo basket

一支竹 (一枝竹) a bamboo stick

大轆竹 Chinese water pipe

盲公竹 (指路者 / 老練的人) guide; old hand

破竹 irresistible force

梅花間竹 in alternative series

勢如破竹 advance with irresistible force; carry all before one; carry everything before one; carry the world before one; like a hot knife cutting through butter; like splitting a bamboo; meet with no resistance; push forward from victory to victory; push onward with overwhelming momentum; with irresistible force; without a hitch

【米】 mai⁵ rice

米已成炊 the die is cast

米水 (洗米水) rice-washing water

米仔蘭 (米蘭花) Chinese rice plant

米白色 (米色) beige

米色 beige

米厘 (毫米) millimetre

米氣 odour of rice

　唔嗅米氣 (不通人情) have no experience of life

米酒 rice wine

米粉 rice noodles
米通（米花糖）crunchy rice candy
米碎（碎米）crushed rice
米飯 cooked rice
　　米飯班主 people from whom one earns a living
米線 rice noodles
米鋪（糧店）grain store

一公斤米（一斤米）a kilogram of rice
一粒米 a grain of rice
一拃米（一把米）a handful of rice
一揸米（一把米）a handful of rice
一執米（一把米）a handful of rice
一嘜米（一杯米）a can of rice
乞米（討飯）very poor
大雞唔食細米（不屑於幹小事）not care about trifles; important person does not bother with trivial matters
石米 crushed stones
好天搵埋落雨米（積穀防饑）gather hay against a rainy day
早造米（早稻米）early season rice
有米（有錢）rich
炒米 fried vermicelli
厘米 centimetre
咬米（吃）eat
星洲炒米 fried vermicelli in Singaporean style
洗米 wash rice
食枉米（白吃飯）a person of no use
食塞米（無能／懵懂）good-for-nothing; idler
食飽無憂米 have nothing to worry about; lead an idle life
倒米（拆台／把事情搞壞）cause others to suffer losses; mess up; stand in one's own light
偷雞唔倒蝕揸米（佔不到便宜，反招致損失）end up with nothing; go for wool and come back shorn
得米（得手）achieve one's goal; meet with success
問米（通靈）communicate with the dead through a witch
粟米（玉米）corn
晚造米（晚稻米）late season rice
越窮越見鬼，肚餓打瀉米（越倒霉，運氣越差）go from bad to worse; misfortunes never come singly
煮重米（說某人的壞話）paint sb in the darkest colour
蝦米 ① small shrimp ② shrimp meat ③ dried shrimp
糯米 glutinous rice
糴米（買米）buy rice; get rice

【羊】joeng⁴ lamb; sheep
羊毛 wool
　　羊毛出在羊身上（做任何事總要付出成本）whatever is given is paid for

羊毛冷（羊毛絨）sheep's wool
羊毛氈 felted wool blanket
羊年 Year of the Sheep; Year of the Goat
羊肉 lamb; lamb meat; mutton
　　唔食羊肉一身臊（事情對自己沒有好處，還惹來一身麻煩）invite unexpected trouble; miss the goat meat and just get the smell of the goat
羊牳（母羊）ewe
羊咩（山羊）goat
羊牯 ①（公羊）ram ②（傻子）fool
羊雜（羊下水）haggis
羊欄 sheepfold

歧路亡羊 a lamb goes astray on forked road; a lamb goes astray at a fork in the road — go astray in a complex situation; a straggling sheep; the highway leads a sheep astray with its numerous turnings
牧羊 shepherd; tend sheep
順手牽羊 go on the scamp; make away with sth

【羽】jy⁵ feather
羽毛 down; feathers; plumes
　　羽毛球 badminton
　　　　打羽毛球 play badminton
羽扇 feather fan
　　羽扇舞 feather-fan dance
羽量級 feather-weight

【老】lau¹ Shanghainese
老鬆（上海人）Shanghainese

【老】lou⁵ old
老一脫（老一代）older generation
老人 old person; old people; the aged; the elderly
　　老人成嫩仔（越活越年青）once a man and twice a child
　　老人家 ① old folks; the aged; the old ② old men ③ old women ④ parents
　　老人院 home for the aged; home for the elderly; old people's home
　　老人院都唔收（絮叨）one's remarks are too superfluous
　　老人問題 problems with the aged
　　老人精（年少老成）a young child of prudence
老千（江湖騙子／騙子）trickster
　　出老千（耍花招）perform a sleight of hand; play tricks; trickish; try it on; up to one's tricks; up to sth
老土（土包子／土氣／過時）old-fashioned
　　老土仔（土氣的男孩）old-fashioned boy
老大 boss; leader
老公（丈夫）hubby; husband

老公仔 (男朋友) steady boyfriend
老公撥扇 (淒涼) miserable
　未來老公 husband-to-be
老友 ① (好朋友) good friend ② (老朋友) old friend
老友記 ① (好朋友) good friend ② (老朋友) old friend
老友鬼鬼 (老朋友了) good friend
　好老友 (夠交情 / 深交誼) very friendly
　唔夠老友 (不夠友好) not friendly enough
老少 old and young
　老少咸宜 suitable for people of all ages; suitable for the old and the young
　老少無欺 be equally honest with the old and the young
　老老少少 old and young; people old and young
老手 experienced person; expert; old hand; old stager
　情場老手 veteran womaniser
老牛聲 (破鑼嗓子) coarse voice
老本 original principal
老外 foreigner
老幼 the old and the young
　扶老攜幼 bring along the old and the young
老母 (母親 / 媽媽) mother
　老母雞 ① old hen ② old bitch
　你老母 (你媽媽) your mother
　佢老母 (他媽媽) his mother
老奸巨猾 as cunning as an old fox
老早 long ago; very early
老死 (老朋友) buddy
老老哋 (有點兒老) a little old
老行尊 (老行家 / 專家) old timer in the line; verteran professional
老西 (西裝) men's suit
老作 (吹牛 / 胡說) lie
老吹 bullshit
老成 experienced
　老成持重 experienced and prudent
　少年老成 young but prudent
　年少老成 (年齡輕但精於世故) an old head on young shoulders
老豆 (父親 / 爸爸) father
　老豆大把 (爸爸很有錢) one's father is loaded
　老豆養仔仔養仔 (無孝心) sons who support their fathers are rare
　唔知老豆姓乜 (過份沉迷某事) one is totally immersed in sth that he doesn't remember anything at all
老來 in one's old age
　老來少 old in age but young at heart
　老來富 live in richness in one's old age
　老來福 live in happiness in one's old age
　老來嬌 (老來俏) old but still beautiful

老到 (老練) experienced; seasoned
老姑婆 (老處女) old maid; old spinster
老定 (從容 / 鎮定 / 穩重) calm; keep one's head; not stir an eyelid
老屈 (誣衊) frame sb
老抽 (紅醬油 / 濃醬油) dark soy sauce
老泥 (污垢) old dirt
　老泥妹 (無所事事，到處遊蕩的青年女孩) bad girl; girl in the hood
　捽老泥 (搓汗垢 / 搓澡) rub off the old dirt on the skin
老虎 tiger
　老虎乸 (母老虎) ① (悍妻) one's shrewish wife; one's wife ② (兇女人 / 悍婦) unyielding woman
　老虎唔發威當病貓 (不發惡便當作是好欺負的) mistake a sleeping wolf for a dead dog
　老虎都會瞌眼瞓 (警剔也有不留神的時候) even a watchful person will fall asleep
　老虎機 ① (停車收費錶) parking meter ② (吃角子機) slot machine
　老虎頭上釘蝨乸 —— 自尋死路 (太歲頭上動土 / 耗子舔貓鼻子 —— 找死) bread the lion in his den; defy the mighty; offend powerful people; provoke a powerful person; provoke sb far superior in power
　老虎蟹 (橫下心 / 鐵了心) no matter what
　冇牙老虎 (只得外表嚇人) toothless tiger
　打老虎 (對付位高權重的人) arrest the high-ranking officials who break the law
　扮豬食老虎 (佯裝愚蠢) feign ignorance; play the fool; pretend to be a fool but to be actually very clever
　紙老虎 paper tiger
老表 (表兄弟 / 表親) cousin
老柴 (老傢伙) old guy; old man
老相好 ex-lover
老軍 uniformed police
老套 (過時 / 土包子 / 土氣) old-fashioned
老差骨 experienced police-officer
老師 teacher
老馬 the experienced
　識途老馬 the experienced know the ropes
老鬼 old person
　呢嗰老鬼 (這個老傢伙) this old guy
老婆 (妻子 / 愛人) wife
　老婆仔 (女朋友) steady girlfriend
　老婆乸 (老婆子) my old woman; old biddy
　娶老婆 (娶媳婦) take a wife
老笠 (搶劫) rob
老粗 vulgar person
老粒 (搶劫) rob

老細 (老闆／僱主) boss; employer; manager; owner

老處 (處子之身) virgin

老雀 (經驗豐富的人) old hand

老頂 (最高層人員) direct boss; immediate superior

老幾 (輩份) status of a person

老牌 old brand

老番 (洋鬼子) foreigner

　老番睇榜 (倒數第一) the first from the bottom

老脾 (脾氣) temper

老媽子 (老媽) mum

老爺 (外父／親家公) the father-in-law of one's child

老當益壯 old and vigorous

老葉 old leaf

　摘去老葉 pick out old leaves

老鼠 (耗子) mouse

　老鼠仔 ① (小老鼠) little mouse ② (小偷) thief
　　③ (二頭肌) bulging biceps

　老鼠尾生瘡 —— 大極有限 (耗子尾巴長瘡 —— 沒多少膿
　　血) there's a ceiling for sth

　老鼠拉龜 —— 冇埞埋手 (狗咬刺猬 —— 下不得嘴／無從
　　下手) at one's wit's end; have no way of doing sth; not
　　know how to start

　老鼠拉鱔魚 —— 一命搏一命 (拼死吃河豚 ——
　　不要命了) risking life in eating puffer fish

　老鼠貨 (後門兒貨) goods illegally obtained
　　and sold

　老鼠跌落天平 —— 自己秤自己 (耗子跌落天秤 ——
　　自己讚自己) sing one's own praise

　沙灘老鼠 (沙灘的小偷) thieves on the beach

　捉老鼠 (抓老鼠) catch a mouse

老實 frank; honest; naive; simple-minded; well-behaved

　老實講 (老實說) to be frank; frankly speaking; speak the
　　truth

老態龍鍾 look old and clumsy

老辣 (老謀深算) experienced and vicious

老遠 a very long distance; far away; very far

老鴇 (娼妓) prostitute

老積 (老成) have an old head on young shoulders; mature;
　young but steady

老舉 (娼妓) prostitute

老餅 (老土) old-fashioned

老謀深算 be experienced and calculating

老貓燒鬚 (老馬失蹄) a good horse stumbles; even Homer
　sometimes nods; sb who has had a bad experience with sth

老頭子 father

老糠 (粗糠) chaff

　老糠搾出油 (排除萬難) (literally) get oil out of rocks,
　　meaning that sb overcomes difficulties to achieve success

老總 boss; chief

老薑 (老練的人) experienced person

老闆 boss; proprietor

　老闆娘 female boss; wife of the boss

　　自己做老闆 be one's own boss

　　後台老闆 backstage boss

　　搵老闆 ① (找老闆) look for a boss ② (找有錢人)
　　　look for a rich person ③ (找個有錢的老公) look for
　　　a rich husband

　　舊老闆 (以前的老闆) former boss

老點 (瞎騙) mislead

老襟 (連襟) maternal cousins

老鵬 (好朋友) buddy; very close friend

老竇 (父親／爸爸) father

　老竇都要多 (貪小便宜) be greedy for gains

老襯 ① (笨蛋／傻人／傻瓜) fool; naive person; stupid
　person; sucker ② relation by marriage

　搵老襯 ① (騙人) fool sb into doing sth; trick ② (冤大
　　頭) a person deceived on account of his generosity

一本 (部) 通書睇到老 (不懂適時變通) adhere to the old
　ways; cling conservatively to the old system; devote to
　conventions; follow a stereotypical routine; get into/
　move in/stay in/be stuck in a rut; go round like a horse
　in a mill; inflexible; stick-in-the-mud; stick to accustomed
　rules/conventions/established practice/outdated ways
　and regulations/the old ways

一時唔偷雞做父老 (平日偷雞摸狗／難得一天無錯／
　便教訓人) a rogue goes so far as to moralize to
　another rogue

人老心不老 young in spirit for one's old age

元老 doyen; senior statesmen

父老 elders

古老 ① ancient ② old-fashioned

好老 very old

年老 aged; old

百年歸老 die of old age

抗老 anti-aging

活到老學到老 a person should study till their dying day; it
　is never too old to learn; keep on learning as long as you
　live; live and learn; never too old to learn; one is never
　too old to learn

長生不老 live a long life and never grow old; perpetual
　youth and longevity

長老 senior

恃老賣老 (倚老賣老) act like a Dutch uncle; flaunt one's
　seniority

鄉親父老 elders and folks

敬老 respect the old

攢錢防老 save up money for one's old age

【考】haau² examine

考到 passed an examination
考起（難倒）baffle; beat; daunt
考試 examination
考牌（考駕照）take a driving test
考慮 consider

思考 think
參考 reference
備考 for reference

【而】ji⁴ but

而後 after that; then
而倚哦哦（絮絮叨叨）shilly-shally
而家（現在）at once; at present; at the moment; for the moment; immediately; now; nowadays; of the moment; presently; right now
　而家幾點（現在幾點鐘）what time is it now
　　由而家起（從現在開始）from now on
　　到而家為止（到目前為止）up to now
　　照而家咁（照現狀看）as it is

反而 but; instead; on the contrary; rather than
繼而 afterwards then

【耳】ji⁵（耳朵）ear

耳仔（耳朵）ear
　耳仔軟（容易順從）be easily persuaded
　耳仔邊（耳朵旁）the "ear"（耳）radical
　　一隻耳仔（一隻耳朵）a ear
　　右耳仔（右耳旁）the "town"（阝）radical
　　左耳仔（左耳旁）the "mound"（阝）radical
　　扭耳仔（擰耳朵）bully sb
　　咬耳仔（密談／耳語）have a word in one's ear; talk secretly; whisper to sb
　　單耳仔（單耳旁）the "single ear"（耳）
　　揸住耳仔（摀着耳朵）cover one's ears
　　撩耳仔（掏耳朵）clean one's ears; pick the ears
耳挖（耳挖子）earpick
耳屎（耳垢）cerumen; earwax
耳珠（耳垂）earlobe
耳筒（耳機）earphone
　耳筒機（隨身聽）walkman
耳殼（耳輪）helix
耳環 earring
　一對耳環（一雙耳環）a pair of earrings
耳窿（耳孔）earhole
　大耳窿（高利貸）loan shark
　耳仔窿（耳孔）earhole

耳邊風 unheeded advice; words treated as unimportant
耳聾 deaf

木耳 wood fungus
好耳（耳朵好）have sharp ears
刺耳 ear-piercing; grating on the ear; harsh; irritating to the ear; jarring; unpleasant to the ear
忠言逆耳 good advice is always unpleasant to the ear
招風耳 flaring ear
油耳（油性耳垢）earwax
肥頭耷耳（肥頭大耳）stupid
借咗聾陳隻耳（假裝聽不到別人說的話）turn a deaf ear to sb
哽耳（逆耳）grating on the ear; irritating to the ear
逆耳 grate on the ear; unpleasant to the ear
兜風耳（招風耳）flaring ear
雪耳 snow fungus; white fungus
雲耳 black fungus
隔牆有耳 walls have ears
膊頭高過耳 skinny person
豬耳 pig's ear
錐耳（打耳洞）pierce the ears
親耳 with one's own ear

【肉】juk⁶ flesh; meat

肉丸（肉丸子）meat ball
肉月（肉月餅）mooncake stuffed with meat
肉批（肉餅子）steamed minced pork
肉赤（心疼／心痛）feel hurt when one lets sth valuable go; grudge; heartbreak
肉刺（心疼）be reluctant to spend
肉麻 feel disgusted
肉參（綁票）kidnap for ransom
肉眼 ① pork rib eye ② beef rib eye ③ naked eyes
肉粒（肉丁）diced pork
肉痛（心疼／心痛）feel hurt when one lets sth valuable go
肉感 sexy
肉緊（揪心／神經緊張）be highly excited; feel anxious; feel very tense
肉酸（不堪入目／肉麻／難看／難聽）creepy-crawly; ugly
　鬼咁肉酸（怪難看的）look quite awful
　唱得好肉酸（不堪入耳／唱得很難聽）one's singing is very poor
肉餅（肉餅子）steamed minced pork
肉檔（肉攤）butcher's; meat stall
肉隨砧板上（任人宰割）be led by the nose
肉類 meat

一個螺一個肉（一個蘿蔔一個坑）each has their own task, and there is nobody to spare; every hole has its own turnip

一嚿肉（一塊肉）a piece of meat

上肩肉 pork shoulder chop

山竹牛肉 beef ball with bean curd skin

五花肉 pork belly; streaky pork

午餐肉 luncheon meat

太公分豬肉（每人平分一份）distribution money where every body gets an equal share

手板係肉，手背又係肉（左右為難）difficult to decide in taking sides as both parties are on good terms; have friendly relation with both parties

牙肉 gum

牛肉 beef

牛脾肉 round steak

去骨肉 boned meat

生肉（長肉）put on weight

好肉 fleshy

羊肉 lamb; lamb meat; mutton

肌肉 muscle

沙爹牛肉 beef with satay sauce

免治牛肉 minced beef

免治豬肉 minced pork

咕嚕肉 sweet and sour pork

炆豬肉 stewed pork

肩肉 beef shoulder

香肉 dog meat

砌生豬肉（偽造罪名陷害）fabricate a charge against sb; frame sb

個螺個肉（一個蘿蔔一個坑）just one for just one

唔生肉（長不胖）lose weight

息肉 polyp

烤肉 roast meat

酒肉 wine and women

骨肉 one's natural children

啖啖肉（利潤豐收）lucrative; profitable

掛羊頭賣狗肉（表裏不一）hang out a sheep's head when what one is selling is dog's meat; hanging up a sheep's head and selling dog's meat; he cries wine, and sells vinegar; offer chaff for grain; sell a pig in a poke; sell dog meat as mutton; sell dog meat under the label of a sheep's head; sell horsemeat as beefsteak; swindle others by making false claims

斬肉 chop the meat

圓肉 dried longan pulp

煙肉 beacon

煨肉 stew meat

瘦肉 lean meat; lean pork

碎肉 minced meat

腩肉 pork belly

鼻哥窿冇肉（驚心動魄）be extremely terrified

賣肉（靠出賣身體維生）offer sex for a living

鴨肉 duck meat

橫肉（面相兇巴巴的）look ugly and ferocious

豬腩肉 pork belly

燒肉 roast pork

燒豬肉 roast pork

錶肉（錶瓤兒 / 手錶機芯）inside mechanism of a watch

龍眼肉 dried longan pulp

戲肉（戲劇的精彩部份）climax; highlight

臀肉 beef rump

雞肉 chicken

雞胸肉 chicken breast

蟹肉 crab meat

癩蛤蟆想食天鵝肉（妄想）estimate oneself; overreach oneself

【肋】lak⁶ ribs

肋骨 ribs

肋條 ① rib ② pork rib

肋軟骨 cartilage ribs

打大赤肋（光膊子）be stripped to the waist; strip oneself to the waist

【肌】gei¹ muscle

肌肉 muscle

肌膚 skin and muscle

肌纖維 muscle fibre

六塊腹肌 six-pack

腹肌 abdominal muscle

【自】zi⁶ oneself

自大 arrogant

自己 oneself

　自己人 one of us

　自己友（自己人）one of us; our own mate

　自己身有屎（自己有不見得光的事）feel compunction

　自己最知自己事（自己最瞭解自己）every person knows himself best; one knows best what one's doing

　你自己 yourself

　佢自己（他 / 她自己）① himself ② herself

　我自己 myself

　信自己 believe in yourself

自不然（自然）a matter of course; naturally; of course; to be sure

自幼（從小）as a child; from childhood
自由 free; freedom
　　自由式（自由泳）free stroke
　　自由行 independent travelling
自在 ①（自由）free ② relaxing
　　有自唔在，攞苦嚟辛（自討苦吃）prefer to do things in a hard way
　　唔自在（不舒服）unwell
自此之後 after that
自助餐 buffet
　　食自助餐（吃自助餐）have buffet
自把自為 decide arbitrarily
自投羅網 put one's own head in the noose
自私 selfish
自便 do as one wishes
自修 self study
自動 automatic
　　自動波（自動擋）automatic shift
　　自動掣（自動開關）automatic switch
　　自動櫃員機 automatic teller machine (ATM); cash machine
自梳女（自願不嫁的女子）a maid making up her mind not to marry all her life
自殺 commit suicide; suicide; take one's own life
　　跳河自殺 commit suicide by jumping into a river; suicide by drowning
自細（從小）as a child; from childhood; since childhood
自然 natural
　　大自然 nature
　　自自然然（自然而然）naturally
　　唔自然（不舒服）unwell
自傳 autobiography
自斟自酌 in the enjoyment of one's own life all by oneself
自僱 self-employed
自製 ① home-made ② do it yourself (DIY)
自學 self-study
自願 voluntary; willing
　　純屬自願 entirely voluntary

一自（一邊／一面）at the same time
妄自 excess presumptuous
私自 without authorization
尚自 still; yet
徑自 without consulting anyone; without leave

【至】zi³（最）at most
至多（大不了／最多）at most; the most
　　至多唔係（大不了）if the worst comes to the worst
至好（最好）had better; it might as well
至低限度（最低限度）at least

至尾 at last
至到（及至）as to
至怕（最怕）fear most
　　至怕嚟唔切（最怕來不及）what is most worrisome is that it might be too late to do sth
至於 as for
至係（才是）only then is
至無… even if
至話（剛剛）just now

冬至 Winter Solstice
先至（剛才）① just; not until; only; then and only then ② just now
免至（免得）in order to avoid; lest; save; so as not to; so as to avoid
沓至（接連而至）come one after another without stop
夏至 June solstice; summer solstice
就至（剛）just now
幾難先至（多難才可以）by the skin of one's teeth; go to a lot of trouble; have a hard time; it takes a lot of time to; not easy at all; with much difficulty
傳真至 fax to

【舌】sit⁶ tongue
舌尖 tip of the tongue
舌痛 glossalgia
舌戰 argue heatedly; debate with verbal confrontation; have a verbal battle with
舌頭 tongue

七嘴八舌 all talking at once
反口覆舌 break one's promise; inconsistent with what one says
牛舌 ox tongue
白費唇舌 speak to the wind; waste one's breath; waste one's words; whistle down the wind
枉費唇舌 a mere waste of breath; waste one's breath
唇舌 ① lips and tongue ②（辯論）argument; persuasion; plausible speech; talking round; words
室口室舌（結結巴巴）stammer nervously
粗口爛舌（愛說粗話）speak coarse language; use a lot of bad language
帽舌 peak of a cap; visor
駁嘴駁舌（頂咀）talk back

【舟】zau¹ boat
舟車 vessel and vehicle

爬龍舟（划龍船）dragonboating

順水推舟 make use of an opportunity to win one's end

漁舟 (漁船) fishing boat

龍舟 (龍船) dragon boat

【色】 sik¹ colour

色士風 (薩克管) saxophone

色中餓鬼 (性慾狂) sex maniac

色水 (顏色) colour

色仔 (骰子) dice

　　扰 / 擲色仔 (擲骰子) throw the dice

色司 (性感) (transliteration) sexy

色字頭上一把刀 womanising is dangerous

色香味 appearance, fragrance, and taste

色狼 (色鬼 / 色情狂) sex maniac

色迷迷 look at a woman with shifty eyes

色情 pornographic; sexy

色魔 lecher; satyr; sex lupine; sex maniac

一粒色 (小個子) short person

七嘢色 (甚麼顏色) what colour

五顏六色 ① a riot of colour; colourful; play of colours ② (病得嚴重) (said of illness) critical

天藍色 sky blue

古銅色 sun-tanned colour

奶白色 beige

打色 ① (擲骰子) throw the dice ② (作主) sb decide

出色 outstanding

甩色 (脫色) fade; lose colour

生色 add colour to; add lustre to

白色 white

好色 lecherous; sex-obsessed

灰色 grey

米白色 beige

米色 beige

走色 (不要醬油) no soy sauce

咖啡色 brown

油顏色 (塗顏色) apply paint

金色 gold

金黃色 golden yellow

青色 light green

染色 colouration; dye; dyeing; staining; tinge

紅色 red

面色 (臉色) facial expression

彩色 multi-coloured

校色 (調配顏色) mix colours; mix paints

桃色 ① peach colour ② symbolic of romance ③ (男女不正當關係) illicit love

茶色 brown

草青色 greyish green

草綠色 green as grass

粉紅色 pink

啡色 brown

病到五顏六色 (病得非常嚴重) be critically ill

淨色 (素色) plain colour

清一色 ① (麻將術語：由同一種花組成的一副牌) (mahjong) royal flush ② (同一性別) of the same gender ③ (同一類) uniformly

蛋黃色 yolk yellow

貨色 (甚麼樣的人) kind of person

景色 scenery

紫色 purple

睇人面色 (看別人臉色) be dependent on other's pleasure

黃色 yellow

黑色 black

綠色 green

銀色 silver

暮色 dusk; gloaming shadow; twilight

橙色 orange

膚色 complexion

顏色 colour

寶藍色 royal blue

藍色 blue

鹹濕好色 (好色) sex-mad; sleazy

【血】 hyut³ blood

血汗 blood and sweat; sweat and toil

　　血汗錢 hard-earned money; money earned by hard toil

血氣 ① disposition ② animal spirits; sap; vigour ③ courage and uprightness

　　血氣方剛 be easily excited; full of animal spirits; full of sap; full of vigour and vitality; full of vim and vigour; hot-tempered; in one's raw youth; in one's salad days; in the green

血淋淋 ① bloody ② naked facts

血淚 blood and tears; extreme sorrow

　　血淚史 heart-rending story; sad story

血債 debt of blood

　　血債血還 blood demands blood; blood for blood; blood must atone for blood; blood will have blood; debts of blood must be paid in blood; demand blood for blood; make sb pay blood for blood; the blood debts must be repaid in kind; the debt in blood must be repaid with blood

血管 blood vessel

　　爆血管 (血管破裂) rupture of blood vessel

血壓 blood pressure

　　血壓低 (低血壓) low blood pressure

　　血壓高 (高血壓) high blood pressure; hypertension

一頸血（損了一大筆錢）lose a great deal of money

大出血（大減價）big sale

止血 stanch bleeding; stop bleeding

出血 bleed

咯血（咳血）cough up blood

捐血 blood donation

流血 bleeding

流鼻血 nosebleeding

屙血 have blood in one's stool

貧血 anemia

嘔心瀝血 take infinite pains

嘔血（吐血）exasperating; exhausted

鼻血 nosebleed

滿地鮮血 blood all over the place

鮮血 blood; fresh blood

雞毛鴨血（一塌糊塗）in a bad situation

【行】hang⁴（走）walk

行一勻（走一次）take a walk

行人 pedestrian

　　行人路（人行路）path; pedestrian crossing

　　行人隧道（地下隧道）underground tunnel

行下（走走／散步／遛躂）take a walk; take an airing

行山（遠足／爬山）hiking; take a walk on the hills; walk the hills

行友（徒步旅行者）hiker

行出啲（往外點兒）move a little outside

行必（巡邏）walk the beat

　　行孖必（一對警察拍檔地巡邏）two police officers walk the beat

行先（先走）go first

　　行先一步（去世）die

　　我行先（我先走）I'll go first

行行企企（無所事事）at loose ends; be engaged in nothing; be occupied with nothing; do nothing; fool about/around; goof (off); hang about/around; have nothing to do; idle about/along/away one's time; kick one's heels; loaf; lost and bewildered; mess about/around; moon about/around; not to do a hand's turn; not to do a stitch of work; not to lift a hand; play about in a foolish way; twiddle/twirl one's thumbs; vegetate

行李 luggage

　　手提行李 hand luggage

　　執行李（收納行李）pack one's luggage

　　報失行李 report the loss of one's luggage

行使 exercise

　　行使權利 exercise one's rights

行咗（去世了）dead

行政費 administration fee

行軍牀（帆布牀）canvas cot

行倒 ①（能走）walkable ②（走得到）can be reached by walking

　　行唔倒（走不到）cannot be reached by walking

　　行得倒（走得到）can be reached by walking

行唔喐（走不動）can't walk

行埋 ①（走近點）come closer ②（有了性關係）have sex

　　行唔埋（合不來）unable to get along with

　　行得埋（合得來）get along well with people; hit it off

行差踏錯 make a mistake

行動 action

　　　聯合行動 united action

行啦 let's go

行得（能走）can walk

行得正，企得正（光明正大）act in a totally proper manner; play fair and square

行船 ①（走船／開船／跑船／駕船）ride in a boat ② make a living as a sailor

　　行船好過灣（不怕慢就怕站）it is better to have a little to do than it is to do none

　　行船爭解纜（帶頭）take the lead

行喇 let's go

行街 ①（逛街／逛商店）stroll around the streets; walk around ② go window-shopping ③ go shopping ④（推銷員）broker; salesperson ⑤（外賣）take away

　　好行街（好逛街／愛逛街）① fond of strolling aound the streets ② fond of window-shopping

　　行街街（逛街）wander around the streets

行開（走開／滾開／離開）go away

　　行開行埋（走來走去）move around; move about; go around; wander; went around; pace up and down

　　行開咗（走開了）not here at the moment; just stepped out for a moment

行經（來月經）menstruate; monthly period

行路（走路／步行）go on foot; walk

　　行路去（走路去）go on foot

　　行路打倒褪（事事不順利）misfortunes never come singly

　　行路唔帶眼（走路不長眼睛）jaywalk

行運（走運）by good luck; devil's luck; fall on one's feet; have fortune on one's side; have good luck; have one's moments; in luck; land on one's feet; luck is on one's side; luck of the devil; luck out; lucky; lucky sb; on the gravy train; one's luck is in; play big luck; strike it lucky; touch luck; you never know your luck; what a stroke of luck

　　行運一條龍 have good fortune

　　行運一條龍，失運一條蟲 a person in luck walks heavy but a person out of luck cowers with humility

　　行大運（運氣極好）enjoy good luck

行好運（走好運）by good luck; devil's luck; fall on one's feet; have fortune on one's side; have good luck; have one's moments; in luck; land on one's feet; luck is on one's side; luck of the devil; luck out; lucky; lucky sb; on the gravy train; one's luck is in; play big luck; strike it lucky; touch luck; you never know your luck; what a stroke of luck

行衰運（走背運）bad luck; have bad luck; suffer an unlucky fate

行雷（打雷）have thunderstorm; thunder
行雷閃電 lightning and thunder

行頭（帶頭）take the lead

行嚟（走過來）come over
行埋（過）嚟（走過來）come over

行 beat（巡邏）walk the beat

一次旅行（一趟旅行）a tour; a trip

十分流行 be in vogue

寸步難行 cannot do anything; cannot go a step; cannot move a single step; difficult for sb to move a single step; difficult to move even one step; find it hard to make a single move; forced into a strait; unable to do a thing; unable to move one inch forward

五行 five basic elements

刊行 print and publish

另行 at some other time; separately

同枱食飯，各自修行 each does what he thinks is right

好行 ① （再見）goodbye ② （保重）take care

好腥（聲）行 ① （再見）goodbye ② （保重）take care

自由行 independent travelling

衣食住行 clothing, food, shelter and means of travel, the four basic needs of everybody; food, clothing, shelter and transportation, basic necessities of life

坐言起行 no sooner said than done

步行 foot it; go on foot; walk

巡行 ① parade ② demonstrate; march

言行 statements and actions; words and deeds

例行 routine

兒女成行 sons and daughters forming a row — have many children

拍埋行（排成一行走路）walk in a row

明知山有虎，偏向虎山行 go into the mountains knowing well that there are tigers there

直行（往直去）go straight ahead

長途旅行 long journey

品行 behaviour; conduct

流行 ① be in vogue; current; fashionable; popular ② go around; rage; rampant; spread

旅行 journey; tour

送行 see sb off on a journey

起行 begin a journey; depart; departure; go on a journey; leave for a place; set out on a journey

蛇無頭不行 without a person in the lead, all the others move no farther

越嚟越流行（越來越流行）become more and more popular

遊行 demonstration march

禍不單行 an evil chance seldom comes alone; an Illiad of woes; bad events rarely come singly; disasters do not come alone; disasters pile up on one another; it never rains but it pours; misery loves company; misfortunes never come singly; one misfortune calls upon another; one misfortune comes on the neck of another; one woe doth tread upon another's heels; when it rains it really pours; when sorrows come, they come not single spies, but in battalions

實行 carry out; practice

運路行（繞道走）detour; go by a roundabout route; go round; make a detour; take a devious route

慢慢行 ① （再見）goodbye ② （慢慢走）walk slowly

履行 act up to; carry out; enforce; execute; fulfill; meet; observe; perform

點行（怎樣走）how to get to

識行（懂走）learn to walk

辭行 say goodbye to sb before setting out on a jurney; take one's leave

【行】hong⁴ ① （行業）trade; industry ② （建起）set up

行內人 expert; insider

行牀（架牀 / 搭個鋪）set up a temporary bed

行家（同行）persons of the same trade

行貨 ① ordinary goods ② （正品 / 正牌貨）standard goods

一行 a line of

一間銀行 a bank

入行（進入某行業）enter a field; join a profession

三句不離本行 cadgers speak of lead saddles; talk about nothing but one's own interests; talk always about one's own line; talk shop; talk shop all the time

三行（泥水 / 木工 / 油漆三種行業的統稱）construction business

內行 expert

分行 branch

本行 one's line; one's profession; one's specialty; one's trade

充內行 pass oneself off as an expert; pose as an expert

同行 ① of the same trade ② of the same profession

在行 be skilled; be well acquainted with a task

有行（有希望／有門兒）there is hope

老本行 old hand

洋行 foreign company; foreign firm

唔在行（外行）out of one's beat; out of one's line

排成一行 stand in a line

朝拆晚行 a bed set up at the evening and dismantled in the morning

經紀行 brokerage

銀行 bank

熟行（在行／對某一事物很熟悉）be skilled; be well acquainted with a task

儲錢入銀行 save one's money with the bank

總行 headquarters

轉行 change one's profession; change one's trade

鐘錶行 clock and watch shop

【衣】ji¹ clothes

衣車（縫紉機）sewing machine

衣服 clothes

執衣服（收拾衣服）pack one's clothes

衣食 clothes and food

衣食父母 employer; those on whom one's livelihood depends

衣食住行 clothing, food, shelter and means of travel, the four basic needs of everybody; food, clothing, shelter and transportation, basic necessities of life

衣食無憂 have no worries about money

方衣食（沒食德）guilty of bad faith

有衣食（有吃有穿）have ample food and clothing

衣着 apparel; attire; clothing; dress; headgear and footwear

衣櫃 wardrobe

小雨衣（避孕套）condom

內衣 underwear

更衣 change dresses; change one's clothes

車衣 sew; stitch

披衣 throw on gown

泳衣 swimming suit

雨衣 raincoat

洗衣（洗衣服）wash clothes

胎衣 afterbirth

食爺飯，着乸衣（食的由爸爸供給，穿的由媽媽供應）be supported by parents

罩衣 dust cloak; overall

葛衣（用葛布製成的衣服）clothing made with linen

睡衣 pajamas

燒衣（燒錢紙）burn nether banknotes

【西】sai¹ west

西人（西方人／老外／洋人／外國人）Westerner

西方 west

西片（外國電影）Western movie

西瓜 water melon

一嚿西瓜（一塊西瓜）a slice of water melon

西米露 sago in coconut milk

西冷 beef sirloin

西芹（西芹菜）celery

西柚 grapefruit

西班牙 Spain

西班牙人 Spanish

西婦（西方女人）Western woman

西斜（西曬）have a western exposure to the hot sun in the afternoon

西梅（乾梅子）prune

西湯 Western soup

西裝 ① （西服）Western-style clothes ② Western suite

西裝友（穿西服的人）man in a suit

一套西裝（一套西服）a suit

着住西裝（穿着西服）wearing a suit

西餅（西式點心／西點）cake; pastry

一件西餅（一塊西點）a cake

西褲（寬鬆長褲）slacks

西餐 ① Western food ② Western meal

西蘭花（洋花菜／青花菜）broccoli

中西 Chinese and Western

老西（西服）men's suit

呃呃西西（懇求）beg a favour of sb

送佛送到西（好事做到底）when you help sb, help him from end to end

單吊西（只有上衣，不配褲子的單件西服）Western-style suite

捹西（馬虎）not serious; scamp one's work; sloppy

睇東睇西（東張西望）gaze this way and that; stare about; watch out furtively to the east and west

歸西（死）die

7 劃

【串】cyun³ ① arrogant; cheeky; cocky ② collude

串字（拼寫）transliterate

串通 collude with sb; plot with sb

串聯 contact; establish; establish a relation with; establish ties with; link up; make contacts with

好串（很囂張）① cocky ② stuck-up
扮晒串（裝囂張）arrogant; vain; boastful
唔好咁串（別要那麼囂張）don't get cocky

【亨】hang¹ tycoon

亨通 go smoothly; prosperous
　　官運亨通 have a successful official career

大亨 tycoon

【些】se¹ some

些少（一點兒）a bit; a bit of; a little; a morsel of; a shade;
　　a streak of; a trifle; faintly; slightly something
些微 a bit; a little

【伯】baak⁸ uncle

伯父（老伯／老漢／老頭兒）old chap; old codger;
　　old man
伯母 auntie
伯仲（兄弟長幼）brothers; older and younger brothers
　　伯仲之間 about the same
　　　　不相伯仲 about the same
伯伯 uncle
伯娘（伯母）aunt
伯爺公（老大爺／老伯／老漢／老頭兒）old chap; old
　　codger; old man
伯爺婆（老太太／老婦）old lady; old woman
伯爵 count; earl

叔伯 paternal uncles
阿伯 ①（伯伯）uncle ②（老頭子）old chap; old codger; old
　　fogey; old man
姻伯 uncle by marriage
瞥伯（偷窺者）peeper

【估】gu³（猜／猜想）a shot in the dark; guess blindly; guess groundlessly; guess wildly; guess without ground; make a random guess; make a wild guess

估中（猜到／猜着）one's guess is right
　　估唔中（猜不到）cannot guess; miss one's guess; unable
　　　　to make out the right answer; unable to reach the right
　　　　answer
　　估得中（猜得到／猜得着）one's guess is right
估估吓（瞎猜）calculate roughly
估計 estimate
　　粗略估計 rough estimate
估倒（猜到／猜着）one's guess is right
　　估唔倒（猜不到）cannot guess; miss one's guess;

unable to make out the right answer; unable to reach
the right answer
　　點都估唔倒（怎樣也猜不到）cannot predict;
　　　　unexpectedly
　　估得倒（猜得到／猜得着）one's guess is right
估值 valuation
估量 appraise; assess; balance; estimate; ponder; value; weigh
估價 ① evaluate ② appraised price

死估估（沒生氣的）poor-witted
低估 disappreciation; underestimate
開估 reveal the answer to the riddle
斷估（猜想）guess; wild guess

【你】nei⁵（您）you

你又係嘅…（你真是…）your're really...
你去埋嘞（你也去吧）why don't you come along
你先（請先）after you
　　你先啦（請先吧）after you
你同我定（別擔心）don't worry, everything will be fine
你好嗎 how are things going; how are you; how are you
　　doing; how goes it; how have you been; how's tricks
你有張良計，我有過牆梯（你有關門計，我有跳牆法）
　　be evenly matched
你有乾坤，我有日月 be on a par with
你我 you and I
　　不分你我 make no distinction between you and I
　　有你冇我（有你沒有我）you and I cannot coexist
　　你有你，我有我（你有你的，我有我的）let's each go
　　　　our own way
　　你走你嘅陽關路，我過我嘅獨木橋（互不相干）each
　　　　goes their own way
你係得嘅（你真行）you're really good
你哋（你們）you
　　你哋嘅（你們的）your
你唔嫌我籮疏，我唔嫌你米碎（互相諒解）be two of
　　a kind
你真係（你真的是）you're really
　　你真係好人氏（你真好）you're very nice
　　你真係有心（謝謝你的關心）thank you for your care
　　你真係有我心（你真關心我）you really care about me
你做初一，我做十五（以牙還牙／以血還血）a tooth
　　for a tooth; an eye for an eye; answer blows with blows;
　　blow for blow; fight fire with fire; give as good as one
　　gets; like for like; measure for measure; meet force by
　　force; repay evil with evil; return blow for blow; return
　　like for like; serve the same sauce to sb; tit for tat; tooth
　　for tooth
你眼望我眼（互相對望）look at each other's eyes

你敬我一尺，我敬你一丈 You scratch my back and I'll scratch yours

你話啦（你話事吧）whatever you say

你嘅（你的）your

打鑼咁搵你（不停地找你）take a lantern to look for you

由得你（隨便你）as you please; as you think fit; do as you like; it's up to you; please yourself; suit yourself; whatever you say

多得你（多虧你）thanks to you

我會掛住你（我會想念你）I'll miss you

恭喜你 congratulations

俾你個頭（不會給你）I'll give you nothing

俾番你（還給你）give sth back to you

迷你 mini

鬼打你（你被迷住了）you are obsessed

呸過你（吓過你）go to blazes; go to hell; the hell you are; up yours

掠死你（嗌死你）strangle you to death

殺你（成交）it's a deal

勞煩晒你（麻煩你了）really sorry to trouble you

話之你（不管你）do what you like

輪到你 it's your turn

廢時睬你（懶理你）don't waste my time on you

錫晒你（愛死你）love sb most dearly

隨便你 as you like; do what you want

點呀你（你還好嗎）how are you

【伴】bun⁶ companion

伴侶 companion
　　理想伴侶 ideal companion
　　終生伴侶 lifelong companion

伴奏 accompaniment; accompany; play an accompaniment
　　鋼琴伴奏 piano accompaniment

伴郎 best man; groomsman

伴娘 bridesmaid

伴唱 ① vocal accompaniment ② accompany a singer

伴舞 dancing partner

伴遊（陪遊）escort

貿易伙伴 trade partner

夥伴 companion; partner

【伸】san¹ stretch

伸一腳（給了一腿 / 打了一頓）beat up

伸手 hold out one's hand; reach out one's hand; stretch out one's hand
　　伸手不見五指 darkness visible; pitchdark; so dark that you can't see your hand in front of you

伸出 extend; project; overhang; reach; runout
　　伸出援手 lend a helping hand
　　伸出嚟（伸出來）stick out

伸展 extend

伸開 extend; spread; stretch out

伸縮 ① expand and contract; lengthen and shorten; stetch out and draw back ② adjustable; elastic; flexible

大丈夫能屈能伸 stretch one's leg according to one's own blanket

兩腳一伸（伸腿兒）death

能屈能伸 able to adapt to circumstances; can either stoop or stand; flexible; know when to eat humble pie and when to hold one's head high; know when to yield and when not; take the rough with the smooth

【似】ci⁵ resemble

似乎 as if; as it appears; it appears that; it looks as if; it looks like; it seems; seem; seemingly

似足（非常像）like a splitting image
　　似到十足（像極了）like a splitting image

似樣 ① (像 / 像話) proper; reasonable; right ② (相像 / 像樣) look alike
　　似模似樣（相像 / 像樣）look alike

互相類似 similar to each other

好似（好像）as if; look like; resemble; seem; seem like

相似 resemble

唔似（不像）unlike

都似（也像）it's possible

極之相似 close resemblance

貌似 in appearance; seemingly

類似 ① kind of; sort of ② similar

【但】daan⁶ but

但凡（凡是）① as long as ② all; any; every; in every case

但係（但是）but; however
　　之但係（但是）but; however

但願 I wish; if only
　　但願如此 be it so; I hope so; I hope that's right; I only hope it is so; I simply wish it to be so; I wish it were true; let it be so; let's hope so; so be it

是但（兩可）anybody will do; as you like it; anything is alright/all right; anything will do

是是但但（模稜兩可 / 隨便了）anybody will do; as you like it; anything is alright/all right; anything will do

【佈】bou³ announce

佈告 bulletin; make public announcement

佈局 layout

佈防 deploy troops in anticipation of an enemy attack; organise the defence

佈景 scenery for stage

佈置 ① make arrangements ② arrange; decorate

宣佈 announce; declare; proclaim

【位】wai⁶ ①（位子）place ②（職位）position

位於 be located; be situated; lie; sit on; stand on

位置 position

一個席位 a seat

上位（升職）be promoted; get promoted

大把位（很多座位）many seats available

水位 price

中間位 middle seat

出位（破格兒）make a name for oneself

出晒位（出風頭／破格兒）beyond expectations

加多個位（加多一個位子）put in an extra seat

卡位 balcony seat

示範單位 show flat

穴位 acupuncture point

名譽地位 fame and status

地位 status

江湖地位 status in the underworld

你係邊位（你是誰）who's calling; who's it; who's on the phone; who's that; who's this

冷氣機位（空調機位）space for air-conditioner

坐位 seat

走廊位 aisle seat

岆個位（霸個位子）occupy a seat

車位 parking space

呢位（這位）this person

易位 change positions

泊位 park a car

物業單位 property unit

保住席位 hold onto a seat; keep a seat

客位 ① seat ② class

帝位 throne

派位 allocate school places

座位 seat

埋位（就位）take one's place

席位 seat

商務客位 business class

執位（轉位）change of position

登機櫃位 check-in counter

連車位 including car park

博士學位 doctorate degree

揢（住個）位（佔座位）occupy a seat

單位 ① unit ② apartment; flat

換位 change places

窗口位 window seat

開位（訂位）book a seat

嗰位（那位）that person

搵位（找座位）find a seat

搏出位（爭取成名）try and make a name for oneself

祿位 official salary and rank

經濟位 economy class seat

經濟客位 economy class

價位 price

調位 swap places

舖位 shopfront

優質單位 grade A flat

學位 ① student place ② degree

機位 aeroplane seat

褪位（移位）move

艙位 passenger berth

櫃位 bar; counter; desk

邊位（誰）who

攝位（抬高自己）self-promoting

霸（個）位（搶座位）grab a seat

攤位 booth

攞位（拿座位）① win status ② get a seat

【低】dai¹ down

低下 low; lowly

低估 disappreciation; underestimate

低低地蹟舖（承認失敗）admit being defeated

低波（低速檔）low gear

低威（自卑）despise oneself; feel oneself inferior; self-abased; slight oneself; underestimate oneself

低格（人格低）ill-bred

低級 ① elementary; lower; primary; rudimentary ② low; vulgar

低能 fool; stupid

低莊（出手低／低下）regardless of one's own social status

低微 humble; lowly

低價 at a low price

低頭 ① bow one's head; hang one's head; lower one's head ② submit; yield

低頭切肉，把眼看人（察言觀色）choose a pigeon to cheat

低檔 ①（低速檔）low gear ② lower end

低 B（低能／愚蠢）feeble-mindedness; incompetent; mental deficiency; retarded

下低（下面）low; under

山高水低 unexpected misfortune

牛唔飲水，唔揼得牛頭低（不可強人所難）(literally) one cannot press down the head of a cow if it does not want to drink water, meaning it is not possible to force sb to do what he or she is not willing to do

出手低（出價低）① low offer ② not so generous with one's money

打低（打敗）defeat

交低（交下）leave behind

伏低（伏下）lie down

血壓低 low blood pressure

坐低（坐下）sit down

抄低（寫下）jot down; write down

放低（放下）leave; put down

狗眼看人低（看不起）despise

砌低（擊敗）beat; defeat

留低（留下）stay behind

做低（殺了）kill

掠低（殺了）kill

泹低（槍殺）gun down

剩低（剩下）be left over; remain

勍低（推倒）push over

睇低（看不起）look down on

貶低 abase; belittle; cry down; denigrate; depreciate; detract from; disparage; play down; run down

跌低（滑倒）fall down

搞低（蹲下）bend down

暈低（暈倒）faint; pass out

碌低（翻滾）tumble

話低（留口訊）leave a message

跣低（滑倒）slip

跪低（跪下）throw oneself on one's knees

跳高踎低（跳高蹲下）jump up and down

酙低（忘記並留下）forget and leave behind sth

踎低（蹲下）squat down

劈低（劈開）chop down

寫低（寫下）write down

撲低（撲倒）lie down

摜低（跌下）fall; stumble; tip over

瞓低（躺下）lie down

踩低（踏下）step down

揿低（擊敗）① beat; defeat ② press down

擒高擒低（爬高爬低）climb up and down

請坐低（請坐下）please sit down

舉得起放得低（能屈能伸）able to advance or retreat; adaptable; flexible

嘥低 finish off

擠／薑低（放下）lay down; put down

講低（留口訊）leave a message

鍊低（擊敗對手）come out on top

躂低（跌倒）fall; tumble

【住】dzy⁶ live

住戶 resident

住宅 apartment

　　服務式住宅 serviced apartment

住所 abode; domicile; dwelling place; home; residence

住客 tenant

住埋（同居）cohabit; cohabitation; live together; shack up with

住喺 live

　　住喺呢度（住在這裏）live in here

�住 watch closely

且住（且慢）hold it; stop it

冚住（遮蓋）cover up

卡住 get stuck; seize

扐住（拿着）holding; taking

扐唔住（拿不起）can't hold it

扐得住（拿得起）can hold it

生蟲拐杖——靠唔住（不可靠）a rail made of rotten rushes – a broken reed; unrealiable

（用膊頭）托住 carry sth on the shoulder

企住（堅持）halt; stand one's ground; stop

因住（估計不超過／小心）① not to exceed the limit ② take care of oneself ③ control one's emotions ④ beware of one's life; watch out

扣住 pin; pin up

吼住（盯住）keep a close watch on

夾住（夾着）① carry under one's arm ② clip

忍唔住（忍受不了）be driven beyond the limits of forbearance; beyond endurance; can't help doing sth; can't put up with sth any longer; cannot bear; cannot stand; cannot tolerate sth any longer; come to the end of one's patience; have enough of; have no time for; not to brook; out of patience with; unable to bear; unable to stand; worn out

扶住（扶着）help by the arm

亞超着褲——焗住（被迫）be forced to do sth

受唔住（受不了）can't stand it

居住 reside

抱住 hold in one's arms

拍得住（比得上）bear comparison with; can compare with; compare favourably with

拎住（拿着）carrying

扡住（帶上）carry with

枕住（持續）continue an action

爭住 (爭奪) compete for; vie with each other for sth or to get sth

近住 (附近) near

阻住 (阻礙) block; in the way; obstruct

咪住 (等一下) hold on

咬住 (堅持) ① bite into; grip with one's teeth ② grip; refuse to let go of; seize; take firm hold of

恃住 (依靠) rely on

揸住 (釘住) pin

指住 (指着) point at

閂住 (關上) close; lock up

閂唔住 (關不上) can't lock up

閂得住 (關得上) can be locked up

倔住 / 掘住 (瞪着) stare at; staring fixedly

套住 cover up

挨住 (俯身靠住) lean

捉住 (抓住) grab

揹住 (背着) carry on the back; carry on the shoulders

兜住 (保護某人免他尷尬) ① hold ② save sb from embarrassment

啱住 (適合居住) fit for living

接住 (接下來) follow

望住 (望着) gaze; stare at

焗住 (被迫) be compelled; be forced to do sth; can't help; involuntary

頂住 (忍住) stand up to; withstand

頂唔住 (忍不住) fail to put up with; unable to hold out; unbearable

頂得住 (忍得住) able to stand

圍住 (圍着) surround

就住 (遷就) take care in a particular situation

揞住 (遮蓋) cover

揪住 grasp sb with force

揸住 (拿住) grip

揸唔住 (拿不住) cannot hold it

揸得住 (拿得住) can hold it

捌 / 撐住 (緊握) catch hold of; grab

睇住 (小心看住 / 看管) keep an eye on; watch

睇唔住 (看不住) cannot watch closely

睇得住 (看得住) can watch closely

順住 (跟着 / 沿着) follow; go along

慌住 (擔心) for fear that; lest; so as not to

搦住 (拿着) holding

搦唔住 (拿不起) can't hold it

搦得住 (拿得起) can hold it

搞住 (妨礙) disturb

照住 ① (保護) back-up; protect ② (照着) according to; after; agreeable to; agreeably to; along; as; at; be based on; be scheduled; by; by any measure; considering; follow, from; in accordance with; in compliance with; in conformity to; in conformity with; in line with; in proportion to; in pursuance of; in the light of; on; on its merits; on the basis of; on the principle of; pursuant to; the way; to; under

跟住 (跟着) accordingly; carry on; follow; following; go on; in the wake of; next; proceed; then

闡住 (停住) stop

對你唔住 (對不起你) I beg your pardon

對唔住 (對不起) excuse me; I'm sorry; pardon me; sorry

對得住 (對得起) worthy of

摟住 (披着) cover; put on

撄住 (拉住) pull

認住 (認着) believe that; feel that

趕住 (趕着) hurry

噎住 be choked with food

搛住 (卡住) get stuck

諗住 (打算) intend; plan

靠唔住 (不可靠) undependendable; unreliable

靠得住 (可靠) dependable; reliable

撳住 press

縛住 (縛着) tie up

錫住 (愛惜) cherish a deep love for sb

隨住 (隨着) along with; in pace with

磲住 (支持着) prop-up; support

輨住 (關進) shut in

擤住 (拿着) holding

戴住 (帶着) carry along

額頭上面寫住 sth can be easily found out

鯁住 (卡着) have a fishbone stuck in one's throat

擺住 (拿着) hold in the hand

瓊住 (凝結) coagulate

顧住 (留心) ① not to exceed the limit ② take care of oneself ③ control one's emotions ④ beware of one's life; watch out

攞住 (拿住) holding; taking

攞唔住 (拿不住) can't hold it

攞得住 (拿得住) can hold it

黐住 (黏住) stick to

纏住 (纏着) entangled; entwined; wind around

驚住 (擔心) anxious; be afraid; take care; worried

攬住 (摟抱) cuddle; embrace; hug

【佑】 jau⁶ bless

佑助 aid; assist; help

庇佑 bless; prosper; protect

拜得神多自有神庇佑 the god will bless one who frequently worships him

【佔】dzim[1] occupy

佔上風 have the advantage of sb

佔便宜 profit at others' expense

佔有 ① have; own; possess ② hold; occupy

佔據 hold; occupy; take over; take

侵佔 encroach upon; invade and occupy; occupy illegally; seize

獨佔 solely own

【何】ho[4] how; what

何不 not see any harm in; why not

何必 there is no need; why

何妨 might as well; there is no harm in; why not

何況 let alone; much less; not to mention; to say nothing of

何苦 not worth; not worth the trouble; why bother; why trouble

何嘗 no question; not that

冇奈何（無何奈何）against one's will; at the end of one's resources; have no alternative (but to do sth) ; have no choice; have no way out; have to; helpless; hopeless; powerless; reluctant; willy-nilly

冇幾何（不常）seldom

任何 any; whatever; whichever

因何 how is it that; what for; why; why is it that; why oh why (used by overly dramatic people when things are out of their control)

好少 / 冇幾何（難得）rarely; seldom

奈何 what is to be done

幾何 often

無論如何 anyway; at any rate

【佛】fat[9]（佛祖）Buddha

佛口蛇心（人面獸心）a beast in human shape; a brute of a man; a brute under a human mask; a fiend in human shape; a man's face but a the heart of a beast; a wolf in sheep's clothing; bear the semblance of a man but have the heart of a beast; gentle in appearance but cruel at heart; have the face of a man but the heart of a beast; kind-mouthed but vicious-hearted; with a human face and the heart of a beast

佛法 ① Buddhist dharma; Buddhist doctrines ② power of the Buddha

佛法無邊 the powers of the Buddha are unlimited

佛堂 Buddhist temple

佛教 Buddhism

佛都有火（佛祖也火了）it would try the patience of a saint

佛爺 the Buddha

佛像 figure of the Buddha; image of the Buddha

佛誕（佛祖生日）Buddha's Birthday

大頭佛 motor-bike helmet

借花敬佛（借花獻佛）make use of the gift from another to show respect to sb

滿天神佛 things are in a mess

攪出個大頭佛 put all the fat in the fire

【作】dzok[8] compose; make

作人一筆（敲人家一筆）extort money; sponge a person; squeeze a person for money

作大（誇大）exaggerate

作反（造反）rebel; revolt; rise up against

作主 ① decide; have the say; make the decision; take the responsibility for a decision ② back up; support

當家作主 master in one's own house

作用 effect

副作用 side-effect

作死（找死）take the road to ruin oneself; threat

作供（作證）act as a witness in court; bear witness; give evidence; testify

作怪 make trouble; scheme

作狀（做作 / 裝模作樣）pretend; put on an act; strike a pose

作威 bossy

作威作福 abuse one's power tyrannically; act like a tyrant; assume great airs; bossy; domineer over; lord it over; play the bully; play the tyrant; ride roughshod over others; sit on the back of; throw one's weight about; throw one's weight around; tyrannically abuse one's power

作品 works

作風 style; style of work; way

作家 author; writer

作動（胎動）fetal movement

作賊心虛 have a guilty conscience

作對 ① act against; choose to be sb's rival; oppose; set oneself against ② match with another in marriage

作嘔 ① about to vomit ② （噁心）make one feel sick

令人作嘔 make one sick

作弊 cheat; indulge in corrupt practices; practice fraud

作樂 enjoy; have a good time; have fun; make merry

作賤（犯賤）cheap

作賤自己 run oneself down

作數（造假賬）cook the books

一份工作 a job

一件工作 a piece of work

人多好做作（人多好辦事）many hands make light work
工作 ① work ② job
分工合作 share out the work and cooperate with one another; work in cooperation with a due division of labour
手作 handicraft
代表作 magnum opus; representative work
合作 cooperate
全職工作 full-time job
老作（說謊）lie
社會工作 social work
冒雨工作 work in the rain
耕作 cultivate; farming; tillage
動作 act; action; motion; movement; start moving
習作 exercise
處女作 debut work
造作 ① make ② affectations; artificial; pretentious; unnatural
睇作（看作）look upon as; regard as
搵人合作（找人合作）find sb to cooperate
著作 ① books; works; writings ② write
製作 fabricate; make; manufacture
輪流工作 work in shifts

【佣】jung⁴ commission
佣金 commission

回佣 kick-back; rebate
抽佣 draw a commission on the sale

【克】hak⁷ conquer
克扣 embezzle part of what should be issued
克制 exercise restraint; restrain
　　自我克制 self-control
克服 conquer; overcome; surmount

不克（不能）unable
休克 coma
坦克（transliteration）tank

【兌】doey³ ① cash a cheque ② exchange currency
兌付 cash a cheque
兌現 cash
　　兌現支票 cash a cheque
兌換 exchange
　　兌換率 exchange rate
　　自由兌換 freely convertible

【免】min⁵ exempt
免至（以免／免得）in order to avoid; lest; save; so as not to; so as to avoid
免找 keep the change; no changed required
免治（肉糜）minced
　　免治牛肉（碎牛肉）minced beef
　　免治豬肉（碎豬肉）minced pork
免息 interest free
免除 ① avoid; prevent ② excuse; exempt; immunize; relieve; remit
免得 in order not to; lest; save; so as not to; so as to avoid
　　免得惹麻煩 so as to avoid causing trouble
免稅 duty free; exemption from duty; free of duty; remission of tax; tax exemption; tax-free
　　免稅店 duty free shop
免費 free of charge
　　免費入場 admission is free; be admitted gratis; free admission
免職 relieve sb of his post; remove sb from office

在所難免 can hardly be avoided; impossible to be avoided; scarcely avoidable; unavoidable
倖免 escape by sheer luck; have a narrow escape
赦免 absolve; excuse; pardon; remit a punishment
錯誤難免 errors are unavoidable
避免 avoid

【兵】bing¹ soldier
兵力 armed forces; military strength; troops
兵來將擋，水來土掩 roll with the punches
兵法 military strategy and tactics; the art of war; warcraft
兵房（兵營）barrack
兵家 ① military strategist in ancient China ② military commander; soldier
兵敗如山倒 a beaten army is like a collapsing mountain; a rout is like a landslide; an army in flight is like a landslide
兵器 armament; arms; weaponry

一列士兵 a row of soldiers
士兵 soldier
子弟兵 army made up of the sons of the people
先禮後兵 a dog often barks before it bites
收兵 withdraw troops
步兵 ① infantry; infantryman ② foot soldier
官兵 officers and men
傘兵 parachute troop; parachute; paratrooper
援兵 reinforcements
賊過興兵 lock the stable door after the horse is stolen

駐兵 station troops
觀音兵 man who runs around looking after a woman

【冷】 laang⁵ cold

冷天 ① (冬天) winter ② (寒冷的日子) cold weather
冷水 cold water
潑冷水 (令人掃興) a wet blanket; dampen sb's
 enthusiasm; dampen sth; discourage sb from
 doing sth; pour cold water on sth; throw cold water
 on sb
冷冰冰 cold; icy
冷汗 cold sweat
 擺冷汗 (出冷汗) break out in a cold sweat
冷巷 (小巷 / 小通道 / 走廊 / 過道) alley; by-street; lane
 冷巷擔竹竿 —— 直出直入 (胡同裏扛木頭 —— 直來直
 去) walking in a lane with a plank on one's shoulder –
 taking an arrow-straight course
冷氣 (空調) air-con; air-conditioning
 冷氣太凍 (空調太冷) the air-con is too cold
 冷氣房 (空調房) air-conditioned room
 冷氣機 (空調機) air-conditioner
 冷氣機位 space for air-conditioner
 開大啲冷氣 (調高空調) turn up the air-con
 開冷氣 (開空調) turn on the air-con
 開細啲冷氣 (調低空調) turn down the air-con
 歎冷氣 (享受冷氣) enjoy air-conditioning
冷馬 (黑馬) dark horse
冷淡 ① indifferent ② lonely; solitary
 假裝冷淡 feign indifference
冷清 deserted; desolate; lonely
 冷冷清清 deserted; desolate; lonely
冷落 treat coldly
 冷落人 (冷待人) give sb the cold shoulder; ice sb out;
 leave sb out in the cold; treat sb with indifference
 俾人冷落 (給人冷待) be given the cold shoulder; be
 left out in the cold; be treated coldly
冷飯 (剩飯) left-over cooked rice
 冷飯菜汁 (殘羹剩飯) leftovers
 炒冷飯 ① heat the left-over rice ② (重複) do or say
 the same old thing
冷酷 callous; cruel; hard; hardhearted; heartless; merciless
 冷酷無情 merciless
冷靜 calm
 冷靜落嚟 (冷靜下來) calm down; cool down; cool off;
 sober down
 保持冷靜 keep calm; keep one's head; maintain calm
冷戰 cold war
冷藏 cold storage
冷親 (着涼) catch cold; has caught a cold

心灰意冷 feel disheartened
生冷 raw or cold food
西冷 beef sirloin
抵冷 (忍受寒冷) suffer from cold
風涼水冷 cool and comfortable
凍冰冰 ice cold; icy; frosty
晒冷 (攤牌) put all one's card on the table; show
 one's hand
寒冷 cold; frigid
發冷 chills
爆 (大) 冷 (不符預期) big upset

【冷】 laang⁵⁻¹ (絨線) knitting wool

冷衫 (毛衣) woollen sweater
 織冷衫 (打毛衣) knit a woollen sweater
冷襪 (毛襪子) woollen shorts

毛冷 sheep's wool
打冷 (吃潮州款式的夜宵) have a night snack in the Chiu
 Chow style
羊毛冷 sheep's wool
夜冷 (二手貨商店) second-hand shop; (transliteration)
 yelling

【初】 tso¹ first

初步 first step; preliminary; tentative
初初 (起初 / 最初) at first; at the beginning; at the outset;
 initial; original
初哥 ① (新手) beginner; new hand ② for the first time
初時 (開始 / 最初) at first; at the beginning; at the outset;
 initial; original
初期 early period
初等 elementary; primary; rudimentary
頭等 first class
初嚟步到 (新來乍到) newly on board
初歸心抱，落地孩兒 bend a tree while it is
 still young
初戀 first love
 初戀情人 first love; first lover

早知今日，何必當初 / 悔不當初 it is too late to ask
 oneself why one has gone astray (to repent for having
 gone astray) when one knows the consequence to be
 so serious

【判】 pun³ ① (包) contract ② sentence

判刑 pass a sentence; sentence
判別 differentiate; discriminate; distinguish
判罰 penalise

判頭（工頭／包工／包工頭）contractor
判斷 assess; decide; determine; judge; size up

批判 criticism
面對面談判 face to face negotiation
評判 judge; referee; umpire
裁判 referee
談判 negotiation

【別】bit⁹ special

別人 ① another person; sb else ② other people; others
別字 ① mispronounced character; wrongly written character ② alias
別開生面 break a new path; break fresh ground; open up a new facet; out of the common road; start sth new; with freshness and novelty
別墅 villa
別緻 new and unusual

不同類別 different categories
分別 ① leave each other; part; separate ② discriminate; differentiate; distinguish ③ differently ④ respectively; separately
判別（辨別）differentiate; discriminate; distinguish
吻別 kiss sb goodbye
告別 farewell
男女有別 a distinction should be made between males and females; between the sexes there should be a prudent reserve; males and females should be distinguished
性別 sex
泣別 part in tears
特別 especial; special
級別 grade; level; rank; rating; scale; sort
區別 differ from/in/with; different from; differentiate (among/between); discern; discriminate; dissimilar from/ to/with; distinct; distinctive; distinguish (between/from); distinguishable from; draw a distinction between; make a distinction between; tell the difference
惜別 hate to see sb go; reluctant to part; unwilling to part
暫別 a short separaton; part for a short time
臨別 at the time of departure; just before parting; on parting
類別 category

【刨】paau⁴⁻² (搲) pare

刨冰 water ice
刨書（啃書本）study hard
刨根 get to the root of the matter
刨馬經（啃馬經）study horse-racing news

鉛筆刨 pencil sharpener
鬚刨 shaver

【利】lei⁶ ① advantage ② interest ③ (鋒利) sharp

利口便辭 have a ready tongue
利口唔利腹（好吃但對健康不好）good for mouth but bad for health
利市 ①（紅包／紅封包）red pocket ②（吉利）luck
利用 make use of
　　充分利用 make the best use of
利好 advantage
　　利好因素 advantageous factors
利事（紅包／紅封包）red pocket
利毒（狠毒）atrocious; brutal; cruel; malicious; venomous; vicious
利是（紅包／紅封包）red pocket
　　利是錢 red pocket money
　　　大吉利是（試圖擋住壞運的話）touch wood
　　　派利是（發紅包）give red pockets
　　　搰利是（討紅包／拿紅包）ask for red pockets; receive red pockets
利害 advantages and disadvantages; gains and losses
　　有一利必有一害 no rose without a thorn
利息 interest
　　利息回扣 interest rebate
　　存款利息 interest on a deposit
　　借款利息 interest on a loan
利益 benefit; interest
　　切身利益 one's immediate interests; one's vital interests
　　局部利益 partial and local interests
　　既得利益 vested interests
利率 interest rate
　　利率調整 interest rate adjustment
　　市場利率 market rate
　　年利率 annual interest rate
　　銀行利率 bank rate
　　最優惠利率 prime rate
　　調整利率 adjust the interest rate
利弊 pros and cons
利潤 gain; profit
　　純利潤 net profit
　　總利潤 gross profit
利疊利（利滾利）at compound interest

一本萬利 ① a small investment brings a ten-thousand-fold profit; gain big profits with a small capital; gain enormous profit out of a small capital investment; make a ten-thousand-fold profit; make big profits with a small capital ② wish you a profitable business

刀唔利（刀不鋒利）the knife is blunt

大吉大利 may you be fortunate

公民權利 civic rights

牙尖嘴利 have a caustic and flippant tongue; have a caustic tongue; have a sharp tongue

功利 material gains; utility

平均獲利 average profit

目光銳利 have a sharp eye

吉利 auspicious; lucky

名利 fame and fortune; fame and gain; fame and wealth

好犀利（好厲害）really terrific; very good

行使權利 exercise one's rights

周身刀冇張利（雜而不精）jack-of-all-trades, master of none

放貴利（放高利貸）work as a loan-shark

便利 convenience

急功近利 anxious to achieve quick success and get instant benefits; eager for quick success and instant benefits; seek quick success and instant benefits

盈利 gains; profit

流利 fluent; smooth

茂利（傻子）idiot

針冇兩頭利（魚與熊掌，不能兼得）one cannot have it both ways; there's no rose without a thorn

追求名利 court fame and fortune

從中牟利 get advantage out of; get some advantage from the mediate position between; have an axe to grind; make a profit for oneself in some deal; make capital out of sth; play both ends against the middle; step in and take the advantage

淨利 net profit

爽利 enliven; in high spirits

勝利 ① triumph; victory; win ② successfully; triumphantly

犀（飛）利（很厲害）excellent; good; terrific; wonderful

貴利（高利貸）loan-sharking

周身刀──冇張利 jack of all trades and master of none

意大利 Italy

福利 benefit; welfare

說話流利 speak with fluency

賬面獲利 book value in profit

勢利 snobbish

精神爽利（心情舒暢）brisk and neat; full of spirit and energy; in good/great/high feather

銳利 keen; pointed; sharp

獲利 make a profit; profits obtained

權利 legal right

蠅頭小利 small profit

【助】dzo[6] help

助人 help others

助人為快樂之本 happiness lies in rendering help to others; service begets happiness

助手 assistant

助長 abet; encourage; foment; foster; give a loose rein to sth bad; indulge; nurture; promote the development of

助理 ① assist ② assistant

助興 add to the amusement; add to the fun; join in merry-making; liven things up

大力協助 provide great help

互助 mutual help

佑助 aid; assist; help

扶助 assist; help; support

協助 assist; give assistance; help; help mutually; provide help

拔刀相助 help others for the sake of justice; take up the cudgels for sb/sth/against an injustice

捐助 contribute; donate; offer

祐助 aid; assist; help

援助 aid; help; support

賢內助 good wife

幫助 help

贊助 donate money; patronize; sponsor; support

【努】nou[5] diligent

努力 exert oneself; make efforts; try hard

努力不倦 strive without ceasing

加倍努力 redouble one's efforts

【劫】gip[8] abduct

劫持 abduct; hijack; hold under duress; kidnap

劫掠 loot; pillage; plunder; ravage; sack

劫獄 break into a prison to rescue a prisoner

劫數 predestined fate

劫數難逃 it is impossible to escape fate; there is no escape from fate

劫機 air piracy; hijack a plane; hijack an aircraft; skyjack

打劫（搶劫）rob; robbery

明火打劫 rob in the light of day

俾人打劫（給人搶劫）be robbed

騎劫 abduct; hold under duress; kidnap

【即】dzik[7] immediately

即日（當天）that very day; the same day

即日來回 same day return

即刻（立刻 / 馬上）as soon as; as quick as a flash; at
　　once; at one stroke; at the drop of a hat; directly; first
　　thing off the bat; here and now; immediately; in a brace
　　of shakes; in a crack; in a flash; in a jiffy; in a minute;
　　in a moment; in no time; just now; lose no time in...;
　　off hand; on the moment; on the nail; out of hand;
　　promptly; pronto; right away; right now; right off the
　　bat; straight away; straight off; this instant; this moment;
　　without a moment's delay; without delay; without
　　hesitation; without loss of time; without thinking
　　much longer

即係（就是）that is
　　即係話（即是）that is to say

即食麵（方便麵 / 快熟麵）instant noodles

即晚（當晚）that evening; that night; the same evening;
　　the same night

立即 at once; immediately; off hand; promptly

亦即 i.e.; namely; that is; viz.

【君】gwan¹ monarch

君子 gentleman
　　君子協定 gentleman's agreement
　　　　先小人後君子 make sure of every trifling matter
　　　　　　before generosity
　　　　有仇不報非君子 demand blood for blood

君主 crowned head; monarch; sovereign

灶君 God of the Kitchen

郎君 my husband

【吞】tan¹ swallow

吞吐 hesitant in speaking
　　半吞半吐 hesitate in speaking
　　吞吞吐吐 hem/hum and haw; hesitate in speech;
　　　　mince words; mutter and mumble; prunes and prism;
　　　　say hesitantly; speak in a halting way; speak of
　　　　things with scruple; speak with reservation; stumble
　　　　over one's words; tick over

吞服 take medicine

吞拿魚（金槍魚）(transliteration) tuna (fish)
　　吞拿魚三文治 tuna sandwich

吞蛋 zero score

吞噍（偷懶）goof off

併吞 annex and absorb; swallow up entirely

炸雲吞 deep-fried shrimp dumplings

淨雲吞 shrimp dumplings in soup

雲吞 shrimp dumplings

煮雲吞 cook shrimp dumplings

慢吞吞（非常慢）very slow

【吟】jam⁴（囉嗦）chant

吟咗一大輪（囉嗦了半天）being lectured for a long time

吟唱 chant; sing

吟詩 hum verse; recite poems
　　吟詩都吟唔甩（沒法逃避）fail to shirk

笑口吟吟 a face radiating with smiles; a smile lit up one's
　　face; all smiles; grin from ear to ear; have a broad smile
　　on one's face; with a beaming face; with a face all smiles

【吠】fai³ bark

吠犬不咬 barking dogs seldom bite; great barkers are
　　no biters

犬吠 bark (of a dog)

【否】fau²（犯規）(transliteration) foul

否決 nix; overrule; reject; veto; vote down

否咗佢出局（淘汰了他）he was eliminated

否定 ① denial; deny; negate ② negative

否認 deny; disclaim; gainsay; give a denial to sth; make a
　　denial of; negate; repudiate
　　一口否認 completely deny; flatly deny; repudiate flatly
　　無可否認 cannot be denied; it is not to be denied
　　　　that; there is no denying; undeniable

【吩】fan¹ instruct

吩咐（囑咐）instruct; tell

【含】ham⁴ hold

含血噴人 smite with the tongue

含沙射影 attack by innuendo/insinuation; hurt others
　　maliciously; insinuate; make insinuations

含冤莫白 suffer an unrighted wrong

含糊 ① ambiguous; vague; unclear ② careless;
　　perfunctory; sloppy

【吮】syn⁵（嘬）suck

吮手指（嘬手指頭）suck one's finger

吮奶（吸奶）① suck milk ② suck the breast

吮吮（吸吮）absorb; suck

【吸】kap⁷ absorb

吸引 attract

吸水紙（吸墨紙）absorbent paper

吸取 absorb; assimilate; draw; drink in; suck up

吸毒 be on drugs; become addicted to narcotics; do drugs; drug abuse/taking; drug use; smoke opium; take drugs; use drugs

吸氣 breathe in; inhale

吸煙 smoke; smoking
    不准吸煙 no smoking

吸塵機 vacuum cleaner

吮吸 absorb; suck

呼吸 breathe

深呼吸 deep breath

【吹】 tsoey¹ blow

吹口哨 whistle

吹毛求疵 captious; carp; censorious; fastidious; faultfinding; find faults deliberately; find faults with; find quarrel in a straw; hair-splitting; hypercritical; (informal) nitpick; persnikety; pettifogging; pick flaws/holes in; pick on sth to find fault with; picky; split hair

吹水 (吹牛 / 瞎説) chat; prevaricate
    吹水唔抹嘴 shoot the breeze
    吹一輪水 have a chat

吹牛 baloney; blow one's own horn/trumpet; boast; brag; draw a/the long bow; (informal) eyewash; (informal) hot air; talk big; tell lies

吹波 (吹風) dry hair with a blower
    吹波仔 (酒精呼氣測試) breath alcohol test

吹笛 (吹笛子) play the bamboo flute

吹漲 ① (氣壞) beside oneself with rage; feel offended ② (無可奈何) have no alternative; have no choice; have no way out
    吹佢唔漲 (拿他沒辦法) cannot provoke him into anger
    吹唔漲 (無可奈何) have no choice
        畀佢吹漲 (被他氣壞了) be provoked by him

吹雞 (吹哨子) ① get help ② blow the whistle

吹鬚碌眼 (吹鬍子瞪眼睛) blow a fuse; blow a gasket; fall into a rage; foam with rage; froth at the mouth and glare with rage; scowl and growl; snort and stare in anger

吹 BB (吹哨子) blow the whistle

老吹 (胡説) bullshit

【吻】 man⁵ kiss

吻合 coincide; dovetail; fit; identical; tally (with)

吻別 kiss sb goodbye

狼吻 smooch

接吻 kiss

【吼】 hau¹ (看) watch

吼下 (喜歡) take a fancy to

吼住 (盯住 / 盯着 / 看住 / 看着) keep a close watch on

吼路 (找破綻) find a flaw

吼實 (盯死) keep a close watch on
    吼實佢 (把他看住) keep a watch on him

冇人吼 (沒人感興趣) nobody is interested

唔吼 (不喜歡) not take a fancy to

【吱】 dzi¹ ① chirp ② noisy; talkative

吱吱喳喳 (説個不停的) ① chirping ② chattering; noisy; talkative

【告】 gou³ tell

告白 (廣告) advertisement
    賣告白 (出廣告) advertise

告示 bulletin; official notice; placard

告別 farewell

告急 ask for emergency help; in an emergency; make an urgent request for help; report an emergency

告密 give secret information against sb; inform against sb; snitch

告票 writ
    違例停車告票 parking ticket

告假 (請假) be absent on leave; apply for leave; ask for leave/leave of absence

告發 blow the whistle; delate; fink on; inform against; lodge an accusation against; peach against; put the finger on; report; split on sb
    告發者 informant; informer; whistle-blower

天氣報告 weather report

正式通告 formal notice

佈告 bulletin; make public announcement

每日報告 daily report

紅色暴雨警告 red rainstorm warning signal

原告 plaintiff

控告 sue

被告 defendant

通告 notice

報告 report

黑色暴雨警告 black rainstorm warning signal

廣告 advertisement

暴雨警告 rainstorm warning signal

勸告 admonish; advise; counsel; exhort; remonstrate; urge

警告 warning

【呀】aa¹ ① ah ② [particle used in questions]

呀然 creaking sound

又點呀（又怎樣）so what
火燭呀（起火了）fire
今日係幾號呀（今天幾號）what is the date today
平啲得唔得呀（便宜些可以嗎）can it be cheaper; can you make it cheaper
佢話乜呀（他說甚麼呀）what does he say
有乜指教呀（我可以怎樣幫你）what can I do for you
有幾何呀（難得呀）not so often; seldom or never
你得未呀（你準備好了嗎）are you ready
咪走呀（別走呀）don't run away
食咗飯未呀（吃飯了嗎）have you eaten
哦呀 oh
救命呀 help
幾多錢呀（多少錢呀）how much is it
貴姓呀 may I know your name
搶嘢呀（搶東西呀）I've been mugged; robbery
點呀（怎樣呀）① how are things ② how is it
點做呀（怎樣做呀）how can you do anything
邊個呀（誰呀）who is it
邊啲最合時呀（哪些最合時）what is in season

【呃】ngak⁷（欺詐／欺騙）cheat; deceive; trick

呃人（欺騙人）deceive sb
　　你呃人 you're cheating people/me
呃呃西西（求某人幫助）beg a favour of sb
呃呃騙騙（欺詐／欺騙）deceive; cheat
呃契爺咁呃（一直騙人）keep on fooling sb
呃神騙鬼／呃鬼食豆腐（引人上當）lure sb into a trap
呃秤（短秤）short weight

打呃／嗝 hiccup
易呃（易受騙）easy to be cheated
靠呃（靠騙）live by getting sth dishonesly

【呆】ngoi⁴ dull

呆板 ① boring; dull; inflexible; rigid; stereotyped ② starchy; stiff
呆傻傻 dazed; stupefied
呆滯 ① dull; inert; lifeless ② idle; slack; sluggish; stagnant
呆賬 bad debt

目定口呆 be struck dumb; be dumbfounded; be dumbstruck; gape; gaping; stand aghast; stare in mute amazement; stare openmouthed; stare with astonishment; strike sb dumb; stunned; stupefied

發呆／發晒呆（因驚嚇而發呆）be shocked; be stunned; be completely shocked
痴呆 ① dull-witted; stupid ② amentia; dementia

【呎】tsek⁸ foot

呎價 price per square foot
　　平均呎價 average price per square foot

【吧】baa¹ bar

吧女 bargirl
吧喳 nagging; talkative

水吧 bar
酒吧 bar; pub
落吧（去酒吧）go to the bar
網吧 internet café

【呔】taai¹ ①（領帶）necktie; tie ②（輪胎）tyre

呔夾（領帶夾子）tie bar

一條呔 a tie
士啤呔（後備輪胎）spare tyre
打呔 tie a tie
打煲呔 wear a bowtie
車呔（車胎）tyre
補呔（補輪胎）mend a tyre; repair a tyre
煲呔 bowtie
領呔 tie
爆呔 ① a tyre blows out; flat tyre ② rip
鬆開領呔 loosen one's tie

【吽】ngau⁶ dull

吽豆（發呆）dull; dumbfounded; in a daze; in a trance; spellbound; stare blankly; stunned; stupefied
　　吽吽豆豆（獸頭獸腦）very dull and boring
　　發吽豆（發獸）in a daze
吽鬼 idiot

【困】kwan³（圈）confine; encircle

困住佢（把他圍困起來）confine him
困身 restrictive in time
困惑 at a loss; bewildered; not knowing what to do; perplexed; puzzled
困境 difficult position; morass; plight; predicament; straits
困難 ① difficulty; hard ② financial difficulties; straitened circumstances
　　困難重重 be beset with difficulties; bristle with difficulties; straitened circumstances

【囱】 tsung¹ chimney

煙囱 chimney

【坊】 fong¹ neighborhood

坊間 on the market

街坊 neighbour

【圾】 saap⁸ garbage; rubbish; waste

一袋垃圾 a bag of rubbish
垃圾 rubbish
狗屎垃圾 crap; rubbish
倒垃圾 dispose (the) rubbish
家庭垃圾 domestic waste
執垃圾 (撿垃圾) pick odds and ends from refuse heaps
揮垃圾 scoop up rubbish with a dustbin

【址】 zi² site

地址 address
改地址 change of address
電郵地址 email address

【均】 gwan¹ even

均勻 even; well-matched
均真 (認真) fair-minded
均等 equal; fair; impartial
均衡 balanced; equalization; even; proportionate

平均 average; on average
唔平均 uneven

【坎】 ham² knock

坎坷 bumpy; rough
坎過 (拼了) risk one's life
　同佢坎過 (跟他拼了) fight against him
　坎不過 (不值得拼了) not worth risking one's life
坎頭埋牆 (把頭撞在牆上) bang one's head against the wall
坎嘅頭 (磕着頭了) knock one's head

【坐】 tso⁵ sit

坐月 (坐月子) confinement in childbirth; lying-in
　坐月婆 (月嫂) confinement nanny
坐正 become head of a unit
坐低 (坐下) sit down
　請坐低 please sit down
坐花廳 (坐大牢) be imprisoned; be jailed; be shut behind

the bars; be taken off to prison; commit a person to prison; go to prison; in jail/prison; lay sb by the heels; put into prison; run in; send to prison
坐夜 (守靈) keep vigil beside the coffin; stand as guards at the bier
坐過龍 (坐過頭) miss one's stop
坐墊 seat cushion
坐監 (坐牢) be imprisoned; be jailed; be shut behind the bars; be taken off to prison; commit a person to prison; go to prison; in jail/prison; lay sb by the heels; put into prison; run in; send to prison
坐盤 hold a position

批個頭俾你當櫈坐 (沒有可能) it's impossible that sth you say will ever happen
排排坐 sit in a row
請坐 please take a seat; please be seated
隨便坐 make yourself at home; please be seated

【坐】 tso⁵ sit

坐一望二 (吃一看二眼觀三) hope for another after gaining one
坐位 (位子) seat
坐定粒六 (極有信心) be sure about sth; have full confidence
坐食山崩 (山食山空) sit idle without work and the whole fortune will be at last used up
坐梗 (穩拿) lie within one's grasp
坐鎮 in the seat of power
坐穩釣魚船 on firm ground

【坑】 haang¹ pit

坑渠 (溝渠) gutter
　坑渠浸死鴨 (陰溝能翻船) fail miserably in a very easy task

水坑 ditch; drain; gaw; gole; gool; gutterway
瓦坑 concave channels of tiling
屎坑 (糞坑) latrine pit
新屎坑 (貪新鮮) new things cease to be attractive once they have become old after a short period of time
亂晒坑 (亂七八糟) at sixes and sevens; be thrown into confusion

【壯】 dzong³ ① strengthen ② strong

壯大 ① robust; strong; sturdy; vigorous ② make better; strengthen ③ big; grand; great; magnificent ④ prime of one's life
壯年 prime of one's life

壯烈 brave; courageous; heroic; on a grand and spectacular scale
　壯烈犧牲 die a glorious death; die a heroic death; die as a martyr; die for one's country; give one's life heroically; sacrifice one's life bravely and gloriously

壯健 healthy

壯膽 boost one's courage; embolden

壯觀 grand; grandiose; magnificent; vast

老當益壯 old and vigorous

強壯 strong

【夾】 gaap⁹⁻² ① （合起來）pool; pool money ② （夾）clip

夾份 （合夥 / 湊份子 / 湊份兒）club together; make up the full amount of money; pool shares

夾住 ① （夾着）carry under one's arm ② （夾）clip

夾板 （膠合板）plywood

夾計 （合謀 / 串通）collude with sb; conspire; gang up with sb; plot together

夾倒 （夾着）be nipped

夾埋 ① （串通）collude; plot with sb ② （合起來）combine
　夾埋一齊（搭伙一起）join as partner

夾帶 （作弊）cheat in an examination

夾棍 / 食夾棍 （大小通吃）cheat

夾硬 （硬要… / 硬幹）by force

夾萬 （保險櫃 / 保險箱）safe
　失匙夾萬 a young person who can hardly obtain money from a rich father

夾錢 （湊錢）make up the full amount of money

夾嚫 （夾着）be nipped

夾 band （合奏）assemble

文件夾 file

好夾 （相處融洽）get along well; hit it off

呔夾 tie bar

衫夾 clothes peg

兼夾 （而且）also; and; and that; as well as; besides; moreover; not only...but also...; what is more

唔夾 （相處不來）can't get along with

萬字夾 （回形針 / 曲別針）paper clip

髮夾 hairpin

頭夾 hair clip

爆夾 （入屋盜竊）burglarize a house

【奀】 ngan¹ thin

奀仔 （瘦男孩）thin boy

奀皮 （頑皮）naughty

奀挑鬼命 （瘦弱）extremely skinny and frail

奀細 / 孻 （瘦小）thin and small

奀裊裊 （又高又瘦）tall and thin

人工好奀 （人工低）the salary is miserable

生得奀 （皮包骨）skinny

賺得好奀 （賺錢少）the profits gained are minimal

【妓】 gei⁶ prostitute

妓女 harlot; (slang) hooker; (slang) hustler; prostitute; streetwalker; strumpet; tart; (slang) tom; troller; trollop; whore
　淪為妓女 be driven to prostitution

妓院 brothel

嫖妓 patronize a prostitute

【妗】 kam⁵ wife of mother's brother

妗母 （舅母）aunt; wife of mother's brother

【妒】 do⁵ jealous

妒忌 feel jealous

妒恨 envy and resent

【妖】 jiu¹ enchanting

妖言 absurd statements; heresies; fallacies
　妖言惑眾 arouse people with wild talks; cheat people with sensational speeches; deceive people with fabulous stories; delude people with strange legends; spread fallacies to deceive people; spread wild rumours to mislead the people; wild rumours mislead the masses

妖怪 bogy; demon; evil spirit; goblin; monster

妖精 ① demon; evil spirit ② alluring woman

妖魔鬼怪 demons and ghosts

人妖 transvestite

【妙】 miu⁶ excellent

妙計 brilliant scheme; excellent plan; good tactics; wonderful idea
　山人自有妙計 I've an excellent solution

妙想天開 （異想天開）a flight of fancy; a stretch of the imagination; ask for the moon; come out with most fantastic ideas; cry for the moon; expect wonders; fanciful; get fancy/fanciful ideas into one's head; give loose to the fancy; give rein to fancy; have bats in the belfry; have bees in the brain/in the head; have fantastic notions; have one's head full of bees; indulge in the wildest fantasy/one's fancy; lend wings to one's imagination; let one's imagination run away with one; one's head is full of bees; vagarious; whimsical; wild hopes; wish for the moon; wishful thinking

妙齡 youthfulness

巧妙 clever; ingenious; skilful; smart; wonderful
奇妙 / 美妙 wonderful
莫名其妙 absurd; all abroad; all adrift; baffled; cannot make anything of it; difficult to guess what it is all about; in a fog; inexplicable; make neither head nor tail of it; odd; puzzling and inexplicable; queer; rather baffling; seem totally in the dark; unable to guess what it is all about; unable to make head or tail of sth; unable to understand; without rhyme or reason
歌聲美妙 the singing is wonderful
橋妙 / 蹺妙 have a knack for sth

【粧】 dzong¹ make up

粧扮 doll up
粧飾 adorn; deck out; decorate; dress up

化粧 apply cosmetics; make up; put on make-up; wear make-up
卸粧 remove make-up and ornaments

【妥】 to⁵ in order

妥善 appropriate; proper; satisfactory; well arranged
妥貼 appropriate; fitting; proper; satisfactory
妥當 appropriate; proper; well-thought-out
妥協 compromise

形住有啲唔妥（感覺不妥當）always feel that there's sth wrong about sth
唔多妥 / 唔妥 not on the right track; not quite right; not well
搞妥 / 攪妥 secure
講妥 come to an agreement

【妨】 fong⁴ obstruct

妨礙 encumber; hamper; handicap; hinder; impede; obstruct; put a crimp in; put a crimp into; stand in the way

不妨 / 何妨 could/may/might as well; not matter; there is no harm in

【孝】 haau² filial piety

孝女 bereaved daughter
孝子 ① devoted child; dutiful son; submissive and obedient son ② bereaved son

孝心 filial piety; love and devotion to one's parents; love toward one's parents
孝男 bereaved son
孝順 filial piety
孝敬 give presents to; piety; show filial respect for

廿四孝 ① twenty-four paragons of filial piety ② caring

【完】 jyn⁴（結束）finish

完全 absolutely; completely; entirely; fully; mere; perfectly; pure; thorough; totally; whole
完成 complete; finish
完美 perfect
完蛋 all over; all up; be busted; be doomed; be done for; be finished; be ruined; collapse
完善 consummate; faultless; improve and perfect; perfect
完喇（結束了）it's over
完整 complete; entire; intact; integrated; undamaged; whole

玩完 ① be played out; game over ② die; pass away ③ end a relationship
食完 eat up
喫 / 吃完 eat up
話口未完 sth happens when one is just talking about it

【尾】 mei⁵ ①（尾巴）tail ② last

尾七 the ninth seven after one's death
尾二（倒數第二）second from the bottom; second last
尾車 / 尾班車（末班車）last train
尾指（小指）little finger
尾站（終點站）bus terminal
尾龍骨（尾骨 / 尾椎骨）spine; tailbone

一頭一尾 ① both ends ② here and there
口水尾 saliva drops
冇（鼇）手尾 fail to put things back after use; leave things about
手尾 ① unfinished job left by sb ② troubles left behind
手指尾 / 小指 little finger
月尾 end of the month
水尾 ①（剩貨）leftover goods; leftovers; remaining goods ② end of a prime time
牛尾 ox tail
包斷尾（治病治斷根）guarantee to remove the root of an illness
半夜食黃瓜──不知頭定尾 make neither head nor tail of sth
由頭到尾 all the way; from A to Z; from beginning to end; from end to end; from first to last; from soup to nuts;

from start to finish; from stem to stern; from the egg to the apple; from (the) head to (the) tail; from tip to toe; from top to bottom; from top to toe; the whole way; through and through; through the whole length

禾尾 ear of rice; spike of rice

吊尾（跟蹤）follow sb

回尾 give back; return; send back

好頭好尾 a good beginning and a good ending

年尾（年底）end of the year; year-end

收／至尾（最後）at last; finally; lastly

有手尾 there's a beginning and an end

行運行到落腳趾尾（非常幸運）very lucky

行運醫生醫病尾 a lucky doctor cures a patient who is in the last stage of recovery

扯／搊貓尾 collaborate with each other to hide the truth from sb; lie one's way out of a problem; two people trying to support each other's stories in order to trick someone

車尾 back of the car

季尾 end of the season

拉尾（最後）finally; in the end; last

拉車尾 just squeeze through

虎頭蛇尾 begin well but fall off towards the close; start out well but cannot continue; have/with a fine start but a poor finish

巷尾 end of a lane

後尾（後來）afterwards; eventually; later; later on; subsequently

耷尾（有始無終）a good beginning and a poor ending

衫尾（衣服後襟）lower hem of a gown

頁尾（頁腳）footer

飛尾（票根）ticket stub

埋尾（收尾）bring to completion

馬尾（hair style）ponytail

執手尾（結束）clean up; deal with the work left over; finish a job for sb; wind up

執頭執尾（做瑣碎工作）do odd jobs

從頭到尾 all the way; at both the end and the beginning; from A to izzard; from A to Z; from beginning to end; from cover to cover; from end to end; from first to last; from hub to tire; from soup to nuts; from start to finish; from stem to stern; from the egg to the apple; from the head to the tail; from the soul of the foot to the crown of the head; from the word go; from tip to toe; from title page to colophon; from top to bottom; from top to toe; the whole way; through and through; through the whole length

搣衫尾（求人給恩惠）beg for sth

斬頭截尾 cut off the head and tail

眼尾 corners of one's eyes

票尾（票根）stub

第尾 the last

貨尾 leftover goods; leftovers

搯尾（搖尾）wag the tail

睇頭睇尾（幫忙）lend a hand

結尾 end

街頭巷尾 everywhere in the streets

塘尾（蜻蜓）dragonfly

腳趾尾（小腳趾）little toe

話頭醒尾（機靈）able to take a hint

跟手尾 complete an unfinshed job left by sb

跟尾 follow after

飲水尾 ①（賣剩的東西）leftovers ②（撈便宜的機會已過）no more chance to take advantage of sth

數尾 balance; odd amount in addition to the round number

踩／踹嘅…條尾 cause offence to sb

樹尾 tip of a tree

頭尾 about; altogether; around; around the time of; one time or another; or so; round about; the time spent on sth

頭頭尾尾 ① odd pieces ② altogether

龍尾 end of a queue

儘尾（最後面）last; the last one

斷尾（完全治癒）be over for good; be thoroughly cured

擸頭撒尾（丟三落四）forgetful; always losing this and forgetting that; forget this, that, and the other; miss this and that

雞尾 chicken bum; chicken's rump

爛尾 give up half-way

【尿】niu⁶ ① urine ② make water; pass water; urinate

尿片（尿布／紙尿片）diaper; nappy
　　成人尿片（成人紙尿片）adult diaper
　　換尿片（換尿布）change the baby's diaper
　　攬尿片（包尿布）wear the diaper

尿布 diaper; napkin; nappy

尿急 urgent urination

尿酸 uric acid

一篤尿／一督尿（一泡尿）pass water

大蛇痾尿（大場面）important deal

急尿（尿急）hold up one's urine

流馬尿（哭）snivel; weep

甜尿（糖尿病）diabetes

勒尿（把尿）help a small child unrinate by holding their legs apart

屙／痾尿（拉尿）urinate; pee; wee; tinkle; piddle (slang) whiz; discharge one's urine; drain one's radiator/one's snake; empty/evacuate one's bladder; go tap a kidney; take/have a leak; have a run off; make (salt) water; micturate; pass urine/water; point Percy at the porcelain; pump ship; see a man about a dog/one's aunt; spend a penny

痾篤尿 take a piss

賴尿 / 瀨尿 wet the bed

臨天光瀨尿（始料不及）there is many a slip twixt/between the cup and the lip

懶人多屎尿 a lazybone cooks up many lame excuses

瀨尿（小便失禁）urinate involuntarily; urinary incontinence

【局】guk⁹ station

局中人 player

局內人 insider

局外人 outsider

局長 director-general

局促 ① cramped; narrow ② short ③ constrain

局限 confine; limit; localization

局面 aspect; phase; prospect; situation
控制局面 control the situation

局部 part; partial

局勢 situation
局勢緊張 the situation is serious
分析局勢 analyze a situation

收拾殘局 clear up a messy situatio/the mess; pick up the pieces; settle a disturbed situation

佈局 layout

否咗佢出局（被趕出局）he was eliminated

格局 arrangement; manner; pattern; setup; structure; style

消防局 fire station

書局 ① stationery shop ② bookstore

結局 end

郵（政）局 post office

郵政總局 general post office

雀局 game of mahjong

稅局 Inland Revenue Department

靜局（冷清）deserted

騙局 fraud; hoax; put-up job; shell game; swindle

警局 police station

【屁】pei³ fart

屁股 backside; behind; bottom; bum; buttocks; (slang) duff; hip; (slang) keister
打屁股 get a slap on the buttocks/a spanking/ punished; receive punishment; spank

屁都唔痾個（碰一鼻子灰）show no sign of having children

一面屁 be rebuffed; meet frustration; meet humiliation; meet rejection; run into a stone wall

把屁 what for

拍馬屁 adulate; brown-nose; butter sb up; crawl to; curry favour; curry favour with sb; eat sb's toads; fawn on; flatter; flatter sb in power; give sb the soft-soap; ingratiate oneself with; kiss sb's ass; lay it on thick; lay it on with a trowel; lick sb's boots; lick sb's shoes; lick sb's spittle; lick the boots of sb; obsequious; play up to; polish the apple; soft-soap; suck up to; sycophancy; toady sb

放 / 屙 / 打屁 ① break wind (backwards/downwards); drop a rose; fart; rip a fart; have gas; pass air/wind; there's a smell of touch bone and whistle ② bullshit; talk nonsense; talk rot; what a crap

狗屁 horseshit; nonsense; rubbish

噴一面屁（碰一鼻子灰）be rejected; be snubbed; be sent off with a flea in one's ear; cold shoulder; get rebuffed; meet rejection; meet with a rebuff

【岌】ngap⁹（晃）hazardous; high; perilous; steep

岌岌 precarious
岌岌可危 be placed in jeopardy; between the beetle and the block; extremely hazardous; hang by a hair/ a single thread; in a critical situation; in a precarious situation; in a tottering position; in great peril; in imminent danger
岌岌貢（晃動 / 搖晃）quake; shake

岌頭（點頭）nod one's head

【迓】ngaa⁴（佔）occupy

迓個位（佔個位子）occupy a seat

迓埞 ①（佔地方）occupy a place ②（霸道）overbearing

【希】hei¹ hope

希罕（珍惜）① rare; scarce; uncommon ② care; cherish; value as a rarity ③ rare thing; rarity

希望 hope

【庇】bei³ shelter

庇佑 bless; prosper; protect

庇護 shelter
庇護站 temporary shelter

蔭庇 patronize; protect

【序】dzoey⁶ order

序文 foreword; preface

序言 preface

序幕 curtain raiser; prelude; prologue
序數 ordinal; ordinal number

公共秩序 public order
次序 arrangement; order; sequence
程序 course; order; procedure; proceeding; process; programme; route; sequence

【延】yin⁴ delay
延長 extend; lengthen; prolong; prolongate; protract
延期 ① be postponed; defer; delay; lay over; postpone; put off; put over ② extend
延誤 delay
延遲 be delayed; defer; delay; hold over; postpone; put off; retard
延續 be continued; continue; go on; last

【廷】ting² court
廷試 imperial examination

宮廷 ① palace ② court; royal court

【弄】lung⁶ make
弄巧反拙 try to outsmart oneself but turn out to be foolish
弄假成真 what was make-believe has become reality
弄權 manipulate power for personal ends

【弟】dai⁶ young brother
弟子 disciple; follower; pupil
弟兄 brothers
弟弟 one's younger brother
弟妹 younger brother and sister
弟婦 (弟媳婦) sister-in-law; younger brother's wife

一世人兩兄弟 / 打死不離親兄弟 (血濃於水) blood is thicker than water
子弟 children; juniors; sons and youngr brothers; young dependents
仁弟 my dear friend
兄弟 brothers
好兄弟 good mates
有酒有肉多兄弟 a heavy purse makes friends come
沙煲兄弟 / 砂煲兄弟 friends in the same boat; good friends
舍弟 my younger brother
表弟 cousin; first cousin; younger male cousin
叔伯兄弟 cousins; sons of paternal uncles
苦過弟弟 (非常困苦) deplorable; go through all kinds of hardship
徒弟 apprentice; disciple

師弟 ① junior male apprentice ② junior male schoolmate ③ younger son of one's master
堂兄弟 cousins
幾係幾係 / 五郎救弟 big names
硯弟 (學弟) junior classmate
疏堂兄弟 cousins on the paternal side
襟兄弟 two men sleeping with the same woman
難兄難弟 fellow sufferers; two of a kind

【形】jing⁴ ① (老覺得) always feel ② form
形式 form; format; formation; layout; modality; shape
形住有啲唔妥 (感覺有點不妥) always feel that there's sth wrong about sth
形成 form; produce as a result; take shape
形狀 shape
形容 describe
　　難以形容 hard to describe
形勢 ① contour; terrain; topographical features ② circumstances; landscape; situation

三角形 triangle
之字形 zigzag
弓形 bow-shaped
正方形 square
身形 bodily form; build; figure
定晒形 (一動不動) be stupefied; stare fixedly; trance oneself
扇形 fan-shaped; sector (technical term)
框形 frame
矩形 rectangle; rectangular
傘形 umbrella type
落形 (消瘦) become thin; slim down
落晒形 (憔悴) downcast
蹄形 horseshoe shape
鵝蛋形 oval shape

【役】ik⁹ slave
役夫 labourer; servant
役役 ① overwork ② servile

奴役 enslave; keep in bondage; slavery

【忌】gei⁶ jealous
忌才 jealous of other people's talent; resent people more able than oneself
忌食 avoid certain food
忌廉 (奶油) cream
忌憚 dread; fear; scruple
　　肆無忌憚 act outrageously/recklessly and care for

nobody; afraid of nothing; behave in a disorderly manner without fear; have no scruples at all; have no respect for anything; in an unrestrained way; indulgent and reckless; make no scruple; reckless and unbridled; run riot; scruple at nothing; stop at nothing; unbridled; unscrupulous; without restraints of any kind; without scruple

妒忌 feel jealous; jealous

威士忌 (transliteration) whisky

真係棹忌 it is too bad; alas; damn it; dread; far from good; good gracious; how terrible; taboo; what bad luck

避忌 ① taboo ② avoid as a taboo ③ abstain from; avoid as harmful

驟忌 (禁忌) taboo

【忍】jan² tolerate

忍心 hardhearted; have the heart to; merciless; steel one's heart; unfeeling

　　於心何忍 how can one bear it in one's heart/bear to do it/have the heart to do it

　　唔忍心 compassionate

忍受 bear

　　難以忍受 hard to bear

忍耐 endure; exercise patience/restraint; put up with; restrain oneself; tolerant of

忍唔住 (忍不住) be driven beyond the limits of forbearance; beyond endurance; can't help doing sth; can't put up with sth any longer; cannot bear/stand/tolerate sth any longer; come to the end of one's patience; have enough of; have no time for; not to brook; out of patience with; unable to bear/stand; worn out

忍氣 restrain one's indignation

　　忍氣吞聲 control oneself and suppress one's indignation; (slang) eat dirt; eat humble pie; eat one's leek; endure without protest; hold back one's anger and say nothing; keep quiet and swallow the insults; pocket an insult; restrain one's anger and abstain from saying anything; restrain one's anger and keep silence; restrain one's indignation; restrain one's temper and say nothing; submit to humiliation; suffer indignities without a protest; suppress one's groans; swallow insult and humiliation silently; swallow one's anger; swallow one's pride and endure in silence; swallow one's resentment and dare say nothing; swallow one's wrath and not dare to speak; swallow the insults in meek submission

忍無可忍 at the end of one's forbearance/one's patience; be driven beyond the limits of forbearance; bear the

unbearable; beyond all bearing; beyond endurance; come to the end of one's patience; enough to try the patience of a saint; it would try the patience of a saint; out of patience; beyond endurance; unable to bear it any longer

殘忍 cruel

【志】dzi³ purpose; will

志同道合 cherish the same ideals and follow the same path; have a common goal; hit if off well together; in the same camp; of one mind; share the same ambition and purpose; share the same view; two minds with but a single thought

志在 (目的在於) aim at; with the intention of

志氣 ambition; aspiration; will

　　冇志氣 without ambition

　　有志氣 full of ambition

　　長他人志氣，滅自己威風 boost the enemy's morale and dampen one's own spirit; laud the spirit of the enemy and belittle that of our own; puff up the enemy's morale and lower one's own

志趣 aspiration and interest; inclination

　　志趣相投 after one's own heart; congenial to; find each other congenial; friends of similar purposes and interests; have similar aspirations and interests; hit it off; like-minded; of like mind

志願 ① aspiration; ideal; wish ② do sth of one's own free will; volunteer; voluntarily

女同志 lesbian

同志 gay; homosexual

男同志 male homosexual

胸懷大志 aim high; cherish high aspirations in one's mind/ high ideals; entertain great ambitions; fly high; have lofty aspirations; think big

惑志 (懷疑) doubt; suspicion

勵志 pursue a goal with determination

【忘】mong⁴ forget

忘本 ① bite the hand that feeds one; ungrateful ② forget one's class origin; forget one's past suffering

忘年交 a friendship in which the difference of years is forgotten; friendship between generations; friendship between old and young people; good friends despite great difference in age; the best of friends in spite of the difference in ages

忘恩 bite the hand that feeds one; devoid of gratitude; ungrateful

忘恩負義 devoid of gratitude; bite the hand that feeds one; forget sb's kindness and turn one's back upon him in return; forgetful of all favours one has been given; have no sense of gratitude and justice; kick down the ladder; kick over the ladder; show ingratitude for favours received; show no sense of gratitude; turn one's back on righteousness and forget kindness; turn on one's friend; ungrateful and act contrary to justice; ungrateful and leave one's benefactor in the lurch

忘記 forget; fail to remember; slip sb's mind

忘懷 forget
　　難以忘懷 hard to forget

令人難忘 unforgettable

永世不忘 remember sth for life; will bear sth in mind for life; will never forget sth

念念不忘 bear in mind constantly

難忘 unforgettable

【快】faai³ fast

快人 person who is frank by nature; straightforward man
　　快人一步 one step ahead of others
　　　快人快語 a person of straightforward disposition is outspoken; a straight talk from an honest person/a straightforward person; an outspoken person speaks their mind; sb who does not mince words

快刀斬亂麻 a swift and ruthless action; cut the Gordian knot; cut a tangled skin of jute with a sharp knife; make lightning decisions; slice through a knot with a sharp knife; take resolute and effective measures to solve a complicated problem in an instant

快手 ①（手快／處事迅速的人）deft of hand ② nimbled-handed person; quick worker

快快（趕快）in a hurry

快佬（資料夾／檔案）file

快活（快樂）happy

快馬 on the double
　　快馬加鞭 accelerate the speed; burn up the road on one's way; do a fast job; posthaste; ride whip and spur; spur the flying horse at high speed; whip one's horse up to a swift trot; with whip and spur

快高長大 may you grow tall and strong

快啲（趕快）be quick; hurry up
　　快啲啦 be quick; hurry up

快勞（文件／文件夾／檔案）(transliteration) file
　　一個快勞 a file
　　入快勞（入檔案）keep on file

快艇 speedboat

快遞 express delivery; fast mail

快樂 feel happy; happy

快趣 ①（爽快）neatly ②（趕快）quickly
　　快快趣趣 ①（爽爽快快）neatly ② quickly

快餐 fast food
　　快餐店 fast food shop

快 D（快點）hurry up

一時口快 speak too quickly

口快快 say sth quickly without thinking

工作愉快 happy work

手急眼快（眼明手快）quick of eye and deft of hand

外快（額外收入）income from an extra job

鬥快（比賽速度）competition of speed

時間過得好快 time flies

祝你旅途愉快 wish you a happy trip

就快 soon

話咁快（很快）before one knows it; very quickly

盡快 as soon as possible

【忙】mang² impatient, restless

忙憎（煩躁）agitated; fidgety; fret; irritable

【成】sing⁴ ① complete ②（成功）success

成日（整天）① all day long ② always
　　成日傍住我（整天在我身邊）sb is with me all day long
　　成日黐住我（老不離開我）sb never leaves me

成世（一輩子／一生人）a lifetime; all one's life; as long as one lives; man and boy; one's whole lifetime; throughout one's life

成功 success

成本 cost

成立 establish

成全 help

成年（整年）all the year round; the whole year; throughout the year
　　成年人 adult

成衣鋪（衣服店）clothes shop

成批（整批）in batches

成身（一身）whole body

成為 become

成個（整個）all; entire; total; whole
　　成個月（整個月）whole month

成套（整套）whole set

成家（全家）the whole family

成班 the whole group

成堆 in heaps

成婚（成親）get married

成揸人（一伙人）a group of people

成棚人 (一大堆人) a large group of people
成晚 (整晚) all night long
成朝 (整個早上) whole morning
成羣 in groups
成數 (比例) it is likely that
成碟 (整碟) whole plate
成盤 ① (成交) clinch/do a deal; close/conclude a transaction ② (整盤) whole pan
成龍配套 fill in the gaps to complete a chain
成績 result; score

一成 ten percent
少年老成 young but prudent
心想事成 may your wishes come true
(打) 擸成 (transliteration) practise boxing
年少老成 an old head on young shoulders
老成 experienced
完成 complete; finish
形成 form; produce as a result; take shape
佳偶天成 a good match as if made in heaven; a happy couple united by heaven; the match is ordained by fate
促成 facilitate; favour; help to bring about; help to materialize; lead on to
現成 ready
組成 be composed of; be made up of; compose; consist of; constitute; form; make from/of
造成 ① bring about; cause; cause to happen; create; effect; engender; give rise to; result in ② build up; complete; compose
睇成 (看作) look upon as; regard as
達成 achieve; conclude; reach
製成 be made from; manufacture
贊成 accede; agree on; agree to; agree with; all for; approve of; assent; be reconciled to; comply; concur; consent to; endorse; favour; give sth a nod; go all the way with sb; go along with sb; hold with; in agreement with; in favour of; see eye to eye with sb; subscribe to
釀成 breed; bring on; lead to

【戒】 gaai³ abstain from

戒口 (忌口 / 忌嘴) avoid certain food; on diet
戒奶 (斷奶) wean
戒指 ring
戒酒 quit drinking
戒煙 quit smoking
　戒咗煙 (戒了煙) have quitted smoking

懲戒 discipline sb as a warning; punish sb to teach him a lesson; take disciplinary action against sb

【我】 ngo⁵ I; me

我行我素 act according to one's will regardless of others' opinions; do things in one's own way; follow one's bigoted course; go one's own way; in a world by oneself/ of one's own; persist in one's old ways; stick to one's old way of doing things; take one's own course
我哋 (我們 / 咱們) us; we
我都冇你咁好氣 (不想多談) I'm not going to talk to you any more
我嗰 agent (我的代理人) my agent

不分你我 make no distinction between you and I
有你冇我 you and I cannot coexist
成日傍住我 (整天在我身邊) sb is with me all day long
成日黐住我 (老離不開我) one never leaves one
你有你，我有我 (各行各路) let's each go our own way
你我 you and I
兩公婆見鬼——唔係你就係我 (不是你就是我) either of the two
咪點我 (別誤導我) don't mislead me
唔好笑我 don't laugh at me
搦返俾我 (帶回給我) bring it back to me
萬大 (事) 有我 even if the sky falls down, I'll hold it up; you have my full support whatever may happen
等埋我 wait for me
激死我 (氣死我) I'm furious
嚦我 push me

【扭】 nau² twist

扭六壬 (絞盡腦汁) rack one's brains
扭曲 contort
扭身扭勢 move one's body to attract attention to oneself
扭計 (不順從 / 鬧彆扭) malcontent; resort to manoevres
扭紋 (不聽話 / 耍脾氣) disobedient; insubordinate; peevish
　扭紋柴 (不聽話的小孩) ① whining child ② little mischief
扭細聲啲 (撳小聲點兒) turn down the volume
扭乾啲水 (把水擰乾) wring out the water
扭傷 have a sprain
扭擰 (扭捏) put on poses; squirm
　刁橋扭擰 (左右刁難) deliberately create obstructions for sb
　扭扭擰擰 (扭扭捏捏) squirm
扭轉 turn back
　扭轉局面 bring about changes in the situation
　扭轉乾坤 bring about a radical change in the situation; retrieve a hopeless situation; reverse the course of events; save a country from disaster
扭嚫 (扭傷) sprained; wrenched
　扭嚫隻腳 (扭傷了腳) sprained one's ankle

【扮】baan⁶（裝扮）pretend

扮串（妄自尊大）arrogant; vain
　　扮晒串 arrogant; boastful
扮相 appearance of an actor or actress in custume and make-up
扮傻（裝蒜／裝傻）play the fool
扮嘢（裝蒜／裝模作樣）pretend; strike an attitude
　　扮晒嘢（裝模作樣）arrogant; boastful
　　識扮嘢（會假裝）know how to feign ignorance
扮演 act the part of sb; be dressed up to represent sb; carry off one's role of sb; dress up as sb; interpret the role of sb; make oneself up as sb; play the role of sb; take on the role of sb
扮靚（打扮）make oneself pretty; make over
　　識扮靚（會打扮）know how to make oneself pretty
扮豬食老虎（披着羊皮吃羊）eat sheep on a sheep's clothing
扮懵（裝蒜／裝傻）play the fool
扮蟹 ① （束手就擒）allow oneself to be arrested without offering any resistance; allow oneself to be seized without putting up a fight; resign oneself to being held as a prisoner; submit to arrest with folded arms ② self-important
　　扮晒蟹（裝傻）self-important
扮蠢 pretend ignorance; pretend to be stupid

粧扮 doll up

【扶】fu⁴（攙扶）support sb with one's hand

扶手 handrail
　　緊握扶手 hold the handrail tightly
扶住（攙扶着）help by the arm
扶助 assist; help; support
扶持 give aid to; help; sustain; lend a hand; support

梳扶（舒服）comfortable

【扯】tse²（回去／拉）pull

扯火（發火）get angry; lose one's temper
扯皮條（皮條客）pimp; procure for prostitutes
扯風（抽風／吸風）draw in air
扯氣（氣喘）pant; out of breath; short of breath
扯落水（拖下水）drag sb down
扯悝（揚帆）hoist the sails; set sail
扯旗（升旗）hoist a flag
扯鼻鼾（打呼嚕）snore
扯線（牽線）establish a relationship for both parties
　　扯線公仔（牽線木偶）puppet
扯蝦（哮喘）① asthma ② breathe with difficulty

扯貓尾（串通／扯後腿／演雙簧）collaborate with each other to hide the truth from sb; lie one's way out of a problem
扯頭纜（帶頭／牽頭）take the lead
扯纜（拉纜）tow a boat

拉扯 prevaricate
拍佢扯 oust sb; send sb packing; send (sb) to the right-about; show sb the door
撩佢扯 drive sb away

【扱】kap⁷（蓋）stamp

扱章（蓋印）stamp with a chop

【扷】jiu¹ pull out

扷心扷肺（令人傷心）break sb's heart

【批】pai¹ ① comment; criticise ② (transliteration) pie

批中（説中）as expected
批皮（削皮）peel
批判 criticism
批卷（批改考卷）mark papers
批個頭俾你當櫈坐 it's impossible that sth you say will ever happen
批准 accede; admit of; allow; approve; authorise; clearance; concede; endorse; let; license; permit; ratify; sanction; give a licence to/sb permission to/sanction to; grant one's request/sb permission to
批核 approval
批發 wholesale
　　批發價 wholesale price
批評 criticism
批踭（用手肘攻擊）move one's elbow to attack sb
批盪（抹灰／粉飾牆壁／塗灰漿／牆皮）wall plastering
　　意大利批盪（濃粧）heavy make-up
批簿（批改練習本）mark scripts

肉批（蒸肉餅）steamed minced pork
成批 in batches
螺絲批（螺絲刀）screwdriver
蘋果批（蘋果派）apple pie

【找】dzaau² ① make out ② seek ③ give change

找晦氣 blame sb to vent one's anger; say sth out of spite; seek a quarrel
找尋 look for; search for; seek
找番（找回）give in change

找番一蚊（找回一塊錢）pay one back one dollar
找數（付錢／找錢／結賬）make out the bill; pay a bill
　找數先（先付賬）pay the bill first
找錢（找贖／找頭兒）give the change
找贖（找錢／找頭兒）give the change

免找 keep the change; no change required
唔使找 keep the change

【技】gei⁶ technique
技工 artificer; artisan; mechanic; skilled worker; technician
技巧 technique
技師 technician
技術 skill; technic; technique; technology
技藝 artistry; skills

科技 science and technology
發展科技 develop science and technology

【抄】tsaau¹ copy
抄低（抄下來）jot down; write down
抄襲 crib; plagiarize

翻抄 reproduce

【扻】man² wipe
扻屎（擦屁股）clean the buttocks; wipe one's ass

【抓】dzaau² ① grab ② scratch ③ arrest ④ take charge of
抓晒頭（慌亂）feeling confused
抓舉 snatch
抓頸就命（忍氣吞聲）patient with the current situation

【把】baa² hold
把口（嘴）one's mouth
　把口瑯過油（油嘴滑舌）smooth-mouthed
　　加把口（插一嘴）cut in with remarks
　　死淨把口（就剩嘴皮子能耐）mere empty talk
　　得把口（只會說／只說不做／只會耍嘴皮子）all talk and no action
把火（非常生氣）be filled with rage; extremely angry; hot with rage
　一把火 be filled with anger; extremely angry
　把鬼／幾火 burn with anger; extremely angry
把屁（有甚麼用）what for
把持 ① control; keep in one's hands; keep under control ② dominate; monopolize
把炮（把握）ability; strength

有乜把炮（有甚麼把握）what's one's strength
把脈（切脈）feel the pulse
把鬼 of no use; pointless; useless
把舦（掌舵）at the helm; operate the rudder; steer a boat; take the tiller
把戲 acrobatics; jugglery
　出／耍把戲（雜耍）play acrobatics
　老把戲 the same old tricks; the same old stuff
把聲（嗓子）one's voice
　把聲拆晒（嗓子都啞了）lose one's voice
把關 ① look out ② gate-keeping

一把 a bunch of; a bundle of; a handful of; a pair of; a wisp of
一把掃把 a broom; a sweeper
大把 a great deal of; a lot of; many; plenty
老豆大把（老爸很多錢）one's father is rich
泵把（保險桿）bumper
掃把 broom; sweeper
掘頭掃把 worn-down sweeper

【投】tou⁴ drop
投入 ① get involved with sb or sth ② dedicated
投注（下注）bet; place a bet; stake
投胎（轉世）be reborn; be reincarnated
　趕住投胎 in a great hurry; in a hot haste; make a hot haste; rush oneself off one's feet
投降 surrender
投票 cast one's vote; vote
　投票反對 vote against
　投票日 polling day
　投票站 polling station
　投票時間 polling hours
　投票通知卡 poll card
　投票資格 one's eligibility to vote
　投票箱 ballot box
投訴 complain
投資 investment
　投資利潤 profit on investment
　投資者 investor
　　長線投資者 long-term investor
　投資風險 investment risk
　投資氣氛 investment climate
　投資組合 investment portfolio
　投資顧問 investment advisor
投影機 projector
投靠 go and seek refuge with sb
投機 speculate
　投機取巧 opportunistic; resort to dubious shifts to further

one's interests; seek private gain by dishonest means; seize every chance to gain advantage by trickery; speculate and take advantage of an opportunity; use every trick in shortcuts/with finesse; wheel and deal; wheeling and dealing

二手交投 secondary transaction
交投 transactions
志趣相投 after one's own heart; congenial; congenial to/ with; find each other congenial; friends of similar purposes and interests; have similar aspirations and interests; hit it off; like-minded; of like mind

【抗】 kong³ resist

抗生素 antibiotic
抗老 anti-aging
抗菌 anti-bacteria

反抗 resist

【抖】 dau² (休息 / 歇) have a rest; rest

抖吓 (歇會兒) rest a while; take a rest
　　抖吓先 (歇一會兒) have a short rest
抖氣 (歇氣) stop for a rest
　　抖大氣 (深呼吸 / 喘氣) take a deep breath
　　抖唔到氣 (透不過氣來) gasp for breath
　　抖啖氣 (歇口氣) take a break; take a rest

【折】 dzit⁸ break

折扣 discount
折服 ① bring into submission; subdue; submit ② acknowledge the superiority of others; be convinced; be filled with admiration
折衷 compromise
折腰 bow; humble oneself
　　不為五斗米折腰 (literally) cannot make courtesies for the salary of five bushels of rice
折實 (實價) actual price; real price
折墮 (作孽) suffer because of the bad things one has done
折磨 cause physical or mental suffering; submit to an ordeal; torment; torture; trials and afflictions
折頭 (折扣) discount
　　有冇折頭 (有沒有折扣) any discount
折舊 depreciation

一波三折 meet with difficulties one after another
八五折 15% discount
八折 20% discount
九折 10% discount

打八折 give a 20% discount
打折 give a discount
曲折 ① circuitous; curving; intricate; tortuous; ups and downs; winding; zigzag ② complications; intricacy; not smooth; not straightforward
骨折 bone fracture; broken bone; fracture

【抑】 jik⁷ restrain

抑制 check; containment; control; curb; inhibition; rejection; repress; restrain; suppression
抑或 maybe; perhaps; or
抑鬱 depression
　　抑鬱症 melancholia

【扰】 dam² (扔 / 捶 / 敲 / 砸) throw

扰一拳 (捶一拳) give sb a punch
扰心扰肺 (很後悔) deeply regret
扰印 (打印 / 蓋圖章) stamp a chop
扰咗佢 (把它扔了) throw it away
扰門 (敲門 / 砸門) pound the door
扰骨 (捶背) pound the back
扰野 (扔東西) throw things away
扰爛佢 (把它砸爛) smash it

【扰】 dam⁶ pound

扰地 (踩地) stamp the ground
扰腳 (踩腳) stamp one's foot

【扽】 dan³ (磕) (顛) yank

扽吓對鞋 (把鞋磕一下) knock the shoes
扽氣 (懷恨) nurse a grievance
扽蝦籠 (掏空口袋) pick sb's pocket

【扲】 kam² strike

扲波 (扣球) smash

【扲】 ham² (撞) smash

扲倒 (撞倒) knock down

【拎】 ngaam⁴ (掏) draw out; take out

拎袋 fish out from one's pocket

【扔】 wing¹ strike

扔咗佢 (扔掉) throw away

【改】 goi² change

改名 ① (起名字) give a name; name ② change a name
改進 better; improve; make better; mend; perfect (one's skills)
改期 change a date

改過 correct one's mistakes; mend one's ways
改錯水（修正液）correction fluid
改編 ① adapt; convert; rearrange; revise; transcribe
　　② reorganise
改變 alter; change; convert; modify; mold; transform; turn
　　死性不改 as stubborn as a mule; not change for the better

更改 alter; change
悔改 repent and mend one's ways
真心悔改 sincerely repent and earnestly reform oneself

【攻】gung¹ irritate
攻打 assail; assault; attack
攻勢 offensive
攻鼻（沖鼻／刺鼻／嗆鼻子）assail one's nostrils; irritate
　　the nose; pungent
攻擊 attack

兩面夾攻 make a pincer attack

【更】gaang¹ ① watch ② change
更夫 night watchman
更正 amend; make corrections
更生 ① regenerate; revive ② renew
更年期 menopause
　　女性更年期 female menopause
　　男性更年期 male menopause
更衣 change dresses; change one's clothes
　　更衣室 changing room; dressing room
更改 alter; change
更動 alter; change; modify
更換 alter; change; exchange; renew
　　需要更換 need replacement

三更 midnight; third watch of the day
中更 middle switch
五更 fifth watch of the night
日更 morning shift
冇哪更（無緣無故）not to the point
半夜三更 in the depth of night; late at night
交更 change shift
我當緊更（我正當值）I'm on duty
夜更／通宵更／睇更 night shift
看更（保安員）security guard; watchman
唔啦更 irrelevant
當更（當值）on duty; on the shift; on watch
落手／筆打三更 begin with a wrong move; make mistakes
　　when starting to do sth; ruin sth as soon as it starts
輪更 in shifts; on duty; by turn; shift duty

【李】lei⁵（李子）pear
李樹 plum tree

手提行李 hand luggage
行李 luggage
桃李 ① one's disciples; one's pupils ② peaches and plums
　　③ beauty of a woman
執行李（收拾行李）pack one's luggage
報失行李 report the loss of one's luggage

【杉】tsaam³ fir
杉木 fir
　　杉木靈牌 —— 唔做得主（丫鬟帶鑰匙 —— 當家不作主）
　　manage a family but without the right to make any
　　decisions
杉樹 cedar

頂心杉（眼中釘）argumentative person
電燈杉（電線桿）① electric pole ② telegraph pole

【杈】tsaa¹ branch; fork
杈子 forked branch

丫／椏杈 forked branch

【杏】hang⁶（杏兒）apricot
杏仁 ① almond ② ground almond
　　杏仁茶／露 sweet ground almond tea/soup
杏林 medical profession
杏壇 teaching profession

【材】tsoi⁴ timber
材料 ingredient

身材 figure
教材 course material
棺材 coffin
量身材 take sb's measurements
影音器材 audio and visual gadgets
題材 subject matter; theme
魔鬼身材（好身材）great body; nice body; perfect figure
蠢材 fool; idiot

【村】tsyn¹ village
村長 village head
村莊 hamlet; village
村落 village

小村莊 small village

獨家村（孤家寡人）lone wolf; unsociable and eccentric person

【杖】dzoeng⁶ walking stick
杖責 punish by caning

拐杖 crutch
權杖 mace

【杜】dou⁶ shut out
杜絕 eradicate completely; put an end to; stop
杜蟲（打蟲子）cure a parasitic disease; take worm medicine

【杞】gei² medlar
杞子（枸杞子）fruit of Chinese wolfberry

【束】tsuk⁷ ① bundle ② control
束手 have one's hands tied; helpless
　束手待斃 die without a fight; fold one's hands and await destruction/wait for death/wait to be slain; resign oneself to extinction; wait for death with hands bound up/with tied hands; wait helplessly for death
　束手就擒 allow oneself to be arrested without offering any resistance; allow oneself to be seized without putting up a fight; resign oneself to being held as a prisoner; submit to arrest with folded arms
　束手無策 at a loss for what to do; have one's hands tied; helpless; no way out; up a stump
束緊 bind up; lace up
束縛 bind up; fetter; restrain; tie
　解除束縛 liberate from bondage

拘束 ill at ease; restrain; restrict
無拘無束 as free as the birds; carefree; completely without restraints; free and easy; free as a bird; make oneself at home; unconstrained; uncontrolled; unfettered; unrestrained; without a worry in the world; without any restraint; without hindrance
結束 ① come to an end ② put an end to; resolve

【杠】gong³ flat pole
杠架（單杠）horizontal bar
　打杠架（盤杠子）exercise on a horizontal bar
杠桿 ① lever ② leverage

敲竹杠 blackmail; extort
蟹杠 nippers of a crab; pincers of a crab

【杆】gon¹ pole; staff
杆子 ① pole; rod ② gang of bandits

擔杆 carrying pole

【步】bou⁶ step
步行 foot it; go on foot; walk
步兵 ① infantry; infantryman ② foot soldier
步步 at every step
　步步為營 act cautiously; advance gradually and entrench oneself at every step; consolidate at every step; make a stand at every step; move carefully every step on the way; pick one's steps; raise a fort at every step
　步步高陞 wish you promotion and success
步級（台階）staircase; steps
步操 formation training
步驟 measure; move; procedure; step

一人行一步 have both sides make a concession
一步 one step
一步一步 step by step
寸步 single step; tiny step
色情架步（色情場所）sex-for-sale den
行先一步 die
快人一步 one step ahead of others
初步 first step; preliminary; tentative
見一步行一步／見步行步 deal with things one step at a time; take things as they come
走步 travelling
唔識駕步 not know what to do
徒步 go on foot
偷步（搶跑）jump the gun
帶隻狗去散步 take one's dog for a walk; walk one's dog
跑一個鐘頭步（跑一小時步）jog for one hour
跑步 jog; jogging; run; running
散步 ① take a walk ② take a stroll
漫步 ramble; roam; stroll
線步（針腳）stitch
緩步 walk slowly
學業進步 Best wishes on your study
讓步 back down; back out of; compromise; give in; give way; make a concession; yield

【每】mooi⁴ every
每日（每天）each day; everyday
　每日四次（每天四次）four times a day
　每日如是 it's the same everyday
每打 every dozen
每月 every month; monthly

每次 at every turn; each time; every time
　　每次一粒 one tablet each time
每年 every year; per annum
每每 often
每周 every week
每況愈下 become worse and worse; get increasingly
　　worse; go downhill; go from bad to worse; make bad
　　trouble worse; on the decline; steadily deteriorate; take a
　　bad turn; take a turn for the worse; worse and worse
每個人 everyone
每逢 on every occasion; when
　　每逢佳節倍思親 each time a festival arrives, one
　　　　thinks all the more of one's close relatives; on festive
　　　　occasions more than ever one thinks of one's dear ones
　　　　far away
每當 each time; every time; whenever
每隔 day at certain intervals; every

【求】 kau⁴ request
求人 seek help from others
　　求人不如求己 ask other people for help is not as good
　　　　as to help oneself; better depend on oneself than ask
　　　　for help from others; better do it yourself than ask for
　　　　help from others; better to seek help from oneself than
　　　　from sb else; God helps those who help themselves;
　　　　it is better to aid oneself than to depend on the aid of
　　　　others; near is my shirt, but nearer is my skin; relying
　　　　on oneself is better than relying on others; self-help is
　　　　better than help from others; the best answer is to roll
　　　　up your sleeves and do the job yourself; turn one's own
　　　　hand to do one's own business
　　　　不求人（抓手）back scratcher
求先（剛才）a moment ago; just now
求其（馬虎／隨便）do things casually; sloppy
　　求求其其（馬馬虎虎／隨隨便便）do things casually; in a
　　　　slapdash manner; sloppy
求和 ① hold out the olive branch; make overtures of
　　reconciliation; seek peace with an enemy; sue for peace;
　　try to end hostilities ② try to draw a match ③ summation
求婚 ask a woman's hand in marriage; ask for a lady's
　　hand; ask sb in marriage; lead a woman to the alter;
　　make a proposal of marriage; make an offer of marrige;
　　make suit to sb; marry; offer one's hand; pay one's
　　addresses to a lady; pay one's court to a woman; plead
　　one's suit with a woman; pop the question; propose
　　marriage (to); seek a marriage alliance; set one's cap at
　　sb; step up to a girl; wed; woo
求情 appeal to mercy; ask for a favour; beg favours from;
　　beg for leniency; intercede; intercession; plead with sb

求學 ① study; attend school; go to college/school;
　　receive education ② pursue one's studies;
　　seek knowledge

供不應求 demand exceeds supply; supply fails to meet
　　the demand; supply falls short of demand; the demand
　　outstrips the supply; the supply can hardly keep pace
　　with the demand; the supply does not meet the demand;
　　the supply is not adequate to the demand; the supply is
　　unable to meet the demand
供求 supply and demand
供過於求 an excess of supply over demand; in excess of
　　demand; pile up in excess of requirement; the supply
　　exceeds the demand/outstrips the demand
要求 request
哀求 appeal pathetically; beg humbly/piteously/pitifully;
　　beseech; entreat; grovel; implore
追求 chase after; desire; pursue
務求 strive for
訪求 search for; seek
夢魅以求 long for even in one's dream
需求 demand; need; requirement

【汪】 wong¹ a body of water
汪汪 tearful
汪洋 a vast expanse of water; boundless; vast

水汪汪 have only a forlorn hope

【決】 kyt⁸ decide
決心 all set; bent on; bent upon; bound; decide;
　　determination; determine; determined; resolution;
　　resolve; resolved; form/make/pass a resolution; make
　　up one's mind; set on/oneself to/one's heart on/one's
　　mind on
決定 decide; make up one's mind
決策 ① decide a policy; make a strategic decision/policy
　　decisions ② decision-making; policy-making
決賽 final; the finals
決議 resolution

民族自決 national self-determination
否決 nix; overrule; reject; veto; vote down

【汽】 hei³ gas; steam; vapour
汽水 ① aerated water ② soft drink
　　汽水樽 beverage bottle
　　汽水罐 beverage can
　　　　一支汽水（一瓶汽水）a bottle of beverage

汽車 automobile; car; vehicle
　汽車零件 automobile parts
汽油 gas; gasoline; petrol

【沌】dan⁶ turbid

瘟瘟沌沌 bewildered; in confusion

【沈】sam² sink

沈沒 sink

林沈 (零碎的東西) odds and ends

【沉】tsam⁴ deep

沉沉 ① heavy ② deep
　死氣沉沉 apathetic; dead atmosphere; dead calm;
　　deadly still; dull and despondent; hopeless and
　　gloomy; lifeless; lifeless air; like a log; lose one's
　　vitality; spiritless; without animation; without vitality
沉沒 sink
沉思 be buried in thought; be lost in thought;
　contemplative; deliberating; meditate; meditative;
　pensive; ponder; reflective
沉重 ① heavy ② critical; serious
沉迷 indulge; wallow
沉悶 ① depressive; oppressive ② depressed; in low spirits
沉靜 calm; quiet; serene
沉默 ① reticent; taciturn ② quiet; silent
　沉默寡言 a person of few words; a regular oyster; a
　　reticent person; not to be given to much speech; of
　　few words; quiet and taciturn in disposition; scanty of
　　words
　保持沉默 bite the tongue; hush; keep a still tongue
　　in one's head; keep mute/silent; preserve silence;
　　remain silent
沉澱 precipitate; sedimentation

浮沉 drift along; now sink, now emerge
陰沉 / 陰陰沉沉 cloudy; dreary; dusky; gloomy; overcast
暮氣沉沉 apathetic

【沐】muk⁹ bathe

沐恩 offer a helping hand

【沖】tsung¹ flush with water

沖水 ① (灌手) fill with water; pour water ② (再裝滿茶壺)
　refill the teapot
沖沖 in a state of excitement
沖走 flush away; wash away

沖洗 rinse
沖茶 ① (沏茶) make tea ② (加滿茶壺) top up
　the teapot
　唔該你沖茶 (請加滿茶壺) please top up my teapot
沖涼 ① (洗澡) bath; shower; take a bath/a shower
　② shampoo
　沖涼房 (浴室) bathroom
　沖涼盆 (洗澡盆 / 浴盆) bathtub
沖曬 (沖洗) develop
　沖曬店 (沖洗店) photo shop

來也沖沖，去也沖沖 flush when you come and flush when
　you go
對沖 hedging

【沙】saa¹ (沙子 / 泥沙) sand

沙井 (沉沙井 / 滲井) seepage pit
沙冚 (擋泥板) fender board
沙池 (沙坑) ① sandpit; sand trap ② bunker
沙沙滾 (連矇帶騙) deceive and swindle sb
沙展 (中士 / 警長 / 警官) (transliteration) sergeant
沙甸魚 ① (沙丁魚) (transliteration) sardine ② (擠得像罐
　頭裏的沙丁魚) be packed like sardine
沙律 (色拉 / 沙拉) (transliteration) salad
　沙律油 (色拉油) salad oil
　沙律兜 (色拉碗) salad bowl
　沙律醬 (色拉醬) salad dressing
沙爹 satay; satay sauce
　沙爹牛肉 beef with satay sauce
沙紙 ① sand paper ② (證明書 / 證書) certificate
沙梨 (梨) sand pear
沙煲 ① earthen pot ② earthen rice-cooker
　沙煲兄弟 / 砂煲兄弟 friends in the same boat; good
　　friends
　沙煲罌撐 household goods
沙葛 (豆薯) yam bean
沙塵 (愛出風頭) boastful
　沙塵白霍 (不可一世) consider oneself a world above
　　others; consider oneself unsurpassed in the world;
　　insufferably arrogant; on the high ropes; ride the high
　　horse; swagger like a conquering hero; think oneself
　　supreme in the world
沙膠 (硬橡皮) hard rubber
沙聲 (沙啞) hoarse
沙膽 (大膽 / 膽子大 / 膽大包天) bold; daring; foolhardy
沙蟬 (蟬) cicada
沙蟲 (跟頭蟲) wriggle
沙灘 beach
沙欖 (橄欖) Chinese olive

一粒沙 a grain of sand
幼沙（細沙）fine sand
豆沙 red bean paste
泥沙 sand
玩泥沙 play with sand
紅豆沙 sweet red bean soup
飛沙（不要糖）no sugar please
細蚊仔玩泥沙（小孩子玩泥沙）not serious about things
跌倒揦番揸沙 put one's fault in the right side
碌地沙（在地上打滾）roll on the ground
綠豆沙 sweet green bean soup
蓮子紅豆沙 sweet red bean soup with lotus seed
撻沙 flatfish
縮沙（退縮）beat a retreat; chicken out; opt out; shrink back; withdraw

【沙】saa³ sand
沙冧（對不起）sorry

【沙】saa¹ sand
沙沙滾（馬虎了事）live a dissolute life; play the field

【沒】mut⁹ not
沒收 confiscate
沒落 decline; wane

沉沒 sink
神出鬼沒 sb who keeps appearing and then disappearing
覆沒 ① capsize and sink ② be annihilated; be overwhelmed; be routed; be wiped out

【灸】gau³ cautery

針灸 acupuncture

【灼】tsoek⁸ ①（涮）blanch ② burn
灼傷（燒傷）burn
灼熱（涮熱）blanch in hot water

白灼 blanch

【災】dzoi¹ calamity
災害 calamities; damages; disasters; fatalities
災情 condition of a disaster
　災情嚴重 the condition of the disaster is serious
災禍 calamities; catastrophes; disasters
　幸災樂禍 chuckle at sb's discomfiture; crow over; delight in the misfortunes of others; derive pleasure from others' misfortune; exult at the misfortune of others; exult in the misfortune of others; exult over the misfortune of others; exult when another meets with mischance; glad when other people are in difficulties; gloat over others' misfortune; laugh at others' troubles; make game of others' calamities; make merry over another's mishap; mock at others' woes; rejoice in the misfortunes of others; Roman holiday; take pleasure in the calamity of others/from the misfortune of others
災難 calamity; disaster
　大災難 holocaust
　多災多難 always dogged by misfortunes/bad luck/; be plagued by frequent ills; calamitous; come upon a series of misfortunes; ill-starred; suffer a chapter of accidents

水災 flood
受人錢財，替人消災 one must be committed to complete the task for which one has been paid
烏狗得食，白狗當災（黑狗得食，白狗當災）carry the can; the black dog eats the meat and the white dog bears the blame
破財擋災 give money in the hope of being freed from trouble; suffer unexpected personal financial losses to remove misfortune
當災 meet with disaster/misfortune; set in the neck; suffer disaster
雹災 disaster caused by hail

【灶】dzou³ ① kitchen ② cooking stove
灶君 God of the Kitchen
　灶君上天 —— 有句講句（灶王爺上天 —— 有啥說啥）be frank with one's opinions; outspoken; say whatever one likes
　灶君老爺 —— 黑口黑面（張飛擺屠案 —— 兇神惡煞）fierce demon and devils

另起爐灶 a new organisation set up to compete with an exisiting one; make a fresh start; start all over again
倒灶 cause trouble while trying to help; do a disservice to; more of a hindrance than a help

【牡】maau⁵ male animal
牡丹 peony

【狂】kong⁴ crazy
狂人 ① kook; lunatic; madman; maniac ② an extremely arrogant and conceited person
狂妄 arrogant; presumptuous

狂野 violent and rough

狂熱 fanatical; feverish; mania; rabid

欣喜若狂 an ecstasy of joy; as happy as a lark; be intoxicated with joy; beside oneself with joy; delirious with delight; ecstasize; exult; fly into raptures; go mad with joy; go wild with joy; in a transport of delight/joy; in raptures; jubilantly happy; jump out of one's skin; leap out of one's skin; leap with joy

【牢】lou⁴ prison

牢固 fast; firm; secure; solid

牢獄 jail; prison

牢騷 complain; discontent; grumble; grumbling; complaint
　　發牢騷 beef about; blow off steam; complain; dissipate one's grief; grouch; grouse; grumble; let off steam; make a sour remark; make bitter complaint; pour out a stream of complaints; whine about; let or blow off steam

亡羊補牢 better late than never; mend the sheepfold after losing the sheep; take precautions after one has suffered loss

地牢 basement

【甫】pou¹ just

甫士 (姿勢) (transliteration) posture
　　甫士咭 (明信片) postcard

【男】naam⁴ male

男人 man; men
　　男人老九 (男子漢) tough man
　　男人味 manliness; masculinity
　　男人婆 / 頭 tomboy
　　男人靠得住，豬乸都會上樹啦 (男人靠得住，母豬會上樹) all men are unreliable
　　一個男人 a man
　　大男人 chauvinist; domineering man
　　住家男人 family man

男大當婚 a grown-up man ought to marry; a man should get married on coming of age; every Jack must have his Jill
　　男大當婚，女大當嫁 when men and women are fully grown, they must marry

男女 men and women
　　男女有別 a distinction should be made between males and females; between the sexes there should be a prudent reserve; males and females should be distinguished

孤男寡女 a single man and a single woman

男子 man
　　男子漢 tough man

男友 boyfriend

男仔 (小伙子 / 男孩子 / 男孩兒) boy; guy
　　男仔頭 (像男孩子的女生) tomboy; woman who acts like a man

男生 ① (男學生) schoolboy ② (男的) male; man

男性 male

男廁 men's toilet

男裝 men's wear

處男 virgin (male)

舞男 gigolo

【甸】din⁶ transliteration of "ding"

甸子地 marshy grassland

布甸 pudding

芒果布甸 mango pudding

蓮蓉焗布甸 baked lotus seed paste pudding

【秀】sau³ beauty

秀才 county graduate
　　秀才人情紙一張 just a small token of appreciation
　　秀才不出門，全知天下事 a scholar does not step outside his gate, yet he knows all the happenings under the sun; a scholar, without going out, can know the affairs in the world; without going outdoor the scholar knows all affairs of the world
　　秀才手巾 —— 包書 (輸) (孔夫子搬家 —— 淨書 (輸)) one will certainly lose in gambling; stand to lose
　　秀才遇老虎 —— 吟詩都吟唔甩 fail to shirk
　　秀才遇着兵 —— 有理講唔清 be unable to persuade sb with reason

秀外慧中 beautiful and intelligent; pretty and intelligent

秀氣 ① delicate; elegant; fine ② refined; urbane ③ delicate and well-made

秀麗 beautiful; elegant; fine; graceful; handsome; pretty

俊秀 handsome; of delicate beauty; pretty

眉清目秀 beautiful and delicate eyes

面貌清秀 have delicate facial features

【私】si¹ private

私人 private
　　私人樓 (私人房屋) private building

私下 in private; in secret; privately; under the rose

私己 (私房錢) private resources; private savings

私己錢 (私房錢) private resources; private savings

私伙 (屬於自己個人的東西) privately owned things

私自 without authorization

私房 private saving

私家 (私人) private

　　私家車 (私人汽車 / 私人轎車) private car

　　私家車牌費 private car licence fee

　　　一架私家車 a private car

　　私家樓 (私人房屋) private building

私校 (私立學校) private school

私隱 (隱私) privacy

自私 selfish

走私 smuggle

無私顯見私 self-reveal one's own guilty conscience in spite of being irrelative with the trouble

緝私 arrest smugglers; anti-smuggling

【罕】hon² rare

罕有 exceptional; rare; unusual

罕見 rare; seldom seen

　　極為罕見 a rarity

希罕 ① rare; scarce; uncommon ② care; cherish; value as a rarity ③ rare thing; rarity

【肚】tou⁵ (肚子) abdomen; belly

肚皮 belly

　　肚皮打鼓 as hungry as a hunter; very hungry

　　人心隔肚皮 no one can read the mind of another person

　　挪高肚皮 (泄露隱私) reveal one's privacy

肚赤 (肚子痛) stomachache

肚屙 (拉肚子 / 拉稀 / 腹瀉) diarrhoea; give the trots; have diarrhoea; have loose bowels; suffer from diarrhoea

肚痛 (肚子痛) stomachache

肚腩 (小肚子 / 大肚皮 / 上腹) belly; pot belly; tummy

　　大肚腩 (大肚子 / 大肚皮) big tummy; pot belly

肚裏蟲 mind-reader

肚餓 (肚子餓) hungry

　　好肚餓 (肚子很餓 / 很餓) very hungry

　　肚唔肚餓 (餓不餓) are you hungry

　　頂 (吓) 肚 (餓) (充飢 / 墊肚子) allay one's hunger with sth; cram one's stomach; eat sth; have a quick snack; satisfy hunger

　　鬼咁肚餓 (非常飢餓) extremely hungry

　　捱肚餓 (捱餓) go hungry; starve; suffer from hunger/starvation

肚臍 belly button; navel

大肚 (懷孕) heavy with child; pregnant

反肚 (死亡) die

老婆大肚 (懷孕) one's wife is pregnant

空肚 (吃飯前) before meal

直腸直肚 (心直口快) outspoken; straight-talking

金錢肚 beef tripe

留番啖氣暖吓肚 (不出聲) button up one's mouth

神仙肚 (不吃飯也不餓) sb who can go without food

啤酒肚 beer tummy; pot belly

屙肚 (拉肚子) have/suffer from diarrhea; have loose bowel movements; have loose stools; have the trots

牽腸掛肚 feel deep anxiety about sb

眼肚 (下眼皮) lower eyelid

腸肚 intestines and stomach

腳肚 calf of the leg

飽肚 after meal

醫肚 (吃飯) have a meal

爆肚 (臨時編台詞) ad-lib; impromptu speech

鐵腳馬眼神仙肚 (不吃不喝也可長時間工作) energetic person who can work long hours without sitting, sleeping, and eating

【肝】gon¹ liver

肝火 irascibility

　　肝火盛 (肝火旺) hot-tempered; irascible

肝炎 hepatitis

肝病 hepatosis; live ailment

肝硬化 cirrhosis of liver

肝癌 hepatocele; liver cancer

肝膽 ① liver and gall bladder ② courage; heroic spirit ③ open-heartedness; sincerity

　　肝膽相照 a genuine meeting of minds between friends; be open-hearted to each other; friends devoted to each other heart and soul; loyal-hearted; show utter devotion to a friend; treat each other with absolute sincerity

肝臟 liver

冇心肝 (粗心大意) forgetful; inattentive; negligent

生仔唔知仔心肝 (動機難測) it is hard to know people's hidden intention

的起心肝 (下決心) decide; determine; be determined to; bestir oneself; brace up; come to a determination/ a resolution; have one's mind made up; make a firm decision/a firm resolve to do sth; make a resolution; make up one's mind; resolve to do sth

珍肝 gizzard and liver

疏肝（沒牽掛）carefree; free from inhibitions

豬肝 pig liver

諗爛心肝（深思熟慮）chew the cud

雞肝 chicken liver

孻仔拉心肝（父母愛最小的兒子）parents lavish most affection on their youngest son

【臣】san⁴⁻² minister

臣服 submit oneself to the rule of

一朝天子一朝臣 a new chief brings in his own trusted followers

（打）卜臣（拳擊）(practise) boxing

拉臣 (transliteration) licence

花臣（花招）(transliteration) gimmick; tricks

箍臣（靠墊）(transliteration) cushion

撚花臣（出花招）play tricks

【良】loeng⁴ good

良心 good heart; conscience

良心發現 draw out the good that is in sb; one's conscience is moved

良心當狗肺 be ungrateful for a favour and regard it as a disservice

冇良心 have no conscience

揸住個良心（違背良心）against one's conscience; have the conscience to do sth

良好 fine; good; well

良知 conscience

立心不良 have an evil plan; ill-disposed

純良 simple and honest

無良 merciless

善良 kind

營養不良 malnutrition; under-nourished

【芋】wu⁶ taro

芋角 deep-fried taro dumpling

芋頭（大芋頭）taro

芋頭仔（小芋頭）eddoes

芋頭點糖——心淡（冬天吃冰棍——心都涼了）one's heart sinks

生水芋頭（傻頭傻腦的人）blockhead; foolish-looking; simpleton

【芒】mong¹ awn

芒刺 prickle

芒果 (transliteration) mango

芒果布甸 mango pudding

【見】gin³ ①（見）see ②（覺得）feel

見人 see others

見人講人話，見鬼講鬼話 speak to a saint like a saint, to a devil like a devil

冇面見人 feel too shamed to face people; fly from the face of men; have no face to show to any person; too ashamed to face anyone/to see others

見工（面試）be interviewed for a job; job interview

見山就拜 taking A for B without making sure

見牙唔見眼 have a hearty laugh

笑到見牙唔見眼（笑得眼睛都瞇縫了）have a hearty laugh

見功（見效）become effective; provide the desired effect

見世面 see the world

經風雨，見世面 brave the storm and face the world

見死 seeing sb in mortal danger

見死不救 bear to see sb die without trying to save them; do nothing to save sb from dying; do nothing to save sb from ruin; fold one's arms and see sb die; fold one's hands and see sb die; leave one to sink; leave one to swim; leave sb in the lurch; not to help a dying man; not to rescue those in mortal danger; refuse to help sb in real trouble; see sb in mortal danger without lifting a finger to save him; shut one's eyes to people who are dying; stand by when sb is in peril; stand calmly by while another is drowning

見步行步／見一步行一步（走一步是一步）deal with things one step at a time; take things as they come

見使（耐用）durable; withstand wear and tear

見怪 mind; take offence; take sth amiss

唔好見怪 don't be offended; don't feel ill at ease; I hope you will not be offended; kindly forgive me; kindly forgive my lack of repect

見者有份（見面分一半）the seer has a share of sth

見客（見客戶）meet a client; see a client

見紅 see blood

見面 meet

見面禮 a gift presented to sb at the first meeting

定時見面 meet regularly

見笑 ① incur ridicule ② laugh at

見笑大方 be laughed at by experts; become a laughing stock of the learned people; expose oneself to ridicule; give an expert cause for laughter; incur the ridicule of experts; make a laughing stock of oneself before experts

見高拜，見低踹（軟的欺負硬的怕／勢利）flatter those above and bully those below; snobbish

見高就拜，見低就踩（軟的欺負硬的怕）flatter those above and bully those below; snobbish

見過 come across
　見過鬼都／就怕黑（驚弓之鳥）learn from bad experience; once bitten, twice shy
見解 idea; opinion; thesis; understanding; view
見微知著 a straw shows which way the wind blows; from one small clue one can see what is to come; from the first small beginnings one can see how things will develop; one may see day at a little hole; recognise the whole through observation of the part
見義勇為 act bravely for a just cause; do boldly what is righteous; help a lame dog over a stile; never hesitate where good is to be done; ready to take up the cudgels for a just cause
見雷響唔見雨落（只説不做）all talk but no action
見機 according to circumstances; as befits the occasion; as the opportunity arises
　見機行事 act according to circumstances; act as circumstances dictate/the occasion demands; act on seeing an opportunity; adapt oneself to circumstances; do as one sees fit; play sth/it by ear; see one's chance and act; use one's own judgment and do what one deemed best
見錢開眼（見錢眼開）be moved at the sight of money; be tempted by money; care for nothing but money; open the eyes wide at the sight of money; one's eyes grow round with delight at the sight of money
見識 gain experience

一陣見（一會兒見）see you soon
己見 one's own opinion
少見 rare; seldom seen; unique
叩門求見 knock at the door and ask for an interview
未見 have not seen; not yet seen
再見 adieu; adios; bye; bye-bye; cheerio; goodbye; farewell; good day to you; have a nice day; see youagain/around; so long
各抒己見 each airs his/her own view; each has his/her say; each one/everybody expresses his/her own views (freely); everybody sets forth his/her own views
好耐冇見（好久不見）haven't seen each other for a long time; haven't seen you for ages; long time no see
罕見 rare; seldom seen
固執己見 abide by one's opinion; adhere stubbornly to one's own ideas; have a will of one's own; hold stubbornly to one's own viewpoint; nail one's colours to the mast; stick to one's guns; stick to one's own view; stubbornly adhere to one's views

前所未見 have never seen before
洞見 see very clearly
唔見（不見）① not see ② lose
偏見 bias; partial opinion; preconception prejudice; slant; warp
意見 advice; opinion
極為罕見 a rarity
夢見 dream of
遲啲見（等會兒見）see you later
撞見 bump into; chance upon; come across/on/upon; cross sb's path; encounter; fall among; meet unexpectedly/by chance/sb by accident; run across/into; (literary) alight on; (literary) light on/upon
聽日見（明天見）see you tomorrow

【角】gok[8] corner
角度 ① angle; degree of an angle ② point of view
角落頭（角落）corner

八角 aniseed
三尖八角（形狀不規則）of irregular shape
三角 triangle
女主角 actress; female lead; leading lady
主角 lead; leading character/player/role;; main actor/actress; major character protagonist
死角 dead angle; dead space
男主角 actor; chief actor; leading man; male lead; male title role
芋角 deep-fried taro dumpling
豆角 string bean
青豆角 green pea
枱角 corner of a table
挖角 headhunt; lure away sb
捉到鹿唔識脱角（錯失良機）fail to make the best use of an opportunity; let the opportunity slip; miss the boat
茸角（鹿角）antler
眼角 eye
鹿角 antler
鈍角 obtuse angle
號角 ① bugle; horn; trumpet ② bugle call
摔角 wrestling
蝦角 deep-fried shrimp dumplings served with salad dressing
墮角 out-of-the-way; remote
縮埋一二角 hide oneself in a corner
爛口角 aphtha
鹹水角 glutinuous rice dumplings with dried shrimp and pork
麟角 rare things

【言】jin⁴ speech

言之成理 present in a reasonable way; say sth with solid judgment; sound reasonable; speak in a rational and convincing way; speak on the strength of reason; (it) stand(s) to reason; talk sense; well reasoned; what one says makes sense

言不及義 indulge in gossip without touching anything serious; make idle talk; never say anything serious; talk frivolously

言字邊 (言字旁) the "speech" (言) radical

言行 statements and actions; words and deeds

言行一致 act in accordance with one's words; actions matching words; as good as one's word; deeds accord with words; fit one's deeds to one's words; live up to one's words; match one's deeds with one's words; match word to deed; match words with deeds; one's actions accord with one's words; one's actions are in keeping with one's promises; one's deeds and words are in accord; one's deeds are consistent with one's words; one's words correspond with one's actions; square one's words with one's conduct; stand by one's word; suit one's actions to one's words; the deeds suit the words; the deeds match the words

言行不一 actions repugnant to one's words; one does not do what one preaches; one's actions are not in keeping with one's promises; one's acts belie one's words; one's conduct disagrees with one's words; one's conduct is at variance with one's words; one's deeds do not match one's words; one's deeds do not square with one's words; one's doings belie one's commitments; one's words and deeds are at complete variance; one's words are at variance with one's deeds; one's words are not matched by deeds; say one thing and do another; talk one way and behave another; words and actions do not match; words and deeds contradict each other; what one does belies one's commitments

坐言起行 no sooner said than done

言過其實 boast; bombastic; brag; come it strong; draw the long bow; exaggerate; give a false colour; go it strong; hyperbolize; inflated; make a mountain out of a molehill; overshoot the truth; overstate; overstate the fact; pile on the agony; pull the long bow; strain the truth; stretch a point; stretch the facts; turn geese into swans

言論 speech; views

言歸正傳 and now to be serious; come back to our story; come to business; get down to business; hark back to the subject; jesting apart; jesting aside; joking apart; joking aside; keep to the record; lead the conversation to serious things; let's resume the narration; resume the thread of one's discourse; return from the digress; return to one's muttons; return to the subject; return to the topic of discussion; revert to the original topic of conversation

言歸於好 be reconciled; become reconciled; bury the hatchet; bury the tomahawk; heal the breach; kiss and be friends; maintain amicable relations hereafter; make friends again; make it up with sb; make one's peace with sb; make peace with; make sb's peace with; make up a quarrel; on good terms again; put up the sword; reconcile; resume friendship; shake and be friends; sink a feud; smoke the pipe of peace; square oneself with; start with a clean slate

言聽計從 act at sb's beck and call; act upon whatever sb says; always follow sb's advice; always listen to sb's words and accept their advice; believe and act upon whatever sb suggests; listen to sb's words and follow their counsel; readily listen to sb's advice and accept it; take sb's advice and adopt their plan

一言 a word; a single word

一派胡言 a bunch of/a lot of malarkey; a load of codswallop/hogwash/rubbish; a pack of lies/nonsense; complete/gross nonsense; sheer rubbish

仗義執言 speak boldly in defence of justice; speak in accordance with justice; speak out from a sense of justice; speak out to uphold justice; speak straightforwardly for justice

名言 famous remark; well-known saying

多種語言 multilingual

有口難言 find it hard to say

序言 preface

妖言 absurd statements; heresies; fallacies

沉默寡言 a person of few words; a regular oyster; a reticent person; quiet and taciturn in disposition; scanty of words

前言 preface

胡言 rave; talk nonsense

美言 put in a word for sb

格言 adage; aphorism; maxim; motto

酒後吐真言 truth is exposed in wine

寓言 allegory; fable; parable

揚言 declare in public; exaggerate; pass the word that; spread words; threaten

敢言 speak out; vocal

慎言 speak cautiously

語言 language

違背諾言 break one's promise

緒言 foreword; introduction; preamble
諾言 promise
默默無言 remain silent
謠言 rumour
臨別贈言 parting advice

【谷】 guk⁷ moody

谷奶（催奶）stimulate the secretion of milk
谷底 valley bottom; valley floor
谷氣（憋氣）bottle up one's rage; in a bad mood
　谷住度氣（憋着一肚子氣）bottle up one's rage; contain one's anger
谷起泡腮（生氣或憂愁的樣子）be out of sorts

催谷 expedite; give sth a great plug; plug
溪谷 canyon; dale; gorge valley
爆谷（爆米花）popcorn

【豆】 dau⁶ bean

豆丁 children; kid
豆奶 soy milk
豆皮／痘皮 ①（麻子）pockmarked ②（麻子臉）a pockmarked face
　豆皮佬／痘皮佬（有麻子的人）sb who has a pockmarked face
豆沙 red bean paste
　豆沙喉（沙嗓子）coarse voice; rough voice
豆角 string bean
豆泥（次／差／差勁／簡陋）poor in quality
豆苗 pea shoots
豆粉（芡粉／澱粉）starch
豆豉醬 black bean paste
豆腐 ① bean curd ② weak
　豆腐刀（優柔寡斷的人）indecisive person
　豆腐刀──兩便面（銅板切豆腐──兩面光）a bean curd knife is sharp on both sides – a fence-sitter
　豆腐花（豆腐腦）jellied bean curd
　豆腐渣 ① bean curd residue ② poor-quality and dangerous constructions
　豆腐飯 rice with bean curd
　豆腐膶 ① bean curd cube ② very small apartment
　豆腐頭（豆腐渣）bean curd residue
　豆腐朥（豆腐泡兒／炸豆腐）deep-fried bean curd
　一磚豆腐 a cube of bean curd
　水豆腐（嫩豆腐）tender bean curd
　冰豆腐（凍豆腐）frozen bean curd
　有乜冬瓜豆腐 if sb was dead
　諕鬼食豆腐 cheat sb into the belief

臉過豆腐 softer than bean curd
豆蓉（豆泥）bean paste
豆漿 soybean milk

一粒豆 a bean
大豆芽 bean sprout
土豆（馬鈴薯）potato
四季豆 seasonal pea
瓜豆（死亡）die
白豆 yellow bean
老豆（父親）father
吽豆 very dull and boring; dumbfounded; in a daze; in a trance; spellbound; stare blankly; stunned; stupefied
芝麻綠豆 trivial
芽豆 sprouted broad bean
青豆 green pea
青春痘 pimple
紅豆 red bean
荷蘭豆 French bean
發吽豆 idling time away; in a trance
飽死荷蘭豆 be ruffled; feel disgusted
糖黐豆 hand and glove; two people who are very close
擺豆 die; meet one's fate
蠶豆 broad bean

【貝】 bui³ shell

貝殼 shell
貝類 shellfish

干貝 dried scallop
扇貝 yesso scallop

【赤】 tsek⁸ ① bare ②（疼痛）ache

赤字 deficit; in the red
赤腳 barefoot
　打赤腳（光着腳）go barefoot; go without shoes
赤膊 bare one's chest
　赤膊上陣 go into battle stripped to the waist; bare one's shoulders and go into battle ; step forward in person without any disguise; come out without any disguise
　打赤膊（光着上身／光膀子）bare one's chest
赤裸 in one's birthday suit; (stark) naked; without a stitch of clothing

肉赤（心疼）feel hurt when ones lose one's valuable things
肚赤（肚子痛）stomachache
頭赤（頭痛）ache in one's head; have a headache

【走】dzau² ① go away ② (跑) run

走人 (溜走) leave stealthily; scarper; slink; slip away; slope off

　　急急腳走人 go away in a hurry; leave in a hurry

走火 (逃避火災) run away from fire

走甩 (跑掉) get away

　　走唔甩 (跑不掉) cannot escape; cannot get away

　　走得甩 (跑得掉) can escape; can get away

走奶 (不加奶) no milk added please

走光 a woman's underwear is shown due to careless dressing or posture

走冰 (不加冰) no ice

走色 (不加醬油) no soy sauce

走私 smuggle

走味 (變味) loss of flavour

走夾唔抖 (拼命走 / 慌忙逃跑) run for one's life

走步 (持球跑) travelling

走佬 (溜走) be on the run

走油 (不加油) no oil

走法律罅 (鑽法律的漏洞) do evil with a legal loophole

走青 (不加蔥) no spring onion; no scallion

走紅 (走紅運) getting famous; have fortune on one's side

走氣 (漏氣) air leakage

走粉 (走私毒品) smuggle heroin

走馬看花 take a scamper through sth

走鬼 (小販逃避警察) illegal hawkers fleeing from policemen to avoid arrest; make a getaway

走埠 (走江湖 / 跑江湖) wander from place to place to earn a living

走堂 (曠課) skip classes

走眼 (看不準 / 看錯 / 看漏了眼) slip from sight

走廊 corridor

　　走廊位 aisle seat

走喇 go; leave

　　係時候走喇 it's time to go

走債 (躲債 / 避債) avoid creditors

走路 (逃跑) run away; take to one's legs

走勢 trend

走盞 (餘地) back out

　　有走盞 (沒有餘地) inflexible; leave no space for sth

走電 (跑電 / 漏電) leakage of electricity

走精面 act selfishly

走辣 (不加辣) no chilli

走數 (逃債) avoid repaying debts

走糖 no sugar

走學 (走讀) attend a day school without living in the hostels

走頭 (開路) go away

走雞 ① (錯過機會) lose an opportunity; miss a chance; miss out on a good thing; miss the boat; miss the opportunity ② (失去 / 走失 / 跑掉) run away; wander away

　　冇走雞 have everything in the bag

走寶 (錯失 / 錯過了好處) miss a valuable chance; miss an opportunity

走難 (逃難) flee from a calamity; flee from disaster; seek refuge from calamities

走趲 (奔跑) run about; rush about on errands

走趲 (餘地) leeway; margin

未學行先學走 learn to run before learning to walk

全走 (不加油和蠔油) no oil and oyster sauce

早少少走 leave a little bit earlier

沖走 flush away; wash away

亞崩叫狗——越叫越走 (肉包子打狗——一去不回) be unable to restrain sb

兩邊走 go back and forth between two places

拎走 (拿走) take sth away

茶走 (奶茶不加糖，加煉奶) tea with condensed milk

逃走 escape; flee; fly away; make one's escape; run away; take flight; take to one's heels

鬥走 (競走) heel-to-toe walking

啡走 (咖啡不加糖，加煉奶) coffee with condensed milk

揦起錢就走 / 撐起錢就走 grab the money and go

趕走 chase away

遠走 go far away

嚇走 scare away

撐走 remove; take away

攞走 take away

雞飛狗走 all the people scatter around

【足】dzuk⁷ ① adequate ② foot

足水 be contented with one's luck; be pleased with oneself

足字邊 (足字旁) the "leg" (足) radical

足夠 adequate; enough

足球 football

　　足球明星 football star

　　足球場 football stadium

　　　打足球 (踢足球) play football

　　　睇足球 watch a football match

人心冇厭足 one is never contented; one is never satisfied

十足 ① exact ② all

不一而足 by no means an isolated case

心足 (心滿意足) feel very pleased with; very/fully/perfectly contented; fully satisfied; to one's heart's content

水頭足（資金充足）a large amount of money

手足 brothers (secret society slang)

立足 achieve a status

百足 centipede

似足／十足 like a splitting image

活力十足 full of energy

美中不足 some slight imperfection

涉足 set foot in

難以立足 difficult to keep a foothold

【身】san¹ body

身亡 die

身子（身體）body

身不由己 do sth not of one's own free will; helpless; incapable of resistance; involuntarily; lose control of oneself; unable to contain oneself; one's limbs no longer obey one; unable to act according to one's own will; unable to contain oneself; under compulsion

身心 body and mind

　身心健康 physically and mentally healthy; sound in body and mind

身手 ① skills; talent ② agility; dexterity

　大顯身手 bring one's talents into full play; come out strong; cut a dashing figure; display one's skill to the full; distinguish oneself; give a good account of oneself; give full play to one's abilities; play one's ace; show one's best; turn one's talents to full account

身水身汗（汗流浹背）all of a sweat; be running with sweat; be soaked with sweat; drip with perspiration; perspire all over; pouring with sweat; stream with sweat; sweat like a pig; sweat like a trooper; sweating heavily; wet through with perspiration; wringing wet

身份 identity

　身份證 identity card

　　一張身份證 an identity card

　　帶身份證 bring one's identity card

　　智能身份證 smart identity card

身在福中不知福 disregard the happy life one enjoys

身光頸靚 dressed up and look sharp

身有屎（有不當行為）filthy behaviour

身材 figure

　身材苗條 slim

　身材豐滿 fleshy

　　量身材 take sb's measurements

　　魔鬼身材 great body; nice body; perfect figure

身壯力健（身強體壯）have a strong body; in good health; in vigorous health

身形（體形）bodily form; build; figure

身受 ① experience personally ② accept personally; receive in person

　感同身受 appreciate it as a personal favour; be deeply affected by … as if one had experienced it oneself; count it as a personal favour; feel indebted as if it were received in person; I shall count it as a personal favour; I would consider it as a personal favour to me

身後事 funeral

　辦身後事 arrange the funeral

身家（家產／家財／家當）personal asset

　身家百倍 a meteoric rise in social status; find oneself substantially elevated in fame and status; have a sudden rise in social status; one's position and reputation shoot up hundred-fold; receive a tremendous boost in one's prestige

　身家清白 have a clean record

身高 height

　量身高 measure one's height

身痕（心癢癢）be addicted to sth; yearn for sth

身敗名裂 be utterly discredited; bring disgrace and ruin upon oneself; lose all standing and reputation; lose one's fortune and honour; one's name is mud

身慶（身體發熱）have a fever; have a temperature

身嬌肉貴 come from a rich family

身邊 at one's side; with one

身體 ① body ② health

　身體虛弱 frail in health

　身體健康 ① good health ② wish you good health

　　祝你身體健康 wish you good health

　身體檢查 body check; medical check-up

　　保重身體 take good care of your health

　　對身體好 good for health

七點（鐘）起身 get up at seven

上身 one's body being possessed by a spirit or ghost

切身 ① directly affect a person; of immediate concern to oneself ② first-hand; one's own; personal

化身 embodiment; incarnate; incarnation

出身 ① one's family background ② begin the world; start earning one's living

失身 lose one's virginity

打一身 beat up

本身 (in) itself; oneself; personally

甩身（脫身）get away from; get rid of a problem

企身（立式）vertical

企起身（站起來）stand up

好早起身（很早起牀）got up very early

好晏起身（很晚起牀）got up late

成身（整個身體）whole body

屹起身（起來）get up; half rise from one's seat

困身 restrictive in time

快啲起身（快些起來）rise and shine

周身 entire body

厚身 thick and solid

度身 take one's measurements

洗身（洗澡）have a bath; take a shower

砌佢一身（痛打一頓）beat sb up; give sb a beating

俾人砌一身（被人痛打一頓）being/get slugged by sb

吵身／揀身（搜身）conduct/make a body search; search a person

紋身 tattoo

起身 rise; get out of bed; get up; hit the deck; (slang) roll out; show a leg; turn out; wake up

鬼上身 be taken over by a ghost; crazy; mad

悔恨終身 regret sth all one's life

挺身 straighten one's back

健身 body building

側身 turn to the side

動身 begin a journey; depart; departure; go on a journey; leave for a place; set out on a journey

啱身（合身）fit for wearing

殺到埋身（迫在眉睫）have to be dealt with imminently

挷佢起身 drag him up

軟身 soft

帽身 body of a hat

捌屎上身／撐屎上身 get oneself into trouble; invite trouble; wake a sleeping dog

替身 ① (in a film) double; replacement; stand-in; substitute; understudy ② scapegoat

硬身 hard

週身（全身）all over the body

試身（試衣服）fit sth on; try on

惹屎上身（惹火燒身）ask for trouble; invite trouble

葬身 be buried

過身／過咗身（死亡）died; meet one's death; pass away

瘦身 stream-line operation; keep-fit

喙濕身 get very wet

熱身 warm-up

親身 in person

薄身 thin

藏身 go into hiding; hide oneself

黐身 clingy

驗身（體檢）have a check-up

攬上身 take on a task

【車】tse[1] ① vehicle ② (吹) lie

車入去（開進去）drive in

車大炮（吹牛／撒謊）boast; brag; baloney; blow one's own horn/trumpet; draw the long bow; hot air; plume oneself; shoot a line/the breeze/the bull/the shit; swing the lead; talk big/through one's hat; tell tall tales

車天車地（吹得天花亂墜）boast; brag

車仔 ① (人力車) rickshaw ② (手推車) trolley
車仔麵 cart noodles

車卡（車廂）car; carriage; coach; compartment
一卡車卡（一節車廂）a railway carriage; a train

車去嗰度（運到那裏去）take sth to that place

車字邊（車字旁）the "carriage" (車) radical

車死（撞死）be knocked down to death by a car

車衣（做衣服／縫製衣服）sew; stitch
車衣舖（縫店）tailor's shop

車位 parking space
連車位 including car park

車呔（車胎／車輪）tyre

車尾 back of the car
車尾箱（後車廂）boot; trunk

車房（車庫）garage

車衫（縫衣服）sewing

車厘子（櫻桃）cherry

車衫（用縫紉機做衣服）sew with a sewing machine

車埋我喇（把我也帶上吧）take me along

車票 ticket
頭等車票 first-class ticket

車匙（車鑰匙）car key

車葉（螺旋槳）propeller

車牌 ① (駕駛執照／駕駛證) driving licence ② (車牌) car plate; licence plate
考車牌 take a driving test
考車牌肥佬（考駕駛證不及格）failed the driving test

車腳（車費／路費）fare

車路（鐵路）rail; railroad; railway

車轆（輪子）wheel

車嚦人（軋着人了）run over sb

一架（輛）私家車 a private car

一架（輛）車 a car

一架（輛）單車 a bicycle

一架（輛）電車 a tram

二手車 second-hand car; used car

十字車（救護車）ambulance

上火車 get on a train

上車 ① get in the car ② (首次置業) first-time flat buyer

下個站落車（下個站下車）get off a bus at the next stop

小心揸車 drive carefully

山頂纜車 peak tram

冇塞車 the traffic is smooth

手車（手推車）trolley

木頭車 handcart; wheelbarrow

火燭車（消防車）fire engine

片車（賽車）race cars

卡車（貨車）lorry; truck

叫白車（召喚救護車）call an ambulance

右軚車 right-hand drive vehicle

失車 ① lost car ② lost a car

左軚車 left-hand drive vehicle

仲未上車 not yet board the bus

吉車（空車）empty car

好塞車 heavy/a lot of traffic; traffic congestion/jam

汽車 automobile; car; vehicle

衣車（縫紉機）sewing machine

舟車 vessel and vehicle

尾車／班車（末班車）last train

私家車 private car

巡邏車 patrol car

押款車 cash escort vehicle

房車 sedan

直通車 through train

油渣車 diesel car

泊車（停車）park a car

泥頭車 dump truck

炒車（撞車）car crash

拖車 trailer

客貨車 van

架車（這輛車）this car

風車 windmill

飛車（飆車）speeding

唔該呢度停車（請在這裏停車）please stop here

校車 school bus

消防車 fire-engine

救傷車（救護車）ambulance

送車 ① see sb off at the station ② give sb a car as a present

停車 ① stop a car ② park a car

接車 pick up sb at the railway station

跑車 sports car

單車 bicycle; bike

換車 ① trade-in a car ② get a new car

揸車 drive

睇車 ① go to a car showroom to find a car ② watch out for cars

開車 ① start a car ② drive a car

開夜車 burn the midnight oil; work late into the night; work overnight

開篷車（敞篷車）open-topped car

黑箱車（靈車）corpse car

塞車 traffic congestion; traffic jam

塞緊車 be stuck in a traffic jam

搭火車 take a train

搭車 ride a car

搭順風車 hitchhiking

暈車 carsickness

逼車（擠上巴士）jam into a bus

落車 alight; get off a vehicle (bus, train, plane); get out of the car

預備上車 get ready to board

電車 tram

電單車（摩托車）motor bicycle; motorbike; motorcycle

踩車／踩單車（騎自行車）cycling; ride a bicycle/a bike

劏泥車（推土機）bulldozer

捷車（賽車）car racing; motor racing

養車 keep a car; maintain a car

撞車 car crash; collision of vehicles

劏車 disassemble a car

輪流開車 drive by turns

靠車（吹牛）boast; brag; baloney; blow one's own horn/trumpet; draw the long bow; hot air; plume oneself; shoot a line/the breeze/the bull/the shit; swing the lead; talk big/through one's hat; tell tall tales

駕車 drive a car

學車 learn how to drive; take driving lessons

曉揸車 know how to drive a car

褪車 back a car; back up a car/a locomotive; move a vehicle backward; reverse a car

頭車（首班車）first train

賽車 motor racing

避車 ① avoid car crashing ② avoid hitting people

鍊車（賽車）car racing

轉車 change trains or buses

轉彎停車 turn the corner and stop

鏟雪車 snowplough

警車 police car

纜車 ① cable car ② peak tram

【車】goey[1] vehicle

車馬費 transportation fee

食咗人隻車（佔人便宜）take advantage of

【辛】san[1] bitter

辛苦（難受）feel awful/bad/ill/unhappy/unwell/pain

辛苦搵嚟自在食 work hard in order to eat at leisure

千辛萬苦 all kinds of hardships/trials and tribulations;

go through thick and thin/untold hardships/ innumerable trials and tribulations; labouriously; numberless sufferings and hardships; set one's shoulders to the wheel; severe toil; spare no pains; suffer all conceivable hardships; untold hardships

好辛苦 (很難受) feel very bad

辛辛苦苦 at great pains to; laboriously; take all the trouble to; take great pains to; with great efforts; with so much toil; work laboriously

辛酸 bitter/miserable (experience); hardships

有自唔在，攞苦嚟辛 (自討苦吃) prefer to do things in a hard way; ask for trouble

【辰】san⁴ a period from seven to nine o'clock in the morning

辰星 ① (晨星) morning star ② (水星) Mercury

辰時 period of the day from 7 a.m. to 9 a.m.
　　辰時卯時 (任何時間) any time of the day

誕辰 birthday

【巡】tsoen⁴ patrol

巡行 (遊行) ① parade ② demonstrate; march

巡查 go on a tour of inspection; make one's rounds; patrol and investigate

巡迴 go the rounds; make a circuit of; tour

巡遊 (遊行) ① parade ② demonstrate; march

巡邏 patrol
　　巡邏車 patrol car

勻巡 (均勻) even

【邑】jap⁷ county; town

邑人 people of the same county

邑邑 depressed

采邑 fief; vassalage

【邪】tse⁴ bad; evil

邪惡 canker; evil; turpitude; vicious; wicked

邪氣 evil atmosphere

邪教 cult; heresy; perverse religious sect

邪牌 lewd girl
　　邪牌電影 (色情電影) pornographic film

治邪 counteract evil force; exorcise evil spirits

信邪 have belief in meeting with misfortune

撞邪 bad luck

【里】lei⁵ village

里程 mileage
　　里程碑 milepost; milestone

里數 mileage

一日千里 advance by leaps and bounds

卡路里 (transliteration) calorie

好事不出門，壞事傳千里 good news goes on clutchers but ill news flies apace

鄉里 fellow villager

鵬程萬里 great future

【防】fong⁴ guard against

防水 waterproof

防火 fire prevention; fire safety

防守 defend; defence; guard; parry

防空 air defence; anti-aircraft defence

防盜 guard against theft; take precautions against burglars

防煙門 fire door

防腐 antiseptic

防範 precaution

防護 defence; guard; proofing; protect

防曬露 / 防曬霜 sun block lotion

佈防 deploy troops in anticipation of an enemy attack; organise the defence

明槍易擋，暗箭難防 better to suffer an attack by overt than by covert

消防 fire-fighting

8 劃

【並】bing³ together

並列 be juxtaposed; put sth on a par with; put sth on an equal footing

並存 co-exist; put side by side; stand side by side

【乳】jy⁵ milk

乳牛 dairy cattle; milch cow

乳名 child's pet name; infant name

乳房 breasts; boobs; bosoms; (slang) bubbies; (a cow's) udders

乳罩 bra; (old-fashioned) brassiere

乳膠 emulsion; latex

乳豬 piglet
　　燒乳豬 (烤乳豬) roasted piglet

乳頭 (slang) diddies; nipple; teat
乳癌 breast cancer
乳鴿 pigeon
　　燒乳鴿 (烤乳鴿) roasted pigeon

一磚腐乳 (一塊腐乳) a lump of fermented bean curd
南乳 fermented taro curd
腐乳 fermented bean curd
髮乳 hair cream

【乖】 gwaai¹ obedient

乖仔 (乖孩子) good child
乖巧 clever; lovely
乖乖 obedient; well-behaved
　　乖乖哋 (順從地) obediently

口乖 (嘴巴甜) honey-mouthed
好乖 very good; very obedient
精乖 smart
賣口乖 (油嘴滑舌) oil one's tongue; sweet-talk

【乸】 naa² ① (母 / 雌) female ② feminine suffix ③ prefix indicating femininity

乸乸哋 effeminate; sissy
乸型 effeminate; sissy
乸脷 (昂貴) extremely expensive; very expensive

牛乸 (母牛) cow
仔乸 (母子) mother and son
後底乸 (繼母) step-mother
老虎乸 (母老虎) ① one's shrewish wife; one's wife ② unyielding woman
羊乸 (母羊) ewe
狗乸 (母狗) female dog
兩仔乸 (兩母子) mother and son
後底乸 (繼母) stepmother
蚤乸 (跳蚤) flea
蛤乸 (青蛙) frog
蝨乸 (蝨子) louse
豬乸 (母豬) sow
貓乸 (母貓) female cat
鴨乸 (母鴨) female duck
雞乸 (母雞) hen

【事】 si⁶ matter

事不宜遲 it permits no delay; one must lose no time in doing sth; the matter brooks no delay; the matter should not be delayed; there is not a moment to lose; there should be no delay; this matter must not be delayed

事不關己，己不勞心 mind one's own business
事頭 (老闆) boss
事出有因 a thing has its cause; everything has its seed; it is by no means accidental; not devoid of truth; there is a reason for it; there is a good cause for it; there is no smoke without fire; this happens not without reason; where there's smoke there's fire
事件 matter
　　緊急事件 emergency
事因 (因為) as a result of; because (of); by; by dint of; by reason of; by right of; by virtue of; due to; for; from; in; in consequence of; in consideration of; in default of; in right of; in that; in the absence of; in view of; in virtue of; inasmuch as; of; on; on account of; on the grounds of/that; on the score of; out of; over; owing to; seeing that; since; thanks to; that; through; what with; with
事在人為 where there is a will, there is a way
事事 everything
　　事事如意 every success; everything answers; everything comes off satisfactorily; everything falls into one's lap
　　無所事事 at loose ends; be engaged in nothing; be occupied with nothing; do nothing; fool about/around; goof (off); hang about/around; have nothing to do; idle about/along/away one's time; kick one's heels; loaf; lost and bewildered; mess about/around; moon about/around; not to do a hand's turn; not to do a stitch of work; not to lift a hand; play about in a foolish way; twiddle/twirl one's thumbs; vegetate
事後孔明 be wise after an event
事急馬行田 (危急關頭不按常規辦事) use exceptional measures in urgent situations
事故 accident; malfunction; mishap; troublesome incident
　　一單事故 (一宗事故) an accident
事業 career
事幹 (事情) affair; event; incident; matter; thing
　　一單事幹 (一件事) a matter
　　冇事幹 (沒事可做) have nothing to do
　　有事幹 (有事做) have sth to do
事態 situation; state of affairs
　　事態嚴重 the situation is serious
事實 fact
　　事實上 in fact
　　事實勝於雄辯 (literally) facts are more eloquent than words; facts are stronger than words/arguments; facts speak louder than words; the effect speaks, the tongue needs not
　　不顧事實 disregard facts; fly in the face of the facts; have no regard for the truth; ignore the facts

面對事實 face up to the facts

諸多事實 a lot of excuses

隱瞞事實 hide facts

事頭（老板／老闆／東主）boss; employer; proprietor

事頭婆（女店主／老板／老闆娘）female boss; lady boss; proprietress

事關（因為）after; as; as a result of; at; because; because of; by; by dint of; by reason of; by right of; by virtue of; due to; failing; for; from; in; in consequence of; in consideration of; in default of; in right of; in that; in the absence of; in view of; in virtue of; inasmuch as; of; on; on account of; on the ground of; on the ground that; on the score of; out of; over; owing to; seeing that; since; thanks to; that; through; wanting; what with; with

一件事 a matter

人事 relationship

乜嘢事（甚麼事）what is the matter

又關我事（關我甚麼事）has this anything to do with me

大件事（大事）a big event

公事 business; work that you do as part of your job

冇本事（沒本事）of no ability

冇事（沒本事）it's alright/all right

世事 affairs of human life; affairs of the world

以前嘅事（以前的事）things of the past

出事 ① cause the accident ② cause the problem

出嚟做事（出來工作）be working

本事 ability; be capable

民事 civil

生事 make trouble

刑事 criminal; penal

同事 colleague

多事 nosy

好人事（友善／和藹可親）affable; helpful; kind-hearted

年事 age

有本事 capable

有事 there's trouble

有錢佬話事（有錢能使鬼推磨）money talks

自己最知自己事 every person knows himself best; one knows best what one's doing

利事（紅包）red pocket

快人（直爽之人）person who is frank by nature; straightforward man

秀才不出門／全知天下事 a scholar does not step outside his gate, yet he knows all the happenings under the sun; a scholar, without going out, can know the affairs in the world; without going outdoors, the scholar knows all affairs of the world

見機行事 act according to circumstances; act as circumstances dictate/the occasion demands; act on seeing an opportunity; adapt oneself to circumstances; do as one sees fit; play sth/it by ear; see one's chance and act; use one's own judgment and do what one deemed best

身後事 funeral

例行公事 a matter of form; a matter of routine; a prescribed course of action; a regular course of official duties; mere formality; perform the routine; regular procedure; routine business; routine work

往事 history; past events; the past; things that have come to past

怕事 afraid of getting into trouble

兩公婆扒艇／兩公婆扒搖櫓──你有你事（各顧各）beat gongs or sell sweets – each has their own line of business

兩回事 another matter; two different things

明人不做暗事 an honest person does not do anything underhand

炊事 kitchen work

故事 story

唔話得事（作不了主）do not have any say

唔關你事（不關你的事）mind your own business

唔關我事（不關我的事）it's got nothing to do with me; it's not my business; that's nothing to do with me

唔關事（無關）has nothing to do with; not sb's concern; no relationship with; sb is unconcerned about sth

做事 work

從事 about; be bound up in; be engaged in; busy with; be occupied in/with; devote oneself to; go in for; occupy oneself with; work on; take up

清官難審家庭事 outsiders find it hard to understand the cause of a family quarrel

累事 ruin sth

斯事（這件事）this matter

無事（沒事）① nothing ② alright/all right

無所事事 at loose ends; be engaged in nothing; be occupied with nothing; do nothing; fool about/around; goof (off); hang about/around; have nothing to do; idle about/along/away one's time; kick one's heels; loaf; lost and bewildered; mess about/around; moon about/around; not to do a hand's turn; not to do a stitch of work; not to lift a hand; play about in a foolish way; twiddle/twirl one's thumbs; vegetate

無情白事／無端白事（無緣無故）without reason or cause

費事 save the trouble; too lazy to do sth; troublesome

喪事 funeral

閒事 unimportant matter

搞事 / 攪事 (製造麻煩) cause trouble

萬事 all things

董事 director

發生乜嘢事 (發生甚麼事) what's going on

照老規矩辦事 do things in the same old way

話事 (作主) be in charge

話晒事 (大權在握) wield the sceptre

話得事 (作得了主) have the say

瑣事 trivial matters

廢事 (浪費時間) a waste of time

諸事 nosy; poke one's nose into; pry into; meddle in other's affairs

領事 consul

憑良心做事 act according to conscience; obey what conscience dictates

憾事 a matter for regret; regrettable thing

懂事 intelligent; reasonable; sensible

辦身後事 arrange the funeral

賽事 compete in a contest; competition; contest; event of competition; have a race; match

礙事 ① hindrance; in the way; keep under sb's feet; obstacle; problem ② matter; of consequence; serious

關你乜事 (關你甚麼事) mind your own business

搞 / 攪事 (製造麻煩) cause trouble; make trouble

【亞】 aa³ ① runner-up; second ② Asia ③ prefix to names

亞姐 tea lady; trolley lady

亞保亞勝 (阿貓阿狗) every Tom, Dick, and Harry

亞洲 Asia

亞茂整餅 —— 有個樣整個樣 (護國寺買駱駝 —— 沒那事 (市)) try to be different from others

亞軍 runner-up; second place

亞崩叫狗 —— 越叫越走 (肉包子打狗 —— 一去不回頭) be unable to restrain sb

亞崩養狗 —— 轉性 have a change of nature

亞崩劏羊 —— 咩都冇得咩 be forced to keep silence; hold one's tongue

亞單睇榜 —— 一眼睇晒 see with half an eye

亞超着褲 —— 焗住 be forced to do sth

亞駝行路 —— 舂舂地 take a mean course

亞駝賣蝦米 —— 大家都唔掂 all play in hard luck

亞聾送殯 —— 唔聽枝死人笛 (老虎推磨 —— 不吃這一套) turn a deaf ear to sb

亞聾燒炮仗 —— 散晒 (聾子放炮仗 —— 散了) meet with a failure

亞蘭賣豬 —— 一千唔賣，賣八百 bargain away sth; be forced to devalue sth

亞蘭嫁亞瑞 —— 大家累鬥累 drag in one another

【享】 hoeng² enjoy

享用 enjoy; enjoy the use of

享受 enjoy

享福 enjoy a happy life; have a blessing; live in ease and comfort

　　有福同享，有禍同當 for better or for worse; go through thick and thin together; happiness and joy we shall share in common and loyally help each other in suffering; share bliss and misfortune together; share happiness as well as trouble; share joys and sorrows; share weal and woe; stick together through thick and thin; we will cast our lot together, all or none

享樂 indulge in creature comforts; lead a life of pleasure

享譽 enjoy a reputation

　　享譽國際 of international stature

有錢冇命享 have a lot of money but no life in which to spend it

【京】 ging¹ capital

京胡 Beijing opera fiddle

京劇 Beijing opera

北京 Beijing; Peking

【佳】 gaai¹ good

佳人 beautiful woman

佳句 beautiful lines in a poem; well-turned phrases

佳音 good tidings

　　報佳音 proclaim good tidings

佳偶 a happily married couple

　　佳偶天成 a good match as if made in heaven; a happy couple united by heaven; the match is ordained by fate

佳期 ① nuptial day; wedding day ② lovers' rendezvous

佳節 festival; happy festival time

佳話 a much told tale; a story on everybody's lips

佳境 the most enjoyable stages

　　漸入佳境 be getting better; be improving; from bad to good conditions; grow better; turn out for the best

佳餚 delicacies

　　佳餚美酒 excellent wine and delicious dishes; good food and excellent wine

佳麗 ① beautiful; good ② beautiful woman; beauty

佳釀 good wine

　　佳釀美餚 good wine and delicacies; vintage wine and choice food

【佻】tiu¹ frivolous

佻巧 frivolous and tricky

佻脫 frivolous; frivolous and careless; undisciplined

佻薄 frivolous; not dignified

輕佻 frivolous

【使】sai² ① instruct ② (用) use ③ spend ④ need

使人（使喚人）order people about

使乜（不用 / 用不着）need not; why is it necessary to

　使乜講（不用說）as a matter of course; go without saying; needless to say

使出 exert; use

　使出渾身解數 bring all one's skill into play; bring forth all the talent one has; do all that one is capable of; do one's best; exert oneself to the utmost to; use all one's skill

使唔使（要不要）do we need to

使得（不錯 / 好 / 棒）effective

　真使得（真行）good; wonderful

使橫手（使出不光彩的手段）accomplish sth by underhand methods; use dirty methods

使錢（花錢）spend money

　先使未來錢（透支）have one's corn in the blade; spend money one has not yet earned; spend money that has yet to be earned

　好使錢（好花錢 / 愛花錢）fond of spending money

　使太多錢（花太多錢）spend too much money

使頸（使性子 / 賭氣）fly into a temper; get angry; get in a rage; in a fit of pique; lose one's temper

大使（揮金如土 / 好花錢）big-spending

牙齒當金使（信守承諾）always true in word and resolute in deed; as good as one's words; keep one's promise; keep one's word

因住錢使（量入為出）don't overspend

行使 exercise

見使（耐用）durable; withstand wear and tear

促使 impel; lead on to; precipitate; spur; urge

唔使（不用）no need to; not necessary to

唔等使（用不着）of no use; useless

唆使 abet; incite; instigate

啱使（實用）convenient to use; fit for use; work well

堪使（耐用）durable; withstand wear and tear

等錢使 in need of money

慳住嚟使（小心使用 / 節約用錢）spend with care; use with care

擇使（不好用）① not easy to use ② troublesome ③ difficult to carry out; put one to inconvenience

【使】si³ ambassador

使命 mission

使者 guard

　護花使者 bodyguard of a lady

使節 diplomatic envoy; envoy; legate

天使 angel

白衣天使 nurse

【來】loi⁴ come

來也沖沖，去也沖沖 flush when you come and flush when you go

來日 ① coming days; days ahead; days to come; time ahead ② tomorrow

　來日方長 have a long future before one; many a day will come yet; there will be a time for that; there will be ample time; there will be plenty of time

來由（原因 / 根據）reason

來回 ① to and fro ② make a return jouney; make a round trip

　來回飛（來回票）return ticket

來者 comer; those who come

　來者不拒 all is fish that comes to his net; all are welcome, none will be turned away; all comers are welcome; keep open door; keep open house; no comer is rejected; refuse nobody; refuse nobody's request; whoever comes will be welcome

　來者不善，善者不來 he could not have come with good intentions; he that fears the gallows shall never be a good thief; he who has come, come with ill intent, certainly not on virtue bent; he who has come is surely strong or he'd never come along; the one who is coming surely has bad intentions; with good intent he would not come

來得切（來得及）can make it; in time

來源 ① origin; source ② originate; stem from

來路 imported

　來路貨 / 嘢（進口貨 / 舶來品）imported goods

來賓 guest; visitor

來頭 powerful back-up

　大有來頭 have powerful backing; very influential socially

　好有來頭 with a powerful back-up

來臨 advent; arrive; approach; at hand; come; nigh; onset

匆匆而來 come in great haste

未來 future

向來 all along; consistently

老來 in one's old age

到頭來 at last; at the end of the day; end up in; finally; in the end; result in

往來 ① back and forth; come and go; go and return; to and fro ② contact; dealings; intercourse

近來 recently

美好未來 glorious future

素來 all along; always; up to the present

鬥起來 piece together

原來 actually; in fact; originally

從來 from the beginning

捲土重來 have a come-back

搰出來 (拉出來) pull out

貿易往來 commercial intercourse; trade contacts

連接起來 join together

適過來 (跨過來) stride over

慕名而來 come to sb because one admires his reputation

歷來 all along; always; constantly; from the old days; since a long time ago

遲來 come late

聯合起來 unite

【侈】 ci² wasteful

侈談 prate about; prattle about; talk glibly about

奢侈 luxurious

【例】 lai⁶ ① example ② conventional

例子 case; example; instance

例外 exception

例如 for example; for instance; such as

例行 routine

例行公事 a matter of form; a matter of routine; a prescribed course of action; a regular course of official duties; mere formality; perform the routine; regular procedure; routine business; routine work

例牌 ① regular size of dish ② (常例／常規) as usual

比例 proportion

先例 precedent

按比例 pro-rata basis

破例 break a rule; make an exception; stretch a point; stretch the rules; waive a rule

規例 regulation; rule

循例 according to convention

違例 break rules and regulations

【侍】 si⁶ serve

侍仔 (服務員) waiter

侍奉 attend on; serve; wait upon

侍候 attend upon; look after; serve; wait upon

侍應 (服務員) ① waiter ② waitress

　侍應生 (服務員) waiter

　女侍應 (女服務員) waitress

妾侍 concubine

【供】 gung¹ (給) give

供水 water supply

　供水管 water pipe

　供水系統 waterworks

供求 supply and demand

　供求關係 supply and demand relationship

　求過於供 an excess of demand over supply; demand outstrips supply; the demand exceeds the supply

　供不應求 demand exceeds supply; supply fails to meet the demand; supply falls short of demand; the demand outstrips the supply; the supply can hardly keep pace with the demand; the supply does not meet the demand; the supply is not adequate to the demand; the supply is unable to meet the demand

　供過於求 an excess of supply over demand; in excess of demand; pile up in excess of requirement; the supply exceeds the demand; the supply outstrips the demand

供樓 (分期付款供樓房) mortgage

供應 supply

口供 evidence; statement; verbal statement

作供 act as a witness in court; bear witness; give evidence; testify

求過於供 an excess of demand over supply; demand outstrips supply; the demand exceeds the supply

招供 confess

落口供 (錄取口供) take deposition

證供 evidence; proof; testimony; witness

【依】 ji¹ depend on

依牙鬆槓 (做出騷擾的行為) clench one's teeth

依依哦哦 (吞吞吐吐地) hem/hum and haw; hesitate in speech; mince words; mutter and mumble; runes and prism; say hesitantly; speak in a halting way; speak of things with scrule speak with reservation; stumble over one's words; tick over

依法 according to law; by operation of law; in conformity with legal provisions

依郁 (動作／動靜) action

依家 (現在) at once; at present; at the moment; for the moment; immediately; now; nowadays; of the moment;

presently; right now

依挹（依偎）amorous behaviour
　　依依挹挹（依偎）amorous behaviour

依時 / 依時依候（按時）on schedule; on time; punctual
　　依時不誤（準時不誤）on time

依傍（依靠）rely on

依靠 depend on; rely on
　　無依無靠 all alone in the world; be left forlorn and without a protector; completely helpless; have no one to depend on; have no one to turn to; have nothing to depend on; helpless; high and dry; with no one to rely on; with no one to turn to; with nothing to support one

依據 ① according to; in the light of; judging by; on the basis of ② basis; foundation

依賴 dependence; dependency; dependent on; rely on

依舊 as before; as usual; in the usual manner; in the usual way; still

唇齒相依 as close as lips and teeth; as close to each other as lips to teeth; as close to each other as the lips are to the teeth; as closely related as the lips and the teeth; as interdependent as lips and teeth; closely related and mutually dependent; closely related to each other like lips and teeth; interdependent; mutually depend on each other as lips and teeth

【佬】lou² ① (男人) guy; man ② vulgar person

口水佬（長篇大論的人）talkative person

土佬（鄉巴佬）boor; bumpkin; churl; country bumpkin country cousin; hayseed; hick; redneck; rustic; yokel

大佬（大哥）① elder brother ② big brother ③ boss; gang leader; triad boss

大食佬（食量大的人）big eater

大隻佬（強壯的人）big guy; hulk; muscular guy; strongly-built person

大粒佬（重要的人）big-shot; influential person; man of mark; very important person; VIP

大舊佬 / 大嚿佬（強壯的人）big man; hulk; strongly-built person

勾佬（勾引男人）pick up a man

巴士佬（巴士司機）bus driver

北佬（北方人）northerner

四眼佬（戴眼鏡的男人）a man wearing glasses; short-sighted guy

外江佬（外地人 / 外省人）people from other provinces

打鐵佬（鐵匠）ironsmith

白頭佬（白頭鴨 / 灰椋鳥）Chinese bulbul; grey starling

仵作佬（以殮葬為業的人）undertaker

光棍佬（單身漢）trickster

光頭佬（光頭男人）bald man

地盤佬（建築地盤工人）construction worker

好佬怕爛佬（富的怕窮的，窮的怕橫的，橫的怕不要命的）a pigeon makes no friends with a hawk

收買佬（收買破爛的）junk collector

有錢佬（富翁）rich man

江湖大佬（黑幫老大）underworld big boss

快佬（文件夾）file

扮闊佬（充豪氣）ostentatious and extravagant; parade one's wealth

考車牌肥佬（考駕照不及格）failed the driving test

豆皮佬（臉上留有疤痕的麻子）pockmarked-faced man

走佬（潛逃）be on the run

咕喱佬（苦力）coolie

和事佬（中間人）mediator; peace-maker

咖啡佬（交通督導員）older male parking warden

垃圾佬（撿破爛兒的）garbage collector; rubbish collector

拐子佬（人口販子）abductor

拖頭佬（駕駛集裝箱車的司機）container trucker driver

泥水佬（泥水匠）bricklayer; mason; plasterer; tiler

的士佬（的士司機）taxi-driver

盲佬（瞎子）blind person

肥佬 ①（胖子）fat guy; fat man ②（不及格）fail in an examination or a test

金魚佬（好色鬼）sleazy man

南嘸佬（道士）Daoist master

契家佬（情夫）adulterer; illicit male lover; male cohabitant; secret husband

契細佬（乾弟弟）adoptive younger brother

客家佬（客家人）hakka

柯佬（口語 / 口試）oral

神經佬（瘋子）crazy man; madman; mentally ill person

軍佬（軍人）armyman; serviceman; soldier

風水佬（風水師）geomancer

飛髮佬（理髮師）barber; hairdresser

差佬（警察）cop; policeman

耕田佬（農夫）farmer

衰佬（壞男人）bad guy

財主佬（財主）rich man

高佬（高大的人）tall guy; tall person

鬥木佬（木工 / 木匠）carpenter

鬼佬（外國人）foreigner; Western guy; Westerner; white male

啞佬（啞巴）dumb man

堂細佬（堂弟）first cousin; younger male cousin

崩嘴佬（患有兔唇的人）cleft-lip man

掃街佬 (清道夫) scavenger; street-cleaner
教書佬 (老師) teacher
細佬 ① (小孩) kid ② (弟弟) younger brother
蛋家佬 (漁民) fisherman
麻甩佬 (外表粗獷／行為猥褻粗魯的男人) dirty dog; mean fellow public nuisance; villain
喃嘸佬 ① (道士) Daoist monk ② (法師) witch
單眼佬 (獨眼的人) one-eyed person
㗎佬 (日本人) Japanese man
報紙佬 (報販子) news vendor
番鬼佬 (外國人) foreigner; Westerner
痘皮佬 (臉上留有疤痕的麻子) pockmark-faced man
睇相佬 (相士) fortune teller
街市佬 (菜市場的檔販) food market hawker
補鞋佬 (補鞋匠) cobbler; shoemaker; shoe repairer
貴利佬 (放高利貸的人) loan-shark
跛手佬 (獨臂的人) arm-disabled person
跛腳佬 (瘸子) lame man
傻佬 (傻子) follish man
搭棚佬 (搭建棚架的工人) scalfolding builder
矮佬 (矮小的人) short fellow; short guy; short man
裝闊佬 (裝闊綽的人) ostentatious and extravagant; parade one's wealth
賊佬 (小偷) thief
鄉下佬 (鄉巴佬) boor; churl; country bumpkin; country cousin; country folk; country-born; farming folk; hayseed; hick; redneck; yokel
鄉巴佬 boor; churl; country bumpkin; country cousin; country folk; country-born; farming folk; hayseed; hick; redneck; yokel
嘀打佬 (吹鼓手) trumpeters and drummers
寡佬 (單身漢) bachelor; middle-aged bachelor
漏口佬 (結巴) stammerer; stutterer
賓佬 (菲律賓人) Filipino guy
影相佬 (攝影師) photographer
撈鬆佬 (北方人) northerner
賤格佬 (下流的人) bad character; scum
醉酒佬 (醉漢) alcoholic; drunk
駝背佬 (駝子) humpback
機佬 (攝影師) cameraman
豬肉佬 (屠夫) butcher
戲子佬 (演員) actor
虧佬 (陽痿的人) impotent man
講古佬 (說書人) storyteller
闊佬 ① (闊綽) generous with money; liberal with money ② (闊綽的人) generous man
擺闊佬 (裝闊綽的人) make a parade of one's wealth
懶佬 (懶惰的人) idler; lazy man; lazybone; sluggard
懵居佬 (傻子) stupid man

鬍鬚佬 (有鬍鬚的人) a man with a beard
鹹濕佬 (好色的人) lecherous man
爛酒佬 (酒鬼) drunkard; inebriate; sot
羅佬 a criminal fleeing the police
聾佬 (失聰的人) deaf man
黐線佬 (瘋子) crazy guy; crazy man; madman
變態佬 (性變態者) sexual pervert
癲佬 (瘋子) crazy man; madman
躝闊佬 (裝闊綽) ostentatious and extravagant; parade one's wealth
戇居佬 (傻子) blockhead; fool; idiot; simpleton

【併】bing³ combine

併合 integrate; unite
併吞 annex and absorb; swallow up entirely
併肩 shoulder to shoulder
併發 occur at the same time

合併 merger

【侄】zat⁶ nephew

侄女 (侄女兒) brother's daughter; nephew
侄仔 (侄子) brother's son; nephew
侄孫 brother's grandson

【兒】ji⁴ child

兒女 children; sons and daughters
　兒女成行 sons and daughters forming a row — have many children
　兒女私情 love affair between a man and a woman
　兒女情長 be immersed in love; love between a man and a woman is long; the lasting affection of boys and girls
　　生兒育女 give birth to children and raise them; multiply the earth; raise children
　　無兒無女 childless; have neither sons nor daughters
兒科 paediatrics
兒孫 descendants; posterity
　兒孫滿堂 have children and grandchildren
兒甥女 (外甥女兒) niece
兒甥仔 ① (外甥) nephew ② (外孫) daughter's son
兒童 children; kids
　兒童節 Children's Day
兒嬉 ① (不扎實／不牢靠) unreliable ② (不認真) not serious

乞兒 (乞丐) beggar
幼兒 child; infant; nestling
妻兒 one's parents, wife and children; the whole family; wife and children

育兒 child rearing

初歸心抱，落地孩兒（教育越早越好）bend a tree while it is still young

胎兒 fetus; embryo; unborn baby

淪為乞兒（淪為乞丐）be reduced to beggary; become a beggar

健兒 player

寧生敗家仔，莫生蠢鈍兒 one would rather have a prodigal son than a stupid one

模特兒 model

樹大有枯枝，族大有乞兒（害羣之馬）there's a black sheep in every fold

嬰兒 baby

寵兒 blue-eyed boy; darling; fair-haired boy; favourite; minion

【兔】tou³（兔子）rabbit

兔仔（兔子）rabbit
　　一隻兔仔（一隻兔子）a rabbit

兔年 Year of the Rabbit

兔嘴（兔唇／缺唇／崩嘴／裂嘴／豁嘴／豁嘴兒）harelipped person

狡兔 wily hare

踢死兔（男士的晚禮服）tuxedo

【兩】loeng⁵ ① two ② tael

兩三 a couple
　　兩三日 a couple of days
　　兩三年 a couple of years

兩公婆（夫婦）husband and wife
　　兩公婆搖櫓——你有你事（敲鑼賣糖——各幹一行）beat gongs or selling sweets – each has their own line of business

兩仔嬤（母子兩人／娘兒）mother and son

兩回事 another matter; two different things

兩次 twice

兩面 both aspects; both sides; double; dual; two sides
　　兩面手法 double-faced tactics
　　兩面光 please both parties
　　兩面夾攻 make a pincer attack
　　兩面派 double dealing
　　兩面黃 golden pancake

兩個 two
　　兩個兩個 by twos; in pairs

兩家（兩人／雙方）both sides

兩梳蕉（兩手空空）visit sb without bringing a gift

兩造（兩季）two crops a year

兩番（of mahjong）two times

兩睇喇（兩説兒）it depends

兩腳一伸（死）death

兩頭 both ends
　　兩頭唔到岸（進退兩難）in a situation where whichever way one turns one will lose out; neither sink nor swim in the middle of the sea; on the horns of a dilemma
　　兩頭唔受中間受（兩邊推讓，自認倒楣）feather one's nest
　　兩頭蛇（兩面派）fence-rider; fence-sitter; servant of two masters; tale teller
　　兩頭騰（非常忙碌）be extremely busy

兩點（二時正）two o'clock
　　兩點半（二時半）half past two

兩騎牛（騎牆）double dealer; sit on the fence

兩邊 both directions; both parties; both places; both sides
　　兩邊走 go back and forth between two places

一兩（一両）one tael

冇斤兩（沒能耐）have no skill in sth

斤兩 ① catty and tael ②（能耐）ability

半斤八兩 as broad as it is long; as long as it is broad; fifty-fifty; half a pound of one and eight ounces of the other; much of a muchness; not much to choose between the two; nothing to choose between the two; six of one and half a dozen of the other; tweedledum and tweedledee; well-match in ability

有斤兩（有能耐）capable

此地無銀三百兩 reveal one's secret unintentionally

你有半斤，我有八兩 six of one and half a dozen of the other

炸兩 rice noodle roll stuffed with deep-fried dough

銀兩 money

雞春摸過輕四兩（靠不住）do damage to whatever sb handles

【其】kei⁴ such

其他 other

其次 ① besides; next; secondly; the next in order; then ② next in importance; of minor importance; secondary
　　退而求其次 be left with nothing better than the second choice; have no alternative but to give up one's preference; have to be content with the second best; seek what is less attractive than one's original objective; the next best thing

其表 appearance of sth
　　虛有其表 a penny plain and twopence coloured; appear better than it is; deceptively handsome; good in appearance; good looks without substantial ability; impressive only in appearance; look impressive but lack real worth; many a fine dish has nothing

on it; merely ornamental without solidity; one's
qualifications are superficial

其實 in fact; in reality

其貌不揚 far from beautiful; far from handsome; far
from pretty; hard-feathered; hard-visaged; ill-favoured;
ill-looking; ill-shaped; not to be much to look at; of
undistinguished appearance; one's appearance is
ungainly; one's face is ugly; physically unattractive; ugly
in appearance

尤其 especially

求其 / 求求其其（隨便 / 隨隨便便）do things casually; in a
slapdash manner; sloppy

【具】geoi⁶ ① tool; ware ② goods

具有 be provided with; have; possess

具備 be equipped with; be provided with; have; possess

具體 concrete; particular; specific

一件玩具 a toy

一副工具 a set of tools

文具 stationary

皮具 leather goods

用具 tool

交通工具 transportation

炊具 cooking utensils; cookware; kitchenware

玩具 plaything; toy

茶具 tea set

面具 mask

食具 tableware

茗具 tea set

釣具 fishng tackle

廚具 kitchenware

餐具 tableware

【典】din² ① canon ② allusion ③ pawn ④ take charge of

典型 archetype; example; model; type; typical

典故 allusion; literary quotation

典雅 elegant; refined

典當 hock; impawn; mortgage; pawn

典範 epitome; example; model; nonesuch; paradigm
樹立典範 set an example for

典禮 ceremony
主持典禮 host a ceremony

典籍 ancient books and records

一本字典 a dictionary

古典 ① classical ② classical allusions

字 / 詞典 dictionary

盛典 big ceremony; grand ceremony; grand occasion

【凭】pang⁴（靠）rely on

凭埋牆（靠着牆）lean on a wall

【刮】gwaat³ scrape

刮除 strike off

刮損皮（擦傷皮膚）hurt one's skin with scraping

刮錢（斂財）obtain money by unfair or illegal means

刮攏 ①（搜刮）reap huge profits ②（刮地皮）batten on
people's properties

【到】dou³ reach

到手 come to one's hands; in one's hands; in one's
possession

到此 so far
到此一遊 have visited this place
到此為止 leave it at that; let's call it a day; rest here; so
much for; that's all for

到家 be excelled in

到埗（到達 / 抵達）arrive at; arrive in

到時 by that time
到期時（到時候）in due time; when the time comes

到處 all about; all over; all over the place; all over the shop;
all over the show; all round; at all places; everywhere;
from place to place; here, there and everywhere; here
and there; high and low; hither and thither; in all
directions; in every place; in every quarter; on all hands;
on all sides; on everyside; on every hand; right and left;
up hill and down dale
到處楊梅一樣花 same trees at all places bear the same
fruit

到喉唔到肺（不滿足）be half satisfied; insufficient; not
enough to satisfy one's appetite; unsatisfying

到期 at maturity; become due; due; expire; fall due; mature
到期日 ① expiry date ② maturity date

到達 arrive; reach
平安到達 arrive safely

到頭來 at last; at the end of the day; end up in; finally; in
the end; result in

一講曹操，曹操就到 talk of the devil and he will appear

大丈夫講得出做得到（一言九鼎）a real man does what he
says

冇料到（沒用）useless

冇嘢到（沒有好處）have no benefit

打到 beat sb until

因住遲到（別遲到）make sure you're on time

早到 arrive ahead of time; arrive early

有料到（有本事）be really something

老到（有經驗）experienced; seasoned

至到…（直至…）as to...

收到 ① receive ② got it

考到 passed an examination

周到（面面俱到）① considerate ② thorough

初嚟步到（初來）newly on board

知道 know

咸起幡竿有鬼到 people will come as soon as they know the location

捉到 be caught

衰到（極壞）extremely bad

笑到（笑成）laugh until

追到 catch up with

做到 work until...

執到（幸運）achieve sth desirable

被人捉到 be caught

報到 ① report for duty ② register ③ check in

睇到（看到）see

睇唔到（看不到）invisible

搵到（找到）have found; have obtained; succeed in finding

搵唔到（找不到）cannot find; fail to find sth

新鮮運到 deliver recently

想唔到（想不到）unexpectedly

想得周到 really considerate

遇到 come across

達到 achieve; amount to; attain; reach; to the amount of

輪到 be one's turn; in one's turn

聞到 smell

撞到 bump into; chance upon; come across; cross sb's path; meet unexpectedly; meet with; run across; run into

遲到 late

遲到好過冇到（遲到總比不到好）rather late than never

遲晒大到（遲很多）very late in arriving

講到（提及）as for

講到做到（說到做到）do what one says

賺到 make a profit

聽到 hear

【制】zai³ ①（限制）limit ②（肯／願意）agree; willing

制止 check; curb; face down; prevent; put an end to; stop

制水（限水）water rationing

制定 draft; draw up; enact; establish; formulate; institute; lay down; set up; work out

制宜 make measures to suit different conditions

因人制宜 suit measures to different people; (literally) treatment chosen according to the variability of physique of an individual

因地制宜 act according to the circumstances; act in accordance with the circumstances; adapt to local conditions; adopt measures suiting local conditions; do sth in line with local conditions; do the right thing at the right place; do what is appropriate according to the regional circumstances; do what is suitable to the environment; hinge on local conditions; suit measures to local conditions; take appropriate measures in accordance with local conditions; take measures suited to local conditions

因事／時制宜 act according to the circumstances/the time; act in accordance with the times; circumstances alter cases; do the right thing at the right time; do what is appropriate according to the circumstances; do what is suitable to the occasion; in a manner suitable to the time; suit measures to circumstances; take measures suitable to the time

制服（工作服）uniform
　　着制服（穿工作服）wear a uniform

制度 institution; system

制唔制 ①（幹不幹）is it a deal; take it or not ②（願不願意）willing or not

制唔過（不值得做／划不來）it does not pay; not worth it
制得過（划得來／值得幹）it is worth doing sth; worthwhile

制裁 punish; sanction

制衡 check and balance

三級制 three-tier system

自我克制 self-control

克制 exercise restraint; restrain

抑制 check; containment; control; curb; inhibition; rejection; repress; restrain; suppression

肯制 willing

帝制 autocratic monarchy; imperial system; monarchy

限制 restrict

唔制／唔肯制（不願意）not willing to do sth

控制 control

幾大都唔制（說甚麼也不願意）won't do it whatever you say

遏制 suppress

幣制 currency system

轉讓限制 alienation restrictions

AA 制（各付各的賬）go Dutch

【制】dzai³（值）worth

制唔過（划不來／不值得／犯不着）not worthwhile

制得過（划得來／合算／犯得着）worthwhile

咪制（不要這樣做）don't do it
唔制（不會這樣做）not do it; won't do it

【刷】caat³ ① eat ② （刷子）brush

刷一餐（大吃一頓）have a square meal
刷牙 brush one's teeth
刷新 ① freshen; refurbish; renovate ② break

一枝／個牙刷 a toothbrush
牙刷 toothbrush
印刷 printing
衫刷 clothes brush

【刺】ci³ prick

刺耳 ear-piercing; grating on the ear; harsh; irritating to the ear; jarring; unpleasant to the ear
刺骨 biting; cut to the bones; piercing; pierce to the bones
刺探 detect; make roundabout inquiries; make secret inquiries; pry; spy
刺眼 ① dazzling ② offending to the eye; unpleasant to look at
刺激 exciting
刺繡 embroidery

肉刺 be reluctant to spend
芒刺 prickle
頭刺（刺）headache; have a bit of headache
離行離刺（兩者並排但相距很遠）wide of the mark

【刻】hak¹ carve

刻不容緩 admit of no delay; brook no delay; cannot be delayed even a moment; demand immediate attention; must not lose a minute; no time to lose; not a moment to be lost; of great urgency; permit of no delay; there is no time to be lost; there is no time to lose; there is not a moment to be lost; urgent
刻字 carve characters on a seal
刻板 ① cut blocks for printing ② inflexible; mechanical; stiff
刻苦 ① assiduous; hardworking; painstaking ② simple and frugal
　刻苦耐勞 industriousness and stamina; work hard without complaint
刻骨 bone-deep; deep-rooted; deeply ingrained
刻劃 depict; describe; portray
刻意 painstakingly; sedulously
刻薄 acerbity; harsh; mean; unkind

立刻 as soon as; as quick as a flash; at once; at one stroke; at the drop of a hat; before one could say Jack Johnson; before you found where you are; directly; first thing off the bat; here and now; immediately; in a brace of shakes; in a crack; in a flash; in a jiffy; in a minute; in a moment; in no time; just now; lose no time in; off hand; on the moment; on the nail; out of hand; promptly; pronto; right away; right now; right off the bat; straight away; straight off; thereupon; this instant; this moment; without a moment's delay; without delay; without hesitation; without loss of time; without thinking much longer
即刻（立刻）as soon as; as quick as a flash; at once; at one stroke; at the drop of a hat; before you found where you are; directly; first thing off he bat; here and now; immediately; in a brace of shakes; in a crack; in a flash; in a jiffy; in a minute; in a moment; in no time; just now; lose no time in...; off hand; on the moment; on the nail; out of hand; promptly; pronto; right away; right now; right off the bat; straight away; straight off; this instant; this moment; without a moment's delay; without delay; without hesitation; without loss of time; without thinking much longer
雕刻 carve; engrave

【刮】gat⁷ （扎）prick

刮個窿（扎個眼兒）prick a hole
刮嚹腳（扎腳了）prick the foot

【卒】zeot¹ ① final ② （Chinese chess） soldier

卒之（終於／最終）at last; end in; eventually; finally; in the end; result in; ultimately
卒仔 ① （跟隨者）follower ② （小人物）small potato

烏卒卒 ① （黑乎乎）pitch black ② （目中無人）entirely ignorant
無名小卒 mere nobody
織卒（蟋蟀）cricket

【協】hip⁶ assist

協力 exert together; in cooperation with; join in a common effort; unite efforts; work in concert
　同心協力 all of one mind; cooperate with one heart; make concerted efforts; of one heart; unit together in a common effort; with one heart; work as one man; work in full cooperation and with unity of purpose
協助 assist; give assistance; help; help mutually; provide help

大力協助 provide great help

協定 agreement
　　正式協定 formal agreement

協商 bargaining; consult; consult with each other; discuss; negotiate; talk things over

協會 association; institute; society

協調 adjust; bring about full coordination; bring into line; bring to harmony; cohere with; concert; coordinate; harmonize; integrate

協議 ① agree on ② deal; treaty ③ discuss; negotiate

妥協 compromise

【卦】gwaa³ divinatory symbols

八卦（三八／好事／好管閒事／愛打探人家秘密／饒舌）gossipy; nosy

中途變卦（中途改變主意）change one's mind in middle course

占卦 divination; divine by the Eight Diagrams; tell by divination

唔好咁八卦（不要好管閒事）don't be so nosy

諸事八卦（好管閒事）nosy

變卦（改變主意）break an agreement; change one's mind; go back on one's words; retract one's promise

【卷】gyun² examination paper; test paper

卷軸 scroll

一碟春卷 a plate of spring rolls

交白卷 fail to accomplish anything

芝麻卷 seet black sesame roll

春卷 spring roll

批卷 mark papers

書卷 books

海鮮卷 seafood roll

債卷 bond

腐皮卷 bean curd sheet roll

鮮竹卷 bean curd roll

證卷 securities

【卸】se³ unload

卸下 disboard; unsnatch

卸粧 remove make-up and ornaments

卸責 shirk the responsibility

卸膊（擺挑子）put the blame on sb; pass the buck; shirk responsibility

拆卸 dismantle; dismount

【叔】suk¹ ① paternal uncle; uncle; younger brothers of one's father ② younger brothers of one's husband ③ general designation for members of one's father's generation who are younger than one's father ④ decline ⑤ a surname

叔丈 one's wife's uncle

叔公 grand uncle

叔父 uncle

叔仔（小叔子）brother-in-law; one's husband's younger brother

叔母（嬸嬸）wife of one's father's younger brother

叔伯 paternal uncles

叔叔 ① uncle (younger brother of one's father) ② uncle (younger brother of one's husband)

叔姪 uncles and nephews

叔祖 granduncle; one's grandfather's younger brother

叔婆 wife of one's grandfather's younger brother

叔舅 one's mother's younger brother

叔嬸 aunt; wife of a junior uncle

叔叔 ① uncle (younger brother of one's father) ② uncle (younger brother of one's husband)

阿叔 uncle

鐸叔（吝嗇的人）miser; niggard

【取】ceoi² take

取代 displace; replace; step into sb's shoes; substitute for; supersede; supplant; take for
　　取而代之 cut out; facilitate a takeover; fill sb's bonnet; fill sb's shoes; nail drives out nail; place oneself in sb's stead; replace; replace sb; step into sb's shoes; substitute sb; supersede; supplant; take over; take sb's place; take the place of; usurp another's position

取決於 be decided by; depend on; depend upon; dependent on; dependent upon; hang on; hang upon; hinge on; it's up to; lie on; rest with ride on; turn on

取消 abandon; abolish; abrogate; annul; be cleared of; be edged out by; call off; cancel; cancellation; cross out; deprive sb of; discard; dispense with; do away with; liquidate; negate; nullify; obliterate; off; put an end to; reject; relinquish; remove; renounce; repeal; repudiate; rescind; revoke; scrap; strip of; write off

取得 achieve; acquire; assume; conquest; gain; get; obtain; win; wrest; yield

取捨 accept or refuse; accept or reject; choose; decide what to adopt and what to discard; make a choice; make one's choice; select

取締 ban; declare a ban on; clampdown; discipline; forbid; interdict; outlaw; prohibit; punish the violator; suppress

取錄（錄取）admit; enroll; recruit

吸取 absorb; assimilate; draw; drink in; suck up

咎由自取 a trouble of one's own making

備取 on the waiting list; put on reserve

提取 withdraw

棄取 be accepted or rejected; take or reject

錄取 admit; enroll; recruit

騙取 cheat sb out of sth; defraud; gain sth by fraud; swindle

竊取 grab; steal; take sth which does not lawfully belong to one; usurp

【受】 sau⁶ ① receive ② endure; suffer

受人二分四（受催於人）work as an employee
　　受人二分四，做到一條氣 one has to work hard as an employee in order to get one's pay

受人錢財，替人消災 one must be committed to complete the task for which one has been paid

受用 ① enjoy ② comfortable; feel good
　　受用不盡 benefit from sth all one's life; enjoy a benefit forever

受唔住（受不了）can't stand it

受氣 suffer wrong; take the rap

受得（受得了）bearable
　　唔受得（受不了）unbearable

受軟唔受硬（吃軟不吃硬）person who is more easily persuaded than coerced

受硬唔受軟（吃硬不吃軟）submit to sb's pressure after first turning down his gentle manners

受傷 be injured; be wounded
　　受咗傷（受了傷）injured; wounded

受溝（接受追求）get picked up

受落（受用）accept sth

切身感受 personal impressions and experience

忍受 bear

身受 ① experience personally ② accept personally; receive in person

享受 enjoy

兩頭唔受中間受（兩邊推讓，自認倒楣）feather one's nest

物質享受 material enjoyment

逆來順受 resign oneself to adversity

授受 give and accept; give and receive; grant and receive

接受 accept

貼錢買難受 get bad service; pay for troubles

樂於接受 accept sth with pleasure

感同身受 appreciate it as a personal favour; be deeply affected by ... as if one had experienced it oneself; count it as a personal favour; feel indebted as if it were received in person; I shall count it as a personal favour; I would consider it as a personal favour to me

感受 feeling

難以忍受 hard to bear

難以接受 hard to accept

難受 feel unhappy

【呢】 ni¹（這）this

呢一層（這一層/這一點/這方面）on this point

呢一輪（這一陣子/這些天）lately; recently

呢手野（這種玩意）this sort of stuff

呢世（這一生）all one's life
　　呢世人 this lifetime

呢次（這次）current; present; this time

呢位（這位）this person

呢度（這兒/這裏）here
　　喺呢度（在這兒）it's here

呢味野（這件事）this thing

呢便 ①（這邊兒）here ② this side ③ this way

呢個（這個）this
　　呢個人（這個人）this person
　　　冇呢個人（沒有這個人）there's no one by that name
　　呢個月（這個月）this month
　　呢個係乜野（這是甚麼東西）what is this

呢條友（這小子）this guy
　　呢條友仔（這小子）this guy

呢停人（這路人/這種人）this kind of people

呢啲（這些）these

呢排（近來/這一陣子/這些日子）lately; recently
　　呢一排（近來/這一陣子/這些日子）lately; recently

呢球波（這一球）this ball

呢處（這兒/這裏）here

呢單野（這件事）this thing

呢種人（這路人/這種人）this kind of people

呢舖話法（這種說法）this kind of view

呢頭（這兒/這裏）here
　　呢頭…嗰頭（這邊…那邊）on the other hand...on the other; this...that
　　呢頭食嗰頭嘔（剛剛吃完就吐了）eat and throw up; one eats and vomits
　　呢頭家（這個家）this family

呢檀野（這件事）this thing

呢籠野（這些東西）this type of thing

邊度係呢（不用客氣）don't mention it

【咗】zo² (了／已經／過) has already

十號風球除咗 (十號風球已除下) typhoon signal number ten has been taken down

十號風球落咗 (十號風球已除下) typhoon signal number ten has been taken down

冇咗 ① (流產) abortion ② (死亡／過世) dead

凹咗 (凹陷) cave in

失咗 (丟失) lose

去咗 ① (去了) has gone to ② (過世) has passed away

打爛咗 (打破了) be broken; be smashed

瓜咗 (死了) dead; die; pass away

甩咗 fall off

丟疏咗 (生疏了／荒廢了) have one's skills go rusty; out of practice

同…行埋咗 (跟…談戀愛了) have made love with sb

扻咗 erase; rub off; rub out; wipe off

有咗 (懷孕了) be pregnant

死咗 (死了) dead

行咗 (死了) dead

行開咗 (離開了一會) not here at the moment; just stepped out for a moment

屈遠咗 (走遠路了) take a long devious route

抹咗 (擦掉了) erase; rub off; rub out; wipe off

枝筆掘咗 (筆尖禿了) the pencil is blunt

肥咗 (胖了) put on weight

阿吱阿咗 (多管閒事) argue; moan; talk back; whine

門鎖壞咗 (門鎖壞了) the door lock is broken

門鐘壞咗 (門鎖壞了) the doorbell doesn't work; the doorbell is broken

雨停咗 (雨停了) the rain has stopped

為咗 (為了) for the purpose of; for the sake of; in order to

閂咗 (關上了) turn off

香咗 ① (死了) dead ② (失敗了) failure

冧咗 (倒塌／崩塌) collapse

唔見咗 (遺失了) ① lost ② mislaid

神咗 (壞了) be out of order

釘咗 (死了) dead

除咗 ① (脫掉了) take off ② (除了) besides; except

崩咗 (破裂了) cracked

得咗 (成功了) come off with flying colours; got it

掂咗 (完成了) it's settled

掉咗 (丟棄了) be thrown away

條頸梗咗 (脖子痠) stiff neck

寄失咗 (寄失了) lost in the post

焗暈咗 (悶熱得快暈了) faint due to suffocation

廁所塞咗 (馬桶塞了) the toilet is clogged

裂咗 (裂開了) come apart; split open; rend

跌咗 (遺失了) lose

跌爛咗 (跌壞了) break sth by dashing it on the ground

塗咗 (刪除了) cross out

暈咗 (暈了) faint and fall; fall in a faint; pass out; swoon

電話壞咗 (電話壞了) the telephone is out of order

溶咗 (溶了) melted

當咗 (當成) believe; consider

預咗 ① (習慣了) calculate in advance; estimate; expect ② (預留) keep; reserve; save

慣咗 (習慣了) be accustomed to

摳埋咗 (混合在一起) mix together

摺咗 (結業了) closed

滾瀉咗 (煮開了) spilt water

漏低咗 (遺漏了) left behind

漏咗 (遺漏了) miss

精歸咗 (長歪了心眼兒) clever only at ill doings

酹咗 lose

撒咗 abandon; cast away

摩打壞咗 (發動機壞了) the motor is out of order

瞓晏咗 (睡過頭了) overslept

遲咗 (遲到了) late

搣咗 (偷了) steal

擗咗 (丟棄了) throw away

橫咗 (搞砸了) screw up

醒咗 (醒了) awake

講好咗 (說好了) have come to an agreement; it's settled

鍾意咗 (愛上了) fall in love

嚇到傻咗 (嚇傻了) be completely shocked

壞咗 (壞了) break down; out of order

鏟咗 (刮掉) scrape off

黐埋咗 (黏在一起) stick together

攣咗 (彎了) curved

癱咗 (癱瘓了) be paralysed

【周】zau¹ revolve

周末 weekend
　周末快樂 have a nice weekend

周刊 weekly magazine

周身 (全身) entire body
　周身刀冇張利 (甚麼都只懂一點) jack-of-all-trades, master of none
　周身屎 ① (劣跡斑斑) notorious ② (很多麻煩) in trouble
　周身唔聚財 (渾身不自在) uneasy
　周身鬆晒 (一身輕) free-hearted
　周身蟻 (一身麻煩) make trouble

周到 ① considerate ② thorough
　想得周到 really considerate

周時 (常常／經常) always; often
　周不時 (常常／經常) always; often

周街（到處／隨處）all about; all over; all over the place; all over the shop; all over the show; all round; at all places; everywhere; from place to place; here, there and everywhere; here and there; high and low; hither and thither; in all directions; in every place; in every quarter; on all hands; on all sides; on every side; on every hand; right and left; up hill and down dale

周圍（到處）all around; everywhere
　周圍貢（到處去）go everywhere
　周圍都係（到處都是）everywhere is

每周 every week

【咎】gau³ blame
咎由自取 a trouble of one's own making
咎無可辭 cannot evade responsibility; the responsibility cannot be shirked

既往不咎 forgive somebody's past misdeeds; it is needless to blame things that are past; let bygones by bygones; let the past be forgotten; let the dead bury their dead; wipe the slate clean

【呱】gwaa¹ cry
呱呱叫 complain; make a lot of noise
呱呱嘈（呱呱叫）make a lot of noise

【味】mei⁶ taste
味道 taste
　味道好正（味道很好）the taste is superb
　冇味道（沒有味道）tasteless
　好味道 delicious; good taste; tasty; yummy
味精 monosodium glutamate (MSG)
　走味精（不加味精）no MSG
味覺 sense of taste
　味覺靈敏 have a sharp sense of taste

一味 ① always; as a rule; commonly; constantly; generally; invariably; usually; without exception ② dish ③ ingredient
口味 taste
分甘同味 share and share alike
廿四味 tea boiled with twenty-four kinds of herbs
吊味（調味）add to the taste; adjust the taste
好好味（很好吃）very tasty
好味（好吃）delicious
有女人味 feminine
有男人味 manly; masculine
有味 revert
有書卷味 have an intellectual demeanour

色香味 appearance, fragrance, and taste
走味 revert
咂滋味 savour; taste
男人味 manliness; masculinity
和味 ①（收入很好）good income ②（好吃）delicious; tasty
品味 savour; taste
津津有味 relish; with good appetite; with great interest; with gusto; with keen interest; with much unction; with relish; with zest
美味 delicious
食過翻尋味（吃過還想吃）would like to try once again
校味（調味）adjust the taste
氣味 odour
海味 ① marine products ② dried seafood
脂粉味 pansy
夠味 have the right flavour
啱口味（對口味）be to one's taste; suit one's taste
幾和味 ①（收入非常好）very good income ②（很好吃）very delicious; very tasty
嗒落有味 the significance of sth becomes clear after careful consideration
滋味 delicious
腥味 fishlike smell
試味 taste
調味 condiment; seasoning
燒味 roast meat; siu mei
獨沽一味 have a strong preference for only one thing
膩味 hate; loathe
臘味 wind-dried pork
變味 rotten smell

【呵】ho¹（安慰）comfort
呵吓佢（安慰安慰他）soothe him

【咕】gu¹ rumble
咕咕聲 have a rumbling stomach
咕喱（苦力／搬運工）(English) coolie
　咕喱佬（苦力／搬運工）coolie
咕嚕肉 sweet and sour pork

死咕咕（沒有生氣）not lively

【咂】zaap³ suck; sip
咂嘴 make clicks

【呷】haap³（喝）sip
呷醋（吃醋／妒忌／嫉妒）be jealous; get angry out of envy; jealousy in a man-woan relationship
　呷乾醋（吃乾醋）be jealous for no reason

【呻】san¹（嘮叨）chatter; garrulous

呻冇錢（嘆沒錢）complain of being short of money

呻呢呻嘮（怨這怨那）always complain about something;
　　if not complaining one thing, one complains about another

呻氣（歎氣）heave a sigh; sigh

呻笨（怨上當了／後悔／懊惱）complain that one has
　　been taken in

呻窮（哭窮）complain of being short of money

【呼】fu¹ ① call ② exhale

呼叫 ① call out; shout ② call; ring

呼吸 breathe

　　深呼吸 deep breath

呼呼 ① snore ② howling of the wind

　　呼呼大睡 snore loudly in one's sleep

　　呼呼聲（呼嘯）scream; whistle

打招呼 greet

招呼 beckon

稱呼 ① address; call ② form of address

**【命】meng⁶ ①（生命）life ②（命運）
destiny; fate**

命大 lucky

命不該絕 be not fated to die

命水（命運）fate

命根（命根子）one's life flood

命理 theories about fate

命硬 tough

二奶命（注定成為後備）always have to settle for second best

人命 life

亡命 ① flee; go into exile; refuge; seek refuge ② desperate

大命 escape with bare life

占卦算命 divine one's fortune

任命 appoint; commission; designate; nominate

同遮唔同柄，同人唔同命（人各有命）the same group of
　　people have different lot

吊命（勉強維持生計）depend on some source of money to
　　survive

老鼠拉鱔魚——一命搏一命（一命拼一命）risking life in
　　eating puffer fish

奀挑鬼命（瘦骨如柴）extremely skinny and frail

抓頸就命（逆來順受）patient with the current situation

奔命 in a desperate hurry

長命 long life

怨命 blame one's fate; submit to one's own destiny

唔要命（不要命）know no shame

害命 kill; murder; take sb's life

恕難從命 one is sorry but one cannot obey; regretably, one's
　　wishes cannot be complied with; we regret that we
　　cannot comply with your wishes

恭敬不如從命 it is better to accept deferentially than to
　　decline courteously; obedience is better than politeness;
　　the best way to show respect is to obey; to accept is
　　better than to stand on ceremony

效命 ① obey orders ② go all out to serve sb regardless of
　　the consequence; pursue an end at the cost of one's life

晒命（炫耀）show off

乘機搏命（趁機拼命）exploit an unusual situation by doing
　　sth not normally permitted

逃命 flee for one's life; run for one's life

從命 obey an order

執番條命（大命不死）escape with bare life

博命（拼命）defy death; fight desperately; go all out; go all
　　out regardless of danger to one's life; try very hard

揸頸就命（逆來順受）bear and forbear to save life; have no
　　choice but to comply

趁你病，攞你命（乘虛而入）do harm to sb when they are
　　already in trouble; drop stones on the person who has
　　fallen into a well; hit a person when he/she is down; pull
　　water on a drowning person; push sb down a well and
　　then drop stones on him

嗌救命（呼叫救命）cry for help

愛靚唔愛命（要美不要命）be more concerned about looking
　　good than being healthy

搏命（拼命）defy death; fight desperately; give one's all to
　　a task; go all out; go all out regardless of danger to one's
　　life; make every effort

搏老命（拼老命）risk one's old age to give one's all to a task

算命 fortune telling

趕頭趕命（催命似的）in a great hurry

賣命 sacrifice oneself

謀財害命 commit murder out of greed; murder sb for his/
　　her money

斃命 get killed; meet a violent death

攞命（要命）kill sb; ride one to death

攪出人命（意外懷孕）have a baby unexpectedly

曬命（炫耀）cry up one's own fortune; flaunt one's
　　possessions; show off; sing one's own glorious song

**【命】ming⁶ ①（生命）life ②（命運）
destiny; fate**

命中 hit the target; score a hit

命令 order

　　下命令 issue an order

　　服從命令 obey orders

　　接受命令 take orders

執行命令 carry out orders; execute orders

命名 name
命名典禮 naming ceremony

命運 destiny; fate

生命 life

使命 mission

性命 one's life

拼命 defy death; fight desperately; go all out; go all out regardless of danger to one's life

革命 revolution

致命 ① causing death; deadly; fatal; lethal; moral; vital ② sacrifice one's life

維他命 (維生素) (English) vitamin

【和】 wo⁴ blend

和平 peace
促進和平 promote peace

和尚 Buddhist monk
和尚食狗肉——一件穢，兩件穢 it is equally disgraceful to do such an ill deed for once or even once more again
打完齋唔要和尚 (唸完經趕和尚) kick down the ladder
兩個和尚擔水食，三個和尚冇水食 (不肯互相幫助 / 一拍兩散) everybody's business is nobody's business

和味 ① (收入很好) good income ② (好吃 / 好味道 / 美味) delicious; tasty
幾和味 ① (收入非常好) very good income ② (很好吃) very delicious; very tasty

和事佬 (中間人) mediator; peacemaker

和稀泥 (毫無原則地調解紛爭) try to smooth things over

和暖 (暖和) warm

和緩 gentle and mild

和諧 harmony

大泡和 (二百五) ① muddle-headed ② absent-minded person

不和 at cross-purposes; at loggerheads with sb; at odds with sb; at outs with sb; at sword's points with sb; at variance with sb; bad blood; discord; disunity; get at cross-purposes; ill blood; not get along well; on bad terms

打和 (打平) draw; tie

求和 ① hold out the olive branch; make overtures of reconciliation; seek peace with an enemy; sue for peace; try to end hostilities ② try to draw a match ③ summation

拌和 blend; mix and stir

柔和 soft

牀頭打交牀尾和 (牀頭吵，牀尾和) a family quarrel which is likely to be settled

溫和 mild; moderate

緩和 allay; calm; diffuse; ease up; itigate; relax

【咖】 gaa³ coffee

咖喱啡 (臨時人員) (origin: "carefree") extra

咖啡 coffee
咖啡仔 (交通督導員) young male parking warden
咖啡好靚 (咖啡質素良好) this coffee is very nice
咖啡色 brown
咖啡佬 (交通督導員) older male parking warden
咖啡妹 (女交通督導員) young female parking warden
咖啡婆 (女交通督導員) older female parking warden
一杯咖啡 a cup of coffee
沖咖啡 (沖泡咖啡) make coffee
歎咖啡 (享用咖啡) enjoy coffee

咖喱 curry
咖喱雞 ① curry chicken ② (吻痕) love bite

【咐】 fu³ direct; instruct

吩咐 instruct; tell

囑咐 exhort

【咁】 gam³ (那 / 那麼 / 這樣) so; that being so

咁仲 (這還得了) how could
咁仲得了 (這還得了) how could this be
咁仲得掂嘅 (這還得了) how could this be

咁多位 (各位 / 諸位) ladies and gentlemen

咁好 (這麼好) so nice

咁啱 (剛好 / 這麼巧 / 湊巧 / 碰巧) by chance; by coincidence; just by chance; what a coincidence
咁啱線 (湊巧 / 碰巧) by chance; by coincidence; just by chance; what a coincidence

咁都得 (這還成) how can this be
咁都得嘅 (這還成) how can this be

咁樣 (這樣) in that case; so; such
咁樣至啱 (這樣才對) this is just right
咁樣嘅話 (那末) in that case

咁橋 (這麼巧) by chance

咁點得㗎 (這怎麼成啊) how can this be

一嚿木咁 (呆頭呆腦) look dumb

一嚿飯咁 (呆頭呆腦) stupid person

不停咁 (不停地) non-stop

打到豬頭咁 (被打慘了) beat severely

如果係咁 (如果是這樣的話) if it were so; if that's the case; in that case

好似平時咁 (跟平常一樣) as usual

好似咁（就像這樣）like this

年年係咁（每年一樣）year in and year out

係咁（不停）active; eager; energetically; enthusiastically; exert all one's strength; go all out; in high spirits; showing much zeal; vigorously; vociferous; with gusto; with zest and vigour; work frantically

唔停咁（不停地）continuously

鬼咁（非常）① extremely; very ② quite; rather

猛咁（不停）active; eager; energetically; enthusiastically; exert all one's strength; go all out; in high spirits; repeatedly; showing much zeal; vigorously; vociferous; with gusto; with zest and vigour; work frantically

就算係咁（就算是這樣）even so

照而家咁（按現在這樣）as it is

攣弓蝦米咁（曲里拐彎）tortuous

【吟】ling⁶ shiny

立立吟（閃亮亮）glossy; shiny

閃閃吟（閃亮亮）glittering

【固】gu³ of course

固定 ① fixed; regular ② fasten; fix; make fast; mount; regularize ③ fix

固執 ① obstinate; stiff neck; stubborn ② cling to; persist in
固執己見 abide by one's opinion; adhere stubbornly to one's own ideas; have a will of one's own; hold stubbornly to one's own viewpoint; nail one's colours to the mast; stick to one's guns; stick to one's own view; stubbornly adhere to one's views

固然之（固然）indeed; it is true; of course; really

牢固 fast; firm; secure; solid

堅固 firm; solid

【坤】kwan¹ earth

坤宅 bride's family

扭轉乾坤 bring about a radical change in the situation; retrieve a hopeless situation; reverse the course of events; save a country from disaster

【坦】taan² flat

坦白 candid; confess; frank; honest; tell the truth
坦白從寬，抗拒從嚴 anyone who comes clean gets treated with leniency; anyone who holds back the truth gets treated harshly; leniency to confessor, but severity to resisters; leniency to those who confess and severity to those who resist

坦克 (English) tank

坦率 blunt; candid; candour; frank; outspoken; straightforward; upfront

坦然 calm; fully at ease; self-possessed; unperturbed; with no misgivings

坦誠 candid

眼坦坦（生氣而無奈）exhausted; in a desperate state

蛋家婆打仔——唔慌你走得上坦（無路可逃）put sb at the dead end

【坷】ho² rough

一生坎坷 a lifetime of frustrations; have hard luck all one's life

坎坷 bumpy; rough

【垂】seoi⁴（滑）slide

垂手 ① obtain sth hands down; within easy reach ② let the hands hang by one's sides; stand with one's hands hanging by the sides
垂手可得 acquire sth easily; acquire sth with a wet finger; at one's fingertips; easy to win; get sth without lifting a finger; win sth hands down; within easy reach

垂危 approaching death; at one's last gasp; close to death; critically ill; near one's end; terminally ill
垂危病人 dying patient
生命垂危 at the gasp

垂死 at the last breath; dying; expiring; fading fast; going; going belly up; going for your tea; have one foot in the grave; knocking on heaven's door; moribund; on one's last legs; receive notice to quit; sinking; slipping
垂死掙扎 conduct desperate struggles; deathbed struggle; flounder desperately before dying; give dying kicks; in one's death throes; in the throes of one's deathbed; make a last desperate stand; on one's last legs; put up a last-ditch fight

垂注 show concern

垂直 vertical

垂涎 covet; drool over; gloat over; hanker after; slaver over
垂涎三尺 bring the water to one's mouth; cast a covetous eye at sth; cast greedy eyes at; cannot hide one's greed; drool with envy; gape after; gape for; hanker for; have one's mouth made up for; lick one's chops; lick one's lips; make sb's mouth water; one's mouth waters after; smack one's lips
垂涎已久 have coveted sth for a long time; one's mouth has long been watering for
垂涎欲滴 keep a covetous eye on; make sb's mouth water

垂滑梯 (去玩滑梯) play the slide
垂落嚟 (滑下來) slide down
垂頭 hang one's head
　　垂頭餒氣 become dejected and despondent; blue about
　　the gills; bury one's head in dejection; down at the
　　mouth; down in the chops; down in the dumps; down
　　in the hips; down in the mouth; hang one's head;
　　have one's tail down; in low spirits; in the dumps; look
　　downcast; mope oneself; one's crest falls; out of heart;
　　out of spirits; out of sorts; sing the blues; take the
　　heart out of sb

【垃】 laap⁶ rubbish

垃圾 rubbish
　　垃圾佬 (撿破爛兒的) garbage collector; rubbish
　　collector
　　垃圾房 garbage room
　　垃圾缸 rubbish bin
　　垃圾站 waste collection point
　　垃圾桶 litter bin; rubbish bin
　　垃圾袋 rubbish bag
　　垃圾婆 (撿破爛兒的) female garbage collector; female
　　rubbish collector
　　垃圾嘢 (垃圾食品) junk food
　　垃圾蟲 litter bug
　　垃圾鏟 garbage shovel
　　　一袋垃圾 a bag of rubbish
　　　倒垃圾 dispose (the) rubbish
　　　家庭垃圾 domestic waste
　　　執垃圾 (撿破爛兒) pick odds and ends from refuse
　　　heaps
垃雜野 (雜七雜八的東西) random things

【坺】 paat⁶ soft mass

一坺 a soft mass of

【夜】 je⁶ ① night ② (晚) late

夜半 (半夜) midnight
夜冷 (二手貨店 / 舊貨店) second-hand shop; (English)
　　yelling
　　夜冷店 (二手貨店 / 舊貨店) second-hand shop
　　夜冷貨 (二手貨 / 舊貨) second-hand goods
夜更 (夜班 / 晚班) night switch
夜長夢多 too long a delay causes hitches
夜鬼 (夜貓子) insomniac; late sleeper; night person
夜晚 (晚上) at night; evening; in the evening; night; night
　　time
　　夜晚黑 (晚上) at night; evening; in the evening; night

夜媽媽 (深夜) very late at night
夜遊神 (夜貓子) night owl
夜瞓 (晚睡) go to bed late
夜總會 nightclub

三更半夜 in the middle of the night
子夜 midnight
午夜 midnight
日夜 day and night
半夜 midnight
平安夜 Christmas Eve
守夜 keep vigil beside the coffin; stand as guards at
　　the bier
坐夜 keep vigil beside the coffin; stand as guards at
　　the bier
宵夜 night snack
消夜 night snack
捱更抵夜 (熬夜) sit up all night to work; work night
　　and day
捱夜 (熬夜) sit up late
捱近午夜 (接近午夜) near midnight
晝夜 day and night
深夜 late in the night; midnight
睇夜 (晚班 / 夜班) on night shift
開夜 (開夜車) burn the midnight oil; work late into the
　　night; work overnight
隔夜 (放置一晚) overnight
漏夜 (連夜) that very night; the same night
漫漫長夜 endless night

【奄】 jim¹ soak

奄尖 (挑剔) fussy
　　奄尖聲悶 (挑剔) choosy; fussy

【奇】 kei⁴ (奇怪) strange

奇士 (親吻) (English) kiss
奇妙 wonderful
奇怪 ① curious; funny; odd; queer; strange; surprising;
　　unusual ② beyond comprehension; hard to
　　understand; puzzling; strange; unexpected
　　③ kaleidoscopic; wonders
　　千奇百怪 a great variety of fantasies; a multitude
　　of wonders; all kinds of strange things; all sorts
　　of strange things; an infinite variety of fantastic
　　phenomena; exceedingly strange; grotesque shapes;
　　numerous strange forms; weird shapes
奇異 ① bizarre; old; queer; strange ② amazed; amaing;
　　curious; surprising
　　奇異果 (獼猴桃) (English) kiwi fruit

奇貨可居 a rare commodity worth hoarding; corner the market; hoard as a rare commodity; keep rare commodities for a better price; make a profit by cornering the market; rare and precious goods; rare commodities which can be hoarded for better prices; rare commodity worth hoarding against a later higher price; wait to sell sth valuable at a high price

奇蹟 miracle

出奇 (特別) extraordinally; unusually
好奇 curious
曲奇 (English) cookie
唔出奇 (不奇怪) not surprising
稀奇 ① rare; strange ② care

【奈】noi⁶ endure
奈何 what is to be done
　　冇奈何 (無可奈何) against one's will; at the end of one's resources; have no alternative; have no choice; have no way out; have to; helpless; hopeless; powerless; reluctant; willy-nilly
　　無可奈何 have no alternative but to do sth

【奉】fung⁶ ① give ② receive ③ wait upon
奉旨 (一定 / 肯定 / 無論如何 / 照例 / 總是) take things for granted
　　奉旨 (子) 成婚 shotgun wedding
奉承 adulate; bow and scrape; fawn upon; flatter; lick the feet of sb; toady
　　奉承上司 play up to one's superiors
　　奉承拍馬 apple-polish; bow the scrape; cajole sb with flattering words; kiss the hem of sb's garment; tickle sb's ears
　　奉承討好 fawn upon sb; flatter; lick the feet of sb; toady
　　奉承話 blarney
　　　　百般奉承 flatter sedulously; sedulous flattery; servile flattery; tirelessly fawn upon
　　　　阿諛奉承 act the yes-man; butter sb; butter up; compliment unduly; curry favour with sb; dance attendance on; eat sb's toads; fawn on sb; flatter and cajole; flatter and toady; flattery; ingratiate oneself into sb's favour; ingratiate oneself with sb; lay it on thick; make much of; make up to; oil one's tongue; polish the apple; praise insincerely in order to please another's vanity; stoop to flattery; tickle sb's ears; toady; try to get sb's favour by flattery

侍奉 attend on; serve; wait upon

【奔】ban¹ run
奔命 in a desperate hurry

裸奔 streak

【妹】mui⁶ (妞兒) younger sister
妹夫 ① brother-in-law ② younger sister's husband
妹妹 younger sister

兄弟姐妹 brothers and sisters
弟妹 younger brother and sister
姊妹 ① sisters ② female friends
姐妹 sisters
舍妹 my younger sister
表妹 cousin; first cousin
金蘭姊妹 good sisters
阿妹 younger sister
師妹 ① junior female apprentice ② junior female schoolmate ③ younger daughter of one's master
堂妹 first cousin; younger female cousin
堂細妹 (堂妹) first cousin; younger female cousin
細妹 (妹妹) younger sister

【妹】mui¹ (妞兒) girl
妹仔 (丫頭) servant girl
　　妹仔大過主人婆 (喧賓奪主) have one's priority wrong; put the trivial above the important; the tail wags the dog
妹釘 (小丫頭 / 小姑娘) little girl; small young girl

一個賓妹 (一個菲律賓女傭) a Filipino maid
八卦妹 (三八) gossipy girl; nosy girl
八妹 (三八) nosy girl
老泥妹 (邊緣少女) bad girl; girl in the hood
竹升妹 (曾經在外國留學的中國女生) young overseas Chinese girl
咖啡妹 (女交通督導員) young female parking warden
肥妹 (胖妞) fat girl
悍雞妹 (牙尖嘴利 / 潑辣的女生) a girl of passionate disposition and violent temper
差妹 (印度女生) Indian girl
泰妹 (泰國女生) Thai girl
鬼妹 (外國女生) young female foreigner
骨妹 (從事按摩行業的女生) massage girl; masseuse
魚蛋妹 (提供色情服務的女生) girls for men to squeeze their breasts
㗎妹 (日本女生) Japanese girl
番鬼妹 (外國女生) young female foreigner
傻妹 (傻女孩) silly girl
鄉下妹 (土包子) country girl

賓妹 ① (菲律賓女生) Filipino girl ② (菲律賓女傭) Filiphino maid

靚妹 (妞兒) little girl

嘲妹 (妞兒) young girl

【妻】 cai[1] one's ball and chain; one's better half; one's carving knife; one's fork and knife; one's formal wife; one's homework; one's legal wife; one's mother of pearl; one's old Dutch; one's wife; wife

妻女 wife and daughters

　淫人妻女 violate another's wife and daughters

妻子 ① one's ball and chain; one's better half; one's carving knife; one's fork and knife; one's homework; one's mother of pearl; one's old Dutch; one's wife ② one's wife and children

妻離子散 a scattered family; be separated from one's family; be separated from one's wife and children; break up a family; families are broken up, with wives separated from their husbands and children separated from their parents; have one's family scattered over different places; one's family is broken up; parents are separated from children, husbands tear themselves away from their wives; the breaking up of a family; the scattering of a family; the wife leaves and the children scatter; with one's family scattered

妻離子散，家破人亡 cause the break-up by death or separation of countless families

妻小 one's wife and children

妻兒 one's parents, wife and children; the whole family; wife and children

　妻兒老小 one's parents, wife and children; a married man's entire family; wife and family

妻妾 wife and concubine

　妻不如妾，妾不如偷 a wife is not as good as a concubine, and a concubine is not as good as a mistress

妻室 one's legal wife; one's wife

妻舅 one's brother-in-law; one's wife's brother

夫妻 husband and wife

未婚妻 fiancée

老夫老妻 an old married couple

兩夫妻 husband and wife

【妾】 cip[3] concubine

妾侍 (小老婆 / 少奶奶) concubine

妾妾 wife and concubine

【姊】 zi[2] elder sister

姊妹 ① sisters ② female friends

　金蘭姊妹 good sisters

【始】 ci[2] beginning

始末 ① from beginning to end ② ins and outs; whole story

始終 all along; first, midst, and last; from beginning to end; from start to finish; remain; throughout

　由始至終 all the time; all the way; all the way through; all the while; at both the end and the beginning; during the whole period; from A to Z; from beginning to end; from cover to cover; from first to last; from start to finish; from the egg to the apple from the very beginning; from top to toe; the whole time; the whole way; throughout

從頭開始 a clean slate; back to square one; back to the beginning; from the jump; from the ground up; from scratch; from the word go; make a fresh start; start all over; start all over again; start anew; take a start from the head

開始 begin; commence

【姐】 ze[2] ① elder sister ② young woman

姐夫 brother-in-law; elder sister's husband

姐手姐腳 (慢吞吞 / 幹活不麻利) clumsy because she is not accustomed in doing heavy work

姐妹 sisters

千金小姐 well-off lady

大妗姐 go-between; match-maker

大姐 big sister

大家姐 (大姐) ① eldest sister ② big sister ③ tough lady

小姐 miss

空中小姐 air hostess

空姐 air hostess; female flight attendant

姑姐 aunt; father's sister

表姐 cousin; first cousin

阿姐 ① (姐姐) big sister ② (能幹的女人) capable woman ③ (服務員) teahouse waitress

促銷小姐 booth bunny

契姐 adoptive elder sister

家姐 elder sister

師姐 ① senior female apprentice ② senior female schoolmate ③ elder daughter of one's master

堂姐 elder female cousin; first cousin

堂家姐 (堂姐) elder female cousin; first cousin

細姐 (小媽) father's concubine

舞小姐 nightclub hostess

鳳姐（妓女）prostitute

【姑】gu¹ female relative

姑丈（姑夫／姑父）uncle

姑仔（小姑子／姑姑）aunt; father's younger sister

姑奶（大姑子）aunt; father's elder sister

姑且 for the time being

姑母（姑媽）aunt

姑妄 see no harm in sth

　　姑妄言之 just talk for talking's sake; just talk for the sake of talking; just venture an opinion; tell sb sth for what it is worth

　　姑妄聽之 just listen leisurely and by no means seriously; just listen to sth without taking it seriously; let him talk and let's just listen; take sth for what it is worth; take sth with a grain of salt; to hear is not to believe; to see no harm in hearing what sb has to say

姑姐（姑姑／姑母／嬸嬸）aunt; father's sister

姑姑 aunt; father's sister

姑表 cousinship

姑娘 ① girl ②（護士）nurse ③（妓女）prostitute

　　叫姑娘（召妓）visit a prostitute

　　灰姑娘 Cinderella

姑息 appease; attention; indulge; tolerate

　　姑息養奸 excessive indulgence breeds traitors; indulge the evildoers; lenient towards villains and let them grow; overindulgence nurtures evil; pardon makes offenders; to tolerate evil is to abet it; tolerant and indulgent

姑婆 ①（老奶奶）old woman ②（姑奶奶）grandfather's sisters

　　老姑婆（老處女）old spinster

姑爺 son-in-law

　　姑爺仔（拉皮條的人）pimp

尼姑／師姑 Buddhist nun

翁姑 woman's parents-in-law

道姑（吸毒上癮的女人）female drug addict

【姓】sing³ ① surname ② whose surname is

姓名 name

　　更改姓名 change one's name

　　貴姓名（尊姓大名）what's your name

　　講低姓名（留下姓名）leave one's name

姓賴（誣賴別人）deny one's guilt

小姓 one's surname is

平民百姓 common people

百姓 common people; people

老百姓 civilians; common people; folks; ordinary

【委】wai² ① entrust ② appoint

委任 appoint

委屈 feel wronged

委員 committee member

委實 indeed; really

【季】gwai³ season

季刊 quarterly; quarterly publication

季尾（季末）end of the season

季度 quarter of a year

季軍 second runner-up; third place; third winner in contest

季節 season

一年四季 four seasons of the year

四季 four seasons

旺季 peak season

雨季 rainy season

夏季 summer; summer season; summertime

換季 change season

【孤】gu¹ lonely

孤注一擲 a long shot gamble; all-or-nothing; ball the jack; bet all on a single throw; bet one's boots on; bet one's last dollar on; bet one's shirt on; bet one's bottom dollar on; cast the die; go for the gloves; go nap over; go the vole; have all one's eggs in one basket; make a last desperate effort; make a spoon or spoil a horn; make or break; make or mar; mend or mar; monkey with a buzz saw; neck or nothing; place one's efforts in a single thing; put all one's eggs in one basket; put the fate of sb/sth at a stake; risk all on a single throw; risk everything on a single venture; risk everything in one effort; send the axe after the helve; shoot one's wad; shoot the works; sink or swim; stake all one's fortune in a single throw; stake all one has; stake everything on a cast of the dice; stake everything on one last throw; stake everything on one attempt; take a great risk; venture on a single chance; venture one's fortune on a single stake; vie money on the turn of a card; win the horse or lose the saddle; win the mare or lose the halter; throw the helve after the hatchet

孤苦伶仃 lonely and poor

孤寒（吝嗇）mean; miserly; stingy

　　孤寒鬼／孤寒種／孤寒鐸（吝嗇鬼）miser; miserly person; stingy person

孤零零 all alone; alone; solitary

孤獨 lonely; solitary

【宗】 zung¹ ① sect ② purpose

宗旨 aim; objective; purpose
宗派 faction; sect
宗師 master of great learning and integrity
宗教 religion
宗廟 ancestral temple of a ruling house

教宗 Pope
萬變不離宗 myriads of changes base themselves on the origin

【官】 gun¹ government official

官方 authority; by the government; of the government; official
官仔骨骨 (衣冠楚楚) well dressed
官司 lawsuit
官字兩個口 (官員權力大，怎樣說都有理) officials can say whatever they like; speak in bureaucratese
官兵 officers and men
官官相衛 devils help devils
官非 (官司) lawsuit
官校 (公立學校) government school; public school
官員 officer; official
官場 official circles; officialdom
官僚 bureaucracy

大官 high-ranking official
父母官 local officials
法官 judge
長官 one's superior in office
軍官 army officer
做慣乞兒懶做官 (討飯三年懶做官) get used to living in idleness
量地官 (失業的人) be out of job; be unemployed
新官 new official
器官 organ

【宙】 zau⁶ cosmos

宙合 all-embracing; all-encompassing

大宇宙 macrocosmos
宇宙 cosmos; universe

【定】 ding⁶ ① (平穩 / 鎮定 / 穩) stable ② (還是) or ③ (準) accurate

定力 (毅力) perserverance
定必 (必定) bound to; sure to
定性 (踏實) stable

冇定性 / 冇啲定性 / 冇釐定性 (一點兒都不踏實 / 心不定 / 不專心) not realistic
定係 (或者 / 還是) or; or rather; whether
定型 set the hair
　定型啫喱 (髮膠) hair gel
　定型噴霧 hair spray
定晒形 (定神 / 愣住了) be stupefied; stare fixedly; trance oneself
定啲嚟 (鎮定點) keep cool; calm
定情 make a pledge of love
定期 time deposit
定過抬油 (心定 / 不慌亂 / 穩當) be completely composed; have full confidence in; have the game in one's hands
定檔 (有把握 / 鎮定) certain; sure
定點 (小數點) decimal point

一口咬定 assert categorically; cling to one's view; hold firm to one's stance; insist emphatically; insist on saying sth; speak in an assertive tone; state categorically; stick to one's statement; stick to what one says; stubbornly assert that; the arbitrary assertion that
一言為定 that's a deal
一定 certainly; must
不一定 not necessarily so; not sure; uncertain
內定 designated
冇一定 (不一定) it is unfixable
冇時定 (不固定) changeful; fluid; unfixed; unstable; unsteadfast
心神不定 a confused state of mind; a restless mood; agitated; an unstable mood; anxious and preoccupied; distracted, feel restless; have no peace of mind; ill at ease; in a state of discomposure; indisposed; out of sorts; wandering in thought
必定 bound to; sure to
正式協定 formal agreement
生死有定 every bullet has its billet
生定 destined; predestined
立定 halt
立場堅定 be firm in one's stand; keep one's stand; take a firm stand
企定 (站定) stand still
老定 (鎮定) calm; keep one's head; not stir an eyelid
你同我定 (不用擔心) don't worry, everything will be fine
君子協定 gentleman's agreement
否定 ① denial; deny; negate ② negative
決定 decide; make up one's mind
制定 draft; draw up; enact; establish; formulate; institute; lay

down; set up; work out

協定 agreement

命中注定 be determined by fate

固定 ① fixed; regular ② fasten; fix; make fast; mount; regularize ③ fix

注定 be decreed

肯定 absolute; affirm; approve; as sure as death; as sure as eggs is eggs; as sure as fate; as sure as hell; as sure as I'm standing here; as sure as you live; ascertain; certain; confident; confirm; definite; for sure; guarantee; in the affirmative; make sure; positive; sure; swear; with absolute certainty

咬定 insist

政治穩定 stable in politics

架車好定 (這輛車子行走得很穩定) this car runs smoothly

界定 delimit

限定 define; determine; fix; limit; prescribe a limit to; restrict; specification; specify

修游淡定 (冷靜 / 鎮定) calm and composed

唔一定 (不一定) it is indefinite

唔定 (不一定) maybe; perhaps

唔話得定 (不一定) can't say for certain

脂油淡定 (冷靜 / 鎮定) calm

酌情而定 be determined by the circumstances; decide according to the circumstances; depend upon the circumstances

停火協定 ceasefire agreement

淡定 calm; unflappable

眼定定 (目不轉睛) stare; stare fixedly

規定 ① lay down a rule ② regulate

睇定 (看準了) be certain about sth

註定 destined; doomed; predestined

滋油淡定 (冷靜 / 鎮定) calm; not panic; slow coach

話定 (說好) agree on; come to an agreement

話唔定 (說不定) can't say for certain; hard to predict; may be; perhaps; probably

話得定 (說定了) agree on; come to an agreement

搵定 (預先找) find in advance

塵埃落定 all is fixed; everything is settled

整定 (注定) destined; predestined

醒定 ① (聰明) clever ② (小心) careful; watch out

醒醒定定 (小心) do the clever thing

確定 confirm

禪定 deep meditation

擬定 draft; draw up; work out

講定 (說好了) agree on

講唔定 (說不定) it's not yet settled

斷定 assert; conclude; decide; form a judgement

臨時協定 provisional agreement

【定】deng⁶ deposit

定金 deposit

落定 (付訂金) pay the deposit

撻定 (取消交易並放棄訂金) forfeit a deposit

【宜】ji⁴ proper

宜人 agreeable; delightful; pleasant

宜於 good for; suitable for

宜得 (巴不得) be only anxious to do sth; earnestly wish

宜然 suitable

小便宜 small gains

不宜 inadvisable; inappropriate; not suitable

因人制宜 suit measures to different people; treatment chosen according to the variability of physique of an individual

因地制宜 act according to the circumstances; act in accordance with the circumstances; adapt to local conditions; adopt measures suiting local conditions; do sth in line with local conditions; do the right thing at the right place; do what is appropriate according to the regional circumstances; do what is suitable to the environment; hinge on local conditions; suit measures to local conditions; take appropriate measures in accordance with local conditions; take measures suited to local conditions

因事制宜 circumstances alter cases; do what is suitable to the occasion; suit measures to different things

因時制宜 act according to the circumstances; act according to the time; act in accordance with the times; do the right thing at the right time; do what is appropriate according to the circumstances; do what is suitable to the occasion; in a manner suitable to the time; take measures suited to the time

老少咸宜 suitable for people of all ages; suitable for the old and the young

佔皮宜 (佔便宜) profit at others' expense

便宜 petty gain

相宜 cheap; inexpensive

攞便宜 (佔便宜) benefit at others' expense

【尚】soeng⁶ monk

尚且 ① even ② still; yet

尚可 ① acceptable; passable ② still permissible; still possible

尚自 still; yet

一種時尚 a social trend
打完齋唔要和尚（過河拆橋）kick down the ladder
和尚 Buddhist monk
迎合時尚 pander to the trend of the times
指住禿奴罵和尚（指桑罵槐）talk at sb
時尚 social trend

【居】geoi¹ reside

居心 harbour evil intentions
居民 resident
居住 reside
　　居住環境 living environment
居留權 right of abode
　　永久居留權 permanent residency
居然 go so far as to; to one's surprise; unexpectedly

分居 live apart; separate without a legal divorce; separation
民居 local dwelling houses
穴居 cave-dwelling; live in caves
奇貨可居 a rare commodity worth hoarding; corner
　　the market; hoard as a rare commodity; keep rare
　　commodities for a better price; make a profit by cornering
　　the market; rare and precious goods; rare commodities
　　which can be hoarded for better prices; rare commodity
　　worth hoarding against a later higher price; wait to sell
　　sth valuable at a high price
茶居 teahouse
窟居 live in a cave
鄰居 neighbour
隱居 hermit; live in seclusion; retire from public life;
　　withdraw from society and live in solitude
舊居 old home
戇居居 ①（傻乎乎／傻裏傻氣）foolish; stupid ②（呆頭呆
　　腦）dull; dull-looking

【屈】wat¹ ①（窩）force; squeeze ②（扣帽子）be branded as; give sb a label; pin a label on sb; put a label on sb; stick a label on; stigmatyize sb as; tag sb with the label of ③（繞）in a roundabout way; make a detour

屈一圈（繞一圈兒）take a turn round
屈水（敲詐金錢）extort money
屈打成招 confess to false accusations under torture
屈曲（使彎曲）twist sth until it is bent
屈尾十（掉頭）turn round and go back
屈服 bow down to; bow to; capitulate; give away; knuckle
　　under; submit to; succumb; surrender; yield to; yielding
屈指 count on one's fingers

屈氣（憋氣）suffer breathing obstruction
屈得就屈（冤枉別人）frame sb
屈從 capitulate; knock under; knuckle under to; submit to;
　　yield to
屈蛇 ①（坐船偷渡）immigrate illegally by hiding in a
　　boat; stow away ②（沒有經批准在大學宿舍住宿）stay
　　overnight in a university hostel without permission
屈就 accept a job too humble for one's position; condescend
　　to take a post offered
屈遠咗（繞遠了）take a long devious route
屈質 ①（地方窄小／侷促／擁擠）cramped ②（雜亂）in a
　　mess; messy

老屈（冤枉別人）frame sb
委屈 feel wronged
明屈 pressure sb
冤屈 false charge
寧死不屈 would rather die than yield

【岳】ngok⁶ mountain peak

岳父 one's father-in-law; one's wife's father
岳母 one's mother-in-law; one's wife's mother
岳高頭（抬起頭／仰起頭）raise one's head

頭岳岳（抬起頭）raise one's head

【岸】ngon⁶ coast; shore

岸上 bank; shore
岸然 gravely; impressive; in a solemn manner; solemn;
　　solemn and dignified look
　　道貌岸然 assume soemn airs; one's imposing bearing;
　　　　pose as a person of high morals; sanctimonious;
　　　　simulate solemnity
岸邊 dockside; quayside

上咗岸（發了財）have made one's fortune
內陸口岸 inland port
兩頭唔到岸（進退維谷）in a situation where whichever way
　　one turns one will lose out; neither sink nor swim in the
　　middle of the sea; on the horns of a dilemma
埋岸（到岸）draw alongside; pull in shore
遲嚟先上岸（晚到的先佔了便宜）the last comer becomes
　　the first goer
攏岸（靠岸）moor to the shore

【岩】ngaam⁴ large rock

岩洞 cave; cavern; grotto
岩嶢（凹凸不平／高低不平）full of bumps and holes;
　　rugged; uneven

岩岩巉巉（凹凸不平／高低不平）full of bumps and
　　holes; rugged; uneven

【幸】hang⁶ luck

幸好 fortunately; just as well; luckily

幸災樂禍 gloat upon others' misfortune

幸免 escape by sheer luck; have a narrow escape
　　幸免於難 a close shave; a narrow shave; a narrow
　　　　squeak; a near squeak; escape by the skin of one's
　　　　teeth; escape death by a hair's breadth; escape death
　　　　by sheer luck

幸運 good luck

幸福 fortune
　　幸福快樂 full of happiness

榮幸 be honoured; have the honour of

【底】dai² ①（底部）base ②（背景）background ③（衣服內襯）inside of clothing

底下（下面）below; under

底衫（內衣）underwear
　　底衫褲（內衣褲）underwear

底貨（剩貨）leftover goods; leftovers

底牌 the opposition's secret

底裙 slip

底褲（內褲）panties; underwear

底薪（基本工資）basic salary

一底（一盤）a large piece of

下底（下面）low; under

天腳底（天邊兒）ends of the earth

心字底 the "heart bottom"（心）radical

包底（包圓兒）promise to pay money until it's enough

加底（另加份量）increase the bulk of food

打底（預先給予心理準備）give sb a hint beforehand

甩底 ①（爽約）break one's appointment; fail to turn up; not
　　turn up for an appointment; stand someone up ②（鞋底
　　掉了）the bottom part of a shoe looses off

好物沉歸底（好東西留到最後）the best comes last; the best
　　fish swim near the bottom

扣底（減少份量）smaller portion of rice or noodles

谷底 valley bottom; valley floor

牀下底（牀底）under a bed

相底（底片）negative

洗底（重新做人）expunge a criminal record

為人為到底 when one helps others, help them to the end

穿櫃桶底（監守自盜）embezzle funds; misappropriate funds

紅底（一百元紙幣）one-hundred-dollar note

臥底 ① undercover agent ② spy

趴底（趴下）lie face down

食碗面，反碗底（吃裏扒外）betray a friend; ungrateful

原底 originally

根底 foundation

案底（犯罪紀錄）criminal record

狷落牀下底（鑽進牀底）get into the bottom of the bed

留案底（留下犯罪紀錄）keep a criminal record

胳肋底（胳肢窩）armpit

脷底（舌下）root of the tongue

起底（揭老底）check up on sb's background

追到天腳底 hunt sb to the end of the earth

貨底（剩貨）leftover goods; leftovers

揭開謎底 ① solve a riddle ② find out the truth

黑底（黑幫成員）member of a triad society

暗啞底（暗地）suffer in silence

腳（板）底（腳板）sole of the foot

摸底（摸清底細）know the real situation; sound sb out

漏底（漏下）let the cat out of the bag

樓底 ① downstairs ② ceiling

蝕底（吃虧）miss out on a chance; suffer losses

鞋底 sole

薦底（墊底）bedding

歸根到底 in the end; in the final analysis; when all is said
　　and done

舊底（以前）before; formerly; in the past; previously

騎樓底（陽台下）pavement; sidewalk

寶物沉歸底（好東西留到最後）the best things come at the
　　end

躓底（跌倒）fall down

謎底 ① answer to a riddle ② truth

【店】dim³ shop

店面 shopfront; storefront

店員 shop assistant

店鋪 shop; store

一間店 a shop

一間酒店 a hotel

士多店 grocery store

小食店 snack shop

五星級酒店 five-star hotel

古董店 antique shop

打店 put up for the night in an inn or a hotel

百年老店 century-old shop

住一晚酒店 stay for one evening in a hotel

快餐店 fast food shop

沖曬店 photo shop

夜冷店（二手貨店／舊貨店）second-hand shop

免稅店 duty free shop
花店 florist; flower shop
訂酒店 book a hotel room
長生店（棺材店）shops selling coffins
門店 retail department
便利店 convenience store
書店 bookstore
旅店 hostel
酒店 hotel
珠寶店 jewellery shop
連鎖店 chain store
傢俬店 furniture shop
零食店 snack bar
影音店 audio visual shop
餅店 cake shop; pastry shop
鴨店 duck shop
禮品店 gift and souvenir shop
寵物店 pet shop
book 酒店（預約酒店）book a hotel room

【庚】gang¹ age

傻庚（傻子）fool
傻傻庚庚（傻傻的）foolish

【府】fu² government office
府上 ① your family; your home ② your native place

政府 government
聯合政府 coalition government
臨時政府 interim government; provisional government

【弦】jin⁴ chord
弦外之音 connotation; implied meaning; overtone
弦歌 ① sing with stringed accompaniment ② schooling
弦樂 string music

唔咬弦（話不投機）out of tune with sb

【彼】bei² that
彼此 both parties; each other; one another; this and that;
　　you and me
　　彼此之間 between you and me
　　彼此彼此 the feeling is mutual; we are alike; we are in a
　　　　similar position
　　　　無分彼此 one for all and all for one

知己知彼 it needs to understand both oneself and others
厚此薄彼 biased; discriminate against one and favour the

other; discriminate against some and favour others;
favour one and be prejudiced against the other; give
handsome treatment to one and niggardly treatment
to the other; give a royal welcome to one and cold
reception to the other; give too much to one and too
little to the other; liberal to one and stingy to the other;
make chaff of one and cheese of the other; make fish of
one and flesh of the other; make invidious distinctions;
partial to one while neglecting the other; say turkey to
one and buzzard to the other; the treatment accorded
to one is out of all proportion to that accorded to the
other; treat one warmly and another coldly; treat with
partiality

【往】wong⁵ past
往日（以前）previously
往年 in bygone years; in former years; in the years past
往事 history; past events; the past; things that have come
　　to past
往來 ① back and forth; come and go; go and return; to and
　　fro ② contact; dealings; intercourse
往陣時（以前）ago; before; former; formerly; in the past;
　　once; previous; prior; used to be
往常 as one used to do previously; as usual; habitually in
　　the past; make it a rule; used to

交往 date
秘密交往 date with sb secretly

【忠】zung¹ loyal
忠心 devotion; faithfulness; loyalty; sincerity
忠忠直直，終須乞食 an honest person will end up
　　begging for livelihood
忠厚 honest and tolerant; kind and big-hearted; sincere and
　　kindly
忠誠 faithful; loyal; truthful
忠實 faithful; reliable; true

效忠 allegiance; devote oneself heart and soul to; loyal to;
　　pledge allegiance; pledge loyalty to

【念】nim⁶ remember
念念不忘 bear in mind constantly
念念有詞 mumble
念頭 idea; thought
念舊 keep old friendships in mind

作為留念 as a souvenir; keep as a keepsake
紀念 commemorate

留念 keep for commemoration
值得紀念 worthy of commemorating
影相留念 take a photo to mark the occasion
簽名留念 autograph to mark the occasion; sign one's name as a memento
繫念 have constantly on one's mind

【忽】fat[1] ① suddenly ② disgard

忽然 suddenly

忽視 blank sb; disregard; give a cold shoulder; ignore; look down on; neglect; overlook

忽略 elude; ignore; lose sight of; neglect; overlook

屎忽（屁股）anus; bottom; buttocks
洗屎忽（清洗屁股）clean one's bottom
崩咗一忽（缺了一塊）missing one piece
喊苦喊忽（呼天搶地）be continually in tears; weep and wail; weeping and wailing; whine with plaintive broken sounds
疏忽 negligence
飄忽 ① fleet; move swiftly ② float

【忿】fan[5] anger; fury; get angry; grudge; hatred

忿忿 angry; furious; indignant
　忿忿不平 indignant and disturbed

忿氣（服氣）be convinced
　唔忿氣（不服氣）be unconvinced; reluctant to give in; unwilling to submit

【怖】bou[3] horror

怖畏／怖禍 afraid; dread; scared

恐怖 horrible

【怕】paa[3]（生怕／擔心）afraid

怕人 ① shy; timid ② awful; frightening; horrible; terrifying
怕死 fear death
怕事 afraid of getting into trouble
怕怕 scared
怕苦 fear hardship
怕唧（怕人胳肢）afraid of being tickled
怕醜（怕羞／害羞／害臊）bashful; feel ashamed; feel shy; shy
　唔使怕醜（不用害羞）don't be shy

冇有怕（別怕／沒甚麼好怕的）don't be afraid
可怕 terrible
至怕（最怕）fear most
唔怕（不怕）have no fear

害怕 afraid for sth; afraid of sb; be frightened; be overcome by fear; be overcome with fear; be scared of; can't say boo to a goose; dread; dreadful; fear; fearful; fly the white feather; for fear of; frighten; frightful; get cold feet; have a dread of; have cold feet; in dread of sb; in dread of sth; in fear of; make one's blood run cold; make one's hair stand on end; quail; shake in one's boots; show the white feather; strike fear into; tremble in one's shoes

恐怕 I'm afraid; might as well; perhaps
鬼都怕（可怕）terrifying
得人怕（可怕）awful; horrible; terrible; terrifying
睇怕（恐怕）I'm afraid; may be; might as well; perhaps; probably
慌怕 for fear that; lest; so as not to
嚇怕 frighten
懼怕 dread; fear

【性】sing[3] nature

性交 act of love; action; amorous congress; amorous rites; aphrodisia; approach; art of pleasure; balling; bonk; caress; carnal acquaintance; carnal connection; carnal engagement; carnal enjoyment; carnal knowledge; carnal relations; carnalize; coitus; compress; concubitus; congress; conjugal relations; conjugal rites; conjugal visit; conjugate; connection; consummation; conversation; copulate; copulation; crouch with; deed of kind; do a kindness to; do it; do some good for oneself; do the chores; effect intromission; enjoy a woman; familiar with; federate; fix her plumbing; foraminate; foregather; fruit that made men wise; funch; game; get it on; get one's leg over; go all the way with sb; go the limit; go the whole route; go to bed with; gratification; grease the wheel; greens; have a bit; have one's will of a woman; have relations; improper intercourse; in Abraham's bosom; in bed; intercourse; intimate with; jump; keeping company; larks in the night; last favours; lewd infusion; lie with; life one's leg; light the lamp; love life; lovemaking; make it; make love; make someone; make out; make time with; marital duty; matinee; meaningful relationships; night work; nookie; on the make; pareunia; perform; play; play at in-and-out; play doctor; please; pluck; possess carnally; rites of love; scale; score; screw the arse off; see; service; sex experience; sexual intercourse; sexual intimacy; sleep together; switch; the bee is in the hive; the facts of life; tie the true lover's knot; union; venereal act; what Eve did with Adam

性別 sex
　性別歧視 sexual discrimination

性命 one's life

性急 quick-tempered
性格 character; personality
　　　有性格 have character
性情 disposition; temper; temperament
性感 sexy

女性 female
冇耳性 (健忘) forgetful; have a memory like a sieve
冇定性 (不穩重) not realistic
冇性 (不講理 / 殘忍) savaged and absurd; unreasonable
冇耐性 (沒有耐性) impatient
冇記性 (沒有記性) foregetful; have a bad memory; have a memory like a sieve; have a poor memory; have a short memory
冇啲定性 (不穩重) not realistic
冇釐定性 (不穩重) not realistic
失去理性 be out of one's senses; lose one's reason
本性 instincts; one's natural character; real nature
生性 (爭氣) have a grown-up understanding
好記性 have a good memory
有耐性 patient
男性 male
亞崩養狗──轉性 (性情改變) have a change of nature
定性 stable
品性 character personality; temperament
耐性 patience
唔生性 (不爭氣) unpromising
唔熟性 (不懂事 / 不通情達理) ignorant; inconsiderate
烈性 strong; violent
記性 memory
悟性 comprehensive; power of understanding
真係生性 (真爭氣) promising
理性 reason; sense
惰性 inertia; laziness
雄性 male
感性 emotional
彈性 flexibility
熟性 considerate; reasonable; sensible
戲劇性 drama
轉 (死) 性 (性情改變) change one's disposition

【怪】 gwaai³ ① strange ② blame

怪人 strange guy
怪之得 (怪不得) no wonder
怪物 ① monster ② eccentric person
怪責 (責怪) blame
怪夢 strange dream
　　　發咗個怪夢 (發了一個怪夢) had a strange dream
怪誕 funny; strange

怪聲怪氣 in an strange voice
怪雞 (奇怪) bizarre

千奇百怪 a great variety of fantasies; a multitude of wonders; all kinds of strange things; all sorts of strange things; an infinite variety of fantastic phenomena; exceedingly strange; grotesque shapes; numerous strange forms; weird shapes
大驚小怪 a storm in a tea cup
少見多怪 a man who has seen little regards many things as strange; comment excitedly on a commonplace thing; consider sth remarkable simply because one has not seen it before; having seen little, one gets excited easily; he who has little experience has many surprises; ignorant people are easily surprised; kick up a fuss; the less a man has seen, the more he has to wonder at; things rarely seen are regarded as strange; things seldom seen seem strange; wonder at what one has not seen; wonder is the daughter of ignorance
古古怪怪 bats; bizzare; cranky; eccentric; erratic; flaky; funky; gnarled; odd; ornery; quaint; queer; quizzical; strange; uncouth; wacky; wayward; whimsical; whimsy; wonder
古怪 (蹊蹺) odd; strange
古靈精怪 (古里古怪 / 稀奇古怪) bizarre; funny; queer
有古怪 (有蹊蹺) that's very extraordinary
有怪莫怪 (請別見怪) beg for one's apology
作怪 make trouble; scheme
妖怪 bogy; demon; evil spirit; goblin; monster
妖魔鬼怪 demons and ghosts
見怪 mind; take offence; take sth amiss
奇怪 ① curious; funny; odd; queer; strange; surprising; unusual ② beyond comprehension; hard to understand; puzzling; strange; unexpected ③ kaleidoscopic; wonders
唔好見怪 (不要見怪) don't be offended; don't take it ill; I hope you will not be offended; kindly forgive me; kindly forgive my lack of repect; you must not take it ill
趣怪 amusing; funny; lively; vivacious
整古做怪 (裝神弄鬼) wrap sth in mystery
醜八怪 very ugly person
醜死怪 (羞死人) disgraceful
醜怪 ugly
禮多人不怪 civility costs nothing
難怪 no wonder

【或】 waak⁶ or

或者 maybe; perhaps
或許 maybe; perhaps

抑或 maybe; perhaps; or

【戾】lai² perverse

戾手（一轉手／跟手）at once; right away

戾氣 disharmony; irregularity; perversity

【房】fong⁴（房間）room

房地產 property; real estate

房地產中介 property agency

房地產市道 real estate market trends

房地產市場 real estate market

房地產業界 real estate sector

房車（小轎車）sedan

房租 rent

房間 room

一間房 a room

入房 enter the room

士多房（雜物房）storeroom

工人房 room for domestic helper

牛房（牛欄）cattle pen

主人房 master bedroom

扒房 ①（主要提供扒類食品的餐廳）steak house
②（相貌醜陋的女性聚集的地方）place with lots of ugly women

兵房 barrack

冷氣房 air-conditioned room

沖涼房（浴室）bathroom

私房 private saving

車房 garage

乳房 apples; bangles; bazoombas; bazungas; beef curtains; blobs; boobs; bosoms; bouncers; bubbies; bumpers; charlies; chestnuts; dairies; easts and wests; fainting fits; female breasts; funbags; jamboree bags; jugs; knobs; knockers; love blobs; milk-jugs; milk-bars; shock absorbers; stonkers; tits; titties; udders; wammers; whammers

垃圾房 garbage room

空房 empty room; vacant room

狗房 kennel

客房 guest room

查房 check the rooms

洗衣房 laundry room

洞房 bridal chamber

訂房 reserve a room

凍房 cold storage

套房 suite

庫房 ① storehouse; storeroom ② treasury

書房 study room

班房 classroom

馬房 callgirl centre

執房 tidy up the room

娶填房（娶繼室）a widower getting a second wife

梗房（板套房）solid-partitioned cubicle

票房 box office

單人房 single room

開房（與情人去酒店開房間）go to a hotel to have sex

黑房 darkroom

填房（繼室）second wife (of a widower)

睡房 bedroom

電壓房 substation

廚房 kitchen

廠房 factory building

監房（監獄）prison cell

瞓房（睡房）bedroom

禪房 mediation room

雜物房 storeroom

雙人房 double room

藥房 drugstore; pharmacy

【所】so² place

所以 hence; therefore

所好 one's inclination; one's likes

各有所好 each follows their own bent; each has their hobby; each has their likes and dislikes; every person has their hobby-horse; everyone to their own taste; every person to their taste; tastes differ; there is no accounting for tastes

投其所好 cater to sb's likes; cater to sb's pleasure; cater to sb's tastes; cater to sb's wishes; cater to the needs of sb; give sb exactly what they like; hit on what sb likes; offer what sb is hankering after; rub sb the right way; suit one's fancy; take a fancy to; take sb's fancy; tickle the ear of sb; to one's liking

所有 ① owe; possess ② possessions ③ all

所長（長處）one's forte; one's strength; one's strong point; what one is good at

所謂 so-called

冇所謂（無所謂）all the same; anything will do; cannot be called; doesn't matter; indifferent; never mind; not care; not deserve the name of; not matter

正所謂 what people said

所難 difficult for sb

強人所難 compel sb to do sth against their will; constrain sb to do things that are beyond a person's power; force some work on a person who is not equal to it; force sb to do sth against their will; force sth down sb's throat; impose a difficult task on sb; impose upon a person a task that they are incapable of doing; saddle sb with a difficult task; try and force people into doing things they don't want to; try to make sb do what is against their will; try to make sb do what is beyond their power; try to make sb do what they are unable to

公眾場所 public places
牙科診所 dental clinic; the dentist; the dentist's
去廁所 go to the toilet
托兒所 child-care centre; nursery; nursery school
住所 abode; domicile; dwelling place; home; residence
拘留所 detention centre
牀位寓所 bedspace apartment
風月場所 place of carnal pleasures
娛樂場所 places for entertainment
廁所 toilet
寓所 one's dwelling
場所 arena; place
診所 clinic
會所 clubhouse

【承】sing⁴ succeed
承包 contract
承先啟後 (承前啟後) inherit the past and usher in the future
承惠 (感謝／承蒙照顧／多承惠顧) appreciate
承認 confess
承辦 agree to do sth; undertake
承諾 acceptance of an offer; promise to undertake; undertake to do sth
承擔 assume; bear; undertake
承繼 ① be adopted as heir to one's uncle ② adopt one's brother's child

百般奉承 flatter sedulously; sedulous flattery; servile flattery; tirelessly fawn upon
托塔都應承 (無條件答應) promise without conditions
奉承 adulate; bow and scrape; fawn upon; flatter; lick the feet of sb; toady
阿諛奉承 act the yes-man; butter sb; butter up; compliment unduly; curry favour with sb; dance attendance on; eat sb's toads; fawn on sb; flatter and cajole; flatter and toady; flattery; ingratiate oneself into sb's favour; ingratiate oneself with sb; lay it on thick; make much of; make up to; oil one's tongue; polish the apple; praise insincerely in order to please another's vanity; stoop to flattery; tickle sb's ears; toady; try to get sb's favour by flattery
紹承 (繼承) inherit; succeed to
應承 (答應) promise
繼承 inherit

【抱】pou⁵ embrace
抱住 hold in one's arms
抱怨 beef about; blow off; chew the rag about; complain; complain about; complain of; grouse; grouse about; grumble; grumble about; grumble at; grumbling; kick against; kick at; murmur against; murmur at; mutter against; mutter at; natter on about; quarrel with; rail against; rail at
抱負 ambition; aspiration
　　實現抱負 fulfill one's ambition; realise one's aspiration
抱歉 feel apologetic; feel sorry; regret
　　非常抱歉 feel very apologetic
抱緊 hold tightly in one's arms
抱頭 cover one's head with one's hands

心抱 (兒媳婦／媳婦) daughter-in-law
水抱 ① (水疱) blister ② (救生圈) life buoy
娶心抱 (娶媳婦) get a daughter-in-law
新抱 (媳婦) daughter-in-law
擁抱 cuddle; embrace; hold in one's arms; hug

【抨】ping¹ attack
抨擊 denounce

【披】pei¹ wear
披甲 put on an armour
披衣 throw on gown
披肩 shawl
披頭散髮 disheveled; have one's hair hanging loose; unkempt

草披 ① grassland ② glassplot; lawn

【抵】dai² (活該／值得) worth
抵打 (該打) deserve punishment
抵死 (活該／該死) serve sb right; you deserve it
　　抵你死 (活該) have only oneself to thank; serve sb right; you deserve it
　　抵佢死 (活的該) have only himself to thank; he deserves it; serve him right
抵佢發 (該他發迹) he deserves getting rich
抵冷 suffer from cold
抵到爛 (太合算了) get a very good deal; get the best value for one's money
抵食 ① (吃得過) cheap for such good food; worth eating ② (合算) deserving; worthwhile
抵唔抵 (值不值得) is it worth it
抵埗 (抵達) arrive; reach

抵消 (扯平) make even

抵得凍 (禁冷) endure cold

抵買 ① (買得過) worth buying ② (合算) deserving; worthwhile

　　好抵買 (買得過) it's worth buying

抵搞 (該搞) deserve being slapped on the face

抵諗 (不斤斤計較 / 肯吃虧 / 能忍讓) can bear the burden of work and complaint

　　抵得諗 (不斤斤計較 / 肯吃虧 / 能忍讓) can bear the burden of work and complaint

抵鬧 (該罵) deserve the scolding

抵賴 find a way to avoid blame

大抵 generally; generally speaking; in the main; most likely; mostly; on the whole; probably; roughly

心甘命抵 (心甘情願) of one's own accord; willing to follow a course of action whatever the consequences

死慳死抵 (省吃儉用) pinch and screw; tighten one's belt

身當命抵 have only oneself to blame

唔抵 (不值) not deserved; not worthwhile

戥你唔抵 (為你感到不值) it's regrettable for you

【抹】maat³ (擦) swipe

抹口 (擦嘴巴) wipe one's mouth

抹地 (擦地板) mop the floor

抹咗 (擦掉) erase; rub off; rub out; wipe off

抹油 (擦油泥) cleaning and oiling

抹枱 (抹桌子) wipe the table

　　抹枱布 (抹布) table-cleaning cloth

抹面 (抹臉 / 擦臉) clean one's face

　　抹吓塊面 (擦把臉) clean one's face

抹乾 (擦乾) dry; wipe dry

抹黑 blacken sb's name; bring shame on; discredit; throw mud at

　　抹黑墨 (抹黑) smear

抹靚 (擦亮) polish

【抽】cau¹ (提) pull

抽水 ① draw water ② (佔便宜) fool around with a girl; take advantage of a girl ③ (抽頭) take a percentage out of the winnings in gambling

抽佣 draw a commission on the sale

抽波 (扣球) smash the ball

抽油 (醬油) soy sauce

　　抽油煙機 kitchen hood; range hood

抽後腳 (抓辮子) pull sb's leg; tease sb by repeating what he says

抽風扇 (排風扇) air ejector fan

抽氣扇 (排風扇 / 換氣扇) air ejector fan; air extractor; ventilation fan

抽高條褲 (把褲子提高點) pull up one's trousers

抽秤 (挑眼) nit-picking

抽絲剝繭 trace a fox to its den

抽筋 (痙攣) cramp; have a cramp

　　悶到抽筋 (非常沈悶) very bored

抽獎 lucky draw

抽頭 (突然轉彎 / 脫身) do a U-turn; run away; withdraw

抽濕機 dehumidifier

一抽 (一串) a bunch of; a cluster of; a rope of; a strand of; a string of

生抽 light soy sauce

老抽 dark soy sauce

勁抽 (厲害) ① excellent; very good ② powerful

熟抽 dark soy sauce

鞋抽 ① jutting lower jaw ② shoehorn; shoe lifter

【押】aat³ give as security

押犯 (押送犯人) escort a criminal; send a criminal away under escort

押後 (延期 / 推遲) be postponed; defer; delay; extend; lay over; postpone; put off; put over

押款車 (解款車) cash escort vehicle

押櫃 (付按金) pay a deposit

大押 (當舖) pawnshop

【拆】caak⁸ ① take apart; tear open ② remove

拆穿西洋鏡 (拆穿騙局) expose the fraud

拆卸 dismantle; dismount

拆息 daily interest rate

　　銀行同業拆息 interbank offered rate

拆骨頭 (去骨頭 / 剔骨頭) boning

拆樓 (拆房子) pull down a building

　　嘈到拆樓 (非常嘈吵) extremely noisy

拆檔 (拆伙 / 散夥) break up a partnership

七除八拆 various deductions; big discounts

朝行晚拆 a bed set up in the morning and dismantled at the evening

【拉】laai¹ (抓) pull

拉人 (抓人) arrest sb

　　拉人返差館 (拉上警局) arrest sb to the police station

　　拉人裙冚自己腳 (沾別人的光) benefit from association with sb or sth

拉上補下 (截長補短) make up for the deficit in one area by using resources from another

拉手仔 (搞對象) be occupied with finding a match; go steady; in love

拉勻 (平均 / 拉平) average; balance up
　拉勻計 (平均算) strike an average

拉尺 (皮尺 / 捲尺) band tape; tape measure

拉牛上樹 (迫使做力不能及的事情) a vain attempt to do sth

拉尾 (末了) finally; in the end; last

拉扯 prevaricate
　拉拉扯扯 prevaricate

拉臣 (駕駛執照) (English) license

拉車尾 (包尾) just squeeze through

拉柴 (死掉) die; meet one's fate

拉埋 drag into
　拉埋天窗 (結婚) get married
　拉埋…落水 (拉…下水) drag sb in; include sb in the subject of conversation

拉掣 (關閘門) pull a switch

拉閘 (關門) stop work
　拉閘放狗 (關門) close the door

拉落水 (拉下水) drag sb into the mire

拉線 (牽線搭橋) act as a go-between; bring both sides together; bring one person into cntact with another; build bridges; foster the relationship between two people; pull strings and build bridges

拉頭馬 (拉着冠軍馬匹) parade a winning horse

拉闊 (現場) (English) live

拉鏈 ① zip ② zipper
　拉拉鏈 zip up

拉纜 eat noodles
　拉頭纜 (牽頭 / 帶頭) lead; take the lead; the first one to start

長拉拉 (長長的) lengthy
軟拉拉 (軟軟的) feathery; soft; velvety
開麥拉 (相機) (Engish) camera
搏拉 (想被拘捕) put oneself in danger of being arrested

【拋】 paau¹ throw

拋生藕 (灌迷湯) colquette with a man; flirt

拋浪頭 (嚇唬) come the bully over sb; show off before a fight

拋錨 stall

鬥拋 (互相嚇唬) show off before a fight by using abusive language

【拌】 bun⁶ mix

拌勻 mix well
拌和 blend; mix and stir
拌麵 noodles in mixed sauce

【拐】 gwaai² kidnap

拐子佬 (人販子 / 拐子 / 騙子) abductor
拐杖 crutch
　生蟲拐杖──靠唔住 (燈草欄杆──不能靠) a rail made of rotten rushes – a broken reed; unrealiable
拐帶 kidnap
拐賣 abduct and traffic
拐騙 ① swindle ② abduct

【拍】 paak³ ① slap ② (攆) drive out; expel; oust; show sb the door

拍手 applaud; clap hands
拍片 (拍電影) make a movie; produce a movie; shoot a movie
拍佢扯 (攆他走) oust sb; send sb packing; send sb to the right-about; show sb the door
拍拖 (談戀愛) date; go on a date; go out for a date; lovers going out hand in hand
拍門 (敲門) knock at a door; knock on the door; rap at the door; rap on the door; tap at the door; tap on the door
拍埋 (拼起來) put together
　拍埋行 (並排走) walk in a row
　拍埋啲 (挪近點兒) move a little closer
拍得住 (比得上) bear comparison with; can compare with; compare favourably with
拍薑咁拍 (欺負) give sb a hard smack
拍檔 (合作者 / 伙伴 / 伙伴兒) partner
　好拍檔 (好伙伴) good partner
　拍吓檔 (協助一下) please help
　拍硬檔 (大力協助 / 通力合作) help each other to work on; work well together

烏蠅拍 (蒼蠅拍) flyswatter; swatter

【拎】 ling¹ ① (拿) carry ② (提 / 提取) take

拎住 (提着) carrying
拎走 (拿去) take sth away

【拒】 keoi⁵ refuse

拒付 refuse payment
拒絕 decline; decline doing sth; decline to do sth; refuse; reject; repulse; throw down; throw over; turn away; turn down

來者不拒 all is fish that comes to his net; all are welcome, none will be turned away; all comers are welcome; keep open door; keep open house; no comer is rejected; refuse nobody; refuse nobody's request; whoever comes will be welcome

【拔】bat⁶ pull

拔刀 draw one's sword
　拔刀相助 draw a sword and render help; help another for the sake of justice; take up the cudgels against an injustice
拔出 draw out; extract; pull out
拔除 eradicate; pluck; pull out; remove; uproot; weed out; wipe out
拔蘭地（白蘭地）(English) brandy

象拔 trunk

【拗】aau³（折 / 撅）bend

拗柴（扭傷）twist one's ankle
拗開兩撅（折成兩段）break into two
拗腰（向後彎腰）bend one's body backward
拗斷（折斷）break; break asunder; break off; rive; snap

【拗】ngaau³ ① obstinate ②（爭論）argue

拗氣（鬥氣）quarrel with
拗數（鬥氣）quarrel with
拗撬（爭議）(English) argue
拗頸（抬槓 / 爭吵）argue; argue against sb; quarrel with
　包拗頸（抬槓）sure to argue to the contrary

口同鼻拗（各執一詞）argue over nothing; it's useless to argue

【拖】to¹ ① lead ② tow

拖友（情人）lover
拖手仔（談戀愛）be in love; be in a relationship
拖卡（拖斗 / 拖車）trailer
拖地（拖地板）mop the floor
拖車 trailer
拖拉手（手拉手）hand in hand
拖板（接線板）extension lead
拖泥帶水 be sloppy in one's work; indecisive
拖肥糖（太妃糖）toffee
拖慢來做（磨洋工）dawdle along; dawdle over one's work; lie down on the job; longer over one's work; loaf on the job; slacking
拖數（拖欠）be behind in payment; be in arrears
拖鞋 flip-flop

着拖鞋（穿拖鞋）put on the slippers
拖頭（集裝箱車）container truck
　拖頭佬（駕駛集裝箱車的司機）container trucker driver

用拖（分手）break up a relationship; lovers no longer dating each other
地拖（拖把）mop; swop
拍拖（約會）date; go on a date; lovers going out hand in hand
單拖（自己一個人）be by oneself
膠拖（拖鞋）plastic flip-flops; plastic slippers

【拕】to¹ drag out

拕仔（懷孕）pregnant
拕住（帶着）carry with
拕累（連累）get sb into trouble; implicate; incriminate; involve
拕錶（掛錶 / 懷錶）pocket watch

【拙】zyut³ clumsy

拙劣 bochy; clumsy; inferior
拙笨 awkward; clumsy; dull; stupid; unskillful
拙稿 my poor manuscript

弄巧反拙 try to outsmart oneself but turn out to be foolish
獻醜不如藏拙 it is wiser to conceal one's stupidity than it is to show oneself up

【拘】keoi¹ take

拘束 ill at ease; restrain; restrict
　無拘無束 as free as the birds; carefree; completely without restraints; free and easy; free as a bird; make oneself at home; unconstrained; uncontrolled; unfettered; unrestrained; without a worry in the world; with any restraint; without hindrance
拘捕 arrest; detain; take in
拘留 detain; detention
　拘留所 detention centre
拘禁 put under arrest; take into custody
　非法拘禁 unlawful incarceration

咪拘（甭想）I won't take it
唔使拘 not to be concerned with
唔拘（不介意）all the same; indifferent; never mind; not care; not matter

【拼】ping³ go all out

拼死無大害 do sth at the risk of
拼命 defy death; fight desperately; go all out; go all out regardless of danger to one's life

拼湊 confect; knock together; piece together; rig up; scrape together

七拼八湊 a patchwork without pattern or order; cobble together; compile from many sources a book; conjoin multifarious elements to form a whole as a patch-quilt; improvise desperately; knock together; piece together; piece together odds and ends; raise money from different sources; rig up; scrape together; scrape together odd amounts to form a sum for a definite purpose

東拼西湊 do patchwork; pitch up from bits; put together from different sources; scrape together; scratchy

拼爛 act shamelessly

【招】 ziu¹ summon

招供 confess

招呼 beckon

打招呼 greet

招架 return blows

有招架之功，無還手之力 can only ward off blows

招風耳 (招風耳朵) flaring ear

招財進寶 wish you a prosperous year

招紙 (招貼／商標紙) trademark tag

招牌 advertisement

招牌菜 chef's recommendation; signature dish

生招牌 a walking advertisement for sth

拆招牌 destroy the good reputation a company/unit has built up

招搖過市 be fond of showing oneself in the streets

招搖撞騙 put on a good bluff

招標 tender

招積 (刺兒頭／傲慢／囂張) disgustingly arrogant

招積仔 (刺兒頭／傲慢的人) arrogant child; arrogant guy

不打自招 make a confession without duress

中招 (上當) be caught in a trap; get hit

出招 make a strategic move

屈打成招 confess to false accusations under torture

鬼拍後尾枕──不打自招 (不打自招) confess without being pressured

街招 bill; notice; placard; poster

【抬】 toi⁴ raise

抬棺材甩褲──失禮死人 (非常尷尬) very embarrassing

抬舉 good favour; good turn; do a good turn

抬頭 ① raise one's head ② upsurge

【扚】 kam² (蓋) cover

扚被 (蓋被子) cover with a quilt

扚賭 (抓賭局) smash a gambling party

【挋】 joeng² (抖) shake

挋吓張被 (把被子抖一抖) shake the quilt

【拃】 zaa⁶ handful

揸拃 (霸道) overbearing

捹一拃 (拿一把) grab a hanful of sth

【放】 fong³ release

放下心頭大石 free from anxiety

放工 (下班) finish work; get off work; knock off

放咗工 (下了班) after work

放心 breathe easy; feel relieved; free from cares; have one's heart at ease; put one's heart at ease; rest assured; rest one's heart; set one's mind at rest; with no worries

放水 ① (小便) urinate ② (給以提示或某種方便) make an exception to favour sb

放生 ① (任由自便) as one likes ② (放人離開) let sb go

放光蟲 (螢火蟲) fire beetle; firefly; glowworm

放低 (放下) leave; put down

放低買路錢 (放下過路費) leave your money before you can pass through this road

放屁 ① backfire; beef-hearts; break wind; break wind backwards; break wind downwards; dropp a rose; fart; have gas; lay fart; let one fly; make a noise; pass air; pass wind; rip off a fart; set a fart; shoot rabbits; sneeze; there's a smell of touch bone and whistle ② bullshit; talk nonsense; talk rot; what a crap

放虎歸山 lay trouble for the future

放長線釣大魚 (做事從長遠打算) wait patiently for a long time in order to get sth big

放風 (把風／散佈消息) be on the lookout for sth/sb; spread the news

放蛇 (臥底) undercover police

放假 on a holiday; on leave

放棄 abandon; give up

永不放棄 never give up

放貴利 (高利貸) work as a loan-shark

放路溪錢──引死人 (十分吸引) very attractive

放過 forgive and let go

有殺錯冇放過 (寧枉勿縱) what is done may be wrong but no one will be allowed to let go

放電 (向人灌迷湯) flirt

放生電 (向人灌迷湯) flirt

放監 (出獄) be discharged from prison; be released from prison

放數 (放債) lend money at a high interest

放盤 (出售) put on sale

放膽 (大膽 / 放心) act boldly

放鬆吔 (放輕鬆) take it easy

推放 (堆積) pile up; stack

開放 open

釋放 release

【斧】fu² axe

斧正 (修正) make corrections

斧頭 axe; hatchet

斧頭打鑿鑿打木 (斧頭吃鑿子，鑿子吃木頭) the axe strikes the chisel, and the chisel strikes the wood – everything has its vanquisher; there is always one thing to conquer another

斧頭邊 (雙耳旁) the "two ears" (阝) radical

板斧 (辦法) solutions to a problem

【於】jyu¹ at

於今 at present; now; since; up to the present

於此 here; in this place

於是乎 (於是) as a result; consequently; hence; so; then; thereafter; therefore; thereupon; thus

一於 ① even; even if ② insist on

不致於 it is unlikely that; unlikely to go so far

由於 as; as a result of; because of; by virtue of; considering; due to; for; for-as-much-as; in consequence of; in consideration of; in that; in the light of; in view of; in virtue of; inasmuch as; on account of; owing to; seeing that; since; take into consideration; thanks to; through; with; with a view to

至於 as for

位於 be located; be situated; lie; sit on; stand on

取決於 be decided by; depend on; depend upon; dependent on; dependent upon; hang on; hang upon; hinge on; it's up to; lie on; rest with ride on; turn on

宜於 good for; suitable for

致力於 apply oneself to; dedicate oneself to; devote oneself to; devote to; engage oneself in; work for

終於 at last; eventually; finally

敢於 bold in; dare to; have the courage to

等於 equal to

樂於 be glad to; be willing to; like to; love to

關於 in relation to

屬於 belong to

【旺】wong⁶ (興旺) bustling; prosperous

旺地 good land; prosperous place

旺季 peak season

旺盛 exuberant; full of vitality; overflowing with life; vigorous

人有三衰六旺 (運氣有好有壞，人生沉浮興衰) a person suffers misfortunes and other times strokes of good fortune

三衰六旺 (人生的禍福) ups and downs of life

生意旺 business is blooming

交投暢旺 a lot of transactions

唔睇旺 (不看好) not optimistic about sth

條街好旺 (這條街很熱鬧) this street is bustling

睇旺 (看好) be optimistic about sth

新屎坑三日旺 (貪新鮮) a new broom sweeps clean

興旺 prosper

【明】ming⁴ (明白) understand

明人 honest person

明人不做暗事 an honest person does not do anything underhand

明刀明槍 before sb's very eyes; do sth openly

明寸 (不轉抹角的嘲諷) deliberately obtuse

明火打劫 rob in the light of day

明月 bright moon

明白 be clear about; realise; understand

明白人 perceptive person

明明白白 as clear as noonday

明屈 (明顯是被冤枉) pressure sb

明明 (明顯) obviously

明明係 (明顯是) clearly; obviously

明知 be fully aware; know perfectly well

明知山有虎，偏向虎山行 go into the mountains knowing well that there are tigers there

明知故犯 break a law on purpose

明知故問 ask while knowing the answer

明信片 postcard

一張明信片 a postcard

明星 ① star ② movie star

崇拜明星 worship stars

想做明星 want to become a star

明眼人 discerning person

明暗 ① light and shade ② openly and secretly

明一套，暗一套 act one way in the open and another way in secret

明智 sagacious; sensible; wise

明解（明白）understand

明槍易擋，暗箭難防 better to suffer an attack by overt than by covert

明蝦（明目張膽地欺負人）bully sb

明顯 clear; distinct; evident; obvious

一理通，百理明（融會貫通）once one has mastered the basic idea, the rest is easy

小聰明 cleverness in trivial matters; good at playing petty tricks; petty shrewdness; petty tricks; sapient; smart in a small way

心知肚明（心照不宣）know in one's heart

月到中秋份外明 the harvest moon is exceptionally bright; the mid-autumn moon is exceptionally bright

牛皮燈籠——點極都唔明（牛皮燈籠——點不透）thick-headed

另請高明 find another better qualified person

守得雲開見月明 wait till the clouds roll by

明解（明白）understand

事後孔明 be wise after an event

恩怨分明 discriminate between love and hate; kindness and hatred are clearly distinguished; make a clear distinction between kindness and hatred

高明 qualified person

發明 invent

睇明（看明白）read and understand

睇唔明（看不明白）cannot read and understand

睇得明（看明白）can read and understand

註明 explain clearly in writing; give clear indication of; make a footnote; mark out

透明 transparent

說明 clarify; explain; expound; illustrate; show

寫明 written clearly

黎明 dawn; daybreak

鄰近黎明 be close to daybreak

聰明 clever

離婚證明 certificate of divorce

聲明 statement

聯合聲明 joint statement

講明（說明）give a clear explanation

講唔明（說不明白）not explain clearly

講得明（說明白）can explain clearly

擺明（明顯地）blatant; obvious

擺到明（明顯地）blatantly; expose one's intention

雞食放光蟲——心知肚明 have a clear mind; know what is what

雞啄放光蟲——心知肚明 a turtledove eating up a firefly – bright in the belly – have a clear understanding of things

證明 proof

聽唔明（聽不明白）not understand

聽得明（聽明白）understand

難以證明 hard to prove

【昏】fan¹ faint

昏花 dim-sighted

昏倒 faint; fall down in a faint; fall unconscious

昏迷 coma

黃昏 evening

【易】ji⁶（容易）easy

易打（容易打）easy to beat

易呃（容易騙）easy to be cheated

易洗（容易洗）easy to wash

易食（容易吃）easy to eat

易做（容易做）easy to do

易發（容易發財）get rich easily

易睇（好看）easy to watch

易搞（容易搞）easy to manage

易話為（好說／隨便）easy-going

易過借火（易如反掌）a piece of cake; as easy as ABC; as easy as child's play; as easy as damn it; as easy as falling off a log; as easy as pie; as easy as turning one's palm over; as easy as turning over one's hand; as easy as winking; easy job

易賣（容易賣）easy to sell

易整（易做）easy to make

易學（容易學）easy to learn

容七易（很容易）it's very easy

容易 apt to; as easy as ABC; as easy as taking pennies from a blind man; as easy as taking toffee from a child; as easy as you know how; easily; easy; easy as pie; easy-peasy; likely, liable to

話咁易（很容易）it's very easy

談何容易 by no means easy; easier said than done; easy to talk, difficult to achieve; how easy it is to talk about it; it's no easy thing; not as easy as it sounds; not as easy as one thinks it to be

【易】jik⁶ ① dealing ② change

易手 change hands

易主 change masters; change owners

易名 change one's name

易位 change positions

冇交易（沒有交易）no dealing can be concluded

交易 dealing; make a deal; transaction
有交易 dealings can be concluded
枱底交易（黑箱作業）under-the-table transaction
貿易 trade
網上交易 online trading
幕後交易 behind-the-scenes deal

【昔】sik¹ former
昔日 in former days
昔者 before; formerly; in ancient times; in former times

士多啤梨奶昔（草莓奶昔）strawberry milkshake
奶昔 milkshake

【朋】pang⁴ friend
朋友 friend
 小朋友 ① little boys; little friends; little girls ② one's
  children
 女朋友 girlfriend
 有少少朋友（有一些朋友）have a few friends
 男朋友 boyfriend
 探朋友 visit a friend
 幾個朋友 several friends
 豬朋狗友（不三不四的朋友）bad companions; bad
  friends; bad mates; friends of bad character; friends
  with bad habits or low morals
朋比為奸 act in collusion with; claw me and I will claw
 thee; claw me, claw thee; collude in doing evil; conspire
 for illegal ends; gang up for evil purposes; join in plotting
 reason; play booty; scratch me and I'll scratch you; scratch
 my back and I'll scratch yours; work hand in glove with sb
 for evil doings
朋輩 friends

【服】fuk⁶ ① be convinced ② dress
服用 take the medicine
 吃飯時服用 to be taken during a meal
 飯前服用 to be taken before a meal
 飯後服用 to be taken after a meal
服從 obey
服務 give service; service
 服務員 attendant
 服務業 service industry
 暫停服務 temporary suspension of service
服裝 clothing
 中式服裝 Chinese clothing
服藥 take the medicine

心服 be convinced

心服口服 be sincerely convinced
令人心服 carry conviction
衣服 clothes
吞服 take medicine
折服 ① bring into submission; subdue; submit
 ② acknowledge the superiority of others; be convinced;
 be filled with admiration
臣服 submit oneself to the rule of
克服 conquer; overcome; surmount
制服 uniform
屈服 bow down to; bow to; capitulate; give away;
 knuckle under; submit to; succumb; surrender; yield to;
 yielding
便服 plain clothes
洋服 foreign style dresses
軍服 military uniform
唔舒服（不舒服）① uneasy ② uncomfortable; unwell
校服 school uniform
執衣服（收拾衣服）pack one's clothes
着制服（穿制服）wear a uniform
舒服 comfortable
舒舒服服 comfortable
禮服 formal dress

【杯】bui¹（杯子）cup
杯茶好濃（茶很釅）the tea is very strong
杯酒 cup of wine
杯葛（抵制）(English) boycott
杯盤（盤子）tray

一杯 a cup
一個杯 a cup; a glass
水杯 glass
茶杯 teacup
唥杯（洗杯）wash a cup
飲杯（乾杯）cheers
飲番杯（喝一杯）cheers

【東】dung¹ east
東方 ① east ② East; Orient
東北 ① northeast ② northeast China
東施效顰 copy others blindly and make oneself look
 foolish; crude imitation; imitate awkwardly; imitate
 others and make oneself foolish and ridiculous; imitate sb
 in certain particulars; play the sedulous ape; take a leaf
 out of sb's book
東家唔打打西家（另謀高就）lose employment on one
 but get a job in another
東邊 east side

乜東東 (甚麼東西) thingummy; what is it

少東 young boss; young master

做東 (請客) play host

廣東 Canton

【板】baan² plank

板斧 (辦法) solutions to a problem

板球 cricket

板塊 plate

板鴨 pressed dried salted duck

天花板 ceiling

手板 (手掌) palm

主板 main board

打手板 (打手掌) hit the palm of the hand

未見官先打三十大板 (未見其利，先見其害) suffer a loss before the gain

甲板 deck; deck armour

包撞板 (保證會碰壁) sure to go wrong

地板 floor

竹板 bamboo lath

呆板 ① boring; dull; inflexible; rigid; stereotyped ② starchy; stiff

夾板 plywood

刻板 ① cut blocks for printing ② inflexible; mechanical; stiff

抹黑板 erase the blackboard

拖板 (接線板) extension lead

波板 (球板) bat; racket

柚木地板 teak floor

梗板 (死板) inflexible; rigid; stereotyped; stiff

牀下底破柴——包撞板 (一定碰壁) be rebuked; meet with a rebuff; run into big trouble

長生板 (棺材) coffin

洗衫板 ① (搓衣板) wash board ② (平胸的女人) woman with a flat chest

砧板 chopping block

賊起牀板 (徹夜思考問題) stay awake thinking about a problem

浮板 bodyboard

紙板 cardboard

魚板 fish cake

黑板 blackboard

朝種樹，晚劈板 (勉強糊口) live from hand to mouth

搖搖板 see-saw

過橋抽板 kick down the ladder

腳板 sole of the foot

撞大板 (犯大錯) make a serious mistake

撞板 (犯錯) get into trouble; make a mistake; run into trouble; screw up

撞晒大板 (犯大錯) make a serious mistake

錶板 (儀表盤) control board

蔗渣板 board made of residual sugar cane fibre

鋸板 saw a piece of board

攤大手板 (張開雙手要錢) open up one's hands to ask for money

蠟板 stencil plate

籃板 backboard

【枉】wong² be wronged

枉死 be wronged and driven to death; die through injustice

枉法 abuse law; pervert the law; twist law to suit one's own purpose

枉費 of no avail; try in vain; waste

　枉費工夫 spend time and work in vain; waste time and energy

　枉費心機 a fool for one's pains; bay at the moon; bark at the moon; bay the moon; beat the air; beat the wind; flog a dead horse; fruitless efforts; futile; go down the drain; go on a wild goose chase; in vain; make futile efforts; rack one's brains in vain; rack one's brains to no purpose; scheme in vain; scheme without avil; try in vain to; waste one's contrivances; waste one's efforts; waste one's labour; waste one's pains; wreck one's brain without results

　枉費唇舌 a mere waste of breath; waste one's breath

　枉費精力 flog a dead horse

　枉費錢財 throw away good money for nothing

冤枉 be wrongly accused of sth

【枋】fong¹ betel nut tree

枋榔樹一條心 (一心一意) love sb heart and soul; single-minded in love

【枕】zam² pillow

枕木 railway sleeper; sleeper; tie

枕住 (一直) continue an action

枕長 ① (一直) all along; throughout ② (經常) always

枕頭 pillow

　枕頭包 (方麵包) pillow-shaped bread

　枕頭袋 pillowcase

　告枕頭狀 (吹枕邊風) lay a complaint against sb in the presence of one's husband

　攝高枕頭想吓 (徹夜思考) sleep over it

枕邊人 (妻子) wife

後尾枕 (後腦勺) back of one's head

【林】lam⁴ forest

林下 in the country
林木 ① forest; woods ② crop; forest tree
林立 a forest of; stand in great numbers
林沈（瑣碎）odds and ends
林柿（柿子）persimmon
林蔭 shade of trees
　　林蔭大道 tree-shaded boulevard

一卷菲林 a roll of film
一筒菲林 a roll of film
杏林 medical profession
武林 circle of boxers
菲林 (Engish) film
嗱林（快點）quickly
園林 garden; park
謀殺菲林 use up all the films

【枝】zi¹ branch

枝椏（枝條）branch; twig
枝筆好稔（筆尖上墨水很多）too much ink at the tip of
　　the writing brush
枝筆掘咗（筆尖禿了）the pencil is blunt
枝節 ① minor matters ② complication; knottiness
　　枝枝節節 complexity and diversity; complications; minor
　　　　issues; digressive
　　節外生枝 bring about extra complications; bring up
　　　　unnecessary ramifications; cause complications;
　　　　complicate matters; create side issues; deliberately
　　　　complicate an issue; give rise to other contingencies;
　　　　inject side issues; new problems crop up unexpectedly;
　　　　proliferate issues and problems; raise obstacles; side
　　　　issues crop up unexpectedly
枝頭 on the branch

一枝 a piece of; a stick of
一紮樹枝（一捆樹枝）a bundle of firewood
竹枝 ① bamboo pole ② dried bean curd stick
花枝 squid
荔枝 lichee
粗鐵枝 large iron rod
椏枝 forking branch
節外生枝 bring about extra complications; bring up
　　unnecessary ramifications; cause complications;
　　complicate matters; create side issues; deliberately
　　complicate an issue; give rise to other contingencies;
　　inject side issues; new problems crop up unexpectedly;
　　proliferate issues and problems; raise obstacles; side
　　issues crop up unexpectedly

酸枝 rosewood
樹大有枯枝（林子大了，甚麼鳥都有）there are good and
　　bad people in every group
樹枝 ① firewood ② branch of a tree
鐵枝 iron rod

【果】gwo² fruit

果子狸 masked civet
果仔（果子／水果）fruit
果占（果醬）jam
果汁 fruit juice
果真 if indeed; really
果欄（水果行）fruit store

一抽蘋果（一袋蘋果）a bag of apples
一籃生果 a basket of fruit
生果 fruit
白果 ① ginko; gingko nut ②（沒有收獲）no business
生白果——腥夾悶（尖酸刻薄）fault-finding; nitpick; picking
　　bones in an egg – overcritical
因果 cause and effect
如果 if
芒果 (English) mango
奇異果（獼猴桃）(English) kiwi fruit
若果 but for; but that; failing; if; in case; in case of; in default
　　of; in the absence of; in the event of; in the event that;
　　on condition that; on the understanding; only that;
　　provided; should; suppose; supposing; unless; wanting;
　　what if; when; where; without
食白果（沒有收獲）① rewardless ② no business
效果 effect
粉果 shrimp and bamboo shoot dumpling
涼果 candied preserved fruit
蛇果 red delicious
殼果 nut
結果 result
開心果 a person who is always happy; a person with a
　　cheerful face
腰果 cashew nut
萬壽果（木瓜）papaya
潮州粉果 shrimp and bamboo shoot dumpling in Chiu Chow
　　style
糖果 sweets
蘋果 apple

【枚】mui⁴ stalk of shrub

枚舉 enumerate

猜枚（猜拳）guessing game

【杰】git⁶ outstanding
杰捷捷 ① (厚重) thick ② (有很大麻煩) in a lot of trouble

鑊鑊杰 everything one does ends in trouble

【欣】jan¹ glad
欣喜 delighted; enjoyable; glad; gratifying; happy; joyful
　欣喜若狂 an ecstasy of joy; as happy as a lark; be intoxicated with joy; beside oneself with joy; delirious with delight; ecstasize; exult; fly into raptures; go mad with joy; go wild with joy; in a transport of delight; in a transport of joy; in raptures; jubilantly happy; jump out of one's skin; leap out of one's skin; leap with joy
欣然 joyfully; with good grace; with pleasure
欣賞 admire; appreciate

【歧】kei⁴ discriminate
歧途 aberration; wrong path; wrong road; wrong track
　走入歧途 deviate from the right path; go astray; go off at a tangent; jump the track; take the wrong turning
　誤入歧途 be misguided; be misled; be misled into the wrong path; devious; fall by the wayside; fall into a wrong path; go astray; off the track; take the wrong road by mistake
歧視 discrimination
歧路 branch road; crossroads; fork in a road; forked road; wrong road
　歧路亡羊 a lamb goes astray on forked road; a lamb goes astray at a fork in the road — go astray in a complex situation; a straggling sheep; the highway leads a sheep astray with its numerous turnings
　歧路徘徊 hesitate at the crossroads
　歧路彷徨 be depressed at the crossroads; hesitant at a road junction; not certain which road to take and remain at the crossroads hesitating; hesitant at the cross-roads as to which way one should go

【武】mou⁵ martial
武力 ① force ② military force; military might
武林 circle of boxers
武術 martial art
　武術師傅 kung fu master; martial art master
武器 armament; armature; arms; weaponry; weapons
武藝 fighting skills
武斷 arbitray decision; assertive

也文也武 (炫耀自己的力量) flaunt one's power; make a show of power

【毒】duk⁹ poison
毒氣 poisonous vapour
毒素 virus
毒鬥毒 (以毒攻毒) pay tit for tat; use poison as an antidote to poison
毒藥 poison
　烈性毒藥 deadly poison

中毒 poison
利毒 atrocious; brutal; cruel; malicious; venomous; vicious
吸毒 be on drugs; become addicted to narcotics; do drugs; drug abuse; drug taking; drug use; smoke opium; take drugs; use drugs
食物中毒 food poisoning
倔毒 merciless
消毒 disinfect; sterilise
狼毒 atrocious; brutal; cruel; malicious; venomous; vicious
病毒 virus
惡毒 wicked
排毒 detoxification
販毒 peddle drugs
陰毒 evil-hearted
黃賭毒 prostitution, drugs, and gambling
墨魚肝肚雞泡心腸──黑夾毒 (墨魚肚腸河豚肝──又黑又毒) the belly and intestines of a cuttlefish and the liver of a puff fish: they are all black and poisonous

【氓】mong⁴ rascal

流氓 ① ganster; hooligan; hoodlum; rascal; scoundrel ② immoral behaviour; indecency; rascal behaviour

【氛】fan¹ atmosphere; prevailing mood
氛圍 atmosphere

投資氣氛 investment climate
氣氛 atmosphere; ambience; climate; mood

【沓】daap⁶ crowded together
沓合 pile one upon another; superimpose
沓至 come one after another without stop
沓沓 ① lax ② chattering and talkative ③ run quickly
沓雜 confused; crowded and mixed

一沓 ① pile ② pillar

【沫】mut⁶ foam
沫子 foam; froth
沫水舂牆 go through fire and water

涎沫 saliva

【沮】zeoi² depressed
沮喪 frustrated

【沱】to⁴ flow
沱茶 compressed mass of tea leaves

真金不怕洪爐火，石獅不怕雨滂沱 a person of integrity can stand severe tests

【油】jau⁴ ① oil ② (上色 / 油漆 / 塗 / 漆) apply paint
油水 ① grease ② profit
　　揩油水 (佔便宜) profit at others' expense
油占多 (奶油果醬吐司) toast with butter and jam
油多 (奶油吐司) toast with butter
油耳 (油耳朵) ear wax
油炸鬼 (油條) deep-fried dough stick
　　隔夜油炸鬼 (脾氣好的人) good-tempered person
油缸 fuel tank
　　打爆油缸 (注滿氣油) fill up the fuel tank
油站 (加油站) filling station; gas station; petrol station
油脂 (小阿飛) ① teddy boy ② teddy girl
　　油脂女 (小阿飛) teddy girl
　　油脂仔 (小阿飛) teddy boy
油紙遮 (油布傘) oilcloth umbrella
油瓶 ① oil bottle ② (女方的繼子) stepchild on mother's side
　　油瓶女 (繼女) step-daughter
　　油瓶仔 (繼子) step-son
　　挽油瓶仔 (拖油瓶) a woman's children by previous marriage; step-children
油渣 ① (柴油 / 柴油) diesel; diesel oil
　　② (豬油渣) lard
　　油渣車 (柴油車) diesel car
油菜 vegetable with oyster sauce
　　一碟油菜 a dish of vegetable with oyster sauce
油漆 oil paint
　　油漆工人 oil painter
　　油漆未乾 wet paint
　　油漆師傅 oil painter
　　油漆掃 (油漆刷) paint brush
油鋪 (油坊) oil mill
油樽 (油瓶兒) oil bottle
油顏色 (上色 / 上顏色) apply paint
油罌 (油罐兒) oil jar
油膩 greasy; oily
　　好油膩 (很油膩) very greasy

一罌豉油 (一罐豉油) an earthen jar of soy sauce
人造牛油 margarine
人哋出雞，你出豉油 (佔人便宜) While the larger part of the expenses is borne by others, one still has to bear a small part of the expenses
入油 refuel
太陽油 (防曬油) suntan lotion
水溝油 (合不來) cannot get along with each other; unfriendly
火上加油 add oil to the flames; pour oil on fire
火油 (煤油) kerosene
牛油 butter
白油 (塗改液) correction fluid
石油 petroleum
加油 ① go ② make extra efforts ③ refuel
生油 cooking oil
老糠搾出油 get oil out of rocks
把口瑯過油 (口甜舌滑) smooth-mouthed
汽油 gas; gasoline; petrol
沙律油 salad oil
走油 (不要油) no oil
走蠔油 (不要蠔油) no oyster sauce
定過抬油 (不慌亂 / 穩當 / 從容鎮定) completely composed; have full confidence in; have the game in one's hands
抹油 cleaning and oiling
抽油 (豉油) soy sauce
芥花籽油 canola oil
花生油 peanut oil
香油 oil-lamp money
指甲油 nail varnish
倒掛臘鴨 ──(滿)嘴油 (動口不動手) have a glib tongue; just by talking
桐油 tung oil
桐油埕裝桐油 (桐油罐子無二用) a tung oil canister is merely for holding the tung oil
脂油 lard
索油 (佔便宜) intend to make a pass at a lady; lecherous man
麻油 sesame oil
偈油 (潤滑油) lubricant oil
捽啲藥油 (塗藥油) apply some herbal ointment
豉油 soy sauce
魚油 cod liver oil
揩油 (佔便宜) molest a woman
菜油 vegetable oil
菠蘿油 pineapple-shaped bun with butter
粟米油 corn oil
搽油 (塗油) apply ointment
植物油 vegetable oil
滋油 (慢悠悠) act or speak leisurely and unhurriedly; slow-paced

滋滋油油 (慢悠悠) unhurriedly

煉油 oil refining; rendering

煤油 kerosene

電油 gasoline; petrol

啤燈賣油 a game worth a candle

漆油 paint

辣油 chilli oil

辣椒 chilli

舔豉油 dip with soy sauce

熟油 cooked oil

豬油 lard

橄欖油 olive oil

點豉油 dip with soy sauce

簽香油 (捐燈油錢) donate money to the oil-lamp

醬油 sauce; soy sauce

蠔油 oyster sauce

蘸豉油 dip with soy sauce

【河】ho⁴ river

河口 estuary; firth; river mouth

河水 river water

　　河水不犯井水 each follows their own bent; each minds their own business; river water does not mix with well water

河流 rivers; streams

河馬 hippo; hippopotamus

河粉 rice noodles

河蝦 river prawn; river shrimp

河邊 river bank

河蟹 river crab

河鰻 river eel

乾炒牛河 dry-fried rice noodles with beef

跳河 commit suicide by throwing oneself into the river; drown oneself

遊車河 car ride; drive around for pleasure; go for a drive in a car; take a car ride for pleasure

遊船河 boat ride; boat trip; cruise trip; take a boat ride for pleasure

過冷河 ① (將煮熟的食物放到冷水中稍浸) blanch ② (離開工作崗位一段時間) sterilisation period before taking up another position

踎水過河 (涉水過河) wade a stream

欄河 balustrade; bannister; railing

【沽】gu¹ sell

沽出 (售出) sell

沽名釣譽 angle for compliment; angle for praise; angle for undeserved fame; buy reputation and fish for praise; cater to publicity by sordid methods; chase fame; court publicity; fish for fame and compliments; fish for fame and reputation; strive for reputation

沽清 (售完 / 售罄) be sold out

【治】zi⁶ administer

治本 deal with a trouble at the source; effect a permanent cure; get at the root; get at the root of a problem; provide fundamental solutions to the problems; take radical measures; treat a matter thoroughly

治安 peace and order of a nation; public order; public security

治邪 (辟邪) counteract evil fore; exorcise evil spirits

治治浸浸 (喊喊喳喳) noise of talking

治理 ① administer; govern; manage; put in order ② bring under control; harness; regulate

治標 cope with the symptoms only; provide temporary solutions to the problems; take stopgap measures

　　治標不治本 cure the symptoms, not the disease; palliatives

治療 cure; treatment

　　治療師 healer

　　　　物理治療師 physiotherapist

　　　　職業治療師 occupational therapist

一份三文治 one sandwich

三文治 (English) sandwich

公司三文治 club sandwich

州治 state government

吞拿魚治 (吞拿魚三文治) tuna sandwich

免治 (English) minced

玩政治 play politics

政治 politics

根治 bring under permanent control; cure once and for all; fundamental solution; radical cure

蛋治 (雞蛋三文治) egg sandwich

統治 dominate; govern; reign; rule

診治 make a diagnosis and give treatment

賓治 (English) punch

腿蛋治 (火腿雞蛋三文治) egg and ham sandwich

雜果賓治 fruit punch

【況】fong³ situation

況且 furthermore

何況 let alone; much less; not to mention; to say nothing of

狀況 condition; state; state of affairs; status

情況 circumstances; situation

現況 current situation; existing state of affairs; present situation; things as they are

境況 circumstances; conditions

【泊】paak³ (停) (English) park

泊位 park a car

泊車 (停車 / 停放車子) park a car

　　泊車咪錶 (停車收費表) parking meter

泊船 moor a boat

【法】faat³ ① law ② method; way

法子 (辦法) method; way

　　冇法子 (沒有辦法) it can't be helped; nothing can be
　　done; there's no way

法文 French

法官 judge

法律 law

法郎 franc

　　瑞士法郎 Swiss francs

法庭 law court

　　臨時法庭 temporary court

法院 court house

法國 France

　　法國人 French

不法 illegal; unlawful

冇晒辦法 (沒有辦法) can't do anything about it

文法 (語法) grammar

方法 means; method; way

句法 ① sentence structure ② syntax

另想辦法 try to find some other ways; try other ways

司法 administration of justice; judicature

犯法 break the law; violate the law

立法 legislate

合法 legal

守法 abide by the law; keep the law; law-abiding; observe
　　the law

佛法 ① Buddhist dharma; Buddhist doctrines ② power of
　　the Buddha

兵法 military strategy and tactics; the art of war; warcraft

依法 according to law; by operation of law; in conformity
　　with legal provisions

兩面手法 double-faced tactics

呢舖話法 (這種說法) this kind of view

枉法 abuse law; pervert the law; twist law to suit one's own
　　purpose

波法 (球技) ball game skills

知法犯法 deliberately break the law; know the law and violate
　　it; know the law but break it; knowingly violate the law;
　　transgress a law knowingly; wilfully commit an offence

非法 illegal

效法 follow the example of; follow the lead of; imitate;
　　model oneself on; learn from; take sb as a model

章法 ① art of composition; presentation of ideas in a piece
　　of writing ② methodicalness; orderly ways

睇法 (看法) perspective; view; way of looking at a thing

違法 against the law; break the law; illegal; unlawful; violate
　　the law

語法 grammar

諗法 (想法) idea; notion; opinion; thinking; view; way of
　　looking at sth; what one has in mind

曆法 calendar

辦法 method; way

講法 (說法) statement; wording

繩之以法 bring sb to justice; keep sb in line by punishments;
　　prosecute according to the law; punish sb according to
　　law; restrain sb by law

【波】bo¹ ① (球) (English) ball ② (女性乳房) woman's breast ③ (風球) typhoon signal

波子 ① (滾珠) ball ② (保時捷) Porsche

　　波子棋 (中國跳棋) Chinese checkers

波士 (老板 / 老闆) (English) boss

波牛 (熱愛踢足球的人) person who is always playing
　　football

波地 (球場) football field

波板 (球拍) bat; racket

　　波板糖 (板兒糖) lollypop

波波 (泡泡) bubbles

　　吹波波 ① (吹泡泡) blow bubbles ② (吹酒精測試儀)
　　breathalyzer test

波法 (球技) ball game skills

波衫 (球衣) sports shirt

波恤 (球衣) sports shirt

波珠 (滾珠) ball

波動 fluctuation

波鈢 (球靴) (English) ball boot

波場 (球場) football field

波幅 volatility

波斯貓 Persian cat

波棍 (變速桿) gear lever

波路 (球路) style of play

波樓 (枱球館) billiard house

波箱 (變速箱) gear box

波鞋 (球鞋 / 運動鞋) sneaker; sports shoes

波罅 (乳溝) cleavage

波蘿 (鳳梨) pineapple

　　波蘿蓋 (膝蓋) knee cap

入波 (進球) score a goal

八號波 (八號風球) typhoon signal 8

十號波 (十號風球) typhoon signal 10

三號波 (三號風球) typhoon signal 3
五五波 (機會均等) a fifty-fifty chance
手動波 (手動檔) manual shift
世界波 (射門很準) good shot at goal
打乒乓波 (打乒乓球) play table-tennis
打波 (打球) play a ball game
打枱波 (打枱球) ① play snooker ② play billiard
打茅波 (作弊) ① bend the rules ② cheat ③ act dumb;
　　pretend to be ignorant of something in order to gloss it
　　over ④ play dirty in a ball game
打假波 (打假球) cheat at soccer
乒乓波 (乒乓球) table tennis
交波 (傳球) pass the ball; passing
好打波 (愛打球) fond of playing ball games
自動波 (自動檔) automatic shift
低波 (低檔) low gear
吹波 dry hair with a blower
吹波波 ① (吹泡泡) blow bubbles ② (吹酒精測試儀)
　　breathalyzer test
扻波 smash
呢球波 (這一球) this ball
抽波 (扣球) smash the ball
後波 reverse gear
枱波 (枱球) ① (English) snooker ② billiard
茅波 (作弊) tricks in a ball game
高波 (高檔) high gear
鬥波 (比拼球技) ① ball game ② play a ball game
掟波 (拋球) throw the ball
棍波 (手動檔) manual shift
睇波 (看球賽) ① watch a ball game ② watch football
開波 (開始) ① start an activity ② serve
傳波 (傳球) pass the ball
斟波 (跳球) jump ball
漾波 (漣漪) ripples
踢波 ① (踢球) kick the ball ② (踢足球) play football
　　③ (推卸責任) pass the buck; slip work
篤波 (打枱球) ① play snooker ② play billiard
篩波 (開出旋轉的球) chopping in playing table-tennis;
　　cutting in playing table-tennis
賭波 (賭球) bet on football; soccer gambling
濤波 (大波浪) billows; great waves
轆地波 (地滾球) ground ball

【泣】jap¹ sob
泣下 one's tears fall
泣不成聲 be choked with tears; choke with sobs; cry one's
　　heart out; cry one's voice out; cry till one's tears dry;
　　weep one's heart out; weep till one's tears dry

泣別 part in tears
泣涕 come to tears for sorrow; weep
泣訴 accuse while weeping; blubber out one's bitter
　　experiences; sob out one's grievances; tell one's sorrows
　　　如泣如訴 pathetic and touching; plaintive; plangent

涕泣 cry in tears

【泡】paau¹ soak
泡打粉 (發粉) baking powder
泡茶 make tea

一鑊泡 (混亂) chaotic; unmanageable
大頸泡 (甲狀腺腫脹) ① big neck ② goiter
水泡 (救生圈) life buoy
起泡 send up bubbles

【泥】nai⁴ ① mud ② clay; earth
泥水佬 (泥瓦匠 / 泥匠) bricklayer; mason; plasterer; tiler
　　泥水佬開門口——過得自己過得人 (心安理得) live and
　　　let live
泥氹 (泥潭) mire; morass; quagmire
泥沙 (沙子) sand
　　玩泥沙 (玩沙子) play with sand
泥屋 (土房) earth house
泥堆 (土堆) mound
泥菩薩過江——自身難保 (連自己也救不了) cannot
　　even protect oneself
泥路 (土路) muddy road
泥塵 (灰塵) ash; dirt; dust
泥磚 (土磚) cob brick
泥頭 (渣土) dregs
　　泥頭車 (砂石車 / 運泥車) mover
泥鯭 rabbit fish
　　釣泥鯭 taxi drivers picking up passengers going to the
　　　same destination and charge them each a fare

一坺泥 (一堆泥) a soft mass of mud
一嚿泥 (一塊泥) a lump of mud
山泥 mountain clay
水泥 cement
地底泥 (沒有價值的東西) ① sb not worthy of respect
　　② sth cheap and nasty
老泥 (汗垢) old dirt
豆泥 (品質差) poor in quality
和稀泥 (毫無原則地調解紛爭) try to smooth things over
紅毛泥 cement
英泥 cement

浮泥 surface dust
鬼食泥 (口吃) mutter incomprehensibly
捽老泥 (挖走汗垢) rub off the old dirt on the skin
棗泥 jujube paste
黃泥 loess
賤泥 (性格不好的人) person of bad character
壅泥 (埋在泥下) bank up with earth
擔泥 (搬運泥土) carry away the mud

【注】 zyu³ bet
注定 be decreed
　　命中注定 be determined by fate
注重 attach importance to; consider to be important; emphasize; lay emphasis on; lay stress on; pay attention to
注射 get a shot; inject
注視 focus one's look on; gaze at; look attentively at; watch
注意 care about; careful; have an eye on; look out; mindful of; notice; on the look-out; on the watch; pay attention to; show application; take care; take note of; watch; watch one's step; watch out
　　引起注意 attract attention; attract sb's attention; bring to sb's attention; call attention; catch sb's eye; draw attention; excite attention

全神貫注 all attention; all ears; all eyes; all eyes and ears; apply the mind to; be absorbed in; be deeply engrossed in sth; be engrossed in; be occupied with; be preoccupied with; be utterly concentrated in; be wholly absorbed in; be wrapped up in; complete mental concentration; concentrate on; concentrate one's attention on; concentrate the whole energy upon; give one's whole attention to; have sth on the brains; have sth on the mind; in complete absorption; pay undivided attention to; rapt; very attentive; with absorbed interest; with all one's mental faculties on the stretch; with all one's soul; with breathless attention; with one's heart and soul; with rapt attention; with undivided attention
投注 bet; place a bet; stake
受到關注 receive attention
垂注 show concern
起尾注 (吃現成兒) usurp ownership; usurp sb's gains
貫注 ① be absorbed in; concentrate on ② be connected in meaning
落注 (下注) place a bet
關注 attention

【泳】 wing⁶ swim
泳手 (游泳選手) swimmer
泳池 (游泳池) swimming pool
　　露天泳池 (室外游泳池) open-air swimming pool
泳衣 (游泳衣) swimming suit
泳褲 swimming trunks
泳灘 (海水浴場) bathing beach

冬泳 winter swimming
仰泳 backstroke
背泳 backstroke
游泳 swim
韻律泳 synchronised swimming

【炎】 jim⁴ ① hot ② inflammation
炎涼 ① change in temperature; hot and cold ② change in attitude toward persons; snobbishness
炎夏 hot summer; summer at its hottest
炎熱 blazing; burning hot; scorching; very hot

肝炎 hepatitis
肺炎 pneumonia
消炎 anti-inflammatory
關節炎 arthritis

【炊】 ceoi¹ cook
炊事 kitchen work
炊具 cooking utensils; cookware; kitchenware
炊煙 smoke from kitchen chimneys

巧婦難為無米之炊 even a clever woman cannot cook a meal without rice; even the cleverest housewife can't cook a meal without rice; if you have no hand, you can't make a fist; one cannot make a silk purse out of a sow's ear; one cannot realise a certain purpose without the necessary means; one can't make bricks without straw; the French would be the best cooks in Europe if they had got any butcher's meat; you cannot make an omelette without breaking eggs; you can't make sth out of nothing
米已成炊 the die is cast

【炆】 man¹ (燜 / 燉) stew over a slow fire
炆牛腩 stew beef brisket

【炕】 kong³ ① (烘) bake ② (烤) roast
炕乾 (烤乾) bake to dry

【炖】 dan⁶ (隔水蒸) heat with fire
炖蛋 (蒸蛋) steam eggs

【炒】caau² ① stir-fry ② (抬高…價) raise the price ③ (投機) speculate ④ (解僱) fire an employee

炒人 (解僱) be dismissed; boot sb out; cast out; discharge; dismiss; fire; fire an employee; fire out; get one's mittimus; get the bag; get the mitten; give sb the air; give sb the axe; give sb the bounce; give sb the chop; give sb the chuck; give sb the mitten; give sb the push; give sb the sack; give the bag to sb; give the bounce; give walking papers to sb; kick out sb; lay off; let out; pay off; sack; send off; stand off; throw sb out of employment; turn away; turn off

炒友 (投機者) speculator

炒外匯 (炒賣外匯) speculate in foreign currencies

炒地皮 (炒賣地皮) speculate in land

炒米 fried vermicelli
　　星洲炒米 fried vermicelli in Singaporean style

炒車 (車禍) car crash

炒金 (炒賣黃金) speculate in gold

炒飛 (抬高票價) lift up the price of the ticket; raise the ticket price; scalp tickets

炒埋一碟 (混在一起) put everything into one package

炒蛋 ① fried egg ② scramble egg

炒飯 fried rice
　　一個炒飯 a plate of fried rice
　　一碟炒飯 a dish of fried rice; a plate of fried rice

炒樓 (炒賣房產) speculate in real estate

炒蝦嚓蟹 (粗言爛語 / 說話粗俗) use vulgar language

炒魷 (解僱) be dismissed; boot sb out; cast out; discharge; dismiss; fire; fire out; get fired; get one's mittmus; get the bag; get the mitten; give sb the air; give sb the axe; give sb the bag; give sb the boot; give sb the bounce; give sb the chop; give sb the chuck; give sb the itten; tive sb the push; give sb the sack; give the bag to sb; give the bounce; give walking papers to sb; kick out sb; lay off; let out; pay off; sack; send off; stand off; throw sb out of employment; turn away; turn off

炒燶 (賠了 / 虧了) loss through speculation

炒麵 fried noodles
　　肉絲炒麵 fried noodles with shredded pork

炒鑊 (炒菜鍋子) frying pan

兜炒 stir-fry quickly

乾炒 dry-fried

搏炒 (想被解僱) inviting dismissal

翻炒 (重複) repeat; reproduce

【爬】paa⁴ clamber; climb; crawl; creep

爬上 climp up; get up; scale; scramble up
　　爬上去 climb up

爬山 mountain climbing

爬落 (爬下) climb down; scramble down

爬頭 ① (超車) overtake other cars on the road ② (超越他人) be ahead of others

爬蟲 reptile

向上爬 ambitious; be intent on personal advancement; careerist; climb to the upper echelon of society; climb up the social ladder; intent on personal advancement; office seeker; social climber

【爭】zaang¹ ① (爭取) fight for ② (欠) own ③ (相差) differ

爭交 stop people from fighting with each other

爭先 compete

爭好多 (差很多) much difference

爭住 (爭奪) compete for; vie with each other in doing sth
　　爭住先 (先欠着) owe sb sth temporarily

爭氣 win respect through success
　　爭一口氣 make a good showing
　　爭返啖氣 (爭一口氣) stand up for oneself

爭啲 (差點兒) nearly

爭崩頭 (競爭激烈) fierce rivalry

爭論 argument; controversy

爭錢 (欠錢) owe sb money
　　爭人錢 (欠別人錢) owe sb money

爭 D 嘢 (欠缺一些東西) something is missing

貧不與富敵，富不與官爭 money speaks louder and kings have long arms

戰爭 war

瘦田冇人耕，耕嘅有人爭 once a wasteland is inhabited, a rush for an occupation is insisted

競爭 competition

【爸】baa¹ father

爸爸 (父親) father; papa
　　佢好似佢爸爸 (他就像他的父親一樣) he is a splitting image of his father

阿爸 (父親) papa

賊亞爸 (向盜賊集團敲竹杠的人) a thief of thieves

【牀】cong⁴ bed

牀下底（牀底下）under a bed
  牀下底放紙鷂——高極有限（牀底下放風箏——不見起）
    flying a kite under a bed, it won't rise
  牀下底破柴——包撞板（半夜叫城門——碰釘子）be
    rebuked; meet with a rebuff; run into big trouble
  牀下底踢毽——高極有限（牀底下放風箏——不見起）
    flying a kite under a bed, it won't rise

牀冚（牀罩）bedspread
牀單 bed sheet
  一張牀單（一條牀單）a bedsheet
牀墊（褥子）mattress
牀褥（褥子）mattress
牀頭 headboard
  牀頭几 bedside table
  牀頭打交牀尾和 a family quarrel which is likely to
    be settled
  牀頭枱（牀頭桌）bedside table
  牀頭櫃 bedside cupboard
牀邊櫃 bedside cabinet

大牀 double bed
上牀 have sex
行軍牀 canvas cot
行牀（鋪牀）set up a temporary bed
竹牀 bamboo bed
臥牀 lie in bed
執牀（收拾牀鋪）make the bed
細牀（小牀）single bed
單人牀 single bed
開牀（收拾牀鋪）make the bed
落牀（下牀）get out of bed
碌架牀（雙層牀）bunk bed
彈弓牀（彈簧牀）spring bed
雙人牀 double bed
薦牀（褥子）mattress

【版】baan² page

版本 edition
版面 ① layout of a printed sheet ② space of a
  whole page
版畫 block print; print; woodcut
版權 copyright

出版 publish
盜版 priated edition
電影版 movie version
頭版 front page

【牧】muk⁶ ① shepherd ② pasture

牧羊 shepherd; tend sheep
  牧羊狗 sheepdog
牧師 priest
牧場 grazing land; pasture
牧童 buffalo boy; cow boy; shepherd boy
牧歌 pastoral song

畜牧 domestic animals

【物】mat⁶ things

物主 owner
物以罕為貴（物以稀為貴）precious things are never
  found in heaps
物以類聚 birds of a feather flock together
物理 physics
  物理治療 physical therapy
  物理學 physics
物業 flat; real property
  物業升值 appreciation in value for flat
  物業市道 property market
  物業保養 property maintenance
  物業面積 area of a property
  物業單位 property unit
  物業價格 price of property
物輕情義重 a gift of trifling value conveys affection
物質 material
  物質享受 material enjoyment
物離鄉貴，人離鄉賤 articles leaving home become
  precious, but people, demeaned

一件禮物 a gift; a present
一物治一物 everything has its superior; one thing is always
  controlled by another; there's always one thing to conquer
  another
七七物物（等等）and so on and so forth
小人物 cipher; nobody; small beer; small fry; small potato
尤物 ① uncommon person ② rare beauty; woman of
  extraordinary beauty
以物交物 barter; exchange of goods; exchange of one
  commodity for another; trade one thing against another
刊物 publication
生日禮物 birthday gift
生物 biology
奶媽抱仔——人家物（老媽抱孩子——人家的）a wet nurse
  holding a baby – sb else's child
交換禮物 exchange gifts
宇宙萬物 myriad things in the universe
池中物 person of mediocre abilities

怪物 ① monster ② eccentric person
食物 food
建築物 ① building ② structure
動物 animal
常見藥物 common medicine
壺中物 drinks; liquor; wine
新年禮物 New Year gift
植物 ① plant ② vegetable
結婚禮物 wedding gift
尋找獵物 hunt for one's prey
聖誕禮物 Christmas present
節日禮物 festive gift
違例建築物 illegal structure
幕後人物 wirepuller
廢物 waste
穀物 cereal; grain
禮物 gift
購物 buy things
藥物 medicine
寵物 pets
礦物 mineral
獵物 prey
囊中物 sth in the bag

【狀】zong⁶ ① shape ② legal

狀元 first in the civil service examination
　　行行出狀元 every profession produces its own leading
　　　authority; every profession produces its own
　　　specialists; every trade has its master; one can be
　　　outstanding in any trade
狀況 condition; state; state of affairs; status
狀師 (律師) lawyer
狀態 condition; situation; state; state of affairs; status

大狀 (律師) barrister
作狀 (裝模作樣) pretend; put on an act; strike a pose
形狀 shape
告枕頭狀 (吹枕邊風) lay a complaint against sb in the
　　presence of one's husband
惡人先告狀 take a preemptive step
症狀 symptom
粒狀 graininess; granular

【狗】gau² dog

狗上瓦桁——有條路 (耗子鑽水溝——各有各的路)
　　rats passing through a sewer – each going their
　　own way
狗公 (公狗) dog; male dog
狗爪邊 (反犬旁 / 犬猶兒) the "dog" (犬) radical

狗主 dog owner
狗仔 (小狗) puppy
　　狗仔隊 paparazzi
狗年 Year of the Dog
狗屁 horseshit; nonsense; rubbish
狗乸 (母狗) female dog
狗房 kennel
狗咬呂洞賓——不識好人心 (狗咬呂洞賓，不知好
　　歹) not know chalk from cheese
狗咬狗骨 (狗咬狗 / 同類相鬥) fighting among members
　　of the same group; put up an internecine fight
狗屎 dog poo; dog shit
　　狗屎垃圾 crap; rubbish
　　　落狗屎 (下大雨) it rains dogs and cats
　　　落狗屎都要去 (即使下大雨也要去) will go regardless
　　　　of weather conditions
狗隻 dog
　　狗隻訓練 dog training
狗帶 dog leash
狗眼看人低 despise
狗蝨 (蛇蚤) dog flea
狗糧 dog food
狗膽包天 monstrous audacity
狗竇 ① (狗窩) doghouse; kennel ② (凌亂的家) untidy
　　home
狗籠 crate

一個熱狗 a hot dog
一隻狗 a dog
土狗 mole cricket
男人老九 (男人) tough man
拉閘放狗 (關門) close the door
牧羊狗 sheepdog
門口狗 (看門狗) guard dog; watchdog
食砒霜土狗 at disadvantage before gaining an advantage
拳師狗 boxer
流浪狗 stray dog
狼過華秀隻狗 (十分兇猛) very ferocious
番狗 (外國品種犬) dog of foreign breed
貴婦狗 poodle
喪家狗 (喪家犬) be seized with fear; in a state of anxiety
嫁雞隨雞，嫁狗隨狗 become a subordinate to one's husband
　　once married
裝假狗 (裝模作樣) make believe; pretend; put on airs
跟尾狗 ① (北京狗) Pekingese ② (裝模作樣的人)
　　obsequious person
養隻狗 keep a dog
賭狗 bet on dogs
熱狗 hot dog

賽狗 dog racing

擦鞋狗 (拍馬屁) flunky

癩皮狗 ① mangy dog ② loathesome creature

癲狗 (憤怒的人 / 兇惡的人 / 瘋子) angry person; furious man; mad man

【狐】 wu⁴ fox

狐狸 fox

　狐狸精 enchantress; seductive woman; seductress; woman of easy virtue; woman who seduces another woman's husband

　　老狐狸 crafty old fox; crafty scoundrel; cunning old person

狐臭 body odour; bromhidrosis

狐疑 doubt; suspicion

臭狐 hircus

【玫】 mui⁴ rose

玫瑰 rose

　玫瑰花 rose

　　一打玫瑰 a dozen roses

【玩】 waan² (玩兒) play

玩一鋪 (玩一次) play a game

玩火 play with fire

玩死 (作弄別人至死) play tricks on sb to cause him/her trouble; play with sb until they are dead or finished

玩完 ① (完蛋 / 結束) be played out; game over ② (去世 / 死) die; pass away ③ (結束關係) end a relationship

玩玩吓 (鬧着玩) horse around; joke

玩殘 (作弄別人至死) play with sb until they are dead or finished

玩牌 play cards

玩野 (鬧事) make trouble

玩餐飽 (玩個夠) have a good time

玩謝 (作弄別人至死) play with sb until the are dead or finished

好玩 amusing; enjoyable; funny; interesting

好玩 fond of playing

唔係講玩 (不是說笑) it is no joke

摟人玩 (找別人玩) ask sb to play

摻埋佢玩 (讓他一塊來玩) let sb play with us

【玩】 wun⁶ plaything

玩具 plaything; toy

　一件玩具 a toy

【畀】 bei² (給) give

畀錢 (付錢 / 給錢) pay cash

嫁畀 (嫁給) marry a man

【疚】 gau³ compunction

疚懷 ashamed

內疚 compunction; guilty conscience

【的】 dik⁷ of

的士 (出租小汽車 / 出租車 / 出租汽車 / 計程車) taxi

　的士司機 taxi driver

　的士佬 (的士司機) taxi driver

　的士站 taxi stand

　的士高 (的是高 / 迪斯科) (English) disco; discotheque

　　一架的士 a taxi

　　上的士 get into a taxi

　　揸的士 (駕駛的士) taxi driver

　　落的士 (下的士) get out of a taxi

的式 / 的的式式 (小巧 / 秀氣 / 標緻 / 嬌小玲瓏) delicate; small; tiny

的確 / 的的確確 definitely

士的 (棒) stick

打的 (乘的士) take a taxi

目的 aim; purpose

紅的 ① (紅色的士) red taxi ② (市區的士) urban taxi

飛的 (趕乘的士) speed up the journey by taking a taxi

搭的 (乘的士) take a cab; take a taxi

達到目的 attain one's goal

漫無目的 aimless

綠的 ① (綠色的士) green taxi ② (新界的士) New Territories taxi

顧客永遠是對的 customers are always right

【盂】 jyu⁴ jar

盂蘭節 Hungry Ghost Festival

【盲】 maang⁴ (瞎) blind

盲人 (瞎子) blind person

盲中中 (沒頭沒腦) absent-minded

盲公 (瞎子) blind man

　盲公竹 (引導者) old hand

　　盲公竹——督人唔督己 (手電筒——對人不對己) a flash light – one who is always strict with others but never with himself

　盲公鏡 (太陽眼鏡 / 墨鏡) sunglasses

盲毛 (傻子) idiot

盲目 blind
　盲目行動 act blindly
盲佬 (盲人 / 瞎子) blind person
　盲佬貼符——倒貼 not getting but giving away money
盲拳打死老師傅 (新手勝老手) a poor hand may put the old master to death
盲炳 (傻子) idiot
盲婆 (女瞎子) blind woman
盲眼 (瞎) blind
盲腸 appendix
盲摸摸 (盲目地 / 瞎摸合眼地) blindly

眼盲 blind
發雞盲 (看不見某東西) blind to sth

【直】 zik⁹ ① straight ② vertical

直升機 helicopter
直去 (直走) go straight
直白 (坦率 / 直率) candid; forthright; frank; outspoken; straightforward
直行 (直走) go straight ahead
直身裙 (連衣裙) one-piece dress
直情 (直接 / 根本) straightway
　直情係喇 (根本就是) this is really true
直接 direct
直通 through
　直通巴 (直通巴士) shuttle bus
　直通車 (直通火車) through train
直畢甩 (直溜溜的) very straight
直程 (直接 / 根本 / 徑直) directly; simply; straightway
直腸直肚 (真性子) outspoken; straight-talking
直腸直腦 (真性子) outspoken; straight-talking
直播 live broadcast
直頭 (直接 / 根本 / 徑直) straightaway
　直頭搵佢 (直接找他) contact him directly
直覺 basic instinct; gut feeling; intuition
直譯 literal translation

打到瞓直 (被打慘了) beat severely
打直 (直放) vertical
瓜直 (死了) die
企直 (站直) stand upright
阿駝都俾你激直 (暴跳如雷) you make sb crazy
垂直 vertical
挺直 erect; straight and upright
船到橋頭自然直 in the end things will mend; let things slide; things at worst will mend; when the boat comes to the bridge underpass, it will go through straight; when things are at the worst, they will mend

蹟直 (完全失敗) be completely defeated; meet a lost cause
攤直 (死 / 直躺) die; have fallen flat
戇直 ① blunt and tactless ② honest

【知】 zi¹ (知道) know

知人口面不知心 be familiar with sb but ignorant of his true nature
知子莫若父 no one knows a boy better than his father
知己知彼 it needs to understand both oneself and others
知到 (知道) know
知其一不知其二 have a smattering of sth or sb
知唔知 (知道…嗎) don't you know that...
知書識墨 (知書識禮) educated and polite person
知埞 (知地兒) know what one is doing
知情識趣 know how to behave oneself to cope with sb's feeling and interest
知無不言，言無不盡 say all what one knows
知道 know
知醒 (睡得醒 / 醒得了) wake up in time
　唔知醒 (睡不醒 / 醒不了) wake up late
知醜 (害羞 / 害臊) bashful; feel ashamed; shy
知識 knowledge
　知識就是力量 knowledge is power
　知識產權 patent right

不知 not know
另行通知 be notified later; issue a separate notice
有所不知 there are things one doesn't know
良知 conscience
明知 be fully aware; know perfectly well
唔知 (不知道) not know
殊不知 (誰知道) who could have realised that; who knows that
茫然不知 utterly ignorant of
鬼知 (誰知道) who knows
假裝唔知 (假裝不知道) pretend not to be aware of; pretend that one does not know
通知 inform; notice
啞仔食黃蓮——有苦自己知 (啞巴吃黃蓮—有苦說不出) swallow the leek
無知 innocent
詐帝唔知 (假裝不知道) pretend not to be aware of; pretend that one does not know
須知 ① have to know; it must be understood; one should know; should know ② note; notice; points for attention
照我所知 (按我知道的) as far as I know
話你知 (告訴你) tell you

話畀你知（告訴你）let me tell you
誰不知（誰知道）who would have thought that
點知（誰知道）who knows

【社】se⁵ society

社女 call girl
社工 social worker
社交 social intercourse
　　社交禮節 social etiquette
社會 society
　　社會工作 social work
　　社會工作者 social worker
　　　黑社會（黑幫）secret society; triad society

旅行社 travel agency

【空】hung¹ empty; vacant

空口講白話（只會説 / 只説不做）all mouth and no
　　action; boasting; words pay no debts
空少（飛機男服務員）air steward
空心 hollow
　　空心老倌（外強中乾的人）a person without real ability
　　and learning; gorgeous in appearance but inwardly
　　insubstantial
空肚 before meal
空房 empty room; vacant room
空姐（飛機女服務員）air hostess; female flight attendant
空軍 air force
空氣 air
　　空氣污染 air pollution
　　空氣清新 the air is fresh
　　新鮮空氣 fresh air
空缺 vacancy
　　職位空缺 vacancy
空郵 air mail
空閒 free; leisure
空檔 free time
空寥寥（空落落的）spacious and desolate; open and
　　desolate; empty

一場歡喜一場空 draw water with a sieve
天空 sky
太空 outer space
防空 air defence; anti-aircraft; anti-craft defence
凌空 be high in the sky; tower aloft
航空 aviation; voyage
真空 pantiless
晴空 bright sky; clear air; clear sky; cloudless sky; serene
笪箕打水——一場空 draw water with a sieve

【者】ze² person

支持者 backer; camp follower; follower; supporter; sympathizer
死者 the deceased
告發者 informant; informer; whistle-blower
社會工作者 social worker
來者 comer; those who come
昔者 before; formerly; in ancient times; in former times
長者 elder; senior
長線投資者 long-term investor
投資者 investor
使者 guard
冒充記者 pass oneself off for a journalist
冒充學者 pose as a scholar
弱者 the weak; the weak and the timid; underdog
記者 journalist; reporter
學者 scholar
護花使者 bodyguard of a lady
譯者 translator
露宿者 street sleeper
讀者 reader

【股】gu² stock

股市 stock market
股息 dividend
股票 equity; share; stock
　　股票市場 stock market
　　股票掛鈎 equity-linked
　　股票經紀 stock broker
　　　一隻股票（一種股票）a stock
　　　炒股票（炒賣股票）speculate in share
　　　賭股票 gamble on shares
股價 share price

打屁股 get a slap on the buttocks; get a spanking; get
　　punished; receive punishment; spank
屁股 backside; behind; boff; bottom; bum; buttocks; cheeks;
　　chuff; duff; fanny; hip; keister
美股 American stock
蚊型股（仙股）penny stock
碎股（零股）odd lot

【肥】fei⁴（胖）fat

肥仔（小胖子 / 胖小子）fat boy; fatty
肥妹（胖妞兒 / 胖姑娘）fat girl
肥肥白白（胖胖白白）fair and plump
肥肥哋（有點兒胖）a little fat; quite fat
肥佬 ①（胖子 / 胖男人）fat guy; fat man ②（不合格）
　　(English origin: fail) fail in an examination or a test

肥咗（胖了）put on weight
肥屍大隻（肥頭大耳的）strongly-built man
肥缺 armchair job
肥婆（胖女人）fat woman
肥嘟嘟（胖胖的）chubby; fat and round
肥頭耷耳（笨笨的）stupid
肥膩 greasy; oily
肥雞餐（遣散費）golden handshake
肥騰騰（胖乎乎的／過度肥胖）overfat

人怕出名豬怕肥（槍打出頭鳥）fame brings trouble
太肥（太胖）too fat
減肥 go on diet; lose weight
痴肥（過重）abnormally fat; obese
落肥（施肥）apply fertilizer; fertilize; spread manure
獨食難肥（人有利益應該與別人分享）one will be more successful if one shares with others
癡肥（過重）abnormally fat; obese

【肩】gin¹ shoulder
肩肉 beef shoulder
肩負 bear; shoulder; take on; undertake
肩痛 omalgia; pain in the shoulder; shoulder pain

口水肩（圍嘴兒）bib; cloth necklet
併肩 shoulder to shoulder
披肩 shawl

【肪】fong¹ fat

脂肪 fat

【肯】hang² agree; consent
肯定 absolute; affirm; approve; as sure as death; as sure as eggs is eggs; as sure as fate; as sure as hell; as sure as I'm standing here; as sure as you live; ascertain; certain; confident; confirm; definite; for sure; guarantee; in the affirmative; make sure; positive; sure; swear; with absolute certainty
肯制（願意）willing
肯肯舞 cancan

【育】juk⁶ raise
育兒 child rearing
育嬰 rear a baby
育齡 childbearing age

孕育 foster; nurse; nurture
成人教育 adult education
培育 breed; cultivate; foster; nurture; raise; rear

強迫教育 compulsory education
教育 education
填鴨式教育 spoon-feeding education

【肺】fai³ lung
肺炎 pneumonia
肺部感染 chest infection
肺癌 lung cancer
肺癆 tuberculosis

入心入肺（刻骨銘心）take sth to heart
甩肺（被打得很厲害）be beaten up badly
扰心扰肺（極度後悔）deeply regret
挵心挵肺（傷透他人的心）break sb's heart
良心當狗肺（好心當成驢肝肺／不知感恩）be ungrateful for a favour and regard it as a disservice
到喉唔到肺（不滿足）be half satisfied; insufficient; not enough to satisfy one's appetite; unsatisfying
俾個心你食都當狗肺（好心當成驢肝肺／不知感恩）be ungrateful for a favour and regard it as a disservice
頂心頂肺（堵心／耿耿於懷）be hurt by others by what they say about one; pain in the neck
照肺（被上司質問）be questioned by the boss
黐肺 exhausted; to an extreme extent

【臥】ngo⁶ rest
臥底 ① （內應）undercover agent ② （間諜）spy
　　臥底行動 undercover operation
臥牀 lie in bed
臥室 bedroom
臥病 be confined to bed; be laid up; bedridden on account of illness

【舍】se³ ① dwelling ② my
舍弟 my younger brother
舍妹 my younger sister
舍監 house master; warden

青年旅舍 youth hostel
旅舍 hostel
神不守舍 absence of mind; absent-minded; n an absent way; in brown study; in the clouds; inattentive; jump the track; nobody home; one's heart is no longer in it; one's mind is not in it; one's mind is occupied with other things; one's wits go woolgathering; out to lunch; preoccupied with sth else; with an abstracted air; with one's mind wandering; with one's thoughts elsewhere; woolgathering
宿舍 hostel

隔籬鄰舍 neighbours

零舍 (特別) especially; extraordinarily; particularly

魂不守舍 lose one's head; out of one's wits

靈舍 (特別) especial; extraordinary; out of the ordinary; particular; special; unusual

【芙】fu⁴ hibiscus

芙蓉 ① hibiscus ② scrambled egg

　　出水芙蓉 ① hibiscus rising out of water; lotus comes into bloom ② pretty girl

【芝】zi¹ sesame

芝士 (奶酪) cheese

　　芝士餅 cheese cake

　　　　一塊芝士 a piece of cheese

芝麻 sesame

　　芝麻卷 seet black sesame roll

　　芝麻綠豆 (小事) trivial

　　芝麻糊 sweet sesame soup

芝蘭 orchid

【芡】hin³ starch

芡粉 starch

打芡 (勺芡) starching

【芥】gaai³ mustard plant

芥花籽油 (菜籽油) canola oil

芥辣 (芥末) ground mustard; mustard

芥醬 (芥末醬料) mustard sauce

芥蘭 (甘藍 / 芥藍菜) kale

醬芥 pickled rutabaga

【芭】baa¹ plantain

芭蕾舞 ballet

【芯】sam¹ pith of rushes

芯子 ① fuse; wick ② forked tongue of a snake

芯片 microchip

一粒電芯 (一粒電池) a battery

一嚿電芯 (一粒電池) a battery

蒜芯 garlic shoot

電芯 (電池) battery

燭芯 candlewick

【花】faa¹ ① flower ② (矇矓不清) blurred ③ (破損痕跡) get scarred; scar ④ (弄髒) make dirty ⑤ (花錢) spend worthlessly

花士令 (凡士林) (Fnglish) vaseline

花心 (二心 / 不專一) disloyal; have many lovers; not to give one's mind to one's lover

　　花心大少 (花花公子) playboy

　　花心蘿蔔 (花花公子) playboy

花王 (花匠 / 園丁) gardener

花市 ① flower market ② Lunar New Year flower market

　　行花市 (逛花市) visit the flower market

花弗 ① (輕挑) flirtatious ② (花俏) gaudy like a peacock

花生 peanut

　　花生油 peanut oil

　　花生醬 peanut butter

　　　　一樽花生醬 a jar of peanut butter

　　　　一粒花生 a peanut

花名 (外號 / 綽號) nickname

　　改花名 (起外號) give sb a nickname

　　起花名 (起外號) give sb a nickname

花多眼亂 (太多選擇) have a dazzling array of choices before one; there are too many to choose; too many choices

花臣 (花樣) (English: fashion) gimmick; tricks

　　撚花臣 (玩花樣) play tricks

花言巧語 fine words; have a sweet tongue

花店 florist; flower shop

花枝 squid

花花公子 dandy; playboy

花紅 (獎金) bonus; dividend

花面 painted face

　　花面貓 dirty face

　　大花面 (大花臉) painted face

花柳 syphilis

花洒 (蓮蓬頭) shower

　　花洒帽 (蓮蓬頭) shower cap

　　花洒頭 (蓮蓬頭) shower head

花冧 (花蕾) bud

花哩碌 (花花碌碌 / 花哨) colourful

　　花哩花碌 (花花碌碌 / 花哨) colourful

花粉症 hay fever

花茶 tea with dried flowers

花瓶 ① flower vase ② pretty woman with no brain

花假 (不實在 / 虛假) fake; false

花椒 Sichuan pepper-corn

花款 (花色 / 花樣) pattern

花階磚 (方磚) ceramic brick

花開富貴 may your wealth bloom like flowers

花碌碌 (花斑斑的) colourful

花花碌碌 colourful

花園 garden
　　遊花園 ① walk around the garden ② go around in circles

花墟 (花市) flower market

花膠 fish maw

花靚 (毛小子 / 臭小子) little boy; little rascal
　　花靚仔 (毛小子 / 臭小子) little boy; little rascal

花樽 (花瓶) ① flower vase; vase ② pretty woman with no brain

花燈 festive lantern
　　睇花燈 (賞燈) watch festive lanterns

花嚫 (年輕小伙子) idle young man
　　花嚫仔 (年輕小伙子) playfellow; youngerster of rascality

花灑 (噴頭 / 蓮蓬頭) shower; sprinkler

一枝花 a spray of flower
一紮花 (一束花) a bundle of flowers
丁香花 lilac
口水花 saliva drops
口花花 (油嘴滑舌) like to tease others; loose-tongued when flirting with girls; sweet talk; talk frivolously
五花 five-flower
天花 ① smallpox ② ceiling
打到開花 (被打慘了) beat severely
生花 flowers; fresh flowers
印花 stamp
百合花 lily
西蘭花 broccoli
豆腐花 jellied bean curd
走馬看花 take a scamper through sth
到處楊梅一樣花 same trees at all places bear same fruits
放煙花 let off fireworks
昏花 dim-sighted
玫瑰花 rose
校花 most beautiful girl in the school
桂花 osmanthus
桃花 peach blossom
浪花 ① spray ② a happy event in one's life
帶花 shot a bullet
梨花 pear blossom
淋花 (澆水) water the flower
荷花 lotus
眼花 dazzled; eyes blurred
眼花花 with blurred vision
魚花 (魚苗) young fry
揩花 (刮花) be scratched
棉花 ① cotton ② medical cotton
窗花 window lattice

菊花 ① chrysanthemum ② dried chrysanthemum
買樓花 (買未建成的住宅單位) buy a flat under construction
椰菜花 cauliflower
煙花 fireworks
葵花 sunflower
葱花 chopped green onion
劃花 (刮花) ruin sth by scratching
種花 cultivate flowers
撚花 (種花) play with flowers and grass
樓花 (未建成的住宅單位) uncompleted residential unit
蓮花 lotus flower
襟花 boutonniere; corsage
獻花 present flowers
蘭花 orchid
櫻花 cherry blossom

【芹】kan⁴ celery

芹菜 Chinese celery

西芹 celery

【芽】ngaa⁴ sprout

芽豆 sprouted broad bean
芽菜 (豆芽兒 / 黃豆芽 / 綠豆芽) bean sprout
　　大豆芽菜 (黃豆芽) soybean sprout
　　細豆芽菜 (綠豆芽) mung bean sprouts

銀芽 bean sprout
嫩芽 delicate shoots

【芫】jyun⁴ coriander

芫茜 (香菜) coriander

【虎】fu² tiger

虎口 tiger's mouth
　　送羊入虎口 a lamb to the slaughter; put sb to death
虎父無犬子 like father, like son
虎年 Year of the Tiger
虎落平陽被犬欺 out of one's sphere of influence, out of one's power
虎頭蛇尾 a brave beginning and weak ending; a brave beginning but a poor ending; a tiger's head and a snake's tail; begin well but fall of towards the close; begin with tigerish energy but peter out towards the end; come out at the small end of the horn; do sth by halves; fine start and poor finish; in like a lion, out like a lamb; start out well but not continue; with a fine start but a poor finish

一山不能藏二虎 at daggers drawn

上得山多終遇虎 the fist that nibbles at every bait will be caught

冇牙老虎 (紙老虎) toothless tiger

打老虎 (拘捕幕後黑手) arrest the high-ranking officials who break the law

老虎 tiger

扮豬食老虎 (大智若愚) feign ignorance; play the fool; pretend to be a fool but to be actually very clever

紙老虎 paper tiger

馬虎 not serious; perfunctory; sloppy

馬馬虎虎 not serious; perfunctory; sloppy

猛龍活虎 alive and kicking; brimming with energy; bursting with energy; dynamic and vigorous; full of life and energy; full of vigour and vitality; full of vim and vigour

【虱】sat¹ bug; louse

虱目魚 milkfish

塘虱 catfish

【迎】jing⁴ welcome

迎合 cater to; pander to; play up to

迎接 greet; meet; receive; welcome
　　迎接大駕 meet sb on his arrival

迎新 welcome the new arrivals
　　迎新晚會 evening party to welcome newcomers
　　　　送舊迎新 bid farewell to the old and welcome the new

迎賓 receive guests

迎難而上 advance against difficulties; press ahead in face of difficulties

大受歡迎 receive great popularity; very popular

列隊歡迎 line up to welcome

曲意逢迎 curry favour with others by roundabout methods; do everything to please sb; flatter by hook or by crook; flatter sb in a hundred and one ways; go out of one's way to curry favour with sb; gratify sb's every whim; lick sb's boots; ply sb with assiduous flattery; submit obsequiously to sb's will

受歡迎 be well received; enjoy great popularity; popular

歡迎 welcome

【近】gan⁶ close

近山不可燒枉柴，近河不可洗枉水 waste not, want not

近水樓台先得月 in a favourable situation

近住 near
　　近住城隍廟求炷好香 hope to curry favour with sb powerful

近官得力 it is much more convenient to have a friend in court

近來 recently

近便 (又近又方便) close and convenient

近排 (近來) lately; of late; recently

近期 (最近) lately; not long ago; of late; recently

近廚得食 in a favourable position to gain advantage

左近 ① (附近) around the corner; in the vicinity; neighbouring; nearby; round the corner ② (大約) roughly

生人勿近 stay away from an obnocious person

附近 nearby; vicinity

挨近 (靠近) close by; close upon; come close to; get close to; get near to; leave a small interval; near to; steal up

最近 recently

咽頭近 (快死了) at death's door; close to the age of death; have one's foot in the grave

新近 newly

遠近 ① far and near; remote or close ② distance

幡竿燈籠——照遠唔照近 benefit any other person than close ones

鄰近 adjacent; adjoining; close; contiguous; near; neighbouring

臨近 close by; close on; close to; draw close; draw near

【返】faan² (回) return

返工 (上班) get to the office; go to office; go to work; start work
　　可以隨時返工 (隨時可以上班) immediately available
　　好早返工 (很早上班) go to work very early
　　夜晚返工 (晚上上班) work at night
　　返夜工 (上夜班) go on night shift; work on a night shift
　　揸車返工 (駕駛上班) drive to work

返去 (回去) go back
　　返去舊時嗰度 (重回舊地) back to the old place

返生 (再世 / 起死回生 / 復活) bring back to life; come alive again; resurgence; resuscitate; revive

返學 (上學) attend school; go to school

返嚟 (回來) come back; return
　　啱啱返嚟 (剛剛回來) just come back

一去不返 be gone without returning

計返 work backward

徒勞往返 hurry back and forth for nothing; make a futile journey; make a trip in vain; make a vain trip

淨返 (剩下) only remain

剩返 (剩下) be left over; remain

擾返 redeem; retrieve

遣返 deport; repatriate; send back; send home

【采】coi² ① mien ② demeanour

采地 fief
采邑 fief; vassalage

一睹風采 take a look at sb's elegant demeanour
風采 ① mien ② demeanour

【金】gam¹ gold

金山（美國）the United States
　金山客（美籍華人）America-born Chinese
　金山橙（美國橙）American orange
　　舊金山（三藩市）San Francisco
金牛（一千元紙幣）one-thousand-dollar note
　一隻金牛（一千元紙幣）one-thousand dollar note
金玉滿堂 house filled with gold and gems
金瓜（南瓜）pumpkin
金字邊（金字旁）the "metal"（金）radical
金色 gold
金盆洗手 hang up one's axe
金針 dried lily flowers
金魚 goldfish
　金魚佬（好色鬼）sleazy man
　金魚缸 ① fish tank ② the Stock Exchange ③ display
　　window for prostitutes
　金魚黃 bright yellow
　　突眼金魚 person with protruding eyes
金絲雀（被包養的女人）a beautiful lady who is financially
　supported by a rich man but has no freedom
金絲貓（年輕的外國女人）young female foreigner
金鈪（金手鐲）gold bracelet
金黃色 golden yellow
金銀 gold and silver
　金銀衣紙（冥紙）paper gold, silver and clothes for
　　burning to the desceased or gods
　金銀珠寶 gold, silver, jewellery, and treasure
　金銀蛋 fried and preserved eggs
　金銀滿屋 wish you abundant wealth
　金銀膶 ① pork wrapped with dried and preserved pig
　　liver ② watch with gold and platinum band
金飾 gold jewellery
金舖（銀樓）gold shop; gold store
金器 gold vessel
金錢 money
　金錢肚 beef tripe
金融 finance
　金融公司 finance company
金龜（富有丈夫）rich husband
　金龜婿（富有丈夫）rich husband
　　釣金龜（找個富有丈夫）hook a rich husband

金鏈（金項鏈）gold necklace

千金 ① a thousand pieces of gold ② daughter
　③ extremely precious
五金 hardware; metals in general
生果金（長者津貼）old age allowance
本金 principal
白金 platinum
百忍成金 patience is a plaster for all sores
佣金 commission
定金 deposit
保證基金 guaranteed fund
按金 deposit
美金 American dollar; US dollar
訂金 deposit
烊金 molten metal
真金 real gold; real money
租金 rent
貢金 aids; tributes
退休金 pension
俾現金（以現金結帳）pay cash
基金 fund
掘金（找快錢）make quick money
救濟金 relief money
現金 cash
強積金 MPF (Mandatory Provident Fund)
透支現金 cash advance
黃金 gold
經紀佣金 brokerage
煉金 alchemy
獎金 prize money
獎學金 scholarship
薪金 salary
禮金 ① bride-price; bethothal gifts ② cash gift

【長】coeng⁴ long

長毛（長頭髮）long hair
　長毛賊（長頭髮的男人）long-haired man
長生 long life
　長生不老 live a long life and never grow old; perpetual
　　youth and longevity
　長生板（棺材）coffin
　　長生店（棺材店）shops selling coffins
長命 long life
　長命債，長命還（慢慢兒還債）a life-long debt is to be
　　settled by a life time
長拉拉（長了呱嘰的）lengthy
長度 length
長枱（長桌子）long table

長衫 ① (大褂) long gown ② (旗袍) woman's dress called *cheongsam*

長倉 long position

長氣 (絮叨／囉嗦) long-winded; talkative
　　長氣袋 (絮叨鬼) long-winded person
　　　鬼咁長氣 (絮叨／囉嗦) long-winded

長袖 long sleeve

長途 long distance
　　長途客 long-distance passenger

長痛不如短痛 better eye out than always ache; better eyes out than ever to ache

長傳 long pass

長腳蜢 (腿長的人) long-legged

長線 (長期) long-term

長頸 (長脖子) long neck
　　長頸鹿 giraffe

長嘴鉗 (尖嘴鉗) long-nose pliers

長龍 (排大隊) long queue
　　排長龍 (排大隊) line up in a long queue; queue up in a long line; stand in a long queue
　　　大排長龍 (排大隊) line up in a long queue; queue up in a long line; stand in a long queue

長櫈 (長木櫈) bench

長壽 longevity

一人計短，二人計長 (一人智，不如兩人議) two heads are better than one

一世流流長 (人生漫長) as long as one lives

一疋布咁長 (長篇大論) it's a long story

太長 too long

水蛇春咁長 (很長) lengthy

加長 lengthen

打得更多夜又長 it wastes time only to talk

枕長 (經常地) ① all along; throughout ② always

來日方長 have a long future before one; many a day will come yet; there will be a time for that; there will be ample time; there will be plenty of time

兒女情長 be immersed in love; love between a man and a woman is long; the lasting affection of boys and girls

所長 (長處) one's forte; one's strength; one's strong point; what one is good at

延長 extend; lengthen; prolong; prolongate; protract

泵長 prolong work unnecessarily

特長 extra long

望到頸都長 (望穿秋水) hanker after

眼眉毛長 (長眉毛) ① very old ② not interesting in doing a long-term job

細水流長 waste not, want not

幾長 how long

等到頸都長 (等很久) wait for a very long time

壽星公吊頸──嫌命長 (活得不耐煩) tempt one's fate

語重心長 meaningful; say in all earnestness; say with deep feeling; sincere words and earnest wishes

講起嚟一疋布咁長 (長篇大論) it is like telling a long story

【長】 zoeng[2] ① senior ② leader ③ grow

長大 grow up; mature

長子 eldest son

長老 senior

長官 one's superior in office

長者 elder; senior
　　長者咭 senior citizen card

長輩 ① elder ② senior generation

一時唔偷雞做保長 a rogue goes so far as to moralize to another rogue

伍長 lead of a five-soldier unit

州長 governor of a state

助長 abet; encourage; foment; foster; give a loose rein to sth bad; indulge; nurture; promote the development of

局長 director-general

村長 village head

家長 parents

庭長 chief justice; presiding judge

校長 headmaster

站長 head of a station

院長 college head; dean; president

族長 chief of a clan

船長 captain

部長 commissioner; head of a department; minister

會長 president

署長 administrator

廠長 factory director; factory manager

機長 captain

館長 curator

廳長 sb sleeping in the living room

【門】 mun[4] door

門口 door; doorway
　　門口狗 (看門狗) guard dog; watchdog
　　　大門口 main doorway

門戶 ① door ② family status
　　另立門戶 live in a separate house
　　　門當戶對 let beggars match with beggars; marry into a proper family; marriage with the two families well-matched in social status

門外漢 layman

門字邊 (門字旁) the "door" (門) radical

門戌 (門閂) bolt

門店 (門市部) retail department

門面 ① shop front ② appearance; façade

門面大 have a large shop front

門面小 have a small shop front

裝門面 maintain an outward show

撐門面 keep up appearances

擺門面 put up a front

門框 (門框兒) door case; doorframe

門拴 (插銷) bolt

門票 admission ticket; entrance ticket

買門票 buy the admission ticket

門路 ① knack; way to do sth ② pull; social connections

有門路 know the right places to go to get sth done

搵到門路 (找到門路) catch the knack of; find the way to do sth; learn the ropes

門鉸 (合頁) hinge

門楫 (門檻兒) door sill

門罅 (門縫兒) crack between a door and its frame

門檻 (門檻兒) door sill

門鎖 door lock

門鎖壞咗 (門鎖壞了) the door lock is broken

門鐘 (門鈴) doorbell

門鐘壞咗 (門鈴壞了) the doorbell doesn't work; the doorbell is broken

一度門 (一扇門) a door

一道門 (一扇門) a door

上天無路, 入地無門 (無路可走) in desperate straits

上門 house call

大門 main door

小心車門 mind the door of the vehicle

五花八門 a motley of variety of; all kinds of; all sorts and kinds; all sorts of; in many different ways; many and manifold; multifarious; of a wide variety; rich in variety

丙門 (蠢人) stupid person

出身名門 come from an illustrious family

出門 ① (外出) away from home; go out ② marry off

叩門 (敲門) knock at the door

司法部門 judicial department

名門 illustrious family

寺門 temple

有關部門 department concerned

竹門對竹門, 木門對木門 (門當戶對) choose a husband/ wife with a similar background

防煙門 fire door

扰門 pound the door

走後門 (靠關係) attain one's goal through personal connection; attain one's goal by improper means; get

things done through the back door

拍門 knock at a door; knock on the door; rap at the door; rap on the door; tap at the door; tap on the door

侯門 gate of a noble house

前門 front door

後門 back door

政府部門 government department

閂門 (關門) close the door; shut the door

閂後門 express one's own poor situation beforehand to stop sb from borrowing money from one

埋門 (逼近球門) get close to the goal

射門 shoot; shoot at the goal; shooting

旁門 side door; sidegate

桃李滿門 have many disciples

窄門 narrow door

送貨上門 send goods to one's doorstep

記得鎖門 remember to lock the door; remember to lock up

專門 specialized

部門 department

窗門 casement; window

偏門 illegal business

率門 bolt the door

開鈕門 (開扣眼兒) cut a buttonhole

鈕門 (扣眼兒) buttonhole

碇開度門 push open the door without using one's hands

撈偏門 (做偏門生意) earn a living from illegal business

橫門 side door; sidegate

澳門 Macau

龍門 ① goal ② goal-keeper

臨門 ① arrive at one's door ② before the goal

鎖門 lock the door

鎖鈕門 (扣眼兒) do a lockstitch on a buttonhole

雙喜臨門 get double happiness; get two pieces of good news

爆冷門 unexpected

【阻】zo² (妨礙 / 阻礙 / 阻攔) obstruct

阻住 (阻止) block; in the way; obstruct

阻唔阻你吖 (妨礙你嗎) excuse me

阻碇 (佔地方 / 礙事兒) occupy a place

阻街 (妨礙交通 / 堵塞街道) cause an obstruction in a public place

阻滯 ① (不順暢 / 阻礙) hindrance ② (麻煩) trouble

有啲阻滯 (不太順暢) not smooth

阻頭阻勢 (推三阻四) decline with all sorts of excuses; fob sb off with excuses; get in the way; give the runaround; make excuses and put obstacles in the way

面阻阻 (互不理睬) not on good terms with

勸阻 advise against; advise sb not to; discourage sb from; dissuade sb from doing sth; talk sb out of; warn sb against

【阿】 aa³ prefix for people's names

阿一 ① (老闆) boss ② (領導) leader ③ (負責人) person-in-charge

阿二 ① (第二) number two ② (妾侍 / 小老婆) mistress; second wife

阿八 duck

阿大 (老大) gang boss

阿公 ① (外公 / 外祖父 / 姥爺) grandpa ② (老伯 / 老漢 / 老頭兒) old chap; old codger; old fogey; old man

阿四 (女傭) maid servant

阿吉 chicken

阿伯 ① (伯父 / 伯伯) uncle ② (大爺 / 老伯 / 老漢 / 老頭兒) old chap; old codger; old fogey; old man

阿吱阿咗 (多管閒事) argue; moan; talk back; whine

阿叔 (叔父 / 叔叔) uncle

阿妹 (妹妹) younger sister

阿姐 ① (姐姐) big sister ② (有能力的女人) capable woman ③ (女服務員) teahouse waitress

阿爸 (父親 / 爸爸) papa

阿陀 (駝子) humpback; hunchback

阿星 (印度人) Indian

阿姨 (姨兒 / 姨媽) aunt

阿茂 (傻瓜) stupid person

阿差 (印度人) Indian

阿哥 (哥哥) elder brother
　　大阿哥 (老大) don; leader of a triad society
　　堂阿哥 (堂哥) elder male cousin; first cousin

阿崩 (兔唇 / 豁嘴 / 豁嘴兒) harelip

阿婆 ① (外祖母 / 姥姥) grandma; grandmother ② (大娘 / 大媽 / 老太太) old lady; old woman

阿蛇 (警察) sir

阿頂 ① (老闆) boss ② (老大) gang boss; triad big brother

阿媽 (母親 / 媽媽) mama; mother; mum

阿嫂 (嫂子 / 嫂嫂) ① elder brother's wife; sister-in-law ② a polite way of addressing a friend's wife

阿爺 (祖父 / 爺爺) grandfather; grandpa

阿嫲 (奶奶 / 祖母) ① paternal grandma; paternal grandmother ② gran; granny; nan; nanna; nanny

阿筲 overscrupulous

阿福 (笨蛋 / 蠢人) fool; sucker
　　阿福阿壽 (張三李四) any person in the street

阿駝 (駝子) humpback; hunchback
　　阿駝行路——中中咘 (不上不下) the state of being in the middle

阿駝都俾你激直 (暴跳如雷) you make sb crazy

阿頭 (頭兒) boss; chief; head

阿豬 (笨蛋 / 蠢人) stupid; stupid person

阿燦 (土包子) boor; churl; country bumpkin; country cousin; country folk; country born, farming folk; hayseed; hick; redneck; yokel

阿嬸 ① (叔母) aunt ② (嬸子 / 嬸嬸) sister-in-law

阿 sir (警察) sir

【陀】 to⁴ ① load ② humpback

陀手唔腳 (拖累) clumsy

陀地 (保護) protection
　　陀地費 (保護費) protection fee

陀衰家 (倒霉得連累家人) a person of rough luck implicates others

陀螺 top
　　打陀螺 (抽陀螺) spin a top

阿陀 (陀背) humpback; hunchback

【附】 fu⁶ additional

附加費 surcharge

附近 nearby; vicinity

【雨】 jyu⁵ rain

雨衣 raincoat
　　小雨衣 (避孕套) condom

雨字頭 the "rain" (雨) radical

雨季 rainy season

雨停咗 (雨停了) the rain has stopped

雨溦 (毛毛雨) drizzle; light rain
　　雨溦溦 drizzle; light rain

雨遮 (雨傘) umbrella
　　雨遮架 (雨傘架) umbrella rack

雨褸 (雨衣) raincoat
　　帶雨褸 (帶雨衣) have a raincoat

及時雨 a much-needed rain; a seasonable rain; a timely help; a timely rain; an opportune rain; help rendered in the nick of time

毛毛雨 drizzle

成日落雨 (整天下雨) it rains all day

冒雨 brave the rain; in spite of the run

屋漏兼逢夜雨 it never rains but pours; misfortunes never come singly

要風得風，要雨得雨 be able to get what one wants

紅雨 (紅色暴雨警告) red rain storm signal

風雨 wind and rain

流星雨 ① meteor shower ② falling stars ③ shooting stars

陣雨 occasional drizzle; passing shower; rain shower; shower; shower of rain

停咗雨（雨停了）the rain has stopped

掘尾龍──攪風攪雨（興風作浪）the person who stirs up strife

細雨（小雨）light rain; sprinkle

睇嚟會落雨（看來將會下雨）it looks like it's going to rain

就嚟落雨（快要下雨）it's going to rain

微雨 drizzle; light rain

落大雨（下大雨）it's pouring

落毛毛雨（下毛毛雨）drizzle

落好濃雨（下大雨）it rains heavy

落雨（下雨）rain

落緊大雨（正在下大雨）it's pouring; it's raining cats and dogs

落緊毛毛雨（正在下毛毛雨）it's drizzling

落緊雨（正在下雨）it's raining

落緊微微雨（正在下微微雨）it's drizzling

腥風腥雨 violent conflict

過雲雨（陣雨）shower

零星小雨 occasional drizzle

撇雨（潲雨）① rain slanted by wind ② get wet by the slanting rain

暴雨 rainstorm

翻風落雨（刮風下雨）when there's any change in weather

攪風攪雨（興風作浪）make trouble; stir up troubles

【青】cing¹ green

青口（貽貝）mussel

青少年 adolescent

青白（蒼白）pale

青瓜（黃瓜）cucumber

青色（綠色）light green

青豆（豇豆／碗豆）green pea
　青豆角 green pea

青春 youth
　青春常駐 may you stay youthful and beautiful
　青春痘（青春疙瘩）pimple
　青春期 puberty

青梅竹馬 a boy and a girl who have known each other since childhood

青啤啤（青不嘰的）① blue ② green

青椒 green bell pepper

青菜 green vegetables; vegetables

青頭仔（處男）male virgin

青蟹（十元紙幣）ten-dollar note

年青 young

走青（不要蔥）no spring onion; no scallion

面青（青）（面色蒼白）① pale ② scared; look frightened

唔使擒擒青（慢慢來）easy does it

殺青 finish shooting a movie

割禾青（在賭局中贏了錢便提早離開）leave a gambling game early with one's winnings

標青（出眾）distinguished; great; outstanding

擒（擒）青（不耐煩／匆匆忙忙）① in a hurry; impatient ② over-eager

臘青（瀝青）asphalt

爐火純青 attain perfection; master one's skills to perfection; reach high perfection; the stove fire is pure green — perfection in one's studies

驚青（驚恐）all in a fluster; be afraid; frightened; panic; run scared

【非】fei¹ object to

非法 illegal

非洲 Africa

非常之（非常／極）very; very much

非禮（調戲）assail with obscenities; flirt with women; indecent assault; molest; play the make on; take liberties with
　非禮少女（調戲少女）take liberties with a girl

口是心非 a hypocrite; affirm with one's lips but deny in one's heart; agree in words but disagree in heart; carry fire in one hand and water in the other; carry two faces under one head; cry with one eye and laugh with the other; double-dealing; double-faced; duplicity; hypocrisy; outwardly agree but inwardly disagree; pay lip service; play a double game; play the hypocrite; right with the mouth but wrong at heart; say one thing and mean another; say yes and mean no; show a false face; the mouth specious and the mind perverse; though one speaks well, one's heart is false

官非 lawsuit

明辨是非 clear about what is right and what is wrong; discern between right and wrong; distinguish between truth and falsehood; distinguish clearly between right and wrong; distinguish right from wrong; know right from wrong

是非 gossip

面目全非 be changed beyond recognition

莫非 can it be that; could it be; is it possible that

無事生非 make trouble out of nothing

誰是誰非 who is in the right who is in the wrong; who is right and who is wrong

搬是搬非（搬弄是非）tell tales

較非（冒險）get sb into trouble

撩是鬥非（惹事生非）provoke a fight; stir up a quarrel; sow the seeds of discord

學是非（說閒話／挑撥是非）cause trouble between people; make trouble

講是非 gossip

顛倒是非 confound right and wrong; confuse truth and falsehood; distort truth; give a false account of the true facts; invert justice; reversal of right and wrong; reverse right and wrong; stand facts on their heads; swear black is white; the perversion of truth; turn right into wrong; turn things upside down; twist the facts

攪是攪非（搬弄是非）cause trouble between people; make trouble

9 劃

【亭】 ting⁴ pavilion
亭子 kiosk; pavilion
亭亭 ① erect ② gracefully slim
　　亭亭玉立 slim and graceful; stand gracefully erect; tall and straight

中亭 medium

【亮】 loeng⁶ bright
亮光 light
亮相 strike a pose on the stage

月亮 moon

【侮】 mou⁵ disgrace
侮辱 insult
侮罵 insult with words

【侯】 hau⁴ ① marquis ② wait
侯門 gate of a noble house
　　侯門似海 the gate of a noble house is like the sea — impassable to the common man; the mansions of the nobility are inaccessible to the common man; the threshold of a noble house is deeper than the sea
侯審 await trial
侯爵 marquess; marquis

【侶】 leoi⁵ companion

伴侶 companion
理想伴侶 ideal companion

終生伴侶 lifelong companion
情侶 couple

【侵】 tsam¹ ① （參加） participate; take part in ② （加） add
侵入 intrude into; invade; make incursions into; sneak in
侵水（加水）add water
侵犯 encroach upon; in violation of; infringe upon; intrude; molestation; violate
侵佔 encroach upon; invade and occupy; occupy illegally; seize
侵略 invade

【便】 bin⁶ ① simple ② excrement
便利 convenience
　　便利店 convenience store
便服 plain clothes
便秘 constipation
便飯 ordinary meal

入便（裏面）inside
上便（上面）above; on the surface of; on top of; over; top; upper surface
下便（下面）at the bottom; below; under
小便 apple and pip; burn the grass; dickydiddle; discharge one's urine; drain one's radiator; drain one's snake; empty one's bladder; evacuate the bladder; go tap a kidney; have a leak; have a quickie; have a run off; life his leg; make number one; make salt water; make water; micturate; pass urine; pass water; pee; piddle; pie and mash; piss; plant a sweet pea; point Percy at the porcelain; pump ship; retire; scatter; see a man about a dog; see one's aunt; shake hands with an old friend; shake the dew off the lily; shoot a lion; spend a penny; take a leak; take a quickie; tap a keg; tinkle; urinate; water the lawn; water the stock; whiz
方便 ① convenient; handy ② go to the bath; go to the bathroom to tidy; go to the toilet
出便（外面／外邊）outside
四便（四面／四周）all round; all sides; four sides; on all sides; on four sides
右手便（右邊／右面）right hand side
右便（右邊）on the right side
外便（外面／外邊）outside
左手便（左面／左邊）left hand side; to the left
左便（左邊／左面）on the left side
自便 do as one wishes
呢便（這邊）① here ② this side ③ this way
近便（又近又方便）close and convenient

前便（前面）ahead; at the head; in front; in front of

後便（後面）at the back; behind; in the rear

後面 at the back; behind; in the rear

枱下便（桌下）under the table

埋便（裏面）inside

側便（旁邊）near by position; next to; right by; side

順便 at one's convenience; conveniently; in passing; while sb is about it; without extra effort; without taking extra trouble

提供方便 provide convenience

開便（外面）outside

嗰便（那邊）over there; there

裏便（裏面）inside

精埋一便（小聰明）clever only at ill doings

邊便（哪邊）where; which side

隨便 ① casual; informal ② help yourself ③ as you like; as you please; feel free ④ anything will do

【便】pin⁴ cheap

便宜 petty gain

小便宜 small gains

攞便宜（佔便宜）benefit at others' expense

【係】hai⁶ ① （是）be ② （是嗎）is that so

係咁（使勁兒地／起勁／拼命）active; eager; energetically; enthusiastically; exert all one's strength; go all out; in high spirits; showing much zeal; vigorously; vociferous; with gusto; with zest and vigour; work frantitically

係咁大（玩完了）it's game over

係咁先（就這樣）that's all for now

係咁啦（就這樣）let it be this way; so be it

係咁意（小意思／做做樣子）as a token gesture; do sth as a token

係咁話（就這樣）that's it

係咩（真的嗎）is that so

係咪（是不是）isn't it

係嘅（真是的）this is true

又係嘅（可也是）this is also true

係囉（就是呀）this is true

唔係囉（可不是）this is really so

一係（要不）or

又係（同樣）also the same

之但係（但是）but; however

之唔係（不是）isn't that

凡係（凡是）all; any; every

父子關係 set membership

正係（剛巧）just happens to be

仲係（仍然）still

如果唔係（不然）otherwise

至多唔係 if the worst comes to the worst

至係 only then is

你真係（你真是）you're really

但係（但是）but; however

我都係（我都是）me too

即係（即是）that is

供求關係 supply and demand relationship

咁又係（那又是）that is also true

周圍都係（周圍都是）everywhere is

定係（還是）or; or rather; whether

明明係（明顯是）clearly; obviously

度度都係（周圍都是）everywhere is

祇係（只是）just; merely; only

唔係（不是）① not ② but for; if not; or; or else; otherwise

特別係（特別是）especially

真係（真是）really

梗係（當然）certainly; definitely; must be

淨係（只是）① alone; barely; merely; no more than; nothing but; only; solely ② always; as a rule; commonly; constantly; generally; invariably; usually; without exception

逢係（每逢是）all; every

單係（單是）alone; barely; merely; no more than; nothing but; only; solely

就係（正是）exactly

硬係 after all; always; any; as a rule; at last; be bound; be certain; be sure; commonly; constantly; eventually; ever; every; frequently; generally; have a habit of; however; invariably; keep doing sth; must; never; no matter; one; some; sooner or later; used to; usually; when; where; will; without exception; would

都係（都是）① still ② also; too

絕對唔係（絕對不是）absolutely not

話名係 in name only

實係（當然是）certainly; definitely; must be

算係（算是）consider as

獨係（只是）just; merely; only

整係 always; as a rule; commonly; constantly; generally; invariably; usually; without exception

關係 connection; relationship; relevance

【促】cuk⁷ quick

促成 facilitate; favour; help to bring about; help to materialize; lead on to

促使 impel; lead on to; precipitate; spur; urge

促進 accelerate; advance; boost; encourage; facilitate; gear up; press forward; promote

促銷 promote the sale

促銷小姐 booth bunny

局促 ① cramped; narrow ② short ③ constrain
倉促 all of a sudden; hastily; hasty; hurriedly

【俊】 zeon³ handsome
俊秀 handsome; of delicate beauty; pretty
俊俏 pretty and charming
俊傑 hero; person of outstanding talent

英俊 handsome
髦俊 man of talent

【俐】 lei⁶ ① easy and quick; facile ② clever; sharp ③ in good roder; neat; tidy

眼唔見為伶俐 (眼不見為乾淨) out of sight, out of mind
精乖伶俐 clever and quick-witted; clever and sensible; ntelligent and smart; quick on the uptake
聰明伶俐 smart and sharp

【俗】 zuk⁶ vulgar
俗人 ① vulgarian; ordinary person ② layman
俗不可耐 atrocity; intolerable vulgarity; too vulgar to be endured; unbearably vulgar; vulgar in the extreme
俗骨 (氣質鄙陋庸俗) in bad taste
俗稱 ① secular name of a monk ② common called; commonly known as; common name
俗語 common saying

民間習俗 folk custom
習俗 custom
雅俗 the refined and the vular; the sophisticated and the simple-minded

【俚】 lei⁵ hide
俚埋 (藏起來) hide oneself; keep out of sight

【保】 bou² guarantee
保安 security
　保安員 ① (保安) security guard ② watchman
　保安人員許可證 security personnel permit
保你大 (服了你了) I concede
保重 take care
保祐 bless
保養 maintenance
　保養期 guarantee period; maintenance period
保險 insurance
　保險經紀 insurance agent
保證 guarantee

保釋外出 (擔保外出) release on bail
保齡 (English) bowling
保護 protect

包保 (保證) guarantee
生保 (陌生) strange; unfamiliar
泥菩薩過江——自身難保 cannot protect oneself
擔保 guarantee
環保 environmental protection
難保 there is no guarantee

【信】 seon³ ① faithful ② (相信) believe
信人 (相信別人) trust others
信心 ① confidence ② faith
　對你有信心 have confidence in you
信用 ① trust ② credit
　信用咭 (信用卡) credit card
　信用咭戶口 credit card account
　信用咭月結單 credit card statement
　有信用 trustworthy
信瓜 (茄子) eggplant
信邪 have belief in meeting with misfortune
信封 envelope
　一個信封 an envelope
　大信封 (解僱信) dismissal letter
信差 messenger
信紙 letter paper
信得過 (可以相信的) can be trusted; reliable; trustworthy
信貸 credit
　信貸評級 credit rating
信箱 mail box

一封信 a letter
口信 message
介紹信 letter of introduction
手信 (禮物) sourvenir; sourvenir bought as a gift
打單信 (請帖) invitation
派信 deliver letters; send letters
相信 believe; trust
唔信 (不相信) not believe
破除迷信 abolish superstition
迷信 superstition
匿名信 anonymous letter
寄信 post a letter
掛號信 registered letter
通信 correspondence
誠信 faith; good faith
擔保信 registered letter
難以置信 hard to believe

【俬】si¹ furniture

木傢俬 wooden furniture
竹傢俬 bamboo furniture
傢俬 furniture
鐵傢俬 metal furniture

【冒】mou⁶ risk

冒犯 affront; offend
　　故意冒犯 offend sb on purpose
冒充 pass off as; pretend to be
冒名 assume another's name
　　冒名頂替 assume the identity of another person
冒雨 brave the rain; in spite of the run
　　冒雨搶修 rush to repair in spite of the rain
冒牌 fake
　　冒牌貨 fraudulent goods; imitation goods;
　　　　pirated goods
冒險 take a risk; take chances

流行性感冒 influenza
感冒 flu; have a cold

【冠】gun¹ champion

冠軍 champion
冠詞 article

后冠 tiara
桂冠 crown of laurels; laurel

【剎】saat³ stop

剎掣 （剎車） put on the brakes to stop a vehicle

【則】zak¹ drawing

則師 （建築師） architect

交通規則 traffic regulations
原則 principle
規則 regulation
條款細則 terms and conditions
畫則 drawing paper
圖則 blueprint; drawing; drawing sheet
雖則 （雖然） although; even though

【剃】tai³ （刮） shave

剃刀 razor
　　即棄剃刀 disposable razor
剃面 （刮臉） shave; shave the face
剃頭 shave one's head

險過剃頭 （九死一生） a hair's breadth; a narrow
　　escape; barely escape danger; hang by a hair; in the
　　hour of peril
剃鬚 （刮鬍子） shave
　　剃鬚膏 shaving cream

鬍鬚頭——難剃 difficult to manage; hard to deal
　　with; tough

【削】soek³ cut

削除 omit; strike out; take out
削膊 （溜肩膀） sloping shoulder
削髮 shave one's head
削薄 （of hair） thin out

瘦削 emaciated; emaciated and frail; thin and weak
薄削 thin and soft

【前】cin⁴ formerly

前一個 the previous one
前七 old piece of machinery
前人種果後人收 descendants reap wheat their
　　ancestors sowed
前日 day before yesterday
前功盡廢 （前功盡棄） all efforts go down the drain; all
　　former achievements are nullified; all labour's lost; all
　　one's earlier achievements are in vain; all one's labout is
　　thrown away; all one's merits count for nothing; all one's
　　previous efforts are wasted; all one's work is wasted; back
　　where one strtd; forfeit all one's former achievements;
　　have one's previous efforts wasted; labour lost; nullify
　　all the advantages of a series of victories; nullify all the
　　previous efforts; one's previous efforts have proved to be
　　useless; turn all the previous labour to nothing; waste all
　　the previous efforts; waste the efforts already made
前世 （前生） previous life
　　前世唔修 （可憐） pitiful; suffer retribution for all the ill
　　　　deeds done in the previous existence
　　前世撈亂骨頭 （兩人關係極差） be hostile to each other
前年 year before last
　　前幾年 a few years ago
前言 preface
　　前言不對後語 one's remarks are incoherent; one's words
　　　　do not hang together
前門 front door
前便 （前面） ahead; at the head; in front; in front of
前面 in front; ahead; at the head
前座 front stall
前排 （前些日子） not long ago

前幾排 / 前嘔排（前些日子）not long ago

前晚（前天晚上）the evening of the day before yesterday

前景 prospect

前閘 front gate

前頭（前面）in front; ahead; at the head

前邊（前面）front side; in front

以前 ago; before; ex-; former; formerly; in the past; old; once; past; previous; prior to; since; used to be

目前 at present; at the moment

向前 ahead; forward; go orward; onward

好耐以前（很久以前）a long time ago; long ago; since the year dot; time out of mind

面前 in front of

從前 a long time ago; as of old; before; "ex-"; former; formerly; in former times; in the old days; in the past; long long ago; many years ago; old; once; once upon a time; some time ago; thousands of years ago; used to be

推前 put forward

飯前 before meal

遙遙領前 enjoy a commanding lead; far ahead; way ahead

【勁】ging⁶ ① great ② （強勁）strong

勁抽 ① （很好）excellent; very good ② （帶勁兒）powerful

勁秋 ① （很好）excellent; very good ② （帶勁兒）powerful

勁料（屬害的東西）excellent stuff

勁野（屬害的東西）things that are excellent

好勁（很屬害）excellent

夠勁（夠屬害）energetic; forceful; vigorous

夠晒勁（夠屬害）energetic; forceful; in high spirits; with great energy and efforts; vigorous

蠻勁 animal strength

【勇】jung⁵ brave

勇氣 courage

勇猛 bold and powerful; brave and fierce; full of valour and vigour

勇敢 bold; brave; courageous; gallant; heroic; valiant

【勉】min⁵ reluctant

勉為其難 agree to do what one knows is beyond one's ability; agree to do what one knows is beyond one's power; be forced to do a difficult thing; contrive with difficulty; do the best one can in a difficult situation; make the best of a bad job; manage to do what is beyond one's power; undertake to do a difficult job as best one can

勉強 reluctant

勉勵 encourage; urge

勉勵上進 exhort one to make progress

有則改之，無則嘉勉 correct the mistakes, if any; and keep the good record if no mistakes have been committed; correct mistakes if you have committed them and avoid them if you have not; correct mistakes if you have made any and guard against them if you have not; if there is any error, correct it; if not, then avoid it

嘉勉 praise and encourage; urge sb to greater efforts with words of encouragement

【南】naam⁴ south

南方 south

南瓜 pumpkin

南乳（紅腐乳 / 紅醬豆腐）fermented taro curd

南嘸佬（法師）Daoist master
　南嘸佬遇鬼迷（張天師被鬼迷）an old horse loses its way

南邊 south

回南（回暖）the weather gets warm

指南 guidebook

越南 Vietnam

講明就陳顯南（一點就明）it is tiresome repetition to make oneself clear

【厘】lei⁴ thousandth part of a tael

厘米 centimetre

米厘 milimetre

【厚】hau⁵ thick

厚身（厚實）thick and solid

厚意 kindness

厚薄 thick and thin
　厚此薄彼 biased; discriminate against one and favour the other; discriminate against some and favour others; favour one and be prejudiced against the other; give handsome treatment to one and niggardly treatment to the other; give a royal welcome to one and cold reception to the other; give too much to one and too little to the other; liberal to one and stingy to the other; make chaff of one and cheese of the other; make fish of one and flesh of the other; make invidious distinctions; partial to one while neglecting the other; say turkey to one and buzzard to the other; the treatment accorded to one is out of all proportion to that accorded to the other; treat one warmly and another coldly; treat with partiality

厚疊疊 very thick

宅心仁厚 of a kindly disposition; settle the mind with benevolence and honesty

忠厚 honest and tolerant; kind and big-hearted; sincere and kindly

面皮 (好厚) (不知羞恥) be shameless; have a thick skin; know no shame; shame on you; thick skin

雄厚 abundant; ample; plentiful; rich; substantial

腰圓背厚 plump

監人賴厚 (硬要別人喜歡自己) shamelessly take oneself for sb's intimate

醇厚 ① mellow ② gentle and kind

濃厚 dense; strong

膽大心細面皮厚 (膽子大，細心，厚臉皮) bold, cautious, and thick-skinned

【咧】le³ grin

咧啡 (隨便) do a sloppy job; sloppy-dressed

咧飯應 (立刻答應) accept another party's demand at once

騎咧 (奇怪) bizarre; odd

【咪】mai⁵ (不用 / 不要 / 別) do not

咪住 (先別 / 慢着) hold on
　　咪住先 (慢着) hold on

咪走呀 (別走呀) don't run away

咪拘 (不用計較 / 別計較) I won't take it

咪急 (不要急 / 別急) take one's time; there's no hurry

咪制 (別幹) don't do it

咪喊 (不要哭 / 別哭) don't cry

咪惡 (不要兇 / 別那麼兇) don't be so horrid

咪嗌 (不要叫 / 別叫) don't shout

咪煩 (不要煩 / 別煩) don't be vexed

咪逼 (不要擠 / 別擠) don't push

咪話 (不用說 / 且不說) let alone; not to mention; not to speak of; to say nothing of

咪嘈 (不要吵 / 別吵 / 別鬧) shut up

咪爭住佢 (別護着他) don't side with sb who is in the wrong

咪嬲 (不要生氣 / 別生氣) don't get angry

咪點我 (別給我胡指) don't mislead me

咪驚 (不要怕 / 別怕) don't be afraid

係咪 (是不是) isn't it

【咪】mai¹ ① (讀書) study ② (麥克風) microphone ③ (英里) mile

咪家 (書呆子) bookish person

咪書 (摳書本 / 啃書本) study hard

咪高峯 (麥克風) microphone

咪錶 ① (里程計) milometer ② (電子計時表) parking meter

一個咪 (一個麥克風) a microphone

無線咪 (無線麥克風) wireless microphone

【咪】mi¹ slow

咪嚟 (慢吞吞) very slow and clumsy
　　咪咪嚟嚟 / 咪嚟咪嚟 (慢吞吞) very slow and clumsy

媽咪 ① (媽媽) mammy; mummy ② (拉皮條的女子) female pimp

【咬】ngaau⁵ bite

咬牙 ① grit one's teeth ② grind one's teech
　　咬牙切齒 clench one's teeth; gnash one's teeth; grind one's teeth; set one's teeth

咬字 enunciate
　　咬字清楚 enunciate clearly; have clear articulation; pronounce every word clearly

咬米 eat

咬住 ① bite into; grip with one's teeth ② grip; refuse to let go of; seize; take firm hold of

咬定 insist
　　一口咬定 assert categorically; cling to one's view; hold firm to one's stance; insist emphatically; insist on saying sth; speak in an assertive tone; state categorically; stick to one's statement; stick to what one says; stubbornly assert that; the arbitrary assertion that

咬唔入 (抓不住把柄) cannot take one's advantage

咬飯 (吃飯) eat

咬實牙齦 (咬緊牙關) endure hardship; tolerate bitterly

吠犬不咬 barking dogs seldom bite; great barkers are no biters

飛擒大咬 over-eager; show one's horn; show one's lustful manner

【咯】lo³ ① final particle ② cough

咯血 cough up blood

該煨咯 (真不幸) what a bad luck

【咳】kat¹ (咳嗽) cough

咳藥丸 (止咳藥丸) cough drops; lozenges

咳藥水 (止咳藥水) cough syrup

止咳 temporary solution to a problem

做到氣咳 (工作忙碌) up to the ears in work

【哀】oi¹ sad

哀求 appeal pathetically; beg; beg humbly; beg piteously; beg pitifully; beseech; entreat; grovel; implore

哀悼 condole with sb upon the death of...; condolence; express one's condolences on the death of sb; grieve; grieve over sb's death; lament; lament sb's death; mourn; mourn for the dead; mourn over sb's death; mourning; wail the dead

哀痛 deep mourning; deep sorrow; feel the anguish of sorrow; feel the pain of grief; great sorrow; grie; profoundly grieved

哀傷 distressed; feel grief; feel sorrw; grieve; mourn; sad; sorrowful

哀愁 grieved; lamentation; sad; sorrowful

悲哀 sad
默哀 stand in silent tribute

【品】ban² behaviour

品行 behaviour; conduct
品味 savour; taste
品性 (性格) character personality; temperament
品格 ① character of a person; one's character and morals ② quality and style
品牌 brand; name brand
品德 moral character
品質 quality

上等禮品 choice present
日用品 articles in daily use
叫甜品 (點甜品) order dessert
必需品 necessity
印刷品 printed matter
作品 works
紀念品 souvenir
食品 food
唔係人咁品 (不是省油的燈) lose one's reason
展品 exhibit; item on display
疵品 inferior work
貢品 articles of tribute
副產品 by-product
產品 product
甜品 dessert
祭品 sacrificial utensil
發財立品 cultivate one's character when one becomes rich
補品 nutritious food; tonic
飲品 beverage; drinks
馴品 (純良) gentle and yielding
製品 manufactured items; products
獎品 prize

應節食品 food for a festival
謝絕禮品 no gifts
禮品 gift; present
贈品 freebie
藏品 object

【哄】hung¹ ① roars of laughter ② hubbub

哄堂 bring the room down; fill the room with laughter
　哄堂大笑 a volley of laughter; burst into a guffaw; burst into uproarious laughter; fall about laughing; laugh uproariously; roar with laughter; the whole room bursts out laughing; the whole room rocking with laughter

哄動 cause a sensation; make a stir
哄然 boisterous; uproarious
哄騙 bamboozle; blandish; cajole; coax; humbug; wheedle

起哄 boo and hoo; jeer

【哇】waa¹ sound of a child's crying

哇哇 cry
　哇哇大哭 cry very loudly

【哈】haa¹ sound of laughter

哈哈 ha ha; haw haw
　哈哈大笑 burst into hearty laughter; burst out into a fit of violent laughter; give a loud guffaw; laugh heartily; roar with laughter
　哈哈鏡 distorting mirror; magic mirror

哈蜜瓜 Hami melon

笑哈哈 laugh

【咭】kat¹ (卡) (English) card

咭片 (卡片 / 名片) calling card; name card
　呢張係我嘅咭片 (這是我的名片) this is my name card

打咭 (打卡) punch a card
生日咭 (生日卡) birthday card
甫士咭 (名信片) postcard
長者咭 (長者卡) senior citizen card
信用咭 (信用卡) credit card
拜年咭 (賀年卡) New Year card
提款咭 (提款卡) ATM (automatic teller machine) card
賀年咭 (賀年卡) New Year card
聖誕咭 (聖誕卡) Christmas card
碌咭 (刷卡) swipe one's card to settle payment
轆咭 (刷卡) swipe one's card to settle payment
鐘咭 (鐘卡) clock card; timecard
post 咭 (名信片) postcard

【咩】me¹ is it

咩野（甚麼）what
你要咩野（你要甚麼）what do you want

好架勢咩（很了不起嗎）nothing patent; what does that matter anyway
羊咩（羊）goat
亞崩劏羊——羊都冇得咩 be forced to keep silence; hold one's tongue
係咩（是嗎）is that so
茄士咩 cashmere
做媒人仲要包生仔咩（要求不合理）over-demanding
想食咗大隻車咩（貪得無厭）hope to get a lot from others
講咁易咩（說易行難）it's easy to talk so

【哋】dei⁶ [adverb; plural]

人哋（人們／其他人）other people; others
佢哋（他們）them; they
劫劫哋（有點累）a little tired
老老哋（有點老）a little old
你哋（你們）you
我哋（我們）us; we
阿駝行路——中中哋（甘居中游）the state of being in the middle
肥肥哋（有點胖）a little fat; quite fat
乖乖哋（挺乖的）obediently
姆姆哋（有點女性化）effeminate; sissy
神神哋（壞了）not right in the mind
爹哋（爸爸）daddy
笑笑哋（微笑）with smiles
鬼鬼哋（看上去像外國人）have the look of a foreigner
偷偷哋（偷偷地）secretly
麻麻哋（普通）neither good nor bad; not too good; so so
室人哋（噎人家）choke others
痕痕哋（有點癢）itchy; ticklish
閒閒哋（最少）① at least; easily; without any difficulties ② at any rate; on any account; the least
傻傻哋（傻傻的）likeable but stupid; not very clever; simple-minded
瘦瘦哋（傻傻的）a little slim; quite slim
暈暈哋（有點暈）a little dizzy
痺痺哋（有點麻痺）have pins and needles
矮矮哋（有點矮）quite short
慳慳哋（節儉）be conomical
憎人哋（討厭他人）hate others
靜靜哋（靜靜地）act in silence; inwardly; quietly; secretly
蠢蠢哋（傻傻的）a little foolish
驚驚哋（有點怕）be frightened somehow

【型】jing⁴ shape

型號 model
最新型號 latest model

台型（有型／好看）good-looking
好型（有型）very stylish
有型 cool; handsome; stylish
典型 archetype; example; model; type; typical
定型 set the hair
姆型（女性化）effeminate; sissy
面型 shape of one's face
高大有型 tall and stylish
蚊型（小型）small size
造型 ① modelling; mould-making ② model; mould
詐型（擺架子）bluff; play the fool; pretend; put on an act
模型 model
髮型 hair style; hairdo
懶有型（裝有型）have pretensions to be stylish
類型 category; sort; type

【奏】zau³ present a memorial to an emperor

奏效 effective; efficacious; get the desired result; have the intended effect; prove effective; successful
奏鳴曲 sonata
奏樂 play music; strike up a tune

三重奏 instrumental trio; trio
先斬後奏 act before reporting
伴奏 accompaniment accompany; play an accompaniment
節奏 rhythm
鋼琴伴奏 piano accompaniment

【契】kai³ adopt

契女（乾女兒）adoptive daughter
契仔 ①（乾兒子）adoptive son ②（笨蛋／傢伙）idiot
契弟（王八蛋／兔崽／沒出息的小子／孫子）bastard
契姐（乾姐姐）adoptive elder sister
契娘（乾娘／乾媽）adoptive mother
契哥（乾哥哥）adoptive elder brother
契家佬（情夫）adulterer; illicit male lover; male cohabitant; secret husband
契家婆（情婦）adulteress; female cohabitant; illicit female lover; secret wife
契媽（乾媽）adoptive mother
契爺 ①（乾爹）adoptive father ②（包養者）sugar-daddy

上契（認乾親）enter into an adoptive relationship
老契（情婦的暱稱）blossom friend

樓宇公契 deed of mutual covenant
默契 tacit agreement

【姜】goeng¹ a surname

姜太公封神——漏咗自己（姜太公封神——忘了自
己）leave out oneself

姜太公釣魚——願者上釣 do sth on a voluntary basis;
swallow the bait of one's own accord

【姦】gaan¹ ① adultery ② rape

姦夫 adulterer; intrigant; paramour
姦婦 adultress; paramour
姦情 adulterous affair
姦淫 ① adultery; illicit sexual relations ② rape; seduce

強姦 rape
輪姦 gang rape
雞姦 buggery; male rape; sodomy

【姨】ji⁴ aunt

姨丈 （姨父 / 姨夫）husband of one's maternal aunt
姨太太 concubine
姨仔 （小姨子）aunt; sister-in-law
姨表 maternal cousin
姨媽 ① （姨母）aunt; mother's sister ② （月經）menstrual
period; monthly period
姨媽姑姐 （七姨兒八姥姥）father's sisters and
mother's sisters
大姨媽 （月經）menstrual period; monthly period

大姨 aunt
阿姨 aunt

【姪】zat⁶ nephew

姪女 niece; one's brother's daughter
姪仔 （姪子）nephew; one's brother's son
姪孫 grandnephew; one's brother's grandson

叔姪 uncles and nephews

【姻】jan¹ marriage

姻母 aunt by marriage
姻伯 uncle by marriage
姻家 ① families of the married couple ② elders of the
families of the married couple
姻戚 relatives by marriage
姻緣 marriage
美滿姻緣 happy marriage
姻親 relatives by marriage

婚姻 marriage

【姿】zi¹ carriage

姿整 （磨蹭）dally; dawdle; move slowly
姿姿整整 （磨磨蹭蹭）dally; dawdle; move slowly

【威】wai¹ （威風 / 神氣）smart

威士 （棉紗頭）cotton waste
威士忌 (English) whisky
威也 （鋼絲繩）wire
吊威也 （吊鋼絲繩）hanging from a wire
威化餅 （維化餅乾）(English) wafer
威水 （威風 / 氣派 / 神氣）awe-inspiring; imposing;
impressive; majestic-looking; spirited
威水史 （不凡經歷）famous achievements
威水吓 （顯顯威風）show one's prowess
好威水 （真厲害）it's really impressive
威吓 （顯一顯）show off one's power and influence
威番吓 （顯一顯）show off
威吔 （鋼絲繩）(English) wire
吊威吔 （吊鋼絲繩）hanging from wire
威到盡 （威風透了）overwhelm sb with one's authority
威勢 （權威）power and influence
係威係勢 （似模似樣）look impressive

下馬威 display one's authority soon after one comes
into power; stamp one's authority over sb at
the outset
去威 （玩樂）go out for a good time; hang about; hang
around; hang out; hang round
失威 （丟臉）humiliate oneself; lose face
示威 demonstration
好失威 （很丟臉）take sb down a peg or two
低威 （拜下風 / 認錯）despise oneself; feel oneself
inferior; self-abased; slight oneself; underestimate
oneself
作威 bossy
迷信權威 have blind faith in authority
夠威 （神氣 / 威風）imposing; majestic
淫威 （濫用權力）abuse of power
揚威 attain eminence; show one's great authority
認低威 （拜下風 / 認錯）admit being inferior; confess to be
unworthy
懶威 （裝威風）cocky
權威 authority

【娃】waa¹ baby; girl

娃娃 ① baby; child ② doll; dolly
娃鬼 （調皮鬼）naughty guy

柴娃娃（不正經）not serious; play a joke
蕩婦淫娃 abandoned and dissolute woman; alley cats

【客】haak³（客人／顧客）guest

客人 guest
客戶 client
客仔（顧客）client; customer; patient; punter; shopper
　　大客仔（大主顧）important client
客位 ① seat ② class
　　商務客位 business class
　　經濟客位 economy class
客房 guest room
客家 ① hakka ② guest
　　客家佔地主（雀巢鳩佔）reverse the positions of the host
　　and the guest
　　客家佬（客家人）hakka
客氣 polite
　　咪客氣 ①（不客氣／不用客氣／別客氣）don't
　　mention it; my pleasure; not at all; you're welcome
　　② don't stand on ceremony; help yourself; make
　　yourself at home
　　唔好客氣 ①（不客氣／不用客氣／別客氣）don't
　　mention it; my pleasure; not at all; you're welcome
　　② don't stand on ceremony; help yourself; make
　　yourself at home
　　唔使客氣 ①（不客氣／不用客氣／別客氣）don't
　　mention it; my pleasure; not at all; you're welcome
　　② don't stand on ceremony; help yourself; make
　　yourself at home
　　諏客氣（裝客氣）pretend to be polite
客貨車 van
客廳 living room; sitting room

人客 guest
水客（走私水貨過境的旅客）parallel trader
水貨客（走私水貨過境的旅客）parallel trader
住客 tenant
見客 meet a client; see a client
長途客 long-distance passenger
姣婆遇着脂粉客（臭味相投）two of a kind
座上客 guest of honour; honoured guest
乘客 passenger
旅客 passenger; traveller
脂粉客（風流子弟）playboy
租客 tenant
偷渡客 stowaway
兜客（兜售客人）scout around for customers
啲客（客戶們）customers
常客 frequent caller

訪客 visitor
稀客 rare visitor
搭客（乘客）passenger
落客（讓乘客下車）let passengers off
遊客 tourist
嫖客 customer of a prostitute; john
熟客 frequent customer; old customer; regular customer
請客 treat sb
顧客 customer

【宣】syun¹ declare

宣佈 announce; declare; proclaim
宣傳 promote

心照不宣 have a tacit understanding

【室】sat¹ room

室內 indoors
　　室內設計 interior design
　　室內設計師 interior designer
　　　　留係室內（留在室內）remain indoors; stay indoors
室外 outdoor; outside
室溫 room temperature

化驗室 laboratory
手術室 operation theatre
冰室（冷飲店）cold drinks shop
更衣室 changing room; dressing room
妻室 one's legal wife; one's wife
急症室 emergency room
候機室 waiting lounge
桌球室（枱球室）billiard room
浴室 bathroom
健身室 gymnasium
試身室 fitting room
會客室 meeting room
課室 classroom
辦公室 office
餐室 restaurant
錄音室 recording room
艙室（飛機艙）cabin

【封】fung¹ seal

封面 ① title-page ② front-cover of a book ③ cover; front cover
封閉 ① close; close down ② seal off; seal up
封嘴 keep one's mouth shut
封鎖 block; seal off

一封 a (letter) (measure phrase)

一個信封 an envelope

大信封（解僱信）dismissal letter

信封 envelope

故步自封 a standpatter and be proud of it; be satisfied with old practices; complacent and conservative; confine oneself to the old method; content with staying where one is; do not want to move a step forward; hold fast to one's established ideas; limit one's own progress; remain where one is; rest complacently on one's laurels; self-satisfaction and conservatism; self-satisfied with being a stick-in-the-mud; stand still and cease to make progress; stand still and refuse to make progress; ultra-conservative and self-satisfied; unwilling to move forward; without desire to advance further

首日封 first-day cover

密封 sealed

雁封 letter; written message

【屋】 uk¹（房子）house

屋主（房東）landlady; landlord

屋仔（小屋）small house

屋企 ①（家 / 家裏）home ②（家庭）family

　　屋企人（家人）family member

　　　返屋企（回家）go home; return home

　　　喺屋企（在家）at home

屋苑 estate

　　大型屋苑 large residential estate

　　大藍籌屋苑 blue chip estate

屋租（房租）rent

屋脊（房脊）roof ridge

屋漏兼逢夜雨 it never rains but pours; misfortunes never come singly

屋價（房價）house price

屋樑（房樑 / 房檁）house beam

一間屋（一間房子）a house

一辣屋（一排房子）a row of houses

丁屋 indigenous villager's house

入屋（進入房子）enter the house

大屋（大房子）big house

引蛇入屋（引狼入室）court disaster

石屋（石房子）brick house

吉屋（空房）unoccupied flat; unoccupied house

泥屋（泥房子）earth house

金銀滿屋 wish you abundant wealth

度假屋 holiday apartment; holiday flat

砌屋（建房子）build a house

起屋（建房子）build a house

租屋（租房子）rent a room

執屋（收拾家裏）tidy up the house

換屋（換房子）change a house; change an apartment

買屋（買房子）buy a house

睇屋（看房子）take a look at the house

間屋（一間房子）① a house ② a room

搬屋（搬家）move house; removal

寮屋 squatter structure

賣屋（賣房子）sell a house

髮型屋（理髮店）hair salon

餓死老婆燻臭屋（養不起老婆）cannot earn enough bread to get married

舊屋（舊房子）old house

爛屋（破房子）dilapidated house

【屍】 si¹ corpse

屍骨 skeleton of a corpse

屍體 cadaver; corpse; dead body; remains

一條屍（一具屍體）a corpse

焚屍 burn sb's body

躝屍（滾開）get out

【屎】 si² ① excrement; poo; faeces ②（差）inferior; poor

屎氹關刀——又唔文（聞）得又唔武（舞）得（狗屎做鞭子——不能文（聞）也不能武（舞））imposing looks but useless

屎坑（毛坑 / 茅坑）latrine pit

　　屎坑關刀——聞唔聞得，武唔武得（狗屎做鞭子——不能文（聞）也不能武（舞））imposing looks but useless

　　新屎坑（貪新鮮）new public toilet

　　新屎坑三日旺（新添馬桶——三日香）a new broom sweeps clean

屎忽（屁股）anus; bottom; buttocks

　　屎忽窿（肛門）anus; asshole

　　洗屎忽（洗屁股）clean one's bottom

屎計（下策 / 餿主意）poor strategy

屎棋（爛棋藝）hard tactics

屎塔（馬桶）toilet

屎橋（餿主意）crap idea; poor scheme

一個仙屎（一分錢）one cent

一啖砂糖一啖屎（胡蘿蔔加大棒）praise is followed by criticism

一篤屎（一陀屎）dung

一腳牛屎（鄉巴佬）boor; churl; country bumpkin; country cousin; country folk; country-born; farming folk; hayseed; hick; redneck; yokel

了鼻屎（挖鼻孔）pick one's nose

大蛇痾屎 important deal
反轉豬肚就係屎（翻臉不認人）change friendship into anger
心中有屎（心中有鬼）have a guilty conscience
火屎（火灰／火星）spark
牛屎 cowpat
牙屎（牙垢）tartar
仙屎（分）(English) cents
石屎（水泥）concrete
耳屎（耳垢）cerumen; earwax
自己身有屎（心裏有鬼）feel compunction
扶屎（擦屁股）clean the buttocks; wipe one's ass
身有屎（心裏有鬼）filthy behaviour
周身屎 ① （臭名昭着）notorious ② （惹來麻煩）in trouble
狗屎 dog poo; dog shit
唔睇白鴿，都睇吓堆屎 a straw shows which way the wind blows
屙屎（大便）① clear one's bowel; defecate; dump; egest; empty the bowels; evacuate one's bowels; go boom-boom; go number two; go potty; have a bowel movement; loose bowels; make little soldiers; move the bowels; relieve oneself; relieve the bowels; shit; sit on the throne; take a shit; the bowel moves; void excrement ② faeces; human excrement; shit; stool; turd
眼屎（眼垢）gum in the eyes; mucus in the eyes
黑癦屎（痣）freckles
煙屎 ① （煙渣）smoke waste ② （撲克牌中的 A 牌）ace
落狗屎（下大雨）it rains dogs and cats
鼻屎（鼻垢）bogey; booger; mucus in the nose; nasal secretion
慶過火屎（十分憤怒）very angry
撩鼻屎（挖鼻孔）pick one's nose
餓狗搶屎（爭前恐後）compete against each other for sth
攔屎（大便失禁）defecate involuntarily; faecal incontinence
瀨屎（大便失禁）defecate involuntarily
癦屎（痣）freckle
蘇州屎（別人留下的麻煩事）the troubles left behind
fen 屎（粉絲）fans
gut 屎（膽量）guts

【坳】aau³ cavity; hollow on the ground

半山坳（山腰）mid-slope of a mountain

【巷】hong⁶（胡同）alley; lane

巷口 entrance to a lane
巷仔（小巷／小胡同）by-street; lane
巷尾 end of a lane

冷巷 alley; by-street; lane

倔頭巷（死胡同）dead-end alley
窄巷 narrow lane
掘頭巷（死胡同）blind alley
趕狗入窮巷（趕盡殺絕）compel sb to strike back in self-defence; force sb into a corner
橫巷 alley; lane; side street
橫街窄巷 side streets and by-lanes

【帝】dai³ emperor; king

帝王 emperor; monarch
帝位 throne
帝制 autocratic monarchy; imperial system; monarchy
帝國 empire

大帝 ① gluttonous idler ② lazy, arrogant, and willful man
土皇帝 local despot
打工皇帝（高薪員工）highly-paid worker
胡天胡帝（言語荒唐／行為放肆）behave foolishly; run wild
皇帝 emperor; king
詐帝／詐詐帝帝（裝模作樣）feign; pretend

【幽】jau¹ dark

幽香 delicate fragrance
幽會 lover's rendezvous; tryst
幽默（English) humour
幽靜 peaceful; placid; quiet and secluded; serene

【度】dou⁶ where

度度（到處／每個地方／隨處）everywhere
　度度都係（到處都是）everywhere is
度假 enjoy a vacation
　度假屋 holiday apartment; holiday flat
度數（分寸）propriety

一年一度 annual; once a year
中度 medium
仆嚟度（跌倒）fall down here
方難度（沒有難度）there is no difficulty
去邊度（去哪兒）where are you going; where to
用腦過度 overtax one's brain
印度 India
有風度 ① gentlemanly ② good-mannered
有番兩度（有兩下子）have it in one; have real skill; have a thing or two; know a few tricks of the trade; know one's staff
至低限度（最少）at least
年華虛度 spend idly the best of one's days
住喺呢度（住在這裏）live in here
角度 ① angle; degree of an angle ② point of view

車去嗰度 (運到那兒) take sth to that place
制度 institution; system
呢度 (這裏) here
季度 quarter of a year
返去舊時嗰度 (重回舊地) back to the old place
長度 length
限度 limits; measures; tethers
流利程度 fluency
風度 ① bearing; demeanour ② manners ③ tolerance
唔喺度 (過世) dead
財政年度 financial year
程度 degree; extent; level
第二度 / 第度 (別的地方) elsewhere
幅度 extent; range; scope
喺度 (在這裏) at this place; be present; on the scene; on the spot
喺呢度 (在這裏) it's here
喺嗰度 (在那裏) it is there
喺邊度 (在哪裏) where is it
幾度 (多少度) what's the temperature
嗰度 (那裏) that place; there
溫度 temperature
態度 attitude
濃度 concentration; strength
擠響度 (放在這裏) lay up here; place it here
濕度 humidity
邊度 (哪兒) where
難度 degree of difficulty
響度 (在這裏) be present

【度】 dok⁶ ① (量度) measure ② (要求) ask for

度下 (量一下) take a measurement of sth
度水 (向人借錢 / 借錢) ask for money; borrow money from others
度身 (量身) take one's measurements
　度身定做 tailor-made
度橋 (找竅門 / 想招兒 / 想辦法) plot; think of a way out; think of the tactics; try to think of a solution
　同我度吓橋 (幫我想辦法) help me find a way out
　度到好橋 (琢磨出高招兒) think up good tactics
　度返度好橋 (想個高招兒) think up some good tactics

端端度度 have evil intention

【建】 gin³ build

建立 establish; set up
建造 construct
建築 architecture

建築公司 construction company
建築材料 building materials
建築物 ① building ② structure
　違例建築物 illegal structure
建築面積 gross floor area
建築師 architect

【建議】 suggest

重建 rebuild
僭建 ① illegal structure ② (隆胸) breast augmentation; have a boob job

【待】 doi⁶ treat

待慢晒嘅 (招待不周全) I've not been a good host
待薄 (虧待) maltreat; treat unfairly

交待 ① account for ② hand over; turn over
老實交待 come clean; make a clean breast of everything
坦白交待 come clean; make a clean breast of one's crimes
耐心等待 wait patiently
急不及待 brook no delay; can wait no onger; hasten to; in haste; lose no time; no sooner...than; too impatient to wait; unable to hold oneself back; unable to wait any longer; with unusual haste
款待 entertain; entertain with courtesy and warmth; treat cordially
等待 wait

【徊】 wui⁴ to and fro

歧路徘徊 hesitate at the crossroads
徘徊 loiter

【律】 leot⁶ rhyme

律己 discipline oneself; self-restraint
律師 lawyer
　律師紙 (法律證明) legal certificate
　律師費 legal fee
　律師樓 law firm
　大律師 barrister

一律 alike; all; uniform; without exception
沙律 (沙拉) salad
法律 law
韻律 rhyme

【後】 hau⁶ back

後人 descendants
後日 (後天) day after tomorrow

後代 descendants

後台 contacts behind the scenes
　　後台硬 powerful contacts behind the scenes
　　　　有後台 have support behind the scenes

後生 ① (年輕) young ② (年輕人) young people;
　　youngster; youth ③ (助理 / 學徒) apprentice;
　　assistant
　　後生女 (小姑娘 / 姑娘) lass; miss; young girl
　　後生仔 (小伙子 / 年青人 / 年輕人) chap; chappy;
　　　kiddo; lad; laddie; laddy; little fellow; sonny; stripling;
　　　young chap; young fellow; young lad; young man;
　　　youngster
　　後生仔女 (小伙子 / 年青人 / 年輕人) young people;
　　　youngster; youth
　　　好後生 (很年青) very young
　　　我後生嗰時 (我年青的時候) when I was young

後年 year after next

後尾 (後來) afterwards; eventually; later; later on;
　　subsequently
　　後尾枕 (後腦勺) back of one's head

後底乸 (後娘 / 繼母) stepmother

後底爺 (繼父) stepfather

後波 (後檔) reverse gear

後門 back door
　　走後門 (靠關係) attain one's goal through personal
　　　connection; attain one's goal by improper means; get
　　　things done through the back door
　　閂後門 express one's own poor situation beforehand to
　　　stop sb from borrowing money from one

後便 (後面) at the back; behind; in the rear

後面 at the back; behind; in the back; in the rear
　　門後面 (門後) behind the door

後悔 regret

後座 back stall

後晚 (後天晚上) the evening of the day after tomorrow

後朝 (後天早上) the morning of the day after tomorrow

後媽 (後娘 / 繼母) stepmother

後數 (後面的付賬) bill to be settled by the person who
　　follows the speaker

後頭 (後面) at the back; behind; in the rear

後邊 (後面) at the back; back

之後 after; then

今後 along the road; down the road; from now on;
　　henceforth; hereafter; in the future; in the days to come

以後 ① after; afterward; from then on; hereafter;
　　later; later on; since then; subsequent to ② at
　　a later date

名門之後 descendant of a notable family

向後 ① backward; towards the back; turn around ② in the
　　future

而後 (然後) after that; then

自此之後 after that

承先啟後 inherit the past and usher in the future

押後 (延後) be postponed; defer; delay; extend; lay over;
　　postpone; put off; put over

從今以後 from now on

最後 at last; finally

然之後 (然後) after that; afterwards; be followed by; in turn;
　　later; next; then

殿後 behind; bring up the rear; close the rear; follow in the
　　rear

落雨擔遮——顧前唔顧後 (慮事不周 / 只顧眼前，不顧將
　　來) pay no regard to the future

落後 underdeveloped

飯後 after meal

幕後 backstage; behind the scenes

瞠乎其後 far behind

褪後 fall backward; move backward

戰後 post-war

續後 (後續) afterward; later

【思】 si¹ think

思考 think

思鄉 homesick
　　思鄉病 homesickness

思想 idea; thought
　　思想流派 schools of thought
　　　中心思想 central idea

思疑 (懷疑 / 疑慮) suspect

思縮 (畏縮) shy and awkward
　　思思縮縮 (行動不果斷) not carry oneself with ease and
　　　confidence; shy and awkward

小意思 a slight token of regard; mere trifle

心思思 (心心念念 / 老惦念着 / 老是想着 / 掛念) have a
　　mind to do sth; keep thinking of; trying to do sth; long
　　for sth

令人深思 make one deep in thought

有意思 meaningful

沉思 be buried in thought; be lost in thought; contemplative;
　　deliberate; in a brown study; meditate; meditative;
　　pensive; ponder; reflective

唔好意思 ① (不好意思) excuse me ② (抱歉) feel
　　apologetic; feel sorry; I'm sorry; sorry ③ embarrass

眠目靜思 close the eyes and meditate

深思 think deep

意思 meaning

【急】gap¹ urgent

急口令（繞口令）tongue twister

急不及待（迫不及待）brook no delay; can wait no longer; hasten to; in haste; lose no time; no sooner...than; too impatient to wait; unable to hold oneself back; unable to wait any longer; with unusual haste

急尿（憋尿）hold up one's urine

急急腳（急急忙忙地）leave in a hurry

急症（急診）accident and emergency
　急症室（急診室）emergency room

急救 first aid

急驚風遇着慢郎中（有急事，卻遇上慢性子的人）be too impatient to wait

人有三急 have one's needs to do; need to go to the toilet; take a leak

十萬火急（非常緊急）very urgent

三急 go for a pee; need to go to the toilet

心急 anxious; short-tempered

危急 hazardous; in a desperate situation; in a state of emergency; pressing; urgent

告急 ask for emergency help; in an emergency; make an urgent request for help; report an emergency

尿急（急於小便）urgent urination

性急 quick-tempered

咪急（不用急）take one's time; there's no hurry

皇帝唔急太監急（皇帝不急太監急）key oneself up over others' business

唔好急（不要急）take one's time; there's no hurry

喉急（性急）desperate; eager; impatient

猴急（性急）anxious; impetuous

緊急 emergency; urgency

濟急（解燃眉之急）give urgent relief

臨急（迫到眉睫）when emergency comes

臨時臨急（迫到眉睫）at the last moment; be hard pressed for time

【怨】jyun³ repine

怨命 blame one's fate; submit to one's own destiny

怨恨 enmity; grudges; hate; ill will; resentment

怨氣 complaints; grievances; resentment

怨聲 cries of discontent
　怨聲載道 complaints are heard everywhere; complaints rise all round; grumblings are heard all over; murmurs of discontent fill the streets; swamp with complaints; voices of discontent are heard everywhere

抱怨 beef about; blow off; chew the rag about; complain; complain about; complain of; grouse; grouse about; grumble; grumble about; grumble at; grumbling; kick against; kick at; murmur against; murmur at; mutter against; mutter at; natter on about; quarrel with; rail against; rail at

埋怨 blame; complain

恩怨 feelings of gratitude and feelings of resentment; grievances; old scores; resentment

【恒】hang⁴ persistent

恒久 constant; endurable; forever; lasting

恒心 perseverance

恒星 fixed star; star

恒溫 constant temperature

撐到恒（劍拔弩張）support to the utmost; at sword's point

【恃】ci⁵（依仗／憑藉）rely on

恃老賣老（倚老賣老）act like a Dutch uncle; flaunt one's seniority

恃住（依仗／憑藉）rely on

恃勢欺人（仗勢欺人）abuse one's power and bully the people; bully others because one has power; bully people on the strength of one's powerful connections; bully the weak on one's power; make use of one's position to bully others; pull one's rank on others; rely on sb else's power to bully people; take advantage of one's own power to bully people; take one's position to lord it over and insult people; throw one's weight about; trust to one's power and insult people

恃熟賣熟 too familiar with each other to stand on ceremony

【恨】han⁶ ① hate ②（渴望）yearn for

恨仔（渴望生兒子）want to have a son

恨死隔離（羨煞旁人）become the envy of others; object of great envy

恨到發燒（非常渴望）want sth desperately

恨咗好耐嘞（盼了很久了）have chased after sth for a long time

恨嫁（想結婚）want to get married

恨錢（想發財）want to get rich

仇恨 animosity; enmity; grudge; hatred; hostility

妒恨 envy and resent

怨恨 enmity; grudges; hate; ill will; resentment

洩恨 give one's grudge; give vent to one's resentment; vent one's anger

悔恨 bitterly remorseful; regret deeply

唔使恨（別指望）cherish no hope for sb; no need to hope; useless

唔恨（不稀罕）not to care about
種族仇恨 race hatred
憎恨 hatred

【恤】seot¹ ① (English) shirt ② help

恤衫（襯衣／襯衫）shirt
　　一件恤衫（一件襯衣）a shirt
　　女裝裇衫（女裝襯衣）blouse
恤髮（做頭髮）do one's hair; have one's hair done at a beauty parlour; style one's hair

波恤（球衣）sports shirt
飛機恤（夾克）jacket
憫恤 pity and help

【恰】hap¹（欺負／欺侮）bully

恰人（欺負人）bully others

【扁】bin² flat

扁鼻（塌鼻樑）flat nose
　　扁鼻佬戴眼鏡——冇得頂（好極了）without equal
扁嘴（瘪嘴）puckered mouth

搓得圓撳得扁（性格溫和）as mild as a dove

【拜】baai³ worship

拜山（掃墓）visit a grave
拜年 pay a New Year visit
　　拜年咭（賀年卡）New Year card
拜拜（再見）bye; bye-bye; goodbye
拜神（拜佛）worship the Buddha
　　拜神唔見雞（口中不停低聲唸着／嘟嘟噥噥）bustle in and out with a murmur; complain with a murmur
　　拜得神多自有神庇佑（佛祖會庇佑拜佛拜得勤的人）the Buddha will bless one who frequently worships him
　　祭灶拜神 offer to the god of kitchen and worship the Buddha

上兩個禮拜（上兩個星期）the week before the last week
上個禮拜（上星期）last week
下個禮拜（下星期）next week
今個禮拜（這個星期）this week
見山就拜（盲目虔誠）taking A for B without making sure
呢個禮拜（這個星期）this week
幾多個禮拜（多少個星期）how many weeks
跪拜 worship on bended knees
激死老豆搵山拜（故意氣壞父親）unfilial son who infuriates his father to death is only looking for a tomb to sweep
禮拜（星期）week

【拮】gaat³（戳）strike lightly

拮住（戳着）pin
拮穿（戳穿）pierce through
拮針（扎針）have an acupuncture treatment
拮窿（戳洞）pierce a hole
拮嚫（扎到）be struck lightly
拮爛（戳壞）pierce

【括】kut³ include

括號 brackets

包括 include
囊括 ① embrace; include ② win all

【拾】sap⁶ ten

拾吓拾吓（傻傻的）foolish
拾遺 appropriate lost property
　　路不拾遺 no one picks up what's left by the wayside

收拾 ① clear away; gather up; put in order; tidy ② get things ready; pack ③ mend; repair ④ punish; settle with; torture
執拾（收拾）tidy up

【持】ci⁴ hold

持久 enduring; lasting; protracted
持平 fair; unbiased
持竿跳（撐竿跳）pole vault
持家 keep house; run one's home
持續 continuance; continued; sustained

支持 at sb's back; at the back of sb; backing; bear; buttress; countenance; for; hold out; stand up for; support; sustain
主持 direct; manage; take charge of
劫持 abduct; hijack; hold under duress; kidnap
扶持 give aid to; help sustain; place a hand on sb for support; support; support with the hand
把持 ① control; keep in one's hands; keep under control ② dominate; monopolize
矜持 reserved; restrained
電台主持 radio host

【按】on³ press

按金（押金）deposit
按揭（抵押）mortgage
　　按揭手續費（抵押手續費）mortgage handling fee
按腳 foot massage

按摩 massage
按樽（押瓶）bottle deposit

次按（次級按揭貸款）sub-prime mortgage

【指】zi² point

指公（手指）finger
　　二指公（食指）index finger
　　三指公（中指）middle finger
　　大指公（大拇指）thumb
　　四指公（無名指）ring finger; third finger
指天椒（五色椒）bird's eye chilli
指天篤地（滿口胡言／語無倫次）sheer rubbish; talk
　　nonsense
指引 guide
指手篤腳 ①（胡亂指揮）order sb about ②（指手劃腳）
　　make gestures with one's hands
指出 point out
指甲 nail
　　指甲油 nail varnish
　　指甲鉗（指甲刀）nail clipper
　　指甲銼 nail file
　　剪指甲 cut the nail
指示 indication
指住 point at
　　指住禿奴罵和尚（指桑罵槐）talk at sb
指南 guidebook
指紋 fingerprint
指教（指點教導）give instructions
　　有乜指教呀（你有甚麼指教）what can I do for you
指意（指望）depend on
指證 prosecute
指擬（指望）count on sb

一味靠指（只靠胡言亂語）rely solely on talking nonsense
勾手指 make a promise by hooking each other's
　　little finger
手指 finger
手指指（向別人指手劃腳）gesture with the finger as if to
　　lecture sb
孖指（六指）hand with six fingers
伸手不見五指 darkness visible; pitch-dark; so dark that you
　　can't see your hand in front of you
吮手指（吸手指）suck one's finger
尾指 little finger
金手指 ①（警方密探）police informer ②（告密者）
　　backbiter; backstabber
染指 come in for a share; encroach on; have a hand in; take
　　a share of sth one is not entitled to

期指 option
鎅𠱁隻手指（切傷手指）cut one's finger

【挑】tiu¹ ① select ②（雕／刻）carve; cut; engrave

挑剔 choosy; fastidious; fussy; picky
挑起把火（挑起怒火）arouse sb's anger
挑起條癮（引起慾望）arouse sb's desire
挑逗 tantalize; tease
挑圖章（刻圖章）engrave a seal; make a chop
　　by carving

擔挑（扁擔）carrying pole
斷擔挑（被生活壓彎了腰）with one's back bent under
　　pressure

【挖】waat³（摳）scoop out

挖角 headhunt; lure away sb
挖鼻 pick one's nose

耳挖 earpick

【捋】laap⁸ twist with hands

捋吓鼓邊（旁敲側擊）sound sb out on a question
捋埋（躲藏）hide oneself

【政】zing³ government

政府 government
　　政府部門 government department
　　聯合政府 coalition government
　　臨時政府 interim government; provisional government
政治 politics
　　政治家 politician
　　政治穩定 stable in politics
　　政治觀 political view
　　玩政治 play politics
政策 policy
政黨 political party
政變 coup
　　密謀政變 plot a coup

干涉內政 interference in domestic affairs; meddle in a
　　country's internal affairs
內政 home affairs; internal affairs
各自為政 each one minds their own business
施政 administer political administration; administrate;
　　execute government orders; govern
財政 finance
處理內政 deal with home affairs

【故】gu³ for this reason

故此（因此／所以）as a result; because of this; consequently; for that reason; hence; on that account; so; therefore; thus

故步自封 be a standpatter and be proud of it; be satisfied with old practices; complacent and conservative; confine oneself to the old method; content with staying where one is; do not want to move a step forward; hold fast to one's established ideas; limit one's own progress; remain where one is; rest complacently on one's laurels; self-satisfaction and conservatism; self-satisfied with being a stick-in-the-mud; stand still and cease to make progress; stand still and refuse to make progress; ultra-conservative and self-satisfied; unwilling to move forward; without desire to advance further

一單事故 an accident

人情世故 ways of the world

老於世故 be experienced in the ways of the world; have seen much of the world

世故 experienced

事故 accident; failure; fault; malfunction; mishap; mistake; trouble; troublesome incident

典故 allusion; literary quotation

掌故 ① historical anecdotes ② national institutions

【施】si¹ enforce

施政 administer political administration; administrate; execute government orders; govern

施施然（慢悠悠）slow-moving

施恩 do favours to others

施恩莫望報 throw one's bread upon the waters

情人眼裏出西施 beauty exists in a lover's eyes; love is blind

措施 measures

設施 facility

【既】gei³ since

既來之，則安之 let's cross the bridge when we come to it; since we are here, we may as well stay and make the best of it; since we have come, let us stay and enjoy it; since you have come, take your ease

既往不咎 forgive somebody's past misdeeds; it is needless to blame things that are past; let bygones by bygones; let the past be forgotten; let the dead bury their dead; wipe the slate clean

既然之（既然）as; after; at all; if; inasmuch as; now; now that; once; seeing; seeing that; since; such being the case; well then; what; when; where

【星】sing¹（星星）stars

星星 stars

星星點點 tiny spots

星軍（胡鬧）kick up a row; make a row; run riot; run wild

星軍仔（小淘氣／小胡鬧）naughty child; urchin

星盆（洗滌槽）sink

星期 week

星期一 Monday

星期二 Tuesday

星期三 Wednesday

星期五 Friday

星期六 Saturday

星期日 Sunday

星期四 Thursday

星期幾 which day of the week

上個星期 last week

下個星期 next week

今個星期（這個星期）this week

呢個星期（這個星期）this week

個個星期（每個星期）every week

幾多個星期（多少個星期）how many weeks

星鐵（馬口鐵）galvanized iron

一代巨星 big star of the generation

一粒星（一顆星）a star

五星 five-star

火星 Mars

巨星 big star

百厭星（頑皮鬼）little horror; mischievous imp; naughty boy

足球明星 football star

辰星 ① morning star ② Mercury

明星 ① star ② movie star

阿星（印度人）Indian

恒星 fixed star; star

紅星（紅角）famous actor or actress; popular star; superstar

倒米壽星（幫倒忙的人）person who causes others to suffer losses; person who stands in his own light

兜巴星（掌摑）slap sb in the face

崇拜明星 worship stars

掃把星（倒霉鬼）a person who always brings in ill fortune

粒粒巨星（星光熠熠）everyone is a big star

想做明星 want to become a star

零星 fragmentary; occasional; odd; scattered; sporadic

電影明星 movie star

電影紅星（電影紅角）popular movie star

歌星 singer

歌影視紅星（歌影視紅角）popular star in singing, movies, and television

壽星 God of Longevity
衛星 satellite
諧星 comedian
濕星（瑣碎）odds and ends
懶星（懶惰鬼）lazy person
艷星（色情演員）porn actress

【春】ceon¹ spring
春天 spring
春卷 spring roll
　一碟春卷 a plate of spring rolls
春宵 have a night of sex
春茗（春節聚會）spring dinner

石春（卵石）cobble
有事鍾無艷，無事夏迎春 once out of danger, cast the deliverer behind one's back
青春 youth
揮春 Spring Festival couplets
魚春（魚卵）roe
新春 Lunar New Year
雞春（雞蛋）egg

【昧】mui⁶ obscure
昧水（潛水／潛泳）dive; go under water

【昨】zok⁶ yesterday
昨日（昨天）yesterday
昨晚 last night

【是】si⁶ be
是必（一定／必定／肯定／勢必）have to; must
　是必要（一定要）have to; must
是但（隨便）anybody will do; as you like it; anything is alright; anything will do
　是但啦（隨便吧）anybody will do; anything is alright; anything will do; as you like it
　是是但但（隨隨便便）anybody will do; as you like it; anything is alright; anything will do
是非 gossip
　是非丁（是非鬼）gossip person; gossiper
　是非不分 cannot tell black from white; confuse right and wrong; confuse truth and falsehood; fail to distinguish good from bad; fail to distinguish right and wrong; make no distinction between right and wrong
　是非只為多開口（多話容易引起是非）loquacity leads to trouble
　是非皆因強出頭（多管閒事的人容易引起是非）a busybody often invites troubles

是非鬼 gossip person; gossiper; scandalmonger
是非啄（是非鬼）gossip person; gossiper; scandalmonger
是非精（是非鬼）gossip person; gossiper; scandalmonger
口是心非 a hypocrite; affirm with one's lips but deny in one's heart; agree in words but disagree in heart; carry fire in one hand and water in the other; carry two faces under one head; cry with one eye and laugh with the other; double-dealing; double-faced; duplicity; hypocrisy; outwardly agree but inwardly disagree; pay lip service; play a double game; play the hypocrite; right with the mouth but wrong at heart; say one thing and mean another; say yes and mean no; show a false face; the mouth specious and the mind perverse; though one speaks well, one's heart is false
來說是非者，便是是非人（說別人是非的人就是搬弄是非的人）the person who speaks ill of others will speak ill of you
明辨是非 clear about what is right and what is wrong; discern between right and wrong; distinguish between truth and falsehood; distinguish clearly between right and wrong; distinguish right from wrong; know right from wrong
是古非今 admire everything ancient and belittle present-day achievements; consider anything old as good and reject everything that is modern; praise antiquity and denounce the present; praise the past to condemn the present
搬是搬非（搬弄是非）tell tales
誰是誰非 who is in the right and who is in the wrong; who is right and who is wrong
講是非（搬弄是非）gossip
撩是鬥非（調三窩四）provoke a fight; stir up a quarrel; sow the seeds of discord
學是非（搬弄是非）cause trouble between people; make trouble
顛倒是非 confound right and wrong; confuse truth and falsehood; distort truth; give a false account of the true facts; invert justice; reversal of right and wrong; reverse right and wrong; stand facts on their heads; swear black is white; the perversion of truth; turn right into wrong; turn things upside down; twist the facts
攪是攪非（搬弄是非）cause trouble between people; make trouble

又是 again; also; in addition to; once again
大吉利是 touch wood
尤其是 especially
只是 ① but; yet ② just; merely; only
利是（紅包）red packet

每日如是 it's the same every day
派利是（派紅包）give red packets
掗利是（討紅包）ask for red packets; receive red packets
話是（作主）have the final say
歷來如是 have been so from the old days
積非成是 accept what is wrong as right when one grows accustomed to it; get used to what is wrong and regard it as right; through practice the erroneous becomes correct; what becomes customary is accepted as right

【枳】zi² plug

枳落 thorn hedge

補鑊唔見枳（手足無措）find oneself in a fix

【架】gaa³ ① frame; rack ② den ③（輛）a (vehicle) (measure word for vehicles)

架子 airs
　架子大 arrogant; assume an air of importance
架生 ①（工具）tools ②（武器）weapons
架步（地下妓院）vice spots
　色情架步（色情行當）sex-for-sale den
架車（這輛汽車）this car
　架車好定（車子走得很穩）this car runs smoothly
架勢（了不起／排場／氣派／神氣）extravagant; terrific
　架勢堂（了不起）extravagant; gorgeous
　好架勢咩（有甚麼了不起）nothing patent; what does that matter anyway
　真係架勢（真有氣派）really gorgeous
　讕架勢（裝排場／擺威風）act lord; make the scene to be splendid
架撑 ①（工具／家當）tools ②（武器）weapons
架樑（中間人）mediator in a dispute
　做架樑（做中間人）mediate in a dispute

一架（一輛）measure word for vehicles
十字架 cross
士碌架（枱球）(English) snooker
打槓架（玩單槓）exercise on a horizontal bar
丟架（丟臉）lose face
槓架（單槓）horizontal bar
招架（抵擋）ward off blows
雨遮架（雨傘架）umbrella rack
相架 photo rack
衫架（衣架）coat hanger
框架 frame; framework; framing
烤架 broiler; gridiron
棚架 scaffold

間架（房屋結構）framework of a house
腳架 tripod
鏡架 spectacles frame

【柿】tsi⁵ persimmon

柿子 persimmon fruit

水柿 persimmon
林柿（柿子）persimmon

【柄】beng³ ① hide ② band ③ rod

柄埋（藏在一旁）hide from public view

同人唔同命，同遮唔同柄（人各有命）no man has the same fortune; no two people's fate is the same
插亂戈柄（說話被打斷／打岔）break the thread of discourse
散柄（解散）disband
話柄（把柄／痛處）excuse
遮柄 ①（雨傘手柄）umbrella rod ②（安全套）condom

【柔】jau⁴ tender

柔和 soft
柔情 soft and sentimental; tender affection; tender feelings; tender thoughts; tenderness; the tender feelings of a lover
柔軟 easily bent; flexible; lithe; soft; yielding
柔順 gentle and agreeable; gentle and yielding; meek; submissive
柔道 judo
柔腸 tender heart

剛柔 hardness and softness
溫柔 tender

【染】jim⁵ dye

染色 colouration; dye; dyeing; staining; tinge
染指 come in for a share; encroach on; have a hand in; take a share of sth one is not entitled to
染病 be infected with a disease; catch a disease; catch an illness; fall ill; get infected
染料 colourant; dye; dyestuff; tincture
染髮 hair dye

污染 pollution
空氣污染 air pollution
肺部感染 chest infection
減低污染 reduce pollution
傳染 infect

感染 infection

漬染 dye

【柑】gam¹（橘子）orange

柑橘 oranges and tangerines

【柳】lau⁵ willow

柳條（直條紋）stripe

柳樹 willow

　　一行柳樹 a line of willows

牛柳 beef tenderloin

花柳 syphilis

風擺柳（拿不定主意）undecided

魚柳 fish fillet

楊柳 willow

豬柳 pork loin

雞柳 shredded chicken breast

【柚】jau⁶（柚子）pomelo

柚木 teakwood

一楷碌柚（一片柚子）a slice of pomelo

西柚 grapefruit

洗羅柚（洗屁股）clean one's bottom

洗囉油（洗屁股）clean one's bottom

洗攞柚（洗屁股）clean one's bottom

碌柚（柚子）pomelo

羅柚（屁股）bottom

囉柚（屁股）bottom; buttocks

攞柚（屁股）bottom

【柜】gwai⁶ cabinet

柜台 bar; counter

柜桶（抽屜）drawer

雪柜（冰箱）fridge; refrigerator

【柯】o¹ stalk

柯打（定單／訂單）order

　　落柯打（下定單／下訂單）place an order

柯佬（口試）(English) oral

【柱】cyu⁵（柱子）post

柱躉（柱石／柱座／柱基石）column base; pillar

台柱①（戲班中的主要演員）important actor in a troupe

　　②（集團中的骨幹成員）important person in an organisation

江瑤柱（乾貝）dried scallop

乾瑤柱（乾貝）dried scallop

【查】caa⁴ ① check; examine ② investigate; look into ③ consult; look up

查出 detect; find out

查房 check the rooms

查家宅（查戶口）make a through and detailed inquiry into sb

查牌 check the license

查詢 enquiry

　　查詢熱線 enquiry hotline

　　如有查詢 for enquiries; if you have any enquiries

查實（其實／實在／實際上）actually; as a matter of fact; in fact; in reality; in truth; really

身體檢查 body check; medical check-up

票站調查 exit poll

訪查 go about making inquiries; investigate

搜查 ransack; rummage; search

調查 investigate

檢查 inspect

矇查查（稀裏糊塗）muddle-headed

【柴】caai⁴ brushwood; firewood

柴可夫（司機）chauffeur; driver

柴台（喊倒好兒／喝倒彩）boo; discourage sb; hoot; make catcalls

柴米油鹽醬醋茶 daily household necessities

柴哇哇（兒戲／鬧着玩兒／瞎起鬨／隨隨便便）not serious; play a joke

柴娃娃（兒戲／鬧着玩兒／瞎起鬨／隨隨便便）not serious; play a joke

柴魚花生粥 congee with dried fish and peanut

一支火柴（一根火柴）a match

一盒火柴 a box of matches

山大斬埋有柴（積少成多）achieve a lot by proceeding in small steps; many a pickle makes a mickle

火柴 match

瓜柴（伸腿兒）collapse completely; die

光棍遇着冇皮柴（騙子遇着騙子）a swindler takes in a swindler

老柴（老男人）old guy; old man

扭紋柴①（哭鬧的孩子）whining child ②（淘氣的孩子）little mischief

拉柴（死）die; meet one's fate

拗柴 (扭傷腳腕) twist one's ankle
破柴 (劈柴) chop firewood
斬柴 chop firewood
落雨收柴 (虎頭蛇尾) do a task carelessly; a fine start but a
　　poor finish
廢柴 (失敗者) crap; good-for-nothing; loser;
　　useless person
標松柴 (貪污) embezzle sb's money
虧柴 ① (身體瀟弱) weak ② (身體瀟弱的人) weak man

【柮】 deot¹ firewood

榾柮 (木柴塊) chopped pieces of wood

【枱】 toi² (桌子) table

枱布 (桌布) table cloth
　　一張枱布 (一塊桌布) a table cloth
枱角 (桌角) corner of a table
枱波 ① (士碌架) (English) snooker ② (枱球) billiard
　　打枱波 (打枱球) ① play snooker ② play billiard
枱面 (桌面) table top
枱腳 (桌腿) leg of a table
枱燈 (桌燈) table lamp
　　一盞枱燈 (一盞桌燈) a table lamp

一張枱 (一張桌子) a table
八仙枱 square table with Eight Immortals
大枱 (大桌子) big table
方枱 (方桌子) square table
抹枱 (擦桌子) wipe the table
長枱 (長桌子) long table
牀頭枱 (牀頭桌) bedside table
訂枱 (訂位) reserve a table
食飯枱 (飯桌) dining table
書枱 (書桌) desk; writing desk
細枱 (小桌子) small table
麻雀枱 (麻將桌) mahjong table
執枱 (收拾桌子) clear the table
開枱 ① (打開摺桌) lay the table; set the table ② (打麻將)
　　play mahjong
挪起張枱 (擺飯桌) set up the table
搭枱 (併桌) share a table in a restaurant with people you
　　don't know
搬枱 (搬桌子) move a table
圓枱 (圓桌) round table
摺枱 (摺桌) folding table
餐枱 (餐桌) dining table
擺上枱 (陷害) set sb up
擺枱 (放置桌子) lay the table

【歪】 me² slant

歪曲 distort; misrepresent; twist
歪風 evil wind; unhealthy trend
歪斜 askew; aslant; crooked
歪嘴 wry mouth

上樑唔正下樑歪 (上樑不正下樑歪) those below will follow
　　the bad example set by those above
借歪 (借開) excuse me

【段】 dyun⁶ section

段落 ① paragraph; section ② conclusion of a part; phase;
　　stage
　　告一段落 come to a conclusion; draw to an end

片段 bit; extract; fragment; part; passage; section; segment
預告片段 preview; trailer

【氈】 zin¹ blanket

氈帽 felt cap; felt hat

一張氈 a blanket

【洋】 joeng⁴ foreign

洋行 foreign company; foreign firm
洋服 foreign-style dresses
　　洋服舖 foreign-style tailor's shop
洋瓷 (搪瓷) enamel
洋貨 foreign goods
　　洋貨舖 (洋貨店) foreign goods shop
洋蔥 onion
洋樓 (洋房) foreign-style house
洋燭 (蠟燭) candle

汪洋 a vast expanse of water; boundless; vast
海洋 ocean

【洒】 saa² wipe away

洒手擰頭 (搖頭擺手) give a flat refusal

花洒 (蓮蓬頭) shower

【洗】 sai² clean; wash

洗手 wash one's hands
　　洗手間 (廁所) lavatory; toilet; washroom; water closet
　　洗手盤 washbasin
洗白白 (洗澡) (兒語) take a bath
洗米 (淘米) wash rice
洗衣 wash clothes

洗衣房 laundry room;
洗衣舖（洗衣店）laundry
洗衣機 washing machine
洗身（洗澡）have a bath; take a shower
洗底（摘帽子）expunge a criminal record
洗衫（洗衣服）wash clothes
　洗衫板 ①（洗衣板／搓板）wash board ②（胸部小的女
　　　性）woman with a flat chest
　洗衫梘（洗衣皂）laundry soap
洗面（洗臉）wash one's face
　洗面盆（臉盆）wash basin
　洗面膏 face wash
　以淚洗面 wash one's face with tears
洗粉（洗衣粉）laundry detergent; washing powder
洗袋（輸光）lost all the money in one's pocket in gambling
洗菜 wash the vegetables
洗黑錢 money-laundering
洗碗 do the washing up; wash the dishes
　洗碗布 dish-washing cloth
　洗碗有相磕（相處久了難免有磨擦、衝突）familiarity
　　　would sometimes have a brush
　洗碗碟機 dish washer
　洗碗機 dish washer
洗腳 cleanse one's foot
　洗腳盆 foot basin
　洗腳唔抹腳（亂花金錢）spend lavishly; spend money
　　　extravagantly; splash one's money about; squander
洗塵 welcoming dinner
洗熨 wash and iron clothes
洗頭 wash one's hair
　洗頭水（洗髮水）shampoo
　洗濕個頭（下了水了）have no way to back down; have
　　　to go through what has been started

沖洗 rinse
易洗（容易洗）easy to wash
唔好洗（不容易洗）difficult to wash
乾洗 dry clean
難洗 difficult to wash

【洞】dung⁶ hole
洞穴 burrow; cave; cavern
洞見 see very clearly
洞房 bridal chamber
　洞房花燭 wedding
洞悉 know clearly; understand thoroughly
洞察 discern; examine thoroughly; have an insight into;
　　have a penetrating insight; see clearly; see through
　　clearly

岩洞 cave; cavern; grotto
堵塞漏洞 block up a hole; plug up a leak; shut up a leak;
　　stop a leak
漏洞 ① hole; leak ② flaw; loophole

【津】zeon¹ subsidy
津津 ① interesting; tasty ②（of water or sweat）overflow
　津津有味 relish; with good appetite; with great interest;
　　　with gusto; with keen interest; with much unction;
　　　with relish; with zest
津貼（補貼）allowance; subsidy

止渴生津 quench thirst and help produce saliva

【洩】sit³ leak
洩恨 give one's grudge; give vent to one's resentment; vent
　　one's anger
洩氣 ① lose strength ② disappointing; discouraging
洩漏 leak out
洩露 disclose; divulge; leak out; reveal

【洱】nei⁵⁻² name of a place in Yunnan
洱水 a river in Yunnan

一壺普洱 a pot of Pu'er tea
普洱 Pu'er tea

【洲】zau¹ continent
洲汀（水中的小島）island in a river
洲際 intercontinental

北美洲 North America
汀洲（水中的小島）islet in a river
亞洲 Asia
非洲 Africa
南美洲 South America
美洲 America
歐洲 Europe
澳洲 Australia

【洽】hap¹ in harmony
洽商 discuss
洽談 consult together; discuss together
洽購 arrange a purchase; make arrangements for
　　buying; purchase after talks; talk over conditions
　　of purchase

融洽 get along well with each other; harmonious with each
　　other

【活】wut⁶ live

活力 energetic
　活力十足 full of energy

活生生 living; real

活到老學到老 a person should study till their dying day; it is never too old to learn; keep on learning as long as you live; live and learn; never too old to learn; one is never too old to learn

活動 ① exercise; move about ② shaky; unsteady ③ mobile; movable ④ activity; going-ons; maneuvre ⑤ use personal influence or irregular means ⑥ behaviour

活潑 ① active; full of life; lively; sprightly; vivacious; vivid ② reactive

活躍 ① active; brisk; dynamic ② animate; enliven; invigorate

生活 ① life ② living ③ livelihood
快活 happy
豪華生活 live in luxury
頭腦靈活 nimble-minded
養活 feed
靈活 agile; flexible; quick-minded

【派】paai³ (發) dispatch

派片 (行賄) grease the palm of sb
派司 (通行證) (English) pass
派位 (分配就讀學校) allocate school places
派信 (送信) deliver letters; send letters
派飛 (分票) dispatch tickets
派彩 (分發獎金給彩票中獎者) dividend
派單張 (發傳單) distribute leaflets
派發 (分發) dispatch; distribute; hand out; issue; serve out
派對 (晚會 / 聚會) party
派糖 (發喜糖) give people wedding candies
派頭 (氣派) (English: pride) extravagant and ostentious display; in grand style
派籌 (發號兒) distribute quota tags

托派 (馬屁精) flunky
兩面派 double dealing
宗派 faction; sect
思想流派 schools of thought
流派 school; sect
夠派 (有派頭) put on a lot of airs; put on a show
幫派 gang; triad gang
鴿派 (溫和派) dove; dove faction
黨派 party

【流】lau⁴ ① flow ② (假) fake

流失 drain; erosion; loss
流血 bleeding
流行 ① be in vogue; current; fashionable; popular ② go around; rage; rampant; spread
　十分流行 be in vogue
　越嚟越流行 (越來越流行) become more and more popular
流利 fluent; smooth
　流利程度 fluency
流沙包 bun with creamy egg yolk
流氓 ① gangster; hooligan; hoodlum; rascal; scoundrel ② immoral behaviour; indecency; rascal behaviour
流星雨 ① meteor shower ② falling stars ③ shooting stars
流派 school; sect
流浪 ① roam about; wander ② stray
　流浪狗 stray dog
　流浪漢 stroller; tramp; wanderer; vagrant
　流浪貓 stray cat
　到處流浪 wander here and there
流料 ① (假消息) false news ② (假東西) fake things
流馬尿 (哭鼻子) snivel; weep
流逝 elapse; pass; passage
　時光流逝 passage of time
流通 circulate
　廣泛流通 extensive circulation
流傳 circulate; go about; hand down; spread; transmit
流落 (流浪) live a homeless life
流野 ① (低等) low-graded ② (劣質品 / 冒牌貨 / 假貨 / 贋品) fake goods; imitation brand goods
流暢 fluent; smooth

一流 first rate; superb; top class
九流 poor quality; very poor
人望高處，水往低流 (奮發向上) everybody hopes to climax himself
交流 exchange; interchange; interflow
回流 back-flow
早晨流流 (一大早) bright and early; early in the morning; the crack of dawn
汗流 sweat
河流 rivers; streams
迎合潮流 go with the current of the times
風流 leisurely and carefree
從善如流 follow good advice as naturally as a river follows its course; follow good advice readily; give the ready ear to wise counsel; readily accept good advice
新年流流 (新年期間) on the day of the new year
源流 ① origin and development source and course ② all the details; full particulars; the whole story

溪流 brook; mountain stream; stream; ravine stream

潮流 trend

輪流 alternately; by rotation; by turns; in rotation; in turn;
take turns

飄流 ① drift ② roam aimlessly

【洇】jan¹ wet

濕洇洇（濕漉漉）drenched; dripping wet

【炮】paau³ bombard

炮仗（鞭炮／爆竹）firecracker
　炮仗頸（火性子）short-tempered
　　炮仗頸——一點就着（皮球性子——一拍就跳）a
　　rubber ball temper – you pat it and it will jump;
　　hot-tempered
　　燒炮仗（放鞭炮／放爆竹）let off firecrackers

炮灰 cannon fodder

炮製 concoct; cook up

炮轟 bombard

一坎炮 a canon

土炮 cheap rice wine

大炮 ①（謊言）lie ② cannon

扎炮（挨餓）have nothing to eat; suffer from hunger

水炮 water-cannon

打響頭炮（率先開始）meet with a first success; kickoff

有乜把炮（有甚麼長處）what's one's strength

把炮（長處）ability; strength

車大炮（吹牛）baloney; blast; blow one's own horn; blow
one's own trumpet; boast; brag; draw a long bow;
eyewash; hot air; plume oneself; shoot a line; shoot the
crap; shoot the breeze; shoot the bull; shoot the shit;
stick it on; swing the lead; talk big; talk horse; talk in
high language; talk through one's hat; tell a lie; tell large
stories

紥炮（挨餓）have no money for food; starve

第一炮（開首活動）the first event

劈炮（辭職）quit one's job

燒枱炮（拍桌大鬧）thump the table and heap abuse
on sb

燒炮仗（放鞭炮／放爆竹）let off firecrackers

【炳】bing² bright

炳然 bright

炳耀 bright and luminous

五行欠炳（欠揍）deserve a scolding

盲炳（笨蛋）idiot

【炸】zaa³ deep-fried

炸兩 rice noodle roll stuffed with deep-fried doughs

炸彈 bomb
　定過抬炸彈（極為從容鎮定）very calm and confident
　紅色炸彈（結婚請帖）wedding invitation card

炸藥 explosive
　烈性炸藥 high explosive

白炸 ①（水母）jellyfish ②（交通警）traffic policeman; traffic
warden

【炭】taan³ charcoal

炭化 carbonize

炭黑 carbon black; black

炭渣（煤渣）cinder

炭筆 charcoal pencil

炭畫 charcoal drawing

炭精（引柴）kindling

一嚿炭（一塊炭）a piece of charcoal

煤炭 anthracite; coal; coke; hard coal

【牯】gu² cow

牯牛 ①（公牛）cow ②（閹割過的公牛）castrated cow

牛牯（公牛）bull; ox

羊牯 ① ram ② fool

【牲】saang¹ livestock

牲口 livestock

牲畜 domestic animals

自我犧牲 self-sacrifice

壯烈犧牲 die a glorious death; die a heroic death; die as a
martyr; die for one's country; give one's life heroically;
sacrifice one's life bravely and gloriously

犧牲 sacrifice

【狡】gaau² cunning

狡兔 wily hare
　狡兔三窟 a wily hare has three burrows — a crafty
　person has more than one hideout; it is a poor mouse
　that has one hole; the cunning hare secures safety with
　three openings to its burrow — have many provisions
　for cunning escape only; the mouse does not trust
　to one hole only; the mouse that has but one hole is
　quickly taken

狡猾 cunning; sly

狡辯 indulge in sophistry; quibble; resort to sophistry

【玲】 ling⁴ tinkling of jade pendants

玲瓏浮突 (優美玲瓏／曲線分明) exquisitely carved

【珊】 saan¹ coral

珊瑚 coral

珊瑚蚌 coral mussel

【珍】 zan¹ treasure

珍肝 (鳥類的胃與肝) gizzard and liver

珍重 ① hold dear; set great store; treasure; value highly ② take good care of yourself

珍珠 pearl

珍珠都無咁真 (比珍珠還真) it's genuine; it's really genuine; it's really real; one hundred per-cent pure

珍珠雞 glutinous rice with chicken wrapped with lotus leaf

禾稈冚珍珠 (財不露白) put on rags over glad rags

珍惜 cherish; treasure; treasure and avoid wasting; value

珍貴 precious; rare; valuable

珍視 cherish; have a high opionion of; prize; treasure; value

珍寶機 (大型飛機) jumbo jet

珍藏 consider valuable and collect appropriately; treasure up

袖珍 pocket; pocket-size

【玻】 bo¹ glass

玻子 (玻璃球) glass ball

打玻子 (玩玻璃球) play with a glass ball

玻璃 glass

一塊玻璃 a pane of glass

鎅玻璃 (切割玻璃) cut glass

【珀】 paak³ amber

琥珀 amber

【甚】 sam⁶ to a high extent

甚至乎 (甚至) as...as; enough; even; even if; far from; go so far as to; if anything; if not more; in fact; indeed; nay; nor yet; not a; not a single; not once; not one; not to say; or more; so far from; so much so that; such... that; very

甚至無 (甚至) as...as; enough; even; even if; far from; go so far as to; if anything; if not more; in fact; indeed; nay; nor yet; not a; not a single; not once; not one; not to say; or more; so far from; so much so that; such... that; very

【界】 gaai³ realm

界定 delimit

界限 ① boundary ② end; limit

界面 interface

大把世界 (很多機會) have many chances to make money

內心世界 one's inner world; the inner world of the heart

仔大仔世界 (兒孫自有兒孫福) children who are grown-up should make their own decisions

世界 world

全世界 all over the whole

好世界 (好日子) happy life

好眼界 good eyesight

有眼界 have a good vision

房地產業界 real estate sector

做世界 (偷竊搶劫) become involved in illegal activities in order to make money

捱世界 (熬日子) struggle hard to make a living

眼界 accuracy

搵世界 (找生活) earn a living

業界 industry

境界 ① boundary ② realm; state ③ the extent reached

撈世界 ① (混日子) make a living through crime ② (闖蕩世界) earn a living

撈過界 (過了界) interfere in sb else's business

歎大把世界 (享受人生／享受生活) live in luxury

歎世界 (享受人生／享樂／享福) enjoy life; have a comfortable existence; live in luxury

踏界 (踩到界線上) line ball

踩界 (踩到界線上) line ball

環遊世界 travel around the world

【畏】 wai³ fear

畏死 afraid of dying; fear death

畏懼 awe; be scared of; dread; fear

怖畏 afraid; dread; scared

【疤】 baa¹ ① scar ② birthmark

疤痕 pit; scar; sore

瘡疤 scar of an ulcer; wound scar

【疥】 gaai³ skin disease

疥蟲 sarcoptic mite

癬疥 skin disease

【皆】gaai¹ all; each and every

皆因（因為）because of; due to

【皇】wong⁴ king

皇天不負有心人 God tempers the wind to the shorn
　　lamb

皇后 queen

皇帝 emperor; king

　　皇帝女──唔憂嫁（不愁嫁不出去）a person who is very
　　　　much sought after

　　皇帝唔急太監急（皇帝不急太監急）key oneself up over
　　　　others' business

　　土皇帝 local despot

皇牌 ace

天皇 celebrity

堂皇 grand; magnificent; stately

【盅】zung¹ bowl; cup

盅頭飯（盅飯）bowl of rice with food on top

冬瓜盅 winter melon soup

唥口盅（漱口杯）rinse mug

揭盅（揭曉）announce the results; bring to light; make
　　known

煙灰盅（煙灰缸）ashtray

【盆】pun⁴（盆子）basin

盆栽（盆景）potted landscape

盆菜 basin hot-pot

盆滿缽滿 make a lot of money

沖涼盆（沐浴盆）bathtub

星盆（水槽）sink

洗面盆 wash basin

洗腳盆 foot basin

面盆 washbasin

揼吓個盆（沖洗盆子）rinse the basin

【盈】jing⁴ full of

盈利 gains; profit

盈餘 abundance; have a favourable balance; have a surplus;
　　profit; surplus

笑盈盈（笑容滿面）smile broadly

【盃】bui¹ cup

面盃（臉盤兒）cast of one's face

【相】soeng³⁻² appearance

相干（關係）relation

　　冇相干（沒關係）never mind; nothing serious

相反 opposite

　　相反方向 opposite direction

相似 resemble

　　極之相似（極相似）close resemblance

相見好，同住難（相處容易，同住困難）it's nice to
　　see each other from time to time, but to live together is
　　difficult; familiarity breeds contempt

相宜（便宜）cheap; inexpensive

相信 believe; trust

相逢 meet each other again

　　山水有相逢 some day we will meet again

相處 get along

相睇（相親）make a blind date

相當之（相當）about; considerably; fairly; quite; rather;
　　somewhat; to a great extent; very

相與（相處）get along with

　　好相與（好相處 / 好商量 / 好說話兒 / 容易共事合作）
　　　　approvable; easy to get along with; personable

　　難相與（相處不來）difficult to get along with

相熟（熟悉）know each other well

相撞 crash together

　　連環相撞 crash involving several cars

【相】soeng³⁻² photo

相片 photo; photograph

　　一張相片 a photo

相底（底片）negative

相架（相片架）photo rack

相紙 photo paper

　　鐳射相紙（激光相紙）laser photo paper

相機 camera

　　一部相機 a camera

　　數碼相機 digital camera

相簿 photo album

　　一本相簿 a photo album

一張相（一張相片）a photo

一幅相（一張相片）a photo

一齊影張相（一起拍張照）take a photo together

了解真相 know the facts

六國大封相（混亂）chaotic situation

扮相（演員裝扮成劇中人物後的相貌）appearance of an
　　actor or actress in custume and make-up

亮相 strike a pose on the stage

真相 inside story; truth

執相（編輯相片）photo editing

異相 (外表奇怪) odd-looking; unsightly

睇相 (算命) fortune-telling

影咗好多相 (拍了很多照) take many photos

影相 (拍照) ① take a photo ② have one's photo taken

影番張相 (拍一張照) take a photo

幫我哋影張相 (幫我們拍一張照) could you take a photo for us

點相 (認人) pick out someone for revenge

點錯相 (認錯人) pick on the wrong person for revenge

鹹濕相 (色情照片) pornographic photograph

曬相 (沖印相片) develop a photo; print a photo

【眈】daam¹ look up

眈天望地 (東張西望) glance this way and that way

【盾】teon⁵ shield

盾牌 ① shield ② excuse; pretext

內心矛盾 mental conflicts

內部矛盾 internal contradictions

矛盾 contradiction

自相矛盾 self-contradictory

解決矛盾 solve a problem

避免矛盾 avoid conflicts

【省】saang² save

省到立立令 (口頭上狠狠地教訓一頓) give sb a dressing down

省城 provincial capital

省鏡 (上鏡／漂亮) beautiful; have a good-looking face

儉省 (節儉) economical; thrifty

【眉】mei⁴ (眉毛／眼眉) eyebrow

眉低額窄，冇厘貴格 (眼眉低、額頭窄的人一生平庸) person with low eyebrows and a narrow forehead lives a mediocre life

眉飛色舞 enraptured

眉清目秀 beautiful and delicate eyes

眉精眼企 (精明能幹) know a trick or two; smart

眉頭 eyebrows

　　眉頭一皺，計上心頭 have a sudden inspiration; hit upon an idea; knit the brows and you will hit upon a stratagem

　　眉頭眼額 (眉高眼低) one's thinking being revealed by one's facial expression

　　　　唔識睇人眉頭眼額 (不懂眉高眼低) not know how to adopt different attitudes and measures under different circumstances

識睇人眉頭眼額 (會看人眉高眼低) good at knowing sb's intentions

皺眉頭 frown

一堂眉 (一道眉毛) eyebrows

巾幗鬚眉 women who act and talk like men

水浸眼眉 (火燒眉毛) a matter of the utmost urgency; about to meet with disaster; at death's door; fire catches the eyebrows – in imminent danger

吐氣揚眉 blow off steam in rejoicing; elated; feel proud; feel proud and elated after one suddenly comes to fame; proud and elated; wealth or good luck; happy and proud; hold one's head high; stand up with head high

剃眼眉 ① (敗壞別人名聲) blacken sb's name ② (丟別人的臉) not to save sb's face

挑通眼眉 (精明) clever person

烏眉 (打瞌睡) sleep

眼眉 eyebrow

愁眉 distressed look; knitted brows

劃眉 (劃眉毛) paint one's eyebrows

壽眉 Shou Mei tea

蹙眉 (皺眉頭) knit one's brows

【看】hon³ look

看風駛悝 run before the wind

值得一看 worth watching

察看 look carefully at; observe; watch

【看】hon¹ watch

看牛不及打馬草 (浪費時間跟閒人聊天) it wastes time for a busy person to have a chat with an idler

看更 (看門／警衞員) security guard; watchman

看護 (護士) nurse

【眅】gap⁶ (盯) fix one's eyes on; gaze at

眅住佢 (盯住他) keep a close watch on him

【矜】ging¹ dignified

矜持 reserved; restrained

矜貴 (貴重／寶貴) treasurable; valuable

【泵】bam¹ (水泵) water pump

泵把 (保險桿) (English) bumper

泵氣 (打氣) inflate; pump up

水泵 water pump

單車泵 bicycle pump

廁所泵 cup plunger

【泵】dam¹ delay

泵長（拖長）prolong work unnecessarily
泵波鐘（拖長時間）play for time
泵泵吓（拖延）procrastinate

【砂】saa¹ sand

砂煲 earthern pot
　　砂煲兄弟（哥們）good friends
　　砂煲罌罉（家當）pots and bottles
砂糖 sugar
　　幼砂糖（細白糖）castor sugar
砂鍋 clay pot

幼砂（細白糖）castor sugar

【砌】cai³ lay

砌句（組句）build sentences
砌生豬肉（扣帽子 / 栽贓）fabricate a charge against sb;
　　frame sb
砌佢一身（揍他一頓 / 剋他一通）beat sb up; give sb a
　　beating
砌低（搞垮 / 幹掉）beat; defeat
砌屋（搭房子）build a house
砌圖（拼圖）jigsaw
砌磚 ①（堆砌磚頭）lay bricks ②（打麻將）play
　　mahjong

【砍】ham² knock

砍埋（撞向）crash into
　　砍頭埋牆（頭撞向牆壁）show repentance for having
　　　been foolish

洗碗有相磕（相處久了難免有磨擦、衝突）familiarity would
　　sometimes have a brush

【砐】ngap⁹（點頭）quake; sway

砐吓砐吓（晃晃悠悠）swaying; unstable
砐砐貢（晃悠）shake from side to side; sway
砐頭（點頭）nod one's head

【衹】zi² merely; only

衹有 only
衹係（衹是）just; merely; only

【祈】kei⁴ pray

祈禱 pray

千祈（千萬）by all means; don't ever; earnestly; it is
　　imperative that; must; sure; whatever you do don't

【秋】cau¹ autumn

秋天 autumn
秋後扇（不再需要的人）someone who is no longer
　　needed
秋葵 lady's finger; okra
秋蟬（蟬）cicada

一年容易又中秋（時光易逝）days in the year go by swiftly
　　and it is mid-autumn again
中秋 mid-autumn
勁秋 ①（很好）excellent; very good ②（厲害）powerful
葉落知秋 one falling leaf is indicative of the coming of
　　autumn; the falling leaves announce the approach of
　　autumn

【科】fo¹ ① section ② subject ③ discipline

科文（領班）(English) foreman
科技 science and technology
　　發展科技 develop science and technology
科學 science
　　科學家 scientist
科頭（科長）section chief

小兒科（小事）peanuts; trivial matters
內科 internal medicine
牙科 dentistry
收科 clean up a mess; end up
兒科 paediatrics
婦科 gynaecology
婦產科 obstetrics and gynaecology
眼科 ophthalmology
搞邊科（做甚麼）what are you trying to do; what's going on
精神科 psychiatry
煞科（收尾 / 完結）end up
攪邊科（做甚麼）what are you trying to do

【秒】miu⁵ second

秒針 second hand of a clock; second hand of a watch
秒錶 chronograph; stopwatch

一秒 one second

【穿】cyun¹ bore; piece through

穿心邊（豎心兒 / 豎心旁）the "heart"（心）radical
穿崩（露出破綻）let the cat out of the bag; let the secret out
穿煲（秘密敗露 / 露餡兒）disclose a secret; let the cat out
　　of the bag; let the secret out; reveal a secret
穿過 penetrate
穿窿（穿孔 / 穿洞）bore a hole; perforate

穿戴〔穿着〕apparel

拮穿〔刺穿〕pierce through

貫穿 ① pierce through ② run through

揭穿〔揭露〕debunk; expose; lay sth bare; show up

睇穿〔看穿〕gain an insight into sth; see through sb

睇唔穿〔看不穿〕not able to gain an insight into sth; not see through sb

睇得穿〔看得穿〕able to gain an insight into sth; can see through sb

鼻屎好食，鼻囊挖穿〔利之所在，人爭趨之〕everybody strives for profitable business

講穿〔說穿〕reveal the truth

撻穿〔打碎〕break; smash

櫃桶底穿〔竊空公款〕the funds of a unit are embezzled

識穿〔洞悉〕reveal; see through

【突】dat⁶〔超出〕exceed

突兀〔愕然〕surprised

突出 outstanding

突破 breakthrough

突然間 all of a sudden; out of the blue; suddenly

打個突〔感到愕然〕be surprised; surprise

有突〔超出〕exceed; odd

玲瓏浮突〔優美玲瓏／曲線分明〕exquisitely carved

唐突 abrupt

核突 ①〔噁心〕disgusting; give sb the creeps ②〔難看〕bad looking; ugly

矮突突〔矮小〕dumpy; pudgy; short and plump; stumpy

【竿】gon¹ pole

釣竿 angling rod; casting rod; fishing pole; fishing rod

【紀】gei² record

紀念 commemorate

　　紀念品 souvenir

　　值得紀念 worthy of commemorating

紀錄 record

世紀 century

年紀 age

有咗身紀〔懷孕〕pregnant

地產經紀 real estate agent; property agent

股票經紀 stock broker

保險經紀 insurance agent

經紀 agent; broker; middleman

綱紀 social order and law

黨紀 party discipline

【約】joek³ around

約莫〔大約〕about; approximately; or so; roughly

約會 dating

合約 contract

租約 tenancy agreement

買賣合約 sale and purchase agreement

預約 make an appointment

締約 conclude a treaty; sign a treaty

臨時買賣合約 provisional sale and purchase agreement

續約 renew a contract

【紅】hung⁴ red

紅人 a favourite of the person in power

紅卜卜〔紅乎乎的〕red

紅毛泥〔水泥／洋灰〕cement

紅包 red packet

紅光滿面 one's face glows with health

紅色 red; red colour

　　紅色暴雨訊號 red rain storm signal

紅汞水〔紅藥水〕mercurochrome

紅豆 red bean

　　紅豆水 red bean soup

　　紅豆沙 sweet red bean soup

　　　蓮子紅豆沙 sweet red bean soup with lotus seed

紅到發紫〔紅得發紫〕enjoy great popularity; extremely popular; extremely successful in the show business

紅底〔一百元紙幣〕one-hundred-dollar note

紅的 ①〔紅色的士〕red taxi ②〔市區的士〕urban taxi

紅雨〔紅色暴雨警告〕red rain storm signal

紅星〔紅角〕famous actor or actress; popular star; superstar

　　電影紅星〔電影紅角〕popular movie star

　　歌影視紅星〔歌影視紅角〕popular star in singing, movies, and television

紅衫魚 ①〔金線魚〕golden threadfin bream ②〔一百元紙幣〕one-hundred-dollar note

紅茶 black tea

紅粉花緋〔紅艷艷〕bright red

紅酒 red wine

　　一箱紅酒 a carton of red wine

紅椒 red bell pepper

紅當當〔紅彤彤／紅通通〕bright red

紅綠燈〔信號燈〕traffic lights

紅藥水 mecurochrome solution

紅簿仔〔銀行存摺〕bank passbook

紅麴 red yeast

紅轟轟 red

紅籌 red chips

紅鬚軍師（狗頭軍師）misadvisor; thoughtless advisor

紅鬚綠眼（外國人）Westerner

紅 van（紅色小巴）red minibus

仇人見面，份外眼紅（仇敵碰在一起，彼此更為激怒）
　　meeting enemies opens old wounds; when two foes
　　meet, there is no mistaking each other

白裏透紅 rosy chin

石榴紅 garnet

好紅 ①（紅通通的）very red ②（很受歡迎）very popular

見紅（流血）see blood

走紅 getting famous; have fortune on one's side

花紅（獎金）bonus; dividend

面青心紅 apparently weak but actually strong and loyal

面紅 ① blush; blush with shyness ② become red in the face;
　　flushed; one's face goes red

桃紅 light red; pink

眼紅（眼饞）feel envy at; get jealous; have green eyes;
　　jealous

當紅 currently popular

豬紅 pig's blood

雞紅 chicken blood

【缸】gong[1] earthern ware

缸仔（小瓦缸）tub

缸瓦（陶器）earthenware
　　缸瓦船打老虎——盡地一煲（沙鍋搗蒜——一捶子買賣）
　　shoot one's last bolt

一個缸 a bowl

打爆油缸（注滿氣油）fill up the fuel tank

垃圾缸 rubbish bin

油缸 fuel tank

金魚缸 ①（魚缸）fish tank ②（股票交易所）the Stock
　　Exchange ③（展示妓女的櫥窗）display window for
　　prostitutes

浴缸 bath tub

浸浴缸 take a bath

潲水缸 swill vat

【美】mei[5] beautiful

美人 beautiful lady
　　美人照鏡（吃光所有食物）eat up all the food on
　　　　the dish
　　大美人 very beautiful lady

美女 beautiful girl; beautiful woman
　　絕世美女 a girl of unparalleled beauty

美中不足 some slight imperfection

美元 American dollar; US dollar

美化 beautify; embellish; prettify
　　美化環境 beautify the environment

美好 fine; glorious; happy

美妙 wonderful

美言 put in a word for sb
　　請你為我美言幾句 please put in a good word for me

美味 delicious
　　美味可口 delicious and tasty

美金 American dollar; US dollar

美股 American stock

美洲 America
　　北美洲 North America
　　南美洲 South America

美食 good food
　　美食天堂 food paradise; gourmet paradise

美容 ① cosmetology ② beauty treatment
　　美容師 beautician

美酒佳餚 good wine and dainty dishes

美國 America; the United States of America
　　美國人 American

美意 good intention; kindness

美感 aesthetic feeling; sense of beauty

美滿 happy; perfectly satisfactory

美夢 fond dream
　　美夢成真 a fond dream comes true

美德 moral excellence; virtue
　　培育美德 cultivate virtue

美麗 beautiful
　　美麗動人 beautiful and charming

美觀 artistic; beautiful; pleasing to the eye
　　美觀耐用 beautiful and durable

十全十美 absolutely perfect; all roses; complete; flawless
　　and perfect; leave nothing to be desired; out of this
　　world; perfect; perfect in every respect; perfect in
　　every way; perfect to the last degree; the acme
　　of perfection; the pink of perfection; up to the
　　knocker

內在美 inner beauty

年輕貌美 young and pretty

完美 perfect

風景優美 beautiful landscape

價廉物美 low price but good quality

讚美 exalt; extol; glorify; praise

【者】ze[2] person

或者 maybe; perhaps

第三者 ① third party ② mistress of a married man

【耐】noi⁶ ① (久) long ② endure

耐不耐 (有時候 / 間中 / 間或 / 隔不多久) at times; from time to time; now and then; occasionally; sometimes

耐中 (有些時候) occasionally; sometimes

　　耐唔中 (有時候 / 隔一段日子) occasionally; sometimes

耐心 patient

耐用 durable

耐性 patience

　　冇耐性 (沒有耐性) impatient

　　有耐性 patient

耐唔耐 (有時候) at times; from time to time; now and then; occasionally; sometimes

冇幾耐 (不久之前) not long ago

未有耐 (早着呢 / 還早) it is still a long time before...

好耐 (很久) for a long time; for yonks; yonks ago

忍耐 endure; exercise patience; exercise restraint; put up with; restrain oneself; tolerant of

俗不可耐 atrocity; intolerable vulgarity; too vulgar to be endured; unbearably vulgar; vulgar in the extreme

要等幾耐 (要等多久) how long do we have to wait

能耐 capability

幾耐 (多久) how long

【耍】saa² play

耍手擰頭 (搖頭擺手) refuse

耍花槍 exchange banter; have a quarrel for fun

耍花樣 behave in a deceitful manner

耍家 (擅長) very accomplished

耍樂 (娛樂) entertain

　　麻雀耍樂 (打麻將) play mahjong

【耶】je⁴ coconut

耶穌 Jesus

　　耶穌受難節 Good Friday

　　耶穌誕 (聖誕節) Christmas

　　講耶穌 (說大道理 / 說教) lecture

甜耶耶 (甜過頭) over-sweet

【耷】dap¹ (低下) droop

耷尾 (垂頭喪氣) be crestfallen

耷頭 (低頭) lower one's head

　　耷頭佬 (詭計多端的人) person of schemes and tricks

　　耷頭耷腦 (垂頭喪氣) listless

　　耷低頭 (低下頭) disheartened; upset

嚡耷 (破舊) shabby

頭耷耷 (低着頭) dejected; keep one's head down

【胃】wai⁶ stomach

胃口 appetite

　　冇胃口 (沒胃口) have no appetite

　　好好胃口 (胃口很好) have very good appetite

胃食 (嘴饞) gluttonous; greedy eater

胃痛 (胃疼) stomachache; stomach pain

胃酸 gastric acid

胃藥 antiacid

反胃 ① stomach upset ② disgusting

令人反胃 nasty

好反胃 (非常反胃) very disgusting

好開胃 (胃口好) have very good appetite

你真開胃 (你胃口真好) avaricious

唔開胃 ① (沒有胃口) have no appetite; unappetizing ② dislike; no interest

益胃 reinforce one's stomach; tonify one's stomach

睇見就唔開胃 (看見就沒有胃口) feel sick upon seeing sth

脾胃 ① stomach ② appetite

開胃 ① (胃口好) have a good appetite ② (異想天開) a flight of fancy; a stretch of the imagination; ask for the moon; come out with most fantastic ideas; cry for the moon; expect wonders; fanciful; fanciful ideas; get fancy ideas into one's head; give loose to the fancy; given rein to fancy; have a maggot in one's head; have bats in the belfry; have bees in the brain; have bees in the head; have fantastic notions; have one's head full of bees; indulge in the wildest fantasy; indulge one's fancy; lend wings to one's imagination; let one's imagination run away with one; one's head is full of bees; vagarious; whimsical; wild hopes; wish for the moon; wishful thinking

瘤胃 rumen

醒胃 (開胃) appetizing

膩胃 (食慾減退) kill one's appetite

【背】bui³ back

背泳 (仰泳) backstroke

背面 overleaf

背頁 overleaf

背脊 (脊背) back

　　背脊向天人所食 all animals can be eaten by human beings

　　篤背脊 (背後中傷) back-stabbing; calumniate sb behind one's back; rip up the back; speak ill of sb behind their back; stab sb in the back; talk behind sb's back

背景 background

背囊 (背包) rucksack

水過鴨背（不留一點痕跡）without a trace
瓦背 roof
寒背（輕微的駝背）bow-backed
椅背 back of a chair
腹背 in front and behind
駝背 hunchback

【背】bui⁶ recite

背書（背課文）learn a lesson by rote; recite a text
　死背書 simply recite a text
背默（默寫）write from memory

死記硬背 mechanical memorizing

【胎】toi¹ embryo

胎衣（胞衣／胎盤）afterbirth
胎兒 fetus; embryo; unborn baby
胎記 birthmark
胎教 antenatal training; foetus education; prenatal
　education
胎盤 placenta

投胎 be reborn; be reincarnated
娘胎 mother's womb
狼胎（狼命／魯莽）ferocious; ferocious and relentless; fierce
棉胎（棉被）cotton quilt
趕住投胎（非常趕急）in a great hurry; in a hot haste; make
　a hot haste; rush oneself off one's feet
餓鬼投胎（狼吞虎嚥）devour like a hungry tiger pouncing
　its prey

【胡】wu⁴ wildly

胡同 alley; alleyway; lane; side road
　小胡同 by-street
　死胡同 blind alley; cul-de-sac; dead end; impasse
胡言 rave; talk nonsense
　胡言亂語 babble; blather; clotted nonsense; codswallop;
　　delirium; flimflam; full of hops; maunder; muck;
　　nonsense; punk; ramble in one's speech; rave;
　　ravings; rigmarole; shoot off one's mouth; shoot the
　　bull; sling the bull; speak at a venture; talk foolishly;
　　talk through one's hat; talk wildly; throw the bull;
　　wander in one's speech; wander in one's talk;
　　wanderings
　　一派胡言 a bunch of malarkey; a load of codswallop; a
　　　load of hogwash; a load of rubbish; a lot of eyewash;
　　　a lot of malarkey; a pack of lies; a pack of nonsense;
　　　complete nonsense; gross nonsense; sheer rubbish
胡帝胡天 behave foolishly; run wild

胡天胡帝 behave foolishly; run wild
胡胡混混（混日子）live an aimless life
胡桃 walnut
胡椒 black pepper; pepper
　胡椒粉 pepper
胡說 baloney; bilge; blather; bullshit; cobblers; cod;
　codswallop; cut the nonsense; don't talk rot; fiddlesticks;
　guff; horseshift; humbug; nonsense; rats; rot it; rubbish;
　shit; stuff and nonsense; what crap
　胡說八道 a pile of shit; all baloney; all my eye; apple
　　sauce; banana oil; broad nonsense; cobblers; cod;
　　drool; flubdub and gulf; full of hops; haver; hooey; lie
　　in one's teeth; lie in one's throat; mere humbug; prate
　　nonsense; pure rubbish; rats; rubbish; sheer nonsense;
　　sling the bull; speak through the back of one's neck;
　　stuff and nonsense; talk bosh; talk foolishly; talk
　　gibberish; talk nonsense; talk rot; talk rubbish; talk
　　sheer nonsense; talk through one's hat; talk through
　　the back of one's neck; talk wet; talk without truth;
　　throw the bull
胡鬧 cause disturbance without obvious reasons; kick up
　a row; make a row; mischievous; raise a row; run riot;
　run wild

京胡 Beijing opera fiddle

【胼】zan¹ callus

手胼（老繭）callus on the hand

【苑】jyun² estate

大型屋苑 large residential estate
大藍籌屋苑 blue chip estate
屋苑 estate

【苔】toi¹ coating

苔癬 lichen

脷苔（舌苔）coating on the tongue

【苗】miu⁴ seedling

苗條 slender; slim
　保持苗條 keep oneself slim
苗頭 suggestion of a new development; symptom of a trend

禾苗 rice seedlings; rice shoot
豆苗 pea sprout
感冒疫苗 cold and flu vaccine

【若】joek⁶ if

若干 certain

若果（如果／要是）but for; but that; failing; if; in case; in case of; in default of; in the absence of; in the event of; in the event that; on condition that; on the understanding; only that; provided; should; suppose; supposing; unless; wanting; what if; when; where; without

若要人不知，除非己莫為（幹了壞事終究無法隱瞞）there are eyes even in the dark; what is done by night will appear by day

若然之（如果／要是）but for; but that; failing; if; in case; in case of; in default of; in the absence of; in the event of; in the event that; on condition that; on the understanding; only that; provided; should; suppose; supposing; unless; wanting; what if; when; where; without

【苦】fu² bitter

苦口苦面（愁眉苦臉）look miserable

苦口婆心 exhort sb repeatedly with good intentions; words importunate but heart compassionate

苦瓜 bitter gourd

苦瓜乾（愁眉苦臉）gloomy face

苦瓜乾咁嘅面口（愁眉苦臉）a face of woe; a face shaded with melancholy; down in the dumps; down in the mouth; draw a long face; gloomy face; have a face as long as a fiddle; have a face like a fiddle; have a worried look; look blue; make a long face; pull a long face; put on a long face; wear a glum countenance; with a long face

苦過弟弟（非常辛苦）deplorable; go through all kinds of hardship

千辛萬苦 all kinds of hardships; all kinds of trials and tribulations; all kinds of untold hardships; go through thick and thin; go through untold hardships; innumerable hardships; innumerable trials and tribulations; labouriously; numberless sufferings and hardships; set one's shoulders to the wheel; severe toil; spare no pains; suffer all conceivable hardships; untold hardships

生活刻苦 lead a simple and frugal life

好辛苦（很辛苦）feel very bad

好苦（很苦）very bitter

何苦 not worth; not worth the trouble; why bother; why trouble

辛辛苦苦 at great pains to; laboriously; take all the trouble to; take great pains to; with great efforts; with so much toil; work laboriously

辛苦 feel awful; feel bad; fee ill; feel unhappy; feel unwell; suffer pain

刻苦 ① assiduous; hardworking; painstaking ② simple and frugal

怕苦 fear hardship

疾苦 difficulties; hardships; sufferings

捱得苦（吃得苦）able to bear hardship

貧苦 badly off; poor; poverty-stricken

痛苦 painful

訴苦 air one's grievance; complain about one's grievances; pour out one's woes; vent on's grievances

【英】jing¹ heroic

英才 talented person

天忌英才 heaven envies talented people

英文 English

英名 good reputation

英名一世，蠢鈍一時（人非聖賢，孰能無過）even Homer sometimes nods; every man has a fool in his sleeve

英年早逝 die when one is still in one's prime

英泥（水泥／洋灰）cement

英俊 handsome

英國 Britain

英國人 British

英雄 hero

英雄一世，蠢鈍一時（人非聖賢，孰能無過）even Homer sometimes nods; every man has a fool in his sleeve

英雄所見略同 great minds think alike

英雄重英雄 like knows like

英雄莫問出處 not every great person was born with a silver spoon in his mouth

識英雄重英雄 like knows like; think highly of each other

英鎊 British pound; sterling pound

石英 quartz

海洛英 heroin

靜英英（寂靜）silent; very quiet

薄英英（很薄）very thin

【苴】zaa² (差) poor

苴斗（低劣／差勁）of low quality; poor

苴貨（次貨）poor goods

苴嘢（次貨）poor things

【茂】mau⁶ exuberant

茂利（傻瓜）idiot

茂盛 exuberant; luxuriant; profuse

阿茂（傻瓜）stupid person

【茄】ke⁴⁻² eggplant

茄士咩 (開士米) cashmere
茄汁 (蕃茄醬) ketchup; tomato sauce
茄呢啡 (臨時演員) (English: carefree) carefree actor;
　carefree actress
茄喱 (小人物) unimportant person
　茄喱啡 (小人物) unimportant person
茄薯 (現金) (English) cash

蕃茄 tomato

【茄】gaa¹ ① root of lotus ② cigar

食雪茄 smoke cigar
雪茄 cigar

【茅】maau⁴ tricky

茅台 Maotai
茅波 (作弊) tricks in a ball game
　打茅波 ① (放寬規定) bend the rules ② (作弊) cheat
　③ (裝瘋子) act dumb; pretend to be ignorant of
　something in order to gloss it over ④ (在球賽上耍花
　招) play dirty in a ball game
茅廁 (茅坑) latrine pit
茅寮 (小茅房) small hut
茅躉 (耍賴) trick

奸茅 (耍賴) rascally; shameless; shameless behaviour;
　unreasonable
唔好咁茅 (不要耍賴) don't play tricks
發茅 (撒野) flurried; flustered
發晒茅 (撒野) flurried; flustered

【表】biu² ① cousin ② meter

表妹 cousin; first cousin
表姐 cousin; first cousin
表弟 cousin; first cousin; younger male cousin
表面 superficial; surface
表哥 (表兄) cousin; elder male cousin; first cousin
表情 expression; facial expression
　表情呆滯 have a dull expression on one's face
　冇晒表情 (沒表情 / 無精打彩) expressionless
　冇釐表情 (沒表情 / 無精打彩) expressionless

工作表 spreadsheet
代表 represent
外表 appearance
生字表 vocabulary list
老表 (表兄弟姐妹) cousin

其表 appearance of sth
姑表 cousinship
姨表 maternal cousin
虛有其表 a penny plain and twopence coloured; appear
　better than it is; deceptively handsome; good in
　appearance; good looks without substantial ability;
　impressive only in appearance; look impressive but lack
　real worth; many a fine dish has nothing on it; merely
　ornamental without solidity; one's qualifications are
　superficial
寒暑表 (溫度計) thermometer
損益表 profit and loss account
履歷表 curriculum vitae; resume

【衫】saam¹ (衣服) clothes

衫夾 (衣服夾子) clothes peg
衫尾 (下擺) lower hem of a gown
衫刷 (刷子) clothes brush
衫架 (衣架) coat hanger
衫衩 (衣衩) slit
衫料 (衣料) dress material
衫袖 (衣袖 / 袖子) sleeve
衫袋 (口袋) pocket
衫腳 (下擺) lower hem of a gown
衫領 (領子) collar
衫褲 (衣服) clothes

一件恤衫 (一件襯衣) a shirt
一件衫 (一件衣服) an item of clothing
一套衫 (一套衣服) a set of clothing
二手衫 (二手衣服) second-hand clothes
上衫 (上衣) blouse
大肚衫 (孕婦裝) maternity wear
女裝袖衫 (女裝襯衣) blouse
冇着衫 (裸體) naked
冷衫 (毛衣) woollen sweater
車衫 (縫紉衣服) sewing
底衫 (內衣) underwear
波衫 (球衣) sports shirt
長衫 ① long gown ② woman's dress called cheongsam
恤衫 (襯衣) shirt
洗衫 (洗衣服) wash clothes
面衫 (外衣) jacket; outerwear
着多件衫 (穿多一件衣服) put on more clothes; wear more
　clothes
着衫 (穿衣) get dressed; put on clothes; wear
除衫 (脫衣) undress
做衫 (做衣服) make clothes
哯衫 (晾衣服) dry clothes in the sun; sun clothes

笠衫 (套頭上衣) sweater
換衫 (換衣服) change clothes
補衫 (修補衣服) mend clothes
買衫 (買衣服) buy clothes
新衫 (新衣服) new clothes
罩衫 dustcoat; overall
試衫 (試衣服) fit sth on; try on
摺衫 (叠衣服) fold clothes
對胸衫 (胸前開襟的外套) Chinese-style jacket with buttons down the front
對襟衫 (胸前開襟的外套) Chinese-style jacket with buttons down the front
搵濕衫 (淋濕上衣) shirt doused by the rain
靚衫 (漂亮的衣服) beautiful clothes
樽領衫 (高領衣服) turtleneck shirt
燙衫 (熨衣服) iron clothes
聯好件衫 (把衣服縫好) stitch the clothes
聯衫 (縫衣服) stitch clothes
舊衫 (舊衣) old clothes
織冷衫 (織毛衣) knit a woollen sweater
攝住件衫 (把衣服塞進褲子) tuck a shirt into one's trousers
曬衫 (曬衣服) dry clothes in the sun
體育衫 (運動服裝) sports wear

【衩】 caa³ slit

衫衩 (衣服開衩兒的地方) slit

【要】 jiu³ have to; must

要人 (重要人物) important person
要生要死 hysterical
要求 request
要面 (要面子) anxious to keep up appearances; keen on face-saving
　唔要面 (不要臉) know no shame
要起手 (要用的時候) when needed
要靚唔要命 (要美不要命) be willing to risk one's life to become more beautiful; beauty has priority over life

一定要 must
主要 chief; main; major
只要 ① want only ② all one has to do is
必要 indispensable; necessary; need
吓吓要 (動不動就要) apt to
次要 less important; minor; next in importance; secondary; subordinate
是必要 (必要) have to; must
為咗要 (為了) in order to
重要 important

唔要 (不要) not want
唔緊要 ① (小問題) minor ② (不要緊) it doesn't matter; it's alright; never mind
唔憂冇人要 (不怕沒人要) not to worry about not having anyone wanting it
須要 have to; must
想要 want
綱要 ① outline; sketch ② compendium; essentials
緊要 (要緊) serious; severe
需要 need
閻羅王嫁女——鬼要 (沒人想要) nobody wants it
撮要 gist; summary
輯要 abstract; summary

【觔】 gan¹ muscle

觔斗 (跟斗) somersault
　翻觔斗 (翻跟斗) somersault; take a somersault

【計】 gai³ (算) calculate

計一計 (算一算) calculate; reckon up
計下 (算一下) figure out; make out
計少 (少算) short-charge
計正 (通常情況下) in the ordinary course of things; under normal circumstances
計多 (多算) over-charge
計返 (算回) work backward
計唔掂 (算不過來) not worthwhile
計埋 (全算上) everything included; taken together
　計埋一齊 (算在一起) taken together
　計埋晒 (全算上) everything included; taken together
計啱 (算對／算準) the calculation is correct
　計啱晒 (全算對了) the calculation is all correct
計落 (算下來／算起來) altogether; in all
計算 calculate
計數 ① (計算) calculate; count ② (算賬) settle a score
　計數機 (計算器) calculator
　計條數 (算一算) settle a score
　　計吓條數 (算一算) calculate
計劃 plan
計錯 (算錯) miscalculate
　計錯數 (算錯) calculate wrongly

千方百計 a thousand schemes; all sorts of schemes; by a thousand ways and a hundred devices; by all kinds of methods; by all means at one's command; by all sorts of means; by all ways and means; by diverse means; by every conceivable means; by every means imaginable; by every possible means; by fair means or foul; by hook or by crook; by one means or another; contrive in every possible way; cut and contrive; do all in one's power; do all one can; do everything one can do; do everything possible; do one's utmost; employ all available means; explore every possible means; explore every avenue; go to all lengths; go to any length; go to qreat lenqths; in a hundred and one ways; in a thousand and one ways; in all manner of ways; in countless ways; in every possible way; inexhaustible in devices and schemes; leave no avenue unexplored; leave no means untried; leave no stone unturned; make every attempt; make every endeavour; make every effort; make every possible effort; move heaven and earth; pull all the stops out; pull out all the stops; resort to every trick; scheme in a thousand and one ways; stop at nothing; take every means; try every means; try a thousand and one ways; try all means; try by all means; try by hook or by crook; try desperately; try every means; try every method; try every possible means; try every possible way; try in a thousand and one ways; try in a thousand ways; try in every possible way; try in every way; try one's utmost; try to...in all sorts of ways; use all one's ingenuity; use all sorts of wiles and methods; use all sorts of wits and methods; use all ways and means; use every means; use every method; use every possible means; use every stratagem; worry out ways

小數怕長計 (數目雖少,但長遠計算則是大數目) carelessness with small amounts leads to big money problems in the long term

山人自有妙計 I've an excellent solution

中計 fall into a set-up; fall into a trap

伙計 (服務員) waiter

共計 add up to

估計 estimate

夾計 (合謀) collude with sb; gang up with sb

妙計 brilliant scheme; excellent plan; good tactics; wonderful idea

扭計 (鬧彆扭) malcontent; resort to manoevres

拉勻計 (平均計算) strike an average

室內設計 interior design

唔使計 (不用計) don't mention it; forget it

將計就計 turn sb's tricks against him

粗略估計 rough estimate

堪計 (難以計算) hard to calculate; hard to work out

統計 ① census; statistics ② add up; count

會計 accounting

照計 (按說) by all accounts; by right; ought to

網頁設計 webpage design

諗計 (想辦法) map out a strategy

點計 (怎樣計算) how much is to be charged

斷斤計 (以一斤為單位計算) calculate by catty

襟計 (花大量金錢) cost a large amount of money

【計】 gai³⁻² (點子) way

計仔 (計策 / 計謀 / 辦法 / 點子) stratagem; trick; way

出計仔 (出點子 / 出謀劃策) offer advice; work out a way to deal with sth/sb

諗計仔 (想辦法 / 出主意) work out a way

冇計 (沒法子 / 沒辦法 / 沒轍) be unable to find a way out; can't be helped; can do nothing about it; can't help it; have no choice but; have no way out but to do sth; nothing can be done about it

冇晒計 (完全沒法子 / 完全沒辦法) can't do anything about it

多計 (多計謀) full of wicked ideas

夾計 (合謀) collude with sb; conspire; gang up with sb; plot together

屎計 (壞點子) poor strategy

敆計 (合謀) collude with sb; conspire; gang up with sb; plot together

矮仔多計 (矮個子的計謀多) a short person has a resourceful mind; a short person is full of tricks; a short person has many strategems

【訂】 deng³ order

訂房 reserve a room

訂金 deposit

訂枱 (訂位子) reserve a table

訂做 made to order

訂飛 (訂票) book a ticket

【訂】 ding³ bind

訂裝 (裝訂) bookbinding

【負】 fu⁶ bear

負累 (連累) get sb into trouble; implicate; incriminate; involve

負責 be in charge

負債 in debt

　　負債比率 gearing

抱負 ambition; aspiration

肩負 bear; shoulder; take on; undertake

欺負 bluff; bluster; browbeat; bulldoze; bully; coerce; insult; intimidate; oppress; overbear; push around; ride roughshod over sb; ridicule; treat sb high-handedly; treat sb rough

辜負 disappoint; fail to live up to; let down; unworthy of

實現抱負 fulfill one's ambition; realise one's aspiration

【趴】paa¹ drop down; fall down

趴台（伏在桌上）bend over the table
趴底（伏下）lie face down
趴係地上面（伏在地上）lie on the ground

【軌】gwai² track

軌道 course; path; track
軌跡 ① locus; path; way ② orbit

電車軌 ① rail track ② （額頭的皺紋）wrinkles on the forehead

【軍】gwan¹ military

軍人 soldier
軍佬（軍人）armyman; serviceman; soldier
軍官 army officer
軍服 military uniform
軍師 military advisor
　狗頭軍師 inapt advisor; villainous advisor
軍隊 army

火頭軍（炊事員）cook
伙頭將軍（廚師）cook
老軍 uniformed police
亞軍 runner-up; second place
季軍 second runner-up; third place; third winner in contest
空軍 air force
冠軍 champion
星軍（挑起事端）kick up a row; make a row; run riot; run wild
兜篤將軍（從後偷襲）rip up the back of sb
海軍 navy
將軍 ① general ② (in Chinese chess) check
陸軍 army
殿軍 ① rear guard ② fourth winner in a contest
濟軍（淘氣鬼）regular mischief
雜牌軍（烏合之眾）ragtag group

【迫】bik¹（擠）crowded

迫人（擁擠）crowded
　太迫人（很擁擠）overcrowded
　好迫人（很擁擠）packed; very crowded

擠迫 crowded
壓迫 oppression

【述】seot⁶ state

述評 commentary; review
述說 give an account of; narrate; recount; state; tell
述職 report; report on one's work

描述 describe
著述 ① compile; write ② books; literary works; writings

【郁】juk¹（動）move

郁手（動手）take action
郁吓就（動不動就）apt to; easily
郁身郁勢（動來動去）show discontent with one's position
郁郁槓（來回動）move back and forth
郁動（活動）move about

心郁郁（心動／起了心／動了心／動心）one's desire is aroused
四方木——踢一踢，郁一郁（木頭人——推一推，動一動）a wooden person never moves without a rush on it; lazybones
依郁（行動）action
唔好郁（不要動）don't move
神主牌都會郁（出乎意料之外的幸運）meet with one's fortune
費事郁（懶得動）not in the mood to move

【重】zung⁶（還）still

重未（還沒有）has not; not yet; still not yet
重要 important

老成持重 experienced and prudent
沉重 ① heavy ② critical; serious
災情嚴重 the condition of the disaster is serious
事態嚴重 the situation is serious
注重 attach importance to; consider to be important; emphasize; lay emphasis on; lay stress on; pay attention to
保重 take care
珍重 ① hold dear; set great store; treasure; value highly ② take good care of yourself
莊重 grave; serious; solemn
尊重 respect
隆重 grand; solemn
慎重 careful; cautious; considerate; discreet; prudent
器重 have a high opinion of; regard highly; think highly of; think much of
嚴重 serious

【重】cung⁴ ① repeat ② double ③ layer

重建 rebuild
重陽節 Chung Yang Festival; Double Ninth Festival
重複 repeat

三重 threefold; treble; triple; tripling

矛盾重重 with many contradictions
困難重重 be beset with difficulties; bristle with difficulties;
　　straitened circumstances

【重】cung⁵ heavy
重皮（成本高）costly; expensive
重秤（壓秤）weigh heavy
重量 weight

千里送鵝毛，物輕情意重 the trifling gift sent from afar
　　conveys deep affection
太重 too heavy
物輕情義重 a gift of trifling value conveys affection
為皮好重（成本重）the cost is heavy
量體重 take the body weight; weigh oneself; weigh sb
落雨賣風爐——越擔越重（雨天挑稻草——越挑越重）one's
　　burden gets greater
過重 overweight
舉重 weight lifting
禮輕情意重 the gift is trifling but the feeling is profound
濕氣重 very humid
體重 body weight

【閂】saan¹（關）bolt
閂住（關上）close; lock up
　　閂唔住（關不住）can't lock up
　　閂得住（關得住）can be locked up
閂咗（關上）turn off
閂門（關門）close the door; shut the door
閂倒（關得上）can be locked up
　　閂唔倒（關不上／關不起來）can't be locked up
　　閂得倒（關得上／關得起來）can be locked up
閂埋（關着）close up
　　閂唔埋（關不住）can't lock up
閂窗（關窗户）close the window
閂掣（剎車）brake a car
閂舖①（商店關門／關店）close for the day
　　②（倒閉）close down
　　未閂舖（未關門）the shop is not closed
　　閂咗舖（關了門）the shop is closed

【陋】lau⁶ humble
陋包（粗笨）bulky; cumbersome; heavy; unwieldy
陋習 bad habits; vice
　　戒除陋習 break off a bad habit

【降】hong⁴ surrender
投降 surrender

【降】gong³ descend
降級 demote
降落（着陸）alight; descend to the ground; land; landing;
　　touch down

升降 hoist and lower; rise and fall
從天而降 appear out of the blue; come down from heaven;
　　come from above; descend out of the blue; drop from
　　the clouds; fall from the sky; sudden unexpected arrival;
　　unexpectedly
禍從天降 a calamity descends from the sky; an unexpected
　　affliction; disaster comes from the sky; misfortune drops
　　from heaven, and falls on sb

【限】haan⁶ limit
限度 limits; measures; tethers
限定 define; determine; fix; limit; prescribe a limit to;
　　restrict; specification; specify
限制 restrict
限期①set a time limit; within a definite time ②deadline;
　　time limit

工作年限 fixed number of years for work
名額有限 limited quota
好人有限（不算是好人）far from being a good person
年限 fixed number of years
老鼠尾生瘡——大極有限（事情再大也有極限）there's a
　　ceiling for sth
局限 confine; limit; localization
牀下底放紙鷂——高極有限（本事再高也枉然）a kite flew
　　under a bed won't rise
牀下底踢毽——高極有限（本事再高也枉然）a shuttlecock
　　kicked under a bed won't rise
界限①boundary ②end; limit
茶瓜送飯——好人有限（不算是好人）far from being a
　　good person
菜瓜餞——好人有限（不算是好人）far from being a
　　good person

【面】min⁶（面子／臉）face
面大（重要）important; influential
面口（相貌／臉色／樣子）face
　　二口六面（當面）face to face
　　三口六面（三頭對面／當面）face-to-face; two parties
　　　and witness confront in court
　　木口木面（木無表情）expressionless; slow-witted;
　　　wooden-faced
　　生面口（陌生）stranger
　　板面口（板起臉）straighten one's face

嚊口嚊面（板起臉孔）look upset

嘸口嘸面（板起臉孔）in a bad mood

睇人口面（看人家臉色）be dependent on other's pleasure

熟口面（熟悉）familiar face

熟口熟面（老相識）familiar face

熟面口（熟悉）familiar

面子 face

面子問題 a matter of face

面巾（洗臉巾／臉巾）face towel; towel; washcloth

面不改容（面不改色）not to change colour; one's countenance betrays nothing; one's face is untroubled; remain calm; undismayed; without batting an eyelid; without changing countenance; without turning a hair

面孔 face

天使面孔 angel face

面左左（雙方互不理睬）be at odds with one another

面皮（臉皮）face; sb's feelings; self-respect

面皮好厚（臉皮厚）shame on you

面皮厚（臉皮厚）be shameless; have a thick skin; know no shame; thick skin

面皮薄（臉皮薄）sensitive; shy; thin-skinned

面目 appearance; face

面目全非 be changed beyond recognition

面色（臉色）facial expression

面色好番（氣色變好）look much better than before;

面色唔好（氣色不佳）look blue about the gills; look green about the gills; look white about the gills; look yellow about the gills; look pale; not to look oneself; off colour;

俾面色人睇（給臉色別人看）let others see one's displeasure

睇人面色（看人臉色）be dependent on other's pleasure

面具 mask

面青 scared

面青口唇白（臉色煞白）white with fear

面青心紅 apparently weak but actually strong and loyal

面青青 ①（臉色蒼白）pale ②（面有懼色）look freightened

面阻阻（雙方互不理睬／形同陌路）not on good terms with

面前 in front of

面型（臉型）shape of one's face

面盆（臉盆）washbasin

面紅 ①（因害羞而臉紅）blush; blush with shyness ②（臉紅）become red in the face; flushed; one's face goes red

面紅面綠（面紅耳赤）as red as a turkey-cook; blush to the roots; blush up to the ears; colour up; crimson with rage; flush red in the face; flush to the ears; flush with

shame; get red in the face; one's face reddens to the ears; red in the face; red with anger

面衫（上衣／外衣）jacket; outerwear

面盃（臉盤兒）cast of one's face

面面 in every way

面面觀 view sth from every angle

面珠（臉蛋兒）face

面珠墩（臉蛋兒）face

面豉（豆醬／黃醬）fermented soybean paste

面善（臉熟）familiar face

面黃骨瘦 skinny and look pale

面對 confront; face

面對面 face to face

面墩（臉蛋兒）face

面積 area

面貌 face

面貌清秀 have delicate facial features

社會面貌 social aspects

面褲（外褲）over-trousers

面臨 be confronted with; be faced with; be up against

面額 denomination

面霜（雪花膏）vanishing cream

面懜懜（臭臉）wear a long face

面懵（難為情）lose face

面懵心精（似傻非傻）appear to be stupid but is actually very smart; play the fool

面懵懵（傻瓜似的）look foolish

唔怕面懵（臉皮厚）thick-skinned

一方面 on one hand

一面 ① one aspect; one side ② at the same time

一塊面（一張臉）a face

二口六面（面對面）face to face

人面 personal relations

入面（裏面）inside

十面 ten-sided

三口六面（面對面）face-to-face; two parties and witness confront in court

上面 above; on the surface of; on top of; over; top; upper surface

下面 below; under

大花面 painted face

口面（口臉）one's look

公開露面 appear in public; make a public appearance; make one's appearance in public; show one's face in public

反面 ① reverse side ② fall out; not on good terms with one; suddenly turn out to be hostile to sb

木口木面（木無表情）expressionless; slow-witted; wooden-faced

牛頭馬面 devils

冇面 (沒面子 / 沒臉 / 丟瞼) have no face; lose face

冇晒面 (沒一點面子) lose face completely

方面 aspect

片面 ① one-sided; single-faceted; unilateral ② lopsided

以淚洗面 wash one's face with tears

出面 (以個人或集體的名義) act on behalf of someone or a group

另一方面 on the other hand; to the right

右手面 right-hand side; to the right

左手面 left-hand side; to the left

生面 (陌生) unfamiliar

瓜子面 (瓜子臉) oval face

好熟口面 (熟悉) look familiar

充撐場面 give one's support

有面 (有面子) enjoy due respect

有頭有面 ① be famous and titled ② person with social status

有關方面 concerned parties

別開生面 break a new path; break fresh ground; open up a new facet; out of the common road; start sth new; with freshness and novelty

坐櫃面 (坐在前枱) serve at the counter

局面 aspect; phase; prospect; situation

扭轉局面 bring about changes in the situation

拋頭露面 make a living in the public eye; show oneself to make a living

灶君老爺──黑口黑面 (板起臉孔) fierce demons and devils

豆腐刀──兩便面 (為人圓滑 / 兩面討好) a bean curd knife is sharp on both sides – a fence-sitter

走精面 (小聰明) act selfishly

見世面 (增長見識) see the world

見面 meet

兩面 both aspects; both sides; double; dual; two sides

定時見面 meet regularly

店面 shopfront; storefront

抹吓塊面 (擦擦臉) clean one's face

抹面 (擦臉) clean one's face

㑂口㑂面 (板起臉孔) in a bad mood

版面 ① layout of a printed sheet ② space of a whole page

花面 painted face

表面 superficial; surface

封面 ① title page ② front cover of a book ③ cover; front cover

門後面 behind the door

門面 ① shop front ② appearance; façade

剃面 (刮臉) shave; shave the face

前面 in front; ahead; at the head

要面 (要面子) anxious to keep up appearances; keen on face-saving

後面 at the back; behind; in the back; in the rear

背面 overleaf

背頁 overleaf

苦口苦面 (愁眉苦臉) look miserable

枱面 (桌上) table top

界面 interface

紅光滿面 one's face glows with health

頁面 page

俾面 (給面子) give face

唔要面 (不要面) know no shame

唔俾面 (不給面子) not to give face

唔睇僧面，都睇吓佛面 (不看僧面看佛面) not for everybody's sake but for sb's sake

桌面 desktop; tabletop

神主牌都會擰轉面 (愧對先人) once one becomes a leper, one brings disgrace on one's fore-fathers

被面 (鋪蓋) quilt cover

馬面 (長臉) long face

國字口面 (方臉) square face

控制局面 control the situation

場面 ① scene ② occasion

㖿口㖿面 (板起臉孔) look upset

捌起塊面 (板起臉孔) assume a displeased look; assume a serious look; have a taut face; pull a long face; with a long face; with a straight face

最後一面 take a last look at a dying person

湖面 lake surface

睇人口面 (看人口臉) be dependent on other's pleasure

朝見口，晚見面 (經常見面) see each other very often

裝門面 maintain an outward show

黑口黑面 ① (非常生氣) very angry ② (板起臉孔) look displeased; pull a long face

黑埋口面 ① (非常生氣) very angry ② (板起臉孔) look displeased; pull a long face

圓面 round face

當面 face to face

落面 (丟別人的臉) be disgraced; feel ashamed; lose face

落…嘅面 (丟…的臉) bring disgrace on sb; make sb lose face

經風雨，見世面 brave the storm and face the world

腳面 instep

裏面 in; inside

路面 road surface

對面 on the other side; opposite; opposite side

層面 aspect; dimension; general characteristic

撐門面 keep up appearances

撞面 (撞上) bump into

樓面 ① (營業範圍) floor ② (服務員) waiter
精彩場面 wonderful scene
熟口面 (熟悉) familiar face
熟口熟面 (熟悉) familiar face
賞面 do sb a favour; favour sb with one's presence; thanks for coming
遮面 (傘面) umbrella fabric
賬面 book value
錶面 face of a watch
擘面 (翻面) break up; fall out; suddenly turn hostile
擰歪面 (扭過臉去) turn one's face
擰轉面 (扭過臉去) turn one's face
擺門面 put up a front
燶起塊面 (板起臉孔) keep a straight face; pull a long face; wear a long face
櫃面 (櫃枱) bar; counter; desk
顏面 ① countenance; face ② honour; prestige
鵝蛋口面 oval face
露面 show up
鐵面 judge

【革】 gaak³ change

革命 revolution
革除 ① abolish; do way with; get rid of ② dismiss; dispel; excommunicate; expel; remove from office
革新 innovation; reform; renovation
革職 discharge from a position; dismiss; remove from office; sack

【韭】 gau² Chinese chive

韭菜 green chive
韭黃 yellow chive

【音】 jam¹ sound

音樂 music
音樂家 musician
音樂會 concert
露天音樂會 open-air concert; outdoor concert
古典音樂 classical music
聽音樂 listen to music
聽吓音樂 (聽音樂) listen to some music
音櫃 (音箱) loudspeaker box; speakers
音響 hi-fi
一套音響 a set of hi-fi
音響組合 hi-fi set

佳音 good tidings
弦外之音 connotation; implied meaning; overtone
發音 pronunciation

報佳音 proclaim good tidings
影音 audio visual
播音 make broadcasts
燈芯敲鐘——冇音 (秤鉈落在棉花上——沒回音) no reply
錄音 record
鐵觀音 Iron Goddess of Mercy tea
觀音 Goddess of Mercy

【頁】 jip⁶ page

頁尾 footer
頁面 page
頁邊 margin

冊頁 alhum of calligraphy; album of paintings
網頁 webpage

【風】 fung¹ ① wind ② (風聲 / 消息) information

風月場所 place of carnal pleasures
風水 ① (transliteration) fung-shui; geomancy ② fortune
風水佬 (風水先生) geomancer
風水佬呃你十年八年，唔呃得一世 (時間證明一切) time can witness to a fact
風水師傅 fung-shui master; geomancy master
風水輪流轉 every dog has his day; fortunes change
風生水起 get rich
睇風水 (看風水) practise geomancy
風吹芫荽——衰 (垂) 到貼地 (爛眼睛招蒼蠅——倒霉透了) reach the pitch of bad fortune
風吹雞蛋殼——財散人安樂 pay a price for one's safety
風車 windmill
風采 ① mien ② demeanour
一睹風采 take a look at sb's elegant demeanour
風雨 wind and rain
要風得風，要雨得雨 be able to get what one wants
腥風腥雨 violent conflict
攪風攪雨 (興風作浪) make trouble; stir up troubles
風度 ① bearing; demeanour ② manners ③ tolerance
有風度 ① gentlemanly ② good-mannered
風流 leisurely and carefree
風扇 fan
開風扇 switch on the fan
風涼水冷 (清涼舒適) cool and comfortable
風球 typhoon signal
一號風球 typhoon signal number one
八號風球 typhoon signal number eight
十號風球 typhoon signal number ten
十號風球除咗 (十號風球已除下) typhoon signal

number ten has been taken down

十號風球落咗 (十號風球已除下) typhoon signal
number ten has been taken down

三號風球 typhoon signal number three

掛三號風球 typhoon signal number three is hoisted

幾號風球 what is the typhoon signal

風景 landscape; scenery

風景優美 beautiful landscape

睇風景 (看風景) watch scenery

風筒 (電吹風) hair dryer

風槍 (氣槍) air gun; air rifle

風趣 witty

風趣幽默 witty and humorous

風險 risk

風頭 ① condition ② limelight

風頭火勢 (事情鬧得正兇的時候) at full throttle; in the
state of full blast

風頭躉 (風雲人物) person who is fond of limelight;
some who enjoys being in the limelight

出風頭 be in the limelight

避風頭 (躲避風吹) stay out of trouble; lie low

風濕 rheumatism

風擺柳 (拿不定主意) undecided

風騷 attractive; sexy

懶風騷 (賣弄風騷) cocky; coquettish

風癱 (癱瘓) paralysis

大少爺作風 (奢華的作風) behaviour typical of the spoiled
son of a rich family; extravagant ways

大風 windy

中風 stroke

手風 (手氣) luck

台風 stage manners

打風 ① typhoon ② have a typhoon

好大風 (風很大) very windy

好猛風 (風很大) the wind is strong

耳邊風 unheeded advice; words treated as unimportant

色士風 saxophone

收到風 (收取消息) gather information about sth; get wind
of sth

收風 (收取消息) gather information about sth; get wind of
sth

佔上風 have the advantage of sb

作風 style; style of work; way

扯風 (通風) draw in air

放風 (放風箏) kite-flying

長他人志氣，滅自己威風 boost the enemy's morale and
dampen one's own spirit; laud the spirit of the enemy
and belittle that of our own; puff up the enemy's morale

and lower one's own

歪風 evil wind; unhealthy trend

食西北風 (喝西北風) have nothing to eat; live in poverty

弱不禁風 so delicate a constitution that one is unable to
stand a qust of wind; on the lift; too frail to stand a gust
of wind

祝你順風 have a fine trip; have a good trip; have a pleasant
journey; have a smooth trip; wish you a nice trip

逆風 go against the wind

馬上風 (性交時死掉) die while having sex

透風 let in air; ventilate

密不透風 airtight

寒風 bleak wind; cold wind

發噏風 (胡說八道) baloney; bilge; blather; bullshit; cobblers;
cod; codswallop; guff; horseshift; humbug; nonsense; rats;
rot it; rubbish; say nonsense; shit; talk nonsense; talk rot;
talk through one's hat

發風 (發麻瘋) leprosy

順風 fine trip

傷風 catch cold; cold; have a cold

當耳邊風 ignore advice

萬事俱備，只欠東風 ready to the last gaiter button

漏口風 blurt out a secret; let slip a secret

漲風 (漲價) upward trend of commodity prices

颱風 typhoon

頭風 ache in one's head; have a headache; headache

樹大招風 a person of reputation is liable to become the envy
of others

翻風 ① gale ② (起風) the wind is getting strong

【飛】 fei[1] ① fly ② (票) (English) fare; ticket ③ (拋棄) get rid of

飛士 (面子) face

飛女 (女阿飛 / 女流氓) teddy girl

飛仔 (阿飛 / 流氓) gangster; teddy boy

飛仔飛女 (流氓阿飛) teddy boys and teddy girls

飛尾 (票尾) ticket stub

飛沙 (不加糖) no sugar please

飛車 (超速) speeding

飛咗佢 (把他剔了) get rid of him

飛來蜢 (意外的好處) unexpected fortune

飛的 (坐出租車趕路) speed up the journey by taking a
taxi

飛個電話去 (趕快打個電話) give sb a quick call

飛釘 (女性衣着內的乳頭凸出輪廓) nip out; smuggle
smarties

飛起 ① (拋棄) get rid of ② (很) extremely

寸到飛起 (很囂張) very arrogant

忙到飛起 (很忙碌) busy to death

貴到飛起 (貴到不得了) exorbitantly expensive; extremely expensive

飛站 (不停站) fail to stop at the bus stop

飛番 (飛回) fly back

飛過 fly over

飛線 (接駁電話) divert the phone call

飛蟻／痱滋 (口腔潰瘍／口瘡) aphtha; mouth ulcer
　生飛蟻 (長口瘡) have a thrush

飛象 the chess "elephant" flying across the river

飛鼠 (蝙蝠) bat

飛劍 flying sword
　放飛劍 (吐痰) spit

飛舞 dance in the sky
　凌空飛舞 fly in the sky

飛髮 (理髮) haircut; have a haircut
　飛髮佬 (理髮師) barber; hairdresser
　飛髮剪 (理髮推子) hair clipper
　飛髮舖 (理髮店) barber's shop

飛機 aeroplane
　飛機友 (經常失約的人) a person who always breaks appointments
　飛機恤 (甲克／夾克) jacket
　飛機師 (飛行員) pilot
　飛機場 (胸部平坦) flat-chested
　一架飛機 an aeroplane
　放飛機 (失約) break a promise; ditch sb; fail to show up for an appointment; fail to turn up for a date; stand sb up
　送飛機 ① see sb off at the airport ② miss the flight ③ give sb an aeroplane as a present
　寄飛機 (空郵) send by air
　搭飛機 (乘飛機) go by air; take a plane
　落飛機 (下飛機) get out of an aeroplane

飛擒大咬 over-eager; show one's horn; show one's lustful manner

飛邊 (去邊兒) remove the edges

飛嚟飛去 (飛來飛去) flying to and fro

一張飛 (一張票) a ticket

大飛 (快速艇) speedboat

水靜河飛 ① (生意慘淡) have no business; the market is dull ② (冷冷清清) silence reigns in the place

好食懶飛 (好吃懶做) eat but do nothing; eat one's head off; lazy

來回飛 (來回票) return ticket

炒飛 (炒賣門票) raise the ticket price; scalp tickets

訂飛 (訂票) book a ticket

派飛 (發放票) dispatch tickets

頂飛 (負責) take responsibility

頂重飛 (擔當重任) star attraction

起飛 take off

退飛 ① (收回票錢) get a refund for a ticket ② (退票) return a ticket ③ (空頭票) dishonoured ticket

臭飛 (臭流氓) dirty teddy boy

粗口橫飛 (滿嘴髒話) use a lot of bad language

船飛 ① (船票) ferry ticket ② (快速渡輪船票) turbo jet ticket

單程飛 (單程票) one-way ticket

插翼難飛 unable to escape

普飛 (自助餐) (English) buffet

幾點飛 (甚麼時候飛) what time is your flight

買飛 (買票) buy a ticket

補飛 (補買票) buy one's ticket after the normal time

罰飛 (罰票) penalty ticket

蒲飛 (自助餐) (English) buffet

遠走高飛 flee far away; fly far and high; fly high and go away; go far away; off to distant parts; slip away to a distant place; take it on the lam; take wing

撲飛 (搶購門票) look everywhere for a ticket

輪飛 (排隊買票) queue up to buy tickets

戲飛 (戲票) play ticket; opera ticket

雙程飛 (來回票) return ticket

【食】sik⁶ (吃) eat

食一餐 (吃一頓) have a meal

食七咁食 (狼吞虎嚥) eat and drink as much as one can; gorge oneself; have a good stomach

食人唔磡骨 (吃人不吐骨頭) greedy for gains

食大餐 (大吃一頓) have a square meal

食少啖多覺瞓 (安全至上) play for safety

食水 ① (飲用水) drinking water ② (吸水) absorb water
　食水深 (謀取暴利) charge excessively

食奶 (喝奶) suck the breast

食冰 (吃冷飲) have cold drinks

食西北風 (喝西北風) have nothing to eat; live in poverty

食字邊 (食字旁) the "food" (食) radical

食死貓 (吃啞巴虧) be accused wrongly; be made a scapegoat; be unjustly blamed; take all the blame
　監人食死貓 (冤枉他人) lay the blame upon sb

食完 (吃完) eat up

食夾棍 (接受兩面的好處) take the wind out of sb's sails

食君之祿，擔君之憂 do one's duty as one is paid

食波餅 (被球擊中臉部) hit by a ball in the face

食具 tableware

食咗人隻車 (想要人家老命) take the wind out of sb's sails

食咗人隻豬 (奪去初夜) have seduced a virgin

食枉米 (白吃飯／不做事) a person of no use

食物 food
　食物中毒 food poisoning

食品 food
　應節食品 food for a festival

食砒霜土狗 (絕處逢生) at a disadvantage before gaining an advantage

食倒 ① (能吃) edible ② (吃到) can be eaten
　食唔倒 ① (不能吃) not edible ② (吃不到) can't be eaten
　食得倒 ① (能吃) edible ② (吃到) can be eaten

食唔落 (吃不下) ① cannot eat any more ② not feel like eating

食埋呢碗 (把這碗也吃了) let me finish eating this bowl of sth

食息 (吃利息) live on interest

食晏 (吃午飯 / 吃午餐) have lunch; lunch
　佢去咗食晏 (他去了吃午飯) he has gone out for lunch
　我哋去邊度食晏 (我們去哪裏吃午飯) where do we go for lunch
　食完晏 (吃完午飯) after lunch

食晒 (吃光) eat up
　食唔晒 (吃不了 / 吃不完) cannot eat it up; cannot finish so much food

食神 (口福) gourmet's luck; luck in having nice food; the luck to get sth nice to eat
　有食神 (有口福) lucky to have sth nice to eat

食得 ① (能吃) edible ② (可以吃) can be eaten
　食得禾米多 (多行不義) have made lots of people fall into one's foolery
　食得是福 being able to eat a lot is a blessing
　食得落 (吃得下) edible
　食得瞓得 (能吃能睡) can eat and sleep
　食得嚟 (吃得來) eatable
　食得鹹魚抵得渴 (敢做敢當) since one has the courage of one's convictions, one must be prepared to accept the consequences
　食得鹹魚，就要抵得渴 (敢做敢當) since one has the courage of one's convictions, one must be prepared to accept the consequences
　唔食得 ① (不能吃) not edible ② (不可以吃) can't be eaten

食剩 (吃剩) leftovers

食蛋 ① (吃蛋) eat an egg ② (零分) obtain a zero mark

食粥 (吃稀飯 / 吃粥) eat congee
　食粥定食飯 (結果是好是壞) the results will be decisive

食飯 (吃飯 / 就餐) have a meal
　食飯枱 (飯桌) dining table
　食咗飯 (吃了飯) have eaten
　　食咗飯未呀 (吃飯了沒) have you eaten

食拖鞋飯 (小白臉) sponge upon one's girlfriend; sponge upon one's wife

食軟飯 (小白臉) live off women's earnings; sponge upon one's girlfriend; sponge upon one's wife

食緊飯 (正吃着) one's having a meal

夠鐘食飯 (到時候吃飯) time to have meal

睇餸食飯 (看菜吃飯) live within one's means
　　睇餸食飯，睇蜀喃嘸 (看菜吃飯) live within one's means

食塞米 (白吃飯了) good-for-nothing; idler

食煙 (吸煙 / 抽煙) smoke; smoke a cigarette
　食煙仔 (吸煙 / 抽煙) smoke; smoke a cigarette
　食口煙 (抽口煙) smoke a cigarette
　食大煙 (抽鴉片) smoke opium
　唔准食煙 (不可抽煙) smoking is not allowed

食爺飯，着嬷衣 (靠父母養) be supported by parents

食過夜粥 (學過武術) have learned the techniques of Chinese martial arts

食過翻尋味 (吃過還想吃) would like to try once again

食碗面，反碗底 (背叛) betray a friend; ungrateful

食葱送飯 (合情合理) stand to sense

食腦 (用智力謀生) earn a living by using one's intelligence

食嘢 (吃東西) eat sth
　食乜嘢 (吃甚麼) eat what

食滯 (吃膩 / 積食) indigestion

食福 (口福) gourmet's luck; luck in having nice food; the luck to have sth nice to eat

食飽 (吃飽) have eaten one's fill
　食飽無憂米 (豐衣足食) have nothing to worry about; lead an idle life

食塵 (落後) be left behind

食糊 (和了) draw; win a game in mahjong
　食天糊 (吃天糊) win a game in mahjong before any tile is played
　食炸糊 (希望落空) fail to attain one's hope
　食頭糊，輸甩褲 (吃頭糊的人會以輸家收場) first game winner in playing mahjong will be the biggest loser in the end
　衰家食尾糊 (輸家贏了最後一局麻將) the unlucky mahjong player wins the last game
　詐糊 (空歡喜) call out a winnng hand in error
　滿糊 (和了滿貫) slam

食穀種 (吃老本) live on one's fat

食餂 (吃轉) fail to receive a spinning ball

食貓麵 (挨吡) be scolded; get it in the neck

食餐飽 (吃個夠) eat one's fill

食齋 (吃素 / 吃齋) eat vegetarian food
　食齋不如講正話 (廢話少說) it is better to have straight talking

食雞（食葷）carnivorous
食藥（吃藥／喝藥／服藥）take Chinese medicine
食鹽（精鹽）tablet salt
　食鹽多過你食飯，行橋多過行路（見多識廣）have seen
　　more elephants
食 lunch（吃午飯）have lunch
食 pizza（吃比薩）have a pizza

乞食（討飯）beg for food
大食（食量大）big-eating; gluttonous
小心飲食 be careful with what you eat
小食（零食）snack
手搵口食（勉強糊口）live from hand to mouth
冇衣食 guilty of bad faith
冇啖好食 ①（沒甚麼好吃的）nothing good to eat ②（沒錢
　可賺）no profits to be gained ③（生活窮困）struggle to
　make a living
冇錢買嘢食（沒錢買東西吃）no money to buy food
白食 get a free meal; have a free meal
出街食（在外面吃）dine out; eat out
出嚟搵食 ①（謀生）come into the world to earn a living
　②（找快錢）make easy money
包埋飲食（包括食物飲料）inclusive of food and drinks
伙食 board; fare; food; meal; mess; table
好大食（食量很大）big eater
好好食（很好吃）delicious; good to eat; tasty; very tasty;
　yummy
好食 ①（好吃）delicious; good to eat; tasty; yummy ②（喜
　歡吃）fond of eating
好睇唔好食（好看但不好吃）good-looking but of no
　practical use
好難食（很難吃）hard to eat
好難搵食 ①（很難謀生）hard to earn a living ②（很難賺錢）
　hardly get a decent pay
有衣食（不浪費糧食而享福壽）have ample food and
　clothing for not wasting food
衣食（衣服和食物）clothes and food
忌食（忌口）avoid certain food
辛苦搵嚟自在食（民以食為天）work hard in order to eat at
　leisure
忠忠直直，終須乞食（忠直的人終會乞討過活）an honest
　person will end up begging for livelihood
抵食 ①（值得吃）cheap for such good food; worth eating
　②（值得的）deserving; worthwhile
易食（容易吃）easy to eat
兩個和尚擔水食，三個和尚冇水食（不肯互相幫助／一拍
　兩散）everybody's business is nobody's business
近廚得食 in a favourable position to gain advantage
美食 good food

胃食（嘴饞）gluttonous; greedy eater
背脊向天人所食（任何動物皆可吃）all animals can be eaten
　by human beings
食七咁食（狼吞虎嚥）eat and drink as much as one can;
　gorge oneself; have a good stomach
食生菜咁食（容易吃）it is as easy as rolling a log
食零食（吃零食）nibble between meals; nibble tidbits; take
　snacks between meals
為食（嘴饞）gluttonous; greedy eater
唔好食（不好吃）hard to eat
捕食 catch and feed on; prey on
素食 ① vegetarian diet ② vegetarian
鬼咁好食（非常好吃）quite delicious
偏食 dietary bias
偷食 ①（偷吃）take food surreptitiously ②（外遇）have a
　brief love affair ③（婚外情）have sex outside marriage
啱食（對口味）suit one's taste; to one's taste
殺食（有優勢／有效）advantageous; effective
添食（請求再要多次／乘勢再做某事）ask for one more; do
　sth again
猛咁食（狂吃）eat with all one's might
細食（吃很少）not eat much
貪威識食（引人注意的人）publicity seeker
喺乞兒兜搲飯食（向乞丐討飯吃）rob the poor; squeeze
　wool for water
黃皮樹鷯哥──唔熟唔食（八哥兒啄柿子──挑軟的）the
　person who swindles money out of his familiar friends
搲食（抓東西來吃）grab sth to eat
揀飲擇食（偏吃）be particular about one's food; choose
　one's food; fussy about food; fussy eater
搭食（搭伙）board out regularly in a place
搵食（謀生）earn a living; make a living
煮到嚟就食（順其自然）deal with things in due course;
　submit oneself to the circumstances
煮食 cook
煞食（吸引）appealing; attractive
節食 on diet
進食 eating
飲食 food and drinks
飲飲食食 eat and drink; wine and dine with sb
零食 between-meal nibbles; snack
嘢食（食物）food
監住佢食（看管他吃飯）force him to eat
暴飲暴食 eat and drink immoderately
熱煮不能熱食（放涼再吃）patient to wait
蔬食 ① vegetarian diet ② simple food
擇食（偏吃）choosy with food; fuzzy eater; picky eater
擔屎都唔偷食（非常誠實）very honest
整嘢食（煮食）cook

燒嘢食（燒烤）barbecue; BBQ

獨食（自私）selfish

餐搵餐食（掙一頓吃一頓）live from hand to mouth

識食（很會吃）eat smart; gourmandize; know how to enjoy food

識飲識食（會吃會喝）enjoy life to the fullest; have a good palate for food; know how to enjoy food and drink

難食（難吃）hard to eat

爛食（貪吃／嘴饞）gluttonous

攤凍嚟食（放涼再吃）go about things steadily and surely; go ahead steadily and strike sure blows; play for safety; proceed steadily and step by step; wage steady and sure struggle; slow and steady

【首】sau² head

首日封 first-day envelope

首本戲（拿手戲）one's specialty

首歌好（好歌）the song is a big hit

首飾 jewellery

羣龍無首 a group of people without a leader; a host of dragons without a head; a multitude without a leader; an army without a general; many dragons without a head; no leader in a host of dragons; sheep that have no shepherd

【香】hoeng¹ ① fragrant ② fail ③ die; pass away

香口膠（口香糖）chewing gum

香水 perfume

　一樽香水（一瓶香水）a bottle of perfume

香片 jasmine tea

　一壺香片 a pot of jasmine tea

香肉（狗肉）dog meat

香咗 ①（死了）dead ②（失敗了）failure

香油（燈油錢）oil-lamp money

　簽香油（捐燈油錢）donate money to the oil-lamp

香料 herb

香梘（香皂）perfumed soap; scented soap; soap; toilet soap

香港 Hong Kong

　香港造（香港製造）made in Hong Kong

　香港腳（腳癬）athlete's foot; ringworm of the foot

香腸 sausage

香噴噴 very fragrant

香蕉 banana

　香蕉皮 banana skin

　一梳香蕉（一把香蕉）a bunch of bananas; a hand of bananas

香檳（English）champagne

香爐 incense burner

　香爐灰（香灰）incense ashes

　香爐躉（獨苗兒）male heir; the only son in the family

丁香 lilac

人爭一口氣，佛爭一爐香 make a good show of oneself

小茴香 cumin

古色古香 air of antiquity; antique; quaint; be beautiful in the traditional style; classic beauty; having an antique flavour; in ancient styles; of ancient flavour; smack of sth classical in its design

好香（很香）it smells good; very fragrant

有麝自然香 good wine needs no bush

近住城隍廟求柱好香（近水樓台先得月）hope to curry favour with sb powerful

幽香 delicate fragrance

桂子飄香 fragrance of the laurel blossoms fills the air

鳥語花香 birds sing and flowers are fragrant

裝香（上香）offer incense

隔籬飯香（隔壁的飯比較香）the grass at the other side of one's own fence looks greener

聞見棺材香（快死了）at the death's door; have one's foot in the grave

賣花讚花香（老黃賣瓜，自賣自誇）make a boast of oneself; sing one's own praises

臨尾香（最後出了差錯）fall at the last fence

馨香（稀罕）be very much sought after; in great demand; popular

鬱金香 tulip

10 劃

【乘】sing⁴ travel by

乘人 take advantage of

　乘人之危 capitalize on sb's difficulties; make use of sb's dilemma; take advantage of sb's precarious position

乘客 passenger

乘虛 catch sb napping; take advantage of a weak point

　乘虛而入 break through at a weak point; get a chance to step in; seize the chance to get in; seize the opportunity to step in; sneak in; take advantage of an opening for a place of entrance

乘勝 exploit a victory; follow up a victory

　乘勝追擊 continue one's victorious pursuit; exploit victories by hot pursuit; follow up a victory with hot pursuit; seize the day and pursue a routed army

乘搭 ride in (a vehicle)

乘興 while one is in high spirits

乘興而來，敗興而歸 come in high spirits but return crestfallen; come in high spirits but go back disheartened; come in high spirits, but return in disappointment; come with great enthusiasm and return disillusioned; set out cheerfully and return disappointed; set out in high spirits and return crestfallen

乘機 take the opportunity to do sth

乘機搏命 (趁人不備從中取利) exploit an unusual situation by doing sth not normally permitted

乘機搏懵 (渾水摸魚) exploit an unusual situation by doing sth not normally permitted; fish in troubled waters

【修】sau¹ cultivate

修女 nun; sister

修理 mend; repair

修游 (過安逸的生活) lead an easy life

修整 (修理) repair

修游淡定 (氣定神閒) calm and composed

入廠大修 (重病入醫院) be hospitalized for a serious illness

自修 self study

冒雨搶修 rush to repair in spite of the rain

前世唔修 (上輩子作了孽) pitiful; suffer retribution for all the ill deeds done in the previous existence

散修修 in pieces; loose

裝修 renovation

維修 maintenance

【俾】bei² ① (給) give; offer ② (讓) allow

俾人 (給人) allow sb; give sb

俾人笑到面黃 (給人取笑感到尷尬) feel embarrassed when being teased by others

俾人砌一身 (給人家摸了一通) being slugged by sb

俾人剝光豬 (給人剝個精光) be stripped to the skin; strip bare; strip sb to the skin

俾低錢 (留下錢) leave some money

俾我睇 (給我看) show me

俾面 (給面子／賞臉) give face

冇面俾 (不給面子) show disrespect

唔俾面 (不給面子) not to give face

俾個心你食都當狗肺 (好心當成驢肝肺／不知感恩) not to know chalk from cheese

俾個頭你 (給你我的頭) I'll give you nothing

俾番你 (還給你) give sth back to you

俾蕉皮人踩 (設局害人) make sb meet with losses; make sb slip up

俾西瓜皮人踩 (設局害人) make sb meet with losses; make sb slip up

俾錢 (給錢) pay

俾 card (信用卡結帳) pay with a credit card

冇面俾 (不給面子) show disrespect

交俾 (交給) hand to sb

【悷】caang⁴ wild

悷雞 (潑辣) shrewish; volubly demanding

悷雞妹 (潑辣的姑娘) a girl of passionate disposition and violent temper

悷雞婆 (潑辣的女人) volubly demanding woman

【倉】cong¹ warehouse

倉底貨 (過時貨) poor-selling goods; slow-selling goods; unsalable goods

倉促 all of a sudden; hastily; hasty; hurriedly

倉庫 depository; depot; repository; stockroom; store; storehouse; warehouse

倉魚 (鯧魚) pomfret

入倉 entry into warehouse

長倉 long position

貨倉 depository; depot; repository; stockroom; store; storehouse; warehouse

短倉 short position

監倉 prison cell

【個】go³ ① individual ② dollar ③ measure word for persons, round objects, and abstract things

個人 individual

個人利益 personal benefit

個三 (一塊三) one dollar and thirty cents

個女 (…的女兒) one's daughter

我個女 (我的女兒) my daughter

個心十五十六 (心裏七上八下) feel very perturbed

個仔 (…的兒子) one's son

我個仔 (我的兒子) my son

個半 (一塊五) one dollar and fifty cents; one dollar fifty

個肚打鼓 very hungry

個個 ① (每個) every ② (每個人) everybody

個個人 (每個人) everybody

個個月 (每個月) every month

個案 (案件／案例／實例) case

個唱 solo concert

個蜆個肉（剛巧足夠）just one for just one

個零（一個多）more than

    個零月（一個來月）more than a month

    個零鐘（一個多小時）more than an hour

一個 ① a; an; one ② a piece of; a word of

一個二個（你們全部人）all of you

三個 three

上一個 one ahead of you

下一個 next in line

下個 next

成個（整個）all; entire; total; whole

屁都唔痾個（沒有懷孕的跡象）show no sign of having children

呢個（這個）this

兩個 two

兩個兩個（兩個一雙）by twos; in pairs

前一個 the previous one

唔知邊個打邊個（不知道哪個是哪個）can't make out which ones match which ones

得個（只剩下）end up with

嗰個（那個）that

黃皮樹鷯哥──熟嗰個食嗰個（八哥兒啄柿子──挑軟的）the person who swindles money out of his familiar friends

邊個 ①（哪個）which ②（哪人）who

【倌】gwun¹ actor

大老倌 famous actor

空心老倌（虛有其表的人）a person without real ability and learning; gorgeous in appearance but inwardly insubstantial

過氣老倌 actor, actress who past their prime

【倍】pui⁵ double

倍加（加倍）double; extraordinarily; extremely; increase by one fold

倍減 demultiply

倍增 redouble

倍數 multiple

身家百倍 a meteoric rise in social status; come up in the world; find oneself substantially elevated in fame and status; have a sudden rise in social status; one's position and reputation shoot up a hundred fold; receive a tremendous boost in one's prestige; rise in the world; rise to high note

雙倍 double

【倒】dou² invert

倒米（拆台／搞亂）cause others to suffer losses; mess up; stand in one's own light

    倒米壽星（拆台的貨）person who causes others to suffer losses; person who stands in his own light

倒灶（幫倒忙）cause trouble while trying to help; do a disservice to; more of a hindrance than a help

倒茶（斟茶）pour tea

倒掛臘鴨──嘴油（狗掀門簾──全憑一張嘴）just by talking

倒閉 closure; shut down

倒塌 collapse

倒塔咁早（一大早）very early in the morning

倒模（鑄模子）mould

倒豎葱（倒立）handstand; stand upside down

倒瀉（倒灑）spill water

    倒瀉水（倒灑水）spill water

    倒瀉籮蟹（狼狽不堪）in a muddle; messy; troublesome

倒翻轉（反過來／倒過來）conversely; turn the other way round

打倒（打着）knock down

打唔倒（打不到）can't knock down

打得倒（打得着）can knock down

扐倒（拿到）have got

扐唔倒（拿不了／拿不到）can't get it

扐得倒（拿得了／拿得到）can get it

地上執到寶，問天問地攞唔倒（地上撿到寶，問天問地拿不到）things that one picks up from the ground cannot be taken away by any means

行倒 ①（適合步行的）walkable ②（可以走去的）can be reached by walking

行唔倒（不能走）cannot be reached by walking

行得倒（能走）can be reached by walking

估倒（猜到）one's guess is right

估唔到（猜不到）cannot guess; miss one's guess; unable to make out the right answer; unable to reach the right answer

估得倒（猜得到）one's guess is right

兵敗如山倒 a beaten army is like a collapsing mountain; a rout is like a landslide; an army in flight is like a landslide

扻倒（撞擊到）knock down

夾倒 be nipped

昏倒 faint; fall down in a faint; fall unconscious

食倒 ①（適宜食用的）edible ②（吃得到）can be eaten

食唔倒 ①（不適宜食用的）not edible ②（吃不到）can't be eaten

食得倒 ①（適宜食用的）edible ②（吃得到）can be eaten

閂倒（關得到）can be locked up

閂唔倒（關不到）can't be locked up
閂得倒（關得到）can be locked up
捉倒（捉到）grab
神魂顛倒 be out of one's head
追唔倒（追不到）can't catch up with
追得倒（追得到）can catch up with
執倒（幸運）by good luck; have fortune on one's side; have good luck; in luck; luck is on one's side; one's luck is in; strike luck; tough luck
揩倒（觸碰到）be rubbed
睇倒（看到）visible
睇得倒①（可以看見的）visible ②（看得到）can be seen
跌倒 fall down
搵倒（找到）found
搵唔倒（找不到）cannot find it
搵得倒（找得到）can find it
搦倒（拿到）have got
搦唔倒（拿不到）can't get it
搦得倒（拿得到）can get it
飲倒①（很能喝／好酒量）have a large capacity for wine ②（可飲用的）drinkable
飲唔倒①（酒量差）have a small capacity for wine ②（不可飲用的）not drinkable
飲得倒①（很能喝／好酒量）have a large capacity for wine ②（可飲用的）drinkable
解倒（能解釋）can be explained
解唔倒（不能解釋）can't be explained
解得倒（能解釋）can be explained
寫倒（能寫）can be written out
寫唔倒（不能寫）cannot be written out
寫得倒（能寫）writable
瞓倒（能睡）can sleep
瞓唔倒（不能睡）cannot sleep
瞓得倒（能睡）can sleep
講倒①（能說）able to speak; able to utter ②（投契）able to get along; on good terms
講唔倒①（不能說）not speakable ②（不投契）cannot get along with sb; on bad terms ③（說不了）unable to speak; unable to utter
講得倒①（能說）able to speak; able to utter ②（投契）able to get along; on good terms
點都估唔倒（怎樣也想不到）cannot predict; unexpectedly
躓倒（絆倒）fall; stumble over
攞倒（拿到）have got
攞唔倒（拿不到）can't get it
攞得倒（拿得到）can get it
聽倒①（聽到）can be heard ②（能聽到並理解到）can hear and understand
聽唔倒①（聽不到）cannot be heard ②（無法聽到和理解）cannot hear and understand
聽得倒①（聽得到）hearable ②（能聽到）can hear

【倒】dou³ reverse
倒吊冇滴墨水（文言）be illiterate
倒吊荷包（自願蝕本）invite losses for oneself
倒掛臘鴨——滿嘴油（口甜舌滑）have a glib tongue
倒褪（倒退）backward movement; go backwards
　打倒褪（倒退）backward movement; go backwards
倒轉（倒過來）turn upside-down

【倔】gwat⁶ ① tough ②（不通）be blocked up
倔住（瞪着）staring fixedly
倔毒（絕情）merciless
倔情（無情／絕情）unamiable
倔擂槌（鈍的）blunt
倔頭（不通）be blocked up
　倔頭巷（死胡同）dead-end alley
　倔頭倔腦 blunt in manner and gruff in speech
　倔頭路（死路）dead-end street

【候】hau⁶ ① borrow ② lend
候機室 waiting lounge
候選人 candidate
候鑊（廚師）chef; cook

小時候 in one's childhood
侍候 attend upon; look after; serve; wait upon
依時依候 on schedule; on time; punctual
係時候（是時候）it's about time
恭候 wait respectfully
時候 time
症候① disease ② symptom
揼時候（拖時間）kill time; pass the time
等候 wait

【倚】ji² count on; depend on; rely on
倚老賣老 act like a Dutch uncle; flaunt one's seniority
倚靠 depend on; rely on

唔使指倚（別指望）have no fond dreams about it

【借】ze³ ① borrow ② lend
借刀殺人 murder with a borrowed knife
借咗聾陳隻耳（假裝聽不到）turn a deaf ear to sb
借花敬佛（借花獻佛）make use of the gift from another to show respect to sb
借歪（讓開）excuse me

借借（借光／勞駕／讓一讓）excuse me
借一借（借光／請讓路／讓一讓）excuse me
借啲意（找個藉口）cook up a lame excuse; make a feeble excuse
借咗啲（借借光）excuse me
借過（借光／勞駕／讓讓）excuse me
借艇割禾（借水行舟）make use of sb to profit oneself
借頭借路（找由頭兒）cook up a lame excuse; use any pretext
借題發揮 make use of the subject under discussion to put across one's ideas

唔該借一借（麻煩讓一下）excuse me; please give way; please let me through
唔該借借（麻煩讓一下）excuse me; please give way; please let me through

【值】zik⁶ worth
值班 on duty; on the shift; on watch
值得 worth
值得一看 worth watching
值勤 on duty
值錢 costly; valuable
好值錢（很值錢）worth a lot of money

升值 appreciate; revaluation
自我增值 upgrade oneself
估值 valuation
物業升值 appreciation in value for flat
淨值 net worth
票面值 face value
貨幣升值 currency revaluation; upward revaluation of currency
貶值 depreciate; devalue; devaluate
當值 on duty; on the shift; on watch
價值 value
增值 ① appreciate; appreciate in price; increase in value; value-added ② add value to an octopus card
幣值 purchasing power of a currency

【倦】gyun⁶ tired
倦容 tired look
倦勤 be tired of work
倦意 sleepiness; tiredness; weariness

努力不倦 strive without ceasing
厭倦 boredom; lassitude; weary of

【倫】leon⁴ ① human relationships ② hurry
倫比（匹敵）equal; rival
無與倫比 beyond compare; beyond comparison; defy all comparison; head and shoulders above the rest; incomparable; matchless; out of comparison; past compare; peerless; stand alone; there is no comparison with; there is none to compare to; unbeatable; unequalled; unique; unparalleled; unrivalled; untouched; without compare; without comparison; without equal; without parallel; without peer; without rival
倫常 human relations
倫理 ethics; moral principles; morals

頻倫（趕急）hurry-scurry; in a hurry; rush
頻頻倫倫（趕趕急急）in great hurry

【兼】gim¹ concurrently
兼任 ① hold a concurrent post ② part-time
兼夾（又／而且／加上／並且／和）also; and; and that; as well as; besides; moreover; not only...but also...; what is more
兼職 concurrent job; moonlight; moonlighting; part-time job; side job
兼顧 give consideration to two or more things

仲兼（還有）what's more

【冧】lam¹ pile up

耍冧（道歉）say sorry

【冧】lam¹ ①（取悅）coax; soothing ② flower bud
冧人（取悅別人）please others
冧巴（號碼／數字）number
冧巴溫（第一）(English) Number one
冧宮頭（寶蓋兒）the "roof top" (宀) radical
冧酒（朗姆酒）(English) rum
冧歌（情歌）romantic songs
冧篷頭（寶蓋兒）the "roof top" (宀) radical

布冧（李子／洋李子／美國李子）(English) plum
花冧（花蕾）bud
嗱嗱冧（趕快）quickly
劏冧（推倒）push over

【冧】lam³ (坍塌) collapse; topple

冧咗 (倒塌) collapse

冧莊 (做莊一方因吃糊而繼續做莊) be the banker again after winning a game in mahjong

冧樓 (房子坍塌) the house has collapsed

冧檔 (倒台) collapse

隊冧 (殺死) kill sb

【准】zeon² allow

准予 approve; authorise; grant; permit

准許 allow; approve; permit

批准 accede; admit of; allow; approve; authorise; clearance; concede; endorse; give a license to; give permission; give sanction to; grant one's request; grant sb permission to; let; license; permit; ratify; sanction

【凌】ling⁴ ① insult ② rise high

凌空 be high in the sky; tower aloft

凌晨 in the small hours of the day

凌雲 aim high; reach the clouds; ride the high clouds; soar to the skies

凌亂 in a mess; in disarray; in total disorder; messy

凌駕 override; place oneself above; rise above others

欺凌 browbeat; bully; bully and humiliate; humiliate; insult; mistreat; ride roughshod over

【凍】dung³ (冷) cold

凍水 (冷水 / 涼水) cold water

　　凍水壺 (涼水壺) cold water bottle

　　凍過水 (沒有希望了) there is no hope

凍冷冷 (冷冰冰) ice old; icy; frosty

凍房 (冷藏庫) cold storage

凍格 (冰格) ice tray

凍飲 (冷飲) cold drinks

凍嚫 (受涼) have a cold

天寒地凍 (冰天雪地) freezing; severe cold and frozen land; the weather is so cold that the ground is frozen; very cold

冰凍 (冰冷) freeze; frost; frozen

好凍 (很冷) very cold

冷氣太凍 (空調太冷) the air-con is too cold

抵得凍 (耐冷) endure cold

陰陰凍 (陰冷陰冷) gloomy and cold

雪凍 (冷凍) chilled

雞凍 (雞果凍) chicken jelly

攤凍 (放涼) cool down

【剔】tik¹ (打勾) tick

剔土邊 (剔土旁 / 提土兒) the "earth" (土) radical

剔手邊 (剔手旁 / 提手旁) the "hand" (手) radical

剔除 eliminate; get rid of; reject;

剔透 ① well-expressed ② keen and perceptive

打剔 (打鈎) tick

光頭剔 (光頭漢) bald man

挑剔 choosy; fastidious; fussy; picky

【剛】gong¹ just

剛才 a moment ago; a while ago; just now

剛柔 hardness and softness

剛剛 ① as soon as; hardly...when; just; no sooner...when ② barely; merely; narrowly

剛強 firm; staunch; unyielding

血氣方剛 be easily excited; full of animal spirits; full of sap; full of vigour and vitality; full of vim and vigour; hot-tempered; in one's raw youth; in one's salad days; in the green

啱啱碰着剛剛 (剛好) coincident

【剝】mok¹ extract

剝牙 (拔牙) extract a tooth; pull out a tooth

剝皮牛 (馬面魚) black scraper

剝皮田雞——死都唔閉眼 (冬天的大蔥——葉黃根枯心不死) die without closing one's eyes

剝光豬 ① (把衣服脫光) strip sb of their clothes ② (推光頭) a thorough loss in chess play; be entirely defeated in chess play

【削】cok³ jerk

削住度氣 (生氣卻被逼接受) be compelled to hold back one's rage; be forced to bear with sth; be forced to submit to humiliation; be forced to swallow the leek

【原】jyun⁴ original

原子 atomic

　　原子粒 (晶體管) transistor

　　原子筆 (圓珠筆) ball pen

　　原子彈 atomic bomb

　　原子襪 (尼龍襪) nylon socks

原本 (本來) at first; from the beginning; in itself; in the first place; it goes without saying; original; originally; properly speaking; should have; used to be

原告 plaintiff

原來 actually; in fact; originally

原底 (原來) originally

原則 principle
原封不動 be kept intact
原諒 forgive
原嚟（原來）originally

【唔】m⁴（不）not

唔三唔四（不三不四）indecent; immoral in character; improper; neither fish, flesh nor fowl

唔切（太急於／忙不及）cannot make it
　走唔切（來不及走）have not enough time to go
　來唔切（來不及）can't make it; won't make it
　食唔切（來不及吃）not have enough time to eat up
　做唔切（做不過來）not have enough time to complete the tasks
　趕唔切（來不及／趕不上）have not enough time to do sth; out of time; too late to catch
　嚟唔切（來不及）there's not enough time to do sth

唔化（死腦筋／執迷不誤／想不開）too stubborn

唔少得（不能少／少不了）cannot dispense with; cannot do without; must be at least; not less than

唔中用（不中用）good-for-nothing; useless

唔及得（比不上／及不上）inferior to; no peer for; not come near; not comparable to; not hold a candle to; not so...as...

唔止（不光是）not only
　唔單止（不光／不但／不僅）not only

唔打唔相識（不打不相識）no discord, no concord; no fight, no acquaintance

唔再（不再）not again; no longer

唔合何尺（不一致／不合拍／不協調）mismatch

唔同（不同）different; various
　唔同床唔知被爛（如人飲水冷暖自知）no one knows what the other side of the world looks like
　咁又唔同（那又不一樣）it is different

唔在行（外行）out of one's beat; out of one's line

唔在講（不但／不僅）not only

唔多（不太）don't...very much
　唔多覺（不太覺得）don't feel very strongly

唔好（不用／不好／不要／別）do not; not good
　唔好打（不好對付）not easy to beat
　唔好咁串（別那麼狂妄）don't get cocky
　唔好咁茅（別耍滑）don't play tricks
　唔好玩我啦（別作弄我了）don't make fun of me
　唔好急（不要急／別急）take one's time; there's no hurry
　唔好洗（不好洗）difficult to wash
　唔好郁（別動）don't move
　唔好食（不好吃／難吃）hard to eat
　唔好笑我（別笑我）don't laugh at me
　唔好做（不好做／難做）hard to make; hard to manage
　唔好乾（不好乾）hard to dry in the sun

唔好喊（不要哭／別哭）don't cry; stop crying
唔好惡（不要兇／別那麼兇）don't be so horrid
唔好睇（不好看／難看）ugly; unattractive; unsightly
唔好搞（不好搞）hard to handle
唔好逼（不要擠／別擠）don't push
唔好嗌（不要叫／別叫）don't shout
唔好煩（不要煩／別煩）don't be vexed
唔好話（不用說／且不說）let alone; not to mention; not to speak of; to say nothing of
唔好嘈（不要吵／別吵／別鬧）shut up
　請大家唔好嘈（請大家安靜）please be quiet; please keep your voices down
唔好嘞（不了）no thank you
唔好賣（不好賣）hard to sell
唔好嬲（不要生氣／別生氣）don't get angry
唔好學（不好學）hard to learn
唔好驚（不要怕／別怕）don't be afraid

唔自在①（不好受）not feel comfortable②（不在乎）not care a bit
　好唔自在（很不好受）feel very uncomfortable

唔自量（不知自量）overrate oneself

唔似（不一樣／不像）unlike
　唔似得（不像）unlike
　唔似樣（不像樣）go too far; it is most improper

唔吼（不要／看不中）not take a fancy to

唔夾（合不來）can't get along with

唔妥（不對頭）not on the right track; not well
　唔多妥（不大對頭／欠妥）not quite right

唔志在（不在乎）not to care a fig

唔見①（沒看到）not see②（丟失）lose
　唔見咗①（丟失）lost②（一時找不到）mislaid
　唔見得光（見不得光）cannot be exposed to the light of day; keep sth secret
　唔見棺材唔流眼淚（大難臨頭，才洞悉問題早在眼前／欠缺危機感）refuse to be convinced until facing the grim reality; oblivious to danger
　唔見過鬼都唔怕黑（好了傷疤忘了痛）once on shore, one prays no more

唔使（不用／不需要／用不着／別）no need to; not necessary to
　唔使旨意（不用指望／別指望）don't count on me
　唔使你加把口（不用你插嘴）there's no need for you to chip in
　唔使找（不用找續）keep the change
　唔使拘（不用計較／別計較）not to be concerned with
　唔使恨（別提了／別指望）cherish no hope for sb; no need to hope; useless
　唔使指倚（不用指望／別指望）have no fond dreams about it

唔使指擬（不用指望／別指望）have no fond dreams about it

唔使計（不用算／別計較）don't mention it; forget it

唔使袋（不要袋子）do not want any bags

唔使喇（不用了）no, thanks

唔使得（不行／沒有用）not work

唔使問亞貴（不用多問）as sure as eggs are eggs; there's no need to inquire

唔使慌 ①（不用害怕／不用擔憂／別慌張）don't be afraid; no need to be afraid ②（別指望）have no fond dreams about it

唔使憂（不用發愁／別擔心）not to worry

唔使錢（不用錢）free of charge; gratis

唔使講（不用說）it goes without saying; needless to say

唔使劃公仔劃出腸（不用說得太白）it goes without saying

唔使擒擒青（不用着急）easy does it

唔使嚟嘞（甭用來了）no need to come

唔使驚（不用怕／不用慌／別慌）don't panic

唔爭在（不差）can do without

唔制（不肯／不幹／不願意）not willing to do sth

唔制得過（不合算／不幹才好）it does not pay to do sth; not worthwhile

唔肯制（不肯／不幹／不願意）not willing to do sth

幾大都唔制（說甚麼也不幹）won't do it whatever you say

唔定（不定／未定）maybe; perhaps

唔一定（不一定）it is indefinite

唔怕（不怕）have no fear

唔怕一萬，至怕萬一（不怕一萬，只怕萬一）contingency is what we are afraid of

唔怕米貴，至怕運滯（不怕白米貴，只怕運氣壞）not afraid of the price of rice going up, but afraid of being unlucky

唔怕官至怕管（不怕官，只怕管）a mouse fears nobody but the cat that would catch it; one's immediate superior is more fearful than the person in charge

唔怕醜（不害羞）shameless; unabashed

唔怪得（怪不得／難怪）little wonder that; no wonder

唔怪之（怪不得／難怪）little wonder that; no wonder

唔怪之得（怪不得／難怪）little wonder that; no wonder

唔怪得之（怪不得／難怪）little wonder that; no wonder

唔抵（不合算／不值得）not deserved; not worthwhile

唔抵得 ①（禁不住）cannot help ②（不服氣／受不了）cannot bear ③（不甘心／眼紅）jealous

唔抵得瘀（看不下去）cannot bear the waste

唔抵得頸（憋不住了）cannot control one's temper

唔抵諗（怕吃虧）calculating

抵唔抵（值不值得）is it worth it

唔拘（不要緊／沒關係／無所謂／隨便）all the same; indifferent; never mind; not care; not matter

唔爭氣（不爭氣）fail to live up to one's expectation

唔知（不知）not know

唔知死（不怕死）unaware of the death ahead

唔知個醜字點寫（不知羞恥）dead to shame; have no sense of shame; thick-skinned

唔知幾（不知多）extremely

唔知醜（不要臉／不害羞／沒羞臊）know no shame; shameless

假裝唔知（假裝不知）pretend not to be aware of; pretend that one does not know

詐帝唔知（假裝不知）pretend not to be aware of; pretend that one does not know

唔係 ①（不是）not ②（不然／要不然）but for; if not; or; or else; otherwise

唔係人咁品（不通人性）lose one's reason

唔係你財唔入你袋（不是你的財，不入你口袋）money goes to the right person

唔係我嗰皮（比不上我）not my match

唔係咁講（不能這樣說）that's not true

唔係嘞（怎麼可能）is that possible

唔係路（不是辦法／不對路／不對勁／不對頭）it is far from good; sth does not look right

唔係嘢少（不那麼簡單）it's not that simple

唔係嘅話（不然的話）or; otherwise

唔係講玩（不是說笑）it is no joke

唔係猛龍唔過江，唔係毒蛇唔打霧（不是猛龍不過江，不是毒蛇不打霧）he who dares to come is surely not a coward

絕對唔係（絕對不是）absolutely not

唔信（不信）not believe

唔信命都信吓塊鏡（不信命，也得信信鏡子）it is wise to know oneself

唔信鏡（不相信真實反映）refuse to believe what is real

唔咬牙（談不來／談不攏）not get along well

唔咬弦（談不來／談不攏）out of tune with sb

唔恨（不渴望／不想要）not to care about

唔相干（沒關係／無關）have nothing to do with; no concern; no relationship; unconcerned

唔紅唔黑（半紅不黑）not enjoy popularity in the show business

唔要（不要）not want

唔要冰（不要冰）no ice

唔要命（不要命）know no danger

唔要就罷（不要就算了）take it or leave it

唔要斧頭唔得柄甩（進退兩難）hold a wolf by the ears

唔計帶（不介意）do not mind

唔食得豬（不是完璧之身）non-virginal

唔埋得個鼻 (臭不可聞) make a long nose

唔衰得 (輸不起) hate to lose; sore to lose

唔衰攞嚟衰 (自找麻煩／自討苦吃) ask for trouble; borrow trouble; bring on trouble; encourage trouble; look for trouble; make a rod for oneself; prepare a rod for one's back; seek trouble for oneself

唔做 (不做) quit

　　唔做中唔做保，唔做媒人三代好 (不做中間人，不做擔保人，不做媒人三代好) one who does not engage himself in the business of a middleman or a guarantor will have worthy descendants for three generations

唔停口 (説過不停) talkative

唔停咁 (不停地) continuously

唔制 (不幹) not do it; won't do it

　　唔制得過 (划不來) it won't pay

唔啦更 (毫無關係) irrelevant

唔啱 (不正確／不對／不適合／合不來) can't get along with

　　唔啱牙 (談不來／談不攏) not get along well

　　唔啱偈 (談不來／談不攏) not get along well

　　唔啱傾 (談不來／談不攏) not get along well

　　唔啱蕎 (談不來／談不攏) do not get along well with each other

　　唔啱 key (談不來／談不攏) not get along well

　　咁樣做唔啱 (這樣做不對) this is not the right thing to do

唔夠 (不夠) insufficient; not enough; shortage

　　唔夠力 (力氣不夠) not have the enough strength

　　唔夠皮 (不夠花) not enough to spend

　　唔夠佢嚟 (鬥不過他) no match for him

　　唔夠好 (欠佳) not good enough

　　唔夠氣 (力氣不足) short of breath

　　唔夠秤 (年齡不夠) not old enough

　　唔夠喉 ① (不過癮) be not satisfied ② (還想吃) one's hunger is not fulfilled

　　唔夠腳 (人數不足) not enough players; one player short

　　唔夠運 (運氣不好) in bad luck; luckless

　　唔夠瞓 (沒睡夠／缺覺) inadequate sleep

唔得 (不可以) be forbidden; cannot

　　唔得了 (不得了) exceedingly; extremely; terrible

　　絕對唔得 (絕對不可以) absolutely not

唔掂 (不好過) it's not alright

　　好唔掂 (很不好過) have a hard time

　　周身唔掂 (很不好過) have a hard time

　　唔得掂 ① (不行了) on the point of collapse ② (闖大禍) get into a big trouble; in a big trouble

唔淨只 (不但／不僅) not only

唔理 (不管) ignore; not pay attention to

　　唔理三七廿一 (不管怎樣) regardless of the consequences

唔理得咁多 (管他呢) cast all caution to the wind

唔着 (不對) not right

唔通 (難道) could it be that

唔喺度 (過世) dead

唔敢 (不敢) not dare to

　　唔敢當 (不敢當) I really don't deserve this; not at all; you're flattering me

唔曾 (不曾／沒有) never; not yet

唔湯唔水 (非驢非馬／不論不類) neither fish nor fowl

唔睇白鴿，都睇吓堆屎 (觀微知著) a straw shows which way the wind blows

唔睇僧面，都睇吓佛面 (不看僧面，也看看佛面) not for everybody's sake but for sb's sake

唔等使 (不中用／不合用／沒用) of no use; useless

唔嗲唔吊 (大大咧咧的) careless; casual

唔慌 (不用擔心) no need to worry

唔經大腦 (不經思考) not to rack one's brains

唔經唔覺 (不知不覺間) without realising it

唔睬佢 (不理睬他／不答理他) pay no heed to sb

唔話得 (沒得説／沒説的／很不錯／夠意思) have nothing to complain of; no complaints against sb who has done a good job

　　唔話得定 (説不定) can't say for certain

唔該 ① excuse me ② (勞駕／謝謝) thank you

　　唔該晒 (非常感謝) many thanks; thank you very much; thanks a lot; very grateful

　　唔該借一借 (麻煩讓一下) excuse me; please give way; please let me through

　　唔該借歪啲 (麻煩讓一下) excuse me

　　唔該借借 (麻煩讓一下) excuse me; please give way; please let me through

　　唔該靜啲 (請安靜) please keep quiet

　　唔該讓開 (麻煩讓一下) please move over

　　唔駛唔該 (不謝／不用謝) don't mention it

　　認真唔該 (非常感謝) many thanks; thank you so much; thank you very much; thanks a lot; very grateful

唔對路 (不對頭) problematic

　　有啲唔對路 (有點不對頭) sth strange; there's sth weird about it

唔對辦 (不對頭) problematic

唔算 (不算) not regarded as

　　唔算數 (食言) go back on one's words

唔聚財 (不舒服) unwell

唔憂 (不愁／不擔心) not to worry

　　唔憂冇人要 (不愁沒人要) not to worry about not having anyone wanting it

唔撈 (不幹) quit one's job

　　最多唔撈 (大不了不幹) it's no big deal to quit one's job

唔論 (不論) it doesn't matter; no matter

唔論幾多（不論多少）no matter how much/many

唔黐家（不喜歡待在家）not to stick to home

唔錯（不錯）not bad; pretty good
　唔錯㗎（不錯哦）not bad

唔嬲就假（不生氣才怪）it would be strange if one does not get angry

唔聲唔盛（不聲不響）make no reply; mute; not making a sound; not utter a word; without saying a word

唔聲唔聲（不吭聲）not speak up

唔識 ①（不認識）don't know sb ②（不會／不懂得／不曉得）be unable to; do not know
　唔識駕步（不內行）not know what to do

唔關事（沒牽扯／沒關係／無關）have nothing to do with; no concern; no relationship; unconcerned
　唔關你事（與你無關）mind your own business
　唔關我事（與我無關）it's got nothing to do with me; it's not my business; that's nothing to do with me

唔覺意（不小心／不留神／沒注意／沒留意）accidentally; take no care; unintentionally

唔攢 ①（不合算）not paying ②（沒錢賺）not earning money

唔聽佢支笛（不聽他那一套）don't listen to what they say

唔 happy（不開心）not happy; unhappy

唔 like（不喜歡）do not like

一定唔（一定不）must not

【員】jyun⁴ staff member
員工 staff

一個售貨員 a salesperson
女售貨員 salesgirl; saleswoman
女演員 actress
工作人員 working staff
公務員 civil servant; government servant
文員 clerk
司令員 commander
打字員 typist
收銀員 cashier
男售貨員 salesman
男演員 actor
委員 committee member
官員 officer; official
店員 shop assistant
服務員 attendant
保安員 ①security guard ②watchman
消防員 fireman
售貨員 salesclerk; salesperson; shop assistant; shop clerk

接待員 receptionist
球員 player
救生員 life guard
救護人員 ambulance corps; relief corps
船員 crew
幅員 size of the country
會員 member of a society
電腦程式員 programmer
運動員 athlete
演員 actor
傳譯員 interpreter
裁員 staff cut
舞蹈員 dancer
僱員 employee
管理員 ①security guard ②management officer
輔導員 counsellor
賣貨員（售貨員）saleman; salesperson; shop assistant; shop clerk
簿記員 accounting clerk; bookkeeper; clerk
職員 clerk; employee; staff
翻譯員 translator
警員 policeman

【哥】go¹ elder brother
哥哥 elder brother
　哥哥仔（年輕男子）young man
哥爾夫（高爾夫）(English) golf
　哥爾夫球（高爾夫球）(English) golf
　　打哥爾夫球（打高爾夫球）play golf

一哥 ①（頭兒）chief; head; number-one person ②（警務處處長）Police Commissioner
大阿哥（老大）don; leader of a triad society
士哥（分數）score
出鷯哥（做手腳，做弊）plot a conspiracy
白鼻哥 ①（小丑）clown; comedian ②（考試不及格的人）person who fails in an examination ③（奸猾的人）cunning person; wicked person
初哥 ①（新手）beginner; new hand ②（初次）for the first time
表哥 cousin; elder male cousin; first cousin
阿哥 elder brother
堂阿哥 elder male cousin; first cousin
契哥（乾哥哥）nominal elder brother
細路哥（小孩）child
新郎哥（新郎）bridesgroom
鼻哥（鼻子）beezer; bugle; nose
篤鼻哥（仗着地位高而得到特許）gain admission on account of one's status

膝頭哥（膝蓋）knee
學生哥（學生）pupil; student
鷯哥（八哥兒）myna

【哦】o² oh
哦呀 oh

而倚哦哦（猶豫不決）shilly-shally
依依哦哦（吞吞吐吐）hem and haw; hesitate in speech; hum and haw; mince words; mutter and mumble; runes and prism; say hesitantly; speak in a halting way; speak of things with scrule speak with reservation; stumble over one's words; tick over

【哨】saau³ protrude
哨牙（大板牙／門牙外露／齙牙）protruding tooth
哨牙蘇（長有齙牙的人）person with protruding teeth

吹口哨 whistle

【哩】lei⁵ ① mile ② sloppy
哩啡（不整齊）slipshod; sloppy; slovenly; untidy

啫哩（果凍）(English) jelly

【哭】huk¹（喊）cry
哭笑 cry and laugh
哭聲 cries

哇哇大哭 cry very loudly

【哮】haau¹ ① pant ② howl
哮喘 asthma

【哲】zit³ philosophy
哲人 philosopher; sage
哲理 philosophical principle; philosophical theory
哲學 philosophy

【哽】gang²（噎）choke
哽心（戳心）break one's heart
哽耳（刺耳）grate on the ear; irritate to the ear
哽腳（硌腳）hurt one's foot
哽嚫（噎到）choked

【唆】so¹ incite; instigate
唆使 abet; incite; instigate
唆擺（教唆）incite; instigate

【唐】tong⁴ Chinese
唐人 Chinese
　唐人街 Chinatown
唐突 abrupt
唐裝 ①（中式衣服）Chinese-style clothes ②（中裝）Chinese suite
唐樓（中式房屋）tenement building
唐餐（中菜）Chinese cuisine

荒唐 absurd; fantastic; preposterous

【唧】zit¹ ①（撓癢）tickle ②（擠）squeeze
唧都唔笑（木訥寡言）over-serious

【哈】lang⁶ onomatopoetic
哈鐘（銅鈴）brass bell

冚唪哈（全部）altogether; one and all

【唇】seon⁴ lip
唇舌 ① lips and tongue ② argument; persuasion; plausible speech; talking round; words
　白費唇舌 speak to the wind; waste one's breath; waste one's words; whistle down the wind
　唇槍舌劍 a battle of repartee; a battle of wits; a war of words; cross verbal swords; engage in a battle of words; exchange heated words; have a tit-for-tat argument with sharp words
唇膏（口紅）lippy; lipstick
　一枝唇膏（一支口紅）a lipstick
唇齒 lips and teeth
　唇齒相依 as close as lips and teeth; as close to each other as lips to teeth; as close to each other as the lips are to the teeth; as closely related as the lips and the teeth; as interdependent as lips and teeth; closely related and mutually dependent; closely related to each other like lips and teeth; interdependent; mutually depend on each other as lips and teeth
　唇亡齒寒 be immediately threatened; if one falls, the other is in danger; if the lips are gone, the teeth are exposed; the teeth are cold when the lips are cold; when the lips are lost, the teeth will be exposed to the cold; share a common lot
　唇紅齒白 have rosy lips and pretty white teeth

口唇 lip
朱唇 red lips

【哟】tsaau¹（搜）search
哟身（搜身）body search; conduct a body search; search a person

【唞】tau² ①（呼吸）breathe ②（休息／歇）rest; take a rest
唞氣（呼吸）breathe
　　唞大氣（深呼吸）take a deep breath
　　唞唔倒氣（吸不過氣來）be unable to breathe
唞涼（乘涼）enjoy the cool weather; relax in a cool place
唞暑（乘涼）enjoy the cool weather; relax in a cool place

早唞 ①（閉嘴）shut up ②（晚安）good night
　　③（走開）go away

【哴】long² rinse
哴口（漱口）gargle; rinse the mouth
　　哴口盅（漱口盅）rinse mug
哴杯（沖杯子）wash a cup

【嗿】cam³ ① layer ② long-winded
嗿氣（囉嗦）long-winded

一嗿（一層）a bed of; a blanket of; a cloak of; a coat of; a curtain of; a deck of; a film of; a flake of; a layer; a layer of; a level of; a line of ; a mantle of; a ring of; a veil of

【啶】ding⁶ what
知啶（有自知之明）know what one is doing

【埋】maai⁴ bury
埋口 ①（合口／收口）heal (wounds) ② sealed
　　埋口信（封口信件）sealed letter
埋手 ①（入手／下手）take as the point of departure ②（動手）tackle
埋牙 ①（交手）come to blows; start to fight ②（發生性行為）have sex
埋去（走近去／過去）go near; go over
埋位（就座）take one's place
　　埋位啦（就座）please proceed to the dining table
埋尾（收尾／掃尾／煞尾）bring to completion
埋岸（靠岸）draw alongside; pull in shore
埋門（逼近球門）get close to the goal
埋便（裏面／裏邊）inside
埋怨 blame; complain
埋站（進站／靠站）enter the station
埋席（入席／就席）take one's seat at a table for a meal
埋啲（靠近點）come closer

埋堆（紮堆）form a small clique; join a group
埋單 ①（結賬／開賬單）pay the bill; settle the bill ②（承擔責任）bear responsibility ③（死亡）die
　　唔該埋單（麻煩結賬）can I have the bill please; could I have the bill please; may I have the bill please; the bill please
埋葬 bury
埋數（結算）balance accounts; close an account; make the final calculation; settle accounts; settle the bill; wind up an account
埋鋪（關門）closed for business
埋頭埋腦（全神貫注）all attention; all ears; all eyes; all eyes and ears; apply the mind to; be absorbed in; be deeply engrossed in sth; be engrossed in; be occupied with; be preoccupied with; be utterly concentrated in; be wholly absorbed in; be wrapped up in; complete mental concentration; concentrate on; concentrate one's attention on; concentrate the whole energy upon; give one's whole attention to; have sth on the brains; have sth on the mind; in complete absorption; pay undivided attention to; very attentive; with absorbed interest; with all one's mental faculties on the stretch; with all one's soul; with breathless attention; with one's heart and soul; with rapt attention; with undivided attention
埋嚟（走近來／過來）come here; come over; come up
埋櫃（店鋪每晚結賬）close the turnover of the day

大纜扯唔埋（風馬牛不相及）cannot meet sb half-way; people or groups who are always in conflict
冚埋（蓋住）cover up
加埋（加起來）add up to
加加埋埋（全都加起來）add together
包埋（包括）include
汁都撈埋（打淨撈乾）consume every possible thing on offer
共埋（全部加起來）add up to; amount to; together
同…行得好埋 on very familiar terms with sb
同埋 ①（以及）and ②（一起）all together; at the same time; in company; in unison; simultaneously; together; together with
收埋（收起）hide; put aside
行埋 ①（走在一起）come closer ②（性交）have sex
行唔埋（合不來）unable to get along with
行得埋（合得來）get along well with people; hit it off
行開行埋（走來走去）move around; move about; go around; wander; went around; pace up and down
住埋（住在一起）cohabit; cohabitation; live together; shack up with
夾埋（共謀）① collude; plot with sb ②（連同）combine
拉埋（拉進去）drag into

拍埋 (拼起來) put together
閂唔埋 (關不上) can't lock up
閂埋 (關上) close up
俚埋 (藏起來) hide oneself; keep out of sight
捌埋 (藏起來) hide oneself
柄埋 (藏起來) hide from public view
砍埋 (撞向) crash into
計埋 (計算所有) everything included; taken together
敨埋 ① (串通) collude; plot with sb ② (合起來) combine
鬥埋 (拼起來) piece together
做埋 (完成他人的工作) finish off one's work
匿埋 (藏起來) hide oneself
措措埋埋 (攢起來) accumulate
連埋 (連同) along with; complete with; together with
捌埋 (甚麼都在內) generally; inclusive
等埋 (等等) wait for me
傾唔埋 (談不來) do not speak the same language
傾得埋 (談得來) get along with sb
搆埋 (混在一起) mix with
腦筍未生埋 (幼稚) childish
葬埋 (埋葬) bury
話唔埋 (說不定) perhaps; who knows
話得埋 (同意) agree on; come to an agreement
鈴鈴鎈鎈都丟埋 (失敗得慘烈不堪) meet with a crushing defeat
預埋 (算進去) you're included
撈埋 (混在一起) blend; mix and stir
撞埋 (撞向) bump into; crash into
積埋 (累積) accumulate
頭都大埋 (腦袋都脹了) addle one's head
擰埋 (扭上) put screws on
攞到骨罅都刺埋 (整天不斷在投訴) make a constant complaint for having paid so much for sth
攞到樹葉都落埋 (整天不斷在埋怨) express one's repentance
聯埋 (縫合) stitch up
聲都沙埋 (聲線都啞了) lose one's voice
繑埋 (繞起來) coil
黐埋 (黏在一起) bond
攙埋 (到處搜集) gather up
攪唔埋 (合不來) unable to get along with
攪得埋 (合得來) get along well with people; hit it off
攬埋 (擁抱) hug sb tight

【城】 sing⁴ town
城巴 city bus
城市 city
　大城市 big city
城隍 city god

城鎮 cities and towns

省城 provincial capital
眾志成城 collective purposes form a fortress; our wills unite like a fortress; union is strength; unity of purpose is a formidable force; unity of will is an impregnable citadel
頻倫唔得入城 (欲速則不達) more haste, less speed

【埃】 aai¹ fine dust
埃及 Egypt

山埃 potassium cyanide

【塽】 long³ (架起) put up
塽高 (架高) elevate; raise

【埗】 bou⁶ dock

生埗 strange; unfamiliar
到埗 arrive at; arrive in
抵埗 arrive; reach

【埕】 cing⁴ (罐子) jar

桐油埕 (桐油罐子) a person who does the same job without any change
酒埕 (酒罐子) earthen wine jar

【夏】 haa⁶ summer
夏天 summer
夏令 ① summer; summertime ② summer weather
夏至 June solstice; summer solstice
夏季 summer; summer season; summertime

炎夏 hot summer; summer at its hottest

【套】 tou³ set
套住 cover up
套房 suite
套料 (套取秘密) try and trick sb into giving away a secret
套現 cash in
套餐 set meal
　午市套餐 set lunch
　晚市套餐 set dinner
　優惠套餐 special set meal

一套 ① a set; a suit ② a pack of; a set of; an article of
一對手套 a pair of gloves

手套 gloves
另搞一套 go one's own way
外套 coat; jacket
安全套 condom
老一套 the same old methods; the same old story; the same old stuff
老套 old-fashioned
冷外套 (開襟毛衣) cardigan
成套 (整套) whole set
成龍配套 (填補缺口 / 湊成完整的系統) fill in the gaps to complete a chain
明一套，暗一套 act one way in the open and another way in secret
褥套 ticking
避孕套 condom

【娘】 noeng⁴ girl

娘子 my wife
娘丙 (過時的) old-fashioned
娘胎 mother's womb
娘娘 ① empress ② imperial concubine ③ goddess
娘家 parents' home of a married woman
娘親 ① relatives on the maternal side ② one's mother

王母娘娘 Heaven Queen
叫姑娘 (召妓) visit a prostitute
有奶便是娘 (誰有奶水，就認誰做娘) he that serves God for money will serve the devil for better wages
灰姑娘 Cinderella
老闆娘 female boss; wife of the boss
伯娘 aunt
伴娘 bridesmaid
姑娘 ① (女子) girl ② (護士) nurse ③ (妓女) prostitute
玩新娘 (鬧洞房) celebrate wedding in the bridal chamber
契娘 (乾娘) adoptive mother
新娘 bride
過埠新娘 a bride married to a man far away
嬸娘 aunt; wife of father's younger brother

【娛】 jyu⁴ entertain

娛人 make sb happy
娛樂 entertainment; recreation
　娛樂圈 entertainment circles
　娛樂場所 places for entertainment

【娩】 min⁵ give birth

娩出 deliver a child; give birth to

分娩 give birth

自然分娩 natural childbirth
無痛分娩 painless delivery

【孫】 syun¹ (孫子) grandchildren

孫女 (孫女兒) granddaughter
孫仔 (孫子) grandson

子子孫孫 children and grandchildren; descendants; posterity
子孫 children and grandchildren; descendants; posterity
百子千孫 have many siblings
侄孫 brother's grandson
兒孫 descendants; posterity
為老不尊，教壞子孫 (為老不尊，為幼不敬) disrespectful old man sets a bad example for his descendants
姪孫 grandnephew; one's brother's grandson
徒子徒孫 (一眾徒弟) disciples and followers
湊孫 (照顧孫子) look after one's grandchildren

【宮】 gung¹ palace

宮廷 ① palace ② court; royal court
宮殿 palace
　一座宮殿 a palace

子宮 uterus; womb

【孭】 me¹ (揹) carry on the back; carry on the shoulders

孭仔 (揹孩子) carry one's child on the back
孭住 (揹着) carry on the back; carry on the shoulders
孭飛 (頂缸 / 負責) take responsibility
　孭重飛 (負重責) star attraction
孭帶 (揹帶) straps
孭實 (揹着) carry on the back; carry on the shoulders
孭數 (背負重債) be heavily in debt
孭鑊 (揹黑鍋) bear the responsibility; carry the can

【害】 hoi⁶ harm

害人 victimization
　害人不淺 cause deep injury to people; cause infinite harm to people; do people great harm; injure the people deeply; no small harm is done; very harmful to people
　害人害己 bite off one's own head; curses come home to roost; harm set, harm get; harm watch, harm catch; he who bites others gets bitten himself
　害人終害己 curses come home to roost; harm set, harm get; harm watch; harm catch; he that mischief hatches mischief catches; hoist with one's own petard; one will injure oneself in injuring others; the damage recoils upon one's own head

害死亞堅（拖累別人）be encumbered by sb

害命 kill; murder; take sb's life

　謀財害命 commit murder out of greed; murder sb for his/her money

害怕 afraid for sth; afraid of sb; be frightened; be overcome by fear; be overcome with fear; be scared of; can't say boo to a goose; dread; dreadful; fear; fearful; fly the white feather; for fear of; frighten; frightful; get cold feet; have a dread of; have cold feet; in dread of sb; in dread of sth; in fear of; make one's blood run cold; make one's hair stand on end; quail; shake in one's boots; show the white feather; strike fear into; tremble in one's shoes

害蟲 destructive insects; injurious insects

冇害（無害）harmless

未見其利，先見其害 suffer a loss before an uncertain gain

有一利必有一害 no rose without a thorn

利害 advantages and disadvantages; gains and losses

災害 calamities; damages; disasters; fatalities

拼死無大害 do sth at the risk of

傷害 hurt

禍害 canker; curse; disaster; scourge

厲害 ① cruel; fierce; severe; sharp ② formidable; serious; terrible

靠害（陷害）lead sb into a trap

謀害 plot a murder

擾害 harass and injure

【宵】siu¹ dark

宵夜（夜宵）night snack

　食宵夜（吃夜宵／吃宵夜）have night snack

宵禁 curfew

元宵 Lantern Festival

年宵 Lunar New Year's Eve

春宵 have a night of sex

通宵 work overnight without a break

【家】gaa¹ family

家人 members of a family

　家人團聚 family reunion

家下（現在）at once; at present; at the moment; for the moment; immediately; now; nowadays; of the moment; presently; right now

家公（公公）father-in-law

家生 ①（工具）tools ②（武器）weapons

家用（家庭開支）family allowance; family expenses

家有一老，如有一寶 an old-timer in the family is an advisor of rich experience

家和萬事興 harmony makes a family prosperous

家姐（姐姐）elder sister

　大家姐 ①（大姐）eldest sister ② big sister ③ tough lady

　堂家姐（堂姐）elder female cousin; first cousin

家肥屋潤 wish you a prosperous year

家長 parents

家家有本難唸的經 each and every family has its own problems

家庭 ① family ② home ③ household

　家庭主婦 housewife

　家庭美滿 have a happy family

　家庭樂趣 family joy; homely pleasure

家務 household chores; housework

　家務助理 domestic helper

家陣（現在）at once; at present; at the moment; for the moment; immediately; now; nowadays; of the moment; presently; right now

家產 family property

　傾家蕩產 sell all one's family property

家婆（婆婆）mother-in-law

家眷（家屬）one's family; one's family dependents; one's household; one's wife and children

家常 domestic trivia

　家常便飯 ① homely food; ordinary meal ② common occurrence

　閒話家常 daily chats

家教 home education

　冇家教（沒家庭教養）lack home education

　冇釐家教（沒家庭教養）lack home education

　有家教（有修養／有教養）have good home education

家嫂（兒媳婦／媳婦）daughter-in-law

家嘈屋閉（家庭不和睦）cause trouble at home

家頭細務（家務）household chores

家醜 family scandal

　家醜不可外傳（家醜不可外揚）not to wash dirty linen in public

一家 a family; one family

一頭家（一個家庭）a family

大家 ① everyone ② you ③ all of us; we ④ together

大撈家 ①（黑幫分子）someone who earns a living from vice ②（事業有成的人）sb successful in business

小家（小氣／小家子氣）mean-spirited; tightfisted

工業家 industrialist

仇家 enemy

內陸國家 landlocked country

冚家（全家）entire family

外家（娘家）parents' home of a married woman

白手興家 achieve success in life with one's own hands; start from scratch

全家 the whole family

而家 (現在) at present; at the moment; now; nowadays; presently; right now

行家 persons of the same trade

作家 author; writer

兵家 ① military strategist in ancient China ② military commander; soldier

私家 private

身家 personal asset

依家 (現在) at present; at the moment; now; nowadays; presently; right now

兩家 both sides

到家 (擅長) be excelled in

呢頭家 (這個家) this family

東家唔打打西家 (另有高就) lose employment on one but get a job in another

老人家 ① old folks; the aged; the old ② old men ③ old women ④ parents

陀衰家 (連累家人) a person of rough luck implicates the family

客家 ① hakka ② guest

咪家 (書呆子) bookish person

姻家 ① families of the married couple ② elders of the families of the married couple

持家 keep house; run one's home

政治家 politician

音樂家 musician

科學家 scientist

耍家 (擅長) very accomplished

唔黐家 (不喜歡待在家) not to stick to home

娘家 parents' home of a married woman

酒家 restaurant

祖家 one's native place; one's old home

做專家 be a specialist; be an expert

國家 country; nation; state

執到襪帶累身家 (因小失大) lose a pound for gaining a penny

執輸行頭，慘過敗家 (錯失先機) it would be disadvantageous not to take an immediate action in time

冤家 ① enemy; opponent ② fall out with sb

專家 expert; specialist

羞家 (恥辱) bring about shame; shame on; shameful

莊家 banker

商家 businessman; merchant; trader

教育家 educationist

蛋家 (漁民) fisherman

畫家 painter

當家 leader

置家 start one's own family

慳家 (節儉) thrifty

管家 ① butler; steward ② housekeep ③ housekeeper; manager

銀行家 banker

撈家 (詐騙者) racketeer

頭家 (頭兒) boss; chief

鋼琴家 pianist

餅家 cake shop; pastry shop

離家 leave home

黐家 sb who likes to stay at home

藝術家 artist

【容】jung⁴ easy

容光 facial expression; general appearance

　容光煥發 be aglow with health; glow with health; look like a million dollars; in radiating health; one's face glows with health; radiant

容易 apt to; as easy as ABC; as easy as taking pennies from a blind man; as easy as taking toffee from a child; as easy as you know how; easily; easy; easy as pie; easy-peasy; likely, liable to

　容乜易 (不難 / 沒甚麼難的 / 很容易) it's very easy

　談何容易 by no means easy; easier said than done; easy to talk, difficult to achieve; how easy it is to talk about it; it's no easy thing; not as easy as it sounds; not as easy as one thinks it to be

容許 allow; concede

容量 capacity; measurement; volume

內容 content

天地不容 heaven and earth do not tolerate; heaven forbid

形容 describe

美容 ① cosmetology ② beauty treatment

笑容 smile on one's face

面不改容 not to change colour; one's countenance betrays nothing; one's face is untroubled; remain calm; undismayed; without batting an eyelid; without changing countenance; without turning a hair

面帶笑容 have a smile on one's face

倦容 tired look

陣容 ① battle array; battle formation ② cast; line-up

愁容 anxious expression; worried look

寵物美容 pet grooming

難以形容 hard to describe

【射】se⁶ shoot

射門 shoot; shoot at the goal; shooting

射喱眼 (斜視) squint

射程 firing range; range of fire; reach; throw

射燈 spotlight
射籃 (投籃) shoot
射擊 ① fire; shoot ② shooting

注射 get a shot; inject

【展】 zin² exhibit

展出 exhibit; put on display; on show
展示 display; exhibit; lay bare; open up before one's eyes; reveal; show
展品 exhibit; item on display
展望 ① look into the distance ② envisage; envision; look ahead; look into the future; outlook
展現 develop; emerge; present before one's eyes; unfold before one's eyes; yield up
展開 ① amplify; decoil; develop; open up; spread; spread out; unfold ② carry out; develop; launch
展銷 exhibit and sell
展覽 exhibit; exhibition
　　展覽會 exhibition

孖展 (保證金) (English) margin
伸展 extend
沙展 (長官) sergeant
舒展 limber up; relax; stretch; unfold
發展 development

【屐】 kek⁶ (木拖鞋 / 木屐) wooden slippers

屐齒 teeth of clogs

木屐 wooden slippers
雪屐 ① roller skate ② ice roller skate
踩雪屐 (溜冰) ice skate

【峯】 fung¹ ① mountain top; summit ② transliteration of "phone"

峯迴路轉 ① the path winds along mountain ridges ② things change drastically
峯頂 crest; summit

咪高峯 (麥克風) (English) microphone

【島】 dou² island

荒島 barren island; desert island; uninhabited island

【差】 caa¹ ① bad ② Indian

差皮 (差勁) poor
　　差一皮 (差一等) a bit worse; on a lower level

差池 (差錯 / 過失) error; fault; miscalculation; mistake; slip
差妹 (印度女生) Indian girl
差唔多 ① (大約) almost; around; nearly ② (差不多) about the same; more or less; much of a muchness; similar
　　差好多 (差得多) entirely different; very different
差啲 ① (差點兒) almost; nearly ② (未夠好) not good enough; not up to the mark
差婆 (印度女人) Indian woman
差遲 (差錯 / 過失) error; fault; miscalculation; mistake; slip

天氣好差 (天氣很差) the weather is very bad
仲差 (更差) worse
阿差 (印度人) Indian
偏差 departure; deviation; divergence; drift; offset; variance
摩囉差 (印度人) Indian
嚤囉差 (印度人) Indian

【差】 caai¹ official duty

差人 (公安 / 民警 / 警察) cop; police
差佬 (公安 / 民警 / 警察) cop; policeman
差婆 (女警) policewoman
差餉 rates
差館 (公安局 / 派出所 / 警察局) police station

出差 (公幹) on a business trip
交差 (馬虎了事) get the work over without enthusiasm
交通差 (交通警) traffic policeman
信差 (郵務員) messenger
郵差 mail carrier; mailman; postie; postman
當差 (做警察) serve as a policeman
雜差 (警探) plaincloth; police detective

【師】 si¹ teacher

師太 (師娘) wife of one's teacher
師父 master
師兄 ① senior male apprentice ② senior male schoolmate; senior schoolmate ③ elder son of one's master
師奶 (大嫂 / 家庭婦女) housewife; middle-aged married woman
　　師奶殺手 (深受婦女歡迎的中年男人) men who are popular among middle-aged married women
師母 (師娘) teacher's wife
師弟 ① junior male apprentice ② junior male schoolmate; junior schoolmate ③ younger son of one's master
師妹 ① junior female apprentice ② junior female schoolmate ③ younger daughter of one's master

師姐 ① senior female apprentice ② senior female schoolmate ③ elder daughter of one's master

師姑 (尼姑) Buddhist nun

師傅 expert; master worker
　水喉師傅 (管道工) plumber
　盲拳打死老師傅 (不講章法 / 亂衝亂撞 / 誤打誤中) a poor hand may put the old master to death
　教車師傅 driving instructor
　電器師傅 electrician

師爺 advisor
　扭計師爺 (詭計多端的人) schemer

大律師 barrister
大師 master
工程師 engineer
中醫師 Chinese medicine practitioner
化裝師 make-up artist
老師 teacher
技師 technician
宗師 master of great learning and integrity
治療師 healer
牧師 priest
物理治療師 physiotherapist
狀師 lawyer
狗頭軍師 (愛給人出主意而不高明的人) inapt advisor; villainous advisor
則師 (建築師) architect
室內設計師 interior designer
紅鬚軍師 (愛給人出主意而不高明的人) misadvisor; thoughtless advisor
美容師 beautician
軍師 military advisor
律師 lawyer
建築師 architect
飛機師 pilot
恩師 one's respected teacher
拳師 boxer; boxing coach; boxing master; expert in the art of boxing
核計師 (審計師) auditor
核數師 (會計師) accountant
偷師 (偷學) pick up a skill by watching in secret
時裝設計師 fashion designer
教師 teacher
訟師 (律師) attorney at law; law practitioner; lawyer
測量師 surveyor
視光師 optometrist
會計師 accountant
緊張大師 (容易緊張的人) nervous person
精算師 actuary

廚師 chef; cook
導師 instructor
樂師 musician
機師 (飛機師) pilot
髮型師 hair stylist
講師 lecturer
職業治療師 occupational therapist
騎師 jockey
藥劑師 pharmacist
嚴師 severe teacher; stern teacher; strict teacher

【席】 zik⁶ ① banquet ② table

席地 on the ground
席位 seat
　一個席位 a seat
　保住席位 hold onto a seat; keep a seat
席捲 take away everything
　席捲全國 sweep over the country

入席 start the banquet
五時恭候，八時入席 reception at 5 p.m. and banquet at 8 p.m.
主席 chairman; chairperson
主家席 head table
名譽主席 honorary chairman; honorary chairperson
訂酒席 make a banquet reservation
缺席 absence
埋席 (入席) take one's seat at a table for a meal
座無虛席 all seats are occupied; every seat is occupied; have a full house; have no empty seat; with every seat taken
酒席 banquet; feast
連任主席 be reelected chairman
開席 dinner is ready
開酒席 prepare a banquet; prepare a feast
擺酒席 give a banquet; hold a banquet

【桅】 lei⁵ sails

有風駛盡桅 (見風使舵) avail oneself of an opportunity to the fullest extent; take advantage of an opportunity to the full extent
看風駛桅 (見風使舵) run before the wind
順風駛桅 (人云亦云) avail oneself of an opportunity; trim the sails

【座】 zo⁶ ① seat ② block ③ flat

座上客 guest of honour; honoured guest
座右銘 maxim; motto; permanent reminder; precept
座位 seat
座椅 seat

座無虛席 all seats are occupied; every seat is occupied; have a full house; have no empty seat; with every seat taken

座談 have an informal discussion

十六座 mini-bus
太座 (自家夫人) my wife (respectful)
叫座 appeal to the audience; draw a large audience; draw well
全院滿座 full house
前座 front stall
後座 back stall
盒座 (錄音帶盒) cassette holder
椅座 (座椅) seat
滿座 all seats are taken; full house; fully booked
戲院滿座 the cinema is full

【庫】fu³ storehouse
庫存 inventory; repertory; reserve; stock
庫房 ① storehouse; storeroom ② treasury
庫藏 have a storage of; have in storage; have in store

地庫 basement
倉庫 depository; depot; repository; stockroom; store; storehouse; warehouse

【庭】ting⁴ court
庭長 (審判長) chief justice; presiding judge
庭院 courtyard; patio
庭園 flower garden; garden

法庭 law court
家庭 ① family ② home ③ household
臨時法庭 temporary court

【弱】joek⁶ weak
弱不禁風 so delicate a constitution that one is unable to stand a gust of wind; on the lift; too frail to stand a gust of wind
弱者 the weak; the weak and the timid; underdog
弱智 moron
弱勢 ① in a relatively weak position ② the disadvantaged
弱點 Achilles' heel; failing; vulnerable point; vulnerable spot; weak point; weak spot; weakness
弱雞 (弱) weak

身體虛弱 frail in health
神經衰弱 nervous breakdown
脆弱 delicate; fragile; frail; frailty; tender; weak
財多身子弱 (一有錢便容易有病痛) rich but in poor health

孱弱 (虛弱) feeble; frail; weak
減弱 weaken
瘦弱 weak
懦弱 coward

【徑】ging³ way
徑自 without consulting anyone; without leave
徑路 route

途徑 approach; avenue; channel; pathway; road; way
捷徑 shortcut
蹊徑 narrow path

【徒】tou⁴ disciple
徒子徒孫 (一眾徒弟) disciples and followers
徒手 bare-handed; empty-handed; freehand; unarmed
徒弟 apprentice; disciple
徒步 go on foot
徒勞 bad job; bark at the moon; bay at the moon; be a fool for one's pains; be sent on a fool's errand; bite on granite; burn daylight; fight a losing game; fruitless labour; futile effort; go for nothing; go on a fool's errand; hold a candle to the sun; in vain; milk the bull; milk the ram; shoe the goose; sleeveless; to no avail; to no purpose; waste; wild-goose chase; without avail
徒勞往返 hurry back and forth for nothing; make a futile journey; make a trip in vain; make a vain trip
徒勞無功 an ass for one's pains; beat the air; draw water in a sieve; drop a bucket into an empty well; flag a dead horse; labour in vain; labour to no purpose; make a futile effort; make useless trouble; milk a he-goat; not to succeed after trying hard; plough the waves; plowing the wave; prove futile; sow the sands; use vain efforts; wasted effort; work to no avail; work without achieving anything
徒勞無益 all to no purpose; come to naught; end in smoke; fish in the air; flog a dead horse; futile; hold a candle to the sun; lash the waves; of no avail; of no purpose; plough the air; plough the sand; shoe a goose; sow beans in the wind; weave a rope of sand; work in vain

亡命之徒 badmen; dead rabbits; desperado; fugitive; refugees from justice; ruffian

【恐】hung² horror
恐怖 horrible
　恐怖主義 terrorism
　恐怖份子 terrorist

恐怕 I'm afraid; might as well; perhaps

恐慌 fright; frightened; panic; scared; terrified

恐龍 dinosaur

恐嚇 threaten

恐懼 afraid of; dread; fear; frightened; terrified

【恩】jan[1] favour

恩人 benefactor

恩仇 debt of gratitude and of revenge

  恩將仇報 bite the hand that feeds one

恩怨 feelings of gratitude and feelings of resentment;
  grievances; old scores; resentment

  恩怨分明 discriminate between love and hate; kindness
    and hatred are clearly distinguished; make a clear
    distinction between kindness and hatred

恩師 one's respected teacher

恩情 great kindness; love; loving-kindness

恩愛 affectionate; conjugal love

忘恩 bite the hand that feeds one; devoid of gratitude;
  ungrateful

施恩 do favours to others

謝恩 express thanks for great favours; thank sb for their
  favour

【息】sik[1]（利息）interest

息口（利率）interest rate

  息口持續低企（利率維持在低水平）interest rate being
    continuously low

息肉（軟纖維瘤）polyp

入息（收入）income

小道消息 hearsay; rumour; the grapevine; the grapevine
  gossip

內部消息 inside information

內幕消息 inside information

冇出息（沒出息）futureless

心息（放棄）give up one's hope forever; have no more
  illusions about the matter; think no more of sth

出息 ① promising ② high-minded

生息（收取利息）bear interest

休息 rest; take a rest

存款利息 interest on a deposit

死心不息 as obstinate as a mule

再度減息 reduce the interest rate again

免息 interest free

利息 interest

姑息 appease; attention; indulge; tolerate

拆息（按日計算的利率）daily interest rate

泄漏消息 leak out the news

股息 dividend

食息（依靠利息生活）live on interest

借款利息 interest on a loan

消息 news

訊息 information; message; news; tidings

喘息 ① gasp for breath; pant; puff ② breather; breathing
  spell; respite

減息 interest rate reduction

歇息 ① have a rest ② go to bed; put u for the night; stay at
  an inn

銀行同業拆息（利息結算利率）interbank offered rate

壞消息 bad news

【恭】gung[1] ① respectfully ② dung

恭候 wait respectfully

恭喜 congratulate

  恭喜你 congratulations

  恭喜晒（恭喜）congratulations

  恭喜發財 wish you a prosperous year

  恭喜發財，利是拉來（恭喜發財，紅包拿來）wish you a
    prosperous year, and give me a red packet

恭賀 congratulate

恭敬 respectful; with great respect

  恭敬不如從命 it is better to accept deferentially than
    to decline courteously; obedience is better than
    politeness; the best way to show respect is to obey;
    to accept is better than to stand on ceremony

  必恭必敬 extremely deferential; reverent and
    respectful

  恭恭敬敬 in an attitude of respect; most respectfully;
    reverently

  畢恭畢敬 cap in hand; extremely deferential; hat in
    hand; in a most respectful attitude; in humble
    reverence; reverent and respectful; with all courtesy
    and respect; with excessive courtesy; with the
    utmost deference

恭維 adulation; butter sb up; compliment; flatter

出恭 ①（如廁）clear one's bowel; defecate; dump;
  egest; empty the bowels; evacuate one's bowels; go
  boom-boom; go number two; go potty; have a bowel
  movement; loose bowels; move the bowels; relieve
  oneself; relieve the bowels; shit; sit on the throne; take a
  shit; the bowel moves; void excrement ②（大便）faeces;
  human excrement; shit; stool; turd

結恭（便秘）constipation; intestinal constipation

謙恭 civility; humility; modest and courteous; modest and
  polite; respectful; unassuming

【恥】ci² shame

廉恥 sense of honour; sense of shame

【悔】fui³ regret

悔改 repent and mend one's ways
　　真心悔改 sincerely repent and earnestly reform oneself
悔恨 bitterly remorseful; regret deely
　　悔恨終身 have a secret regret all one's life; nurse a secret
　　　regret all one's life; regret sth all one's life
悔過 penitence; repent one's error; repentant
　　悔過自新 express one's repentance and determination
　　　to turn over a new leaf; repent and make a fresh start;
　　　repent and start anew; repent and start with a clean
　　　slate repent and turn over a new leaf

後悔 regret

【悟】ng⁵ enlighten

悟性 comprehensive; power of understanding
悟道 awake to truth
悟禪 come to understand the principle of Zen

穎悟 clever

【戙】dung⁶（立／豎）stand upright; vertical

戙企（豎放）stand upright
　　戙企水魚（油葫蘆）fat person
戙起（豎起來）erect
　　戙起牀板（不眠不休，思考問題）stay awake thinking
　　　about a problem
　　戙起幡竿有鬼到 people will come as soon as they know
　　　the location
　　戙起嚟（豎起來）erect
戙篤企（直立／直着放／豎着）place upright

一戙（一疊）a pile of; a stack of
一畫一戙（一橫一豎）a horizontal stroke and a vertical
　　stroke
毛管戙（起雞皮疙瘩）get the creeps; make one's flesh crawl
打戙（豎放）set upright

【扇】sin³（扇子）fan

扇貝 yesso scallop
扇形 sector

大葵扇 go-between; match-maker
羽扇 feather fan

老公撥扇（淒涼；可憐）miserable
抽風扇 air ejector fan
抽氣扇 air ejector fan; air extractor; ventilation fan
秋後扇（不再需要的人）someone who is no longer
　　needed
風扇 fan
揸大葵扇（做媒人）act as a go-between; match-maker
開風扇 switch on the fan
葵扇 palm-leaf fan
撥大葵扇（做媒人）act as a go-between; act as a
　　matchmaker; play cupid
撥扇 fan with a fan

【挙】ung²（推）push

挙我（推我）push me

【拳】kyun⁴ fist

拳不離手，曲不離口（熟能生巧）boxing cannot
　　dispense with the hand, nor songs the mouth; keep
　　one's eye in; keep one's hand in; no day without a line;
　　one cannot strike without the hand, nor sing without the
　　mouth; practice makes perfect
拳手 boxer
拳王 boxing champion
拳打 strike with fists
　　拳打腳踢 beat and kick; beat up; box and kick; cuff and
　　　kick; give sb a good beating; strike and kick
拳師 boxer; boxing coach; boxing master; expert in the art
　　of boxing
　　拳師狗 boxer
　　後備拳師——聽打（等着挨打）sb who will be beaten by
　　　others
拳頭 fist
拳賽 boxing match

打拳 boxing; play boxing; spar
扰一拳（打一拳）give sb a punch
猜拳 finger-guessing drinking game
單手獨拳 pull a lone oar
揼佢一拳（打他一拳）give him a punch
餉以老拳（暴打一拳）give sb a sound thrashing

【拿】naa⁴ take

拿手 good at; strong suit
　　拿手好戲 one's strong suit
拿拿聲（趕忙）make haste to do sth; quickly

士巴拿（扳手）(English) spanner
大拿拿（大數目）quite a large amount

去桑拿 go to have a sauna

有咩揸拿（有甚麼保證）there's no assurance

桑拿 sauna

揸拿（保證）assurance

雲呢拿（香草）(English) vanilla

【挈】kit³ take along

挈挈（急切）urgent

帶挈（提攜）look after sb

【挨】aai¹（靠）lean

挨住（靠着）lean

挨近（靠近）close by; close upon; come close to; get close to; get near to; leave a small interval; near to; steal up

挨晚（傍晚）at dusk; at nightfall; dusk; late in the afternoon; nightfall; towards evening; twilight

【挹】jap¹（招手）wave one's hand

挹手（招手）wave one's hand

依依挹挹（男女間打情罵俏）amorous behaviour

依挹（男女間偷情）amorous behavior; affair

【挽】waan⁵（拿／提）carry

挽下手（突然）abruptly; all at once; all of a sudden; by the run; cap the climax; out of the blue; short; suddenly; unexpectedly; with a run; with suddenness; without any warning

挽手（提手）handle

挽水（提水）carry water

挽起手（突然）abruptly; all at once; all of a sudden; by the run; cap the climax; out of the blue; short; suddenly; unexpectedly; with a run; with suddenness; without any warning

挽鞋（提鞋）perform some menial task for someone

【挺】ting⁵ endure; erect

挺身 straighten one's back

挺身而出 bell the cat; bolster oneself up; come forward courageously; come out boldly; stand up and volunteer to help; step forth bravely; step forward boldly; step forward bravely; thrust oneself forward to face a challenge

挺直 erect; straight and upright

挺舉 clean and jerk

中挺（中等）medium

【捋】lyut³ rub

捋汗（尷尬）be embarrassed

捋起衫袖（捋起袖子）push up one's sleeve

烏捋捋（黑黑滑滑）black and shiny

滑捋捋（滑溜溜）slick; slippery; smooth

【捉】zuk¹（抓）catch

捉用神（揣測）make a guess at sth

捉錯用神（誤會別人的用意）misunderstand sb's intention

捉字蝨（摳字眼兒）fool others with words one uses; pick fault with the words one uses; play with the meaning of a word used by someone

捉住（抓住／抓着）grab

捉住佢（抓住他）catch him

捉依因（捉迷藏）play hide-and-seek

捉兒人（捉迷藏）play hide-and-seek

捉到 be caught

捉到鹿唔識脫角（拿着燒餅當枕頭）fail to make the best use of an opportunity; let the opportunity slip; miss the boat

被人捉到 be caught

捉倒（抓到）grab

捉蛇 ①（逮住躲懶的員工）catch workers who are shirking; find out the lazy employees ②（逮住大學裏的非法留宿者）find out students who stay overnight at a university hostel without permission ③（逮住非法入境者）catch illegal immigrants

捉魚（捕魚）catch fish

捉棋（下棋）play chess

捉黃腳雞（捉姦）catch sb having illicit sex; extort money from a man by setting up a sex-trap

捉路（預測對手的下一步）predict the strategy of one's opponent

捉賊（抓賊）catch a thief

捉摸 pin down

難以捉摸 hard to pin down

捉蟲（惹上麻煩）get into difficulties; get into trouble

【挾】gaap³ grip

挾餸（挾菜）take food

逼挾 cramped

【捕】bou⁶ capture

捕風捉影 act on hearsay evidence; catch at shadows; indulge in groundless suspicion; grasp at a shadow; lay hold on the wind; run after a shadow

捕食 catch and feed on; prey on

捕殺 catch and kill; capture and kill
捕魚 catch fish; fishing
捕獲 ① acquire; arrest; capture; catch; seize; succeed in catching ② trapping

拘捕 arrest; detain; take in
圍捕 surround to capture

【捐】gyun[1]（鑽）pass through

捐血（獻血）blood donation
捐助 contribute; donate; offer
捐款 ① contribute money; donate a sum; gift ② contribution; donation; subscription
捐錢 donate money
捐窿（鑽洞）bore
捐窿捐罅（尋找每個角落）search high and low for a place
捐贈 contribute; donate; offer

【挏】dau[3]（碰 / 觸動）touch

挏嘢（碰東西 / 動東西）touch sth

【效】haau[6] effect

效力 ① render a service to; serve ② effect; efficacy; potence ③ avail; effect; force
效尤 follow a bad example
以儆效尤 as a warning to others; in order to warn against bad examples; so as to deter anyone from committing the same crime; warn others against following a bad example; warn others against making the same mistake
效用 effectiveness; utility; usefulness
效命 ① obey orders ② go all out to serve sb regardless of the consequence; pursue an end at the cost of one's life
效忠 allegiance; devote oneself heart and soul to; loyal to; pledge allegiance; pledge loyalty to
效法 follow the example of; follow the lead of; imitate; model oneself on; learn from; take sb as a model
效果 effect
效益 achievements; beneficial result; benefit; effectiveness
效率 effect; effectiveness; efficiency; productivity
效勞 bear a hand; can I help you; do sb a favour; give a hand; I am at your service; lend a hand; render service; what can I do for you; work for
效應 action; effect; influence

冇效（無效）null
有效 effective
見功 become effective; provide the desired effect
奏效 effective; efficacious; get the desired result; have the intended effect; prove effective; successful
降低療效 weaken the curative effect
報效 free of charge
影響療效 affect the treatment
療效 curative effect

【敆】gaap[8]（湊）pool; pool money

敆份（合夥 / 湊份子 / 湊份兒）club together; make up the full amount of money; pool shares
敆計（合謀 / 串通）collude with sb; conspire; gang up with sb; plot together
敆埋 ①（串通）collude; plot with sb ②（合起來）combine
敆錢（湊錢）make up the full amount of money

【料】liu[6] ① material ②（消息）information ③（才能 / 本事）ability

料理 ① cooking; dish ② attend to; manage; take care
料理家務 manage household matters
日本料理 Japanese cooking; Japanese dish
西式料理 Western cooking
料想 expect; presume; think

乜料 ①（甚麼）what is it ②（有甚麼特別）what is special
冇乜料（沒甚麼本事）nothing special
冇料 ①（沒本事 / 沒本領）nothing special ②（沒學問）ill-educated
加料 ①（加勁）make a greater effort ②（添額外菜餚）add in extra dish
史料 historical data; historical materials
有料（有本事）capable
收料（收集情報）get some information
西式料理 Western cooking
材料 ingredient
勁料（令人意外的消息）excellent stuff
染料 colourant; dye; dyestuff; tincture
香料 herb
建築材料 building materials
流料 ①（假消息）false news ②（假東西）fake things
衫料（衣料）dress material
套料（套取秘密）try and trick sb into giving away a secret
料理家務 manage household matters
堅料 ①（真消息）true information ②（真東西）real thing
猛料（令人震驚的消息）brilliant stuff; great stuff; stunning stuff
斬料（買燒肉吃）buy cooked meat
提料（提取某物）extract materials; reclaim
碎料（小意思）trivial matters
資料 ① data ② information

預料 predict
醃料 marinade
調味料 condiments
難以預料 hard to predict
難料 difficult situation
顏料 colour; dyestuff; pigment
爆料 (洩露秘密) disclose a secret; have a scoop

【旁】pong⁴ side

旁人 other people; others
旁及 take up
旁支 collateral branch
旁白 aside; narration; speak aside; voice-over
旁門 side door; sidegate
　　旁門左道 heresy; all sorts of back doors; unorthodox
　　　　ways
旁證 circumstantial evidence; collateral evidence; side
　　witness
旁聽 audit; visitor at a meeting
旁邊 beside; by the side of
旁觀 look on; observe from the sidelines; on-looker
　　旁觀者清 a bystander is always clear-minded; a spectator
　　　　sees clearly; an onlooker sees clearly; bystanders see
　　　　more than players; lookers-on see more than players;
　　　　lookers-on see most of the game; the onlooker sees
　　　　most of the game; the onlooker sees the game best;
　　　　the outsider sees the best of the game; the spectator
　　　　sees most clearly; the spectator sees most of the sport
　　冷眼旁觀 stay aloof
　　袖手旁觀 fold one's arms; fold one's arms and look
　　　　on; hold the ring; look on and do nothing; look on
　　　　indifferently; look on with folded arms; praise the
　　　　sea but stay on land; put one's hands in one's sleeves
　　　　and look on; remain an indifferent spectator; sit
　　　　around with folded arms; sit out; stand aside; stand by;
　　　　stand by with folded arms; stand idle; stand idly by;
　　　　watch indifferently without lending a hand; watch with
　　　　folded arms

【旅】leoi⁵ travel

旅行 (旅遊) journey; tour
　　旅行社 travel agency
　　旅行喼 (旅行箱) suitcase
　　一次旅行 a tour; a trip
　　長途旅行 long journey
旅店 hostel
旅舍 hostel
　　青年旅舍 youth hostel
旅客 passenger; traveller

旅途 trip
　　祝你旅途愉快 wish you a happy trip
旅程 itinerary; journey; route; trip
　　縮短旅程 shorten one's journey
旅遊 travel
　　旅遊巴 (旅遊巴士) sightseeing bus
　　旅遊勝地 tourist resort
　　觀光旅遊 sightseeing tour

【晏】aan³ (晚 / 遲) late

晏晝 (中午) high noon; midday; noon; noonday
　　晏晝飯 (午飯) lunch
晏覺 (午睡) afternoon nap

佢去咗食晏 (他去了吃午飯) he has gone out for lunch
我哋去邊度食晏 (我們去哪裏吃午飯) where do we go for
　　lunch
食完晏 (吃完午飯) after lunch
食晏 (吃午飯) have lunch; lunch

【時】si⁴ time

時下 nowadays
時不時 (有時候) at times; now and then; occasionally;
　　sometimes
時尚 social trend
　　一種時尚 a social trend
　　迎合時尚 pander to the trend of the times
時候 time
　　小時候 in one's childhood
　　依時依候 (按時按候) on time
　　係時候 (是時候) it's about time
　　搵時候 (磨時間) kill time; pass the time
時時 (常常 / 時常 / 經常) always; often
　　時時都 (經常) always
　　一時時 (有時) occasionally
時款 (新式 / 新款) fashionable; new style
時間 time
　　時間過得好快 (時間過得很快) time flies
　　冇時間 (沒空兒) have no time; time is not on one's side
　　立時間 (一時間) for a time
　　有冇時間 (有空嗎) spare sb a few minutes
　　同一時間 at the same time
　　因吓時間 (算算時間) estimate the time
　　抽時間 (抽空) manage to find time
　　泵時間 (磨時間) play for time
　　唔夠時間 (時間不夠) not enough time
　　第一時間 (馬上) as soon as; as quick as a flash; at once;
　　　　at one stroke; at the drop of a hat; before you found
　　　　where you are; directly; first thing off the bat; here and

now; immediately; in a brace of shakes; in a crack; in a flash; in a jiffy; in a minute; in a moment; in no time; just now; lose no time in; off hand; on the moment; on the nail; out of hand; promptly; pronto; right away; right now; right off the bat; straight away; straight off; this instant; this moment; without a moment's delay; without delay; without hesitation; without loss of time; without thinking much longer

嘥時間（浪費時間）waste the time

搶時間（與時間競賽）race against time

趕時間 in a hurry; in haste

慳時間（省時間）save time

時裝 fashion; fashionable dress

時裝表演 fashion show

時裝設計師 fashion designer

時髦 fashion

趕時髦 follow the fashion

時價 current price

時興（時尚／時髦）fashionable

一時 a period of time; briefly; for a short while; momentarily

一時時（一時）for a single moment; sometimes

刁時（平局）(English) deuce

大熱天時（大熱天）on a hot day

冇時（無時／無時無刻）all the time; at all times; every hour and moment; every minute; incessanty; without a moment's pause

及時 at a most opportune moment; at the right time; in due course; in due time; in good season; in good time; in season; in the nick of time; in time; promptly; timely; without delay

天時 climate; weather

平時 usually

合時 in season

同時 at the same time; simultaneously

好多時（經常）very often

好準時（很準時）very punctual

守時 on time; punctual

戌時 the period between seven and nine p.m.

有時 sometimes

有陣時（有時）sometimes

此時 at present; for the time being; now; right now; this moment

先時（以前）ago; before; former; formerly; in the past; once; previous; prior; used to be

我後生嗰時（我年輕的時候）when I was young

初時（起初）at first

辰時 period of the day from 7 a.m. to 9 a.m.

辰時卯時 any time of the day

依時 on schedule

到時 by that time

到期時（到時候）in due time; when the time comes

周不時（經常）always; often

周時（經常）always

往陣時（以前）ago; before; former; formerly; in the past; once; previous; prior; used to be

英名一世，蠢鈍一時（人非聖賢，孰能無過）even Homer sometimes nods; every man has a fool in his sleeve

英雄一世，蠢鈍一時（人非聖賢，孰能無過）even Homer sometimes nods; every man has a fool in his sleeve

第時（以後）at a later date

細時（年輕時）as a child; during one's childhood; in childhood; when one was young

斯時（此時）presently; such a time; this time

幾時 at what time; when

登時（立刻）at once; immediately; in no time

過時（超時）overtime

頓時（立刻）at once; forthwith; immediately; suddenly

準時 punctual

嗰陣時（那時候）at that time

較早時（早些時候）in earlier times

廢時 a waste of time

暫時 temporary

霎時 in the twinkling of an eye; instant; moment; very short time

臨時 temporary

聰明一世，糊塗一時（聰明一輩子，偶爾犯糊塗起來）a clever person has their stupid moments; a lifetime of cleverness can be interrupted by moments of stupidity; clever all one's life, but stupid this once; smart as a rule, but this time a fool

聰明一世，蠢鈍一時（聰明一輩子，偶爾卻蠢鈍起來）clever all the time but become a fool this once

舊時（以前）before; formerly; in the old days; in the past; previously

舊陣時（以前）ago; before; former; formerly; in the past; once; previous; prior; used to be

【晒】saai³ ① finish ② brag to ③ flaunt; show off

晒冷（亮底牌）put all one's cards on the table; show one's hand

晒命（炫耀）show off

一天光晒（雨過天晴）all is bright and clear; the trouble is over

一句講晒（一言以蔽之）in a word

化晒（看透了）be disillusioned with this human world; see through the emptiness of the material world; see through the vanity of life; see through the vanity of the world; understand and despise worldly affairs; world-weary

心都涼晒（對別人的不幸感到高興）gloat over one's enemy's misfortune

心都淡晒（心灰意冷）lose heart

心都實晒（悶悶不樂）downhearted

冇晒（完了）come to an end

白晒晒（白色）just white

生骨大頭菜——縱（種）壞晒 be spoiled

生番晒（精神過來）resume one's spirits

扐唔晒（拿不完）can't take all; too many to be taken away

扐晒（拿光／拿完）be all taken; be taken up

丟生晒（生疏）out of practice; show neglect of one's skill

充生晒（裝作全都知道）pretend to know sth

多到十隻手指都數唔晒（多得數不過來）too many to be counted

多謝晒（非常感謝）thank you so much

好返晒（完全康復）be fully recovered

扒到花晒（刪得很凌亂）cross out messily

把聲拆晒（聲音啞了）lose one's voice

亞單睇榜——一眼睇晒（一目瞭然）see with half an eye

亞聾燒炮仗——散晒（只能看到，卻聽不到）meet with a failure; perceive with sight without hearing

周身鬆晒（身心放鬆）free-hearted

計埋晒（全算上）everything included; taken together

計啱晒（全算對了）the calculation is all correct

食唔晒（吃不完）cannot eat it up; cannot finish so much food

食晒（吃完）eat up

唔該晒（謝謝）many thanks; thank you very much; thanks a lot; very grateful

恭喜晒（恭喜）congratulations

做得嗮（做完了）can be completed

唱生晒（說是非）gossip; spread a rumour

啱晒 ①（全對）all correct; that's right ②（適合）suitable ③（極好）wonderful

夠晒 ①（足夠）enough ②（非常）really

掹行晒（促進／推進／催促）urge; push to the limit

條氣順晒（心情很舒暢）ease of mind; enjoy ease of mind; feel happy; have one's mind at ease; in a merry mood

窒住晒（不斷打斷）keep interrupting

麻煩晒（麻煩你）thank you

喝生晒（胡亂大叫）shout blindly

喫晒（吃光）eat up

單眼仔睇老婆——一眼見晒（一目瞭然）clear at a glance; see with half an eye

單筷箸挾豆腐——攪喎晒（弄得一團糟）make a mess of things

散晒（累透）exhausted

睇化晒（全都看透了）know thoroughly

睇唔晒（看不完）cannot finish reading sth

睇晒（看完）finish reading sth

睇得晒（看得完）can finish reading sth

亂晒（全都亂了）be thrown into confusion

嗌生晒（吵鬧）clamour

搦唔晒（拿不去）can't take all; too many to be taken away

搦晒（全都拿去了）be all taken; be taken up

溶晒（全都溶掉了）be completely dissolved

當堂唔同晒（完全不一樣）it's immediately totally different

話晒（說到底）after all; at bottom; in the final analysis; in the last analysis; in the ultimate analysis

嘈生晒（吵吵鬧鬧）make much voice; very noisy; vociferous

滾攪晒 ①（打擾）disturb ②（不好意思／打擾了）sorry to trouble you

彈生晒（諸多批評）criticise blindly

撤晒（全都拿去了）take away all

騷擾晒（打擾你）sorry to trouble you

攞唔晒（拿不完）can't take all; too many to be taken away

攞晒（拿光）be all taken; be taken up

攪掂晒（全都辦妥了）everything is settled; it's settled

攣埋晒（捲曲）contracted

【書】syu¹ book

書友 ex-classmate

書仔（小冊子）booklet

書包 school bag

　一個書包 a school bag

　拋書包（顯擺學問）show off one's knowledge

書局 ①（文具店）stationary shop ②（書店）bookstore

書店 bookstore

書房 study room

書卷 books

書枱（書桌）desk; writing desk

書院女（書院女學生）schoolgirl

書櫃（書櫥）book cabinet

書蟲（書呆子）bookworm

一本書 a book

一命二運三風水，四積陰功五讀書（知識改變命運）education can change one's destiny

一個秘書 a secretary

一戙書（一疊書）a pile of books

一部書（一本書）a book

公仔書 children's book; comics

天書 success key book

剝書（啃書本）study hard

死背書 simply recite a text

咪書（啃書本）study hard

背書 learn a lesson by rote; recite a text

授權書 authorization letter

秘書 secretary
售樓說明書 property sales brochure
教書 teach
陪太子讀書 (侍從作伴) bear sb company; some not given much chance of winning
睇吓書 (看看書) do some reading
睇書 (看書) read books
溫書 review one's lessons
番書 (外國書籍) foreign books
著書 author a book
搴開書 (打開書) open the book
歌書 songbook
曆書 almanac
罄竹難書 one's crimes are too numerous to be recorded
鍾意睇書 (喜歡看書) like reading
攆書 (翻書頁) leaf through a book
藏書 book collection
證書 certificate
繼續讀書 continue one's study
鹹書 (色情書籍) pornographic book
聽書 (上課) attend a lecture; sit in on a class
讀書 ① attend school; go to school ② study ③ read books
讀壞詩書 (斯文敗類) well-read but bad in behaviour

【栗】 leot⁶ chestnut

楓栗 chestnut

【核】 hat⁶ check

核子 ① nuclear ② nucleon
核心 centre; core; crux; heart; kernel; nucleus
核計師 (審計師) auditor
核對 check; collate; verify
核實 check; verify
核數師 (會計師) accountant

批核 approval

【核】 wat⁶ kernel

核突 ① (噁心) disgusting; give sb the creeps ② (樣子難看) bad looking; ugly

眼核 (眼球) eyeball
喉核 (喉結) Adam's Apple

【校】 haau⁶ school

校工 (工友) manual worker in a school
校巴 school bus
校車 school bus

校花 most beautiful girl in the school
校服 school uniform
校長 headmaster
校草 best-looking boy in the school
校園 campus
　漫步校園 take a walk on campus

一間學校 a school
大專院校 tertiary institutions
中小學校 primary and secondary schools
母校 alma mater
民辦學校 school run by the local people
私校 private school
官校 government school; public school
院校 schools and institutions
國際學校 international school
野雞學校 (文憑工廠) non-recognised school
學校 school
離校 leave school

【校】 gaau³ (校正 / 調節) adjust

校水 (調節水溫) adjust the warmth of the water
校台 (調頻道) tune the channels
校奶 (調牛奶) adjust the warmth of the milk
校色 (調色) mix colours; mix paints
校味 (調味兒) adjust the taste
校啱 (校好 / 調好) adjust well
校細聲啲 (弄小聲點兒) turn down the volume
校錶 (撥錶) set the watch
校鐘 (調鐘) set the clock

【根】 gan¹ foundation; root

根本 at all; essence; fundamental; not care a hoot; not give a damn; not the least; once for all; simply; thoroughly
根底 foundation
根治 bring under permanent control; cure once and for all; fundamental solution; radical cure
根除 do away with; eliminate; eradicate; exterminate; root out; uproot
根源 bottom; fountain; fountainhead; grass roots; origin; root; source
根據 base on; evidence
　冇根冇據 (沒有根據) without evidence
　有根有據 be based on evidence

刨根 get to the root of the matter
命根 one's lifeblood
脷根 (舌根) root of the tongue
葉落歸根 an apple does not fall far from the apple tree; the

fruit falls near the branch; the leaves always fall toward the root

慧根 root of wisdom that can lead one to the truth

樹高千丈，落葉歸根 no matter whether it is east or west, home is the best

斷窮根（飛黃騰達）not to live in poverty any more; strike oil

黐脷根（大舌頭）lisp; lisper

【格】gaak³ compare

格仔（格子）check

格外 all the more; especially; exceptionally; extraordinarily

格式 form; format; layout; mode; style

格肋底（腋窩）armpit

格言 adage; aphorism; maxim; motto

格局 arrangement; manner; pattern; setup; structure; style

格格不入 alien to; cannot get along with others; feel out of one's element; ill-adapted to; incompatible with; jar with; like a square peg in a round hole; misfits; out of one's elements; out of tune with

格價（比較價錢）compare prices

格調 style

人格 personality

及格 pass an examination

合格 pass

有性格 have character

低格（粗魯）ill-bred

投票資格 one's eligibility to vote

協商價格 negotiated price

性格 character; personality

物業價格 price of property

品格 ① character of a person; one's character and morals ② quality and style

眉低額窄，冇厘貴格（眼眉低、額頭窄的人一生平庸）person with low eyebrows and a narrow forehead lives a mediocre life

凍格（冰格）ice tray

勉強合格 scrape through the examination

唔及格（不及格）clutch the gunny; fail; fail in an examination

唔合格（不及格）fail

衰格（人品壞）of bad character

間格 ①（打格子）draw a rectangular grid ②（方格圖案）check

暗格（隱密的空間）secret place

填寫表格 fill in a form

落格（獨吞財物）line one's own pockets; take money illegally

資格 qualification

零售價格 retail price

緊緊合格（剛好及格）just pass the examination

價格 price

賤格（下流）bad character; base-minded; miserable wretch; scum

爆格（入屋偷竊）(English) burglary; break in

【案】on³ record

案件 case

案底（作案記錄 / 前科）criminal record
留案底（保存作案記錄）keep a criminal record

案情 details of a case; facts of a case; ins and outs of a crime; record of a case

個案 case

備案 enter into the records; keep on record; put on record; register; serve as a record

答案 answer

罪案 criminal case

審案（審理案件）try a case

竊案 burglary; theft case

【桌】coek³ desk

桌上舞 table dance

桌面 desktop; tabletop

桌球 ①（士碌架）(English) snooker ② billiards
桌球室 billiard room

【桑】song¹ mulberry

桑土 mulberry fields; mulberry grounds

桑田 plantation of mulberry trees

桑拿 sauna
去桑拿 go to have a sauna

桑葉 mulberry leaf

桑圍 mulberry field

桑樹 mulberry tree

【栽】zoi¹ ① plant ② fall

栽培 ① plant and cultivate; tend ② educate; foster; train ③ give special favour; receive special favour

栽植 plant; raise; transplant

栽種 grow; plant

盆栽 potted landscape

【桂】gwai³ cassia

桂子飄香 fragrance of the laurel blossoms fills the air

桂皮 cinnamon bark

桂花 osmanthus
　桂花蚌 osmanthus mussel
　桂花魚 mandarin fish
桂冠 crown of laurels; laurel
桂魚 mandarin fish
桂圓 longan

蘭桂 orchid and cassia

【桃】tou⁴（桃子）peach
桃木 peachwood
桃色 ① peach colour ② symbolic of romance
　　③ illicit love
桃李 ① one's disciples; one's pupils ② peaches and plums
　　③ beauty of a woman
　桃李滿門 have many disciples
桃花 peach blossom
　桃花運 success in romantic adventures
桃紅 light red; pink
桃樹 peach tree

合桃 shelled walnut; walnut
胡桃 walnut
楊桃 star fruit

【桄】gwong¹ coir-palm
桄榔樹——一條心（對愛情專一）love sb with heart and soul; single-minded in love
桄關（門閂）latch

【框】kwaang¹ ①（梗兒）stem ② frame
框形 frame
框架 frame; framework; framing
框框 ① frame ② restriction

方框 rectangular frame
四方框 square frame
門框 door case; doorframe
菜框（菜梗兒）vegetable stem

【桐】tung⁴ paulownia; tung tree
桐油 tung oil
　桐油灰（油灰／膩子）putty
　桐油埕（桐油罐子）a person doing the same job without any change
　　桐油埕裝桐油（桐油罐子無二用）a tung oil canister is merely for holding the tung oil
桐葉 leaves of a tung tree
桐樹 tung tree

【桔】gat¹ orange
桔仔（桔子）small mandarin orange
桔餅 mandarin orange cake

得個桔（甚麼都得不到）come to nothing; draw water with a sieve; end up with nothing; get nothing
跌咗個橙，執番個桔（聊勝於無）half a loaf is better than no bread
籮底桔（賣剩的）leftover

【殊】syu⁴ special
殊不知（沒想到）who could have realised that; who knows that
殊死（生死攸關）desperate; life-and-death
　殊死戰（一決生死的戰鬥）desperate fight; fight to the last man; life-or-death battle
殊異（特異／特別）extraordinary; special

【氣】hei³ air
氣味 odour
氣氛 atmosphere; ambience; climate; mood
氣頂（氣壞了／憋氣）bottle up one's rage
氣勢 grand feeling
氣溫 temperature
　最低氣溫 lowest temperature
　最高氣溫 highest temperature
氣墊船 hovercraft
氣質 grace
氣羅氣喘（喘不過氣）gasp for breath; out of breath

一口氣 a breath; at a breath; at a stretch; at a whack; at one fling; at one go; at one sitting; in one breath; right off the reel; straight off the reed; without a break; without stopping
一肚氣（一肚子氣）a stomachful of grudge; full of complaints; full of grievances; strong emotions
一泡氣（一肚子氣）a stomachful of grudge; full of complaints; full of grievances; strong emotions
一條氣（一口氣）at a breath; at a stretch; at a whack; at one fling; at one go; at one sitting; in one breath; right off the reel; straight off the reed; without a break; without stopping
一啖氣（一口氣）at one breath
一氣（一口氣）at one go; in one breath; without a break
人氣 ① popularity ② liveliness ③ with lots of people
上氣唔接下氣（喘氣）be out of breath; pant
下氣（卑微恭順）humble oneself; humble one's pride
土氣 rustic
士氣 morale

小氣 narrow-minded; petty

小腸氣 hernia

中氣 lung power

丹田之氣 deep breath controlled by the diaphragm

元氣 strength; vigor; vitality

冇志氣 (沒有志氣) without ambition

冇厘神氣 (無精打彩) looking out of sorts

冇氣 ① (喘不過氣來) exhausted; out of breath ② (死了) die; pass away

冇神氣 (無精打彩) looking out of sorts

冇聲氣 ① (沒消息) no news ② (沒希望) beyond hope

冇聲冇氣 ① (沒消息) no news ② (沒希望) beyond hope

天氣 weather

手氣 luck; luck in gambling

火氣 bad temper; temper

牛脾氣 ① bad-tempered ② stubborn

出返啖氣 (出口氣) vent one's spleen on

出氣 ① release gas ② let off steam by losing one's temper; vent one's anger; vent one's disgust on sb; vent one's spleen

出番啖氣 (出口氣) get one's own back

打氣 (鼓勵) give support to

石油氣 butane gas

同一鼻哥窿出氣 (同一鼻孔出氣) breathe through the same nostrils; have the same opinion; in tune with; sing the same tune; talk exactly one like the other

同聲同氣 (意見一致) of the same opinion

名氣 fame; name; reputation

吐氣 give vent to pent-up feelings

吊頸都要透氣 (再忙也要歇一歇) need to have an opportunity to relax no matter how busy one is

好手氣 luck in gambling

好氣 ① (健談) talkative ② (有耐性) patient

好脾氣 good-tempered

好激氣 (很生氣) very angry

好聲好氣 (心平氣和) speak in a kindly manner

有乜聲氣 (有甚麼新聞) any news

有志氣 full of ambition

有神冇氣 (有氣無力) breath is present but vigour is absent; faint; feeble; listless; slack; weak; wearily

有骨氣 have guts; have moral backbone

有啲名氣 (有些名氣) enjoy some reputation

有義氣 have loyalty; loyal

有聲氣 (有希望) there is hope

死死地氣 (勉為其難) reluctant but have no alternative

死死自氣 (勉為其難) reluctant but have no alternative

死死氣 (勉為其難) reluctant but have no alternative

米氣 odour of rice

血氣 ① disposition ② animal spirits; sap; vigour ③ courage and uprightness

低聲下氣 put one's pride in one's pocket

冷氣 air-con; air-conditioning

忍氣 (容忍) restrain one's indignation

志氣 ambition; aspiration; will

烏煙瘴氣 (亂七八糟) chaos

秀氣 ① delicate; elegant; fine ② refined; urbane ③ delicate and well-made

吸氣 breathe in; inhale

我都冇你咁好氣 (我不想再跟你談了) I'm not going to talk to you any more

扯氣 (抽氣) pant; out of breath; short of breath

找晦氣 (算帳) go to blame sb to vent one's spite; seek a quarrel

抖大氣 (深呼吸) take a deep breath

抖唔到氣 (不能呼吸) gasp for breath

抖氣 (歇息) stop for a rest

抖啖氣 (歇息) take a break; take a rest

忳氣 (憋氣) nurse a grievance

走氣 (漏氣) air leakage

谷住度氣 (憋着一肚子氣) bottle up one's rage; contain one's anger; eat the leek

谷氣 (窩氣) bottle up one's rage; in a bad mood

邪氣 evil atmosphere

垂頭餒氣 (垂頭喪氣) become dejected and despondent; blue about the gills; bury one's head in dejection; down at the mouth; down in the chops; down in the dumps; down in the hips; down in the mouth; hang one's head; have one's tail down; in low spirits; in the dumps; look downcast; mope oneself; one's crest falls; out of heart; out of spirits; out of sorts; sing the blues; take the heart out of sb

使乜咁勞氣 (不用這麼動氣) there's no need to lose your temper

受人二分四，做到一條氣 (受僱於人，幹活幹得很累) one has to work hard as an employee in order to get one's pay

受氣 suffer wrong; take the rap

呻氣 (歎氣) heave a sigh; sigh

屈氣 (憋一肚子氣) bottle up one's rage

忿氣 (服氣) be convinced

怪聲怪氣 in an strange voice

戾氣 disharmony; irregularity; perversity

拗氣 (賭氣) quarrel with; in a snit

放聲氣 (放消息) leak out information; spread information

毒氣 poisonous vapour

㧒聲㧒氣 (娘娘腔) effeminate voice

爭一口氣 make a good showing

爭返啖氣 (爭一口氣) stand up for oneself

爭氣 win respect through success

空氣 air

洩氣 ① lose strength ② disappointing; discouraging

長氣 (絮叨／囉嗦) long-winded; talkative

勇氣 courage

咪客氣 (不用客氣) don't mention it; my pleasure; not at all; you're welcome ② don't stand on ceremony; help yourself; make yourself at home

客氣 polite

怨氣 complaints; grievances; resentment

泵氣 (充氣) inflate; pump up

剒住度氣 (生氣卻被逼接受) be compelled to hold back one's rage; be forced to submit to humiliation; be forced to swallow the leek; forced to bear with sth

唔好客氣 ① (不用客氣) don't mention it; my pleasure; not at all; you're welcome ② (不用拘束) don't stand on ceremony; help yourself; make yourself at home

唔使客氣 ① (不用客氣) don't mention it; my pleasure; not at all; you're welcome ② (不用拘束) don't stand on ceremony; help yourself; make yourself at home

唔忿氣 (不服氣) be unconvinced; reluctant to give in; unwilling to submit

唔爭氣 (不爭氣) fail to live up to one's expectation

唔夠氣 (不夠氣) short of breath

唔通氣 (不知趣／不識相) irritate in some ways; not considerate; not to know how to behave in a delicate situation

唔嗅米氣 (不懂人情世故) have no experience of life; unworldly

嗌氣 (絮叨／囉嗦) long-winded

唞大氣 (吸一大口氣) take a deep breath

唞唔倒氣 (不能呼吸) be unable to breathe

唞氣 (呼吸) breathe

氧氣 oxygen

烏煙瘴氣 (亂七八糟) all in a muddle; foul atmosphere; chaos

珠光寶氣 be adorned with brilliant jewels and pearls; be richly bejeweled; bedecked with jewels

益氣 stimulate the vital forces

神氣 spirit

索氣 ① (吸氣) inhale ② (氣喘) short of breath ③ (吃力) exhausting

酒色財氣 wine, sex, money, and power

骨氣 moral backbone

鬥氣 (賭氣) on bad terms; in a snit

鬼咁長氣 (絮叨／囉嗦) long-winded

鬼聲鬼氣 ① (陰陽怪氣) speak in a strange voice; strange-sounding voice ② (裝風洋化) speak with a foreign accent

做到一條氣 (不停地工作) up to the ears in work

夠氣 with good lungs

夠義氣 loyal

夠鑊氣 (炒得香) long duration and high degree of cooking

冤氣 (心懷不滿) nurse a grudge

捱義氣 (賣義氣) do a favour out of loyalty

掬氣 (受氣) choke with resentment

晦氣 (不忿) show sb a querulous and discontent attitude

條氣 (心情) one's mind; one's mood

室住條氣 (插嘴) interrupt someone

通氣 (知趣) do what is expected without being asked

連氣 (一連) at a stretch; in a row; in succession; on end; running

陰聲細氣 (低聲細語) have a buzz of talk; in a whisper; speak softly and tenderly

勞氣 (動氣) angry; fly into a temper

喘氣 gasp; pant

發氣 (發脾氣) blow a fuse; blow a gasket; blow one's fuse; blow one's lid off; blow one's top; blow up; cut up rough; flare up; flay into a rage; fly into a temper; get angry; get one's hackles up; have sb's hackles up; hit the ceiling; let oneself go; lose one's temper; make sb's hackles rise; out of temper; vent one's spleen; with one's hackles rising; with one's hackles up

發脾氣 blow a fuse; blow a gasket; blow one's fuse; blow one's lid off; blow one's top; blow up; cut up rough; flare up; flay into a rage; fly into a temper; get angry; get one's hackles up; have sb's hackles up; hit the ceiling; let oneself go; lose one's temper; make sb's hackles rise; out of temper; vent one's spleen; with one's hackles rising; with one's hackles up

發熱氣 (發燒) suffer from internal heat

脾氣 temper

費事同你嗌氣 (不跟你白費唇舌) won't waste my breath with you

開大啲冷氣 (把空調調高一點) turn up the air-con

開冷氣 turn on the air-con

開細啲冷氣 (把空調調低一點) turn down the air-con

傲氣 air of arrogance; conceit; haughtiness

嗲聲嗲氣 (嬌聲嬌氣) coquettish voice

喺氣 (喘氣) lose one's breath; out of breath; tired out

嘥氣 (喘氣) gasp; pant

新鮮空氣 fresh air

暑氣 heat of summer; scorching heat

煤氣 gas

瑞氣 celestial phenomena auguring peace and prosperity

嘥啲氣 (浪費氣力) fruitless; futile; have no use; in vain; no good; no use; of no use; spend effort in vain; to to purpose; useless

義氣 loyalty

腥氣 (腥味) smell of fish or seafood

運氣 luck

過氣 past one's prime

語氣 ① manner of speaking; tone; tone of voice ② mood

碰吓運氣 (碰運氣) try one's luck

雷氣 (義氣) loyalty to friends

嘥氣 (白費唇舌) waste one's breath

嘥聲壞氣 (白費唇舌) speak to the wind; waste one's breath; waste one's words; whistle down the wind

塵氣 (擺架子) arrogant; put on airs

慳番啖氣 (不值得浪費唇舌) save your breath

滲氣 (絮叨／囉嗦) long-winded; wordy

漏氣 ① gas leakage ② slow in doing things; slow to act

漏煤氣 (泄漏煤氣) gas leakage

颯氣 (心中氣悶) exhausted and frustrated

嘈氣 (磨叨) repeat oneself

撐腰打氣 bolster and pep up; bolster and support; in an effort to back up

暮氣 apathy; lethargy

歎冷氣 (涼冷氣) enjoy air-conditioning

歎氣 sigh

潮氣 (輕佻) flirtatious

熱氣 heat; inflammation

賣魚佬洗身——冇晒聲氣 (沒有消息) there's no news

激氣 (生氣) angry; annoy; feel frustrated

賭氣 do sth in a fit of pique

嘵氣 (吵架) argue

濕氣 humidity; moisture

翳氣 (心中氣悶) be vexed; unhappy

聲氣 (消息) news

譖氣 (能言善道) have the gift of the gab; loquacious; talkative

鑊氣 (火候) duration and degree of cooking

闊客氣 (裝客氣) pretend to be polite

鬥氣 (賭氣) at odds with sb; have the sulks; in a snit

【氧】 joeng⁵ oxygen

氧化 oxidation

氧氣 oxygen

【泰】 taai³ Thai

泰妹 (泰國女孩) Thai girl

泰國 Thailand

　泰國菜 Thai food

泰銖 Thai baht

泰傭 (泰國傭人) Thai maid

【浦】 pou² shore

浦頭 (露面) show up

喪浦 (厮混) hang out; fool aorund

【浪】 long⁶ wave

浪人 ① vagrant ② dismissed courtier ③ jobless person; unemployed

浪口 (漱口) rinse one's mouth

浪子 bum; dissipater; loafer; prodigal; rakehell; rounder; wastrel

浪花 ① spray ② a happy event in one's life

浪費 waste

浪漫 romantic

　浪漫色彩 romantic colours

浪潮 bandwagon; tide; wave

浪濤 billow; great wave; surge; wave

一浪接一浪 waves after waves

到處流浪 wander here and there

流浪 ① roam about; wander ② stray

無風三尺浪 (無風起浪) make touble out of nothing

滑浪 surf

暈車浪 (暈車) carsickness

暈浪 ① (暈頭轉向) feel giddy ② (迷住) be entranced by the beauty of a woman; fall under the spell of a beautiful woman ③ (入迷／神魂顛倒) be entranced by the flattery of a beautiful woman

暈晒大浪 (被某人迷住) fall under sb's spell

暈船浪 (暈船) seasickness

暈機浪 (暈飛機) airsickness

褲浪 (褲檔) crotch of trousers

【浴】 juk⁶ bath

浴巾 bath towel

浴室 bathroom

浴缸 (洗澡盆／浴盆) bath tub

　浸浴缸 (泡澡) take a bath

浴簾 shower curtain

【浮】 fau⁴ ① (露) expose; reveal; surface ② (輕浮) frivolous

浮沉 drift along; now sink, now emerge

浮板 bodyboard

浮泥 (浮土／虛土) surface dust

浮現 appear before one's eyes; drift; emerge; occur; raise

浮華 flashy; foppish rococo; ostentatious; showy; vain

浮雲 floating clouds

浮動 ① drift; float; ripple ② fluctuate; unstable; unsteady ③ float ④ flexibility

浮頭 (露面) make one's appearance; show up

　浮頭魚——死梗 (服毒又上吊——死定了) taking poison and hanging oneself – sure to die

浮雕 boss; cameo; enchase; relief

浮躁 flighty and rash; impetuous; impulsive

輕浮 frivolous

【海】hoi² sea

海上無魚蝦自大 (一葉障目) a dwarf in Lilliput would be thought a superbeing

海水沖倒龍王廟 (自家人不認自家人) not to know the person(s) belong to the same group

海皮 (海岸 / 海濱 / 海邊) seafront; seaside; waterfront

海味 ① (海產) marine products ② dried seafood
　　海味舖 dried seafood shop

海洋 ocean
　　海洋公園 Ocean Park

海洛英 (海洛因) heroin

海軍 navy

海參 sea cucumber

海產 marine products

海豚 dolphin

海傍 (海邊) seafront; seaside

海景 sea view

海港 seaport

海報 poster

海蜇皮 (海蜇) jellyfish

海嘯 tsunami

海膽 sea urchin

海鮮 seafood
　　海鮮炒飯 fried rice with seafood
　　海鮮卷 seafood roll
　　生猛海鮮 fresh seafood
　　游水海鮮 fresh seafood

海邊 seashore; seaside

海關 custom

海灘 beach

海鷗 seagull

人山人海 a sea of faces; huge crowds of people

上海 Shanghai

下海 (從事色情行業) begin one's career as a prostitute

大海 big sea

五湖四海 different places of the country

出海 go out to the sea

地中海 ① Mediterranean Sea ② (禿頭) bald in the middle of the head

侯門似海 (門禁森嚴) the gate of a noble house is like the sea — impassable to the common man; the mansions of the nobility are inaccessible to the common man; the threshold of a noble house is deeper than the sea

航海 navigation; voyage

處女下海 (首次嘗試) the first time a prostitute goes with a client

湖海 lakes and seas

過海 cross the sea

腦海 brain; mind

瞞天過海 do sth secretly

蹈海 (跳海自殺) kill oneself by jumping into the sea

【浸】zam³ soak

浸水 (淹水 / 溺水) flood; submerge

浸吓佢 (把它泡泡) soak it

浸死 (淹死) drown

一浸 (一層) a bed of; a blanket of; a cloak of; a coat of; a curtain of; a deck of; a film of; a flake of; a layer; a layer of; a level of; a line of ; a mantle of; a ring of; a veil of

水浸 (水淹) flood

治治浸浸 (咕咕噥噥) noise of talking; murmur

涼浸浸 (涼涼的) chilly

銀行水浸 (銀行儲備太多) too much money is deposited in the bank

【涉】sip³ involve

涉水 wade; wade into the water

涉及 deal with; involve; refer to; relate to; touch upon

涉足 set foot in

涉嫌 suspect

涉獵 browse; dabble in; do desultory reading; read cursorily

干涉 butt in on sth; butt into sth; interfere in; interfere with; intervene in; meddle in; mess in; nose into; poke one's nose into sth; poke into sth; thrust one's nose into

外力干涉 external intervention

牽涉 involve

隔涉 (偏僻) remote

【消】siu¹ relieve

消化 digest
　　消化藥 digestant

消失 disappear

消防 fire-fighting
　　消防局 fire station
　　消防車 fire-engine
　　消防員 fireman
　　消防喉 fire hose

消炎 anti-inflammatory

消夜 (夜宵 / 夜餐) night snack

消毒 disinfect; sterilise
　　消毒藥膏 antiseptic cream

消息 news
　消息靈通 well-informed
　內部消息 inside information
　泄漏消息 leak out the news
　壞消息 bad news
消耗 consumption
消費 spending
　消費力 spending power
　　內部消費力 domestic spending power
　最低消費 minimum charge
消滯 (消食) relieve stagnation
消遣 pastime

抵消 make even
取消 abandon; abolish; abrogate; annul; be cleared of; be
　edged out by; call off; cancel; cancellation; cross out;
　deprive sb of; discard; dispense with; do away with;
　liquidate; negate; nullify; obliterate; off; put an end to;
　reject; relinquish; remove; renounce; repeal; repudiate;
　rescind; revoke; scrap; strip of; write off

【涎】jin⁴ saliva

涎沫 saliva

垂涎 covet; drool over; gloat over; hanker after; slaver over
痰涎 expectoration; phlegm spittle

【涕】tai³ snivel

涕泣 cry in tears
涕淚 tears
涕零 shed tears

泣涕 come to tears for sorrow; weep
鼻涕 nasal discharge

【烏】wu¹ black; dark

烏吓烏吓 (傻乎乎) dim-witted
烏狗得食，白狗當災 carry the can
烏眉 (睡覺) sleep
　烏眉恰睡 (昏昏欲睡) sleepy; drowsy
烏捋捋 (烏亮 / 烏墨發亮) black and shiny
烏啄啄 ① (茫無所知) at a complete loss; entirely
　ignorant; in the dark ② (稀裏糊塗) muddled
烏蛇蛇 ① (茫無所知) at a complete loss; entirely
　ignorant; in the dark ② (稀裏糊塗) muddled
烏喱馬扠 (亂七八糟) illegible and sloppy; in a mess
烏喱單刀 (一塌糊塗 / 烏七八糟 / 亂七八糟) chaotic;
　disorder; get everything mixed up; in a mess; muddled
烏煙瘴氣 (亂七八糟) all in a muddle; foul atmosphere; chaos

烏賊 (墨魚) cuttlefish
烏鴉 crow
　烏鴉嘴 (壞事一說就靈的臭嘴) whammy
　天下烏鴉一樣黑 all crows are equally black; all crows
　　under the sun are black; crows are black all the world
　　over; devils everywhere are devils of the same kind;
　　evil people are bad all over the world; in every country
　　dogs bit; they are all bad
烏燈黑火 (一片漆黑，黑燈瞎火) completely dark;
　pitch-dark
烏頭 (鯔) grey mullet
烏龍 ① (昏庸) muddle-headed ② (糊塗) absent-minded
　③ (烏龍茶) Oolong tea
　烏龍王 (糊塗蟲) addle-brained; airhead; muddled
　　person; nitwit
　擺烏龍 ① (給搞糊塗了) get confused ② (弄錯 / 做錯)
　　confuse black and white; make a mistake
烏龜 ① tortoise ② (皮條客) pimp; procure for prostitutes
　縮頭烏龜 (怕死鬼) coward
　縮頭龜 (怕死鬼) coward
烏蠅 (蒼蠅) fly
　烏蠅拍 (蒼蠅拍) flyswatter; swatter
　烏蠅摟馬尾——一拍兩散 (兩敗俱傷) smash up a
　　monopoly; both sides suffer
　冇頭烏蠅 (亂碰亂闖) act helter-skelter
　打烏蠅 ① (拍蒼蠅) flap a fly; swat a fly ② (拘捕低級官
　　員) arrest the low-ranking officials
　拍烏蠅 ① (拍蒼蠅) flap a fly; swat a fly ② (生意冷淡)
　　business is bad; have a dull market; have no business
　拍晒烏蠅 (生意很差) have absolutely no business
　盲頭烏蠅 (無頭蒼蠅) a bull in a china shop; act in a
　　chaotic manner

丫烏 (樣子醜陋的人) ugly devil
吔吔烏 (差勁) very bad

【烈】lit⁶ intense

烈士 martyr
烈日 burning sun; scorching sun
烈性 strong; violent
　烈性酒 strong liquor

壯烈 brave; couraeous; heroic; on a grand and spectacular
　scale
劇烈 acute; fierce; severe; violent
興高采烈 above oneself; as jolly as a sandboy; blithe;
　boisterous; buoyant; cheerful; cheery; effervescence;
　elated; elated and overjoyed; excited; exhilarated;
　expansive; exultant; feel one's oats; full of beans; full of

spirits and elated; go into raptures; have a hectic time; in a bright humour; in buoyant spirits; in exuberant spirits; in good form; in good spirits; in great delight; in great spirits; in high glee; in high spirits; in one's altitudes; in the pride of one's heart; joyful bustle; jubilant; on the high ropes; on top of the world; on wings; sparkling with joy; tails up; with great gusto; with rapturous joy

頭崩額烈 (焦頭爛額) be scorched by the flames; badly battered; beat sb's head off; be bruised and battered; be scorched and burned; in a sorry plight; in a terrible fix; smash heads and scorch brows; utterly exhausted from overwork

轟轟烈烈 achieve great things

【烊】 joeng⁴ melt
烊金 (金屬溶液) molten metal

打烊 (關店門) finish business

【烤】 haau¹ roasted
烤火 warm oneself by a fire
烤肉 roast meat
烤架 broiler; gridiron
烤餅 baked cake
烤箱 oven
烤鴨 roasted duck
　　烤鴨條 roasted duck strips
烤爐 brazier; grill; oven; roaster

【焓】 saap³ boil
焓蛋 (煮蛋) boiled egg
焓熟狗頭 (煮熟的狗頭——咧嘴逢迎) smiling stupidly

白焓 (水煮) boil without seasoning
慶焓焓 ① (燒熱) burning hot ② (非常生氣) very angry
鞋焓焓 (粗糙) coarse

【爹】 de¹ dad; father; pa
爹哋 (父親 / 爸爸) daddy
爹媽 (爹娘) father and mother

收爹 (閉嘴) shut up
(沙爹 / 沙嗲) satay; satay sauce

【特】 dak⁶ exceptional
特大 extra large
特別 especial; special
　　特別係 (特別是) especially
特長 extra long

特登 ① (故意) deliberately; intentionally; on purpose ② (專門 / 特地 / 特意) specially
特細 (特小) extra small
特價 special price

打特 (心感愕然) be startled
黑古勒特 (黑不溜秋) very dark
鬍鬚勒特 (滿臉鬍子) heavy-bearded

【狼】 long⁴ ① wolf ② (兇狼 / 狠) ferocious ③ (太貪心) too covetous
狼忙 (趕忙) in a hurry; in a hurry-skurry
狼死 (兇狠) unscrupulous
狼吻 (熱烈擁吻) smooch
狼毒 (狠毒) atrocious; brutal; cruel; malicious; venomous; vicious
狼胎 (兇狠 / 兇蠻 / 蠻橫) ferocious; ferocious and relentless; fierce
狼過華秀隻狗 (非常兇猛) very ferocious
狼膽 (狼子野心) fierce guts

色狼 sex maniac
勢兇夾狼 (野心大) act outrageously and ferociously; rapacious ambition

【狷】 gyun³ (鑽) get into
狷落牀下底 (鑽到牀底下) get into the bottom of the bed

【狸】 lei⁴ fox

老狐狸 crafty old fox; crafty scoundrel; cunning old person
果子狸 masked civet
狐狸 fox

【珠】 zyu¹ pearl
珠末 (珍珠粉) pearl powder
珠淚 (淚珠) tears
珠算 calculation with an abacus; operation on the abacus; reckoning by the abacus
珠聯璧合 excellent combination; excellent match; happy combination; perfect pair; strings of pearls and girdles of jade
珠璣 exquisite wording of a piece of writing; gems; graceful writings; pearls
珠寶 jewellery
　　珠寶店 jewellery shop
　　珠寶首飾 jewellery, accessories, and adornments
　　珠光寶氣 be adorned with brilliant jewels and pearls; be richly bejeweled; bedecked with jewels

一粒珠 (一粒珍珠) a pearl

禾稈冚珍珠 (財不露白) hide one's true wealth; rich people pretending to be poor

吐明珠 (刷牙) brush the teeth

有眼無珠 (沒長眼珠子) blind; misvalue sb

耳珠 (耳垂) earlobe

波珠 (滾珠) ball

珍珠 pearl

面珠 (臉蛋) face

啜面珠 (親臉蛋) kiss the face

淚珠 teardrops

眼珠 (眼球) pupils of the eyes

雪珠 (霰) soft hail; graupel

睛珠 (眼球) eyeball; pupil of the eye

養珠 (養殖珍珠) cultured pearl

攪珠 (抽獎) lottery

【班】 baan¹ ① class ② deploy

班房 (教室 / 課室) classroom

班馬 (請救兵) call for back up; call for more persons; call more people to come and help; gang up with more persons

班戟 (薄餅) (English) pancake

班機 (航班) scheduled flight

一班 a class of; a group of; a squad of; a troupe of

下班 come off work; go off work; knock off

大班 (老闆) boss

未夠班 (不夠格) not good enough

加班 work overtime

同班 classmate

早班 morning shift

成班 (整班) the whole group

值班 on duty; on the shift; on watch

留班 (留級) fail to go up to the next grade; stay down; stay in the same grade

航班 flight

夠班 (夠格) up to the right level

超班 (實力超羣) extremely clever; outclass

跟班 (手下) follower

輪班 in shifts; on duty by turn

臨班 (留級) repeat a year at school

【畜】 cuk¹ (畜牲) animal

畜牧 domestic animals

六畜 six domestic animals

牲畜 domestic animals

【留】 lau⁴ remain; stay

留心 be careful; be cautious; bear in mind; pay attention to; take care; take heed; take note

留低 (留下) stay behind

留念 keep for commemoration

作為留念 as a souvenir; keep as a keepsake

留神 be careful; look out; pay attention; take care

留起 reserve

留班 (留級) fail to go up to the next grade; stay down; stay in the same grade

留堂 (留校) get detention; stay behind after class; stay behind after school

留得青山在，哪怕有柴燒 (留得青山在，不怕沒柴燒) life is safe and gains will surely be safe; where there is life there is hope

留番 (留下) leave behind

留番啖氣暖吓肚 (不白費唇舌) button up one's mouth

留番嚟攝灶罅 (女兒嫁不出去，留她在家無所用之) let one's own daughter stay unmarried

留意 (注意) pay attention to

留學 study abroad

留醫 (住醫院) be hospitalised; in hospital

留辮 (留辮子) wear plaits

留戀 yearn

留 message (留信息) left a message

一嚿留 (一團) a lump

不留 all along; consistently; frequently; for always

扣留 be caught and detained by police

拘留 detain; detention

逗留 stay; stick around; stop

羈留 detain; hold in custody

【疹】 can² rashes

疹子 measles

出疹 (出疹子 / 出麻疹) suffer from measles

麻疹 measles

【疼】 tang⁴ ① ache; hurt ② be fond of; dote on

疼錫 (疼愛) love dearly

【疾】 zat⁶ ① (疾病) disease; illness; suffering ② detest; hate ③ fast; quick

疾苦 difficulties; hardships; sufferings

疾病 illness

常見疾病 common disease

痢疾 dysentery

【病】beng⁶ ① (生病) be ill; be sick ② (疾病) disease; illness

病字頭 (病字旁／病當兒) the "sickness" (病) radical

病毒 virus

病鬼 sickly person

病假 sick leave

　　請病假 take sick leave

病患 illness

病貓 (病包兒／病鬼) sickly person

大病 serious illness

小毛病 glitch

心肺病 cardiac-pulmonary disease

心病 (不和) sore point; secret trouble

心臟病 heart disease

毛病 ① breakdown ② defect; fault; mistake; shortcoming ③ bad habit ④ illness

牙周病 periodontal disease; periodonotosis

年老多病 old and be troubled by illness

死於愛滋病 die of AIDS

肝病 hepatosis; live ailment

臥病 be confined to bed; be laid up; bedridden on account of illness

思鄉病 homesickness

染病 be infected with a disese; catch a disease; catch an illness; fall ill; get infected

疾病 illness

神經病 mental disease

起病 come on

得閒死，唔得閒病 (忙到沒空生病) as busy as one can possibly be; awfully busy; have one's hands full; have one's work cut out; have too much on one's plate; not to have a moment one can call one's own; terribly busy; up to one's ears in work; up to one's eyes in work; up to one's neck in work

常見疾病 common disease

患病 get ill; get sick; suffer from an illness

腎病 kidney disease; nephralgia

睇病 ① (看醫生) consult a doctor; go to see a doctor; see a doctor ② (看病人) see a patient

診病 diagnose a disease

傳染病 infectious disease

愛滋病 AIDS

暗病 sexual disease

精神病 mental disease; psychosis

糖尿病 diabetes

癌病 cancer

醫病 (治病) cure the sickness; treat an ailment; treat a disease

【症】zing³ disease; illness

症狀 symptom

症候 ① disease ② symptom

大熱症 typhoid fever

抑鬱症 depression; melancholia

花粉症 hay fever

急症 accident and emergency

睇街症 (到門診部看病) see a doctor at a government hospital

絕症 incurable disease; terminal illness

街症 (門診部) outpatient service

頑症 chronic disease

癌症 cancer

【疵】ci¹ defect; flaw

疵品 (瑕疵品) inferior work

疵點 (瑕疵) blemish; defect; fault; flaw; weak spot

吹毛求疵 blow aside the fur to seek for faults; blow upon the hair trying to discover a mole; captious; carp; censorious; fastidious; faultfinding; find faults deliberately; find faults with; find quarrel in a straw; hair-splitting; hypercritical; nitpick; persnickety; pettifogging; pick flaws; pick holes in; pick on sth to find fault with; picky; pull sth to pieces; split hair; squeamish; very fastidious

【痱】fei² heat rash

痱子 heat rash

出熱痱 (長熱痱) have prickly heat

生熱痱 (長熱痱) have prickly heat

發熱痱 (長熱痱) have prickly heat

熱痱 heat rash; heat spot; prickly heat

癲痱 (瘋癲) crazy

癲癲痱痱 (瘋瘋癲癲) crazy

【益】jek¹ benefit

益友 beneficial friends; helping friends; useful friends

益胃 reinforce one's stomach; tonify one's stomach

益氣 stimulate the vital forces

益處 advantage; benefit

益發 all the more; ever more; increasingly more and more

益智 grow in intelligence

益壽 lengthen one's life

延年益壽 extend one's years; lengthen one's life; prolong life; promise longevity

益蟲 beneficial insect

切身利益 one's immediate interests; one's vital interests

冇益 (沒好處) do no good; not beneficial

有益 advantageous

利益 benefit; interest

局部利益 partial and local interests

既得利益 vested interests

個人利益 personal benefit

徒勞無益 all to no purpose; come to naught; end in smoke; fish in the air; flog a dead horse; futile; hold a candle to the sun; lash the waves; of no avail; of no purpose; plough the air; plough the sand; shoe a goose; sow beans in the wind; weave a rope of sand; work in vain

效益 achievements; beneficial result; benefit; effectiveness

國家利益 country interest

得益 benefit from

【眠】min⁴ sleep

眠目 close one's eyes
眠目靜思 close the eyes and meditate

失眠 insomnia

【眨】zaap³ (閃) wink

眨吓雙眼 (眨眼) make a wink; wink at sb

眨吓眨吓 (一閃一閃) wink

眨吓眼 (一眨眼) in a wink

眨眨吓 (一眨一眨) twinkle

眼眨眨 (眨眼) blink one's eyes

【真】zan¹ real

真人 the person himself/herself
真人表演 live show

真正 real

真定假 true or false

真空 (不穿內衣物) pantiless
真空上陣 (不穿內衣穿上裸露的衣服) wear revealing clothes; pantiless

真金 real gold; real money
真金不怕洪爐火，石獅不怕雨滂沱 (真金不怕火煉) a person of integrity can stand severe tests; true blue will never stain
真金白銀 real money

真係 (真是) really

真係巴閉 (真了不得) it's really remarkable

真係冇眼睇 (真看不下去) can't continue to watch

真係叻 (真棒) you're great

真係折墮 (真造孽) it's really evil

真係奇嘞 (真怪) very strange

真係啱喇 (真巧) what a coincidence

真係慘嘞 (真夠受的) it's really hard to bear

真相 inside story; truth
了解真相 know the facts

均真 (公私分明) fair-minded

弄假成真 what was make-believe has become reality

果真 (當真) if indeed; really

珍珠都無咁真 (真實無誤) it's genuine; it's really genuine; it's really real; one hundred per-cent true

美夢成真 a fond dream comes true

純真 genuine; pure; sincere; unsophisticated

睇真 (看清楚) see clearly

睇唔真 (看不清楚) can't see clearly

睇得真 (看得清楚) can see clearly

稟神都冇句真 (老是說謊) live a lie

傳真 fax

圖文傳真 fax line

認真 seriously

寫真 photographs of scantily clad women

夢想成真 a dream come true; realise one's dream

講真 (說真) to say the truth

嚟真 (認真) serious; not kidding

【睷】laap⁸ glance

睷一眼 (瞟一眼) take a glance

【矩】geoi² regulation

矩形 rectangle; rectangular

老規矩 convention; follow the same old practice; old practices; old rules and regulations; the old way of doing things

規矩 regulation

【砧】zam¹ anvil

砧板 chopping block

【破】po³ break; chop

破口 ① cut ② get a cut
破口大罵 abuse roundly; bawl out abuse; curse freely; give vent to a torrent of abuse; heap abuse on; hurl all kinds of abuse against; let loose a flood of abuse; pour out a whole ocean of abuse over; pour out torrents of

abuse; raise hail Columbia; rave widely against; shout abuse; swear home; swear like a trooper; swear one's way through swear one's way through a stone wall; swear through a two-inch board; vociferate oaths

破天荒 (史無前例) occur for the first time; take the extraordinary step; unheard of; unprecedented

破竹 irresistible force
　勢如破竹 advance with irresistible force; carry all before one; carry everything before one; carry the world before one; like a hot knife cutting through butter; like splitting a bamboo; meet with no resistance; push forward from victory to victory; push onward with overwhelming momentum; with irresistible force; without a hitch

破例 break a rule; make an exception; stretch a point; stretch the rules; waive a rule

破除 abolish; break with; do away with; eradicate; get rid of

破柴 (劈柴) chop firewood

破財 lose money
　破財擋災 give money in the hope of being freed from trouble; suffer unexpected personal financial losses to remove misfortune

破產 ① bankrupt; become impoverished; become insolvent; go bankrupt; go broke; go into bankruptcy; go to the wall ② come to naught; fall through; wrecked

破碎 ① broken; tattered ② break into pieces; crush; smash sth into pieces; tear into shreds

破綻 ① burst seam ② flaw; weak point
　破綻百出 full of flaws; full of holes; full of loopholes; ragged; rags and tatters

破壞 damage; decompose; destroy; do damage to; failure; wreck

破舊 dilapidated; old and shabby; outdated; worn-out
　破舊立新 abolish the old and build up the new; destroy the old and establish the new; discard the old and create sth new; disrupt the old roder and establish a new one; eradicate the old and foster the new; the destruction of the old and the establishing of the new

破爛 ① dilapidated; ragged; tattered; worn-out ② junk; scrap

突破 breakthrough
撕破 rip; tear

【砵】but³ bowl

打爛齋砵 (違背宗旨 / 破了戒) break one's fast

【砣】to⁴ scale

公不離婆，秤不離砣 (形影不離) husbands are in pair with wives, just like sliding weights are inseparable from scales

秤砣 scale

【祐】jau⁶ bless
祐助 aid; assist; help

保祐 bless

【祖】zou² ancestor
祖先 ancestor
祖家 (老家) one's native place; one's old home
祖國 motherland

二世祖 (紈絝子弟) big-spending son; fop
叔祖 granduncle; one's grandfather's younger brother

【祝】zuk¹ wish
祝酒 drink a toast; toast
祝捷 celebrate a victory
祝壽 celebrate sb's birthday; offer birthday congratulations; wish sb a happy birthday
祝賀 congratulate; felicitate
祝福 benediction; blessing; wish happiness to
祝願 wish

慶祝 celebrate
廟祝 temple attendant in charge of incense and religious service
熱烈慶祝 grandly celebrate

【神】san⁴ spirit
神女 (妓女) prostitute
神不守舍 (心不在焉) absence of mind; absent-minded; in an absent way; in brown study; in the clouds; inattentive; jump the track; nobody home; one's heart is no longer in it; one's mind is not in it; one's mind is occupied with other things; one's wits go woolgathering; out to lunch; preoccupied with sth else; with an abstracted air; with one's mind wandering; with one's thoughts elsewhere; woolgathering
神心 (虔誠) devout; pious
神化 (古怪) strange
　神神化化 (古裏古怪) not quite right in the mind; silly and curious; strange
神父 father

神主牌 (神主／神位／牌位) memorial tablet; spirit tablet
　神主牌都會郁 (出乎意料的大幸運) meet with one's
　　fortune
　神主牌都會擰轉面 (愧對先人) once one becomes a
　　leper, one brings disgrace on one's fore-fathers
神仙 fairy
　神仙肚 (不用吃飯也不餓的肚子) sb who can go without
　　food
　生神仙 (活神仙／算命師傅) fortune-telling person
神咗 (壞了) be out of order
神前桔——陰乾 (金錢愈積愈少) (said of money)
　become less and less slowly; the longer the sum of
　money is saved, the smaller and smaller it becomes
神枱貓屎——神憎鬼厭 (人人討厭) accused target;
　person who is hated by all
神氣 expression
　冇厘神氣 (無精打彩) look out of sorts
　冇神氣 (無精打彩) look out of sorts
　有神冇氣 (有氣無力) breath is present but vigour is
　　absent; faint; feeble; listless; slack; weak; wearily
神神哋 (發瘋) not right in the mind
　神神哋經 (發瘋) not right in the mind
神秘 mysterious
神鬼 gods and ghosts
　神不知鬼不覺 (不為人知) without anybody knowing it
　神出鬼沒 sb who keeps appearing and then disappearing
　神推鬼㧬 (神差鬼使) in spite of oneself
　神憎鬼厭 (人人討厭) accused target; person who is
　　hated by all
　呃神騙鬼 (行騙) lure sb into a trap
神棍 (騙子) fraud
神經 ① nerve ② (發瘋) crazy; insane
　神經佬 (瘋子) crazy man; madman; mentally ill person
　神經衰弱 nervous breakdown
　神經病 (精神病) mental disease
　神神經經 (發瘋) crazy
　發神經 (發瘋) go berserk; go crazy
神魂顛倒 be out of one's head
神鏡 (變焦鏡頭) zoom lens

入屋叫人，入廟拜神 (入鄉隨俗) do whatever you're
　supposed to do; do in Rome as the Romans do
女神 goddess
心神 mood; state of mind
冇厘精神 (沒精打彩) a cup too low; disheartened; dispirited
　and discouraged; have a fit of blues; in low spirits; in the
　blues; in the dumps; lackadaisical; listless; out of humour;
　out of sorts; out of spirits; seedy; spiritless; with little
　enthusiasm; with the wind taken out of one's sails

手神 (手氣) one's luck
日頭唔好講人，夜晚唔好講神 (一說曹操，曹操就到) talk
　of the devil and he will appear
毛神神 (毛茸茸) very hairy
失驚無神 (冷不防) be seized with panic
打醒十二個精神 (抖擻精神) raise one's spirits
有食神 (有口福) lucky to have sth nice to eat
夜遊神 (夜貓子) night owl
拜神 worship the Buddha
食神 (口福) gourmet's luck; luck in having nice food; the
　luck to get sth nice to eat
唔係幾精神 (不太精神) not feel well
唔夠精神 (不太精神) not energetic enough
唔精神 (不精神) not feel well; sick; unwell
留神 be careful; look out; pay attention; take care
財神 God of Wealth
捉用神 (揣測) make a guess at sth
捉錯用神 (誤會別人的用意) misunderstand sb's intention
衰神 (倒霉蛋) jinx
財可通神 money makes the mare go; money talks
祭灶拜神 offer to the god of kitchen and worship the Buddha
提神 (振奮精神) raise one's spirit; refresh
貼錯門神 (反貼門神——意見相左) at odds with each other;
　become hostile; can't get along with each other
黑面神 (臭臉的人) person with an angry face
笡箕冚鬼一窩神 (蛇鼠一窩) be hand and glove with each
　other
解渴提神 quench one's thirst and raise one's spirit
團隊精神 team spirit
精神 spirit
撞手神 (碰手氣) ① have a stroke of luck; try one's luck
　② try one's luck in gambling
瘟神 god of plague
賭神 god of gamblers
學神 (初學開車的人) learner-driver
醒神 (神采奕奕) brighten up
龍馬精神 ① as vigorous as a dragon or a horse ② wish you
　good health
還神 (酬神) redeem a vow to a god
鶴神 (壞蛋) damn guy

【崇】seoi⁶ afflict; haunt

鬼鬼祟祟 look sneaky

【秘】bei³ private; secret
秘書 secretary
　一個秘書 a secretary
秘密 secret

保守秘密 keep a secret
洩露秘密 disclose a secret
秘撈（兼職／賺外快）do part-time job; moonlight

便秘 constipation
神秘 mysterious

【租】zou¹ rent
租用 rent
租金 rent
租客（房客）tenant
租屋（租房子）rent a room
租約 tenancy agreement
租樓（租房子）rent a room

出租 for rent; to let
交租 pay the rent
房租 rent
屋租 rent
起租（加租）increase the rent
鋪租 rent

【秧】joeng¹ seedling
秧歌 songs sung when transplanting rice seedlings

禾秧 rice seedlings; rice shoot
搣秧（拔秧）pull up seedlings

【秤】cing³ ① weigh ②（提）take
秤砣 scale

一把秤 a steelyard
未夠秤（未成年）not old enough
呃秤（缺斤短兩）short weight
抽秤（挑剔）nit-picking
重秤（份量重）weigh heavy
唔夠秤（未成年）not old enough
隔夜素馨釐釐戥秤（貴細藥材得細細稱量）the outmoded are sometimes outvalued

【窄】zaak³（狹窄）cramped; narrow
窄小 small and narrow
窄巷 narrow lane
窄門 narrow door

心胸狹窄 narrow-minded
地方淺窄 the room is too small
冤家路窄（狹路相逢）enemies are bound to meet
淺窄 cramped; narrow; small

眼闊肚窄（眼饞肚飽）bite off more than one can chew

【站】zaam⁶ station; stop
站立 on one's feet; stand
站長 head of a station

小巴站 minibus station
巴士站 bus stop
巴士總站 bus terminal
水費站（洗手間）toilet
火車站 train station
地鐵站 MTR (Mass Transit Railway) station
孖站（共站）co-station
行去巴士站（走去巴士站）walk to the bus stop
庇護站（臨時庇護所）temporary shelter
尾站（總站）bus terminal
投票站 polling station
垃圾站 waste collection point
的士站 taxi stand
油站 filling station; gas station; petrol station
近地鐵站 close to the MTR station
飛站（過站）fail to stop at the bus stop
埋站（靠站）enter the station
票站 polling station
發電站 ①（發電廠）power station ②（賣弄風騷的女性）flirtatious woman
電車站 tram stop
網站 website
頭站（起點站）origin station
總站 terminal; terminal station; terminus
纜車站 ① cable car station ② peak tram station

【笆】baa¹ bamboo fence
笆簍 basket

雪笆 (English) sorbet
籬笆 bamboo fence; hedge; hurdle; wattle

【笈】kap¹ case

藤笈 rattan case

【笑】siu³ smile
笑口 in smile
　笑口吟吟（笑容滿面）a face radiating with smiles; a smile lit up one's face; all smiles; grin from ear to ear; have a broad smile on one's face; with a beaming face; with a face all smiles
　笑口常開 ①（笑顏常開）beam with smiles at all times

② may you be happy all the time

笑口騎騎（嬉皮笑臉）behave in a noisy, gay and boisterous manner; grinning and smiling; grinning cheekily; grinning mischievously; smiling and grimacing; with a cunning smile; with an oily smile

笑口噬噬（張開嘴笑）roar with laughter; uproarious laughter

笑大人個口（貽笑大方）to be laughed at

笑笑口 ①（說笑）joking ②（微微笑）with a smiling face
笑笑口話（笑着說）say with a smile

笑吓（笑一笑）smile

笑到 laugh until

笑到見牙唔見眼（開懷大笑）laugh happily; grin from ear to ear

笑到肚刺（笑疼了肚子）laugh one's head off

笑到轆地（捧腹大笑）burst out laughing; laugh your head off

笑哈哈 laugh

笑容 smile on one's face
面帶笑容 have a smile on one's face

笑盈盈 smile broadly

笑笑哋（面帶笑容）with smiles

笑淫淫（不懷好意地笑）leer

笑眯眯（眯着眼睛笑）narrow one's eyes into a smile

笑話 joke

笑騎騎（笑哈哈）giggle; laugh heartily; with a laugh

笑爆嘴（咧嘴大笑）laugh loudly

皮笑肉不笑 put on a false smile; insincere smile

奸笑 sinister smile

有講有笑 ①（有說有笑）chat and laugh; chattering and laughing; have a pleasant talk together; talking and laughing ②（相處融洽）get along with

你講笑（你開玩笑）you're kidding

見笑 ①（被人取笑）incur ridicule ②（笑話）laugh at

哄堂大笑 a volley of laughter; burst into a guffaw; burst into uproarious laughter; fall about laughing; laugh uproariously; roar with laughter; the whole room bursts out laughing; the whole room rocks with laughter

哈哈大笑 burst into hearty laughter; burst out into a fit of violent laughter; give a loud guffaw; laugh heartily; roar with laughter

哭笑（又哭又笑）cry and laugh

唥都唔笑（木訥寡言）over-serious

訕笑 laugh; slander; sneer

偷笑 chuckle; laugh behind sb's back; laugh in one's heart; laugh in one's sleeve; laugh up one's sleeve; snicker; snigger

得啖笑 ①（純娛樂）just for fun ②（一無所獲）gain nothing

陰陰笑（偷笑）smile to oneself privately

陰陰嘴笑（偷笑）smile to oneself privately; smirk

揞住嘴嚟笑（掩口而笑）laugh at sb in one's sleeve

棟篤笑（單口喜劇）stand-up comedy

微笑 smile

搞笑（逗人發笑）joke

嘲笑 tease

賣笑（賣淫）work as a prostitute

賺到笑（賺大錢）earn lots of money

講笑 ①（開玩笑 / 說笑 / 說着玩兒）joke; kidding; tease ②（邊聊邊笑）chatting and laughing

攪笑（逗人發笑）joke

【笋】seon² bamboo shoot

笋工（夢寐以求的工作）dream job

笋尖 tips of bamboo shoots

笋嘢（好東西）good things

【粉】fan² ① powder ② rice noodles

粉皮 bean jelly sheet

粉板字——唔啱就抹咗佢（忘掉不愉快）forget it if what is said is incorrect

粉果 shrimp and bamboo shoot dumpling
潮州粉果 shrimp and bamboo shoot dumpling in Chiu Chow style

粉紅色 pink

粉絲 ①（粉絲）bean vermicelli ②（⋯迷 / 狂熱愛好者 / 熱烈崇拜者）(English) fans

粉擦（板擦 / 粉筆刷 / 黑板擦）eraser

叉燒腸粉 steamed rice roll with barbeque pork

中筋麵粉 plain flour

火腿通粉（火腿通心粉）macaroni with ham

牛肉腸粉 steamed rice roll with beef

古月粉（胡椒粉）ground pepper

奶粉 dried milk; milk powder; powdered milk

生粉 corn flour

白粉（海洛因 / 海洛英）heroin

米粉 rice vermicelli

河粉 flat rice noodles

泡打粉（發酵粉 / 發粉）baking powder

豆粉（澱粉）starch

走粉（走私海洛因）smuggle heroin

芡粉（澱粉）starch

洗粉（洗衣粉）laundry detergent; washing powder

胡椒粉 pepper

食白粉（服用海洛因）take heroin

脂粉（化粧品）cosmetics

梳打粉（發酵粉 / 發粉）baking powder

梘粉（洗衣粉）detergent; soap powder; washing powder
爽身粉（滑石粉）talcum powder
涼粉 bean jelly
通心粉（通心麵）macaroni
粟米粉（玉米粉 / 玉米澱粉 / 粟粉）cornflour
粟粉（玉米粉 / 玉米澱粉 / 粟粉）corn starch
塗脂抹粉 apply cosmetics; apply facial makeup; apply power and paint; deck oneself out; deck up; make up; paint and powder oneself
意大利粉（意大利麵）spaghetti
腸粉 steamed rice roll
搽粉（塗粉）apply powder to one's face
搽脂蕩粉（塗脂抹粉）apply powder
搓粉（揉麵粉 / 擀麵團）knead the flour
搓麵粉（揉麵粉 / 擀麵團）knead the flour
澱粉 starch
嬰兒爽身粉 baby powder
蟹粉 crab roe
蘇打粉（發酵粉 / 發粉）baking soda
麵粉 flour
鷹粟粉（玉米粉 / 玉米澱粉 / 粟粉）starch

【粑】baa¹ cake

鍋粑（鍋巴 / 米鍋巴）puff rice

【紋】man⁴ lines; veins

紋身（刺青）tattoo
紋路（條理）orderliness
　　有紋路（有條理）in good order

手紋（掌紋）palm print
扭紋（不服從 / 不聽話 / 頑皮）disobedient; insubordinate; peevish
指紋 fingerprint
魚尾紋（皺紋眼睛）wrinkles around the eyes
裂紋 crack; crackle

【紐】nau² New Zealand

紐元（紐西蘭元 / 紐西蘭幣）New Zealand dollar
紐帶 bond; link; tie

【純】seon⁴ pure

純正 pure
純良 simple and honest
純真 genuine; pure; sincere; unsophisticated
純種 pure breed
純潔 chaste; clean and honest; pure; virginal
純熟 fluent; practiced; skilful; well versed

純樸 honest; simple; unsophisticated
純屬 purely; simply

【紗】saa¹ gauze

紗十（棉紗頭）cotton waste
紗布 gauge
紗紙（證書 / 文憑）certificate; diploma

幼紗（細紗）fine thread

【紙】zi² paper

紙巾（手巾紙 / 面紙）tissue; tissue paper
　　一包紙巾 a packet of tissue paper
　　濕紙巾（濕面紙）wet tissue; wipe
紙皮（馬糞紙）straw board
　　紙皮石（馬賽克）mosaic
　　紙皮箱 carton box
紙板 cardboard
紙紮下扒——口輕輕（下巴掛鈴鐺——想（響）到哪說到哪兒）talk at random
紙袋 paper bag
紙鷂（風箏）kite
　　放紙鷂（放風箏）fly a kite

一沓銀紙（一堆鈔票 / 一疊鈔票）a pile of banknotes
一張紙 a sheet of paper
一張報紙（一份報章）a newspaper
一毫紙（一毛錢）ten cents
人情薄過紙（人情如紙薄）human decency is rare in relationships between people
入伙紙（入住證明書）occupation permit; Certificate of Compliance
仄紙（支票）cheque
冇散紙（沒有碎銀 / 沒有小硬幣 / 沒有零錢）have no small notes
出水紙（提貨單）bill of lading
出世紙（出生證明）birth certificate
卡紙（紙板 / 硬紙板）cardboard
打針紙（注射記錄 / 注射證明）injection record
瓦通紙（瓦楞紙）corrugated paper
再造紙（再生紙）recycled paper
印水紙 waterjet paper
吸水紙 absorbent paper
沙紙 ① sand paper ②（證書 / 成績合格證書 / 畢業證書）certificate
招紙（商標標籤）trademark tag
金銀衣紙（冥錢 / 冥鏹）paper gold; silver and clothes for burning to the deceased or gods
信紙 letter paper

封箱膠紙 duct tape
律師紙 (法律證明書) legal certificate
相紙 (照相紙) photo paper
針紙 (接種證明書) vaccination certificate
陰司紙 (冥錢 / 冥鏹 / 陰司錢) nether banknotes
報紙 (報章) newspaper
廁紙 (衛生紙) toilet paper
散紙 (零錢 / 碎銀 / 碎錢) change; small change; small notes
港紙 (港幣) Hong Kong currency; Hong Kong dollar
睇報紙 (看報紙) read a newspaper
搣紙 (撕紙) tear paper to shreds
碎紙 ① (零錢) coins; small change ② (撕碎的紙) shred paper
落貨紙 (下貨紙 / 卸貨單) landing order
過底紙 (碳式複寫紙) carbon paper
暢 / 唱散紙 (換零錢) change small notes
歌紙 (歌譜) music score of a song
碳紙 carbon paper
銀紙 ① (鈔票 / 紙幣 / 紙鈔) banknote ② (錢) money
影印紙 (複印紙) copy paper
膠紙 (膠帶) cellotape; sticky tape
賣報紙 (在報紙上宣佈) make an announcement in a newspaper
貓紙 ① (作弊紙) paper used in cheating in an examination ② (提示) prompt
噻過沙紙 (非常粗糙) extremely rough
擘紙 (撕紙) tear paper
牆紙 wallpaper
點心紙 (點心訂單) dimsum order form
鉸紙 (剪紙) cut paper
醫生紙 (病假證明) sick-leave certificate
雞皮紙 (牛皮紙) kraft paper
攝紙 (插入紙張) insert paper
鐳射相紙 (激光相紙) laser photo paper
驗身紙 (身體檢查文件) body check document
驗樓紙 (樓宇檢查記錄) flat inspection record

【級】 kap¹ steps

級別 grade; level; rank; rating; scale; sort
級數 (等級) array; progress; series

三級 (第三類) Category III; X-rated
上級 superior
中等階級 middle class
五星級 five-star
升級 advance to a higher grade; be promoted to a higher class; go up one grade in school
打工階級 (工人階級) working class

石級 (石階) staircase; steps; stone steps
年級 grade; year
羽量級 feather-weight
低年級 junior grade
低級 ① (初級) elementary; lower; primary; rudimentary ② (低 / 庸俗) low; vulgar
步級 (樓梯) staircase; steps
信貸評級 credit rating
高年級 senior grade
高級 high class
降級 demote
梯級 (階梯) staircase; steps

【素】 sou³ ① (簡單 / 樸素) plain ② (素食) vegetarian

素月 (素月餅) vegetarian mooncake
素仰 have always admired; have always looked up to
素來 (一直 / 總是 / 至今為止) all along; always; up to the present
素食 ① (素食) vegetarian diet ② (素) vegetarian
素菜 vegetarian diet; vegetable dishes
素餐 ① (素菜餐) vegetable meal ② (素食) vegetarian ③ (尸位素餐) not work for one's living

內在因素 internal factor
利好因素 advantageous factors
我行我素 act according to one's will regardless of others' opinions; do things one's own way; follow one's bigoted course; gang one's own gait; go one's own way; in a world by oneself; in a world of one's own; in one's own sweet way; persist in one's old ways; stick to one's old way of doing things; take one's own course
抗生素 antibiotic
毒素 virus
胰島素 insulin
葉綠素 chlorophyll
質素 (素質) quality
樸素 simple and plain
護髮素 conditioner

【索】 sok³ ① (吸) sniff ② (尖銳) (English) sharp ③ (漂亮) beautiful; gorgeous; pretty

索女 (漂亮的女人) babe; dazzling girl; hottie
索水 (吸水) absorb water
索油 (佔女性便宜 / 好色的男人) intend to make a pass at a lady; lecherous man
索氣 ① (吸氣) inhale ② (氣喘) short of breath ③ (吃力) exhausting

一子錯滿盤皆落索（一招不慎，滿盤皆輸）a wrong step causes a masty tumble; one careless move loses the whole game

向人勒索 impose blackmail on sb

勒索 blackmail; extort

零星落索（零零落落／七零八落）all in a hideous mess; all upside down; at sixes and sevens; chaotic; everything is upside down; fall apart into seven or eight pieces; in a state of confusion; in disorder; in great disorder; in ruin; in scattered confusion; scatter about in all directions; scattered here and there; scattering

摸索 feel about; try to find out

【紮】zaat³ tie

紮起（走紅）be in favour; be in vogue; get famous

紮馬（劈馬步）firm stance

紮帶（繫帶子）tie a belt

紮亂（打斷）interrupt

紮辮（編辮子）braid one's hair; plait one's hair; tie up one's plait

【缺】kyut³ ① (缺乏) lack ② (空缺) vacancy

缺口 ①（突破口／漏洞）breach; gap; loophole; opening ②（不足／短缺）deficiency; insufficiency; shortage

缺少 absence; deficient in; lack; short of

缺乏 lack of

缺席 absence

缺陷 blemish; defect; drawback; fault; flaw

缺漏 gaps and omissions

缺課 absent from class; absent from school; miss a class

缺點 shortcoming

空缺 vacancy

肥缺（高收入職位）armchair job

職位空缺 vacancy

【翁】jung¹ old man

翁姑（公婆）woman's parents-in-law

富翁 rich man

【翅】ci³ fin

翅膀 wings

魚翅 shark's fin

碗仔翅（仿魚翅羹）shark fine soup

鞘翅 coleoptera

【耕】gaang¹ (種) farm

耕田（莊稼／種田／種地）farm; ploughing

耕田佬（莊稼人／種田人／農民）farmer

耕作 cultivate; farming; tillage

耕種 cultivate

耕織 farming and weaving

【耗】hou³ consume

耗費 consume; cost; expend

耗損 consume; deplete; lose; waste

耗資 consume funds

耗盡 burn up; consume; deplete; exhaust; impoverish; use up

消耗 consumption

【胭】jin¹ rouge

胭脂 blusher; cochineal; rouge

胭脂馬——難騎（無法控制的人）uncontrollable person

【胰】ji⁴ pancreas

胰島素 insulin

【胱】gwong¹ bladder

膀胱 bladder

【胸】hung¹ ① (胸部) chest ② (乳房) breast

胸口 ①（胸部中間）middle of the chest ②（胃部對上的位置）pit in the upper part of the stomach

胸口痛 chest pain

胸毛 chest hair

胸部 bosom; breast; bust; chest; thorax

胸圍（乳罩／胸罩）bra

胸罩（乳罩／緊身胸衣）bra; brassiere; breast shield; bust bodice

胸膛 breast; chest

挺起胸膛 stand straight in gesture of self-confidence; stick out one's chest

胸懷 mind

胸懷大志（志在千里／志向遠大）aim high; cherish high aspirations in one's mind; cherish high ideals; cherish lofty designs in one's bosom; entertain great ambitions; fly a high pitch; fly at high game; fly at higher game; fly high; have lofty aspirations; hitch one's wagon to a star; think big

胸襟 breadth of mind; mind

心胸 mind

雞胸（雞胸肉）chicken breast

【能】 nang⁴ possible

能人 able person
能力 ability
　缺乏能力 lack the ability
能屈能伸 able to adapt to circumstances; can either stoop
　or stand; flexible; know when to eat humble pie and
　when to hold one's head high; know when to yield and
　when not; take the rough with the smooth
能者多勞 able people are given more work to do; all lay
　loads on the willing horse; an able man has many burdens;
　an able person is always busy; the abler a person, the
　busier he gets; the capable ones are always busy
能耐 capability
能夠 able to; can
能量 energy
　正能量 positive energy
能幹 able; capable; competent; have a lot on the ball

才能 talent
冇七可能 (不太可能) it's out of the question; unlikely
冇可能 (不可能) it's out of the question; unlikely
出於本能 by instinct
功能 function
可能 possible
本能 instinct
好可能 (很可能) likely
有可能 be on the cards
低能 fool; stupid
欲罷不能 can't help carrying on; cannot refrain from going
　on; try to stop but cannot; unable to stop even though
　one wants to; want to stop but unable to do so
智能 brain power; intellect; intellectual ability; intelligence;
　knowledge and ability; mind
無能 impotent
萬能 multi-purpose
懦弱無能 weak and useless
雜崩能 (什錦 / 雜 / 雜物) bits and pieces; miscellaneous;
　mixed; odds and ends

【脂】 zi¹ cosmetics

脂油 (豬油) lard
　脂油淡定 (慢條斯理) calm
脂肪 fat
脂粉 (胭脂水粉) cosmetics
　脂粉味 pansy
　脂粉客 playboy
　塗脂抹粉 apply cosmetics; apply facial makeup; apply
　　power and paint; deck oneself out; deck up; make up;
　　paint and powder oneself

油脂 ① (古惑仔) teddy boy ② (飛女 / 太妹) teddy girl
胭脂 blusher; cochineal; rouge

【脆】 ceoi³ crisp

脆卜卜 (繃脆) crispy
脆皮 (皮兒薄的) crispy
　脆皮乳豬 crispy roasted piglet
脆弱 delicate; fragile; frail; frailty; tender; weak

卜卜脆 (鬆脆) crispy
爽脆 (脆 / 香脆) crispy; crunchy
鬆脆 crunchy

【脈】 mak⁶ pulse

脈搏 pulse
脈壓 pulse pressure

把脈 feel the pulse
探脈 feel sb's pulse; take sb's pulse
掊脈 (按脈) feel the pulse
睇脈 ① (看中醫) see a doctor of Chinese medicine ② (診脈)
　feel the pulse
搭脈 (按脈) feel sb's pulse; take sb's pulse
點脈 (點穴) hit at a certain acupoint

【脊】 zek³ ① (脊柱) spine ② (脊) ridges

脊神經 spinal nerve
脊骨 (脊梁骨) backbone; spine

屋脊 roof ridge
背脊 (脊背) back
督 / 篤背脊 (在別人背後誹謗) back-stabbing; calumniate sb
　behind one's back; rip up the back; speak ill of sb behind
　their back; stab sb in the back; talk behind sb's back

【胳】 gaak³ armpit

胳肋底 (夾肢窩 / 胳肢窩 / 腋下 / 腋窩) armpit

【脷】 lei⁶ (舌頭) tongue

脷底 (舌根) root of the tongue
脷苔 (舌苔) coating on the tongue
脷根 (舌根) root of the tongue

三口兩脷 (輕率) play fast and loose
牛脷 (牛舌頭) ox tongue
嚹脷 (極端昂貴 / 非常昂貴) extremely expensive; very
　expensive
捹脷 (價錢高昂 / 價錢高昂，不能負擔) high-priced; the
　price is too high to be affordable

龍脷（龍利魚）sole

繑脷（舌頭打結）awkward-sounding; hard to pronounce; twist the tongue

【臭】cau³ foul; smelly; stinking

臭丸（樟腦丸／衞生球）moth ball

臭口（口臭）smelly breath

臭坑出臭草（本性難移）a smelly ditch grows smelly grass

臭狐（狐臭）hircus

臭飛（臭阿飛／臭飛仔）dirty teddy boy

臭崩崩（臭烘烘的）foul-smelling; smelly; stinking

臭檔（壞脾氣）bad-tempered; notorious

又鹹又臭（又髒又臭）dirty and stinky

口臭 ① (口臭) bad breath ② (語言粗鄙) irritating

好臭（很臭）very smelly

狐臭 body odour; bromhidrosis

廁所好臭（廁所很臭）the toilet is very smelly

冤臭（很臭）foul smell

冤崩爛臭（臭氣沖天）smelly; stinking

發臭 stink

腥臭 stinking smell of rotten fish

數臭（臭罵）scold

鬧臭（公開責罵）scold sb in public

【致】zi³ devote

致力 take special aim at

　　致力於 apply oneself to; dedicate oneself to; devote oneself to; devote to; engage oneself in; work for

致命 ① (造成死亡／致死) causing death; deadly; fatal; lethal; moral; vital ② (犧牲一個人的生命) sacrifice one's life

致富（獲得財富／脫貧致富／變得富有）achieve prosperity; acquire wealth; become prosperous; become rich

致賀 congratulate; extend congratulations; offer one's congratulations

致敬 pay homage; pay one's respects to; pay tribute to; salute

致意 convey one's best regards; convey one's best wishes; give one's regards; present one's compliments; salutation; salute; send one's greeting; with the compliments of

致電 call

致謝 convey thanks; express one's thanks; extend thanks to; offer thanks; thank

致癌 cancer-causing; carcinogenic

言行一致 act in accordance with one's words; actions matching words; as good as one's word; deeds accord with words; fit one's deeds to one's words; live up to one's words; match one's deeds with one's words; match word to deed; match words with deeds; one's actions accord with one's words; one's actions are keeping with one's promises; one's deeds and words are in accord; one's deeds are consistent with one's words; one's words correspond with one's actions; square one's words with one's conduct; stand by one's word; suit one's actions to one's words; the deeds suit the words; the deeds match the words

淋漓盡致 completely; incisively; thoroughly

【航】hong⁴ vessel

航空 aviation; voyage

航海 navigation; voyage

航班 flight

　　航班延誤 the flight is delayed

航線 air route; itinerary; navigation route; route; way

航機 flight

宇航（航天）astronautical; space travel

【般】bun¹ general

般配（匹配）match each other; well matched

一般 common; general

【舦】taai⁵（舵）helm

舦盤（方向盤）steering wheel

把舦（掌舵／操作方向盤）at the helm; operate the rudder; steer a boat; take the tiller

硬晒舦（陷入僵局）bring to a deadlock

揸舦（掌舵／操作方向盤）at the helm; operate the rudder; steer a boat; take the tiller

擺舦（掌舵／操作方向盤）at the helm; operate the rudder; steer a boat; take the tiller

【茗】ming⁵ ①（茶）tea ②（茶點）refreshments

茗具（茶具）tea set

春茗 spring dinner

【荔】lai⁶ lichee

荔枝 lichee

一抽荔枝（一束荔枝）a bunch of lichees

【茫】mong⁴ ① (漫漫) boundless ② (愚昧) ignorant; in the dark

茫茫 boundless and indistinct
　茫茫大地 boundless land
茫然 in the dark
　茫然不知 utterly ignorant of

大海茫茫 a vast expanse of sea

【茶】caa⁴ ① (茶) tea ② (湯藥) liquid and medication

茶几 coffee table
茶水 tea or boiled water
茶瓜 (醬瓜 / 酸黃瓜) pickled cucumber
　茶瓜送飯——好人有限 (遠不是一個好人) far from
　　being a good person
茶包 (袋泡茶) tea bag
茶色 (棕色) brown
　茶色玻璃 brown glass
茶走 (港式奶茶) tea with condensed milk
茶具 / 茶餐 tea set
茶杯 teacup
　茶杯碟 (茶托 / 茶盤) saucer
茶居 (茶館) teahouse
茶匙 teaspoon
茶壺 teapot
茶葉 ① (茶) tea ② (茶葉) tea leaf
茶錢 (茶費) charge for the tea
茶樓 (酒家 / 酒樓) Cantonese restaurant; Chinese
　restaurant; teahouse
茶餐 afternoon tea set
　茶餐廳 (港式茶餐廳) Hong-Kong-style restaurant;
　　local café
　　一間茶餐廳 a local café

一杯茶 a cup of tea
下午茶 afternoon tea
口水多過茶 (非常健談 / 廢話連篇) all mouth and no action;
　shoot off one's mouth; talk too much; very talkative; wag
　one's tongue
中國茶 Chinese tea
五花茶 five-flower tea
日本綠茶 Japanese green tea
水仙茶 narcissus tea
半杯茶 half a cup of tea
打瀉茶 (望門寡 / 喪偶的女子) widowed maiden
奶茶 milk tea; tea with milk
珍珠奶茶 pearl milk tea
花茶 tea with dried flowers

紅茶 black tea
杏仁茶 sweep ground almond tea
沖茶 ① (沏茶) make tea ② (加滿茶壺) top up the teapot
泡茶 make tea
沱茶 (茶磚 / 茶餅 / 茶塊) compressed mass of tea leaves
凍奶茶 (冰奶茶) iced tea with milk
凍檸茶 (凍檸檬茶 / 冷泡檸檬茶) cold lemon tea
柴米油鹽醬醋茶 (日常生活必需品) daily household necessities
倒茶 pour tea
唔該你沖茶 (請替我加滿茶壺) please top up my teapot
鬼佬涼茶 (啤酒) beer
涼茶 herbal tea
焗茶 (沏茶 / 泡茶) make tea
菊花茶 chrysanthemum tea
斟茶 (倒茶進杯子) fill the cup with tea
煲茶 (泡茶) brew tea
飲下午茶 (喝下午茶) have afternoon tea
飲奶茶 (喝奶茶) drink tea with milk
飲完茶 (喝完了茶) after finishing tea
飲咗門官茶——大笑不止 (大笑不止) always wear a smile
　on one's face
飲杯茶 (喝杯茶) have a cup of tea
飲茶 ① (喝茶) drink tea ② (吃點心) have dimsum lunch;
　have tea and refreshments; (transliteration) yum cha
飲啖茶 (喝一口茶) have a sip of tea
歎茶 (享受茶) enjoy tea
綠茶 green tea
熱檸茶 (熱檸檬茶) hot lemon tea
請飲茶 ① (請喝茶) have a cup of tea, please ② (請人吃點
　心) treat sb with a dim-sum lunch
檸茶 (檸檬茶) lemon tea; tea with lemon

【茸】jung⁴ ① (細膩柔軟) fine and soft ② (糊狀物) paste

茸角 (鹿茸) antler

蒜茸 (蒜泥) garlic paste; mashed garlic

【草】cou² grass

草皮 (草地 / 草坪 / 草坡地) grassland
　鋪草皮 (在賽馬中賠錢) lose money in horse-racing
草地 grassland
　一幅草地 (一片草地) a piece of grassland
草坡 ① (草地) grassland ② (草坪 / 草坡地)
　glassplot; lawn
草花頭 (草字頭 / 草頭兒) the "grass" (草) radical
草青色 (灰綠色) grayish green
草屋 (草房 / 茅草屋) thatched hut
草菇 (鮮蘑菇) straw mushroom

草綠 (如草般綠) green as grass
草蜢 (蚱蜢) grasshopper

一條水草 (一根水草) a blade of waterweed
一紮草 (一捆草) a bundle of grass
大草 (大寫字母) block letter; capital letter
水草 waterweed
牛嚼牡丹——唔知花定草 (豬八戒吃人參果——不知啥滋味)
　　cannot appreciate good food; not know chalk from cheese
甘草 licorice
禾草 / 禾稈草 (稻草) rice straw
好馬不食回頭草 (好馬不吃回頭草) a bird flying away from
　　the cage will never come back to be fed
看牛不及打馬草 (浪費時間與閒人聊天) it wastes time for a
　　busy person to have a chat with an idler
校草 (在學校裏最好看的男孩) best-looking boy in the school
茜草 madder
起草 (草擬) draft; make a draft
臭坑出臭草 (本性難移) a smelly ditch grows smelly grass
剪草 cutting grass
斬草 cut down grass; mow
着草 (逃逸 / 逃走 / 逃跑) escape; flee
嫩草 delicate grass
算死草 (算計 / 吝嗇 / 刮削) miserly person; pinch and scrape
稻草 rice straw
頭大冇腦，腦大生草 (頭大無腦，腦大長草 / 沒有智慧的蠢
　　人) stupid person without intelligence

【荒】 fong¹ ridiculous
荒地 no man's land; wasteland
荒唐 absurd; fantastic; preposterous
荒島 barren island; desert island; uninhabited island
荒涼 bleak and desolate; wild
荒淫 debauched; dissolute; licentious
荒廢 fall into disuse; fall into disrepair; lie waste; out of
　　practice
荒誕 absurd; incredible; unbelievable
荒謬 ridiculous

破天荒 occur for the first time; take the extraordinary step;
　　unheard of; unprecedented

【荏】 jam⁵ soft
軟荏荏 (軟綿綿 / 柔軟) feathery; soft; velvety

【茜】 sai¹ parsley
茜草 madder

芫茜 (香菜) coriander

【茭】 gaau¹ dry grass
茭筍 (茭白) wild grass stem

【蚌】 pong⁵ mussel
蚌殼 (壯蠣殼) oyster shell

珊瑚蚌 (珊瑚貽貝) coral mussel
桂花蚌 (桂花貽貝) osmanthus mussel
象拔蚌 (象鼻蛤蜊) elephant-trunk clam; geoduck

【蚊】 man¹ ① (蚊子) mosquito ② (元) dollar
蚊仔 (蚊子) mosquito
蚊型 (小型) small size
　　蚊型股 (小型股票) penny stock
蚊帳 mosquito net
　　一堂蚊帳 (一頂蚊帳) a mosquito net
蚊滋 (小蚊子) tiny mosquito
　　蚊滋咁細聲 (微弱的聲音) weak voice of a person
蚊瞓 (太晚了) too late
　　蚊都瞓 (太晚了 / 為時已晚) it would be too late to;
　　　　too late
蚊髀同牛髀 (小巫見大巫 / 沒法相比) by long chalks;
　　no comparison between; one cannot be compared to the
　　other; pale into insignificance by comparison; the moon is
　　not seen where the sun shines; when the sun shines, the
　　light of stars is not seen; when the sun shines, the moon
　　has nought to do

一千蚊 (一千元) one thousand dollars
一百蚊 (一百元) one hundred dollars
一蚊 (一元) one dollar
一萬蚊 (一萬元) ten thousand dollars
十蚊 (十元) ten dollars
十幾蚊 (十幾元) ten odd dollars
千幾蚊 (一千多元) a thousand something dollars
百幾蚊 (一百多元 a hundred something dollars
找番一蚊 (找回一元) pay back one dollar
幾十蚊 (幾十元) several tens of dollars

【蚪】 dau² tadpole

蝌蚪 tadpole

【蚤】 zou² flea
蚤嫲 (跳蚤) flea

跳蚤 flea

【衰】seoi¹ (壞) bad
衰人 (缺德鬼／壞人／壞傢伙／壞蛋) bad guy; bad person
　　做衰人 (頂罪／替罪羊) scapegoat
衰女 (壞女孩) naughty girl
衰公 (壞人／壞傢伙) bad man
衰仔／衰仔頭 (小傢伙／兔崽子／混小子／搗蛋鬼／小
　　流氓) little brat; little rascal
衰佬 (壞傢伙／流氓) bad guy
衰到 (壞得很) extremely bad
　　衰到冇人有 (壞透了／壞極了) extremely bad
　　衰到冇得頂 (壞得非常討厭) extremely obnoxious
　　衰到死 (壞透了／壞極了) extremely bad
　　衰到貼地 (壞得令人討厭) extremely nasty
衰退 go into decline; recession
衰格 (下賤／缺德) bad character
衰神 (王八蛋／瘟神／壞蛋) bad apple; bad egg; bad guy;
　　baddie; bogeyman; dirtbag; rotten apple
衰鬼 ① (討厭鬼／該死) bigbore; damnable person; git;
　　mush; pest ② (愛人／蜜糖兒／甜心) (woman calling
　　her lover) darling; honey; sweetheart
衰婆 (壞女人) bad woman
衰運 (背運／霉運) unlucky fate
衰野 (壞東西／壞分子) inferior goods
衰樣 (鬼樣子) ugly face

口衰 (滿嘴髒話) foul-mouthed
大舊衰 (恃強凌弱／以大欺小) big bully
有咁衰講到咁衰 (詆毀／抹黑) paint sb/sth in dark colour
仲衰 (更壞) worse
好衰唔衰 (不幸) sth is really bad; unfortunately; unluckily
高大衰 (笨蛋／笨頭笨腦) lummox
唔衰攞嚟衰 (惹禍／自找麻煩／自討苦吃) ask for trouble;
　　borrow trouble; bring on trouble; encourage trouble; look
　　for trouble; make a rod for oneself; prepare a rod for
　　one's back; seek trouble for oneself
鬼咁衰 (非常壞／非常討厭) very bad; very nasty
唱衰 (中傷／誹謗／說人壞話) bad-mouth
陸雲庭睇相──唔衰攞嚟衰 (為自己帶來恥辱／令人丟臉)
　　bring disgrace to oneself; feign oneself to be poor
睇衰 (不看好) look down on sb
詐衰 (給人惹麻煩) get sb into trouble
當衰 (不幸) unlucky
影衰 (使人臉上無光) be overshadowed
樣衰 (樣子不好／臉目醜陋) bad looking; ugly face
樣衰衰 (長得難看) bad looking; ugly face

【衷】cung¹ sincere
衷心 cordial; heartfelt
衷情 feelings in one's heart; heartfelt emotion; inner feelings

折衷 (妥協／和解) compromise

【袍】pou⁴ Chinese style gown
袍澤 (同袍) comrades in arms

罩袍 dust-gown; dust-robe
旗袍 cheongsam

【袒】taan² protect
袒護 (偏愛／翼庇／蔭庇) give protection to; partial to;
　　protect; shield; side with

偏袒 (偏心／偏私／偏護) bias for; discriminate in favour
　　of; favour; partial to; partial to and side with; take sides
　　with; weigh

【袖】zau⁶ sleeves
袖口 cuff; wristband
　　袖口鈕 (袖扣) cuff link
袖珍 (口袋大小) pocket; pocket-size

衫袖 (袖／袖子) sleeve
手袖 (袖套) oversleeve
長袖 long sleeve
捋起衫袖 (捲起衣袖) push up one's sleeve
短袖 short sleeve
攦衫袖 (捲起衣袖) roll up one's sleeves

【被】bei⁶ (被子) quilt
被冚 (被單／床單) bedsheet
被告 defendant
被面 (被套) quilt cover
被袋 (被套) bedding bag
被鋪 (鋪蓋／被套) quilt cover
被櫃 (被子櫃) quilt cabinet
被竇 (被窩) folded quilt

三幅被 (唱老調／老調重彈) harp on the same string; harp
　　on the shopworn theme; play the same old tune; sing the
　　same song; strike up a hackneyed tune; strike up an old
　　tune
冚被 (蓋上毯子) cover with a blanket
抑被 (蓋上被子) cover with a quilt
抌吓張被 (把被子抖一抖) shake the quilt
執被 (折疊被子) fold the quilt
摺被 (折疊被子) fold up a quilt
聯被 (縫被) stitch the quilt
講嚟講去都係三幅被 (說來說去都是老話題) sing the song
　　of burden

攃被 (抬起被子) lift the quilt
攃被 (捲在被子裏) tuck in a quilt

【衲】naap⁶ jacket

棉衲 (棉襖) cotton-padded jacket
爛棉衲 (爛棉襖) rotten cotton-padded jacket

【討】tou² demand

討好 blandish; butter up; cotton up to; curry favour with; fawn on; fawn upon; get in with; ingratiate oneself with; keep sb sweet; make up to; play up to; please; polish the apple; shine up to; suck up to; sweeten up; throw oneself at; throw oneself at sb's head
兩面討好 please both parties

討厭 (麻煩 / 傷腦筋) abhorrent of; adverse to; allergic to; antipathetic to; averse to; bad news; be annoyed with; be annoyed at; be browned-off with; be disgusted at; be disgusted by; be disgusted with; be fed up with; bore; detest; disagreeable; disgusting; dislike; hate; have a dislike for; have a distaste for; have a horror of; have an aversion to; have no time for; have no use for; hold sth in abomination; indisposed; loathe; nasty; nuisance; pain in the neck; repugnant to; sick of; take a dislike to; tired of; trouble; troublesome
討厭鬼 disgusting person

討價 ask a price; name a price
討價還價 bargain; bargain with sb for a supply of sth; dicker; drive a bargain; haggle about a price; haggle for a price; haggle over a price; haggle with sb over the price of sth

討論 discussion

【訊】seon³ message

訊息 (信息 / 音信 / 新聞) information; message; news; tidings
訊問 ① (詰問 / 審問) interrogate; question ② (對應 / 通訊) correspondence

口訊 ① (信息) message ② (口信) voice message
發短訊 send short mail
短訊 short mail; short message

【訓】fan³ lesson

訓示 ① (告誡) admonish ② (指導) instructions
訓話 exhort; lecture
訓練 (操練) coach; discipline; drill; train
訓導 teach and guide

培訓 cultivate; train
教訓 lesson; exhortation

【訕】saan³ slander; sneer

訕上 (誹謗上級) slander one's superior
訕笑 (嘲笑 / 誹謗) laugh at; slander; sneer

搭訕 (聊天) chat up

【記】gei³ memorise; remember

記事簿 (記事本) note book
記性 (記憶) memory
　冇記性 (記憶力差 / 健忘) forgetful; have a bad memory; have a memory like a sieve; have a poor memory; have a short memory
　好記性 have a good memory
記者 (新聞記者 / 新聞從業員) journalist; reporter
　冒充記者 pass oneself off for a journalist
記起 (想起) recall
　記番起 (回憶 / 回想) recall
記得 (想起 / 記憶 / 想到) remember
　唔記得 (忘了 / 忘記 / 記不住) do not remember; forget
記掛 (惦記 / 想念) miss sb
記認 (記號) sign

日記 diary
牛記 (牛仔褲) jeans
牛記笠記 (便裝) casual style of dress
伙記 ① (職員) employee ② (侍應生) waiter
老友記 ① (好朋友) good friend ② (老朋友) old friend
住宅摩貨登記 (住宅單位的確認交易) confirmor transaction on residential flat
忘記 escape from sb's mind; escape sb; escape sb's memory; fail to remember; forget; get sth out of one's head; get sth out of one's mind; go out of sb's mind; have sth off one's mind; pass out of sb's mind; slip sb's memory; slip sb's mind
胎記 birthmark
速記 shorthand
筆記 notes
買賣登記 sale and purchase registration
傳記 biography; life story
緊記 remember
摩貨登記 (確認人交易登記) registration of confirmor transaction
臨記 extra
簿記 bookkeeping

【豈】 hei² ① (怎麼) how ② (甚麼) what

豈有此理 (胡說八道 / 離譜) can anything be more absurd; how absurd; hw absurd it is; how can this be right; how could such a thing be possible; how could that be; how unreasonable; how unreasonable all this is; that's absurd; that's ridiculous; this is arrant nonsense; this is outrageous; this is sheer effrontery; what a thing to say; what nonsense

【豹】 paau³ (豹子) leopard

豹死留皮 a leopard leaves behind its skin when it dies

【貢】 gung³ ① (獻給) tribute ② (周圍走) go everywhere

貢金 aids; tributes
貢品 articles of tribute
貢獻 contribution

四圍貢 (四處走動) go around everywhere
岌岌貢 (周圍看) look around
周圍貢 (到處去) go everywhere
兀兀貢 (搖擺不定) shake from side to side; sway
啷啷貢 (不斷亂動) move about

【財】 coi⁴ wealth

財不可露眼 (錢財不要讓別人看到) don't flaunt your wealth; opportunity makes the thief
財主佬 (大財主 / 財主) rich man
財可通神 money makes the mare go; money talks
財多身子弱 (富裕但健康不佳) rich but in poor health
財到光棍手——有去冇回頭 (錢財到了騙子手中就很難取回) give a bone to a dog
　　財到光棍手——易放難收 (錢財到了騙子手中就很難取回) once money goes to the hands of a conman, it's difficult to get it back from him
財政 finance
　　財政年度 financial year
財神 God of Wealth
財務 financial matters
　　財務顧問 financial consultant
財產 property
財富 wealth
　　追求財富 pursue wealth
財散人安樂 (花了錢令人安心 / 花錢安人心) when money is spent, peace of mind is possible
財源廣進 (祝你有豐富的財富) wish you abundant wealth
財路 (賺錢的方式) way of making money
財勢 wealth and power
　　有財有勢 rich and powerful

力不到不為財 (一分耕耘一分收穫) no pain, no gain
水為財 water is money
周身唔聚財 (渾身彆扭 / 渾身不舒服) uneasy
枉費錢財 (浪費金錢) throw away good money for nothing
唔聚財 (不適) unwell
恭喜發財 wish you a prosperous year
恭喜發財，利是拿來 (恭喜發財，紅包拿來) wish you a prosperous year, and give me a red packet
破財 (賠錢) lose money
理財 banking
勒索錢財 extort money from sb
週身唔聚財 (渾身彆扭 / 渾身不舒服) uneasy all over
發財 (變得富有) become rich; make a fortune
網上理財 internet banking
橫財 (不循正途取得的金錢 / 不義之財) ill-gotten wealth
錢財 money; riches; wealth

【起】 hei² ① (漲) increase ② (蓋) build

起好 (建好 / 完成施工) complete the construction
起行 (動身 / 出發) begin a journey; depart; departure; go on a journey; leave for a place; set out on a journey
起尾注 (吃現成兒 / 篡奪某人的收益) usurp ownership; usurp sb's gains
起步槍 (發令槍 / 發號槍) starting gun
起底 (偵查某人的背景) check up on sb's background
起泡 send up bubbles
起身 (起床 / 起來) get off; get out of bed; get up; hit the deck; rise; roll out; show a leg; stir; turn out; wake up
　　七點起身 (七點起床) get up at seven
　　好早起身 (很早起床) got up very early
　　好晏起身 (很遲起床) got up late
　　快啲起身 (趕快起床) rise and shine
起屋 (蓋房子 / 造房子 / 蓋樓房) build a house
起哄 boo and hoo; jeer
起飛 (飛起) take off
　　起飛腳 (過河拆橋) fly high over sb
起病 (發病) come on
起租 (加租 / 漲租金) increase the rent
起草 draft; make a draft
起釘 (收取利息) collect an interest payment
起骨 (去骨頭 / 剔骨頭) boning
起眼 (搶眼 / 吸引注意) draw attention; eye-catching
起貨 ① (完工) complete a project; finish doing sth ② (交貨) deliver goods
起菜 ① (上菜) serve food; serve the dishes ② (性愛) have sex with a girl
起程 depart for; start a journey
起勢 (使勁兒地 / 起勁 / 拼命) active; eager; energetically; enthusiastically; exert all one's strength; go all out; in

high spirits; show much zeal; vigorously; vociferous; with gusto; with zest and vigour; work frantically

起源 origin

起痰 ①（被一個女性吸引）be sexually attracted to a woman ②（有強烈的願望）have a strong desire for ③（有痰）have phlegm

起筷（勸客進食）help youself to the food
　　起筷啦（我們開始吃了／開吃吧）let's start eating

起價（漲價）raise prices; rise in price

起模（做模子／做模型）make a mould

起樓（蓋房子／蓋樓房）build a building

起碼（至少）at least

起頭（起先／起初）at first; in the beginning

起牆（建牆／壘牆）build a wall

起瞨（長水皰）get blisters

起鑊（燒鍋）heat the frying pan

一波未平，一波又起 one trouble is followed by another; troubles come one after another

寸到飛起（非常傲慢）very arrogant

引起 arise from; arise out of; arouse; bring about; bring down the house; bring on; bring to; call forth; cause; create; engender; evoke; give rise to; induce; lead to; lead up to; produce; set off; stir up; touch off; trigger

冇醒起（忘記了／記不起來）didn't remember

升起 rise

比起（相比／比較）compare to

火起（生氣／發火／惱火）angry; be ablaze with anger; fire up; fit to be tied; flare up; get angry; get shirty; lose one's temper

凸起 convex

由而家起（從現在開始）from now on

忙到飛起（非常忙碌／忙不過來）busy to death

扣起（扣除）deduct

考起（擊敗對手／嚇倒對手）baffle; beat; daunt

風生水起（致富／發財）get rich

飛起 ①（擺脫）get rid of ②（非常）very

戙起（直立／豎立）erect

紮起（越來越盛行／越來越出名）be in favour; be in vogue; getting famous

留起（預留）reserve

唔醒起（忘記了／想不起來）didn't remember

記起（想起／回想／回憶）recall

記番起（想起／回想起／回憶起）recall

從頭做起（從頭開始）do it all over again; start a new life; start all over again; start all over again from the beginning; start from a clean slate; start from the beginning; turn over a new leaf

掘起（挖掘）dig up

梳起（決意不結婚的女性）a woman who is determined not to get married

殺起（立意／決心）make up one's mind

提起 mention

登起（舉起／撩起／擎）hold up; lift up

睇唔起（看不上眼／看不起）look down on

睇起（看得起／評價很高）have a high opinion of sb; take a bright view of sb

睇得起（評價很高）have a high opinion of sb

貴到飛起（貴得很／非常昂貴）exorbitantly expensive; extremely expensive

撈起 ①（飛黃騰達）have a rise in life ②（發達／致富）become rich; make a fortune

豎起 erect; hoist; hold up

諗起（想起／記起）remember

醒唔起（想不起）unable to call to mind

醒起（突然想起）it suddenly occurs to one

醒得起（想得起）able to call to mind

嬲到彈起（非常憤怒）hit the roof

繞起（擊敗某人）beat sb

攊起（抬起）lift up

臚起（捲起）push up sth

【趷】gat⁶ ①（探／爬）get up ②（蹺）lift up

趷個頭出去（把頭探出去）stretch out one's head

趷起身（探起身子）get up

趷腳（跛腳／瘸腿）lame
　　趷高腳（踮起腳）on the tips of one's toes

趷路（滾蛋）get out

有嘰趷（不和／爭吵）at cross-purposes; at loggerheads with sb; at odds; at outs with sb; not get along well; on bad terms

嘰趷（意見不一／有矛盾）at cross-purposes; at loggerheads with sb; at odds; at outs with sb; not get along well; on bad terms

嘰嘰趷趷（口吃／說不清楚）stutter out

【辱】juk⁶ humiliate

辱罵 abuse; abuse and insult; call sb name; hurl insults

侮辱 insult

【迴】wui⁴ rounds

迴光反照 a reflected ray of the setting sun — the transient reviving of a dying person; an illumination before death; the last radiance of the setting sun — moment of consciousness just before death; the sun's reflected light at the evening — brief glow of health before passing away

迴避 ① (躲避) avoid meeting another person; avoidance
② (撤離) withdraw ③ (拒絕) decline an offer
④ (逃避) evade

巡迴 (巡遊) go the rounds; make a circuit of; tour

【迷】 mai⁴ ① (困惑) be confused ② (被迷住了) be fascinated by ③ (迷) fan

迷人 charming; enchanting
迷你 (微型) mini
　　迷你裙 (超短裙) miniskirt
迷信 superstition
　　破除迷信 abolish superstition
迷途 ① (失去方向) lose one's way ② (走錯路) wrong path
　　誤入迷途 take the wrong path by mistake
迷惑 (困擾 / 困惑) baffle; confuse; perplex; puzzle
　　令人迷惑 (擾亂判斷) disturb the judgement
迷路 (迷失方向) go astray; lose one's way; get lost
迷頭迷腦 (全神貫注) indulge oneself in; immerse oneself in
迷戀 be infatuated with

小樂迷 child music fan
色迷迷 look at a woman with shifty eyes
沉迷 (沉溺) indulge; wallow
昏迷 coma
南嘸佬遇鬼迷 (張天師被鬼迷 / 迷途老馬) an old horse loses its way
經濟低迷 the economy is sluggish
影迷 movie fan
樂迷 music fan; music lover

【追】 zeoi¹ ① (趕) chase ② (追求) chase after

追台 (調台 / 調整頻道) tune the channels
追求 (追逐 / 慾望) chase after; desire; pursue
追到 catch up with
　　追到天腳底 (追尋某人至天涯海角) hunt sb to the end of the earth
　　追到瘦 (追亡逐北) put the squeeze on sb
追唔上 (趕不上) can't catch up with
　　追得上 (趕得上) can catch up with
追唔倒 (趕不上 / 趕不及) can't catch up with
　　追得倒 (趕得上 / 趕上) can catch up with
追數 (追債) dun for debt

一龍去，二龍追 (來回追趕) while one goes to look for sb along a route, that person comes back along the other

窮寇莫追 not to try to run after the hard-pressed enemy

【退】 teoi³ return

退休 retire
　　退休人士 retired person
　　退休金 pension
退飛 ① (獲得退款) get a refund for a ticket
② (退票) return a ticket
退款 refund
退學 leave school
　　勒令退學 order a student to leave school
退燒 (退熱) bring down a fever
　　退燒藥 antipyretic

衰退 (不景氣) go into decline; recession
撤退 retreat
辭退 (解僱) discharge; dismiss; give sb the air; turn away

【送】 sung³ send

送外賣 delivery
送行 see sb off on a journey
　　送行酒 (歡送晚宴 / 餞別宴) farewell dinner
送車 ① (在車站送別) see sb off at the station ② (送一輛車給人作禮物) give sb a car as a present
送佛送到西 (幫忙到底) when you help sb, help him from end to end
送貨 delivery; delivery of goods
　　送貨上門 send goods to one's doorstep
　　免費送貨 delivery is free of charge; free delivery
送船 ① (在碼頭送別) see sb off at the pier ② (送一艘船給人作禮物) give sb a boat as a present
送飯 (下飯) go with rice
送樓 (送一層樓給人作禮物) give sb an apartment as a present
送禮 give a present

傳送 (輸送 / 運送) convey
葬送 burial; waste
運送 transport; ship; convey
遞送 deliver; send
遣送 repatriate; send away; send back; send sb away forcibly

【逃】 tou⁴ escape

逃亡 abscond; become a fugitive; escape; flee from home; fly; go into exile; run away
逃生 escape; escape with one's life; flee for one's life
　　死裏逃生 be saved from death; be snatched from the jaws of death; close call; close shave; escape by a hairbreadth; escape by the skin of one's teeth; escape

death by a narrow margin; escape with one's bare life; hairbreadth escape; have a close bout with death; miss death by a hair's breadth; narrow escape from death; narrow shave; near thing

逃走 escape; flee; fly away; make one's escape; run away; take flight; take to one's heels

逃命 flee for one's life; run for one's life

逃脫 break away; break free; escape from; free oneself from; get clear of; make good one's escape; succeed in escaping from

逃跑 abscond; break away; buzz off; cop a heel; cut and run; cut away; cut loose; cut one's stick; decamp; duck; escape; flee; get away; get out; give leg bail; make good one's escape; make off; make one's escape; make one's getaway; move off; run away; run off; scarper; show a clean pair of heels; show legs; show one's heels; slip away; take leg bail; take to flight; take to one's heels; take to one's legs

逃稅 avoid paying tax; evade taxes; tax avoidance; tax evasion

逃課 (逃學) cut class; ditch class; play truant; skip class

逃學 bunk off; cut class; escape school; hooky; play hookey; play hooky; play truant; skip school; skive off; truancy; truant

逃避 dodge; escape; evade; run away from; shirk

逃離 flee for one's life; run for one's life

逃難 flee from a calamity; seek refuge from calamities

大限難逃 (死期將至) meet one's fate; pay one's debt to nature

劫數難逃 (難逃厄運) it is impossible to escape fate; there is no escape from fate

【逆】jik⁶ inverse

逆水 (逆流而上) go against the current

逆耳 grate on the ear; be unpleasant to the ear
　　忠言逆耳 good advice is always unpleasant to the ear

逆來順受 resign oneself to adversity

逆風 go against the wind

逆境 adverse circumstances; adversity
　　逆境求存 try to survive in adverse circumstances
　　身處逆境 in adversity

逆轉 deteriorate; take a turn for the worse
　　不可逆轉 impossible to reverse the trend

【迾】laat⁶ row

一坺迾 (弄得一塌糊塗) as thick as paste; be all muddled up; make a mess of sth

【郎】long⁴ man

郎中 (醫生) doctor; physician trained in herbal medicine

郎君 (我的丈夫) my husband

郎當 ① (不適當) unfit ② (委靡) dejected; dispirited ③ (不稂不莠) good-for-nothing; worthless
　　吊兒郎當 bugger about; careless and casual; dillydally; do a milk; dodge the column; dog it; fool around; goof off; idle about; slovenly; take a devil-may-care attitude; take things easy; undisciplined; untidy; utterly carefree

牛郎 (男妓) gigolo; male prostitute; rent boy; renter; ring-snatcher

令郎 (你的兒子) your son

法郎 (法國貨幣) franc

伴郎 (男儐相) best man; groomsman

馬鮫郎 (馬鮫魚) spanish mackerel

新郎 bridgegroom

瑞士法郎 (瑞士貨幣) Swiss francs

應召女郎 (妓女) prostitute

【酌】zoek³ serve wine

酌情 act according to circumstances; take into consideration the circumstances; use one's discretion
　　酌情而定 be determined by the circumstances; decide according to the circumstances; depend upon the circumstances
　　酌情處理 act according to one's judgement; act after full consideration of the actual situation; act at one's discretion; deal with sth on the merits of each case; depend upon circumstances; do as one thinks fit; exercise discretion in light of the circumstances; handle as one sees fit; settle a matter as one sees fit

酌量 weigh and consider

自斟自酌 in the enjoyment of one's own life all by oneself

【配】pui³ match

配搭 ① (搭配) co-ordinate ② (擺列) collocate

配襯 (相配 / 相稱) fit each other; match each other; match up; match well; match with; mesh with

交配 mating

般配 (匹配) match each other; well matched

許配 affiance; be affianced to; be bethrothed to; betroth one's daughter to

【酒】zau² wine

酒凹 (酒窩) dimple

酒色財氣 wine, sex, money, and power

酒肉 wine and women
　有酒有肉多兄弟 (酒肉朋友) a heavy purse makes
　　friends come
酒吧 bar; pub
酒店 ① (飯店 / 旅館) hotel ② (酒家 / 酒館) winehouse
酒店大堂 hotel lobby
　一間酒店 a hotel
　大酒店 (殯儀館) funeral parlour
　五星級酒店 five-star hotel
　住一晚酒店 (酒店住宿一晚) stay for one evening in a hotel
　訂酒店 (訂飯店) book a hotel room
酒後吐真言 truth is exposed in wine
酒席 banquet; feast
　訂酒席 make a banquet reservation
　開酒席 (辦酒席) prepare a banquet; prepare a feast
　擺酒席 (設宴 / 辦酒席) give a banquet
酒家 (飯店 / 飯莊 / 飯館 / 餐廳) restaurant
酒埕 (酒罌子) earthen wine jar
酒鬼 (醉酒的人 / 酒徒) alcoholic; alkie; bar fly; bibber;
　caner; drinker; drunkard; gargler; tippler; toper; wine bibber
酒渣 (酒釀 / 醪糟) sweet fermented glutinous rice wine
　酒渣鼻 (酒糟鼻) rosacea
酒菜 (酒食 / 飲食) food and drink
酒會 cocktail party
酒樓 (飯館 / 飯店) Chinese restaurant
　一間酒樓 a Chinese restaurant
酒精 alcohol
　酒精測試 breath alcohol test
酒醉三分醒 be in wine but still a little conscious
酒樽 (酒瓶兒) wine bottle
酒辦 (酒樣品 / 樣品酒) miniature wine
酒餅 (酒曲 / 酒藥) distiller's yeast; yeast for brewing rice
　wine or fermenting glutinous rice
酒罌 (酒罐兒) wine jar
酒釀 fermented glutinous rice

一支酒 (一瓶酒) a bottle of wine
一埕酒 (一罐酒) a jar of wine
一箱紅酒 a carton of red wine
一箱啤酒 a case of beer
一樽酒 a bottle of wine
一圍酒 (一圍酒席) a table for Chinese banquet
火酒 (酒精) alcohol
去飲 (喝喜酒) go to a wedding banquet
白酒 white wine
好酒 / 好飲酒 (喜歡喝酒) fond of the bottle
米酒 rice wine
戒酒 quit drinking
佳餚美酒 excellent wine and delicious dishes; good food and

excellent wine
一杯酒 cup of wine
紅酒 red wine
冧酒 (朗姆酒) (English) rum
烈性酒 (烈酒) strong liquor
祝酒 drink a toast; toast
送行酒 (餞別酒 / 歡送晚宴) farewell dinner
啤酒 beer
缽酒 (波特酒) (English) port; porto; port wine
喜酒 (婚宴) wedding banquet
隊酒 (喪飲酒) drink alcohol
嗒酒 (淺嚐) have a sip of wine
敬酒 drink a toast
飲花酒 (去夜總會) go night-clubbing
飲酒 (喝酒) drink alcohol; drink beer; drink wine; have a drink
飲啤酒 (喝啤酒) drink beer
飲喜酒 ① (參加婚宴) go to a wedding banquet ② (在婚宴
　上喝酒) drink wine at a wedding banquet
飲悶酒 (喝悶酒) drink alone
飲醉酒 (喝醉) get drunk
一滴酒 a drop of wine
劈酒 (瘋狂地喝酒) drink alcohol
醉酒 (喝醉) drunk
燒酒 (蒸餾米酒) rice wine
醒酒 dispel the effects of alcohol
氈酒 (杜松子酒) (English) gin
擺酒 (辦酒席) give a banquet
擺滿月酒 (辦滿月酒) banquet to celebrate a baby's first
　month birthday
雞尾酒 cocktail
釀酒 make wine

【釘】 deng[1] ① (釘子) nail ② (釘住) nail ③ (死) die; pass away ④ (甄選) pick on ⑤ (跟蹤) follow; keep an eye on

釘仔 (小釘子) small nail
釘咗 (嗚呼了 / 死了) dead
釘書釘 (釘書針) staple
　釘書機 stapler
釘牌 (吊銷牌照) have one's licence suspended
釘鈕 (釘扣子) stitch a buttonhole
釘裝 (裝釘 / 裝訂) bind
　釘裝機 (裝釘機 / 裝訂機) binding machine
釘蓋 (死) die

一口釘 (一枚釘子) a nail
一眼釘 (一枚釘子) a nail
打書釘 (看白書 / 光看不買) spend a long time in a
　bookstore reading books

死妹釘（壞女孩）hussy; you selfish girl; you naughty girl

妹釘（小丫頭 / 小姑娘）little girl; small young girl

飛釘（露出乳頭）nip out; smuggle smarties

起釘（收取利息）collect an interest payment

眼中釘（眼中刺）a pain in the neck; a thorn in one's flesh

摸門釘（到訪不遇）go to visit sb but not find him/her at home; miss the doorpost

窩釘（鉚釘）rivet

撳釘（圖釘）drawing pin; thumbtack

爛船拆埋都有三斤釘 / 爛船都有三斤釘（船破還有三斤釘 / 具剩餘價值）even the wrecks of a boat are still of some surplus value

【針】zam[1] needle

針冇兩頭利（甘蔗沒有兩頭甜 / 不能兩全其美）one cannot have it both ways; there's no rose without a thorn

針灸 acupuncture

針唔拮到肉唔知痛（切膚之痛）no one but the wearer knows better where the shoe pinches

針紙（注射證明 / 疫苗接種證書）vaccination certificate

針筒（針管 / 注射器）syringe

針鼻削鐵（只向微中取利）gain the narrowest margin of profit

針嘴（針頭）needle head

一口針 / 一支針 / 一眼針（一枚針）a needle

大海撈針 look for a needle in a haystack

大頭針（別針）pin

心口針 / 襟針（胸針）brooch

方針 guiding principle; orientation; policy

生眼挑針（長麥粒腫）have a stye

打針（注射）give an injection; have an injection

扣針（胸針）brooch

快過打針（很快）very fast

金針（金針菜）dried lily flowers

拮針（注射）have an acupuncture treatment

秒針 second hand of a clock; second hand of a watch

探熱針（體溫計 / 體溫錶）clinical thermometer; medical thermometer

眼挑針 eye pick

溫度針 thermometer

聯針（縫針）stitch

織針 knitting needle

鐵杵磨成針 little strokes fell great oaks

【閃】sim[2] flash; sparkle

閃閃吟（亮光光的）glittering

閃電 ① （打閃）lightning ② （急速）rapidly

　　閃電戀 fling

閃縮（鬼祟）furtive

　　閃閃縮縮（躲躲閃閃）furtive

【陞】sing[1] advancement

步步高陞 wish you promotion and success

【院】jyun[6] ① （家）home ② （醫院）hospital

院士 academician

院長 college head; dean; president

院校 schools and institutions

　　大專院校 colleges and universities; tertiary institutions

一間醫院 a hospital

入咗醫院（住進了醫院）be hospitalised

入院（住院）be admitted to hospital; be hospitalised; go into a hospital

出院 be discharged from the hospital

宅院（房子）house; house with a courtyard

安老院（養老院 / 敬老院）home for the elderly

寺院 monastery; temple

老人院 home for the aged; home for the elderly; old people's home

妓院 brothel

法院 court house

庭院 courtyard; patio

學院 college; institute

療養院 sanitarium

戲院 ① （電影院）cinema ② （劇院）theatre

醫院 hospital

【陣】zan[6] ① （部隊列陣）file of troops ② （一會兒）moment; while

陣亡 be killed in action; fall in action; fall in battle

陣地 battle field; position

陣雨 occasional drizzle; passing shower; rain shower; shower; shower of rain

陣容 ① （戰鬥陣型）battle array; battle formation ② （排隊）cast; line-up

陣陣（間歇）at intervals; by fits and starts; intermittently; now and again; repeatedly; spasmodically

陣線 alignment; front; line of battle

陣腳 ① （前線）front line ② （情況）circumstances; position; situation

　　亂咗陣腳（亂了陣腳 / 打亂步伐）break one's stride; keep sb off their stride; knock sb off stride; put sb off their stride; throw sb off stride

一陣（一會兒）a little while; a short while; in a jiffy; in a

moment; presently

一陣陣 a while; sometimes for a single moment

打頭陣（率先）take the lead

企一陣（站一會兒）stand for a while

有頭威，冇尾陣（虎頭蛇尾）a brave beginning and a weak ending; a brave beginning but a poor ending; a tiger's head and a snake's tail; begin well but fall off towards the close; begin with tigerish energy but peter out towards the end; come out at the small end of the horn; do sth by halves; fine start and poor finish; in like a lion, out like a lamb; start out well but not continue; with a fine start but a poor finish

赤膊上陣（輕裝上陣／親自上場）come out into the open; come out pugnaciously; come out without any disguise; emerge into the open; go into battle stripped to the waist; go into battle with bared shoulders; step forward in person without any disguise; strip off all disguise and come to the fore; take the field oneself undisguised; throw away all disguise

阻你一陣（稍候片刻）keep you for a moment

家陣（現在／目前）at present; now

唔隱陣（不安全／靠不住）insecure

真空上陣（不穿內衣／穿上裸露的衣服）wear revealing clothes; pantiless

頂頭陣（率先／帶領／當先鋒）act as a pioneer; take the lead

等一陣（等一下／等一會／等一會兒／等一等）wait a moment

等陣（等一下／等一會／等一會兒／等一等）wait a moment

嗰陣（那時候／當初）at that time

暈得一陣／暈得一陣陣（被一個人的美麗迷住／頭暈／眩暈）be intoxicated by one's beauty; dizziness; giddiness; fall under sb's spell

瞓一陣（睡一會兒／小睡一下／打盹兒）take a nap

瞓陣（小憩／睡覺／打盹兒）nap

衝鋒陷陣（出生入死／赴湯蹈火）breach and storm the enemy's citadel; break into enemy ranks; charge against enemy fire; charge an enemy's position; charge and shatter enemy's positions; charge forward; charge the enemy lines; dash bravely to the front of the battle; make frontal attacks on; press boldly forward; rush on the enemy and break the line; rush on the hostile ranks; smash into the enemy ranks; storm and break up the enemy's front; storm and shatter the enemy's position; strike into the enemy ranks

穩陣（可靠／安全／穩定）reliable; safe; secure; stable

穩穩陣陣（穩定／穩固／安穩／安定）stable

【除】ceoi⁴ ①（擺脫）get rid of ②（脫）take off

除夕 Chinese New Year's Eve

除咗 ①（脫掉）take off ②（除了）besides; except

除衫（脫衣服）undress

除笨有精（吃小虧佔大便宜）problems apart, there are still advantages to a particular activity

除落嚟（脫下來）take it off

除裙（脫裙子）take off a skirt

除褲（脫褲子）take off one's trousers

　除褲放屁——多此一舉（脫褲子放屁）do sth which is unnecessary

除鞋（脫鞋）remove one's shoes; take off one's shoes

除襪（脫襪子）remove one's socks; take off one's socks

扣除 deduct; take off

刮除（打掉／罷工）strike off

免除 ①（避免／防止）avoid; prevent ②（豁免／緩解）excuse; exempt; immunize; relieve; remit

拔除（根除／去掉／刪除）eradicate; pluck; pull out; remove; uproot; weed out; wipe out

削除 omit; strike out; take out

革除 ①（廢除）abolish; do way with; get rid of ②（解僱／驅逐）dismiss; dispel; excommunicate; expel; remove from office

剔除 eliminate; get rid of; reject

根除（廢除／消除／刪除）do away with; eliminate; eradicate; exterminate; root out; uproot

破除（打破／廢除／根除）abolish; break with; do away with; eradicate; get rid of

開除（解僱）dismiss; fire; sack

剷除（根除）eradicate; root out

鏟除（清除／消除／刪除）clear off; eliminate; uproot

【隻】zek³ ① a/an; one ② measure word for animals, boat, and one of a pair

隻手（單手）single-handed

　隻手遮天（一手遮天／隱瞞真相）hide the truth from the masses; hoodwink the public; pull the wool over the eye of the public

隻字（一個字／簡要說明）brief note; single character; single word

　隻字不提（一個字都不說／保持沉默／對某事沒有說一句話／根本沒有提到）keep mum; keep silent about; make no mention of; not a word is said about; not a word slips from one's mouth about; not breathe a word about sth; not drop a word; there is no mention at all of

雙眼開，雙眼閉 （閉上眼睛／視而不見）shut one's eyes to; turn a blind eye to

雙揪 （一對一的打鬥）one-against-one fight

一隻 a; an; one
人影都冇隻／鬼影都冇隻 （沒有人／一個人也沒有／連個鬼影都沒有）there's nobody
大隻 （大塊頭／肌肉發達／強壯）big guy; bulky; muscular; tough; well build
好大隻 （很強壯）strong; robust; sturdy; very big
狗隻 （狗／犬）dog
肥屍大隻 （強壯的男人）strongly-built man
得小貓三四隻 （只有少數人）only a few people
豬欄報數——又一隻 （又死一人／三長兩短／兩腳一伸）one more has died

【馬】maa⁵ sloppy

馬虎／馬馬虎虎 （不認真／敷衍／稀鬆）not serious; perfunctory; sloppy

【馬】maa⁵ horse

馬上 （立刻／立即）at once; immediately; right away
馬上風 （在做愛時死亡）die while having sex
馬主 （馬主人）horse owner
馬仔 ① （侍從）attendant ② （打手／保鏢）bodyguard; hatchet man; henchman ③ （手下／初級員工／下屬）junior employee; subordinate ④ （薩其瑪）candied rice fritter
馬字邊 （馬字旁）the "horse" （馬）radical
馬年 Year of the Horse
馬死落地行 （沒有依賴後就需要自力更生）have to get oneself through a difficulty without help
馬伕 （拉皮條／促成賣淫）pander; pimp; procure for prostitution
馬屁 （奉承／吹捧／阿諛奉承）flatter
　拍馬屁 （諂媚／討好／奉承／吻某人的屁股／舔某人的鞋子）adulate; brown-nose; butter sb up; crawl to; curry favour; curry favour with sb; eat sb's toads; fawn on; flatter; flatter sb in power; give sb the soft-soap; ingratiate oneself with; kiss sb's ass; lay it on thick; lay it on with a trowel; lick sb's boots; lick sb's shoes; lick sb's spittle; lick the boots of sb; obsequious; play up to; polish the apple; soft-soap; suck up to; sycophancy
馬尾 （紮辮子）(hair style) ponytail
馬拉糕 Malay sponge cake
馬房 （妓館）call girl centre
馬面 （長臉／長臉型）long face
馬桶 toilet bowl

馬場 （跑馬場）horse race course; race course; race track; racing course
馬會 （賽馬會）horse club
馬路 （路／街）road; street
　過馬路 cross the street
馬鈴薯 （土豆／薯仔）potato
馬蹄 （荸薺）water chestnut
馬戲 （馬戲團）circus
馬鮫郎 （馬鮫魚）spanish mackerel
馬騮 ① （猴子）monkey ② （頑皮的孩子）naughty kid
　馬騮精 （調皮鬼／頑皮的孩子）naughty child
　馬騮戲 （猴戲）monkey show
　甩繩馬騮 （不受管控的調皮鬼／非常頑皮的孩子）on the loose; very naughty child

一字馬 （劈叉）the splits
一隻馬 （一匹馬）a horse
八字馬 splay-foot
上馬 ① （騎上馬背）riding on horseback ② （上班／動工）take on a job
水馬 （充水塑料路障）water-filled plastic barricade
出馬 （處理／解決問題／參加比賽）deal with; tackle a problem; tackle a situation; take the field
去馬 （上馬／前進）go ahead
好賭馬 （喜歡賭馬）fond of betting on horses
老馬 （經驗豐富）the experienced
冷馬 （黑馬）dark horse
快馬 （趕緊）on the double
奉承拍馬 （奉承／吹捧／阿諛奉承／恭維話語）apple-polish; bow the scrape; cajole sb with flattering words; kiss the hem of sb's garment; tickle sb's ears
拉頭馬 （拉着勝利的馬巡遊）parade a winning horse
河馬 hippo; hippopotamus
青梅竹馬 a boy and a girl who have known each other since childhood
班馬 （呼籲更多人前來幫忙／與更多人聯手）call for back up; call for more persons; call more people to come and help; gang up with more persons
紮馬 （紮馬步）firm stance
鬼馬 （滑稽／扮小丑／詼諧／充滿幽默感）comical; play the clown; witty; witty and full of humour
鬼鬼馬馬 （滑稽／扮小丑／詼諧而充滿幽默感）comical; play the clown; witty and full of humour
做牛做馬 （做艱苦的工作）do hard work
紮馬／紮晒馬 （準備打架）prepare for a fight
造馬 ① （造馬）fixing races ② （搞貪污）engage in embezzlement ③ （修復）a fix
斑馬 zebra

跑馬（賽馬）horse racing

買馬（賭馬）bet on horses

超班馬（才能超出同齡人的人）person who is at a level beyond their peers

開明車馬（心胸開闊 / 公開表達自己的意圖）open-hearted; state one's intention openly

撞死馬（走路急匆匆趕路的人）person who jostles his way in hot haste

親自出馬（親自處理）take up a matter by oneself

賭馬 bet on horses

頭馬（最得力的助手）top assistant

擘一字馬（劈叉）do the splits

擘八字馬 split the splayed feet

賽馬 horse racing

擺明車馬 put all one's cards on the table

騎牛搵馬（在堅持自己的同時追求更好）seek for the better while holding on to one; work in one job but look out for a better one

騎馬 ride on horseback

騎硫磺馬（將某人的錢轉移為己用）divert sb's money to one's own purpose

騎膊馬（一個孩子騎在大人肩膀上）a child sitting on the shoulders of an adult

識途老馬（老馬識途）the experienced knows the ropes

鐵馬 ①（警察摩托車）police motorbike ②（鐵欄杆）iron railing ③（鐵路障）iron road block

【骨】gwat¹（骨頭）bone

骨子（精巧 / 精緻）delicate and exquisite

骨肉（親生子女）one's natural children

骨折（骨頭斷裂）bone fracture; broken bone; fracture

骨妹（按摩女郎）massage girl; masseuse

骨氣（道德）moral backbone

    有骨氣（具道德）have guts; have moral backbone

骨場（按摩院）massage parlour

骨痛（骨頭疼）pain in the bones

骨裂（骨折 / 斷裂）bone fracture; crack in the bone

骨痹（令人肉麻 / 肉麻）cause sb to be disgusting; feel unnatural

骨頭 bone

    骨頭打鼓（人死了很久）died a long time ago

    硬骨頭（無畏不屈的人）dauntless and unyielding person

    賤骨頭（惡棍 / 壞人 / 壞蛋 / 無賴）scoundrel

骨骹（關節）joint

一個骨 ①（十五分鐘）fifteen minutes ②（四分之一）a quarter

一棚骨（一排骨頭）a bag of bones

一點一個骨（一點十五分）a quarter past one; one fifteen

一點三個骨（一點四十五分）a quarter to two; one forty-five

一嚿骨（一塊骨頭）a bone

三個骨（四十五分鐘 / 四分之三個小時）forty-five minutes; three quarters of an hour

反骨（背叛 / 叛逆 / 忘恩負義）bite the hand that feeds one; quit love with hate; rebellious; repay love with hate; requite kindness with enmity; return evil for good; return kindness with ingratitude; treat one's benefactor as one's enemy

冇腰骨（沒骨氣 / 靠不住）cowardly; spineless; undependable; unreliable

出骨（露骨）undisguised

去骨（去掉骨頭）boned

打腳骨（敲竹槓 / 勒索金錢）extort money; fleece; fleece sb of his money; make advantage of sb's being in a weak position to overcharge him; make an exorbitant charge for services rendered; make sb pay through the nose; make sb squeal; overcharge; put the lug on; soak; sponge a person; sponge on sb; squeeze a person for money; sting; that is as good as blackmail; that is highway robbery

甩皮甩骨（皮開骨散 / 散了架子）in bad shape

有骨（諷刺 / 譏諷 / 挖苦 / 冷言冷語）have a sting in one's words; sarcastic

有腰骨（信得過 / 靠得住）reliable; trustworthy

收買路錢打腳骨（搶劫旅客）rob travellers

老差骨（經驗豐富的警察）experienced police officer

肋骨 ribs

肋軟骨（軟骨肋骨）cartilage ribs

尾龍骨（脊柱 / 尾骨）spine; tailbone

枕骨 pound the back

刺骨 biting; cut to the bones; piercing; pierce to the bones

刻骨（根深蒂固）bone-deep; deep-rooted; deeply ingrained

官仔骨骨（衣冠楚楚）well dressed

狗咬狗骨（狗咬狗 / 同類相鬥）fight among members of the same group; put up an internecine fight

俗骨（氣質鄙陋庸俗）in bad taste

屍骨 skeleton of a corpse

食人唔𩗴骨（貪得無厭）greedy for gains

起骨（剔骨）boning

脊骨 backbone; spine

排骨 ①（排骨）spare ribs ②（枯瘦 / 皮包骨）skinny ③（瘦小的人）skinny person

梅子蒸排骨 steamed spareribs with plum sauce

趾骨 phalanges; phalanx of the foot

魚骨 fishbone

揸骨（捏骨頭）pinch the bones

鈒骨（鎖邊）stitch edges

揼骨（捶背 / 按摩）pound sb's back; massage

筋骨 bones and muscles

腕骨 wrist bone

腰骨 ① (盆腔 / 骨盆 / 髖) pelvic ② (性格強烈 / 骨氣) strong character

腳骨 leg bone

䐃骨 cheekbone

過骨 (打通 / 考試及格 / 刮透) get through; pass a test; scrape through

精到出骨 (巧妙地從自私的動機中採取行動) act cleverly from selfish motives

銅皮鐵骨 (銅筋鐵骨) iron constitution; brass muscles and iron bones; strong and solid body; tough and strong as iron and steel; with vigorous skin and bones and strong muscles

遮骨 (傘骨) ribs of an umbrella

駁骨 (接骨) set a fracture

嚟骨 (啃骨頭) gnaw a bone

豬骨 pigbone

豬頭骨 (糟糕的工作 / 無利可圖的業務) bad job; unprofitable business

頸骨 (頸椎) neck bone

鋼骨 (鋼筋) reinforcing steel

縮骨 (從自私的動機行事 / 自私和狡猾 / 偷懶) act from selfish motives; selfish and cunning; shirker

䐃骨 (吐出骨頭) spit out the bones

骾骨 (魚刺卡在喉嚨裏) fishbone stuck in the throat

鬆吓腳骨 (放鬆一下腿) relax one's legs

鬆骨 (按摩) massage

蹺嘥腰骨 (跌倒時腰部受傷) hurt the waist in a tumble

露骨 (不含蓄) embarrassingly direct

聽落有骨 (意在言外 / 諷刺) more is meant than meets the ear

【高】gou¹ high; tall

高大 (高個子 / 高個兒) well-built
　高大有型 (高大時尚) tall and stylish
　高大衰 (傻大個兒 / 笨拙愚蠢的人) lummox
　高大威猛 huge and tough; tall and majestic; tall and stout
　神高神大 (高個子 / 高個兒) well-built

高不成，低不就 (既不適合更高的職位，也不願意從事更低的職位) neither unfit for a higher position nor willing to take a lower one

高中 senior middle school; high school

高手 (專家 / 大師) expert; master
　武林高手 (武術世界的大師) master in the world of martial art

高水平 high levels; premium

高佬 (高個子) tall guy; tall person

高明 (有資格的人) qualified person
　另請高明 (找另一個更有資格的人) find another better

qualified person

高波 (高速檔) high gear

高級 high class

高高瘦瘦 tall and slim

高啲 (高一點) higher up

高就 (更好的工作) better job

高貴 elegant; noble

高買 (三隻手 / 偷商品 / 小偷 / 賊) pickpocket

高矮 height
　唔高唔矮 (中等身高 / 不高不低) of medium height

高踭鞋 (高跟鞋) high-heeled shoes

高爾夫球 golf
　打高爾夫球 play golf

高鼻 (高鼻樑) high nose

高樓大廈 tall buildings

高瘦 / 又高又瘦 / 高高瘦瘦 tall and slim

高興 feel happy

高壓煲 (高壓鍋 / 壓力鍋) pressure cooker

高檔 ① (高速檔) high gear ② (高等貨物) upper end

高櫃 (大立櫃) high cabinet

高竇 (自高自大 / 看不起人 / 架子大 / 清高 / 瞧不起人) as proud as a peacock; proud and look down on others; snobbish
　高竇貓 (勢利) snobbish

上高 (當局) authorities

心頭高 (心志太高 / 期待太多 / 過於雄心勃勃 / 定下的目標太高了) expecting too much; over-ambitious; set one's goal too high

年事已高 (年紀大 / 年老) be advanced in years

血壓高 high blood pressure; hypertension

身高 height

的士高 (迪斯科 / 迪斯科舞廳) (English) disco; discotheque

埞高 (提升 / 提高) elevate; raise

眼角高 ① (有很高的要求 / 挑剔) have high demands; picky ② (選擇配偶時要高標準) set a high standard in choosing one's spouse

量身高 measure one's height

跳高 ① (跳高) high jump ② (跳得高) jump high

跳得好高 can jump very high

擒高 (爬上 / 攀上) climb up

樓底高 (天花板很高) the ceiling is high

【鬥】dau³ ① (比賽) contest ② (拼合 / 拼湊在一起) piece together

鬥木 (做木工活兒) carpentry; woodwork
　鬥木佬 (木工 / 木匠) carpenter

鬥叻 (比本事 / 衡量一個人的技能) measure one's skill against one's rival

鬥字（拼字／拼寫）orthography

鬥快（比快）competition of speed

鬥抛（通過使用侮辱性語言在戰鬥前炫耀）show off before a fight by using abusive language

鬥走（競步走／賽步）heel-to-heel walking

鬥波 ①（賽球）ball game ②（打一場球賽）play a ball game

鬥埋（拼起來）piece together

鬥氣 on bad terms

鬥起來（拼起來／拼湊在一起）piece together

鬥靚（比美／選美賽）beauty contest

鬥雞眼（對眼）cross-eyed

【鬼】gwai² ghost

鬼上身 be taken over by a ghost; crazy; mad

鬼火咁靚（十分漂亮）very beautiful

鬼古（鬼故事）ghost story
　講鬼古（講鬼故事）tell a ghost story

鬼打你（活見鬼）you are obsessed

鬼打鬼（狗咬狗／內鬨）at odds with each other; gangsters arguing among themselves; in-fighting

鬼打都冇咁醒（保持警惕）be on the alert

鬼仔（洋男孩兒／外國男孩）young foreigner; young Westerner
　番鬼仔（洋男孩兒／外國男孩）young foreigner; young Westerner

鬼佬（老外／洋人／外國人）foreigner; Western guy; Westerner; white male

鬼拍後尾枕——不打自招 confess without being pressured

鬼咁 ①（非常）extremely; very ②（怪…的）quite; rather
　鬼咁好（很好）very good
　鬼咁衰（很糟糕）very bad; very nasty

鬼妹（外國女孩）young female foreigner
　番鬼妹（外國女孩）young female foreigner

鬼知（誰知道）who knows

鬼食泥（嘀嘀咕咕）mutter incomprehensibly
　鬼食泥噉聲（怨聲地嘀咕）groan; moan; murmur against

鬼馬／鬼鬼馬馬（不正經的／滑頭／機靈／滑稽／詼諧而充滿幽默感）comical; play the clown; witty; witty and full of humour
　鬼五馬六 ①（油頭滑腦）act in a grotesque way; act strangely ②（輕佻的）frivolous ③（污穢的）messy

鬼鬼哋（像外國人的樣子）have the look of a foreigner

鬼鬼祟祟 look sneaky

鬼混 ①（調情）flirt with ②（嫖妓）visit prostitutes

鬼殺咁嘈（大吵大嚷／大聲吵鬧）extremely noisy; very noisy

鬼婆／番鬼婆（洋女人／白種女人／白人女子）Caucasian woman; white woman
　鬼都怕（可怕的／嚇人的／恐怖／駭人的）terrifying

鬼揞眼（無法看到某事）fail to find sth

鬼話（惡意八卦／壞話）malicious gossip
　鬼話連篇（說謊／大話連篇）tell lies

鬼猾（狡猾）as crafty as a fox; crafty

鬼鼠（鬼祟）furtive; sneaky
　鬼鬼鼠鼠（鬼鬼祟祟）furtive; sneaky; stealthy

鬼劃符（難以辨認的筆跡／手寫字寫得不好）illegible handwriting; poor handwriting

鬼槍（洋槍）rifle

鬼影都冇隻（一個人影都沒有）there's nobody

鬼遮眼（看不見要找的東西）fail to find sth

鬼頭（魔鬼妖怪／惡魔）devil
　鬼頭仔（內奸／告密／賣國賊）hidden traitor; informer; quisling
　小鬼頭（小鬼／小惡魔／惡作劇的孩子）buster; little devil; mischievous child; imp

七鬼（那是甚麼）what is it

大炮鬼（吹牛／說謊者）braggart; liar; teller of tall stories

大鬼（王牌）joker

大話鬼（說謊者／騙子）liar

大頭鬼（大人物）big-spending person

大懵鬼（心不在焉的人）absent-minded person

內鬼（間諜）spy on the inside

打靶鬼（沒用的人）useless person

生鬼（滑稽／詼諧）comical; funny; jocular

白鬼（白種人）Caucasians

白粥油炸鬼（白粥配油條）plain rice congee with deep-fried dough stick

充大頭鬼（假裝一個富有或強大的人／穿上一個有錢人的外表）pretend that one is rich or powerful; put on the appearance of a man of wealth

吊靴鬼（跟蹤者／跟屁蟲）limpet

多個香爐多隻鬼（競爭對手越多，競爭越激烈）the more the competitors, the keener the competition

好鬼（好／十分）very

好猛鬼（滿是鬼）full of ghosts

有鬼 there's sth fishy

老友鬼鬼（好朋友）good friend

老鬼（老頭／老人）old person

色中餓鬼（色情狂／色魔）sex maniac

死鬼 ①（死者）deceased ②（魔鬼／妖怪）devil

呃神騙鬼（行騙／裝神弄鬼）lure sb into a trap

吽鬼（白痴／呆子）idiot

把鬼（沒用／無意義／無用）of no use; pointless; useless

走鬼（無牌小販躲避警察／逃避追捕）illegal hawkers
　　fleeing from policemen to avoid arrest; make a getaway
油炸鬼（油條）deep-fried dough stick
呢嗰老鬼（這個老傢伙）this old guy
夜鬼（夜貓子）insomniac; late sleeper; night person
孤寒鬼（吝嗇鬼）miser; miserly person; stingy person
娃鬼（頑皮的傢伙）naughty guy
是非鬼（八卦／說閒話／講是非）gossip person; gossiper;
　　scandalmonger
為食鬼（饞嘴）glutton; greedy eater
酒鬼（醉翁）alcoholic; alky; barfly; bibber; cancer; drinker;
　　drunkard; gargler; tippler; toper; wine bibber
病鬼（體弱多病的人）sickly person
神鬼（神與鬼）gods and ghosts
衰鬼 ①（該死的人）big bore; damnable person; git; mush;
　　pest ②（甜心／蜜糖／愛人）（女性稱呼她的愛人）
　　(woman calling her lover) darling; honey; sweetheart
討厭鬼（噁心的人）disgusting person
冤鬼（死纏爛打）stalker
細鬼（王牌）jokers
替死鬼（替罪羊／替代受害者）fall guy; scapegoat;
　　substitute victim; whipping boy
番鬼（洋鬼子／外國人）foreign devil; foreigner
黑過鬼（倒霉）have bad luck
搖鬼（沒有人）no one
搞鬼（製造麻煩／搞鬼）make trouble; play tricks
煮鬼（扯掉某人的背影）rip up the back of sb
盞鬼（可愛）cute
隔夜油炸鬼（好脾氣的人）good-tempered person
嘩鬼（淘氣鬼／調皮鬼）naughty; noise-maker
撞鬼（活見鬼／運氣差／不幸的）be haunted by a ghost;
　　down on one's luck; unfortunate
窮鬼（窮光蛋／身無分文的流浪漢）pauper; penniless
　　vagrant; poor wretch; ragamuffin
厲鬼 ①（殘忍／激烈／嚴重／尖銳）cruel; fierce; severe;
　　sharp ②（強大／嚴重／可怕）formidable; serious; terrible
賭鬼（賭徒）gambler
餓鬼（飢餓的鬼）hungry ghost
醜死鬼（羞死人）feel really embarrassed
懶鬼（懶惰的人）lazy person
鹹濕鬼（好色的男人）lecherous man
魔鬼 devil
爛鬼（壞蛋／惡棍／壞人／無賴）rascal
爛賭鬼（病態賭徒／賭鬼）compulsive gambler
攢鬼 ①（合算／有好處）good ②（賺錢）earn money; save
　　up money
攪七鬼（攪甚麼／做甚麼）what gives
攪鬼（製造麻煩／搗亂／鬧事／惹事／生事）make trouble

11 劃

【乾】gon¹ dry

乾衣機（烘乾機）clothes dryer
乾炒 dry-fried
　　乾炒牛河 dry-fried rice noodles with beef
乾洗 dry clean
乾時緊月（捉襟見肘）hard up for money
乾淨（清潔）clean
　　洗乾淨 wash clean
　　揩乾淨（擦乾淨）wipe clean
　　整乾淨（清理）clean up
　　擦乾淨（抹乾淨）wipe clean
乾貨 seasonings and dehydrated food
　　乾貨舖（乾貨店）stall selling seasonings and
　　　dehydrated food
乾萌萌（乾巴巴地）dull and dry; insipid
乾塘 ①（抽乾池塘）drain a pond ②（缺錢）broke; fall
　　short of money
乾電（直流電）direct current
乾瑤柱（乾貝）dried scallop
乾燥 dry
　　好乾燥（十分乾燥）very dry
乾濕褸（風雨衣／雨衣）mackintosh

一塊餅乾 a biscuit
口乾（口渴）thirsty
牛肉乾 ①（牛肉乾）beef jerky ②（停車票）parking
　　ticket
抹乾（擦乾）dry; wipe dry
油漆未乾 wet paint
炕乾（烤乾）bake to dry
苦瓜乾（愁眉苦臉）gloomy face
唔好乾（在陽光下難以曬乾）hard to dry in the sun
神前桔──陰乾（金錢愈積愈少）(said of money) become
　　less and less slowly; the longer the sum of money is
　　saved, the smaller it becomes
晾乾（在陽光下曬乾）dry in the sun
陰乾（慢慢乾涸）dry up slowly
提子乾（葡萄乾）dried grapes; raisin
焙乾（烤乾）dry by a fire
菜乾 dried cabbage
撚乾（擠乾）squeeze dry
餅乾 biscuit
蝦乾 dried shrimp
燂乾（用火燒乾）dry by a fire
難乾（不好乾）hard to dry in the sun
瓊乾（滴乾）drip dry

【假】gaa² fake

假牙 false teeth
　　一隻假牙（一顆假牙）a false tooth

假設 assume

假貨（偽製品）counterfeit; fake goods

假裝 pretend

假野（冒牌貨 / 假貨）imitation brand goods

假膊（墊肩）shoulder pad

乜都係假（它無法幫助）it can't be helped

乜都假（好歹 / 在任何情況下）in any case

丟假（丟臉 / 丟人 / 丟面子）lose face

放暑假 have a summer vacation

花假（假 / 偽裝 / 偽造）fake

唔嬲就假（不生氣才奇怪）it would be strange if one does not get angry

真定假（真或假）true or false

暑假 summer vacation

虛假（假 / 虛偽的 / 虛幻）false; insincere; sham; unreal

【假】gaa² leave

假期 holiday; vacation

休假 ①（去度假 / 有個假期）go on a vacation; have a holiday; take a vacation ②（休假 / 請假）on leave; take a leave

年假 annual leave

告假（請假 / 休假 / 申請休假）be absent on leave; apply for leave; ask for leave; ask for leave of absence; leave of absence

度假 enjoy a vacation

放假 on a holiday; on leave

病假 sick leave

產假 maternity leave

暑假 summer vacation

請病假 take sick leave

【偈】gai⁶ chat; talk

偈油（潤滑油）lubricant oil

大偈（船主 / 首席）chief officer; first mate

好啱偈（談得來 / 相互融洽）be congenial to each other

唔啱偈（談不攏 / 相處不合）not get along well

傾吓偈（聊聊天）have a little chat

傾偈（聊天 / 閒聊 / 談話）chat; chit-chat; have a chat; have a good chat; talk

傾密偈（密斟 / 密談）have a personal chat

傾閒偈（聊天 / 閒談）have a chat

【偉】wai⁵ great

偉人 great man; great personage

偉大 great; mighty

偉績 brilliant achievements; glorious achievements; great achievements; great exploits; great feats

【偏】pin¹ partial

偏心（偏袒 / 偏愛）show partiality to sb

偏見 bias; partial opinion; preconception; prejudice; slant; warp

偏門（非法經營）illegal business
　　撈偏 / 撈偏門（靠非法生意謀生）earn a living from illegal business

偏食 dietary bias

偏差 departure; deviation; divergence; drift; offset; variance

偏偏（故意 / 只是 / 只要）deliberately; just; only

偏袒（偏向）bias for; discriminate in favour of; favour; partial to; partial to and side with take sides with; weigh

偏愛 affect; favour; go overboard; have a predilection for; have a preference for; have partiality for sth; love one more than another; partial to; play favourites; predilection; show favouritism to sb; take sides

偏遠（遠處 / 遠程）faraway; remote

偏離 deflect; departure; diverge; deviate; skew

【做】zou⁶ do

做一輪（做一段時間）work for a period

做人 behave as a person; conduct oneself
　　點做人呀（你怎麼能做任何事情）how can you do anything

做七（斷七 / 人們死後七週的悼念儀式）memorial ceremony for the dead seven weeks after their death

做又三十六，唔做又三十六（無論是勤勞還是懶惰，都能得到同樣的報酬）one gets the same pay whether one is hardworking or lazy

做乜 / 做乜嘢（為甚麼 / 怎麼會 / 怎麼樣 / 做甚麼的 / 為甚麼會這樣）how come; how is it that; what for; why; why is it that; why oh why

做一日和尚唸一日經（做一天和尚撞一天鐘 / 過一日算一日）wear through the day

做牛做馬（做苦工）do hard work

做冬（過冬至 / 慶祝冬至節）celebrate the Winter Solstice Festival

做瓜（幹掉 / 殺 / 殺死 / 殺害）kill
　　做瓜佢（把他幹掉 / 把他殺死 / 把他殺害）kill him

做好做醜（又唱紅臉又唱白臉）coax and coerce

做低（打倒 / 搞垮 / 幹掉 / 殺死 / 殺害）kill

做事（工作）work

出嚟做事 (外出工作) be working

憑良心做事 (按照良心行事) act according to conscience; obey what conscience dictates

做到 work until...

做到一條氣 (忙得透不過氣來) up to the ears in work

做到隻展嗽 (工作很辛苦) work very hard

做到氣咳 (忙得透不過氣來) up to the ears in work

做咗鬼會迷人 (小人得志) once a beggar is set on horse back, he will work for devils

做東 (請客) play host

做衫 (做衣服) make a dress

做埋 (做完／幹完) finish off one's work

做起未 (做好了嗎) have you finished doing sth

做鬼都唔靈 (無法提供任何幫助／沒有用處) cannot offer any help; good-for-naught

做得 (可以做／能做) can be done

做得好 well done

做得好好 (做得非常好) well done

做得嗮 (做得完) can be completed

做得嚟 (做得來) can be done

唔做得 (不可以做／不能做) can't be done

做莊 (做莊家) be a banker in a gambling game

做節 (過節日) celebrate a festival

做野 ① (行動) take action ② (幹活兒) work

冇做嘢 (沒有工作／沒工做) not working

做廠 (開工廠) set up a factory

做數 (做賬) keep accounts

做鴨 (男妓) work as a gigolo

做薑唔辣，做醋唔酸 (遠遠不夠) it is far from sufficient for the purpose

做戲 ① (演戲) act in a play ② (做戲／演出) put on a show

做醜人 (唱紅臉兒／當和事老) carry the can

做嚟湊 (做着看) do it for show

做雞 (做妓女) work as a prostitute

做騷 (表演) do a show

做 facial (臉部美容) have a facial

做 gym (在健身房鍛煉身體) exercise in a gym

做 show (表演) perform in a show

做 spa (做水療) have a spa

人心肉做 (有良心／人們本質上是富有同情心的) have a good conscience; people are by nature compassionate

出嚟做 (做妓女) start a career as a prostitute

叫做 (叫做／所謂) is called; so-called

生安白做 (胡編亂造) fabricate; invent a story

好人難做 a sage is often regarded as a savage

好心唔怕做 (不怕做善事) not afraid to do good deeds; have

one's heart in the right place

好做唔做 (應該做不去做，沒有做需要做的事) not doing what needs to be done

年三十晚謝竈——好做唔做 (沒有做自己應該做的事情) do not do what one should do

死做爛做 (不斷重複做自己的工作) tire oneself out through overwork; work oneself to death

拖慢來做 (磨蹭／磨洋工／偷懶／消極怠工) dawdle along; dawdle over one's work; lie down on the job; linger over one's work; loaf on the job; slacking

易做 (容易做) easy to do

度身定做 tailor-made

訂做 made to order

唔好做 (很難做／很難處理) hard to make; hard to manage

唔做 (放棄／退出) quit

執正嚟做 (按照原則行事) act according to principles; act on principles

惡做 (難以管理／難以對付／強硬) difficult to manage; hard to deal with; tough

揸正來做 (按本子辦事) go by the book

搵工做 (找工作做) look for a job

搵嘢做 (找一份工作做) find a job; look for a job

識唔識做 (你知不知道怎樣做是最好的) do you know what is best to do

識做 (知道怎樣做最好) know what is best to do

難做 (艱鉅的工作／難以管理) a tough job to do; hard to manage

霸住嚟做 (自己承擔一切) take on everything by oneself

驚住唔識做 (恐怕不會做) worry that one may not be able to do sth

【停】 ting⁴ stop

停止 (暫停) stop

停水 (暫停供水) suspension of water supply

停火 (停戰／休戰) ceasefire

停火協定 (停戰協定／休戰協定) ceasefire agreement

停車 ① (停車) stop a car ② (停泊汽車／泊車) park a car

停車處 parking

停車場 car park

公眾停車場 public car park

停車熄匙 (汽車停止時關閉發動機／停車熄火) switch off the engine when the car stops

唔該呢度停車 (請停在這裏／請停車) please stop here

轉彎停車 (拐彎停車) turn the corner and stop

停咗雨 (雨停了) the rain has stopped

停電 (燈火管制) blackout

停頓 (暫停／中止／中斷／停止) suspend

不停（不斷）non-stop
中停（介質／中／中等／中號）medium
手停口停（不做事就沒飯吃）if a person doesn't work he/she has no food to eat; no work no food
街口停（停在街道交叉口）stop at the street intersection
調停（調解／斡旋）mediation

【健】gin⁶ healthy

健身（健美運動／健身運動）bodybuilding
　健身室（健身房）gymnasium
健兒（競賽者）player
健康 health
　健康舞（健美操）aerobics
　追求健康 pursue health
健談 talkative

身壯力健 have a strong body; in good health; in vigorous health
壯健／康健 healthy

【側】zak¹ side

側身（轉向一邊）turn to the side
側便（旁邊）near by position; next to; right by; side
側側膊（繞過規則／避開正途）get round the rules
側跟（旁邊／側面）near by position; right by; side
側頭（歪脖子／扭脖子）wry neck
側邊（旁邊）beside; by the side of
側轉（側過來／轉向側面）turn sideward

打側（側放／斜的／傾斜）sidelong; slant
閘側（轉向側面／側向轉）turn sideward

【偶】ngau⁵ idol

偶然（意外地／不經意）by accident
偶像 idol
　大眾偶像（受歡迎的偶像）popular idol
　崇拜偶像 worship idols
木偶（傀儡）puppet
佳偶（一對幸福的已婚夫婦）a happily married couple

【偷】tau¹ steal

偷呃拐騙（偷訛拐騙）steal, cheat, kidnap, and swindle
偷步（搶跑）jump the gun
偷食 ①（偷吃）take food surreptitiously ②（短暫的戀情）have a brief love affair ③（婚外情）have sex outside marriage
　偷食唔抹嘴（留下做錯事的證據）leave behind evidence of one's wrongdoing
偷師（偷學）pick up a skill by watching

偷笑（暗笑／在某人的背後笑／在一個人的心裏笑）chuckle; laugh behind sb's back; laugh in one's heart; laugh in one's sleeve; laugh up one's sleeve; snicker; snigger
偷偷哋（暗自／暗地裏）secretly
偷偷摸摸（悄悄地行動）act stealthily
偷渡客（偷渡者）stowaway
偷嘢（偷東西／偷竊）steal things; theft
　俾人偷嘢（被人偷東西／東西被盜）things are stolen
偷龍轉鳳（秘密替代／狸貓換太子）make a secret substitution
偷薄（削薄／把頭髮弄薄了）thin out the hair
偷雞（偷懶／抓住機會避免工作）take a chance to avoid work
　偷雞唔倒蝕揸米（偷不着雞丟把米／沒有任何得益）end up with nothing; go for wool and come back shorn
偷懶（忽視一個人的工作）loaf on the job; neglect one's work

妻不如妾，妾不如偷（妻子不如妾，妾不如情婦）a wife is not as good as a concubine, and a concubine is not as good as a mistress
熟讀唐詩三百首，唔會吟詩也會偷（技能來自不斷的練習／熟能生巧）skill comes from constant practice

【兜】dau¹ ①（杓）ladle ②（招攬生意）solicit business ③（捧）hold

兜一兜（炒一炒）stir-fry once
兜巴星（打了一巴掌）slap sb in the face
兜住 ①（捧着）hold ②（從尷尬中解脫出來）save sb from embarrassment
兜炒（快炒）stir-fry quickly
兜客（招攬客戶）scout around for customers
兜風耳（招風耳朵）flaring ear
兜路（繞路）go the long way round
兜踎（貧困／邋遢／破舊）poverty-stricken; scruffy; shabby

沙律兜（沙拉碗）salad bowl
現兜兜（以現金的形式）in the form of cash
揸兜（做乞丐／失業）be a beggar; be unemployed
踎兜（失業／失業人士）unemployed
豬兜 ①（白痴／呆子）idiot ②（給料機／料斗／飼料槽）feeder; hopper; manger

【副】fu³ assistant

副手（副）deputy
副本 copy

一副 measure word for spectacles, games, etc.

【剪】zin² cut

剪刀 scissors; shears
剪草 (剪頭髮) cut hair
剪彩 cut the ribbon at an opening ceremony
剪裁 ① (裁縫) cut out a garment; tailor ② (從一篇文章中刪剪不需要的材料) cut out unwanted material from a piece of writing; prune
剪影 ① (剪紙剪影) paper-cut silhouette ② (草圖 / 大綱) sketch; outline ③ (黑色半身側面剪影) silhouette

一把鉸剪 (一把剪刀) a pair of scissors
一把較剪 (一把剪刀) a pair of scissors
飛髮剪 (理髮剪) hair clipper
較剪 (剪刀) scissors
鉸剪 (剪刀) scissors

【勒】lak⁶ ① (緊縮 / 拉緊) tighten ② (迫使) compel; force

勒尿 (把尿 / 幫助小孩小便) help a small child urinate by holding their legs apart
勒索 blackmail; extort
　勒索錢財 extort money from sb
　向人勒索 impose blackmail on sb
勒勒卡卡 (結結巴巴 / 吞吞吐吐) hesitate in speaking; stammer; stammer out; stumble over; stutter

【務】mou⁶ matters

務必 (無論如何 / 必須) be sure to; by all means; must
務求 strive for
務實 deal with concrete matters relating to work

公用事務 (公用事業) utilities
巴士服務 bus services
任務 (職務 / 工作 / 責任) assignment; duties; job; mission; responsibility; task
免除債務 remit a debt
服務 give service; service
家務 household chores; housework
家頭細務 (家務) household chores
財務 financial matters
業務 business activities; official functions; professional work; vocational work
義務 obligation
電話留言服務 voice mail box
債務 debt; liabilities
履行義務 fulfill one's obligations
暫停服務 temporary suspension of service

【動】dung⁶ movement

動人 moving; touching
動力 dynamic power; motive power
動心 (激起了慾望) one's desire is aroused
動向 tendency; trend
動作 act; action; motion; movement; start moving
動身 (開始旅程 / 出發去旅行) begin a journey; depart; departure; go on a journey; leave for a place; set out on a journey
動物 animal
　動物園 zoo
動粗 (動武 / 訴諸武力 / 開始戰鬥 / 使用武力) come to blows; resort to force; start a fight; use force
動畫 animation
動亂 (騷亂 / 動盪) disturbance; turbulence; turmoil; upheaval
動搖 (搖擺不定) shake; waver and falter
動機 (意向) intention; motivation; motive
動靜 ① (某事的聲音) sound of sth astir ② (活動 / 條件 / 事件 / 發生的事情) activities; conditions; events; happenings; movements
動盪 (不穩定的) in a flux; turbulence; unrest; unstable; upheaval
動議 motion; move; proposal
動聽 interesting to listen to; moving; persuasive; pleasant to listen to

手動 manual
主動 (個人意見 / 主動) of one's own accord; take the initiative
好少運動 (很少運動) seldom do exercise
自動 automatic
行動 action
作動 (胎動) fetal movement
更動 (改變 / 更改 / 修改) alter; change; modify
波動 fluctuation
盲目行動 act blindly
哄動 cause a sensation; make a stir
臥底行動 (秘密行動) undercover operation
活動 ① (動一動) exercise; move about ② (搖搖欲墜 / 不穩定) shaky; unsteady ③ (移動 / 活動) mobile; movable ④ (演習) activity; going-ons; maneuver ⑤ (運用個人影響力或不正當手段) use personal influence or irregular means ⑥ (行為 / 特性 / 表現 / 做法) behaviour
郁動 (動一下 / 走動 / 活動) move about
原封不動 (保持完整) be kept intact
浮動 ① (漂移) drift; float; ripple ② (波動 / 不穩定) fluctuate; unstable; unsteady ③ (浮動 / 漂浮) float ④ (靈活性 / 伸縮性 / 機動性) flexibility
做運動 exercise

採取主動 take the initiative
移動 move
勞動 (勞工) labour
嘟動 (擊中 / 移動 / 觸摸) hit; move; touch
揮動 (揮舞) brandish; wave
策動 engineer instigate; stir up
運動 ① (運動) sport ② (練習 / 鍛煉 / 活動) exercise
熱身運動 warm-up
撼動 (搖擺 / 抖動) rock; shake
聯合行動 united action
震動 (振動) vibration
鬨動 (引起轟動) cause a sensation

【匙】si⁴ spoon

匙羹 (勺子) ladle; spoon
　一隻匙羹 (一把勺子) a spoon
　木匙羹 (木勺) wooden ladle

一抽鎖匙 (一串鑰匙) a string of keys
一條鎖匙 (一把鑰匙 / 一管鑰匙) a key
車匙 (車鑰匙) car key
茶匙 (茶勺) teaspoon
停車熄匙 (汽車停止時關閉發動機 / 停車熄火) switch off
　the engine when the car stops
鎖匙 (鑰匙) key

【匿】nik¹ (躲 / 藏) conceal; hide

匿名 anonymous
　匿名信 anonymous letter
匿埋 (躲起來 / 藏起來) hide oneself

【區】keoi¹ district

區分 (標定 / 辨析) demarcate; differentiate; differentiate
between; discriminate; distinguish; make a distinction
between; set apart
區別 (與…不同 / 不同的 / 不同於 / 區分 / 辨別 / 辨析 /
劃清界限 / 分辨其中的不同之處) differ from; differ in;
differ with; different from; differentiate; differentiate
among; differentiate between; discern; discriminate;
dissimilar from; dissimilar to; dissimilar with; distinct;
distinctive; distinguish; distinguish between; distinguish
distinction; distinguish from; distinguishable from; draw a
distinction between; make a distinction between; tell the
difference
區區 (瑣碎 / 不重要的) poor present; shabby gift; trifling;
trivial
　區區小事，何足掛齒 (微不足道的事情幾乎不值得一提)
　don't mention such small things; such a trifling matter
　is hardly worth mentioning

區域 district

市區 urban area
地區 area
局部地區 parts of an area
鄰近地區 neighbourhood

【參】caam¹ participate

參加 participate; take part in
參考 reference
參與 participation
參觀 visit
　免費參觀 free visit; visit without charge

【參】sam¹ ransom

參商 ① (兩兄弟之間的敵意) animosity between two
brothers ② (彼此隔絕) morning and evening stars

肉參 (綁票) kidnap for ransom
海參 sea cucumber
標參 (綁架) hold sb to ransom; kidnap
贖參 (支付綁匪贖金) pay the ransom

【售】sau⁶ sell

售出 (賣 / 成功銷售) sell; succeed in selling
售票 sell tickets
售貨 sell goods
　售貨員 (銷售業務員 / 營業員 / 店員) sales clerk;
　salesperson; shop assistant; shop clerk
　　一個售貨員 (一名銷售員) a salesperson
　　女售貨員 salesgirl; saleswoman
　　男售貨員 salesman
售價 (價錢) price; selling price
售樓 (出售房屋 / 出售房產) sale of property
　售樓說明書 (物業銷售手冊) property sales brochure
售罄 (售完) be sold out

出售 (賣 / 銷售) sale
廉價出售 (以便宜的價格出售) be sold at a bargain
零售 retail
銷售 sale

【唱】coeng³ ① (唱歌) sing ② (說人壞話) badmouth others

唱反調 sing a different tune
唱片 record; disc; disk
　白金唱片 platinum record
　金唱片 golden record
唱生晒 (瞎嚷嚷 / 八卦 / 傳播謠言) gossip; spread a rumour

唱好 (說某人某事的好話) say sth good about sth/sb

唱衰 (說某人某事的壞話) bad-mouth; speak ill of
　唱衰人 (說別人壞話) bad-mouth others
　唱衰佢 (說得他一文不值) say that sb is worthless

唱對台戲 (進入競爭 / 與對手比賽) enter into rivalry; put on a rival show

唱歌 ① (唱歌) sing songs ② (唱) sing; singing
　唱歌唱得好好聽 (唱得很動聽) one sings very well
　唱隻歌 (唱首歌) sing a song

唱碟 (唱片 / 唱盤) record; disc; disk
　一隻唱碟 (一張唱片) a record; a disc; a disk

唱錢 ① (更換 / 轉換) (English) change ② (兌換錢幣) exchange; exchange money

唱雙簧 (兩個人一起策劃) two people scheming together

唱 K (在卡拉 OK 唱歌) sing songs at a karaoke

三重唱 (三人唱 / 聲樂三人組) trio; vocal trio

冇呢枝歌仔唱 (過去有過的好事) such a good thing is a thing of the past

伴唱 ① (幫腔) vocal accompaniment ② (伴唱) accompany a singer

吟唱 (詠唱) chant; sing

個唱 (個人演唱會 / 獨奏音樂會) solo concert

演唱 sing in a performance

【啡】 fe[1] coffee

啡色 (棕色) brown

啡走 (咖啡加煉乳) coffee with condensed milk

一杯咖啡 a cup of coffee

沖咖啡 (煮咖啡) make coffee

咖喱啡 (臨時人員) extra

咖啡 coffee

茄喱啡 (小人物) unimportant person

咧啡 (處事草率 / 衣冠不整) do a sloppy job; sloppy-dressed

哩啡 (粗製濫造 / 馬虎 / 不修邊幅) slipshod; sloppy; slovenly; untidy

齋啡 (黑咖啡) black coffee

歎咖啡 (享受咖啡) enjoy coffee

【啄】 doek[3] slander

啄木鳥 woodpecker

是非啄 (八卦人) gossip person; gossiper; scandalmonger

烏啄啄 ① (傻乎乎) at a complete loss; entirely ignorant; in the dark ② (糊塗) muddled

【商】 soeng[1] business; commerce

商人 businessman; merchant; trader

商家 (商人) businessman; merchant; trader

商埠 (商港) trading port

商場 shopping mall

商會 (工會) trade union

商業 business; commerce

商標 (牌子) trade mark

協商 (討價還價 / 互相討論 / 談判) bargaining; consult; consult with each other; discuss; negotiate; talk things over

洽商 (討論 / 商討 / 洽談) discuss

參商 ① (兩兄弟之間的敵意) animosity between two brothers ② (彼此隔絕) morning and evening stars

帽商 (製帽商) hatter

發展商 developer

零售商 retailer

廠商 firm; manufacturer

【問】 man[6] ask

問人 (問別人) ask people
　問吓人 (問一下別人) ask someone

問米 (通過女巫與死者溝通) communicate with the dead through a witch

問你死未 (看你怎麼辦 / 看你如何處理它) we'll see how you would handle it

問和尚借梳——實冇 (和尚廟裏借梳子——走錯門了 / 問錯人) ask the wrong person for sth; come to the wrong shop

問師姑攞梳——實冇 (和尚廟裏借梳子——走錯門了 / 問錯人) ask the wrong person for sth; come to the wrong shop

問路 ask for direction

問題 question
　一個問題 a question
　一條問題 (一個問題) a question
　冇問題 (沒問題) no problem; not trouble at all

一門學問 (研究課題) a subject of study

投資顧問 investment advisor

明知故問 ask while knowing the answer

訊問 ① (訊問) interrogate; question ② (對應) correspondence

財務顧問 financial consultant

訪問 ① (面試) call by; call on; interview; pay a call; visit ② (訪問) access

詢問 ① (查詢) enquire ② (審問) interrogate

請問 (你可以告訴我嗎 / 我可以問) could you tell me; may I ask

慰問（轉達問候／表達同情和關懷）convey greetings to; express sympathy and solicitude for; extend one's regards to; salute

盤問 cross-examine

學問（學習／研究）learning; study

顧問 consultant

【啤】be¹ ①（啤酒）beer ②（模壓）mould pressing

啤一啤（喝啤酒）have a beer

啤令（滾珠軸承）bearing

啤酒 beer
　啤酒肚 beer tummy; pot belly
　一箱啤酒 a case of beer
　飲啤酒（喝啤酒）drink beer

啤梨（梨／洋梨／澳洲梨）pear
　士多啤梨（草莓）(English) strawberry

啤啤佢（我們喝啤酒吧）let's have beer

啤膠機（熱壓機）hot press

啤機（模壓機／衝壓機）mould press

士啤（備用／備件／後補）(English) spare

生啤 draught beer

青啤啤 ①（藍色）blue ②（綠色）green

淋啤啤（軟綿綿）very soft

眼啤啤（盯／瞪／凝視）stare

隊啤（喝啤酒）drink beer

煉啤啤（搗碎／稀爛）mashed; pulpy

【啤】pe¹ poker

啤友（情侶／戀人）lovers

啤牌（撲克）playing cards; (English) poker
　賭啤牌（用撲克賭博）gamble at cards

打啤（打撲克）play poker

【啦】laa¹ final particle

啦啦隊（歡呼隊）cheering team

啦啦聲（很快地／短時間內採取行動）action within a short time; quickly

山卡啦（荒涼的地方）deserted place

冇計啦（沒辦法啦）can't be helped

去死啦（見鬼／滾蛋／該死）go to hell

平啲啦（便宜一點兒吧）cheaper, please; make it cheaper

行啦（可以了）let's go

你先啦（你先請）after you

你話啦（不管你說甚麼／無論你怎麼說）whatever you say

快啲啦（快點／趕快）be quick; hurry up

男人靠得住，豬乸都會上樹啦（所有的男人都靠不住／男人靠得住，母豬會上樹）all men are unreliable

係咁啦（就這樣吧）let it be this way; so be it

是但啦（任何人都會這樣做／甚麼都行／如你所願）anybody will do; anything is alright; anything will do; as you like it

起筷啦（我們開始吃了／開吃吧）let's start eating

埋位啦（請前往餐桌）please proceed to the dining table

唔好玩我啦（不要取笑我）don't make fun of me

得啦（行／好吧／好的）all right

添飯啦（多吃一點飯）have some more rice

蛇都死啦（為時已晚）it would be too late to do sth

無啦啦（沒原因／無緣無故／沒有理由）for no reason

慳啲啦（胡謅）cut the crap

算係咁啦（一般般／不好不壞）so so

算啦（算了吧／沒關係）forget it; never mind; take it easy

算數啦（算了吧／沒關係）forget it; never mind

講少的啦（話說得越少越好）few words are best; the less said about it, the better

嚟啦（來吧／加油）come on

【啱】ngaam¹ ①（正確／對）correct; proper; right ②（適合）suit sb; suitable ③（剛才）just now

啱牙（合得來／談得來／談得攏）get along well with people; hit it off

啱用（合用／好使）convenient to use; fit for use; work well

啱先（剛才）just now

啱好（剛才／碰巧）by chance

啱巧（剛才／碰巧）by chance

啱住（合住／好住）fit for living

啱身（合身）fit for wearing

啱使（合用）convenient to use; fit for use; work well

啱食（合胃口）suit one's taste; to one's taste

啱晒 ①（全對）all correct; that's right ②（合適）suitable ③（太好了）wonderful

啱啱（剛好／剛剛）by coincidence; just; only
　啱啱好（正好／剛剛好／恰到好處）as right as nails; just right
　啱啱碰着剛剛（在關鍵時刻）at the critical moment
　啱唔啱（對嗎／對不對）is it correct; is it right

啱着（合身／合穿）fit well

啱傾（合得來／談得來／談得攏）get along well with people; hit it off

啱蕎（合得來／談得來／談得攏）get along well with people; hit it off

啱聽（中聽／愛聽／喜歡聽／耳朵很舒服）agreeable to the hearer; enjoy listening to; pleasant to the ear

啱 key（很合得來／一拍即合）get along well; hit it off

咁啱（剛好／這麼巧／湊巧／碰巧）by chance; by coincidence; just by chance; what a coincidence

咁樣至啱（這樣才對）this is just right

咁樣做唔啱（這不是正確的做法／這樣做不對）this is not the right thing to do

計啱（算對／算準）the calculation is correct

唔啱（不正確／不對／不適合／合不來）can't get along with

校啱（調整好）adjust well

湊啱 ①（不巧／碰巧）as luck would have it; by coincidence ②（只是／正好）exactly right; just; just right

睇唔啱（不要看中／看不上）not take a fancy

睇啱（看中）take a fancy

睇得啱（看得準）take a fancy

碰啱（偶然／碰巧）as luck would have it; by chance; by coincidence

撞啱（偶然／碰巧／偏巧）by chance

【啖】daam⁶ mouthful

啖啖肉（吃的每口都是肉／利潤豐厚／有利可圖）lucrative; profitable

一啖（一口／一口氣）a mouthful of

反口咬一啖（反咬一口／回身反擊）turn around and hit back

呷一啖（喝一口／唆一口）have a sip; take a sip

咬一啖（咬一口）have a bite

嘴啖（給一個吻）give a kiss

噬咗一啖（被咬傷）be bitten

錫佢一啖（給他一個吻）give him a kiss

【啞】aa² dumb; mute

啞仔（啞巴）dumb

啞仔食雲吞——心中有數（啞巴吃餃子——心裏有數）know what to do

啞仔食黃蓮——有苦自己知（啞巴吃黃蓮——有苦難言）swallow the leek

啞仔食湯丸——心中有數（啞巴吃餃子——心裏有數）know what to do

啞佬（啞巴）dumb man

啞婆（啞巴）dumb woman

又聾又啞（在外國時既不懂當地語言，又不能說母語）can neither understand or speak the native language when in a foreign country

口啞（舌頭打結／口齒不清）tongue-tied

口啞啞（舌頭打結／口齒不清）tongue-tied

聾啞（聾啞人）deaf and mute

【唸】nim⁶ recite

唸口簧 ①（背誦）rote learning ②（說順口溜）chant a doggerel

【啜】zyut³（嘬）suck

啜奶（嘬奶／吸奶）suck milk

啜面珠（吻臉／親親臉蛋）kiss the face

啜嘴（接吻）kiss

啜爆（熱吻）seriously make out

【啋】coi¹ bah

啋過你（去你的／去死吧）go to blazes; go to hell; the hell you are; up yours

【啲】di¹（一點兒）few; little; some

啲水好濁（水很渾／水很渾濁）the water is turbid

啲打（嗩吶）suona horn

　吹啲打（吹嗩吶）play the souna horn

啲咁多（一丁點兒／一點點）a little bit; a wee bit

啲客（顧客）customers

啲啲（一丁點兒／一點點）a wee bit

一啲（一些）some

平啲（便宜點）cheaper

企入啲（站入裏面一點）stand a little inside

企埋啲（站得近一點）stand closer to each other

多啲（多一些／多一點）more

好啲（更好／優勝）better

有啲 ①（一些）some ②（有些）rather; somewhat

行出啲（向外面移動一點）move a little outside

快啲（快點／趕快）be quick; hurry up

扭細聲啲（調低音量）turn down the volume

呢啲（這些）these

拍埋啲（挪近點兒）move a little closer

放鬆啲（放輕鬆／別緊張）take it easy

爭啲（幾乎／差不多／將近）nearly

玩開心啲（玩得開心些）enjoy yourself; have fun

借歪啲（勞駕／對不起／請問）excuse me

差啲 ①（幾乎）almost; nearly ②（還不夠好／未達標）not good enough; not up to the mark

唔該借歪啲（勞駕讓開／請讓一讓）excuse me

唔該靜啲（請保持安靜）please keep quiet

埋啲（靠近點）come closer

校細聲啲（調低音量）turn down the volume

高啲（再高點）higher up

第二啲（其他）other

第啲（其他）other

細力啲（減少力量／輕一點）less force; lighter

細聲啲（小聲點兒）lower than one's voice

逐啲（一點一點地）little by little; point by point

喐啲（動不動）at every move; at every turn; at the drop of a hat; at the slightest provocation; easily; frequently; on every occasion

嗰啲（那些）those

裝多啲（用更多的米飯填滿碗）fill a bowl with more rice

諗真啲（想一想）think sth through

揸實啲（拉緊一些）hold tighter

遲啲（晚些時候）afterwards; by and by; later

醒定啲（小心 / 照顧自己）be careful; take care

嚼爛啲（深深地咀嚼）chew deeply

邊啲（哪些）which

攪勻啲（使⋯均勻）make sth evenly distributed

【啩】gwaa³ final particle implying probability

唔係啩（不會吧 / 那可能嗎）is that possible

講吓笑都得啩（開玩笑而已）it's alright to crack a joke

【國】gwok³ country; nation

國文（中文 / 中國語文）Chinese

國家 country; nation; state
國家利益 country interest
內陸國家 landlocked country

國語（普通話）Mandarin; Putonghua
國語片（國語電影）Mandarin movie

國際 international

國慶（國慶日）National Day

亡國 ①（一個國家的淪陷）fall of a nation ②（戰敗國）conquered nation

中立國 neutral nation

中國 China

外國 foreign country

全國（全國 / 國民 / 整個國家 / 在全國各地）countrywide; nationwide; national; the entire country; throughout the country

同行如敵國（同一行業的人們之間存在着激烈的對抗和仇恨）bitter rivalries and hatreds exist among people in the same profession; two of a trade never agree

法國 France

帝國 empire

美國（美利堅合眾國）America; the United States of America

英國 Britain

祖國（故國）motherland

泰國 Thailand

席捲全國 sweep over the country

愛國 patriotic

德國 Germany

澤國 ①（一片充滿河流和湖泊的土地 / 沼澤）a land that abounds in rivers and lakes; marsh; swamp ②（被淹沒的地區）inundated areas

韓國 Korea

【域】wik⁶ district

域名 domain name

區域 district

領域 domain; field; realm; sphere

【圈】hyun¹ circle

圈中人（圈內人）insider

圈外人 outsider

屈一圈（繞一圈兒）take a turn around

娛樂圈 entertainment circles

眼圈（眼窩）eye socket

圓圈 circle

滿肚密圈（滿腹計謀）full of wrinkles

【培】pui⁴ cultivate

培育 breed; cultivate; foster; nurture; raise; rear

培訓（培育 / 培養）cultivate; train

培植（培育 / 教育 / 提高 / 培養）cultivate; culture; educate; foster; raise; train

培養（培育 / 開發 / 教育 / 培養）breed; cultivate; culture; develop; educate; foster; train

栽培 ①（植物栽培）plant and cultivate; tend ②（教育 / 培育 / 培養）educate; foster; train ③（給予特別的好感）give special favour; receive special favour

【埠】fau⁶（城市）city

埠頭（渡口 / 碼頭）pier; wharf

走埠（從一個地方到另一個地方謀生）wander from place to place to earn a living

商埠 trading port

遊埠 ①（旅行 / 旅遊）travel ②（白日夢）daydream

過埠（出國）go abroad

【執】zap¹ ①（收拾 / 拾 / 拾起 / 撿）pick up ②（倒閉）shut down

執二攤 ①（使用二手貨）use second-hand goods ②（約會別人的前男友或前女友）date sb's ex-boyfriend or ex-girlfriend

執仔（接生 / 助產）midwifery

執仔婆（接生婆／助產士）midwife
執正（衣着打扮得體）dress properly
　執正嚟做（按原則辦事）act according to principles; act on principles
　執到正（衣着打扮得體）dress properly
執生（見機行事／隨機應變）act according to circumstances; act as circumstances dictate; act as the occasion demands; act on seeing an opportunity; adapt oneself to circumstances; do as one sees fit; play sth by ear; lay to the score; profit by the occasion; see one's chance and act; take things as they come; use one's own judgment and do what one deemed best
　自己執生（謹慎行事／用自己的判斷做自己認為最好的事情）tread carefully; use one's own judgment and do what one deems best
執禾（撿稻穗兒）pick up the ears of rice
執好（整潔／整理）make neat; tidy up
執字粒（排字）typeset
執位（換位子）change of position
執身彩（有好運）have good fortune
執到（檢到／實現理想的某事）achieve sth desirable
　執到寶（檢着便宜了）achieve a desirable aim
　執到襪帶累身家（撿了芝麻掉了西瓜）lose a pound for gaining a penny
執牀（收拾牀鋪）make the bed
執房（收拾房間）tidy up the room
執屋（收拾房子）tidy up the house
執拾（收拾／整理）tidy up
執枱（收拾桌子）clear the table
執相（編輯相片）photo editing
執倒（走運／好運）by good luck; have fortune on one's side; have good luck; in luck; luck is on one's side; one's luck is in; strike luck; tough luck
執笠 ①（倒閉）close down; shut down ②（破產倒閉）go bankrupt; go bust
執被（疊被子）fold the quilt
執番條命（檢回一條命）escape with bare life
執媽（接生婆／助產士）midwife
執漏（堵漏／檢漏／補漏）repair the leaky part of roof
執頭執尾（打雜）do odd jobs
執輸 ①（落後）fall behind ②（佔下風／吃虧）at a disadvantage; lose; miss out
　執輸行頭，慘過敗家（慢人一步，失去先機）it would be disadvantageous not to take an immediate action in time
　唔執輸（不落人後）not fall behind
執雞（帶走別人丟失或扔掉的東西）take sth which has lost or thrown away
　執死雞 ①（幸運得了便宜）take sth which has lost or thrown away ②（檢現成）score an easy goal after a

shot has been blocked by the goalkeeper
執籌（抽籤）by lot; draw lots
執藥（抓藥）get Chinese herbs

一執 ①（少數）a handful of ②（一大堆）a tuft of
固執 ①（頑固／硬頸／倔強）obstinate; stiff neck; stubborn ②（堅持）cling to; persist in

【基】gei¹ gay
基金 fund
　保證基金（保本基金）guaranteed fund
基督教 Christianity
基礎 foundation

田基 balk; rand

【堂】tong⁴ hall
堂口（幫口／黑社會幫派）underworld gang
堂兄 elder male cousin; first cousin
堂主（幫主）underworld gang leader
堂妹 first cousin; younger female cousin
堂姐 elder female cousin; first cousin
堂皇（華麗／莊嚴）grand; magnificent; stately

一堂（一段時間）a period of; a set of
一間禮拜堂 a church
上堂 ①（上課）attend a class; attend class; go to a class; take a class ②（上一堂課）conduct a class; give a lesson
大堂 lobby; lounge
子孫滿堂 have many children and grandchildren
天堂 heaven
手板堂（手心）palm of the hand
去教堂 go to church
禾堂（曬穀物的地面）grain-sunning ground
名堂（項目）item
企堂 ①（服務員／侍應生）waiter ②（女服務員／女侍應生）waitress
佛堂 Buddhist temple
走堂（逃課）skip classes
兒孫滿堂 have children and grandchildren
金玉滿堂（房子裏裝滿了金子和寶石）house filled with gold and gems
哄堂（笑聲瀰漫在房間裏）bring the room down; fill the room with laughter
架勢堂（華麗）extravagant; gorgeous
美食天堂 food paradise; gourmet paradise
酒店大堂 hotel lobby
留堂（下課後留下來）get detention; stay behind after class; stay behind after school

庵堂〈修道院／尼姑庵〉convent; nunnery

教堂 church

提堂〈帶上法庭審判〉bring sb up for trial

疏堂 relations between cousins

貼堂〈張貼在教室的牆上〉post sth on the wall of the classroom

當堂 ①〈立刻／立即／馬上〉at once; immediately; right away ②〈當場〉on the spot; right there; there and then

聖堂〈教堂〉church

殿堂〈宮殿〉palace

落堂〈下課〉after class; come off from class; dismissed class; finish class; get out of class

腳板堂〈足弓〉arch of the foot

電梯大堂 lift lobby

飯堂〈食堂〉canteen

學堂 ①〈學校〉school ②〈警察學院〉police academy

禮拜堂〈教堂〉church

禮堂 auditorium

轉堂 change class

靈堂 funeral hall

【堅】gin¹〈真〉genuine; real

堅固 firm; solid

堅料 ①〈真消息〉true information ②〈真東西〉real thing

堅嘢〈真貨／正宗商品／正品〉authentic goods; genuine; genuine goods; the real thing; true

害死亞堅〈被某人困擾〉be encumbered by sb

【堆】deoi¹ pile

堆放〈積累〉pile up; stack

堆積〈積累／累積〉accumulate; cumulate; heap up; pile up; upbuilding

禾稈堆 stack of rice straw

冷手執個熱煎堆〈拾到個天上飛來的餡餅〉have an unexpected stroke of good fortune

成堆 in heaps

泥堆 mound

埋堆〈攢聚一起／搞小圈子〉form a small clique; join a group

惡到凸堆〈欺負者／小霸王〉play the bully

煎堆 deep-fried sesame balls

牆倒眾人推〈落井下石〉everybody hits the person when he is down; everybody kicks the man who is down; everyone gives a shove to a falling wall; everyone hits a person who is down; if a wall starts tottering, everyone gives it a shove; lick sb when he is down; make things worse for others who are already in difficulties; the wall tottering, the crowd contributes to its collapse by pushing it; when a man is going down-hill, everyone will give him a push; when a wall is about to collapse, everybody gives it a push

【埞】deng⁶ place

【夠】gau³ enough

夠力〈有足夠的力量〉have enough strength

夠本〈足夠〉enough; enough to cover the costs; have had enough; sufficient

夠皮〈足夠〉nough; enough to cover the costs; have had enough; sufficient

夠味〈合適的味道〉have the right flavour

夠勁〈帶勁兒／精力充沛的／有力／蓬勃〉energetic; forceful; vigorous

夠派〈有派頭／很派／很有體面〉put on a lot of airs; put on a show

夠威〈神氣／威風／氣勢／雄偉〉imposing; majestic

夠晒 ①〈足夠〉enough ②〈非常〉really

　夠晒勁〈真帶勁／精力充沛的／有力〉energetic; forceful; in high spirits; with great energy and efforts; vigorous

　夠晒數〈齊了／完整了〉it's complete

夠班〈夠格／達到合適的水平〉up to the right level

夠氣〈中氣足〉with good lungs

夠傑〈夠麻煩／棘手／傷腦筋〉troublesome

夠喉〈過癮〉thrilled

夠喇〈這就足夠了〉that's enough

夠照〈有派頭／很派／很有體面〉put on a lot of airs; put on a show

夠腳〈夠人打麻將／有足夠的玩家〉enough players (for a game of mahjong)

夠運〈好運氣／幸好／幸運〉in luck; luck out; lucky

夠算〈足夠／滿意〉enough; satisfied

夠數〈足夠／尚可以／夠數量／充足〉adequate; enough; sufficient in quantity

夠薑〈有種／有勇氣／有膽量〉have courage; have guts

夠膽〈有種／有膽量／夠勇敢／有勇氣〉dare; have courage; have guts

夠膴〈有種／有膽量／夠勇敢／有勇氣〉dare; have courage; have guts

夠鐘〈到時候／到時間了／到點／時間到了／是時候了〉it's time to; time's up

　未夠鐘〈現在還不是時候〉it's not time yet

　啱啱夠鐘〈及時／正好〉just in time

足夠〈充足〉adequate; enough

唔夠〈不足／不夠／短缺〉insufficient; not enough; shortage

能夠〈可以〉able to; can

【婆】po⁴ grandmother

婆仔數 (微不足道的金額) insignificant sums

婆乸 (婦人 / 心胸狹窄的老太太) small-minded old woman

婆家 (丈夫的家人) one's husband's family

婆婆 ① (奶奶) one's husband's mother; one's mother-in-law ② (外祖母) grandmother

婆媽 (過分客氣) over-polite

婆媽數 (微不足道的數量) trivial amount

婆婆媽媽 (優柔寡斷) womanishly fussy

大肚婆 (孕婦) pregnant woman

大婆 (合法的妻子) legal wife

公婆 (夫妻 / 夫婦) husband and wife

太婆 great-grandmother

包租婆 (女房東 / 房東太太) sub-landlady

四眼婆 (戴眼鏡的女人 / 近視的女人) a woman wearing glasses; short-sighted woman

外婆 (姥姥) maternal grandma; maternal grandmother

百爺婆 (老太太 / 老婦人) old lady; old woman

老姑婆 (老處女) old maid; old spinster

伯爺婆 (老太太 / 婦人) old lady; old woman

坐月婆 (月嫂 / 坐月子保姆) confinement nanny

男人婆 (假小子) tomboy

豆腐婆 (女同性戀) lesbian

事頭婆 (女老闆 / 老闆娘) female boss; lady boss; proprietress

兩公婆 (夫妻 / 已婚夫婦) husband and wife; married couple

叔婆 (祖父弟弟的妻子) wife of one's grandfather's younger brother

垃圾婆 (女性垃圾收集員) female garbage collector; female rubbish collector

妹仔大過主人婆 (把不重要的事情放在重要的事情上面) have one's priority wrong; put the trivial above the important; the tail wags the dog

姑婆 ① (未結婚過的老女人) old woman ② (姑婆) grandfather's sisters

阿婆 ① (外婆 / 姥姥) grandma; grandmother ② (老奶奶 / 老婆婆) old lady; old woman

家婆 (婆婆 / 家姑) mother-in-law

啞婆 (女啞巴) dumb woman

執生婆 (助產士 / 接生婆) midwife

娶老婆 (娶妻 / 娶媳婦) take a wife

媒人婆 (女媒人) go-between; match-maker

媒婆 (女媒人) woman matchmaker

黃面婆 (一個人的妻子) one's wife

煮飯婆 (家庭主婦) housewife

鄉下婆 (鄉下女人 / 農婦) country woman

寡母婆 (寡婦 / 孀婦) widow

聾婆 (女聾人) deaf woman

【娶】ceoi³ marry a female

娶親 (結婚 / 娶妻) get married; take a wife; tie the knot

【婚】fan¹ marriage

婚姻 marriage

婚姻美滿 enjoy conjugal happiness

婚禮 wedding ceremony

主持婚禮 host a wedding ceremony

參加婚禮 attend a wedding ceremony

舉行婚禮 hold a wedding ceremony

已婚 married

失婚 (離異 / 離婚) divorce

合法離婚 be legally divorced

成婚 (結婚) get married

求婚 ask a woman's hand in marriage; ask for a lady's hand; ask sb in marriage; lead a woman to the altar; make a proposal of marriage; make an offer of marrige; make suit to sb; marry; offer one's hand; pay one's addresses to a lady; pay one's court to a woman; plead one's suit with a woman; pop the question; propose; propose a marriage; propose marriage to; seek a marriage alliance; set one's cap at sb; step up to a girl; sue to; sue for a woman's hand in marriage; wed; woo

男大當婚 (男人應該在成年後結婚) a grown-up man ought to marry; a man should get married on coming of age; every Jack must have his Jill

協議離婚 (經雙方同意下離婚) divorce by consent

奉旨 (子) 成婚 shotgun wedding

結婚 get married

離婚 divorce

【婦】fu⁵ woman

婦人 (已婚婦人) married woman

婦女 (女人 / 女性 / 女子) women

婦女節 Women's Day

婦科 gynaecology

婦產科 obstetrics and gynaecology

一對夫婦 a couple

夫婦 husband and wife

孕婦 pregnant woman

巧婦 (聰明的女人) clever woman

西婦 Western women

弟婦 sister-in-law; younger brother's wife

兩夫婦 married couple
家庭主婦 housewife
貴婦 ①（有錢的女人／富婆）rich woman ②（優雅的女人）elegant woman
媳婦 daughter-in-law

【婄】pau³ soft

鬆婄（柔軟／鬆軟）soft

【冤】jyun¹（不公正／做出錯誤的指控）injustice; make a false accusation

冤有頭，債有主（某人要對錯誤負責／做錯事的人要為此付出代價）there must be an agent for what is done; sb is responsible for a wrong and they will pay for it
冤枉（被錯誤地指責）be wrongly accused of sth
　冤枉嚟瘟疫去（當作大病一場）ill gotten, ill spent
冤屈 false charge
冤家 ①（敵人／對手）enemy; opponent ②（鬧翻）fall out with sb
　冤家宜解不宜結（仇人應早日冰釋前嫌，不應繼續結仇）it is better to bury the hatchet
　冤家路窄（敵人狹路相逢）enemies are bound to meet
冤氣（懷恨在心）nurse a grudge
冤鬼（死纏爛打）stalker
冤臭（惡臭）foul smell
冤崩爛臭（惡臭）smelly; stinking
冤屈（冤枉）frame
冤豬頭都有盟鼻菩薩（臭豬頭有爛鼻子來聞／情人眼裏出西施）a lover has no judge of beauty
冤孽 evil connection

死冤（死纏爛打）stick like a limpet
眼冤（不順眼）eyesore
睇見就眼冤（看不順眼某人做某事）one's heart aches when sb sees sth

【密】mat⁶ hidden

密不透風 airtight
密切 close
密友 close friend
密底算盤——冇蛛漏（鐵公雞——一毛不拔／孤寒小氣／拒絕貢獻一分錢）as close as a clam; as mean as a miser; as tight as a drum; close-fisted; not give a cent; not lift a finger; not stir a finger; not turn a finger; refuse to contribute a single cent; stingy; too stingy to pull out a hair; unwilling to give up even a hair; unwilling to sacrifice even a single hair

密封 sealed
密食當三番（積少成多）a lot of small gains is as good as one big gain
密密手（手勤／勤奮／用功／勤勞）diligent; hardworking; industrious
密密麻麻（非常密集）as thick as huckleberries; as thick as stalks in a field of flax; close and numerous; thickly dotted; very dense
密密摸（閒不住／總是保持忙碌／拒絕閒着）always keep oneself busy; refuse to stay idle
密斟（密商／密談）talk secretly
密集 concentrated; crowded together
密實 ①（嚴密）tight ②（嘴緊）tight-mouthed ③（稠密／厚）dense; thick
　密實姑娘假正經（戀愛中的女子假裝嘴巴嚴密，不說真話）a girl of few words may not be so serious as she should be
密質質（密匝匝／稠密／人山人海）dense; packed; very crowded
密碼 code; secret code
密謀（合謀）conspire; plot; scheme
密籠（密封）seal up; sealed
密鑼緊鼓（下大力氣）make great efforts; the noose is hanging

口密（能保守秘密／言語謹慎）able to keep a secret; cautious about speech; discreet in speech
冚到密（阻止信息的傳遞）block the passage of information; keep one's mouth shut
告密（告發秘密事件）give secret information against sb; inform against sb; snitch
保守秘密 keep a secret
洩露秘密 disclose a secret
秘密 secret
緻密 ①（細膩／精細）close; delicate; fine ②（適當／小心）appropriate; careful
親密 close; intimate
頻密 frequent

【宿】suk¹ ①（居留）reside ②（餿）sour

宿舍（旅館）hostel

寄宿 boarding
酸宿（難聞的氣味）stingy
露宿 sleep in the open

【寂】zik⁶ lonely

寂寞 lonely; lonesome

【寄】gei³ ① (發送) send ② (郵寄) post

寄失咗 (寄失郵件) lost in the post

寄生蟲 parasite

寄信 post a letter

寄宿 boarding

寄船 (通過船發送) send by ship

【專】zyun¹ special

專利權 monopoly

專門 specialized

專家 expert; specialist
　做專家 (成為專家) be a specialist; be an expert

專登 (故意 / 專門) deliberately; intentionally

專業 ① (職業) profession ② (專業的) professional

【將】zoeng³ get hold of

將心比己 (易地而處) measure another's foot by one's own last

將佢拳頭抆佢嘴 (以牙還牙) pay sb back in his own coin; return like for like

將計就計 (用對方的計策,反過來對付對方) turn sb's tricks against him

將軍 ① (將軍) general ② (最後一關) (in Chinese chess) check
　兜篤將軍 (給予出其不意的打擊) rip up the back of sb

將就 (湊合着用 / 忍受 / 容忍) make do with; make the best of; put up with; tolerate

將錯就錯 (事情做錯了,順着錯誤做下去) make the best of a bad job; make the best of a mistake; over shoes over boots

正將 (刺中) sting

蝦兵蟹將 (不重要的人 / 小人物) unimportant person

【屙】o¹ (拉 / 撒) ease nature

屙血 (便血) have blood in one's stool

屙尿 (小便 / 拉尿 / 撒尿) apple and pip; burn the grass; dickydiddle; discharge one's urine; drain one's radiator; drain one's snake; empty one's bladder; evacuate the bladder; go tap a kidney; have a leak; have a quickie; have a run off; life his leg; make number one; make salt water; make water; micturate; pass urine; pass water; pee; piddle; pie and mash; piss; plant a sweet pea; point Percy at the porcelain; pump ship; retire; scatter; see a man about a dog; see one's aunt; shake hands with an old friend; shake the dew off the lily; shoot a lion; spend a penny; take a leak; take a quickie; tap a keg; tinkle; urinate; water the lawn; water the stock; whiz

屙爛屎 (便溏 / 大便稀溏) loose stool

屙屁 (放屁) backfire; beef-hearts; break wind; break wind backwards; break wind downwards; drop a rose; fart; have gas; lay fart; let one fly; make a noise; pass air; pass wind; rip off a fart; set a fart; shoot rabbits; sneeze; there's a smell of touch bone and whistle

屙肚 (拉肚子 / 腹瀉) diarrhoea; have diarrhea; have loose bowels; have the trots; suffer from diarrhoea

屙屎 (排便 / 大便 / 拉屎) ① clear one's bowel; defecate; dump; egest; empty the bowels; evacuate one's bowels; go boom-boom; go number two; go potty; have a bowel movement; loose bowels; make little soldiers; move the bowels; relieve oneself; relieve the bowels; shit; sit on the throne; take a shit; the bowel moves; void excrement ② (糞便 / 排泄物) faeces; human excrement; shit; stool; turd
　屙屎唔出賴地硬 (拉不出屎賴茅房) blame others for your own mistakes

屙唔出 (拉不出來) cannot pull out the excrement

屙得出 (拉得出) can pull out the excrement

屙痢 (拉痢疾) suffer from dysentery

屙嘔 (吐瀉) vomiting and purging
　又屙又嘔 (上吐下瀉) suffer from vomiting and diarrhoea; vomit and have a water stool; vomiting and purging

肚屙 (腹瀉) diarrhoea; give the trots; have diarrhoea; have loose bowels; suffer from diarrhoea

【崩】bang¹ (崩裂) broken; burst

崩口 (兔唇 / 缺唇 / 裂嘴 / 豁嘴 / 豁嘴兒) harelipped person
　崩口人忌崩口碗 (當着矮子別說短話 / 避免提及可能傷害他人的某事) avoid mentioning sth that may hurt other people; avoid touching sb on the raw

崩牙 goofy teeth

崩咗 (崩掉) cracked
　崩咗一忽 (缺了一塊兒) missing one piece

崩嘴 (兔唇 / 缺唇 / 裂嘴 / 豁嘴 / 豁嘴兒) harelipped person
　崩嘴佬 (豁嘴 / 豁嘴兒) cleff-lip man

坐食山崩 (坐吃山空) sit idle without work and the whole fortune will be at last used up

阿崩 (兔唇 / 豁嘴 / 豁嘴兒) harelip

穿崩 (露出破綻) let the cat out of the bag; let the secret out

臭崩崩 (臭烘烘) foul-smelling; smelly; stinking

硬崩崩 (堅硬) unyielding

硬淨 (硬朗 / 結實) tough

硬碰硬 (真家伙 / 強中自有強中手) confront the tough with toughness; diamond cut diamond

硬橛橛 (非常硬) very hard

硬頸 (頑固 / 固執 / 倔強 / 執拗) stubborn; unyielding

好硬頸 (非常固執) very stubborn

口硬 ① (嘴硬) refuse to admit a mistake; stubborn and reluctant to admit mistakes or defeats ② (口氣強硬) talk toughly

手瓜硬 (胳膊粗) have power; have real power

手硬 (有本事) smart person

石地堂鐵掃把——硬打硬 (石頭打着烏鴉嘴——硬碰硬 / 石地板,鐵掃把——硬碰硬 / 石板上釘釘子——硬碰硬 / 鐮刀對斧頭——硬碰硬 / 烏龜碰石頭——硬碰硬) a tortoise pounding a slabstone – a case of the tough confronting the tough

死硬 (死定了) have no hope

夾硬 (勉強 / 硬來) by force

受軟唔受硬 (吃軟不吃硬) person who is more easily persuaded than coerced

命硬 tough

後台硬 powerful contacts behind the scenes

梗硬 (勉強 / 硬來) by force

屙屎唔出賴地硬 (拉不出屎賴茅房) don't blame others for your own mistakes

監硬 (勉強 / 硬來) by force

賴地硬 (找借口 / 怨天尤人) make excuses

攞硬 (勢在必得) lie within one's grasp

鑑硬 (魯莽) act recklessly

12 劃

【揼】dam¹ (擊) strike

揼石仔 (處理繁瑣的工作) handle complicated work

揼死 (殺死) kill

揼骨 (捶背 / 按摩) pound sb's back; massage

揼濕 (淋濕) get very wet
　揼濕身 (淋濕全身) get very wet
　揼濕衫 (淋濕上衣) get very wet

揼爛 (粉碎 / 砸碎) smash to a pulp

【硯】jin⁶⁻² inkslab; slab

硯友 (同學) classmate; fellow student

硯兄 (學長) elder classmate

硯弟 (學弟) junior classmate

硯盒 case for an inkslab

墨硯 (硯台) inkslab

【稍】saau² slightly

稍為 (稍稍 / 稍微) slightly

【稀】hei¹ thin

稀少 few; few and far between; little; rare; scarce; sparse

稀有 one in a million; rare; uncommon; unusual

稀奇 (罕見 / 稀有 / 奇特) rare; strange

稀客 rare visitor

稀粥 (稀飯) thin congee

【稅】soey³ tax

稅局 (稅務局) Income Revenue Department
　稅務局 Inland Revenue Department

稅單 tax notice

入息稅 income tax

印花稅 stamp duty

地稅 rates bill

免稅 duty free; exemption from duty; free of duty; remission of tax; tax exemption; tax-free

逃稅 avoid paying tax; evade taxes; tax avoidance; tax evasion

瞞稅 conceal facts to proper taxation

繳稅 pay taxes

【稈】gon² stalk; stem

稈稻 (稻稈) stalk of rice

禾稈 (稻稈) rice straw

【程】tsing⁴ way

程式 ① form; pattern ② programme; programming

程序 course; order; procedure; proceeding; process; programme; route; sequence

程度 degree; extent; level

程數 (可能性) probability

一項工程 a construction

人生歷程 life journey

工程 engineering

里程 mileage

直程 (直接 / 根本 / 徑直) directly; simply; straightaway

重複療程 repeat a treatment

射程 firing range; range of fire; reach; throw

旅程 itinerary; journey; route; trip

起程 depart for; start a journey

章程 (法規 / 規則 / 律例) regulations; rules; statutes

途程 (路途 / 路程) course; road; way

單程 one-way

運程 (運氣 / 運勢) one's fortune; one's luck

路程 distance; journey; route

課程 ① course ② curriculum

歷程 course; procedure

療程 course of treatment

雙程 return; two-way

縮短旅程 shorten one's journey

縮短路程 shorten one's route

【稔】 nam⁵ ripe

枝筆好稔 (筆頭太多墨水) too much ink at the tip of the writing brush

瞓得稔 (睡得安穩) sleep like a log; sleep soundly

【窗】 tsoeng¹ (窗戶) window

窗口 (窗戶) window
　窗口位 (靠窗座位) window seat

窗台 ① bay window ② window ledge; windowsill

窗花 (窗格子) window lattice

窗門 (窗戶) casement; window

窗鈎 window catch

窗簾 curtain
　窗簾布 curtain

一隻窗 (一扇窗) a window

拉埋天窗 (結婚) get married

閂窗 (關窗) close the window

【童】 tung⁴ child

童裝 children's wear

童養媳 child bride

童黨 child gang

兒童 children; kids

牧童 buffalo boy; cow boy; shepherd boy

頑童 naughty child; urchin

【筆】 bat⁷ ① pen ② brush

筆升 (筆筒) brush pot; pen container

筆名 pen name

筆芯電 (五號電池) AA battery

筆記 notes

筆塔 (筆套) cap of a pen; cap of a writing brush

筆跡 sb's handwriting

筆嘴 (筆尖兒) tip of a writing brush

一枝毛筆 a writing brush

一枝筆 ① a pen ② a writing brush

一筆 one sum; one stroke

一筆還一筆 (一事歸一事 / 就事論事) treat two things separately

一橛鉛筆 (一段鉛筆 / 一截鉛筆) a section of a pencil

毛筆 writing brush

作人一筆 (敲詐別人錢財) extort money; sponge off sb; squeeze a person for money

刨鉛筆 (削鉛筆) sharpen a pencil

炭筆 charcoal pencil

原子筆 (圓珠筆) ball pen

揸筆 (握筆) hold a writing brush; hold a pen

鉛筆 pencil

墨水筆 (自來水筆 / 鋼筆) fountain pen

墨筆 (毛筆) writing brush

顏色筆 (彩筆) colour pencil

鐵筆 (鋼釺) steel drill

蠟筆 crayon

【筍】 soen² (竹筍) bamboo shoot

筍嘢 ① (便宜貨) real bargain ② (上等貨 / 好東西 / 好貨) genuine stuff; great stuff

冬筍 bamboo shoot

竹筍 bamboo shoot

茭筍 (茭白) wild grass stem

萵筍 celtuce

腦筍 (囟門) fontanelle

蘆筍 asparagus

露筍 (蘆筍) asparagus

【等】 dang² wait

等我嚟 (讓我來) let me

等到頸都長 (等很久) wait for a very long time

等於 equal to

等待 wait
　耐心等待 wait patiently

等候 wait

等埋 (等等) wait for me
　等埋我 (等等我) wait for me

等陣 (等一下 / 等一會 / 等一會兒 / 等一等) wait a moment
　等一陣 (等一下 / 等一會 / 等一會兒 / 等一等) wait a moment

等等 ① wait a moment ② hold on
　唔該等等 (請等一會兒) please wait a moment
　請等等 hold on, please

等錢使 (缺錢花) in need of money

一等 first class

二等 second class
三等 third class
中等 middle class
丙等 C grade; the third class
劣等 low-grade; of inferior quality; poor
次等 inferior; second-class; second-rate
均等 equal; fair; impartial
初等 elementary; primary; rudimentary
頭等 first class

【筒】tung⁴⁻² roll
筒管（綫軸）bobbin

一枝飲筒（一根吸管）a drinking straw
大花筒（花錢如流水／亂花錢）big spender; extravagant spender
耳筒（耳機）earphone
風筒（電吹風／吹風機）hair dryer
針筒（針管兒／注射器）syringe
蛋筒（蛋卷）egg roll
郵筒（郵政信箱）post box
甜筒（冰淇淋甜筒）ice cream drumstick
滅火筒（滅火器）fire extinguisher
電筒（手電筒）torch
飲筒（吸管）drinking straw
筷子筒 chopstick holder
聽筒（話筒）telephone speaker

【筋】gan¹ muscle
筋疲力盡 be totally exhausted
筋骨 bones and muscles

抽筋（痙攣）cramp; have a cramp
悶到抽筋（無聊透頂）very bored
腦筋 ① brain ② idea
橡筋（橡皮筋／鬆緊帶）elastic cord; rubber band
顧得頭嚟腳反筋（扶得東來西又倒／顧此失彼）attend to one thing and neglect another

【答】daap⁸ answer
答口（搭碴兒）pick up the thread of a conversation and take part in it
答案 answer
答應 promise
答嘴（搭碴兒）pick up the thread of a conversation and take part in it

【策】tsaak⁸ policy
策動 engineer; instigate; stir up
策略（戰略／戰術）strategy; tactic
策劃 engineer; plan; plot; scheme

束手無策 at a loss of what to do; have one's hands tied; helpless; no way out; up a stump
決策 ① decide a policy; make a strategic decision; make policy ② decision-making; policy-making
政策 policy
鞭策 encourage; goad on; spur on; urge on

【粟】suk⁷ millet
粟米（玉米／玉蜀黍）corn
　粟米油（玉米油）corn oil
　粟米粉（玉米粉／玉米麵）cornflour
　粟米羹（玉米羹）thick corn soup
粟粉（玉米粉／玉米澱粉／鷹粟粉）corn starch

包粟（玉米）millet
罌粟 opium poppy

【粥】dzuk⁷（稀飯）congee; porridge; rice congee; rice gruel; rice porridge
粥水（粥湯）congee soup
粥麵舖（粥麵館）congee and noodles shop

一煲粥（一個煲鍋的粥）a pot of congee
一鑊粥（一鍋粥／一團糟）chaotic situation
冇米粥（無米之粥／微不足道）sth that will never amount to anything
牛肉粥 congee with beef
白粥 congee; gruel; plain congee; plain rice congee; porridge
皮蛋瘦肉粥 congee with lean pork and century egg
食過夜粥（學過武術／有兩下子）have learned the techniques of Chinese martial arts
食粥（喝粥／吃粥）eat congee
柴魚花生粥 congee with dried fish and peanut
魚片粥 congee with fish slices
傑粥（稠粥）thick congee
喫粥（喝粥／吃粥）eat congee
稀粥（稀飯）thin congee
煲冇米粥（做無米之炊／說空話／說沒影的事兒）all talk; discuss something that will never amount to anything; make an idle talk
煲粥 ①（煮粥／熬粥）cook congee; make congee; make porridge ②（煲電話粥／談很久電話）natter on the phone; on the phone for a long time; talk for hours on the telephone

煲電話粥（泡蘑菇／聊大天）have a marathon talk on the phone; natter on the phone; on the phone for a long time; shoot the breeze on the phone

艇仔粥 boat congee; sampan congee

潮州粥 Chiu Chow congee

【粵】jyt⁹（廣東）Cantonese

粵式 Cantonese style

粵菜 Cantonese cuisine

粵語 Cantonese dialect

粵劇 Cantonese opera

【粧】dzong¹ make-up

粧扮 doll up

落粧（下粧／卸裝）remove make-up and costume

【結】git⁸ form

結他（吉他）guitar
  彈結他（彈吉他）play the guitar

結尾 end

結局 end

結束 ① come to an end ② put an end to; resolve

結果 result

結恭（便秘）constipation; intestinal constipation

結婚 get married
  結婚禮物 wedding gift

結單（通知書）statement

結焦（結痂）form a scab

結數（結算／結賬）balance accounts; close an account; make the final calculation; settle accounts; settle the bill; wind up an account

結論 conclusion

結霜（下霜）frost has occurred

了結 bring to an end; bring to conclusion; finish; get through with; settle; wind up

十拿九結（十拿九穩）hold the cards in one's hand

巴結 be all over sb; bootlick; brown-nose; buddy up; butter up sb; cotton up to; cozy up to; curry favour with sb; fawn on; flatter; get in with sb; lay on the butter; lay the butter on; lick sb's boots; lick sb's shoes; make up to; play up to; polish the apple; soak sb down; stand in with sb; suck up to; toady to sb; try hard to please

死結 fast knot

連結（鏈接／連接／聯繫）link

冤家宜解不宜結 it is better to bury the hatchet

超連結（超鏈接）hyperlink

團結 unite

締結 conclude; establish

總結 conclude; summarise

【絕】dzyt⁹ cease

絕交 break off friendship

絕症 incurable disease; terminal illness

絕情（無情）heartless; inexorable; merciless; ruthless

杜絕 eradicate completely; put an end to; stop

命不該絕 be not fated to die

拒絕 decline; decline doing sth; decline to do sth; refuse; reject; repulse; throw down; throw over; turn away; turn down

絡繹不絕 come and go in a continuous stream; come in a continuous stream; come one after the other; flock in an endless stream; go to and fro in constant streams; in a continuous line; in an endless stream; proceed in a steady stream

綿綿不絕 remain unbroken

【絡】lok³ net

絡繹 in an endless stream
  絡繹不絕 come and go in a continuous stream; come in a continuous stream; come one after the other; flock in an endless stream; go to and fro in constant streams; in a continuous line; in an endless stream; proceed in a steady stream

失去聯絡 lose contact

保持聯絡 keep in touch

網絡 network

聯絡 ① contact; liaison ② come into contact with; get in touch with

籠絡 entice; tempt

【絨】jung⁴⁻²（呢子）woollen cloth

絨布 cotton flannel

絲絨 velvet

【統】tung² all

統一 unification

統治 dominate; govern; reign; rule

統計 ① census; statistics ② add up; count

統籌 plan as a whole

供水系統 waterworks

傳統 tradition

總統 president

襪統（襪筒）leg of a stocking
籠統 general; sweeping

【紫】dzi² purple
紫色 purple; purple colour
紫羅蘭 pansy; violet

大紅大紫 at the height of one's power and influence; at the zenith of one's fame; enjoy great popularity; extremely popular; extremely successful in the show business; very popular
紅到發紫（紅得發紫）enjoy great popularity; extremely popular; extremely successful in the show business

【絲】si¹ silk
絲絨 velvet
絲帽（螺帽）nut
絲襪 pantyhose

火腿絲 shredded ham
食螺絲（吃螺絲／講錯話／張口結舌）make a mistake when reading out a script
甜絲絲（甜蜜／很甜）pleasantly sweet; very sweet
粉絲 ①（粉絲）bean vermicelli ②（…迷／狂熱愛好者）(English) fans
摩絲（頭髮定型劑／定型水）hair spray
慕絲（慕斯蛋糕）(English) mousse
膠絲（尼龍絲）nylon yarn
薑絲 ginger shreds; shredded ginger
雞絲 shredded chicken
螺絲（螺釘）screw

【㤱】jap⁷ agree
㤱手（招手）beckon with the hand; wave one's hand
㤱眼（眨眼）blink; twinkle; wink

【脹】dzoeng³ swelling
脹卜卜（鼓脹／鼓鼓囊囊的）bulging out

腫脹 swell
腹脹 abdominal distension; meteorism

【腌】jip⁸ pickle
腌尖（挑剔）cavil; choosy; fastidious; fussy; hypercritical; nitpick; pick and choose; pick fault; picky; upbraid
　腌尖腥悶（眾口難調／難以取悅）hard to please
腌悶（煩惱／心煩意亂／沮喪）upset; vex oneself

小腌（肋下）intercostal

【腎】san⁶ kidney
腎病（腎炎）kidney disease; nephralgia
腎虛 asthenia of the kidney; kidney deficiency
腎臟 kidney

鴨腎 duck kidney
雞腎 chicken kidney

【腑】fu² entrails; viscera
腑臟 ① viscera ② one's integrity

臟腑 ① viscera ② one's integrity

【腕】wun² wrist
腕骨 wrist bone

手腕 wrist

【脾】bei²（腿）leg
脾胃 ① stomach ② appetite

【脾】pei⁴ temper
脾氣 temper
　牛脾氣 ① bad-tempered ② stubborn
　好脾氣（脾氣好）good-tempered
　耍脾氣 get into a huff
　發脾氣 blow a fuse; blow a gasket; blow one's fuse; blow one's lid off; blow one's top; blow up; cut up rough; flare up; fly into a rage; fly into a temper; get angry; get one's hackles up; have sb's hackles up; hit the ceiling; let oneself go; lose one's temper; make sb's hackles rise; out of temper; vent one's spleen; with one's hackles rising; with one's hackles up

老脾（脾氣）temper
炸雞脾（炸雞腿）deep-fried chicken leg; deep-fried drumstick
發老脾（發脾氣）lose one's temper
雞脾（雞腿）chicken leg

【腚】ding⁶ buttock

喉嚨腚（小舌／懸雍垂）little red tongue; uvula

【舒】sy¹ unhurried
舒服 comfortable
　唔舒服 ①（不安）uneasy ②（不舒服／不適）uncomfortable; unwell
　舒舒服服 comfortable

舒展 limber up; relax; stretch; unfold

舒適 comfortable; cosy; snug

舒暢 ① comfortable; free from worry; happy; pleasant
② leisurely and harmonious

【莽】 mong⁵ rash; reckless

莽撞 crude and impetuous

魯莽 careless; discourteous; rash; reckless; rough; rude; uncivil

【菊】 guk⁷ chrysanthemum

菊花 ① chrysanthemum ② dried chrysanthemum
菊花茶 chrysanthemum tea

菊普 (菊花普洱茶) Pu'er tea with dried chrysanthemum

【菌】 kwan² bacteria

菌種 type culture

抗菌 anti-bacteria

桿菌 bacillus

細菌 bacteria

微菌 (細菌) bacteria; germ

【菜】 tsoi³ ① (蔬菜) greens; vegetables ② (食物) food ③ (料理) course; dish

菜刀 kitchen knife

菜心 (菜薹) flowering Chinese cabbage

菜瓜 snake melon
菜瓜餿飯——好人有限 (沙鍋滾下山——沒好的) far from being a good person

菜油 vegetable oil

菜框 (菜梗) vegetable stem

菜乾 (乾菜) dried cabbage

菜脯 (鹽漬蘿蔔) salted preserved sweet turnip

菜販 (蔬菜商) greengrocer

菜牌 (菜單) menu

菜葉綠 (如菜葉般綠) green like vegetable leaves

菜腳 (剩菜) leftovers

菜餃 vegetable dumpling

菜檔 (蔬菜攤) vegetable stall

菜館 (餐館) restaurant
上海菜館 Shanghainese restaurant
素菜館 vegetarian restaurant

菜欄 (蔬菜行) vegetable store

菜攤 vegetable stall

一棵生菜 a lettuce

一棵白菜 a Chinese cabbage

一棵菜 a vegetable

一碟油菜 a dish of vegetable with oyster sauce

一齋菜 (一棵菜) a vegetable

一擔菜 two baskets of vegetables carried on a shoulder pole

上海菜 Shanghainese food

大豆芽菜 (黃豆芽) soybean sprout

小棠菜 (上海青) Shanghai cabbage

小菜 common dishes; plain dishes; side dishes

川菜 Sichuan food

中菜 (中國菜) Chinese food

中國菜 Chinese dishes; Chinese food

日本菜 Japanese food

主菜 main course; main dish

北京菜 Beijing food

叫多個菜 (多點道菜) order one more dish

叫菜 (點菜) order dishes

台灣菜 Taiwanese food

正菜 (美女) good-looking girl

生菜 lettuce

白菜 Chinese cabbage

印度菜 Indian food

招牌菜 chef's recommendation; signature dish

油菜 vegetable with oyster sauce

芹菜 Chinese celery

芽菜 (豆芽) bean sprout

青菜 green vegetables; vegetables

洗菜 wash the vegetables

盆菜 basin hot-pot

韭菜 green chive

素菜 vegetarian diet; vegetable dishes

食生菜 (容易 / 易如反掌) as easy as pie; sth easy to do

泰國菜 Thai food

唐生菜 (萵苣) Chinese lettuce

酒菜 (酒食 / 飲食) food and drink

起菜 ① (上菜) serve food; serve the dishes ② (性愛) have sex with a girl

越南菜 Vietnamese food

越菜 (越南菜) Vietnamese food

細豆芽菜 (綠豆芽) mung bean sprouts

紹菜 (大白菜) celery cabbage

莧菜 Chinese spinach

通心菜 (蕹菜 / 空心菜) water spinach

通菜 (蕹菜 / 空心菜) water spinach

雪菜 (雪里蕻) potherb mustard; preserved vegetable

菠菜 spinach

意大利菜 Italian food

廣東菜 (粵菜) Cantonese dishes; Cantonese food

粵菜 Cantonese cuisine

椰菜 (包心菜 / 洋白菜 / 卷心菜 / 圓白菜) cabbage

飯菜 dishes to go with rice

種菜 grow vegetables

誓願當食生菜 (隨口發誓卻從不履行 / 起誓當白饒) take an easy oath

蔬菜 vegetables

霉菜 (梅菜 / 梅乾菜) molded dried vegetable

點菜 order dishes; order food

齋菜 (素菜) vegetarian food

蕹菜 (空心菜) water spinach

韓國菜 Korean food

鹹魚白菜 (簡單的菜) humble meal; simple meal

鹹菜 crumpled clothes

鹹酸菜 (醃菜) salted vegetable

【菠】 bo¹ spinach

菠菜 spinach

菠蘿 ① (鳳梨) pineapple ② (土製炸彈) home-made bomb

菠蘿包 pineapple-shaped bun

菠蘿汁 pineapple juice

菠蘿油 (菠蘿包夾牛油) pineapple-shaped bun with butter

菠蘿蓋 (膝蓋) kneecap

金菠蘿 (寶貝兒孫) one's darling children; one's darling grandchildren

【華】 waa⁴ brilliance

華而不實 arty and crafty; flashy and without substance; have all one's goods in the window; have everything in the window; flashiness without substance; gewgaw; gimcrack; meretricious; pomposity; showy but not substantial

華爾滋 (圓舞曲 / 華爾茲) (English) waltz

華麗 gorgeous; magnificent; resplendent

才華 talent

中華 China

有才華 have talent

年華 time; year

浮華 flashy; foppish rococo; ostentatious; showy; vain

豪華 luxurious

嘉年華 (遊藝會) carnival

【菇】 gu¹ mushroom

冬菇 (香菇) dried mushroom

草菇 (鮮蘑菇) straw mushroom

燉冬菇 (降級) demotion

蘑菇 button mushroom

【菲】 fei¹ ① thin ② Filipino

菲林 (膠卷) (English) film

一卷菲林 (一個膠卷 / 一卷膠卷) a roll of film

一筒菲林 (一個膠卷 / 一捲膠卷) a roll of film

謀殺菲林 (吸引所有人拍照) use up all the films

菲傭 (菲律賓傭人) Filipino maid

一個菲傭 a Filipino maid

【萌】 mang⁴ sprout

萌塞 (頑固 / 冥頑不靈) inflexible; stubborn

乾萌萌 (乾巴巴) dull and dry; insipid

黑眯萌 (黑咕隆咚 / 黑糊糊) dusky; rather dark

【菩】 pou⁴ fragrant herb

菩提子 (葡萄) grape

一抽菩提子 (一串葡萄) a bunch of grapes

菩薩 Buddha

【虛】 hoey¹ hollow

虛名 bubble reputation; empty reputation; false reputation; undeserved reputation

虛榮 empty glory; vain glory; vanity

虛榮心 vanity

虛假 (假 / 虛偽的 / 虛幻) false; insincere; sham; unreal

虛偽 false; hypocritical; insincere; sham; spurious

作賊心虛 have a guilty conscience

乘虛 catch sb napping; take advantage of a weak point

謙虛 humble

【蛙】 waa¹ frog

蛙人 frogman

蛙式 breast stroke

蛙魚 (蟾蜍魚) toadfish

【街】 gaai¹ (街道) street

街口 (路口) corner of the street; road junction; street intersection; street junction

街口停 (在路口停) stop at the street intersection

街市 (菜市場) market

街市佬 (菜市小販) food market hawker

濕貨街市 (濕貨市場) wet market

街坊 (鄰居) neighbour

街招 (招貼) bill; notice; placard; poster

街症 (門診部) outpatient service

街渡 (小型渡輪) ferry boat

街數 (外賬) debt; overdue bill

街燈 (路燈) road lamp; street lamp; street light

一盞街燈 (一盞路燈) a street lamp

街線 (外線) outside line

街頭 street

　　街頭巷尾 everywhere in the streets

　　流浪街頭 roam the streets; run the streets; wander
　　　　around the streets

　　橫死街頭 be dead in the street

街邊 (路旁 / 路邊) roadside

　　街邊檔 (小攤兒) booth; road-side stall; stall; vendor's
　　　　stand

一個人出街 (一個人逛街) go out into the street alone

一條街 a street

出咗街 (出去了) has gone out

出街 ① (外出 / 上街) go out; go out into the street
　　② (播映) (said of TV show) broadcast; on air ③ (出版)
　　(said of publications) put on the market for sale

去街 ① (上街) go into the street; go on the street
　　② (外出) go out

好行街 ① (喜歡逛街) fond of strolling aound the streets
　　② (喜歡只看不買) fond of window-shopping

行街 ① (逛街) stroll around the streets; walk around
　　② (只看不買) go window-shopping ③ (購物) go
　　shopping ④ (經紀人 / 售貨員) broker; salesperson

行街街 (在街上亂逛) wander around the streets

周街 (到處 / 隨處) all about; all over; all over the place;
　　all over the shop; all over the show; all round; at all
　　places; everywhere; from place to place; here, there and
　　everywhere; here and there; high and low; hither and
　　thither; in all directions; in every place; in every quarter;
　　on all hands; on all sides; on every side; on every hand;
　　right and left; up hill and down dale

阻街 (妨礙交通 / 堵塞街道) cause an obstruction in a public
　　place

唐人街 Chinatown

帶街 (導遊) tour guide

通街 (到處 / 隨處 / 到處都是) all about; all over; all over
　　the place; all over the shop; all over the show; all round;
　　at all places; everywhere; from place to place; here, there
　　and everywhere; here and there; high and low; hither
　　and thither; in all directions; in every place; in every
　　quarter; on all hands; on all sides; on everyside; on every
　　hand; right and left; up hill and down dale

嗌通街 (與左鄰右舍都吵過架) bandy words with everyone

落街 ① (上街) go into the street ② (購物) go shopping

踎街 (流落街頭 / 無家可歸) homeless

瞓街 (睡馬路) sleep on the road

鬧通街 (舊聞) old news

橫街 (橫馬路) by-street; side street

罵街 (在街上亂罵) shout abuse in the street

擺街 (擺地攤 / 擺攤) set up a stall in the street

躝街 (在街上亂逛) hang around on the street

【裁】 tsoi⁴ reduce

裁判 referee

　　裁判司 (裁判法官) magistrate

裁員 staff cut

裁減 cut; reduce

裁縫 tailor

制裁 punish; sanction

剪裁 ① (裁縫) cut out a garment; tailor ② (從一篇文章中
　　刪減不需要的材料) cut out unwanted material from a
　　piece of writing; prune

總裁 company director

【裂】 lit⁹ split

裂口 crack; gap; split

裂咗 (裂開了) come apart; split open; rend

裂紋 crack; crackle

裂開 cleave; crack; rend; split

裂縫 breach; chink; cleavage; crack; crevice; fissure;
　　fracture; rift; split

　　修補裂縫 mend a split

人格分裂 disintegration of personality

分裂 break up; cleavage; disintegrate; dissociate; disunity;
　　divide; smash; split; tear

四分五裂 be rent by disunity; be smashed to bits; be split
　　up; be torn apart; break into pieces; come apart at the
　　seams; come to pieces; fall apart; fall to pieces; scattered
　　and disunited; split up

身敗名裂 be utterly discredited; bring disgrace and ruin
　　upon oneself; lose all standing and reputation; lose one's
　　fortune and honour; one's name is mud

骨裂 (骨折 / 骨頭斷裂) bone fracture; crack in the bone

爆裂 (裂開) burst open

【裙】 kwan⁴ (裙子) skirt

裙拉褲甩 (急急忙忙) in a great hurry

裙腳仔 (依賴母親的男孩) a boy who is dependent on his
　　mum

一條裙 (一條裙子) a skirt

半截裙 (半身裙) skirt

底裙 (襯裙) slip

直身裙 (連衣裙) one-piece dress

迷你裙 (超短裙) miniskirt

除裙（脫裙子）take off a skirt
圍裙 apron
着裙（穿裙子）wear a skirt

【補】bou² ① add to ② repair

補水（津貼／補助／補錢）payment for overtime work
補呔（補胎）mend a tyre; repair a tyre
補品 nutritious food; tonic
補衫（補衣服）mend clothes
補飛（補票）buy one's ticket after the normal time
補數 ①（補錢）make up the money ②（補償）do sth as a
　　sort of remedy
　　補番數（補足錢）make it up; make up for
補鞋佬（補鞋匠）cobbler; shoemaker; shoe repairer
補鐘（補課）make up missed classes; make-up classes
補鑊（補救）get a problem fixed
　　補鑊唔見枳（手足無措／尷尬／狼狽）find oneself in a
　　fix

互補 complement each other; supplement each other
多除少補（多退少補）return the overcharge and demand
　　payment of the shortage; return the surplus and charge
　　the balance; the balances will be paid to either side as
　　the case may be
惡補（參加速成班）take a crash course

【袱】fuk⁹ bundle wrapped in cloth

包袱 ① a bundle wrapped in cloth ② burden; liability; load;
　　weight
執包袱（捲鋪蓋）be fired

【裇】soet⁷ shirt

裇衫 shirt

t 裇（短袖汗衫）t-shirt

【視】si⁶ view

視力 eyesight; power of vision; sight; vision
視光師（驗光師）optometrist
視野（眼界／地平線）field of vision; horizon; visual field
視像（視頻）video

注視 focus one's look on; gaze at; look attentively at; watch
忽視 blank sb; disregard; give a cold shoulder; ignore; look
　　down on; neglect; overlook
性別歧視 sexual discrimination
歧視 discrimination
珍視 cherish; have a high opionion of; prize; treasure; value

睇電視（看電視）watch television
透視 see through
開電視 turn on the television
電視 television
漠視 ignore; overlook
熄電視（關電視）turn off the television

【診】tsan² diagnose

診治 make a diagnosis and give treatment
診病 diagnose a disease
診所 clinic
診斷 diagnose; diagnosis

【註】dzy⁶ register

註定 destined; doomed; predestined
註冊 register
註明 explain clearly in writing; give clear indication of;
　　make a footnote; mark out
註釋 annotation; commentary; explanatory note; note

【訴】sou³ complain

訴苦 air one's grievance; complain about one's grievances;
　　pour out one's woes; vent one's grievances
訴訟 lawsuit; litigation; suit
訴說 ① air grievances; complain ② narrate; recount; relate;
　　tell

上訴 appeal to a higher court
申訴 appeal; complain
如泣如訴 pathetic and touching; plaintive; plangent
有冤無路訴 have no one to complain about one's injustice
投訴 complain
泣訴 accuse while weeping; blubber out one's bitter
　　experiences; sob out one's grievances; tell one's sorrows

【詐】zaa³（裝）pretend

詐帝（裝模作樣／裝蒜／假裝）feign; pretend
　　詐詐帝帝（裝模作樣／假惺惺地）feign; pretend
詐型（擺架子／擺款）bluff; play the fool; pretend; put on
　　an act
詐假意（開玩笑／假裝）make a joke; make believe;
　　pretend
詐嗲（撒嬌）sulk
詐傻（裝傻）act stupid; play the fool
　　詐傻扮懵（裝傻充愣）act stupid; play the fool
詐嬌（撒嬌）behave like a spoiled child; sulk
詐諦（裝蒜／假裝）feign; make a pretence of ignorance;
　　pretend
詐戇（裝傻）act stupid; play the fool

欺詐 cheat; deceive; hoodwink; swindle

【詐】dzaa³ quick
詐詐淋（快速地）quickly

【評】ping⁴ comment
評判（評判員）judge; referee; umpire
評語 comment
評講（講評）comment on and appraise

批評 criticism
述評（敘述評論）commentary; review

【詞】tsi⁴ statement
詞典 dictionary
詞彙 vocabulary
詞語 terms; words and expressions

一面之詞 one-sided statement
介詞 preposition
片面之詞 one-sided statement
代詞 pronoun
字詞 words and phrases
念念有詞 mumble
冠詞 article
欲加之罪，何患無詞 a staff is quickly found to beat a dog with; any stick will do to beat a dog with; he who has a mind to beat his dog will easily find his stick; if one is out to condemn sb, one can always trump up a charge; if you want a pretence to hip a dog, say that he ate the frying-pan; it is easy to find a stick to beat a dog
眾口一詞（異口同聲）all agree in saying; all tell the same story; everyone says so; in the same story; say of one accord; speak with one voice; unanimously; with one voice
詩詞 poetry and rhymed prose
謂詞（謂語）predicate

【象】dzoeng⁶ elephant
象牙 ivory
　象牙塔（大學校園）university campus
象拔（象鼻子）trunk
　象拔蚌（象鼻蛤蜊）elephant trunk clam; geoduck
象腿 ① elephant's leg ② thick leg

人心不足蛇吞象 human beings are never satisfied with what they have; no person is contented with their own possessions

大笨象 ①（大象）elephant ②（胖子）fat person
冇乜印象（沒甚麼印象）not have any impression of sth or sb
印象 impression
飛象 the chess "elephant" flying across the river
跡象 indication; sign; straw in the wind; token
險象 dangerous sign or phenomenon
蟻多摟死象（弱者人多而齊心，可以戰勝強者／團結就是力量）a large number of weak individuals can overwhelm a very strong individual; union is strength; unity is strength

【貴】gwai³ expensive
貴人 people who can help
貴夾唔飽（質量差，不實用）not good value and not practical
貴利（高利）loan-sharking
　貴利佬（放高利貸的人）loan-shark
貴姓呀 may I know your surname
貴婦 ①（有錢的女人／富婆）rich woman ②（優雅的女人）elegant woman
　貴婦狗 poodle
貴得滯（太貴）too expensive
貴貨（高價貨）expensive goods
　貴價貨（高價貨）expensive goods
貴嘢（高價貨）expensive goods

人間富貴（世上的財富）wealth in this world
大富大貴 rich and honoured
以和為貴 make peace
功名富貴 fame and fortune; fame, riches, and honours; officialdom, wealth, and fame; rank, success, fame, and riches
冚家富貴（混蛋）you bastard
名貴 famous and precious
有平有貴（有便宜的，也有貴的）have expensive ones and cheap ones
身嬌肉貴（金尊玉貴）come from a rich family
花開富貴 may your wealth bloom like flowers
物以罕為貴（物以稀爲貴）precious things are never found in heaps
珍貴 precious; rare; valuable
矜貴（貴重／寶貴）treasurable; valuable
唔使問亞貴（顯而易見／無需多言）as sure as eggs are eggs; there's no need to inquire
高貴 elegant; noble
富貴（富裕）rich and honoured; wealthy

【貶】bin² blink
貶低 abase; belittle; cry down; denigrate; depreciate; detract from; disparage; play down; run down

貶值 depreciate; devalue; devaluate

眼貶貶 (眨眼睛) blink

【買】maai⁵ buy

買一送一 buy one get one free
買入 (買進) buy in
買少見少 (越來越少) become increasingly scarce
買水咁嘅頭 (垂頭喪氣) crestfallen; dejected; sing the blues
買主 buyer; purchaser
買田 (買地) buy land
買生不如買熟 (買東西去熟悉的店) feel secure to make a purchase in a familiar shop
買屋 (買房子) buy a house
買衫 (買衣服) buy clothes
買飛 (買票) buy a ticket
買馬 (賭馬) bet on horses
買嘢 (購物) buy; go shopping; shopping
　好買嘢 (愛買東西) like shopping
　鍾意買嘢 (喜歡購物) like shopping
買樓 (買樓房) buy a flat
　買踏樓 (買層樓) buy a flat
買賣 buying and selling
　買賣合約 (買賣合同) sale and purchase agreement
　　臨時買賣合約 (臨時買賣合同) provisional sale and purchase agreement
　買賣登記 sale and purchase registration
　低買高賣 buy low, sell high
　炒買炒賣 (投機倒把 / 倒買倒賣) play the market; speculate; speculation and profiteering
買餸 (買菜 / 點菜) buy groceries; buy meat and vegetables for meal

好抵買 (值得買) it's worth buying
抵買 ① (值得買) worth buying ② (合算) deserving; worthwhile
高買 (店舖盜竊) pickpocket
搵鬼買 (找鬼買 / 沒人買) no one is willing to buy it
閻羅王揸攤 —— 鬼買 (沒人買) nobody buys
購買 acquire; buy; purchase

【貸】taai³ loan

貸款 loan
　貸款額 loan amount

信貸 credit

【費】fai³ fee

費用 cost; expenses; fee
　分擔費用 share the expenses
費事 (省得 / 懶得) save the trouble; too lazy to do sth; troublesome
　費事郁 (懶得動) not in the mood to move
　費事喇 (省得麻煩了) let it avoid trouble
費解 hard to understand
　令人費解 elude understanding

小費 gratuity; tip
月費 monthly fee
水費 water bill
加一服務費 (收一成服務費) ten per-cent service charge
皮費 (成本) expenses; overheads
交水費 (小便) urinate
交通費 transportation fee
交學費 ① pay tuition fees ② (受教訓) be taught a lesson
年費 annual fee
行政費 administration fee
私家車牌費 private car licence fee
車馬費 transportation fee
免費 free of charge
枉費 of no avail; try in vain; waste
陀地費 (保護費) protection fee
附加費 surcharge
律師費 legal fee
按揭手續費 (抵押手續費) mortgage handling fee
掩口費 (封口費) hush money
掟煲費 (分手費) payment for severing a relationship
浪費 waste
消費 spending
耗費 consume; cost; expend
頂手費 (轉讓費) fee for transfer possession
揸口費 (封口費) hush money
最低消費 minimum charge
湯藥費 (醫藥費) medical bill; medical expenses
煤氣費 gas bill
郵費 (郵資) postage
經費 expenditure
電費 electricity bill
電話費 telephone bill
管理費 management fee
牌費 (牌照費) licence fee
經紀費 (中介費) agent's fee
稿費 contribution fee
學費 tuition fee
雜費 sundry expenses
醫藥費 medical expenses

繳費 payment

【貼】tip⁸ paste

貼上 stick on

貼士 ① (小賬／小費) (English) tips ② (提示) hint; prompt

貼堂 (張貼在教室的牆上) post sth on the wall of the classroom

貼現價 (打折) on discount

貼錢買難受 (花錢買氣受) get bad service; pay for troubles

貼錯門神 (反貼門神——意見相左) at odds with each other; become hostile; can't get along with each other

妥貼 appropriate; fitting; proper; satisfactory

盲佬貼符——倒貼 (倒貼錢) not getting but giving away money

津貼 (補貼) allowance; subsidy

溫柔體貼 tender and considerate

鍋貼 (煎餃) fried meat dumpling

【賀】ho⁶ congratulate

賀年咭 (賀年片) new year card

賀歲片 movies shown during the Lunar New Year

賀禮 congratulatory gift

　一份賀禮 a congratulatory gift

恭賀 congratulate

祝賀 congratulate; felicitate

致賀 congratulate; extend congratulations; offer one's congratulations

【貿】mau⁶ trade

貿易 trade

　貿易伙伴 trade partner

　貿易往來 commercial intercourse; trade contacts

　貿易發達 (貿易興旺) prosperous trade

　擴大貿易 extend trade

貿然 (輕率地) hastily; rashly; without careful consideration

　貿貿然 (輕率地) hastily; rashly; without careful consideration

【趁】tsan³ ① take advantage ② take the chance of

趁手 (趁便／趁機會／順手) take the opportunity

趁你病，攞你命 (乘虛而入／落井下石) do harm to sb when they are already in trouble; drop stones on the person who has fallen into a well; hit a person when he/she is down; pull water on a drowning person; push sb down a well and then drop stones on him

趁墟 (趕集) go to the market

【超】tsiu¹ surpass

超班 (實力超羣) extremely clever; outclass

　超班馬 (才能超出同齡人的人) person who is at a level beyond their peers

超速 speeding

大細超 (偏心／不公平) show favouritism

眼超超 (敵視別人／以敵對的方式凝視) stare in a hostile way

順超 (贊同) agreeable

黑超 (太陽眼鏡／墨鏡) sunglasses

【越】jyt⁹ the more

越多越好 as much as possible; the more, the better

越南 Vietnam

　越南菜 Vietnamese food

越菜 (越南菜) Vietnamese food

越窮越見鬼，肚餓打瀉米 (屋漏偏逢連夜雨) go from bad to worse; misfortunes never come singly

越嚟 (越來越) more and more

　越嚟越多 (越來越多) more and more

【跌】dit⁸ cut; down; fall; fall down

跌低 (跌落／跌倒) fall down

跌咗 (丟了／丟失／掉了) lose

　跌咗個橙，執番個桔 (塞翁失馬，焉知非福) lose at sunrise and gain at sunset

　跌咗嘢 (丟東西) drop sth

　跌爛咗 (摔破了) break sth by dashing it on the ground

跌倒 fall down

　跌倒捊番揸沙 (為免尷尬找爛藉口) put one's fault in the right side

跌落 drop; fall

　跌落水 (掉到水裏) fall into water

　跌落嚟 (摔下來) fall down

跌跤 ① (摔跤) wrestling ② (跌倒) fall down

跌價 (降價) cut down prices; go down in price; mark down; on sale; price breaks; price out; reduce the price

跌嚫 (摔傷) get hurt in a fall

升跌 (起落) rise and fall

無升跌 (沒起落) constant

㧐跌 (推倒) push over

【跎】to⁴ stumble

跎仔 (懷孕) be pregnant

跎衰 (連累) get sb into trouble

歲月蹉跎 idle away one's time; let time slip by without accomplishing anything; the years drift by

【跑】paau² run
跑步 jog; jogging; run; running
　　跑一個鐘頭步（跑步一個小時）jog for one hour
跑車 sports car
跑馬（賽馬）horse racing

逃跑 abscond; break away; buzz off; cut and run; cut away; cut loose; cut one's stick; decamp; duck; escape; flee; get away; get out; give leg bail; make good one's escape; make off; make one's escape; make one's getaway; move off; run away; run off; scarper; show a clean pair of heels; show legs; show one's heels; slip away; take leg bail; take to flight; take to one's heels; take to one's legs
緩步跑（慢跑）canter; jog

【跛】bai¹（瘸）lame
跛手佬（拐子／獨臂的人）arm-disabled person
跛腳（瘸腿）lame
　　跛腳佬（瘸子）lame man
　　跛腳婆（瘸腿女人）lame woman
　　跛腳鴨 lame duck
　　跛腳鷯哥自有飛來蜢（呆人有呆福／傻人有傻福／再不濟的人也會有好運氣）God tempers the wind to the shorn lamb
　　俾人打破腳（腿給打瘸了）be crippled
　　跛咗腳（腿瘸了）be crippled

趷跛跛（單腳跳）hop
毆跛（打斷）break; smash

【距】koey⁵ distance
距離 distance
　　遠距離 long distance

【軸】dzuk⁹ ① axis ② scroll
軸心 axis

卷軸 scroll

【軚】lip¹（升降機／電梯）lift
搭軚（搭升降機／乘電梯）take the elevator; take the lift
壞軚（升降機故障／電梯故障）the lift is out of order

【辜】gu¹ guilt
辜負 disappoint; fail to live up to; let down; unworthy of

死有餘辜 death would not expiate all one's crimes
無辜辜（無端／平白無故／無緣無故）for no reason

【週】dzau¹ all over
週身（全身／渾身）all over the body
　　週身刀——冇張利（甚麼都只懂一點）jack of all trades and master of none
　　週身唔自然（渾身彆扭／渾身不舒服）feel uneasy all over
　　週身唔聚財（渾身彆扭／渾身不舒服）feel uneasy all over

【進】dzoen³ advance
進入 enter
進食 eating

上進 ambitious
先進 advanced
改進 better; improve; make better; mend; perfect
促進 accelerate; advance; boost; encourage; facilitate; gear up; press forward; promote
勉勵上進 exhort one to make progress
財源廣進（祝你有豐富的財富）wish you abundant wealth
跟進 follow up

【都】dou¹（也）also
都似（都可能）it's possible
都有（都可能）it's possible
都係 ①（還是）still ②（也是）also; too
　　都係唔好嘞（還是不了）I would not do it anyway
　　我都係（我也是）me too

一向都 have always been
亦都（也都）also
時時都（一直／總是）always
從來都 have always been

【酥】sou¹ crisp; crunchy
酥餅 pastry

叉燒酥 barbeque pork pastry
合桃酥（核桃酥）walnut cake

【酡】to⁴ flushed

暈酡酡（頭暈／暈眩／暈暈忽忽）dizzy

【量】loeng⁴ measure
量地（失業）out of job; unemployed
　　量地官（失業者）out of job; unemployed

估量 appraise; assess; balance; estimate; ponder; value; weigh
容量 capacity; measurement; volume
測量 survey

【量】loeng⁶ calculate

量入為出 cut the coat according to one's cloth; keep one's expenditures within one's limits of income; live within one's means; measure one's needs to one's income

量力 do sth according to one's capability
量力而為 do sth according to one's capability

力量 ① physical strength ② force; power; strength
少量 a few; a little; a small amount; a sprinkling of
分散力量 scatter one's forces
正能量 positive energy
收細音量（降低音量）turn down the sound volume
知識就是力量 knowledge is power
重量 weight
唔自量（不自量）not understand oneself
能量 energy
酌量 weigh and consider
集中力量 concentrate one's efforts
極其量（充其量）at best; at most
飯量 appetite
數量 quantity
質量 ① mass ② quality
衡量 assess; judge; measure
劑量 dosage

【鈔】tsaau¹ money

鈔票（紙幣）bank note; paper money

偽鈔（偽幣）counterfeit money

【鈍】doen⁶ slow-witted

鈍角 obtuse angle

腦筋遲鈍 have slow wits

【鈕】nau² button

鈕門（扣眼／鈕扣孔）buttonhole
　開鈕門（開扣眼兒）cut a buttonhole
　鎖鈕門（鎖扣眼兒）do a lockstitch on a buttonhole

扣鈕 button up
釘鈕（釘鈕扣）stitch a buttonhole
袖口鈕（袖扣）cuff link

【鈒】dzaap⁹ stitch

鈒骨（鎖邊）stitch edges

【鈎】ngau¹ hook

鈎鼻（鷹鈎鼻）acquiline nose

甩鈎 disconnect; unhook
股票掛鈎 equity-linked
掛鈎 peg; peg up
窗鈎 window catch

【鈪】aak⁸⁻² bracelet

手鈪（手鐲）bracelet
玉鈪（玉鐲）jade bracelet
金鈪（金手鐲）gold bracelet

【開】hoi¹ open

開刀 ①（動手術）perform an operation on a patient ②（作出行動）take action
開叉 slit
開口 ① open one's mouth ② unsealed
　開口及着脷／開口夾着脷（一說話就惹惱別人／口無遮攔）annoy others as soon as one starts talking; talk at sb as soon as one starts talking
　開口信 unsealed letter
　開口埋口（張口閉口）always talk about
　　開口埋口都話（一張嘴就是…／張口閉口都說）always sing the same old tune; whenever one speaks, one says that
開大價（張大口）open one's mouth wide
開工（開始工作）start work
　有工開（有工作做／有工作）① have work to do ② have a job to earn a living
開心（高興）happy
　開心見誠（開誠相見）open-hearted
　開心果 ① pistachio ② a barrel of laughs; a person who is always happy; a person with a cheerful face
　好開心 really happy
　玩開心啲（玩得開心點）enjoy yourself; have fun
　開開心心 very happy
開天索價（漫天要價）ask a sky-high price; ask an exorbitant price
　開天索價，落地還錢（漫天要價，坐地還錢）drive a hard bargain over sth
開火 argue; fight; start a war; start gunfire
開方（開藥方）write out a prescription
開片（打羣架／鬥毆／械鬥）fight with weapons between groups of people; scuffle
開奶（調奶／調乳）adjust the warmth of the milk
開正佢個槓（正對他的勁）it's his forte
開年 scold sb during the Lunar New Year time
開估（公開謎底）reveal the answer to the riddle
開位（訂座位）book a seat
開車 ① start a car ② drive a car

輪流開車 drive by turns

開始 begin; commence

開放 open
開放時間 opening hours

開門見山 come straight to the point; not to mince one's words; put it bluntly

開明車馬 (公開戰略 / 講明用意 / 開宗明義) open-hearted; state one's intention openly

開波 ① (開始) start an activity ② (發球 / 開球) serve

開牀 (鋪牀) make the bed

開夜 (熬夜 / 開夜車) burn the midnight oil; work late into the night; work overnight
開夜車 (熬夜) burn the midnight oil; work late into the night; work overnight

開房 (與情人去酒店開房間) go to a hotel to have sex

開枝散葉 ① produce offspring ② expand business

開便 (外面 / 外邊) outside

開枱 ① (擺桌子) lay the table; set the table ② (打麻將) play mahjong

開胃 ① (胃口好) have a good appetite ② (異想天開) a flight of fancy; a stretch of the imagination; ask for the moon; come out with most fantastic ideas; cry for the moon; expect wonders; fanciful; fanciful ideas; get fancy ideas into one's head; give loose to the fancy; given rein to fancy; have a maggot in one's head; have bats in the belfry; have bees in the brain; have bees in the head; have fantastic notions; have one's head full of bees; indulge in the wildest fantasy; indulge one's fancy; lend wings to one's imagination; let one's imagination run away with one; one's head is full of bees; vagarious; whimsical; wild hopes; wish for the moon; wishful thinking
開胃消滯 (消食開胃) whet the appetite and ease indigestion
好開胃 (胃口好) have very good appetite
你真開胃 (你真貪心) avaricious
唔開胃 ① (沒胃口) have no appetite; unappetising ② (不喜歡 / 不想要 / 沒興趣) dislike; no interest

開席 (入席) dinner is ready

開埋井俾人食水 (努力創業卻任人坐享其成) do pioneering work with labour but let sb sit with folded arms to enjoy the results

開除 (解僱) dismiss; sack

開麥拉 (相機) (English) camera

開彩 (開獎) draw the winning numbers of a lottery; run a lottery

開通 (開悟) be enlightened; liberal

開單 (寫收據 / 開發票) make out a bill; write a receipt

開張 (開門營業 / 開業) open for business; start business

開荒牛 (先鋒 / 開闢者) pioneer in a particular field

開襠褲 (開檔褲) open-seat pants; split pants

開飯 serve a meal
開飯喇 (飯已準備好了 / 吃飯了) dinner is ready; let us eat; serve the meal

開會 ① have a meeting; hold a meeting ② start a meeting
十點開會 the meeting starts at ten

開閘 (開門) open the gate

開盤 ① (開售) be on sale ② (股市開盤) opening
開盤價 opening price

開遮 (撐傘 / 打傘) open an umbrella; spread an umbrella; unfurl an umbrella

開幕 opening
開幕典禮 opening ceremony

開燈 turn on the light

開舖 (商店開門 / 開店) open for business; start business

開學 start school; the new term begins

開餐 (開吃) have a meal

開頭 (最初) at first; at the beginning; at the outset; initial; original
一開頭 at first

開齋 ① (進行一天的首宗交易) conclude an initial transaction of the day ② (打破連敗) break a losing streak; get an initial win after losing a lot; win after repeated failures

開檔 ① (設攤兒 / 擺攤) operate a stall; set up a stall in the street; set up a stall in the market ② (開店 / 開始做生意) start one's business
開攤檔 (設攤兒 / 擺攤) operate a stall; set up a stall in the street; set up a stall in the market

開篷車 (敞篷車) open-topped car

開聲 (作聲 / 說話) say sth; speak up; talk

開講有話 (常言道 / 俗話說) as the saying goes

開關掣 (開關) switch

開鏡 (開拍) start shooting a movie

開籠雀 (不停說話的人 / 嚼舌) someone who chatters all the time; wag one's tongue

開鑼 (賽季開始) start of a season

開 OT (加班) work an extra shift; work extra hours; work overtime

開 P (聚會) have a party; hold a party

開 party (聚會) have a party; hold a party

開 show (開演唱會) have a concert; hold a concert

分開 break up; divide; isolate; part; partition; segregate; separate; sort

分隔開 separate from

召開 convene; convoke

有工開 ① (有工作要做) have work to do ② (有工做) have

a job to earn a living

行開（走開）go away

伸開 extend; spread; stretch out

妙想天開（異想天開／奇思妙想／天馬行空）a flight of fancy; a stretch of the imagination; ask for the moon; come out with most fantastic ideas; cry for the moon; expect wonders; fanciful; fanciful ideas; get fancy ideas into one's head; give loose to the fancy; give rein to fancy; have a maggot in one's head; have bats in the belfry; have bees in the brain; have bees in the head; have fantastic notions; have one's head full of bees; indulge in the wildest fantasy; indulge one's fancy; lend wings to one's imagination; let one's imagination run away with one; one's head is full of bees; vagarious; whimsical; wild hopes; wish for the moon; wishful thinking

唔該讓開（麻煩讓一下）please move over

展開 ① amplify; decoil; develop; open up; spread; spread out; unfold ② carry out; develop; launch

笑口常開 ① beam with smiles at all times ② may you be happy all the time

提前召開 convene before the due date

揚開（抖開）shake out

揭開（透露／打開／揭示／揭露）disclose; open; reveal; uncover

揀開（丟棄／拋棄／扔掉）throw away

揄開（剝開）peel off

掏開 ①（扔掉）throw away ②（甩開）throw off

異想天開（奇思妙想／天馬行空）a flight of fancy; a stretch of the imagination; ask for the moon; come out with most fantastic ideas; cry for the moon; expect wonders; fanciful; fanciful ideas; get fancy ideas into one's head; give loose to the fancy; give rein to fancy; have a maggot in one's head; have bats in the belfry; have bees in the brain; have bees in the head; have fantastic notions; have one's head full of bees; indulge in the wildest fantasy; indulge one's fancy; lend wings to one's imagination; let one's imagination run away with one; one's head is full of bees; vagarious; whimsical; wild hopes; wish for the moon; wishful thinking

睇唔開（看不開／想不開）cannot get over something; can't let go

睇得開（看得開／想得開）come to accept an unpleasant fact; get over sth

睇開（看開／想開）be tolerant of sth

裂開 cleave; crack; rend; split

勷開（推開）push open

間開（隔開）partition; separate

想唔開（想不開）take a matter to heart; take things too hard

想得開 not take to heart

搬開 remove

趌開（推開）push off

對開（對面）on the other side

撇開 get rid of

撕開 rip open; tear open

諗唔開（想不開）at the end of one's tether

擰開 unscrew

㩒開（撐開）open; prop-up

縮開（挪開／移開）move away

講開（講到／提及）mentioning; talking about

離開 depart from; deviate from; keep away from; leave; separate from

斷開 break into

鬆開（解開）loosen

讓開 get out of the way; make way; step aside

蹈開（滾開／走開）get lost; go away

【間】gaan¹ space

間中（有時／有時候）at times; every so often; occasionally; sometimes

　間唔中（間或）at times; every so often; occasionally; sometimes

間尺（尺子）ruler

　一把間尺（一把尺子）a ruler

間花腩（五花肉）pork belly; streaky pork

間屋 ①（房子）house ②（房間）room

間唔中（間或）now and then; occasionally; once in a while; sometimes

間格 ①（打格子）draw a rectangular grid ②（方格圖案）check

間條（條紋）stripe

間接 indirect

間開（隔開）partition; separate

間隔（間架）ledge

間諜 undercover

一息間（一瞬間）a little while; in a moment

一陣間（一瞬間／一會兒）a little while; a short while; in a jiffy; in a moment; presently

一間 measure word for a room

工作時間 working hours

冇時間（沒時間）have no time; time is not on one's side

中間 centre; in the middle of; middle

民間 ① among the people ② non-governmental

立時間（一時間）for a time

同一時間 at the same time

因吓時間（算算時間）estimate the time

有冇時間（有沒有時間）spare sb a few minutes; do you have time

伯仲之間 about the same

投票時間 polling hours

抽時間（抽空）manage to find time

突然間 all of a sudden; out of the blue; suddenly

挑撥離間 alienate; drive a wedge between; drive a wedge into; set one party against another; sow discord; turn sb against another

洗手間（廁所）lavatory; toilet; washroom; water closet

時間 time

泵時間（磨時間／拖時間）play for time

唔夠時間（時間不夠）not enough time

第一時間（馬上）as soon as; as quick as a flash; at once; at one stroke; at the drop of a hat; before you find where you are; directly; first thing off the bat; here and now; immediately; in a brace of shakes; in a crack; in a flash; in a jiffy; in a minute; in a moment; in no time; just now; lose no time in; off hand; on the moment; on the nail; out of hand; promptly; pronto; right away; right now; right off the bat; straight away; straight off; this instant; this moment; without a moment's delay; without delay; without hesitation; without loss of time; without thinking much longer

揬時間（磨時間／拖時間）stall for time

等一陣間（等一會兒）wait for a moment

開放時間 opening hours

嗰陣間（那時候）at that time

嘥時間（浪費時間）waste the time

搶時間（趕時間）race against time

慳時間（省時間）save time

趕時間 in a hurry; in haste

辦公時間 office hours

離間 alienate; drive a wedge between; drive a wedge into; set one party against another; sow discord; turn sb against another

【間】gaan³ occasional

間架（房屋結構）framework of a house

化粧間 powder room

坊間 on the market

彼此之間 between you and me

房間 room

【閏】joen⁶ intercalary

閏月 intercalary month

閏年 intercalary year

十年唔逢一閏（千載難逢）once in a blue moon; the chance of a lifetime; very rare

【閒】haan⁴ free

閒日（平常日子／星期一至五）Monday to Friday; weekdays

閒事（小事兒）unimportant matter

閒閒哋 ①（最起碼）at least; easily; without any difficulties ②（至少）at any rate; on any account; the least

好閒（沒事）it's nothing; never mind

空閒 free; leisure

唔得閒（沒空）busy; have no time; not free

得閒（有空）free; have time; when one's available

【陽】joeng⁴ sun

陽台 veranda

　大陽台 terrace

陽光 sunlight

　好好陽光（陽光充沛）very sunny

夕陽 setting sun

太陽 sun

好好太陽（陽光充沛）very sunny

曬太陽（日光浴）sunbathe

【隆】lung⁴ bloom

隆重 grand; solemn

生意興隆 wish you a blooming business

【隊】doey⁶ team

隊冧（殺死）kill sb

隊酒（灌酒）drink alcohol

隊啤（喝啤酒）drink beer

三羣五隊（三五成羣）in groups

列隊 fall into rank; file; line up; rank

狗仔隊 paparazzi

軍隊 army

啦啦隊（歡呼隊）cheering team

排隊 line up; queue

球隊 team

敢死隊 suicide squad

團隊 team

聯羣結隊（成羣結隊）band together; in crowds; in flocks; in groups; in throngs

艦隊 fleet

【階】gaai¹ steps

階磚（方片兒／方塊兒／地磚）floor brick

【隍】wong⁴ dry moat

水鬼升城隍（升職）get a promotion
城隍 city god

【雄】hung⁴ ① male ② hero

雄性 male
雄厚 abundant; ample; plentiful; rich; substantial

巾幗英雄 female hero; heroine
英雄重英雄（惺惺相惜）like knows like
識英雄重英雄（惺惺相惜）like knows like; think highly of each other

【雁】ngaan⁶（大雁）wild goose

雁封（雁書／書信）letter; written message

【雅】ngaa⁵ elegant

雅俗 the refined and the vulgar; the sophisticated and the simple-minded
　雅俗共賞 appeal to all; appeal to both the sophisticated and the simple-minded; appeal to highbrows and lowbrows; be admired by scholars and laymen alike; be enjoyed by both the educated and the common people; both the refined and the vulgar can take pleasure in; everyone can enjoy; for the enjoyment of both the educated and the common; highbrows and lowbrows alike can enjoy; suit all tastes; suit both refined and popular tastes; the uneducated as well as the educated can appreciate it
雅興 aesthetic mood; refined interest
雅觀 graceful and elegant in appearance; in good taste; nice appearance; nice-looking; refined

典雅 elegant; refined

【集】dzaap⁹ collect

集合 assemble
集郵 stamp collecting
集資 fund-raising

人口密集 be densely populated
卡通片集（動畫片集）cartoon series
召集 call together; convene; draw together
密集 concentrated; crowded together
搜集 collect; gather; seek and gather
聚集 aggregation; assemble; collect; gather
續集 sequel

【雲】wan⁴（雲彩）cloud

雲石（大理石）marble
雲耳（白木耳／銀耳）black fungus
雲吞（餛飩）shrimp dumpling
　雲吞麵（餛飩麵）shrimp dumpling noodles
　炸雲吞（炸餛飩）deep-fried shrimp dumplings
　淨雲吞（餛飩）shrimp dumplings in soup
　煮雲吞（煮餛飩）cook shrimp dumplings
雲呢拿（香草）(English) vanilla

一嚿雲（不知所措）all at sea
朵朵白雲 clusters of cloud
凌雲 aim high; reach the clouds; ride the high clouds; soar to the sky
浮雲 floating clouds
亂過一嚿雲（亂成一鍋粥／不知所措）in great chaos

【韌】ngan⁶⁻¹ tenacious

韌皮（頑皮）naughty

煙韌 ①（有韌性）sticky ②（如膠似漆／親密）intimate behaviour

【項】hong⁶ nape of the neck

項目 item; project

款項 ① a sum of money; fund ② section of an article in a legal document
債項（債務）debt
雞項（雲英雞／小母雞）virgin chicken

【順】soen⁶ smooth

順口 read smoothly
順水人情（不費力的人情）the favour done at one's convenience
順水推舟 make use of an opportunity to win one's end
順手 handy; sth that can be done easily in the course of things; without extra trouble
　順手牽羊 go on the scamp; make away with sth
順住（沿着）follow; go along
順便（順道）at one's convenience; conveniently; in passing; while sb is about it; without extra effort; without taking extra trouble
順風 fine trip
　順風駛悝（見風駛舵／人云亦云）avail oneself of an opportunity; trim the sails
　祝你順風（一路順風）have a fine trip; have a good trip; have a pleasant journey; have a smooth trip; wish you a nice trip

順得哥情失嫂意 (左右為難) find it hard to be partial to either side of the two

順眼 (悦目／賞心悦目) pleasing to the eyes

順喉 (潤喉) mild to the throat

順景 (順利／景況好) good times; happy days

順超 (贊同) agreeable

順德 (得) 人 (不會拒絕的人) a person who never refuses

順攤 (順利／順當) easy-going

手風順 (手氣好) have luck

同花順 straight flush

孝順 filial piety

柔順 gentle and agreeable; gentle and yielding; meek; submissive

條氣唔順 (心情不舒暢) feel unhappy; not convinced

頂唔順 (吃不消／受不了／無法忍受) be too much for one to do sth; cannot bear it; cannot stand sth; cannot stick with it; more than one can bear; unable to stand; unable to tolerate

頂得順 (吃得消／受得了) able to stand

【須】 soey¹ necessary

須知 ① have to know; it must be understood; one should know; should know ② note; notice; points for attention

須要 have to; must

必須 cannot do without; have to; it is imperative for; it is necessary that; must; ought to

終須 (終究／畢竟／最終) after all; eventually; in the end

【黃】 wong⁴ yellow

黃大仙——有求必應 (土地廟的橫批——有求必應) one who always accepts others' requests

黃毛 (黃頭髮) yellow-haired

黃牙白 (大白菜) Chinese lettuce

黃牛 (非法中介／不當得利) profiteer
黃牛黨 (倒票) scalpers

黃犬 (蚯蚓) earthworm

黃皮樹鷯哥——唔熟唔食 (八哥兒啄柿子——挑軟的) the person who swindles money out of his familiar friends

黃皮樹鷯哥——熟嗰個食嗰個 (老太太吃柿子——挑軟的) the person who swindles money out of his familiar friends

黃立鱠 (金鯧魚) pompano

黃色 yellow; yellow colour

黃昏 evening

黃泡髧熟 (黃而浮腫) a swollen face with yellow complexion

黃泥 (黃土) loess

黃花魚 (黃魚) yellow croaker

黃芽白 (大白菜) Chinese lettuce

黃金 gold

黃面婆 (黃臉婆) one's wife

黃馬褂 ① clerk related to the boss ② relatives of the boss

黃猄 (鹿) muntjac

黃魚 yellow croaker

黃腫腳——不消蹄 (提) (沒有提到／沒有提及) make no mention of sth

黃蜂 (螞蜂) hornet
黃蜂腰 (蜂腰) lady's well-proportioned waist

黃線 yellow line

黃糖 (紅糖) brown sugar

黃賭毒 prostitution, drugs, and gambling

黃燦燦 bright yellow

黃黚黚 (黃乎乎) yellow

黃藥水 (雷弗諾爾／利凡諾) acrinol solution

黃蟮 (蚯蚓) earthworm

黃鱔 ricefield eel

牛黃 (暴燥的) bad-tempered

金魚黃 bright yellow

韭黃 yellow chive

俾人笑到面黃 (被人笑到面紅耳赤) feel embarrassed when being teased by others

淺黃 light yellow

掃黃 (反色情／打擊副業) anti-pornography; clamp down on the vice-trade

嫩黃 light yellow

檸檬黃 lemon yellow

【黑】 hak⁷ ① black ② (背運／運氣不好) hard luck; unlucky

黑口黑面 ① (死眉瞪眼) very angry ② (不滿的樣子／板起臉) look displeased; pull a long face
口黑面黑 ① (死眉瞪眼) very angry ② (不滿的樣子／板起臉) look displeased; pull a long face
黑埋口面 ① (死眉瞪眼) very angry ② (不滿的樣子／板起臉) look displeased; pull a long face

黑工 (非法勞工) illegal worker

黑心 (心腸不好) evil-minded

黑仔 ① (倒霉) unlucky ② (倒霉蛋) bad-luck guy

黑古勒特 (黑咕隆咚／黑不溜秋) very dark

黑市 black market

黑吃黑 a struggle among different triad groups

黑孖孖 (黑漆漆) very dark

黑色 black; black colour

黑底 (黑幫成員) member of a triad society

黑板 blackboard

　抹黑板（擦黑板）erase the blackboard

黑房（暗房 / 暗室）darkroom

黑狗得食白狗當災（一人得到好處，另一人遭殃）the white dog eats the meat and the black dog bears the blame

黑面神（臭臉的人）person with an angry face

黑麻麻（黑漆漆）pitch dark

黑超（太陽眼鏡 / 墨鏡）sunglasses

黑媽媽（黑漆漆）very dark

黑暗 dark

黑話 triad society language

黑過鬼（倒霉）have bad luck

黑過墨斗（倒霉）have bad luck

黑墨墨（黑糊糊）very dark

黑箱車（收屍車）corpse car

黑瞇萌（黑咕隆咚 / 黑糊糊）dusky; rather dark

黑錢（賄賂錢）bribery money

黑癭屎（痣）freckles

黑鑊（不幸 / 倒霉）misfortune

一日到黑（從早到晚）all day; all day long; as the day is long; from dawn to dusk; from morning till night; the whole day

口黑面黑 ①（死眉瞪眼）very angry ②（不滿的樣子 / 板起臉）look displeased; pull a long face

天下烏鴉一樣黑（天下烏鴉一般黑）all crows are equally black; all crows under the sun are black; crows are black all the world over; devils everywhere are devils of the same kind; evil people are bad all over the world; in every country dogs bite; they are all bad

天黑 the sky becomes dark

好黑 ① it's dark ② very dark

見過鬼都怕黑（吃一塹，長一智）learn from bad experience; once bitten, twice shy; a burnt child dreads the fire

見過鬼就怕黑（吃一塹，長一智）learn from bad experience; once bitten, twice shy; a burnt child dreads the fire

夜晚黑（晚上）evening; night

抹黑 blacken sb's name; bring shame on; discredit; throw mud at

炭黑 carbon black; black

唔見過鬼都唔怕黑（好了傷疤忘了痛）once on shore, one prays no more

唔紅唔黑（半紅不黑）not enjoying popularity in the show business

晚黑（晚上）at night; evening; in the evening; night

晚頭黑（晚上）at night; evening; in the evening; night

幾點天黑（天甚麼時候黑）what time will it get dark

當黑（不幸 / 倒霉 / 背運 / 運氣不好）down on one's luck;

out of luck; unlucky

摸黑 grope one's way on a dark night

頭頭碰着黑（處處碰釘子 / 諸事不順）everything goes wrong; meet with difficulties whatever one does; strike a snag everywhere

聽晚黑（明晚）tomorrow evening; tomorrow night

13 劃

【亂】lyn[6] disorderly

亂七八糟 at sixes and sevens; chaotic; in a mess; in confusion; in extreme disorder

亂打亂撞（歪打正着）score a lucky hit

亂立立（亂哄哄）in a hubbub; in an uproar; in noisy disorder; tumultuous

亂咁春（四處遊蕩 / 瞎跑）wander around

亂晒（全都亂了）be thrown into confusion

　亂晒坑（七上八下 / 全都亂了）at sixes and sevens; be thrown into confusion

亂過一嚿雲（亂成一鍋粥 / 不知所措）in great chaos

亂寫 write without ground

亂撞一通（漫無目標 / 漫無目的）aimlessly

亂噏（胡扯 / 胡說 / 胡謅 / 亂說）talk nonsense; talk rubbish

　亂噏廿四（瞎說八道 / 胡說八道）talk nonsense; talk rubbish

　亂噏無為（瞎說一氣 / 亂說一氣）talk nonsense; talk rubbish

亂糟糟 messy

亂講（胡說 / 胡謅）speak nonsense; talk rubbish; talk without ground

　亂講廿四（瞎說八道 / 胡說八道）talk nonsense; talk rubbish

亂嚟（胡來）do things irresponsibly; mess things up

亂籠（亂了套）make a mess of sth; out of whack

　亂晒籠（亂了套）chaos; disorder

　亂晒大籠（全亂套了）in great chaos; in great disorder

人多手腳亂（人多誤事）too many cooks spoil the broth

七國咁亂（亂作一團）chaotic; in a disorderly situation; in a very confusing and messy situation; messy; very messy

內亂 civil strife; internal disorder

手忙腳亂 all in a hustle of excitement; be thrown into a panic; be thrown into confusion; in a great flurry; in disarray

平息內亂 put down the internal disorder

立立亂（亂哄哄）all in a muddle; messy

立亂（亂哄哄）messy

好亂 very messy

花多眼亂（眼花繚亂）have a dazzling array of choices before one; there are too many to choose; too many choices

個腦好亂（腦子好亂）cannot think straight

凌亂 in a mess; in disarray; in total disorder; messy

紊亂（打亂／打斷）interrupt

動亂（騷亂／動盪）disturbance; turbulence; turmoil; upheaval

從中搗亂（從中作梗）throw a spanner into the works

混亂 chaotic; confused; messy

博亂（渾水摸魚）gain some advantage; make a hand of; profiteer; rake in profit; reap some profit

惑亂（迷惑／欺騙／困擾）confuse; delude; puzzle

間屋好亂（這間屋子好亂）the house is really messy

搏亂（渾水摸魚）fish in troubled water; take advantage of a chaotic situation

搆亂（弄亂）mix up

搗亂（搗蛋）make trouble

撈亂（弄亂／搞亂）mix up

整亂（弄亂）mess

霍亂 cholera

擾亂 disturb

穢亂 debauched; wanton

【催】tsoey¹ hasten; urge

催谷（推動／加強）expedite; give sth a great plug; plug

催命符 message to press others to complete sth

【傭】jung² ①（佣金）commission ②（傭人）maid; servent

傭人 servant

傭工 hired labourer; servant

一個菲傭 a Filipino maid

女傭 maid

印傭（印尼傭人）Indonesian maid

泰傭（泰國傭人）Thai maid

菲傭（菲律賓傭人）Filipino maid

【傲】ngou⁶ proud

傲氣 air of arrogance; conceit; haughtiness

傲慢 haughty and overbearing; impudent

驕傲 arrogant; big-headed; cock-a-hoop; cock-sure; cocky; conceited; get uppish; get too big for one's breeches; have a big head; pride oneself on; proud; snooty; stuck up; take pride in; too big for one's shoes; uppish; uppity; vain of

【傳】tsyn⁴ pass

傳波（傳球）pass the ball

傳染 infect

傳染病 infectious disease

傳真 fax

傳真至 fax to

傳真機 fax machine

圖文傳真 fax line

傳送（輸送／運送）convey

傳媒 mass media

傳統 tradition

傳說 legend

民間傳說 popular legend

傳播 transmit

傳譯（口譯）interpret

傳譯員（口譯員）interpreter

民間流傳 circulate among the people

長傳 long pass

宣傳 promote

家醜不可外傳（家醜不可外揚）not wash dirty linen in public

流傳 circulate; go about; hand down; spread; transmit

謠傳 hearsay; rumour

【傳】dzyn⁶⁻² biography

傳記 biography; life story

自傳 autobiography

言歸正傳 and now to be serious; come back to our story; come to business; get down to business; hark back to the subject; jesting apart; jesting aside; joking apart; joking aside; keep to the record; lead the conversation to serious things; let's resume the narration; resume the thread of one's discourse; return from the digress; return to one's muttons; return to the subject; return to the topic of discussion; revert to the original topic of conversation

【債】dzaai³ debt

債仔（債務人）debtor

債卷（債券）bond

債項（債務）debt

債務 debt; liabilities

免除債務 release from debt

血債 debt of blood

走債（逃債）avoid creditors

負債 in debt

還債 pay one's debt

【傷】 soeng¹ injury
傷口 wound
傷心 sad; sorrowful
傷風 (感冒) catch cold; cold; have a cold
傷害 hurt

中傷 defame
元氣大傷 one's constitution is greatly undermined; sap one's vitality
扭傷 have a sprain
灼傷 (燒傷) burn
受咗傷 (受了傷) injured; wounded
受傷 be injured; be wounded
哀傷 distressed; feel grief; feel sorrw; grieve; mourn; sad; sorrowful
損傷 injury
燒傷 burn
痨傷 (勞傷) be weakened by overexertion
嚴重損傷 severe injury

【傾】 king¹ (談 / 聊) chat; talk
傾吓 (聊聊 / 談談) have a chat
　傾吓問吓 (有問有答) ask and answer
傾唔埋 (談不來 / 談不攏) do not speak the same language
　傾唔埋欄 (無法表述觀點) fail to carry one's point
　傾得埋 (談得來 / 談得攏) get along with sb
傾偈 (聊天 / 閒聊 / 談話) chat; chit-chat; have a chat; have a good chat; talk
　傾吓偈 (聊聊天) have a little chat
　傾密偈 (密斟 / 密談) have a personal chat
　傾閒偈 (聊天 / 閒聊) have a chat

冇得傾 (沒門兒 / 沒得說) unnegotiable
好傾 (談得來 / 談得攏) get along with sb
唔啱傾 (談不來 / 談不攏) not get along well
啱傾 (談得來 / 談得攏) get along well with people; hit it off

【僅】 gan² just
僅僅 merely

【傻】 so⁴ foolish
傻人 (傻蛋) silly person
　傻人有傻福 the foolish are often lucky
傻女 (傻姑娘) silly girl
傻仔 ① (傻子) silly boy; silly fellow ② (笨蛋) fool; simpleton
傻瓜 (傻子) dopey; fool; silly fool

傻夾戇 (缺心眼兒) candid; careless; frank; lack of calculation; mindless
傻庚 (傻子) fool
　傻傻庚庚 (傻裏傻氣) foolish
傻妹 (傻妞兒) silly girl
傻佬 (傻子) foolish man
傻婆 (傻女人) silly woman
傻傻哋 (傻傻的) likeable but stupid; not very clever; simple-minded
傻豬 (蠢貨 / 小傻子) silly fool; you silly kid

呆傻傻 (呆呆的) dazed; stupefied
扮傻 (裝傻) play the fool
詐傻 (裝傻) act stupid; play the fool
睬佢都傻 (管他是多餘的 / 誰會理他呀 / 傻子都懶得理他) not bother to pay any attention to sb; who would pay attention to him

【鏟】 tsaan² (刮) scrape
鏟平 level; level to the ground
鏟泥車 (推土機) bulldozer
鏟除 (根除) eradicate; root out

【勢】 sai³ situation
勢不兩立 absolutely antagonistic; at daggers drawn; at enmity; at the opposite pole to; completely incompatible; diametrically opposed to; extremely antagonistic to; implacable hostility; irreconcilable with; swear not to coexist with; unable to coexist
勢必 be bound to; certainly will; undoubtedly
勢兇夾狼 (心狠手辣 / 窮兇極惡) act outrageously and ferociously
勢利 snobbish
勢均力敵 all square; balance in power; balance of forces; diamond cut diamond; equal in authority and power; equal scale; even scale; evenly matched; in an equilibrium; level; level-pegging; match each other in strength; neck and neck; nip and tuck; well-matched; well-matched in strength

三兩吓手勢 (手又快又巧) quickly and skillfully
分析局勢 analyze a situation
手勢 ① (做菜能力) skill at cooking ② (運勢) one's luck
仗勢 take advantage of one's power or connection with influential people
劣勢 inferior position; inferior strength
有財有勢 rich and powerful
形勢 ① contour; terrain; topographical features ② circumstances; landscape; situation

局勢 situation

扭身扭勢（吸引注意力／搔首弄姿）attract attention to oneself

攻勢 offensive

走勢 trend

阻頭阻勢（推三阻四／礙事）decline with all sorts of excuses; fob sb off with excuses; get in the way; give the runaround; make excuses and put obstacles in the way

係威係勢（像模像樣／夠氣派）look impressive

威勢（權威）power and influence

架勢（了不起／排場／氣派／神氣）extravagant; terrific

郁身郁勢（動來動去）show discontent with one's position

風頭火勢（事情鬧得正兇的時候）at full throttle; in the state of full blast

弱勢 ① in a relatively weak position ② the disadvantaged

真係架勢（真有氣派）really gorgeous

氣勢 grand feeling

財勢 wealth and power

起勢（使勁兒地／起勁／拼命）active; eager; energetically; enthusiastically; exert all one's strength; go all out; in high spirits; showing much zeal; vigorously; vociferous; with gusto; with zest and vigour; work frantically

窒頭窒勢（礙手礙腳／頂心頂肺）interrupt with discouraging comments

造勢 media hype; spin

捹手唔成勢（臨時抱佛腳／突如其來的事，不懂得應付）be tied up in knots due to lack of preview

睇頭勢（看風頭）find out how the wind blows; see how things stand; see which way the wind blows

態勢 ① situation; state ② posture

趨炎附勢 a follower of the rich and powerful; a snob who plays up to those in power; approach the bustling place and cleave to the strong; attach oneself as subordinate to those in power; cater to those in power; climb on the bandwagon; creep into the good grace of; curry favour with the powerful; curry favour with those in power; fawn upon the rich and powerful persons; to where there is anything to be got; gravitate to those rising in the world; hail the rising sun; hang on to the sleeves of those in power; hurry to the glorious and hang on to the influential; jump on the bandwagon; play up to those in power; please and flatter wealthy and influential persons; run round persons in warm comfortable circumstances and flatter to the powerful; serve the time; worship the rising sun

趨勢 tendency

黐身黐勢（黏人）cling to sb

攬身攬勢（摟摟抱抱）hug each other; lovey-dovey

謅架勢（裝排場／擺威風）act lord; make the scene to be splendid

【勤】kan⁴ diligent

勤力（用功／勤奮）diligent; hardworking; studious

勤工獎（全勤獎）attendance bonus

地勤 ground service

值勤 on duty

倦勤 be tried of work

【匯】wui⁶ converge

匯率 exchange rate

匯票（銀行匯票）bank draft

匯款 remittance

外匯 foreign exchange

炒外匯（炒賣外匯）speculate in foreign currencies

詞匯 vocabulary

電匯 telegraphic transfer

賭外匯 gamble on foreign exchange

【嗎】maa¹ particle used in questions

你好嗎 how are things going; how are you; how are you doing; how goes it; how have you been; how's tricks

【嗒】daap⁷ lick; sip

嗒低頭（垂頭喪氣）disheartened upset

嗒酒（呷一口酒／淺嚐）have a sip of wine

嗒得杯落（有吸引力）attractive

嗒落有味（仔細考慮後發現某物很重要）the significance of sth becomes clear after careful consideration

嗒糖 ①（感到開心）happy about sth ②（對異性有吸引力）be sexually attracted to sb

　　嗒晒糖（被異性吸引）be sexually attracted to sb

頭嗒嗒（垂頭喪氣）depressed

【嗜】si³ neat

嗜正（整齊／端莊）neat

【嗤】tsi¹ sneeze

打乞嗤（打噴嚏）sneeze

【嗍】sok⁸（吸氣）breathe in; inhale

嗍氣（吸氣／喘氣）gasp; pant

【嗱】naa⁴ pick up

嗱林（迅速地）quickly

嗱嗱臨（迅速地）quickly

嗻嗻聲 (迅速地) quickly

冇渣嗻 (沒有保證) gain no guarantee against loss; no guarantee

無嗻嗻 (無端 / 平白無故 / 無緣無故) without reason or cause

【嘥】 saai¹ (花 / 浪費) waste

嘥士 (尺碼) (English) size

嘥晒 (可惜 / 浪費) waste entirely

嘥氣 (白費唇舌) waste one's breath

　盞嘥氣 (徒勞 / 白費力氣) fruitless; futile; have no use; in vain; no good; no use; of no use; spend effort in vain; to no purpose; useless

　費事同你嘥氣 (不跟你白費唇舌) won't waste my breath with you

　嘥鬼氣嘿 (白費口舌 / 白費唇舌) waste one's words

　嘥聲壞氣 (白費口舌 / 白費唇舌) speak to the wind; waste one's breath; waste one's words; whistle down the wind

嘥腳力 (費腳力) waste energy by walking

嘥燈賣油 (費燈賣油 / 小往大來) a game worth a candle

嘥揬 (浪費) go to waste

大嘥 (靡費) extravagant

鬭嘥 (互相誹謗) calumniate each other; defame each other; slander each other

【嗲】 de² finicky

嗲吊 (做事漫不經心 / 不緊不慢) sluggish and dilatory

　唔嗲唔吊 (大大咧咧) casual

　嗲嗲吊 (不負責任) irresponsible

收嗲 (閉嘴) shut up

詐嗲 (撒嬌) sulk

搭嗲 (插話) interrupt a conversation

嬌嗲 (嬌滴滴) delicate and pretty

【嗖】 so¹ sniff

嗖氣 (喘氣) lose one's breath; out of breath; tired out

【嗰】 go² (那) that

嗰次 (那次) that time

嗰位 (那位) that person

嗰便 (那邊) over there; there

嗰度 (那兒 / 那裏) that place; there

　喺嗰度 (在那兒 / 在那裏) it is there

嗰隻野 (那個人) that person

　嗰隻衰野 (那個討厭鬼) that nasty person

嗰個 (那個) that

嗰個人 (那個人) that person

　嗰個嘢 (那個人) that person

嗰陣 (那時候) at that time

　嗰陣時 (那時候) at that time

　嗰陣間 (那時候) at that time

嗰條友 (那個傢伙) that guy

　嗰條友仔 (那個小子) that guy

嗰啲 (那些) those

　嗰啲嘢 ① (鬼) ghosts ② (像那些東西) stuff like that

嗰排 (那一陣子) for a period of time; that time

嗰處 (那裏 / 那兒 / 那邊) there

嗰輪 (那一陣子) at that time; for a period of time; that time

　嗰一輪 (那一陣子) at that time; for a period of time; that time

嗰頭 (那兒 / 那裏) that place; there

嗰頭近 (快死了 / 翻白眼兒了) at death's door; close to the age of death; have one's foot in the grave

嗰 sales ① (那個售貨員) the salesman ② (那個女售貨員) the saleswoman

痀嗰 (笨死了) very clumsy

【嗌】 aai³ (叫) shout; yell

嗌人 (叫人) cry for sb

嗌生晒 (瞎叫唤) clamour

嗌交 (吵架 / 爭吵 / 對罵) argument; bicker; make a row; quarrel; wrangle

嗌救命 (叫救命 / 喊救命) cry for help

嗌通街 (與左鄰右舍的都吵過架) bandy words with everyone

嗌霎 (爭吵 / 鬥嘴) have a serious argument

嗌餸 (點菜) order dishes; order food

大嗌 (大喊大叫) yell out

咪嗌 (不要叫 / 別叫) don't shout

唔好嗌 (不要叫 / 別叫) don't shout

撩交嗌 (吵架) provoke an argument with sth

【嗯】 nang⁴ (連) join

嗯埋一齊 (連在一起) join together

一抽二嗯 (大包小包的) carry lots of different things

冇哪嗯 (沒事做 / 無所事事) have nothing to do with

【園】 jyn⁴ garden

園地 ① garden plot ② field; scope

園林 garden; park

園遊會 (遊園會) garden party

園藝 garden husbandry; gardening; horticulture

公園 park
幼兒園 kindergarten; nursery school; pre-school
幼稚園（幼兒園）kindergarten; nursery school; pre-school
田園 countryside; fields and gardens
宅園（私家花園）private garden
行公園（逛公園）walk in the park
海洋公園 ocean park
花園 garden
庭園 flower garden; garden
校園 campus
桑園 mulberry field
動物園 zoo
梨園（戲曲界）operatic circles
漫步校園 take a walk on campus
遊花園 ①（逛花園）walk around the garden ②（打圈圈）go around in circles
蕉園（香蕉園）banana plantation

【圓】jyn⁴ round
圓肉（桂圓肉）dried longan pulp
圓枱（圓桌）round table
圓面（圓臉）round face
圓圈 circle
圓揉朵（圓乎乎的）chubby
圓滑 diplomatic
圓領 round collar

日圓 Japanese yen
桂圓 longan

【塊】faai³ a piece of
塊頭 hulky; large

一塊 a piece of; a sheet of; a slice of; a tablet of
板塊 plate
炸雞塊 chicken nugget
雞塊 chicken piece

【塌】taap⁸ collapse
塌落嚟（塌下來）collapse

倒塌 collapse

【塑】sok⁸ plastic
塑膠（塑料）plastic material; plastics

【塔】taap⁸ ① pagoda ②（缸）jar; vat
塔頂（寶塔的頂部）top of a pagoda

屎塔（馬桶）toilet
筆塔（筆套）cap of a pen; cap of a writing brush
象牙塔（大學校園）university campus
穩如鐵塔（穩如泰山）as firm as it is founded on the rock

【塘】tong⁴ pool
塘水滾塘魚（同一集團的成員互相獲利／左手交右手）members of the same group gain profits from each other; people do business among themselves
塘尾（蜻蜓）dragonfly
塘虱（鯰魚）catfish
塘蒿（茼蒿／蒿子稈）garland chrysanthemum
塘蝨（鯰魚）catfish
塘邊鶴（等待機會的旁觀者）the person who hastens to make away with his gains

水塘 ① reservoir ② pool
禾塘（曬穀場）grain-sunning ground
地塘（曬穀場）grain-sunning ground
池塘 pond
乾塘 ①（抽乾池塘）drain a pond ②（破產／缺錢）broke; fall short of money
避風塘（避風港）habour; haven

【塗】tou⁴ blot out; cross out; efface; erase; obliterate
塗改液（修正液）correction fluid
塗咗（塗掉）cross out

糊塗 confused; muddled

【塞】sak⁷（曾孫）great grandchildren
塞古盟憎（突然）all of a sudden
塞車（堵車）traffic congestion; traffic jam
冇塞車（交通順暢）the traffic is smooth
好塞車（交通堵塞）the traffic is congested; there's a heavy traffic jam
塞緊車（正在塞車）be stuck in a traffic jam
塞實窿（小孩）a little child

水松塞（木塞）cork
瓶塞 bottle plug; bottle stopper; cork
萌塞（頑固／冥頑不靈）inflexible; stubborn
盟塞（思想閉塞／落後／死腦筋）as stupid as an owl; poor at understanding
鼻塞（鼻子不通氣）nasal congestion; stuffy nose

【填】 tin⁴ fill in

填氹 (填補虧空) replace money that one has taken
　　secretly
填房 (續絃 / 繼室) second wife (of a widower)
　　娶填房 (續絃 / 娶繼室) a widower getting a second wife
填數 (填補盜走的錢) replace money that one has taken
　　secretly
填寫 fill in
　　填寫表格 fill in a form
填鴨 ① (烤鴨) roast duck ② (強行灌輸) spoon-feeding

漏填 fail to fill in; forget to fill in

【奧】 ou³ mystery

奧運會 Olympic Games

【嫁】 gaa³ marry

嫁畀 (嫁給) marry a man
嫁雞隨雞，嫁狗隨狗 become a subordinate to one's
　　husband once married

男大當婚，女大當嫁 when men and women are fully
　　grown, they must marry
恨嫁 want to get married
皇帝女──唔憂嫁 (皇帝的女兒不愁嫁) a person who is
　　very much sought after

【嫂】 sou² sister-in-law

嫂夫人 your wife

兄嫂 one's elder brother and his wife
阿嫂 ① (嫂子 / 嫂嫂) elder brother's wife; sister-in-law
　　② (嫂子 / 嫂嫂) a polite way of addressing a friend's wife
家嫂 (兒媳婦) daughter-in-law

【媳】 sik⁷ daughter-in-law

媳婦 (兒媳婦) daughter-in-law

童養媳 child bride

【媽】 maa¹ (媽媽) mother

媽咪 ① (母親 / 媽媽) mammy; mummy ② (拉皮條的女
　　子) female pimp
媽媽 ma; mama; mammy; mother; mum; mummy
　　媽媽生 (老鴇 / 操控性工作者 / 皮條客) female pimp
　　媽媽聲 (滿嘴粗話) swear; swear like a pirate; swear like
　　　　a trooper

大姨媽 (月經 / 女性生理期) menstrual period; monthly period

奶媽 wet nurse
夜媽媽 (深夜) very late at night
阿媽 (母親 / 媽媽) mama; mother; mum
契媽 (養母) adoptive mother
姨媽 ① (姨母) aunt; mother's sister ② (月經) menstrual
　　period; monthly period
後媽 (後娘 / 繼母) stepmother
爹媽 (爹娘) father and mother
執媽 (接生婆 / 助產士 / 產婆) midwife
婆婆媽媽 (女人般挑剔) womanishly fussy
婆媽 (過分客氣) over-polite
黑媽媽 (黑漆漆) very dark

【媾】 gau³ pick up

媾女 (追求女生) pick up a girl
　　媾女王 (花花公子) playboy
媾仔 (追求男生) pick up a man

【嫌】 jim⁴ detest

嫌棄 turn a cold shoulder to sb

涉嫌 suspect
釋嫌 ① dispel suspicion ② dispel ill feelings

【幹】 gon³ do

幹部 (支幹部) cadre

一單事幹 (一件事情) a matter
才幹 ability; caliber; capability; competence; management ability
冇事幹 (沒事幹) have nothing to do
有事幹 have sth to do
事幹 (事情) affair; event; incident; matter; thing
能幹 able; capable; competent; have a lot on the ball
諸多事幹 (許多事情 / 八卦) nosy

【廈】 haa⁶ building

大廈 building
多層大廈 multi-storey building
高樓大廈 tall buildings

【廉】 lim⁴ honest

廉恥 sense of honour; sense of shame
廉價 cheap; inexpensive; low-priced
　　廉價出售 be sold at a bargain
　　廉價出讓 be sold at a low price
廉潔 honest; whitehanded; with clean hands

忌廉 (奶油 / 黃油) butter; cream

【廊】long⁴ corridor
廊檐 eaves of a veranda

走廊 corridor

【微】mei⁴ tiny
微波爐 microwave oven

微雨（小雨）drizzle; light rain

微笑 smile

微菌（細菌）bacteria; germ

式微 decline

低微 humble; lowly

些微 a bit; a little

酸微微 ①（酸溜溜）sour; tart ②（嫉妒）envious; jealous

【想】soeng² wish
想去 wish to go to

想要 want

想食咗大隻車咩（貪得無厭）hope to get a lot from others

想唔到（想不到）unexpectedly

想唔開（想不開）take a matter to heart; take things too hard
　想得開 not take to heart

想當然 take for granted

想話（正想 / 正想說 / 打算）be just going to; just want to say

想像 imagine
　不可想像 cannot be imagined; inconceivable; unthinkable

不堪設想（很難成像 / 無法想像）can hardly be imagined; cannot be imagined; dreadful to contemplate; hard to imagine; unthinkable

中心思想 central idea

幻想 fantasy; imagine

充滿幻想 full of fancies

好想 eager to

妄想 absurd pursuit; daydream; delusion; forlorn hope; kink; vain hope; wishful thinking

思想 idea; thought

料想 expect; presume; think

崇高理想 lofty ideal

理想 ideal

設想 ①（假設 / 構想 / 想像）assume; conceive; envisage; imagine ②（想法 / 粗略計劃）idea; rough plan; scheme; tentative idea; tentative plan

痴心妄想 fond dream; wishful thinking

實現理想 realise one's ideal

夢想 ① dream of ② vain hope; wishful thinking

【愁】sau⁴ sorrow
愁眉 distressed look; knitted brows
　愁眉苦臉 a face of woe; a face shaded with melancholy; down in the dumps; down in the mouth; draw a long face; gloomy face; have a face as long as a fiddle; have a face like a fiddle; have a worried look; look blue; make a long face; pull a long face; put on a long face; wear a glum countenance; with a long face

愁容 anxious expression; worried look

哀愁 grieved; lamentation; sad; sorrowful

【惹】je⁵ ①（招惹）stir up ②（傳染）contagious
惹火（火辣 / 性感）sexy

惹屎上身（自找麻煩 / 惹禍上身）ask for trouble; invite trouble

惹眼（醒目 / 顯眼）attract attention; eye-catching; sharp

惹蟻（招螞蟻）attract ants

【意】ji³ idea
意大利 Italy
　意大利人 Italian
　意大利文 Italian
　意大利粉（意大利麵）spaghetti
　意大利菜 Italian food

意中人 the person one is in love with

意見 advice; opinion

意思 meaning
　小意思 a slight token of regard; mere trifle
　有意思 meaningful
　唔好意思 ①（不好意思）excuse me ②（很抱歉 / 過意不去）feel apologetic; feel sorry; I'm sorry; sorry ③（尷尬）embarrass

意粉（意大利麵）spaghetti

意頭（兆頭 / 彩頭）auspicious sign; good luck; omen
　好意頭（有彩頭）auspicious omen
　　唔好意頭（意頭不好）inauspicious omen
　攞意頭（討個彩頭）do sth for the sake of good luck; get an auspicious sign

一單生意（一宗生意）a business transaction

入口生意（進口生意）import business

三心兩意 dillydally; in two minds

大安旨意（過份放心而不加過問）choose to ignore any risk or danger

大食有旨意（奢侈行為有堅實後盾）have a firm backing to do such a deed for one's extravagance

大意（粗心）careless

小本生意 small business

不必介意 not care a rush

不成敬意 just a little token to show my respect to you; just a trifle

不為意（不在意）without paying much attention to

中意 like; satisfied

介意 mind

分外寫意（格外愜意）especially contented

天意 destiny; fate

引起注意 attract attention; attract sb's attention; bring to sb's attention; call attention; catch sb's eye; draw attention; excite attention

主意 idea

令人滿意 be entirely satisfactory

出入口生意（進出口生意）import and export business

出口生意 export business

另打主意 make some other plans

打錯主意 get a wrong idea into one's head

民意 popular sentiment; will of the people

生意 business

示意 drop a hint; give a sign; hint; indicate one's wish; motion; signal

同意 agree; consent

在意 use caution

好主意 good idea; that's a brilliant idea; that's a good idea; that's a marvelous idea; that's a practical idea; that's a wonderful idea; that's an excellent idea; what a capital idea

好生意 do a brisk business; good business

旨意（依靠）depend on; rely on

曲意 make a special concession to achieve others' goals

改變主意 change one's mind

事事如意 every success; everything answers; everything comes off satisfactorily; everything falls into one's lap

刻意 painstakingly; sedulously

咁又幾得意（那樣很有趣）that's interesting

注意 care about; careful; have an eye on; look out; mindful of; notice; on the look-out; on the watch; pay attention to; show application; take care; take note of; watch; watch one's step; watch out

係咁意（小意思／做做樣子）as a token gesture; do sth as a token

指意（依靠）depend on

為意（在意）pay attention to

厚意 kindness

故意 by design; by intention; deliberately; go out of one's way; intentionally; of set purpose; on purpose; willfully

美意 good intention; kindness

借啲意（找個藉口）cook up a lame excuse; make a feeble excuse

倦意 sleepiness; tiredness; weariness

唔在意（不在意）not careful

唔使旨意（不用指望／別指望）don't count on me

唔覺意（不小心／不留神／沒注意／沒留意）accidentally; take no care; unintentionally

留意（注意）pay attention to

致意 convey one's best regards; convey one's best wishes; give one's regards; present one's compliments; salutation; salute; send one's greeting; with the compliments of

做生意 conduct business; do business; do business transactions; run a business

得意 ①（好玩／有趣）interesting ②（可愛）cute ③（新奇）strange

粗心大意（不夠細心／粗心／馬虎）careless; inadvertent; negligent; remiss; scatterbrain; slipshod; thoughtless; want of care

貪得意（貪好玩）curious

創意（創造力／創造性）creative idea; creativity

寓意（隱含意義）allegoric meaning; implied meaning; import; message; moral

最鍾意（最喜歡／最愛）favourite

揸主意（打定主意／下決定）make a decision; make up one's mind

盛意（盛情）generosity; great kindness

詐假意（開玩笑／假裝）make a joke; make believe; pretend

順得哥情失嫂意（左右為難）find it hard to be partial to either side of the two

順從民意 obey the will of the people

萬事勝意（萬事如意）may things get better than what you expect

傾生意（談生意）solicit business

嗰 BB 好得意（這個寶寶真可愛）this baby is very cute

斟生意（談生意）negotiate business

會錯意（誤會對方意思）misunderstand sb's intention

敬意 esteem; regard; respect; salute; tribute

誠意 good faith; sincerity

達意 convey one's ideas; express one's ideas

摟生意（招攬生意）solicit business; solicit trade

歉意 apologies; regrets

滿意 satisfied

蓄意 deliberate; harbour certain intentions; premeditated

寫意（愜意）comfortable; contented; easy; free and happy; gratified; pleased; satisfied

樂意 glad to

銳意 determination; eager intention; sharp will

鍾意（喜愛／喜歡）favour; like; love

願意 willing

【愚】jy⁴ foolish

愚人節 April Fools' Day

愚不可及 abysmal ignorance; could not be more foolish; crass stupidity; hopelessly stupid; most foolish; the height of folly

愚笨（笨拙／愚蠢）clumsy; foolish; imbecile; stupid

愚蠢 as nutty as a fruitcake; chuckle-headed; dull; foolish; silly; stupid

【感】gam² feel

感受 feeling
　　切身感受 personal impressions and experience

感恩節 Thanksgiving Day

感性 emotional

感染 infection

感冒 flu; have a cold
　　感冒疫苗 cold and flu vaccine
　　流行性感冒 influenza

感情 ①（情懷）feelings ②（關係）relationship
　　聯繫感情 keep a good relationship

感激 grateful

感覺 feeling

皮膚敏感 skin allergy

好感 favourable impression

肉感（性感）sexy

性感 sexy

美感 aesthetic feeling; sense of beauty

敏感 ①（過敏的）allergic ②（心思細密）sensitive

禽流感 bird flu

【愛】oi³ ①（喜愛）love ②（要）want

愛人 lover

愛國 patriotic

愛情 love

愛滋 AIDS
　　愛滋病 AIDS
　　死於愛滋病 die of AIDS

愛靚（愛美）be concerned about looking good
　　愛靚唔愛命（要美不要命）be more concerned about looking good than being healthy

愛錫（疼愛／愛惜）be fond of; love dearly

可愛 likable; lovable; lovely

母愛 maternal love; mother love

相親相愛 love and care for each other; mutual love

恩愛 affectionate; conjugal love

偏愛 affect; favour; go overboard; have a predilection for; have a preference for; have partiality for sth; love one more than another; partial to; play favourites; predilection; show favouritism to sb; take sides

溺愛 dote on

慈愛 affection; gentle; gentleness; kindness; love

憐愛 have tender affection for; love tenderly; show tender care for

親愛 dear; love

鍾愛 cherish; dote on; love deeply

寵愛 cosset; dote on; make a pet of sb; receive favour from a superior; think the world of sb; think the world of sth

戀愛 love

【慎】san⁶ prudent

慎言 speak cautiously

慎重 careful; cautious; considerate; discreet; prudent

慎終追遠（依禮慎重辦理父母喪事，祭祀要誠心追念遠祖）carefully attend to the funeral rites of parents and follow them when gone with due sacrifices; conduct the funeral of one's parents with meticulous care and let not sacrifices to one's remote ancestors be forgotten

審慎（慎重）prudent

【慌】fong¹ panicky

慌失失（慌裏慌張／慌慌張張）all in a fluster; higgledy-piggledy; in a hurried and confused manner; in a rush; lose one's head; nervous; on the rush
　　失失慌（慌裏慌張／慌慌張張）all in a fluster
　　慌慌失失（慌裏慌張／慌慌張張）nervous

慌死（生怕）for fear that; lest; so as not to

慌住（生怕／擔心）for fear that; lest; so as not to

慌怕（生怕／擔心）for fear that; lest; so as not to

不必驚慌 there is no need to panic; there is no cause for alarm

唔使慌 ①（不用害怕／不用擔憂／別慌張）don't be afraid ②（別指望）have no fond dreams about it

唔慌（不用擔心）no need to worry

恐慌 fright; frightened; panic; scared; terrified

悶到發慌（無聊）be bored beyond endurance

驚慌 panic

【戥】dang² （為／替）for

戥你唔抵（為你可惜）it's regrettable for you

戥穿石（伴郎）best man; men helping the bridegroom at his wedding

戥興（幸災樂禍）take pleasure in other people's misfortune

【損】 syn² (破) injure

損友 (壞朋友) vicious companion
損手 (傷了手) injured
　損手爛腳 ① (頭破血流) be beaten; be crushed; be seriously injured; head broken and bleeding; injured; run into bumps and bruises ② (損失慘重) suffer heavy losses
　整損手 (弄傷手) one's hand is injured
損益表 profit and loss account
損傷 injury
　嚴重損傷 severe injury
損毀 damage
損壞 damage

耗損 consume; deplete; lose; waste
磨損 wear and tear
整損 (受傷) hurt
擦損 (擦傷) bruise; graze

【撈】 kau³ (混和 / 摻和) blend; mingle; mix

撈水 (兌水) mix with water
撈埋 (兌上 / 混合 / 摻和) mix with
撈亂 (弄亂) mix up

【搏】 bok⁸ (拼) risk

搏一搏 take a risk
搏打 (討打) put oneself in danger of being punched
搏拉 (想被拘捕) put oneself in danger of being arrested
搏命 (拼命) defy death; fight desperately; give one's all to a task; go all out; go all out regardless of danger to one's life; make every effort
　搏老命 (拼老命) risk one's old age to give one's all to a task
搏炒 (想被解僱) invite dismissal
搏唔過 (不值一搏) it is not worthwhile running such a risk
搏彩 ① (碰運氣) chance one's luck; depend upon luck; pot luck; stand one's chance; take a chance; try one's luck ② (賭錢) gamble with money
搏殺 (拼搏 / 拼殺) take risks to achieve one's goal
搏過 (比拼) compete
搏亂 (渾水摸魚) fish in troubled water; take advantage of a chaotic situation
搏盡 (拼盡) exert oneself to the utmost; make one's best exertions
搏鬧 (招罵) incur abuses
搏懵 (佔便宜) take advantage of one's inattention

脈搏 pulse

【搔】 sou¹ scratch

搔癢 scratch the itch; scratch the itching place

冇人搔 (沒人搭理) nobody pays any attention to sb

【搾】 dzaa³ press; squeeze

搾出 squeeze out
搾汁 liquidise
　搾汁機 juicer

【搓】 tsaai¹ ① (揉) rub between the hands ② (托) twist up

搓粉 (揉麵粉 / 擀麵團) knead the flour
搓得圓撳得扁 (性格溫和) as mild as a dove
搓麵 (揉麵) knead dough

【搽】 tsaa⁴ (抹) apply ointment or powder

搽油 (塗油) apply ointment
搽脂蕩粉 (塗脂抹粉) apply powder
搽粉 (抹粉 / 塗粉) apply powder to one's face
搽梘 (擦肥皂) apply soap
搽藥 (抹藥 / 塗藥) apply ointment to the affected area

【搗】 dou² beat

搗亂 (搗蛋) make trouble

【搖】 jiu⁴ rock

搖勻 shake up
搖搖板 (蹺蹺板) see-saw

動搖 (搖擺不定) shake; waver and falter

【搜】 sau² search

搜身 conduct a body search
搜查 ransack; rummage; search
搜集 collect; gather; seek and gather
搜尋 look for; search for; seek; seek and find

【搭】 daap⁸ (坐 / 乘) take; to go by

搭上 hook up
搭手 (幫助) assist; help
搭沉船 (一個人的靈運影響其他人) join a doomed venture; one's bad luck implicates others
搭車 (乘車) ride a car
　搭順風車 (坐順風車) hitchhiking
搭的 (打的 / 乘出租汽車) take a cab; take a taxi
　搭的士 (打的 / 乘出租汽車) take a cab; take a taxi
搭客 (乘客) passenger

搭枱（拼桌／併桌）share a table in a restaurant with people you don't know

搭食（搭伙／搭夥）eat regularly in a place

搭脈（號脈）feel sb's pulse; take sb's pulse

搭訕（聊天）chat up

搭船（坐船／乘船）take a ferry

搭單（搭夥／捎帶）join as a partner

搭棚（搭腳手架）scalfold

　　搭棚佬（搭棚工人）scalfolding builder

搭軬（搭升降機／乘電梯）take the elevator; take the lift

搭嗲（插嘴）interrupt a conversation

搭膊（墊肩）shoulder pad

搭嘴（插嘴）interrupt a conversation

搭錯賊船（上錯賊船）be misled to suffer a loss

搭錯線 ①（打錯電話／串線）dial a wrong number; have the wrong number ②（誤會）misunderstand sth

搭霎（正經／關心）care

　　冇搭霎 ①（不負責任／沒章法）irresponsible ②（沒正經）have no sense of propriety

　　冇釐搭霎 ①（不負責任／沒章法）irresponsible ②（沒正經）have no sense of propriety

搭檔 ①（合夥）go into partnership ②（聯手合作）join forces

勾搭 find a lover; pick up someone

乘搭 ride in (a vehicle)

配搭 ①（搭配）co-ordinate ②（擺列）collocate

蘇州過後冇艇搭（過了這村就沒這店／機不可失，失不再來）an opportunity missed is an opportunity lost; opportunities never come twice; the opportunity once missed will never come back

【搶】tsoeng² rob; take by force

搶手（搶着買／暢銷）big hit; in great demand; sell like hot cakes; sell well; the cat's meow

　　搶手貨（暢銷貨）a commodity in great demand; goods in great demand; grabbed items; hot consumer goods; shopping-rush goods; the cat's meow; very popular item

　　非常搶手 go like hot cakes; sell like hot cakes; the cat's meow

搶眼（醒目／顯眼）attract attention; attractive; eye-catching; sharp

搶閘（搶着做）rush to do sth

搶嘢（搶劫）loot; plunder; rob

　　搶嘢呀（搶劫呀）I've been mugged; robbery

搶錢 ask for too much money like robbery

搶購 rush to buy

搶鏡 photogenic; steal the show

好過去搶（比搶劫好）what one gets is better than robbing others

【搬】bun¹ move

搬去 move to

　　搬入去（搬進去）move in

　　搬去新地方 move to a new place

搬枱（搬桌子）move a table

搬屋（搬家）move house; removal

搬開 remove

搬運 removal

　　搬運工人 carrier

【搵】wan² ①（找）find; look for; search ②（拜訪）visit

搵丁（騙人）trick

搵人（找人）look for sb

搵工（找工作）find a job; job-hunting; look for a job

　　搵工做（找工作）look for a job

　　搵份工（找一份工作）find a job; look for a job

　　搵緊工（正在找一份工作）looking for a job; trying to find a job

搵水（掙錢）make money

搵米路（找方法掙大錢）find a way to get big profits

搵位（找座位）find a seat

搵到（找到）have found; have obtained; succeed in finding

　　搵唔到（找不到）cannot find; fail to find sth

搵定（提前找好）find in advance

搵兩餐（混飯吃）make a living

搵周公（找周公／去睡覺）go to sleep

搵食（找飯吃／謀生）earn a living; make a living

　　出嚟搵食 ①（謀生）come into the world to earn a living ②（掙快錢）make easy money

　　好難搵食 ①（很難謀生）hard to earn a living ②（很難賺錢）hardly get a decent pay

搵倒（找到）found

　　搵唔倒（找不到）cannot find it

　　搵得倒（找得到）can find it

搵埋佢嘅（把他也叫上）ask him to join us

搵鬼（找鬼／沒有人）no one

　　搵鬼買（找鬼買／沒人買）no one is willing to buy it

　　搵鬼幫手（找鬼做幫手／無人願意來幫忙）no one is willing to help someone in need

　　搵鬼幫襯（找鬼幫襯／瀕死的企業）a company that is doomed to fail

搵笨（騙人）fool sb into doing sth; rip sb off; take advantage of sb; trick sb

　　搵人笨（愚弄某人做某事／矇騙別人／佔人便宜）fool sb into doing sth; rip sb off; take advantage of sb; trick sb

搵得嚟使得去（能掙能花）easy come, easy go; light come, light go

搵朝唔得晚（生活僅夠糊口）live from hand to mouth

搵番（找回）retrieve
搵番嚟（找回來了）find it back; get it back

搵野（找東西）search for things
搵野做（找工作／找活兒幹）find a job; look for a job

搵銀（掙錢／賺錢）make money
搵銀良機（掙錢良機）opportunity to make profit

搵錢（掙錢／賺錢）make a living; make money
搵快錢（掙快錢／賺快錢）make a fast buck; make money quickly

好搵（掙大錢／賺大錢）make a lot of money

【搗】wu¹（捂）prostrate
搗低（俯下／俯身向下）bend down

【搞】gaau²（弄）arrange
搞住（干擾）disturb
搞妥（弄好）secure
搞事（挑起事端／製造麻煩）make trouble
搞笑（逗樂／逗趣／滑稽）joke
搞鬼（挑起事端／製造麻煩）make trouble; play tricks
搞掂（順利完成／解決／辦妥）be done smoothly; make a good job of; settle sth; solve a problem; the task is done
搞唔掂（搞不定／辦不妥）can't settle sth; unable to solve a problem
搞得掂（搞得定／辦得妥）able to solve a problem; settle sth
搞喎（破壞／摧毀／銷毀／毀滅）destroy
搞亂檔（製造混亂）cause chaos
搞搞震（挑起事端／製造麻煩／搞鬼）make trouble
搞野（挑起事端／製造麻煩）make trouble
搞錯（弄錯）make a mistake
有冇搞錯（有沒有弄錯）what a ridiculous thing; you're kidding
搞邊科（做甚麼）what are you trying to do; what's going on
搞攣（挑起事端／製造麻煩）cause problems; make trouble

易搞（容易搞）easy to manage
唔好搞（不好搞／難搞）hard to handle
撈搞（麻煩）troublesome
難搞（難以處理）hard to handle

【搣】mit⁷（剝／撕／掰／捏）peel
搣人（撏人）pinch others
搣皮（剝皮）peel; peel off the skin
搣佢面珠墩（捏她的臉蛋兒）pinch her face

搣紙（撕紙）tear paper to shreds
搣開兩邊（掰開兩半）pull apart into halves with one's hands
搣爛（扯壞／撕壞）tear apart; tear asunder

【撳】gam⁶（按下）cover
撳地游水（安全至上）play for safety; play safe
撳鵪鶉（藉優勢敲詐勒索）use one's advantage to practice extortion

【搕】kap¹（蓋）affix a seal; stamp
搕印（蓋印）affix one's seal
搕單（在賬單上戳上印章）affix one's seal on a bill

【搦】lik⁷（拿）take
搦住（拿住／拿着）holding
搦住桶水（提着一桶水）carrying a bucket of water
搦唔住（拿不住）can't hold it
搦得住（拿得住）can hold it
搦返俾我（拿來給我）bring it back to me
搦晒（拿光／拿完）be all taken; be taken up
搦唔晒（拿不完）can't take all; too many to be taken away
搦唔嘟（拿不動）can't move
搦得嘟（拿得動）can be moved
搦倒（拿到）have got
搦唔倒（拿不了／拿不到）can't get it
搦得倒（拿得了／拿到）can get it

【撝】waa²（抓）scratch
撝損皮（把皮膚抓破）scratch the skin
撝嚫（劃傷）be scratched

【敬】ging³ respect
敬老 respect the old
敬酒 drink a toast
敬意 esteem; regard; respect; salute; tribute
不成敬意 just a little token to show my respect to you; just a trifle

必恭必敬 extremely deferential; reverent and respectful
孝敬 give presents to; piety; show filial respect for
恭恭敬敬 in an attitude of respect; most respectfully; reverently
恭敬 respectful; with great respect
致敬 pay homage; pay one's respects to; pay tribute to; salute
畢恭畢敬 cap in hand; extremely deferential; hat in hand; in a most respectful attitude; in humble reverence; reverent and respectful; with all courtesy and respect; with excessive courtesy; with the utmost deference
尊敬 respect

【斟】dzam¹ ① (倒) pour ② (商量 / 商談) confer; discuss; talk over

斟水 (倒水) pour water

斟波 (跳球) jump ball

斟茶 (倒茶) fill the cup with tea

　斟茶認錯 (承認錯誤道歉) offer tea as an admission of wrongdoing or as an apology

斟盤 (洽談 / 談判) hold talks with sb; negotiation

斟瀉 (倒灑了) overfill the cup

冇得斟 (沒商量的餘地) no room for discussion

密斟 (密商 / 密談) talk secretly

【新】san¹ new

新人 newlywed

新手 beginner; novice

新仔 (新手 / 新入行的人) new recruit

新加坡元 Singaporean dollar

新正頭 (新年裏) during the New Year

新年 New Year

　新年快樂 Happy New Year

　新年流流 (大過年的) on the day of the new year

　新年禮物 New Year gift

　新曆新年 (元旦) New Year's Day

　農曆新年 (春節 / 舊曆年) Lunar New Year

新抱 (兒媳婦) daughter-in-law

新官 new official

　新官上場三把火 (新官上任三把火) a new broom sweeps clean; a new official applies strict measures; new brooms sweep clean

　新官上場整色水 (新官上任三把火) a new broom sweeps clean; a new official applies strict measures; new brooms sweep clean

新近 newly

新春 Lunar New Year

　新春假期 (春節假期) Lunar New Year holidays

新郎 bridegroom

　新郎哥 (新郎 / 新郎官) bridesgroom

新衫 (新衣服) new clothes

新娘 bride

　玩新娘 (鬧洞房) celebrate wedding in the bridal chamber

　過埠新娘 (嫁去他地的新娘) a bride married to a man far away

新淨 (嶄新) brand-new

新款 new model; new style

新聞 news

　新聞報導 news reporting

　新聞廣播 news broadcast

小道新聞 grapevine news

財經新聞 financial news

睇新聞 (看新聞) watch the news

煲水新聞 (八卦新聞) gossip news

新潮 trendy

新曆 (陽曆) solar calendar

　新曆年 (元旦) New Year's Day

新鮮 fresh

　新鮮運到 (新近運到 / 剛運到) deliver recently

　新鮮滾熱辣 (又新鮮又熱和) fresh and warm

　新鮮熱辣 (又新鮮又熱和) fresh and warm

新嚟嘅 (新來的) newcomer

刷新 ① freshen; refurbish; renovate ② break

迎新 welcome the new arrivals

革新 innovation; reform; renovation

悔過自新 express one's repentance and determination to turn over a new leaf; repent and make a fresh start; repent and start anew; repent and start with a clean slate; repent and turn over a new leaf

破舊立新 (推陳出新) abolish the old and build up the new; destroy the old and establish the new; discard the old and create sth new; disrupt the old roder and establish a new one; eradicate the old and foster the new; the destruction of the old and the establishing of the new

送舊迎新 (辭舊迎新) bid farewell to the old and welcome the new

嘗新 taste a new delicacy

【暈】wan⁴ (昏 / 暈眩) dizzy; faint

暈低 (昏迷 / 暈倒) faint; pass out

暈車 carsickness

暈咗 (暈倒) faint and fall; fall in a faint; pass out; swoon

暈浪 ① (暈頭轉向) feel giddy ② (對美女神魂顛倒) be entranced by the beauty of a woman; fall under the spell of a beautiful woman ③ (着迷於美女的魅語) be entranced by the flattery of a beautiful woman

　暈浪丸 (暈車藥 / 暈船藥) motion sickness medicine; seasick pill

　暈車浪 (暈車) carsickness

　暈晒大浪 (神魂顛倒) fall under sb's spell

　暈船浪 (暈船) seasickness

　暈機浪 (暈飛機) airsickness

暈得一陣 (神魂顛倒 / 暈頭轉向) be intoxicated by one's beauty; fall under sb's spell

　暈得一陣陣 (神魂顛倒 / 暈頭轉向) fall under sb's spell

暈船 seasick

暈酡酡 (頭暈 / 暈眩 / 暈暈忽忽) dizzy

暈暈哋 (有點暈) a little dizzy

靚到暈（漂亮極了）absolutely gorgeous; stunning; very beautiful

頭暈 dizziness

頭暈暈（頭暈）feel dizzy

嚇暈（嚇昏）be frightened into fits; faint from fear

【暑】 sy² heat

暑氣 heat of summer; scorching heat

暑假 summer vacation

暑期 ① summer ② summer vacation; summer vacation time

暑熱 heat of summer; hot summer weather; scorching heat

中暑 sun stroke

唞暑（避暑）enjoy the cool weather; relax in a cool place

清暑（祛暑／消暑）relieve heat

【暗】 am³ dim

暗示 infer

暗病（性病）sexual disease

暗格（隱秘的空間）secret place

暗渠（暗溝／陰溝）underground channel

暗瘡（粉刺／痤瘡）acne

明暗 ① light and shade ② openly and secretly

黑暗 dark

【暗】 am³ cover

暗住良心（昧着良心）go aginst one's conscience

【暗】 am³ secret

暗啞底（不作聲獨自忍受）suffer in silence

【暖】 nyn⁵（溫暖／暖和）warm

暖水（溫水）warm water

　暖水袋（熱水袋）hot-water bag

　暖水壺（暖水瓶／暖壺／熱水瓶）thermos bottle; thermos flask

暖笠笠（暖烘烘／溫暖舒適）warm and comfortable

暖爐 heater

好暖（好暖和）very warm

和暖（暖和）warm

溫暖 warm

【會】 wui⁶ party

會長 president

會客室（會議室）meeting room

會計 accounting

會計師 accountant

　會計師樓（會計師事務所）accounting firm

會所 clubhouse

會員 member of a society

　會員證（會員卡）membership card

會議 conference; meeting

　主持會議 hold a meeting

　召開會議 call a meeting; convene a meeting

十點開會 the meeting starts at ten

三合會 triad society

大食會（盛筵）food feast

切身體會 direct experience; first-hand experience; have intimate experience of; intimate experience; intimate knowledge; keenly aware of; one's own experience; personal understanding

生日會 birthday party

休會 adjourn a meeting

再會 goodbye; see you again

有機會 have a chance

協會 association; institute; society

社會 society

夜總會 nightclub

迎新晚會 evening party to welcome newcomers

幽會 lover's rendezvous; tryst

音樂會 concert

約會 dating

展覽會 exhibition

酒會 cocktail party

馬會（賽馬會）horse club

參加舞會 join a dancing party

商會（工會）trade union

趁機會 take the opportunity

開生日會 hold a birthday party

開會 ① have a meeting; hold a meeting ② start a meeting

黑社會（黑幫）secret society; triad society

散會 adjourn a meeting

園遊會（遊園會）garden party

奧運會 Olympic Games

遊艇會 yacht club

運動會 sports day

嘉年華會 carnival

演唱會 singing concert

聚會 ① get together; meet ② assembly; beanfeast; bunfight; gathering; meeting

舞會 dancing party

誤會 get one's wires crossed; misunderstanding; misapprehend; misconstrue; mistake; misunderstand

廟會 temple fair

賣物會 (市場／義賣會) bazaar
點會 (怎麼會) how come
機會 chance; opportunity
融會 (融匯) blend harmoniously
驚住會 (擔心會) feel anxious that
體會 realise
議會 assembly; congress; council; parliament
露天音樂會 open-air concert; outdoor concert
露天舞會 open-air dance party

【會】 wui⁵ understand
會錯意 (誤會對方意思) misunderstand sb's intention

【椰】 je⁴ coconut
椰子 coconut
椰奶 (椰子奶) coconut milk
椰青水 (椰子水) coconut water
椰菜 (包心菜／洋白菜／卷心菜／圓白菜) cabbage
　椰菜花 (花菜／花椰菜／菜花) cauliflower
　椰菜頭 (波浪卷) curly hair

【楓】 fung¹ maple
楓栗 (栗子) chestnut
楓葉 maple leaf
楓樹 maple

【楊】 joeng⁴ willow
楊枝甘露 sweet mango soup with pomelo and sago
楊柳 willow
楊桃 star fruit
楊梅 arbutus

【楚】 tso² clear
楚楚 ① bright and clear; neat; tidy ② luxuriant ③ delicate
　楚楚可憐 delicate and touching
　楚楚動人 delicate and attractive; lovingly pathetic; moving the heart of all those who see her

咬字清楚 enunciate clearly; have clear articulation; pronounce every word clearly
唔清唔楚 (不清不楚／不明不白) doubtful; dubious; for no clear reason whatever; obscure; unclear
清楚 clear

【業】 jip⁹ trade
業主 ① (產權所有人) property owner ② (房東) landlord
　原業主 original owner; original property owner
業界 industry
業務 business activities; official functions; professional work; vocational work
業績 performance
　過往業績 past performance

大學畢業 graduate from the university
工業 industry
失業 out of job; unemployed
市民置業 (市民買房) citizens buying flats
企業 corporation
事業 career
物業 flat; real property
服務業 service industry
商業 business; commerce
專業 ① (職業) profession ② (專業的) professional
產業 ① (房地產／財產) estate; property ② (行業／工業) industry
畢業 graduate
創業 set up one's business
漁業 fishery; fishery industry; fishing industry
銀行業 banking industry
學業 study
置業 (買房) buy real estates
營業 business operation
職業 calling; career; occupation; profession; vocation

【極】 gik⁹ extreme
極力子 (離合器) (English) clutch
極之 (極其) exceedingly; extremely; very
極其量 (充其量) at best; at most
極端 extreme

太極 Chinese shadow boxing
好到極 (太棒了) excellent; great
耍太極 ① (打太極) play shadow boxing ② (敷衍搪塞) give the runaround
態度積極 positive attitude

【歇】 hit⁸ cease
歇後語 end-clipper
歇息 ① have a rest ② go to bed; put up for the night; stay at an inn
歇腳 rest the feet after walking; stop on the way for a rest

勿歇 (不斷) unceasingly

【歲】 soey³ age
歲月 ① times and seasons ② years
　歲月不待人 time and tide wait for no man; time marches on

歲月蹉跎 idle away one's time; let time slip by without accomplishing anything; the years drift by

蹉跎歲月 dawdle one's life; dawdle one's time; fool one's time away; fritter one's time away; idle about; idle away one's time; lead an idle life; let time slip by without accomplishing anything; live an idle life; live in idleness; on the racket; profane the precious time; spend one's time in dissipation; spend one's time in frolic; trifle away one's time; waste time; while away one's time

歲數 age

二十幾歲 (二十多歲) twenty sth

四十幾歲 (四十多歲) forty sth; in one's forties; more than forty years old

幾歲 (多大歲數 / 多大了) how old are you

對歲 (周歲) one full year of life

【殛】gik⁷ kill by thundering

好心着雷殛 (好心遭雷劈 / 好心沒好報) bite the hand that feeds one; recompense good with evil

【殿】din⁶ palace

殿後 behind; bring up the rear; close the rear; follow in the rear

殿軍 ① rear guard ② fourth winner in a contest

殿堂 (宮殿) palace

一座宮殿 a palace

宮殿 palace

無事不登三寶殿 (沒事不上門) have an axe to grind

【毀】wai² damage

毀屍滅跡 burn the corpse to destroy the evidence; bury the corpse in order to destroy all traces of one's crime; chop up a corpse and obliterate all traces; reduce the corpse to ashes in order to destroy all traces of one's crime

毀滅 destroy; exterminate; ruin

毀壞 damage; destroy; injure

損毀 damage

【溫】wan¹ warm

溫和 mild; moderate

溫度 temperature

溫度針 (溫度表 / 溫度計) thermometer

溫柔 tender

溫柔體貼 tender and considerate

溫書 (溫習 / 復習) review one's lessons

溫習 revise lessons

溫溫燉燉 (渾渾噩噩) muddle-headed

溫暖 warm

溫暖牌 (愛人織的毛衣) sweater made by one's wife or lover

溫馨 heart-warming

室溫 room temperature

恒溫 constant temperature

冧巴溫 (第一) (English) number one

氣溫 temperature

最低氣溫 lowest temperature

最高氣溫 highest temperature

量體溫 take sb's temperature

諗巴溫 (第一) (English) number one

體溫 temperature

【源】jyn⁴ source

源本 origin of an event

源流 ① origin and development source and course ② all the details; full particulars; the whole story

源頭 fountainhead; head; headstream; headwater; source of a stream

人力資源 human resources

來源 ① origin; source ② originate; stem from

根源 bottom; fountain; fountainhead; grass roots; origin; root; source

起源 origin

資源 resources

【溝】kau¹ ① ditch ② pick up

溝女 (追求女生) make friends with girls; pick up a girl

溝女王 (花花公子) playboy

溝仔 (追求男生) pick up a man

溝渠 (陽溝 / 明渠) ditch; open drain

受溝 (接受追求) get picked up

【溜】lau⁶ ① slide ② skate

溜口 (結巴) stammer; stutter

溜冰 skate; skate on the ice; staking

不溜 (總是) all along; always; at all times; consistently; for alwalys

滑溜 (光滑) glossy; sleek

【準】dzoen² certain
準決賽（半決賽）semi-final
準時 punctual
　　好準時（很準時）very punctual
準備（籌備／醞釀）prepare
　　及早準備 make preparations as soon as possible

冇定準（不一定／沒準兒）not sure; the chances of success
　　are uncertain
冇準（不一定／沒準兒）not sure; the chances of success are
　　uncertain
標準 standard
聲大夾冇準（只會瞎嚷嚷）much cry and little wool; talk
　　nonsense

【溪】kai¹ brook
溪水 water of a mountain stream
溪谷 canyon; dale; gorge valley
溪流 brook; mountain stream; stream; ravine stream
溪錢（紙錢）nether banknote

【溺】nik⁹ ① drown ② be addicted to
溺死 be drowned
溺愛 dote on
　　溺愛子女 spoil one's children
溺職（瀆職／失職／玩忽職守）dereliction; neglect of duty

【溶】jung⁴（溶化）dissolve; melt
溶咗（溶化）melted
溶晒（全溶化了）be completely dissolved
溶溶爛爛（稀爛）pulpy

【滅】mit⁹ exterminate
滅亡 become extinct; die out
滅火筒（滅火器）fire extinguisher

人不為己，天誅地滅 everyone for themselves; look after
　　one's own interests
人道毀滅（安樂死）euthanasia
毀滅 destroy; exterminate; ruin

【滋】dzi¹ leisurely
滋味（好吃／美味）delicious
　　咂滋味（細細品嚐）savour; taste
滋油（慢悠悠／慢條斯理）act or speak leisurely and
　　unhurriedly; slow-paced
　　滋油淡定（不慌不忙／優游從容）calm; not panic; slow
　　　　coach
　　滋滋油油（慢條斯理）unhurriedly

滋事婆（長舌婦）garrulous woman; gossipmonger
滋陰 nourish body's essential fluid

蚊滋（小蚊子）tiny mosquito
華爾滋（圓舞曲／華爾茲）(English) waltz
愛滋 AIDS

【滑】waat⁹ slippery
滑水 water ski
滑牙（滑扣）stripping
滑浪（衝浪）surf
　　滑浪風帆（帆板）windsurfing
滑捋捋（滑溜溜）slick; slippery; smooth
滑梯 slide
滑脫脫（滑溜溜／絲般柔軟）silky soft
滑雪 ski
滑溜（光滑）glossy; sleek
滑鼠（鼠標）mouse
　　滑鼠墊（鼠標墊）mouse pad
滑頭 ① slick ② sly fellow
　　滑頭蛇（處事圓滑／不老實）slick operator
滑潺潺（滑膩）wet and slippery

口甜舌滑（油嘴滑舌）oil one's tongue; sweet talk
口滑（說話隨便／脫口而出）flattering tongue; glib; glib-
　　tongued; have a well-oiled tongue; mealy-mouthed;
　　oily-mouthed; slimy-tongued; smooth tongue; smooth-
　　tongued
小心地滑 beware of slippery floor
皮光肉滑（膚如凝脂／冰肌玉膚）smooth skin
光滑 glossy; sleek; slick; smooth
魚滑（魚肉泥）minced fish
圓滑 diplomatic
蝦滑（蝦肉泥）minced shrimp
墨魚滑（墨魚肉泥）minced cuttlefish

【溦】mei⁴⁻¹ small
溦溦雨（細雨／毛毛雨）occasional drizzle; passing
　　shower; rain shower; shower; shower of rain

雨溦（細雨／毛毛雨）drizzle; light rain
雨溦溦（細雨／毛毛雨）drizzle; light rain
執人口水溦（拾人牙慧）parrot sb's words
落雨溦（細雨／毛毛雨）drizzle

【煉】lin⁶ smelt
煉金 alchemy
煉奶（煉乳）condensed milk
煉油 oil refining; rendering

煉鋼 steelmaking

【煙】jin¹ smoke

煙士（撲克牌中的 A 牌／愛司）ace
煙仔（香煙）cigarette
　　煙仔嘜（香煙罐兒）cigarette box
　　煙仔檔（香煙攤兒）cigarette stall
　　一包煙仔（一包香煙）a pack of cigarettes
煙灰盅（煙灰缸）ashtray
煙肉（薰肉）beacon
煙囪（煙筒）chimney
煙花（煙火）fireworks
　　放煙花（放煙火）let off fireworks
煙屎 ①（煙灰）smoke waste ②（撲克牌中的 A 牌／愛司）ace
煙韌 ①（有韌性）sticky ②（如膠似漆／親密）intimate behaviour
煙塵（塵土）dust
　　煙塵滾滾（塵土飛揚）clouds of dust flying up; dust rises high in the air
煙頭（煙蒂）cigarette end
煙鏟（煙鬼）cigarette addict; heavy smoker
煙癮 craving for tobacco

一支煙 a cigarette
一嚿煙（一道煙）a trail of smoke
一頭煙（非常忙）extremely busy
七竅生煙 fly into a rage
不准吸煙（不准抽煙）no smoking
切菜刀剃頭──牙煙（剃頭刀擦屁股──懸得乎）dangerous; horrible
牙煙（危險）dangerous; horrible
好煙 fond of smoking
年晚錢，飯後煙（尋常人享受的樂事）things that ordinary people enjoy
吸煙（抽煙）smoke; smoking
戒咗煙（戒了煙）have quitted smoking
戒煙 quit smoking
炊煙 smoke from kitchen chimneys
食口煙（吸口煙／抽口煙）smoke a cigarette
食大煙（抽大煙／抽鴉片）smoke opium
食煙（吸煙／抽煙）smoke; smoke a cigarette
唔准食煙（不准吸煙／不准抽煙）smoking is not allowed
喫大煙（抽大煙／抽鴉片）smoke opium
喫煙（吸煙／抽煙）smoke; smoke a cigarette
睇見就牙煙（看着真懸）it looks dangerous
禁煙 smoking is not allowed
煲煙（吸煙／抽煙）smoke
頭殼頂出煙（七竅生煙／非常生氣）get very angry

【煤】mui⁴ coal

煤油 kerosene
煤炭 anthracite; coal; coke; hard coal
煤氣 gas
　　煤氣費 gas bill
　　煤氣喉（煤氣管道）gas pipe
　　煤氣掣（煤氣閘）gas lock
　　煤氣爐 gas stove
　　漏煤氣（煤氣泄漏）gas leakage
煤渣 cinder clinker; coal cinders; coal slag

【煨】wui¹ bake

煨肉（燉肉）stew meat

該煨（糟糕）what a shame

【煩】faan⁴（心煩）vexed

煩勞（麻煩／煩惱）trouble
煩悶（不快樂／鬱悶／苦悶）unhappy; worried
煩惱 fret over; vexed; worried
煩躁 agitated; fidgety; in a fret; irritable

心煩（心緒不寧）be vexed; flutter; in a disturbed state of mind; in a flutter; in a state of agitation; one's state of mind is not at ease
好麻煩（頭疼／傷腦筋）troublesome
免得惹麻煩 so as to avoid causing trouble
咪煩（別煩）don't be vexed
唔好煩（不要煩／別煩）don't be vexed
麻煩 trouble; troublesome
勞煩（麻煩／煩勞）bother sb; encumber; give sb trouble; inconvenience sb; lead sb a dance; make trouble for sb; play up on sb; play up sb; put sb to trouble; trouble sb
憚煩（嫌煩）afraid of trouble; dislike taking the trouble
膩煩 ① be bored; be fed up ② hate; loathe

【煮】dzy² cook

煮人一鑊（説人家壞話）badmouth others
煮死（捉到）catch
煮到嚟就食（順其自然／隨遇而安）deal with things in due course; submit oneself to the circumstances
煮食（開伙）cook
　　煮食爐（灶具）cooking stove
煮重米（説某人的壞話／背後使壞）paint sb in the darkest colour
煮鬼（説某人的壞話／背後使壞）rip up the back of sb
煮飯（做飯）cook
　　煮飯仔（煮飯做菜）cook a simple meal
　　　玩煮飯仔（玩過家家）cook for fun

煮飯婆（家庭主婦）housewife
煮緊飯（正在做飯）cooking

煮麵（下麵）cook noodles
煮個麵（下個麵）cook some noodles

【煎】dzin¹ fry

煎堆（油煎糯粑／麻團）deep-fried sesame balls
年晚煎堆——人有我有（藥裏的甘草——總有份兒）possess oneself of the same as others do
冷手執個熱煎堆（有一個意想不到的好運／天上掉餡餅／冷鍋裏撿了個熱栗子）have an unexpected stroke of good fortune

煎蛋 fry eggs
煎蛋牛肉飯 rice with beef and fried egg
煎雙蛋 double sunny side up

【煲】bou¹ ①（熬）boil ②（砂鍋／壺／鍋／鍋子）casserole

煲大（討好）play up
煲水 ①（燒水）boil water ②（瞎編）indulge in petty gossip
煲仔（小砂鍋）clay pot
煲老藕（娶老女人）marry an aged woman
煲呔（領結）(English) bowtie
打煲呔（繫領結）wear a bowtie
煲茶（泡茶／煎茶）brew tea
煲湯（熬湯）make soup; stew for broth
煲粥 ①（煮粥／熬粥）cook congee; make congee; make porridge ②（煲電話粥／談很久電話）natter on the phone; on the phone for a long time; talk for hours on the telephone
煲冇米粥（說空話／說沒影的事兒）all talk; discuss something that will never amount to anything; make an idle talk
煲電話粥（泡蘑菇／聊大天）have a marathon talk on the phone; natter on the phone; on the phone for a long time; shoot the breeze on the phone
煲煙（吸煙／抽煙）smoke
煲碟（長時間看影碟）watch video compact disks for a long time
煲蓋（鍋蓋）pot cover
煲滾（煮沸）bring to the boil
煲藥（熬藥）decoct medicinal herbs

一個煲（一個鍋）a pot
一煲（一鍋）a pot of
大煲（大問題）big problem
水煲（水鍋）kettle
瓦煲（砂鍋）earthenware pot

同撈同煲（同甘共苦）live together through fair and foul; stick together through adversity
吊沙煲（斷炊／因失業斷絕生活來源）can't afford the next meal; go hungry; starve
吊煲（斷炊／因失業斷絕生活來源）go hungry
沙煲 ①（砂鍋）earthen pot ②（煮飯砂鍋）earthen rice-cooker
穿煲（泄露秘密／揭穿內幕）disclose a secret; let the cat out of the bag; let the secret out; reveal a secret
缸瓦船打老虎——盡地一煲（破釜沉舟／孤注一擲）shoot one's last bolt
砂煲（砂鍋）earthen pot
高壓煲（高壓鍋／壓力鍋）pressure cooker
掟煲（戀情告吹／戀人分手）break up; break-up of a relationship; end a relationship
單料銅煲（一見如故／與陌生人首次見面就像很熟絡）the person who instantly makes friends with a stranger
揩煲（刷鍋）brush clean the pot
賊佬試砂煲（不懷好意，試探虛實）put forth a feeler; put out feelers
飯煲（飯鍋）rice cooker
電水煲（電熱水壺）electric kettle
電飯煲（電飯鍋）electric rice cooker
盡地一煲（破釜沉舟／孤注一擲）risk everything on one bet
箍煲（言歸於好）repair a broken relationship
銻煲（鋁鍋）aluminium casserole
爆煲 ①（敗露）exposed ②（超過極限）go over the limit
藥煲 ①（煎藥用的砂鍋）pot for decocting herbal medicine ②（久病之人）chronic invalid

【煞】saat⁸ ① evil spirit ② stop

煞科（收尾／完結）end up
煞食（討人喜歡）appealing; attractive

兇神惡煞 fiendish and devilish; look furious

【照】dziu³（戳）shine

照住 ①（保護／照顧）back-up; protect ②（按照／照着）according as; according to; after; agreeable to; agreeably to; along; as; at; be based on; be scheduled; by; by any measure; considering; follow, from; in; in accordance with; in compliance with; in conformity to; in conformity with; in line with; in proportion as; in proportion to; in pursuance of; in the light of; on; on its merits; on the basis of; on the principle of; pursuant to; the way; to; under
照我所知（據我所知）as far as I know
照板煮碗（照方抓藥）copy; follow the beaten track; imitate

照計 (按理説／照理説) by all accounts; by right; ought to
照肺 (被上司責罵) be questioned by the boss
照常 as usual
照殺 (照做不誤) do as usual
照單執藥 (照方抓藥) follow instructions; follow the beaten track
照樣 repeat an action
照 X 光 (拍 X 光／X 光檢查) take an X-ray

大家心照 (心照不宣) have a tacit understanding
心照 (心照不宣) understand what is meant without needing explicit explanation
肝膽相照 a genuine meeting of minds between friends; be open-hearted to each other; friends devoted to each other heart and soul; loyal-hearted; show utter devotion to a friend; treat each other with absolute sincerity
迴光反照 a reflected ray of the setting sun — the transient reviving of a dying person; an illumination before death; the last radiance of the setting sun — moment of consciousness just before death; the sun's reflected light at the evening — brief glow of health before passing away
夠照 (有派頭／很有體面) put on a lot of airs; put on a show
牌照 (執照／許可證) licence
關照 look after
駕駛執照 (駕照) driving licence
護照 passport

【燂】tsam² (軟) mashed
燂啤啤 (蔫呼呼的／稀爛) mashed; pulpy
燂善 (善良／溫厚) good; good and kind; good-natured; well-behaved

【爺】je⁴ grandfather
爺爺 grandfather; grandpa

大少爺 ① eldest son of a rich family ② eldest son of one's master ③ spendthrift; spoilt son of a rich family
大資爺 (傲慢的人) arrogant person
大舅爺 one's wife's elder brother
少爺 young master of the house
太子爺 ① young master ② eldest son of a rich family ③ eldest son of one's master ④ spoilt son of a rich family
仔爺 (父子) father and son
老爺 father
佛爺 the Buddha
扭計師爺 (出謀劃策的人／狗頭軍師) schemer
兩仔爺 (父子兩人／爺兒倆) father and son

姑爺 son-in-law
阿爺 (祖父／爺爺) grandfather; grandpa
契爺 ① (乾爹) adoptive father ② (包養者) sugar-daddy
後底爺 (繼父) stepfather
師爺 advisor
頂爺 (黑社會老大) triad boss
惡爺 (惡人／惡棍) extremely cruel and violent person; fierce and nasty person; villain
親家老爺 (親家公) one's child's father-in-law
蠱蟲師爺 (出餿主意／作繭自縛) a person who always offers bad solutions to problems; a person who is caught in his own trap

【獅】si¹ dragon
獅子 lion
　獅子開大口 (獅子大開口) over-demanding
　獅子鼻 (翹鼻) pug nose

舞獅 (舞獅子) dragon dance

【猾】waat⁹ cunning
猾賊 (奸狡) glib rascal

老奸巨猾 as cunning as an old fox
狡猾 cunning; sly
鬼猾 (狡猾) as crafty as a fox; crafty

【瑞】soey⁶ auspicious; fortunate; lucky
瑞氣 celestial phenomena portending peace and prosperity

祥瑞 (吉祥的跡象／吉祥的預兆) auspicious sign; propitious omen

【瑚】wu⁴ coral
珊瑚 coral

【畸】kei¹ odd
畸士 (案子／事件／情況) (English) case

【當】dong¹ ① (當…時) fill in a post ② (當作) work as
當心 beware of
當打 (強大) formidable
當災 (遭殃) meet with disaster; meet with misfortune; set in the neck; suffer; suffer disaster
當更 (值班) on duty; on the shift; on watch
　我當緊更 (我在值班) I'm on duty
當值 (值班) on duty; on the shift; on watch

當紅 currently popular
當面 face to face
當家 leader
當差 (當警察) serve as a policeman
當時得令 (正當時宜) in season
當衰 (合該倒霉) unlucky
當堂 ① (立刻 / 立即 / 馬上) at once; immediately; right away ② (當場 / 在那裏 / 那時候) on the spot; right there; there and then
當堂唔同晒 (完全不一樣) it's immediately totally different
當紮 ① (等待被提拔) waiting to be promoted ② (現在) current
當眼 (突出 / 醒目 / 引人注目) conspicuous; eye-catching; in plain sight; showy; striking
當造 (應時 / 時令 / 當季 / 當令) in season
當然 of course
當黑 (不幸 / 倒霉 / 背運 / 運氣不好) down on one's luck; out of luck; unlucky

一人做事一人當 one is responsible for what one does
吊兒郎當 bugger about; careless and casual; dilly-dally; dodge the column; dog it; fool around; goof off; idle about; slovenly; take a devil-may-care attitude; take things easy; undisciplined; untidy; utterly carefree
有福同享，有禍同當 (有福同享，有難同當) for better or for worse; go through thick and thin together; happiness and joy we shall share in common and loyally; help each other in suffering; share bliss and misfortune together; share happiness as well as trouble; share joys and sorrows; share weal and woe; stick together through thick and thin; we will cast our lot together, all or none
妥當 appropriate; proper; well-thought-out
每當 each time; every time; whenever
紅當當 (紅彤彤 / 紅通通) bright red
唔敢當 (不敢當) I really don't deserve this; not at all; you're flattering me
郎當 ① (不適當) unfit ② (委靡) dejected; dispirited ③ (不稂不莠) good-for-nothing; worthless
領當 (上當) be duped; be fooled; be taken in; be tricked
旗鼓相當 equally matched
銳不可當 cannot be held back; full of fighting spirit as to be irresistible; irresistible; no force can stop

【當】dong³ treat as
當耳邊風 (當耳旁風) ignore advice
當咗 (當成 / 當作) believe; consider
當票 (典當票) pawn ticket
當舖 pawn shop

上當 be duped; be fooled; be taken in
勾當 business; deal
好定當 (冷靜 / 沉穩) calmly; deliberately; keep a level head; keep one's head; neither alarmed nor excited; take one's time; unhurried; with full composure; without haste or confusion; without hurry or bustle
典當 hock; impawn; mortgage; pawn
適當 proper

【痾】o¹ defecate; urinate
痾尿 (小便 / 拉尿 / 撒尿) apple and pip; burn the grass; dickydiddle; discharge one's urine; drain one's radiator; drain one's snake; empty one's bladder; evacuate the bladder; go tap a kidney; have a leak; have a quickie; have a run off; lift his leg; make number one; make salt water; make water; micturate; pass urine; pass water; pee; piddle; pie and mash; piss; plant a sweet pea; point Percy at the porcelain; pump ship; retire; scatter; see a man about a dog; see one's aunt; shake hands with an old friend; shake the dew off the lily; shoot a lion; spend a penny; take a leak; take a quickie; tap a keg; tinkle; urinate; water the lawn; water the stock; whiz
大蛇痾尿 (大場面) important deal
痾篤尿 (撒泡尿) take a piss
痾屎 (排便 / 大便 / 拉屎) defecate
大蛇痾屎 (大場面) important deal
痾嘢 (笨死了) very clumsy

【痰】taam⁴ phlegm
痰火 phlegm-fire
痰涎 expectoration; phlegm spittle
痰罐 (痰盂) spittoon

一篤痰 (一口痰) a mouthful of phlegm; a spit of phlegm
化痰 reduce phlegm
吐痰 spit
起痰 ① (被一個女性吸引) be sexually attracted to a woman ② (有強烈的願望) have a strong desire for ③ (有痰) have phlegm
禁止吐痰 spitting is prohibited

【痹】bei³ (發麻) numb; paralysis; tingle
痹痹哋 (麻酥酥的) have pins and needles

手痹 (手發麻) paralysis of hands
骨痹 (令人肉麻 / 肉麻) cause sb to be disgusting; feel unnatural
麻痹 numb
腳痹 (腳發麻) paralysis of feet

靚到瘀（漂亮極了）absolutely gorgeous; stunning; very beautiful

【瘀】jy¹ ① （淤血）bruise ② （困窘）embarrass ③ （丟臉）lose face

瘀皮（丟臉）lose face

唔抵得瘀（看不下去）cannot bear the waste

【瘁】soey⁶ weary

累瘁（憔悴 / 枯槁）haggard; thin and pallid; wan and sallow

【痴】tsi¹ idiot

痴心 infatuation
　痴心妄想 fond dream; wishful thinking
痴呆 ① （呆傻）dull-witted; stupid ② （失智症）amentia; dementia
痴肥（過重）abnormally fat; obese
痴情 blind passion; infatuated; infatuation

白痴 idiot; stupid

【瘟】mang² （怒）annoyed

瘟憎（惱怒 / 煩惱）annoyed

【盞】dzaan² ① （徒勞）waste time ② （好）good ③ （量詞）measure word for lamps and lights

盞俾人鬧（肯定要挨罵的）it will surely be blamed
盞鬼（可愛）cute
盞嘢（上好東西）excellent stuff
盞攪（浪費時間和精力）a waste of time and effort
　盞攪嘅啫（這只是浪費時間和精力）it's just a waste of time and effort

一盞 measure word for lamps and lights
冇走盞（沒有迴旋的餘地）inflexible; leave no space for sth
走盞（迴旋餘地）room for manoeuvre

【盟】mang⁴ swear

盟塞（思想閉塞 / 落後 / 死腦筋）as stupid as an owl; poor at understanding
盟鼻（鼻塞）nasal congestion
盟誓（起誓 / 發誓）make a pledge; take an oath

結成聯盟（結盟）enter into an alliance
聯盟 alliance; coalition; league; union

【睛】dzing¹ eyeball

睛珠（眼球 / 眼珠）eyeball; pupil of the eye

眼睛 eyes

【睡】soey⁶ sleep

睡衣 pajamas
睡房（臥室）bedroom

入睡 go to sleep
呼呼大睡 snore loudly in one's sleep
烏眉恰睡（昏昏欲睡）sleepy; drowsy
難以入睡 hard to go to sleep

【睬】tsoi² （理睬）pay attention to; take notice of

睬佢都傻（管他是多餘的 / 誰會理他呀 / 傻子都懶得理他）not bother to pay any attention to sb; who would pay attention to him

【督】duk⁷ direct

督背脊（背後中傷 / 打小報告 / 戳脊樑骨）back-stabbing; calumniate sb behind one's back; rip up the back; speak ill of sb behind their back; stab sb in the back; talk behind sb's back
督眼督鼻（眼中釘）a thorn in one's eye; eyesore; irritate the eyes
督察（警官）sergeant

【䁥】gwat⁶ （瞟）glance; look askance

䁥吓佢（瞟他一眼）glance at him

【睩】luk⁹ （瞪）glare; stare at

睩大眼（睜大眼睛 / 瞪大眼睛）open one's eyes wide
睩地（滾地）roll on the ground
睩起對眼（圓睜雙眼 / 瞪着某人 / 怒視某人）glare at sb

【矮】ai² short

矮仔（矮個子）dwarf; short person
　矮仔上樓梯——步步高升（腳踏樓梯板——步步高升）climb up step by step in one's career
　矮仔多計（矮子矮，一肚怪）a short person has a resourceful mind; a short person is full of tricks; a short person has many stratagems
矮瓜（茄子）eggplant
矮佬（矮子）short fellow; short guy; short man
矮突突（矮墩墩的）dumpy; pudgy; short and plump; stumpy
矮細（又矮又小）short and small

矮矮細細（又矮又小）short and small

矮矮哋（挺矮的）quite short

矮磨磨（非常矮）very short

矮樹（灌木）shrub

唔高唔矮（中等身高 / 不高不低）of medium height

高矮 height

樓底矮（天花板低）the ceiling is low

【碌】luk⁷ ① pass through ② measure word for stick

碌木（傻子）idiot

碌地沙（滾地）roll on the ground

碌低（滾倒）tumble

碌咭（刷卡）swipe one's card to settle payment

碌柚（柚子）pomelo

　　一楷碌柚（一瓣兒柚子）a slice of pomelo

碌架牀（雙層牀）bunk bed

碌葛（傻子）idiot

碌蔗（傻子）idiot

碌 card（刷卡）pay by credit card

一扑一碌（跌跌撞撞）in a great hurry

一碌（一條）(a measure word)

忙忙碌碌 as busy as a bee; busy going about one's work

忙碌 all go; be engaged in doing sth; be engaged in sth; be occupied with; be swamped with work; bustle; bustle about; busy; get one's hands full; have much to do; have one's hands full; on one's toes; on the go; on the run; one's hands are full; up to one's eyes in work; up to the ears in work

花花碌碌（花花綠綠 / 花哨）colourful

花哩花碌（花花綠綠 / 花哨）colourful

花哩碌（花花綠綠 / 花哨）colourful

花碌碌（花花綠綠 / 花哨）colourful

眼仔碌碌（眼睛圓圓）have cute eyes

眼碌碌（直瞪瞪地 / 怒視某人）glower at sb; stare in a hostile way

符碌（蒙混過關）(English) fluke; stroke of luck

蝦碌（倒霉 / 出糗）(English) hard luck; bizarre

磨碌（圓矮笨重）short and fat

【碑】bei¹ upright stone tablet

碑文 inscription on a tablet

口碑 word of mouth

里程碑 milepost; milestone

墓碑 gravestone; tombstone

【碎】soey³ fragmented

碎肉（肉末）minced meat

碎股（零星股）odd lot

碎料（小意思）trivial matters

碎紙 ①（硬幣 / 零鈔 / 零票 / 零錢）coins; small change
　　②（碎紙片）shred paper
　　碎紙機 paper shredder

碎銀（硬幣 / 零鈔 / 零票 / 零錢）coins; small change

碎濕濕（碎得很）bits and pieces; fragmentary; odds and ends; piecemeal; scrappy

米碎（碎米粒）crushed rice

你唔嫌我籮疏，我唔嫌你米碎（相互諒解 / 互不挑剔 / 一團和氣）be two of a kind

破碎 ① broken; tattered ② break into pieces; crush; smash sth into pieces; tear into shreds

零碎 fragmentary; odds and ends; piecemeal; scrappy

零零碎碎 piecemeal

瑣碎 trifling

撕碎 tear to pieces

濕碎（零碎）piecemeal

濕濕碎 ①（零碎）a small amount of money ②（小意思）trivial matter

濕濕碎碎（零七八碎）miscellaneous and trifling things; miscellaneous trifles; odds and ends; scattered and disorderly

雞碎（雞胃）chicken's stomach

【碰】pung³ collide

碰彩（碰運氣 / 賭運氣）try one's luck

碰啱（碰巧）as luck would have it; by chance; by coincidence

【碗】wun² bowl

碗仔（小碗）small bowl
　　碗仔翅（仿魚翅羹）imitation shark's fin soup
　　一個碗仔（一個小碗）a small bowl
　　一隻碗仔（一個小碗）a small bowl

碗櫃 cupboard

一隻碗 a bowl

打爛飯碗（丟掉工作）lose one's job

爭飯碗（競爭工作）compete for jobs

金飯碗（高薪工作）highly-paid job; high-salary job

保住飯碗（保住工作）keep one's job

洗碗 do the washing up; wash the dishes

食埋呢碗（吃完這碗）let me finish eating this bowl of sth

崩口人忌崩口碗（當着矮子別說短話 / 避免提及可能傷害他人的某事）avoid mentioning sth that may hurt other people; avoid touching sb on the raw

捧碗（拿碗）hold a bowl

細碗（小碗）small bowl
照板煮碗（照方抓藥）copy; follow the beaten track; imitate
飯碗 ①（盛飯的碗）rice bowl ②（工作）job
鐵飯碗（穩定的工作）secure job

【祿】luk⁹ blessing
祿位（官位俸祿）official salary and rank

無功不受祿 refuse to be paid for doing nothing

【禁】gam³ prohibitions
禁止 prohibit
禁煙 smoking is not allowed

入境問禁（入鄉隨俗）do in Rome as the Romans do
拘禁（拘捕／拘押）put under arrest; take into custody
非法拘禁（非法拘捕／非法拘押）unlawful incarceration
宵禁 curfew

【禽】kam⁴ bird
禽流感 bird flu

【稟】ban² report
稟神咁聲（嘟嘟嚷嚷地）murmur indistinctly
稟神都冇句真（求神都沒句真話／沒句話可信的／老是說謊）live a lie

【稚】dzi⁶ childish
稚女（幼女）young girl
稚嫩 ① tender and delicate ② young and tender

幼稚 childish; naive; puerile

【窟】fat⁷ hole
窟居（住在洞穴）live in a cave

一窟（一小片）a small piece of
狡兔三窟 a wily hare has three burrows — a crafty person has more than one hideout; it is a poor mouse that has one hole; the cunning hare secures safety with three openings to its burrow — have many provisions for cunning escape only; the mouse does not trust to one hole only; the mouse that has but one hole is quickly taken

【笪】saau¹ basket
笪箕打水——一場空（什籃打水——一場空）draw water with a sieve
笪箕冚鬼一窩神（蛇鼠一窩）be hand and glove with each other

【筷】faai³ chopstick
筷子 chopstick
　筷子筒 chopstick holder
　一隻筷子（一根筷子）a chopstick
　一對筷子（一雙筷子）a pair of chopsticks
　揸筷子（握筷子）hold a pair of chopsticks
　淥吓筷子（把筷子燙一燙）rinse the chopsticks in hot water

起筷（勸客進食）help youself to the food

【節】dzit⁸ section
節日 festival
　節日禮物 festive gift
　民間節日 folk festival
　喜慶節日 festive days
節瓜（毛瓜）fuzzy melon; hairy gourd
節目 programme
節哀順變 restrain one's grief and accommodate the change; suppress one's sorrow and accept the change
節奏 rhythm
節食 on diet

中秋節 Mid-autumn Festival
五月節（端午節）Dragon Boat Festival
元宵節 Lantern Festival
父親節 Father's Day
外交禮節 diplomatic propriety
母親節 Mother's Day
合乎禮節 be according to protocol
佳節 festival; happy festival time
使節 diplomatic envoy; envoy; legate
兒童節 Children's Day
季節 season
枝枝節節（零零碎碎的事情）complexity and diversity; complications; minor issues; digressive
枝節 ①（旁枝末節）minor matters ②（糾紛）complication; knottiness
社交禮節 social etiquette
按照禮節 in accordance with protocol
盂蘭節 Hungry Ghost Festival
耶穌受難節 Good Friday
重陽節 Double Ninth Festival
做節（過節日）celebrate a festival
婦女節 Women's Day
情人節 St. Valentine's Day
清明節 Ching Ming Festival
細節 detail
勞動節 Labour Day

復活節 Easter
萬聖節 (鬼節) Halloween
愚人節 April Fools' Day
過節 ① (彆扭) uncomfortable ② (仇恨 / 怨恨 / 積怨) animosity; enmity; grudge; hatred; hostility ③ (過假日) pass a holiday ④ (慶祝節日) celebrate a festival
聖誕節 Christmas
感恩節 Thanksgiving Day
違反禮節 impropriety
端午節 Dragon Boat Festival
颱風季節 typhoon season
禮節 ceremony; civility; courtesy; etiquette; protocol; rules of politeness

【綁】 bong² tie up

綁帶 (繫帶子) tie a belt
綁票 (劫持) kidnap

打腳綁 (打綁腿) wear leg wrappings
腳綁 (綁腿) leg wrappings

【經】 ging¹ pass by

經已 (已經) has already
經紀 (中間人 / 代理商) agent; broker; middleman
　經紀行 (中間人業務) brokerage
　經紀佣金 (中介費) brokerage
　經紀費 (中介費) agent's fee
經唔經 (經不經過) do you pass through (a certain street)
經理 manager
　總經理 general manager
經費 expenditure
經過 pass by
經濟 economy
　經濟位 (二等座位) economy class seat
　經濟低迷 the economy is sluggish
　經濟利益 economic benefit
　經濟復甦 economic recovery
　經濟艙 (二等艙) economy class
經驗 experience

一經 as soon as; once
三字經 foul language; swear words
冇釐正經 (沒正經) joke about serious matters; not so decent as one should be
月經 period
正經 serious
行經 (月經來潮) menstruate; monthly period
刨馬經 (研究賽馬新聞) study horse-racing news
神神哋經 (腦子不正常) not right in the mind

神神經經 (發瘋) crazy
神經 ① (神經) nerve ② (發瘋) crazy; insane
家家有本難唸的經 (各家有各家的難處與苦衷) each and every family has its own problems
脊神經 spinal nerve
做日和尚唸日經 (做一天和尚撞一天鐘) wear through the day
密實姑娘假正經 (戀愛中的女子假裝嘴巴嚴密，不說真話) a girl of few words may not be so serious as she should be
曾經 have already
途經 approach; avenue; channel; pathway; road; way
發神經 (發瘋) go berserk; go crazy; go mad
聖經 Bible
經濟利益 economic benefit
諷正經 (裝正經 / 假正經) pretend to be serious

【罩】 dzaau³ cover

罩衣 dust cloak; overall
罩衫 dustcoat; overall
罩袍 dust-gown; dust-robe

口罩 mask
奶罩 (乳罩 / 胸罩) bra
乳罩 (乳罩) bra; brassiere
胸罩 (乳罩 / 緊身胸衣) bra; brassiere; breast shield; bust bodice
戴口罩 wear a mask
餸罩 (飯罩 / 菜罩) dish cover

【罪】 dzoey⁶ ① crime ② sin

罪犯 criminal
罪名 accusation; charge
　罪名成立 be proved to be guilty
罪案 (犯罪案件) criminal case

犯罪 commit a crime; commit an offence; crime; offence
得罪 offend; provoke
赦罪 (原諒罪犯 / 赦免某人) absolve sb from guilt; forgive an offender; pardon sb
輕枷重罪 (一時承受大量工作) be burdened with the work of a moment
謝罪 apologise; apologise for an offence; offer an apology

【置】 dzi³ establish

置家 (成家) start one's own family
置業 (買房) buy real estates
　置業人士 (買房人士) property buyer
　市民置業 (市民買房) citizens buying flats

佈置 ① make arrangements ② arrange; decorate
位置 position
棄置 cast aside; discard; throw aside

【羣】kwan⁴ group

羣眾 crowd; mob
羣策羣力 club ideas and exertions; collective wisdom and efforts; draw upon collective wisdom and strength of the masses as a source of power; lay heads together and work in concert; pool everybody's wisdom and efforts; pool the wisdom and strength of the masses; pool the wisdom and effort of all the people; put heads together and work in concert; united strength and wisdom; with collective wisdom and efforts; with everybody contributing his ideas and strength; with united wisdom and strength; work and pull together; work as a team
羣情 (公眾情緒) feelings of the masses; public sentiment
羣龍無首 a group of people without a leader; a host of dragons without a head; a multitude without a leader; an army without a general; many dragons without a head; no leader in a host of dragons; sheep that have no shepherd

成羣 in groups
蜂羣 a cluster of bees; a swarm of bees

【義】ji⁶ loyalty; righteous

義工 (義務工) volunteer worker
　做義工 do volunteer work
義氣 loyalty
　義氣搏兒戲 (冒忠於潛在叛徒的風險) take the risk of being loyal to a potential traitor
　有義氣 have loyalty; loyal
　�義氣 (賣義氣) do a favour out of loyalty
　夠義氣 loyal
義務 obligation
　履行義務 fulfill one's obligations

仁義 kindheartedness and justice
仗義 rely on a sense of justice
名義 name
江湖道義 code of ethics of the underworld
忘恩負義 devoid of gratitude; bite the hand that feeds one; forget sb's kindness and turn one's back upon him in return; forgetful of all favours one has been given; have no sense of gratitude and justice; kick down the ladder; kick over the ladder; show ingratitude for favours received; show no sense of gratitude; turn one's back on righteousness and forget kindness; turn on one's

friend; ungrateful; ungrateful and act contrary to justice; ungrateful and leave one's benefactor in the lurch
言不及義 (詞不達意) indulge in gossip without touching anything serious; make idle talk; never say anything serious; talk frivolously
恐怖主義 terrorism

【聖】sing³ sacred

聖堂 (教堂) church
聖經 Bible
聖誕 (聖誕節) Christmas
　聖誕卡 (聖誕賀卡) Christmas card
　聖誕老人 Father Christmas; Santa Claus
　聖誕快樂 Merry Christmas
　聖誕咭 (聖誕賀卡) Christmas card
　聖誕節 Christmas
　聖誕歌 Christmas carol
　　唱聖誕歌 sing Christmas carols
　聖誕燈飾 Christmas illumination
　聖誕樹 Christmas tree
　　一棵聖誕樹 a Christmas tree
　聖誕禮物 Christmas present
　白色聖誕 (白色聖誕節) white Christmas

朝聖 pilgrimage

【聘】ping³ hire

聘請 hire
聘禮 betrothal gift

【腥】seng¹ fishlike smelly

腥味 fishlike smell
腥氣 (腥味) smell of fish or seafood
腥臭 stinking smell of rotten fish
腥鰛鰛 (魚腥氣很濃) stinking smell of fish

辟腥 (去腥) remove the fishlike smell

【腦】nou⁵ (腦子) brain

腦汁 (腦漿) brain
　絞盡腦汁 rack one's brains
腦海 brain; mind
　腦海一片空白 have a blank mind
腦囟 (囟門) fontanelle
　腦囟未生埋 (幼稚) childish
腦筋 ① brain ② idea
　腦筋遲鈍 have slow wits

一部電腦 (一台電腦 / 一部計算機) a computer

人頭豬腦（蠢笨）as stupid as a pig; stupid

冇腦（沒腦子）brainless

手提電腦（筆記本電腦）laptop computer

主腦（主謀 / 頭目）boss; chief; leader; mastermind

用腦 use one's brain

有腦（腦筋轉得快）have quick wits; keen and sharp in thinking

直腸直腦（真性子）outspoken; straight-talking

耷頭耷腦（垂頭喪氣）listless

食腦（用智力謀生）earn a living by using one's intelligence

倔頭倔腦（說話、態度固執生硬）blunt in manner and gruff in speech

唔經大腦（不經思考 / 不經大腦）not rack one's brains

埋頭埋腦（全神貫注）all attention; all ears; all eyes; all eyes and ears; apply the mind to; be absorbed in; be deeply engrossed in sth; be engrossed in; be occupied with; be preoccupied with; be utterly concentrated in; be wholly absorbed in; be wrapped up in; complete mental concentration; concentrate on; concentrate one's attention on; concentrate the whole energy upon; give one's whole attention to; have sth on the brains; have sth on the mind; in complete absorption; pay undivided attention to; very attentive; with absorbed interest; with all one's mental faculties on the stretch; with all one's soul; with breathless attention; with one's heart and soul; with rapt attention; with undivided attention

迷頭迷腦（全神貫注）indulge oneself in; immerse oneself in

笨頭笨腦 block-headed

微型電腦（微型計算機）micro-computer

電腦（計算機）computer

賊頭賊腦 stealthy

壽頭壽腦（呆頭呆腦 / 傻裏傻氣）muddle-headed

幕後主腦（幕後主使）master-mind

頭大冇腦（頭大無腦 / 愚蠢）stupid

頭腦 brain

薯頭薯腦（呆頭呆腦 / 傻裏傻氣）stupid

【腫】dzung² swollen

腫脹 swell

腫瘤 tumor

口腫面腫（嘴腫臉腫）swollen face

【腰】jiu¹ waist

腰果 cashew nut

腰骨 ① （盆腔 / 骨盆 / 髖）pelvic ② （性格強烈 / 骨氣）strong character

　冇腰骨（沒骨氣 / 靠不住）cowardly; spineless; undependable; unreliable

有腰骨（信得過 / 靠得住）dependable; reliable; trustworthy

腰圍（腰身）waist

　腰圍廿三吋（腰圍二十三英寸）one's waist measures twenty-three inches

　量腰圍 take the waist measure

腰圓背厚（豐滿）plump

不為五斗米折腰 cannot make courtesies for the salary of five bushels of rice

有人撐腰 be backed by sb; have sb at one's back

折腰 bow; humble oneself

拗腰（向後彎腰）bend one's body backward

黃蜂腰（蜂腰）lady's well-proportioned waist

撐腰 back up; bolster up; support

攤攤腰 ① （非常疲憊）very tired ② （在很大程度上）to a great extent

【腳】goek⁸ （腿）leg

腳巾（洗腳布）foot-cleaning cloth

腳甲（腳指甲 / 腳趾甲）toenail

腳瓜（小腿肚 / 腿肚子）calf of the leg

　腳瓜囊（小腿肚 / 腿肚子）calf of the leg

腳肚（小腿肚 / 腿肚子）calf of the leg

腳板（腳掌）sole of the foot

　腳板底（腳板 / 腳掌）sole of the foot

　腳板堂（腳心 / 足弓）arch of the foot

腳底（腳板 / 腳掌）sole of the foot

腳架（三腳架）tripod

腳面（腳背）instep

腳骨 leg bone

　腳骨力（腳力）strength of one's legs

　打腳骨（敲竹槓 / 勒索金錢）rob sb in the street

　收買路錢打腳骨（搶劫旅客）rob travellers

　鬆吓腳骨（放鬆一下腿）relax one's legs

腳眼（腳踝）ankle

腳趾 toe

　腳趾公（大腳趾）big toe

　腳趾尾（小腳趾）little toe

　　行運行到落腳趾尾（鴻運當頭）very lucky

　腳趾罅（腳指縫）space between the two toes

腳軟（膝蓋無力 / 腿軟）weak at the knees

　企到腳軟（站到腿軟 / 腿因長時間站立而疲憊不堪）one's legs are tired from standing for a long time; one's legs are weak from standing so long

腳掣（剎車 / 腳制動 / 行車制動器）brake; foot brake; service brake

腳痹（腳發麻）paralysis of feet

腳綁（綁腿）leg wrappings

打腳綁（打綁腿）wear leg wrappings

腳睜（腳後跟／腳制動）heel

腳踏（腳蹬）pedal

腳瘓（腿僵硬）paralysis of the feet

腳頭（腳勁兒／運氣）fortune; luck

　腳頭好（運氣好）bring good fortune

　腳頭壞（運氣差）bring ill fortune

　好腳頭（帶好運）come with good luck to sb

腳骹（腳踝）ankle

一手一腳（獨自做事）do sth all by oneself

一隻腳 a leg

一對腳（一雙腳）a pair of legs

一腳 one foot

小手小腳（小氣／膽小）stingy; timid

山腳 base of a mountain; bottom of a mountain; foot of a
　mountain

丑腳（小丑／喜劇演員）clown; comedian

手腳 hands and feet

毛手毛腳 inappropriate fondling or touching

水腳（路費／運費）toll

四隻腳（麻將玩家）four players of a game of mahjong

打赤腳（光腳丫／光着腳）go barefoot; go without shoes

印印腳①（放鬆）relaxed ②（享受生活）enjoy life

地腳（地基）foundation; ground

多手多腳（亂摸東西）touch things one likes

托大腳（拍馬屁／奉承討好／吹捧／溜溝子／抬轎子）
　adulate; brown-nose; butter sb up; crawl to; curry favour;
　curry favour with sb; eat sb's toads; fawn on; flatter; give
　sb the soft-soap; ingratiate oneself with; kiss sb's ass; lay
　it on thick; lay it on with a trowel; lick sb's boots; lick sb's
　shoes; lick sb's spittle; lick the boots of sb; obsequious;
　play up to; polish the apple; soft-soap; suck up to;
　sycophancy; toady sb

有人做咗手腳（有人做了手腳）sb has secretly got up to
　little tricks

伸一腳（毆打）beat up

夾手夾腳（一起動手）co-operate closely with each other;
　work well together

扭噚隻腳（扭傷腳）sprained one's ankle

扰腳（踩腳）stamp one's foot

赤腳 barefoot

車腳（車輪）fare

刮噚腳（扎腳了）prick the foot

姐手姐腳（慢吞吞／幹活不麻利）clumsy because he/she is
　not accustomed in doing heavy work

抽後腳（抓辮子）pull sb's leg; tease sb by repeating what he
　says

拉人裙冚自己腳（沾別人的光）benefit from association with

sb or sth

阻手阻腳（阻礙／礙手礙腳）a hindrance to sb; a nuisance
　to sb; an encumbrance to sb; cumbersome; cumbrous; get
　in the way of sb; hinder; impede; in the way; obstructive;
　one too many; stand in sb's way; stand in the way of

陀手嗱腳（拖累）clumsy

急急腳（急急忙忙地）leave in a hurry

急時抱佛腳（臨時抱佛腳）seek help at the last moment

按腳 foot massage

指手篤腳①（指手劃腳）order sb about ②（做手勢）make
　gestures with one's hands

枱腳（桌腿）leg of a table

洗腳 cleanse one's foot

洗腳唔抹腳（揮金如土）spend lavishly; spend money
　extravagantly; splash one's money about; squander

衫腳（下擺）lower hem of a gown

食雞腳（吃雞爪）eat chicken feet

香港腳（腳氣／腳癬）athlete's foot; ringworm of the foot

香雞腳（瘦長腿）long thin legs

俾人打破腳（腿給打瘸了）be crippled

俾人揸住痛腳（給人抓辮子／被人抓住把柄）give sb a
　handle

凌空一腳 kick the ball high up in the air

唔好手腳（手腳不乾淨）have a tendency of stealing

唔係我手腳（不是我的對手）not one's equal

唔夠腳（人數不足）not enough players; one player short

哽腳（硌腳）hurt one's foot

捉人痛腳（抓人辮子）exploit the weakness of others

捉痛腳（抓辮子）go for the weak spot

砣手嗱腳（累累贅贅）burdensome

起飛腳（過河拆橋）fly high over sb

趷高腳（踮起腳）on the tips of one's toes

趷腳（跛腳／瘸）lame

陣腳①（前線）front line ②（情況）circumstances; position;
　situation

做咗手腳（搞了鬼把戲）do some tricks

夠腳（夠人打麻將／足夠的玩家）enough players (for a
　game of mahjong)

從頭到腳（從上到下／由頭至尾）from face to foot; from
　head to foot; from the sole of the foot to the crown of the
　head; from top to toe

捽吓隻腳（揉一下腳／按摩腳）massage the foot

笨手笨腳 stumblebum

粗手粗腳（笨手笨腳）have clumsy fingers

貨腳（路費／運費）freight

乾手淨腳①（乾淨利落）crispy; dapper; efficient; neat; neat
　and tidy; neatly; smooth and clean; trim; very efficient
　②（一勞永逸）finished and done with, once for all

痛腳（把柄／過失／辮子）weak spot

菜腳（剩菜）leftovers
就腳（行走方便／便利／交通方便的地方）convenient; easily accessible places
跛咗腳（腿瘸了）be crippled
跛腳（瘸腿）lame
亂咗陣腳（亂了陣腳／打亂步伐）break one's stride; keep sb off their stride; knock sb off stride; put sb off their stride; throw sb off stride
損手爛腳 ①（頭破血流）be beaten; be crushed; be seriously injured; head broken and bleeding; injured; run into bumps and bruises ②（損失慘重）suffer heavy losses
歇腳 rest the feet after walking; stop on the way for a rest
落手落腳（親力親為）do sth oneself; do the actual work oneself
落腳（住宿）hang out
趷高腳（踮着腳）on tiptoe
踩嘥腳（踩着腳了）step on one's foot
較腳（開溜／撒丫子）escape; flee
過水濕腳（經手三分肥／水過地皮濕）draw water to one's mill; take a commission
運腳（路費／運費）freight
滾水淥腳（火燒火燎地）go quickly; hurry off
竭竭腳（歇歇腳）take a rest
聚腳（聚首）hang out together
蹺蹺腳（生活得很好）lead a rose-coloured life; live well
駁腳（跑腿）intermediary
撐枱腳（桌腿）have a meal; have a meal with one's lover
撬牆腳 ①（挖角）lure sb away from a job ②（橫刀奪愛）seduce sb away from a lover
褲腳（褲腿）bottom of a trouser leg
踢晒腳（手忙腳亂）very busy
踢腳（手忙腳亂）very busy
鬢腳（鬢邊／鬢腳）sideburns
豬腳（豬後蹄）pork trotter
頭痛醫頭，腳痛醫腳（只顧眼前的問題，不解決問題的根本）a defensive stopgap measure; cure only the symptoms; sporadic and piecemeal steps; take only a stopgap measure, not a radical one; take only palliative measures for one's illness; treat symptoms but not the disease; treat the head when the head aches, treat the foot when the foot hurts
鴨乸腳（平足）flat feet
擘腳（叉開腳）with feet apart
踹腳（腳下打滑／腳踩不穩）slip
轆嘥腳（碾着腳了）one's foot is being rolled over
雞手鴨腳（七手八腳）clumsy; have two left feet
雞咁腳（穿兔子鞋似的）fleet of foot; take to one's legs
雞腳 ①（雞爪子）chicken feet ②（把柄／過失／辮子）weak spot
餸腳（剩菜）leftovers
露出馬腳 incautiously let out one's fault; incautiously let out one's secret; show the cloven foot
露馬腳 incautiously let out one's fault; incautiously let out one's secret; show the cloven foot
讀壞詩書包壞腳（迂腐）pedantic

【腱】gin³ tendon
腱鞘 tendon sheath

牛腱 beef gristle

【腍】nam⁴（爛熟）boiled
腍善（善良温柔）kind and gentle

【腸】tsoeng⁴（腸子）intestines
腸仔（香腸）sausage
腸肚（腸胃）intestines and stomach
腸粉 steamed rice roll

一孖臘腸（一對香腸／兩根香腸）a pair of sausages
一抽臘腸（一串香腸）a string of sausages
叉腸（叉燒腸粉）steamed rice roll with barbeque pork
心腸 heart
牛腸（牛肉腸粉）steamed rice roll with beef
立實心腸（硬起心腸）make up one's mind
盲腸 appendix
香腸 sausage
唔使劃公仔劃出腸（不用說得太白）it goes without saying
橫丫腸（盲腸）caecum
豬大腸（豬腸子）pork intestines
豬腸（豬腸子）pork intestines
齋腸（豬腸粉）plain rice roll
蝦腸（蝦腸粉）shrimp rice roll
膶腸（臘肝腸）liver sausage
雞腸 ①（雞腸子）chicken intestine ②（書面英文）written English
臘腸（香腸）sausage

【腹】fuk⁷ belly
腹肌 abdominal muscle
　六塊腹肌 six-pack
腹背 in front and behind
　腹背受敵 be attacked both from behind and in front; be caught between two fires; between the devil and the deep sea; between the hammer and the anvil; have enemies in front and rear
腹部 abdomen midriff; stomach
腹脹 abdominal distension; meteorism

利口唔利腹（好吃但對身體無益）good for mouth but bad for health

推心置腹（對某人充滿信心）place confidence in sb

【腍】nau⁶（膩）greasy

腍喉（甜美的聲音）sweet voice

【腩】naam⁵ brisket

腩肉（五花肉）pork belly

大肚腩 big tummy; pot belly
五花腩（五花肉）pork belly; streaky pork
牛腩 beef brisket; belly beef; brisket
肚腩 belly; pot belly; tummy
炆牛腩（燉牛腩）stew beef brisket
清湯牛腩 beef brisket in plain soup
魚腩 ①（魚腩）fishing rod; belly ②（打麻將經常輸掉的玩家 / 賭徒）frequent loser in mahjong games; incompetent gambler
間花腩（五花肉）pork belly; streaky pork
鯇魚腩（草魚腹）grass carp belly

【腺】sin³ gland

腺瘤 adenoma

甲狀腺 thyroid gland
汗腺 apocrine sweat gland; sweat gland

【腮】soi¹ ① cheek ② gills of a fish

腮骨 cheekbone

生痄腮（患腮腺炎）have mumps; suffer from epidemic parotitis
谷起泡腮（鼓起腮幫子 / 不合適）be out of sorts
鼓埋泡腮（鼓起腮幫子 / 耷拉着臉）pull a long face

【舅】kau⁵ uncle

舅父（舅舅）mother's brother; uncle
舅仔（小舅子）brother-in-law; wife's younger brother
舅母（舅媽）aunt; wife of mother's brother

大舅 one's wife's elder brother
叔舅 one's mother's younger brother
妻舅 one's brother-in-law; one's wife's brother

【與】jy⁵ and

與及（以及）along with; and; as well as; including; together with
與別不同（與眾不同）different from all others; different from other people; different from the common run; different from the rest; distinctive; extraordinary; flaky; not like others; not the same as others; out of the common; out of the ordinary; peculiar; uncommon; unlike others; unusual

好相與（好相處 / 好商量 / 好說話兒 / 容易共事合作）approvable; easy to get along with; personable
相與（相處）get along with
參與 participation
難相與（相處不來）difficult to get along with

【艇】teng⁵（小船）small boat

艇仔（小船）boat; small boat
　艇仔粥 boat people congee
　扒艇仔（划船）row a boat

反艇（死）die
扒艇（划船）boating; go boating; paddle a boat; row a boat
快艇 speedboat
棹艇（划小船 / 搖船）row a boat
遊艇 yacht
撐艇（划船）boating; go boating; paddle a boat; row a boat

【萬】maan⁶ ten thousand

萬一 in case
萬大有我（天塌我頂着）even if the sky falls down, I'll hold it up
萬中無一 most unlikely
萬字夾（曲別針 / 迴形針）paper clip
萬事 all things
　萬事俱備，只欠東風 ready to the last gaiter button
　萬事起頭難（萬事開頭難）it is difficult to begin a new business; all things are difficult before they are easy
　萬事勝意（萬事如意）may things get better than what you expect
　萬大事有我（天塌下來我頂着）you have my full support whatever may happen
萬能 multi-purpose
　萬能蘇（三通 / 萬能插）universal plug
萬無一失 as sure as a surefooted horse
萬聖節（鬼節）Halloween
萬壽果（木瓜）papaya
萬變不離宗（萬變不離其宗）myriads of changes base themselves on the origin

一萬 ten thousand
十萬 one hundred thousand
四萬 forty thousand

失匙夾萬（沒鑰匙的保險箱／依靠有錢父母生活的二世祖，看的到錢卻拿不到）a young person who can hardly obtain money from a rich father

夾萬（保險箱）safe

【萵】wo¹ lettuce

萵筍（萵苣）lettuce

【落】lok⁹ ① （下）alight from; go down ② （上）go up ③ （放）add; put in

落力（下力氣／賣力）spare no effort

落口供（錄口供）take deposition

落手（下手）begin; put one's hand to the plough

　　落手打三更（剛開始工作就出現失誤）begin with a wrong move; make mistakes when starting to do sth; ruin sth as soon as it starts

落井下石 persecute sb while he is down

落牙（拔牙）extract a tooth; pull out a tooth

落仔（墮胎）induced abortion

落台（下台）step down

落本（下本錢／投入了時間、金錢和精力）put in time, money, and effort

落皮（下本錢）put in time, money, and effort

落去（下去）go down

落田（下地）go farming in the field

落伍 outdated

落名（署名）put down one's signature

　　落你個名（簽上你的名）put down your name

落吧（去酒吧）go to the bar

落形（憔悴）become thin; slim down

　　落晒形（憔悴不堪）downcast

落足嘴頭（用盡唇舌）make a long harangue

落車（下車）alight; get down from a car; get off a car; get off a vehicle; get out of the car

　　下個站落車（下一站下車）get off at the next stop

落定（付訂金／給定金／給定錢）pay the deposit

落注（下注）place a bet

落肥（施肥）apply fertiliser; fertiliser; spread manure

落雨（下雨）rain

　　落雨收柴（虎頭蛇尾）do a task carelessly; a fine start but a poor finish

　　落雨微（細雨／毛毛雨）drizzle

　　落雨絲濕（下雨路滑）roads becoming slippery due to raining

　　落雨賣風爐——越擔越重（雨天挑稻草——越挑越重）one's burden becomes greater

　　落雨擔遮——顧前唔顧後（慮事不周／只顧眼前，不顧將來）pay no regard to the future

　　成日落雨（整天下雨）it rains all day

就嚟落雨（快要下雨）it's going to rain

睇嚟會落雨（看來會下雨）it looks like it's going to rain

落大雨（下大雨）it's pouring

落好濃雨（下大雨）it rains heavy

落緊大雨（正在下大雨）it's pouring; it's raining cats and dogs

落緊毛毛雨（正在下毛毛雨）it's drizzling

落雨（正在下雨）it's raining

落緊微微雨（正在下毛毛雨）it's drizzling

落客（讓乘客下車）let passengers off

落牀（下牀）get out of bed

落後 under-developed

落面（丟臉）be disgraced; feel ashamed; lose face

　　落⋯嘅面（丟⋯的臉）bring disgrace on sb; make sb lose face

落格（私吞錢財／獨吞財物）line one's own pockets; take money illegally

落堂（下課）after class; come off from class; dismiss class; finish class; get out of class

落得（結束／完結）end in

落莊（從委員會卸任）step down from a committee

落貨（卸貨）unload goods

　　落貨紙（下貨紙／卸貨單）landing order

落雪（下雪）snow

落船 ① （上船）board a ship ② （下船）disembark a ship

落單 ① （叫菜）order food ② （下訂單）place an order

落湯雞（渾身濕透）completely drenched

落筆打三更（一上手就搞壞了）begin with a wrong move; make mistakes when starting to do sth; ruin sth as soon as it starts

落粧（下粧／卸裝）remove make-up and costume

落畫（結束放映／下架）off the board; off screen

落袋（放入口袋）put sth into one's pocket

落街 ① （上街）go into the street ② （購物）go shopping

落葬（下葬／安葬）bury

落腳 hang out

落旗（起錶）flag fall

落雹（下冰雹）hail

落嘴頭（哄騙某人）cajole sb

落樓（下樓）go downstairs

　　落三樓（下到三樓）go down to the third floor

落機（下飛機）get off a plane; get out from an aeroplane

落糖（加糖）add sugar

落霜（下霜）frost has occurred

落嚟（下來）come down

落霧（下霧／起霧）fog has fallen

落疊（參加／下注）agree to a deal

落 club（去夜總會）go to a nightclub

落 D（去迪廳）go to a discotheque

七零八落 in disorder

日落 sunset

巴士站有落 (公交站有人下車) get off at the bus stop

巨星殞落 death of a big star

有落 (有人下車) I want to get off

冷落 treat coldly

告一段落 come to a conclusion; draw to an end

村落 village

沒落 decline; wane

見雷響唔見雨落 (雷聲大雨點小) all talk but no action

受落 (受用) accept sth

爬落 (爬下) climb down; scramble down

枳落 (刺籬笆) thorn hedge

降落 (着陸) alight; descend to the ground; land; landing; touch down

前面有落 (前面有人下車) please stop in front; please stop over there; would like to get off over there

段落 ① paragraph; section ② conclusion of a part; phase; stage

流落 (流浪) live a homeless life

計落 (算下來／算起來) altogether; in all

食唔落 ① (吃不下) cannot eat any more ② (不想吃) not feel like eating

食得落 (吃得下) edible

俾人冷落 (受人冷落) be given the cold shoulder; be left out in the cold; be treated coldly

睇落 (看上去／看起來) have the look of

疏落 (疏遠) alienate; become estranged; drift apart; estrange; keep at a distance; not close; not in close touch

跌落 drop; fall

跳上跳落 (跳上跳下) jump up and down

嗒得杯落 (有吸引力) attractive

淪落 (摔倒／跌得很低) be reduced to; fall down; fall low

葉落 leaves fall

路口有落 (路口有人下車) I want to get off at the intersection

話落 (離開前吩咐) leave words before one's departure

飲得杯落 (可以開懷暢飲了) drink to one's heart's content

飲得落 (喝得下) drinkable

寥落 sparse

慳落 (省下) save money

對落 (下面) below; under

鳳凰無寶不落 (不做對自己無利可圖的事) draw water to one's mill

擒上擒落 (爬上爬下) rush up and down

寫得落 (寫得下) can be written

熟落 (不生疏／熟悉) on familiar terms with sb; very familiar with

諗落 (想起來) when we come to think of it

闊落 (地方大／寬敞／寬闊) spacious

轉彎有落 (轉彎有人下車) I want to get off at the corner

騰上騰落 (爬上爬下) rush around

【葉】jip⁹ leaf

葦落 leaves fall

葉落知秋 one falling leaf is indicative of the coming of autumn; the falling leaves announce the approach of autumn

葉落歸根 an apple does not fall far from the apple tree; the fruit falls near the branch; the leaves always fall toward the root

葉綠素 chlorophyll

一塊葉 (一片葉子) a leaf

月桂葉 bay leaf

牛栢葉 (牛胃) beef tripe

老葉 old leaf

車葉 (螺旋槳) propeller

桑葉 mulberry leaf

桐葉 leaves of a tung tree

茶葉 ① (茶) tea ② (茶葉) tea leaf

粗枝大葉 crude and careless

開枝散葉 ① produce offspring ② expand business

楓葉 maple leaf

綠葉 green leaves

嫩葉 tender leaves

摘去老葉 pick out old leaves

賣花姑娘插竹葉 (賣花女自己只能插竹葉) a tailor makes the man but he clothes himself in rags

【著】dzy³ ① author ② famous ③ work; writing

著名 famous

著作 ① books; works; writings ② write

著述 ① compile; write ② books; literary works; writings

著書 author a book

巨著 great work; monumental work

名著 famous work

見微知著 a straw shows which way the wind blows; from one small clue one can see what is to come; from the first small beginnings one can see how things will develop; one may see day at a little hole; recognise the whole through observation of the part

【葛】got⁸ dolichos

葛衣 clothing made with linen

沙葛 (涼薯／豆薯) yam bean

杯葛（抵制）(English) boycott
碌葛（傻子）idiot

【董】dung² direct
董事 director
　　董事總經理 managing director

一件古董 an antique
古董 ① antique; curio ② old fogey
老古董 ① antique; museum piece; old-fashioned article
　　② fuddy-duddy; old fogey; ultra-conservative

【葬】dzong³ bury
葬身 be buried
葬埋（埋葬）bury
葬送 bury; waste
葬禮 funeral service; funeral rites; obsequies

火葬 cremation
埋葬 bury
落葬（下葬／安葬）bury

【葵】kwai⁴ sunflower
葵花（向日葵）sunflower
葵扇 palm-leaf fan

秋葵 lady's finger; okra

【葱】tsung¹ onion
葱白 scallion
葱花 chopped green onion
葱綠 light green
葱頭（洋葱）onion

一條葱（一棵葱）a piece of green onion
倒豎葱（倒立）handstand; stand upside down

【號】hou⁶ ① number ② mark ③ date ④ days of the month
號令 order; verbal command; whistle
號外 extra of a newspaper
號召 appeal; call; draw
號角 ① bugle; horn; trumpet ② bugle call
號碼 number

三號 No.3
口號 slogan
井號 pound sign
今日幾月幾號（今天幾月幾號）what is today's date

分號 ① semicolon ② branch of a firm
引號 inverted comma; quotation mark; speech mark
句號 full point; full stop; period
件號 piece number
字號 company
老字號 established company
型號 model
括號 brackets
紅色暴雨訊號 red rain storm signal
單引號 single quotation marks
幾多號 ①（哪一天／哪一日）what day of the month; which date ②（號碼是多少）what number
幾號 ①（哪一天／哪一日）what day of the month; which date ②（號碼是多少）what number
掛號 register
最新型號 latest model
頓號 punctuation mark placed between several proper names
編號 ① arrange under numbers; number ② number; serial number
雙引號 double quotation marks

【蜂】fung¹ hornet
蜂王 ① queen bee ② queen wasp
蜂羣 a cluster of bees; a swarm of bees
蜂蜜 honey
蜂巢 beehive; honeycomb; nest

黃蜂（螞蜂）hornet

【蜆】hin²（蜆子／蛤蜊）freshwater clam

【蜇】dzit⁸ jellyfish
蜇皮（海蜇）jellyfish

【裊】niu⁵ thin
裊裊 ① curling up ② continuous

夭裊裊（高高瘦瘦）tall and thin

【裏】lei⁵ inside
裏便（裏面／裏邊）inside
裏面 in; inside
裏頭（裏面／裏邊）inside

蒙在鼓裏 be kept in the dark

【裝】dzong¹ ① equip ②（盛）fill sth
裝入 install
裝多啲（多盛點兒）fill a bowl with more rice

裝修 renovation
裝香（上香）offer incense
裝假狗（裝假／裝模作樣）make believe; pretend; put on airs
裝飯（盛飯）fill up a bowl with rice
裝傻扮懵（裝瘋賣傻）play the fool
裝滿 fill up

一套西裝 a suit
人要衣裝，佛要金裝（人靠衣裝馬靠鞍）fine feathers make fine birds; the tailor makes the man
女裝 women's wear
中式服裝 Chinese clothing
化裝 make up; wear make-up
古裝 ancient costume
孕婦裝 maternity clothes
西裝 ① Western-style clothes ② Western suite
男裝 men's wear
服裝 clothing
訂裝（裝訂）bookbinding
唐裝 ① Chinese-style clothes ② Chinese suite
時裝 fashion; fashionable dress
釘裝（裝釘／裝訂）bind
假裝 pretend
瓶裝 bottled
盒裝 boxed
着住西裝（穿着西裝）wearing a suit
無上裝（赤裸上身）topless
童裝 children's wear
罐裝 canned

【裸】lo² naked; nude
裸奔 streak
裸露 exposed; nudity; uncovered
裸體 naked; nude

赤裸 in one's birthday suit; naked; stark naked; without a stitch of clothing

【褂】gwaa³ jacket
褂子 gown; overcoat; robe

黃馬褂 ① clerk related to the boss ② relatives of the boss

【解】gaai² （解釋）explain
解倒（能解釋）can be explained
解唔倒（不能解釋）can't be explained
解得倒（能解釋）can be explained

解渴 quench one's thirst

解渴提神 quench one's thirst and raise one's spirit
解散 adjourn
解釋 ① explain ② interpret

了解 know clearly; understand
分解 ① decompose; resolution; resolve ② disclose; recount
冇解（不像話／沒道理／無法解釋）it is unreasonable that
互相諒解 make allowance for each other; understand each other
令人費解 elude understanding
瓦解 breakdown; collapse; crumble; disintegrate; disorganized; fall apart; fall into pieces
見解 idea; opinion; thesis; understanding; view
直接了解 know directly
理解 understand
費解 hard to understand
諒解 forgiveness; make allowance for; understanding
點解（為甚麼／甚麼原因）how is it that; what for; why; why is it that; why oh why
難分難解（難捨難分）be locked together
難以理解 hard to understand

【詢】soen¹ enquire
詢問 ① （查詢）enquire ② （審問）interrogate
詢價（問價）enquiry

如有查詢 for enquiries; if you have any enquiries
查詢 enquiry

【試】si³ try
試用期 probationary period
試吓（試一下）have a try
　試吓得唔得（我可以嘗試一下嗎／我可以試試嗎）can I try it on
試身（試穿）fit sth on; try on
　試身室（試衣間／試衣室）fitting room
試味（嚐味兒）taste
試衫（試穿）fit sth on; try on
試過（有過／曾經）has tried
試驗 experiment

入學試（入學考試）entrance examination
又試（再試試看）again; also; in addition to; once again
再試（再試試看）again; also; in addition to; once again
考試 examination
廷試 imperial examination
酒精測試 breath alcohol test
路試（路考）road test
嘗試 try

【詩】si¹ poem

詩人 poet
詩詞 poetry and rhymed prose
詩歌 poems and songs; poetry

吟詩 hum verse; recite poems

【詫】tsaa³ surprised

詫異 amaze

【話】waa⁶⁻² ① (說) say ② (批評) criticise

話人 (說別人) bad-mouth others; talk behind one's back
話口 (話頭) thread of a discourse
　話口未完 (話還沒落音) sth happens when one is just talking about it
話之佢 ① (隨便他／管他的) as you like; as you please ② (不在乎) couldn't care less
話之你 (隨便你) do what you like
話吓佢 (說說他) lecture sb
話名 (名義上) in name; nominally
　話名係 (叫做／說的是) by the name; in name only
話你知 (告訴你) tell you
　話界你知 (告訴你) let me tell you
話低 (留下話) leave a message
話咁快 (很快) before one knows it; very quickly
話咁易 (很容易) it's very easy
話定 (說定／說好) agree on; come to an agreement
　話唔定 (說不定) can't say for certain; hard to predict; may be; perhaps; probably
　話得定 (說得定) agree on; come to an agreement
話事 (作主／說了算／掌權) be in charge; have the say
　話事人 (主事的) person in charge
　唔話得事 (沒甚麼說的) do not have any say
　話晒事 (主事) wield the sceptre
　話得事 (作主) have the say
話柄 (把柄／痛處) excuse
話是 (說了算／作主) have the final say
話晒 (說完／說到底) after all; at bottom; in the final analysis; in the last analysis; in the ultimate analysis
話唔埋 (說不定) perhaps; who knows
　話得埋 (說得定) agree on; come to an agreement
話時話 (順便說／附帶說說) by the way
話落 (離開前吩咐) leave words before one's departure
話實 (說定) confirm; make sure that
話齋 (正如某人所說) as sb says

一於咁話 (說定了) so it's settled
一部手提電話 (一部手機) a mobile phone
土話 (家鄉話) native dialect

大家咁話 (與你一樣) the same to you
大話 lie
冇人聽電話 (沒人接電話) no one answered the phone
冇話 (從不) never ever
手提電話 (手機) mobile phone
正話 ① (剛才) just now ② (正在) in the midst of doing sth
打個電話 call; make a phone call; make a telephone call
打電話 call; make a phone call; make a telephone call
全城熱話 (全城討論) talk of the town
同朋友傾電話 (和朋友打電話) chat with one's friend on the phone
好話 (好說) not at all; you're welcome
至話 (剛剛) just now
即係話 (就是說) that is to say
見人講人話，見鬼講鬼話 speak to a saint like a saint, to a devil like a devil
佳話 a much-told tale; a story on everybody's lips
咁樣嘅話 (如果是這樣的話／那麼) in that case
奉承話 blarney
空口講白話 (只會說／只說不做) all mouth and no action; boasting; words pay no debts
長途電話 long-distance call
係咁話 (就這樣) that's it
咪話 (不用說／且不說) let alone; not to mention; not to speak of; to say nothing of
食齋不如講正話 (廢話少說) it is better to have straight talking
唔好話 (不用說／且不說) let alone; not to mention; not to speak of; to say nothing of
唔係嘅話 (不然的話) or; otherwise
笑笑口話 (笑着說) say with a smile
笑話 joke
訓話 exhort; lecture
鬼話 (壞話) malicious gossip
接聽電話 handle calls; receive calls
流動電話 (移動電話) mobile phone
喋話 (日語) Japanese language
普通話 ① Putonghua ② Mandarin
發吟發話 (胡說八道) talk nonsense; talk rubbish
視像電話 (視頻電話) visual mobile phone
開口埋口都話 (一張嘴就是…／張口閉口都說) always sing the same old tune; whenever one speaks, one says that
開講有話 (常言道／俗話說) as the saying goes
黑話 triad society language
傾電話 (打電話／講電話) be on the phone; chat on the phone
想話 (正想／正想說／打算) be just going to; just want to say
電話 telephone
說話 (話語／講話) say; speak; talk
廢話 nonsense

對話 conversation; dialogue
熱話 (熱門話題) hot gossip
談話 ① chat; colloquy; conversation; talk ② say; state
廣東話 (粵語) Cantonese; Cantonese dialect
點話 (怎麼說) what to say
講大話 (說大話) lie; tell a lie
講好話 praise; say good things about
講到話 (至於 / 說到) as for
講倒話 (說反話) say to the contrary
講話 (說話) say; speak; talk
講電話 (打電話 / 接電話) be on the phone
講廢話 talk bullshit; talk nonsense
講壞話 say bad things about; speak ill of sb
識少少廣東話 (聽得懂一點廣東話) know a little Cantonese
鹹濕笑話 (黃色笑話) dirty joke; lewd joke
聽晒你話 (全聽你的) at your command
聽話 ① (順從) obedient; subordinate to ② (聽說) be said; be told; hear of
聽電話 (接電話) answer the phone
聽聞話 (聽說) I was told
聽講話 (聽說) be told that

【誠】 sing⁴ honest

誠心 sincere desire; wholeheartedness
誠信 faith; good faith
誠意 good faith; sincerity
誠實 honest

坦誠 candid
忠誠 faithful; loyal; truthful
開心見誠 (開誠相見) open-hearted

【該】 goi¹ ought

該死 deserve it
該釘就釘，該鐵就鐵 (直言不諱) call a spade a spade
該煨 (糟糕) what a shame
　　該煨咯 (糟糕了) what a bad luck

唔該 ① (不好意思) excuse me ② (勞駕 / 謝謝) thank you
唔駛唔該 (不謝 / 不用謝) don't mention it
認真唔該 (非常感謝) many thanks; thank you so much; thank you very much; thanks a lot; very grateful
應該 ought to; should

【誇】 kwaa¹ exaggerate

誇口 boast; brag; talk big
誇大 exaggerate
誇獎 commend; compliment sb on; praise
誇耀 boast of; brag about; flaunt; show off

【資】 zi¹ subsidy

資本 capital
　　資本市場 capital market
資格 qualification
資料 ① (數據) data ② (信息) information
　　資料輸入 (數據輸入) data entry; data input
資產 ① (財產 / 房地產) property; real estate ② (資本) capital ③ (資產) asset
　　資產管理 asset management
　　負資產 negative equity
　　流動資產 liquid asset
資源 resources

投資 investment
耗資 consume funds
集資 fund-raising

【賊】 tsaak⁹ bandit; burglar; robber; thief

賊人 (賊) thief
賊公計，狀元才 (小偷才智有如狀元) know a trick worth two of that
賊仔 (小偷) thief
賊亞爸 (向盜賊集團敲竹杠的人) a thief of thieves
賊佬 (小偷) thief
　　賊佬試砂煲 (不懷好意，試探虛實) put forth a feeler; put out feelers
賊眉賊眼 (賊頭賊腦 / 賊眉鼠眼) look like a thief
賊婆 (女賊) female thief
賊喊捉賊 cover up the misdeed of oneself by shifting the blame onto others
賊過興兵 lock the stable door after the horse is stolen
賊頭賊腦 stealthy

長毛賊 (長頭髮的男人) long-haired man
捉賊 (抓賊) catch a thief
船頭慌鬼，船尾慌賊 (膽小怕事) get into a hobble; timid and overcautious
船頭驚鬼，船尾驚賊 (膽小怕事) get into a hobble; timid and overcautious
烏賊 (墨魚) cuttlefish
盜賊 bandit; robber; thief
猾賊 (奸狡) glib rascal

【趀】 gat⁹ (拐) limp

趀高腳 (踮着腳) on tiptoe
趀跛跛 (單腳跳) hop
趀開 (推開) push off
趀路 (滾蛋) go away

【跟】gan¹ follow

跟手（接着／跟着）carry on; follow; go on; in the wake of; proceed

跟吓眼（盯着點兒／留意／關照）keep an eye on

跟住（接着／跟着／隨後）accordingly; carry on; follow; following; go on; in the wake of; next; proceed; then

跟尾（尾隨）follow after

　跟尾狗 ①（哈巴狗）Pekingese ②（裝模作樣的人）obsequious person

跟紅頂白（趨炎附勢）flatter those in power and hurt those in bad luck

跟埋我去（跟我一起去）come along with me

跟班（手下）follower

跟進 follow up

側跟（旁邊／側面）near by position; right by; side

【跡】dzik⁷ trace

跡象 indication; sign; straw in the wind; token

軌跡 ① locus; path; way ② orbit

筆跡 sb's handwriting

毀屍滅跡 burn the corpse to destroy the evidence; bury the corpse in order to destroy all traces of one's crime; chop up a corpse and obliterate all traces; reduce the corpse to ashes in order to destroy all traces of one's crime

【踩】tsaai² (踩) step on; trample; tread on

踩嚟腳（踩着腳了）step on one's foot

【跣】sin² (滑) trick

跣人（誣陷別人）trick sb

跣低（滑倒）slip

【跪】gwai⁶ kneel

跪地餵豬乸——睇錢份上（人在屋簷下，不得不低頭）money makes the mare go; money makes the world go round; suffer disgrace and insults in order to get money

跪低（跪下）throw oneself on one's knees

跪拜 worship on bended knees

【路】lou⁶ (道路) road

路人 passer-by

路口 crossing; road intersection; road junction

　十字路口 at crossroads

　三岔路口 fork in the road; junction of three roads

路少車多 many vehicles and few roads

路向（方向）direction

路面 road surface

路程 distance; journey; route

　縮短路程 shorten one's route

路試（路考）road test

路數 ①（門路）way of making money ②（社會關係）social connections

　有路數（有辦法／有線索）there's a way

路線 course; itinerary; route

路邊 roadside

　路邊雞（娼妓）streetwalker

一甫路（十英里路）a distance of ten miles

一條路 a road

一路 ① all along; all the time; all the way; all the while; all through; always; as ever; as the day is long; constantly; continuously; ever since; from...till now; hold; keep; on end; till; to this day; until; used to be ② during the whole journey

上路 die

大細路（心境年輕的老人／老小孩）older person who is young at heart

公路 road

天無絕人之路 it is a long lane that has no turning; there is always a way out

火路（火候）duration and degree of cooking

冇紋路（沒正經／沒章法）have no sense of propriety

氹細路（哄小孩）coax a child

打喊路（打哈欠）yawn

末路 dead end; impasse

同⋯⋯有路（和⋯⋯有一腿）have illicit intercourse with sb

有門路 know the right places to go to get sth done

有紋路（有條理）in good order

有啲唔對路（有點不對頭）sth strange; there's sth weird about it

有路（有一腿）have an affair with sb

死人尋舊路（走老路）follow one's own old tracks

死路 blind alley; the road to ruin

老虎頭上釘蝨乸——自尋死路（太歲頭上動土）bread the lion in his den; defy the mighty; offend powerful people; provoke a powerful person; provoke sb far superior in power

行人路（人行道）path; pedestrian crossing

行路（走路）go on foot; walk

吼路（找人破綻）find a flaw

走路（跑路）run away; take to one's legs

車路（車道／軌道）rail; railroad; railway

來路 imported

歧路 branch road; crossroads; fork in a road; forked road; wrong road

波路（球路）style of play

泥路（土路）muddy road

狗上瓦桁——有條路（耗子鑽水溝——各有各的路）rats passing through a sewer – each going their own way

門路 ① knack; way to do sth ② pull; social connections

食鹽多過食飯，行橋多過行路（見多識廣）have seen more elephants

倔頭路（死路）dead-end street

借頭借路（找由頭兒）cook up a lame excuse; use any pretext

唔係路（不是辦法／不對路／不對勁／不對頭）it is far from good; sth does not look right

唔對路（不對頭）problematic

徑路（小路）route

捉路（預測對手的下一步）predict the strategy of one's opponent

紋路（條理）orderliness

財路（賺錢的方式）way of making money

趷路（滾蛋）get out

迷路（迷失方向）go astray; lose one's way; get lost

馬路 road; street

高速公路 highway

兜路（繞路）go the long way round

掘頭路（死胡同）dead end

探路（收集信息）collect information

教路（出點子／指點）instruct; teach

斜路（坡路／斜坡）slope

細路 ① （小孩／小孩兒）child; kid ② （陰莖）penis

蛇有蛇路，鼠有鼠路（人各有生存或解決問題的出路或途徑）play a lone hand

問路 ask for direction

單程路（單行線）one way

睇路（看路）watch out

搵米路（找方法掙大錢）find a way to get big profits

搵到門路（找到門路）catch the knack of; find the way to do sth; learn the ropes

搵窿路（搵門路）solicit help from potential backers

趯路（滾蛋）go away

過馬路 cross the street

對路（對頭）correct; on the right track

趕路 hurry on with one's journey

數還數路還路（人情是人情，數目要算清）balance accounts with sb no matter who they are

銷路 sale

鋪路 pave a road

築路 build roads

蕩失路（迷路）lose one's way; one is lost

頭路（路）pull; way

竅 ① （方法／途徑）channel; knack; know-how; outlet; trick of the trade; way ② （門路）way of making money

識路（認識路）know one's way

彎路 roundabout way

鐵路 railway

讓路 get out of the way; give way; give sb the right of way; make way for sb; make way for sth; step aside

趲路（趕路）hurry in a journey

【跳】 tiu³ jump

跳上 jump up
　跳上棵樹（跳上這棵樹）jump up the tree
　跳上跳落（跳上跳下）jump up and down

跳水 diving

跳皮（調皮）mischievous; naughty

跳灰（賣白面兒）sell heroin

跳河（投河）commit suicide by throwing oneself into the river; drown oneself

跳蚤 flea
　跳蚤市場 flea market

跳高 ① （跳高）high jump ② （跳得高）jump high
　跳高踎低（跳上跳下）jump up and down
　跳得好高 can jump very high

跳舞 dance
　跳草裙舞 ① （跳呼拉舞）have a hula hula dance ② （鬧情緒）make a fuss
　跳隻舞（跳個舞）have a dance; shake a leg

跳樓 jump off a building to commit suicide
　跳樓貨（最低價出售）sell at rock-bottom prices

跳槽（換工作）switch jobs

卜卜跳（怦怦跳）heart beating

三級跳 ① hop, skip, and jump; triple jump ② quick promotion

心跳 heart beating

扎扎跳（跑跑跳跳／蹦蹦跳）bouncing and vivacious; hot with rage

生蝦咁跳（熱鍋上的螞蟻）furious; have ants in one's pants

有尾學人跳，冇尾又學人跳（盲從）blindly imitate sb

持竿跳（撐竿跳）pole vault

笨豬跳（波比跳）bumpee jump

紮紮跳（憤怒／生氣）be livid with rage

激到生蝦咁跳（氣得直哆嗦）tremble with anger

嚇一跳 be astonished; be shaken; be shocked; be surprised

嚇咗一跳（嚇了一跳）be astonished; be shaken; be shocked; be surprised

邊有咁大隻蛤乸隨街跳（那有這麼便宜的事／天上不會掉餡餅）good cheap is dear

【跤】 gaau¹ wrestle

跌跤 ① （摔跤）wrestling ② （跌倒）fall down

蹟跤（摔跤）wrestling

【躲】do² avoid; dodge
躲懶（偷懶）take a chance to avoid work

【較】gaau³ compare
較早時（早些時候）in earlier times
較非（冒險）get sb into trouble
較為（比較）by comparison; compare; compare with; comparatively; contrast; fairly; in comparison; in comparison with; in contrast to; somewhat
較剪（剪刀）scissors
　一把較剪（一把剪刀）a pair of scissors
較腳（開溜／撤丫子）escape; flee

斤斤計較 calculating; calculating and unwilling to make the smallest sacrifice; excessively mean in one's dealings; haggle over every ounce; mindful of narrow personal gains and losses; palter with a person about sth; particular about; reckon up every iota; split hairs; split straws; stand on little points; skin a flint; weigh and balance every detail; weigh up every detail
比較 ① compare ② comparatively
牙較（牙關）jaw
打牙較（閒聊）bull session; chat; chat idly; chew the rag; chinwag; gossip; have a chat; have small talk; natter; schmooze; shoot the breeze
甩牙較（下巴脫臼）dislocated jaw

【辟】pik⁷ keep away
辟腥（去腥）remove the fishlike smell

【農】nung⁴ farm
農夫 farmer
農民 farmer
農場 farm
農曆 lunar calendar

【逼】bik⁷（擁擠）cramped
逼人（擁擠）crowded
　好逼人（好擠）very crowded
逼力（剎車）(English) brake
逼車（擠車）jam into a bus
逼挾（狹窄／逼仄）cramped

好逼 ①（好擠）very crowded ②（狹窄／逼仄）cramped
咪逼（不要擠／別擠）don't push
唔好逼（不要擠／別擠）don't push

【遇】jy⁶ meet
遇見 bump into; come across; meet; run into
遇到 come across
遇險 in danger; in distress; meet with a mishap; meet with danger
遇難 ① die in an accident; get killed in an accident ② be murdered

際遇 favourable or unfavourable turns in life; spells of good or bad fortune

【遊】jau⁴ travel
遊行 demonstration; march
遊車河（坐車玩／兜風／乘車兜風）car ride; drive around for pleasure; go for a drive in a car; take a car ride for pleasure
遊客 tourist
遊埠 ①（旅行／旅遊）travel ②（白日夢）day-dream
遊船河（乘船兜風）boat ride; boat trip; cruise trip; take a boat ride for pleasure
遊艇 yacht
　遊艇會 yacht club
遊樂場 playground
遊學 study tour
遊戲 game
　遊戲機 video game

伴遊（護送）escort
巡遊 ① parade ② demonstrate; march
到此一遊 have visited this place
旅遊 travel
漫遊 roam; wander
觀光旅遊 sightseeing tour

【運】wan⁶ luck
運氣 luck
　碰吓運氣（碰碰運氣）try one's luck
運送 carry
運動 ①（運動）sport ②（練習／鍛煉／活動）exercise
　運動員 athlete
　運動會 sports day
　運動場（體育場）stadium
　好少運動（很少運動）seldom do exercise
　做運動 exercise
運程（運氣／運勢）one's fortune; one's luck
運腳（路費／運費）freight
運路行（繞道走）detour; go by a roundabout route; go round; make a detour; take a devious route
運滯（倒運／走背運／運氣壞）hard luck

運輸 transport
　運輸公司 transport company

交好運（有好運）run into good fortune
好運 good fortune
行大運（走好運）enjoy good luck
行好運（走好運）by good luck; devil's luck; fall on one's feet;
　have fortune on one's side; have good luck; have one's
　moments; in luck; land on one's feet; luck is on one's side;
　luck of the devil; luck out; lucky; lucky sb; on the gravy
　train; one's luck is in; play big luck; strike luck; touch luck;
　you never know your luck; what a stroke of luck
行衰運（走壞運）bad luck; have bad luck; suffer an unlucky
　fate
行運（走運）by good luck; devil's luck; fall on one's feet;
　have fortune on one's side; have good luck; have one's
　moments; in luck; land on one's feet; luck is on one's side;
　luck of the devil; luck out; lucky; lucky sb; on the gravy
　train; one's luck is in; play big luck; strike luck; touch luck;
　you never know your luck; what a stroke of luck
命運 destiny; fate
幸運 good luck
桃花運 success in romantic adventures
唔夠運（運氣不好）in bad luck; luckless
衰運（背運 / 霉運）unlucky fate
祝你好運 good luck; good luck to you
夠運（好運氣 / 幸好 / 幸運）in luck; luck out; lucky
貨運（貨物運輸）cargo transportation
販運（運輸貨物待售）traffic; transport goods for sale
晨運①（晨練）morning exercise ②（晨運）do morning
　exercises
搬運 removal

【遍】pin³ all over
遍地 everywhere; throughout the land

普遍 common

【過】gwo³ cross
過口癮（過嘴癮）speak for the sake of speaking; talk
　nonsense
過火（過頭 / 過分）go too far; overstep the bounds
過日晨（做些事來打發時間）do sth to pass the time
過水①（給錢）give sb money; grease sb's hand; pay sb
　②（沖洗）rinse
　過水濕腳（經手三分肥 / 水過地皮濕）draw water to
　　one's mill; take a commission
過手（經手）deal with; handle
過主（滾蛋）go away

過去 in the past
　留戀過去 yearn for the past
過份 do too much; go too far; overstep the bounds
過江龍（外國專家 / 強大的局外人）foreign expert;
　powerful outsider
過冷河①（將煮熱的食物放到冷水中稍浸）blanch ②（離
　開工作崗位一段時間）sterilisation period before taking
　up another position
過身（去世 / 死了 / 逝世）die; meet one's death; pass
　away
　過咗身（去世 / 死了 / 逝世）died; passed away
過夾吊頸（小心翼翼）handle everything with great care
過來人 experienced person
過底紙（碳式複寫紙）carbon paper
過重 overweight
過海 cross the sea
　八仙過海——各顯神通（每個人都展示自己的才能 /
　　每個人都有自己的優點 / 相互提升，相互競爭）each
　　displays their ability; each has their merits; try to
　　outshine each other; vie with each other
　過咗海就係神仙（為求目的，不擇手段）using whatever
　　means would be alright as long as goals are achieved
　瞞天過海 do sth secretly
過時（超時）overtime
過氣（過時）past one's prime
　過氣老倌（過氣演員）actor/actress who past their prime
過骨（過關）get through; pass a test; scrape through
過埠（出國）go abroad
過帶（複製）copy
過得去 not too bad; passable
過敏症（過敏）allergy
過幾日（過幾天）for a couple of days
過期 expired; overdue
過雲雨（陣雨）occasional drizzle; passing shower; rain
　shower; shower; shower of rain
過節①（彆扭）uncomfortable ②（仇恨 / 怨恨 / 積怨）
　animosity; enmity; grudge; hatred; hostility ③（過假日）
　pass a holiday ④（慶祝節日）celebrate a festival
過電①（傳電）conduct electricity ②（被女人的調情所征
　服）be conquered by the flirt of a woman
過數（轉錢）transfer money
過獎 be flattered; I'm flattered
　你過獎啫（你誇獎 / 你過獎了）you're flattering me
過磅①（稱重）weigh ②（超重）overweight
過橋（當跳板）as a jumping board
　過橋抽板（過河拆橋）kick down the ladder
過膠（層壓）laminate
　過膠機（層壓機）laminator
過頭（太）excessively; much; over; too

叻過頭（太聰明）too smart
凍過頭（太冷）too cold
貴過頭（太貴）too expensive
熱過頭（太熱）too hot
熟過頭（太熟）① over-cooked ② over-ripe
過龍（過頭）exceed; go beyond the limit; in excess; overdo
過檔（換單位）change jobs
過嚟（過來）come over here
過鐘（過時了／過點）past the appointed time
過癮 satisfy a craving; thrilled
　　鬼咁過癮（太過癮了）really exciting
　　過口癮（過嘴癮）speak for the sake of speaking; talk
　　　　nonsense

一次過 all at once; at one dash; at one go; in one breath;
　　once for all
大步躪過（逃避不幸）escape from misfortune
之不過（只不過）but; just that
太過（太）excessively; much; over; too
少過（少於）less than
日子難過 have a hard time; lead a hard life
片過（打架）have a fight
功過 merits and demerits
未驚過（沒害怕過）know no fear
同佢坎過（跟他打架）fight against him
好過 be better than
有殺錯冇放過（寧枉勿縱／寧可錯殺不能放過）what is
　　done may be wrong but no one will be allowed to
　　let go
年關難過（難以過年）it is difficult to pass the end of the
　　year
坎不過（不值得冒一個人的生命）not worth risking
　　one's life
坎過（冒一個人的生命）risk one's life
改過 correct one's mistakes; mend one's ways
見過 come across
制唔過（不值得做／划不來）it does not pay; not worth it
制得過（划得來／值得幹）it is worth doing sth; worthwhile
放過 forgive and let go
信得過（可以相信的）can be trusted; reliable; trustworthy
為得過（還合算）worthwhile
穿過 penetrate
飛過 fly over
借過（借光／勞駕／讓讓）excuse me
悔過 penitence; repent one's error; repentant
唔制得過（不合算／划不來）it does not pay to do sth; not
　　worthwhile
唔制得過（划不來）it won't pay
制唔過（划不來／不值得／犯不着）worthwhile

制得過（划得來／合算／犯得着）not worthwhile
得過且過 muddle along
赦過（赦免過失）pardon a fault
睇唔過（看不下去）not stand the sight of
睇得過（值得看）worth seeing
睇過（看看）look through; take a look
感到難過 feel sorry for
搏唔過（不值一搏）it is not worthwhile running such
　　a risk
經過 pass by
試過（有過／曾經）has tried
諗過（想想看）think about it
繞過 bypass; pass over in a roundabout manner
難過 ① have a hard time ② feel sorry

【遏】aat⁸ suppress
遏制 suppress

【道】dou⁶ ① way ② drug
道友（吸毒者）drug addict; druggie
道姑（女吸毒者）female drug addict
道高一尺魔高一丈 offenders are a stroke above law-
　　makers
道理 reason
　　講得有道理（你說的話聽起來合情合理）what you said
　　　　sounds reasonable
道歉 apologise

一道 a beam of; a coat of; a flash of; a line of; a shaft of; a
　　streak of; a trail of
大行其道 in the trend; prevail throughout
小道 branch; pass; passageway; path; pathway; trail;
　　walkway
冇味道（沒有味道）tasteless
公道 reasonable
主持公道 unhold justice
市道（市場狀況）market conditions
好味道 delicious; good taste; tasty; yummy
行人隧道（人行隧道）underground tunnel
走火通道（逃生通道）fire exist
味道 taste
林蔭大道 tree-shaded boulevard
知道 know
房地產市道（房地產市場狀況）real estate market
物業市道（物業市場狀況）property market
怨聲載道 complaints are heard everywhere; complaints
　　rise all round; grumblings are heard all over; murmurs of
　　discontent fill the streets; swamp with complaints; voices
　　of discontent are heard everywhere

柔道 judo

胡說八道 all baloney; all my eye; apple sauce; banana oil; broad nonsense; cobblers; cod; drool; flubdub and gulf; full of hops; haver; hooey; lie in one's teeth; lie in one's throat; mere humbug; prate nonsense; pure rubbish; rats; rubbish; sheer nonsense; sling the bull; speak through the back of one's neck; stuff and nonsense; talk bosh; talk foolishly; talk gibberish; talk nonsense; talk rot; talk rubbish; talk sheer nonsense; talk through one's hat; talk through the back of one's neck; talk wet; talk without truth; throw the bull

軌道 course; path; track

悟道 awake to truth

旁門左道 heresy; all sorts of back doors; unorthodox ways

通道 ①（通路）passage ②（出口）exit

渠道 ① irrigation ditch ② channel of communication

睇市道（看市場狀況）watch the market conditions

橫行霸道 play the bully

隧道 tunnel

繞道 detour; go by a roundabout route; make a detour

離境通道（登機口）departure gate

翻渣茶葉──冇釐味道（涼水沏茶──沒味兒）as insipid as water

【達】daat⁹ reach

達人 ① expert; master ② wise person
美食達人 food expert; gourmet

達成 achieve; conclude; reach

達到 achieve; amount to; attain reach; to the amount of

達意 convey one's ideas; express one's ideas

平安到達 arrive safely

到達 arrive; reach

無端端發達（一夜暴富／一夜成名）strike oil

發咗達（發了跡）has made a fortune

發達 ①（發跡）get rich; make a fortune ②（繁榮）prosperous

貿易發達（貿易興旺）prosperous trade

【違】wai⁴ violate

違反 act against; contradict; disregard; infringe; run counter to; transgress; violate

違法 against the law; break the law; illegal; unlawful; violate the law

違例（違章）break rules and regulations

違規（違反規定）against regulations

【遖】naam³（跨）straddle

遖過來（跨過來）stride over

【鄉】hoeng¹ home village

鄉下 ① country side ② home village
鄉下仔（鄉巴佬）boor; churl; country bumpkin; country cousin; country folk; country-born; farming folk; hayseed; hick; redneck; yokel
鄉下佬（鄉巴佬）boor; churl; country bumpkin; country cousin; country folk; country-born; farming folk; hayseed; hick; redneck; yokel
鄉下妹（土包子）country girl
鄉下婆（鄉下女人／農婦）country woman
返鄉下（回老家）go to one's home town; return home

鄉巴佬 boor; churl; country bumpkin; country cousin; country folk; country-born; farming folk; hayseed; hick; redneck; yokel

鄉村 village

鄉里（同鄉／老鄉）fellow villager

他鄉 alien land; other lands; place far away from home

客死他鄉 die abroad; die in a strange land

思鄉 homesick

淪落異鄉 get lost in a strange land

【鈴】ling⁴⁻¹ bell

鈴鈴（小鈴鐺）small bell
鈴鈴霖霖（匆匆忙忙）in a big hurry
鈴鈴鎈鎈都丟埋（丟盔卸甲／失敗得慘烈不堪／慘敗）meet with a crushing defeat

【鉗】kim⁴（鉗子）clipper; pliers

鉗仔（鉗子）forceps; pincers; pliers

長嘴鉗（尖嘴鉗）long-nose pliers

指甲鉗（指甲刀）nail clipper

【鉛】jyn⁴ lead

鉛筆 pencil
鉛筆刨（鉛筆刀／卷筆刀）pencil sharpener
鉛筆盒 pencil box
一梳鉛筆（一段鉛筆／一截鉛筆）a section of a pencil
刨鉛筆（削鉛筆）sharpen a pencil

【鉈】to⁴ short spear

冇尾飛鉈（斷線風箏）a person without any trace

【閘】dzaap⁹ ①（柵欄）railings ② fence

閘口 gate

閘住（停住）stop
閘住先（先卡一卡）block it first

閘側（轉向側面／側向轉）turn sideward

入閘 pass through an entry gate
拉閘（關門）stop work
前閘（前門）front gate
開閘（開門）open the gate
搶閘（搶着做）rush to do sth
鐵閘（鐵柵欄）① iron gate ② grated door

【隔】gaak⁸ interval

隔山買牛（瞎碰／不靠譜／閉着眼睛走南牆）buy sth
　　without seeing it first
隔日（隔天）every other day
隔夜（放置一晚）overnight
　　隔夜素馨鏖戥秤（貴重藥材得細細稱量）the outmoded
　　　　are sometimes outvalued
　　隔夜錢（剩錢）money left over for use
　　隔夜餸（剩菜）leftovers
隔岸觀火 show indifference towards sb's trouble
隔涉（偏僻）remote
隔渣（濾渣）filter residue
隔靴搯痕（隔靴搔癢）hit beside the mark
隔牆有耳 walls have ears
隔斷（隔開）cut off; separate
隔籬（隔壁）adjoining; neighbouring; next door; next to
　　隔籬左右（鄰居）neighbours
　　隔籬飯香（隔壁的飯比較香）the grass at the other side
　　　　of one's own fence looks greener
　　隔籬鄰舍（左右四鄰／鄰居）neighbours

每隔 day at certain intervals; every
間隔（間架）ledge
飯隔（蒸架）steaming rack

【雹】bok⁹ hail

雹災 disaster caused by hail

落雹（下冰雹）hail

【零】ling⁴ zero

零丁（餘下零數）odd cents
零比零（沒有分數）love all; no score
零用錢（零花錢）pocket money
零件 component parts; part; spare parts
　　備用零件 spare parts
零舍（分外／格外／特別）especially; extraordinarily;
　　particularly
　　零舍唔同（與眾不同）in a different class
零食 between-meal nibbles; snack
　　零食店 snack bar
　　食零食（吃零食／吃零嘴）eat snacks; have snacks;

nibble between meals; nibble tidbit; take snacks
　　between meals
零星 fragmentary; occasional; odd; scattered; sporadic
　　零星小雨 occasional drizzle
　　零星落索（零零落落／七零八落）all in a hideous
　　　　mess; all upside down; at sixes and sevens; chaotic;
　　　　everything is upside down; fall apart into seven or
　　　　eight pieces; in a state of confusion; in disorder; in
　　　　great disorder; in ruin; in scattered confusion; scatter
　　　　about in all directions; scattered here and there;
　　　　scattering
零蛋（零分／零鴨蛋）zero mark
　　零雞蛋（零分／零鴨蛋）zero mark
零售 retail; sell at retail
　　零售商 retailer
　　零售價格 retail price
　　零售網（零售網絡）retail network
零碎 fragmentary; odds and ends; piecemeal; scrappy
　　零零碎碎 piecemeal
零零丁丁（孤零零的）all alone; lone; solitary
零錢 odd change; petty cash; small change
零點一 zero point one
零點五 zero point five

斗零（五分錢）five cents
孤零零 all alone; alone; solitary
個零（一個多）more than
泥零 shed tears

【雷】loey⁴ thunder

雷氣（義氣）loyalty to friends
雷暴 thunderstorm

地雷 ① mine ② animal shit on the road
行雷（打雷）have thunderstorm; thunder

【電】din⁶ electricity

電力 electricity
電子 electronic
電工（電器技師）electrician
電水煲（電熱水壺）electric kettle
電台 radio station
　　電台主持 radio host
　　電台節目主持人 radio host
電池 car battery
電車 tram
　　電車站 tram stop
　　電車軌 ①（電車軌道）rail track ②（額頭皺紋）wrinkles
　　　　on the forehead

一架電車 a tram

電油（汽油）gasoline; petrol

電芯（電池）battery
　一粒電芯（一節電池）a battery
　一嚿電芯（一節電池）a battery

電郵（電子郵件）email
　電郵地址 email address
　睇電郵（查看電子郵件）check email

電梯 elevator; lift
　電梯大堂 lift lobby
　自動電梯（電動扶梯）escalator
　扶手電梯（電動扶梯）escalator
　搭電梯（乘電梯）take the lift

電眼（監視器）monitor

電椅 electric chair

電筒（手電筒）torch

電費 electricity bill

電船（飛艇／飛船）airship

電掣 ①（電源開關）electrical power supply ②（電閘）electric brake ③（電鈕）button

電單車（摩托車）motorcar

電視 television
　電視機 television; television set
　　等離子電視機 plasma TV
　電視劇 TV drama
　　一套電視劇 a TV drama
　睇電視（看電視）watch television
　開電視 turn on the television
　熄電視（關電視）turn off the television

電報 telegram
　打電報（給一個提示）give a hint

電匯 telegraphic transfer

電腦（計算機）computer
　電腦公司（計算機公司）computer company
　電腦軟件（計算機軟件）computer software
　電腦程式員（計算機程序員）programmer
　一部電腦（一台電腦／一部計算機）a computer
　手提電腦（筆記本電腦）laptop computer
　微型電腦（微型計算機）micro-computer

電話 telephone
　電話冇人聽（沒人接電話）no one answered the phone
　電話卡 calling card
　　IDD 電話卡（國際直撥電話卡）IDD (International Direct Dialling) calling card
　電話充電器（手機充電器）phone charger
　電話好矇（電話聽不清楚）the line is blurred
　電話唔通（電話佔線／線路正忙）the line is busy
　電話留言服務（語音信箱）voice mail box
　電話接線生（電話接線員）telephone operator

電話費 telephone bill
電話斷咗線（電話斷線）the line was disconnected
電話簿 telephone directory
　一本電話簿 a telephone directory
電話壞咗（電話壞了）the telephone is out of order
手提電話（手機）mobile phone
　手提電話差電器（手機充電器）mobile phone charger
　一部手提電話（一部手機）a mobile phone
打個電話 call; make a phone call; make a telephone call
打電話 call; make a phone call; make a telephone call
長途電話 long-distance call
流動電話（移動電話）mobile phone
接聽電話 handle calls; receive calls
傾電話（打電話／講電話）be on the phone; chat on the phone
　同朋友傾電話（和朋友打電話）chat with one's friend on the phone
視像電話（視頻電話）visual mobile phone
講電話（打電話／接電話）be on the phone
聽電話（接電話）answer the phone
　冇人聽電話（沒人接電話）no one answered the phone

電影 movie
　電影明星 movie star
　電影版 movie version
　一套電影（一部電影）a movie
　一齣電影（一場電影）a film; a movie
　睇電影（看電影）see a movie

電線 cable

電髮（燙頭髮／燙髮）give a permanent wave; perm; wave hair

電器 electrical appliances
　電器師傅（電工）electrician
　電器舖（電器店）electrical appliances shop

電燈 electric light
　電燈杉 ①（電線桿）electric pole ②（電話線杆）telegraph pole
　電燈掣（電總開關）electricity main switch
　電燈膽（電燈泡）electric light bulb
　　電燈膽——唔通氣（電燈泡——不通氣）not to stand to sense; tactless person

電壓房（變電站／變電所）substation

電聯（電話聯絡）keep in touch by telephone

電鐘（電鈴）electric bell

一支細電（一節三號電池）an A-size battery
一嚿電（一節電池）a battery
大電（一號電池）D-size battery
中電（二號電池）C-size battery
手機冇電（手機沒電）one's cell phone battery is dead

充電 ① recharge ② recharge the batteries
行雷閃電 (打雷閃電) lightning and thunder
走電 (停電) leakage of electricity
放生電 (向人灌迷湯) flirt
放電 (向人灌迷湯) flirt
致電 call
閃電 ① (閃電) lightning ② (急速) rapidly
停電 (燈火管制) blackout
乾電 (直流電) direct current
細電 (三號電池) A-size battery
筆芯電 (五號電池) AA battery
過電 ① (傳電) conduct electricity ② (被女人的調情所征服) be conquered by the flirt of a woman
慳電 (省電) save electricity
漏電 electrical leakage
嘔電 (吐血) throw up
濕電 (交流電) alternating current

【靴】hoe¹ boots
靴子 boots

水靴 (雨靴) rubber boots for wet weather

【靶】baa² target
靶心 bull's-eye

打靶 ① (沒用的人) useless person ② (槍決 / 槍斃) execute by shooting; shoot to death

【預】jy⁶ ① (估計) estimate ② (保留) reserve
預先 in advance
預早 (提早 / 預先) ahead of schedule; in advance; shift to an earlier time
預告片 trailer
預咗 ① (預計到) calculate in advance; estimate; expect ② (預留) keep; reserve; save
預約 make an appointment
預埋 (算進去) you're included
預料 predict
難以預料 hard to predict
預測 predict
預期 expect
預備 prepare
預繳 (預付) pay in advance

【頑】waan⁴ ① naughty ② stubborn
頑皮 naughty
頑症 (宿疾) chronic disease
頑童 naughty child; urchin

【頓】doen⁶ stop
頓時 (立刻) at once; forthwith; immediately; suddenly
頓號 punctuation mark placed between several proper names

停頓 (暫停 / 中斷) suspend

【飲】jam² (喝) drink
飲大 (喝大了 / 喝醉了) drink and get drunk
　飲到大大地 (喝大了 / 喝醉了) drink and get drunk
飲水 (喝水) drink water
　飲水尾 (喝剩湯) drink the left-over soup
　飲水機 (水機) water dispenser
飲冰 (吃冷飲) have cold drinks
飲杯 (乾杯) cheers
　飲杯嘢 (喝一杯) have a drink
　飲得杯落 (可以開懷暢飲了) drink to one's heart's content
　飲番杯 (喝一杯) cheers
飲品 beverage; drinks
飲食 food and drinks
　飲食男女 men and women interested in eating and drinking
　小心飲食 be careful with what you eat
　包埋飲食 (吃喝兒全包) inclusive of food and drinks
　揀飲擇食 (偏吃 / 挑食) be particular about one's food; choose one's food; fussy about food; fussy eater
　飲飲食食 (吃吃喝喝) eat and drink; wine and dine with sb
　暴飲暴食 eat and drink immoderately
飲倒 ① (很能喝 / 好酒量) have a large capacity for wine ② (可飲用的) drinkable
　飲唔倒 ① (酒量差) have a small capacity for wine ② (不可飲用的) not drinkable
　飲得倒 ① (很能喝 / 好酒量) have a large capacity for wine ② (可飲用的) drinkable
飲茶 ① (喝茶) drink tea ② (吃點心) have dimsum lunch; have tea and refreshments; (transliteration) yum cha
　飲完茶 (喝完茶) after finishing tea
　飲咗門官茶 (大笑不止) always wear a smile on one's face
　飲杯茶 (喝杯茶) have a cup of tea
　飲啖茶 (喝口茶) have a sip of tea
　請飲茶 ① (請喝茶) have a cup of tea, please ② (請人吃點心) treat sb with a dim-sum lunch
飲凍嘢 (喝冷飲) have cold drinks
飲酒 (喝酒) drink alcohol; drink beer; drink wine; have a drink
　好飲酒 (好喝酒) fond of the cup

飲花酒（去夜總會）go night-clubbing

飲悶酒（喝悶酒）drink alone

飲得 ①（很能喝／好酒量）have a large capacity for wine ②（可飲用的）drinkable

　飲得倒 ①（很能喝／好酒量）have a large capacity for wine ②（可飲用的）drinkable

　飲得落（喝得下）drinkable

　飲得嚟（喝得來）drinkable

　好飲得（可以喝很多）can drink a lot

　唔飲得 ①（酒量差）have a small capacity for wine ②（不可飲用的）not drinkable

飲筒（吸管）drinking straw

　一枝飲筒（一根吸管）a drinking straw

飲勝（一飲而盡／乾杯／舉杯暢飲）bottoms up; cheers; drink a toast; drink to; let's drink up; propose a toast; to

　飲勝佢（乾杯）bottoms up; cheers; drink a toast; drink to; let's drink up; to

飲歌（最擅長的歌）one's best song in karaoke

飲飽食醉（吃飽喝足）good meal and many drinks; have had one's fill of food and drink

飲野（喝一杯）have a drink

飲醉（喝醉）drunk; tipsy

　飲醉酒（喝醉）get drunk

飲頭啖湯（拔頭籌／第一個吃螃蟹的人）gain the initial advantage

飲藥（喝藥）drink Chinese medicine

好好飲（好好喝）very tasty

好飲（好喝）tasty

有得飲（有個宴會要去）have a banquet to attend

凍飲（冷飲）cold drinks

熱飲 hot drinks

請飲（宴請／請客）hold a banquet

識飲（會喝）know how to drink smartly

【飯】faan⁶（米飯）cooked rice; rice

飯前 before meal

飯後 after meal

飯桶 ①（飯桶）rice bucket ②（食量大）big eater ③（傻瓜／白痴）fathead; good-for-nothing; idiot

飯盒（午餐盒）lunch box

　一盒飯盒（一個飯盒／一個午餐盒）a lunch box

　食飯盒（吃飯盒／吃午餐）have lunch box

飯堂（食堂）canteen

飯票 rice ticket

　長期飯票（可以長期蹭飯的人／丈夫）husband

飯量 appetite

飯焦（鍋巴）rice crust

飯菜 dishes to go with rice

飯殼（飯勺）rice ladle

飯煲（飯鍋）rice cooker

　電飯煲（電飯鍋）electric rice cooker

飯碗 ①（盛飯的碗）rice bowl ②（工作）job

　打爛飯碗（丟掉工作）lose one's job

　爭飯碗（競爭工作）compete for jobs

　金飯碗（高薪工作）highly-paid job; high-salary job

　保住飯碗（保住工作）keep one's job

　鐵飯碗（穩定的工作）secure job

飯隔（蒸架）steaming rack

飯蓋（鍋蓋）rice-cooker cover

飯餸（飯菜）dishes of food

飯鏟頭（眼鏡蛇）cobra

飯廳 dining room

一個炒飯（一盤炒飯）a plate of fried rice

一兜飯（一盆飯）a plate of cooked rice

一啖飯（一口飯）a mouthful of rice

一殼飯（一勺飯）a ladle of rice

一碗白飯 a bowl of steamed rice

一煲飯（一鍋飯）a pot of rice

一碟炒飯 a dish of fried rice; a plate of fried rice

一餐飯（一頓飯）a meal

一嚿飯 ①（一塊飯）a lump of cooked rice ②（蠢人）stupid person

大茶飯（大案）big deal

大鑊飯 ①（大鍋飯）cooked rice in a big pot ②（大混亂）big mess

乞飯（討飯）beg for food

叉雞飯（叉燒雞飯）rice with barbeque pork and chicken

牛扒飯 rice with beef steak

扒飯 eat one's rice very fast

白飯 plain cooked rice

吔飯（吃飯）eat

米飯 cooked rice

冷飯 left-over cooked rice

豆腐飯 rice with bean curd

咖喱雞飯 curry chicken with rice

炒冷飯 ①（熱左右餘的飯）heat the left-over rice ②（do or say the same old thing; serve a standing dish

炒飯 fried rice

便飯 ordinary meal

咬飯（吃飯）eat

盅頭飯（盅飯／蓋飯）bowl of rice with food on top

食大鑊飯（吃大鍋飯）use resources from the government

食咗飯（吃過飯了）have eaten

食拖鞋飯（小白臉）sponge upon one's girlfriend; sponge upon one's wife

食晚飯（吃晚飯）have dinner

食軟飯（吃軟飯／小白臉）live off women's earnings; sponge upon one's girlfriend; sponge upon one's wife

食粥定食飯（結果是好是壞）the results will be decisive

食飯（吃飯／就餐）have a meal

食葱送飯（合情合理）stand to sense

食緊飯（正吃着）one's having a meal

食霸王飯（吃霸王餐／吃飯不給錢）eat a free meal

家常便飯 ① homely food; ordinary meal ② common occurrence

晏晝飯（午飯）lunch

海南雞飯 Hainan chicken with rice

海鮮炒飯 fried rice with seafood

送飯（下飯）go with rice

夠鐘食飯（到時候吃飯）time to have lunch

帶飯（帶午餐）take lunch

淡飯 simple meal

添飯（再盛一次飯）take another bowl of rice

焗石斑飯 baked rice with garoupa

焗飯 baked rice

荷葉飯 steamed glutinous rice in lotus-leaf wrapping

粗茶淡飯（飲食簡單／生活簡樸）plain tea and simple meal

魚翅撈飯（吃一頓豐盛的飯／打牙祭）have a sumptuous meal

喫飯（吃飯／就餐）eat a meal; have a meal

晚飯 dinner

睇餸食飯（看菜吃飯）live within one's means

煮飯（做飯）cook

煮緊飯（正在做飯）cooking

開飯 serve a meal

裝飯（盛飯）fill up a bowl with rice

煎蛋牛肉飯 rice with beef and fried egg

碟頭飯（蓋飯）plate of rice with food on top

團年飯（年夜飯）New Year Eve's dinner

寧食開眉粥，莫食愁眉飯（寧窮而開心，不富而憂慮）would rather be poor but happy than become rich but anxious

撞板多過食飯（成功少，碰壁多）keep making mistakes

撈飯（和飯／拌飯）mix with rice

揮飯（盛飯）fill a bowl with rice

鳳爪排骨飯 rice with chicken feet and spare ribs

熱氣飯（難題）difficult job

豬扒飯 rice with pork chop

鴛鴦飯 fried rice with white and red sauces

嚓飯（吃飯）have a meal

舊飯（剩飯）left-over cooked rice

雞飯 chicken with rice

餵飯 feed sb with rice

臘味飯（臘肉飯）rice with wind-dried pork

鹹魚肉餅飯 rice with salted fish and meat cake

爛飯（軟飯）thoroughly cooked rice

【馳】tsi⁴ hurry

馳名 ① spread one's fame ② famous; renowned; well-known

為口奔馳（為生活奔忙）work hard to make a living

【馴】seon⁴（馴服）tamed

馴品（柔順／溫順）gentle and yielding

【鼓】gu² bulge

鼓埋泡腮（鼓起腮幫子／耷拉着臉）pull a long face

鼓氣袋（性格內向／言語不多的人）introvert; person of few words

鼓勵 encourage

打退堂鼓 back out one's promise

肚皮打鼓（肚子很餓）as hungry as a hunter; very hungry

個肚打鼓（肚子很餓）very hungry

骨頭打鼓（人死了很久）died a long time ago

密鑼緊鼓（下大力氣）make great efforts; the noose is hanging

搲鼓（繃鼓面／愁眉苦臉）pull a long face

鑼鼓 gongs and drums

【鼠】sy² ① mouse ②（偷）steal

鼠入嚟（溜進來）steal into

鼠年 Year of the Rat

鼠摸（小偷）burglar

鼠嘢（偷東西）steal things

鼠輩 scoundrels

老鼠 mouse

沙灘老鼠（沙灘小偷）thieves on the beach

飛鼠（蝙蝠）bat

捉老鼠 catch a mouse

鬼鬼鼠鼠（鬼鬼祟祟）furtive; sneaky; stealthy

鬼鼠（鬼祟）furtive; sneaky

豚鼠 guinea pig

袋鼠 kangaroo

滑鼠（鼠標）mouse

14 劃

【像】dzoeng⁶ image; photo

像片（相片）photo; photograph

大眾偶像（受歡迎的偶像）popular idol

不可想像 cannot be imagined; inconceivable; unthinkable

佛像 figure of the Buddha; image of the Buddha
偶像 idol
崇拜偶像 worhip idols
視像（視頻）video
想像 imagine
雕像 effigy; monument; statue

【僚】liu⁴ staff
僚屬 officials under sb in authority; staff; subordinates

官僚 bureaucracy
幕僚 aids and staff; assistant to a ranking official or general in old China

【偽】ngai⁶ bogus; fake
偽鈔（偽幣）counterfeit money

虛偽 false; hypocritical; insincere; sham spurious

【僭】tsim³ usurp
僭建 ①（違法建築）illegal structure ②（隆胸）breast augmentation; have a boob job

【僱】gu³ employ
僱主 employer
僱員 employee

自僱（個体經營的）self-employed

【凳】dang³（椅子）chair
凳子 bench; stool

三腳凳 ①（靠不住）unreliable ②（靠不住的人）unreliable person
摺凳（摺椅）folding chair
踎凳（入獄）in jail

【劃】waak⁹ design
劃花（劃壞／刮花）ruin sth by scratching
劃眉（劃眉毛）paint one's eyebrows

十劃 ten strokes
列入計劃 be incorporated in the plan
計劃 plan
策劃 engineer; plan; plot; scheme
擬定計劃 map out a plan

【劏】tsaam⁵（扎了刺）get a thorn
劏嚫手（手上扎了刺）get a thorn in one's hand

【厭】jim³ disgust
厭倦 boredom; lassitude; weary of

百厭（頑皮）mischievous; naughty; playful
神枱貓屎──神憎鬼厭（人人討厭／過街老鼠，人人喊打）accused target; person who is hated by all
神憎鬼厭（人人討厭／過街老鼠，人人喊打）accused target; person who is hated by all
討厭（麻煩／傷腦筋）abhorrent of; adverse to; allergic to; antipathetic to; averse to; bad news; be annoyed with; be annoyed at; be browned-off with; be disgusted at; be disgusted by; be disgusted with; be fed up with; bore; detest; disagreeable; disgusting; dislike; hate; have a dislike for; have a distaste for; have a horror of; have an aversion to; have no time for; have no use for; hold sth in abomination; indisposed; loathe; nasty; nuisance; pain in the neck; repugnant to; sick of; take a dislike to; tired of; trouble; troublesome
貪得無厭 too greedy for gains

【嘅】ge³（的）[possessive]

又係嘅（也對）this is also the same
又會咁嘅（怎麼會這樣）how can this be
冇事嘅（沒事的）it's all right
冇計嘅（沒說的）have nothing to be criticised
冇壞嘅（沒有壞處的）there's no harm in doing sth
你又係嘅（你真是）your're really...
你係得嘅（你真棒）you're really good
你哋嘅（你們的）your
你嘅（你的）your
佢哋嘅（他們的／她們的／它們的）their
佢嘅 ① his ② her ③ its
咁仲得掂嘅（這還得了）how could this be
新嚟嘅（新來的）newcomer
諗落又係嘅（細想一下也對）when you come to think of it, it's right

【嘈】tsou⁴（嘈雜）noisy
嘈生晒（吵吵鬧鬧）make much voice; very noisy; vociferous
嘈交（吵架）have a row; quarrel; wrangle
嘈到拆天（非常吵鬧）extremely noisy
嘈喧巴閉（吵吵嚷嚷／吵鬧／喧鬧）clamour; make a lot of noise; noisy

太嘈（太吵）too noisy
呱呱嘈（呱呱叫）make a lot of noise
咪嘈（不要吵／別吵／別鬧）shut up
唔好嘈（不要吵／別吵／別鬧）shut up

鬼殺咁嘈 (大吵大嚷 / 大聲吵鬧) extremely noisy; very noisy

勞嘈 (發出吵鬧的叫聲) make noisy clamour

發嘮嘈 (發牢騷) beef; beef about; blow off steam; chew the rag; complain; grouch; grouse; grumble; grumble about; grumble at; grumble over; let off steam; make a sour remark; murmur; natter; say devil's paternoster; whine about; work off steam

嘮嘈 (牢騷) complain; grieve; grumble; grumbling

【嘉】gaa¹ praise

嘉年華 (遊藝會) carnival

嘉勉 praise and encourage; urge sb to greater efforts with words of encouragement

　　有則改之，無則嘉勉 correct the mistakes, if any; and keep the good record if no mistakes have been committed; correct mistakes if you have committed them and avoid them if you have not; correct mistakes if you have made any and guard against them if you have not; if there is any error, correct it; if not, then avoid it

嘉賓 honourable guest

嘉獎 cite; commend

【嘔】au² (嘔吐) throw up; vomit

嘔心 (痛心) distressed; grieved; painful

　　嘔心瀝血 take infinite pains

嘔奶 (吐奶 / 漾奶) throw up milk; vomit milk from repletion

嘔吐 vomit

　　引起嘔吐 cause vomiting

嘔血 (吐血) exasperating; exhausted

嘔電 (吐血) throw up

嘔藥 (吐藥) throw up medicine

又屙又嘔 (上吐下瀉) suffer from vomiting and diarrhoea; vomit and have a water stool; vomiting and purging

令人作嘔 make one sick

作嘔 ① about to vomit ② make one feel sick

呢頭食嘔頭嘔 (剛剛吃完就吐了) eat and throw up; one eats and vomits

屙嘔 (吐瀉) vomiting and purging

【嘗】soeng⁴ try

嘗新 taste a new delicacy

嘗試 try

何嘗 no question; not that

【嘜】mak⁷ ① (牌) mark ② (罐) (English) mug

嘜頭 ① (商標) trade mark ② (樣子) look

士嘜 (聰明) (English) smart

牛奶嘜 (牛奶罐兒) milk jar

煙仔嘜 (香煙罐兒) cigarette box

豬嘜 ① (笨人) fool; idiot ② (蠢豬) stupid

豬頭嘜 (蠢豬) idiot

薯嘜 (呆 / 笨) (English: schmuck) stupid

雜嘜 (雜牌) fake brand goods

鐵嘜 (鐵罐) can; tin

【嘢】je⁵ ① (東西) thing ② (事) matter ③ (貨) goods

嘢可以亂食，說話唔可以亂講 (飯可以亂吃，話不能亂講) watch what one says

嘢食 (食物) food

一戚嘢 (一百元) one hundred dollars

一條嘢 (十元) ten dollars

一粒嘢 (一萬元) ten thousand dollars

乜嘢 (甚麼) what; whatever; why

乜嘢物嘢 (等等等等) and so on and so forth

三張嘢 (三十多歲) thirty something

大枝嘢 (傲慢的人) arrogant person

大粒嘢 (重要人物) important person

大嘢 (傲慢) arrogant

大鑊嘢 (大混亂) big mess

五張嘢 (五十多歲) fifty something

及嘢 (窺視) peep

水嘢 (次貨) defective goods; inferior goods; substandard goods

冇乜嘢 (沒事兒 / 沒甚麼) it doesn't matter; it's nothing; never mind; that's all right

冇做嘢 (沒有工作 / 沒工做) not working

冇嘢 (沒事兒 / 沒甚麼) it doesn't matter; it's nothing; never mind; that's all right

四張嘢 (四十多歲) forty something

平嘢 (便宜貨) bargain; cheap stuff; schlock

平嘢冇好嘢 (便宜沒好貨) cheap things are not good things

扑嘢 (性交) have sex with

正嘢 (上等貨 / 正品 / 好東西 / 好貨) genuine stuff; great stuff

立雜嘢 (垃圾食品) junk food

印嘢 (打印東西) print

好買嘢 (愛買東西) like shopping

好嘢 ① (好樣的) great ② (好東西) good stuff; good things

托住啲嘢 (扛些東西) carry sth on the shoulder

老嘢 (老傢伙) battle axe; biddy; buffer; codger; crone; gaffer; goat; old bag; old bat; old dog; old fish; old fogey; old folks; old guys; old geezer; old people; old prune; old-timer; old trout; seniors; wrinkled; wrinkly

你好嘢 (你好棒) you're really great

你要咩嘢 (你要甚麼) what do you want

扰嘢 (扔東西) throw things away

扮晒嘢 (裝模做樣) arrogant; boastful

扮嘢 (假裝) pretend; strike an attitude

來路嘢 (進口貨物／進口商品／舶來品) imported goods

呢手嘢 (這種玩意) this sort of stuff

呢味嘢 (這件事) this thing

呢個係乜嘢 (這是甚麼) what is this

呢單嘢 (這件事) this thing

呢檀嘢 (這件事) this thing

呢籠嘢 (這類東西) this type of thing

垃圾嘢 (垃圾食品) junk food

垃雜嘢 (零食) snack

玩嘢 (鬧事) make trouble

勁嘢 (厲害的東西) things that are excellent

咩嘢 (甚麼) what

流嘢 ① (低等) low-graded ② (劣質品／冒牌貨／假貨／贋品) fake goods; imitation brand goods

為乜嘢 (為甚麼) how is it that; what for; why; why is it that; why oh why

苴嘢 (次貨) poor things

食乜嘢 (吃甚麼) what to eat

食嘢 (吃東西) eat sth

俾人偷嘢 (被人偷東西／東西被盜) things being stolen

唔好講嘢 (不要講話) stop talking

捴嘢 (碰東西／動東西) touch sth

真好嘢 (真棒) it's really great

笋嘢 (好東西) good things

衰嘢 (壞東西／壞分子) inferior goods

假嘢 (冒牌貨／假貨) imitation brand goods

做乜嘢 (為甚麼／怎麼會／怎麼樣／做甚麼的／為甚麼會這樣) how is it that; what for; why; why is it that; why oh why

做嘢 ① (行動) take action ② (幹活兒) work

偷嘢 (偷東西／偷竊) steal things; theft

堅嘢 (真貨／正宗商品／正品) authentic goods; genuine; genuine goods; the real thing; true

笠嘢 (偷／竊取／偷竊) steal

軟嘢 (放着鈔票的紅包) red pocket with a banknote

喫嘢 (吃東西) eat sth

渣嘢 (下品貨) cheap goods; low-graded; low-levelled; of poor quality

筍嘢 ① (便宜貨) real bargain ② (上等貨／好東西／好貨) genuine stuff; great stuff

買嘢 (購物) buy; go shopping; shopping

貴嘢 (高價貨) expensive goods

跌咗嘢 (丟東西) drop sth

嗰隻衰嘢 (那個討厭鬼) that nasty person

嗰隻嘢 (那個人) that person

嗰個嘢 (那個人) that person

嗰啲嘢 ① (鬼) ghosts ② (像那些東西) stuff like that

飲杯嘢 (喝一杯) have a drink

飲凍嘢 (喝冷飲) have cold drinks

飲嘢 (喝一杯) have a drink

搵嘢 (找東西) search for things

搶嘢 (搶劫) loot; plunder; rob

想食啲乜嘢 (想吃些甚麼) what would you like to have

揲嘢 (翻找東西) search things

演嘢 (炫耀／賣弄) parade in the limelight; show off

辣嘢 (辣的東西) spicy food

領嘢 (上當／上套兒) swallow the bait; victim of sth

樣樣嘢 (每樣東西) everything

靚嘢 (好東西) good things

賣嘢 (賣東西) sell things

撻嘢 (偷東西／騙東西) steal things

賴嘢 (掉入陷阱) fall into a trap

擠嘢 (放東西／擱東西／擺東西) lay down things; put down things

撐住啲嘢 (拿着東西) holding things

碌我買嘢 (纏着我買東西) pester me to buy sth for sb

講嘢 (說話) say; speak; talk

鍾意買嘢 (喜歡購物) like shopping

嚇嘢 (碰上麻煩事) be cheated

擱低咗嘢 (落下東西了) leave sth behind

識扮嘢 (會裝無知) know how to feign ignorance

識穿佢槓嘢 (看穿他的詭計) know his tricks

識嘢 (懂事) intelligent

薑嘢 (放東西／擱東西／擺東西) lay down things; put down things

爛鬼嘢 (破玩意) lousy gadget

攪嘢 (製造麻煩) make trouble

曬嘢 (炫耀) show off

讕有嘢 (炫耀／賣弄) cry up one's own fortune; flaunt one's possessions; sing one's own glorious song

do 嘢 (做愛) have sex

【嘞】laa¹ (啦) final particle for polite refusal

又試嚟嘞 (又來這一套了) there you go again

多得你唔少嘞 (多虧了你) it owes much to you

多得你嘞 (多虧了你) thanks to you

好番嘞 (恢復了) have recovered

好話嘞（說的沒錯）that's right
好嘞（好吧）well
死嘞（該死的）damn it
你去埋嘞（你為甚麼不來）why don't you come along
恨咗好耐嘞（盼了很久了）have chased after sth for a long time
唔好嘞（不了）no thank you
唔使嚟嘞（不用來了）no need to come
真係奇嘞（真怪）very strange
真係啱喇（真巧）what a coincidence
真係慘嘞（真夠受的）it's really hard to bear
勞煩你嘛（麻煩你了）if you don't mind; sorry to trouble you
都係唔好嘞（還是不了）I would not do it anyway
搵埋佢嘞（把他也叫上）ask him to join us
弊嘞（幹了）alas; it's awful; oh dear; oh heck
虢礫嘩嘞（雜物）odds and ends

【嘛】maa⁴ final particle for exclamation

之嘛（只要／就這樣）only; that's all
你無事吖嘛（你沒事吧／你還好嗎）are you alright
幾好吖嘛（你好嗎／你怎麼樣／挺好的吧）how are you
棺材舖拜神──想人死啫嘛（棺材店裏咬牙──恨人不死）gritting one's teeth in a coffin shop – laying a curse upon all who are not dying

【嘀】dik⁹ sound of a trumpet

嘀打佬（吹鼓手）trumpeters and drummers

【喱】lei¹ syllable

喱士（花邊）(English) lace

定型啫喱（髮膠）hair gel
咕喱（苦力／搬運工）coolie
咖喱 curry
茄喱（小人物）unimportant person

【嘟】dou¹ pout

嘟嘴（噘嘴）pout one's lips

肥嘟嘟 chubby; fat and round

【圖】tou⁴ map

圖則（圖紙）blueprint; drawing; drawing sheet
圖書館 library

一幅地圖 a map
火警路線圖（消防安全路線）fire safety route
企圖 intention

地圖 map
砌圖（拼圖）jigsaw

【團】tyn⁴ group; reunion

團年（吃年夜飯）New Year Eve's dinner
　團年飯（年夜飯）New Year Eve's dinner
團結 unite
團隊 team
　團隊精神 team spirit

代表團 contingent; delegation; deputation; mission
豬仔團（宰客旅行團）tour group whose members are cheated by its travel agent

【墓】mou⁶ grave

墓地 cemetery
墓碑 gravestone; tombstone

墳墓 tomb

【塵】tsan⁴ ① dust ② （驕傲）boastful

塵埃落定 all is fixed; everything is settled
塵氣（傲慢／擺架子）arrogant; put on airs

灰塵 ① ash; dirt; dust ② spindrift
沙塵 boastful
泥塵（灰塵）ash; dirt; dust
洗塵 welcoming dinner
食塵（落後）be left behind
煙塵（塵土）dust

【境】ging² situation

境況 circumstances; conditions
境界 ① boundary ② realm; state ③ the extent reached

困境 difficult position; morass; plight; predicament; straits
身處逆境 in adversity
佳境 the most enjoyable stages
居住環境 living environment
附近環境 the environment in its vicinity
美化環境 beautify the environment
逆境 adverse circumstances; adversity
移民入境 immigration
環境 ① environment ② situation
離境（出境）leave a country; leave a place

【墅】soey⁵ resort

別墅 villa

【墊】 din³ cushion
墊平 (升級) level up
墊褥 (牀褥 / 褥子) mattress

坐墊 seat cushion
牀墊 (褥子) mattress
椅墊 (坐墊) seat cushion
滑鼠墊 (鼠標墊) mouse pad
餐墊 placemat

【壽】 sau⁶ long-life
壽仔 (不懂人情世故的小孩) fool; idiot
壽司 (Japanese) sushi
壽星 God of Longevity
　壽星女 birthday girl
　壽星公 (老壽星) birthday boy
　　壽星公吊頸——嫌命長 (壽星老兒上吊——活膩了) tempt one's fate
　壽星仔 (小壽星) birthday boy
壽眉 (貢眉) Shou Mei tea
壽頭 (傻子) blockhead; idiot
　壽頭壽腦 (呆頭呆腦 / 傻裏傻氣) muddle-headed
壽瘢 (壽斑) senile plagues

阿福阿壽 (張三李四) any person in the street
延年益壽 extend one's years; lengthen one's life; prolong life; promise longevity
長壽 longevity
益壽 lengthen one's life
祝壽 celebrate sb's birthday; offer birthday congratulations; wish sb a happy birthday
擺大壽 (辦六十大壽宴會) hold a sixtieth birthday banquet

【夢】 mung⁶ dream
夢幻 illusion; reverie
夢見 dream of
　夢見故土 dream of one's hometown
夢想 ① dream of ② vain hope; wishful thinking
　夢想成真 a dream come true; realise one's dream
夢魅以求 long for even in one's dream

托夢 appear in one's dream and make a request
怪夢 strange dream
美夢 fond dream
惡夢 nightmare
發咗個怪夢 (做了一個怪夢) had a strange dream
發惡夢 (做噩夢) have a nightmare; nighmare
發開口夢 (說夢話) ① talk nonsense ② be naively optimistic

發夢 ① (作夢 / 做夢) dream; have a dream ② (做白日夢) day-dreaming
噩夢 nightmare

【夥】 fo² assistant; companion; partner
夥伴 companion; partner

一夥 a company of

【獎】 dzoeng² ① prize ② bonus
獎金 prize money
獎品 prize
獎牌 medal
　囊括所有獎牌 win all the medals
獎學金 scholarship
獎勵 reward

中咗頭獎 (中頭獎) won the first prize
抽獎 lucky draw
誇獎 commend; compliment sb on; praise
過獎 be flattered; I'm flattered
勤工獎 (全勤獎) attendance bonus
嘉獎 cite; commend
頭獎 first prize
獲獎 bring down the persimmon; get an award; prize-winning; receive an award; win an award; win the prize

【嫖】 piu⁴ visit prostitutes
嫖妓 (打炮) patronise a prostitute
嫖客 customer of a prostitute

【嫩】 nyn⁶ tender
嫩口 (稚嫩) someone who lacks experience
嫩芽 delicate shoots
嫩草 delicate grass
嫩黃 light yellow
嫩葉 tender leaves
嫩綠 tender green

稚嫩 ① tender and delicate ② young and tender
鮮嫩 fresh and tender

【嘛】 maa⁴ paternal grandmother
嘛嘛 (奶奶) paternal grandmother

阿嘛 ① (奶奶 / 祖母) paternal grandma; paternal grandmother ② (奶奶 / 祖母) gran; granny; nan; nanna; nanny

【寞】mok⁹ lonely

寂寞 lonesome

【察】tsaat⁸ investigate
察看 look carefully at; observe; watch
察覺 become aware of

交通警察 traffic policeman
叫警察 call the police
冒充警察 pretend to be a policeman
洞察 discern; examine thoroughly; have an insight into; have penetrating insight; see clearly; see through clearly
秘密警察 secret policeman
督察（警官）sergeant
諒察（請某人理解並原諒自己）ask sb to understand and forgive oneself
警察 police
觀察 observe

【寧】ning⁴ would rather
寧可 would rather
寧犯天條，莫犯眾憎（不要冒犯公眾）it is wise not to offend the public
寧死 would rather die
　寧死不屈 would rather die than yield
寧食開眉粥，莫食愁眉飯（寧窮而開心，不富而憂慮）had rather be poor but happy than become rich but anxious
寧欺白鬚公，莫欺鼻涕蟲（莫欺少年窮）a colt may make a good horse
寧靜 calm; serene
寧願 prefer; would rather

【寡】gwaa² widowed
寡母婆（寡婦／孀婦）widow
　寡母婆死仔——冇晒希望（老太太哭大妞兒——沒盼兒）be driven to despair
　寡母婆咁多心（三心兩意）in two minds
寡佬（光棍兒／單身漢／鰥夫）bachelor; middle-aged bachelor

守寡 keep living as a widow; live in widowhood; remain a widow; remain in widowhood

【寥】liu⁴ empty
寥落 sparse

空寥寥（空落落的）spacious and desolate; open and desolate; empty

【實】sat⁹ ① （硬）hard ② （緊）tight ③ （堅固／實在）solid
實牙實齒（板上釘釘）certain
實用 practical
　實用面積 net usable area; usable area
實行 carry out; practice
實係（一定是／肯定是／當然是）certainly; definitely; must be
實食冇黐牙（手到擒來）sure win
實情（其實／實在／實際上）in reality
實淨（堅實／結實）strong; tough
實鼓實鑿（真刀真槍）neither garish nor gaudy
實鄭（結實／硬掙）serviceable
實 Q（保安員）security guard; security personnel

一口咬實（一口咬定）hold firm to one's stance; speak in an assertive tone
不顧事實 disregard facts; fly in the face of the facts; have no regard for the truth; ignore the facts
心都實（悶悶不樂）downhearted
心實（失望）disappointed
冚到實（不要對某事說一句話）not to breathe a word about sth
史實 historical facts
列舉事實 cite facts
名符其實 the name matches the reality
多事實（愛管閒事的女孩）nosy girls
有名無實 in name but not in reality
死口咬實（一口咬定）stand by one's guns; stick to what one says
老實 frank; honest; naive; simple-minded; well-behaved
吼實（密切關注）keep a close watch on
折實（實際價格）actual price; real price
言過其實 boast; bombastic; brag; come it strong; draw the long bow; exaggerate; give a false colour; go it strong; hyperbolise; inflated; make a mountain out of a molehill; overshoot the truth; overstate; overstate the fact; pile on the agony; pull the long bow; strain the truth; stretch a point; stretch the facts; turn geese into swans
事實 fact
其實 in fact; in reality
委實（着實）indeed; really
忠實 faithful; reliable; true
查實（其實／實在／實際上）actually; as a matter of fact; in fact; in reality; in truth; really
面對事實 face up to the facts
面對現實（正視事實）face reality; face up to the fact
孭實（揹着）carry on the back; carry on the shoulders
核實 check; verify

務實 deal with concrete matters relating to work

密實 ① (嚴密) tight ② (嘴緊) tight-mouthed ③ (稠密) dense; thick

現實 reality

睇實 (把關) check on; guarantee

華而不實 arty and crafty; flashy and without substance; have all one's goods in the window; have everything in the window; flashiness without substance; gewgaw; gimcrack; meretricious; pomposity; showy but not substantial

話實 (說定) confirm; make sure that

攬實 (扒住) cling to; hold on to

誠實 honest

確實 confirm

諸多事實 (許多藉口) a lot of excuses

樸實 ① plain; simple ② down-to-earth; guileless; sincere and honest

劏實 (塞緊) stuff firmly

講實 (說好 / 說定 / 說準了) it's settled

隱瞞事實 hide facts

攬實 (摟緊點兒) hold tight

【搴】 hin¹ (掀) lift with the hands; raise

搴開書 (打開書) open the book

【對】 doey³ ① (正確) right ② (對聯) couplet ③ (量詞) measure word for a pair of objects

對上 (上面) above; on the surface of; on top of; over; top; upper surface

對手 competitor

對方 counterpart; opposite side

對牛彈琴 sing to a mule; speak to the wrong audience

對沖 hedging

對面 on the other side; opposite; opposite side

對唔住 (對不起) excuse me; I'm sorry; pardon me; sorry
　　對你唔住 (對不起你) I beg your pardon
　　對得住 (對得起) worthy of

對胸衫 (對襟衣) Chinese-style jacket with buttons down the front

對開 (對面) on the other side

對落 (下面) below; under

對話 conversation; dialogue

對歲 (周歲) one full year of life

對路 (對頭) correct; on the right track

對撼 (對打) fight with

對辦 (對頭) correct; on the right track

對襟衫 (對襟衣) Chinese-style jacket with buttons down the front

對鐘 (對時間 / 對錶) synchronise a watch

一個對 (二十四小時) twenty-four hours

一對 a pair; pair

反對 argue against; be against; be opposed to; buck against; combat; come out against; conspire against; cry against; cry out against; declare against; deery; demonstrate against; demur at; fight; fight against; go against; have an objection to; have an opposition to; in opposition to; make an objection to; object to; objection; oppose; protest against; react against; set against; set one's face against; set oneself against; show opposition to; side against; speak against; stand against; take opposition to; vote against

比對 balance; comparison; contrast

生日派對 birthday party

作對 ① act against; choose to be sb's rival; oppose; set oneself against ② match with another in marriage

投票反對 vote against

門當戶對 let beggars match with beggars

派對 (晚會 / 聚會) party

面對 confront; face

核對 check; collate; verify

登對 (配合 / 般配) well-matched

敵對 antagonistic; hostile; oppose

【幕】 mok⁹ screen

幕後 backstage; behind the scenes
　　幕後主腦 (幕後主使) master-mind
　　幕後黑手 person who controls everything from behind the scenes

幕僚 aids and staff; assistant to a ranking official or general in old China

內幕 inside story

字幕 caption; subtitle; title

序幕 curtain raiser; prelude; prologue

泄漏內幕 give the show away

帳幕 (帳篷) tent

閉幕 closing

開幕 opening

螢幕 (屏幕) screen

營幕 (營帳) tent sheet

謝幕 acknowledge the applause; answer a curtain call; curtain call; respond to a curtain call

簾幕 curtain

【幗】 gwok⁸ woman

巾幗 ① ancient woman's headdress ② woman

【慈】tsi⁴ kind
慈父 loving father; father
慈母 loving mother
慈祥 (和睦友善) amicable; kind
慈悲 (仁慈／憐憫) benevolent; mercy
慈善 charity
慈愛 affection; gentle; gentleness; kindness; love

仁慈 kind; merciful

【態】taai³ state
態度 attitude
　　態度冷淡 cold in manner
　　態度積極 positive attitude
態勢 ① situation; state ② posture

心態 (心理) mentality
世態 ways of the world
事態 situation; state of affairs
狀態 condition; situation; state; state of affairs; status
媚態 (撒嬌／賣弄風情) coquetry; subservience
變態 perverted

【慘】tsaam² miserable; tragic
慘情 (可憐／淒涼) pitiful

累得我好慘 (害得我真苦) cause deep injury to me

【慢】maan⁶ slow
慢工出細貨 (慢工出細活) if one works slowly, one would produce quality goods; slow work yields fine products; soft fire makes sweet malt
慢手 (慢) slow
慢吓手 (弄不好) if things are messed up
慢吞吞 (慢騰騰) very slow
慢條斯理 (悠閒／從容不迫／不慌不忙) leisurely; slowly; unhurriedly
慢慢 ① (慢慢地) slowly ② (不要急) take it easy ③ (慢慢來) take your time
　　慢慢行 ① (慢走) goodbye ② (慢慢走) walk slowly
　　慢慢都唔遲 (慢慢來) take your time

且慢 hold it; wait a minute
傲慢 haughty and overbearing; impudent

【慣】gwaan³ (習慣) be accustomed to
慣咗 (習慣了) be accustomed to
慣喇 (習慣了) be used to
　　我慣嘿喇 (我已經習慣了) I'm used to it

慣熟 (熟悉) familiar

習慣 habit
睇唔慣 (看不慣) cannot bear the sight of

【慨】koi³ generous
慨歎 lament with sighs

丈夫氣慨 (丈夫氣概) manliness
慷慨 generous

【慷】hong² generous
慷慨 generous

【慳】haan¹ ① (節省) save ② (節儉) thrifty
慳力 (省力) save efforts
慳水 (省水) save water
　　慳水慳力 (以次充好) shoddy
　　慳水又慳力 (以次充好) shoddy
慳皮 (省本錢) save money
慳的啦 (胡謅) cut the crap
慳家 (節儉) thrifty
慳得過就慳 (能省就省) be frugal as far as possible
慳番 (省回／省掉) save
　　慳番啖氣 (不值得浪費唇舌) save one's breath
慳電 (省電) save electricity
　　慳電膽 (省電燈炮／節能燈泡) energy-saving light bulb; energy-saver light bulb
慳落 (省下) save money
慳慳哋 (省一點兒／節儉) be economical
慳儉 (節儉) thrifty
　　知慳識儉 ① (省吃儉用) eat sparingly and spend frugally; economical in everyday spending; go slow with; live frugally; pinch and scrape; practice austerity; save money on food and expenses; scrape and screw; skimp and save; stint oneself ② (精打細算) careful calculation and strict budgeting
慳錢 (省錢) save money

【截】dzit⁹ cut
截止 close; end
截然 completely; entirely; sharply
截稿 deadline for the submission of a manuscript
截擊 ① intercept ② interception

二叔公割禾——望下截 (往回看) look back on

【摑】gwaak⁸ slap

摑佢一巴（摑他一巴掌）give sb a slap

抵摑（該摑）deserve being slapped on the face

【摟】lau¹ ①（披／蓋）put on ②（找）find

摟人玩（約別人玩）ask sb to play

摟打（討打）want to engage in a fight

摟住（披着／蓋着）cover; put on

　　摟住個頭（披在頭上）drape sth over one's head

摟蓆（成為乞丐）become a beggar

摟錯人皮（披錯人皮／像野獸一樣）behave oneself like a beast

不摟（總是）all along; always; at all times; consistently; for alwalys

【摔】soet⁷ throw to the ground

摔角（摔跤）wrestling

【摳】kau¹（混）mix

摳埋咗（混在一起了）mix together

摳啲水添（多加點水／再兌點水）add more water

【摺】dzip³（疊）fold

摺咗（結業了）closed

摺枱（摺桌）folding table

摺衫（摺疊衣服）fold clothes

摺被（疊被子）fold up a quilt

摺凳（摺椅）folding chair

存摺 bankbook; passbook

【摸】mo² grope

摸底（摸清底細）know the real situation; sound sb out

摸盲雞（騎瞎馬）do sth aimlessly

摸門釘（訪友不遇／撞鎖了）go to visit sb but not find him/her at home; miss the doorpost

摸索 feel about; try to find out

摸黑 grope one's way on a dark night

盲摸摸（盲目地／瞎摸合眼地）blindly

偷偷摸摸（悄悄地行動）act stealthily

密密摸（閒不住／總是保持忙碌／拒絕閒着）always keep oneself busy; refuse to stay idle

捉摸 pin down

鼠摸（小偷）burglar

難以捉摸 hard to pin down

觸摸 touch

【摽】biu¹ throw out

摽汗（冒汗）sweat

【摻】tsaam¹（攪）mingle; mix

摻埋佢玩（讓他來一塊玩）let sb play with us

摻啲水（攪點兒水）mix with some water

【捷】lin²（掐）pinch

捷住條頸（掐着脖子）have sb by the throat

捷車（賽車）car racing; motor racing

【摱】maan¹（攀）cling to; hold

摱上去（攀上去）climb up

摱住（扳住）pull

摱返（挽回）redeem; retrieve

摱實（扒住）cling to; hold on to

冇得摱（無法挽回）past remedy

【搟】hang¹（敲）beat

搟爛（敲壞）ruin by beating

【撨】tsiu⁶（掏）search

撨身（搜身）body search; conduct a body search; make a body search; search a person

撨袋（掏口袋）draw out from one's pocket

撨野（翻找東西）search things

【撪】pang¹（轟）drive away

撪佢扯（把他轟走）drive sb away

【敲】haau¹ beat

敲竹杠 blackmail; extort

敲鼓邊（敲邊鼓／從旁幫腔）sound sb out on a question

【旗】kei⁴ flag

旗袍 cheongsam

旗鼓相當 equally matched

一支旗（一面旗）a flag

冚國旗（為國捐軀）die

冚旗 ①（死）die ②（的士休班）(taxi) out of service

扯旗（昇旗）hoist a flag

祭旗（承擔過錯／承擔責任）take the blame

揸大旗（主管）be in charge

揸旗（主管）be in charge

落旗（起錶）flag fall

擔大旗（扛大旗）person in charge

【暢】tsoeng³ (English) change
暢錢（找零）(English) change

流暢 fluent; smooth
舒暢 ① comfortable; free from worry; happy; pleasant
　　② leisurely and harmonious

【榔】long⁴ betel nut
榔頭 hammer

檳榔 areca nut; betel nut

【榨】dzaa³ squeeze
榨汁機 juice extractor

【榜】bong² list of successful candidates
榜樣 example; model

老番睇榜（倒數第一）the first from the bottom

【榴】lau⁴ pomegranate
榴蓮 durian

石榴 pomegranate
蕃石榴 / 番石榴（芭樂）guava

【榮】wing⁴ glorious
榮幸 be honoured; have the honour of
榮耀 glory; honour; splendour

虛榮 empty glory; vain glory; vanity
繁榮 prosperous

【槌】tsoey⁴ wooden hammer
槌球（門球）croquet

倔擂槌（鈍的）blunt
頭槌（頭球）header
靈神不用多致燭，好鼓不用多槌（響鼓不用重錘敲）a word
　　is enough to the wise

【槍】tsoeng¹ gun
槍手 ①（代寫）ghost-writer ②（射擊手）one who does
　　homework, sit examinations, or write essays for someone
　　else
　　做槍手（幫人代寫）ask sb to do sth for a person
槍頭（槍）gun
　　調轉槍頭（反戈一擊）turn around to criticise fellow
　　members

刀槍 sword and spear; weapons
手槍 handgun; pistol
回馬槍 back thrust
明刀明槍 before sb's very eyes; do sth openly
耍花槍（耍虛招）exchange banter; have a quarrel for fun
風槍（氣槍）air gun; air rifle
真刀真槍 in real earnest; real swords and spears – the real
　　thing; with swords out of sheaths
起步槍（發令槍 / 發號槍）starting gun
鬼槍（洋槍）rifle
替槍（槍替 / 代考 / 槍手）sit for an examination in place of
　　another person
舞槍（耍槍）play with a spear
請槍 ①（請人槍替）ghost-write ②（找人代考）ask sb to sit
　　for an examination in place of another person
機關槍 ① machine gun ② fire words at sb like a machine
　　gun
燒槍（打槍）fire with a pistol

【槓】gung³ trunk
槓桿比率 leverage

未食五月糭，寒衣不入槓（未吃端午糭，寒衣不可送）don't
　　put one's winter clothes into the chest before the fifth
　　month of the year
依牙鬆槓（做出騷擾的行為）clench one's teeth
郁郁槓（來回動）move back and forth
開正佢個槓（正對他的勁）it's his forte
樟木槓（樟木箱）camphorwood trunk

【榾】gwat⁷ pieces of wood
榾柮（木柴塊）chopped pieces of wood

硬榾榾（非常硬）very hard

【樑】loeng⁴ beam
樑上君子（小偷）thief

屋樑（房樑 / 房檁）house beam
架樑（中間人）mediate in a dispute
做架樑（做中間人）mediate in a dispute
橋樑 bridge

【歉】hip⁸ apology
歉意 apologies; regrets

抱歉 feel apologetic; feel sorry; regret
非常抱歉 feel very apologetic
道歉 apologise

【歌】go¹ song

歌手 singer
　　流行歌手 pop singer

歌仔（小曲／歌兒）song

歌曲 song
　　流行歌曲 popular songs

歌星 singer

歌書（歌本／音樂書）songbook

歌紙（歌譜）music score of a song

歌喉（歌聲）one's voice

歌劇 opera

歌聲 singing
　　歌聲美妙 the singing is wonderful

歌廳 lounge

九因歌（九九乘法表）multiplication table rhyme

民歌 folk song

弦歌 ① sing with stringed accompaniment ② schooling

牧歌 pastoral song

冧歌（情歌）romantic songs

秧歌 songs sung when transplanting rice seedlings

唱民歌 sing folk songs

唱隻歌（唱首歌）sing a song

唱聖誕歌 sing Christmas carols

唱歌 ①（唱歌）sing songs ②（唱）sing; singing

飲歌（最擅長的歌）one's best song in karaoke

聖誕歌 Christmas carol

詩歌 poems and songs; poetry

靚歌（好歌）good song

聽歌 listen to songs

【滯】dzai⁶（消化不良）indigestion

滯口 ①（胃口不好）poor appetite ②（不順利）not smooth

目光呆滯 have fishy eyes; have glassy eyes

有啲阻滯（不太順暢）not smooth

呆滯 ① dull; inert; lifeless ② idle; slack; sluggish; stagnant

表情呆滯 have a dull expression on one's face

阻滯 ①（不順暢／阻礙）hindrance ②（麻煩）trouble

唔怕米貴，至怕運滯（不怕白米貴，只怕運氣壞）not afraid of the price of rice going up, but afraid of being unlucky

消滯（消食）relieve stagnation

得滯（過度）excessively; much; over; too

貴得滯（太貴）too expensive

開胃消滯（消食開胃）whet the appetite and ease indigestion

運滯（倒運／走背運／運氣壞）hard luck

銷路呆滯（銷售緩慢）slow in sale

濕滯 ①（麻煩／撓頭／纏手）difficult to deal with; difficult

to tackle; headache; meet with a hitch; messed-up ②（濕熱）hot and damp; warm and humid

翳翳滯滯（食慾不振）have a poor appetite; one's appetite is poor

【滲】sam³ long-winded

滲水 water leakage; water seepage

滲氣（絮叨／囉嗦）long-winded; wordy

【滴】dik⁹ drop

滴下 drip

滴水（鬢角）hair on the temples

滴酒 a drop of wine

垂涎欲滴 keep a covetous eye on; make sb's mouth water

軟滴滴（軟乎乎的）soft

【滾】gwan² ①（沸騰）boil ②（鬼混）fool about; fool around; lead an aimless or irregular existence; play about; potter about; run around ③（欺騙）cheat; deceive

滾人（曦人家）swindle others

滾下（滾一滾）boil for a minute

滾友 ①（訪問妓女的人）one who visits prostitutes ②（冒名頂替者）imposter; swindler ③（不負責任的人）irresponsible person ④（說謊的人）liar

滾水 ①（開水）boiling water ②（沸過的水）boiled water ③（熱水）hot water
　　滾水淥腳（火燒火燎地）go quickly; hurry off
　　滾水淥豬腸——兩頭縮（罈子裏養王八——越養越抽抽）become less; lose out on both sides
　　一壺滾水（一壺開水）a pot of boiling water; a pot of hot water
　　白滾水（白開水）plain boiled water
　　沖滾水（倒開水）pour boiled water
　　凍滾水（涼開水／涼白開）cold boiled water
　　飲滾水（喝開水）drink boiled water

滾紅滾綠 ①（淫蕩好色）lecherous ②（胡說八道）speak nonsense; talk nonsense

滾蛋（滾開）piss off

滾湯（煮湯／煲湯）make a soup

滾熱辣 ①（滾燙／熱騰騰的）boiling hot; piping hot; steaming hot ②（最新新聞）latest news

滾瀉（沸到溢出來）spilling of boiling water
　　滾瀉咗（沸到溢出來了）spilt boiling water

滾攪 ①（打擾）disturb ②（打擾了）sorry to trouble you
　　滾攪晒 ①（打擾）disturb ②（打擾了）sorry to trouble you

一味靠滾（一味靠作弊）always rely on cheating
火滾（生氣 / 發火 / 氣憤 / 惱火）angry; indignant
沙沙滾（欺騙和詐騙某人）deceive and swindle sb
煲滾（煮沸）bring to the boil
煙塵滾滾（塵土飛揚）clouds of dust flying up; dust rises high in the air

【滿】mun⁵ full

滿天神佛 things are in a mess
滿月 a baby's completion of its first month of life
　擺滿月酒（辦滿月酒）banquet to celebrate a baby's first month birthday
滿肚密圈（滿腹計謀）full of schemes
滿座 all seats are taken; full house; fully booked
　全院滿座 full house
滿意 satisfied
　令人滿意 be entirely satisfactory
滿瀉（滿溢）overflow

生活美滿 lead a happy life
身材豐滿 fleshy
美滿 happy; perfectly satisfactory
盆滿缽滿 make a lot of money
家庭美滿 have a happy family
婚姻美滿 enjoy conjugal happiness
裝滿 fill up
盤滿缽滿（盆滿缽滿 / 大冚滿小冚流）full to the brim
豐滿 ① plentiful ② full and round; full-grown; well-developed; well-endowed; well-equipped; well-heeled; well-loaded; well-stacked
爆滿（滿座）full house

【漁】jy⁴ fishery

漁夫 fisher; fisherman
漁民 fisherman
漁舟 fishing boat
漁港 fishing port
漁業 fishery; fishery industry; fishing industry

【漆】tsat⁷ paint

漆油（油漆）paint

油漆 oil paint

【漏】lau⁶ stammer

漏口（口吃 / 結巴 / 結結巴巴）stammer; stutter
　漏口佬（口吃 / 結巴）stammerer; stutterer

【漏】lau⁶ leak

漏口風（透露口風）blurt out a secret; let slip a secret
漏水 water leakage
漏低咗（遺漏了）left behind
漏咗（遺漏了）miss
漏底（露餡兒）let the cat out of the bag
漏夜（連夜）that very night; the same night
漏洞 ① hole; leak ② flaw; loophole
　堵塞漏洞 block up a hole; plug up a leak; shut up a leak; stop a leak
漏氣 ①（氣體泄露）gas leakage ②（拖拉）slow in doing things; slow to act
漏填 fail to fill in; forget to fill in
漏電 electrical leakage
漏寫 fail to write; forget to write
漏罅（漏縫兒）loophole; miss out

天網恢恢，疏而不漏 justice has long arms
洩漏 leak out
缺漏 gaps and omissions
執漏（堵漏 / 檢漏 / 補漏）repair the leaky part of the roof
密底算盤——冇罅漏（鐵公雞——一毛不拔 / 作為吝嗇鬼的意思 / 拒絕貢獻一分錢）as close as a clam; as mean as a miser; as tight as a drum; close-fisted; not give a cent; not lift a finger; not stir a finger; not turn a finger; refuse to contribute a single cent; stingy; too stingy to pull out a hair; unwilling to give up even a hair; unwilling to sacrifice even a single hair; penny pincher

【漚】au³（浸泡）soak

漚爛（泡爛）soak sth until softened

【演】jin² perform

演員 actor
　女演員 actress
　男演員 actor
演唱 sing in a performance
　演唱會 singing concert
演野（炫耀 / 賣弄）parade in the limelight; show off
演講 speech; talk

扮演 act; act sb; act the part of sb; be dressed up to represent sb; carry off one's role of sb; dress up as sb; interpret the role of sb; in the character of sb; make oneself up as sb; play sb; play the role of sb; take on the role of sb
真人表演 live show
時裝表演（時裝秀）fashion show
導演 movie director

【漠】mok⁹ indifferent

漠視 ignore; overlook

漠然 apathetically; indifferently; with unconcern

漠漠 ① (有霧) foggy; misty ② (浩瀚而孤獨) vast and lonely

【漢】hon³ man

漢字 Chinese character

漢奸 traitor

漢語 Chinese; Chinese language

漢堡包 hamburger

男子漢 tough man

門外漢 layman

流浪漢 stroller; tramp; wanderer; vagrant

【漫】maan⁶ overflowing

漫步 ramble; roam; stroll

漫畫 comic

漫遊 roam; wander

漫漫 very long

　漫漫長夜 endless night

浪漫 romantic

瀾漫 (滿溢) overflowing

【漬】dzik⁷ stains

漬染 (染) dye

水漬 water stain

生漬 (產生污漬) generate stains

【漱】sau³ rinse

漱口水 mouthwash

【漲】dzoeng² rise

漲風 (漲價) upward trend of commodity prices

漲幅 (增長率) rate of increase

漲價 raise prices

漲潮 flood tide

吹佢唔漲 (不能激怒他) cannot provoke him into anger

吹唔漲 (不能激怒) cannot be provoked into anger

吹漲 ① (感到被冒犯) beside oneself with rage; feel offended ② (別無選擇) have no alternative; have no choice; have no way out

畀佢吹漲 (被他激怒) be provoked by him

【漾】joeng⁶ ripple

漾波 (漣漪) ripples

盪漾 be tossed about gently; ripple

【漸】dzim⁶ gradual

漸漸 gradually

【澎】biu¹ ① (冒) sweat ② (躥) go up suddenly

澎出去 (躥了出去) go up and dash out suddenly

澎汗 (冒汗) sweat

【熊】hung⁴ bear

熊人 (狗熊) black bear

熊貓 ① panda ② eyes with shadows

　熊貓眼 (黑眼圈) eyes with shadows

樹熊 (考拉 / 樹袋熊) koala

【熄】sik⁷ turn off

熄燈 (滅燈 / 關燈) put out the light; turn off the light

【煽】sin³ stir up

煽風點火 stir up troubles; whip up waves

【爾】ji⁵ that

爾爾 (普通) so so

出爾反爾 go back on one's words

【獄】juk⁹ prison

獄犯 (牢犯 / 囚犯) convict

一間監獄 a prison

地獄 hell

劫獄 break into a prison to rescue a prisoner

牢獄 jail; prison

監獄 prison

繫獄 (入獄) be imprisoned; imprison

【瑣】so² petty

瑣事 trivial matters

瑣碎 trifling

猥瑣 vulgar

【瑰】gwai³ jasper
瑰寶 gem; treasure

一打玫瑰 a dozen roses
玫瑰 rose

【疑】ji⁴ suspect
疑犯 suspect
疑寶 cause of suspicion

令人懷疑 arouse suspicion
半信半疑 be not quite convinced
狐疑 doubt; suspicion
思疑 (懷疑 / 疑慮) suspect
猶疑 hesitate
懷疑 suspect

【瘓】wun⁶ paralysis

癱瘓 paralyze

【盡】dzoen⁶ exhaust
盡力而為 do one's best; make one's utmost efforts
　我盡力而為 I'll do my best
盡地一煲 (破釜沉舟 / 孤注一擲) risk everything on one bet
盡快 as soon as possible
盡責 (盡職 / 負責任) dutiful; responsible

一言難盡 it's a long story
一網打盡 make a clean sweep
山窮水盡 at the end of one's rope
用盡 run out; use up
受用不盡 benefit from sth all one's life; enjoy a benefit forever
知無不言，言無不盡 say all what one knows
威到盡 (威風透了) overwhelm sb with one's authority
耗盡 burn up; consume; deplete; exhaust; impoverish; use up
博到盡 (竭盡全力 / 不遺餘力) do one's utmost
筋疲力盡 be totally exhausted
論鬼盡 (麻煩) troublesome
論論盡盡 (非常麻煩) very clumsy
論盡 ① (累贅) clumsy ② (麻煩) troublesome

【監】gaam¹ ① (牢) prison ② (坐監) go into prison ③ (強逼) force
監人賴厚 (硬要別人喜歡自己) shamelessly take oneself for sb's intimate
監生 (活生生) alive
　監生打死 (活活打死) be beaten to death alive
　監生壅 (活埋) bury alive

監犯 (囚犯 / 犯人) prisoner
監住佢食 (逼著他吃) force him to eat
監房 (監獄 / 牢房) prison cell
監倉 (牢房 / 監牢) prison cell
監粗嚟 (胡來 / 硬幹 / 硬撐着幹) mess things up; run wild
監硬 (勉強 / 硬來) by force
　監硬搋我去 (硬把我拽去) drag me in by force
　監硬嚟 (硬來 / 蠻幹) do sth forcibly
監獄 prison
　一間監獄 a prison
監躉 (囚犯) prisoner

放監 (出獄) be discharged from prison; be released from prison
舍監 (宿管) house master; warden
踎監 (入獄) in prison

【瞇】mei¹ (合上眼 / 合上口) close
瞇埋個嘴 (把嘴合上) shut up

【罰】fat⁹ fine; penalise; punish
罰企 (罰站) to be made to stand still as a punishment
罰飛 (罰票) penalty fare
罰錢 fine; to be fined

刑罰 criminal penalty; penalty; punishment
判罰 (判決處罰) penalise
懲罰 punish
體罰 corporal punishment

【署】tsy⁵ station
署長 administrator
署理 act as deputy; acting

部署 ① (安排 / 佈局) arrange; lay out; map out ② (部署 / 處理) deploy; dispose
警署 (公安局 / 派出所 / 警察局) police station

【碳】taan³ carbon
碳紙 (複寫紙) carbon paper
碳粉盒 (硒鼓) toner cartridge

【碟】dip⁹⁻² ① (盤子) saucer ② (碟子) dish; plate ③ (光碟) compact disk
碟仔 (小盤子 / 碟子) saucer
碟頭飯 (蓋飯) plate of rice with food on top

一個碟 ① (一個碟子) a plate ② (一個茶碟) a saucer
一隻唱碟 (一張唱片) a record; a disc; a disk
大碟 ① (大盤子) large saucer ② (大專輯) large album

打碟 (播放磁盤) play disks

光碟 (光盤) light disk

有碗話碗，有碟話碟 (直言不諱) call a spade a spade

成碟 (全菜) whole dish

炒埋一碟 (混在一起 / 大雜燴) put everything into one
　　package

茶杯碟 (茶托 / 茶盤) saucer

唱碟 (唱片 / 唱盤) record; disk

豉油碟 (醬油碟) saucer

細碟 ① (小盤子 / 小碟) saucer ② (小唱片) small album

睇碟 (看影碟) watch a video disk

煲碟 (長時間看影碟) watch video disks for a long time

影碟 video disk

磁碟 (磁盤) disk

鐳射碟 (激光視盤) laser disk

【禍】 wo⁶ calamity

禍不單行 an evil chance seldom comes alone; an Iliad of
　　woes; bad events rarely come singly; disasters do not come
　　alone; disasters pile up on one another; it never rains but
　　it pours; misery loves company; misfortunes never come
　　singly; one misfortune calls upon another; one misfortune
　　comes on the neck of another; one woe doth tread upon
　　another's heels; when it rains, it pours; when sorrows
　　come, they come not single spies, but in battalions

禍從天降 a calamity descends from the sky; an
　　unexpected affliction; disaster comes from the sky;
　　misfortune drops from heaven, and falls on sb

禍害 canker; curse; disaster; scourge

禍患 (災害) calamity; disaster
　　禍患無窮 constant cause of trouble; incessant calamities;
　　　　with consequences of maximum seriousness

禍福 disaster and happiness; fortunes and misfortunes
　　因禍得福 a blessing in disguise; a fault on the right side;
　　　　an affliction works out a blessing; derive gain from
　　　　misfortune; get good out of misfortune; good comes out
　　　　of evil; profit by misfortune; profit from a misfortune

扠禍 (毀壞) ruin

災禍 calamities; catastrophes; disasters

幸災樂禍 chuckle at sb's discomfiture; crow over; delight in
　　the misfortunes of others; derive pleasure from others'
　　misfortune; exult at the misfortune of others; exult in
　　the misfortune of others; exult over the misfortune of
　　others; exult when another meets with mischance; glad
　　when other people are in difficulties; gloat over others'
　　misfortune; laugh at others' troubles; make game of
　　others' calamities; make merry over another's mishap;
　　mock at others' woes; rejoice in the misfortunes of

others; Roman holiday; take pleasure in the calamity of
　　others; take pleasure from the misfortune of others

怖禍 (害怕 / 擔心) afraid; dread; scared

福禍 fortune and calamity

橫禍 unexpected calamity

【福】 fuk⁷ good fortune

福利 benefit; welfare

福禍 fortune and calamity

福頭 (笨蛋 / 蠢人) fool; sucker

大難不死，必有後福 one's escape from death will certainly
　　bring one good fortune

牛耕田馬食穀——父賺錢仔享福 (老子打洞——兒子受用)
　　the father earns, the son spends

因禍得福 a blessing in disguise; a fault on the right side;
　　an affliction works out a blessing; derive gain from
　　misfortune; get good out of misfortune; good comes out
　　of evil; profit by misfortune; profit from a misfortune

老來福 (晚年幸福) live in happiness in one's old age

作威作福 abuse one's power tyrannically; act like a tyrant;
　　assume great airs; bossy; domineer over; lord it over; play
　　the bully; play the tyrant; ride roughshod over others; sit
　　on the back of; throw one's weight about; throw one's
　　weight around; tyrannically abuse one's power

身在福中不知福 disregard the happy life one enjoys

享福 enjoy a happy life; have a blessing; live in ease and
　　comfort

幸福 fortune

阿福 (笨蛋 / 蠢人) fool; sucker

食得是福 (能吃是福) being able to eat a lot is a blessing

食福 (口福) gourmet's luck; luck in having nice food; the
　　luck to have sth nice to eat

祝福 benediction; blessing; wish happiness to

焉知非福 how could you know that it is not a blessing

發福 (發胖) become plump; burst one's buttons; gain flesh;
　　get fat; grow stout; put on weight; round out

傻人有傻福 the foolish are often lucky

辣撻人有辣撻福 (傻人有傻福) happiness often comes to
　　mediocre persons

禍福 disaster and happiness; fortunes and misfortunes

賜福 blessing

艷福 good fortune in love affairs

【種】 dzung² ① seed ② mate ③ species

種子 seed
　　一粒種子 a seed

種族 race
　　種族仇恨 race hatred

種種 a variety of; all kinds of; all sorts of

小家種（吝嗇的人）miserly person
打種（配種）breed
孤寒種（吝嗇鬼）miser; miserly person; stingy person
食穀種（吃老本）live on one's fat
純種 pure breed
搲穀種（吃老本 / 以過去的收益為生）live off one's past gains; live on one's own fat; rest on one's laurels; rest on past achievements
陳村種（揮金如土）a fop with money to burn a hole in his/her pocket
混種（雜交）crossbreed
雪種（製冷劑 / 冷卻劑）refrigerant
菌種 type culture
賤種（賤人）person of bad character
孽種 son of a concubine

【種】dzung³ plant

種花 cultivate flowers
種菜 grow vegetables
種樹 plant trees

栽種 grow; plant
耕種 cultivate

【稱】tsing¹ declare

稱王 declare oneself king
稱呼 ① address; call ② form of address
稱霸 dominate; seek hegemony
稱讚 acclaim; commend; compliment; pat sb on the back; praise; slap sb on the back

俗稱 ① secular name of a monk ② commonly called; commonly known as; common name
聲稱 declare; proclaim

【窩】wo¹ cave

窩心（暖心）warm-hearted
窩釘（鉚釘）rivet
窩輪（保證）(English) warrant
窩藏 harbour; shelter

安樂窩 home sweet home
蛇鼠一窩（朋比為奸 / 狼狽為奸）a bad group of people; act in collusion with; collude in doing evil; conspire for illegal ends; gang up for evil purposes; gang up with each other; join in plotting reason; play booty; work hand in glove with sb for evil doings

【竭】kit⁸ rest

竭竭腳（歇歇腳）take a rest

【端】dyn¹ end

端午節 Dragon Boat Festival
端正 ① regular; upright ② correct; proper ③ correct; rectify; straighten
端莊（嫻靜 / 矜持 / 凝重 / 穩重）decorum; demure; dignified; sedate
端端度度（有不好的企圖）have evil intention

尖端 ① acme; external centre; peak; tip ② apex; frontier; leading edge; the most advanced; the sophisticated
無端端（無端 / 平白無故 / 無緣無故）for no reason
極端 extreme

【箍】ku¹ hoop

箍臣（沙發墊）(English) cushion
箍煲（言歸於好）repair a broken relationship
箍頸（勒脖子）seize sb by the throat

橡筋箍（橡皮筋）elastic band; rubber band

【算】syn³ calculate

算死草（鐵公雞）miserly person; pinch and scrape
算命 fortune-telling
　算命師傅（算命先生）fortune-teller
算係（算是）consider as
　算係咁啦（一般般 / 如此）so so
算帳（結算 / 結算賬戶）settle accounts
算啦（算了吧 / 沒關係）forget it; never mind; take it easy
算數 ① （計算）count in ② （算了）forget it; never mind
　算數啦（算了吧 / 沒關係）foreget it; never mind
算盤 abacus
　小算盤 selfish calculations
　打如意算盤 work out a plan advantageous to oneself
　打錯算盤 make a wrong decision
　密底算盤——冇罅漏（鐵公雞——一毛不拔 / 作為吝嗇鬼的意思 / 拒絕貢獻一分錢）as close as a clam; as mean as a miser; as tight as a drum; close-fisted; not give a cent; not lift a finger; not stir a finger; not turn a finger; refuse to contribute a single cent; stingy; too stingy to pull out a hair; unwilling to give up even a hair; unwilling to sacrifice even a single hair; penny pincher

人算不如天算 circumstances often defeat human expectation; man proposes, God disposes; the fate decides all

化算（值得／合算）deserving; worthwhile

另有打算 have some other plans; try to find some other ways

打算 intend; plan

老謀深算 be experienced and calculating

計算 calculate

唔化算（不值得／不合算）not worthwhile

唔知點算（不知道怎麼辦）don't know what to do

唔算（不算）not regarded as

珠算 calculation with an abacus; operation on the abacus; reckoning by the abacus

夠算（足夠／滿意）enough; satisfied

勝算（確保成功的戰略／穩操勝券）stratagem which ensures success; sure of success

就算（甚至／即使）even; even if

精打細算 pinch and scrape

點算（怎麼辦）what is to be done

講咗就算（說了就算）one means what one says

【管】gun² ① be in charge of ② control

管工（水管工人）plumber

管家 ① butler; steward ② housekeeper ③ manager

管教 control; subject sb to discipline

管理 manage

管理員 ① security guard ② management officer

管理處（管理辦公室）management office

管理費 management fee

管樂 wind music

三不管（無人管）nobody's business

毛管（毛孔）sweat pores

冇王管（沒人管）a chaotic situation where there is no one in charge

主管 ① leader ② supervisor

光管（日光燈／燈管）fluorescent lamp; tube light

有王管（有人管）sb is in charge

血管 blood vessel

供水管 water pipe

唔怕官至怕管（不怕官，只怕管）a mouse fears nobody but the cat that would catch it; one's immediate superior is more fearful than the person in charge

喉管（水管）water pipe

筒管（線軸）bobbin

爆血管 rupture of blood vessel

【筒】gwo¹ piece

阿筒（過分潦草）over-scrupulous

【精】dzeng¹ clever

精人出口，笨人出手（言語比行動更聰明）smart people get stupid people to do annoying tasks for them; words are cleverer than action

精仔（精明的人）smart guy

精叻（精明能幹）bright; capable; intelligent; smart

精到出骨（精於為自己打算的自私人）act cleverly from selfish motives

精乖（聰明懂事）smart

精乖伶俐（聰明伶俐）clever and quick-witted; clever and sensible; intelligent and smart; quick on the uptake

精埋一便（小聰明）clever only at ill doings

精歸咗（長歪了心眼兒）clever only at ill doings

妖精 ① demon; evil spirit ② alluring woman

面懵心精（似傻非傻／大智若愚）appear to be stupid but is actually very smart; play the fool

除笨有精（吃小虧佔大便宜）problems apart, there are still advantages to a particular activity

【精】dzing¹ spirit

精打細算 pinch and scrape

精神 spirit

精神科 psychiatry

精神面貌 mental attitude

精神病 mental disease; psychosis

精神病人 mental disease patient; psychiatric patient

精神爽利（神清目爽／精神飽滿）brisk and neat; full of spirit and energy; in good feather; in great feather; in high feather

冇厘精神（沒精打彩）a cup too low; disheartened; dispirited and discouraged; have a fit of blues; in low spirits; in the blues; in the dumps; lackadaisical; listless; out of humour; out of sorts; out of spirits; seedy; spiritless; with little enthusiasm; with the wind taken out of one's sails

打醒十二個精神（打起十二分精神／抖擻精神）raise one's spirits

唔係幾精神（不太精神）not feel well

唔夠精神（不太精神）not energetic enough

唔精神（不精神）not feel well; sick; unwell

精算師 actuary

精靈（機敏）alert and resourceful; smart and lovely

大話精（謊話精）liar

牛精（牛脾氣／倔小子／倔強）behave like a bully; unreasonable

生雞精（光澤）luster

老人精（年齡小但精於世故）a young child of prudence

走味精 (不加味精) no MSG

味精 monosodium glutamate (MSG)

狐狸精 enchantress; seductive woman; seductress; woman of easy virtue; woman who seduces another woman's husband

是非精 (八卦鬼) gossip person; gossiper; scandalmonger

炭精 (引柴) kindling

酒精 alcohol

馬騮精 (調皮鬼 / 頑皮的孩子) naughty child

排骨精 (瘦子) skinny man

敗家精 (敗家子 / 害羣之馬 / 家庭的恥辱 / 浪子) black sheep; disgrace to the family; prodigal son; spendthrift; wastrel

魂精 (太陽穴) temple

賤精 (賤人) person of bad character

【粽】 dzung³⁻² dumpling

粽子 glutinous rice dumpling

裹蒸粽 wrapped dumpling with pork

鹹肉粽 steamed glutinous rice dumpling with pork wrapped in lotus leaves

【綠】 luk⁹ green

綠色 green; green colour

綠豆 green bean

　綠豆水 (綠豆湯) green bean soup

　綠豆沙 (綠豆湯) sweet green bean soup

綠的 ① (綠色的士) green taxi ② (新界的士) New Territories taxi

綠茶 green tea

　日本綠茶 Japanese green tea

綠葉 green leaves

綠燈 get the go ahead; green light

綠 van (綠色小型公共汽車) green minibus

火紅火綠 (怒氣沖沖) in a frenzy

交通燈——點紅點綠 (瞎指揮) person who fools others into doing sth at one time and other things at other times

面紅面綠 (面紅耳赤) as red as a turkey-cook; blush to the roots of sb's hair; blush up to the ears; colour up; crimson with rage; flush red in the face; flush to the ears; flush with shame; get red in the face; one's face reddens to the ears; red in the face; red with anger

菜葉綠 (如菜葉般綠) green like vegetable leaves

葱綠 light green

嫩綠 tender green

滾紅滾綠 ① (淫蕩好色) lecherous ② (胡說八道) speak nonsense; talk nonsense

翠綠 bluish green; emerald

蘋果綠 apple green

【綢】 tsau⁴ silk

綢子 silk fabric

燥燥都係羊肉，爛爛都係絲綢 (金子是金子，無論它是否發光) gold is gold no matter whether it glitters or not

【維】 wai⁴ maintain

維他命 (維生素) (English) vitamin

　維他命丸 (維生素丸) vitamin pill

維修 maintenance

　維修工人 (修理人員) repairman

肌纖維 muscle fibre

【綱】 gong¹ outline

綱紀 social order and law

綱要 ① outline; sketch ② compendium; essentials

綱領 outline

大綱 outline

擔綱 (負責 / 擔當) assume; take on; undertake

【網】 mong⁵ net

網上 online

　網上交易 online trading

網友 internet friend

網吧 internet café

網頁 webpage

　網頁設計 webpage design

網站 website

網球 tennis

　網球場 tennis court

　打網球 play tennis

網絡 network

　局部網絡 (局域網) local area network

上網 access the Internet; surf the net

互聯網 internet

自投羅網 put one's own head in the noose

零售網 (零售網絡) retail network

蠄蟧絲網 (蜘蛛網) spider web

鐵絲網 wire fence; wire mesh; wire netting

【綻】 dzaan⁶ flaw

破綻 ① burst seam ② flaw; weak point

【綽】 tsoek⁸ spacious

綽頭（手法）gimmick

闊綽 generous; liberal with money

【綿】 min⁴ cotton

綿羊仔 ①（綿羊）sheep ②（摩托車）motorcycle
綿綿 continuous; unbroken
　綿綿不絕 remain unbroken

纏綿 exceedingly sentimental

【緊】 gan² tense

緊急 emergency; urgency
緊要（要緊）serious; severe
　唔緊要 ①（很小事）minor ②（不要緊）it doesn't matter;
　　it's alright; never mind
緊記 remember
緊張 nervous
　緊張大師（緊張的人）nervous person
緊緊（剛剛）just
　緊緊合格（剛剛及格）just pass the examination

口緊（嘴巴嚴）able to keep a secret; cautious about speech;
　discreet in speech
太緊 too tight
手緊（手頭緊）out at elbows; short of money
肉緊（緊張／揪心／乾着急）be highly excited; feel anxious;
　feel very tense
束緊（繫緊）bind up; lace up
抱緊 hold tightly in one's arms
搵搵緊（緊巴巴的）barely enough
着緊（着急）be worried about
講緊（電話佔線）the line is engaged
嚟緊（馬上來）coming
擸擸緊（缺錢）out at elbows; short of money

【緋】 fei¹ red

緋聞 scandal

紅粉花緋（紅艷艷）bright red

【翠】 tsoey³ emerald

翠綠 bluish green; emerald

翡翠 emerald

【翡】 fei² emerald

翡翠 emerald

【聚】 dzoey⁶ gather

聚合 ① get together ② polymerisation
聚集 aggregation; assemble; collect; gather
聚會 ① get together; meet ② assembly; beanfeast;
　hunfight; gathering; meeting
聚腳（聚首）hang out together

物以類聚 birds of a feather flock together
家人團聚 family reunion
攢聚（聚集在一起）gather together

【聞】 man⁴ ① hear ② smell

聞名 ① distinguished; famous; renowned; well-known
　② familiar with sb's name; know sb by repute
聞到 smell
聞所未聞 have never even heard of sth; have never
　heard of such a thing; hear of sth extremely unusual;
　unheard of

小道新聞 grapevine news
地產新聞 property news
財經新聞 financial news
睇新聞（看新聞）watch the news
新聞 news
煲水新聞（八卦新聞）gossip news
緋聞 pink news
醜聞 scandal
聽聞（聽說）be said; be told; hear; hear of

【腐】 fu⁶ bean curd

腐皮（油皮）bean curd sheet
　腐皮卷 bean curd sheet roll
腐乳（豆腐乳／醬豆腐）fermented bean curd
　一磚腐乳（一塊腐乳）a lump of fermented bean curd
腐敗 corrupt; decay

一磚豆腐（一塊豆腐）a cube of bean curd
水豆腐（嫩豆腐）tender bean curd
冬瓜豆腐（死）die
冰豆腐（凍豆腐）frozen bean curd
有七冬瓜豆腐（若然死了）if sb was dead
呃鬼食豆腐（誘入陷阱）lure sb into a trap
豆腐 ① bean curd ② weak
防腐 antiseptic
魚腐（魚豆腐）braised fish curd
腍過豆腐（比豆腐軟）softer than bean curd
諗鬼食豆腐（欺騙信仰）cheat sb into the belief

【腿】toey² leg
腿毛 hair on legs
腿蛋治（火腿雞蛋三文治）egg and ham sandwich

大腿 thigh
小腿 lower leg; shank
火腿 ham
象腿 ① elephant's leg ② thick leg
劈腿（出軌）cheat on

【膀】pong⁴ ① wing ② bladder
膀胱 bladder

翅膀 wings

【膏】gou¹ ointment
膏火（燈火）lamp oil
膏藥 medicated plaster; patch; plaster

一支藥膏（一管膏藥）a tube of ointment
一枝唇膏（一支口紅）a lipstick
口唇膏（唇膏）lippy; lipstick
牙膏 toothpaste
打石膏 apply a plaster cast
石膏 plaster cast
剃鬚膏 shaving cream
洗面膏（洗面奶）face wash
唇膏（口紅）lippy; lipstick
消毒藥膏（抗菌乳膏）antiseptic cream
唧牙膏（擠牙膏）squeeze toothpaste out from the tube
豬膏（豬板油）pig's oil
藥膏 ointment
蟹膏（蟹黃）crab roe
黐身藥膏（狗皮膏藥）cling to sb closely

【膊】bok⁸（肩膀）shoulder
膊頭（肩膀）shoulder
　膊頭高過耳（瘦小的人）skinny person
　拍膊頭（在某人的肩膀上哭泣／拍拍肩膀／輕拍肩膀）
　　cry on sb's shoulder; pat on the shoulder; tap sb on
　　the shoulder

打赤膊 bare one's chest
赤膊 bare one's chest
削膊（溜肩膀）sloping shoulder
卸膊（摺挑子）put the blame on sb; pass the buck; shirk
　responsibility
假膊（墊肩）shoulder pad
側側膊（繞過規則／避開正途）get round the rules

搭膊（墊肩）shoulder pad
轉膊 ①（換肩）shift the burden from one shoulder to
　another ②（靈活）flexible

【脈】dzin²（肌肉）muscle

手瓜起脈（胳膊粗）have strong and muscular arms

【舔】tim² lick
舔一舔 taste by licking

【舞】mou⁵ dance
舞小姐（舞女）nightclub hostess
舞女 nightclub hostess
舞台 stage
　臨時舞台 makeshift stage
舞男 gigolo
舞唔掂（玩不轉／做不好）not work
　舞嚟舞去舞唔掂（無論多麼努力地嘗試，仍然沒用）
　　no matter how hard one tries, still it does
　　not work
舞會 dancing party
　參加舞會 join a dancing party
　露天舞會 open-air dance party
舞獅（舞獅子）dragon dance
舞槍（耍槍）play with a spear
舞蹈 dancing
　舞蹈員（舞蹈演員）dancer
舞廳 cabaret; dance hall

交際舞 social dance
羽扇舞 feather-fan dance
伴舞 dancing partner
肯肯舞（康康舞／大腿舞）cancan
芭蕾舞 ballet
凌空飛舞 fly in the sky
眉飛色舞 enraptured
飛舞 dance in the sky
桌上舞 table dance
健康舞（健美操）aerobics
揮舞（揮動／掄／舞弄）brandish; wave; wield
跳草裙舞 ①（跳呼拉舞）have a hula hula dance ②（鬧情緒）
　make a fuss
跳隻舞（跳個舞）have a dance; shake a leg
跳舞 dance
爵士舞 jazz dance

【蒙】mung⁴ cover
蒙在鼓裏 be kept in the dark
蒙混（欺騙）deceive
　　蒙混過關 get by under false pretences
蒙騙 cheat; deceive; hoodwink

荷爾蒙 hormone

【蒜】syn³ garlic
蒜子（蒜瓣兒）garlic clove
蒜芯 garlic shoot
蒜茸（蒜泥）garlic paste; mashed garlic
蒜蓉（蒜泥）garlic paste; mashed garlic
蒜頭（大蒜／蒜）garlic
　　一個蒜頭（一頭蒜）a bulb of garlic
　　一粒蒜頭（一瓣蒜）a clove of garlic

大蒜 garlic

【蒲】pou⁴ rushes
蒲士卡（名信片）(English) postcard
蒲飛（自助餐）(English) buffet
蒲頭 ①（浮上來／浮在水上）float on water ②（出現／露臉了）turn up
蒲點（聚集的地點）place to hang out

出嚟蒲（從事非法行業）make a living in the criminal underworld
去蒲（玩樂）go out for a good time; hang about; hang around; hang out; hang round
四圍蒲（四處玩樂）hang around on the streets

【蒸】dzing¹ steam
蒸生瓜（不成熟穩重）not alert
蒸魚 steamed fish
蒸餾水 distilled water
蒸籠 steamer
　　小蒸籠 small steamer

【蒿】hou¹ mugwort
蒿子（艾蒿）mugwort

塘蒿（茼蒿／蒿子稈）garland chrysanthemum

【蓄】tsuk⁷ save
蓄意 deliberate; harbour certain intentions; premediated
蓄髮（留長髮）grow long hair

儲蓄 save; savings

【蓆】dzek⁹ ①（吃）eat ②（蓆子）mattress
蓆咗佢（得到她）get her

一張蓆（一張草蓆）a straw mattress
摟蓆（成為乞丐）become a beggar

【蓉】jung⁴ ①（漿糊）paste ②（溶化）melt away
蓉爛（破爛）ragged; worn-out

出水芙蓉 ① hibiscus rising out of water; lotus comes into bloom ② pretty girl
豆蓉（豆瓣醬）bean paste
芙蓉 ① hibiscus ② scrambled egg
細蓉（小碗雲吞麵）small bowl of shrimp dumplings
蓮子蓉（蓮蓉）lotus seed paste
蓮蓉（蓮子泥）lotus seed paste
蒜蓉（蒜泥）garlic paste; mashed garlic
薑蓉（薑泥）minced ginger
爛蓉蓉（破爛／稀巴爛）smashed beyond repair; soggy

【蓋】goi³ cover
蓋世 matchless; unparalleled
　　蓋世無雙 have no equal on earth; matchless; peerless; stand without peer in one's generation; the best one in the whole world; unparalleled; without an equal in the world
蓋章（蓋印）affix one's seal; seal; stamp

十個甕缸九個蓋（不能收支平衡）fail to make both ends meet
冚蓋（蓋蓋兒）cover with a lid
死雞撐飯蓋（明知有錯仍不願悔改）shabby-genteel
波籮蓋（膝蓋）knee cap
釘蓋（死）die
荷蘭水蓋（勳章）medal of honour
煲蓋（鍋蓋）pot cover
飯蓋（鍋蓋）rice-cooker cover
菠蘿蓋（膝蓋）kneecap
箱蓋 case cover; cover
錶蓋（錶蒙子）watch cover
鑊蓋（鍋蓋）pan cover

【蜜】mat⁹ honey
蜜月 honey moon
蜜瓜（白蘭瓜）honey dew melon
蜜糖 honey

蜂蜜 honey
檸蜜（蜂蜜檸檬水）honey lemonade

【蝌】fo¹ tadpole
蝌蚪 tadpole

【蜢】maang⁵ (蝗蟲 / 攔蚱) grasshopper

長腳蜢 (腿長的人) long-legged
飛來蜢 (意外的好處) unexpected fortune
草蜢 (蚱蜢) grasshopper
跛腳鷯哥自有飛來蜢 (呆人有呆福 / 傻人有傻福) God tempers the wind to the shorn lamb
瘦蜢蜢 (很瘦) very thin

【蝕】sit⁹ ① (侵蝕) erode ② (虧損) lose

蝕水 (虧錢) lose money
蝕本 (虧本) lose money in business; lose one's capital; suffer a deficit
　蝕大本 (賠了老本) lose money greatly in business
蝕底 (吃虧) miss out on a chance; suffer losses

白蝕 (白斑病) leukoderma; white spots
輸蝕 (比不上別人 / 吃虧) let sb gain the wind; miss out

【裹】gwo² bind; wrap
裹蒸粽 wrapped dumpling with pork

包裹 parcel

【製】dzai³ create; make; manufacture; produce
製作 make; manufacture
製成 be made from; manufacture
製品 manufactured items; products
製造 (製作 / 生產) make; manufacture

仿製 be modelled
自製 ① home-made ② do it yourself (DIY)
炮製 concoct; cook up
複製 copy; duplicate; replicate; reproduce

【複】fuk⁷ repeat
複印 copy; duplicate; photocopy; xerox
複製 copy; duplicate; replicate; reproduce
複雜 complex; complicated; intricate; sophisticated

重複 repeat

【認】jing⁶ admit; recognise
認叻 (炫耀) boast; brag
認住 (認為 / 覺得) believe that; feel that

認低威 (自認不行 / 認下風 / 認輸) admit being inferior; confess to be unworthy
認屎認屁 (假裝知識淵博) pretend to be knowledgeable
認真 (真是 / 確實) seriously
認得 (認識 / 曉得 / 懂得) know
認賬 acknowledge what one has said or done
認數 (承認債務) acknowledge the debt

一口否認 completely deny; flatly deny; repudiate flatly
六親不認 turn one's back on all one's relations
否認 deny; disclaim; gainsay; give a denial to sth; make a denial of; negate; repudiate
承認 confess
記認 (記號) sign
無可否認 cannot be denied; it is not to be denied that; there is no denying; undeniable

【誌】dzi³ records
誌慶 (道賀) offer congratulations

一本雜誌 a magazine
八卦雜誌 gossip magazine; tabloid magazine
交通標誌 traffic sign
雜誌 magazine

【誓】sai⁶ oath
誓死 pledge one's life
誓神劈願 (矢口發誓) swear solemn oath; take an oath and call God to witness
誓願 (起誓 / 發誓) take an oath
　誓願當食生菜 (隨口發誓卻從不履行承諾 / 起誓當白饒) take an easy oath

發誓 swear
盟誓 (起誓 / 發誓) make a pledge; take an oath

【誕】daan³ birth
誕生 birth
誕辰 birthday

七姐誕 (七夕節) Double Seventh Festival
天后誕 Birthday of the Heaven Queen
孔聖誕 (孔子誕辰日) Birthday of Confucius
白色聖誕 (白色聖誕節) white Christmas
佛誕 Buddha's Birthday
怪誕 funny; strange
耶穌誕 (聖誕節) Christmas
荒誕 absurd; incredible; unbelievable
猴王誕 Monkey God Festival

聖誕 (聖誕節) Christmas
譚公誕 Birthday of Tam Kung
觀音誕 Birthday of the Goddess of Mercy
關公誕 Birthday of Lord Kwan
關帝誕 Birthday of Kwan Tai

【誘】jau⁵ tempt

誘人 attract
誘因 incentive; inducement; remote cause
誘惑 temptation
誘導 guide; induce; lead

引誘 accost; attract; cajole; entice; induce; lead on; lure; persuade; seduce; tempt

【語】jy⁵ ① words ② language

語言 language
　多種語言 multilingual
語法 grammar
語重心長 meaningful; say in all earnestness; say with deep feeling; sincere words and earnest wishes
語氣 ① manner of speaking; tone; tone of voice ② mood
語無倫次 babble in one's statement; babble like an idiot; go off at score; ramble in one's statement; speak incoherently; use indecent language; want of order in one's speech

母語 mother tongue
快人快語 a person of straightforward disposition is outspoken; a straight talk from an honest person; a straightforward talk from a straightforward person; an outspoken person speaks their mind; sb who does not mince their words
花言巧語 fine words; have a sweet tongue
俗語 common saying
前言不對後語 (前言不搭後語) one's remarks are incoherent; one's words do not hang together
胡言亂語 babble; blather; clotted nonsense; codswallop; delirium; flimflam; full of hops; maunder; muck; nonsense; punk; ramble in one's speech; rave; ravings; rigmarole; shoot off one's mouth; shoot the bull; sling the bull; speak at a venture; talk foolishly; talk through one's hat; talk wildly; throw the bull; wander in one's speech; wander in one's talk; wanderings
國語 (普通話) Mandarin; Putonghua
術語 (行內話) jargon; terminology
鳥語 (鳥叫) bird call
評語 comment

詞語 terms; words and expressions
粵語 Cantonese dialect
歇後語 end-clipper
漢語 Chinese; Chinese language
謂語 predicate
謎語 riddle

【誤】ng⁶ error

誤人 harm people
誤用 misuse
誤會 get one's wires crossed; misunderstanding; misapprehend; misconstrue; mistake; misunderstand
誤點 (晚點) be delayed

局部錯誤 local error
延誤 delay
依時不誤 (準時不誤) on time
航班延誤 the flight is delayed
錯誤 error; mistake
聰明反被聰明誤 a wise person can be ruined by their own wisdom; clever people may be victims of their own cleverness; cleverness may overreach itself; every person has a fool in their sleeve; suffer for one's wisdom
謬誤 error; mistake; falsehood

【說】syt⁸ say; speak; talk; utter

說明 clarify; explain; expound; illustrate; show
說教 (傳道 / 機械地闡述 / 宣講) deliver a sermon; expound sth mechanically; preach; talk rubbish
說話 (話 / 話語 / 講話) say; speak; talk
　說話流利 speak with fluency

小說 fiction; novel
民間傳說 popular legend
武俠小說 martial art novel
胡說 baloney; bilge; blather; bullshit; cobblers; cod; codswallop; cut the nonsense; don't talk rot; fiddlesticks; guff; horseshift; humbug; nonsense; rats; rot it; rubbish; shit; stuff and nonsense; what the crap
述說 give an account of; narrate; recount; state; tell
訴說 ① air grievances; complain ② narrate; recount; relate; tell
傳說 legend
據說 a story is going around that; according to hearsay; as the story goes; allegedly; by all accounts; I hear that; it is said; people say that; the story goes that; the story runs that; they say

【豪】hou⁴ brave

豪宅 luxurious apartment
　　買豪宅 buy a luxurious apartment
豪雨（大雨／暴雨）torrent
豪爽 generous
豪華 luxurious
　　豪華生活 live in luxury
　　豪華艙（頭等艙）first-class

大富豪 tycoon
富豪 rich and powerful people

【貌】maau⁶ facial expression

貌似 in appearance; seemingly

冇禮貌（沒禮貌）be wanting in politeness; have bad
　　manners; have no manners; impolite
好有禮貌（很有禮貌）be all courtesy
有禮貌 courteous; have good manners; have manners; polite
社會面貌 social aspects
面貌 face
精神面貌 mental attitude
禮貌 politeness

【賒】se¹ buy and sell on credit

賒數（賒賬）on account; on credit

【賓】ban¹ ① guest ② Filipino

賓佬（菲律賓男人）Filipino guy
賓治（潘趣酒）(English) punch
　　雜果賓治（水果雞尾酒）fruit punch
賓妹 ①（菲律賓女生）Filipino girl ②（菲律賓女傭）
　　Filipino maid
　　一個賓妹（一名菲傭）a Filipino maid
賓館 guesthouse

來賓 guest; visitor
迎賓 receive guests
嘉賓 honourable guest

【趕】gon² hurry to

趕上 catch up with
趕工（趕任務／趕活兒）work overtime
趕住（匆忙）hurry
趕走 chase away
趕狗入窮巷（趕盡殺絕）compel sb to strike back in self-
　　defence; force sb into a corner
趕得切（趕得上）have enough time to do sth
趕路 hurry on with one's journey

趕頭趕命（催命似的）in a great hurry
趕鴨仔（跟着一羣人匆忙）hurry along a group

【踎】mau¹（蹲）squat down

踎低（蹲下）squat down
踎兜（失業／失業人士）unemployed
踎街（流落街頭／無家可歸）homeless
踎凳（入獄）in jail
踎監（入獄）in prison
踎躉（失業）out of work; unemployed

地踎（非常便宜的餐廳）very cheap restaurant
兜踎（貧困／邋遢／破舊）poverty-stricken; scruffy;
　　shabby

【踬】an³（抖）shake

踬踬腳（生活得很好）lead a rose-coloured life; live well

【輔】fu⁶ counsel

輔導 counsel
　　輔導員 counsellor

【輕】hing¹ light

輕佻 frivolous
輕枷重罪（一時承受大量工作）be burdened with the
　　work of a moment
輕浮 frivolous
輕鐵 light rail transit
輕飄飄 ① light as a feather ② buoyant

下扒輕輕／下巴輕輕 ①（說空話）talk at random; talk with
　　no real meaning ②（答應做不到的事情）make promises
　　too easily
口輕輕（答應做不到的事情）glib; make easy promises
年輕 young
紙紮下巴——口輕輕（下巴掛鈴鐺——想（響）到哪說到哪
　　兒）talk at random
無官一身輕 free from office, free from care; without burden,
　　without worriment
無債一身輕 feel relieved if one is not in debt; out of debt,
　　out of burden
睇輕（看輕）look down on
頭重腳輕 top-heavy

【辣】laat⁸ ①（辣味）hot; spicy ②（排）a row of ③（狠毒）cruel

辣手（難以對付）hard to deal with
辣低（擊落）shoot down
辣油（辣椒油）chilli oil

辣椒 pepper
　辣椒仔（橫蠻無理）unreasonable person
　辣椒油 chilli oil
　辣椒醬 chilli sauce
　紅辣椒 red chilli
辣着（激怒）make angry; provoke
辣野（辣的東西）spicy food
辣興（激怒）make angry; provoke
辣撻（邋遢）dirty; soiled
　辣撻人有辣撻福（傻人有傻福）happiness often comes to
　　mediocre persons
辣覥（辣傷）get hurt

一辣（一排）a row of
巴辣（潑辣）fierce
本地薑唔辣（牆裏開花牆外香）grass is always greener on
　　the other side of the fence; local things or talents are not
　　as valued as foreign ones
好辣 very spicy
有辣有唔辣（各有長短）each has its own advantages and
　　weak points; there are pros and cons
芥辣（芥末）ground mustard; mustard
老辣（經驗豐富且惡毒）experienced and vicious
走辣（不要辣）no chilli
麻辣（辛辣）spicy
甜酸苦辣 all the sweet and bitter experiences of life
新鮮滾熱辣（又新鮮又熱和）fresh and warm
新鮮熱辣（又新鮮又熱和）fresh and warm
滾熱辣 ①（熱騰騰的）boiling hot; piping hot; steaming hot
　②（最新新聞）latest news
潑辣 shrewish and violent
熱辣辣（熱呼呼的）burning hot; hot; piping hot; scorching
薑越老越辣（薑還是老的辣）the older, the wiser

【遙】jiu⁴ far

遙遙領前（遙遙領先）enjoy a commanding lead; far
　ahead; way ahead

【遞】dai⁶ delivery

遞交 deliver; hand over
遞送 deliver; send
遞減 decrease by degrees; decrease progressively; reduce
　progressively
遞增 increase by degrees; increase progressively

快遞 express delivery; fast mail
特快郵遞（快遞送貨）express mail delivery
郵遞（郵件派送／郵件投遞）mail delivery

【遠】jyn⁵ far

遠大 ambitious; broad; long-range; very promising
遠方 distant place; remote place
遠走 go far away
　遠走高飛 flee far away; fly far and high; fly high and go
　　away; go far away; off to distant parts; slip away to
　　distant place; take it on the lam; take wing
遠近 ① far and near; remote or close ② distance
遠親 distant relatives; remote kinsfolk
　遠親不如近鄰 a close neighbour means more than a
　　distant relative; a distant relative is not as good as a
　　near neighbour; a near neighbour is better than a far-
　　dwelling kinsman; a relative far away is not as helpful
　　as a neighbour close by; a relative far off is less helpful
　　than a neighbour close by; an afar off relative is not as
　　helpful as a near neighbour; better is a neighbour that
　　is near than a brother far off; distant relatives are not
　　as helpful as close neighbours; distant relatives are of
　　less account than near neighbours

山高皇帝遠（王法管轄不到）run one's own affairs without
　　interference from a distant centre of authority; while the
　　cat is away, the mice will play
冇雷公咁遠（遙遠的地方）remote place
永遠 ever
好遠 very far
老遠（很遠）a very long distance; far away; very far
相距好遠 far away from
偏遠（遠處／遠程）faraway; remote
幾遠（多遠）how far
慎終追遠（依禮慎重辦理父母喪事，祭祀要誠心追念遠祖）
　　carefully attend to the funeral rites of parents and
　　follow them when gone with due sacrifices; conduct the
　　funeral of one's parents with meticulous care and let not
　　sacrifices to one's remote ancestors be forgotten
離開好遠 be far away; be far off

【遢】taat⁸ dirty

污糟邋遢（骯髒邋遢）dirty; soiled

【遣】hin² dispatch; send

遣返 deport; repatriate; send back; send home
遣送 repatriate; send away; send back; send sb away
　forcibly
遣散 disband; dismiss; send away

消遣 pastime

【醒】 tsing⁴ (罐子) earthenware jar

醋醒 (醋罐子) vinegar jar

【酷】 huk⁹ cruel

酷熱 very hot

冷酷 callous; cruel; hard; hardhearted; heartless; merciless

【酸】 syn¹ ① acid ② sour

酸枝 (紅木) rosewood
酸宿 (酸臭) stingy
酸梅 plum
酸微微 ① (酸溜溜) sour; tart ② (嫉妒) envious; jealous
酸辣湯 hot and sour soup

心酸 be deeply grieved
好酸 very sour
肉酸 (噁心 / 難看 / 難聽) creepy-crawly; ugly
尿酸 uric acid
辛酸 bitter; hardships; miserable; sad; the bitters of life
胃酸 gatric acid
鬼咁肉酸 (難看 / 醜陋) look quite awful
做嘢唔辣，做醋唔酸 (遠遠不夠) it is far from sufficient for the purpose
唱得好肉酸 (唱歌很難聽) one's singing is very poor
寒酸 (破舊) miserable and shabby; shabby; sorry; scrubby
磺酸 (亞硫酸) sulfonic acid

【醛】 lyt⁶ lose

醛低 (忘記了而留下) forget and leave behind sth
醛咗 (遺忘了 / 遺漏了) lose; leave out; leave behind

【銀】 ngan⁴⁻² ① (銀子) silver ② (錢) money

銀仔 (硬幣 / 銅鏰兒) coin; hard currency
銀包 (錢包) purse; wallet
　一個銀包 (一個錢包) a purse
銀行 bank
　銀行月結單 (銀行每月通知書) bank monthly statement
　銀行家 banker
　銀行業 banking industry
　一間銀行 (一家銀行) a bank
銀色 silver
銀兩 money
銀芽 (綠豆芽) bean sprout
銀紙 ① (鈔票 / 紙幣 / 紙鈔) banknote ② (錢) money
　銀紙縮水 (鈔票貶值) currency depreciation; currency devaluation
　一沓銀紙 (一堆鈔票 / 一疊鈔票) a pile of banknotes

銀碼 (金額) amount of money; sum of money
　外幣銀碼 (外幣金額) currency amount
　港幣銀碼 (港幣金額) Hong Kong dollar amount
銀雞 (哨子) whistle
　吹銀雞 (吹哨子) blow the whistle

冇散銀 (沒硬幣 / 沒零錢) no coins
本銀 (本錢) principal
白銀 silver
收銀 collect cash
金銀 gold and silver
真金白銀 real money
現銀 (現金) cash
港銀 (港幣 / 港元) Hong Kong currency; Hong Kong dollar
散銀 (硬幣 / 零錢) coins
搵銀 (掙錢 / 賺錢) make money
碎銀 (硬幣 / 零鈔 / 零票 / 零錢) coins; small change

【鉸】 gaau³ ① hinge ② scissors

鉸剪 (剪刀 / 剪子) scissors
　一把鉸剪 (一把剪刀) a pair of scissors
門鉸 (合頁) hinge

【銅】 tung⁴ copper

銅皮鐵骨 (銅筋鐵骨) iron constitution; brass muscles and iron bones; strong and solid body; tough and strong as iron and steel; with vigorous skin and bones and strong muscles
銅銀買病豬——大家偷歡喜 (互相欺騙) each of the two hugs himself on having cheated the other

【銖】 dzy¹ ancient coinage

銖積寸累 (積少成多 / 慢慢積累起來) build up slowly

泰銖 Thai baht

【銘】 ming⁴ inscription

座右銘 maxim; motto; permanent reminder; precept

【銜】 haam⁴ title

銜頭 (頭銜 / 職稱) official title of a person

名銜 (名稱 / 稱號) designation
領銜 (主演) act the leading role

【閣】 gok⁸ attic

閣仔 (閣樓) attic; penthouse
閣樓 cockloft

內閣 cabinet
解散內閣 disband the cabinet

【隙】gwik[7] crack
隙縫 (縫隙) crack; crevice; fissure

罅隙 (縫隙) cleft; crack

【際】dzai[3] boundary
際遇 favourable or unfavourable turns in life; spells of good or bad fortune

交際 social intercourse
州際 interstate
享譽國際 of international stature
洲際 intercontinental
國際 international

【障】dzoeng[3] obstacle
障礙 ① barrier; hurdle; obstacle; obstruction ② handicap; malfunction

故障 accident; blunder; breakdown; bug; conk; defect; do not work; do not work properly; failure; fault; hitch; inaction; ineffective; malfunction; out of gear; out of order; sth wrong; stoppage; trouble

【需】soey[1] need
需求 demand; need; requirement
需要 need

必需 essential; indispensable

【領】ling[5] ① (領取) receive ② (領子) collar
領土 territory
領先 have a lead; lead; take the lead
　　稍稍領先 have a slight lead
領呔 (領帶) tie
領事 consul
　　領事館 consulate
領域 domain; field; realm; sphere
領當 (上當) be duped; be fooled; be taken in; be tricked
領野 (上當 / 上套兒) swallow the bait; fall victim of sth
領銜 (主演) act the leading role
領導 ① guide; lead ② leader
　　領導人 leader

心領 no, thank you
企領 (立領) stand collar; stand-up collar

衫領 (衣領) collar
圓領 round collar
綱領 outline
樽領 (高領) choker

【颯】saap[8] waste
颯氣 (心中氣悶 / 費神) waste of energy; exhausted and frustrated

【颱】toi[4] typhoon
颱風 typhoon
　　颱風季節 typhoon season

【飽】baau[2] full
飽死 (臭吹 / 臭美) be exasperated against sb; feel disgusted
　　飽死荷蘭豆 (覺得討厭) be ruffled; feel disgusted
飽肚 (飯後) after meal
飽唔死餓唔嚟 (僅能糊口) earn no more than what one needs

有情飲水飽 (感情足夠深，喝水也能飽) people in love could satisfy their hunger by drinking water
玩餐飽 (玩個夠) have a good time
食飽 (吃飽) have eaten one's fill
食餐飽 (吃個夠) eat one's fill
貴夾唔飽 (質量差，不實用) not good value and not practical

【飾】sik[7] decoration
飾櫃 (展示櫥窗) display window; show window

粧飾 (裝飾) adorn; deck out; decorate; dress up
金飾 gold jewellery
首飾 jewellery
珠寶首飾 jewellery, accessories, and adornments
聖誕燈飾 Christmas illumination

【駁】bok[8] connect; disagree
駁火 (交火) fire fight
駁骨 (接骨 / 接骨頭) set a fracture
　　駁骨頭 (接骨 / 接骨頭) set a fracture
駁腳 (跑腿) sb who runs errands
駁嘴 (強嘴 / 頂嘴) answer back; talk back
　　駁嘴駁舌 (頂嘴) talk back
駁線 (接線) connect a wire; wiring

反駁 confute; contradict; controvert; countercharge; counterplea; disprove; gainsay; refute; retort

接駁（連接／結合／鏈接）annex; attach; be connected; be joined; clasp; combine; connect; connet with; couple; draw together; fasten; join; link; link up; linkage; put together; unite

辯駁（反駁）confute; contradict; controvert; countercharge; counterplea; disproof; gainsay; refute; retort

【骰】tau⁴（骰子）dice

打骰（負責）be in charge
揸骰（負責）be in charge

【髦】mou⁴ man of talent

髦俊（才智傑出）man of talent

時髦（時尚）fashion
趕時髦（追隨時尚）follow the fashion

【魂】wan⁴ soul

魂不守舍 lose one's head; out of one's wits
魂不附體（魂不守舍）lose one's head; out of one's wits
魂精（太陽穴）temple
魂魄 soul
　魂魄都唔齊（魂不守舍）be entranced with fear; be frightened out of one's wits; be scared out of one's wits; be scared to death
　三魂唔見咗七魄（三魂丟了七魄／魂不守舍）be entranced with fear; be frightened out of one's wits; be scared out of one's wits; be scared to death
出賣靈魂 sell one's soul
失魂（丟了魂兒／冒失／精神恍惚）absent-minded; distracted; in a trance; lose one's soul
嚇失魂（嚇破了膽）be scared out of one's wits; be scared stiff
靈魂 soul

【鳳】fung⁶ phoenix

鳳爪（雞爪／雞爪子）chicken feet; chicken's paws
　鳳爪排骨飯 rice with chicken feet and spare ribs
鳳尾魚 anchovy
鳳姐（妓女）prostitute
鳳凰無寶不落（不做對自己無利可圖的事）draw water to one's mill

一樓一鳳（一個住宅單位中只有一名妓女）one-woman brothel
天花龍鳳（天花亂墜）bluff
偷龍轉鳳（秘密替代／狸貓換太子）make a secret substitution
終須有日龍穿鳳（莫欺少年窮）every cloud has a silver lining; every dog has its day

【鳴】ming⁴ cry

鳴謝 acknowledge one's thanks

一雞死一雞鳴（事情結束後，就自然地有另一事情發生）persons of a kind come forth in succession; successors come forth one after another; when one person leaves a business, another will take it up
蟬鳴 shrill sound of a cicada

【鼻】bei⁶ nose

鼻大（大鼻子）big nose
鼻水（鼻涕）nasal mucus; snivel
　流鼻水（流鼻涕）have a runny nose
　　有咳同流鼻水（有咳嗽，也有流鼻涕）have a cough and a runny nose
鼻血 nosebleed
　流鼻血 nosebleeding
鼻屎（鼻垢）bogey; booger; mucus in the nose; nasal secretion
　鼻屎好食，鼻囊挖穿（利之所在，人爭趨之）everybody strives for profitable business
　了鼻屎（挖鼻孔）pick one's nose
　撩鼻屎（挖鼻孔）pick one's nose
鼻哥（鼻子）beezer; bugle; nose
　鼻哥尖（鼻尖兒）tip of the nose
　鼻哥窿（鼻孔）nares; nostrils
　鼻哥窿冇肉（非常驚恐）be extremely terrified
　篤鼻哥（仗着地位高而得到特許）gain admission on account of one's status
鼻涕 nasal discharge
　鼻涕蟲 snot-nosed kid
鼻塞（鼻子不通氣）nasal congestion; stuffy nose
鼻鼾（呼嚕）snore
　鼻鼾聲（呼嚕聲）snore
　打鼻鼾（打呼嚕）snore
　扯鼻鼾（打呼嚕）snore

大鼻 ①（傲慢）arrogant; haughty; putting on airs; snob; snobbish ②（大鼻子）big nose
弓鼻（刺鼻）irritate the nose
佢好大鼻（他好傲慢）he is very arrogant
攻鼻（刺鼻）assail one's nostrils; irritate the nose; pungent
扁鼻（塌鼻樑）flat nose
挖鼻 pick one's nose
唔埋得個鼻（臭不可聞）make a long nose
酒渣鼻（酒糟鼻）rosacea
高鼻（高鼻樑）high nose
揞住個鼻（捂鼻子）cover one's nose with one's hand
鈎鼻（鷹鈎鼻）acquiline nose

獅子鼻（翹鼻）pug nose

盟鼻（鼻塞）nasal congestion

督眼督鼻（眼中釘）a thorn in one's eye; eyesore; irritate the eyes

篤門篤鼻（看不順眼／指着鼻子罵）scold sb with the finger pointing at him

篤眼篤鼻（看不順眼／指着鼻子罵）scold sb with the finger pointing at him

豬鼻（豬鼻子）pig's nose

【鼾】hon⁶ snore

打鼻鼾（打呼嚕）snore

扯鼻鼾（打呼嚕）snore

鼻鼾（呼嚕）snore

【齊】tsai⁴ ① together ② round up to

齊人（人來得齊）all the people are present

齊全（齊備）complete

齊齊（一起）all together; at the same time; in company; in unison; simultaneously; together

齊緝緝（很整齊／齊茸兒）neat

齊頭數 ①（整數）round figure; round number ②（巨款）round sum

齊整（整齊）neat

一齊（一起）all together; at the same time; in company; in unison; simultaneously; together

三十六度板斧都出齊（智窮力竭／黔驢技窮）at the end of one's wits

夾埋一齊（合夥）join as partner

計埋一齊（算在一起）taken together

睇齊（看齊）keep up with

唭埋一齊（連在一起）join together

魂魄都唔齊（魂不守舍）be entranced with fear; be frightened out of one's wits; be scared out of one's wits; be scared to death

擺埋一齊（擺在一起）bring together

黐埋一齊（黏在一起）stick together

15 劃

【價】gaa³ price

價位（價格）price

價值 value

價格 price

　協商價格 negotiated price

價廉物美 low price but good quality

價錢 price

　價錢牌（價格標籤）price tag

大減價（大甩賣）big sale; sale

不二價 one price only

付出代價 pay a price

代價 cost; price

出價 offer

加價（漲價）increase the price; raise prices; rise in price

半價 half price

市價 market price

叫價（要價）asked price; asking price

平價（廉價）cheap; inexpensive

打死狗講價（趁火打劫）fish in troubled waters

打價（定價）fix a price

地價 land price

收市價（收盤價格）closing price

估價 ① evaluate ② appraised price

低價 at a low price

呎價（每平方呎價格）price per square foot

批發價 wholesale price

每方呎叫價（每平方呎要價）asked price per square foot

股價 share price

屋價（房價）house price

格價（比較價錢）compare prices

時價（現時市價）current price

討價 ask a price; name a price

討價還價 bargain; bargain with sb for a supply of sth; chaffer; dicker; drive a bargain; haggle about a price; haggle for a price; haggle over a price; haggle with sb over the price of sth; palter

起價（漲價）raise prices; rise in price

特價 special price

售價（價錢）price; selling price

票價 price of a ticket

減價（跌價／降價）cut down prices; go down in price; mark down; on sale; price breaks; price out; reduce the price

貼現價（打折）on discount

跌價（降價）cut down prices; go down in price; mark down; on sale; price breaks; price out; reduce the price

開大價（張大口）open one's mouth wide

開天索價（漫天要價）ask a sky-high price; ask an exorbitant price

開盤價 opening price

廉價 cheap; inexpensive; low-priced

補地價（向政府支付土地溢價）pay a premium to the government

詢價（問價）enquiry

漲價 raise prices
還價 counteroffer
講價 (討價還價 / 談價錢) bargain; haggle over a price; negotiate the price
議價 (價格協商) price negotiation

【儀】ji⁴ ceremony
儀式 ceremony
儀器 instrument

禮儀 decorum; etiquette; protocol

【憼】ging² (小心) warn
憼住嚟使 (節約用錢) spend with care; use with care
憼錫 (愛惜 / 愛護) care

【儉】gim⁶ frugal
儉省 (節儉) economical; thrifty
儉模 economical; thrifty and simple

知慳識儉 ① (省吃儉用) eat sparingly and spend frugally; economical in everyday spending; go slow with; live frugally; pinch and scrape; practice austerity; save money on food and expenses; scrape and screw; skimp and save; stint oneself ② (精打細算) careful calculation and strict budgeting
慳儉 (節儉) thrifty

【劇】kek⁹ opera
劇本 drama; play; script
劇烈 acute; fierce; severe; violent
劇場 theatre

一套電視劇 a TV drama
一場鬧劇 a farce
川劇 Sichuan opera
日劇 Japanese drama
古裝劇 costume drama
京劇 Beijing opera
喜劇 comedy
湘劇 Hunan opera
電視劇 TV drama
歌劇 opera
粵劇 Cantonese opera
鬧劇 farce
歷史劇 historical play
諧劇 (鬧劇) farce
韓劇 Korean drama

【劈】pek⁸ chop up
劈低 (砍倒) chop down
劈炮 (甩手兒 / 摞挑子 / 辭職) quit one's job
　劈炮唔撈 (甩手兒 / 摞挑子 / 辭職) give up one's job
劈酒 (瘋狂地喝酒) drink alcohol to drown the sorrow
劈腿 (出軌) cheat on

【劉】lau⁴ a surname
劉備借荊州——有借冇回頭 (劉備借荊州——有借無還) money or things borrowed are never returned; the loan once given never comes back

【劍】gim³ sword
劍術 (擊劍) fencing; swordsmanship
劍蘭 gladiolus

一把劍 a sword
刀劍 knives and swords
放飛劍 (吐痰) spit
飛劍 flying sword
唇槍舌劍 a battle of repartee; a battle of wits; a war of words; cross verbal swords; engage in a battle of words; exchange heated words; have a tit-for-tat argument with sharp words

【劏】tong¹ ① (殺) kill; slaughter ② (拆) disassemble ③ (剖開) slice apart
劏牛 (宰牛) slaughter a cow
劏死牛 (打槓子 / 路上強搶) highjack; mug; rob
劏光豬 (下棋時棋子全被對方吃光) all the pieces (chessmen) have been taken by the opponent
劏車 (拆車) disassemble a car
劏豬 (殺豬) butcher pigs; kill pigs; slaughter pigs
　劏豬咁聲 (殺豬叫) sing in a terrible way, like a pig being slaughtered
　劏豬櫈——上嚟就死 (老肥豬上屠場——挨刀的貨) a fat pig going to the butchery – sure to die
劏雞 ① (殺雞) kill a chicken ② (拉小提琴像殺雞) play the violin badly
　劏雞殺鴨 (殺雞殺鴨) kill chickens and ducks
　劏雞嚇馬騮 (殺雞嚇猴 / 殺雞儆猴) kill the chicken to frighten the monkey – punish sb as a warning to others; make an example of a few to frighten all the rest

生劏 (活生生殺死) kill alive

【厲】lai⁶ fierce

厲害 ① cruel; fierce; severe; sharp ② formidable; serious; terrible

厲鬼 ①（殘忍／激烈／嚴重／尖銳）cruel; fierce; severe; sharp ②（強大／嚴重／可怕）foridable; serious; terrible

冤厲（冤枉）frame
發嘲厲（大發雷霆）suddenly fly into a rage; throw one's temper all of a sudden

【嘩】waa¹ ① shout ② wow

嘩鬼（淘氣／噪音製造者）naughty; noise-maker
嘩嘩聲（嘩然）in a uproar; loudly

【嘯】siu³ tsunami

海嘯 tsunami

【噏】ngap⁷（胡扯／亂說）babble; chat; gossip

噏三噏四（說三道四）chatter away; gossip
噏耷（破舊）shabby
噏得就噏（胡扯／亂說）bullshit

口噏噏（口吃）stammer
亂噏（胡扯／胡說／胡謅／亂說）talk nonsense; talk rubbish
豬噏（胡扯／胡說／胡謅／亂說）talk nonsense
齋噏（胡扯／亂說）bullshit

【噓】hoey¹ sigh

噓噓聲（很快）very quickly

【嘮】lou⁴ grumble

嘮嘈（牢騷）complain; grieve; grumble; grumbling
發嘮嘈（發牢騷）beef; beef about; blow off steam; chew the rag; complain; grouch; grouse; grumble; grumble about; grumble at; grumble over; let off steam; make a sour remark; murmur; natter; say devil's paternoster; whine about; work off steam

呻呢呻嘮（怨這怨那）always complain about something; if not complaining one thing, one complains about another

【嘰】gei¹ talk indistinctly

嘰哩咕嚕（嘰嘰咕咕）incomprehensible talk
嘰趷（意見不一／不和）at cross-purposes; at loggerheads with sb; at odds; at outs with sb; not get along well; on bad terms

有嘰趷（不和／爭吵）at cross-purposes; at loggerheads with sb; at odds; at outs with sb; not get along well; on bad terms

嘰嘰趷趷（口吃／說不清楚）stutter out

【嘲】dzaau¹ tease

嘲笑 tease

【嘴】dzoey² mouth

嘴巴 mouth
　自打嘴巴 contradict oneself
嘴尖（嘴刁）particular about food
嘴啖（給一個吻）give a kiss
嘴廟廟（用嘴巴表示不滿的樣子）pout

一把嘴（一張嘴）a mouth
一輪嘴（滔滔不絕／花言巧語／一口氣說完）a volley of words; talk continuously; wag one's tongue
刀嘴（刀尖）point of a knife
木嘴（噘嘴）pursed mouth
火嘴（火花塞／電嘴）ignition plug; spark plug; sparking plug
牛頭唔對馬嘴（牛頭不對馬嘴）beside the point
奶嘴 dummy
吊嘴（吊墜）pendant
尖嘴 ① sharp mouth ② particular about food
吹水唔抹嘴（吹牛不交稅）tell big lies
沐嘴（蠢蛋）fool
咂嘴 make clicks
兔嘴（兔唇／缺唇／崩嘴／裂嘴／豁嘴／豁嘴兒）harelipped person
封嘴 keep one's mouth shut
扁嘴（癟嘴）puckered mouth
歪嘴 wry mouth
笑爆嘴（咧嘴大笑）laugh loudly
針嘴（針頭）needle head
烏鴉嘴（壞事一說就靈的臭嘴）foul-mouthed
偷食唔抹嘴（留下一個人做錯事的證據）leave behind evidence of one's wrongdoing
啜嘴（接吻）kiss
將佢拳頭扷佢嘴（用他自己的硬幣買回來／一報還一報）pay sb back in his/her own coin; return like for like
崩嘴（兔唇／缺唇／裂嘴／豁嘴／豁嘴兒）harelipped person
得把嘴（只會說）boasting; go on cackling without laying an egg
接嘴（接茬／打斷對話）butt into a conversation; interrupt a conversation
喉嘴（氣門）air door; air valve

渺嘴（撇嘴）pout one's lips

筆嘴（筆尖兒）tip of a writing brush

答嘴（搭碴兒）pick up the thread of a conversation and take part in it

搭嘴（插嘴）interrupt a conversation

嘟嘴（噘嘴）pout one's lips

暗埋個嘴（把嘴合上）shut up

撅嘴 pout

箭嘴（箭頭）arrowhead

遮嘴（傘尖兒）tip of an umbrella

鞋嘴（鞋尖）toe cap

應嘴（頂嘴）answer back; backchat; backtalk; reply defiantly; talk back

講漏嘴（說漏嘴）a slip of the tongue

【嘸】mou⁵ unclear

喃嘸 ①（僧侶）monk ②（祭神祈禱）pray

發嘸（發霉）mould

睇餸食飯，睇蠋喃嘸（看茶吃飯）live within one's means

【噗】pok⁸ burst

吞噗（偷懶）goof off

【噎】jit⁸ hiccup

噎住 be choked with food

打思噎（打嗝兒）① burp ② get hiccups; have hiccups; hiccup

打噎（打嗝）① hiccup ② belch; burp

【噍】dziu³（咀嚼）chew

噍爛（嚼碎）chew; masticate; munch

【噚】kam⁴ last

噚日（昨天）yesterday

噚晚（昨晚）last night

【噚】tsam⁴ yesterday

噚日（昨天）yesterday

噚日朝（昨天早上）yesterday morning

噚晚（昨晚）last night

【噚】tsam³ talk in a boring way

噚氣（磨叨／囉嗦）repeat oneself

【嚩】bo³ final particle for emphasis

又係嚩（可也是）this is also true

係嚩（真是的）this is true

待慢晒嚩（招待不周全）I've not been a good host

唔錯嚩（不錯哦）not bad

【嗙】paang⁴（趕／攆）drive out; expel; oust; show sb the door

嗙出去（趕出去／攆出去）drive sb away; drive sb out of the door; expel; kick out of; kick sb downstairs; oust; put sb to the door; see the back of sb; send sb about his/her business; send sb packing; send sb to the right-about; show sb the door; throw out; turn out sb; turn sb out of doors; turn sb out of the house

【噉】gam² ① such ②（那麼）well then

做到隻屐噉（工作很辛苦）work very hard

【墟】hoey¹（集）market

墟冚（人山人海／熱鬧）as bustling as a market; in a bustle

墟場（集市）market

三個女人一個墟（三個女人一台戲）when women get together they make a lot of noise chattering

花墟（花市）flower market

趁墟（趕集）go to the market

【墜】dzoey⁶ relieve

墜火（去火／敗火）relieve heat; relieve inflammation

【增】dzang¹ add

增加 increase

增值 ① appreciate; appreciate in price; increase in value; value-added ② add value to an octopus card

自我增值 upgrade oneself

倍增 redouble

遞增 increase by degrees; increase progressively

【墨】mak⁹ ink

墨七（小偷）burglar; thief

墨水 ink

墨水筆（自來水筆／鋼筆）fountain pen

墨魚（烏賊）cuttlefish

墨魚肝肚雞泡心腸——黑夾毒（墨魚肚腸河豚肝——又黑又毒）the belly and intestines of a cuttlefish and the liver of a pufffish: they are all black and poisonous

墨魚滑（墨魚肉泥）minced cuttlefish
墨盒 ①（墨盒）ink box ②（噴墨墨盒）inkjet cartridge
墨硯（硯台）inkslab
墨筆（毛筆）writing brush

一枝墨（一塊墨）a slab of ink
知書識墨（知書識禮）educated and polite person
抹黑墨（抹黑）smear
黑墨墨（黑糊糊）very dark
磨墨 grind the ink

【墩】dan¹ block of stone
墩布 mop; swab

一墩（石堆）block of stone
面珠墩（臉蛋兒）face
面墩（臉蛋兒）face
搣佢面珠墩（捏他的臉蛋兒）pinch sb's face

【墮】do⁶ fall down
墮角（偏僻）out-of-the-way; remote

折墮（造孽）obtain one's deserts; suffer because of the bad
    things one has done
真係折墮（真造孽）it's really evil

【嬉】hei¹ play
嬉戲 frolic; have fun; make merry; play; romp; sport

兒嬉 ①（不扎實 / 不牢靠）unreliable ②（不認真）not
    serious

【嬌】giu¹ beautiful and loveable
嬌媚 ①（嬌媚）coquettish ②（甜美迷人）sweet and
    charming
嬌嗲（嬌滴滴）delicate and pretty

老來嬌（年老卻嬌媚）old but still beautiful
詐嬌（撒嬌）behave like a spoiled child; sulk
矄眼嬌（第一眼好看）a woman who seems attractive at first
    sight but is in fact not especially attractive; appear to be
    beautiful at a glance

【審】sam² ① examine ② try
審案（審理案件）try a case
審慎（慎重）prudent

候審 await trial

【寫】se² write
寫字 writing
    寫字台 writing desk
    寫字樓（辦公室）office
        一座寫字樓（一座辦公大樓）an office block
        一間寫字樓（一間辦公室）an office
        搬寫字樓（搬辦公室）move office
寫低（寫下）write down
    寫低你個名（寫下你的名字）write down your name
寫明 written clearly
寫倒（寫得來）can be written out
寫唔倒（寫不來）cannot be written out
寫真 photographs of scantily clad women
寫得 ①（擅長寫作）good at writing ②（可以寫）can be
    written out
    寫得倒（能寫）writable
    寫得落（寫得下）can be written
    寫得嚟（寫得來）can write
寫意（愜意）comfortable; contented; easy; free and happy;
    gratified; pleased; satisfied
    分外寫意（格外愜意）especially contented
寫錯 write sth wrongly

唔知個醜字點寫（不知羞恥）dead to shame; have no sense
    of shame; thick-skinned
描寫（寫真 / 描述）describe; portray
填寫 fill in
亂寫 write without ground
漏寫 fail to write; forget to write
撮寫（縮寫）abbreviation

【寮】liu⁴ hut
寮屋（鐵皮屋 / 木屋）squatter structure

茅寮（小茅房）small hut
棚寮（茅棚）thatched shed

【層】tsang⁴ layer
層面 aspect; dimension; general characteristic
層層 layer upon layer; ring upon ring; tier upon tier

一層 ① one floor; one storey ② a stratum ③ a bed of; a
    blanket of; a cloak of; a coat of; a curtain of; a deck of; a
    film of; a flake of; a floor of; a floor of; a layer; a layer of; a
    level of; a line of; a mantle of; a ring of; a storey; a storey
    of; a veil of
千層 multi-layer
呢一層（這一層 / 這一點 / 這方面）on this point

【履】lei⁵ ① shoes ② tread on
履行 act up to; carry out; enforce; execute; fulfill; meet; observe; perform
履歷表 curriculum vitae; resume

【幡】faan¹ pennant
幡竿燈籠──照遠唔照近（丈八燈台──照遠不照近）benefit any other person than close ones

【幣】bai⁶ currency
幣制 currency system
幣值 purchasing power of a currency

人民幣 Renminbi
外幣 foreign currency
換外幣 exchange foreign currency
港幣（港元）Hong Kong currency; Hong Kong dollar
貨幣 currency

【廚】tsy⁴ chef
廚房 kitchen
廚具 kitchen ware
廚師 chef; cook

大廚 chef
齋廚（素菜館）vegetarian restaurant

【廟】miu⁶⁻² ① temple ② pout
廟宇 temple
廟祝 temple attendant in charge of incense and religious service
廟會 temple fair

寺廟 temple
宗廟 ancestral temple of a ruling house
海水沖倒龍王廟（大水衝了龍王廟，自家人不認自家人）not know who belongs to the same group
祭五臟廟（填飽肚子）eat
嘴廟廟（噘嘴）pout

【廠】tsong² (工廠) factory
廠房 factory building
廠長 factory director; factory manager
廠商 firm; manufacturer

入廠（入院）be hospitalised
山寨廠（山寨工廠）cottage factory; squatter factory
做廠（開工廠）set up a factory
賺粒糖，蝕間廠（撿了芝麻，丟了西瓜）while seeking a small gain, one could suffer a big loss

【廢】fai³ (沒用) waste
廢事（浪費時間）a waste of time
廢物 waste
廢柴（廢人）crap; good-for-nothing; loser; useless person
廢時 a waste of time
　廢時睬你（不想浪費時間理你）don't want to waste time with you
廢話 nonsense
　廢話少講（廢話少說）cut the crap
　講廢話 talk bullshit; talk nonsense

大癲大廢（舉止瘋狂）act in a crazy manner; playsome
前功盡廢（前功盡棄）all efforts go down the drain; all former achievements are nullified; all labour's lost; all one's earlier achievements are in vain; all one's labour is thrown away; all one's merits count for nothing; all one's previous efforts are wasted; all one's work is wasted; back where one started; forfeit all one's former achievements; have one's previous efforts wasted; labour lost; nullify al the advantages of a series of victories; nullify all the previous efforts; one's previous efforts have proved to be useless; turn all the previous labour to nothing; waste all the previous efforts; waste the efforts already made
荒廢 fall into disuse; fall into disrepair; lie waste; out of practice
殘廢（殘疾）disabled

【廣】gwong² ① (廣泛) wide ② (廣州) Canton; Guangzhou
廣州 Guangzhou
廣告 advertisement
廣東 Canton
　廣東人 Cantonese; Cantonese people
　廣東菜（粵菜）Cantonese dishes; Cantonese food
　廣東話（粵語）Cantonese; Cantonese dialect
　　識少少廣東話（聽得懂一點廣東話）know a little Cantonese
廣場（商場）mall
廣播 broadcast; broadcasting
　廣播名人 on-air personality; radio personality

人面廣（人緣廣）be well connected
產品推廣 product promotion

【弊】bai⁶ (糟糕) alas; awful; oh dear; oh heck
弊傢伙（可幹了）how terrible; oh dear; what a bad luck
弊嘞（幹了）alas; it's awful; oh dear; oh heck

作弊 cheat; indulge in corrupt practices; practice fraud
利弊 pros and cons

【彈】 daan⁶ ① **shoot** ② **draw back** ③ **missile**

彈丸之地 tiny little place

彈弓（彈簧）spring
　　彈弓牀（彈簧牀）spring bed
　　裝彈弓（使圈套）make an ambush; set a trap

彈性 flexibility

彈票（空頭支票 / 退回拒付支票）bounced cheque; return a dishonoured cheque

一枝導彈（一枚導彈）a missile
一粒子彈（一顆子彈）a bullet
子彈 ①（子彈）bullet ②（錢）money
反彈 bounce back; rebound
有讚冇彈（只表揚不批評）just praise without criticism
定過抬炸彈（極為從容鎮定）very calm and confident
炸彈 bomb
紅色炸彈（結婚請帖）wedding invitation card
原子彈 atomic bomb
掟手榴彈（扔手榴彈）throw a grenade
蛋家婆打醮——冇彈（壇）（沒有抱怨 / 無投訴）above criticism; no complaints
導彈 guided missile; missile

【彈】 taan⁴（批評 / 指責）criticise

彈人（批評別人 / 指責別人）criticise others
彈生晒（瞎批評）criticise blindly

冇得彈 ①（沒說的 / 無法挑剔的）above criticism; beyond reproach ②（好極了）couldn't be better; excellent; second to none; very good; wonderful
濕水棉胎——冇得彈（帽子破了邊——頂好）①（沒說的 / 無法挑剔的）above criticism; beyond reproach ②（好極了）couldn't be better; excellent; second to none; very good; wonderful

【影】 jing² ①**（影子 / 蹤影）shadow** ②**（照相）take a photo**

影友（攝影愛好者）shutterbug
影印（複印）copy; photocopy
　　影印紙（復印紙）copy paper
　　影印機（複印機）copying machine; photocopier
影相（照相）① take a photo ② have one's photo taken
　　影相佬（攝影師）photographer
　　影相留念（照相紀念）take a photo to mark the occasion
　　影相機（照相機）camera
　　影相館（照相館）photo studio
　　影相舖（照相館）photo studio
　　一間影相舖（一家照相館）a photo studio

一齊影張相（一起拍張照）take a photo together
影咗好多相（拍了很多照）take many photos
影番張相（拍一張照）take a photo
幫我哋影張相（幫我們拍一張照）could you take a photo for us

影音（音像）audio-visual
　　影音店（音像店）audio-visual shop
　　影音器材（音像器材）audio and visual gadgets
影衰（使人臉上無光）be overshadowed
影迷（電影迷）movie fan
影帶（錄像帶）videotape
　　睇影帶（看錄像帶）watch a videotape
影碟 video disk
　　影碟機 video disk player
影畫戲（電影）cinema
影壇 filmdom
影響 affect; impact; influence
　　影響力 influence
　　大受影響 be seriously affected
一套電影（一部電影）a movie
一齣電影（一場電影）a film; a movie
人影 human shadow
刀光劍影 be engaged in a fierce battle; flashing with knives and swords; sabre-rattling; the flashes and shadows of swords; the glint and flash of cold steel
三級電影 Category III movie; X-rated movie
古裝電影 costume movie
含沙射影 be attacked by innuendo; be attacked by insinuation; hurt others maliciously; insinuate; make insinuations
邪牌電影（色情電影）pornographic film
捕風捉影 act on hearsay evidence; catch at shadows — indulge in groundless suspicion; grasp at a shadow; lay hold on the wind; run after a shadow
剪影 ①（剪紙剪影）paper-cut silhouette ②（草圖 / 大綱）sketch; outline ③（黑色半身側面剪影）cucoloris
睇電影（看電影）see a movie
電影 movie
踩水影（踏水）tread water
錄影（錄像）video record

【德】 dak⁷ virtue

德文 German
德國 Germany
　　德國人 German

仁義道德 benevolence, righteousness, and virtue; humanity, justice, and virtue; justice and morality; kindness and magnanimity; virtue and morality

品德 moral character
美德 moral excellence; virtue
培育美德 cultivate virtue
關公細佬──亦得（翼德）（後腦勺留鬍子──隨便）as
    you like

【慫】sung² urge
慫恿 urge

【慧】wai³ wisdom
慧根 root of wisdom that can lead one to the truth
慧眼 eye of wisdom

智慧 wisdom
聰慧 astute; bright; clever; intelligent

【慰】wai³ console
慰勞 appreciate sb's services and present gifts; send
    one's best wishes to sb in recognition of their services
    rendered
慰問（轉達問候／表達同情和關懷）convey greetings to;
    express sympathy and solicitude for; extend one's regards
    to; salute

安慰 comfort; console

【慾】juk⁹ desire
慾火 passion; the fire of lust
慾望 desire

【慕】mou⁶ envy
慕名 long for fame
    慕名而來 come to sb because one admires his/her
        reputation
慕絲（慕斯蛋糕）(English) mousse

仰慕 admire; admire and respect; adore; look up to; regard
    with admiration

【憂】jau¹（憂慮）worry
憂心（擔心）worry
憂慮 worry
    無憂無慮 carefree

衣食無憂 have no worries about money
食君之祿，擔君之憂 do one's duty as one is paid
唔使憂（不用發愁／別擔心）not to worry
唔憂（不愁／不擔心）not to worry

【慮】loey⁶ worry
慮患（擔心麻煩）apprehensive of trouble

考慮 consider
智慮（智慧）wisdom
無憂無慮 carefree
憂慮 worry

【慶】hing³ ①（慶祝）celebrate ②（熱）hot ③（興奮）excited
慶烚烚 ①（熱騰騰）burning hot ②（非常生氣）very angry
慶祝 celebrate
    熱烈慶祝 grandly celebrate
慶過火屎（十分憤怒）very angry
慶過辣雞（十分憤怒）very angry

身慶（感冒）have a fever; have a temperature
國慶（國慶日）National Day
誌慶（道賀）offer congratulations
頭慶（頭發熱）hot-headed
攞景定贈慶（幸災樂禍）take advantage of one's vulnerability

【憐】lin⁴ pity
憐愛 have tender affection for; love tenderly; show tender
    care for
憐憫 commiserate; take pity on

可憐 miserable; pity
扮可憐 ① play pitiful; pretend to be pitiful ② play miserable;
    pretend to be miserable
唔抵可憐（不值得可憐）not deserve one's sympathy
楚楚可憐 delicate and touching

【憎】dzang¹（討厭）hate
憎人哋（恨人家）hate others
憎人富貴厭人貧（嫉妒富人，鄙視窮人）envy the rich
    people and despise the poor
憎佢（恨他）hate sb
    憎死佢（恨死他）hate sb deeply
憎恨 hatred

乞人憎（惡心）disgusting; nuisance
犯眾憎（惹公憤）sb who is hated by everyone
忟憎（焦慮不安）agitated; fidgety; in a fret; irritable
發拃憎（心中惱怒，給人臉色／擺臭臉）be vexed and
    lose one's temper; in a temper; quarrel with one's own
    shadow
發盟憎（因煩惱而發脾氣）be vexed and lose one's temper;
    in a temper; quarrel with one's own shadow

塞古盟憎（意想不到的突然）all of a sudden
瘟憎（惱怒／煩惱）annoyed
寧犯天條，莫犯眾憎（不要冒犯公眾）it is wise not to
　　offend the public

【憚】daan⁶ fear

憚煩（嫌煩）afraid of trouble; dislike taking the trouble

忌憚 dread; fear; scruple
肆無忌憚 act outrageously; act recklessly and care for
　　nobody; afraid of nothing; behave in a disorderly
　　manner without fear; have no scruples at all; have no
　　respect for anything; in an unrestrained way; indulgent
　　and reckless; make no scruple; reckless and unbridled;
　　run riot; scruble at nothing; stop at nothing; unbridled;
　　unscrupulous; without restraints of any kind; without
　　scruple

【憫】man⁵ pity

憫恤（憐憫體恤）pity and help

憐憫 commiserate; take pity on

【摩】mo¹ touch

摩打（馬達／電動機）motor
　　摩打壞咗（發動機壞了）the motor is out of order
摩登（時尚／時髦）(English) modern
摩貨（確認交易）confirmor transaction
　　摩貨成交（確認交易成交）complete a confirmor
　　　　transaction
　　摩貨登記（確認人交易登記）registration of confirmor
　　　　transaction
　　住宅摩貨（住宅單位的確認交易）confirmor transaction
　　　　on residential flat
　　住宅摩貨登記（住宅單位的確認交易）confirmor
　　　　transaction on residential flat
摩絲（頭髮定型劑／定型水）hair spray
摩囉差（印度人）Indian
　　摩囉差拜神——睇天（小碗吃飯——靠天（添））it
　　　　depends on the weather; under the mercy of God

按摩 massage

【撇】kyt⁸ snap

撇嘴 pout

水瓜打狗——唔見咗一撇（肉包子打狗——一去不回）half
　　of sth is lost
拗開兩撇（折成兩段）break into two

【撐】tsaang¹ prop up; support

撐到恒（劍拔弩張）support to the utmost
撐枱腳（桌腿）have a meal; have a meal with one's lover
撐腰 back up; bolster up; support
　　撐腰打氣 bolster and pep up; bolster and support; in an
　　　　effort to back up
　　有人撐腰 be backed by sb; have sb at one's back
撐艇（划船）boating; go boating; paddle a boat; row
　　a boat
　　撐艇仔（走之兒）the "walking" (辶) radical
撐雞（撒潑）act hysterically and refuse to see reason;
　　behave rudely; in a tantrum; shrewish and make a scene;
　　unreasonable and make a scene
　　撐雞婆（令人討厭的女人／潑婦／母老虎）fishwife;
　　　　harridan; harpy; shrew; shrewish woman; vixen

支撐 bracing; crutch; prop up; support; sustain; timbering
死撐 refuse to admit a mistake; stubborn and reluctant to
　　admit mistakes or defeats
沙煲罌撐（鍋碗瓢盆）household goods
架撐 ①（工具／家當）tools ②（武器）weapons
篤篤撐（咚咚鏘）clang, clang, clang

【撈】lou¹ ①（謀生）earn a living ②（混合）mix

撈女（妓女）prostitute; street-walker
撈勻（拌勻）mix thoroughly
撈汁（拌菜汁兒）stir and mix with sauce from the dishes
撈佬（北方人）northerner
撈埋（混在一起／拌合）blend; mix and stir
撈起 ①（提升生命）have a rise in life ②（發達／致富）
　　become rich; make a fortune
撈家（詐騙者）racketeer
　　撈家仔（偷拐詐騙的流氓）person who earns dishonest
　　　　profits; racketeer
　　撈家婆（賺取不合法利潤的女人）woman who earns
　　　　dishonest profits
　　大撈家 ①（黑幫分子）sb who earns a living from vice
　　　　②（事業有成的人）sb successful in business
撈偏（靠非法生意謀生）earn a living from illegal business
撈湯（混湯）mix with soup
撈亂（弄亂／搞亂）mix up
撈過界（過了界／串地盤）interfere in sb else's business
撈飯（和飯／拌飯）mix with rice
撈靜水（吃獨門兒）live on one's special skill
撈鬆（北方人）northerner
　　撈鬆佬（北方人）northerner
撈麵（拌麵）noodles in mixed sauce
撈攪（麻煩／沒條理／亂騰）confused; messy; upset

冇得撈（沒活兒幹）be unemployed

出嚟撈 ①（從事非法行業）drift about in the world to engage in dishonest work ②（做妓女）prostitute oneself

唔撈（不幹）quit one's job

秘撈（兼職／賺外快）do part-time job; moonlight

最多唔撈（大不了不幹）it's no big deal to quit one's job

劈炮唔撈（甩手兒／摺挑子／辭職）give up one's job

識撈（會混）know what is best to do

【撈】laau⁴ dredge; scoop out of water

撈搞（麻煩）troublesome

【撒】saat⁸ disperse

撒手鐧 one's trump card

撒賴（耍無賴／蠻橫胡鬧）make a scene with an intention to shift the blame to other shoulders; raise hell

【撤】tsit⁸ retreat

撤出 evacuate; withdraw

撤退 retreat

撤職 be dismissed from office; be removed from one's office; dismiss sb from his post; remove sb from office

【撥】but⁹（搧）fan

撥大葵扇（做媒人）act as a go-between; act as a matchmaker; play cupid

撥扇（搧扇子）fan with a fan

三扒二撥（匆匆完成／三兩下）hurry through; in no time at all

水撥（刮水器）wiper

【撳】gam⁶ press

撳錢（由自動提款機取錢）withdraw from an automatic teller machine (ATM)

【撇】pit⁸（甩）stroke

撇甩（甩掉）dump; get rid of

　撇甩佢（把他甩掉）get rid of him

撇咗（拋棄了）abandon; cast away

撇雨 ①（潲雨）rain slanted by wind ②（被潲雨打濕）get wet by the slanting rain

撇脫（行動要迅速）prompt in action

　撇撇脫脫（行動要迅速）prompt in action

撇開 get rid of

　撇開佢（把他甩掉）get rid of him

撇檔（分手）end a partnership

一撇（一千）one thousand

十劃未有一撇（八字還沒一撇）have barely started a large project

【撚】nip⁹ ① be good at ②（作弄／玩弄／算計）play tricks on; toy with

撚手（拿手）of high quality

　撚手小菜（拿手小菜）good dishes

撚化（捉弄／愚弄）deceive sb; play a trick on sb

　撚化人（算計人家）play a trick on sb

　專登撚化人（故意作弄人）deliberately play tricks on others

撚死（掐死）choke to death by strangling with hands

撚花（種花草）play with flowers and grass

撚乾（擰乾）squeeze dry

撚雀（玩鳥兒）play with birds

撚頸（卡脖子）grab the neck

撚爛（捏破）break by squeezing

【撕】si¹ tear

撕破 rip; tear

撕開 rip open; tear open

撕碎 tear to pieces

【撞】dzong⁶ ①（碰撞）collide; crash; run into ②（瞎猜）random guess; wild guess

撞火（生氣／發火／發怒／惱火）be ablaze with anger; feel angry; fire up; fit to be tied; flare up; get angry; get shirty; lose one's temper

撞手神（碰手氣）① have a stroke of luck; try one's luck ② try one's luck in gambling

撞正（剛好）by a curious coincidence; by chance

　撞到正（剛好）by chance

撞死馬（走路急匆匆趕路的人）person who jostles his way in hot haste

撞見（碰見／遇見）alight on; alight upon; bump into; chance upon; come across; come on; come upon; cross sb's path; cross the path of sb; encounter; fall across; fall among; fall in with; light on; light upon; meet by chance; meet unexpectedly; meet with; meet sb by accident; run across; run into

撞車 car crash; collision of vehicles

撞到（碰到）bump into; chance upon; come across; cross sb's path; meet unexpectedly; meet with; run across; run into

撞板（捅婁子／碰釘子／犯錯）get into trouble; make a mistake; run into trouble; screw up

　撞板多過食飯（成功少碰壁多）keep making mistakes

　包撞板（保證會碰壁）sure to go wrong

　撞大板（犯大錯）make a serious mistake

撞晒大板（犯大錯）make a serious mistake

撞面（碰面）bump into

撞埋（撞向）bump into; crash into

撞彩（碰運氣）achieve sth by luck; chance one's luck; depend upon luck; pot luck; stand one's chance; take a chance; try one's luck

撞啱（偶然／碰巧／偏巧）by chance

撞棍（撞彩／中獎／遇見好運氣）trickster

撞頭（相衝／衝突）confront

撞嚫 ①（撞着）be hurt by sth heavy ②（撞倒）knock down

撞聾（聽覺不靈）play deaf

撞爛 smash in collision

白撞（冒充某人以欺騙他人）pass off as sb in order to cheat others

相撞 crash together

頂撞（得罪某人）offend sb

連環相撞 crash involving several cars

莽撞 crude and impetuous

亂打亂撞（歪打正着）score a lucky hit

橫衝直撞 collide in every direction

【撞】zong⁶ collide

撞邪（見鬼）bad luck

撞鬼（活見鬼／倒霉／着邪）be haunted by a ghost; down on one's luck; unfortunate

【撬】giu² （撬）pry

撬甩（撬掉）pry away

【播】bo³ ① sow ② spread

播出 airing; broadcast

播音 make broadcasts

主播 anchor of the show

直播 live broadcast

傳播 transmit

新聞主播 news anchor

新聞廣播 news broadcast

電視主播 TV anchor

廣播 broadcast; broadcasting

【撩】liu⁴⁻² ①（挑）poke; stir up ②（挑逗）arouse amorous desires; seduce; tantalise; tease

撩下 ①（挑一下／撥一下／攪一下）stir ②（挑逗一下）tease

撩牙（剔牙）pick one's teeth

撩交打（挑起事情打架）provoke sb into fighting

撩交嗌（吵架）provoke an argument with sth

撩耳仔（掏耳朵）pick the ears

撩返出嚟（挑了出來）pick sth out

【撬】giu⁶ （挖人）prise up

撬牆腳（挖牆腳）① lure sb away from a job ② seduce sb away from a lover

拗撬（爭議）(English) argue

【撲】pok⁸ rush

撲水（籌錢）go for rush money; raise money

撲低（趴下）lie down

撲飛（奔票）look everywhere for a ticket

撲倒瞓（俯卧）lie prostrate in sleeping

頻撲（忙碌／奔波／匆忙）in a hurry all the time; rush around; shuttle back and forth for one's living

【撮】tsyt⁸ abbreviate

撮要（總結）gist; summary

撮寫（縮寫）abbreviation

【揤】bat⁷ ①（舀）ladle ②（撮）scoop up

揤垃圾（用簸箕裝垃圾）scoop up rubbish with a dustin

揤湯（舀湯）ladle out soup

揤飯（盛飯）fill a bowl with rice

【撼】ham⁵ （撞）bump against

撼牆（撞牆）bump one's head against the wall

撼嚫（撞傷）injure by bumping

【撠】gik⁷ （卡）block; check

撠住（卡住）get stuck

【摜】gwaan³ fall

摜低（跌倒）fall; stumble; tip over

【敵】dik⁹ enemy

敵人 enemy

迷惑敵人 confuse the enemy

敵對 antagonistic; hostile; oppose

不敵 be defeated; no match for

死敵 arch rival; deadly enemy

勢均力敵 all square; balance in power; balance of forces; diamond cut diamond; equal in authority and power; equal scale; even scale; evenly matched; in an equilibrium; level; lever-pegging; match each other in strength; neck and neck; nip and tuck; well-matched; well-matched in strength

腹背受敵 be attacked both from behind and in front; be caught between two fires; between the devil and the deep sea; between the hammer and the anvil; have enemies in front and rear

斃敵（殲敵）kill enemy troops

【數】sou² counting

數一數二 reckon as one of the very best; the best; the most famous

數臭（臭罵）scold

【數】sou³ ①（數）number ②（賬目）account ③（錢）money

數口（算術很快）quick with figures

數字 figure

數尾（尾數 / 零頭）balance; odd amount in addition to the round number

數量 quantity

數學 mathematics

數據 data

數還數路還路（人情是人情，數目要算清）balance accounts with sb no matter who they are

數簿（賬本）account book

一條數（總計）a sum

入我數（算我的 / 記我賬上）my treat; put it to my account

入數 ①（存錢）deposit money ②（記賬）put it to one's account ③（算賬）put the blame on

口數（心算）do sums in one's head; mental arithmetic

分數（打算）propriety

少數 minority

心中有數 know what is what

日數（天數）number of days

比數（比分）score

出公數（公家報銷）apply for reimbursement from an organisation

平均持貨日數（平均持有天數）average holding days

打咗輸數（作好不成功的心理準備）be mentally prepared for a loss

打定輸數（作好不成功的心理準備）be mentally prepared for a loss

打輸數（作好不成功的心理準備）give up for loss

多數 for the most part; mostly

收數（收債）collect debts

有分數（心裏有打算）have a good sense of propriety; know how to manage sth; know what to do and what not to do

有着數（合算 / 有便宜可佔）profit from a deal

有路數（有辦法 / 有線索）there's a way

死人燈籠報大數（拉長弓）pull a long bow

自有分數（知道該做甚麼）I know what to do and what not to do

作數（做假賬）cook the books

劫數 predestined fate

序數 ordinal; ordinal number

成數（很可能）it is likely that

找數（開賬單 / 付賬單）make out the bill; pay a bill

污染指數 pollution index

走數（逃債 / 躲債）avoid repaying debts

里數 mileage

使出渾身解數 bring all one's skill into play; bring forth all the talent one has; do all that one is capable of; do one's best; exert oneself to the utmost; use all one's skill

拗數（鬥氣）quarrel with

拖數（拖欠）be behind in payment; be in arrears

放數（放債）lend money at a high interest

度數（分寸）propriety

後數（後面的付賬）bill to be settled by the person who follows the speaker

計吓條數（算一算）calculate

計條數（算一算）settle a score

計錯數（算錯）calculate wrongly

計數 ①（計算）calculate; count ②（算賬）settle a score

倍數 multiple

唔算數（食言）go back on one's words

埋數（結算）balance accounts; close an account; make the final calculation; settle accounts; settle the bill; wind up an account

級數（等級）array; progress; series

孭數（揹負重債）be heavily in debt

追數（追債）dun for debt

做數（做賬）keep accounts

啞仔食雲吞——心中有數（啞巴吃餃子——心裏有數）know what to do

夠晒數（齊了 / 完整了）it's complete

夠數（足夠 / 尚可以 / 夠數量 / 充足）adequate; enough; sufficient in quantity

婆仔數（微不足道的金額）insignificant sums

婆媽數（微不足道的數量）trivial amount

彩數（運氣）luck

清數（結清賬目）settle; square up

術數 ①（治國方式）ways of administering a nation ②（算命）fortune-telling

頂數（抵債）pay a debt in kind or by labour

單數（奇數）odd number

揸數（簿記員）book-keeper

程數（可能性）probability
睇數（付賬）pay the bill; the bill please
着數 ①（划算／好處／佔便宜／得便宜／得益）advantage ②（利益）benefit; profitable
結數（結算／結賬）balance accounts; close an account; make the final calculation; settle accounts; settle the bill; wind up an account
街數（外賬）debt; overdue bill
補番數（補足錢）make it up; make up for
補數 ①（補錢）make up the money ②（補償）do sth as a sort of remedy
填數（填補盜走的錢）replace money that one has taken secretly
搵着數（佔便宜）take advantage of sb
過數（轉錢）transfer money
路數 ①（門路）way of making money ②（社會關係）social connections
歲數 age
算數 ①（計算）count in ②（算了）forget it; never mind
認數（承認債務）acknowledge the debt
賒數（賒賬）on account; on credit
齊頭數 ①（整數）round figure; round number ②（巨款）round sum
諗縮數（打小算盤）petty and scheming
撻數（賴賬）repudiate a debt
篤數（虛報數字）inflate the numbers; record a false set of figures
賴數 ①（賴賬）repudiate a debt ②（毀約）break one's promise
縮數（小算盤）scheme to make money; selfish calculations
總數 total
講過算數（說話算話）a verbal promise has to be kept; as good as one's word; honour one's own words; keep one's word; live up to one's word; one means what one says; true to one's word
講數（達成協議／談判／談條件）negotiate; settle a dispute
點數（檢查數目）check the number
雙數（偶數）even number
鐘數（時間）time
攞着數（佔便宜）profit from a deal

【暮】mou⁶ dusk
暮色 dusk; gloaming shadow; twilight
暮氣 apathy; lethargy
　暮氣沉沉 apathetic

【暫】dzaam⁶ temporary
暫別 a short separation; part for a short time
暫時 temporary

【暴】bou⁶ sudden
暴雨 rainstorm
　暴雨警告 rainstorm warning signal
　　紅色暴雨警告 red rainstorm warning signal
　　黑色暴雨警告 black rainstorm warning signal
暴富難睇（暴發戶不可一世，令人厭惡）set a beggar on horse-back and he'll ride to the devil

雷暴 thunderstorm

【槧】tsim³ wooden tablet
槧本（雕版印本）books made of engravings

門槧（門檻兒）door sill

【樂】lok⁹ entertain
樂於 be glad to; be willing to; like to; love to
　樂於助人 be willing to help; like to help others
樂意 glad to
樂趣 enjoyment; fun; pleasure
　增加樂趣 heighten the enjoyment
樂觀 optimistic

生日快樂 happy birthday
安樂 comfortable
吃喝玩樂 beer and skittles; cakes and ale; eat, drink, and be merry; feasting and reveling; gluttony and pleasure-seeking; idle away one's time in pleasure-seeking
作樂 enjoy; have a good time; have fun; make merry
快樂 feel happy; happy
享樂 indulge in creature comforts; lead a life of pleasure
周末快樂 have a nice weekend
奏樂 play music; strike up a tune
耍樂（娛樂）entertain
風吹雞蛋殼——財散人安樂（花錢令人安心）pay a price for one's safety
凍檸樂（冰可樂加檸檬）iced coke with lemon
娛樂 entertainment; recreation
財散人安樂（花了錢令人安心／花錢安人心）when money is spent, peace of mind is possible
麻雀耍樂（打麻將）play mahjong
悶悶不樂（鬱悶／苦悶／鬱鬱寡歡）depressed
復活節快樂 Happy Easter
聖誕快樂 Merry Christmas
新年快樂 Happy New Year
熱檸樂（熱可樂加檸檬）hot coke with lemon
鞋底沙——抌乾淨至安樂（眼中釘——拔掉了才舒坦）you won't feel comfortable until the sting in one's eyes is pulled out

檸樂（可樂加檸檬）coke with lemon
鬱鬱不樂（悶悶不樂）a cup too low; dejected; depressed; despondent; disconsolate; down in the dumps; down in the mouth; downhearted; have a fit of blues; have the blues; in a dismal mood; in the doldrums; jobless; look blue; out of spirits; sing the blues

【樂】ngok⁹ music
樂師 musician
樂迷（音樂迷）music fan; music lover
　小樂迷 child music fan

古典音樂 classical music
幸福快樂 full of happiness
弦樂 string music
音樂 music
管樂 wind music
聽吓音樂（聽一聽音樂）listen to some music
聽音樂 listen to music
爵士樂 jazz music

【槽】tsou⁴ groove
槽口（凹口）notch

水槽（下水管）downpipe; downspout
跳槽（換工作）switch jobs

【樟】dzoeng¹ camphor
樟木槓（樟木箱）camphorwood trunk

【樓】lau⁴⁻²（樓房）building
樓上 the floor above; upstairs
樓下 ① downstairs; the floor below ②（以下／以內）(said of prices) below; within
樓市 property market
樓宇（樓房）building
　樓宇公契（大廈公契）deed of mutual covenant
　樓宇按揭（抵押／典押）mortgage
樓底 ①（樓下）downstairs ②（天花板）ceiling
　樓底下（樓下）downstairs
　樓底高（天花板高）the ceiling is high
　樓底矮（天花板低）the ceiling is low
樓花（期房／未建成的住宅單位）uncompleted residential unit
　買樓花（買期房／買未建成的住宅單位）buy a flat under construction
樓面 ①（營業範圍）floor ②（服務員）waiter
　樓面面積 floor area
樓梯 staircase

　一堂樓梯（一條樓梯）a ladder
　行樓梯（走樓梯）take the stairs
　呢堂樓梯（這道樓梯）this staircase
樓齡（房齡）age of building

一沓樓（一棟樓）a building
一座寫字樓（一座辦公大樓）an office block
一間酒樓 a Chinese restaurant
一間寫字樓（一間辦公室）an office
一棟樓 a building
一層樓 ① a flat ② a storey
二手樓 second-hand property
上樓（住在大樓裏）live in a building
千金難買向南樓 south-facing flats are hard to buy
石屎樓（鋼筋混凝土大樓）building constructed of concrete and steel
交樓（交房）hand over a completed unit
私人樓（私人住宅）private building
私家樓（私人住宅）private building
供樓（分期付款供樓房）mortgage
拆樓（拆房子）pull down a building
波樓（枱球館）billiard house
炒樓（炒賣房產）speculate in real estate
律師樓（律師事務所）law firm
洋樓（洋房）foreign-style house
冧樓（房子坍塌）the house has collapsed
酒樓（飯館／飯店）Chinese restaurant
租樓（租房子）rent a room
茶樓（酒家／酒樓）Cantonese restaurant; Chinese restaurant; teahouse
送樓（送一層樓給人作禮物）give sb an apartment as a present
起樓（蓋房子／蓋樓房）build a building
售樓（出售房屋／出售房產）sale of property
提早贖樓（提前還清購房貸款）early redemption
換樓（換房子）change a house; change an apartment
睇樓（看房子）see the flat; take a look at the house
買樓（買樓房）buy a flat
買踏樓（買層樓）buy a flat
會計師樓（會計師事務所）accounting firm
落三樓（下去三樓）go down to the third floor
落樓（下樓）go downstairs
跳樓 jump off a building to commit suicide
嘈到拆樓（非常嘈吵）extremely noisy
搬寫字樓（搬辦公室）move office
寫字樓（辦公室）office
閣樓 cockloft
賣樓（賣房子）sell a flat
騎樓（陽台）balcony

鹹水樓〔危房〕dangerous building
贖樓〔還清購房貸款〕redemption of the property
驗樓〔樓宇檢查〕flat inspection

【標】biu¹ ① snatch ② symbol

標水〔噴水〕water spray
標汗〔冒汗〕perspire; sweat
標奇立異〔標新立異〕create sth new and original; do sth unconventional; do sth unorthodox; strain after novelty
標青〔出彩 / 出眾 / 拔尖 / 傑出〕distinguished; great; outstanding
標松柴〔貪污〕embezzle sb's money
標參〔綁架〕hold sb to ransom; kidnap
標準 standard

目標 target
招標 tender
治標 cope with the symptoms only; provide temporary solutions to the problems; take stopgap measures
長遠目標 long-term goal
追求目標 pursue one's goal
商標 trade mark
濕水欖核——兩頭標〔水裏的葫蘆——兩邊擺〕fleet of foot

【模】mou⁴ mould

模仿 imitate
模型 model
模特兒 model
模樣 appearance
　一模一樣 be exactly alike; identical
　大模廝樣〔大模大樣〕haughty; proudly; with full composure
　裝模作樣 pretend to be a know-it-all
模範 model
　模範作用 exemplary role
模糊 blurred; dim; indistinct; vague
　模糊不清 blurred and indistinct

工模〔模具〕mould
手指模〔指印〕fingerprint
名模 famous model
倒模〔鑄模子〕mould
起模〔做模子 / 做模型〕make a mould

【樣】joeng⁶ kinds; sorts

樣辦〔樣品〕prototype; sample; specimen
樣樣 all kinds of; all sorts of
　樣樣嘢〔每樣東西〕everything

平時一樣 as usual
各式各樣 all kinds of; all sorts of; every kind of; in every shape and form; of every description; of every hue; of various descriptions
榜樣 example; model

【樣】joeng⁶⁻² 〔模樣 / 樣子〕appearance

樣衰〔樣子不好 / 臉目醜陋〕bad-looking; ugly face
　樣衰衰〔長得難看〕bad-looking; ugly face
樣靚身材正〔模樣漂亮身材棒〕pretty face with a nice body

一時一樣〔變幻無常〕fickle
一模一樣 be exactly alike; identical
一樣 same
大模廝樣〔大模大樣〕haughty; proudly; with full composure
冇嗰樣整嗰樣〔畫蛇添足〕do sth unnecessary
好樣 good-looking
式樣 mode; model; style; type
有樣學樣 follow a bad example
似模似樣〔像模像樣〕look alike
似樣 ①〔像樣〕proper; reasonable; right ②〔外表相似〕look alike
亞茂整餅——冇嗰樣整嗰樣〔阿茂整餅——沒那樣就做那樣〕try to be different from others
咁樣〔這樣〕in that case; so; such
耍花樣 behave in a deceitful manner
唔似樣〔不像樣〕go too far; it is most improper
衰樣〔鬼樣子〕lousy look
得個樣〔虛有其表〕seemingly powerful but actually lacking real substance
無論點樣〔無論如何〕anyhow
睇你個貓樣〔看你這德行〕you're disgusting
照樣 repeat an action
裝模作樣 pretend to be a know-it-all
模樣 appearance
橫掂都喺一樣〔橫豎都一樣〕it is all the same to sb
貓樣〔鬼樣子〕ugly face
講笑搵第樣〔別開這樣的玩笑〕this is no laughing matter
勁醜樣〔太醜了〕mega ugly; very ugly
醜樣〔醜陋 / 難看〕ugly
點樣〔怎麼樣 / 怎樣〕how; how is it
識就鴛鴦，唔識就兩樣〔區分不出兩者之間的差別〕be unable to appreciate the difference between two things

【歎】taan³ 〔享受〕enjoy

歎吓〔享受一下〕enjoy
歎茶〔品茶〕enjoy tea
歎氣 sigh

火燒棺材——大歎 (炭) (盡可能享受生活) enjoy life as much as possible

火燒旗竿——長歎 (炭) (盡可能享受生活) enjoy life as long as possible; live in clover forever

慨歎 lament with sighs

【歐】au¹ (享受) European

歐元 Euro

歐化 Europeanised

歐洲 Europe

歐羅 (歐元) (English) Euro

【扁】po¹ measure word for plants or trees

一扁 (一棵) a head of; a tuft of

【毆】au¹ beat

毆打 beat up

毆跛 (打斷) break; smash

【漿】dzoeng¹ starch

漿糊 paste

豆漿 soybean milk

【潔】git³ clean

潔白 clean and white

純潔 chaste; clean and honest; pure; virginal

清潔 clean

廉潔 honest; whitehanded; with clean hands

【潑】put⁸ spill

潑婦 (狡猾的女人 / 令人討厭的女人 / 母老虎) fishwife; harridan; harpy; shrew; shrewish woman; vixen

潑辣 shrewish and violent

活潑 ① active; full of life; lively; sprightly; vivacious; vivid ② reactive

【潛】tsim⁴ dive

潛水 diving

潛質 (潛能) potential

　有潛質 (好苗子) have good potential

【潤】joen⁶ ① (增潤) enrich ② (挖苦) give sb ironical remarks

潤吓佢 (挖苦他) give sb sarcastic remarks

潤膚霜 moisturising cream

利潤 gain; profit

投資利潤 profit on investment

家肥屋潤 (家庭和睦，有禮且富) wish you a prosperous year

純利潤 (淨利潤) net profit

豬潤 (豬肝) pork's liver

賬面利潤 book value in profit

銷售利潤 profit on the sale

總利潤 (毛利潤) gross profit

【潭】taam⁴ pool

潭水 deep water

鱷魚潭 (龍潭虎穴) dangerous place

【潮】tsiu⁴ ① tide ② Chiu Chow

潮州 Chiu Chow

　潮州音樂——自己顧自己 (老西兒拉胡琴——自顧自) Chiu Chow music —— everyone for themselves; pay one's bill for oneself

　潮州粥 Chiu Chow congee

潮流 trend

　迎合潮流 go with the current of the times

潮氣 (輕佻) flirtatious

潮濕 humid; moisture

　好潮濕 very humid

人潮 crowd of people

新潮 trendy

熱潮 boom

【潺】saan⁴ trouble

潺潺 gurgling of the flowing water

白鱔上沙灘——唔死一身潺 (死定了) get out of distress but into trouble

滑潺潺 (滑膩) wet and slippery

【潲】saau³ hogwash; swill

潲水 (泔水) hogwash; swill

　潲水缸 (泔水桶) swill vat

豬潲 (豬食) hogwash; pig feed; swill

【熠】saap⁹ ① (水煮) boil ② (明亮) luminous

熠蛋 (煮雞蛋) boil eggs; boiled egg

熠熟狗頭 (煮熟的狗頭——咧嘴逢迎) on the broad grin

【熟】suk⁹ cooked

熟人 acquaintance; friend
　熟人買破鑊 (被朋友出賣) be sold a pup by one's friend

熟手 (老練 / 熟練) adept at a particular task; experienced; skilled

熟行 (內行 / 在行 / 知行情 / 懂行規) be skilled; be well acquainted with a task

熟性 (懂事) considerate; reasonable; sensible
　唔熟性 (不懂世故 / 不懂事) ignorant; inconsiderate

熟抽 (紅醬油 / 濃醬油) dark soy sauce

熟油 cooked oil

熟客 (老主顧) frequent customer; old customer; regular customer
　熟客仔 (老主顧) frequent customer; old customer; regular customer

熟食檔 (熟食攤兒) cooked food stall

熟能生巧 practice makes perfect

熟落 (不生疏 / 熟悉) on familiar terms with sb; very familiar with

熟檔 (非常瞭解) know a lot about sth

熟識 familiar with

熟餸 (熟食) cooked food

熟讀唐詩三百首，唔會吟詩也會偷 (熟能生巧) skill comes from constant practice

熟鹽 (精鹽) refined salt; table salt

一次生兩次熟 (一回生二回熟) clumsy at first but skillful later on; people get used to things quickly

一鑊熟 ① (一鍋煮) cook everything in one pot ② (一鍋端) all come to an end; all perish together; end up in common ruin; get killed at one and the same time; perish together

人生路不熟 (人生地不熟) be a complete stranger

工多藝熟 (熟能生巧) practice makes perfect

半生熟 (半熟) medium; medium-cooked

生熟 (生人和熟人) a stranger and a friend

早熟 ① ripen early ② reach puberty early ③ precocious

恃熟賣熟 (仗着與友人關係好，而變得不客氣) too familiar with each other to stand on ceremony

相熟 (熟悉) know each other well

淥熟 (燙熟) blanch

純熟 fluent; practiced; skillful; well versed

焗熟 (燜熟) braised until done

軟熟 (柔軟 / 軟和) soft

買生不如買熟 (買東西去熟悉的店) feel secure to make a purchase in a familiar shop

黃泡髧熟 (黃而浮腫) a swollen face with yellow complexion

慣熟 (熟悉) familiar

養唔熟 (養不熟) disobedient

燉熟 stew until done

【熱】jit⁹ hot

熱心 enthusiastic; zeal

熱水 hot water
　熱水壺 ① (熱水壺) hot-water pot ② (暖壺 / 熱水瓶 / 保溫瓶) thermos bottle; thermos flask
　電熱水壺 electric air pot
　熱水爐 (熱水器) water heater

熱天 (夏天) summer time
　大熱天時 (大熱天) on a hot day

熱手貨 (熱門貨 / 暢銷的商品 / 流行的商品) brisk sale; goods in great demand; goods which sell well; hot item; popular ware

熱身 (做準備動作) warm-up
　熱身運動 (準備活動) warm-up

熱狗 hot dog
　一個熱狗 a hot dog

熱氣 (上火 / 火氣) heat; inflammation
　熱氣飯 (難題) difficult job
　發熱氣 (上火) suffer from internal heat

熱痱 (痱子) heat rash; heat spot; prickly heat
　出熱痱 (長痱子) have prickly heat
　生熱痱 (長痱子) have prickly heat
　發熱痱 (長痱子) have prickly heat

熱帶 tropical

熱情 passion

熱煮不能熱食 (心急吃不了熱豆腐) patient to wait

熱話 (熱門話題) hot gossip
　全城熱話 (全城討論) talk of the town

熱飲 hot drinks

熱辣辣 (熱呼呼的) burning hot; hot; piping hot; scorching

熱潮 boom

熱線 hotline

熱鬧 bustle; excitement; hustle and bustle; lively
　一片熱鬧 all busy and bustling
　湊熱鬧 go along the fun; join in the fun; take part in the merry-making
　睇熱鬧 (看熱鬧) watch the excitement; watch the fun; watch the scene of bustle

熱頭 (太陽) sun
　曬熱頭 (曬太陽) bask in the sun; be exposed to the sun; sunbathe

熱戀 be head over heels in love

大熱 (大熱門) big hit

天氣炎熱 it's hot

天時暑熱 (天氣炎熱) the weather is hot

天時熱 (天氣熱) the weather is hot

天氣酷熱 it's very hot

打鐵趁熱 strike the iron while it is hot

好熱 very hot
灼熱 blanch in hot water
狂熱 fanatical; feverish; mania; rabid
炎熱 blazing; burning hot; scorching; very hot
探熱 (量體溫) take sb's temperature
焗熱 (燜熱 / 熏蒸) suffocating
酷熱 very hot
濕熱 ① (潮濕悶熱) hot and damp; warm and humid
　　② (麻煩 / 撓頭 / 纏手) difficult to deal with; difficult to tackle; headache; meet with a hitch; messed-up
燥熱 hot and dry

【璃】 lei¹ glass

一塊玻璃 a pane of glass
玻璃 glass
鎅玻璃 (切割玻璃) cut glass

【瘟】 wan¹ plague

瘟神 god of plague
瘟瘟沌沌 (糊糊塗塗 / 頭腦不清醒) lose one's consciousness

發台瘟 (舞台表演糟糕) give a poor performance in a live show
發瘟 (發瘋) crazy
發雞瘟 (發瘋) crazy; insane

【瘡】 tsong¹ boil

瘡疤 scar of an ulcer; wound scar

生瘡 form a boil
老鼠尾生瘡——大極有限 (事情再大也有極限) there's a ceiling for sth
暗瘡 (粉刺 / 痤瘡) acne
爆瘡 (爆痘痘) breakout in spots

【瘦】 sau³ thin

瘦田冇人耕，耕嚟有人爭 (不肯努力，只佔便宜) once a wasteland is inhabited, a rush for an occupation is insisted
瘦肉 lean meat; lean pork
瘦身 stream-line operation
瘦削 (瘦弱) emaciated; emaciated and frail; thin and weak
瘦弱 weak
瘦骨仙 (瘦猴兒) very thin
瘦瘦哋 (有點兒瘦) a little slim; quite slim
瘦蜢蜢 (很瘦) very thin

又高又瘦 tall and slim
面黃骨瘦 (面黃肌瘦) skinny and look pale
高高瘦瘦 tall and slim
高瘦 tall and slim
追到瘦 (追亡逐北) put the squeeze on sb

【瘤】 lau⁴ tumour

瘤胃 rumen

腺瘤 adenoma
腫瘤 tumor

【盤】 pun⁴⁻² site

盤問 cross-examine
盤滿缽滿 (盆滿缽滿 / 大圓滿小圓流) full to the brim
盤盤聲 (以萬計算) by ten thousands

上車盤 (第一次購房) first-timer flat
小算盤 selfish calculations
打如意算盤 work out a plan advantageous to oneself
打錯算盤 make a wrong decision
生果盤 (水果盤) fresh fruit platter
地產樓盤 units for sale
地盤 ① (建築工地) building site; construction site ② (黑社會勢力範圍) triad society district
收盤 close a business; close down; go out of business; stop doing business; suspense of business; termination of business; wind up business
坐盤 (持倉) hold a position
成盤 ① (達成交易) clinch a bargain; clinch a deal; close a bargain; conclude a bargain; conclude a transation; settle a bargain; strike a bargain ② (整板) whole plate
放盤 (出售) put on sale
杯盤 (盤子) tray
爭地盤 fight for territory
洗手盤 (臉盆) washbasin
胎盤 placenta
建築地盤 building site; construction site
軚盤 (方向盤) steering wheel
探盤 (摸底) sound out a deal
清盤 (破產 / 清賬 / 結算賬戶) balance the book; clear an account; pay off all one's debts; settle an account; square an account; wind up
密底算盤——冇罅漏 (鐵公雞——一毛不拔 / 作為吝嗇鬼的意思 / 拒絕貢獻一分錢) as close as a clam; as mean as a miser; as tight as a drum; close-fisted; not give a cent; not lift a finger; not stir a finger; not turn a finger; refuse to contribute a single cent; stingy; too stingy to pull out a hair; unwilling to give up even a hair; unwilling

to sacrifice even a single hair; penny pincher

軚盤（駕駛盤／方向盤）steering wheel

開盤 ① （開售）be on sale ② （股市開盤）opening

斟盤（洽談／談判）hold talks with sb; negotiation

算盤 abacus

輪盤 roulette

頭盤（頭道菜）① appetiser; starter ② first course

鍵盤 keyboard

【瞌】 hap⁷ ① （睡）sleep ② （瞇）close the eyes

瞌吓（打盹兒）nap
　瞌一吓（打個盹兒）take a nap

瞌埋眼（閉上眼睛／闔上眼睛／閉上眼）close one's eyes

瞌陣（小憩／睡覺／打盹兒）nap
　瞌一陣（睡一會兒／小睡一下／打個盹兒）take a nap

【瞓】 fan³ （睡）sleep

瞓低（躺下）lie down

瞓厲頸（落枕）stiff neck caused by an awkward sleeping posture

瞓房（臥室／睡房）bedroom

瞓個身落去（整副家產投進去）put all one's investment into sth

瞓倒（能睡）can sleep
　瞓唔倒（睡不着）cannot sleep
　瞓得倒（睡得着）can sleep

瞓晏咗（睡過頭了）overslept

瞓得（睡得着）can sleep
　瞓得唔好（睡得不好）did not sleep very well
　瞓得稔（睡得安穩）sleep like a log; sleep soundly

瞓着（睡着）doze off; get to sleep
　瞓着眼（打瞌睡／睡着）doze off; get to sleep
　瞓唔着（睡不着）cannot sleep; unable to get to sleep

瞓街（睡馬路）sleep on the road

瞓過籠（睡過頭）oversleep

瞓醒（睡醒）wake up

瞓覺（睡覺）sleep
　大覺瞓 ① （不擔心）not be worried; not to care a pin ② （睡大覺／睡得很熟）enjoy a sound sleep
　冇覺好瞓（沒睡好覺）not have a sound sleep
　日頭瞓覺（白天睡覺）sleep during the daytime
　平時幾點瞓覺（平時幾點睡覺）what time do you usually go to bed
　瞓晏覺（睡午覺）take an afternoon nap

大覺瞓 ① （不擔心）not be worried; not care a pin ② （睡大覺／睡得很熟）enjoy a sound sleep

冇覺好瞓（沒睡好覺）not have a sound sleep

反昂瞓（仰臥）lie on one's back in sleeping

打昂瞓（仰臥）lie on one's back in sleeping

打側瞓（側臥）lie on the side in sleeping

好眼瞓（很睏）very sleepy

好醒瞓（淺眠）wake up at the slightest thing

好瞓（睡得安穩）sound sleep

有得震冇得瞓（膽戰心驚）tremble with fear

老虎都會瞌眼瞓（老虎也會打瞌睡／馬有失蹄）even a watchful person will fall asleep

夜瞓（晚睡）go to bed late

食少啖多覺瞓（安全至上）play for safety

唔夠瞓（沒睡夠／缺覺）inadequate sleep

蚊都瞓（太遲了）it would be too late to; too late

蚊瞓（太晚了）too late

眼瞓（發睏／昏昏欲睡）sleepy

捱眼瞓（熬夜）stay up late or all night

撲倒瞓（俯臥）lie prostrate when sleeping

瞌眼瞓（打個盹兒／打瞌睡／感覺困了／小睡一下）doze off; fall asleep; feel sleepy; take a nap

醒瞓（淺眠）wake up at the slightest thing

爛瞓（嗜睡）person who likes to sleep

【瞇】 mei¹ close one's eyes

瞇埋眼（瞇上眼睛）close one's eyes
　瞇埋雙眼（瞇上眼睛）close one's eyes

【確】 kok⁸ confirm

確定 confirm

確實 confirm

千真萬確 as sure as fate

正確 correct; exact; right

的的確確 definitely

的確 definitely

【碼】 maa⁵ size

碼子 system of numerical symbols used in business

十二碼 penalty kick

大碼 large size

中碼 medium; medium size

尺碼 size

加大碼（加大號）extra large size

加細碼（加小號）extra small

細碼（小碼）small; small size

銀碼（金額）amount of money; sum of money

鞋碼（鞋釘）shoe nail

籌碼 chip; counter

【碼】maa⁵ stack up
碼頭 ① pier ② rich husband ③ rich partner

一個碼（一個尺寸）one size
外幣銀碼（外幣金額）currency amount
加細碼（加小號）extra small size
起碼（至少）at least
密碼 code; secret code
港幣銀碼（港幣金額）Hong Kong dollar amount
號碼 number

【磁】tsi⁴ ① magnetism ② porcelain
磁石（磁鐵）magnetic iron
磁碟（磁盤）disk

【磅】bong⁶ ① pound ② （過磅）weigh
磅水（付錢／給錢）give sb the money; pay cash; pay sb;
　　pay up

過磅 ① （稱重）weigh ② （超重）overweight

【穀】guk⁷ grain
穀物 cereal; grain

上屋搬下屋，唔見一籮穀（滾石不生苔）a rolling stone
　　gathers no moss

【稿】gou² manuscript
稿件 manuscript
稿費 contribution fee

拙稿 my poor manuscript
截稿 deadline for the submission of a manuscript

【稻】dou⁶ rice
稻田 paddy field; rice field
稻草 rice straw

稈稻（稻稈）stalk of rice

【窮】kung⁴ poor
窮人 poor people
窮光蛋 poor person
窮到燶（赤貧）as poor as a church mouse; very poor
窮鬼（窮光蛋）pauper; penniless vagrant; poor wretch;
　　ragamuffin
窮寇莫追 not to run after the hard-pressed enemy

人窮志不窮 poor but ambitious

三三不盡，六六無窮（無窮無盡）never-ending
六六無窮（無窮無盡）never-ending
好窮 very poor
呻窮（哭窮）complain of being short of money
貧窮 poor
禍患無窮 constant cause of trouble; incessant calamities;
　　with consequences of maximum seriousness

【箱】soeng¹ box; trunk
箱子 box; case; chest; trunk
箱蓋 case cover; cover

一個箱（一個箱子）a case
公仔箱（電視機）television set
投票箱 ballot box
車尾箱（後備箱）boot; trunk
波箱（變速箱／齒輪箱）gear box
信箱 mail box
烤箱 oven
紙皮箱（硬紙盒）carton box
郵箱 mail box
棚尾拉箱（活動結束後清場／終止活動緊急撤離／爛尾）
　　come to a disgraceful end; meet with an ignominious fate

【箭】dzin³ arrow
箭嘴（箭頭）arrowhead
箭頭 arrowhead; arrow point; arrow tip

一弓射兩箭（一石二鳥／一箭雙雕）kill two birds with one
　　stone
弓箭 bows and arrows
火箭 rocket
揸住雞毛當令箭（拿着雞毛當令箭／狐假虎威／仗勢欺
　　人）steal the show of an authority

【範】faan⁶ model
範本 model for calligraphy or painting
範圍（邊界／限制）ambit; boundary; confine; extent; limit;
　　range; scope; spectrum
範疇 ambit; category; domain; realm; scope

防範 precaution
典範 epitome; example; model; nonesuch; paradigm
模範 model
樹立典範 set an example for

【篇】pin¹ passage
篇章 canto; literary piece; sections and chapters
篇幅 space; length

鬼話連篇（說謊／大話連篇）tell lies

【篋】haap⁹ case

篋篋（錦繡前程）long and thin

皮篋（皮箱）leather case

【糊】wu⁴ paste

糊口 eke out a living; make a living to feed the family
糊塗 confused; muddled

含糊 ① ambiguous; vague; unclear ② careless; perfunctory;
  sloppy
芝麻糊 sweet sesame soup
食天糊（吃天糊）win a game in mahjong before any tile is
  played
食炸糊（詐糊／希望落空）fail to attain one's hope
食糊（吃糊／和了）draw; win a game in mahjong
衰家食尾糊（輸家贏了最後一局麻將）the unlucky mahjong
  player wins the last game
詐糊（空歡喜）call out a winnng hand in error
滿糊（和了滿貫）slam
模糊 blurred; dim; indistinct; vague
漿糊 paste
蟮糊 eel paste

【糭】dzung³⁻²（糭子）glutinous rice dumpling

糭子（粽子）glutinous rice dumpling

梘水糭（鹼水粽）alkaline water glutinous rice dumpling

【糍】tsi⁴ rice dumpling

糯米糍 glutinous rice dumpling

【緒】soey⁵ mental state

緒言 foreword; introduction; preamble; preface

情緒 emotion

【線】sin³ thread

線人（眼目）informer
線口（線頭）end of a thread
線步（針腳）stitch
線眼（眼線）informer
線報（信息／情報）information; intelligence

內線 extension

天線 antenna
水平線 horizon
水線（地線）ground wire
牙線 dental floss
生命線 lifeline
曲線 curve
收線（掛電話）hang up; hang up the phone
死線（截止期限）deadline
米線 rice noodles
扯線（牽線）establish a relationship for both parties
咁啱線（湊巧／碰巧）by chance; by coincidence; just by
  chance; what a coincidence
拉線（牽線搭橋）act as a go-between; bring both sides
  together; bring one person into contact with another;
  build bridges; foster the relationship between two
  people; pull strings and build bridges
長線（長期）long-term
查詢熱線 enquiry hotline
飛線（接駁電話）divert the phone call
航線 air route; itinerary; navigation route; route; way
陣線 alignment; front; line of battle
釣線（釣魚線／魚線）fishing line
短線（短期）short-term
無線 wireless
斑馬線（橫道線）pedestrian crossing; zebra crossing
街線（外線）outside line
黃線 yellow line
搭錯線 ①（打錯電話／串線）dial a wrong number;
  have the wrong number ②（誤會）misunderstand
  sth
電話斷咗線（電話斷線）the line was disconnected
電線 cable
路線 course; itinerary; route
駁線（接線）connect a wire; wiring
熱線 hotline
膠線（塑料繩）plastic cord
踩線 ① foot fault ② step on the line
踩鋼線（走鋼絲）wirewalking
鋼線（鋼絲）steel wire
黐線（神經錯亂）insane; mad
機場快線 airport express
聲線（嗓門兒／嗓音）one's voice
轉線（換線）change the lane
鐵線（鐵絲）iron wire
黐線 ①（神經失常／神經病／神經錯亂／發瘋）crazy;
  insane; mentally deranged; mixed up; nervous
  breakdown; off the rails ②（串線）wrong number
cut 線 ①（換線）change the lane ②（線路被切斷）the line
  is cut

【緝】tsap⁷ sew in close stitches
緝私 arrest smugglers; anti-smuggling

齊緝緝 (很整齊 / 齊茬兒) neat

【締】dai³ ① form ② conclude
締交 ① establish diplomatic relations ② contract a friendship; form a friendship
締約 conclude a treaty; sign a treaty
締結 conclude; establish
　締結良緣 form marital ties

取締 ban; declare a ban on; clampdown; discipline; forbid; interdict; outlaw; prohibit; punish the violator; suppress

【緣】jyn⁴ fate
緣木求魚 (完全浪費時間 / 完全不可能 / 刻舟求劍) a complete waste of time; climb a tree to catch a fish — a fruitless approach; fish in the air; get blood from a stone; get blood from a turnip; it is very hard to shave an egg; milk the bull, milk the pigeon; utterly impossible; wring water from a flint
緣份 destiny; fate

一面之緣 have a face-to-face meeting with sb
人夾人緣 (人與人之間的關係講求互相配合) whether people get along with one another or not depends on the compatibility of their characters
天賜良緣 heaven-sent marriage
美滿姻緣 happy marriage
姻緣 marriage
締結良緣 form marital ties

【編】pin¹ edit
編輯 editor
編號 ① arrange under numbers ② number; serial number

改編 ① adapt; convert; rearrange; revise; transcribe ② redesignate; reorganise

【緩】wun⁶ slow
緩步 (慢走) walk slowly
　緩步跑 (慢跑) canter; jog
緩和 allay; calm; diffuse; ease up; mitigate; relax

刻不容緩 admit of no delay; brook no delay; cannot be delayed even a moment; demand immediate attention; must not lose a minute; no time to lose; not a moment to be lost; of great urgency; permit of no delay; there is no time to be lost; there is no time to lose; there is not a moment to be lost; urgent
和緩 gentle and mild

【練】lin⁶ practise
練球 practise a ball game
練習 practice
　練習簿 (練習本) exercise book
　經常練習 practice constantly

狗隻訓練 dog training
訓練 (操練) coach; discipline; drill; train
教練 coach; instructor; trainer
磨練 temper oneself

【緻】dzi³ detailed
緻密 ① (細膩 / 精細) close; delicate; fine ② (適當 / 小心) appropriate; careful

別緻 new and unusual
細緻 in detail
趣緻 (可愛 / 有趣 / 逗人喜歡) cute; likeable

【罷】baa⁶ let go
罷就 (罷了 / 算了) let a matter drop

唔要就罷 (不要就算了) take it or leave it

【羹】gang¹ soup
羹湯 thick soup

一隻匙羹 (一把勺子 / 一個勺子) a spoon
木匙羹 (木勺) wooden ladle
粟米羹 (玉米羹) thick corn soup
匙羹 (勺子 / 湯匙) ladle; spoon

【膚】fu¹ skin
膚色 complexion
膚淺 shallow; superficial

皮膚 skin
肌膚 skin and muscle

【膝】sat⁷ knee
膝頭 (膝蓋) knee
　膝頭大過髀 (很瘦) very skinny
　膝頭哥 (膝蓋) knee
　　膝頭哥揩眼淚 (犯了大錯，流下眼淚) make a big mistake and shed tears

跌損咗個膝頭哥（摔破膝蓋）fell down and had a scratch on one's knee

【膠】gaau¹（橡膠 / 塑料）plastic

膠水 glue
膠布 ①（塑料布）plastic cloth ②（膏藥）sticking plaster
膠拖（塑料拖鞋）plastic flip-flops; plastic slippers
膠紙（膠帶）cellotape; sticky tape
　　封箱膠紙（膠帶）duct tape
膠通（塑料管）plastic tube
膠袋（塑料袋）plastic bag
膠盒（塑料盒）plastic box
膠喉（塑料管）plastic tube
膠絲（尼龍絲）nylon yarn
膠線（塑料繩）plastic cord
膠鞋（塑料鞋）plastic shoes
膠輪（橡皮輪子 / 塑料輪子）plastic wheel
膠擦（橡皮）rubber eraser
膠轆（橡皮輪子 / 塑料輪子）plastic wheel

沙膠（硬橡膠）hard rubber
乳膠（膠乳）emulsion; latex
花膠 fish maw
香口膠（口香糖）chewing gum
發泡膠（泡沫塑料）foam rubber
塑膠（塑料）plastic material; plastics
過膠（層壓）laminate
擦紙膠（橡皮擦）rubber eraser
擦膠（橡皮擦）rubber eraser

【膛】tong⁴ chest

挺起胸膛 stand straight in gesture of self-confidence; stick out one's chest
胸膛 breast; chest

【興】hing³ pleasure

興高采烈 above oneself; as jolly as a sandboy; blithe; boisterous; buoyant; cheerful; cheery; effervescence; elated; elated and overjoyed; excited; exhilarated; expansive; exultant; feel one's oats; full of beans; full of spirits and elated; go into raptures; have a hectic time; in a bright humour; in buoyant spirits; in exuberant spirits; in good form; in good spirits; in great delight; in great spirits; in high glee; in high spirits; in one's altitudes; in the pride of one's heart; joyful bustle; jubilant; on the high ropes; on top of the world; on wings; sparkling with joy; tails up; with great gusto; with rapturous joy
興趣 interest

助興 add to the amusement; add to the fun; join in merry-making; liven things up
乘興 while one is in high spirits
高興 feel happy
逢場作興（逢場作戲）join in the enjoyment on occasion
雅興 aesthetic mood; refined interest
戥興（幸災樂禍）take pleasure in other people's misfortune
辣興（激怒）make angry; provoke
贈興（幸災樂禍）take pleasure in other people's misfortune

【興】hing¹（時興 / 盛行）become flourish; popular; prosper; rise; thrive

興旺 prosper
興辦 establish; found; initiate; set up

古老當時興（老式的被視為時尚）the old-fashioned is treated as the trendy
家和萬事興 harmony makes a family prosperous
時興（時尚 / 時髦）fashionable
復興（回復繁榮）return to prosperity; revival

【舖】pou³ shop

舖位（店舖）shopfront
舖租（租金）rent
舖頭（店舖 / 商店 / 舖子）shop; store
　　一間舖頭（一間店舖）a shop
　　打理舖頭（看店）take care of the shop
　　開舖頭（開店）open a shop

一間影相舖（一家照相館）a photo studio
工商舖（工商部門）industrial and commercial premises
五金舖（五金店）hardware store
未門舖（沒關門）the shop is not closed
米舖（糧食店）grain store
低低地蹟舖（承認失敗）admit being defeated
成衣舖 clothes shop
車衣舖（裁縫舖）tailor's shop
店舖 shop; store
油舖（油坊）oil mill
金舖（金飾店）gold shop; gold store
洋服舖（洋裝店）foreign-style tailor's shop
洋貨舖（洋貨店）foreign goods shop
洗衣舖（洗衣店）laundry
門咗舖（關門了）the shop is closed
門舖 ①（商店關門 / 關店）close for the day ②（倒閉）close down
飛髮舖（理髮店）barber's shop
埋舖（關門）closed for business
海味舖（海產店 / 乾貨店）dried seafood shop

涼茶舖（涼茶館）herbal tea house
眼鏡舖（眼鏡店）optical shop
桶舖（製桶店）coopery
乾貨舖（乾貨店）stall selling seasonings and dehydrated food
粥麵舖（粥麵館）congee and noddle shop
開舖（商店開門／開店）open for business; start business
當舖 pawn shop
電器舖（電器店）electrical appliances shop
鞋舖（鞋店）shoe shop
影相舖（照相館）photo studio
髮型舖（理髮店）hair salon
齋舖（素菜館）vegetarian restaurant
機舖（電玩中心／電子遊戲機中心）video game centre
雜貨舖（雜貨店）grocery store
藥材舖（中藥店）Chinese drugstore
曬相舖（照片打印店）photo printing shop

【蓮】lin⁴ lotus

蓮子 lotus seed
　蓮子蓉（蓮蓉）lotus seed paste
　蓮子蓉咁口（甜美的笑容）very sweet smile
蓮花（荷花）lotus flower
蓮蓉（蓮子泥）lotus seed paste
　蓮蓉包 lotus seed paste bun
　蓮蓉焗布甸（蓮蓉焗布丁）baked lotus seed paste pudding
　一籠蓮蓉包 a basket of lotus seed paste buns
蓮藕（藕）lotus root
　一節蓮藕（一節藕）one section of lotus root

榴蓮／榴槤 durian

【蔥】tsung¹ spring onion

蔥爆 deep-fried with spring onion

洋蔥 onion
薑蔥（蔥薑）ginger and spring onion

【蔬】so¹ vegetables

蔬食 ①（素食）vegetarian diet ②（簡單的食物）simple food
蔬菜 vegetables

【蔔】buk⁷ radish

白蘿蔔 turnip
花心蘿蔔（花花公子）playboy
紅蘿蔔（胡蘿蔔）carrot
蘿蔔 radish

【蔭】jam³ shade

蔭庇 patronise; protect
蔭蔽 conceal; cover

林蔭 shade of trees

【虢】gwik⁷ odds

虢礫嘩啦（什物）odds and ends

【蝦】haa¹ ① shrimp ② prawn ③（欺負／欺侮）bully

蝦人（欺負人）bully others
蝦公（大蝦／蝦子）prawn
蝦毛 ①（小蝦）small shrimps ②（小人物）unimportant person
蝦米 ①（小蝦）small shrimp ②（蝦仁／蝦肉）shrimp meat ③（乾蝦）dried shrimp
蝦兵蟹將（不重要的人／小人物）unimportant person
蝦角（蝦餃）deep-fried shrimp dumpling served with salad dressing
蝦乾（乾蝦）dried shrimp
蝦滑（蝦肉泥）minced shrimp
蝦腸（蝦腸粉）shrimp rice roll
蝦碌（倒霉／出糗）(English) hard luck; bizarre
蝦餃 dumpling with shrimp meat; shrimp dumpling; steamed shrimp dumpling
　一籠蝦餃 a basket of shrimp dumpling
蝦醬 shrimp paste
蝦霸（欺負／欺侮／欺凌）bully; bully and humiliate
　蝦蝦霸霸（欺負人）bully; bully and humiliate

一斤白灼蝦 a catty of blanched shrimps
大頭蝦（心不在焉的人）absent-minded person
大蝦 prawn
白灼蝦 blanched shrimps
扯蝦 ①（哮喘）asthma ②（呼吸困難）breathe with difficulty
明蝦 prawn
河蝦 river prawn; river shrimp
焗龍蝦 baked lobster
躁蝦（小孩／嬰兒）baby
瀨尿蝦 ①（皮皮蝦）mantis shrimp; yabbies ②（尿牀）bed-wetter
蘇蝦（小孩）baby
龍蝦 lobster

【蝨】sat⁷ flea; louse

蝨乸（蝨子）louse

一物治一物，糯米治木蝨（一物降一物）one thing is always controlled by another

木蝨（牀蝨）bedbug
好眉好貌生沙蝨（面善心狠）a fair face hides a foul heart
狗蝨（虼蚤）dog flea
捉木蝨（捉牀蝨）catch the bedbug
捉字蝨（摳字眼兒）fool others with words one uses; pick fault with the words one uses; play with the meaning of a word used by sb
塘蝨（鯰魚）catfish

【蝴】wu⁴ butterfly
蝴蝶 butterfly
　蝴蝶式（蝶泳）butterfly stroke

【蝶】dip⁹⁻² butterfly

蝴蝶 butterfly

【衝】tsung¹ charge forward
衝出 rush out
衝鋒 assault; charge
　衝鋒陷陣（出生入死／赴湯蹈火）breach and storm the enemy's citadel; break into enemy ranks; charge against enemy fire; charge an enemy's position; charge and shatter enemy positions; charge forward; charge the enemy lines; dash bravely to the front of the battle; make frontal attacks on; press boldly forward; rush on the enemy and break the line; rush on the hostile ranks; smash into the enemy ranks; storm and break up the enemy's front; storm and shatter the enemy's position; strike into the enemy ranks
衝擊 impact

【褥】juk⁹⁻² mattress
褥套（床罩）ticking

牀褥（褥子）mattress
墊褥（牀褥／褥兒）mattress

【褲】fu³（褲子）trousers
褲穿窿（窮得叮噹響）have no money
褲浪（褲襠）croth of trousers
褲袋（褲兜／口袋）pocket
褲腳（褲腿）bottom of a trouser leg
褲頭（褲衩／褲腰）waistband
　褲頭帶（腰帶／褲腰帶）trouser belt
　勒實褲頭帶（勒緊褲腰帶）tighten one's belt
　紮褲頭帶（繫褲帶）tie the trouser belt

　綁紮褲頭帶（繫褲帶）tie the trouser belt
　勒緊褲頭（勒緊褲腰帶）tighten one's belt
褲髀（褲腿）trouser legs

一條牛仔褲 a pair of jeans
一條褲（一條褲子）a pair of trousers
三角褲 briefs
內衣褲 underwear
牛仔褲 jeans
牛頭褲（牛仔褲）jeans
西褲 slacks
底衫褲（內衣褲）underwear
底褲（打底褲／內衣褲）panties; underwear
抽高條褲（提起褲子）pull up one's trousers
衫褲（衣服）clothes
面褲（外褲）overtrousers
食頭糊，輸甩褲（吃頭糊的人會以輸家收場）first game winner in playing mahjong will be the biggest loser in the end
泳褲 swimming trunks
除褲（脫褲子）take off one's trousers
游水褲（游泳褲）swimming trunks
連裲褲（連衣褲）child's pants with no slit in the seat
開裲褲（開襠褲）open-seat pants; split pants
短褲 shorts
碌爆咗條褲（褲子被繃開）the trousers have burst open
優褲（提褲子）lift up the trousers
虧佬褲（長內衣褲）long-johns
襪褲（連褲襪）pantyhose

【課】fo³ class
課本 textbook
課室（教室）classroom
課程 ① course ② curriculum

一堂課（一節課）a class
代課 substitute teacher
功課 homework
缺課（曠課）absent from class; absent from school; miss a class
逃課（逃學）cut class; ditch class; play truant; skip class
做功課 do schoolwork
授課（教課）give instructions; give lessons; teach; teach a class; tutor
備課 prepare lessons

【誰】soey⁴ who
誰不知（誰知道）who would have thought that

【誼】ji⁴ good relationship

友誼 friendship
促進友誼 promote friendship

【調】diu⁶ turn around

調位（交換位置）swap places
調查 investigate
調轉（倒過來）turn upside-down
　調轉頭（反過來／倒過頭來／對調／調換處境／調轉方向／翻過來）change the direction; turn the other way round
　調轉嚟（倒過來）turn the other way round
　調轉嚟講（反過來說）conversely

格調 style
唱反調 sing a different tune
強調 emphasise
聲調 tone

【調】tiu⁴ mix

調味（佐料）condiment; seasoning
　調味料（佐料兒）condiments
調停（調解／斡旋）mediation

協調 adjust; bring about full coordination; bring into line; bring to harmony; cohere with; concert; coordinate; harmonise; integrate
眼眉調（眼跳／眼瞼抽搐）twitching of the eyelid

【談】taam⁴ talk

談吐 manner of speaking; style of conversation; the way a person talks
談判 negotiation
　面對面談判 face-to-face negotiation
談話 ① chat; colloquy; conversation; talk ② say; state

老生常談（陳詞濫調）banal remark; commonplace; cut and dried; home truth; mere platitude; platitudes; platitudes of an old scholar; Queen Anne is dead; stale news; standing dish; Sunday-school truth; the Dutch have taken Holland; trite remarks; truism; truth
侈談 prate about; prattle about; talk glibly about
洽談 consult together; discuss together
座談 have an informal discussion
健談 talkative
常談（老生常談）platitude
訪談（晤面）interview

【請】tseng² invite

請人（招人）recruit people
請坐 please take a seat; please be seated
請客 treat sb
請教 ask
請問 could you tell me; may I ask
請請（再見）goodbye
請飲（宴請／請客）dinner invitation; hold a banquet
請槍 ①（請人槍替）ghost-write ②（找人代考）ask sb to sit for an examination in place of another person
請願 petition

申請 apply
聘請 hire
邀請 invite

【諒】loeng⁶ forgive

諒解 forgiveness; make allowance for; understanding
　互相諒解 make allowance for each other; understand each other
諒察（請某人理解並原諒自己）ask sb to understand and forgive oneself

原諒 forgive

【論】loen⁴ discuss

論文 thesis
論點 argument; opinion; point
論盡 ①（累贅）clumsy ②（麻煩）troublesome
　論鬼盡（麻煩）troublesome
　乜咁論盡㗎（為甚麼你這麼笨拙）why you're so clumsy
　論論盡盡（非常麻煩）very clumsy
論據 argument; bases for argument; grounds for argument

一種理論 a theory
勿論（別說）let alone; regardless
言論 speech; views
姑勿論（更別說）let alone; not to mention; not to speak of; to say nothing of
爭論 argument; controversy
唔論（不論）it doesn't matter; no matter
格殺勿論 capture and summarily execute; kill on the spot with the authority of the law; kill with lawful authority; no matter if killed
討論 discussion
理論 theory
結論 conclusion

辯論 debate
謬論 fallacy; false theory
議論 comment; discuss; talk

【諗】nam² (想) consider; think; think about; think over

諗巴 (數字) number
    諗巴溫 (第一) (English) number one
諗住 (打算 / 準備) intend; plan
諗法 (想法) idea; notion; opinion; thinking; view; way of looking at sth; what one has in mind
諗起 (想起 / 記起) remember
諗計 (想辦法) map out a strategy
諗真 (想清楚) think sth through
    諗真啲 (好好想想) think sth through
諗唔開 (想不開) at the end of one's tether
諗條橋 (想個點子) work out a trick
諗掂 (解決問題) sort things out
諗落 (想起來) when we come to think of it
    諗落又係嘅 (細想一下也對) when you come to think of it, it's right
諗過 (想想看) think about it
    諗過先 (先想想看) think about it first
    諗過度過先 (先琢磨琢磨) think it through first
諗頭 (想法) idea; notion; opinion; thinking; view; way of looking at sth; what one has in mind
    大諗頭 (好大喜功) hot oneself up with ambition; over-ambitious
    有乜諗頭 (有甚麼想法) any ideas
諗縮數 (打小算盤) petty and scheming

心諗 (心想) I think to myself
冇得諗 (別想了) leave sth out of consideration
有得諗 (值得想) be worth consideration
你點諗 (你怎麼想) what do you think
抵得諗 (不斤斤計較 / 肯吃虧) can bear the burden of work and complaint
抵諗 (不斤斤計較 / 肯吃虧) can bear the burden of work and complaint
唔抵得諗 (斤斤計較) calculating
堪諗 (絞盡腦汁) rack one's brains; turn over in one's mind
點諗 (怎麼想) what does one think
襟諗 (費思量 / 費腦筋) crack one's head; turn over in one's mind

【豎】sy⁶ vertical

豎心邊 (豎心兒 / 豎心旁) the "heart" (心) radical
豎立 erect; set upright; stand
豎起 erect; hoist; hold up

【賜】tsi³ give

賜教 (紆尊教導) condescend to teach; grant instruction
賜福 blessing

天賜 endowed by heaven; given by heaven
惠賜 (慷慨地賜予) bestow sth graciously; kind enough to give

【賞】soeng² reward

賞月 enjoy the moonlight
賞面 (賞臉) do sb a favour; favour sb with one's presence; thanks for coming

打賞 (給賞錢) give tips
欣賞 admire; appreciate
雅俗共賞 appeal to all; appeal to both the sophisticated and the simple-minded; appeal to highbrows and lowbrows; be admired by scholars and laymen alike; be enjoyed by both the educated and the common people; both the refined and the vulgar can take pleasure in; everyone can enjoy; for the enjoyment of both the educated and the common; highbrows and lowbrows alike can enjoy; suit all tastes; suit both refined and popular tastes; the uneducated as well as the educated can appreciate it
讚賞 praise

【賠】pui⁴ compensate

賠水 (賠錢) pay compensation
賠湯藥 (賠醫藥費) pay sb the medical expenses
賠錢 indemnify with money
賠償 compensate

有殺有賠 (純獲利) net profits without any loss

【賢】jin⁴ virtuous

賢內助 good wife

【賣】maai⁶ sell

賣大包 (大甩賣) bargain away; offer a good bargain to buyers; sell sth cheaply
賣口乖 (賣嘴) oil one's tongue; sweet-talk
賣仔莫摸頭 (賣兒莫摸頭) express regret at being forced to sell one's favourite
賣生藕 (調情) flirt
賣肉 (賣淫) offer sex for a living
賣花姑娘插竹葉 (賣花女自己只能插竹葉) a tailor makes the man but he clothes himself in rags
賣花讚花香 (王婆賣瓜，自賣自誇) make a boast of oneself; sing one's own praises

賣命 sacrifice oneself
賣物會 (義賣會) bazzar
賣面光 (賣好) curry favour with sb
賣屋 (賣房子) sell a house
賣晒 (售完 / 售罄) be sold out
賣笑 (賣淫) work as a prostitute
賣貨員 (售貨員) saleman; salesperson; shop assistant; shop clerk
賣魚佬洗身——冇晒聲氣 (沒有消息) there's no news
賣剩蔗 (剩女) a girl who remains unmarried
賣嘢 (賣東西) sell things
賣樓 (賣房子) sell a flat
賣鹹酸菜——畀面 (給面子) give face to sb

一籠燒賣 a basket of pork dumplings
二手買賣 secondary market
大賣特賣 sell like hot cakes
出賣 betray
外賣 takeaway
平賣 (便宜賣) selling cheap
吊起嚟賣 (囤積更高的價格) hoard up for a higher price; increase prices when things are in great demand; speculate by hoarding a commodity
好好賣 (銷量好) sell very well
好賣 (銷量好) sell well
你嗰槓嘢我都有得出賣 (這是兩個人可以玩的遊戲) that is a game two people can play
低買高賣 buy low, sell high
拐賣 abduct and traffic
易賣 (容易賣) easy to sell
炒買炒賣 (投機倒把 / 倒買倒賣) play the market; speculate; speculation and profiteering
唔好賣 (不好賣 / 難賣) hard to sell
送外賣 delivery
斬件賣 (分件售賣) sell by the piece
販賣 (兜售 / 出售 / 銷售) market; peddle; sell; traffic
散賣 (零售 / 零賣) sell by the piece; sell in small quantities
買賣 buying and selling
點賣 (怎麼賣) at what price are you selling it; how much is it
燒賣 pork dumpling
難賣 (不好賣) hard to sell

【賤】 dzin⁶ cheap
賤人 vulgar person
賤友 (賤人) vulgar person
賤生 (粗生) easy to grow

賤泥 (賤人) person of bad character
賤格 (下賤 / 缺德 / 賤骨頭) bad character; base-minded; miserable wretch; scum
　賤格佬 (下賤 / 缺德 / 賤骨頭) bad character; scum
賤精 (賤人) person of bad character
賤種 (賤人) person of bad character

犯賤 demean oneself
作賤 cheap
佢死佢賤 (管他 / 她的) not give a damn
物離鄉貴，人離鄉賤 articles leaving home become precious, but people, demeaned
淫賤 promiscuous
爛賤 (不值錢) cheap; low-priced; worthless
攞嚟賤 (自找麻煩 / 自討苦吃) get oneself into trouble; work for one's destruction

【質】 dzat⁷ material
質地 quality; texture
質素 (素質) quality
質量 ① mass ② quality

支質 (囉嗦) wordy
劣質 of poor quality
有潛質 (好苗子) have good potential
屈質 ① (地方窄小 / 侷促 / 擁擠) cramped ② (雜亂) in a mess; messy
品質 quality
氣質 grace
密質質 (密匝匝 / 稠密 / 人山人海) dense; packed; very crowded
蛋白質 protein
物質 material
潛質 (潛能) potential
糟質 (糟踏) play the fool of sb; slander sb

【質】 dzi³ hostage

人質 hostage

【賬】 dzoeng³ debt
賬面 book value
　賬面利潤 book value in profit
　賬面獲利 (賬面利潤) book value in profit
　賬面賺幅 (賬面利潤) book value in profit

五五分賬 fifty-fifty
分賬 ① split the cost ② split the bill
呆賬 (壞賬) bad debt

通賬（通貨膨脹）inflation
認賬 acknowledge what one has said or done
壞賬（倒賬）bad debt

【賍】dzaang¹（欠）owe

賍人錢（欠人家錢）owe sb money

【趣】tsoey³ interesting

趣怪（活潑有趣）amusing; funny; lively; vivacious
趣緻（可愛／有趣／逗人喜歡）cute; likeable
趣趣地（讓個意思）for fun

旨趣 objective; purport
志趣 aspiration and interest; inclination
快快趣趣 ①（整齊地）neatly ②（迅速）quickly
快趣 ①（整齊地）neatly ②（迅速）quickly
知情識趣 know how to behave oneself to cope with sb's feeling and interest
風趣 witty
家庭樂趣 family joy; homely pleasure
情趣 delight; fun; joy
興趣 interest
增加樂趣 heighten the enjoyment
樂趣 enjoyment; fun; pleasure
諧趣 fun; humour
識趣 know what is best to do

【趟】tong³ ① take a journey ②（次）measure word for time

去一趟（去一次）make a trip

【踏】daap⁹ exact

踏正（正好）exactly; just in time
　踏正十二點（正好十二時）twelve o'clock sharp
踏兩頭船（腳踏兩隻船）attempt to profit oneself in two ways; play both ends against the middle
踏界（壓線）line ball

腳踏（腳蹬）pedal

【踢】tek⁸ kick

踢死兔（晚禮服／燕尾服）tuxedo
踢波 ①（踢球）kick the ball ②（踢足球）play football ③（推工作／推卸責任）pass the buck; slip work
踢腳（手忙腳亂）very busy
　踢晒腳（手忙腳亂）very busy
踢燕（踢毽子）kick the shuttlecock

踢檔（突襲賭館）raid a vice den
踢爆（揭穿／洩密／揭露某人的秘密）debunk; disclose a secret; expose sb's secret
踢寶 ①（突襲某地）raid premises ②（捉姦）act adultery in the act

一腳踢（單幹）do everything by oneself; jack-of-all-trades; one-man band
拳打腳踢 beat and kick; beat up; box and kick; cuff and kick; give sb a good beating; strike and kick

【踩】tsaai² ①（踏）step on ② petal ③ backstab sb

踩入（踏進）step into
踩水（踏水）tread water
　踩水影（踏水）tread water
踩冰（溜冰）ice-skate
踩死蟻（慢得像蝸牛）snail-slow; walk at a snail's pace
踩低（踏下）step down
踩車（騎車）ride a bicycle; ride a bike
踩界（壓線）line ball
踩着芋莢都當蛇（杯弓蛇影）take every bush for a bugbear
踩線 ① foot fault ② step on the line
踩鋼線（走鋼絲）wirewalking

踩嗰…條尾（冒犯別人）cause offence to sb
一沉百踩（牆倒眾人推）everybody hits a person who is down; once sb falls from power, other people are eager to criticise
見高就拜，見低就踩（媚上欺下）flatter those above and bully those below; snobbish
俾西瓜皮人踩（設局害人）make sb meet with losses; make sb slip up
俾蕉皮人踩（設局害人）make sb meet with losses; make sb slip up
鬮踩（互相誹謗）calumniate each other; defame each other; slander each other

【踭】dzaang¹ elbow

手踭（胳膊肘）elbow
托手踭（推託／攔胳膊）give sb a flat refusal; refuse sb's request; refuse to help
批踭（手肘）elbow
腳踭（腳後跟／腳跟）heel
鞋踭（鞋後跟／鞋跟）heel of a shoe
豬踭（豬蹄／豬肘子）pig's elbow

【輩】bui³ generation

輩出 appear one after another; come forth in large numbers; come out in succession

輩份 difference in seniority; seniority in a clan; seniority in a family

朋輩 (朋友) friends
長輩 ① elder ② senior generation
鼠輩 scoundrels
疇輩 (同輩) people of the same generation

【輪】loen⁴ alternate

輪更 (輪班 / 輪值) in shifts; on duty by turn; shift duty
輪到 be one's turn; in one's turn
　　輪到你 it's your turn
輪姦 gang rape
輪飛 (排隊買票) queue up to buy tickets
輪候 (排隊) queue up
輪班 (輪值) in shifts; on duty by turn
輪流 alternately; by rotation; by turns; in rotation; in turn; take turns
輪盤 roulette
輪籌 (排號兒) register

小輪 (小型輪船) ferry; ferry boat
火輪 (渡輪) ferry boat
先啱輪 (早前) earlier on; early on; not long ago
吟咗一大輪 (被說教了很長時間) be lectured for a long time
呢一輪 (這一陣子) lately; recently
做一輪 (工作一段時間) work for a period
郵輪 liner
渡海小輪 ferry
渡輪 ferry; ferry boat
嗰一輪 (那一陣子) at that time; for a period of time; that time; at that time
嗰輪 (那一陣子) at that time; for a period of time; that time
窩輪 (權證) (English) warrant
膠輪 (橡皮輪子 / 塑料輪子) plastic wheel
齒輪 gear

【適】sik⁷ suit

適才 (剛才) just now
適合 appropriate; suitable
　　唔適合 (不適合) inappropriate
適當 proper

合適 appropriate
各適其適 (各取所需) each takes what he needs
舒適 comfortable; cosy; snug

【遮】dze¹ ① cover ② (雨傘 / 傘) umbrella

遮柄 ① (雨傘手柄) umbrella rod ② (安全套 / 避孕套) condom
遮面 (傘面) umbrella fabric
遮骨 (傘骨 / 傘架) ribs of an umbrella
遮嘴 (傘尖兒) tip of an umbrella
遮頭 (傘把兒) head of an umbrella

一把遮 (一把傘) an umbrella
油紙遮 (油紙傘) oilcloth umbrella
雨遮 (雨傘) umbrella
帶遮 (帶傘) have an umbrella
開遮 (撐傘 / 打傘) open an umbrella; spread an umbrella; unfurl an umbrella
擔遮 (撐傘) hold an umbrella
縮骨遮 (摺傘 / 摺疊傘) folding umbrella

【鄭】dzeng⁶ solid

實鄭 (結實 / 硬掙) serviceable

【鄰】loen⁴ neighbour

鄰居 neighbour
鄰近 adjacent; adjoining; close; contiguous; near; neighbouring

遠親不如近鄰 a close neighbour means more than a distant relative; a distant relative is not as good as a near neighbour; a near neighbour is better than a far-dwelling kinsman; a relative far away is not as helpful as a neighbour close by; a relative far off is less helpful than a neighbour close by; an afar off relative is not as helpful as a near neighbour; better is a neighbour that is near than a brother far off; distant relatives are not as helpful as close neighbours; distant relatives are of less account than near neighbour

【醃】jim¹ ① (蜇) sting ② (調味) season

醃尖 (挑剔) cavil; choosy; fastidious; fussy; hypercritical; nitpick; pick and choose; pick fault; picky; upbraid
醃料 marinade
醃眼 (蜇眼睛) sting the eyes

【醇】soen⁴ rich wine

醇厚 ① mellow ② gentle and kind

膽固醇 cholesterol

【醉】dzoey³ drunk

醉酒（喝醉）drunk
　　醉酒佬（醉漢／醉鬼）alcoholic; drunkard
醉貓（醉鬼）drunkard
醉醺醺 very drunk

今朝有酒今朝醉 don't worry today about what you're going to eat tomorrow; enjoy the pleasures of drinking wine here and now; enjoy while one can
自我陶醉（自滿／自戀）have self-complacence; narcissism; self-intoxicated
局部麻醉 local anesthesia
麻醉 anaesthesia
陶醉 be intoxicated with; drink in; revel in
飲飽食醉（吃飽喝足）good meal and many drinks; have had one's fill of food and drink
飲醉（喝醉）drunk; tipsy

【醋】tsou³ vinegar

醋埕（醋罐子）vinegar jar
　　打爛醋埕（打翻醋罐子）lovers getting very jealous

加鹽加醋（添油加醋）exaggerate; lay on thicker colours
白醋 white vinegar
呷乾醋（吃乾醋）be jealous for no reason
呷醋（吃醋／妒忌／嫉妒）be jealous; get angry out of envy; jealousy in a man-woman relationship
糖醋 sweet and sour sauce

【銳】joey⁶ sharp

銳不可當 cannot be held back; full of fighting spirit as to be irresistible; irresistible; no force can stop
銳利 keen; pointed; sharp
銳意 determination; eager intention; sharp will

尖銳 incisive; keen; penetrating; sharp; sharp-pointed

【銷】siu¹ eliminate

銷售 sale
　　銷售利潤 profit on the sale
銷路 sale
　　銷路呆滯（銷售緩慢）slow in sale

一筆勾銷 eliminate at one stroke
勾銷 eliminate
促銷 promote the sale
展銷 exhibit and sell

【銻】tai¹ ① antimony ② aluminium

銻煲（鋁鍋）aluminium casserole
銻鑊（鋁鍋）aluminium frying pan

【鋅】san¹ zinc

鋅鐵（馬口鐵）galvanised iron

【鋒】fung¹ sharp

衝鋒 assault; charge

【鋤】tso⁴ hoe

鋤大地（大老二）Big two
鋤頭 hoe

【銼】tso³ file

指甲銼 nail file

【鋪】pou¹ bed

鋪路 pave a road

打地鋪 make up a bed on the ground; sleep on the floor
孖鋪（兩人睡一張牀）two persons sleeping on one bed
玩一鋪（玩一次）play a game
被鋪（鋪蓋／被套）quilt cover

【震】dzan³ shake; shiver

震動（振動）vibration
震騰騰（膽戰心驚）tremble with fear

手騰腳震（渾身哆嗦）tremble all over
打冷震（發抖／顫抖）shiver; tremble
打震（發抖／顫抖）quiver; shake; shiver; tremble
地震 ① earthquake ② shake-up in a large company
搞搞震（挑起事端／製造麻煩／搞鬼）make trouble
騰騰震（膽戰心驚）tremble with fear
攪攪震（挑起事端／製造麻煩／搞鬼）make trouble

【霉】mui⁴ molded

霉菜（梅菜／霉乾菜）molded dried vegetable
霉爛 mildew and rot

【靚】leng³ ①（美麗／漂亮）beautiful; pretty ②（俊俏）handsome ③（好）good ④（美）aesthetic; artistic

靚女（美女／漂亮的姑娘）beautiful girl; beautiful lady; pretty girl
靚太（美麗的太太）beautiful wife

靚仔 ① (俊小子 / 帥哥) handsome boy; handsome guy; handsome man ② (小子) buster
　　好靚仔 (很英俊) very handsome

靚到死 (漂亮極了) absolutely gorgeous; stunning; very beautiful

靚到痹 (漂亮極了) absolutely gorgeous; stunning; very beautiful

靚到暈 (漂亮極了) absolutely gorgeous; stunning; very beautiful

靚衫 (漂亮衣服) beautiful clothes

靚嘢 (好東西) good thing

靚歌 (好歌) good song

靚爆鏡 (非常有吸引力) very attractive

又平又靚 (物美價廉) cheap but good

生得好靚 (生得美麗) sb is beautiful

好靚 (好美) very beautiful; very pretty

貪靚 (愛美) fond of making oneself pretty

你好靚 (你好美) you are very beautiful

扮靚 (打扮得美) make oneself pretty; make over

身光頸靚 (衣着很好看) dressed up and look sharp

咖啡好靚 (咖啡很棒) this coffee is very nice

抹靚 (打扮) polish

花靚 (小流氓) little rascal

彩色好靚 (這顏色好美) the colours are beautiful

鬥靚 (鬥艷 / 選美賽) beauty contest

鬼火咁靚 (太美了) very beautiful

最靚 (最美) most beautiful

愛靚 (愛美) be concerned about looking good

識扮靚 (會打扮) know how to make oneself pretty

靈舍靚 (特別美) specially beautiful

【靚】leng³ young

靚仔 (小伙子 / 毛小子 / 臭小子) little boy; little rascal

靚妹 (小丫頭 / 妞兒) little girl

花靚 (小流氓) little boy; little rascal

【靠】kaau³ rely on

靠山 sponsor; supporter
　　搵靠山 (找靠山) look for a powerful supporter

靠呃 (矇騙) live by getting sth on the cross

靠車 (吹牛) baloney; blast; blow one's own horn; blow ones own trumpet; boast; brag; draw a long bow; eyewash; hot air; plume oneself; shoot a line; shoot crap; shoot the breeze; shoot the bull; shoot the shit; stick it on; swing the lead; talk big; talk horse; talk in high language; talk through one's hat; tell a lie; tell large stories; tell tall tales

靠害 (陷害 / 坑害) lead sb into a trap

靠得住 dependable; reliable
　　靠唔住 (不可靠 / 靠不住) undependendable; unreliable

靠諦 (談論某人) talk at sb

可靠 dependable; reliable; trustworthy

依靠 depend on; rely on

倚靠 depend on; rely on

無依無靠 all alone in the world; be left forlorn and without a protector; completely helpless; have no one to depend on; have no one to turn to; have nothing to depend on; helpless; high and dry; with no one to rely on; with no one to turn to; with nothing to support one

【鞋】haai⁴ ① (鞋子) shoes ② (歎氣) sighing

鞋底 sole
　　鞋底沙——抌乾淨至安樂 (眼中釘——拔掉了才舒坦) you won't feel comfortable until the sting in one's eyes is pulled out

鞋抽 ① (下顎突出) jutting lower jaw ② (鞋拔子) shoehorn; shoe lifter

鞋烚烚 (粗糙) coarse

鞋帶 shoelace
　　紮鞋帶 (繫鞋帶) tie one's shoelace
　　綁鞋帶 (繫鞋帶) tie one's shoelace

鞋嘴 (鞋尖) toe cap

鞋踭 (鞋後跟 / 鞋跟) heel of a shoe

鞋碼 (鞋釘) shoe nail

鞋舖 (鞋店) shoe shop

鞋頭 (鞋尖) toe cap

鞋擦 (鞋刷) shoe brush

鞋櫃 shoe cabinet

鞋薦 (鞋墊) shoe pad

一對鞋 (一雙鞋) a pair of shoes

水鞋 (雨鞋) rain shoes

皮鞋 leather shoes

抌吓對鞋 (敲鞋子) knock the shoes

拖鞋 flip-flop

波鞋 (球鞋 / 運動鞋) sneaker; sports shoes

高踭鞋 (高跟鞋) high-heeled shoes

除鞋 (脫鞋) remove one's shoes; take off one's shoes

挽鞋 (提鞋) perform some menial task for sb

涼鞋 sandals; slip-ons

着拖鞋 (穿拖鞋) put on the slippers

着鞋 (穿鞋) wear one's shoes

膠鞋 (塑料鞋) plastic shoes

擦鞋 ① (擦鞋子) shine shoes ② (吹捧奉承 / 拍馬屁 / 抱粗腿) adulate; brown-nose; butter sb up; crawl to; curry favour; curry favour with sb; eat sb's toads; fawn on; flatter; give sb the soft-soap; ingratiate oneself with; kiss sb's ass; lay it on thick; lay it on with a trowel; lick sb's boots; lick sb's shoes; lick sb's spittle; lick the boots of sb; obsequious; play up to; polish the apple; soft-soap; suck up to; sycophancy; toady sb

擦錯鞋（馬屁拍到馬蹄上）fail to please one's boss; stroke the fur the wrong way

舊鞋 ①（舊鞋子）old shoes ②（前女友）ex-girlfriend

鬆糕鞋 thick high-heeled shoes

懶佬鞋（帆船鞋 / 懶漢鞋）loafers

【餃】gaau² dumpling

餃子 dumpling

一籠蝦餃 a basket of shrimp dumpling

水餃（餃子）dumpling

菜餃 vegetable dumpling

蝦餃 dumpling with shrimp meat; shrimp dumpling; steamed shrimp dumpling

灌湯餃 dumpling stuffed with pork and chicken soup

【餉】hoeng² duties paid

餉以老拳（暴打一拳）give sb a sound thrashing

差餉 rates

【養】joeng⁵ raise

養大 bring up

養車 keep a car; maintain a car

養活 feed

養唔熟（養不熟）disobedient

養珠（養殖珍珠）cultured pearl

養隻狗（養條狗）keep a dog

養隻貓 keep a cat

物業保養 property maintenance

保養 maintenance

培養（培育 / 開發 / 教育）breed; cultivate; culture; develop; educate; foster; train

營養 nutrition

療養 convalesce; recuperate

【駐】dzy³ stay

駐兵 station troops

駐守 garrison

駐顏 preserve a youthful complexion; retain youth looks

青春常駐 may you stay youthful and beautiful

【駕】gaa³ drive

駕車 drive a car

駕駛 driving

　駕駛執照（駕照）driving licence

迎接大駕 meet sb on his arrival

凌駕 override; place oneself above; rise above others

【駛】sai² ① drive ② spend ③ need

駛牛（騎牛）drive a cow

駛田（犁田）till fields

駛錢（省錢）spend money

　駛黑錢（賄賂）bribe

大駛（花大錢）big-spending

魯莽駕駛 reckless driving

駕駛 driving

【駝】to⁴ hunchback

駝背（羅鍋兒）hunchback

　駝背佬（駝子）humpback

駝鳥 ostrich

阿駝（駝子）humpback; hunchback

【髮】faat⁸ hair

髮夾 hairpin

髮乳（髮膠）hair cream

髮型 hair style; hairdo

　髮型屋（理髮店）hair salon

　髮型師（理髮師）hair stylist

　髮型舖（理髮店）hair salon

髮腳（髮邊 / 鬢腳）sideburns

一執頭髮（一綹頭髮）a coil of hair

甩頭髮（掉頭髮）lose one's hair

披頭散髮 disheveled; have one's hair hanging loose; unkempt

長頭髮 long hair

削髮 shave one's head

短頭髮 short hair

恤髮（做頭髮）do one's hair; have one's hair done at a beauty parlour; style one's hair

染髮 hair dye

飛髮（剪頭髮 / 理髮）haircut; have a haircut

剪頭髮 have a hair cut

脫髮 alopecia; baldness; falling out of hair; lose one's hair

電髮（燙頭髮 / 燙髮）give a permanent wave; perm; wave hair

蓄髮（留長髮）grow long hair
頭髮 hair
辮髮（編頭髮）plaited hair

【鬧】naau⁶（罵）scold

鬧人（罵人）give sb a good dressing down; give sb a good
　　wigging; give sb a scolding; give sb a piece of one's
　　mind; give sb the edge of one's tongue; haul sb over the
　　coals; load sb with insults; mutter insults against; rake sb
　　over the coals; reprove; revile; sail into; scold; swear at;
　　take sb to task; tell one off

鬧交（拌嘴兒／吵架）argue; quarrel
鬧臭（公開罵人）scold sb in public
鬧通街（舊聞）old news
鬧劇 farce
　　一場鬧劇 a farce
鬧鐘 alarm clock

一片熱鬧 all busy and bustling
抵鬧（該罵）deserve the scolding
胡鬧 cause disturbance without obvious reasons; kick up a
　　raw; make a row; mischievous; raise a row; run riot; run
　　wild
湊熱鬧 go along the fun; join in the fun; take part in the
　　merry-making
睇熱鬧（看熱鬧）watch the excitement; watch the fun;
　　watch the scene of bustle
搏鬧（招罵）incur abuses
盞俾人鬧（肯定要挨罵的）it will surely be blamed
熱鬧 bustle; excitement; hustle and bustle; lively

【魄】paak⁸ soul

魄力 boldness; daring and resolute

三魂唔見咗七魄（三魂丟了七魄／魂不守舍）be entranced
　　with fear; be frightened out of one's wits; be scared out
　　of one's wits; be scared to death
失魂落魄 stand aghast
魂魄 soul

【魅】mei⁶ ① goblin ② charm

魅力 attractiveness; charm; charisma; spell
　　增添魅力 add charm to

【魷】jau⁴ squid

魷魚 squid
　　炒老闆魷魚（辭工／辭職）quit one's job on one's own
　　　accord
　　炒佢魷魚（把他解僱）fire sb

炒魷魚（解僱／被開除／遣散／失業）boot sb out; cast
　　out; discharge; dismiss; fire; fire out; get fired; get
　　one's mittimus; get the bag; get the mitten; give sb
　　the air; give sb the axe; give sb the bag; five sb the
　　boot; give sb the bounce; give sb the chop; give sb the
　　chuck; give sb the mitten; give sb the push; give sb the
　　sack; give the bag to sb; give the bounce; give walking
　　papers to sb; kick out sb; lay off; let out; pay off; sack;
　　send off; stand off; throw sb out of employment; turn
　　away; turn off

炒魷（解僱）be dismissed; boot sb out; cast out; discharge;
　　dismiss; fire; fire out; get fired; get one's mittimus; get
　　the bag; get the mitten; give sb the air; give sb the axe;
　　give sb the bag; give sb the boot; give sb the bounce;
　　give sb the chop; give sb the chuck; give sb the mitten;
　　give sb the push; give sb the sack; give the bag to sb;
　　give the bounce; give walking papers to sb; kick out sb;
　　lay off; let out; pay off; sack; send off; stand off; throw sb
　　out of employment; turn away; turn off

【魯】lou⁵ rough

魯莽 careless; discourteous; rash; reckless; rough; rude;
　　uncivil
　　魯莽駕駛 reckless driving

粗魯 rough and rude

【鴇】bou² prospitute

鴇母（老鴇）procuress

老鴇 prostitute

【鴉】aa¹ crow

鴉烏婆（醜女人）ugly woman

烏鴉 crow

【黎】lai⁴ dawn

黎明 dawn; daybreak
　　鄰近黎明（接近黎明）be close to daybreak

【齒】tsi² tooth

齒寒（因別人的失敗而受苦）suffer due to others' failure
齒輪 gear

口齒（承諾）guarantee; promise
冇口齒（不講信用）break a promise; break one's promise;
　　break one's words; go back from one's word; go back on

one's word; untrustworthy; violate one's promise

冇齮口齒（不講信用）break a promise; break one's promise; break one's words; go back from one's word; go back on one's word; untrustworthy; violate one's promise

牙齒 tooth

有口齒（講信用）keep one's promise; keep one's word

咬牙切齒 clench one's teeth; gnash one's teeth; grind one's teeth; set one's teeth

唇齒 lips and teeth

屐齒 teeth of clogs

區區小事，何足掛齒 don't mention such small things; such a trifling matter is hardly worth mentioning

實牙實齒（板上釘釘）certain

講口齒（講信用）keep one's word; keep one's word

16 劃

【劑】dzai¹ dose
劑量 dosage

一劑 a dose of

大劑（大問題）big trouble

止汗劑 deodorant

頭劑（頭煎）first dose of herbal medicine

鎮靜劑（鎮定劑）sedative

藥劑 pharmacy

【器】hei³ instrument; vessel
器官 organ

器重 have a high opinion of; regard highly; think highly of; think much of

一副機器（一台機器）a machine

小家器（小家子氣）mean-spirited

小器 narrow-minded

手提電話差電器（手機充電器）mobile phone charger

玉器 jadeware

兵器 armament; arms; weaponry

武器 armament; armature; arms; weaponry; weapons

金器 gold vessel

瓷器 porcelain

陶器 china; crockery; earthenware; pottery

電器 electrical appliances

儀器 instrument

機器 machine

【噩】ngok⁹ shocking
噩夢 nightmare

混混噩噩（無知／思想糊塗）ignorant; muddle-headed; without a clear aim

混噩（無知／思想糊塗）ignorant; muddle-headed; without a clear aim

【噬】sai⁶（咬）bite
噬咗一啖（咬了一口）be bitten

笑口噬噬（張開嘴笑／開口大笑）roar with laughter; uproarious laughter

眼噬噬（側身看某人為了防止他做某事）look sideways at sb in order to prevent him from doing sth

【噹】dong¹ ding-dong
噹噹 clank

叮噹 clank; clatter

【噴】pan³ spurt
噴一面屎（碰一鼻子灰）be rejected; be snubbed; be sent off with a flea in one's ear; cold shoulder; get rebuffed; meet rejection; meet with a rebuff

噴射船（噴射水翼船）jet foil

香噴噴 very fragrant

【圜】waan⁴ circle
韓圜 Korean won

【墳】fan⁴ grave
墳場（公墓）cementery

墳墓 tomb

山墳 grave

【壁】bik⁷ wall
壁球 squash
　打壁球 play squash

壁畫 fresco; mural; mural painting

爛泥扶唔上壁（爛泥扶不上牆）people of bad character will not be able to change

【壅】 ung¹ heap fertiliser around the roots
壅泥〈埋在泥下〉bank up with earth

監生壅〈活埋〉bury alive

【壇】 taan⁴ ① platform ② hall
壇子 earthen jar
壇場〈祭壇〉area of an altar

杏壇 teaching profession
祭壇 altar; sacrificial altar
影壇 filmdom
藝壇 art circle

【壆】 bok⁸ 〈堤壩〉dam

【學】 hok⁹ learn
學士 bachelor
　文學士 bachelor of arts
　理學士 bachelor of science
學友仔〈同學〉classmate
學生 student
　學生哥〈學生〉pupil; student
　大學生 university student
　小學生 primary school student
　中學生 secondary school student
學位 ①〈學額〉student place ②〈教育文憑〉degree
學你話齋〈像你說的〉as you say
學車〈學開車 / 學駕駛〉learn how to drive; take driving lessons
學者 scholar
　冒充學者 pose as a scholar
學校 school
　一間學校〈一所學校〉a school
　中小學校 primary and secondary schools
　民辦學校 school run by the local people
　國際學校 international school
學神〈學車者〉learner-driver
學師仔〈學徒〉apprentice; trainee
學院 college; institute
學堂 ①〈學校〉school ②〈警察學院〉police academy
學習 learn
學問〈學習 / 研究〉learning; study
　一門學問〈研究課題〉a subject of study
學費 tuition fee
　交學費 ① pay tuition fees ②〈受教訓〉be taught a lesson
學業 study
　學業進步 best wishes on your study

學護〈實習護士〉student nurse

一間中學 a secondary school
入學 enter a school
大學 university
小學 primary school
中學 secondary school
化學 ① chemistry ② feeble; fragile; not long-lasting; undurable
文學 literature
史學 historiography
生物學 biology
同班同學 classmate
同學 fellow student
名牌大學 prestigious university
自學 self-study
求學 ① attend school; go to college; go to school; receive education; study ② pursue one's studies; seek knowledge
走學〈走讀〉attend a day school
易學〈容易學〉easy to learn
返學〈上學〉attend school; go to school
科學 science
哲學 philosophy
唔好學〈不好學 / 難學〉hard to learn
留學 study abroad
退學 leave school
逃學 bunk off; cut class; escape school; hooky; play hookey; play hooky; play truant; skip school; skive off; truancy; truant
勒令退學 order a student to leave school
湊個仔返學〈送孩子上學〉take one's child to school
物理學 physics
開學 start school; the new term begins
遊學 study tour
數學 mathematics
舊同學 former classmate
難學〈不好學〉hard to learn
讀緊大學〈正在讀大學〉be studying at university

【導】 dou⁶ guide
導師 instructor
導演 movie director
導彈 guided missile; missile
　一枝導彈〈一枚導彈〉a missile

訓導 teach and guide
新聞報導 news reporting
領導 ① guide; lead ② leader
循循善導〈循循善誘〉good at giving methodical and patient

guidance; lead one gradually into good practices; teach with skill and patience; lead sb gradually and patiently to the right path

誘導 guide; induce; lead

輔導 counsell

【憑】pang⁴（靠着）depend on

憑據 evidence; proof

文憑 diploma

【憶】jik⁷ memory

憶及 call to mind; recollect; remember

失憶 lapse of memory

【憾】ham⁶ regret

憾事 a matter for regret; regrettable thing

遺憾 regret

【懂】dung² know

懂事 intelligent; reasonable; sensible

懂得（掌握／知道／了解／明白）grasp; know; understand

老懵懂（老糊塗）muddle-head old guy; dotard; old forgetful person

懵懂（糊塗）foolish; muddled

【戰】dzin³ war

戰爭 war

戰後 post-war

戰艦（軍艦）warship

　一隻戰艦（一艘軍艦）a warship

內戰 civil war

反戰 anti-war

打竹戰（打麻將）play mahjong

打野戰（在戶外做愛）have sex out-of-doors

竹戰（打麻將）play mahjong

舌戰 argue heatedly; debate with verbal confrontation; have a verbal battle with

冷戰 cold war

殊死戰（一決生死的戰鬥）desperate fight; fight to the last man; life-or-death battle

野戰（叢林戰）jungle warfare

割喉式減價戰（惡性價格戰）cut-throat price war

結束內戰 end a civil war

悶戰（拖延戰術／緩兵之計）stalling tactics

【撻】taat⁸ ①（展開）lay out ②（順手牽羊）steal sth; take at will

撻朵（主動把自己的身份或地位告知別人）name dropping

撻低佢（把他摔倒）knock him down

撻沙 ①（比目魚）flatfish ②（拖鞋）slippers ③（唯一）sole

撻咗（拿走／偷走）steal

撻定（取消訂單）forfeit a deposit

撻嘢（偷東西／騙東西）steal things

撻數（賴賬）repudiate a debt

撻錢（偷錢／騙錢）steal money

撻頭（光頭／禿頭）bald

翻撻（復合）get back together; reunite

鞭撻 castigate; lash

【撻】taat⁷ strike

撻火（點火）ignite

撻着 ①（發動）get started; start ②（擊中）hit off

　撻唔着 ①（打不着火）can't ignite ②（沒打中）fail to hit off

年廿八，洗辣撻（大年二十八，洗淨不邋遢）do the year-end clean-up two days before the Lunar New Year

污糟辣撻（骯髒）dirty; soiled

杰撻撻 ①（厚重）thick ②（有很大麻煩）in a lot of trouble

蛋撻（蛋塔）egg custard tart; egg tart

傑撻撻 ①（厚重）thick ②（有很大麻煩）in a lot of trouble

嘥撻（浪費）go to waste

辣撻（邋遢／骯髒）dirty; soiled

【撼】ham⁶ fight

撼動（搖擺／抖動）rock; shake

對撼（對打）fight with

【擂】loey⁴ beat; hit

擂台 arena; ring

　打擂台 rise to the challenge; take up the challenge

　擺擂台（打擂台）give an open challenge

【擁】jung² support

擁有 be armed with; come into possession of; come into sb's possession; conquer; get possession of sth; have; hold; in possession of; in the possession of; occupy; of; own; possess

擁抱 cuddle; embrace; hold in one's arms; hug

擁護 advocate; back; endorse; support; uphold

擁躉（捧場的人）fans; supporters

擠擁（擁擠）crowded

【操】tsou[1] (練) drill

操吓佢 (幫他練一練) help to drill him

操縱 manipulate

　　幕後操縱 pull the strings behind the scenes

步操 formation training

曹操 (一個代表「壞人」的名字) a name that stands for "bad man"

韻律操 (花樣體操) rhythmic gymnastics

【擔】daam[1] (挑 / 拿) carry

擔大旗 (扛大旗) person in charge

擔天望地 (東張西望) gaze this way and that; stare about; watch out furtively to the east and west

擔心 feel worried; worried

擔水 (挑水) carry water

擔正 (擔任主角) act the leading role

擔杆 (扁擔) carrying pole

擔泥 (挑土) carry away the mud

擔保 guarantee

　　擔保出外 (擔保外出) bail

　　擔保信 (掛號信) registered letter

擔挑 (扁擔) carrying pole

擔屎都唔偷食 (非常誠實) very honest

擔高手 (抬起手) raise one's hand

擔高頭 (抬起頭) raise one's head

擔梯 ① (扛梯子) carry a ladder ② (在參加公開考試時獲得最低的「H」等級) obtain the lowest "H" grade for a subject when taking a public examination

擔綱 (負責 / 擔當) assume; take on; undertake

擔遮 (打傘 / 撐傘) hold an umbrella

擔擔 (挑擔) cornice

擔頭 (抬頭) raise one's head

擔櫈 (端櫈子) carry a stool

擔旛買水 / 擔幡買水 (扶靈送葬) carry the hearse and escort a funeral

擔戴 (擔責) undertake responsibility

一擔擔 (一個樣) two of a kind

士擔 (郵票 / 印花) (English) stamp

分擔 share the responsibility

平均分擔 share and share alike; take equal shares

承擔 assume; bear; undertake

【擇】dzaak[8] choose

擇食 (挑食) choosy with food; fuzzy eater; picky eater

擇使 ① (不好用) not easy to use ② (傷腦筋) troublesome ③ (不好辦 / 難搞) difficult to carry out; put one to inconvenience

揀擇 (挑選 / 選擇) choose

選擇 choice

【擒】kam[4] (攀爬) climb

擒上去 (爬上去) climb up

擒上擒落 (爬上爬下) rush up and down

擒青 ① (匆忙) in a hurry; impatient ② (毛里毛躁 / 急於求成) over-eager

　　擒擒青 ① (匆忙) in a hurry; impatient ② (毛里毛躁 / 急於求成) over-eager

擒高 (爬高) climb up

　　擒高擒低 (爬上爬下) climb up and down

擒落嚟 (爬下來) climb down

擒嚟擒去 (爬來爬去) climb all over

束手就擒 allow oneself to be arrested without offering any resistance; allow oneself to be seized without putting up a fight; resign oneself to being held as a prisoner; submit to arrest with folded arms

喉擒 (心急 / 沒耐性 / 急於 / 着急) desperate; eager; impatient

猴猴擒擒 (焦急) anxious; impetuous

猴擒 (焦急) anxious; impetuous

【據】goey[3] according to

據為己有 appropriate to oneself; have all to oneself; make sth his own; pocket; seize sth for oneself; take forcible possession of sth for oneself

據說 a story is going around that; according to hearsay; as the story goes; allegedly; by all accounts; I hear that; it is said; people say that; the story goes that; the story runs that; they say

據點 fortified point; stronghold

冇根冇據 (無憑無據) without evidence

有根有據 (有憑有據) be based on evidence

收據 receipt

佔據 hold; occupy; take over; take

依據 ① according to; in the light of; judging by; on the basis of ② basis; foundation

根據 base on; evidence

數據 data

論據 argument; bases for argument; grounds for argument

憑據 evidence; proof

證據 evidence; proof

【擗】pek[9] (扔) throw away

擗咗 (扔掉) throw away

　　擗咗佢 (把它扔了) throw it away

【撳】gam⁶ (按 / 摁) press

撳住 (按 / 摁) press

撳低 ① (搞垮 / 幹掉) beat; defeat ② (按下去) press down

撳釘 (圖釘) drawing pin; thumbtack

撳掣 (按鈕 / 按開關) push the button

撳機 (從自動提款機取錢) draw money from an automatic teller machine

撳鐘 (按門鈴 / 按鈴 / 摁鈴) press the bell; push the bell

　　撳門鐘 (按門鈴 / 摁門鈴) press the door bell

【揰】mang¹ (拔 / 揪 / 拽) pull out

揰出嚟 (拔出來) pull sth out

揰耳仔 (揪耳朵) pull one's ear

揰埋佢去 (把他也拽去) get him along

揰實啲 (拽緊點兒) hold tighter

【擙】ou¹ (搖) shake

【整】dzing² ① (做) make ② (修理) repair

整古 (捉弄) trick

　　整古做怪 (裝神弄鬼) wrap sth in mystery

整多碗添 (多吃一碗) have another bowl of sth

整色整水 ① (裝門面) put on a show; put on an act ② (賣俏 / 矯揉造作) flirt; play the coquette

整定 (注定) destined; predestined

整係 (總是) always; as a rule; commonly; constantly; generally; invariably; usually; without exception

整損 (弄傷) hurt

　　整損手 (弄傷手) hurt one's hand

整亂 (弄亂) mess

整嘢食 (做飯吃) cook

整嚫 (弄傷) get hurt

整餸 (做菜) prepare the dishes

整爛 (弄爛) break

整蠱 (捉弄 / 愚弄) play a trick on sb

　　整蠱人 (捉弄人家) play tricks on people

支整 (講究打扮) fastidious

利率調整 interest rate adjustment

完整 complete; entire; intact; integrated; undamaged; whole

易整 (易做) easy to make

姿姿整整 (磨磨蹭蹭) dally; dawdle; move slowly

姿整 (磨蹭) dally; dawdle; move slowly

修整 (修理) repair

齊整 (整齊) neat

難整 (難做) hard to make; hard to manage

【曆】lik⁹ calendar

曆法 calendar

曆書 almanac

日曆 calendar

月曆 calendar

新曆 (陽曆) solar calendar

農曆 lunar calendar

舊曆 (黃曆 / 夏曆) lunar calendar

【曉】hiu² ① (懂) understand ② (會) know

曉未吖 (會了沒有) have you understood

曉得 (會) know

【樸】pok⁸ simple

樸素 simple and plain

樸實 ① plain; simple ② down-to-earth; guileless; sincere and honest

純樸 honest; simple; unsophisticated

儉樸 economical; thrifty and simple

【橄】gam² olive

橄欖 olive

　　橄欖油 olive oil

【樽】dzoen¹ ① (瓶子) bottle; jar ② high

樽仔 (小瓶子) small bottle

樽領 (高領) choker

　　樽領衫 (高領衣服) turtleneck shirt

一個樽 (一個瓶子) a bottle

一樽 (一瓶) a bottle of

入樽 ① (倒入瓶子) pour into a bottle ② (灌籃) slam-dunk

水樽 (水瓶) water bottle

奶樽 (奶瓶) baby's bottle; milk bottle

回樽 (歸還瓶子) return the bottle

汽水樽 (汽水瓶) beverage bottle

油樽 (油瓶兒) oil bottle

花樽 (花瓶) ① flower vase; vase ② (無腦的漂亮女人) pretty woman with no brain

豉油樽 (醬油瓶) soy sauce bottle

按樽 (瓶子抵押費) bottle deposit

酒樽 (酒瓶) wine bottle

藥樽 (藥瓶) medicine bottle

【樹】sy⁶ tree

樹大招風 a person of reputation is liable to become the envy of others

樹皮 (香紙) joss paper

樹尾 (樹梢) tip of a tree

樹枝 ① firewood ② branch of a tree
- 一枝樹枝 (一根樹枝) a branch of tree
- 一紮樹枝 (一捆樹枝) a bundle of firewood
- 樹大有枯枝 (林子大了，甚麼鳥都有) there are good and bad people in every group
- 樹大有枯枝，族大有乞兒 (害羣之馬) there's a black sheep in every flock

樹倒猢猻散 (一哄而散) rats leave a sinking ship

樹高千丈，落葉歸根 no matter whether it is east or west, home is the best

樹椏 (樹杈) forking branch of a tree

樹熊 (考拉 / 樹袋熊) koala

樹頭 (樹根) tree stump

一行柳樹 (一排柳樹) a line of willows

一棵聖誕樹 a Christmas tree

一棵樹 a tree

刀仔鋸大樹 (以小博大) manage to cut down a big tree with a small knife

李樹 plum tree

杉樹 cedar

拉牛上樹 (迫使做力不能及的事情) a vain attempt to do sth

柳樹 willow

桑樹 mulberry tree

桃樹 peach tree

桐樹 tung tree

梨樹 pear

植樹 plant trees

楓樹 maple

矮樹 (灌木) shrub

聖誕樹 Christmas tree

跳上棵樹 (跳上那棵樹) jump up the tree

種樹 plant trees

橘樹 tangerine tree

【橋】kiu⁴⁻² (辦法 / 點子 / 竅) tactics

橋妙 (奧妙) secret power

好啱橋 (相互融洽) be congenial to each other

好橋 (好戰術) good tactic

有咁啱得咁橋 (不巧) as luck would have it

咁橋 (好巧) by chance

屎橋 (餿主意) crap idea; poor scheme

度到好橋 (琢磨出高招兒) think up good tactics

度返度好橋 (想個高招兒) think up some good tactics

度橋 (找竅門 / 想招兒 / 想辦法) plot; think of a way out; think of the tactics; try to think of a solution

過橋 (當跳板) as a jumping board

諗條橋 (想個點子) work out a trick

【橋】kiu⁴ bridge

橋下 below the bridge; under the bridge

橋牌 bridge

橋樑 bridge

橋頭 bridgehead; either end of a bridge
- 船到橋頭自然直 in the end, things will mend; let things slide; things at worst will mend; when the boat comes to the bridge underpass, it will go through straight; when things are at the worst, they will mend

橋躉 (橋墩) bridge pier

一度橋 (一座橋) a bridge

一條橋 (一座橋) a bridge

天橋 flyover

同我度吓橋 (幫我想辦法) help me find a way out

行人天橋 (人行天橋) footbridge

行天橋 (貓步) catwalk

行車天橋 (高架橋) flyover

你走你嘅陽關路，我過我嘅獨木橋 (你走你的陽光道，我過我的獨木橋) each goes their own way

過橋 (當跳板) as a jumping board

【橙】tsaang⁴⁻² (橙 / 橘子) orange

橙汁 (柳橙汁) orange juice
- 鮮橙汁 (鮮榨柳橙汁) fresh orange juice

橙色 orange; orange colour

一個橙 (一個橙子) an orange

金山橙 (美國橙) American orange

籮底橙 ① (挑剩的東西 / 殘貨) left-over; remaining goods ② (成績最差的學生) worst students

【橘】gwat⁷ tangerine

橘樹 tangerine tree

柑橘 oranges and tangerines

【橡】dzoeng⁶ elastic

橡筋 (橡皮筋 / 鬆緊帶) elastic cord; rubber band
- 橡筋箍 (橡皮筋) elastic band; rubber band

【機】gei¹ ① machine ② chance

機位（飛機座位）aeroplane seat

機長 captain

機師（飛機師）pilot

機票（飛機票）air ticket

　　來回機票（往返機票）return ticket

　　訂機票（預訂機票）book an air ticket

　　電子機票 e-ticket

機場（飛機場）airport

　　機場巴士 airport bus

　　機場快線 airport express

　　機場穿梭巴士 airport shuttle bus

　　民用機場 civil airport

機會 chance; opportunity

　　有機會 have a chance

　　趁機會 take the opportunity

機鋪（電玩中心／電子遊戲機中心）video game centre

機器 machine

　　一副機器（一台機器）a machine

機關槍 ① machine gun ② fire words at sb like a machine gun

一架收音機（一台收音機）a radio

一架飛機 an aeroplane

一部相機 a camera

上機（登機）board a plane

心機 mood

手機 cell; cellular phone; hand phone; handset; mobile; mobile phone

火機（打火機）lighter

升降機（電梯）lift

司機 driver

打火機 lighter

打印機 printer

打字機 typewriter

打我手機 call me on my mobile phone

打機（打遊戲機）play video games

打窿機（打孔機／打洞機）hole-puncher; puncher

打爆機（打到遊戲的最高關卡）get to the highest level of a video game

白費心機 waste one's efforts

危機 crisis

收音機 radio

有心機（有心情）in the mood for sth

老虎機 ① parking meter ② slot machine

耳筒機（隨身聽）walkman

自動櫃員機（ATM 機）automatic teller machine (ATM); cash machine

冷氣機（空調）air-conditioner

劫機 air piracy; hijack a plane; hijack an aircraft; skyjack

吸塵機（吸塵器）vacuum cleaner

投影機（投影儀）projector

投機 speculate

見機 according to circumstances; as befits the occasion; as the opportunity arises

抽油煙機 kitchen hood; range hood

抽濕機 dehumidifier

放飛機（失約）break a promise; ditch sb; fail to show up for an appointment; fail to turn up for a date; stand sb up

枉費心機 a fool for one's pains; bay at the moon; bark at the moon; bay the moon; beat the air; beat the wind; flog a dead horse; fruitless efforts; futile; go down the drain; go on a wild goose chase; in vain; make futile efforts; rack one's brains in vain; rack one's brains to no purpose; scheme in vain; scheme without avail; try in vain to; waste one's contrivances; waste one's efforts; waste one's labour; waste one's pains; wreck one's brain without results

的士司機（計程車司機／出租車司機）taxi driver

直升機 helicopter

洗衣機 washing machine

洗碗碟機（洗碗機）dish washer

洗碗機 dish washer

珍寶機（噴氣客機）jumbo jet

相機 camera

計數機（計算器）calculator

飛機 aeroplane

班機（航班）scheduled flight

送飛機 ①（送機）see sb off at the airport ②（錯過航班）miss the flight ③（送飛機）give sb an aeroplane as a present

乘機 take the opportunity to do sth

登機 boarding

釘書機 stapler

釘裝機（裝釘機／裝訂機）binding machine

航機（飛機）flight

動機（意向）intention; motivation; motive

啤膠機（熱壓機）hot press

啤機（模壓機／衝壓機）mould press

寄飛機（空郵）send by air

掃描機（掃描儀）scanner

接飛機 pick up sb from the airport

接機 pick up sb from the airport

搾汁機 juicer

搵銀良機（掙錢良機）opportunity to make profit

碎紙機 paper shredder

等離子電視機 plasma TV

乾衣機（烘乾機）clothes dryer

開收音機 turn on the radio
傳真機 fax machine
搭飛機（乘飛機）go by air; take a plane
落飛機（下飛機）get out of an aeroplane
落機（下飛機）get off a plane; get out of an aeroplane
過膠機（層壓機）laminator
電視機 television; television set
飲水機（水機）water dispenser
遊戲機 video game
榨汁機 juice extractor
熄手機（關手機）switch off the mobile phone; turn off your mobile
影印機（複印機）copying machine; photocopier
影相機（照相機）camera
影碟機 video disk player
數碼相機 digital camera
噴墨打印機 inkjet printer
㩒機（從自動提款機取錢）draw money from an automatic teller machine
標籤打印機 label maker
錄音機 recorder
錄影機（錄像機）video recorder
攝錄機（攝像機）video recorder
鐳射打印機 laser printer
攪拌機（攪拌器）blender
BB 機（傳呼機）pager
call 機（傳呼機）pager

【橫】waang⁴ horizontal

橫丫腸（盲腸）caecum
橫手（不光彩的手段）the person who acts underhand for sb
橫肉（醜陋）look ugly and ferocious
橫行霸道 play the bully
橫咗（搞砸了）screw up
橫門（旁門／側門）side door; side gate
橫巷（小巷／小胡同）alley; lane; side street
橫財（不循正途取得的金錢／不義之財）ill-gotten wealth
橫掂（無論如何／橫豎）anyway; as it happens; in any case
　橫掂都喺一樣（橫豎都一樣）it is all the same to sb
　橫九掂十（任何情況）in any case; such being the case
　橫死掂死（橫豎都是死）it doesn't make any difference either way
橫街（橫馬路）by-street; side street
　橫街窄巷 side streets and by-lanes
橫禍 unexpected calamity
橫衝直撞 collide in every direction
橫額（橫幅）banner; streamer
橫蠻無理 savage like a beast

打橫（橫放／橫着）lie horizontally
蠻橫 arbitrary; impervious to reason; peremptory; rude and unreasonable

【概】kyt⁹ section

一概（一節）a section of

【歷】lik⁹ experience

歷史 history
　歷史事件 historical event
　歷史悠久 have a long history
　歷史劇 historical play
　歪曲歷史 distort history; garble history
歷來 all along; always; constantly; from the old days; since a long time ago
　歷來如是（歷來如此）have been so from the old days
歷程 course; procedure
　人生歷程 life journey

【澤】dzaak⁹ marsh

澤民 benefit the people
澤國 ①（一片充滿河流和湖泊的土地／沼澤）a land that abounds in rivers and lakes; marsh; swamp ②（被淹沒的地區）inundated areas

袍澤（同袍）comrades in arms

【澱】din⁶ sedimentation

澱粉 starch
澱積（沉積）deposition

沉澱 precipitate; sedimentation

【澳】ou³ Australia

澳元 Australian dollar
澳門 Macau
澳洲（澳大利亞）Australia
　澳洲人（澳大利亞人）Aussie; Australian

【激】gik⁷（氣）irritate

激死（氣壞）annoy sb
　激死人（氣死人）annoying; irritating
　激死老豆搵山拜（故意氣壞父親）unfilial son who infuriates his father to death is only looking for a tomb to sweep
　激死我（氣壞了）I'm furious
激到一把火（氣得一肚子火）a stomachful of anger
激到生蝦咁跳（氣得直哆嗦）tremble with anger
激氣（生氣）angry; annoy; feel frustrated

好激氣（好生氣）very angry

激嬲（氣壞）irritate

激嚇（被氣到了）be irritated

刺激 exciting

感激 grateful

【濁】dzuk⁹（嗆）choke

濁嚇（嗆着 / 噎着）be choked

啲水好濁（水很渾濁）the water is turbid

【濃】nung⁴ ①（釅）strong ②（密）dense

濃度 concentration; strength

濃厚 dense; strong

濃縮 concentrate

太濃 too strong

杯茶好濃（這杯茶好濃）the tea is very strong

茶太濃 the tea is too strong

【燈】dang¹ lamp

燈芯敲鐘——有音（秤鉈落在棉花上——沒回音）no reply

燈芯撐成鐵 a straw shows its weight when it is carried a long way

燈油火蠟（運營成本）overheads; running costs of a business

燈掣（燈開關 / 電燈開關）lamp switch; light switch

燈謎 lantern riddles; riddles written on lanterns
估燈謎（猜謎）guess a lantern riddle

燈膽（燈泡）light bulb

燈籠 lantern
燈籠椒（青椒 / 柿子椒）bell pepper
玩燈籠 play with lanterns

一眼燈（一盞燈）a lamp

一盞枱燈（一盞桌燈）a table lamp

一盞街燈（一盞路燈）a street lamp

一盞燈 a lamp

大光燈（汽燈）gas lamp

幻燈 ① slide show ② magic lantern; slide project

水晶燈 crystal light

火水燈（煤油燈）kerosene lamp

交通燈 traffic lights

吊燈 pendant lamp

花燈 festive lantern

枱燈（桌燈）table lamp

紅綠燈（信號燈）traffic lights

射燈（聚光燈）spotlight

睇花燈（看花燈）watch festive lanterns

睇燈（看交通燈）watch the traffic lights

着燈（點燈）turn on the light

街燈（路燈）road lamp; street lamp; street light

開燈 turn on the light

綠燈 get the go ahead; green light

電燈 electric light

熄燈（滅燈 / 關燈）put out the light; turn off the light

爆燈（很高）very high

【燉】dan⁶ stew

燉熟 stew until it is done

溫溫燉燉（渾渾噩噩）muddle-headed

【燒】siu¹ ① burn ②（烤）roast

燒衣（燒紙錢）burn nether banknotes

燒肉（烤肉）roast pork

燒冷竈（燒冷灶）back the wrong horse

燒味 roast meat; siu mei

燒枱炮（拍桌大鬧）thump the table and heap abuse on sb

燒酒（蒸餾米酒）rice wine

燒傷 burn

燒槍（打槍）fire with a pistol

燒野食（燒烤）barbecue; BBQ

燒賣 pork dumpling
一籠燒賣 a basket of pork dumplings

燒鴨（烤鴨）roast duck

燒雞（烤雞）roast chicken

燒鵝（烤鵝）roasted goose
食燒鵝（吃烤鵝）eat roasted goose

燒臘（烤製肉食）barbecue

叉燒 barbeque pork

恨到發燒（非常渴望）want sth desperately

留得青山在，哪怕冇柴燒（留得青山在，不怕沒柴燒）life is safe, and gains will surely be safe

退燒（退熱）bring down a fever

焚燒 burn; incineration; set on fire

發高燒 have a high fever

發燒（發熱）have a fever; run a fever; run a temperature

頭痛發燒（小病痛）minor diseases

【燕】jin³ ① swallow ②（毽子）shuttlecock

燕子 swallow

燕雀 bramble finch

燕梳（保險）(English) insurance

打燕（踢毽子）kick the shuttlecock

踢燕（踢毽子）kick the shuttlecock

【燙】tong³ iron
燙斗（熨斗）iron
燙衫（熨衣服）iron clothes

洗熨 wash and iron clothes

【燂】taam⁴（烤）bake; roast
燂火（烤火）warm oneself by a fire
燂乾（烤乾）dry by a fire

【獨】duk⁹ independent
獨一無二 unique
獨生女（獨生女兒）only daughter
獨生仔（獨生兒子）only son
獨立 independent
獨佔 solely own
獨沽一味（對一件事情有強烈的偏好）have a strong
　　preference for only one thing
獨係（只是）just; merely; only
獨食（自顧自／獨吃／獨吞）selfish
　　獨食難肥（人有利益應該與別人分享）one will be more
　　　　successful if one shares with others
獨家村（孤僻離羣的人）lone wolf; unsociable and
　　eccentric person

木木獨獨（木無表情）expressionless
木獨（木訥／遲鈍）(English) moody; socially inept;
　　unsociable
孤獨 lonely; solitary
發木獨（發呆）in a trance

【璣】gei¹ jade

珠璣 exquisite wording of a piece of writing; gems; graceful
　　writings; pearls

【瘸】ke⁴ lame
瘸子 the crippled; the lame

手瘸（手僵硬）paralysis of the hands
腳瘸（腿僵硬）paralysis of the feet

【瞞】mun⁴ deceive
瞞稅 conceal facts to proper taxation
瞞騙 cheat; deceive

好女兩頭瞞（充分利用兩邊）a smart girl lies to both sides
　　to keep everyone happy
隱瞞 conceal; cover up; hide; hide the truth; hold back

【瞠】tsaang¹ dazzling
瞠乎其後（遠遠落後）far behind

光瞠瞠（亮堂堂）dazzling; very bright

【磨】mo⁴ grind
磨心（受到爭議者投訴的調解員）mediator suffering from
　　complaints from disputants
　　做磨心（兩難）in a dilemma
磨礴（圓矮笨重）short and fat
磨損 wear and tear
磨練 temper oneself
磨墨 grind the ink
磨擦 clash; friction; rub

有錢使得鬼推磨（有錢能使鬼推磨）money makes the mare
　　go; money makes the world go round
折磨 cause physical or mental suffering; submit to an ordeal;
　　torment; torture; trials and afflictions
惡人自有惡人磨（惡有惡報／壞人終不會有好下場）devils
　　devil devils
矮磨磨（非常矮）very short
襟磨（耐磨）wear-resistant

【磚】dzyn¹（磚頭）brick
磚瓦 bricks and tiles
磚頭 brick
　　一砂磚頭（一堆磚頭）a heap of bricks
　　一嚿磚頭（一塊磚頭）a brick

一戙磚（一堆磚頭）a stack of bricks
一磚（一小塊）a small block of
叩門磚（敲門磚）a means to find favour with an influential
　　person; a stepping stone to one's purpose
泥磚（土磚）cob brick
花階磚（陶瓷磚）ceramic brick
砌磚 ①（堆砌磚頭）lay bricks ②（打麻將）play mahjong
瓷磚 ceramic tile
階磚（方片兒／方塊兒／地磚）ground tile

【穌】sou¹ revive

耶穌 Jesus
講耶穌（說大道理／說教）lecture

【積】dzik⁷ accumulate
積木 building blocks; juggle
砌積木（搭積木）juggle; pile up the building blocks
積非成是（習非成是）accept what is wrong as right when

one grows accustomed to it; get used to what is wrong and regard it as right; through practice the erroneous becomes correct; what becomes customary is accepted as right

積埋 (積起來 / 累積) accumulate

內籠面積 (內部建築面積) internal floor area
出售面積 saleable area
生積 (消化功能紊亂) have digestive disorders
老積 (少年老成) have an old head on young shoulders; mature; young but steady
招積 (刺兒頭 / 傲慢 / 囂張) disgustingly arrogant
物業面積 area of a property
面積 area
堆積 (積累 / 累積) accumulate; cumulate; heap up; pile up; upbuilding
單位面積 area of the flat; property area
焦積 (刺兒頭 / 傲慢) arrogant
建築面積 gross floor area
實用面積 net usable area; usable area
樓面面積 floor area
澱積 (沉積) deposition

【築】 zuk¹ build

築土 (建立一個填土結構) build an earth-fill structure
築路 build roads

建築 architecture

【篤】 duk⁷ (戳) stab

篤口篤鼻 (指着鼻子罵) scold sb with the finger pointing at him
篤吓佢 (戳他一下) stab him once
篤低 (最底下 / 最裏頭 / 盡頭) the end
篤波 ① (打桌球) play snooker ② (打枱球) play billiard
篤眼篤鼻 (指着鼻子罵) scold sb with the finger pointing at him
篤數 (虛報數字) inflate the numbers; record a false set of figures
篤篤撐 (咚咚鏘) clang, clang, clang
篤爆 (拆穿 / 戳穿) betray a secret; debunk; let out a secret

一篤 (一個水坑) a puddle
打爛砂盆問到篤 (打破沙鍋問到底) go to the bottom of the matter

【篙】 gou¹ boat pole

篙人 (船工) boatman

竹篙 bamboo pole; bamboo stick

【篩】 sai¹ ① (篩子) sieve; sifter ② (淘汰) eliminate; get rid of

篩波 (削球) chopping in playing table-tennis; cutting in playing table-tennis

食篩 (吃轉) fail to receive a spinned ball

【糕】 gou¹ cake

糕餅 cake; confectionery; pastry
糕點 pastry

千層糕 multi-layered cake
生日蛋糕 birthday cake
年糕 rice cake
芝士蛋糕 cheese cake
馬拉糕 Malay sponge cake
雪糕 (冰淇淋 / 冰激凌) ice cream
蛋糕 cake
鬆糕 Cantonese sponge cake; fluffy cake
蘿蔔糕 radish cake

【糖】 tong⁴ ① sugar ② (糖果) sweets

糖不甩 glutinous rice flour balls with peanuts and coconuts in syrup
糖水 (甜品) sweet soup
糖尿病 diabetes
糖果 sweets
　糖果罌 (糖果罐兒) candy jar
糖醋 sweet and sour sauce
糖罌 (糖罐兒) sugar vase
糖黐豆 (如膠似漆) hand and glove; two people who are very close

一粒糖 (一顆糖) a sweet
止咳糖 cough drop; cough lozenge; cough sweet
幼砂糖 (細白糖) castor sugar
冰糖 rock sugar
走糖 (不要加糖) no sugar
拖肥糖 (太妃糖) toffee
波板糖 (棒棒糖) lollypop
派糖 (發喜糖) give people wedding candies
砂糖 sugar
喉糖 (潤喉糖) throat drop
棉花糖 marshmallow
黃糖 (紅糖) brown sugar
嗒晒糖 (被異性吸引) be sexually attracted to sb
嗒糖 ① (感到開心) happy about sth ② (對異性有吸引力) be sexually attracted to sb
落糖 (加糖) add sugar

蜜糖 honey
蔗糖 cane sugar; sugar from cane; table sugar

【縛】bok⁸ tie
縛住 (綁住) tie up

束縛 bind up; fetter; restrain; tie
解除束縛 liberate from bondage

【膩】nei⁶ greasy; oily
膩味 hate; loathe
膩胃 (食慾減退) kill one's appetite
膩煩 ① be bored; be fed up ② hate; loathe

好油膩 very greasy
油膩 greasy; oily
肥膩 greasy; oily

【膶】joen² liver
膶腸 (臘肝腸) liver sausage

豆腐膶 ① (豆腐乾) bean curd cube ② (特小型公寓) very small apartment
金銀膶 ① (肥豬肉釀進豬肝內的臘味) pork wrapped with dried and preserved pig liver ② (金銀鋼帶手錶) watch with gold and platinum band

【舉】goey² raise
舉止 demeanour
　舉止有禮 courteous in one's demeanour
舉重 weight lifting
舉得起放得低 (拿得起放得下) able to advance or retreat; adaptable; flexible
舉辦 hold; organise

不舉 sexually impotent
列舉 cite; enumerate; list
老舉 (妓女) prostitute
抓舉 (搶奪) snatch
抬舉 good favour; good turn; do a good turn
枚舉 enumerate
挺舉 clean and jerk
除褲放屁——多此一舉 (脫褲子放屁) do sth which is unnecessary
選舉 election

【艙】tsong¹ cabin
艙位 (客運泊位) passenger berth
艙室 (飛機艙) cabin

經濟艙 (二等艙) economy class
豪華艙 (頭等艙) first-class seat

【蔽】bai⁶ conceal
蔽目 blindfold; cover the eyes
蔽體 cover the body

蔭蔽 conceal; cover

【蕃】faan¹ barbarian; foreign
蕃石榴 (芭樂) guava
　蕃石榴汁 (芭樂汁) guava juice
蕃茄 (西紅柿) tomato
　蕃茄汁 (西紅柿汁) tomato juice

【蕉】dziu¹ (香蕉) banana
蕉園 (香蕉園) banana plantation

一梳香蕉 (一把香蕉) a bunch of bananas; a hand of bananas
一梳蕉 (一把香蕉) a bunch of bananas; a hand of bananas
大蕉 (香蕉) banana; plantain
兩梳蕉 (兩手空空) visit sb without bringing a gift
香蕉 banana

【蕎】kiu⁴⁻² buckwheat
蕎麥 (苦蕎 / 苦蕎麥) buckwheat

唔啱蕎 (談不來 / 談不攏) do not get along well with each other
啱蕎 (談得來 / 談得攏) get along well with people; hit it off

【蕩】dong⁶ stroll
蕩失路 (迷路) lose one's way; one is lost

錯蕩 (榮幸出席 / 榮幸受邀) be glad to have the undeserved presence; be honoured by the undeserved visit

【螃】pong⁴ crab
螃蟹 mud crab

【融】jung⁴ harmonious
融合 amalgamate; blend; coalesce; compromise; fuse; harmonise; mix together
融洽 get along well with each other; harmonious with each other
融會 (融匯) blend harmoniously

融會貫通（充分和透徹的理解）be well versed in;
digest; gain a thorough understanding of the subject
through mastery of all relevant material; have a full
and thorough understanding through a comprehensive
study of the subject; thoroughly acquainted with

企業金融 corporate finance
金融 finance
通融（繞過規則／破例）get round the rules; make an
accommodation; stretch a point

【螢】jing⁴ firefly
螢火蟲 fire beetle; firefly; glow-worm; lighting bug
螢光 fluorescence
螢幕（屏幕）screen

【蝨】dzi¹ louse

生飛蝨／生痱滋（長口瘡）have a thrush
生蝨（長疥瘡）have scabies
飛蝨（口腔潰瘍／口瘡）aphtha

【衛】wai⁶ defend; protect
衛生 hygiene
　　衛生巾 sanitary napkin
衛星 satellite

官官相衛（官官相護）devils help devils

【衡】hang⁴ ①（緊繃）tight ②（快）fast; quick
衡量 assess; judge; measure

平衡 balance
均衡 balanced; equalisation; even; proportionate
制衡 check and balance

【褸】loey⁵ coat

大褸（大衣）overcloth; overcoat; topcloth
中褸（短大衣）short overcoat
牛仔褸（牛仔衫）denim jacket
皮褸（皮衣）leather overcoat
雨褸（雨衣）raincoat
帶雨褸（帶雨衣）have a raincoat
乾濕褸（風雨衣／雨衣）mackintosh

【褪】tan³（退）reverse
褪一日（順延一天）put off a day accordingly
褪出 slip out

褪位（挪動）move
褪車（倒車）back a car; back up a car; back up a
locomotive; move a vehicle backward; reverse; reverse a
car
褪後（退後）fall backward; move backward
褪軟（退縮）back down; retreat from one's position when
confronted by a change in circumstances

打到褪（倒退）retrogressive
打倒褪（倒退）backward movement; go backwards
行路打倒褪（倒霉透頂）fortunes never come singly
倒褪（倒退）backward movement; go backwards

【親】tsan¹ relatives
親人 relative
親力親為（親自動手）do sth all by oneself
親手 with one's own hand
親生仔不如近身錢（親生兒不如傍身錢）money is the
nearest relation; one's own son is not as good as money
on hand
親自出馬（親自處理）take up a matter by oneself
親耳 with one's own ear
親身 in person
親密 close; intimate
親戚 relatives
　　親戚朋友 friends and relatives
　　一個親戚 a relative
　　探親戚（走親戚）visit relatives
　　睇親戚（走親戚）visit relatives
　　認親認戚（稱兄道弟）overly familiar with sb
　　親朋戚友（親戚朋友）friends and relatives
親眼 see with one's own eyes
親愛 dear; love
　　相親相愛 love and care for each other; mutual love

六親 one's kin; the six relations: father, mother, elder
brothers, younger brothers, wife, and children
父母親 parents
父親 father
母親 mother
同姓三分親 people with the same surname are somehow
related
每逢佳節倍思親 each time a festival arrives, one thinks all
the more of one's close relatives; on festive occasions
more than ever one thinks of one's dear ones far away
姻親 relatives by marriage
娘親 ① relatives on the maternal side ② one's mother
娶親（結婚／娶妻）get married; take a wife; tie the knot
探親（省親）pay a visit to one's parents or elders

遠親 distant relatives; remote kinsfolk
幫理不幫親 fair-minded

【諜】 dip⁹ undercover
諜犬 setter
諜報（情報）intelligence report

間諜 undercover

【諦】 dai³ attentive
諦聽 listen attentively

詐諦（裝蒜 / 假裝）feign; make a pretence of ignorance; pretend
靠諦（談論某人）talk at sb

【諧】 haai⁴ harmony
諧星 comedian
諧趣 fun; humour
諧劇（鬧劇）farce

和諧 harmony

【諸】 dzy¹ all; various
諸如此類 sth like that
諸多事幹（好管閒事）nosy
諸事（好事）nosy; poke and pry
　諸事丁（好事鬼）meddler; nosy person
　諸事八卦（好管閒事）nosy
　諸事理（愛管閒事的人）meddler; nosy person
　諸事婆（好管閒事的女人 / 饒舌的女人）gossipy woman

【諾】 nok⁹ promise
諾言 promise
　違背諾言 break one's promise

承諾 acceptance of an offer; promise to undertake; undertake to do sth

【謀】 mau⁴ ① scheme ② collude with ③ work for
謀生 make a living
謀害 plot a murder
謀殺 murder

六耳不同謀（兩人成伴，三人不和）two's company, three's none
密謀 conspire; plot; scheme
陰謀 conspiracy

【謂】 wai⁶ be called
謂詞（謂語）predicate
謂語 predicate

冇所謂（無所謂）all the same; anything will do; cannot be called; doesn't matter; indifferent; never mind; not care; not deserve the name of; not matter
正所謂 what people said
所謂 so-called
喊都無謂（說也沒用）there is no point in crying over sth one cannot change
無謂 ①（不必要 / 沒有必要）no need ②（犯不上 / 沒意思）not worth
講多無謂（說多無用）talk is cheap

【豬】 dzy¹ pig
豬大腸（豬腸子）pork intestines
豬公（公豬）boar
豬手（豬前蹄）pork knuckle
　鹹豬手（毛手毛腳）nasty hands
豬仔（小豬）piglet
　豬仔團（宰客旅行團）tour group whose members are cheated by its travel agent
　賣豬仔（販賣勞工 / 騙賣勞力）sell sb like a piglet
　畀人賣豬仔（被人利用或佔便宜）be cheated and taken advantage of by others; be sold like a piglet
豬扒 ①（豬排）pork chop ②（肥婆）fat woman; nottie
　豬扒飯 rice with pork chop
豬耳（豬耳朵）pig's ear
豬年 Year of the Pig
豬肉 pork
　豬肉佬（屠夫）butcher
　炆豬肉（紅燒肉 / 燉肉）stewed pork
　燒豬肉（燒豬肉）roast pork
豬肝 pig liver
豬油 lard
　豬油包（移動或反應緩慢的人）sb who moves or reacts slowly
豬乸（母豬）sow
豬柳（里脊肉）pork loin
豬紅（豬血）pig's blood
豬脷（豬舌 / 豬舌頭）pig's tongue
豬骨（豬骨頭）pigbone
豬兜 ①（蠢貨）idiot ②（食槽）feeder; hopper; manger
豬腳（豬後蹄）pork trotter
豬腸（豬腸子）pork intestines
豬腩肉（豬五花肉）pork belly
豬膏（豬板油）pig's oil
豬噏 ①（笨人）fool; idiot ②（蠢豬）stupid

豬鼻（豬鼻子）pig's nose

豬噏（胡扯／胡說／胡謅／亂說）talk nonsense

豬潲（豬食）hogwash; pig feed; swill

豬潤（豬肝）pork's liver

豬橫脷（豬胰臟）pig's pancreas

豬蹄（豬蹄／豬肘子）pig's elbow

豬頭 be badly beaten

　豬頭丙（蠢人）blockhead; dumb head; fool

　豬頭骨（糟糕的工作／無利可圖的業務）bad job; unprofitable business

　豬頭嘜（蠢豬）idiot

　發過豬頭（賺大錢）make a lot of money; very rich

豬蹄 pig's hoof

　發過豬蹄（賺大錢）make a lot of money; very rich

豬雜（豬下水）pig offal

豬髀（豬蹄膀）pork shank

豬欄（豬圈）pigpen; sty

　豬欄報數——又一隻（又死一人／三長兩短／兩腳一伸）one more has died

豬籠入水（錢財廣進）have lots of money pouring in; have many different ways to make money; hit the jacket; make wads of money; one's financial resources come from all directions

一隻豬 a pig

一竇豬（一窩豬）a nest of pigs

山豬（野豬）boar; wild boar

阿豬（笨蛋／蠢人）stupid; stupid person

乳豬 piglet

俾人剝光豬（給人剝個精光）be stripped to the skin; strip bare; strip sb to the skin

剝光豬 ①（把衣服脫光）strip sb of their clothes ②（推光頭）a thorough loss in chess play; be entirely defeated in chess play

脆皮乳豬 crispy roasted piglet

傻豬（蠢貨／小傻子）silly fool; you silly kid

劏光豬（下棋時棋子全被對方吃光）(chessmen) all the pieces have been taken by the opponent

劏豬（殺豬）butcher pigs; kill pigs; slaughter pigs

燒乳豬（烤乳豬）roasted piglet

懶豬（懶人）lazy person

覺覺豬（睡覺）go to sleep; go sleepy-byes

爛瞓豬（嗜睡的人）person who likes to sleep

蠢過隻豬（比豬還蠢）very foolish; very stupid

蠢豬 fool; stupid like a pig; stupid person; stupid pig

【貓】maau¹ cat

貓公（雄貓）tomcat

貓仔（小貓）kitten

一竇貓仔（一窩小貓）a litter of kitten

貓衣毛——順揈（迎合某人的傾向）cater to sb's tendency; stroke the fur the right way

貓乸（母貓）damcat

貓哭老鼠——假慈悲（貓哭耗子——假慈悲）shed crocodile tears

貓紙 ①（作弊紙）paper used in cheating in an examination ②（提示）prompt

貓樣（鬼樣子）ugly face

貓糧 cat food

一隻貓 a cat

小貓 kitten

出貓（考試作弊）cheat in an examination; exercise fraud in an examination

打貓（偷吃）sneak a taste of food

奸賴貓（狡猾）cunning; dishonest; tricky

污糟貓（小花貓）untidy person

老虎唔發威當病貓（老虎不發威，當我是病貓）mistake a sleeping wolf for a dead dog

波斯貓 Persian cat

花面貓（小花臉）dirty face

流浪貓 stray cat

為食貓（饞鬼／貪吃鬼）glutton; greedy eater

食死貓（吃啞巴虧）be accused wrongly; be made a scapegoat; be unjustly blamed; take all the blame

病貓（病包兒／病鬼）sickly person

高竇貓（勢利）snobbish

監人食死貓（冤枉他人）lay the blame upon sb

養隻貓 keep a cat

醉貓（醉鬼）drunkard

賴貓（不認賬／賴皮）avoid taking the blame; deny mistakes; disavow; make a denial; make a disavowal; shirk responsibilities

熊貓 ① panda ② eyes with shadows

邋遢貓（泥猴兒）dirty person

【賭】dou² ① gamble ② bet on; gamble on

賭王 gambling king

賭仔（賭徒）gambler

賭波（賭球）bet on football; soccer gambling

賭狗 bet on dogs

賭氣 do sth in a fit of pique

賭神 god of gamblers

賭馬 bet on horses

　好賭馬（喜歡賭馬）fond of betting on horses

賭鬼（賭徒）gambler

賭場 casino

賭錢（賭博）gamble with money

鍾意賭錢（愛賭博）like gambling

賭檔（賭窟）gambling den

冚賭（抓賭局）smash a gambling party
好賭 fond of gambling
揪賭（抓賭局）smash a gambling party
輸賭（打賭）accept a bet; accept a wager; bet; betting; have a bet with sb; lay a wager on; lay a wager; risk money on sth; take up a bet; take up a wager; wager
爛賭（好賭／嗜賭）be addicted to gambling

【賴】laai⁶（抵賴）evade

賴人（怪人家）blame others
賴地硬（找借口／怨天尤人）make excuses
賴死（不願意做某事）reluctant to do sth one is supposed to do
賴尿（尿牀）wet the bed
賴嘢（掉入陷阱）fall into a trap
賴數 ①（賴賬）repudiate a debt ②（毀約）break one's promise
賴貓（不認賬／賴皮）avoid taking the blame; deny mistakes; disvow; make a denial; make a disavowal; shirk responsibilities

百無聊賴 be overcome with boredom; bored; bored stiff; bored to death; feel extremely bored; find time hang heavy on one's hands; idle along; in dreary and cheerless circumstances; suffer from boredom; the day is long to those who do not know how to use it; thoroughly bored; while away one's time aimlessly
奸賴 cunning; dishonest; tricky
托賴（感激不盡）be indebted to
依賴 dependence; dependency; dependent on; rely on
姓賴（拒不認罪）deny one's guilt
抵賴 find a way to avoid blame
聊賴（為…而活／依靠…）sth to live for; sth to rely upon
無聊賴（無聊）dispirited; feel bored
撒賴（耍無賴／蠻橫胡鬧）make a scene with an intention to shift the blame to other shoulders; raise hell

【蹄】tai⁴ hoof

蹄形 horseshoe shape

人有失手，馬有失蹄 there's always a slip-up in a person's job
元蹄（豬肘）pig's elbow
馬蹄（荸薺）water chestnut
發軟蹄（膝蓋發軟）go weak at the knees
發過豬蹄（賺大錢）make a lot of money; very rich

豬蹄 pig's hoof
鴨乸蹄（平足）flat feet
薰蹄（煙熏肘子）smoked pork knuckle

【踹】tsaai² trample

踹嘅你條尾（冒犯別人）cause offence to sb

見高拜，見低踹（媚上欺下）flatter those above and bully those below; snobbish

【蹦】naam³（跨）stride

蹦得過去（能跨過去）can overcome sth

【輯】tsap⁷ ① collect; compile ② edit

輯要 abstract; summary
輯錄 compile

編輯 editor
邏輯 logic

【輸】sy¹ lose

輸梗（輸定了）sure loss
輸蝕（比不上別人／吃虧／虧損）let sb gain the wind; miss out
輸賭（打賭）accept a bet; accept a wager; bet; betting; have a bet with sb; lay a wager on; lay a wager; risk money on sth; take up a bet; take up a wager; wager
輸錢 lose money

十賭九輸 lose nine out of ten cases in gambling
打輸（輸了）be defeated
秀才手巾——包輸（書）one will certainly lose in gambling; stand to lose
唔執輸（不落人後）not fall behind
執輸 ①（落後）fall behind ②（佔下風／吃虧）at a disadvantage; lose; miss out
運輸 transport

【辦】baan⁶（樣品）sample

辦公 attend to business; do office work; handle official business; work
　辦公室 office
　　辦公室助理 office assistant
　辦公時間 office hours
辦法 method; way
　冇晒辦法（沒有辦法）can't do anything about it
　另想辦法 try to find some other ways; try other ways

布辦（布樣品）cloth sample

民辦 be run by the local people
承辦 agree to do sth; undertake
唔對辦（不對頭）problematic
酒辦（酒樣品／樣品酒）miniature wine
創辦 found; set up
貨不對辦（名不副實）the name does not match the reality; the title and the reality do not tally; unworthy of the name
貨辦（貨樣／樣品）sample; sample goods
對辦（對頭）correct; on the right track
興辦 establish; found; initiate; set up
舉辦 hold; organise
樣辦（樣品）prototype; sample; specimen
幫辦（警官）police inspector
籌辦 make arrangements; make preparations; on the anvil; plan; prepare; upon the anvil

【遲】tsi⁴ late
遲下（過些時候）later; later on
遲吓（過些時候）later; later on
遲早（早晚）sooner or later
遲到 late
　遲到好過冇到（遲到總比不到好）rather late than never
　遲晒大到（遲到很久）very late in arriving
遲咗（遲到了）late
遲來（來遲）come late
遲啲（晚些時候）afterwards; by and by; later
　遲啲見（待會見）see you later
遲嚟先上岸（來得早不如來得巧）the last comer becomes the first goer

好遲 very late
有心唔怕遲（好飯不怕晚）do sth even though they are late
事不宜遲 delays are dangerous; it permits of no delay; one must lose no time in doing sth; the matter brooks no delay; the matter should not be delayed; there is not a moment to lose; there should be no delay; this matter must not be delayed
延遲 be delayed; defer; delay; hold over; postpone; put off; retard
差遲（差錯／過失）error; fault; miscalculation; mistake; slip
船到江心補漏遲（於事無補／悔之已晚／書到用時方恨少）it is too late to mend
慢慢都唔遲（慢慢來）take your time

【選】syn² choose
選手 player
選票 ballot paper
選舉 election

選擇 choice

揀選（挑選／選擇）choose

【遺】wai⁶ leave behind
遺憾 regret
遺囑 will

拾遺 appropriate lost property
路不拾遺 no one picks up what's left by the wayside

【醒】seng² awake
醒咗（醒了）awake
醒瞓（淺眠）wake up at the slightest thing
　好醒瞓（淺眠）wake up at the slightest thing

扎醒（驚醒）wake up with a start
知醒（睡得醒／醒得了）wake up in time
唔知醒（睡不醒／醒不了）wake up late
酒醉三分醒 be in wine but still a little conscious
甦醒 come back to life; come to; revive
瞓醒（睡醒）wake up
點醒 give the right advice

【醒】sing²（機靈）clever; quick-witted; smart
醒水 ①（領悟／醒悟）quick to realise ②（機警／警覺）alarmed; alert
醒目 ① catch the eye ②（機靈／靈活）clever; intelligent; quick-witted; smart
　醒目女（機靈的女孩）smart girl; smart lady
　醒目仔（機靈的男孩）clever boy; smart guy; smart kid
醒定 ①（聰明）clever ②（小心／注意）careful; watch out
　醒定啲（小心／照顧自己）be careful; take care
　醒醒定定（小心）do the clever thing
醒胃（開胃）appetising
醒酒 dispel the effects of alcohol
醒神（神采奕奕）brighten up
醒起（突然想起）it suddenly occurs to one
　冇醒起（忘記了／記不起來）didn't remember
　唔醒起（忘記了／記不起來）didn't remember
　醒唔起（想不起）unable to call to mind
　醒得起（想得起）able to call to mind
醒覺（睡醒）awake

好醒（好聰明）very smart
鬼打都冇咁醒（保持警惕）be on the alert
清醒 awake
讕醒（自作聰明／逞強）bravado; cocky; flaunt one's superiority; throw one's weight round

【鋸】goe³ (鋸子) saw

鋸木 saw wood

【鋼】gong³ steel

鋼骨 (鋼筋) reinforcing steel
鋼條 (瘦而強壯) (said of a person) thin but strong
鋼琴 piano
　鋼琴家 pianist
鋼線 (鋼絲) steel wire

煉鋼 steelmaking

【錄】luk⁹ record

錄用 employ; take sb on the staff
錄取 admit; enroll; recruit
錄音 record
　錄音室 recording room
　錄音機 recorder
錄影 (錄像) video record
　錄影帶 (錄像帶) videotape
　錄影機 (錄像機) video recorder

目錄 catalogue
取錄 (錄取) admit; enroll; recruit
紀錄 record
票房紀錄 (售票紀錄) box office records
輯錄 compile

【錐】dzoey¹ bore

錐耳 (打耳洞) pierce the ears
錐窿 (錐洞) bore a hole
錐爛 (錐破) damage by boring

【錘】tsoey⁴ hammer

錘仔 (錘子) hammer

鐵錘 iron hammer

【錢】tsin⁴ money

錢七 (超齡車) old car
錢包 purse; wallet
錢財 money; riches; wealth
錢罌 (錢盒子 / 錢罐子) cash box; money box; saving box
　豬仔錢罌 (小豬存錢罐) piggy bank

入錢 (存錢) put money into
下欄錢 (小費) tips
大把錢 (很多錢) a lot of money; rich
乞錢 (討錢) beg for money

五行欠金——冇錢 (五行缺金——沒錢) broke; in need of money; penniless
冇錢 (沒錢) no money
冇賺錢 (沒利潤) do not make any profit
欠人錢 owe sb a debt
欠錢 owe sb a debt
先使未來錢 (預支消費) have one's corn in the blade; spend money one has not yet earned
吓吓要使錢 (容易花錢) apt to spend money
好大筆錢 (一大筆錢) large amount of money
好有錢 very rich
好使錢 (喜歡花錢) fond of spending money
好值錢 (很值錢) worth a lot of money
存錢 ① deposit ② save
收錢 charge
有錢 have money
血汗錢 hard-earned money; money earned by hard toil
利是錢 (紅包錢) red packet money
夾錢 (補齊錢) make up the full amount of money
找錢 (找零) give the change
私己錢 (私房錢) private resources; private savings
使太多錢 (花太多錢) spend too much money
使錢 (花錢) spend money
刮錢 (斂財) obtain money by unfair or illegal means
呻冇錢 (抱怨缺錢) complain of being short of money
放低買路錢 (留下買路錢) leave your money before you can pass through this road
爭人錢 (欠別人錢) owe sb money
爭錢 (欠錢) owe sb money
畀錢 (付錢 / 給錢) pay cash
金錢 money
恨錢 (想發財) want to get rich
洗黑錢 (洗錢) money-laundering
值錢 costly; valuable
唔使錢 (不用錢) free of charge; gratis
捐錢 donate money
茶錢 (茶費) charge for the tea
俾低錢 (留下些錢) leave some money
俾現錢 (給現金) pay cash
俾錢 (給錢) pay
夠錢 (湊錢) make up the full amount of money
唱錢 ① (更換 / 轉換) (English) change ② (兌換錢幣) exchange; exchange money
掠錢 (收取過高的價格) charge an excessive price for sth
措錢 (攢錢 / 囤錢 / 存錢) hoard money; save money
現錢 (現金) cash
換錢 change money
幾錢 (多少錢) how much
散錢 (零錢) change; loose change; small sum of money

開天索價，落地還錢（漫天要價，坐地還錢）drive a hard bargain over sth

黑錢（賄賂錢）bribery money

搶錢 ask for too much money like robbers

搵快錢（掙快錢／賺快錢）make a fast buck; make money quickly

搵錢（掙錢／賺錢）make a living; make money

溪錢（紙錢）nether banknote

隔夜錢（剩錢）money left over for use

罰錢 fine; to be fined

零用錢（零花錢）pocket money

零錢 odd change; petty cash; small change

慳錢（省錢）save money

暢錢（找零）(English) change

撳錢（由自動提款機取錢）withdraw from an automatic teller machine (ATM)

賠錢 indemnify with money

啋人錢（欠人家錢）owe sb money

駛黑錢（賄賂）bribe

駛錢（花錢）spend money

儲錢（存錢）save money

撻錢（偷錢／騙錢）steal money

親生仔不如近身錢（親生兒不如傍身錢）money is the nearest relation; one's own son is not as good as money on hand

輸錢 lose money

賭錢（賭博）gamble with money

鍾意賭錢（愛賭博）like gambling

賺大錢 earn lots of money

賺錢 earn money

贏錢 win money

攢錢 save up money

攞①（拿錢）get money ②（取錢）withdraw money ③（要錢）ask for money

claim 錢（報銷）apply for reimbursement

【錫】sek[8] ①（疼愛）love; pamper ②（親）kiss

錫一啖（親一下）give a kiss

錫住（深愛）cherish a deep love for sb

錫晒你（最疼你）love sb most dearly

疼錫（疼愛）love dearly

愛錫（疼愛／愛惜）be fond of; love dearly

徼錫（愛惜／愛護）care

【錯】tso[3] wrong

錯有錯着（犯錯而意外得到好結果／錯了也有錯了的好處）have a fault on the right side; mistakes can turn out to be useful

錯愕（驚訝／驚呆／目瞪口呆）astonished; dumbfounded; flabbergasted; stunned

錯誤 error; mistake

錯誤難免 errors are unavoidable

局部錯誤 local error

錯蕩（榮幸出席／榮幸受邀）be glad to have the undeserved presence; be honoured by the undeserved visit

冇錯（沒錯）① no mistake ② it's right; that's right; you're right

打錯 wrong number

忙中有錯 error is always made in haste; haste is of the devil; haste makes waste

有冇搞錯（有沒有弄錯）what a ridiculous thing; you're kidding

有冇攪錯（有沒有弄錯）what a ridiculous thing; you're kidding

行差踏錯（犯錯）make a mistake

計錯（算錯）miscalculate

將錯就錯（充分利用錯誤）make the best of a bad job; make the best of a mistake; over shoes over boots

睇錯①（看錯）mistake sth ②（錯看）judge wrongly

搞錯（弄錯）make a mistake

斟茶認錯（承認錯誤道歉）offer tea as an admission of wrongdoing or as an apology

寫錯 write sth wrongly

聽錯 hear sth wrongly

攪錯（弄錯）make a mistake

釀成大錯 breed big mistakes

【錶】biu[2] watch

錶肉（錶瓤）inside mechanism of a watch

錶板（儀表盤／儀器板）control board

錶面（錶盤）face of a watch

錶蓋（錶蒙子）watch cover

錶鏈（錶帶）watch band

一個手錶（一塊手錶）a watch

一個錶（一塊錶）a watch

一隻手錶（一塊手錶）a watch

手錶 watch

扚錶（掛錶／懷錶）pocket watch

泊車咪錶（停車收費表）parking meter

咪錶①（里程計）milometer ②（電子計時錶）parking meter

秒錶 chronograph; stopwatch

校錶（撥錶）set the watch

【閻】jim⁴ hell

閻羅王 the King of Hell
閻羅王探病——問你死未（閻王下帖子——真要命）
drive sb to his death; like the King of Hell dispatching
invitation cards
閻羅王揸攤——鬼買（沒人買）nobody buys
閻羅王嫁女——鬼要（沒人要）nobody wants it

【閹】jim¹ castrate; emasculate

閹痘（種牛痘）get smallpox vaccination

翻閹（唱老調）do the old job once again; sing the same old tune

【隨】tsoey⁴ follow

隨住（隨着）along with; in pace with
隨便 ① casual; informal ② help yourself ③ as you like; as
you please; feel free ④ anything will do
隨便你 as you like; do what you want
隨便坐 make yourself at home; please be seated
隨便睇（隨便看）feel free to look around
隨得（隨便）as one likes; as one sees fit
隨處（到處 / 隨處 / 隨地）everywhere
隨街（到處 / 隨處）all about; all over; all over the place;
all over the shop; all over the show; all round; at all
places; everywhere; from place to place; here, there and
everywhere; here and there; high and low; hither and
thither; in all directions; in every place; in every quarter;
on all hands; on all sides; on every side; on every hand;
right and left; up hill and down dale

連隨（接着 / 跟着 / 繼續 / 跟隨）carry on; follow; go on; in
the wake of; proceed

【隧】soey⁶ tunnel

隧巴（隧道巴士）tunnel bus
隧道 tunnel
隧道巴士 tunnel bus

蹊隧（路徑）path; trail

【險】him² danger

險象 dangerous sign on phenomenon
險象環生 beset with danger; dangers lurking on all sides;
incessant crises; incessant occurrence of crises; signs of
danger appearing everywhere
險勝 edge out; narrow victory; nose out; win by a narrow
margin; win by a neck; win by a whisker

危險 danger

投資風險 investment risk
保險 insurance
冒險 take a risk; take chances
風險 risk
遇險 in danger; in distress; meet with a mishap; meet
with danger

【雕】diu¹ engrave

雕工 carver; grinder
雕刻 carve; engrave
雕像 effigy; monument; statue

浮雕 boss; cameo; enchase; relief

【霍】fok⁸ ① quickly ② suddenly

霍然 ①（忽然）quickly; rapidly; suddenly ②（疾病迅速去
除）be cured quickly
霍亂 cholera

白霍（吹噓自己）make a boast of oneself
沙塵白霍（不可一世）consider oneself a world above others;
consider oneself unsurpassed in the world; insufferably
arrogant; on the high ropes; ride the high horse;
swagger like a conquering hero; think oneself supreme in
the world

【霎】saap⁸（閃 / 晃）dazzle

霎吓霎吓（一晃一晃）appear and disappear very quickly
霎時（霎時間）in the twinkling of an eye; instant; moment;
very short time
霎氣（鬥氣 / 吵架）argue
霎眼（眨眼）blink; twinkle; wink
霎眼嬌（第一眼好看）a woman who seems attractive at
first sight but is in fact not especially attractive; appear
to be beautiful at a glance
霎戇 ①（混蛋）bastard ②（傻）stupid

冇搭霎 ①（不負責任 / 沒章法）irresponsible ②（沒正經）
have no sense of propriety
冇釐搭霎 ①（不負責任 / 沒章法）irresponsible ②（沒正經）
have no sense of propriety
嗌霎（爭吵 / 鬥嘴）have a serious argument
搭霎（正經 / 關心）care

【霖】lam⁴ ① continuous heavy rain ② rush

霖霖 raining continuously

鈴鈴霖霖（匆匆忙忙）in a big hurry

【靜】dzing⁶ quiet

靜局（背靜／清靜／寂靜）deserted

靜英英（僻靜／靜悄悄的）silent; very quiet

靜靜吔（悄悄地／暗地裏／靜靜地）act in silence;
　　inwardly; quietly; secretly

靜靜雞（悄悄地／暗地裏）act in silence; inwardly; quietly;
　　quietly and secretly; secretly; stealthily

靜雞雞（悄悄地／暗地裏）act in silence; inwardly; quietly;
　　quietly and secretly; secretly; stealthily

內心平靜 have inner peace of mind

好靜（好安靜）very quiet

冷靜 calm

沉靜 calm; quiet; serene

保持冷靜 keep calm; keep one's head; maintain calm

幽靜 peaceful; placid; quiet and secluded; serene

動靜 ①（某事的聲音）sound of sth astir ②（活動／事件／
　　發生的事情）activities; conditions; events; happenings;
　　movements

善靜（親切而安靜）kind and quiet

寧靜 calm; serene

頭腦冷靜 be composed in mind; cool-headed; have a cool
　　head; level-headed; sober-minded

【鞘】sau¹ sheath

鞘翅 wing cover

腱鞘 tendon sheath

【穎】wing⁶ novel

穎悟 clever

式樣新穎 in a novel style; stylish

【頭】tau⁴ head

頭一勻（頭一趟）the first time

頭七 the first seven days after sb's death

頭大 ①（頭疼／頭痛）have a headache ②（傷腦筋）
　　difficult to solve; knotty; troublesome

　頭大冇腦（頭大無腦／愚蠢）stupid

　頭大冇腦，腦大生草（頭大無腦，腦大長草／沒有智慧
　　的蠢人）stupid person without intelligence

頭水貨（頭等貨）first-rate goods

頭手貨（頭等貨）first-rate goods

頭皮（頭屑）dandruff

頭先（剛才）a little while ago; a moment ago; just now

頭尾（來龍去脈／始末／前後）about; altogether; around;
　　around the time of; one time or another; or so; round
　　about; the time spent on sth

頭尾三日（前後三天）about three days altogether

一頭一尾（徹頭徹尾）① both ends ② here and there

由頭到尾（從頭到尾）all the way; at both the end and
　　the beginning; from A to Z; from beginning to end;
　　from end to end; from first to last; from hub to tire;
　　from soup to nuts; from start to finish; from stem to
　　stern; from the egg to the apple; from the head to
　　the tail; from the sole of the foot to the crown of the
　　head; from tip to toe; from top to bottom; from top to
　　toe; the whole way; through and through; through the
　　whole length

好頭好尾（善始善終）a good beginning and a good
　　ending

話頭醒尾（頭腦靈活）able to take a hint

頭頭尾尾 ①（零零碎碎）odd pieces ②（全部一起）
　　altogether

攊頭撒尾（丟三落四）always getting things; always
　　losing this and forgetting that; forget this, that, and the
　　other; forgetful; miss this and that

頭夾（髮卡）hair clip

頭赤（頭痛）ache in one's head; have a headache;
　　headache

頭車（頭班車）first train

頭刺（頭疼）headache

　頭刺刺（頭有點疼）have a bit of headache

頭岳岳（東張西望）look around

頭版 front page

頭重腳輕 top-heavy

頭風（頭痛）ache in one's head; have a headache; headache

頭耷耷（耷拉着腦袋／垂頭喪氣）dejected; keep one's
　　head down

　頭耷耷眼濕濕（垂頭喪氣）become dejected and
　　despondent; blue about the gills; bury one's head in
　　dejection; down at the mouth; down in the chops;
　　down in the dumps; down in the hips; down in the
　　mouth; hang one's head; have one's tail down; in low
　　spirits; in the dumps; look downcast; mope about;
　　one's crest falls; out of heart; out of spirits; out of sorts;
　　sing the blues; take the heart out of sb

頭家（頭兒）boss; chief

頭站（起點站／起始站）origin station

頭馬（首席助理）top assistant

頭喋湯（拔頭籌／敢為人先／第一個吃螃蟹的人）the first
　　person to get into a profitable business

頭崩額烈（焦頭爛額）be scorched by the flames; badly
　　battered; beat sb's head off; be bruised and battered; be
　　scorched and burned; in a sorry plight; in a terrible fix;
　　smash heads and scorch brows; utterly exhausted from
　　overwork

頭痕（遇到煩心事）having a difficult problem

頭都大埋（腦袋都脹了／頭都大了）addle one's head

頭痛 headache
頭痛發燒（小病痛）minor diseases
頭痛醫頭，腳痛醫腳（被動應付，對問題不作根本徹底的解決）a defensive stopgap measure; cure only the symptoms; sporadic and piecemeal steps; take only a stopgap measure, not a radical one; take only palliative measures for one's illness; treat symptoms but not the disease; treat the head when getting a headache, treat the foot when the foot hurts

頭等 first class

頭殼（頭骨／腦袋）bonce; head
頭殼頂出煙（七竅生煙／非常生氣）get very angry

頭暈 dizziness
頭暈暈（頭暈）feeling dizzy

頭路（門路）pull; way

頭嗒嗒（垂頭喪氣）depressed

頭腦 brain
頭腦冷靜 be composed in mind; cool-headed; have a cool head; level-headed; sober-minded
頭腦簡單（傻乎乎）simple-minded
頭腦靈活 nimble-minded
笨頭笨腦 block-headed
薯頭薯腦（呆頭呆腦／傻裏傻氣）stupid

頭槌（頭球）header

頭獎 first prize
中咗頭獎（中頭獎）won the first prize

頭慶（頭發熱）hot-headed

頭盤（頭道菜）① appetiser; starter ② first course

頭髮 hair
頭髮灰白 have grizzled hair
頭髮尾浸浸涼（幸災樂禍）gloat over sb's enemy's misfortune
一執頭髮（一綹頭髮）a coil of hair
甩頭髮（掉頭髮）lose one's hair
長頭髮 long hair
短頭髮 short hair
剪頭髮 have a hair cut

頭劑（頭煎）first decoction

頭頭（最初）at first; at the beginning; at the outset; initial; original
頭頭碰着黑（處處碰釘子／諸事不順）everything goes wrong; meet with difficulties whatever one does; strike a snag everywhere

頭擰擰（失望的樣子）disappointed look

頭臘（髮蠟）pomade

一件頭（單件裝）one-piece outfit

一個蒜頭（一頭蒜）a bulb of garlic

一個鐘頭（一個小時）one hour

一粒蒜頭（一瓣蒜）a clove of garlic

一開頭（起初）at first

一間舖頭（一間店舖）a shop

一磈磚頭（一堆磚頭）a heap of bricks

一頭 ① a headful of ② a; an; one

一嚿石頭（一塊石頭）a rock

一嚿磚頭（一塊磚頭）a brick

人頭 head

三件頭（三件套）three-piece suit

上頭 ① boss; superior ② above; on the surface of; on top of; over; top; upper surface

下頭 below; under

大有來頭 have powerful backing; very socially influential

大堆頭（大量）in a large quantity

大頭 big head

大諗頭（好大喜功）hot oneself up with ambition; over-ambitious

小鬼頭（小鬼／小惡魔／惡作劇的孩子）buster; little devil; mischievous child; imp

工頭 foreman; overlooker; overseer; supervisor; task master

及早回頭 lose no time in mending one's ways; make haste to reform; mend one's ways without delay; repent before it is too late

手頭 the money one has at a certain time

日頭 ① (太陽) sun ② (白天) day; daytime

月頭（月初）beginning of the month

水頭（錢款）money

水龍頭 faucet

火車頭 engine

牛王頭（蠻不講理的人）unreasonable person

牛頭 cow's head

冇厘頭（不知所謂）pointless behaviour or talk

冇得番轉頭（不能回頭）no turning back

冇睇頭（沒看頭兒）nothing interesting to see

冇話頭（沒得說）nothing to be said

冇癮頭 ① (沒趣) bored ② (沒勁) disappointed

出風頭 be in the limelight

出頭 take the lead

半個鐘頭（半個小時）half an hour

叻過頭（太聰明）too smart

叩頭（磕頭）kowtow

叮噹馬頭（實力相當）difficult to tell which one has outdone the other; very hard to tell which one is better

奶頭 nipple; teat

巨頭 baron; magnate; tycoon

扒頭（超車）overtake; overtaking

打斧頭（揩油水）① cheat sb when buying sth on their

behalf ② cook up an expense account to line one's pockets

打穿頭 (打破腦袋) break one's head

打崩頭 (打破頭) break one's head

打理舖頭 (看店) take care of the shop

正月頭 (正月裏) during the New Year

生水芋頭 (傻瓜) block-head; block-headed; foolish-looking; simpleton

矛頭 bunt; spearhead; spear point

石頭 rock; stone

禾稈頭 (稻稈) rice straw

禾頭 (稻稈) rice straw

伙頭 (廚師) cook

兆頭 omen; portent; sign

先頭 (最初) at first; in the beginning

光頭 bald

地頭 (地域) sphere of operation; territory

好有來頭 (大有來頭) with a powerful back-up

好食爭崩頭 (瘋搶便宜貨) grab sth when it is cheap

好意頭 (有彩頭) auspicious omen

好腳頭 (帶好運) come with good luck to sb

好戲在後頭 there will be sth interesting to see a little later

年頭 beginning of the year

有乜諗頭 (有甚麼想法) any ideas

有冇折頭 (有沒有折扣) any discount

有瓦遮頭 (有地方住) have a place to live

死人頭 (蠢貨) idiot

死對頭 (仇敵) rival

竹花頭 (竹字頭) the "bamboo" (竹) radical

舌頭 tongue

行返轉頭 (掉頭) turn back

行頭 (領頭) take the lead

低頭 ① bow one's head; hang one's head; lower one's head ② submit; yield

判頭 (承包商) contractor

坎嘞頭 (敲腦袋) knock one's head

炭頭 (點頭) nod one's head

抓晒頭 (抓耳撓腮) feeling confused

折頭 (折扣) discount

拋浪頭 (嚇唬) come the bully over sb; show off before a fight

男人頭 (假小子) tomboy

男仔頭 (假小子) tomboy; woman who acts like a man

芋頭 taro

角落頭 (角落) corner

豆腐頭 (豆腐渣) bean curd residue

走頭 (滾開) go away

乳頭 ① diddies; nipple; teat; tit; tittie; titty ② papilla

事頭 (老闆 / 僱主) boss; employer; proprietor

來頭 powerful back-up

兩頭 both ends

垂頭 hang one's head

呢頭 (這兒 / 這裏) here

呢頭…嗰頭 (這邊…那邊) on the other hand...on the other; this...that

岳高頭 (抬起頭 / 仰起頭) raise one's head

念頭 idea; thought

抱頭 cover one's head with one's hands

抽頭 (突然轉彎 / 脫身) do a U-turn; run away; withdraw

拆骨頭 (去骨頭 / 剔骨頭) boning

拍膊頭 (在某人的肩膀上哭泣 / 拍拍肩膀 / 輕拍肩膀) cry on sb's shoulder; pat on the shoulder; tap sb on the shoulder

拖頭 (集裝箱車) container truck

抬頭 ① raise one's head ② upsurge

斧頭 axe; hatchet

枕頭 pillow

枝頭 on the branch

泥頭 (渣土) dregs

爬頭 ① (超車) overtake other cars on the road ② (超越他人) be ahead of others

爭崩頭 (競爭激烈) fierce rivalry

直頭 (直接 / 根本 / 徑直) straight away

花灑頭 (蓮蓬頭) shower head

阿頭 (頭兒) boss; chief; head

雨字頭 the "rain" (雨) radical

剃頭 shave one's head

前世撈亂骨頭 (兩人關係極差) be hostile to each other

前頭 (前面) in front; ahead; at the head

是非皆因強出頭 (多管閒事的人容易引起是非) a busybody often invites troubles

耍手擰頭 (搖頭擺手) give a flat refusal

洗頭 wash one's hair

洗濕個頭 (下了水了) have no way to back down; have to go through what has been started

派頭 extravagant and ostentious display; in grand style; (English) pride

拳頭 fist

流浪街頭 roam the streets; run the streets; wander about the streets

眉頭 eyebrows

眉頭一皺，計上心頭 have a sudden inspiration; hit upon an idea; knit the brows and you will hit upon a stratagem

砓頭 (點頭) nod one's head

科頭 (科長) section chief

耍手擰頭 (搖頭擺手) refuse

耷低頭 (低下頭) disheartened; upset

耷頭 (低頭) lower one's head

苗頭 suggestion of a new development; symptom of a trend

風頭 ① condition ② limelight

倔頭 (不通) be blocked up

冧宮頭 (禿寶蓋) the "roof top" (宀) radical

冧篷頭 (禿寶蓋) the "roof top" (宀) radical

凍過頭 (太冷) too cold

唔好意頭 (意頭不好) inauspicious omen

浦頭 (露面) show up

浮頭 (露面) make one's appearance; show up

烏頭 (鯔魚) grey mullet

焓熟狗頭 (煮熟的狗頭——咧嘴逢迎) smiling stupidly

病字頭 (病字旁 / 病旁兒) the "sickness" (疒) radical

衰仔頭 (小傢伙 / 兔崽子 / 混小子 / 搗蛋鬼 / 小流氓) little brat; little rascal

草花頭 (草字頭 / 草字兒) the "grass" (艸) radical

財到光棍手——有去冇回頭 (錢財到了騙子手中就很難取回) give a bone to a dog

起頭 (起先 / 起初) at first; in the beginning

骨頭 bone

鬼頭 (魔鬼妖怪 / 惡魔) devil

側頭 (歪脖子 / 扭脖子) wry neck

勒緊褲頭 (勒緊褲腰帶) tighten one's belt

埠頭 (渡口 / 碼頭) pier; wharf

夠水頭 (錢款充足) have enough money

從頭 ① (從一開始) from the beginning; from the top ② (重新 / 再來一次) anew; once again

掃把頭 (頭髮不整齊的人) a person with unruly hair

掉頭 (調頭) turn to face the other way; U-turn

望番轉頭 (回頭望) look back

梅頭 (豬肩扒) pork shoulder chops

梳頭 (梳理一個人的頭髮) comb one's hair

斬頭 (斬首 / 殺頭) behead; decapitate

渡頭 (港口) harbour; port

甜頭 (利益 / 好處) sweetener

眼頭 (大眼角) great canthus

笠頭 (套頭) cover the head

笨頭 (愚蠢) stupid person

細佬哥剃頭 (就快就快 / 很快完成) will be finished in no time

蛇頭 (非法移民 / 走私犯首領) illegal immigrant smuggler

缽頭 (缽兒) small rice bowl

麥頭 (麥茬 / 大麥茶) barley tea

㗎頭 (日本人) Japanese person

幾百萬未開頭 (胡亂花錢) spend as if one were a billionaire

插蘇頭 (插座 / 插銷 / 插頭) plug

掬頭 (搖頭) shake one's head

朝頭 (早上) early in the morning; early morning; morning

貴過頭 (太貴) too expensive

無厘頭 (莫名其妙) silly talk

畫頭 (加片) trailer

發過豬頭 (賺大錢) make a lot of money; very rich

硬骨頭 (無畏不屈的人) dauntless and unyielding person

街頭 street

番轉頭 (回頭) turn back

買水咁嘅頭 (垂頭喪氣) crestfallen; dejected; sing the blues

開舖頭 (開店) open a shop

開頭 (最初) at first; at the beginning; at the outset; initial; original

嗒低頭 (垂頭喪氣) disheartened; upset

嗰頭 (那兒 / 那裏) that place; there

塊頭 hulky; large

意頭 (兆頭 / 彩頭) auspicious sign; good luck; omen

新正頭 (正月期間) during the New Year

椰菜頭 (波浪卷) curly hair

源頭 fountainhead; head; headstream; headwater; source of a stream

滑頭 ① slick ② sly fellow

煙頭 (煙蒂) cigarette end

腳頭 (腳勁兒 / 運氣) fortune; luck

落足嘴頭 (用盡唇舌) make a long harangue

落嘴頭 (哄騙某人) cajole sb

葱頭 (洋葱) onion

裏頭 (裏面 / 裏邊) inside

過頭 (太) excessively; much; over; too

飯鏟頭 (眼鏡蛇) cobra

壽頭 (傻子) blockhead; idiot

嘜頭 ① (商標) trade mark ② (樣子) look

摟住個頭 (披在頭上) drape sth over one's head

榔頭 hammer

槍頭 (槍) gun

福頭 (笨蛋 / 蠢人) fool; sucker

熟過頭 (太熟) ① over-cooked ② over-ripe

綽頭 (手法) gimmick

膊頭 (肩膀) shoulder

蒜頭 (大蒜 / 蒜) garlic

銜頭 (頭銜 / 職稱) official title of a person

調轉頭 (反過來 / 倒過來 / 對調 / 調換處境 / 調轉方向 / 翻過來) change the direction; turn the other way round

駁骨頭 (接骨 / 接骨頭) set a fracture

劉備借荊州——有借冇回頭 (劉備借荊州——有借無還) money or things borrowed are never returned; the loan once given never comes back

撞頭 (相衝 / 衝突) confront

熠熟狗頭 (煮熟的狗頭——咧嘴逢迎) on the broad grin

熱過頭 (太熱) too hot

熱頭 (太陽) sun

碼頭 ① pier ② rich husband ③ rich partner

箭頭 arrowhead; arrow point; arrow tip

皺眉頭 frown

膝頭 (膝蓋) knee

舖頭 (店舖 / 商店 / 舖子) shop; store

褲頭 (褲衩 / 褲腰) waistband

調轉槍頭 (反戈一擊) turn around to criticise fellow
　　members

諗頭 (計劃 / 想法) idea; notion; opinion; thinking; view;
　　way of looking at sth; what one has in mind

賣仔莫摸頭 (賣兒莫摸頭) express regret at being forced to
　　sell one's favourite

賤骨頭 (惡棍 / 壞人 / 壞蛋 / 無賴) scoundrel

鋤頭 hoe

遮頭 (傘把兒) head of an umbrella

鞋頭 (鞋尖) toe cap

撻頭 (光頭 / 禿頭) bald

擰高頭 (抬起頭) raise one's head

擰頭 (抬頭) raise one's head

樹頭 (樹根) tree stump

橋頭 bridgehead; either end of a bridge

橫死街頭 be dead in the street

磚頭 brick

豬頭 be badly beaten

險過剃頭 (九死一生) a hair's breadth; a narrow escape;
　　barely escape danger; hang by a hair; in the hour of peril

龍頭 (隊首) head of a queue

擰頭 (搖頭) shake one's head

擰擰頭 (搖搖頭) shake one's head

牆頭 the crest of a fence; the top of a wall

講返轉頭 (話說回來) return to the main topic

避風頭 (躲避風吹) stay out of trouble

擽頭 (打腦袋 / 打頭) hit sb on the head

繡花枕頭 ① ginger bread ② beautiful in appearance but
　　lacking inner talents

薯頭 (呆 / 笨) stupid

轉頭 ① (一會兒) later ② (回頭) turn about

雞春砍石頭 (以卵擊石) like an egg dashing itself against a
　　rock – courting destruction

額頭 (前額) forehead

襪頭 (襪口) welt

鐘頭 (小時) hour

鏡頭 ① camera lens; lens ② scene; shot

關頭 ① critical juncture ② critical moment

饅頭 steamed bun

髆頭 (肩膀) shoulder

攞意頭 (討個彩頭) do sth for the sake of good luck; get an
　　auspicious sign

癮頭 addiction; strong interest

鑊頭 (大鐵鍋) frying pan

曬熱頭 (曬太陽) bask in the sun; be exposed to the sun;
　　sunbathe

灘頭 beachhead

蘿白頭 (日本人) Japanese

罐頭 can; canning; tin

鱷魚頭 (殘酷的人) cruel person

【頸】geng² (脖子) neck

頸巾 (圍巾) scarf
　　一條頸巾 (一條圍巾) a scarf
　　攬頸巾 (圍圍巾) wear a scarf

頸骨 (脖子) neck

頸梗膞痛 (脖子痠肩膀疼) stiff neck and pain in the
　　shoulder

頸喉 (喉嚨) throat

頸渴 (口渴) thirsty
　　頸唔頸渴 (口渴不渴 / 你渴不渴) are you thirsty

頸鏈 (項鏈) necklace

牛頸 (倔強) obstinate; stubborn; unbending; unyielding

包拗頸 (抬槓) sure to argue to the contrary

吊頸 (上吊) commit suicide by hanging; hang oneself

好硬頸 (非常固執) very stubborn

死牛一便頸 (非常固執) stick to one's guns; stubborn;
　　unyielding

使頸 (使性子 / 賭氣) fly into a temper; get angry; get in a
　　rage; in a fit of pique; lose one's temper

拗頸 (抬槓 / 爭吵) argue; argue against sb; quarrel with

長頸 (脖子長) long neck

炮仗頸 (火性子) short-tempered

唔抵得頸 (憋不住了) cannot control one's temper

望長條頸 (渴望過去 / 望穿秋水) hanker after

頂頸 (爭論 / 頂撞 / 頂嘴 / 回嘴 / 爭論 / 爭吵) answer
　　back; argue; backchat; backtalk; go against another;
　　quarrel; reply defiantly; talk back

揸頸 ① (掐住脖子) grab the neck ② (被霸凌) be bullied

割頸 (自刎 / 抹脖子) cut one's throat

短頸 (脖子短) short neck

硬頸 (頑固 / 固執 / 倔強 / 執拗) stubborn; unyielding

揼住條頸 (掐着脖子) have sb by the throat

蒲頭 ① (浮上來 / 浮在水上) float on water ② (出現 / 露
　　臉了) turn up

箍頸 (勒脖子) seize sb by the throat

瞓戾頸 (落枕) stiff neck caused by an awkward sleeping posture

撚頸 (卡脖子) grab the neck

鯁頸 ① (魚骨鯁着咽喉) have a fishbone stuck in one's
　　throat ② (事情不順利) do things without success

攬頭攬頸 (摟摟抱抱) be very close; on intimate terms with
　　each other

【頻】pan⁴ urgent

頻倫 (忽忙 / 急促 / 倉促) hurry-scurry; in a hurry; rush
　頻倫唔得入城 (欲速則不達) more haste, less speed
　頻頻倫倫 (趕趕急急 / 急急忙忙) in great hurry

頻能 (恐慌) (English) panic

頻密 (頻繁) frequent

頻撲 (忙碌 / 奔波 / 忽忙) in a hurry all the time; rush
　around; shuttle back and forth for one's living

【餐】caan¹ meal; regular meal

餐刀 table knife

餐巾 napkin

餐卡 (餐車) buffet car; dining car; restaurant car

餐具 tableware

餐室 (餐廳) restaurant

餐枱 (飯桌 / 餐桌) dining table

餐單 (菜單) menu

餐湯 (膳食湯) soup for the meal

餐牌 (菜單 / 菜譜) menu

餐搵餐食 (掙一頓吃一頓) live from hand to mouth

餐墊 placemat

餐廳 restaurant
　一間餐廳 a restaurant

一個早餐 (一頓早餐) a breakfast

二人餐 two-person meal

六人餐 six-person meal

午市套餐 (午餐套餐) set lunch

午餐 lunch; luncheon

去野餐 (去郊遊) go for a picnic

西餐 ① Western food ② Western meal

早餐 breakfast

自助午餐 lunch buffet

自助餐 buffet

快餐 fast food

免費午餐 free lunch

刷一餐 (大吃一頓) have a square meal

肥雞餐 (遣散費) golden handshake

為兩餐 (討生活) try and make a living

食一餐 (吃一頓) have a meal

食大餐 (吃大餐) have a square meal

食早餐 (吃早餐) have breakfast

食自助餐 (吃自助餐) have buffet

唐餐 (中菜) Chinese cuisine

套餐 set meal

茶餐 (下午茶) afternoon tea set

素餐 ① (素菜餐) vegetable meal ② (素食) vegetarian
　③ (尸位素餐) not work for one's living

野餐 (郊遊) picnic

揩一餐 (罵一頓) give sb a dressing-down

晚市套餐 (晚餐套餐) set dinner

晚餐 (晚飯) dinner

開餐 (開吃) have a meal

搵兩餐 (混飯吃) make a living

優惠套餐 special set meal

藕餐 (擾頓飯吃) sponge off one's friends

【餓】ngo⁶ hungry

餓死 starve to death
　餓死老婆燻臭屋 (養不起老婆) cannot earn enough
　　bread to get married

餓狗搶屎 (爭前恐後) compete against each other for sth

餓唔餓 (餓不餓) hungry or not
　你餓唔餓 (你餓不餓) are you hungry

餓鬼 (餓死鬼) hungry ghost
　餓鬼投胎 (狼吞虎嚥) devour like a hungry tiger pouncing
　　its prey

好肚餓 (肚子好餓) very hungry

肚唔肚餓 (你餓不餓) are you hungry

肚餓 (肚子餓) hungry

鬼咁肚餓 (非常餓) extremely hungry

揦肚餓 (餓肚子) go hungry; starve; suffer from hunger;
　suffer from starvation

頂肚餓 (墊肚子) allay one's hunger with sth; cram one's
　stomach; eat sth; have a quick snack; satisfy hunger

飢餓 hungry

【餘】jy⁴ remain

餘地 alternative; leeway; margin; room; spare space;
　latitude

餘額 ① vacancies yet to be filled ② remaining sum; surplus

比上不足，比下有餘 be worse as compared with the best
　but better as compared with the worst

多餘 redundant

年年有餘 may there be surpluses every year

盈餘 abundance; have a favourable balance; have a surplus;
　profit; surplus

剩餘 (盈餘 / 過剩) remainder; surplus

【罵】maa⁶ insult

罵人 abuse; call one names; condemn; curse; give sb a
　good dressing down; give sb a good wigging; give sb a
　scolding; give sb a piece of one's mind; give sb the edge
　of one's tongue; haul sb over the coals; load sb with
　insults; mutter insults against; rake sb over the coals;
　reprove; revile; sail into; scold; swear at; take sb to task;

tell one off

罵街（在街上亂罵）shout abuses in the street

侮罵 insult with words

破口大罵 abuse roundly; bawl abuse; curse freely; give vent to a torrent of abuse; heap abuse on; hurl all kinds of abuse against; let loose a flood of abuse; pour out a whole ocean of abuse over; pour out torrents of abuse; raise hail Columbia; rave widely against; shout abuse; swear home; swear like a trooper; swear one's way through swear one's way through a stone wall; swear through a two-inch board; vociferate oaths

辱罵 abuse; abuse and insult; call sb name; hurl insults

【骹】gaau³（鉸鏈）hinge

手骹（手腕）wrist

打牙骹（聊天）chat; engage in friendly banter; have a chat with friends; have a chat with sb; tattle

甩骹（脫臼）broken joint; dislocate

骨骹（關節）joint

腳骹（腳踝）ankle

【髻】gai³（髮髻）topknot

髻年（青少年）childhood; youth

梳髻（梳髮髻）comb a knot out of one's hair

擰頭擰髻（搖頭晃腦）nod one's head – assume an air of self-approbation

鬟髻 woman's hair with a topknot

【鬨】hung³ fighting

鬨動（引起轟動）cause a sensation

內鬨（內訌）internal conflict; internal dissension; internal disorder; internal strife

挑起內鬨（挑起內訌）stir up internal strife

避免內鬨（避免內訌）avoid internal strife

【鮑】baau¹ abalone

鮑人（皮匠）tanner

鮑魚 abalone

【鴛】jyn¹ mandarin ducks

鴛鴦 ①（鴛鴦鳥）mandarin ducks ②（不成對的）unpaired ③（鴛鴦奶茶）coffee mixed with tea

鴛鴦飯 fried rice with white and red sauces

識就鴛鴦，唔識就兩樣（區分不出兩者之間的區別）be unable to appreciate the difference between two things

【鴣】gu¹ pigeon

鴣鴒（鴿子）pigeon

撳鷯鴣（藉優勢敲詐勒索）take sb at advantage to practice extortion

【鴦】joeng¹ mandarin ducks

鴛鴦 ①（鴛鴦鳥）mandarin ducks ②（不成對的）unpaired ③（鴛鴦奶茶）coffee mixed with tea; unpaired

【鴨】aap⁸ ①（鴨子）duck ②（男妓）gigolo; male prostitute; maud; rent boy; renter; ring-snatcher

鴨公（公鴨）drake

鴨片 duck slice

鴨仔 ①（小鴨）duckling ②（旅行團遊客）member of a tour group ③（學生遊客）student passengers taking a nanny van

鴨肉 duck meat

鴨店 duck shop

鴨乸（母鴨）female duck

　鴨乸腳（平足）flat feet

　鴨乸蹄（平足）flat feet

鴨腎 duck kidney

鴨殼（鴨骨架）duck bones

鴨嘴梨（鴨梨）pear

鴨嘴帽（鴨舌帽）casquette; peaked cap

一隻鴨（一隻鴨子）a duck

子鴨（綠鴨）green duck

北京填鴨（北京烤鴨）Peking duck

坑渠浸死鴨（陰溝裏翻船）fail miserably in a very easy task

板鴨 pressed dried salted duck

烤鴨 roasted duck

做鴨（做男妓）work as a gigolo

掛臘鴨（上吊自盡／吊死鬼）hang oneself; kill oneself by hanging

跛腳鴨 lame duck

填鴨 ①（烤鴨）roast duck ②（強行灌輸）spoon-feeding

劏雞殺鴨（殺雞殺鴨）kill chickens and ducks

燒鴨（烤鴨）roast duck

雞鴨 chickens and ducks

臘鴨 cured duck

【默】mak⁹ ① dictate ② silent

默哀 stand in silent tribute

　默哀一分鐘 observe one minute's silence

默契 tacit agreement

默默 silent

　默默無言 remain silent

沉默 ① reticent; taciturn ② quiet; silent

保持沉默 bite the tongue; hush; keep a still tongue in one's head; keep mute; keep silent; mute; preserve silence; remain silent

幽默 (English) humour

背默 (默寫) write from memory

風趣幽默 witty and humorous

懶幽默 (試着幽默) try to be funny

讀默 (聽寫) dictate

【龍】lung⁴ ① dragon ② queue

龍井 Lung Ching tea

龍年 Year of the Dragon

龍舟 dragon boat

　龍舟比賽 dragon boat race

　爬龍舟 (賽龍舟) dragon boating

　游龍舟水 swim while dragon boating

龍床唔似狗竇 (金窩銀窩不如自己的狗窩) there is no place sweeter than home

龍尾 (隊尾) end of a queue

龍門 ① (球門) goal ② (守門員) goal-keeper

龍𦠿 (龍利魚) sole

龍馬精神 ① as vigorous as a dragon or a horse ② wish you good health

龍眼 (桂圓) longan

　龍眼肉 (桂圓肉) dried longan pulp

龍船 (龍舟) dragon boat

　扒龍船 (賽龍舟) dragon boat competition; dragon boating

龍游淺水遭蝦戲 (虎落平陽被犬欺) no man is a hero to his valet

龍精虎猛 (充滿活力 / 充滿力量) full of energy; full of strength

龍蝦 lobster

　焗龍蝦 baked lobster

龍頭 (隊首) head of a queue

龍躉 (大石斑魚) giant garoupa

一條龍 ① one queue ② one-way through ③ one-stop service

大排長龍 (排長隊) line up in a long queue; queue up in a long line; stand in a long queue

化骨龍 (孩子) dependent child

尼龍 nylon

地頭龍 (地頭蛇) powerful figure in a particular area

托水龍 (貪污) embezzle; embezzle sb's money; run away with the money entrusted to sb

行運一條龍 (非常幸運) have good fortune

坐過龍 (坐過站) miss one's stop

長龍 (排長隊) long queue

恐龍 dinosaur

烏龍 ① (昏庸) muddle-headed ② (糊塗) absent-minded ③ (烏龍茶) Oolong tea

排長龍 (排長隊) line up in a long queue; stand in a long queue

過江龍 (外國專家 / 強大的局外人) foreign expert; powerful outsider

過龍 (過頭) exceed; go beyond the limit; in excess; overdo

擺烏龍 ① (給搞糊塗了) get confused ② (弄錯 / 做錯) confuse black and white; make a mistake

【龜】gwai¹ tortoise

龜公 ① (老鴇) pimp; procuress ② (妓院的男老板) man running a brothel ③ (王八) man whose wife has an affair with another man

龜蛋 (王八蛋) bad person; fool; idiot; son of a bitch

金龜 (富有丈夫) rich husband

烏龜 ① (烏龜) tortoise ② (皮條客) pimp; procure for prostitutes

釣金龜 (找個富有丈夫) hook a rich husband

縮頭烏龜 (怕死鬼) coward

縮頭龜 (怕死鬼) coward

17 劃

【償】soeng⁴ compensate

償還 pay back; repay

賠償 compensate

【優】jau¹ ① excellent ② pull up

優先 priority

優異生 (優秀生) excellent student

優褲 (提褲子) lift up the trousers

優點 merit

左優 (左撇子) left-hander

【劗】dzat⁷ (塞) fill in; squeeze in; stuff

劗入去 (強塞進去) stuff in

劗實 (塞緊) stuff firmly

【勵】lai⁶ encourage

勵志 pursue a goal with determination

勉勵 encourage; urge

鼓勵 encourage
獎勵 reward

【嚇】haak⁸ (嚇唬) scare; threaten

嚇一跳 be astonished; be shaken; be shocked; be surprised
  嚇咗一跳 (嚇了一跳) be astonished; be shaken; be shocked; be surprised
嚇死 scare to death
嚇我一驚 (嚇我一跳) be astonished; be taken aback
嚇走 scare away
嚇到傻咗 (嚇傻了) be completely shocked
嚇怕 frighten
嚇窒 (嚇呆／嚇退／嚇倒) freak out; frighten; scare
嚇暈 (嚇昏) be frightened into fits; faint from fear
嚇嚫 (受驚) be frightened; be shocked; scare; suffer a mental shock

恐嚇 threaten

【嚼】dziu⁶ (完) finish

嚼低 (玩完) finish off

【嚼】dziu⁶ (嚼) chew

嚼爛啲 (嚼爛點) chew deeply

【嗼】loen¹ (啃) bite; gnaw; nib

嗼骨 (啃骨頭) gnaw a bone

【嚤】mo¹ clumsy

咪咪嚤嚤 (慢吞吞) very slow and clumsy
咪嚤 (慢吞吞) very slow and clumsy
咪嚤咪嚤 (慢吞吞) very slow and clumsy

【嚓】tsaat⁸ eat

嚓飯 (吃飯) have a meal

【壓】aat⁸ threaten

壓力 pressure; stress
壓死 press to death
壓迫 oppression
壓爛 crush; smash

血壓 blood pressure
脈壓 pulse pressure
掌上壓 (俯臥撐) press-up; push-up
減壓 stress relief

【嬰】jing¹ baby

嬰兒 baby
  嬰兒爽身粉 baby powder

育嬰 rear a baby

【嬲】nau¹ ① (生氣) angry ② (討厭) hate

嬲死 (氣死) very angry
  嬲死佢 (可生他的氣了／恨之入骨／恨死他) very angry with sb
嬲到彈起 (非常憤怒) hit the roof
嬲爆爆 (怒沖沖／氣沖沖) be filled with anger; very angry

咪嬲 (不要生氣／別生氣) don't get angry
唔好嬲 (不要生氣／別生氣) don't get angry
發嬲 (生氣) angry; angry about sth; angry at sb; be filled with fury; become angry; beside oneself with anger; blow one's top; boil over; boil with rage; bridle with anger; burn with anger; burn with wrath; enraged; fall into a rage; fire up; flare up; fly into a rage; fly into a temper; furious; get angry at sb; go off the top; livid; lose one's temper; slip off the handle; white with rage
激嬲 (氣壞) irritate
點解咁嬲 (為甚麼這麼生氣) why are you so angry

【孺】jy⁴ slow

孺子 boy; child

立孺 (反應遲鈍) slow to react

【孻】laai¹ final

孻女 (最小的女兒) youngest daughter
孻仔 (最小的兒子) youngest son
  孻仔拉心肝 (最小的兒子最得疼愛) parents lavish most affection on their youngest son
  孻仔拉心肝，孻女拉五臟 (最小的兒女最得疼愛) parents lavish most affection on their youngest son, but they just lavish much affection on their youngest daughter
  孻尾 (末尾／最後) last; the last one

【幫】bong¹ help

幫口 (幫人講話) put in a few words for sb
幫手 (幫忙／幫助) assist; help
  使唔使幫手 (需不需要幫忙) do you need any help
  幫吓手 (搭把手) lend sb a hand
  幫幫手 (搭把手) lend sb a hand
幫忙 help
  樂於幫忙 be glad to help; be willing to give a hand

幫吓口（説好話）put in a good word for sb
幫吓眼（幫下眼／幫助某人留意某事）help sb to keep an eye on sb/sth
幫助 help
幫派 gang; triad gang
幫理不幫親 fair-minded
幫辦（警官）police inspector
幫襯（光顧）patronise

【應】jing³ should

應付 deal with
應召 work as a prostitute
　　應召女郎（妓女）prostitute
應嘴（頂嘴）answer back; backchat; backtalk; reply defiantly; talk back

女侍應（女服務員）waitress
反應 reaction; response
回應 response
侍應 ①（男服務員）waiter ②（女服務員）waitress
供應 supply
咧飯應（立刻答應）accept another party's demand at once
效應 action; effect; influence
減息效應 effects of reducing the interest rate
答應 promise
黃大仙——有求必應（土地廟的橫批——有求必應）one who always accepts others' requests

【應】jing¹ promise

應份（本分／應該）ought to; should
應承（答應）promise
　　托塔都應承（無條件答應）give promise easily
應該 ought to; should

本應 ought to have; should have

【懦】no⁶ cowardice

懦夫 coward
懦弱 coward
　　懦弱無能 weak and useless

【戲】hei³ play

戲子（演員）actor
　　戲子佬（演員）actor
戲曲 Chinese opera
戲肉（戲劇高潮）climax; highlight
戲飛（戲票）play ticket; opera ticket
戲院 ①（電影院）cinema ②（戲院）theatre
　　戲院滿座 the cinema is full

戲票（電影票）movie ticket
戲劇 drama
　　戲劇性 dramatic

一套戲 ① a movie ② a play
大戲（粵劇）Cantonese opera
出把戲（玩雜技）play acrobatics
古裝戲 costume play
老把戲 the same old tricks; the same old stuff
把戲 acrobatics; jugglery
拿手好戲 one's strong suit
首本戲（拿手戲）one's specialty
耍把戲（玩雜技）play acrobatics
馬戲（馬戲團）circus
馬騮戲（猴戲）monkey show
做戲 ①（演戲）act in a play ②（做戲／演出）put on a show
唱對台戲（進入競爭／與對手比賽）enter into rivalry; put on a rival show
睇大戲（看粵劇）watch a Cantonese opera
睇套戲（看場電影）see a movie
睇戲 ①（看電影）see a movie ②（看戲）go to the theatre
義氣搏兒戲（冒忠於潛在叛徒的風險）take the risk of being loyal to a potential traitor
遊戲 game
嬉戲 frolic; have fun; make merry; play; romp; sport
影畫戲（電影）movie
龍游淺水遭蝦戲（虎落平陽被犬欺）no man is a hero to his valet
戲劇 drama

【擊】gik⁷ strike

擊中 hit the target
擊敗 beat; defeat
擊掌 clap one's hands

入市追擊（通過輸入交易獲利）profit by entering transactions
大受打擊 suffer a big shock
不堪一擊 be finished off at one blow; cannot withstand a single blow; collapse at the first blow
反擊 counter-attack
打擊 hit
目擊 see with one's own eyes; witness
伏擊 ambuscade; ambush; still-hunt; waylay
攻擊 attack
抨擊 denounce
射擊 ① fire; shoot ② shooting
乘勝追擊 continue one's victorious pursuit; exploit victories by hot pursuit; follow up a victory with hot pursuit; seize the day and pursue a routed army

截擊 ① intercept ② interception
衝擊 impact
襲擊 attack by surprise; come at; fly at sb's throat; make a
　　raid; make a surprise attack on; raid; surprise attack

【擎】king⁴ lift up
擎天 prop up the sky

引擎 engine
靈擎（靈驗）effective; efficacious

【擘】maak⁸ ①（張開）pull part ②（掰）be torn into halves ③（撕）tear
擘口（張嘴）open one's mouth
　　擘大口（把嘴張大）open one's mouth wide
擘面（翻臉 / 撕破臉）break up; fall out; suddenly turn
　　hostile
擘紙（撕紙）tear paper
擘梯（人字梯）herring bone ladder
擘眼（張開眼）open one's eyes
　　擘大眼（睜大眼睛）open one's eyes wide
　　擘大雙眼（睜大眼睛）open one's eyes wide
擘開兩邊（扯開兩半）be torn into halves
擘腳（叉開腳）with feet apart
擘網巾（掰了）break off friendly relations with sb; sever
　　connections with sb
擘髀（叉開大腿）with legs apart
擘爛（撕破）shred into pieces

【擠】dzai¹ ① crowded ②（放 / 擱 / 擺）place
擠低（放下 / 擱下）lay down; put down
擠響度（放在這裏）lay up here; place it here
擠迫（擁擠）crowded
擠提（擠兌）a run on a bank
擠嘢（放東西 / 擱東西 / 擺東西）lay down things; put
　　down things
擠擁（擁擠）crowded

【擬】ji⁵ count on
擬定 draft; draw up; work out
　　擬定計劃 map out a plan
擬聲 onomatopoeia

指擬（指望）count on sb
唔使指擬（不用指望 / 別指望）have no fond dreams
　　about it

【擯】ban³ braid
擯辮（梳辮子）braid one's hair

【擦】tsaat⁸ ①（刷）chafe; rub; scrape ②（塞）fill; fill in; satiate; squeeze in; squeeze into; stuff
擦牙（刷牙）brush one's teeth
擦損（擦傷）bruise; graze
擦飽未吖（塞飽了嗎）have you eaten to the full
擦膠（橡皮擦）rubber eraser
　　擦紙膠（橡皮擦）rubber eraser
擦鞋 ①（擦鞋子）shine shoes ②（吹捧奉承 / 拍馬屁 / 抱
　　粗腿）adulate; brown-nose; butter sb up; crawl to; curry
　　favour; curry favour with sb; eat sb's toads; fawn on;
　　flatter; give sb the soft-soap; ingratiate oneself with; kiss
　　sb's ass; lay it on thick; lay it on with a trowel; lick sb's
　　boots; lick sb's shoes; lick sb's spittle; lick the boots of sb;
　　obsequious; play up to; polish the apple; soft-soap; suck
　　up to; sycophancy; toady sb
　　擦鞋仔（馬屁精）flunky
　　擦鞋狗（馬屁精）flunky
　　擦錯鞋（馬屁拍到馬蹄上）fail to please one's boss;
　　　　stroke the fur the wrong way

牙擦 ①（狂妄 / 炫耀自己 / 傲慢）boastful ②（牙刷）
　　toothbrush
牙擦擦 ①（狂妄 / 炫耀自己 / 傲慢）boastful ②（狂妄的
　　人）boastful person
粉擦（板擦 / 粉筆刷 / 黑板擦）eraser
膠擦（橡皮）rubber eraser
鞋擦（鞋刷）shoe brush
磨擦 clash; friction; rub

【擤】sang³ blow the nose
擤到骨罉都剌埋（整天不斷在投訴）make a constant
　　complaint for having paid so much for sth
擤到樹葉都落埋（整天不斷在抱怨）express one's
　　repentance for having paid for sth worthless
擤笨（錯過機會感到遺憾）feel sorry for having missed the
　　opportunity

【擰】ning⁶ ①（扭）twist ②（拿）hold
擰住（拿着）holding
　　擰住啲嘢（拿着東西）holding things
擰走（拿走）remove; take away
擰歪面（扭過臉去）turn one's face
擰埋（扭上）put screws on
擰開 unscrew
擰頭（搖頭）shake one's head
　　擰頭擰髻（搖頭晃腦）nod one's head – assume an air of
　　　　self-approbation
　　擰擰頭（搖搖頭）shake one's head

擰轉面（扭過臉去）turn one's face

刁橋扭擰（左右刁難）deliberately create obstructions for sb
扭扭擰擰（扭扭捏捏）squirm
扭擰（扭捏）put on poses; squirm
頭擰擰（失望的樣子）disappointed look

【檐】jim⁴ eaves

檐蛇（壁虎）house lizard; wall gecko
檐眼（眼皮 / 瞼）eyelid
　　單檐眼（單眼皮）single-fold eyelid
　　雙檐眼（雙眼皮）double-fold eyelid

瓦檐 tile eaves
眼檐（上眼皮）upper eyelid
單眼檐（單眼皮）single-fold eyelid
廊檐 eaves of a veranda
雙眼檐（雙眼皮）double-fold eyelid

【檔】dong³ stall

檔口（攤子）booth; stall; vendor's stand
檔次 gradation; scale

大排檔 Cantonese open-air restaurant
大牌檔（大排檔）Cantonese open-air restaurant
大檔（賭窟）gambling den
中檔 average
冚檔（查封 / 倒閉）close down
生果檔（水果攤）fruit stall
地檔（地攤）street-floor stall
好拍檔（好伙伴）good partner
收檔①（收攤）close the shop for the night ②（停業）shut down
　　a business ③（不再做）not to do it any more ④（死）die
肉檔（肉舖 / 肉攤）butcher's; meat stall
低檔①low gear ②lower end
定檔（有把握 / 鎮定）certain; sure
拆檔（拆伙 / 散夥）break up a partnership
拍吓檔（協助一下）please help
拍硬檔（大力協助 / 通力合作）help each other to work on;
　　work well together
拍檔（合作者 / 伙伴 / 伙伴兒）partner
空檔 free time
冧檔（倒台）collapse
臭檔（壞脾氣）bad-tempered; notorious
高檔①（高速檔）high gear ②（高等貨物）high-end
掂檔（好 / 做得好）okay
頂檔（頂替 / 湊合用 / 湊數 / 作為權宜之計）serve as a
　　stopgap
魚檔（魚攤 / 魚販）fish stall; fishmonger's

散檔（散伙 / 散夥）break up a partner; disband
菜檔（蔬菜攤）vegetable stall
睇檔（看店）look after a stall
報紙檔（報攤）newsstand
街邊檔（小攤兒）booth; road-side stall; stall; vendor's stand
開檔①（設攤兒 / 擺攤）operate a stall; set up a stall in the
　　street; set up a stall in the market ②（開店 / 開始做生
　　意）start one's business
開攤檔（設攤兒 / 擺攤）operate a stall; set up a stall in the
　　street; set up a stall in the market
搭檔①（合夥）go into partnership ②（聯手合作）join forces
搞亂檔（製造混亂）cause chaos
煙仔檔（香煙攤兒）cigarette stall
過檔（換單位）change jobs
撇檔（分手）end a partnership
熟食檔（熟食攤兒）cooked food stall
熟檔（非常瞭解）know a lot about sth
踢檔（突襲賭館）raid a vice den
賭檔（賭窟）gambling den
擺檔（擺攤兒）set up a stall in the market
攤檔（攤子）booth; stall; vendor's stand
攪亂檔（製造混亂）cause chaos

【檢】gim² take

檢查 inspect
檢控（控告 / 控告 / 指控）accuse
檢獲（查獲）hunt down and seize

一地兩檢 co-location clearance

【氈】dzin¹ ①（毯子）blanket ② felt

氈酒（杜松子酒 / 琴酒）(English) gin
氈帽（呢帽）woollen hat

一張地氈（一張地毯）a carpet
一塊地氈（一塊地毯）a carpet
毛氈（毛毯子）blanket
地氈（地毯）carpet
羊毛氈（羊毛毯）felted wool blanket

【濛】mung⁴ misty

濛濛光（蒙蒙亮）daybreak

白濛濛 all white

【澀】sap⁷ harsh; rough

澀口（澀嘴）astringent; pucker

嗶澀澀（非常粗糙）very rough

【濟】dzai³ aid

濟急（解燃眉之急）give urgent relief

濟軍（淘氣鬼）regular mischief

濟貧（幫助窮人／幫助陷入困境的人）give help to the
poor; help people in distress; help the poor; relieve
people in distress; relieve the poor

救濟 relief

【濤】tou⁴ wave

濤波（大波浪）billows; great waves

濤聲 sound of roaring billows; surf

浪濤 billow; great wave; surge; wave

【濕】sap⁷ ①（潮濕）wet ②（零敲碎打）piecemeal

濕水棉胎——冇得彈（帽子破了邊——頂好）①（沒說
的／無法挑剔的）above criticism; beyond reproach ②（好
極了）couldn't be better; excellent; second to none; very
good; wonderful

濕水欖核——兩頭標（水裏的葫蘆——兩邊擺）fleet of
foot

濕吓濕吓（零敲碎打）odds and ends

濕咗水（沾水了）has soaked in water

濕度 humidity

濕洇洇（濕淋淋／濕漉漉）drenched; dripping wet

濕星（瑣碎）odds and ends

濕氣 humidity; moisture

　濕氣重 very humid

濕碎（零碎）piecemeal

　濕濕碎 ①（零碎）a small amount of money ②（小意思）
　trivial matter

　濕濕碎碎（零七八碎）miscellaneous and trifling things;
　miscellaneous trifles; odds and ends; scattered and
　disorderly

濕電（交流電）alternating current

濕滯 ①（麻煩／撓頭／纏手）difficult to deal with; difficult
to tackle; headache; meet with a hitch; messed-up ②（濕
熱）hot and damp; warm and humid

濕熱 ①（潮濕悶熱）hot and damp; warm and humid ②（麻
煩／撓頭／纏手）difficult to deal with; difficult to tackle;
headache; meet with a hitch; messed-up

濕濕地（很濕）damp

扑濕（身體受傷害）assault physically

好潮濕 very humid

風濕 rheumatism

眼濕濕（淚水盈眶／眼睛紅紅的）one's eyes are filled with
tears; with eyes full of tears; with tears in one's eyes

陰陰濕濕（狡猾／陰險／奸詐／惡毒）cunning; treacherous;
vicious

陰濕（狡猾／陰險／奸詐／惡毒）cunning; treacherous;
vicious

落雨絲濕（下雨路滑）roads becoming slippery due to raining

碎濕濕（碎得很）bits and pieces; fragmentary; odds and
ends; piecemeal; scrappy

喙濕（淋濕）get very wet

潮濕 humid; moisture

頭耷耷眼濕濕（垂頭喪氣）become dejected and
despondent; blue about the gills; bury one's head in
dejection; down at the mouth; down in the chops; down
in the dumps; down in the hips; down in the mouth; hang
one's head; have one's tail down; in low spirits; in the
dumps; look downcast; mope about; one's crest falls; out
of heart; out of spirits; out of sorts; sing the blues; take
the heart out of sb

燥濕（炎熱潮濕）hot and moist

鹹濕（下流／淫穢）bawdy; dirty; dirty-minded; lascivious;
lecherous; nasty; randy; salacious; sleazy

【營】jing⁴ camp

營業 business operation

　營業收入 operating income

　營業額 turnover

營養 nutrition

　營養不良 malnutrition; under-nourished

營幕（營帳）tent sheet

扎營 encamp; pitch a camp; pitch a tent

步步為營 a bastion at every step; act cautiously; advance
gradually and entrench oneself at every step; consolidate
at every step; make a stand at every step; move carefully
every step on the way; pick one's steps; raise a fort at
every step

露營（野營）camping

【燦】tsaan³ bright

燦然 brightly; brilliantly; gloriously

燦爛 bright; glorious; magnificent; resplendent; splendid

阿燦（土包子）comrade

黃燦燦 bright yellow

【燥】tsou³ parched

燥火（上火）get angry

燥熱 hot and dry

燥濕（炎熱潮濕）hot and moist

內容枯燥 dull in content
好朝燥 (好乾燥) very dry
朝燥 (乾燥) dry

【燭】dzuk⁷ candle

燭台 candlestick
燭光 candlelight
燭芯 (燈芯) candlewick

元寶蠟燭 paper ingots and candles
火燭 (着火) fire; on fire
洋燭 (蠟燭) candle
洞房花燭 wedding
蠟燭 candle

【燶】nung¹ burn; scorch

燶起塊面 (板着臉 / 繃着臉) keep a straight face; pull a
　　long face; wear a long face

炒燶 (賠了 / 蝕了) loss through speculation
面燶燶 (臭臉) look angry
窮到燶 (赤貧) as poor as a church mouse; very poor

【牆】tsoeng⁴ wall

牆倒眾人推 everybody hits the person when he is down;
　　everybody kicks the man who is down; everyone gives
　　a shove to a falling wall; everyone hits a person who is
　　down; if a wall starts tottering, everyone gives it a shove;
　　lick sb when he is down; make things worse for others
　　who are already in difficulties; the wall tottering, the
　　crowd contributes to its collapse by pushing it; when a
　　man is going down-hill, everyone will give him a push;
　　when a wall is about to collapse, everybody gives it
　　a push
牆紙 (壁紙) wallpaper
牆頭 the crest of a fence; the top of a wall

一埲牆 (一面牆) a wall
一椑牆 (一面牆) a wall
內牆 internal wall
外牆 external wall
坎頭埋牆 (將頭撞向牆壁) bang one's head against
　　the wall
凭埋牆 (靠着牆) lean on a wall
沬水舂牆 (赴湯蹈火) go through fire and water
起牆 (建牆 / 疊牆) build a wall
粉飾外牆 paint external walls
圍牆 enclosing wall
撞牆 (撞牆) bump one's head against the wall

【獲】wok⁹ obtain

獲利 make a profit; profits obtained
　　平均獲利 average profit
獲得 (實現 / 贏得) achieve; acquire; earn; gain; obtain;
　　win
獲勝 (拔得頭籌 / 勝利 / 得勝 / 贏得勝利) come out on
　　top; triumph; victorious; win victory
獲獎 bring down the persimmon; get an award; prize-
　　winning; receive an award; win an award; win the prize

收獲 harvest
捕獲 ① acquire; arrest; capture; catch; seize; succeed in
　　catching ② trapping
斬獲 (獲得利潤) obtain a profit
檢獲 (查獲) hunt down and seize

【環】waan⁴ surrounding

環保 environmental protection
環球 ① (環遊世界) round the world ② (地球) the earth;
　　the whole world
環境 ① environment ② situation
　　附近環境 the environment in its vicinity
環顧 look around

一對耳環 a pair of earrings
耳環 earring

【療】liu⁴ cure

療效 curative effect
　　降低療效 weaken the curative effect
　　影響療效 affect the treatment
療程 course of treatment
　　重複療程 repeat a treatment
療養 convalesce; recuperate
　　療養院 sanitarium

治療 cure; treatment
物理治療 physical therapy

【癌】ngaam⁴ cancer

癌病 (癌症) cancer
癌症 cancer

子宮頸癌 cervical cancer
子宮癌 cancer of the uterus; cancer of the womb; uterine cancer
肝癌 hepatocele; liver cancer
乳癌 breast cancer
肺癌 lung cancer
致癌 cancer-causing; carcinogenic

【癆】lou⁴ tuberculosis

癆傷（勞傷）be weakened by overexertion

肺癆 tuberculosis

【盪】dong⁶ toss about

盪漾 be tossed about gently; ripple

批盪（抹灰）wall plastering

動盪（不穩定的）in a flux; turbulence; unrest; unstable;
　upheaval

意大利批盪（濃粧）heavy make-up

【瞥】pit⁸ peep

瞥伯（偷窺者）peeper

【矃】tsaang³（晃）dazzle

矃眼（晃眼）dazzlingly bright

【磺】wong⁴ sulphur

磺酸（亞硫酸）sulfonic acid

蛇見硫磺（蛇見硫磺——動也不敢動）diamond cut diamond

【𥔤】dzoeng² prop-up; support

𥔤住（撐着）prop-up; support
𥔤開（撐開）open; prop-up

【禪】sim⁴ Zen

禪定 deep meditation
禪房 mediation room

悟禪 come to understand the principle of Zen

【窿】lung¹（洞 / 窟窿）cave; hole

窿仔（小洞）small hole
窿路 ①（方法 / 途徑）channel; knack; know-how; outlet;
　trick of the trade; way ②（門路）way of making money
　搵窿路（找門路）solicit help from potential backers

窿對窿（零比零）zero all
　上半場窿對窿（上半場零比零）it was zero all for the first
　half of the match

窿窿蠄蠄（小孔和縫隙）in every nook and cranny; nook
　and corner

上半場窿對窿（上半場零比零）it was zero all for the first
　half of the match
大耳窿（高利貸者）loan shark
山窿（山洞）cave; cavern

捐窿（鑽洞）bore
耳仔窿（耳洞）ear hole
耳窿（耳洞）ear hole
刮個窿（扎個眼兒）prick a hole
拮窿（戳洞）pierce a hole
屎忽窿（肛門）anus; asshole
穿窿（穿孔 / 穿洞）bore a hole; perforate
掘個窿（挖個洞兒）dig a hole
掘窿（挖洞兒）dig a hole
通窿（穿孔 / 鑽孔 / 刺穿 / 打個洞）bore a hole; perforate;
　pierce; punch a hole
塞竇窿（小孩）a little child
鼻哥窿（鼻孔）nares; nostrils
褲穿窿（窮得叮噹響）have no money
錐窿（錐洞）bore a hole
鎖匙窿（鑰匙孔）key hole
鑿窿（開孔）bore a hole

【簋】gwai² bamboo basket for holding grain

九大簋（盛筵）lavish banquet
食九大簋（享用盛筵）have a sumptuous meal

【簍】lau⁵ bamboo basket

簍休（不修邊幅）slovenly

笆簍（簍子）basket

【糝】sam²（撒）sprinkle

糝鹽（撒鹽）sprinkle salt

【糟】dzou¹ dregs

糟質（糟踏）play the fool of sb; slander sb

污糟（骯髒）dirty; soiled
亂七八糟 at sixes and sevens; chaotic; in a mess; in
　confusion; in extreme disorder
亂糟糟 messy
整污糟（弄髒）stain

【糠】hong¹ bran; chaff; crumb

木糠（鋸末）sawdust
玉糠（細糠）bran shorts
幼糠（細糠）bran shorts
老糠（糠）chaff
麥糠 oatmeal
麵包糠（麵包屑）bread crumbs; crumbly bread; crumbs

【縫】fung⁴ stitch

縫合 sew up

修補裂縫 mend a split

裂縫 breach; chink; cleavage; crack; crevice; fissure; fracture; rift; split

裁縫 tailor

隙縫（縫隙）crack; crevice; fissure

【縱】dzung³（寵愛）bestow favour on; dote on; pamper; spoil

縱仔女（寵孩子）dote on one's children

縱壞（寵壞）spoil

幕後操縱 pull the strings behind the scenes

操縱 manipulate

【縮】suk⁷ shrink

縮手（躲開手）draw back one's hand

縮水 ①（減少開支）reduce one's costs ②（縮小）shrink ③（貶值）depreciation

縮皮（減少開支）cut back expenses

縮沙（退縮／當退兵／褪套兒）beat a retreat; chicken out; cop out; shrink back; withdraw

縮埋一二角（退至陰暗角落）hide oneself in a corner

縮埋一嚿（縮作一團）curl up into a ball; huddle

縮骨（狡猾／靠不住）act from selfish motives; selfish and cunning; shirker

　縮骨遮（摺傘／摺疊傘）folding umbrella

縮開（挪開／移開）move away

縮數（小算盤）scheme to make money; selfish calculations

古縮（古板）conservative; old-fashioned; old-fashioned and inflexible; quiet and unsocial

伸縮 ① expand and contract; lengthen and shorten; stretch out and draw back ② adjustable; elastic; flexible

思思縮縮（行動不果斷）not carry oneself with ease and confidence; shy and awkward

思縮（畏縮）shy and awkward

通縮（通貨緊縮）deflation

閃閃縮縮（躲躲閃閃）furtive

閃縮（鬼祟）furtive

滾水淥豬腸——兩頭縮（罈子裏養王八——越養越抽抽）become less; lose out on both sides

濃縮 concentrate

【總】dzung² total

總而言之（總之）all things considered; at any rate; by and large; cut a long story short; first and last; in a few words; in a nutshell; in a word; in brief; in fine; in one word; in short; in sum; in the lump; make a long story short; on the whole; put it briefly; take it all in all; taking one thing with another; the long and the short of it; to conclude; to make a long story short; to sum up

總行（總部）headquarters

總站（終點站）terminal; terminal station; terminus

總部 headquarters

總結 conclude; summarise

總統 president

總掣（總開關）main switch

總裁 company director

總數 total

老總 boss; chief

攏總（攏共）add up; all told; altogether; in all; sum up

【繁】faan⁴ numerous

繁忙 busy

繁榮 prosperous

繁殖 breeding

【績】dzik⁷ performance

績分（績點）credit

成績 result; score

偉績 brilliant achievements; glorious achievements; great achievements; great exploits; great feats

過往業績 past performance

業績 performance

【繃】bang¹ band

繃帶 bandage

【繑】kiu⁵⁻²①（交叉）cross ②（繞）coil; wind

繑口（拗口）awkward-sounding; hard to pronounce; twist the tongue

繑埋（繞起來）coil

繑起對手（交叉着手）cross one's arms

繑脷（拗口／舌頭打結）awkward-sounding; hard to pronounce; twist the tongue

繑絲邊（亂絞絲兒／絞絲旁）the "silk"（糸）radical

繑繩（繞繩子）wind a rope

繚繑（潦草）in a slipshod way

【罄】 hing³ exhaust; use up

罄竹難書 one's crimes are too numerous to be recorded

售罄 (售完) be sold out

【罅】 laa³ (縫隙) chink; crack; cranny; slit

罅隙 (縫隙) cleft; crack

一條罅 (一道縫) a gap
山卡罅 ① (荒涼的地方) deserted place ② (山谷) mountain valley
山罅 (裂紋) crack; cranny
手指罅 (手指縫) space between two fingers
牙罅 (牙縫) crevice between teeth
卡罅 ① (模棱兩可) equivocal ② (兩件東西間的縫隙) the crevice between two things
走法律罅 (鑽法律的空子) do evil with a legal loophole
波罅 (乳溝) cleavage
門罅 (門縫兒) crack between a door and its frame
飛唔過我手指罅 (逃不過我手心) can't escape from my control
捐窿捐罅 (尋找每個角落) search high and low for a place
留番嚟攝灶罅 (女兒嫁不出去，留她在家無所用之) let one's own daughter stay unmarried
睇開啲罅 (看開點兒吧) turn a blind eye to it
腳趾罅 (腳指縫) space between the two toes
漏罅 (漏縫兒) loophole; miss out
窿窿罅罅 (小孔和縫隙) in every nook and cranny; nook and corner
髀罅 (大腿間縫隙) thigh gap

【翳】 ai³ ① stuffy ② distress

翳氣 (心中氣悶) be vexed; unhappy
翳焗 (悶熱) hot and stuffy; stuffy
翳翳滯滯 (食慾不振) have a poor appetite; one's appetite is poor

心口翳 (胸悶) chest distress
心翳 (胸悶) depressed
使乜閉翳 (用不着發愁 / 沒有必要擔心) there's no need to worry
閉翳 (心境不開朗 / 發愁 / 憂慮 / 變得悲傷 / 鬱悶 / 憂鬱 / 煩亂 / 煩惱) anxious; become sad; depressed; sullen; upset; vexed; worried

【翼】 jik⁹ wing

翼護 shelter and protect

右翼 right wing
有毛有翼 (獨立) independent; uncontrollable
雞翼 (雞翅膀) chicken wing
鬆毛鬆翼 (洋洋得意) burst with joy; sing and dance for joy

【聯】 lyn⁴ (縫) stitch

聯合 united
　聯合起來 unite
聯衫 (縫衣服) stitch clothes
　聯好件衫 (把衣服縫好) stitch the clothes
聯埋 (縫起來 / 縫合) stitch up
聯針 (縫針) stitch
聯被 (縫被子) stitch the quilt
聯絡 ① contact; liaison ② come into contact with; get in touch with
　聯絡感情 maintain a good relationship
　失去聯絡 lose contact
　保持聯絡 keep in touch
聯盟 alliance; coalition; league; union
　結成聯盟 (結盟) enter into an alliance
聯羣結隊 (成羣結隊) band together; in crowds; in flocks; in groups; in throngs
聯繫 communication; connection; contact; link
　保持聯繫 maintain contact

串聯 contact; establish; establish a relation with establish ties with; link up; make contacts with
電聯 (電話聯絡) keep in touch by telephone

【聰】 tsung¹ clever

聰明 clever
　聰明一世，糊塗一時 a clever person has their stupid moments; a lifetime of cleverness can be interrupted by moments of stupidity; clever all one's life, but stupid this once; smart as a rule, but this time a fool
　聰明一世，蠢鈍一時 (聰明一世，糊塗一時) clever all the time but become a fool this once
　聰明反被聰明誤 a wise person can be ruined by their own wisdom; clever people may be victims of their own cleverness; cleverness may overreach itself; every person has a fool in their sleeve; suffer for one's wisdom
　聰明伶俐 smart and sharp
　小聰明 cleverness in trivial matters; good at playing petty tricks; petty shrewdness; petty tricks; sapient; smart in a small way
聰慧 astute; bright; clever; intelligent

【聲】 seng¹ (聲音) voice

聲大夾冇準 (只會喑嚷嚷) much cry and little wool; talk nonsense

聲大夾惡 (惡聲惡氣 / 盛氣凌人) come the bully over sb

聲明 statement
聯合聲明 joint statement

聲氣 (音信 / 消息) news
冇聲氣 ① (沒消息) no news ② (沒希望) beyond hope
冇釐聲氣 ① (沒消息) no news ② (沒希望) beyond hope
同聲同氣 (意見一致) of the same opinion
好聲好氣 (心平氣和) speak in a kindly manner
有乜聲氣 (有甚麼消息) any news
有聲氣 (有希望) there is hope
低聲下氣 put one's pride in one's pocket
放聲氣 (放消息) leak out information; spread information
嬲聲嬲氣 (娘娘腔) effeminate voice
鬼聲鬼氣 ① (陰陽怪氣) speak in a strange voice; strange-sounding voice ② (裝風洋化) speak with a foreign accent
陰聲細氣 (低聲細語) have a buzz of talk; in a whisper; speak softly and tenderly
嗲聲嗲氣 (嬌聲嬌氣) alluring voice

聲都沙埋 (嗓子都啞了) lose one's voice

聲喉 (嗓子 / 嗓門兒 / 聲音) one's voice

聲線 (嗓門兒 / 嗓音) one's voice

聲調 tone

一把聲 (一道聲音) a voice

大聲 in a loud voice; loud

牙痛咁聲 (直哼哼 / 直嚷嚷) groan with pain to show one's reluctance to do sth; grumble to show one's reluctance to do sth

出聲 ① (吭聲) raise one's voice; voice; utter a word ② (說出來) speak out

叭叭聲 (剎那間) in a flash

名聲 reputation

收聲 shut up; stop talking

好聲 (小心) careful; take care

老牛聲 (粗聲) coarse voice

忍氣吞聲 control oneself and suppress one's indignation; eat dirt; eat humble pie; eat one's leek; endure without protest; hold back one's anger and say nothing; keep quiet and swallow the insults; pocket an insult; restrain one's anger and abstain from saying anything; restrain one's anger and keep silence; restrain one's indignation; restrain one's temper and say nothing; submit to humiliation; suffer indignities without a protest; suppress one's groans; swallow insult and humiliation silently; swallow one's anger; swallow one's pride and endure in silence; swallow one's resentment and dare say nothing; swallow one's wrath and not dare to speak; swallow the insults in meek submission

把聲 (聲音) one's voice

沙聲 (聲音沙啞) hoarse

咕咕聲 (肚子咕咕叫) have a rumbling stomach

呼呼聲 (呼嘯) scream; whistle

泣不成聲 be choked with tears; choke with sobs; cry one's heart out; cry one's voice out; cry till one's tears dry; weep one's heart out; weep till one's tears dry

怨聲 cries of discontent

哭聲 cries

唔出聲 (不吭聲) keep silent; remain silent

唔好出聲 (不要吭聲) keep quiet; keep silent

唔聲唔聲 (不吭聲) not speak up

拿拿聲 (趕忙) make haste to do sth; quickly

蚊滋咁細聲 (微弱的聲音) weak voice of a person

鬼食泥噉聲 (怨聲地嘀咕) groan; moan; murmur against

啦啦聲 (很快地 / 短時間內採取行動) action within a short time; quickly

得把聲 (只會說) boasting; go on cackling without laying an egg

細聲 (小聲 / 低聲 / 悄聲) in a low voice

單聲 (給某人一個信息) give sb a message

掌聲 (拍掌 / 鼓掌) applause; clapping; the sound of clapping

揚聲 (吭聲) raise one's voice

開聲 (作聲 / 說話) say sth; talk

嘩嘩聲 (迅速地) quickly

媽媽聲 (發誓) swear; swear like a pirate; swear like a trooper

禀神咁聲 (嘟嘟嚷嚷地) murmur indistinctly

歌聲 singing

鼻鼾聲 (呼嚕聲) snore

劏豬咁聲 (殺豬叫) sing in a terrible way, like a pig being slaughtered

嘩嘩聲 (嘩然) in an uproar; loudly

嘘嘘聲 (很快) very quickly

盤盤聲 (以萬計算) by ten thousands

擬聲 onomatopoeia

濤聲 sound of roaring billows; surf

雞仔聲 (聲音微弱) weak voice

驚到唔識出聲 (嚇得說不出話來) too panic to make any utterance

【聲】 sing¹ claim

聲稱 declare; proclaim

【膽】daam² gall-bladder

膽大心細（辦事果斷，考慮周密）bold but cautious; courageous and cautious
　　膽大心細面皮厚（膽子大 / 細心 / 厚臉皮）bold, cautious, and thick-skinned
膽生毛（膽子大）audacious
膽石 gallstone
　　膽生石（膽結石）cholelithiasis
膽正命平（為正義不怕死）have too much spunk to care for one's own life
膽固醇 cholesterol
膽粗粗（大膽 / 膽子大）fearless
膽搏膽（冒險）take risks
膽囊 gall bladder

大膽 daring; very brave
冇膽（膽小）chicken; do not have the guts; no guts
斗膽 make bold; of great courage; venture
生人唔生膽（膽小）as timid as a hare; be intimidated
地膽 ①（在某地生活很久，熟悉當地的人）sb who knows a particular area well ②（當地黑幫）local gangster ③（地頭蛇）a cock on its own dunghill
有膽 have the guts
壯膽 boost one's courage; embolden
沙膽（大膽）bold; daring; foolhardy
肝膽 ① liver and gall bladder ② courage; heroic spirit ③ open-heartedness; sincerity
放膽（大膽 / 放心）act boldly
海膽 sea urchin
狼膽（狼子野心）fierce guts
夠膽（有種 / 有膽量 / 夠勇敢 / 有勇氣）dare; have courage; have guts
瓶膽 glass liner
細膽（膽小 / 懦弱）cowardly; timid
提心吊膽（心驚膽戰）have one's heart in one's mouth
電燈膽（電燈炮）electric light bulb
慳電膽（省電燈炮 / 節能燈泡）energy-saving light bulb; energy-saver light bulb
燈膽（燈炮）light bulb
攞膽（嚇死）frightening; take away one's life

【膾】kui² minced meat

膾炙人口 on everybody's lips

市膾 materialistic

【臀】tyn⁴ bottom

臀肉（牛臀肉）beef rump

【臂】bei³ arm

臂章（袖章）armband
臂部 hip

三頭六臂 extraordinarily able person; very capable person
手臂（胳膊）arm
麒麟臂（粗手臂）thick arm

【臆】jik⁷ chest

臆測 conjecture; guess; speculate

打思臆（打噎兒）① burp ② get hiccups; have hiccups; hiccup

【臉】lim⁵ face

臉孔 face

小白臉 a man who lives off the earnings of a woman
洗臉 wash one's face
愁眉苦臉 a face of woe; a face shaded with melancholy; down on the dumps; down in the mouth draw a long face; gloomy face; have a face as long as a fiddle; have a face like a fiddle; have a worried look; look blue; make a long face; pull a long face; put on a long face; wear a glum countenance; with a long face

【臊】sou¹（分娩）childbirth

臊蝦（小孩 / 嬰兒）baby
　　臊蝦女（女嬰）baby girl
　　臊蝦仔（男嬰）baby boy
臊臊都係羊肉，爛爛都係絲綢（金子是金子，無論它是否發光）gold is gold no matter whether it glitters or not

唔食羊肉——身臊（無端被牽連）invite unexpected trouble; miss the goat meat and just get the smell of the goat

【臨】lam⁴ descend

臨工（臨時工）temporary worker
臨天光瀨尿（全盤皆輸）there is many a slip twixt the cup and the lip
臨老學吹打（為時已晚）an old dog begins to learn new tricks; an old man learning a new skill
臨別 at the time of departure; just before parting; on parting
　　臨別贈言 parting advice
臨尾香（最後出了差錯 / 功虧一簣）fall at the last fence
臨近 close by; close on; close to; draw close; draw near
臨門 ①（到達家門）arrive at one's door ②（帶球至球門前 / 緊要關頭）before the goal; the critical moment
臨急（迫到眉睫）when emergency comes
　　臨急抱佛腳（臨時抱佛腳）seek help at the last moment

臨急臨忙（迫到眉睫）in a great rush

臨時臨急（迫到眉睫）at the last moment; be hard
　　pressed for time

臨時 temporary

臨時工 temporary job

臨時協定 provisional agreement

臨時牌（臨時車牌）provisional driving license

臨班（留級）repeat a year at school

臨記（臨時演員）extra

臨終 at one's deathbed; at the point of death; just before
　　one's death; on the point of breathing one's last

光臨 arrive

來臨 advent; arrive; approach; at hand; come; nigh; onset

面臨 be confronted with; be faced with; be up against

【瓅】loe² ① （吐）spit ② （滾）roll ③ （纏磨）pester

瓅地（在地上滾／滾地）roll on the ground

瓅我買嘢（纏着我買東西）pester me to buy sth for sb

瓅骨（吐骨頭）spit out the bones

【薄】bok⁹ thin

薄切切（非常薄）very thin

薄皮 prone be blush

薄身（薄）thin

薄削 thin and soft

薄英英（很薄／薄乎乎的）very thin

薄餅（披薩）pizza

薄禮 humble present; trifling gift

尖酸刻薄 mean and cruel

妄自菲薄 excessively humble; have a sense of inferiority;
　　have too low an opinion of oneself; improperly belittle
　　oneself; look down upon oneself; think lightly of oneself;
　　think too lowly of oneself; underestimate oneself;
　　undervalue oneself; unduly humble oneself

佻薄（輕浮）frivolous; not dignified

刻薄 acerbity; harsh; mean; unkind

削薄 (said of hair) thin out

厚薄 thick and thin

待薄（虧待）maltreat; treat unfairly

面皮薄（臉皮薄）sensitive; shy; thin-skinned

偷薄（削薄／把頭髮弄薄）thin out the hair

【薑】goeng¹ ① ginger ② gutsy

薑水（薑汁）ginger water

薑汁 ginger sauce

薑絲 ginger shreds; shredded ginger

薑越老越辣（薑還是老的辣）the older, the wiser

薑蓉（薑泥）minced ginger

薑蔥（蔥薑）ginger and spring onion

　　薑蔥焗蟹 baked crab with ginger and spring onion

一嚿薑（一塊薑）a piece of ginger

子薑（沒經驗）tender ginger; young ginger

老薑（經驗老道）experienced person

夠薑（有種／有勇氣／有膽量）have courage; have guts

【薦】dzin³ recommend

薦底（墊底）bedding

薦褓（褥子）mattress

推薦 recommend

鞋薦（鞋墊）shoe pad

【薪】san¹ salary; wage

薪水 earnings; pay; salary; wage

薪金（薪水）salary

欠薪 salary in arrears

底薪（基本工資）basic salary

減薪 reduce wages; salary cut

【蔗】dze³ （甘蔗）sugar cane

蔗心 centre stem of a cane

蔗汁（甘蔗汁）cane juice; sugarcane juice

蔗渣板 board made of residual sugar cane fibre

蔗糖 cane sugar; sugar from cane; table sugar

一條蔗（一根甘蔗）a sugar cane

一碌蔗（一節甘蔗）a segment of sugar cane; a stick of
　　sugar cane

一橛蔗（一節甘蔗）a section of sugar cane

一轆蔗（一節甘蔗）a segment of sugar cane; a stick of
　　sugar cane

掂過碌蔗（好好的／真的很好）come off well; really good

碌蔗（傻子）idiot

賣剩蔗（剩女）a girl who remains unmarried off

【虧】kwai¹ ① （陽痿）impotent; asynodia ② （虛弱）weak

虧佬（陽痿的人）impotent man

　　虧佬褲（長內衣褲）long-johns

虧柴 ① （身體屏弱）weak ② （體弱多病的人）weak man

吃虧 ① come to grief; get a beating; get the worst of it;
　　suffer losses; take a beating ② at a disadvantage; in an

unfavourable situation

好漢不吃眼前虧 it is better to avoid visible loss than to brave it out

腎虧 weak

【螺】lo⁴（泥螺）conch; river snail

螺絲（螺釘）screw

螺絲批（改錐／起子／螺絲刀）screwdriver

食螺絲（講錯話）make a mistake when reading out a script

打陀螺（抽陀螺）spin a top

田螺 river snail

陀螺 top

【蟀】soet⁷ cricket

爛頭蟀（打架特別凶狠、不要命的流氓）tough guy

【蟆】maa⁴ toad

癩蛤蟆 toad

【謎】mai⁴ riddle

謎底 ① answer to a riddle ② truth

揭開謎底 ① solve a riddle ② find out the truth

謎語 riddle

估燈謎（猜燈謎）guess a lantern riddle

燈謎 lantern riddles; riddles written on lanterns

【謙】him¹ humble

謙恭 civility; humility; modest and courteous; modest and polite; respectful; unassuming

謙虛 humble

謙讓 modestly decline; modestly yield precedence to others; yield from modesty

【講】gong²（說）say; talk

講一套，做一套 one does not do what one preaches; one's actions are not in keeping with one's promises; one's acts belie one's words; one's conduct disagrees with one's words; one's conduct is at variance with one's words; one's deeds do not match one's words; one's deeds do not square with one's words; one's doings belie one's commitments; one's words and deeds are at complete variance; one's words are at variance with one's deeds; one's words are not matched by deeds; say one thing but do another; talk one way and behave another; words and actions do not match; words and deeds contradict each other; what one does belies one's commitments

講一輪（講一通）talk for a while

講三講四（說三道四）gossip

講口齒（講信用）keep one's word

講中（說中）as expected

講少的啦（少說點吧）few words are best; the less said about it, the better

講心啫（大家交心）have a heart-to-heart talk; take each other to bosom

講古（講故事）storytelling

講古仔（講故事）tell a story

講古佬（說書人）storyteller

講好（說好）come to an agreement

講好咗（說好了）have come to an agreement; it's settled

講吓啫（說說而已／閒話而已）just a few casual remarks

講多無謂（說多無用）talk is cheap

講多錯多（多說多錯）the least said, the soonest mended; the more one says, the more mistakes one makes

講低（留下話）leave a message

講妥（說妥）come to an agreement

講定（說定）agree on

講唔定（說不定）it's not yet settled

講咁易咩（說易行難／說的倒容易）it's easy to talk so

講咗就算（說了就算）one means what one says

講到（至於／說到）as for

講到做到（說到做到）do what one says

講到話（至於／說到）as for

講明（說清楚）give a clear explanation

講明就陳顯南（一說就明白）understand without having to explain all the details

講唔明（說不清楚）not explain clearly

講得明（說得清楚）can explain clearly

講法（說法）statement; wording

講返轉頭（話說回來）return to the main topic

講穿（說穿）reveal the truth

講起嚟一疋布咁長（說起來一言難盡）it is like telling a long story

講真（說真的／說實話）to say the truth

講倒 ①（能說）able to speak; able to utter ②（投契）able to get along; on good terms

講倒話（說反話）say to the contrary

講唔倒 ①（不能說）not speakable ②（不投契）cannot get along with sb; on bad terms ③（說不了）unable to speak; unable to utter

講得倒 ①（能說）able to speak; able to utter ②（說得來）able to get along; on good terms

講笑 ① (開玩笑／説笑／説着玩兒) joke; kidding; tease ② (邊聊邊笑) chatting and laughing

講笑搵第樣 (別開這樣的玩笑) this is no laughing matter

有講有笑 ① (有説有笑) chat and laugh; chattering and laughing; have a pleasant talk together; talking and laughing ② (相處融洽) get along with

你講笑 (你開玩笑) you're kidding

呢樣笑認真唔講得 (這不是個該笑的問題) this is not a matter to be laughed at

講吓笑都得㗎 (開開玩笑總可以吧) it's alright to crack a joke

講唔出 (講不出來) cannot say

講唔埋欄 (達不成共識) unable to reach a consensus

講師 lecturer

講得口響 (説得好聽) fine words; make an unpleasant fact sound attractive; says you; talk fine; use fine-sounding phrases

講得出就講 (嘴巴不牢) have a loose tongue

講得過去 (説得過去) justifiable

講情 (説情) plead for mercy for sb

講理 (説理) argue; reason things out

講開 (講到／提及) mentioning; talking about

講開又講 (順便説説) by the way

講就易，做就難 (知之非難，行之不易) easier said than done

講過算數 (説話算話) a verbal promise has to be kept; as good as one's word; honour one's own words; keep one's word; live up to one's word; one means what one says; true to one's word

講話 (説話) say; speak; talk

講好話 praise; say good things about

講壞話 say bad things about; speak ill of sb

講嘢 (説話) say; speak; talk

唔好講嘢 (不要講話) stop talking

講漏嘴 (説漏嘴) a slip of the tongue

講緊 (電話佔線) the line is engaged

講實 (説好／説定／説準了) it's settled

講價 (討價還價／講價錢) bargain; haggle over a price; negotiate the price

講數 (達成協議／談判／談條件) negotiate; settle a dispute

講講吓 (説着説着) as one talks

講嚟講去都係三幅被 (説來説去) sing the song of burden

一般嚟講 (一般來説) generally speaking; usually

人講你又講 (鸚鵡學舌) parrot what other people say

大隻講 ① (説大話) all talk and no action ② (自誇) boastful person

冇話好講 (無話好説) be stuck for an answer

在我嚟講 (對我來説) as for me; for me

有得講 (可以溝通的) negotiable

老實講 to be frank; frankly speaking; speak the truth

使乜講 (不用説) as a matter of course; go without saying; needless to say

唔在講 (不但／不僅) not only

唔使講 (不用説) it goes without saying; needless to say

唔係咁講 (不能這樣説) that's not true

得閒至講 (有空再説) we'll chat when we are free

評講 (講評) comment on and appraise

亂講 (胡説／胡謅) speak nonsense; talk rubbish; talk without ground

嘢可以亂食，説話唔可以亂講 (飯可以亂吃，話不能亂講) watch what one says

廢話少講 (廢話少説) cut the crap

演講 speech; talk

調轉嚟講 (反過來説) conversely

點解咁講 (為甚麼這麼説) why do you say so

點講 (怎麼説) what to say

雞同鴨講 people failing to communicate; unable to communicate

識講 (會説) good at talking

攞嚟講 (找話題來説／説廢話) talk for the sake of talking

聽聞講 (聽説) be said; be told; hear of

聽講 (聽説) be told that

【謝】dze[6] wither

謝皮 (死) die

謝恩 express thanks for great favours; thank sb for their favour

謝罪 apologise; apologise for an offence; offer an apology

謝幕 acknowledge the applause; answer a curtain call; curtain call respond to a curtain call

多謝 thank you

玩謝 (作弄別人至死) play with sb until they are dead or finished

致謝 convey thanks; express one's thanks; extend thanks to; offer thanks; thank

鳴謝 acknowledge one's thanks

【謠】jiu[4] rumour

謠言 rumour

謠傳 hearsay; rumour

造謠 cook up a story and spread it around; start a rumour

【賺】 dzaan⁶ earn

賺到 make a profit

賺到笑（賺大錢）earn lots of money

賺得好丟（沒甚麼賺頭）the profits gained are minimal

賺粒糖，蝕間廠（撿了芝麻，丟了西瓜）while seeking a small gain, one could suffer a big loss

賺錢 earn money

有賺錢（沒利潤）do not make any profit

賺大錢 earn lots of money

【購】 kau³ buy; purchase

購物 buy things

購票 buy a ticket

購買 acquire; buy; purchase

洽購 arrange a purchase; make arrangements for buying purchase after talks; talk over conditions of purchase

搶購 rush to buy

【賽】 tsoi³ competition

賽車 motor racing

賽車手 racing driver

賽狗 dog racing

賽事（比賽）compete in a contest; competition; contest; event of competition; have a race; match

賽馬 horse racing

友誼賽 friendly match

比賽 competition; match

打比賽（進行比賽）have a game

決賽 final; the finals

拳賽 boxing match

參加比賽 participate in a competition

球賽 ball game; ball match; game; match

準決賽（半決賽）semi-final

邀請賽 invitation match

龍舟比賽 dragon boat race

【趨】 tsoey¹ trend

趨向 ① direction; tendency; trend ② incline to; tend to

趨勢 tendency

趨炎附勢 a follower of the rich and powerful; a snob who plays up to those in power; approach the bustling place and cleave to the strong; attach oneself as subordinate to those in power; cater to those in power; climb on the bandwagon; creep into the good grace of; curry favour with the powerful; curry favour with those in power; fawn upon the rich and powerful persons; to where there is anything to be got; gravitate to those rising in the world; hail the rising sun; hang on to the sleeves of those in power; hurry to the glorious and hang on to the influential; jump on the bandwagon; play up to those in power; please and flatter wealthy and influential persons; run round persons in warm comfortable circumstances and flatter to the powerful; serve the time; worship the rising sun

【蹈】 dou⁶ tread

蹈海（跳海自殺）kill oneself by jumping into the sea

蹈襲（盲目跟隨）follow slavishly

舞蹈 dancing

【蹊】 kai¹ trail

蹊徑 narrow path

蹊隧（路徑）path; trail

有蹊蹺（有蹊蹺）there are some tricks

蹊蹺（蹊蹺）trick

【蹁】 sin³（滑）slip and fall down

蹁腳（腳下打滑／腳踩不穩）slip

【輼】 wan¹（關）shut in

輼住（關着）shut in

【避】 bei⁶ avoid

避孕 contraception

避孕套 condom

避忌（忌諱）① taboo ② avoid as a taboo ③ abstain from; avoid as harmful

避車（讓車）① avoid car crashing ② avoid hitting people

避免 avoid

避風塘（避風港）harbour; haven

避無可避 unavoidable

迴避 ①（躲避）avoid meeting another person; avoidance ②（撤離）withdraw ③（拒絕）decline an offer ④（逃避）evade

逃避 dodge; escape; evade; run away from; shirk

【邀】 jiu¹ invite

邀功 take credit for sb else's achievements

邀請 invite

邀請賽 invitation match

【還】waan⁴ repay

還神〔還願／酬神〕redeem a vow to a god
　還得神落〔可以還願去了〕can redeem a vow to a god
還清〔清償／付清〕pay off
還款 ① payment ② repayment
　還款單 repayment slip
還番〔歸還〕return
還債 pay one's debt
還價 counteroffer
還禮 ① present a gift in return ② return the courtesy of sb

交還 return
長命債，長命還〔慢慢兒還債〕a life-long debt is to be
　settled by a life time
償還 pay back; repay
擲還〔歸還〕return sth to sb
璧還〔感激歸還〕return with thanks

【醜】tsau² ugly; unsightly

醜人〔壞人〕bad guy
　搵我做醜人〔要我當罵人的〕ask me to act as the bad guy
醜死鬼〔羞死人〕feel really embarrassed
醜怪〔醜陋／難看〕ugly
　醜八怪 very ugly person
　醜死怪〔羞死人〕disgraceful
醜聞 scandal
醜樣〔醜陋／難看〕ugly
　勁醜樣〔太醜了〕mega ugly; very ugly

一個做好一個做醜〔一個扮紅臉，一個扮白臉〕one plays
　the role of a gentleman while the other plays the role of
　a villain
出醜 incur disgrace
怕醜〔怕羞／害羞／害臊〕bashful; feel ashamed; feel shy;
　shy
知醜〔害羞／害臊〕bashful; feel ashamed; shy
家醜 family scandal
唔知醜〔不要臉／不害羞／沒羞臊〕know no shame;
　shameless
唔怕醜〔不害羞〕shameless; unabashed
唔使怕醜〔不用害羞〕don't be shy
做好做醜〔又唱紅臉又唱白臉〕coax and coerce

【鍊】lin⁶⁻² race

鍊車〔鬥飆車〕car racing
鍊低〔排在首位〕come out on top

一條手鍊 a bracelet
手鍊 bracelet

【錨】maau⁴ practice

錨船 anchor boat

拋錨 stall

【鍋】wo¹ frying pan

鍋粑〔鍋巴／米鍋巴〕puff rice
鍋貼〔煎餃〕fried meat dumpling

火鍋 hotpot
砂鍋 clay pot
食火鍋〔吃火鍋〕have hotpot

【鍵】gin⁶ key

鍵控〔鍵接〕keying
鍵盤 keyboard

【鍾】dzung¹ practice

鍾情 deeply in love; fall in love
鍾意〔喜愛／喜歡〕favour; like; love
　鍾意咗〔愛上了〕fall in love
　最鍾意〔最喜歡／最愛〕favourite
鍾愛 cherish; dote on; love deeply

老態龍鍾 look old and clumsy

【鋸】sing¹ rusty

生鋸〔生鏽〕get rusty

【鍘】gaai³ ①〔裁〕cut ②〔鋸開〕saw

鍘女〔引誘挑逗女性〕pick up a girl
鍘木〔鋸木頭〕saw a piece of wood
鍘板〔鋸板〕saw a piece of board
鍘紙〔裁紙〕cut paper
鍘嚫〔劃破〕be lacerated

【闊】fut⁸ ①〔寬〕wide ② big-spending; generous

闊大〔寬闊〕spacious
闊太 big-spending woman
闊佬 ①〔闊綽〕generous with money; liberal with
　money ②〔闊綽的人〕generous man
　闊佬懶理〔懶得管〕not interested; not to bother with
　　others; won't bother to heed it
　扮闊佬〔充豪氣／擺闊〕ostentatious and extravagant;
　　parade one's wealth
　裝闊佬〔擺闊〕ostentatious and extravagant; parade
　　one's wealth

讕闊佬（擺闊）ostentatious and extravagant; parade
　　one's wealth
擺闊佬（擺闊氣）make a parade of one's wealth
闊落（地方大 / 寬敞 / 寬闊 / 寬鬆）spacious
闊綽 generous; liberal with money
闊銀幕（寬銀幕）wide screen

天空海闊 of boundless capacity
拉闊（現場）(English) live

【闆】baan² boss

老闆 boss; proprietor
自己做老闆 be one's own boss
後台老闆 backstage boss
搵老闆 ①（找老闆）look for a boss ②（找個有錢人）look
　　for a rich person ③（找個有錢丈夫）look for a rich
　　husband
舊老闆（前任老闆）former boss

【隱】jan² private

隱居 hermit; live in seclusion; retire from public life;
　　withdraw from society and live in solitude
隱瞞 conceal; cover up; hide; hide the truth; hold back
隱藏 hide

私隱（隱私）privacy

【雖】soey¹ although

雖則（雖然）although
雖然 although; even though

【霜】soeng¹ frost

霜天 bleak sky
霜雪 ①（霜和雪）frost and snow ②（雪白）snowwhite

面霜（雪花膏）vanishing cream
結霜（下霜）frost has occurred
落霜（下霜）frost has occurred
潤膚霜 moisturising cream

【韓】hon⁴ a surname

韓信點兵──多多益善（越多越好）the more, the
　　better
韓國 Korea
　　韓國菜 Korean food
韓劇 Korean drama
韓圜 Korean won

【餅】beng² cake

餅印（一模一樣）look alike
　　一個餅印（一個模子上刻出來的）a copy of sb; a splitting
　　　　image of sb; as like as two eas; cut from the same
　　　　cloth; exactly alike; exactly the same; identical; like
　　　　two peas in a pod; look the same
餅店（糕餅店）cake shop; pastry shop
餅家（餅店 / 糕餅店）cake shop; pastry shop
餅乾 biscuit
　　一塊餅乾 a biscuit

一件西餅（一塊蛋糕）a cake
一餅（一卡帶的）a cassette of
大餅（一元硬幣）one-dollar coin
月餅 moon cake
打晒蛇餅（很長的人龍）line up with many people like a
　　curling snake
打蛇餅（很長的人龍）line up with many people; long queue
曲奇餅 cookie
老餅（老式）old-fashioned
西餅（蛋糕）cake; pastry
肉餅 steamed minced pork
芝士餅 cheese cake
威化餅（維化餅乾）(English) wafer
洗大餅（洗盤子）clean dishes
食月餅（吃月餅）eat moon cakes
食波餅（被球打中臉）hit by a ball in the face
桔餅（桔子餅）mandarin orange cake
烤餅 baked cake
酒餅（酒曲 / 酒藥）distiller's yeast; yeast for brewing rice
　　wine or fermenting glutinous rice
酥餅 pastry
糕餅 cake; confectionery; pastry
薄餅（披薩）pizza
雞仔餅（小鳳餅）salty and sweet biscuit
藥餅（藥片）pill; tablet

【餚】ngaau⁴ food

佳餚 delicacies
佳釀美餚（美酒佳餚）good wine and delicacies; vintage
　　wine and choice food
美酒佳餚 good wine and dainty dishes

【館】gun² ① hotel ② studio

館長 curator

上海菜館 Shanghainese restaurant
太空館 Space Museum

竹館（麻將館）mahjong parlour
拉人返差館（拉上警局）arrest sb to the police station
差館（公安局／派出所／警察局）police station
素菜館 vegetarian restaurant
麻雀館（麻將館）mahjong parlour
菜館（餐館）restaurant
圖書館 library
領事館 consulate
影相館（照相館）photo studio
賓館 guesthouse

【骾】gang² fishbone etc stuck in the throat

骾骨（魚刺卡在喉嚨裏）fishbone stuck in the throat

【鬁】lei¹ favus

有頭毛冇人想生鬁鬁（被迫做出愚蠢的舉動）be driven to
　　such a stupid move
有頭髮邊個想做鬁鬁（無能為力）can't do anything about sth
鬁鬁（頭癬）favus of the scalp

【鮮】sin¹ ① fresh ② （鮮艷）bright-coloured

鮮竹卷 bean curd roll
鮮血 blood; fresh blood
　　滿地鮮血 blood all over the place
鮮奶 fresh milk
鮮甜（新鮮甜美）delicious and tasty
鮮嫩 fresh and tender

生猛海鮮 fresh seafood
光鮮 clean and tidy; neat; neat and clean; prim; tidy and pretty
海鮮 seafood
游水海鮮（生鮮海鮮）fresh seafood
新鮮 fresh

【鴿】gap⁸⁻² pigeon

鴿子 pigeon
鴿派（溫和派）dove; dove faction

白鴿 dove; pigeon
放白鴿（以女色為誘餌設騙局）conspire to trick with
　　females as the baits
乳鴿 pigeon
燒乳鴿（烤乳鴿）roasted pigeon
鵓鴿（鴿子）pigeon

【點】dim² ① （怎麼）how ② o'clock

點心（transliteration）dimsum; light refreshments
　　點心紙（點心訂單）dimsum order form
　　一籠點心 a basket of dim sum
點名 call the roll; make a roll-call; roll-call
點行（怎麼走）how to get to
點呀（怎麼樣）① how are things ② how is it
　　點呀你（你怎麼樣）how are you
點知（誰知）who knows
點相（認人）pick out sb for revenge
　　點錯相（認錯人）pick on the wrong person for revenge
點計（怎麼算）how much is to be charged
點脈（點穴）hit at a certain acupoint
點得（怎麼可以）how is it possible
　　點得吖（怎麼行啊）how can it be
點搞㗎（這是怎麼回事）what's all this about
點菜 order dishes; order food
點睇（怎麼看）how do you see it
點解（為甚麼／甚麼原因）how is it that; what for; why;
　　why is it that; why oh why
　　點解咁講（為甚麼這麼說）why do you say so
　　點解咁嬲（為甚麼這麼生氣）why are you so angry
　　點解唔好（為甚麼不好）why not
點會（怎麼會）how come
點話（怎麼說）what to say
　　點話點好（隨你怎麼說都好）as you please
點算（怎麼辦）what is to be done
　　點算好（怎麼辦才好）what shall we do
　　唔知點算（不知道怎麼辦）don't know what to do
點樣（怎麼樣／怎樣）how; how is it
　　無論點樣（無論如何）anyhow
點數（檢查數目）check the number
點諗（怎麼想）what does one think
　　你點諗（你怎麼想）what do you think
點賣（怎麼賣）at what price are you selling it; how much is
　　it
點醒 give the right advice
點講（怎麼說）what to say
點餸（點菜）order dishes; order food
點鐘 ① hour（小時）② （…點鐘）o'clock

一點 one o'clock
丁點 a tiny bit
七點 seven o'clock
九點 nine o'clock
二點 two o'clock
八點 eight o'clock
十一點 eleven o'clock
十二點 twelve o'clock
十三點 giggly; not ladylike
十點 ten o'clock
三點 ① three points ② three o'clock

五點 five o'clock

六點 six o'clock

中午十二點 noon

廿一點（二十一點）blackjack; pontoon

冇七點（沒甚麼特別）nothing out of the ordinary; nothing special; nothing unusual

凸點（聰明豆）smarties

四點 four o'clock

交叉點 crossing; intersection; junction

地點 location

污點 black mark; blemish; blot; defect; flaw; flick; smear; smirch; smotch; smudge; smut; smutch; spot; stain

老點（誤導）mislead

而家幾點（現在幾點）what time is it now

兩點 two o'clock

定點（小數點）decimal point

星星點點 tiny spots

疵點（瑕疵）blemish; defect; fault; flaw; weak spot

弱點 Achilles' heel; failing; vulnerable point; vulnerable spot; weak point; weak spot; weakness

缺點 shortcoming

逗點（逗號）comma

斑點 dot; fleck; freckle; mottle; speckle; spot; stain

焦點 focus

景點 attraction; beauty spot; scenic spot

睇吓點（看下怎麼辦）depending on circumstances

幾點（幾點了／甚麼時候）what time

蒲點（聚集的地點）hang out

誤點（晚點）be delayed

論點 argument; opinion; point

踏正十二點（正好十二點）twelve o'clock sharp

據點 fortified point; stronghold

糕點 pastry

優點 merit

鐘點（小時工）part-time

露二點（沒穿上衣）topless, with breasts exposed

露三點（全裸）full frontal nudity

觀點 point of view

【點】kim⁴ yellowish black

黃點點（黃乎乎）yellow

【齋】zaai¹ ① go without meat; vegetarian ② exclusively; only

齋啡（黑咖啡）black coffee

齋菜（素菜）vegetarian food

齋腸（豬腸粉）plain rice roll

齋廚（素菜館）vegetarian restaurant

齋噏（胡扯／亂說）bullshit

齋舖（素菜館）vegetarian restaurant

齋麵（素麵）plain noodles

打齋（做法事）perform Buddhist rites

食齋（吃素／吃齋）eat vegetarian food

開齋 ① conclude an initial transaction of the day ② break a losing streak; get an initial win after losing a lot; win after repeated failures

話齋（正如某人所說）as sb says

學你話齋（像你說的）as you say

18 劃

【儲】tsy⁵ save

儲存 deposit

儲蓄 save; savings

儲錢（存錢）save money
　　儲錢入銀行（把錢存進銀行）save one's money with the bank

【嚤】mo¹ ① Indian ②（慢）slow

嚤囉差（印度人）Indian

【嚕】lou¹ mumbling

嚕蘇（囉嗦）verbose

嘰哩咕嚕（嘰嘰咕咕）incomprehensible talk

【嚟】lai⁴（來）come

嚟真（認真）serious, not kidding

嚟得切（來得及）able to do sth within time; in time; there's still time

嚟啦（來吧／加油）come on

嚟緊（馬上來）coming
　　我嚟緊喇（我在路上／我在途中）I'm on my way

入嚟（進來）come in

上嚟（上來）come up

凸出嚟（凸出來）stick out

本嚟（本來）at first; from the beginning; in itself; in the first lace; it goes without saying; original; originally; properly speaking; should have; used to be

出嚟（出來）go out

打橫嚟（不講理）impervious to all reasons

合得嚟（合得來）get along well

行埋嚟（走過來）come over

行過嚟（走過來）come over
行嚟（過來）come over
伸出嚟（伸出來）stick out
冷靜落嚟（冷靜下來）calm down; cool down; cool off; sober down
定啲嚟（鎮定點）keep cool; calm
返嚟（回來）come back; return
垂落嚟（滑下來）slide down
食得嚟（吃得來）eatable
原嚟（原來）originally
唔夠佢嚟（鬥不過他）no match for him
埋嚟（走近來／過來）come here; come over; come up
戙起嚟（豎起來）erect
除落嚟（脫下來）take it off
做得嚟（做得來）can be done
啱啱返嚟（剛剛回來）just come back
搖過嚟（拉過來／拉攏）rope in
逐啲嚟（一點一點地）little by little
就嚟（快要／馬上／就要／很快）be going to; soon; will...quite soon; will soon
揼落嚟（掉下來）fall down
睇得嚟（看得來）visible
睇嚟（看來）it looks as if; it seems
等我嚟（讓我來）let me
越嚟（越來越）more and more
跌落嚟（摔下來）fallen down
亂嚟（胡來）do things irresponsibly; mess things up
塌落嚟（塌下來）collapse
搵番嚟（找回來了）find it back; get it back
落嚟（下來）come down
過嚟（過來）come over here
飲得嚟（喝得來）drinkable
鼠入嚟（溜進來）steal into
監粗嚟（胡來／硬幹／硬撐着幹）mess things up; run wild
監硬嚟（硬來／蠻幹）do sth forcibly
撩返出嚟（挑了出來）pick sth out
寫得嚟（寫得來）can write
調轉嚟（倒過來）turn the other way round
擒落嚟（爬下來）climb down
掹出嚟（拔出來）pull sth out
瀉出嚟（溢出來）spill over
爆出嚟（揭出來）expose it
聽得嚟（聽得來）upon hearing
攞出嚟（拿出來）bring out

【嘥】haai⁴（不光滑／毛糙／粗糙）rough
嘥過沙紙（粗糙過砂紙）extremely rough
嘥澀澀（非常粗糙）very rough

【靚】leng³（小）small
靚女（黃毛丫頭）teenager girl
靚仔（青少年）teenager
靚妹（少女）young girl
　　靚妹仔（少女）young girl

花靚（年輕小伙子）idle young man

【壘】loey⁵ base
壘手（壘球運動員）baseman
壘球 baseball
　　打壘球 play baseball

堡壘（炮樓／城堡／要塞／據點）bastion; blockhouse; bulwark; citadel; fortress; stronghold

【嬸】sam² aunt
嬸母（嬸嬸）aunt; wife of father's younger brother
嬸娘（嬸嬸）aunt; wife of father's younger brother
嬸嬸 aunt; wife of father's younger brother

叔嬸 aunt; wife of a junior uncle
阿嬸 ①（叔母）aunt ②（嬸子／嬸嬸）sister-in-law

【戴】daai³ put on; wear on the head
戴住（戴着）carry along
戴帽 wear a hat
　　戴四方帽（畢業並獲得大學學位）graduate with a university degree
　　戴高帽（奉承的對象）object of flattery
　　戴綠帽 be cuckolded; cuckold

穿戴（穿着）apparel
擔戴（擔責）undertake responsibility

【擲】dzaak⁹ throw
擲交（遞交）hand over
擲還（歸還）return sth to sb

孤注一擲 a long shot gamble; all-or-nothing; ball the jack; bet all on a single throw; bet one's boots on; bet one's last dollar on; bet one's shirt on; bet one's bottom dollar on; cast the die; go for the gloves; go nap over; go the vole; have all one's eggs in one basket; make a last desperate effort; make a spoon or spoil a horn; make or break; make or mar; mend or mar; monkey with a buzz saw; neck or nothing; place one's efforts in a single thing; put all one's eggs in one basket; put the fate of sb/sth at a stake; risk all on a single throw; risk everything on a single venture; risk everything in one effort; send the axe after the helve; shoot one's wad; shoot the works; sink or swim; stake all one's fortune in a single throw; stake all one has; stake everything on a cast of the dice; stake everything on one last throw; stake everything on one attempt; take a great rish; venture on a single chance; venture one's fortune on a single stake; vie money on the turn of a card; win the horse or lose the saddle; win the mare or lose the halter; throw the helve after the hatchet

【擺】baai² arrange

擺大壽 (辦六十大壽宴會) hold a sixtieth birthday banquet
擺平 ①（平息）calm a situation; settle an argument ②（收拾）punish
　擺平佢（擺平他）punish sb
擺甫士（擺姿勢）pose
擺明（明擺）blatant; obvious
　擺明車馬 put all one's cards on the table
　擺到明（明顯地）blatantly; expose one's intention
擺枱（放置桌子）lay the table
擺酒（設宴 / 辦酒席）give a banquet; hold a banquet
擺舦（掌舵 / 操作方向盤）at the helm; operate the rudder; steer a boat; take the tiller
擺款（擺架子）arrogant; boastful; put on airs
擺街（擺地攤 / 擺攤）set up a stall in the street
　擺街邊（擺地攤 / 擺攤）set up a stall in the street
擺檔（擺攤兒）set up a stall in the market

大搖大擺 swagger about
唆擺（教唆）incite; instigate

【擾】jiu² disturb

擾民 harass the people
擾害 harass and injure
擾亂 disturb

干擾 backdrop; disturb; interfere; lapse; obstruct; tamper; trouble; upset

【攞】laap⁸ ①（收集）collect ②（拿）take

攞走（拿走）take away
攞衫袖（捲起衣袖）roll up one's sleeves
攞理（到處搜集）gather up
攞晒（全都拿去了 / 拿光）take away all

【撲】bok⁷（敲打 / 擊打）hit

撲成（拳擊）(English) boxing
　打撲成（打拳擊）practice boxing
撲穿（打破）break; smash

撲帽（瓜皮帽）skullcap
撲頭（打腦袋 / 打頭）hit sb on the head

【搣】dzit⁷（擠）tickle

【斃】bai⁶ die

斃命 get killed; meet a violent death
斃敵（殲敵）kill enemy troops

束手待斃（束手待擒 / 坐以待斃）die without a fight; fold one's hands and await destruction; fold one's hands and wait for death; fold one's hands and wait to be slain; resign oneself to extinction; wait for death with hands bound up; wait for death with tied hands; wait helplessly for death

【斷】dyn³ abstain from

斷斤計（論斤算）calculate by catty
斷估（估計 / 瞎猜）guess; wild guess
斷定 assert; conclude; decide; form a judgement

一刀兩斷 make a clean break; sever ties with sb
不斷 unceasingly
判斷 assess; decide; determine; judge; size up
武斷 arbitrary decision; assertive
推斷 infer
診斷 diagnose; diagnosis

【斷】tyn⁵ cut off

斷市（脫銷 / 斷檔）be out of stock; be sold out
斷正（逮個正着）be caught red-handed
斷交 ① break off a friendship ② break off diplomatic relations; sever diplomatic relations
斷尾（斷根）be over for good; be thoroughly cured
斷開 break into
斷窮根（飛黃騰達）not to live in poverty any more; strike oil
斷擔挑（被生活壓彎了腰）with one's back bent under pressure

拗斷（折斷）break; break asunder; break off; rive; snap
搣斷（拉斷 / 扯斷）pull apart
隔斷（隔開）cut off; separate
雞啄唔斷（沒完沒了）keep chattering on; rattle on without stopping

【櫈】dang³（櫈子）stool

櫈仔（櫈子）stool

一張櫈（一張櫈子）a stool

長櫈（長木櫈）bench
擔櫈（端櫈子）carry a stool
攞櫈（拿櫈子）take a stool
BB 櫈（嬰兒櫈）baby chair

【檸】ning⁴ lemon

檸水（檸檬水）lemon water
　凍檸水（冰檸檬水）cold lemon water
　熱檸水（熱檸檬水）hot lemon water
檸茶（檸檬茶）lemon tea
　凍檸茶（冰檸檬茶）cold lemon tea
　熱檸茶（熱檸檬茶）hot lemon tea
檸蜜（蜂蜜檸檬水）honey lemonade
檸樂（可樂加檸檬）coke with lemon
　凍檸樂（冰可樂加檸檬）ice coke with lemon
　熱檸樂（熱可樂加檸檬）hot coke with lemon
檸檬 ①（檸檬）(English) lemon ②（拒絕邀請）turn down
　an invitation
　檸檬水 lemon water
　檸檬茶 lemon tea; tea with lemon
　檸檬黃 lemon yellow
　食檸檬 ①（邀請被拒絕）being declined an invitation
　　②（告白被拒絕）get turned down by a girl

【樣】mung¹ lemon

食檸檬 ①（邀請被拒絕）being declined an invitation ② get
　turned down by a girl
檸檬 ①（檸檬）(English) lemon ②（拒絕邀請）turn down
　an invitation

【檻】laam⁶ cupboard

門檻 door sill

【櫃】gwai⁶ cupboard

櫃台 counter
櫃位（櫃台）bar; counter; desk
　登機櫃位（登機櫃台）check-in counter
櫃面（櫃台）bar; counter; desk
　坐櫃面（坐在前枱）serve at the counter
櫃桶（抽屜）anus; drawer
　櫃桶底穿（竊空公款）the funds of a unit are embezzled
　穿櫃桶（虧空公款）embezzle funds; misappropriate
　　funds
　穿櫃桶底（虧空公款）embezzle funds; misappropriate
　　funds

入牆櫃（內置衣櫃）built-in wardrobe

五筒櫃（五抽櫃）five-drawer cabinet
吊櫃 hanging cabinet
衣櫃 wardrobe
押櫃（支付押金 / 付按金）pay a deposit
牀頭櫃 bedside cupboard
牀邊櫃（牀頭櫃）bedside cabinet
音櫃（揚聲器 / 音箱）loudspeaker box; speakers
埋櫃（店舖每晚結賬）close the turnover of the day
被櫃（被櫥）quilt cabinet
書櫃（書櫥）book cabinet
高櫃（大立櫃）high cabinet
缽櫃（酒櫃）wine cabinet
貨櫃（集裝箱）container
雪櫃（冰箱 / 電冰箱）fridge; refrigerator
碗櫃 cupboard
飾櫃（展示櫥窗）display window; show window
鞋櫃 shoe cabinet

【檳】ban¹ areca

檳榔 areca nut; betel nut

香檳 (English) champagne

【歸】gwai¹ return

歸一（不散亂 / 整齊）neat; tidy
歸西（死亡）die
歸根到底（歸根結底）in the end; in the final analysis;
　when all is said and done

乘興而來，敗興而歸 come in high spirits but return
　crestfallen; come in high spirits but go back disheartened;
　come in high spirits, but return in disappointment; come
　with great enthusiasm and return disillusioned; set out
　cheerfully and return disappointed; set out in high spirits
　and return crestfallen
眾望所歸（受人歡迎）command public respect and support;
　enjoy popular confidence; stand high in popular favour; the
　object of public esteem; the people's hope is centred on
終歸（終究 / 畢竟 / 最終）after all; eventually; in the end
無家可歸 homeless

【瀉】se³（溢）overspill

瀉出嚟（溢出來）spill over

山泥傾瀉（泥石流）landslide
倒瀉（倒灑）spill water
斟瀉（裝到滿溢）overfill the cup
滾瀉（沸到溢出來）spilling of boiling water
滿瀉（滿溢）overflow

【瀏】lau⁴ take a glance

瀏覽 browse; glance over

【爵】dzoek⁸ ① peer ② wine pitcher

爵士 ① sir ② jazz
　　爵士樂 jazz music
　　爵士舞 jazz dance

伯爵 count; earl
侯爵 marquess; marquis

【獵】lip⁹ hunt

獵狗終須山上喪 (玩火自焚/引火焚身) he who plays with fire will get burned at last
獵物 prey
　　尋找獵物 hunt for one's prey
獵場 (狩獵場) hunting ground

涉獵 browse; dabble in; do desultory reading; read cursorily

【璧】bik⁷ jade

璧玉 (美玉) jade
璧合 perfect match
璧還 (感激歸還) return with thanks

雙劍合璧 cooperation of two capable persons

【癐】gui⁴ (累) tired

癐到死/劫到死 (累得要命) be tired to death

【磬】faak⁸ (抽) lash; thrash; whip

磬嘅 (抽着) lash

【礎】tso² stone base

基礎 foundation

【禮】lai⁵ courtesy

禮多人不怪 civility costs nothing
禮衣邊 (示字旁/示補兒) the "rite" (示) radical
禮服 formal dress
禮物 gift
　　一件禮物 a gift; a present
　　交換禮物 exchange gifts
禮金 ① (聘金/聘禮) bride-price; bethothal gifts ② (現金禮物) cash gift
禮品 gift; present
　　禮品店 gift and souvenir shop
　　上等禮品 premium present

謝絕禮品 no gifts
禮拜 (星期) week
　　禮拜一 (星期一) Monday
　　禮拜二 (星期二) Tuesday
　　禮拜三 (星期三) Wednesday
　　禮拜五 (星期五) Friday
　　禮拜六 (星期六) Saturday
　　禮拜日 (星期天) Sunday
　　禮拜四 (星期四) Thursday
　　禮拜堂 (教堂) church
　　　　一間禮拜堂 (一間教堂) a church
　　禮拜幾 (星期幾) which day of the week
　　上二個禮拜 (上二個星期) the week before the last week
　　上個禮拜 (上個星期) last week
　　下個禮拜 (下個星期) next week
　　今個禮拜 (這個星期) this week
　　呢個禮拜 (這個星期) this week
　　幾多個禮拜 (多少個星期) how many weeks
　　第個禮拜 (下個星期) next week
禮堂 auditorium
禮單 (禮物清單) list of gifts
禮節 ceremony; civility; courtesy; etiquette; protocol; rules of politeness
　　合乎禮節 be according to protocol
　　按照禮節 in accordance with protocol
　　違反禮節 impropriety
禮貌 politeness
　　冇禮貌 (沒禮貌) be wanting in politeness; have bad manners; have no manners; impolite
　　有禮貌 courteous; have good manners; have manners; polite
　　　　好有禮貌 (很有禮貌) be all courtesy
禮儀 decorum; etiquette; protocol
禮輕情意重 the gift is trifling but the feeling is profound

一份賀禮 a congratulatory gift
下水禮 (啓動儀式) launching ceremony
主持典禮 host a ceremony
主持婚禮 host a wedding ceremony
失禮 (不禮貌/丟人) be disgraced; bring shame on oneself; lose face; lose one's decorum; make a breach of etiquette
回禮 ① send a return gift ② return the courtesy of sb
見面禮 a gift presented to sb at the first meeting
典禮 ceremony
命名典禮 naming ceremony
非禮 (調戲) assail with obscenities; flirt with women; indecent assault; molest; play the make on; take liberties with

送禮 give a present
參加婚禮 attend a wedding ceremony
婚禮 wedding ceremony
畢業典禮 graduation ceremony
閉幕典禮 (閉幕儀式) closing ceremony
喪禮 (喪葬) funeral
賀禮 congratulatory gift
開幕典禮 opening ceremony
葬禮 funeral service; funeral rites; obsequies
聘禮 betrothal gift
舉止有禮 courteous in one's demeanour
舉行喪禮 hold a funeral
舉行婚禮 hold a wedding ceremony
薄禮 humble present; trifling gift
還禮 ① present a gift in return ② return the courtesy of sb

【穢】wai³ dirty
穢亂 debauched; wanton

和尚食狗肉——一件穢，兩件穢 (不當行為做了一次還是兩次，都是同樣可恥的) it is equally disgraceful to do such an ill deed for once or even once more again

【簡】gaan² simplified
簡短 brief
簡筆字 (簡體字) simplified Chinese character

郵簡 aerogram

【簧】wong⁴ spring
簧片 reed

唱雙簧 (兩個人一起策劃) two people scheming together
唸口簧 ① (背誦) rote learning ② (說順口溜) chant a
　　doggerel

【糧】loeng⁴ grains
糧地官 (失業) be unemployed
糧單 (工資單) salary slip

出糧 (發工資 / 發薪) pay salary; pay wages
年尾雙糧 (年底雙薪) double pay at the end of the year
狗糧 dog food
貓糧 cat food
雙糧 (雙薪) double pay

【織】dzik⁷ knit; weave
織卒 (蟋蟀) cricket
織針 (毛衣針) knitting needle

耕織 farming and weaving
組織 (構成 / 形成) constitute; form; organise; texture; tissue

【繚】liu⁴ (潦草) in a slipshod way
繚繞 (潦草) in a slipshod way

【繞】jiu² beat sb
繞起 (難倒) beat sb
繞過 bypass; pass over in a roundabout manner
繞道 detour; go by a roundabout route; make a detour

【繡】sau³ embroidery
繡花枕頭 ① ginger bread ② beautiful in appearance but
　　lacking inner talents

刺繡 embroidery

【鐺】tsaang¹ pot
瓦鐺 (砂鍋) clay pot
砂煲罌鐺 (鍋碗瓢盆) pots and bottles

【翻】faan¹ turn around; turn over
翻生 (復活) bring back to life; resuscitate
翻抄 (重新製作) reproduce
翻炒 (重複 / 炒冷飯) repeat; reproduce
翻風 ① (颱風) gale ② (風勢變強) the wing is getting strong
　　翻風落雨 (刮風下雨) when there's any change in weather
翻渣 (二煎 / 重複煎藥) second decoction
　　翻渣茶葉——冇釐味道 (涼水沏茶——沒味兒) as insipid
　　　as water
翻揸 (復合) get back together; reunite
翻閹 (唱老調) do the old job once again; sing the same
　　old tune
翻譯 translate
　　翻譯員 translator

打大翻 (打空翻) forward somersault

【職】dzik⁷ post
職員 clerk; employee; staff
職責 (義務 / 責任) duty; obligation; responsibility
職業 calling; career; occupation; profession; vocation

升職 promotion
在職 at one's post; hold a position; in-service; on the job
免職 relieve sb of his post; remove sb from office
述職 report; report on one's work
革職 discharge from a position; dismiss; remove from office; sack

兼職 concurrent job; moonlight; moonlighting; part-time job; side job

紮職 (升職) be promoted

撤職 be dismissed from office; be removed from one's office; dismiss sb from his post; remove sb from office

辭職 resign from a position

【臍】 tsi⁴ naval

臍帶 umbilical cord

肚臍 belly button; naval

【舊】 gau⁶ (以前的) old

舊生 (以前的學生) former student

舊交 old acquaintance

舊年 (去年) last year

舊底 (以前 / 從前 / 過去) before; formerly; in the past; previously

舊居 old home

舊金山 (三藩市 / 聖弗朗西斯科) San Francisco

舊屋 (老房子 / 舊房子) old house

舊衫 (舊衣服) old clothes

舊時 (以前 / 從前) before; formerly; in the old days; in the past; previously

　舊陣時 (以前 / 從前) ago; before; former; formerly; in the past; once; previous; prior; used to be

舊貨 (破爛 / 廢棄物 / 二手貨) junk; second-hand goods

舊惡 (舊怨) old grievances

舊飯 (剩飯) left-over cooked rice

舊鞋 ① (舊鞋子) old shoes ② (前女友) ex-girlfriend

舊曆 (黃曆 / 夏曆) lunar calendar

　舊曆年 (黃曆 / 夏曆) lunar calendar

守舊 adhere to past practices; conservative; resistant to advances; stick to old ways

折舊 depreciation

依舊 as before; as usual; in the usual manner; in the usual way; still

念舊 keep old friendships in mind

破舊 dilapidated; old and shabby; outdated; worn-out

殘舊 (破舊) worn-out

懷舊 nostalgic

【薩】 saat⁸ boddhisatva

薩爾瓦多 (English) El Salvador

冤豬頭都有盟鼻菩薩 (臭豬頭有爛鼻子來聞 / 情人眼裏出西施) a lover has no judge of beauty

菩薩 Buddha

【薯】 sy⁴ (馬鈴薯) potato

薯片 potato chips

薯仔 ① (土豆 / 馬鈴薯) potato ② (傻瓜) fool

薯條 French fries; fries

　一包薯條 a bag of French fries

薯嘜 (呆 / 笨) (English) schmuck; stupid

薯頭 (呆 / 笨) stupid

大番薯 (大笨蛋) fat and stupid person; fool; idiot

炕番薯 (烤白薯) roast yam

茄薯 (現金) (English) cash

馬鈴薯 (土豆 / 薯仔) potato

荷蘭薯 (馬鈴薯 / 土豆 / 薯仔) potato

番薯 ① (白薯 / 地瓜 / 紅薯) yam ② (傻子) stupid person

煨番薯 (烤白薯) roast yam

【薰】 fan¹ cauterise

薰蹄 (煙熏肘子) smoked pork knuckle

【藉】 dzik⁹ pretext

藉口 excuse

【藍】 laam⁴ blue

藍本 blueprint

藍色 blue

藍藥水 (紫藥水) gentian violet solution; methyl violet solution

藍籌 (藍籌股) blue chips

湖水藍 acid blue

【蟬】 sim⁴ cicada

蟬鳴 shrill sound of a cicada

沙蟬 (蟬) cicada

秋蟬 (蟬) cicada

【蟲】 tsung⁴ (蟲子) insect; worm

蟲仔 (蟲子) insect; worm

蟲蟲 (蟲子) insect; worm

大懶蟲 (懶惰鬼) lazy person

生蟲 (長寄生蟲) have a parasitic disease

甲蟲 beetle

地頭蟲 (熟悉當地情況的人) sb who knows a particular area well

老鹹蟲 (老色狼) dirty old man; old goat

行運一條龍，失運一條蟲 (走好運像條龍，倒霉運像條蟲) a person in luck walks heavy but a person out of luck cowers with humility

杜蟲 (打蟲) cure a parasitic disease; take worm medicine

沙蟲 wriggle

肚裏蟲 (肚子裏的蛔蟲) mind-reader

垃圾蟲 litter bug

放光蟲 (螢火蟲) fire beetle; firefly; glowworm

爬蟲 (爬行動物) reptile

疥蟲 (疥蟎) sarcoptic mite

害蟲 destructive insects; injurious insects

捉蟲 (惹上麻煩) get into difficulties; get into trouble

書蟲 (書呆子) bookworm

益蟲 beneficial insect

斬腳趾避沙蟲 (截趾適履) trim the toes to fit the shoes

淫蟲 (淫亂的人) sexually immoral person

寄生蟲 parasite

猛虎不及地頭蟲 (強龍不如地頭蛇) a mighty dragon is no match for the native serpent

蛀米大蟲 (好吃懶做的人) sb who has nothing to do but to eat

蛀書蟲 (蠹魚 / 書呆子) bookworm

笨屎蟲 (屎殼郎 / 蜣螂) dung beetle

寧欺白鬚公，莫欺鼻涕蟲 (莫欺少年窮) a colt may make a good horse

鼻涕蟲 snot-nosed kid

螢火蟲 fire beetle; firefly; glow-worm; lighting bug

雞蟲 (蜈蚣) centipede

懶蟲 (懶惰鬼) bedsteader; do-nothing; faineant; gold brick; gentleman of leisure; lady of leisure; layabout; lazy person; lazy guy; lazybones; lounger; sleepyhead; value of resters

鹹蟲 (色狼) dirty man; dirty-minded man; lecherous man; lecherous person

蠶蟲 (蠶) silkworm

【蟮】 sin⁶ eel

蟮糊 eel paste

死蛇爛蟮 (一動不動 / 懶惰) ① too lazy to stir a finger ② lazy person

【蟧】 lou⁴⁻² spider

蟛蟧 (蜘蛛) spider

【蟝】 koey⁴⁻² toad

蟝蟝 (蟾蜍 / 癩蛤蟆) toad

【襟】 kam¹ ① lapel ② durable

襟用 (耐用) durable

襟花 (胸花) boutonniere; corsage

襟計 (花大量金錢) a large amount of money

襟針 (胸針) brooch

襟章 (徽章 / 證章) badge
　一隻襟章 (一枚徽章) a badge

襟着 (耐穿 / 經穿) can stand wear and tear; durable; wear well

襟諗 (費思量 / 費腦筋) crack one's head; turn over in one's mind

襟磨 (耐磨) wear-resistant

老襟 (表親) maternal cousins

胸襟 breadth of mind; mind

【覆】 fuk⁷ repeat

覆亡 demise; fall

覆沒 ① capsize and sink ② be annihilated; be overwhelmed; be routed; be wiped out

反反覆覆 again and again; like the burden of a song; over and over again; repeatedly

反覆 again and again; once and again; over and over; over and over again; iterative; time after time; time and again

【謬】 mau⁶ ridiculous

謬誤 error; mistake; falsehood

謬論 fallacy; false theory

荒謬 ridiculous

【豐】 fung¹ plentiful

豐收 abundant harvest; bumper harvest

豐富 (充沛 / 充足 / 充分 / 豐厚) abundant

豐滿 ① plentiful ② full and round; full-grown; well-developed; well-endowed; well-equipped; well-heeled; well-loaded; well-stacked

【蹟】 dzik⁷ relics

名勝古蹟 scenic spots and historical relics

奇蹟 miracle

【蹎】 gwaan³ fall; stumble over

蹎底 (摔倒) fall down

蹎直 (完全失敗) be completely defeated; meet a lost cause

蹎倒 (絆倒 / 跌倒) fall; stumble over

蹎跤 (摔跤) wrestling

【轉】dzyn³ ① (拐) turn ② (轉乘) take a transfer

轉口 (改口) withdraw one's previous remark

轉工 (換工作) change a job

轉介 (轉診) medical referral

轉台 (換頻道) switch over

轉右 (右拐彎兒) turn right

轉左 (左拐彎兒) turn left

轉名 (過戶) change the name of owner; transfer

轉行 (改行) change one's profession; change one's trade

轉車 (換車) change trains or buses

轉性 (性情改變) change one's disposition
　　轉死性 (性情改變) change one's disposition

轉堂 (換課) change class

轉眼 (眨眼間 / 像眨眼一樣) in a wink
　　轉吓眼 (一轉眼) in a wink; in a wink of an eye; like winking

轉軚 (改變態度) change one's attitude; change one's mind; shift one's ground

轉發球 (換發球) change of service; change service

轉膊 ① (換肩) shift the burden from one shoulder to another ② (靈活) flexible

轉線 (換線) change the lane

轉頭 ① (一會兒) later ② (回頭) turn about
　　行返轉頭 (掉頭) turn back
　　番轉頭 (回頭) turn back
　　　　冇得番轉頭 (不能回頭) no turning back
　　　　望番轉頭 (回頭望) look back

轉彎 (拐彎兒) turn the corner

轉讓 alienation
　　轉讓限制 alienation restrictions

不可逆轉 impossible to reverse the trend

仆轉 (倒扣) turn sth over

反轉 reverse

冇彎轉 (沒法打開僵局) there is no way to break a deadlock

右轉 (右拐) turn right

左轉 (左拐) turn left

世界輪流轉 (風水輪流轉) everybody has the turn of the wheel; fortunes change

打個白鴿轉 (打個轉就回來) turn around

氹氹轉 (團團轉) in a confused haste; turn round and round

扭轉 turn back

風水輪流轉 every dog has his day; fortunes change

倒翻轉 (反過來 / 倒過來) conversely; turn the other way round

倒轉 (倒過來) turn upside down

峯迴路轉 ① the path winds along mountain ridges ② things change drastically

逆轉 deteriorate; take a turn for the worse

側轉 (側過來 / 轉向側面) turn sideward

掉翻轉 (反過來 / 倒過來 / 倒轉) conversely; turn the other way round

調轉 (倒過來) turn upside-down

【轆】luk⁷ (輾) ① pass through ② (根 / 條) a stick of

轆地 (在地上打滾) roll on the ground
　　轆地波 (滾地球) ground ball

轆咭 (刷卡) swipe one's card to settle payment

轆親腳 (碾着腳了) one's foot is being rolled over

一轆 (一節) a stick of

牛輾 (牛腱) beef shank

車轆 (車輪) wheel

眼轆轆 (直瞪瞪地 / 在怒視某人) glower at sb; stare in a hostile way

【醫】ji¹ (醫治) cure; heal

醫生 doctor; medical doctor; physician
　　醫生紙 (病假紙 / 請假單 / 醫生證明) sick-leave certificate
　　行運醫生醫病尾 (幸運的醫生醫治正在恢復的病人) a lucky doctor cures a patient who is in the last stage of recovery
　　私家醫生 (私人醫生) private doctor
　　冒牌醫生 quack doctor
　　黃綠醫生 (蒙古大夫) charlatan; quack; quack physician
　　睇醫生 (看病) consult a doctor; go to see a doctor; see a doctor

醫肚 (充飢 / 墊肚子) have a meal

醫病 (治病) cure the sickness; treat an ailment; treat a disease

醫院 hospital
　　一間醫院 a hospital
　　入咗醫院 (住進了醫院) be hospitalised

醫藥費 medical expenses

人嚇人冇藥醫 (人嚇人沒藥醫) there's no remedy to cure a person horrified by others

人蠢冇藥醫 (人蠢沒藥醫) there's no remedy to cure the stupidity of a person

久病成醫 prolonged illness makes a doctor of a patient

中醫 Chinese medicine

冇藥醫 (沒藥醫) no remedy for one's behaviour

牙醫 dental surgeon; dentist

有得醫 (有得治) can be cured; curable

留醫 (住院) be hospitalised; in hospital

睇中醫 (看中醫) see a doctor of Chinese medicine
睇牙醫 (看牙醫) see a dentist
睇獸醫 (看獸醫) see a vet
獸醫 vet; veterinarian

【醬】dzoeng³ sauce

醬汁 sauce
醬瓜 (醬黃瓜) soy sauced cucumber
醬油 sauce; soy sauce
醬芥 (醬芥菜) pickled rutabaga

一樽花生醬 (一瓶花生醬) a jar of peanut butter
沙律醬 (沙拉醬) salad dressing
豆豉醬 black bean paste
芥醬 (芥末醬) mustard sauce
花生醬 peanut butter
魚子醬 caviar
甜麵醬 sweet bean paste
辣椒醬 chilli sauce
蝦醬 shrimp paste

【鎖】so² lock

鎖你 (對不起) (English) sorry
鎖門 lock the door
　記得鎖門 remember to lock the door; remember to lock up
鎖匙 (鑰匙 / 關鍵) key
　鎖匙扣 (鑰匙圈兒) key holder; key ring
　鎖匙窿 (鑰匙孔) key hole
　一抽鎖匙 (一串鑰匙) a string of keys
　一條鎖匙 (一把鑰匙 / 一管鑰匙) a key
鎖鏈 (鐵鏈) iron chain

一把鎖 a lock
門鎖 door lock
封鎖 block; seal off

【鎊】bong⁶ pound

英鎊 British pound; sterling pound

【鎚】tsoey⁴ hammer

鎚仔 (鎚子) hammer

一個鎚 (一把鎚子) a hammer

【鎮】dzan³ lock

鎮靜劑 (鎮定劑) sedative

市鎮 town

坐鎮 in the seat of power
城鎮 cities and towns

【鎯】long⁴ hammer

鎯鎯 (小銅鈴) small brass bell

【雙】soeng¹ double

雙人房 double room
雙人牀 double bed
雙方 both sides
雙加大 (加加大 / 特大號) extra extra large size
雙皮奶 double-boiled milk and egg white
雙企人 (雙人旁 / 雙立人) the "two persons" (亻) radical
雙面人 (兩面派) double-dealer; double-faced person
雙倍 double
雙氧水 oxydol
雙眼 eyes
　放長雙眼睇吓 (等着瞧 / 拭目以待 / 觀望) wait and see
雙喜 double happiness
　雙喜臨門 get double happiness; get two pieces of good news
雙程 return; two-way
　雙程飛 (雙程票) return ticket
雙劍合璧 cooperation of two capable persons
雙數 (偶數) even number
雙糧 (雙薪) double pay
　年尾雙糧 (年底雙薪) double pay at the end of the year

一三五七九——無傷 (雙) one, two, three, five, and six – nothing goes amiss
一雙 a pair of
蓋世無雙 have no equal on earth; matchless; peerless; stand without peer in one's generation; the best one in the whole world; unparalleled; without an equal in the world

【雜】dzaap⁹ miscellaneous

雜物房 storeroom
雜差 (打雜 / 便衣警察) plaincloth; police detective
雜崩能 (什錦 / 雜物) bits and pieces; miscellaneous; mixed; odds and ends
雜貨鋪 (雜貨店) grocery store
雜牌 less known and inferior brand
　雜牌軍 (烏合之眾) ragtag group
雜費 sundry expenses
雜嘜 (雜牌) fake brand goods
　雜嘜貨 (假冒品牌商品 / 仿牌貨) fake brand goods
雜誌 magazine
　一本雜誌 a magazine
　八卦雜誌 gossip magazine; tabloid magazine

雜種仔（小雜種）bastard

牛雜（牛下水）beef offal
打雜 ① do odd jobs ② odd-job man
羊雜（羊下水）haggis
沓雜（困惑／擁擠）confused; crowded and mixed
食雜（食葷）carnivorous
複雜 complex; complicated; intricate; sophisticated
豬雜（豬下水）pig offal
雞雜（雞下水）chicken giblets

【鶴】hok⁶⁻² crank

鶴神（壞蛋）damn guy

塘邊鶴（等待機會的旁觀者）the person who hastens to
　　make away with his gains

【雞】gai¹ ① chicken ② (哨子) whistle

雞丁 chicken cube
雞子（雞腰子）chicken's kidney
雞公（公雞）cock
雞扎（四寶雞扎）chicken bundle
雞毛 chicken feather
　　雞毛掃（雞毛撣子）feather duster
　　雞毛蒜皮 trivial matter
雞仔（小雞）chicken; springer
　　雞仔唔管管麻鷹（該管的不管，不該管的倒去管）mind
　　　　one's own business
　　雞仔媒人（愛管閒事的人）go-between; nosy
　　　　intermediator
　　雞仔餅（小鳳餅）salty and sweet biscuit
　　雞仔聲（聲音微弱）weak voice
雞皮 ① chicken skin ② goosebumps
　　雞皮紙（牛皮紙）kraft paper
雞年 Year of the Chicken
雞肉 chicken
雞尾（雞屁股）chicken bum; chicken's rump
　　雞尾包 cocktail bun
　　雞尾酒 cocktail
雞肝 chicken liver
雞乸（母雞）hen
　　雞乸咁大隻字（斗大的字）very large characters
　　癲雞乸（瘋婆子）furious woman
雞泡魚（河豚）blowfish; puffer
雞春（雞蛋）egg
　　雞春咁密都褓出仔（世上沒有密不透風的牆）no secret
　　　　can be kept
　　雞春砍石頭（以卵擊石）like an egg dashing itself against
　　　　a rock – courting destruction

雞春摸過輕四兩（靠不住）do damage to whatever sb
　　handles
雞柳 shredded chicken breast
雞飛狗走（雞飛狗跳）all the people scatter around
雞食放光蟲──心知肚明（斑鳩吃螢光蟲──肚事
　　明）have a clear mind; know what is what
雞紅（雞血）chicken blood
雞凍（雞肉凍）chicken jelly
雞胸（雞胸肉）chicken breast
　　雞胸肉 chicken breast
雞啄放光蟲──心知肚明（斑鳩吃螢光蟲──肚裏
　　明）a turtledove eating up a firefly – bright in the belly;
　　have a clear understanding of things
雞啄唔斷（沒完沒了）keep chattering on; rattle on
　　without stopping
雞蛋 egg
　　紅雞蛋 red-dyed egg
　　剝殼雞蛋 ①（剝去殼的蛋）shelled egg ②（光滑的皮膚）
　　　　smooth skin
雞眼（疣／厚繭）corns on a person's foot
雞腎（雞腰）chicken kidney
雞項（雲英雞／小母雞）virgin chicken
雞球（雞塊）chicken piece
雞絲 shredded chicken
雞塊 chicken piece
　　炸雞塊 chicken nugget
雞腸 ①（雞腸子）chicken intestine ②（書面英文）written
　　English
雞腳 ①（雞爪子）chicken feet ②（把柄／過失／辮子）
　　weak spot
　　食雞腳（吃雞爪）eat chicken feet
　　香雞腳（瘦長腿）long thin legs
　　雞咁腳（穿兔子鞋似的）fleet of foot; take to one's legs
雞碎（雞胃）chicken's stomach
　　雞碎咁多（一點兒／很少）a few; a little; a small amount
　　　　of sth; chicken feed; peanuts
雞飯 chicken with rice
　　叉雞飯（叉燒雞飯）rice with barbeque pork
　　　　and chicken
　　咖喱雞飯 curry chicken with rice
　　海南雞飯 Hainan chicken with rice
雞鴨 chickens and ducks
　　雞毛鴨血（雞犬不寧）in a bad situation
　　雞同鴨講 people failing to communicate; unable to
　　　　communicate
雞翼（雞翅膀）chicken wing
雞雜（雞下水）chicken giblets
雞蟲（蜈蚣）centipede
雞髀（雞腿）chicken leg

雞髀打人牙骹軟（拿人手短，吃人嘴軟／說服某人的最好方法就是給予一些利益）beat a dog with a bone and it will not howl; the best way to persuade sb is to offer them sth pleasant

炸雞髀（炸雞腿）deep-fried chicken leg; deep-fried drumstick

一蚊雞（一元）one dollar

一隻雞 a chicken

二撇雞（八字鬍）man with a beard

三腳雞（三輪車）car with three wheels

大眼雞（鱔魚）big eye

大雞 big chicken

山雞（野雞／雉雞）pheasant

冇走雞（十拿九穩／不會錯失／必家得到／跑不了）have everything in the bag; in the bag

田雞（青蛙）frog

生雞（沒閹過的公雞）chick; cockalorum; cockerel

白切雞 poached chicken; steamed chicken

白斬雞 poached chicken; steamed chicken

吊雞（起重機）hoist

老母雞 ①（老母雞）old hen ②（老婊子）old bitch

吹銀雞（吹哨子）blow the whistle

吹雞 ①（獲得幫助）get help ②（吹哨子）blow the whistle

走雞 ①（錯失良機）lose an opportunity; miss a chance; miss out on a good thing; miss the boat; miss the opportunity ②（溜走）run away; wander away

咖喱雞 ①（咖喱雞肉）curry chicken ②（吻痕）love bite

怪雞（奇怪）bizarre

珍珠雞（荷葉糯米雞）glutinous rice with chicken wrapped with lotus leaf

拜神唔見雞（口中不停低聲唸着／嘟嘟噥噥）bustle in and out with a murmur; complain with a murmur

食無情雞（炒魷魚／被解僱）be fired; get the sack

悵雞（潑辣）shrewish; volubly demanding

弱雞（弱）weak

捉黃腳雞（捉姦／仙人跳／色情敲詐）catch sb having illicit sex; extort money from a man by setting up a sex-trap

偷雞（偷懶／抓住機會避免工作）take a chance to avoid work

執死雞 ①（幸運得了便宜／撿便宜）take sth which has lost or thrown away ②（撿現成）score an easy goal after a shot has been blocked by the goalkeeper

執雞（帶走別人丟失或扔掉的東西）take sth which has lost or thrown away

春瘟雞（不假思索地行事／盲目從事）sb who acts without thinking

豉油雞（醬油雞）chicken in soy sauce

野雞（街頭妓女／流鶯）street prostitute

悵雞（潑辣）shrewish; volubly demanding

焗雞（燻雞）smoked chicken

無情雞（炒魷魚／被解僱）be fired

落湯雞（渾身濕透）completely drenched

路邊雞（娼妓）streetwalker

摸盲雞（騎瞎馬）do sth aimlessly

銀雞（哨子）whistle

劏雞 ①（殺雞）kill a chicken ②（拉小提琴像殺雞）play the violin badly

慶過辣雞（十分憤怒）very angry

撑雞（撒潑）act hysterically and refuse to see reason; behave rudely; in a tantrum; shrewish and make a scene; unreasonable and make a scene

燒雞（烤雞）roast chicken

靜靜雞（悄悄地／暗地裏）act in silence; inwardly; quietly; quietly and secretly; secretly; stealthily

靜雞雞（悄悄地／暗地裏）act in silence; inwardly; quietly; quietly and secretly; secretly; stealthily

騰雞（慌亂／手足無措）frightened; nervous

鐵嘴雞（辯才一流）a difficult opponent in an argument

癲雞（瘋女人）crazy woman

【鞭】bin¹ whip

鞭打 flagellate; flog; lash; thrash; whip

鞭策 encourage; goad on; spur on; urge on

鞭撻 castigate; lash

快馬加鞭 accelerate the speed; burn up the road on one's way; do a fast job; posthaste; ride whip and spur; spur the flying horse at high speed; whip one's horse up to a swift trot; with whip and spur

【鞦】tsau¹ swing

打鞦韆（盪鞦韆）get on a swing; have a swing; play on the swing

鞦韆（鞦韆）swing

【額】ngaak⁹ forehead

額外 extra

額頭（前額）forehead

　　額頭上面寫住（額頭上寫字——明擺着）sth can be easily found out

內定名額 officially decided quota

份額 share

名額 quota of people

眉頭眼額（眉高眼低）one's thinking being revealed by one's facial expression

面額（面值）denomination

唔識睇人眉頭眼額（不懂眉高眼低）not know how to adopt different attitudes and measures under different circumstances

款額（總金額）amount of money

睇人眉頭眼額（看人眉高眼低）at sb's disposal

貸款額 loan amount

橫額（橫幅）banner; streamer

餘額 ① vacancies yet to be filled ② remaining sum; surplus

營業額 turnover

識睇人眉頭眼額（會看人眉高眼低）good at knowing sb's intentions

【題】tai⁴ question

題目 question
　一條題目（一道題目）a question

題名 ① autograph; inscribe one's name ② subject; title; topic ③ entitle; name a work

題材 subject matter; theme

一個問題 a question

一條問題（一個問題）a question

心臟有問題 heart problem

冇問題（沒問題）no problem; no trouble at all

老人問題（老齡化問題）problems with the aged

面子問題 a matter of face

情緒問題 emotional problem

問題 question

解決難題 solve a difficult problem

離題 deviate from the main theme; digress; digress from one's topic; drift away from the subject

難題 difficult problem

【顏】ngaan⁴ colour

顏色 colour
　顏色筆（彩筆）colour pencil

顏面 ① countenance; face ② honour; prestige

顏料 colour; dyestuff; pigment

駐顏 preserve a youthful complexion; retaining youth looks

【餵】wai³ ① feed ② feed with food

餵奶 breastfeed

餵飯 feed sb with rice

【騎】ke⁴ ride

騎牛搵牛（騎馬找馬）look for an ox while sitting on one

騎牛搵馬（騎驢找馬）seek for the better while holding on to one; work in one job but look out for a better one

騎劫（劫持）abduct; hold under duress; kidnap

騎咧（古怪／奇怪）bizarre; odd

騎師 jockey

騎馬 ride on horseback
　騎硫磺馬（將某人的錢轉移為己用）divert sb's money to one's own purpose
　騎膊馬（小孩騎在大人肩膀上）a child sitting on the shoulders of an adult

騎樓（陽台）balcony
　騎樓底（過街樓下的人行道／陽台下）pavement; sidewalk

笑口騎騎（嬉皮笑臉）behave in a noisy, gay and boisterous manner; grinning and smiling; grinning cheekily; grinning mischievously; smiling and grimacing; with a cunning smile; with an oily smile

笑騎騎（笑哈哈）giggle; laugh heartily; with a laugh

胭脂馬——難騎（無法控制的人）uncontrollable person

【髀】bei² ① （腿）leg ② thigh

髀罅（大腿間縫隙）thigh gap

大髀（大腿）thigh

蚊髀同牛髀（小巫見大巫／沒法相比）by long chalks; no comparison between; one cannot be compared to the other; pale into insignificance by comparison; the moon is not seen where the sun shines; when the sun shines, the light of stars is not seen; when the sun shines, the moon has nought to do

褲髀（褲腿）trouser legs

膝頭大過髀（很瘦）very skinny

豬髀（豬蹄髈）pork shank

擘髀（叉開大腿）with legs apart

雞髀（雞腿）chicken leg

【鬆】sung¹ loosen

鬆人（開溜／溜之大吉／溜走）get away; sneak away

鬆化（酥脆）crisp

鬆毛鬆翼（洋洋得意）burst with joy and complacency; sing and dance for joy

鬆脆 crunchy

鬆骨（按摩）massage

鬆焙（柔軟／鬆軟）soft

鬆開（解開）loosen
　鬆開領呔（解開領帶）loosen one's tie

鬆糕 Cantonese sponge cake; fluffy cake
　鬆糕鞋 thick high-heeled shoes

太鬆 too loose

老鬆（上海人）Shanghainese

撈鬆（北方人）northerner

【鯇】waan⁵ grass carp

鯇魚（草魚）grass carp
　鯇魚腩（草魚腹）grass carp belly

【鯁】kang² have a fishbone stuck in one's throat

鯁住（鯁着）have a fishbone stuck in one's throat
鯁落去（硬咽下去）swallow sth in a hard way
鯁頸 ①（魚骨鯁着咽喉）have a fishbone stuck in one's throat ②（事情不順利）do things without success
鯁嚫（鯁着）have a fishbone stuck in one's throat

惡鯁（難下嚥／很難對付）difficult to deal with

【鯊】saa¹ shark

鯊魚 shark

【鵝】ngo⁴ goose

鵝公喉（公鴨嗓）low and hoarse voice
鵝蛋形（橢圓形）oval shape

一隻天鵝 a goose; a swan
天鵝 goose; swan
日鵝夜鵝（嘮叨不停）nag day and night
企鵝 penguin
食燒鵝（吃烤鵝）eat roasted goose
黑天鵝 black swan
燒鵝（烤鵝）roasted goose

【鵡】mou⁵ parrot

鸚鵡 parrot

19 劃

【嚨】lung⁴ throat

喉嚨（嗓子）larynx; throat

【嚫】tsan¹ aspect marker of injury

冷嚫（受涼）catch cold; has caught a cold
扭嚫（扭到）sprained; wrenched
夾嚫（夾到）be nipped
拮嚫（扎到）be struck lightly
凍嚫（受涼）have a cold

哽嚫（噎到）choked
掂嚫（碰到）touched
辣嚫（辣傷）scalded
淥嚫（燙傷）burnt by hot liquid
焗嚫（中暑）have a sunstroke; heat exhaustion; heatstroke
逢嚫 ①（凡是／所有／一切）all; every ②（每逢／在任何場合／甚麼時候）on every occasion; when
揩嚫（受傷）be harmed; be hurt
啷嚫（動不動／動輒／容易／經常）at every move; at every turn; at the drop of a hat; at the slightest provocation; easily; frequenty; on every occasion
焫嚫（火燒傷）burn; scald
跌嚫（摔傷）get hurt in a fall
悶嚫（太煩悶了／太無聊了）it's so boring
搲嚫（劃傷）be scratched
飽唔死餓唔嚫（收入不超過所需）earn no more than what one needs
撞嚫 ①（撞着）be hurt by sth heavy ②（撞倒）knock down
撇嚫（撞傷）injure by bumping
濁嚫（嗆着／噎着）be choked
激嚫（被氣到了）be irritated
整嚫（弄傷）get hurt
嚇嚫（受驚）be frightened; be shocked; scare; suffer a mental shock
鎅嚫（劃破）be lacerated
鯁嚫（鯁着）have a fishbone stuck in one's throat

【嚦】lik⁹ sound

讕嚦／讕叻（自作聰明／逞能）act up; parade one's ability; show off one's ability; show off one's skill

【嚟】laai⁶（舐）lick

嚟乾淨（舐乾淨）lick clean
嚟野（碰上麻煩事）be cheated

【嚙】tsoey⁴（氣味）smell

一嘅嚙（一股味道）a trail of smell; an odour trail

【壞】waai⁶ bad

壞人 bad guy; bad man; bad people; bad person; baddie; baddy
壞到加零一（壞透了）extremely bad
壞咗（壞了）break down; out of order
壞較（升降機故障／電梯故障）the lift is out of order
壞賬（倒賬）bad debt

破壞 damage; decompose; destroy; do damage to; failure; wreck

損壞 damage

毀壞 damage; destroy; injure

腳頭壞 (運氣差) bring ill fortune

縱壞 (寵壞) spoil

【寵】 tsung² favour

寵兒 blue-eyed boy; darling; fair-haired boy; favourite; minion

寵物 pets

寵物店 pet shop

寵物美容 pet grooming

寵愛 cosset; dote on; make a pet of sb; receive favour from a superior; think the world of sb; think the world of sth

得寵 in favour

【寶】 bou² treasure

寶石 gem; precious stone
紅寶石 ruby
藍寶石 sapphire

寶物沉歸底 (好東西留到最後) the best things come at the end

寶藍色 royal blue

元寶 paper ingot

出盡八寶 (使盡法寶 / 使盡渾身解數) have exerted one's utmost skill

有寶 (了不起 / 有本領) amazing; extraordinary; far from common; proud and overweening; terrific

走寶 (錯失良機) miss a valuable chance; miss an opportunity

招財進寶 wish you a prosperous year

金銀珠寶 gold, silver, jewellery, and treasure

家有一老，如有一寶 an old-timer in the family is an advisor of rich experience

珠寶 jewellery

執到寶 (撿着便宜了) achieve a desirable aim

瑰寶 gem; treasure

懶有寶 (自以為很了不起) have a high opinion of oneself; play the big-shot

謂有寶 (自以為很了不起) as if one's far from common

【懲】 tsing⁴ punish

懲戒 discipline sb as a warning; punish sb to teach him a lesson; take disciplinary action against sb

懲罰 punish

【懷】 waai⁴ mind

懷孕 pregnant

懷疑 suspect
令人懷疑 arouse suspicion

懷舊 nostalgic

介懷 care about; get annoyed; mind; take offense

忘懷 forget

疚懷 (愧疚) ashamed

胸懷 mind

難以忘懷 hard to forget

【懶】 laan⁵ lazy

懶人 bedsteader; do-nothing; fainéant; gold brick; gentleman of leisure; lady of leisure; layabout; lazy person; lazybones; lounger; sleepyhead; value of resters

懶人多屎尿 (懶驢上磨屎尿多) a lazybone cooks up many lame excuses

懶佬 (懶漢) idler; lazy man; lazybone; sluggard
懶佬工夫 (不費勁的工作) the work that saves labour
懶佬椅 (躺椅) reclining chair
懶佬鞋 (帆船鞋 / 懶漢鞋) loafers

懶到出汁 (極懶) be extremely lazy

懶星 (懶惰鬼) lazy person

懶鬼 (懶人 / 懶蛋) lazy person

懶理 (不管 / 懶得管) won't bother to heed it

懶蛇 (懶人 / 懶骨頭 / 懶漢) idler; lazy man; lazybones; sluggard

懶惰 (懶洋洋 / 怠惰) lazy

懶散 (懶洋洋的) idle; languid; lethargic; listless
懶懶散散 (懶洋洋的) idle; languid; lethargic; listless

懶豬 (懶人) lazy person

懶蟲 (懶惰鬼) bedsteader; do-nothing; fainéant; gold brick; gentleman of leisure; lady of leisure; layabout; lazy guy; lazy person; lazybones; lounger; sleepyhead; value of resters
大懶蟲 (懶惰鬼) lazy person

大食懶 (懶骨頭) lazybone

好懶 very lazy

偷懶 loaf on the job; neglect one's work

躲懶 (偷懶) take a chance to avoid work

【懶】 laan⁵ pretend

懶叻 (臭美 / 自以為是) play the smart guy

懶威 (裝威風) cocky

懶幽默 (試着幽默) try to be funny

懶得戚 (傲慢 / 自大 / 高傲) arrogant

【懵】mung² (懵懵) foolish

懵仔 (傻子) fool

懵佬 (傻子) stupid man

懵閉閉 (不清醒 / 稀裏糊塗 / 蒙在鼓裏) foolish

懵盛盛 (不清醒 / 渾頭渾腦 / 稀裏糊塗) ignorant; muddle-headed

懵懂 (糊塗) foolish; muddled
　老懵懂 (老糊塗) muddle-headed old guy; dotard; old forgetful person

懵懵閉 (渾頭渾腦) ignorant; muddle-headed

大懵 (心不在焉) absent-minded person; blunder head; muddle-headed

扮懵 (裝傻) play the fool

面懵 (難為情) lose face

面懵懵 (傻瓜似的) look foolish

唔怕面懵 (臉皮厚) thick-skinned

乘機搏懵 (渾水摸魚) exploit an unusual situation by doing sth not normally permitted

發懵 (發呆) abstractedness; dumbfounded; in a daze; in a trance; spellbound; stare blankly; stunned; stupefied

博懵 ① (鑽空子) take advantage of a loophole ② (假裝不知) pretend not to be aware of; pretend that one does not know

詐傻扮懵 (裝傻充愣) act stupid; play the fool

博懵 (佔便宜) take advantage of one's inattention

裝傻扮懵 (裝瘋賣傻) play the fool

【攏】lung⁵ together

攏共 (總共) all told; altogether; in all

攏岸 (靠岸) moor to the shore

攏總 (攏共) add up; all told; altogether; in all; sum up

刮攏 ① (搜刮) reap huge profits ② (刮地皮) batten on people's properties

【攔】laai⁶ (落) leave behind

攔低咗野 (落下東西了) leave sth behind

攔尿 (尿褲子) wet the bed

攔屎 (拉一褲子屎) defecate involuntarily; faecal incontinence

【搦】lik⁹ hold

搦住 (握住) hold in the hand

搦起 (抬起) lift up

【攓】kin² turn

攓書 (翻書) leaf through a book

攓被 (揭被子) lift the quilt

【瀟】siu¹ sound of beating wind and rain

瀟湘 (窈窕 / 秀氣) slim; beautiful

【瀨】laai⁶ water rushing by

瀨尿 (尿褲子) urinate involuntarily; urinary incontinence
　瀨尿蝦 ① (皮皮蝦) mantis shrimp; yabbies ② (尿牀) bed-wetter

瀨屎 (大便失禁) defecate involuntarily

【爆】baau³ ① (爆炸) explode ② (爆炒) quick fry

爆人陰司 (揭人家老底兒) reveal the secrets of others

爆大鑊 (揭底兒) reveal a big secret

爆火 (生氣 / 發火 / 惱火) angry; be ablaze with anger; fire up; fit to be tied; flare up; get angry; get shirty; lose one's temper

爆出嚟 (揭出來) expose it

爆石 (拉屎) have a poo

爆冷 (出冷門) upset
　爆冷門 (出冷門) upset
　爆大冷 (大冷門) big upset

爆呔 ① (車胎爆裂) a tyre blows out; flat tyre ② (褲子爆裂) rip

爆夾 (盜竊一所房子) burglarise a house

爆谷 (爆米花) popcorn

爆肚 (現編) ad-lib; impromptu speech

爆格 (入屋偷竊) (English) burglary; break in

爆料 (洩露秘密) disclose a secret; have a scoop

爆粗 (粗言穢語衝口而出) swear in anger

爆棚 ① (滿滿當當) full house ② (擠爆) very crowded
　爆晒棚 ① (滿滿當當) full house ② (擠爆) very crowded

爆裂 (裂開) burst open

爆煲 ① (敗露) exposed ② (超過極限) go over the limit

爆滿 (滿座) full house

爆燈 (很高) very high

爆瘡 (爆痘痘) breakout in spots

爆響口 (走漏風聲) disclose a secret

爆竊 (偷盜 / 盜竊) burglary; pilferage; steal

火爆 (剛烈 / 暴躁 / 急躁) ① intense; sharp ② impetuous; lose one's temper

打爆 (打破) beat up; destroy

正爆 (超級性感) irresistibly sexy

眼火爆 (氣憤至極 / 怒火中燒) extremely angry to see; eyes blazing with anger; see red

睇見就眼火爆 (看見就火冒三丈) one bursts into a fury when one catches sight of sth/sb

蔥爆 deep-fried with spring onion

嗓爆 (認真應付) seriously make out

踢爆（揭穿／洩密／揭露某人的秘密）debunk; disclose a
secret; expose sb's secret

篤爆（拆穿／戳穿）betray a secret; debunk; let out a secret

嬲爆爆（怒沖沖／氣沖沖）be filled with anger; very angry

【獸】sau³ beast

獸醫 vet; veterinarian
獸醫中心 veterinary centre
睇獸醫（看獸醫）see a vet

鳥獸 birds and animals

【爇】jyt⁹（燙）burn; scald

爇手（燙手）① scald one's hand ② difficult to manage
好爇手（燙得很）it really scalds one's hand
爇嚫手（燙傷手）one's hand is burnt

【瓊】king⁴ ①（滴）drip ②（凝結）condense; coagulate; congeal; curdle

瓊住（凝結住）coagulate
瓊埋一嚿（凝成一塊了）clot
瓊乾（滴乾）drip dry

【疇】tsau⁴ scope

疇輩（同輩）people of the same generation

範疇 ambit; category; domain; realm; scope

【癡】tsi¹ crazy; foolish; idiotic; insane; senseless; silly; stupid

癡心 ① blind love; blind passion; infatuation ② silly wish
癡肥（過重）abnormally fat; obese
癡纏（纏綿）exceedingly sentimental

【矇】mung⁴ ①（不清楚）blurred ②（稀裏糊塗）muddle-headed

矇查查（稀裏糊塗）muddle-headed
矇眼仔（蠢人）stupid boy
眼矇矇（睡眼矇矓／睡眼惺忪）unable to see clearly

電話好矇（電話聽不清楚）the line is blurred

【礙】ngoi⁶ obstruct

礙事 ① hindrance; in the way; keep under sb's feet; obstacle; problem ② matter; of consequence; serious
礙眼 be an eyesore; offend the eye

冇礙（無礙）nothng is seriously wrong

妨礙 emcumber; hamper; handicap; hinder; impede; obstruct;
put a crimp in; put a crimp into; stand in the way

障礙 ① barrier; hurdle; obstacle; obstruction ② handicap;
malfunction

【禱】tou² pray

祈禱 pray

【穩】wan² firm; steady

穩打穩紮（穩紮穩打）play safe; take no risk
穩如鐵塔（穩如泰山）as firm as it is founded on the rock
穩陣（可靠／安全／穩定）reliable; safe; secure; stable
唔穩陣（不安全／靠不住）insecure
穩穩陣陣（穩定／穩固／安穩／安定）stable

十拿九穩 a sure thing for; almost certain; as sure as a gun; in
the bag; it's dollar to buttons; ninety per-cent sure; pretty
sure; ten to one; very sure of success

三六滾一滾，神仙都企唔穩（聞到狗肉香，神仙也跳牆）
when dog meat is cooked, even a god is attracted by the
fragrance and cannot stand firm

企穩（站穩）come to a stop; stand firm; take a firm stand

【簽】tsim¹ sign

簽字 affix one's signature to; attach one's signature to;
autograph; put a signature to; put down one's signature;
put one's name to; put one's signature to; set one's hand
to; set one's name to; sign; sign one's name to; signature
簽字儀式 signing ceremony

簽名 affix one's signature to; attach one's signature to;
autograph; put a signature to; put down one's signature;
put one's name to; put one's signature to; set one's
hand to; set one's name to; sign; sign one's name to;
signature
簽名留念 autograph to mark the occasion; sign one's
name as a memento
喺呢度簽名（在這裏簽名）sign here
幫我簽個名 could I have your autograph

簽證 visa
入境簽證 entry visa

一枝牙簽／一枝牙籤（一根牙簽／一根牙籤）a toothpick
牙簽／牙籤 toothpick

【簾】lim⁴ curtain

簾幕 curtain

百葉簾（百葉窗）shutter
竹簾 bamboo curtain; bamboo screen

浴簾 shower curtain
窗簾 curtain

【簿】bou⁶⁻² (本子) book

簿冊 books and files; lists
簿記 bookkeeping
   簿記員 accounting clerk; bookkeeper; clerk

一本相簿 (一本相冊) a photo album
一本電話簿 a telephone directory
支票簿 cheque book
打簿 (存折補登) update passbook
批簿 mark scripts
相簿 (相冊) photo album
記事簿 (記事本) note book
單行簿 (橫格本) lined pad
電話簿 telephone directory
數簿 (賬本) account book
練習簿 (練習本) exercise book

【繩】sing⁴ (繩子) rope

繩之以法 bring sb to justice; keep sb in line by
   punishments; prosecute according to the law; punish sb
   according to law; restrain sb by law
繩仔 (繩子) small cord; small string

一條繩 (一根繩子) a string
一朝俾蛇咬,三年怕草繩 (一朝被蛇咬,十年怕井繩)
   a burnt child dreads the fire; once bitten by a snake,
   one shies at a coiled rope for the next three years;
   once bitten, twice shy; the scalded dog fears
   cold water
搰繩 (扯繩子) pull the rope
繑繩 (繞繩子) wind a rope

【繳】giu² ① pay ② surrender

繳稅 pay taxes
繳款 payment
繳款日期 payment due date
繳費 payment

預繳 (預付) pay in advance

【繹】jik⁶ continuous

繹繹 (絡繹) continuous

絡繹 in an endless stream

【繫】hai⁶ tie

繫念 (掛念) have constantly on one's mind
繫掛 (關心 / 許多擔憂) be concerned about; many worries
繫獄 (入獄) be imprisoned; imprison

保持聯繫 maintain contact
聯繫 communication; connection; contact; link

【繭】gaan² cocoon

抽絲剝繭 trace a fox to its den

【羅】lo⁴⁻¹ bottom

羅柚 (屁股) bottom
   洗羅柚 (洗屁股) clean one's bottom
羅通掃北 (橫掃千軍) make a clean sweep of everything

歐羅 (歐元) (English) Euro

【臘】laap⁹ wax

臘味 (臘肉) wind-dried pork
   臘味飯 (臘肉飯) rice with wind-dried pork
臘青 (瀝青) asphalt
臘起 (捲起) beat sb
臘腸 (香腸) sausage
   一孖臘腸 (一對香腸 / 兩根香腸) a pair of sausages
臘鴨 cured duck
   掛臘鴨 (上吊自盡 / 吊死鬼) hang oneself; kill oneself
     by hanging

燒臘 (烤制肉食) barbecued meat
頭臘 (髮蠟) pomade

【膔】pok⁷ (泡) blister

豆腐膔 (豆腐泡) deep-fried bean curd
起膔 (長水皰) get blisters
夠膔 (有種 / 有膽量 / 夠勇敢 / 有勇氣) dare; have
   courage; have guts

【藕】ngau⁵ lotus root

藕斷絲連 lotus roots break, but the fibres still hold
   together

一節蓮藕 one section of lotus root
拋生藕 (灌迷湯) colquette with a man; flirt
煲老藕 (娶老女人) marry an aged woman
蓮藕 (藕) lotus root
賣生藕 (調情) flirt

【藝】ngai⁶ art

藝人 actor; artist; entertainer
藝名 professional name; stage name
藝術 art
    藝術中心 arts centre
藝術家 artist
藝壇 art circle

十八般武藝 be skilled in wielding the eighteen kinds of
    weapons – be skilled in various types of combat
才藝 talent and skill
冇細藝（沒事兒幹）at a loose end; have nothing to do
手工藝 handicraft
多才多藝 able to put one's hand to many things; gifted in
    many ways; have ability in many different ways; have
    much talent; versatile; with much talent and much artistry
技藝 artistry; skills
武藝 fighting skills
園藝 garden husbandry; gardening; horticulture

【藤】tang⁴ rattan

藤掅瓜，瓜掅藤（唇齒相依）get entangled with
    each other
藤篋（藤篋 / 藤箱子）rattan case
藤條 rattan stick

【藥】joek⁹ medicine

藥丸 pill; tablet
    一粒藥丸 a pill
藥水 liquid medicine; syrup
    藥水梘（藥皂 / 藥用肥皂）medicated soap; medicinal
        soap
    一樽藥水（一瓶藥水）a bottle of liquid medicine
    消毒藥水 antiseptic liquid
藥材鋪（中藥店）Chinese drugstore
藥房 drugstore; pharmacy
藥物 medicine
    常見藥物 common medicine
藥煲 ①（煎藥用的砂鍋）pot for decocting herbal medicine
    ②（久病之人）chronic invalid
藥膏 ointment
    一支藥膏（一管藥膏）a tube of ointment
藥劑 pharmacy
    藥劑師 pharmacist
藥樽（藥瓶）medicine bottle
藥餅（藥片）pill; tablet
藥罐 medicine tin

一隻藥（一種藥）a kind of medicine

一劑藥 a dose of medicine
山草藥（草藥）herbal medicine
止痛藥 painkiller
止嘔藥（止吐藥）antinausea drug
止瀉藥 anti-diarrhoea
火藥 gunpowder
生草藥（中草藥）Chinese herbal medicine
吞咗火藥（吃槍藥了）be hot with rage; fly into a fury
服藥 take the medicine
炸藥 explosive
毒藥 poison
胃藥 antacid
食咗火藥（吃槍藥了）be hot with rage; fly into a fury
食藥（吃藥 / 喝藥 / 服藥）take Chinese medicine
消化藥 digestant
烈性炸藥 high explosive
烈性毒藥 deadly poison
退燒藥 antipyretic
麻醉藥（麻醉劑）anaesthetic
執藥（抓藥）get Chinese herbs
湯藥（醫藥）healing drugs
搽藥（抹藥 / 塗藥）apply ointment to the affected area
煲藥（熬藥）decoct medicinal herbs
照單執藥（照方抓藥）follow instructions; follow the beaten track
飲藥（喝藥）drink Chinese medicine
嘔藥（吐藥）throw up medicine
膏藥 medicated plaster; patch; plaster
賠湯藥（賠醫藥費）pay sb the medical expenses
贈醫施藥 give free consultation and free medicine
驅蟲藥（殺蟲劑）insect repellent

【蕹】ung³ water spinach

蕹菜（空心菜）water spinach

【蟹】haai⁵（螃蟹）crab

蟹民（投資失利的股民）people who lost money in the
    stock market
蟹肉 crab meat
蟹杜（蟹鉗）nippers of a crab; pincers of a crab
蟹粉（蟹黃）crab roe
蟹膏（蟹黃）crab roe

一蟹不如一蟹（一個不如一個）become worse and worse;
    get increasingly worse; go downhill; go from bad to
    worse; make bad trouble worse; on the decline; steadily
    deteriorate; take a bad turn; take a turn for the worse;
    worse and worse
大石責死蟹（屈服於壓力強權下）be crushed by force;
    pressure sb into doing sth

老虎蟹 (不管如何) no matter what

扮晒蟹 (充大頭鬼 / 裝傻) pretend; act dumb

扮蟹 ① (不反抗被五花大綁) allow oneself to be arrested without offering any resistance; allow oneself to be seized without putting up a fight; resign oneself to being held as a prisoner; submit to arrest with folded arms ② (自大) self-important

河蟹 river crab

青蟹 (十元紙幣) ten-dollar note

倒瀉籮蟹 (狼狽不堪 / 手忙腳亂) in a muddle; messy; troublesome

軟腳蟹 (房事太多以至身體衰弱) weak due to too much sex

螃蟹 mud crab

薑蔥焗蟹 baked crab with ginger and spring onion

【蟶】 tsing¹ razor clam

蟶子 razor clam

【蟲】 kam⁴ spider

蟲螞 (蜘蛛) spider

蟲螞絲網 (蜘蛛網) spider web

蟲蟑 (蟾蜍 / 癩蛤蟆) toad

【蟻】 ngai⁵ (螞蟻) ant

蟻多摟死象 (弱者人多而齊心，可以戰勝強者 / 團結就是力量) a large number of weak individuals can overwhelm one very strong individual; union is strength; unity is strength

蟻竇 (螞蟻窩 / 蟻穴) ant nest

一身蟻 (一身臊 / 麻煩纏身) get into trouble; in a great deal of trouble; in a troublesome situation

周身蟻 (一身麻煩) make trouble

惹蟻 (招螞蟻) attract ants

踩死蟻 (慢得像蝸牛) snail-alow; walk at a snail's pace

蠱蟻 (滅蟻) eradicate the ants

【蠅】 jing¹ fly

蠅頭小利 small profit

冇頭烏蠅 (無頭蒼蠅 / 亂碰亂闖) act helter-skelter

打烏蠅 ① (拍蒼蠅) flap a fly; swat a fly ② (拘捕低級官員) arrest the low-ranking officials

拍烏蠅 ① (拍蒼蠅) flap a fly; swat a fly ② (生意冷淡) business is bad; have a dull market; have no business

拍晒烏蠅 (生意很差) have absolutely no business

盲頭烏蠅 (無頭蒼蠅) a bull in a china shop; act in a chaotic manner

烏蠅 (蒼蠅) fly

【證】 dzing³ certificate

證人 witness

證供 (證據) evidence; proof; testimony; witness

證明 proof

　難以證明 hard to prove

證卷 (證券) securities

證書 certificate

證據 evidence; proof

一張身份證 an identity card

入境簽證 entry visa

工作簽證 working visa

死亡證 (死亡證明) death certificate

身份證 identity card

保安人員許可證 security personnel permit

保證 guarantee

指證 prosecute

旁證 circumstantial evidence; collateral evidence; side witness

球證 (裁判 / 裁判員) judge; referee; umpire

帶身份證 bring one's identity card

頂證 (作證 / 指證 / 對證 / 成為證人 / 提供證據) become a witness; produce evidence

智能身份證 smart identity card

會員證 (會員卡) membership card

簽證 visa

【譖】 tsam³ slander

譖氣 (磨叼 / 囉嗦) have the gift of the gab; loquacious; talkative

【識】 sik⁷ ① (認識) know ② (會) be able to

識人 (交朋友 / 認識人) make friends

識字 (認識字兒) literate

識行 (會走路) learn to walk

識穿 (洞悉 / 看穿 / 識破) reveal; see through

　識穿佢槓嘢 (看穿他的詭計) know his tricks

識食 (很會吃) eat smart; gourmandise; know how to enjoy food

　識飲識食 (會吃會喝) enjoy life to the full; have a good palate for food; know how to enjoy food and drink

識唔識 (知不知道) do you know

識貨 (辨別好壞 / 辨別真偽 / 辨識能力) have a good eye for sth; have good taste; know what is good

識做 (知道怎樣做最好) know what is best to do

識唔識做 (你知不知道怎樣做是最好的) do you know what is best to do

識得 ① (認得 / 認識 / 曉得 / 懂得) know ② (能夠 / 可以) be able to

識得佢（認識他）know him
識路（認識路）know one's way
識飲（會喝）know how to drink smartly
識嘢（懂事）intelligent
識撈（會混）know what is best to do
識趣 know what is best to do
識 do（會處理）know what is best to do

不打不相識 build up friendship after an exchange of blows
見識 gain experience
知識 knowledge
唔打唔相識（不打不相識）no discord, no concord; no fight, no acquaintance
唔識 ①（不認識）don't know sb ②（不會／不懂得／不曉得）be unable to; do not know
常識 common sense
熟識 familiar with

【譚】taam⁴ ① talk ② surname
譚公誕 Birthday of Tam Kung

【譜】pou² （歌譜）score
譜子 musical score

五線譜 musical score using the staff notation; staff
冇譜（不像話／亂來）break the routine; incoherent
離晒大譜（太過離譜）go too far; ridiculous
離晒譜（太離譜）go too far; ridiculous
離譜（不像話）a bit too much; far away from what is acceptable; far away from what is normal; far off the beam; go too far; outrageous; over the top; ridiculous; unreasonable

【贈】dzang⁶ give a present
贈品 freebie
贈興（幸災樂禍）take pleasure in other people's misfortune
贈醫施藥 give free consultation and free medicine

回贈 rebate
捐贈 contribute; donate; offer

【贊】dzaan³ praise
贊同 agree with; approve of; be all for; consent to; countenance; endorse; go along with
贊成 accede; agree on; agree to; agree with; all for; approve of; assent; be reconciled to; comply; concur; consent to; endorse; favour; give sth a nod; go all the way with sb; go along with sb; hold with; in agreement with; in favour of; see eye to eye with sb; subscribe to
贊美 exalt; extol; glorify; praise
贊助 donate money; patronise; sponsor; support

【蹺】hiu¹ coincidental
蹺口（拗口）difficult to pronounce
蹺口杉手（難處理）hard to deal with
蹺妙（巧妙）have a knack for sth
蹺蹊（蹊蹺）trick
　有蹺蹊（有蹊蹺）there are some tricks

湊蹺（一致／巧合／湊巧）coincidence

【辭】tsi⁴ word
辭去 resign
辭行 say goodbye to sb before setting out on a jurney; take one's leave
辭退（解僱）discharge; dismiss; give sb the air; turn away
辭職 resign from a position

利口便辭（伶牙俐齒）have a ready tongue
咎無可辭（難辭其咎）cannot evade responsibility; the responsibility cannot be shirked

【邊】bin¹ ① side ② （哪）which
邊年（哪一年）which year
邊位（哪一位）who
　你係邊位（你是哪位）who's calling; who's it; who's on the phone; who's that; who's this
邊便（哪邊）where; which side
邊度（哪兒／哪裏）where
　邊度係呢（不用客氣／哪裏哪裏）don't mention it
　去邊度（去哪兒／去哪裏）where are you going; where to
　喺邊度（在哪兒／在哪裏）where is it
邊個 ①（哪個）which ②（誰）who
　邊個月（哪個月）which month
邊個呀（是誰呀）who is it
唔知邊個打邊個（不知道哪個是哪個）can make out which ones match which ones
邊啲（哪些）which
邊處（哪裏／哪兒／何處）where
邊邊（哪一邊）which side

刀字邊（立刀旁）the "knife"（刀）radical
上邊 above
下邊 below; under
口字邊（口字旁）the "mouth"（口）radical

女字邊（女字旁）the "woman"（女）radical
反文邊（反文旁）the "rap"（攵）radical
日字邊（日字旁）the "sun"（日）radical
月字邊（月字旁）the "moon"（月）radical
木字邊（木字旁）the "tree"（木）radical
火字邊（火字旁）the "fire"（火）radical
犬字邊（犬文邊）the "dog"（犬）radical
王字邊（王字旁）the "king"（王）radical
出邊（外面／外邊）outside
北邊 ① north ② northern part
右邊 on the right; right-hand side; right side
外邊 outside
玉字邊（玉字旁）the "jade"（玉）radical
企人邊（單人旁／人字旁）the "person"（人）radical
企埋一邊（站在一旁）stand back
目字邊（目字旁）the "eye"（目）radical
石字邊（石字旁）the "stone"（石）radical
禾字邊（禾字旁）the "rice straw"（禾）radical
耳仔邊（雙耳旁）the "ear"（耳）radical
佛法無邊 the powers of the Buddha are unlimited
足字邊（足字旁）the "leg"（足）radical
身邊 at one's side; with one
車字邊（車字旁）the "carriage"（車）radical
言字邊（言字旁）the "speech"（言）radical
兩邊 both directions; both parties; both places; both sides
岸邊 dockside; quayside
東邊 east side
河邊 river back
狗爪邊（反犬旁／犬猶兒）the "dog"（犬）radical
斧頭邊（雙耳旁）the "two ears"（阝）radical
金字邊（金字旁）the "metal"（金）radical
門字邊（門字框）the "door"（門）radical
前邊（前面）front side; in front
南邊 south
後邊（後面）at the back; back
捌吓鼓邊（旁敲側擊）sound sb out on a question
穿心邊（豎心兒／豎心旁）the "heart"（心）radical
頁邊 margin
飛邊（去邊兒）remove the edges
食字邊（食字旁）the "food"（食）radical
剔土邊（剔土旁／提土旁）the "earth"（土）radical
剔手邊（剔手旁／提手旁）the "hand"（手）radical
旁邊 beside; by the side of
海邊 seashore; seaside
馬字邊（馬字旁）the "horse"（馬）radical
側邊（旁邊的）beside; by the side of
搊車邊（沾別人的光／托賴關照）benefit from association with sb or sth
蛋家婆打仔——睇你走去邊（大缸擲骰子——沒跑兒／無路

可逃）put sb at the dead end
喉口唇邊（話在舌尖上）have sth at the tip of one's tongue
街邊（路旁／路邊）roadside
搣開兩邊（掰開兩半）pull apart into halves with one's hands
路邊 roadside
敲鼓邊（敲邊鼓／從旁幫腔）sound sb out on a question
豎心邊（豎心兒／豎心旁）the "heart"（心）radical
擘開兩邊（扯開兩半）be torn into halves
擺街邊（擺地攤／擺攤）set up a stall in the street
禮衣邊（示字旁／示補兒）the "rite"（示）radical
繑絲邊（亂絞絲兒／絞絲旁）the "silk"（糸）radical

【邋】laat⁸ dirty
邋遢貓（泥猴兒）dirty person

【鏈】lin⁶⁻² （鏈子）chain
鏈冚（鏈罩）chain cover; chain guard

上鏈（上發條）wind
拉拉鏈 zip up
拉鏈 ① zip ② zipper
金鏈（金項鏈）gold necklace
錶鏈（錶帶）watch band
頸鏈（項鏈）necklace
鎖鏈（鐵鏈）iron chain
鐵鏈（鐵鏈）iron chain

【鏟】tsaan² ①（鏟）shovel ②（刮）scrape
鏟咗（刮掉）scrape off
鏟除（清除／消除／剷除）clear off; eliminate; uproot
鏟雪車（掃雪車）snowplough

垃圾鏟（簸箕／畚箕）garbage shovel
揸鑊鏟（拿鍋鏟／當廚師）be a cook
煙鏟（煙鬼）cigarette addict; heavy smoker
鑊鏟（鍋鏟／鏟子）scoop; shovel; spatula

【鏡】geng³（鏡子）mirror
鏡片 lens
鏡架（眼鏡框／鏡框）spectacles frame
鏡頭 ① camera lens; lens ② scene; shot

一個鏡（一面鏡子）a mirror
一副眼鏡 a pair of spectacles
一塊鏡（一面鏡子）a mirror
上鏡 photogenic
太陽眼鏡 sunglasses
太陽鏡 sunglasses
有色眼鏡（偏見）prejudice

拆穿西洋鏡 (拆穿騙局) expose the fraud

盲公鏡 (太陽眼鏡 / 墨鏡) sunglasses

哈哈鏡 distorting mirror; magic mirror

美人照鏡 (吃光所有食物) eat up all the food on the dish

省鏡 (上鏡 / 漂亮) beautiful; have a good-looking face

唔信命都信吓塊鏡 (不信命，也得信信鏡子) it is wise to know oneself

唔信鏡 (不相信真實) refuse to believe what is real

神鏡 (變焦鏡頭) zoom lens

除眼鏡 (摘下眼鏡) take off one's glasses

眼鏡 ① (眼鏡) eyeglasses; glasses; spectacles ② (胸罩 / 胸圍) bra

跌眼鏡 (走了眼 / 判斷錯誤 / 看走眼 / 出乎意料) make a wrong guess; make an error in judgement; come as a surprise as wrong guess or error in judgement is made

開鏡 (開拍) start shooting a movie

搶鏡 photogenic; steal the show

靚爆鏡 (非常有吸引力) very attractive

戴眼鏡 ① (戴眼鏡) wear glasses ② (戴胸罩) wear a bra

隱形眼鏡 contact lens

攞鏡 (拍照) take a snap; take photographs

【關】 gwaan¹ concern

關人 (懶得理) it has nothing to do with me; none of one's business; not bother with matters that do not concern one

關刀 (大刀) broadsword

舞關刀 (耍大刀) wave a broadsword

關公 Lord Kwan

關公細佬——亦得 (翼德) (後腦勺留鬍子——隨便) as you like

關公誕 Birthday of Lord Kwan

關心 care about

關斗 (斤斗 / 筋斗) somersault

打關斗 (前身翻) somersault; take a somersault

關乎 (涉及) bear upon; relate to

關你乜事 (與你無關) mind your own business

關於 in relation to

關注 attention

受到關注 receive attention

關係 connection; relationship; relevance

關係密切 close connections

關帝誕 Birthday of Kwan Tai

關照 look after

關節炎 arthritis

關頭 ① critical juncture ② critical moment

公關 public relations

交關 (夠戲 / 厲害 / 程度深) extremely; exceedingly

年關 end of the year

把關 ① look out ② gate-keeping

事關 after; as; as a result of; at; because; because of; by; by dint of; by reason of; by right of; by virtue of; due to; failing; for; from; in; in consequence of; in consideration of; in default of; in right of; in that; in the absence of; in view of; in virtue of; inasmuch as; of; on; on account of; on the ground of; on the ground that; on the score of; out of; over; owing to; seeing that; since; thanks to; that; through; wanting; what with; with

度過難關 overcome the crisis

桄關 (門閂) latch

海關 custom

蒙混過關 get by under false pretences

戰勝難關 clear away all difficulties

難關 crisis; difficulty

【離】 lei⁴ away from

離任 leave office; leave one's post; resign from one's office; retire from one's office

離行離剌 (毫不相關 / 東倒西歪) wide of the mark

離家 leave home

離校 leave school

離婚 divorce

離婚證明 certificate of divorce

合法離婚 be legally divorced

協議離婚 (經雙方同意下離婚) divorce by consent

離開 depart from; deviate from; keep away from; leave; separate from

離開好遠 be far away; be far off

離間 alienate; drive a wedge between; drive a wedge into; set one party against another; sow discord; turn sb against another

挑撥離間 alienate; drive a wedge between; drive a wedge into; set one party against another; sow discord; turn sb against another

離鄉別井 (背井離鄉) away from one's home-town

離境 (出境) leave a country; leave a place

離題 deviate from the main theme; digress; digress from one's topic; drift away from the subject

離譜 (不像話) a bit too much; far away from what is acceptable; far away from what is normal; far off the beam; go too far; outrageous; over the top; ridiculous; unreasonable

離晒大譜 (太過離譜) go too far; ridiculous

離晒譜 (太離譜) go too far; ridiculous

恨死隔離 (羨煞旁人) become the envy of others; object of great envy

逃離 flee for one's life; run for one's life

偏離 deflect; departure; diverge; deviate; skew

脫離 ①（擺脫／割捨）be divorced from; breakaway; break away from; separate oneself from ②（遠離）away from; not within; out of

距離 distance

遠距離 long distance

【難】naan⁴ difficult

難上難（難上加難）all the more difficult

難分難解（難捨難分）be locked together

難以 difficult to; hard to
　難以立足 difficult to keep a foothold
　難以置信 hard to believe

難打（不好打）not easy to beat

難忘 unforgettable
　令人難忘 unforgettable

難受 feel unhappy

難怪 no wonder

難保 there is no guarantee

難度 degree of difficulty
　冇難度（沒有難度）there is no difficulty

難洗（不好洗）difficult to wash

難為情（尷尬）embarrassed
　感到難為情（不好意思／感到尷尬）feel embarrassed

難食（不好吃／難吃）unpalatable; hard to eat

難料（困境）difficult situation

難做（艱鉅的工作／難以管理）a tough job to do; hard to manage

難得（很少／不常）seldom

難頂（難以忍受）intolerable

難乾（不好乾）hard to dry in the sun

難堪（尷尬）embarrassed
　令人難堪（處境尷尬）put sb in an awkward position

難發（難發財）hard to get rich

難睇（難看）ugly; unsightly

難搞（難以處理）hard to handle

難過 ① have a hard time ② feel sorry
　感到難過 feel sorry for

難賣（不好賣）hard to sell

難學（不好學）hard to learn

難整（難做）hard to make; hard to manage

難題 difficult problem
　解決難題 solve a difficult problem

難關 crisis; difficulty
　度過難關 overcome the crisis
　戰勝難關 clear away all difficulties

難聽 ① unpleasant to hear ② offensive ③ scandalous

刁難 create difficulties; deliberately put obstacles in sb's way; make things difficult

左右做人難（左右為難）be stuck between a rock and a hard place; between the devil and the deep blue sea; between two fires; get into a fix; in a bind; in a box; in a dilemma; in a quandary about; in an awkward predicament; in the middle; on the horns of a dilemma; stand at a nonplus; torn between

困難 ① difficulty; hard ② financial difficulties; straitened circumstances

所難 difficult for sb

勉為其難 agree to do what one knows is beyond one's ability; agree to do what one knows is beyond one's power; be forced to do a difficult thing; contrive with difficulty; do the best one can in a difficult situation; make the best of a bad job; manage to do what is beyond one's power; undertake to do a difficult job as best one can

故意刁難 deliberately place obstacles

相見好，同住難（相處容易，同住困難）it's nice to see each other from time to time, but to live together is difficult; familiarity breeds contempt

強人所難 compel sb to do sth against their will; constrain sb to do things that are beyond a person's power; force some work on a person who is not equal to it; force sb to do sth against their will; force sth down sb's throat; impose a difficult task on sb; impose upon a person a task that they are incapable of doing; saddle sb with a difficult task; try and force people into doing things they don't want to; try to make sb do what is against their will; try to make sb do what is beyond their power; try to make sb do what they are unable to

萬事起頭難（萬事開頭難）it is difficult to begin a new business; all things are difficult before they are easy

講就易，做就難（知之非難，行之不易）easier said than done

【難】naan⁶ ① disaster ② blame

難友（難兄難弟）fellow sufferer

難民 refugee
　遣返難民 repatriate refugees

大災難 holocaust

大難（死）death

甩難（擺脫麻煩）got out of trouble

多災多難 always dogged by misfortunes; be dogged by bad luck; be dogged with misfortunes and mishaps; be plagued by frequent ills; calamitous; come upon a series of misfortunes; ill-starred; suffer a chapter of accidents

災難 calamity; disaster

走難（逃難）flee from a calamity; flee from disaster; seek refuge from calamities

幸免於難 a close shave; a narrow shave; a narrow squeak; a near squeak; escape by the skin of one's teeth; escape death by a hair's breadth; escape death by sheer luck

逃難 flee from a calamity; seek refuge from calamities

患難 adversity; trials and tribulations; troubles

遇難 ① die in an accident; get killed in an accident ② be murdered

【霧】mou⁶ ① dew ② fog

霧水（露水）dew

一頭霧水（不摸頭／摸不着頭腦）be confused; be puzzled; become lost; cannot understand; can't make the head or tail of sth; in bewilderment; in confusion

大霧 foggy

好大霧（霧很大）very foggy

定型噴霧（髮膠）hair spray

唔係猛龍唔過江，唔係壽蛇唔打霧（不是猛龍不過江，不是壽蛇不打霧）he who dares to come is surely not a coward

落霧（下霧／起霧）fog has fallen

【韻】wan⁵ rhyme

韻律 rhyme

韻律泳（花樣游泳）synchronised swimming

韻律操（花樣體操）rhythmic gymnastics

【願】jyn⁶ wish

願望 aspiration; desire; wish

願意 willing

自願 voluntary; willing

但願 I wish; if only

志願 ① aspiration; ideal; wish ② do sth of one's own free will; volunteer; voluntarily

兩相情願（兩人都願意）both are willing

祝願 wish

純屬自願 entirely voluntary

得償所願（如願以償／達到目的）attain one's end; obtain ones heart's desire

情願（寧願／更樂於）prefer; rather; would rather

許願 make a wish

寧願 prefer; would rather

誓神劈願（矢口發誓）swear solemn oath; take an oath and call God to witness

誓願（起誓／發誓）take an oath

請願 petition

【類】loey⁶ type

類似 ① kind of; sort of ② similar

類似事件 similar incidents

互相類似 similar to each other

類別 category

不同類別 different categories

類型 category; sort; type

人類 mankind

分門別類 arrange under categories; be arranged into sorts; be divided into classes and divisions; classify; classify according to subjects; divided into different classes; put into different categories; sort out into categories

分類 classify; ledger; sort; sorting; taxonomy

肉類 meat

貝類 shellfish

諸如此類 sth like that

【餸】sung³ ① (菜) groceries ② dish

餸罩（飯罩／菜罩）dish cover

餸腳（剩菜）leftovers

一味餸（一道菜）a dish of food

一個餸（一道菜）a dish of food

加餸（加菜）add more dishes

挾餸（挾菜）take food

剩餸（剩菜／剩菜剩飯）leftovers

買餸（買菜／點菜）buy groceries; buy meat and vegetables for meal

嗌餸（點菜）order dishes; order food

飯餸（飯菜）dishes of food

隔夜餸（剩菜）leftovers

熟餸（熟食）cooked food

整餸（做菜）prepare the dishes

點餸（點菜）order dishes; order food

鹹餸（鹹味菜）briny dishes

【騙】pin³ cheat

騙子 blackleg; blagger; charlatan; cheater; con artist; conman; crook; double crosser; faker; fiddler; flimflammer; humbug; hustler; imposter; phony; swindler; trickster

騙局 fraud; hoax; put-up job; shell game; swindle

騙取 cheat sb out of sth; defraud; gain sth by fraud; swindle

騙術（欺騙性的伎倆／騙局／狡計）deceitful trick; hoax; ruse

呃呃騙騙（坑蒙拐騙／招搖撞騙）deceive; cheat

拐騙 ① swindle ② abduct

招搖撞騙 put on a good bluff

哄騙 bamboozle; blandish; cajole; coax; humbug; wheedle

偷呃拐騙 (偷訛拐騙) steal, cheat, kidnap, and swindle

棍騙 (哄騙) bamboozle; blandish; cajole; coax; humbug; wheedle

欺騙 bamboozle; be done in by; beguile; cajoke; cheat; chicanery; come around; come round; come over sb; cozen; cross sb up; deceit; deceive; deception; defraud; delude; diddle; do sb down; do the dirty on sb; draw the wool over sb's eyes; dupe; fool; get over sb; give a flap with a foxtail; gum; have sb on; have sb over sth; hocus-pocus; hoodwink; impose on sb; jiggery-pockery; lead sb up the garden path; make a fool of; play a trick on sb; play sb false; play the old soldier over sb; play upon; pluck; practise on sb; pull a fast one over; pull the wool over sb's eyes; put it across on sb; put on sb; put upon sb; rope along sb; see sb coming; sell sb down the river; set one's cap; string along sb; swindle; take advantage of; take in; take sb for a ride; trick; throw dust in the eyes of; throw mud into the eyes of; throw sb a curve; wheedle

蒙騙 cheat; deceive; hoodwink

瞞騙 cheat; deceive

【鬎】 laat⁸ favus

鬎鬁 (頭癬) favus of the scalp

鬎鬁頭擔遮——無法 (髮) 無天 (和尚打傘——無法 (髮) 無天) lawless and godless

鬎鬁頭——難剃 (難題) (凍豆腐——難辦) difficult to manage; hard to deal with; tough

有頭髮邊個想做鬎鬁 (無能為力) can't do anything about sth

【鬍】 wu⁴ (鬍子) bread

鬍鬚 (鬍子) bread

鬍鬚佬 (大鬍子) a man with a beard

鬍鬚勒特 (鬍子拉碴) heavy-bearded

捋鬍鬚 (捋鬍子) stroke one's beard

【鯨】 king³ whale

鯨魚 whale

【鯪】 ling⁴ dace

鯪魚 dace

鯪魚骨炒飯——唔食餓死，食又哽死 (武大郎服毒——吃也死,不吃也死) just like Wu Dalang taking poison – he will die anyway

鯪魚球 (鯪魚肉丸) minced dace ball

【鰈】 mang³ rabbit fish

泥鰈 (褐藍子魚) rabbit fish

釣泥鰈 (併車) taxi drivers picking up passengers going to the same destination and charge them each a fare

【鵬】 paang⁴ roc

鵬程萬里 great future

老鵬 (死黨 / 密友) buddy; very close friend

【麒】 kei⁴ unicorn

麒麟 unicorn

麒麟臂 (粗手臂) thick arm

火麒麟——週身癮 (各種上癮) a slave to many vices; the person who is addicted to all kinds of lusts

【麗】 lai⁴ beautiful

麗人 beauty

秀麗 beautiful; elegant; fine; graceful; handsome; pretty

佳麗 ① beautiful; good ② beautiful woman; beauty

美麗 beautiful

華麗 gorgeous; magnificent; resplendent

艷麗 bright-coloured and beautiful; captivating; charming; gorgeous; magnificent; radiantly beautiful

【麴】 kuk⁷ yeast for brewing wine

紅麴 red yeast

20 劃

【勸】 hyn³ mediate; persuade

勸交 (勸架) mediate a quarrel; mediate between two quarrelling parties; try to patch up a quarrel; try to stop people from fighting each other

勸告 admonish; advise; counsel; exhort; remonstrate; urge

勸阻 advise against; advise sb not to; discourage sb from; dissuade sb from doing sth; talk sb out of; warn sb against

【嚴】 jim⁴ serious

嚴父 ① stern father ② my father

嚴重 serious

嚴師 severe teacher; stern teacher; strict teacher

嚴寒 severe cold

民族尊嚴 national dignity

坦白從寬，抗拒從嚴 anyone who comes clean gets treated with leniency; anyone who holds back the truth gets treated harshly; leniency to confessor, but severity to resisters; leniency to those who confess and severity to those who resist

莊嚴（凝重／端莊）dignified; solemn; stately

【巉】tsaam⁴ rugged

岩岩巉巉（凹凸不平／高低不平）full of bumps and holes; rugged; uneven

岩巉（凹凸不平／高低不平）full of bumps and holes; rugged; uneven

【瀾】laan⁴ waves

瀾漫（滿溢）overflowing

推波助瀾（興風作浪／添油加醋）make waves; pour oil on the flames

【爐】lou⁴（爐子）burner; cooker; fireplace; hearth; oven; stove

爐火純青 attain perfection; master one's skills to perfection; reach high perfection; the stove fire is pure green — perfection in one's studies

爐灶 stove

另起爐灶 a new organisation set up to compete with an exisiting one; make a fresh start; start all over again

火水爐（煤油爐）kerosene stove

火爐 fire place

出爐 come out newly

打邊爐（吃火鍋／涮鍋子）have hot-pot

多士爐（烤麵包機）toaster

香爐 incense burner

烤爐 brazier; grill; oven; roaster

焗爐（烘箱／烤箱）oven

焚化爐 cremator; destructor; garbage furnace; incinerator; refuse burner; refuse incinerator

煮食爐（灶具）cooking stove

微波爐 microwave oven

新鮮出爐 fresh from the oven

電焗爐（電烤箱）electric oven

暖爐 heater

煤氣爐 gas stove

熱水爐（熱水器）water heater

霸爐（佔爐子）grab a stove

gas 爐（煤氣爐）gas oven

【犠】hei¹ sacrifice

犧牲 sacrifice

自我犧牲 self-sacrifice

【獻】hin³ offer

獻世（丟人現眼／現世）be disgraced; bring shame on oneself; lose face; make a fool of oneself; make a spectacle of oneself

獻花 present flowers

獻醜不如藏拙 it is wiser to conceal one's stupidity than it is to show oneself up

貢獻 contribution

【瓏】lung⁴ dragon-shaped jade

眼眉毛雕通瓏（十分機警）sharp-witted; up to snuff

【癢】joeng⁵ itch

癢癢（發癢的）itchy

痕癢（癢）itch

搔癢 scratch the itch; scratch the itching place

【癍】mak⁹（痣）birthmark; mole

癍屎（痣）freckle

大粒癍（大痦子）person with a big mole

壽癍（壽斑）senile plagues

【瞓】lai⁶（怒視）stare in anger

眼瞓瞓（盯着某人／敵視某人）keep staring at sth; look sideways at sb in order to stop him from doing sth

【礦】kwong³ mineral

礦泉水 mineral water

礦物 mineral

【竇】dau³（窩）den; nest

竇口（安樂窩／巢穴）hang out

一竇（一窩）a brood of; a litter of

冚竇（停業／倒閉）close down

老竇（父親）father

狗竇 ①（狗窩）doghouse; kennel ②（凌亂的家）untidy home

被竇（被窩）folded quilt

高竇 (自高自大 / 看不起人 / 架子大 / 清高 / 瞧不起人)
    as proud as a peacock; proud and look down on others;
    snobbish

雀仔竇 (鳥窩 / 鳥巢) birds-nest

蛇竇 (藏身之地 / 隱藏處) hiding place

疑竇 cause of suspicion

踢竇 ① (襲擊了一處) raid a premises ② (捉姦) act
    adultery in the act

龍床唔似狗竇 (金窩銀窩不如自己的狗窩) there is no place
    sweeter than home

蟻竇 (螞蟻窩 / 蟻穴) ant nest

【競】 ging⁶ compete
競爭 competition

【籃】 laam⁴ (籃子) basket
籃板 backboard

籃球 basketball
    籃球場 basketball court
    打籃球 play basketball

竹籃 bamboo basket

射籃 (投籃) shoot

【籌】 tsau⁴⁻² chips
籌款 fund raising

籌碼 chip; counter

籌辦 make arrangements; make preparations; on the anvil;
    plan; prepare; upon the anvil

派籌 (發號兒) distribute quota tags

紅籌 (紅籌股) red chips

執籌 (抽籤) by lot; draw lots

統籌 plan as a whole

輪籌 (排號兒) register

藍籌 (藍籌股) blue chips

攞籌 (拿號兒) take a number

【籍】 dzik⁹ books
籍貫 one's native place

典籍 ancient books and records

【糯】 no⁶ glutinous rice
糯米 glutinous rice
    糯米糍 glutinous rice dumpling
    糯米雞 glutinous rice with chicken wrapped with
        lotus leaf

【辮】 bin⁶ (辮子) plait
辮髮 (編頭髮) plaited hair

留辮 (留辮子) wear plaits

紮辮 (編辮子) braid one's hair; plait one's hair

眼眉毛長過辮 (非常懶惰) not to stir a finger; very lazy

擯辮 (梳辮子) braid one's hair

【繼】 gai³ ① continue; follow; succeed ② afterwards; then
繼而 afterwards then

繼承 inherit

繼續 continue

承繼 ① be adopted as heir to one's uncle ② adopt one's
    brother's child

【罌】 aang¹ (瓦罐兒) earthen jar
罌粟 opium poppy

一個罌 (一個瓦罐) an earthen jar

油罌 (油罐兒) oil jar

酒罌 (酒罐兒) wine jar

錢罌 (錢盒子 / 錢罐子) cash box; money box; saving box

糖果罌 (糖果罐兒) candy jar

糖罌 (糖罐兒) sugar vase

豬仔錢罌 (小豬存錢罐) piggy bank

鹽罌 (鹽罐兒) salt jar

【耀】 jiu⁶ luminous
耀光 (閃閃發光) sparkle; sparkling

耀目 dazzle

耀眼 (刺眼 / 眩目) dazzling

炳耀 (顯示光芒 / 照耀) bright and luminous

榮耀 glory; honour; splendour

誇耀 boast of; brag about; flaunt; show off

【艦】 laam⁶ warship
艦隊 fleet
    一隻戰艦 (一艘軍艦) a warship

戰艦 (軍艦) warship

【蘑】 mo⁴ mushroom
蘑菇 button mushroom

【蘆】 lou⁴ reed
蘆筍 asparagus

【孽】jip⁹ evil
孽種 son of a concubine

冤孽 evil connection

【蘇】sou¹ revive
蘇打 (English) soda
　　蘇打粉 (發酵粉 / 發粉) baking soda
蘇州屎 (別人留下的麻煩事) the troubles left behind
蘇州過後冇艇搭 (過了這村就沒這店 / 機不可失，失
　　不再來) an opportunity missed is an opportunity lost;
　　opportunities never come twice; the opportunity once
　　missed will never come back
蘇蝦 (小孩) baby
　　蘇蝦女 (小丫頭) baby girl
　　蘇蝦仔 (男嬰) baby boy

牙擦蘇 (自負的人) boastful person
哨牙蘇 (齙牙) person with protruding teeth
插蘇 (插座 / 插銷 / 插頭) plug; socket
萬能蘇 (三孔插座 / 三通 / 萬能插) universal plug
轉頭插蘇 (轉換插頭 / 適配器) adapter

【蘋】ping⁴ apple
蘋果 apple
　　蘋果汁 apple juice
　　蘋果批 (蘋果派) apple pie
　　蘋果綠 apple green
　　一抽蘋果 (一袋蘋果) a bag of apples

【蠔】hou⁴ (牡蠣) oyster
蠔油 oyster sauce
　　走蠔油 (不要蠔油) no oyster sauce
蠔豉 (乾貼貝) dried mussel

【藏】tsong⁴ hide
藏身 go into hiding; hide oneself
藏品 object
藏書 book collection

冷藏 cold storage
珍藏 consider valuable and collect appropriately;
　　treasure up
庫藏 have a storage of; have in storage; have in store
被人雪藏 (給打入冷宮 / 隱藏) banish to the cold palace; be
　　left out in the cold; consign to the back shelf; fallen into
　　disfavour; out of favour; out in the cold; put on the back
　　shelf; turn out in the cold

雪藏 ① (擱置不用) be kept out of the public gaze ② (冰鎮)
　　snow; frozen
窩藏 harbour; shelter
隱藏 hide

【襪】mat⁹ (襪子) socks
襪統 (襪筒) leg of a stocking
襪褲 (連褲襪) pantyhose
襪頭 (襪口) welt

一對手襪 (一雙手套) a pair of gloves
一對襪 (一雙襪子) a pair of socks
手襪 (手套) gloves
冷襪 (厚襪子) woollen shorts
原子襪 (尼龍襪) nylon socks
除襪 (脫襪子) remove socks; take off socks
絲襪 pantyhose
着襪 (穿襪子) wear socks

【覺】gaau³ sleep
覺覺豬 (睡覺) go to sleep; go sleepy-byes

日頭瞓覺 (白天睡覺) sleep during the day time
平時幾點瞓覺 (平時幾點睡覺) what time do you usually go
　　to bed
晏覺 (午睡) afternoon nap
瞓晏覺 (睡午覺) take an afternoon nap
瞓覺 (睡覺) sleep
醒覺 (睡醒) awake

【覺】gok⁸ feel
覺得 (感覺 / 認為) feel; think
覺眼 (保持睜大眼睛 / 留意) keep one's eyes open
　　唔覺眼 (不注意 / 沒有注意到 / 粗心大意) not notice;
　　　　not to keep one's eyes open

不知不覺 unconsciously; without realising it
幻覺 delusion; hallucination; illusion
味覺 sense of taste
直覺 basic instinct; gut feeling; intuition
唔多覺 (不太覺得) don't feel very strongly
唔經唔覺 (不知不覺間) without realising it
神不知鬼不覺 (不為人知) without anybody knowing it
產生幻覺 has an illusion; see things
感覺 feeling
察覺 become aware of

【觸】dzuk[7] touch

觸摸 touch
　　秘密接觸 get in touch with sb confidentially

接觸 touch

【議】ji[5] discuss

議會 assembly; congress; council; parliament
議價 (價格協商) price negotiation
議論 comment; discuss; talk

主持會議 hold a meeting
召開會議 call a meeting; convene a meeting
決議 resolution
協議 ① agree on ② deal; treaty ③ discuss; negotiate
建議 suggest
動議 motion; move; proposal
從長計議 (進一步思考並稍後討論) be considered
　　slowly and carefully; be talked about at length; be
　　treated with careful deliberation; consider careful
　　before making a decision; give the matter further
　　thought and discuss it later; take more time to
　　consider; take one's time in reaching a decision; talk
　　over at length
會議 conference; meeting

【警】ging[2] ① alert ② police

警犬 police dog
警告 warning
警局 (公安局 / 派出所 / 警察局) police station
警車 police car
警匪片 detective movie
警員 policeman
警署 (公安局 / 派出所 / 警察局) police station
警察 (公安) police
　　警察局 police station
　　叫警察 call the police
　　冒充警察 pretend to be a policeman
　　秘密警察 secret policeman
警鐘 alarm

女警 policewoman
火警 fire
交通警 (交通警察) traffic policeman
走火警 (消防演習) fire drill
報警 ① (報警) call the police ② (舉報案件 / 向警方報案)
　　report a case; report to the police

【譯】jik[6] translate

譯者 translator

直譯 literal translation
傳譯 (口譯) interpret
翻譯 translate

【贏】jing[4] win

贏錢 win money

【躁】tsou[3] impetuous; rash

躁火 (燥熱) dryness-heat

浮躁 flighty and rash; impetuous; impulsive
煩躁 agitated; fidgety; in a fret; irritable

【薑】dan[2] (放 / 擱 / 擺) put

薑低 (放下 / 擱下) lay down; put down
薑嘢 (放東西 / 擱東西 / 擺東西) lay down things; put
　　down things

打薑 (經常停留在一個地方) frequent a place
柱薑 (柱石 / 柱座 / 柱基石) column base; pillar
茅薑 (耍賴) trick
風頭薑 (風雲人物) person who is fond of limelight; some
　　who enjoys being in the limelight
香爐薑 (獨苗兒) male heir; the only son in the family
監薑 (囚犯) prisoner
跎薑 (失業) out of work; unemployed
擁薑 (捧場的人) fans; supporters
橋薑 (橋墩) bridge pier
龍薑 (石斑魚) giant garoupa

【蹬】daat[8] (摔) fall; tumble

蹬低 (跌倒) fall; tumble
蹬嚫腰骨 (把腰蹬着了) hurt the waist in a tumble

【釋】sik[7] explain

釋放 release
釋嫌 ① dispel suspicion ② dispel ill feelings

註釋 annotation; commentary; explanatory note; note
解釋 ① explain ② interpret

【鐘】dzung[1] ① (鬧鐘) clock ② (鈴) bell

鐘咭 (出勤卡) clock card; timecard
鐘數 (時間) time
鐘錶行 clock and watch shop
鐘頭 (小時) hour

一個鐘頭（一個小時）one hour
半個鐘頭（半個小時）half an hour

鐘點（小時工）part-time
　鐘點工（計時工）worker paid by the hour
　鐘點工人 ①（計時工）part-time worker ②（鐘點家傭）
　　part-time maid

一分鐘 one minute
一句鐘（一個小時）one hour
一秒鐘 one second
一個鐘 ①（一個小時）one hour ②（一座鐘）a clock
一粒鐘（一個小時）one hour
一點鐘 one o'clock
七點鐘 seven o'clock
九點鐘 nine o'clock
二點鐘 two o'clock
八點鐘 eight o'clock
十一點鐘 eleven o'clock
十二點鐘 twelve o'clock
十點鐘 ten o'clock
三點鐘 three o'clock
五點鐘 five o'clock
六點鐘 six o'clock
分分鐘（隨時／每時每刻／時時刻刻）all the time; any time;
　as the occasion demands; at all times; at any time; whenever
半個鐘（半個小時）half an hour
半粒鐘（半個小時）half an hour
半點鐘（半個小時）half an hour
四點鐘 four o'clock
打咭鐘（考勤機）roll machine
未夠鐘（還沒到時候）it's not time yet
吊鐘 ①（小舌）little red tongue; uvula ②（倒掛金鐘／燈籠
　海棠）fuchsia
門鐘（門鈴）door bell
泵波鐘（拖長時間）play for time
個零鐘（一個多小時）more than an hour
吟鐘（銅鈴）brass bell
校鐘（調鐘）set the clock
幾點鐘（幾點／甚麼時候）at what time
夠鐘（到時間了／到點／是時候了）it's time to; time's up
啱啱夠鐘（及時／正好）just in time
揼波鐘（磨時間／拖時間）stall for time
補鐘（補課）make up missed classes; make-up classes
電鐘（電鈴）electric bell
過鐘（過時了／過點）past the appointed time
對鐘（對時間／對錶）synchronise a watch
鬧鐘 alarm clock
撳門鐘（按門鈴／揿門鈴）press the door bell
撳鐘（按門鈴／按鈴／揿鈴）press the bell; push the bell

默哀一分鐘 observe one minute's silence
點鐘（小時）① hour ② o'clock
警鐘 alarm

【鐐】liu⁵ cuffs

手鐐（手銬）cuffs; handcuffs

【鐧】gaan³ rapier

殺手鐧（絕招）one's trump card
撒手鐧（絕招）one's trump card

【露】lou⁶ ① reveal ② sweet soup

露二點（沒穿上衣）topless, with breasts exposed
露三點（全裸）full frontal nudity
露天 in the open; in the open air; outdoors
露台（陽台）balcony
露面 show up
　公開露面 appear in public; make a public appearance;
　　make one's appearance in public; show one's face in
　　public
　拋頭露面 make a living in the public eye; show oneself
　　to make a living
露馬腳 incautiously let out one's fault; incautiously let out
　one's secret; show the cloven foot
　露出馬腳 incautiously let out one's fault; incautiously let
　　out one's secret; show the cloven foot
露骨（令人尷尬）embarrassingly direct
露宿 sleep in the open
　露宿者 street sleeper
露筍（蘆筍）asparagus
露營（野營）camping

合桃露（核桃露）sweet walnut soup
吐露 confess; disclose; reveal; tell
西米露 sago in coconut milk
杏仁露 sweet ground almond soup
防曬露（防曬霜）sun block lotion
洩露 disclose; divulge; leak out; reveal
原形畢露（揭示一個人的真實面貌）be revealed for what
　one is; be revealed in one's true colours; betray oneself;
　completely exposed; completely unmasked; present one's
　naked self; reveal one's real appearance; reveal the true
　nature completely; show one's true colours; show oneself
　in one's true colours; show the cloven hoof; show what
　one really is
畢露（充分顯露）be fully revealed
魚露 fish sauce

揭露 bring to light; disclose; expose; ferret sth out; lay sth bare; show sth up; uncover

楊枝甘露 sweet mango soup with pomelo and sago

裸露 exposed; nudity; uncovered

【飄】piu¹ float

飄出 blow out

飄忽 ①（艦隊／快速移動）fleet; move swiftly ②（漂浮）float

飄流 ① drift ② roam aimlessly

輕飄飄 ① light as a feather ② buoyant

【饅】maan⁶ steamed bun

饅頭 steamed bun

【響】hoeng² ①（聲響）sound ②（在）be present

響朵（有人主動地把自己的身份或地位告知別人）give props to

響度（在這裏）be present

一套音響 a set of hi-fi

一條鎖匙聞唔聲，兩條鎖匙冷冷響（一個巴掌拍不響）one bowl is quiet while two bowls make a row

大受影響 be seriously affected

口響（說得好聽／誇誇其談／天花亂墜）glib

音響 hi-fi

影響 affect; impact; influence

講得口響（說得好聽）fine words; make an unpleasant fact sound attractive; says you; talk fine; use fine-sounding phrases

【馨】hing¹ fragrance

馨香（稀罕／吃香）be very much sought after; in great demand; popular

康乃馨 carnation

溫馨 heart-warming

【騰】tang⁴ bounce

騰上騰落（爬上爬下）rush around

騰雞（慌亂／手足無措）frightened; nervous

騰騰震（膽戰心驚）tremble with fear

左騰右騰（瞎忙）rushing about

兩頭騰（非常忙碌）be extremely busy

肥騰騰（胖乎乎的／過度肥胖）overfat

發 T 騰（膽戰心驚）(English) frightened

震騰騰（膽戰心驚）tremble with fear

【騷】sou¹ ①（表演）(English) show ②（理睬）pay attention to

騷擾晒（打擾了）sorry to trouble you

牢騷 complain; discontent; grumble; grumbling; complaint

風騷 attractive; sexy

做騷（表演）do a show

發牢騷 beef; beef about; blow off steam chew the rag; complain; dissipate one's grief; grouch; grouse; grumble; grumble about; grumble at; grumble over; let off steam; make a sour remark; make bitter complaint; murmur; natter; pour out a stream of complaints; say devil's paternoster; whine about; work off steam

睇騷（看表演）watch a show

懶風騷（賣弄風騷）cocky

【騮】lau⁴ moneky

甩繩馬騮（不受管控的調皮鬼／非常頑皮的孩子）on the loose; very naughty child

馬騮 ①（猴子）monkey ②（頑皮的孩子）naughty kid

劏雞嚇馬騮（殺雞嚇猴／殺雞儆猴）kill the chicken to frighten the monkey – punish sb as a warning to others; make an example of a few to frighten all the rest

【髆】bok⁸ shoulder

髆頭（肩膀）shoulder

【鯽】dzik⁷ carp

鯽魚 crucian carp

【鯿】bin¹ bream

鯿魚（白鰱魚）bream

【鹹】haam⁴ ① salty ②（髒）dirty ③（色情）erotic; pornographic

鹹水（外國）foreign

鹹水角 glutinous rice dumpling with dried shrimp and pork

鹹水貨（違禁品／走私貨）contraband goods; smuggled goods

鹹水魚（海水魚）saltwater fish

鹹水樓（危房）dangerous buiding

浸鹹水（出國留學）spend time abroad; study abroad

浸過鹹水（曾經出國留學）spent time abroad; studied abroad

鹹片（色情電影）pornographic film

鹹古（色情故事）pornographic story

鹹肉粽 steamed glutinous rice dumpling with pork wrapped in lotus leaves

鹹書（色情書籍）pornographic book

鹹帶（色情錄像帶）pornographic videotape

鹹蛋（鹹鴨蛋）salted egg
　　賣鹹鴨蛋（死亡／去世）die; pass away

鹹魚 ①（鹹魚）dried salted fish; salted fish
　　②（屍體）corpse; dead body
　　鹹魚白菜（簡單的菜）humble meal; simple meal
　　鹹魚肉餅飯 rice with salted fish and meat cake
　　鹹魚翻生 ① escape unexpectedly from a difficulty
　　　　② a person back in favour

鹹菜 crumpled clothes
　　鹹酸菜（醃菜）salted vegetable

鹹濕（下流／淫穢）bawdy; dirty; dirty-minded; lascivious; lecherous; nasty; randy; salacious; sleazy
　　鹹濕仔（下流好色的人）lecherous young man
　　鹹濕好色（下流／淫穢）sex-mad; sleazy
　　鹹濕佬（下流鬼／色鬼）lecherous man
　　鹹濕故仔（色情故事）pornographic story
　　鹹濕笑話（黃色笑話）dirty joke; lewd joke
　　鹹濕鬼（下流鬼／色鬼）lecherous man
　　鹹濕相（色情照片）pornographic photograph

鹹蟲（色狼）dirty man; dirty-minded man; lecherous man; lecherous person
　　老鹹蟲（老色狼）dirty old man; old goat

鹹餸（鹹味菜）briny dishes

好鹹 very salty

【麵】min⁶（麵條）noodles

麵包 bread
　　麵包店 bakery
　　麵包糠（麵包屑）bread crumbs; crumbly bread; crumbs
　　炕麵包（烤麵包）bake bread

麵粉 flour
　　中筋麵粉 plain flour
　　搓麵粉（揉麵粉／擀麵團）knead the flour

麵豉（豆醬／黃醬）fermented soybean paste

麵醬（豆醬／黃醬）bean paste
　　甜麵醬 sweet bean paste

一包麵（一包麵條）a pack of noodles

一窩湯麵（一大碗湯麵）a big bowl of noodles in soup

公仔麵（速食麵／方便麵）instant noodles

牛肉麵 beef noodles

牛腩麵 beef brisket noodles

四川擔擔麵 Sichuan spicy noodles

肉絲炒麵 fried noodles with shredded pork

即食麵（速食麵／方便麵）instant noodles

車仔麵 cart noodles

拌麵 noodles in mixed sauce

炒麵 fried noodles

食貓麵（挨呲）be scolded; get it in the neck

淨麵（素麵／清湯麵）plain noodles

淥麵（煮麵／下麵條）cook noodles

湯麵 noodles in soup

雲吞麵（餛飩麵）shrimp dumpling noodles

搓麵（揉麵）knead dough

煮個麵（下個麵）cook some noodles

煮麵（下麵）cook noodles

撈麵（拌麵）noodles in mixed sauce

齋麵（素麵）plain noodles

麵醬（豆醬／黃醬）bean paste

【黨】dong² ① gang ② party

黨派 party

黨紀 party discipline

黨章 party constitution

反對黨 opposition party

死黨 best friend; bosom friend; very close friend

政黨 political party

童黨 child gang

黃牛黨（倒票）scalpers

【齡】ling⁴ age

入學年齡 age of admission

年齡 age

妙齡 youthfulness

法定年齡 legal age

育齡 childbearing age

保齡（保齡球）(English) bowling

樓齡（房齡）age of building

21 劃

【嚿】gau⁶ a lump of

一嚿（一塊）a cake of; a piece of; a lump of

瓊埋一嚿（凝成一塊了）clot

縮埋一嚿（縮作一團）curl up into a ball; huddle

【屬】suk⁹ belong

屬於 belong to

有情人終成眷屬 the lovers finally got married
純屬 purely; simply
眷屬（家屬）family dependant
僚屬 officials under sb in authority; staff; subordinates

【懼】goey⁶ fear

懼內 henpecked
懼怕 dread; fear

畏懼 awe; be scared of; dread; fear
恐懼 afraid of; dread; fear; frightened; terrified

【攝】sip⁸ ①（調節）regulate ②（塞）fill in; squeeze in; stuff

攝入（塞入）stuff in
攝石（磁石／磁鐵）magnet
　　攝石人（搶鏡的人）sb who tries to hog the limelight
攝位（自我推銷）self-promoting
　　攝住件衫（把衣服塞進褲子）tuck a shirt into one's trousers
攝紙（塞紙）insert paper
攝被（披被子）tuck in a quilt
攝錄機（攝像機）video recorder

【欄】laan⁴⁻¹ ① railing ② store

欄河（欄杆）balustrade; bannister; railing

下欄 ①（外快）extra income; tips ②（雜活）leftovers
牛欄（牛圈）lair
冚辦欄（全部）all; all of a lump; any and every; by the lump; complete; entire; full; in a lump; in one lump; in the lump; lock, stock, and barrel; one and all; the entire shoot; the whole whole; total; without exception; whole
羊欄（羊圈）sheepfold
果欄（水果行／水果店）fruit store
魚欄（水產行）fish store
菜欄（蔬菜行）vegetable store
傾唔埋欄（無法表述觀點）fail to carry one's point
豬欄（豬圈）pigpen; sty
講唔埋欄（達不成共識）unable to reach a consensus

【櫻】jing¹ cherry

櫻花 cherry blossom

【灌】gwun³ pour into

灌湯餃 dumpling stuffed with pork and chicken soup

【爛】laan⁶ ①（破）broken ②（破爛）damaged ③（腐爛）rotten ④（耗盡）worn out

爛口（罵下流話）bad language; coarse language; foul-mouthed; obscene language; swearing; swearing all the time; swear word; vulgar language
　　爛口角（口角炎）aphatha
爛牙（蛀牙）carious tooth; decayed tooth; rotten tooth
　　一隻爛牙（一顆爛牙）a decayed tooth; a rotten tooth
爛市（滯銷）dull of sale
爛仔（二流子／無賴／痞子）hooligan
爛打（好鬥）bellicose
爛生（粗生）easy to grow
爛朵朵（破破爛爛的）dilapidated
爛尾（中途而廢）give up half-way
爛身爛世（破破爛爛）wear shabby clothes
爛泥扶唔上壁（爛泥扶不上牆）people of bad character will not be able to change
爛命一條（這條命不值錢）live a worthless life and have nothing to lose
爛屋（破房子）dilapidated house
爛食（貪吃／嘴饞）gluttonous
爛酒佬（醉鬼／酒鬼）drunkard; inebriate; sot
爛鬼（壞蛋／惡棍／壞人／無賴）rascal
　　爛鬼嘢（破玩意）lousy gadget
爛鬥爛（針鋒相對）give tit for tat
爛笪（不擇手段／不法／無良／毫無顧忌）unscrupulous
　　爛笪笪（不擇手段／不法／無良／毫無顧忌）make no scrupple; unscrupulous
爛船拆埋都有三斤釘（船破還有三斤釘／具剩餘價值）ven the wrecks of a boat are still of some surplus value
爛船都有三斤釘（船破還有三斤釘／具剩餘價值）even the wrecks of a boat are still of some surplus value
爛喉痧（猩紅熱／丹痧）scarlet fever
爛飯（軟飯）thoroughly cooked rice
爛銅爛鐵（破銅爛鐵）scrap metal
爛瞓（嗜睡）person who likes to sleep
　　爛瞓豬（嗜睡的人）person who likes to sleep
爛賤（不值錢）cheap; low-priced; worthless
爛賭（好賭／嗜賭）be addicted to gambling
　　爛賭鬼（病態賭徒／賭鬼）compulsive gambler
爛頭蟀（打架特別凶狠、不要命的流氓）tough guy
爛蓉蓉（破爛／稀巴爛）smashed beyond repair; soggy
爛癮（着迷／癮頭大）be addicted to; have a strong craving

冇穿冇爛（過得去／還好）everything is alright; without a scratch
勾爛（勾破）hang on and break sth

平到爛（非常便宜）very cheap

打爛（打破）break

抵到爛（太合算了）get a very good deal; get the best value for one's money

拼爛（無恥地行事）act shamelessly

拮爛（戳壞）pierce

唔同床唔知被爛（如人飲水，冷暖自知）no one knows what the other side of the world looks like

破爛 ① dilapidated; ragged; tattered; worn-out

　　② junk; scrap

着爛（穿爛／穿破）wear out; worn-out

㪘爛（粉碎／砸碎）smash

搣爛（扯壞／撕壞）tear apart; tear asunder

溶溶爛爛（稀爛）pulpy

摼爛（敲壞）ruin by beating

撞爛 smash in collision

漚爛（泡爛）soak sth until softened

蓉爛（破爛）ragged; worn-out

噍爛（嚼碎）chew; masticate; munch

揀爛（粉碎／砸碎）smash to a pulp

撚爛（捏破）break by squeezing

霉爛 mildew and rot

整爛（弄爛）break

錐爛（錐破）damage by boring

擘爛（撕破）shred into pieces

壓爛 crush; smash

燦爛 bright; glorious; magnificent; resplendent; splendid

【癩】laai³ toad

癩皮狗 ① mangy dog ② loathsome creature

癩尿蝦（蝦姑／皮皮蝦）yabbies

癩蛤蟆 toad

　　癩蛤蟆想食天鵝肉（癩蛤蟆想吃天鵝肉／不自量力）estimate oneself; overreach oneself

【癪】dzik⁷（疳癪）malnutrition

生癪（嬰兒營養不良）infantile malnutrition

【竈】dzou³ stove

燒冷竈（燒冷灶）back the wrong horse

【籐】tang⁴ rattan

籐唅（籐籃）rattan case

【續】dzuk⁹ wind around

續約 renew a contract

續後（後續）afterward; later

續集 sequel

延續 be continued; continue; go on; last

持續 continuance; continued; sustained

連續（陸續）at a stretch; continuous; in succession; on a stretch; on end; running; successive

陸續（連續／相繼／先後／一個接一個）continuous; in succession; one after another; one by one

繼續 continue

【纏】tsin⁴ wind around

纏住 entangled; entwined; wind around

纏綿 exceedingly sentimental

黏纏（難捨難分）loathe to part from each other

癡纏（纏綿）exceedingly sentimental

【蘭】laan⁴ orchid

蘭花 orchid

蘭桂 orchid and cassia

白蘭 gardenia flower

米仔蘭（樹蘭）Chinese rice plant

芝蘭 orchid

芥蘭（甘藍／芥藍菜）kale

荷蘭 Holland

劍蘭 gladiolus

紫羅蘭 pansy

【蠟】laap⁹ wax

蠟板（鋼板）stencil plate

蠟筆 crayon

蠟燭 candle

燈油火蠟（運營成本）overheads; running costs of a business

【蠢】tsoen²（笨）stupid

蠢人 blockhead; fool; idiot; stupid person

蠢材（笨蛋）fool; idiot

蠢笨（尷尬／笨拙）awkward; clumsy

蠢豬 fool; stupid like a pig; stupid person; stupid pig

蠢過隻豬（比豬還蠢）very foolish; very stupid

蠢蠢哋（有點蠢）a little foolish

扮蠢（裝蠢）pretend ignorance; pretend to be stupid

愚蠢 as nutty as a fruitcake; chuckle-headed; dull; foolish silly; stupid

【覽】laam⁵ view
覽古〔遊覽古蹟〕tour ancient relics

展覽 exhibit; exhibition
瀏覽 browse; glance over

【護】wu⁶ nurse
護士 nurse
護照 passport
護髮素 conditioner

庇護 shelter
防護 defence; guard; proofing; protect
保護 protect
看護〔護士〕nurse
學護〔實習護士〕student nurse
擁護 advocate; back; endorse; support; uphold
翼護 shelter and protect

【譽】jy⁶ reputation
譽滿天下 one's reputation is known throughout
　　the world

名譽 ① fame; reputation ② honorary
享譽 enjoy a reputation
沽名釣譽 angle for compliment; angle for praise; angle for
　　undeserved fame; buy reputation and fish for praise;
　　cater to publicity by sordid methods; chase fame; court
　　publicity; fish for fame and compliments; fish for fame
　　and reputation; strive for reputation

【轟】gwang¹ noise
轟轟烈烈 achieve great things

有景轟〔有蹊蹺〕there must be an inside story
炮轟 bombard
景轟〔蹊蹺〕secret motive
紅轟轟 red

【辯】bin⁶ argue; debate; dispute
辯駁〔反駁〕confute; contradict; controvert;
　　countercharge; counterplea; disproof; gainsay;
　　refute; retort
辯論 debate

事實勝於雄辯 facts are more eloquent than words; facts are
　　stronger than arguments; facts speak louder than words;
　　the effect speaks, the tongue needs not

狡辯 indulge in sophistry; quibble; resort to sophistry

【醺】fan¹ drunk
醺醺 tipsy
　　醉醺醺 very drunk

【鐮】lim⁴ sickle
鐮刀 sickle

禾鐮 sickle for cutting rice straws

【鐵】tit⁸ iron
鐵人 strong man
鐵沙梨——咬唔入〔斗大的饅頭——吃不下嘴〕
　　very stingy
鐵杵磨成針 little strokes fell great oaks
鐵枝〔鐵條〕iron rod
　　粗鐵枝〔鐵棍〕large iron rod
鐵面 judge
鐵馬 ①〔警察摩托車〕police motorbike ②〔鐵欄桿〕iron
　　railing ③〔鐵路障〕iron road block
鐵通〔鐵管〕iron pipe; iron tube
鐵筆〔鋼針〕steel drill
鐵絲網 wire fence; wire mesh; wire netting
鐵腳馬眼神仙肚〔廢寢忘食地不停工作〕energetic
　　person who can work long hours without sitting,
　　sleeping, and eating
鐵路 railway
鐵閘 ①〔鐵柵欄〕iron gate ②〔鐵閘門〕grated door
鐵嘜〔鐵罐〕can; tin
鐵嘴雞〔辯才一流〕a difficult opponent in an argument
鐵線〔鐵絲〕iron wire
鐵錘 iron hammer
鐵鏈〔鐵鍊〕iron chain
鐵鑊〔鐵鍋〕iron frying pan
鐵罐 can; tin
鐵觀音 Iron Goddess of Mercy tea

水喉鐵〔鐵水管〕iron water pipe
打鐵 strike the iron
地下鐵 MTR (Mass Transit Railway)
地鐵 ① MTR (Mass Transit Railway) ② subway;
　　underground railway
星鐵〔馬口鐵〕galvanised iron
針鼻削鐵〔只向微中取利〕gain the narrowest margin
　　of profit
該釘就釘，該鐵就鐵〔直言不諱〕call a spade a spade
搭地鐵〔坐地鐵〕take the MTR (Mass Transit Railway)

輕鐵 light rail transit
鋅鐵 (馬口鐵) galvanised iron
燈芯擰成鐵 a straw shows its weight when it is carried a long way
爛銅爛鐵 (破銅爛鐵) scrap metal

【鐸】dok⁹ bell
鐸叔 (吝嗇的人) miser; niggard

孤寒鐸 (吝嗇鬼) miser; miserly person; stingy person

【鐳】loey⁴ radium
鐳射碟 (激光視盤) laser disk

【霸】baa³ occupy
霸王 (霸道) overbearing; high-handed; rule by force
　食霸王飯 (吃霸王餐／吃飯不給錢) eat a free meal
霸位 (佔個位子／搶座位) grab a seat
　霸個位 (搶個座位) grab a seat
霸住嚟做 (攬着自己做) take on everything by oneself
霸拙 (專制／扮小霸王) despotic; play the bully
霸爐 (佔爐子) grab a stove

惡霸 (暴君／獨裁者) tyrant
稱霸 dominate; seek hegemony
蝦蝦霸霸 (欺負人) bully; bully and humiliate
蝦霸 (欺負／欺侮／欺凌) bully; bully and humiliate
籮霸 (肥臀／大臀) large bottom

【顧】gu³ look
顧住 ① (不要超過限度) not to exceed the limit ② (小心) take care of oneself ③ (控制情緒) control one's emotions ④ (當心) beware of one's life; watch out
顧客 customer
　顧客永遠是對的 customers are always right
顧得頭嚟腳反筋 (扶得東來西又倒／顧此失彼) attend to one thing and neglect another
顧問 consultant

主顧 client; customer
兼顧 give consideration to two or more things
眷顧 (關心／關懷／照顧) care for; concern
惠顧 your patronage
環顧 look around

【驅】koey¹ ① drive ② expel
驅蟲藥 (殺蟲劑) insect repellent

【魔】mo¹ ① (妖魔) devil ② magic
魔鬼 devil
魔術 magic
　表演魔術 perform magic
　玩魔術 play magic
魔掌 (魔爪) devil's talons

色魔 lecher; satyr; sex lupine; sex maniac
淫魔 (色狼) lecher; satyr; sex lupine; sex maniac

【鰛】wan¹ sardine
腥鰛鰛 (魚腥氣很濃) stinking smell of fish

【鯧】tsoeng¹ (鰛) pomfret
鯧魚 (鰛魚) silvery pomfret

黃立鯧 (金鯧魚) pompano

【鷂】jiu⁶ kite
鷂鷹 hawk

放紙鷂 (放風箏) fly a kite
紙鷂 (風箏) kite

【齦】ngan⁴ gum

咬實牙齦 (咬緊牙關) endure hardship; tolerate bitterly

22 劃

【囉】lo¹ chatter
囉柚 (屁股) bottom; buttocks
　洗囉油 (洗屁股) clean one's bottom
囉攣 (擔心) worried
　囉囉攣 (鬧騰) be restless with anxiety; worried
囉嗦 (囉嗦) chatter; long-winded
　囉囉嗦嗦 (囉里囉嗦) chatter

係囉 (就是呀) this is true
唔係囉 (可不是) this is really so

【囊】nong⁴ bag; sack
囊中物 sth in the bag
囊括 ① embrace; include ② win all
　囊括一切 make a clean sweep; sweep up everything

背囊（背包）rucksack
腳瓜囊（小腿肚／腿肚子）calf of the leg
膽囊 gall bladder

【彎】waan¹ bend
彎曲 meandering; winding; zigzag
彎路 roundabout way

轉彎 turn the corner

【攢】dzaan² ① accumulate ② gather together
攢鬼 ①（合算／有好處）good ②（賺錢）earn money; save up money
攢聚（聚集在一起）gather together
攢錢 save up money
　　攢錢防老 save up money for one's old age

唔攢 ①（不合算）not paying ②（沒錢賺）not earning money

【攤】taan¹ ① stall ②（躺）lie
攤位 booth
攤直（死／直躺）die; have fallen flat
攤凍（放涼）cool down
　　攤凍嚟食（穩紮穩打）go about things steadily and surely; go ahead steadily and strike sure blows; play for safety; proceed steadily and step by step; wage steady and sure struggle; slow and steady
攤販（街頭小販）street pedlar
攤牌 have a showdown
攤檔（攤子）booth; stall; vendor's stand
攤攤腰 ①（非常疲憊）very tired ②（在很大程度上）to a great extent

執二攤 ①（使用二手貨）use second-hand goods ②（約會別人的前男友或前女友）date sb's ex-boyfriend or ex-girlfried
魚攤 fish stall
番攤（源自廣州的賭博方式）fantan
菜攤 vegetable stall
順攤（順利／順當）easy-going

【攞】lo² ① collect ② fetch ③（拿）bring; get; take
攞出嚟（拿出來）bring out
攞皮宜（撈好處／佔便宜／撿便宜）jolly with sb to amuse oneself
攞住（拿着）holding; taking
　　攞唔住（拿不住）can't hold it

攞得住（拿得住）can hold it
攞豆（見閻王爺）die; meet one's fate
攞位 ①（贏得地位）win status ②（得到座位）get a seat
攞命（要命）kill sb; ride one to death
攞枱（拿桌子）get a table
攞晒（拿光／拿完）be all taken; be taken up
　　攞唔晒（拿不完）can't take all; too many to be taken away
攞苦嚟辛（自找苦吃）ask for trouble
攞唔喐（拿不動）can't move
攞得喐（拿得動）can be moved
攞倒（拿到）have got
　　攞唔倒（拿不了／拿不到）can't get it
　　攞得倒（拿得了／拿得到）can get it
攞彩（獲得榮耀）gain glory
攞貨（拿貨／取貨）take goods
攞朝唔得晚（生活僅夠糊口）live from hand to mouth
攞景 ①（取景）look for the right spot to take a photo ②（起鬨／找茬／搗亂）hit sb when they are down
　　攞景定贈慶（幸災樂禍）take advantage of one's vulnerability
攞硬（勢在必得）lie within one's grasp
攞錢 ①（拿錢）get money ②（取錢）withdraw money ③（要錢）ask for money
攞膽（嚇壞）frightening; take away one's life
攞櫈（拿櫈子）take a stool
攞嚟衰（自找麻煩／自討苦吃）bring disgrace on oneself; get oneself into trouble
攞嚟賤（自找麻煩／自討苦吃）get oneself into trouble; work for one's destruction
攞嚟講（找話題來說／說廢話）talk for the sake of talking
攞嚟攪（瞎折騰）fool around; mess about
攞鏡（拍照）take a snap; take photographs
攞籌（拿號兒）take a number

【摵】din¹ roll
摵地（滾地）roll on the ground

【權】kyn⁴ power
權力 authority
權利 legal right
權杖 mace
權威 authority
　　迷信權威 have blind faith in authority

人權 human rights
民權 civil rights
永久居留權 permanent residency
弄權 manipulate power for personal ends
居留權 right of abode

版權 copyright
知識產權 patent right
保障民權 safeguard civil rights
授權 authorise
專利權 monopoly
揸大權 (手握大權) in power
棄權 abstain
期權 option
認沽期權 put
認購期權 call

【歡】fun¹ happy
歡迎 welcome
　　受歡迎 be well received; enjoy great popularity; popular
　　大受歡迎 receive great popularity; very popular
歡喜 ① (喜愛) fond of; keen on; like; love; prefer ② (欣喜的) be filled with joy; delighted; elated; happy

【灑】saa² sprinkle
灑脫 (隨意而無憂無慮) casual and carefree; free and easy; graceful

花灑 (噴頭 / 蓮蓬頭) shower; sprinkler

【灘】taan¹ beach
灘頭 beachhead

沙灘 beach
泳灘 (海水浴場) bathing beach
海灘 beach

【疊】dip⁹ fold; pile up
疊好 fold up

厚疊疊 (厚厚一疊) very thick
落疊 (參加 / 下注) agree to a deal

【癮】jan⁵ craving
癮頭 addiction; strong interest

上癮 be addicted
火麒麟——週身癮 (各種上癮) a slave to many vices; the person who is addicted to all kinds of lusts
冇癮 ① (沒興趣 / 沒趣) bored ② (沒勁) disappointed
吊癮 (對嗜好略加滿足 / 毒品用完了) not to satisfy the craving for the time being; run out of drugs
有癮 (隨心所欲 / 盡情享受) do sth to one's heart's content; enjoy oneself to the full; satisfy a carving
挑起條癮 (引起慾望) arouse sb's desire

鬼咁過癮 (太過癮了) really exciting
煙癮 craving for tobacco
過口癮 (過嘴癮) speak for the sake of speaking; talk nonsense
過癮 satisfy a craving; thrilled
爛癮 (着迷 / 癮頭大) be addicted to; have a strong craving

【癬】sin² lichen
癬疥 skin disease

苔癬 lichen

【竊】sit⁸ steal
竊取 grab; steal; take sth which does not lawfully belong to one; usurp
竊案 (盜竊案) burglary; theft case
竊聽 eavesdropping

盜竊 theft
爆竊 (偷盜 / 盜竊) burglary; pilferage; steal

【籠】lung⁴ ① (籠子) cage ② basket
籠絡 entice; tempt
籠統 general; sweeping
籠裏雞作反 (窩裏鬥 / 內訌) have an internal dissension; internal rift

一籠 a basket of; a small steamer basket of
小蒸籠 small steamer
內籠 (內部) internal
冇掩雞籠 (自由出入) a coop without a flap; a place where people are free to come and go
出籠 (推出市面) product released on the market
扽蝦籠 (偷東西) pick sb's pocket
狗籠 crate
玩燈籠 play with lanterns
雀籠 (鳥籠) bird cage
密籠 (密封) seal up; sealed
眼大睇過籠 (心粗看不細 / 粗心大意) be too careless to see anything
頂籠 (最多 / 上限) at most; reach the limit
鳥籠 birdcage
亂晒大籠 (全亂套了) in great chaos; in great disorder
亂晒籠 (亂了套) chaos; disorder
亂籠 (亂了套) make a mess of sth; out of whack
蒸籠 steamer
瞓過籠 (睡過頭) oversleep
燈籠 lantern

【糴】dek⁹ run away; rush

糴米（買米）buy rice; get rice

糴佬（躲避警察的罪犯）a criminal fleeing the police

【聽】ting¹ listen

聽一聽（稍候一會兒）wait for a while

聽日（明天）tomorrow

　聽日見（明天見）see you tomorrow

聽到（聽見）hear

聽倒 ①（聽到）can be heard ②（能聽到並理解到）can hear and understand

聽唔倒 ①（聽不到）cannot be heard ②（無法聽到）cannot hear

聽唔明（聽不懂）not understand

聽得明（聽得懂）understand

聽晒你話（全聽你的）at your command

聽得 ①（能聽）audible ②（可以聽）can hear

　聽得倒 ①（聽得到）audible ②（能聽到）can hear

　聽得嚟（聽得來）upon hearing

聽帶（聽錄音帶）listen to a recorder tape

聽書（上課／聽課）attend a lecture; sit in on a class

聽晚（明晚）tomorrow evening; tomorrow night

　聽晚黑（明晚）tomorrow evening; tomorrow night

聽朝（明早）tomorrow morning

　聽朝早（明早）tomorrow morning

聽筒（話筒）telephone speaker

聽話 ①（順從）obedient; subordinate to ②（聽説）be said; be told; hear of

　聽晒你話（全聽你的）take all your advice

聽落有骨（意在言外／諷刺）more is meant than meets the ear

聽歌 listen to songs

聽聞（聽説）be said; be told; hear; hear of

聽聞話（聽説）I was told

聽聞講（聽説）be said; be told; hear of

聽價唔聽斗（只重價錢，不重質量）care for whether the price is cheap or high but neglect the quality or quantity

聽錯 hear sth wrongly

聽講（聽説）be told that; hear

　聽講話（聽説）be told that; hear

冇耳聽（不想聽）do not want to hear sth

好話唔好聽（説得難聽一點）frankly speaking; to be blunt

旁聽 audit; visitor at a meeting

動聽 interesting to listen to; moving; persuasive; pleasant to listen to

唱歌唱得好好聽（唱得很動聽）one sings very well

啱聽（中聽／愛聽／喜歡聽）agreeable to the hearer; enjoy listening to; pleasant to the ear

電話冇人聽（沒人接電話）no one answered the phone

【聽】ting³ wait

聽死（陷入困境）get into trouble

諦聽 listen attentively

竊聽 eavesdropping

【聾】lung⁴ deaf

聾佬（聾子）deaf man

聾啞（聾啞人）deaf and mute

　又聾又啞（在外國時既不懂當地語言又不能説母語）can neither understand or speak the native language when in a foreign country

聾婆（聾女人）deaf woman

耳聾 deaf

撞聾（聽覺不靈）play deaf

【臟】dzong⁶ intestines

臟腑 ① viscera ② one's integrity

內臟 intestines

心臟 heart

肝臟 liver

腎臟 kidney

腑臟 ① viscera ② one's integrity

孻仔拉心肝，孻女拉五臟（最小的兒女最得疼愛）parents lavish most affection on their youngest son, but they just lavish much affection on their youngest daughter

【蟓】hin²（蚯蚓）earthworm

黃蟓（蚯蚓）earthworm

【襲】dzaap⁹ assail

襲用 follow a practice; take over

襲擊 attack by surprise; come at; fly at sb's throat; make a raid; make a surprise attack on; raid; surprise attack

抄襲 crib; plagiarise

蹈襲（盲目跟隨）follow slavishly

【襯】tsan³ supplement

瓜老襯（伸腿瞪眼了／死了）die; fall flat; meet with one's death

合襯（合適／般配）well-matched

好襯（合適／般配）good match; match well with

老襯 ①（易受騙者）naive person; sucker ②（姻親）relation by marriage

配襯（相配／相稱）fit each other; match each other; match up; match well; match with; mesh with

搵老襯 ①（欺騙別人）fool sb into doing sth; trick ②（因慷慨而受騙）a person deceived on account of his generosity

搵鬼幫襯（找鬼幫襯／瀕死的企業）a company that is doomed to fail

幫襯（光顧）patronise

【讀】duk⁹ read

讀者 reader

讀書 ① attend school; go to school ② study ③ read books

　陪太子讀書（侍從作伴）bear sb company; some not given much chance of winning

　繼續讀書 continue one's study

讀默（聽寫）dictate

讀壞詩書（斯文敗類）well-read but bad in behaviour

　讀壞詩書包壞腳（迂腐）pedantic

朗讀 read aloud

【贖】dzuk⁶ pay

贖參（贖票／支付綁匪贖金）pay the ransom

贖樓（還清購房貸款）redemption of the property

　提早贖樓（提前還清購房貸款）early redemption

找贖 give the change

【鑊】wok⁹（煎鍋／鍋）frying pan

鑊氣（火候）duration and degree of cooking

　夠鑊氣（炒得香）long duration and high degree of cooking

鑊蓋（鍋蓋）pan cover

鑊頭（大鐵鍋）frying pan

鑊鏟（鍋鏟／鏟子）scoop; shovel; spatula

　揸鑊鏟（拿鍋鏟／當廚師）be a cook

鑊鑊杰（每次都是爛攤子）everything one does ends in trouble

一隻鑊（一口鍋）a pan

一鑊（一鍋）a pot of

大鑊（大簍子）big trouble

丙一鑊（痛毆）beat up thoroughly

丙鑊（痛毆）beat up

炒鑊（炒菜鍋子）frying pan

候鑊（廚師）chef; cook

起鑊（熗鍋）heat the frying pan

孭鑊（揹黑鍋）bear the responsibility; carry the can

補鑊（補救）get a problem fixed

黑鑊（不幸／倒霉）misfortune

煮人一鑊（說人家壞話）badmouth others

熟人買破鑊（被朋友出賣）be sold a pup by one's friend

鋁鑊（鋁鍋）aluminum frying pan

爆大鑊（揭底兒）reveal a big secret

鐵鑊（鐵鍋）iron frying pan

【鑑】gaam¹ by force

鑑粗（動粗／用武力達致目的）by force; do sth at one's insistence

鑑硬（魯莽）act recklessly

【驕】giu¹ proud

驕兵 proud troops

　驕兵必敗（一支充滿驕傲的軍隊必然會遭到失敗）an army puffed up with pride is bound to lose; an army which is cocksure about its invincibility is doomed to defeat; pride goes before a fall; proud troops will certainly be beaten; the self-conceited troops are destined to failure

驕傲 arrogant; big-headed; cock-a-hoop; cock-sure; cocky; conceited; get uppish; get too big for one's breeches; have a big head; pride oneself on; proud; snooty; stuck up; take pride in; too big for one's shoes; uppish; uppity; vain of

　驕傲自大 be bloated with pride; be puffed up; be swollen with pride; conceited and arrogant; cocky; feel high and mighty; have a swelled head; get a swelled head; give oneself airs; self-important; stuck-up

【鬚】sou¹ mustache

鬚刨（剃鬚刀）shaver

鬚後水（護臉油）after-shave; shaving lotion

二撇鬚（八字鬍）man with a beard

八字鬚（八字鬍）moustache that resembles the Chinese character "eight"

甩鬚（丟臉）feel ashamed; lose face; unbecoming

老貓燒鬚（老馬失蹄）a good horse stumbles; even Homer sometimes nods; sb who has had a bad experience with sth

剃鬚（刮鬍子）shave

捋鬍鬚（捋鬍子）stroke one's beard

鬍鬚（鬍子）bread

【鰻】maan⁶ eel

鰻魚 eel

河鰻 river eel

【鱈】syt⁸ cod fish

鱈魚 cod fish

【鷗】au¹ gull

海鷗 seagull

【黐】tsi¹ (黏) be mixed up; glutinous; stick to

黐牙 (黏着牙齒) stick to one's teeth

黐立立 (黏巴巴) sticky

黐住 (黏住) stick to

黐身 (黏人) clingy

　黐身藥膏 (狗皮膏藥) cling to sb closely

　黐身黐勢 (黏人) cling to sb

黐肺 (精疲力竭 / 要命) exhausted; to an extreme extent

黐埋 (黏在一起) bond

黐埋一齊 (黏在一起) stick together

黐埋咗 (黏上了) stick together

黐家 (喜歡在家) sb who likes to stay at home

黐脷根 (大舌頭) lisp; lisper

黐線 ① (神經失常 / 神經病 / 神經錯亂 / 發瘋) crazy; insane; mentally deranged; mixed up; nervous breakdown; off the rails ② (串線) wrong number

　黐線仔 (神經兮兮的人) crazy kid

　黐線佬 (瘋子) crazy guy; crazy man; madman

黐纏 (難捨難分) loathe to part from each other

黐餐 (擾頓飯吃) sponge off one's friends

　黐餐飯吃 (擾一頓飯) get a free meal

23 劃

【嗉】sou¹ long-winded

嚕嗉 (囉嗦) verbose

囉嗉 (囉嗦) chatter; long-winded

囉囉嗉嗉 (囉里囉嗦) chatter

【戀】lyun² ① love ② attachment

戀人 lover; sweetheart

戀情 romantic love

　男女戀情 love between man and woman

戀愛 love

三角戀 love triangle

失戀 be crossed in love

同性戀 gay love; homosexuality

初戀 first love

留戀 yearn

迷戀 be infatuated with

眷戀 sentimentally attached to a person or a place

單戀 unrequited love

熱戀 be head over heels in love

【攣】lyn⁴ (彎曲) curved

攣弓 (拱起 / 蜷曲) coil; curl; hump up

　攣弓蝦米咁 (曲里拐彎的) tortuous

攣毛 (捲毛) curl

攣咗 (彎了) curved

攣埋晒 (攣縮 / 捲曲) contracted

囉攣 (擔心) worried

囉囉攣 (鬧騰) be restless with anxiety; worried

【攪】gaau² (搞) arrange

攪勻 (搞和) mix; mix thoroughly

　攪勻啲 (弄勻和些) make sth evenly distributed

攪手 ① (贊助人) sponsor ② (創始人) initiator

攪出個大頭佛 (好端端的事情被弄糟了) put all the fat in the fire

攪妥 (確保) secure

攪拌機 (攪拌器) blender

攪事 (鬧事) make trouble

攪屎棍 the person who stirs up trouble

攪唔埋 (合不來) unable to get along with

攪得埋 (合得來) get along well with people; hit it off

攪笑 (逗人發笑) joke

攪珠 (搖獎) lottery

攪鬼 (製造麻煩 / 搞亂 / 鬧事 / 惹事 / 生事) make trouble

攪乜鬼 (攪甚麼 / 做甚麼) what gives

攪掂 (行了 / 得了 / 辦妥) settle sth

　攪掂晒 (全好了 / 行了) everything is settled; it's settled

　攪唔掂 (弄不了 / 弄不好) cannot get sth done; unmanageable

　攪得掂 (弄得好) can get sth done

攪㗎 (破壞 / 摧毀 / 銷毀 / 毀滅) destroy

攪亂檔 (製造混亂) cause chaos

攪腸痧 (絞腸痧) intestinal obstruction

攪野 (製造麻煩) make trouble

攪錯（弄錯）make a mistake
　　有冇攪錯（有沒有弄錯）what a ridiculous thing; you're kidding
攪邊科（做甚麼）what are you trying to do
攪攪震（挑起事端／製造麻煩／搞鬼）make trouble
攪撐（弄糟）cause problems; make trouble

打攪 bother; disturb
盞攪（浪費時間和精力）a waste of time and effort
滾攪（打攪／添麻煩）sorry to trouble you
撈攪（麻煩／沒條理／亂騰）confused; messy; upset
攞嚟攪（瞎折騰）fool around; mess about

【曬】 saai³ display
曬士（大小／尺寸）(English) size
曬命（炫耀／賣弄）cry up one's own fortune; flaunt one's possessions; show off; sing one's own glorious song
曬相（沖印相片）develop a photo; print a photo
　　曬相舖（照片打印店）photo printing shop
曬衫（曬衣服）dry clothes in the sun
曬棚（天台）flat roof
曬野（炫耀）show off

生曬（新鮮曬乾）be dried in the sun while sth is alive
白曬曬（白花花）snowy white
沖曬（沖印）develop

【蘸】 dzaam³ dip
蘸汁 dipping sauce

【蘿】 lo⁴ turnip
蘿白頭（日本人）Japanese
蘿蔔 radish
　　蘿蔔仔（凍瘡）chilblain
　　蘿蔔糕 radish cake
　　白蘿蔔 turnip
　　紅蘿蔔（胡蘿蔔）carrot

金菠蘿（寶貝兒孫）one's darling children; one's darling grandchildren
菠蘿 ①（鳳梨）pineapple ②（土製炸彈）home-made bomb

【蠱】 gu² trick
蠱惑（狡猾／滑頭）crafty; cunning; tricky
　　蠱惑女（女小滑頭）young female villain
　　蠱惑友（奸詐的人）tricky person
　　蠱惑仔（小滑頭／痞子）gangster; young villain
　　出蠱惑（耍滑頭／使壞／試圖推卸責任）act in a slick way; at fast and loose; play fast and loose; try to shirk responsibility

整蠱（捉弄／愚弄）play a trick on sb

【變】 bin³ transform
變化 change
　　千變萬化 full of changes
變幻 change
變味 rotten smell
變卦（改變主意／毀約）break an agreement; change one's mind; go back on one's words; retract one's promise
　　中途變卦（中途改變主意）change one's mind in middle course
變態 perverted
　　變態佬（性變態者）sexual pervert
　　變態婆（異常的女人）abnormal woman

二四六八單——冇得變（變不了）it is unchangeable
女大十八變 a girl changes eighteen times before reaching womanhood; a girl changes fast in physical appearance from childhood to adulthood; a growing girl changes a great deal; girls change a lot when growing up
五時花六時變（變化無常／反復無常／善變）change one's mind easily; changeable; have an unstable temperament
改變 alter; change; convert; modify; mold; transform; turn
政變 coup
密謀政變 plot a coup
無氈無扇，神仙難變（巧婦難爲無米之炊）no one can make bricks without straw; no one can make changes without resources
節哀順變 restrain one's grief and accommodate the change; suppress one's sorrow and accept the change

【轆】 lou⁴ pulley
喉轆（消防龍頭／消防栓）fire hydrant
膠轆（橡皮輪子／塑料輪子）plastic wheel

【邏】 lo⁴ patrol
邏輯 logic

巡邏 patrol

【顯】 hin² reveal
顯示 show

明顯 clear; distinct; evident; obvious

【驗】jim⁶ check

驗身（檢查身體／體檢）have a check-up
　　驗身紙（體檢證明）body check document
驗樓（樓宇檢查）flat inspection
　　驗樓紙（樓宇檢查記錄）flat inspection record

化驗 laboratory test
測驗（考試）quiz; test
經驗 experience
試驗 experiment

【驚】geng¹（害怕）be afraid; fear; sacred

驚乜（怕甚麼）what is to be feared
驚死（怕死／嚇壞）be terrified
驚住（生怕／恐怕／擔心）anxious; be afraid; take care;
　　worried
　　驚住會（擔心會）feel anxious that
　　驚住唔識做（恐怕不會做）worry that one may not be
　　　　able to do sth
驚到唔出得聲（嚇到說不出話來）be speechless with
　　shock
驚青（驚恐／害怕／慌張）all in a fluster; be afraid;
　　frightened; panic; run scared
驚咩喎（慌甚麼）what's to be feared
驚慌 panic
　　不必驚慌 there is no need to panic; there is no cause for
　　　　alarm
驚驚地（有點怕）be frightened somehow

咪驚（不要怕／別怕）don't be afraid
唔好驚（不要怕／別怕）don't be afraid
唔使驚（不用怕／不用慌／別慌）don't panic
得人驚（令人害怕）awful; horrible; terrible; terrifying
幾得人驚（挺嚇人的／非常可怕）quite scary
嚇我一驚（嚇我一跳）be astonished; be taken aback

【體】tai² body

體育衫（運動服）sportswear
體重 body weight
　　量體重 take the body weight; weigh oneself; weigh sb
體會 realise
　　切身體會 direct experience; first-hand experience; have
　　　　intimate experience of; intimate experience; intimate
　　　　knowledge; keenly aware of; one's own experience;
　　　　personal understanding
體溫 temperature
　　量體溫 take sb's temperature
體罰 corporal punishment

天體（裸體）naked
身體 ① body ② health
具體 concrete; particular; specific
保重身體 take good care of your health
屍體 cadaver; corpse; dead body; remains
液體 liquid
媒體（大眾傳媒／媒介）mass media; medium
晶體 crystal
裸體 naked; nude
魂不附體（魂不守舍）lose one's head; out of one's wits
蔽體 cover the body

【鬟】waan⁴ maid; servant girl

鬟髻 woman's hair with a topknot

丫鬟 female slave; servant girl; slave girl

【鱔】sin⁵ eel

鱔魚 eel

黃鱔 ricefield eel

【鱗】loen⁴ scales

鱗片 scales

魚鱗 scales

【鷯】liu¹ wren

鷯哥（九宮鳥）myna

【麟】loen⁴ unicorn

麟角 rare things

麒麟 unicorn

24 劃

【囑】dzuk⁷ exhort

囑咐 exhort

千叮萬囑 exhort sb repeatedly; give advice repeatedly;
　　give many exhortations to sb; warn again and
　　again
叮囑 exhort; repeatedly advise; urge again and
　　again; warn
遺囑 will

【攬】laam⁵ ① (抱／摟) embrace ② (戴) wear

攬上身 (包在身上) take on a task
攬住 (抱着／摟抱) cuddle; embrace; hug
　　攬住一齊死 (同歸於盡) end in common ruin
　　攬住死 (一起死) get into trouble together
攬身攬勢 (摟摟抱抱) hug each other; lovey-dovey
攬埋 (擁抱／抱緊) hug sb tight
攬實 (摟緊點兒) hold tight
攬頭攬頸 (摟摟抱抱) be very close; on intimate terms
　　with each other

【癲】din¹ (瘋) crazy

癲佬 (瘋子) crazy man; madman
癲狗 (憤怒的人／兇惡的人／瘋子) angry person; furious
　　man; mad man
癲癇 (瘋瘋) crazy
　　癲癲癇癇 (瘋瘋癲癲) crazy
癲喪 (瘋瘋癲癲) loopy
癲癲得得 (瘋／瘋癲) crazy

發癲 (發狂／發瘋) become mad; become insane; go
　　bonkers; go crazy; go mad; go nuts; go out of one's mind;
　　lose one's mind; lose one's reason; lose one's senses;
　　mad; round the bend; round the twist

【癱】taan² (癱瘓) be paralysed

癱咗 (癱瘓了) be paralysed
癱瘓 paralyze

風癱 (癱瘓) paralysis
眼癱癱 (乾瞪眼／無奈地看着) look on helplessly; look on
　　in despair
躝癱 (無法行走，在地上爬) creep

【罐】gun³ can; container

罐裝 canned
罐頭 can; canning; tin

火水罐 (煤油罐) kerosene container
汽水罐 beverage can
痰罐 (痰盂) spittoon
鐵罐 can; tin
藥罐 medicine tin

【羈】gei¹ custody

羈留 (拘留) detain; hold in custody

【艷】jim⁶ beautiful

艷星 (色情演員) porn actress
艷福 good fortune in love affairs
艷麗 bright-coloured and beautiful; captivating; charming;
　　gorgeous; magnificent; radiantly beautiful

【蠶】tsaam⁴ silkworm

蠶豆 broad bean
蠶蟲 (蠶) silkworm
　　蠶蟲師爺 (出餿主意／作繭自縛) a person who always
　　　　offers bad solutions to problems; a person who is
　　　　caught in his own trap

【蠹】dou³ eradicate

蠹蟻 (滅蟻) eradicate the ants

【讕】laan⁴ (賣弄／裝扮) flaunt

讕叻 (逞能) act up; parade one's ability; show off one's
　　ability; show off one's skill
讕有野 (炫耀／賣弄) cry up one's own fortune; flaunt
　　one's possessions; sing one's own glorious song
讕醒 (自作聰明／逞強) bravado; cocky; flaunt one's
　　superiority; throw one's weight round
讕㗎 (自作聰明／逞能) act up; parade one's ability; show
　　off one's ability; show off one's skill

【讓】joeng⁶ let

讓步 back down; back out of; compromise; give in; give
　　way; make a concession; yield
讓開 get out of the way; make way; step aside
讓路 get out of the way; give way; give sb the right of way;
　　make way for sb; make way for sth; step aside

頂讓 (出讓) sell
廉價出讓 be sold at a low price
謙讓 modestly decline; modestly yeld precedence to others;
　　yield from modesty
轉讓 alienation

【躝】laan¹ (爬) creep

躝出去 (滾出去) go away
躝開 (滾出去／滾開) get lost; go away
躝街 (在街上亂逛) hang around on the street
躝癱 (無法行走，在地上爬) creep

【釀】joeng⁶ ferment

釀成 breed; bring on; lead to
　　釀成大患 (帶來巨大的災難) bring on a great calamity
　　釀成大錯 breed big mistakes

釀酒 make wine
釀造 brew; make

佳釀 good wine
酒釀 fermented glutinous rice

【靂】lik[7] a sudden peal of thunder

晴天霹靂 a bolt from the blue; a sudden thunder from a clear sky; a thunderbolt out of a clear sky; a thunderclap from a blue sky

【靈】ling[4-1] (靈驗) effective spirit

靈舍（特別）especial; extraordinary; out of the ordinary; particular; special; unusual
靈舍唔同（大不相同）entirely and totally different; quite a different pair of shoes
靈舍唔同過人（跟別人大不相同）be entirely and totally different from others
靈舍靚（特別美）specially beautiful
靈活 agile; flexible; quick-minded
靈神不用多致燭，好鼓不用多槌（響鼓不用重錘敲）a word is enough to the wise
靈堂 funeral hall
靈敏 acute; active; agile; nimble; sensitive
靈魂 soul
出賣靈魂 sell one's soul
靈機一觸（靈機一動）a flash of wit; a sudden inspiration; hit on a bright idea; suddenly have a brain wave
靈擎（靈驗）effective; efficacious

人老精，鬼老靈（年齡大的人經歷多，考慮周到）experienced and thoughtful
失靈 break down
做鬼都唔靈（無法提供任何幫助／好換化為烏有）cannot offer any help; good-for-naught
精靈（機敏）alert and resourceful; smart and lovely

【韆】tsin[1] swing

韆鞦（鞦韆）swing
打韆鞦（盪鞦韆）get on a swing; have a swing; play on the swing

【顰】pan[4] frown

顰眉（皺眉頭）knit one's brows

東施效顰 copy others blindly and make oneself look foolish; crude imitation; imitate awkwardly; imitate others and make oneself foolish and ridiculous; imitate sb in certain particulars; play the sedulous ape; take a leaf out of sb's book

【驟】dzaau[6] gallop

驟忌（禁忌）taboo
驟雨（陣雨）occasional drizzle; passing shower; rain shower; shower; shower of rain

步驟 measure; move; procedure; step

【鬭】dau[3] struggle

鬭氣（賭氣）at odds with sb; have the sulks
鬭啀（互相誹謗）calumniate each other; defame each other; slander each other
鬭踩（互相誹謗）calumniate each other; defame each other; slander each other

【鷹】jing[1] eagle

鷹粟粉（玉米粉／玉米澱粉／粟粉）starch

麻鷹（老鷹）eagle
雞仔唔管管麻鷹（該管的不管，不該管的倒去管）mind one's own business
鷂鷹 hawk

25 劃

【廳】teng[1] (客廳) living room

廳長（睡客廳的人）sb sleeping in the living room

一間茶餐廳 a local café
一間餐廳 a restaurant
坐花廳（坐大牢）be imprisoned; be jailed; be shut behind the bars; be taken off to prison; commit a person to prison; go to prison; in jail; in prison; lay sb by the heels; put into prison; run in; send to prison
客廳 living room; sitting room
茶餐廳（港式茶餐廳）Hong Kong-style restaurant; local café
飯廳 dining room
歌廳 lounge
舞廳 cabaret; dance hall
餐廳 restaurant

【欖】laam[5-2] (橄欖) olive

欖球（橄欖球）rugby

白欖（橄欖）Chinese white olive

沙欖（青欖）Chinese olive
喉欖（喉結）Adam's Apple
橄欖 olive

【攣】waan⁵（無序）out of order

搞攣（挑起事端 / 製造麻煩）cause problems; make trouble
攪攣（弄糟）cause problems; make trouble

【灣】waan¹ bay

灣水（失業）be unemployed

入鄉隨俗，出水隨灣 do in Rome as the Romans do
台灣 Taiwan
行船好過灣（不怕慢，就怕站）it is better to have a little to
　　do than to do none

【籬】lei⁴ bamboo basket

籬笆 bamboo fence; hedge; hurdle; wattle

隔籬（隔壁）adjoining; neighbouring; next door; next to

【䐀】lo⁴⁻¹ arse; bottom

䐀柚（屁股）bottom
　　洗䐀柚（洗屁股）clean one's bottom
䐀霸（肥臀 / 大臀）large bottom

【籮】lo⁴ bamboo basket

籮底桔（賣剩的）leftover
籮底橙 ①（挑剩的東西 / 殘貨）left-over; remaining goods
　　②（成績最差的學生）worst students

多籮籮（很多）many; very much
波籮 / 菠蘿（鳳梨）pineapple

【蠻】maan⁴ savage

蠻勁 animal strength
蠻橫 arbitrary; impervious to reason; peremptory; rude and
　　unreasonable

刁蠻 impervious to reason; obstinate; unruly
野蠻（不理智 / 不理性）barbarous; irrational

【觀】gun¹ look at

觀光 sightseeing
觀音 Goddess of Mercy
　　觀音兵（自願為女子做跟班的男子 / 特別熱衷於為女性
　　　奔走效勞的男人）man who runs around looking after
　　　a woman

觀音誕 Birthday of the Goddess of Mercy
觀察 observe
觀點 point of view

主觀 subjective
寺觀 Buddhist and Daoist temples
式樣美觀 attractive fashion
壯觀 grand; grandiose; magnificent; vast
免費參觀 visit without charge
面面觀 view sth from every angle
政治觀 political view
旁觀 look on; observe from the sidelines; on-looker
美觀 artistic; beautiful; pleasing to the eye
參觀 visit
悲觀 pessimistic
雅觀 graceful and elegant in appearance; in good taste; nice
　　appearance; nice-looking; refined
樂觀 optimistic

【鹽】jim⁴ salt

鹽蛇（壁虎）lizard
鹽墨（鹽罐兒）salt jar
　　一墨鹽（一罐鹽）a clay jar of salt; an earthern jar of salt;
　　　a pottery container of salt

生鹽（粗鹽）coarse salt
幼鹽（細鹽）fine salt
食鹽（精鹽）tablet salt
淮鹽 spicy salt
椒鹽 spiced salt
摻鹽（撒鹽）sprinkle salt
熟鹽（精鹽）refined salt; table salt

26 劃

【讚】dzaan³ praise

讚人（表揚）commend; praise
讚不絕口 praise without stopping
讚賞 praise

有彈冇讚（有貶無褒）just criticism without praise
有彈有讚（有褒有貶）criticise and praise
稱讚 acclaim; commend; compliment; pat sb on the back
　　praise; slap sb on the back

【趲】dzaan² ① hurry through ② urge
趲路（趲路）hurry in a journey

走趲（作通融／餘地）leeway; margin

27 劃

【纜】laam⁶（戴）wear
纜住頸巾（戴着圍巾）wear a scarf
纜車 ① cable car ② peak tram
　　纜車站 ① cable car station ② peak tram station
　　山頂纜車 peak tram

大纜（粗大的纜繩）thick rope
升降機電纜（電梯電纜）lift cable
行船爭解纜（爭做領頭人）take the lead
扯大纜（拔河）tug-of-war
扯頭纜（爭做領頭人）take the lead
扯纜（拉縴）tow a boat
拉大纜（拔河）tug-of-war
拉頭纜（牽頭／帶頭）lead; take the lead; the first one
　　to start
拉纜（吃麵）eat noodles
斬纜（一刀兩斷）break off with sb

【鑼】lo⁴ gong
鑼鼓 gongs and drums

打鑼（敲鑼）beat the gong
開鑼（賽季開始）start of a season

【鑽】dzyn³ ①（刺穿）pierce ②（寶石）
diamond ③（鑽孔）drill
鑽石 diamond

火鑽（紅寶石）ruby

【鱸】lou⁴ weasel
鱸魚探蝦毛——冇好心（黃鼠狼給雞拜年——不安
　好心）a weasel giving new year's greetings to a hen
　has ulterior motives; a yellow weasel goes to pay New
　Year's call to a hen – not with the best of intentions; the
　weasel goes to pay its respects to the hen – not with the
　best of intentions

【鱷】ngok⁹ crocodile
鱷魚 crocodile
　　鱷魚淚（鱷魚的眼淚／偽裝的同情）crocodile tears
　　鱷魚潭（龍潭虎穴）dangerous place
　　鱷魚頭（殘酷的人）cruel person

大鱷（財雄勢強的人）master swindler
鹹水大鱷（海外資產大鱷）foreign swindler

28 劃

【攣】maan¹（補救）remedy
攣唔番（救不回）beyond remedy
攣攣緊（缺錢）out at elbows; short of money

【戇】ngong⁶（傻）stupid
戇居 ①（傻乎乎／傻裏傻氣）foolish, stupid ②（呆頭呆腦）
　dull; dull-looking
　　戇居佬（呆子／傻瓜）blockhead; fool; idiot; simpleton
　　戇居居 ①（傻乎乎／傻裏傻氣）foolish, stupid ②（呆頭
　　呆腦）dull; dull-looking
戇直 ① blunt and tactless ② honest

詐戇（裝傻）act stupid; play the fool
傻夾戇（缺心眼兒）candid; careless; frank; lack of
　calculation; mindless
霎戇 ①（混蛋）bastard ②（傻）stupid

【攣】lyn⁴⁻¹ curled
攣毛（捲頭髮）curled hair

【鑿】dzok⁹（鑿子）chisel
鑿大（言過其實／誇大）overstate sth
鑿窿（開孔）bore a hole

實鼓實鑿（真刀真槍）neither garish nor gaudy

【鸚】jing¹ parrot
鸚鵡 parrot

【鬱】wat⁷ hold in check
鬱金香 tulip
鬱鬱 ① lush; luxuriant ② depressed; gloomy; melancholy
　③ strongly fragrant ④ elegant; refined

鬱鬱不樂（悶悶不樂）a cup too low; dejected; depressed; despondent; disconsolate; down in the dumps; down in the mouth; downhearted; have a fit of blues; have the blues; in a dismal mood; in the doldrums; jobless; look blue; out of spirits; sing the blues

抑鬱 depression

字母開始的字頭

【a】
A 出口 exit A

AA 制（平均分擔費用 / 各付各的）go Dutch

【b】
B 出口 exit B

ball 場（舞廳）dancing hall

bb ①（嬰兒 / 寶寶）baby ②（哨子）whistle

bb 女（女嬰）baby girl

bb 仔 ①（嬰兒）baby ②（男嬰）baby boy

bb 房（嬰兒房）room for the baby

bb 椅（嬰兒椅）baby chair

bb 機（傳呼機）pager

bb 櫈（嬰兒櫈）baby chair

book 酒店（預約酒店）book a hotel room

book 張枱（訂位）book a table

book 場（訂場地）book a court

【c】
C 出口 exit C

call phone（打電話）

call 台（電召服務中心 / 通信中心）communication centre

call 的（電召出租汽車）call the taxi

call 機（傳呼機）pager

calli（資格）qualification

cancel 個會（取消會議）cancel the meeting

case（案件 / 案例 / 實例）case

CD 鋪（音像店）CD shop

check 吓（檢查一下）check

claim 錢（報銷）apply for reimbursement

confirm 張票（確認門票）confirm the ticket

copy 封信（複製封信）copy the letter

cut 線 ①（換線）change the lane ②（線路被切斷）the line is cut

【d】
D 出口 exit D

do 野（做愛）have sex

DQ（取消資格）disqualified

面臨 DQ（面臨被取消資格）face disqualification

dub 碟（拷貝磁盤）copy a disk

dump 時間（磨時間）kill time

DVD（數碼多功能影音光碟）digital video disk

【e】
E 出口 exit E

email 俾我（發電子郵件給我）send it to me by email

encore 咗二次（安可了兩次）encore twice

【f】
fax 士（傳真）fax

fan 屎（粉絲）fans; worshippers

fan 過大打 band（朋友親密過樂隊）close friends

friend 過打 band（朋友親密過樂隊）close friends

fit 晒（身體狀況最佳）one's health is in the best conditions

free 晒士（自由尺寸 / 可調尺寸）free size

【g】
gas 爐（煤氣爐）gas oven

gut 屎（膽量）guts

【h】
hea（無所事事 / 無聊 / 清閒 / 漫不經心 / 懶散 / 隨意閒玩蹓躂）hang around; idle away; lounge around

hi-fi（高保真）hi-fi

【i】
IQ 好高（智商很高）have a very high IQ

IT 公司（信息技術公司）information and technology firm

【k】
k（卡拉 OK / 自動伴奏錄音）karaoka

k 士（案件）case

k 場（卡拉 OK 酒吧）karaoke bar

k lunch（卡拉 OK 午餐）karaoke lunch

keep fit（健身）keep fit

【m】
marketing 好多人讀（很多人主修市場營銷專業）many people major in marketing

Miss（小姐 / 女士）miss

【o】

o 唔 ok （你還好嗎）are you ok

【p】

pa 唔 pass （你通過了嗎）did you pass
post 咭 （明信片）postcard

【q】

q （可愛）cute

【s】

service 好差 （服務很差）the service is very poor
set 頭 （紮頭髮）have one's hair set
show quali （炫耀／賣弄）show off
size 太大 （尺寸太大）this size is too large for me
su 唔 sure （你確定嗎）are you sure
summer 好熱 （夏天好熱）it is hot in summer

【t】

t 裇 （t 恤／短袖汗衫）t-shirt

【v】

van 仔 （小巴）minibus
　　一架 van 仔 （一輛小巴）a minibus
VCD （影音光碟）video compact disk
Visa 卡 （維薩卡）Visa card

【w】

warm-up （熱身／做準備動作）warm-up

【x】

XO 醬 XO sauce

【y】

yen （日圓）Japanese yen